# THE VAMPIRE ARCHIVES

## THE MOST COMPLETE VOLUME OF VAMPIRE TALES EVER PUBLISHED

### Edited with an introduction by

# OTTO PENZLER

FOREWORD BY KIM NEWMAN

PREFACE BY NEIL GAIMAN

VINTAGE CRIME/BLACK LIZARD
Vintage Books
A Division of Random House, Inc.
New York

A VINTAGE CRIME/BLACK LIZARD ORIGINAL, OCTOBER 2009

*Introduction and compilation copyright © 2009 by Otto Penzler*
*Foreword copyright © 2009 by Kim Newman*
*Preface copyright © 2009 by Neil Gaiman*

Owing to limitations of space, permissions to reprint previously
published material appear on pages 1031–1034.

Library of Congress Cataloging-in-Publication Data:
The vampire archives / edited by Otto Penzler.
p.  cm.
ISBN 978-0-307-47389-9
1. Vampires—Fiction.   2. Horror tales, American.   I. Penzler, Otto.
PS648.V35V25 2009
813'.0873808375—dc22
2009008864

*Book design by Christopher M. Zucker*

w w w . v i n t a g e b o o k s . c o m

Printed in the United States of America
10  9  8  7  6  5  4  3  2  1

*For my friend Harlan Ellison,
whose integrity and decency
are the antithesis of the
subject of this book*

# Contents

## Pre-Dracula

## Graveyards, Castles, Churches, Ruins

## True Stories

## That's Poetic

# CONTENTS

# CONTENTS

## This Is War

## Modern Masters

# Foreword

## KIM NEWMAN

So, why *vampires*?

Theoretically, vampire stories—whether novels, films, TV series and episodes, short stories, operas, songs, or anecdotes—are a subgenre of horror fiction. For a long time, the vampire was just one of several key players or major themes in horror, sharing a dark pantheon with the werewolf (whose metamorphoses extend to his city cousin Dr. Jekyll), the Frankenstein monster (whose kin range from golems to cyborgs), the ghost (and its haunted house), the mummy, the zombie, the mad murderer, and a few others, all with their own subdivisions and anthologies to explore—though we are still awaiting a *Mammoth Book of Hunchbacked Minions* to complete the set.

Stephen King calls these mainstays the Tarot, but there are other catchall terms. Being the age I am, I think of them as the Aurora monsters, after the glow-in-the-dark hobby kits ("frightening lightning strikes!") kids glued together in the 1960s and '70s. The Aurora vampire was, of course, Bela Lugosi as Dracula, the image Universal Pictures has effectively registered as a trademark. Lugosi's vampire cuts a dashing figure in opera cloak, tailcoat, medallion, and white tie, the outfit that prompts George Hamilton in *Love at First Bite* to muse, "How would you like to spend five hundred years dressed like a headwaiter?" Besides curious cadences ("I . . . am . . . *Draaahcyulah*") and highlighted eyes, Lugosi brought to the role the hypnotic hand gestures Martin Landau explains in *Ed Wood* with "You have to be double-jointed and Hungarian."

It took centuries for this vampire image to evolve. Folkloric roots are deep and various, with bloodsucking revenants, demons, or shape-shifters appearing in almost every culture. In the late eighteenth century, the vampire of legend crossed over into romantic literature, informing the fatal men and femmes fatales of gothic prose and poetry. These attractive villains often struck poses we now associate with vampires, even if they can't strictly be classified as such. They live in decrepit castles, plot to destroy young innocents, exert mesmeric influence over victims and minions, affect black clothing (with the occasional white shroud), are pale and thin, take their interior decoration tips from crypts and catacombs, labor under family curses, strike Faustian bargains, shrink from (or blaspheme against) religious objects, are mostly seen at night, etc.

John Polidori's Lord Ruthven, who appears in *The Vampyre*, is a typical gothic villain but deserves to be remembered as the first vampire. I'll repeat that, with emphasis: *Lord Ruthven is the first vampire*. You can junk all the folklore, the blood-drinking snake-women, Peter Plaujewitz, Vlad the Impaler, and those South American bats. They might be interesting and influential, but they aren't *vampires* in the sense we're talking about. Lord Ruthven is. The overwhelming majority of subsequent fictional vampires derive from him—except, maybe, the blood-drinking plants that crop up in H. G. Wells's "The Flowering of the Strange Orchid" or *Little Shop of Horrors* and the car that runs on blood in Josef Nesvadba's "Vampires, Ltd." Before Ruthven, vampirism was something a bad person or monster did or was said to do—as in "now I could drink hot blood"; after *The Vampyre* (1819), a vampire was a particular type of creature, a specific subcategory of gothic literary villain. He isn't the muddy, repulsive Middle European peasant zombie of Dom Augustin Calmet's treatise, but a coldhearted, sophisticated, aristocratic fashion plate who indulges in a style of melodramatic villainy old-fashioned even in 1819.

It's worth remembering Polidori was trying to be funny. The story is a lampoon of his employer-friend Lord Byron, implying that the poet's manners and morals are those of a vampire in the same way cartoonists would later draw, say, Margaret Thatcher with fangs. Many readers missed the joke but embraced the image—if anything, Byron became *more* popular after he was facetiously accused of drinking the blood of the ladies he swept away as fast as his gammy leg would allow. Eighty years before Bram Stoker's *Dracula*, Ruthven became a franchise character—appearing in sequels by other hands and multiple theatrical adaptations (with or without music) and inspiring low-grade rip-offs like the penny dreadful *Varney the Vampyre*. Ruthven might have savage foreign habits—like Byron, vampires have a Greek connection—but he's English (in some plays, he's a tartan-kilted Scot); this is why the very British Christopher Lee, whose Dracula owes much to Ruthven, sounds as valid a vampire as the Hungarian Lugosi. Stoker gives his vampire appalling dress sense (he's seen "in a straw hat which suits him not"), but Lugosi's

stage and screen Dracula inherits his nattiness from Byron via Ruthven. Indeed, the business about the vampire insinuating himself into polite society—Stoker's Dracula comes through the window, but Lugosi's presents a calling card and strides into a drawing room—comes from Polidori, too, though the satirical implication of *The Vampyre* is that predatory blood-drinking is typical of "the haut ton" rather than an intrusion into it.

Of course, the picture wasn't complete until there was a female vampire role model. She finally came along in Sheridan Le Fanu's "Carmilla" (1871), in which the vampire is a sham innocent cuckoo-in-the-nest who exerts a seductive fascination over her victims. Actually, Le Fanu—a better writer than many—comes up with something subtler than the dominatrix *belle dame sans merci* we're used to in on-screen female vampires: Carmilla is a passive-aggressive monster, clinging and desperate, a helpless invalid who sucks the life out of those who make the mistake of trying to look after her (her opposite is E. F. Benson's Mrs. Amworth, the nurse whose patients don't get better). Le Fanu was the first to give much thought to matters later crucial to the vampire story—how to get rid of the things. His remedy (a stake through the heart), drawn from the Calmet-approved body of Eastern European lore, has become much more commonplace than, say, the Varney solution (a suicidal leap into a volcano). In *Dracula* (1897), Stoker encapsulates the various vampires who have come before his villain, borrowing from Polidori and Le Fanu. Count Dracula, his male monster, is surrounded by shrouded brides and acolytes.

It's possible that without Stoker's book, vampires would never have gained the dominance in the field that they now command. Perhaps gorgons, ghouls, or chimeras would have emerged from the pack and proliferated to fill the gap. *Dracula* was not immediately a huge sensation: Stoker's initial sales didn't match those of Robert Louis Stevenson's *The Strange Case of Dr. Jekyll and Mr. Hyde* or H. Rider Haggard's *She*, and he didn't attain the literary reputation Oscar Wilde secured with *The Picture of Dorian Gray* or the enormous popular response that greeted Arthur Conan Doyle's

Sherlock Holmes stories. Arguably, the breakout hit vampire novel of 1898 was H. G. Wells's *The War of the Worlds*—the Martians, remember, come to Earth to siphon human blood. Gradually, with stage and then film adaptations, *Dracula* became a standard, then a classic, then an all-pervasive cultural phenomenon. The Dracula who survives to this day isn't strictly Stoker's, but a mélange of Lord Ruthven, Varney, Stoker, Max Schreck's Nosferatu, Lugosi, Lee, Gary Oldman, Jack Palance, Frank Langella, Count Chocula, Jamie Gillis in *Dracula Sucks*, Fred Saberhagen, Gene Colan's *Tomb of Dracula* artwork, Anne Rice's Lestat, McNally and Florescu's Vlad the Impaler, Stephen King's Barlow, Heathcliff, Byron himself, Henry Irving, Jack the Ripper, those hobby kits (and much other Universal Pictures merchandise), and many, many other onion layers.

When I came to write my own take on the Vampire Dracula in *Anno Dracula* and related novels and stories, I was forced to conclude Dracula was all these things, people, and images rather than one set, fixed being. Stoker established that Dracula could become a wolf, a bat, or mist—and others have proved that Dracula can be at once cheery old Grandpa Munster, Klaus Kinski's ailing rat-faced romantic, and an incarnation of Absolute Evil. At the time of writing, the last great addition to the character is Daniel Day-Lewis's take on Upton Sinclair's oil exploiter Daniel Plainview in Paul Thomas Anderson's *There Will Be Blood*: Day-Lewis and Anderson admit that Plainview, who sleeps like the dead on wooden floors and declaims "I drink your milk shake" with Lugosi-like relish, is a combination of John Huston and Count Dracula—though I detect a rasp of Jack Palance's count in Day-Lewis's whispery, cajoling threats as he plans to suck the lifeblood from a parched land.

F. W. Murnau's *Nosferatu* (1922) was a commercially marginal effort, even in the context of the German film industry of the time—and attained its notoriety partially thanks to Mrs. Bram Stoker's tenacious attempts to suppress or get money out of it. Carl Theodor Dreyer's *Vampyr* (1932), notionally adapted from "Carmilla," was even further out of the mainstream. Tod Browning's *Dracula* (1931), the biggest hit of the first half-century of vampire movies, didn't make the impact James Whale's *Frankenstein* did later that year. In subsequent monster movies, Universal plainly saw the monster as their "A" bogeyman, with Dracula as a tagalong (which is how John Carradine plays the count in a brace of 1940s monster rallies where he jostles for attention with the monster, the wolf man, and mad scientists, and is even upstaged by hunchbacked minions); this even carried over into the treatment of the studio's horror stars, with Boris Karloff—the man behind the monster—always getting the plums that eluded Lugosi. Only at the very end of the cycle, with Lugosi's return in *Abbott and Costello Meet Frankenstein* (1948), was the count allowed to dominate the pack, and even in that case note that the title isn't *Abbott and Costello Meet Dracula*.

When Hammer Films revived the gothic monster movie, they reversed the Universal pattern and started with *The Curse of Frankenstein* (1957), then followed up with *Dracula* (1958). But by the time of Francis Ford Coppola's *Bram Stoker's Dracula* (1992)—which would inevitably lead to Kenneth Branagh's *Mary Shelley's Frankenstein* (1994)—the pecking order had been reversed. In the interim, vampire movies had outnumbered and outgrossed Frankenstein films by something like ten to one. A post-*Dracula* drought of vampire novels—relieved only by radical works like Richard Matheson's *I Am Legend* (1954), Simon Raven's *Doctors Wear Scarlet* (1960), and Theodore Sturgeon's *Some of Your Blood* (1961)—gave way to a deluge that got going in the mid-'70s. The three important books that reestablished the vampire novel are Stephen King's *Salem's Lot* (1975), which mashes up the plot of *Dracula* and the milieu of Grace Metalious's *Peyton Place*; Fred Saberhagen's *The Dracula Tape* (1975), which gives the count's side of the story (and remains prime among many, many novels and films that pick new meaning out of Stoker's material), and Anne Rice's *Interview with the Vampire* (1976), which is set almost entirely among vampires (one of Rice's innovations is the idea that vampires might have relationships, differences of opinion, and variant character traits).

All these important books draw on incarnations of *Dracula* but pull the material in fresh directions, opening the way for vampire romances, vampire alternate histories, vampire detectives, vampire team-ups (Saberhagen also wrote *The Holmes-Dracula File*, 1978), vampire pets, vampire romantic comedy, vampirism as a metaphor for drug addiction or sexual nonconformism or venereal disease (Stoker touched on all these themes, as it happens), vampire humor, vampire kung fu, postapocalyptic science-fiction vampires, vampire erotica (and, frankly, vampire porn), punk vampires, goth vampires (obviously), lesbian vampires, ironic postmodern vampires, slacker vampires, Republican vampires, vampire role-playing games,

vampire fashions, and even a few stray horror vampires. It's possible vampire fiction is now a larger publishing category than horror—and, indeed, many recent vampire novels, comics, and films aren't that interested in the primary purpose of horror (i.e., being scary) and owe more to the various brands of wish fulfillment found in the romance, action, or superhero sections of the bookstore or DVD rental outlet.

Though few vampires would admit it, they are in rude good health—other fashions in monstrosity come and go (zombies are "in" at the moment, but serial killers are passé), but vampires remain, whether eternally youthful like Lestat and Carmilla or eternally decrepit like Nosferatu. This whacking great collection of vampire stories goes a long way toward explaining why that is.

# Preface

## NEIL GAIMAN

We get the vampires we deserve, after all.

I remember, even as a small boy, growing up, craving vampires. The first vampire fiction I ever read was *Dracula*, on Christopher Harris's dad's bookshelf, and it was a struggle, even if I was a bright eight-year-old. I wanted more. I wanted vampires, like the ones in the opening sequence, not boring vampire hunters writing interminable letters to one another. I wanted to see the fangs come out. I wanted action.

The first horror film I ever watched was *Son of Dracula*, with Lon Chaney Jr. as the count, plotting evil in the Bayou. I watched him transform into a bat, watched him sleep in a coffin, and I loved him even as I feared him. I had believed before that closing a door would keep the monsters out, but Dracula slipped under doors in the form of smoke, and that terrified me. Doors did not work, even when closed.

Seven years later, on East Croydon station, I picked up a copy of Stephen King's novel *Salem's Lot*, its cover a black pressed-out child's face, with one red teardrop at the corner of the mouth. I remember the excitement with which I read it, as I first suspected it was a vampire story, then the delight when my suspicions were confirmed. Indeed, it was a vampire story, a big one, the kind I had wanted to read since I was a boy. And now, looking back, I do not know how much of my excitement was simply because there *weren't* vampire novels in 1975, or not ones that were crossing my teenage path. The short stories that showed up from time to time in *The Pan Book of Horror Stories* and such had only served to whet my appetite, and I was too young to be allowed into late-night screenings of the breasts-and-blondes Hammer vampire offerings of the time, so I imagined them, and would, in time, be disappointed by how far short of my imaginings the real things would prove.

I wanted vampires. I missed them. A few years later, as a young writer, I would plot vampire stories because I wanted to read them, and because nobody else was writing the stories I wanted to read. (This is a very good reason to write, by the way.) I wrote great reviews of bad movies if they had vampires in them. In the mid-nineties I sold a vampire TV series, and then, when I was told I couldn't control what it looked like, couldn't make sure that it looked and felt grown-up, worried that it might be played for laughs or for camp, I took my vampires and went home. Because I didn't want to sell them short. Because I cared.

And then, one day, they were everywhere. You couldn't move for vampires. There were paranormal vampire romances and junior paranormal vampire romances. There were vampires on TV and vampires in the movies and vampires in the bedrooms and sad strange lonely people with their own custom-made teeth in the shadows at conventions. Everywhere vampires, stripped down like a simple metaphor for genitalia-free relationships. Vampires, as Stephen King said, taking Erica Jong's phrase, were the ultimate zipless fuck.

But there's life in the undead yet. You can't kill a vampire, after all, not even with one of those cool, fake-retro Victorian vampire–killing kits they sell on eBay, with stakes and fresh garlic and perhaps some silver bullets in case you run into a werewolf on the way. They wouldn't be popular if there hadn't been over a hundred years of fine vampire literature as a foundation. Whether as metaphor or as something else—something that stirs the blood, makes you dream of immortality and night, that rustles the counterpanes, or just leaves you glancing nervously at a locked door, because after all, they can move as mist—vampires will always be with us.

So wait until dark, and begin to read . . .

# Introduction

## OTTO PENZLER

# THEY WILL HAVE BLOOD

Most everything you think you know about vampires is true. Or not. Trying to understand the myth of vampirism is like trying to understand the concept of God. All depends upon the culture, the era, and even an individual's imagination and gullibility, or faith.

In the contemporary Western world, the generally accepted notion of a vampire derives from Bram Stoker's iconic Victorian novel, *Dracula*. To most readers and filmgoers, a vampire is an immortal bloodsucking creature with supernatural powers, able to transform itself into other natural forms, such as a bat, a wolf, or other animal. It sleeps during daylight hours, usually in a coffin or grave, and arises to prey when darkness falls or when the moon rises, usually by biting a neck and drinking its victim's blood. It cannot be harmed during those waking hours, although it may be repelled with a cross, holy water, or garlic. When it is resting, it may be killed with a wooden (or silver) stake through the heart or by being decapitated.

The vampire myth actually dates back to ancient times in Eastern as well as Western culture. In ancient Jewish legend, Lilith, Adam's first wife, sucked the blood of men and attacked infants, turning them into Lilam, or children of Lilith, who then grew to feast on blood as well. This myth lasted into the Middle Ages.

In ancient Greece, vampires were the children of Hecate: beautiful women who seduced and drained the blood of innocents. As often depicted in other parts of the world, they had the power to transform themselves into various kinds of animals. They were able to attack during daylight hours as well as at night. Also part of ancient Greece's mythological terror was Lamia, a humble monster with a Gorgon's face, fangs, and snake-like tongue who specialized in killing children for their blood.

Other variations of the myth that date back two millennia are the vampiric creature feared by American Indian tribes, with a trumpet-shaped mouth designed to suck out the brains of sleeping victims through their ears; the Chinese monster Kian-si, with blazing green eyes and enormously long talons, causing great pain when it walked, so it is generally described as hopping from place to place in order to attack its victims, ripping their heads off; the Hindu vampires of India, who focus on drunk or insane women, though they pale compared with Kali, whose bloodlust is so overpowering that, failing to find a victim, she will tear open her own throat to drink blood; the Scottish Glaistig, who will take the form of a beautiful young woman and dance with a man until he is exhausted, whereupon she will suck the blood out of him; and the *jararaca* of Brazil, who will slip into a house in the dark of night and drink the milk as well as the blood of sleeping women. It is safe to say that there do not appear to be any cultures in which the myth of the bloodsucking creature with supernatural powers has not existed.

Naturally (or, perhaps more accurately, unnaturally) under these circumstances, with such a universal belief in some variation of the vampire myth, there are numerous examples of real people who exhibited some of the classic symptoms of the vampire, solidifying the belief in the minds of many.

Among the most heinous of real-life vampires was Countess Elizabeth Bathory, whose family castle was on the border of Hungary, Austria, and the Slovak Republic, where she resided most of the time from 1560 to 1614. She began her life of terror by torturing her servants, any trivial transgression serving as an excuse to visit upon them the most vicious cruelty, including sewing closed the lips of a girl who spoke while performing her duties, submerging another in an icy river in the winter, throwing a naked girl into the snow and pouring ice water over her until she froze to death, and sticking long pins into various parts of her servants' anatomy, including under their fingernails.

On one occasion, when a young girl accidentally pulled her hair while brushing it, the countess hit her so hard that she drew blood, which fell on her own hand. When she wiped it off, she was certain that her aging skin had acquired the moist freshness of her servant's. She immediately had her male servants bring the prettiest young virgins to her and slash their throats, collecting the blood in a giant vat in which she bathed. Convinced that this was restoring her youthful beauty, she soon needed more victims and sent emissaries to the nearby village, promising good jobs as maids and servants to beautiful young virgins. It did not take long for the villagers to suspect that the castle was home to vampirism, as bodies drained of blood were found dumped on the ground outside its walls. It also did not take long for the countess

to realize that the blood baths were not working very well, so her companion, a witch, stated that she needed a better quality of blood, available only from nobility. She was able to attract twenty-five destitute young noblewomen to come to the castle with promises of comfort and instruction in the finer things of life. Within two weeks, all but two had been dispatched. When none of the village girls were ever seen again, convictions increased that they had become the victims of vampires, so complaints by the villagers and the local minister were sent to Parliament. Prime Minister Thurzo of Hungary, a cousin of the countess's, attacked her castle and discovered the veritable abattoir with its mutilated victims as well as several caged girls awaiting their fate. He ordered her confined to a single room in the castle, bricking up the doors and windows, leaving only a small slit through which food could be passed. Unrepentant, the countess lived in this manner for three years, having caused the death of as many as 650 young women and girls.

If there can be evidence of a man being an undying vampire, it surely applies to Rasputin, who famously withstood poisoning sufficient to kill ten men, numerous bullets to the chest, and severe bludgeoning. He survived all of it. Only when he was wrapped in a sheet and thrown into a frozen river did he finally succumb. When his corpse was pulled from the water, his frozen arms were outstretched, apparently trying to claw through the ice that wouldn't allow him to escape. The cause of death was drowning, although the autopsy showed the presence of the poison and the bullets, either of which should have done the job. Part of the vampire legend is that running water cannot be tolerated, adding to the conviction that Rasputin was killed in one of the few ways in which it was possible to accomplish the deed.

The most famous individual associated with the myth of the vampire is the former ruler of Walachia, a province on the border of Transylvania (now Romania), Vlad III, known as the Impaler. Having been involved in the Crusades against the expansionist Ottoman Empire, he led an army against the Turks to drive them from the Danube

Valley. A fierce and skilled warrior, he was moderately successful, but badly outnumbered by the powerful Islamic army, he retreated to his castle, poisoning all the wells and burning his own villages along the way so that the Turks would find neither food nor water as they pursued him. When they approached his castle, they saw the heads of twenty thousand Turkish prisoners impaled on spikes along both sides of the road, a sight so frightening that the Turks turned away and refused to continue the pursuit.

No allegations or evidence suggest that Vlad the Impaler was a vampire, but the undoubted cruelty and extremity of his bloodletting, with an estimated thirty to forty thousand victims, including women, children, and even animals in addition to the Turkish soldiers, have conspired to make him the ideal role model for the ultimate Dracula figure. Stoker recognized this and enhanced the image by modeling Count Dracula's castle on Vlad's forbidding mountain residence, built on the backs of hundreds of laborers who died during its construction.

While *Dracula* is certainly the most famous vampire story, it is not the first, having been preceded by John Polidori's *The Vampyre* (1819). This story was invented on perhaps the most significant single moment in the history of supernatural literature. As Lord Byron read "Christabel," Samuel Taylor Coleridge's vampire poem, to his friend Percy Bysshe Shelley, his wife, Mary Wollstonecraft Shelley, and their physician, Dr. Polidori, he challenged the group to come up with an equally frightening story. Mary Shelley conceived the story of *Frankenstein* that night, and Polidori, clearly an untalented hack, was inspired to write the first English-language vampire story, which is, alas, far too tedious to include in this collection.

None of these works to any significant degree inspired Stoker to write *Dracula*, an honor that fell to the great author of macabre fiction, Sheridan Le Fanu, whose novelette "Carmilla" (1871) featured a lesbian vampire with the ability to transform herself into a gigantic cat, scandalizing Victorian readers.

The great gothic tradition of ruined castles and abbeys whose rooms and crypts serve as resting places for vampires is well represented in this volume. There are numerous spires, clouds passing in front of full moons, handsome men in full evening dress coming to bite the neck of a beautiful and innocent young woman in the dead of night, and coffin lids being raised to reveal their horrible residents.

But vampires come in many guises, and they do here, too: some that look pretty much like the rest of us, some who have frustrating, even occasionally humorous difficulties, and some who are not interested in blood at all, merely wanting to suck the life out of their victims in a metaphorical way. There are stories here by men and women, from every literary era of the past century and a half, right up to the most talented writers of the present day. There are familiar classic stories here, and a few that you are unlikely to have encountered previously.

Also, at the back of this very large volume, you will find the most comprehensive bibliography of vampire fiction ever assembled, a task of staggering scholarship and persistence on the part of Daniel Seitler, who did the heavy lifting in compiling this invaluable reference source.

No matter whether you decide to approach the reading of this tome in small bites or as a gigantic feast, I hope it provides you with a bloody good read.

# GOOD LADY DUCAYNE

# M. E. Braddon

Mary Elizabeth Braddon (1835–1915) was born in Soho, London, and attempted a career on the stage at the age of seventeen under the name Mary Seyton but quit after writing her first novel, *The Octoroon; or, The Lily of Louisiana* (1859). The following year her play *The Loves of Arcadia* was performed at the Strand Theatre. After her second novel, *Three Times Dead; or, The Secret of the Heath* (1860), was published, she met and fell in love with the publisher John Maxwell, moving in with and eventually marrying him.

She became known as the Queen of Sensation, producing more than eighty novels, and was the most popular female writer in the circulating libraries that sprang up in England. Her most famous novel, *Lady Audley's Secret* (1862), was reprinted endlessly and became a long-running theatrical sensation. At the peak of her productivity during the 1860s, she wrote as many as three novels a year, most long enough to be published in three volumes. An accomplished plotter, she was not known for the high quality of her prose. William Makepeace Thackeray, an admirer, said, "If I could plot like Miss Braddon, I would be the greatest writer in the English language."

Although most of her novels were mystery, sensation, and adventure stories, as well as domestic fiction, she wrote occasional supernatural novels and short stories.

"Good Lady Ducayne" was first published in the February 1896 issue of *The Strand Magazine*; frequently anthologized, it was never collected in any of her books.

# Good Lady Ducayne

## M. E. BRADDON

Bella Rolleston had made up her mind that her only chance of earning her bread and helping her mother to an occasional crust was by going out into the great unknown world as companion to a lady. She was willing to go to any lady rich enough to pay her a salary and so eccentric as to wish for a hired companion. Five shillings told off reluctantly from one of those sovereigns which were so rare with the mother and daughter, and which melted away so quickly, five solid shillings, had been handed to a smartly-dressed lady in an office in Harbeck Street, London, W., in the hope that this very Superior Person would find a situation and a salary for Miss Rolleston.

The Superior Person glanced at the two half-crowns as they lay on the table where Bella's hand had placed them, to make sure they were neither of them florins, before she wrote a description of Bella's qualifications and requirements in a formidable-looking ledger.

"Age?" she asked, curtly.

"Eighteen, last July."

"Any accomplishments?"

"No; I am not at all accomplished. If I were I should want to be a governess—a companion seems the lowest stage."

"We have some highly accomplished ladies on our books as companions, or chaperon companions."

"Oh, I know!" babbled Bella, loquacious in her youthful candor. "But that is quite a different thing. Mother hasn't been able to afford a piano since I was twelve years old, so I'm afraid I've forgotten how to play. And I have had to help mother with her needlework, so there hasn't been much time to study."

"Please don't waste time upon explaining what you can't do, but kindly tell me anything you can do," said the Superior Person, crushingly, with her pen poised between delicate fingers waiting to write. "Can you read aloud for two or three hours at a stretch? Are you active and handy, an early riser, a good walker, sweet tempered, and obliging?"

"I can say yes to all those questions except about the sweetness. I think I have a pretty good temper, and I should be anxious to oblige anybody who paid for my services. I should want them to feel that I was really earning my salary."

"The kind of ladies who come to me would not care for a talkative companion," said the Person, severely, having finished writing in her book. "My connection lies chiefly among the aristocracy, and in that class considerable deference is expected."

"Oh, of course," said Bella, "but it's quite different when I'm talking to you. I want to tell you all about myself once and forever."

"I am glad it is to be only once!" said the Person, with the edges of her lips.

The Person was of uncertain age, tightly laced in a black silk gown. She had a powdery complexion and a handsome clump of somebody else's hair on the top of her head. It may be that Bella's girlish freshness and vivacity had an irritating effect upon nerves weakened by an eight-hour day in that overheated second floor in Harbeck Street. To Bella the official apartment, with its Brussels carpet, velvet curtains and velvet chairs, and French clock, ticking loud on the marble chimney-piece, suggested the luxury of a palace, as compared with another second floor in Walworth where Mrs. Rolleston and her daughter had managed to exist for the last six years.

"Do you think you have anything on your books that would suit me?" faltered Bella, after a pause.

"Oh, dear, no; I have nothing in view at present," answered the Person, who had swept Bella's half-crowns into a drawer, absent-mindedly, with the tips of her fingers. "You see, you are so very unformed—so much too young to be companion to a lady of position. It is a pity you have not enough education for a nursery governess; that would be more in your line."

"And do you think it will be very long before you can get me a situation?" asked Bella, doubtfully.

"I really cannot say. Have you any particular reason for being so impatient—not a love affair, I hope?"

"A love affair!" cried Bella, with flaming cheeks. "What utter nonsense. I want a situation because mother is poor, and I hate being a burden to her. I want a salary that I can share with her."

"There won't be much margin for sharing in the salary you are likely to get at your age—and with your—very—unformed manners," said the Person, who found Bella's peony cheeks, bright eyes, and unbridled vivacity more and more oppressive.

"Perhaps if you'd be kind enough to give me back the fee I could take it to an agency where the connection isn't quite so aristocratic," said Bella, who—as she told her mother in her recital of the interview—was determined not to be sat upon.

"You will find no agency that can do more for you than mine," replied the Person, whose harpy fingers never relinquished coin. "You will have to wait for your opportunity. Yours is an exceptional case: but I will bear you in mind, and if anything suitable offers I will write to you. I cannot say more than that."

The half-contemptuous bend of the stately head, weighted with borrowed hair, indicated the end of the interview. Bella went back to Walworth—tramped sturdily every inch of the way in the September afternoon—and "took off" the Superior Person for the amusement of her mother and the landlady, who lingered in the shabby little sitting-room after bringing in the tea-tray, to applaud Miss Rolleston's "taking off."

"Dear, dear, what a mimic she is!" said the landlady. "You ought to have let her go on the stage, mum. She might have made her fortune as an actress."

# II

Bella waited and hoped, and listened for the postman's knocks which brought such store of letters for the parlors and the first floor, and so few for that humble second floor, where mother and daughter sat sewing with hand and with wheel and treadle, for the greater part of the day. Mrs. Rolleston was a lady by birth and education; but it had been her bad fortune to marry a scoundrel; for the last half-dozen years she had been that worst of widows, a wife whose husband had deserted her. Happily, she was courageous, industrious, and a clever needlewoman; and she had been able just to earn a living for herself and her only child, by making mantles and cloaks for a West-end house. It was not a luxurious living. Cheap lodgings in a shabby street off the Walworth Road, scanty dinners, homely food, well-worn raiment, had been the portion of mother and daughter; but they loved each other so dearly, and Nature had made them both so light-hearted, that they had contrived somehow to be happy.

But now this idea of going out into the world as companion to some fine lady had rooted itself into Bella's mind, and although she idolized her mother, and although the parting of mother and daughter must needs tear two loving hearts into shreds, the girl longed for enterprise and change and excitement, as the pages of old longed to be knights, and to start for the Holy Land to break a lance with the infidel.

She grew tired of racing downstairs every time the postman knocked, only to be told "nothing for you, miss," by the smudgy-faced drudge who picked up the letters from the passage floor. "Nothing for you, miss," grinned the lodging-house drudge, till at last Bella took heart of grace and walked up to Harbeck Street, and asked the Superior Person how it was that no situation had been found for her.

"You are too young," said the Person, "and you want a salary."

"Of course I do," answered Bella. "Don't other people want salaries?"

"Young ladies of your age generally want a comfortable home."

"I don't," snapped Bella. "I want to help mother."

"You can call again this day week," said the Person, "or, if I hear of anything in the meantime, I will write to you."

No letter came from the Person, and in exactly a week Bella put on her nearest hat, the one that had been seldomest caught in the rain, and trudged off to Harbeck Street.

It was a dull October afternoon, and there was a greyness in the air which might turn to fog before night. The Walworth Road shops gleamed brightly through that grey atmosphere, and though to a young lady reared in Mayfair or Belgravia such shop-windows would have been unworthy of a glance, they were a snare and temptation for Bella. There were so many things that she longed for, and would never be able to buy.

Harbeck Street is apt to be empty at this dead season of the year, a long, long street, an endless perspective of eminently respectable houses. The Person's office was at the further end, and Bella looked down that long, grey vista almost despairingly, more tired than usual with the trudge from Walworth. As she looked, a carriage passed her, an old-fashioned, yellow chariot, on cee springs, drawn by a pair of high grey horses, with the stateliest of coachmen driving them, and a tall footman sitting by his side.

"It looks like the fairy godmother's coach," thought Bella. "I shouldn't wonder if it began by being a pumpkin."

It was a surprise when she reached the Person's door to find the yellow chariot standing before it, and the tall footman waiting near the doorstep. She was almost afraid to go in and meet the owner of that splendid carriage. She had caught only a glimpse of its occupant as the chariot rolled by, a plumed bonnet, a patch of ermine.

The Person's smart page ushered her upstairs and knocked at the official door. "Miss Rolleston," he announced, apologetically, while Bella waited outside.

"Show her in," said the Person, quickly; and then Bella heard her murmuring something in a low voice to her client.

Bella went in fresh, blooming, a living image of youth and hope, and before she looked at the Person her gaze was riveted by the owner of the chariot.

Never had she seen anyone as old as the old lady sitting by the Person's fire: a little old figure, wrapped from chin to feet in an ermine mantle; a withered, old face under a plumed bonnet—a face so wasted by age that it seemed only a pair of eyes and a peaked chin. The nose was peaked, too, but between the sharply pointed chin and the great, shining eyes, the small, aquiline nose was hardly visible.

"This is Miss Rolleston, Lady Ducayne."

Claw-like fingers, flashing with jewels, lifted a double eyeglass to Lady Ducayne's shining black eyes, and through the glasses Bella saw those unnaturally bright eyes magnified to a gigantic size, and glaring at her awfully.

"Miss Torpinter has told me all about you,"

said the old voice that belonged to the eyes. "Have you good health? Are you strong and active, able to eat well, sleep well, walk well, able to enjoy all that there is good in life?"

"I have never known what it is to be ill, or idle," answered Bella.

"Then I think you will do for me."

"Of course, in the event of references being perfectly satisfactory," put in the Person.

"I don't want references. The young woman looks frank and innocent. I'll take her on trust."

"So like you, dear Lady Ducayne," murmured Miss Torpinter.

"I want a strong young woman whose health will give me no trouble."

"You have been so unfortunate in that respect," cooed the Person, whose voice and manner were subdued to a melting sweetness by the old woman's presence.

"Yes, I've been rather unlucky," grunted Lady Ducayne.

"But I am sure Miss Rolleston will not disappoint you, though certainly after your unpleasant experience with Miss Tomson, who looked the picture of health—and Miss Blandy, who said she had never seen a doctor since she was vaccinated—"

"Lies, no doubt," muttered Lady Ducayne, and then turning to Bella, she asked, curtly, "You don't mind spending the winter in Italy, I suppose?"

In Italy! The very word was magical. Bella's fair young face flushed crimson.

"It has been the dream of my life to see Italy," she gasped.

From Walworth to Italy! How far, how impossible such a journey had seemed to that romantic dreamer.

"Well, your dream will be realized. Get yourself ready to leave Charing Cross by the train deluxe this day week at eleven. Be sure you are at the station a quarter before the hour. My people will look after you and your luggage."

Lady Ducayne rose from her chair, assisted by her crutch-stick, and Miss Torpinter escorted her to the door.

"And with regard to salary?" questioned the Person on the way.

"Salary, oh, the same as usual—and if the young woman wants a quarter's pay in advance you can write to me for a check," Lady Ducayne answered, carelessly.

Miss Torpinter went all the way downstairs with her client, and waited to see her seated in the yellow chariot. When she came upstairs again she was slightly out of breath, and she had resumed that superior manner which Bella had found so crushing.

"You may think yourself uncommonly lucky, Miss Rolleston," she said. "I have dozens of young ladies on my books whom I might have recommended for this situation—but I remembered having told you to call this afternoon—and I thought I would give you a chance. Old Lady Ducayne is one of the best people on my books. She gives her companion a hundred a year, and pays all the travelling expenses. You will live in the lap of luxury."

"A hundred a year! How too lovely! Shall I have to dress very grandly? Does Lady Ducayne keep much company?"

"At her age! No, she lives in seclusion—in her own apartments—her French maid, her footman, her medical attendant, her courier."

"Why did those other companions leave her?" asked Bella.

"Their health broke down!"

"Poor things, and so they had to leave?"

"Yes, they had to leave. I suppose you would like a quarter's salary in advance?"

"Oh, yes, please. I shall have things to buy."

"Very well, I will write for Lady Ducayne's check, and I will send you the balance—after deducting my commission for the year."

"To be sure, I had forgotten the commission."

"You don't suppose I keep this office for pleasure."

"Of course not," murmured Bella, remembering the five shillings entrance fee; but nobody could expect a hundred a year and a winter in Italy for five shillings.

7

# III

From Miss Rolleston, at Cap Ferrino, to Mrs. Rolleston, in Beresford Street, Walworth, London.

*How I wish you could see this place, dearest; the blue sky, the olive woods, the orange and lemon orchards between the cliffs and the sea—sheltering in the hollow of the great hills—and with summer waves dancing up to the narrow ridge of pebbles and weeds which is the Italian idea of a beach! Oh, how I wish you could see it all, mother dear, and bask in this sunshine, that makes it so difficult to believe the date at the head of this paper. November! The air is like an English June—the sun is so hot that I can't walk a few yards without an umbrella. And to think of you at Walworth while I am here! I could cry at the thought that perhaps you will never see this lovely coast, this wonderful sea, these summer flowers that bloom in winter. There is a hedge of pink geraniums under my window, mother—a thick, rank hedge, as if the flowers grew wild—and there are Dijon roses climbing over arches and palisades all along the terrace—a rose garden full of bloom in November! Just picture it all! You could never imagine the luxury of this hotel. It is nearly new, and has been built and decorated regardless of expense. Our rooms are uphol-stered in pale blue satin, which shows up Lady Ducayne's parchment complexion; but as she sits all day in a corner of the balcony basking in the sun, except when she is in her carriage, and all the evening in her armchair close to the fire, and never sees anyone but her own people, her complexion matters very little.*

*She has the handsomest suite of rooms in the hotel. My bedroom is inside hers, the sweet-est room—all blue satin and white lace—white enamelled furniture, looking-glasses on every wall, till I know my pert little profile as I never knew it before. The room was really meant for Lady Ducayne's dressing-room, but she ordered one of the blue satin couches to be arranged as a bed for me—the prettiest little bed, which I can wheel near the window on sunny mornings, as it is on castors and easily moved about. I feel as if Lady Ducayne were a funny old grand-mother, who had suddenly appeared in my life, very, very rich, and very, very kind.*

*She is not at all exacting. I read aloud to her a good deal, and she dozes and nods while I read. Sometimes I hear her moaning in her sleep—as if she had troublesome dreams. When she is tired of my reading she orders Francine, her maid, to read a French novel to her, and I hear her chuckle and groan now and then, as if she were more interested in those books than in Dickens or Scott. My French is not good enough to follow Francine, who reads very quickly. I have a great deal of liberty, for Lady Ducayne often tells me to run away and amuse myself; I roam about the hills for hours. Every-thing is so lovely. I lose myself in olive woods, always climbing up and up towards the pine woods above—and above the pines there are the snow mountains that just show their white peaks above the dark hills. Oh, you poor dear, how can I ever make you understand what this place is like—you, whose poor, tired eyes have only the opposite side of Beresford Street? Some-times I go no farther than the terrace in front of the hotel, which is a favorite lounging-place with everybody. The gardens lie below, and the tennis courts where I sometimes play with a very nice girl, the only person in the hotel with whom I have made friends. She is a year older than I, and has come to Cap Ferrino with her brother, a doctor—or a medical student, who is going to be a doctor. He passed his M.B. exam at Edinburgh just before they left home, Lotta told me. He came to Italy entirely on his sister's account. She had a troublesome chest attack last summer and was ordered to winter abroad. They are orphans, quite alone in the world, and so fond of each other. It is very nice for me to have such a friend as Lotta. She is so thoroughly respectable. I can't help using that* word, for some of the girls in this hotel go on in a way that I know you would shudder at. Lotta was brought up by an aunt, deep down in the country, and knows hardly anything about life. Her brother won't allow her to read a novel, French or English, that he has not read and approved.

"He treats me like a child," she told me, "but I don't mind, for it's nice to know somebody loves me, and cares about what I do, and even about my thoughts."

Perhaps this is what makes some girls so eager to marry—the want of someone strong and brave and honest and true to care for them and order them about. I want no one, mother darling, for I have you, and you are all the world to me. No husband could ever come between us two. If I ever were to marry he would have only the second place in my heart. But I don't suppose I ever shall marry, or even know what it is like to have an offer of marriage. No young man can afford to marry a penniless girl nowadays. Life is too expensive.

Mr. Stafford, Lotta's brother, is very clever, and very kind. He thinks it is rather hard for me to have to live with such an old woman as Lady Ducayne, but then he does not know how poor we are—you and I—and what a wonderful life this seems to me in this lovely place. I feel a selfish wretch for enjoying all my luxuries, while you, who want them so much more than I, have none of them—hardly know what they are like—do you, dearest?—for my scamp of a father began to go to the dogs soon after you were married, and since then life has been all trouble and care and struggle for you.

This letter was written when Bella had been less than a month at Cap Ferrino, before the novelty had worn off the landscape, and before the pleasure of luxurious surroundings had begun to cloy. She wrote to her mother every week, such long letters as girls who have lived in closest companionship with a mother alone can write; letters that are like a diary of heart and mind. She wrote gaily

always, but when the new year began Mrs. Rolleston thought she detected a note of melancholy under all those lively details about the place and the people.

"My poor girl is getting homesick," she thought. "Her heart is in Beresford Street."

It might be that she missed her new friend and companion, Lotta Stafford, who had gone with her brother for a little tour to Genoa and Spezia, and as far as Pisa. They were to return before February; but in the meantime Bella might naturally feel very solitary among all those strangers, whose manners and doings she described so well.

The mother's instinct had been true. Bella was not so happy as she had been in that first flush of wonder and delight which followed the change from Walworth to the Riviera. Somehow, she knew not how, lassitude had crept upon her. She no longer loved to climb the hills, no longer flourished her orange stick in sheer gladness of heart as her light feet skipped over the rough ground and the coarse grass on the mountain side. The odor of rosemary and thyme, the fresh breath of the sea no longer filled her with rapture. She thought of Beresford Street and her mother's face with a sick longing. They were so far—so far away! And then she thought of Lady Ducayne, sitting by the heaped-up olive logs in the overheated salon—thought of that wizened-nutcracker profile, and those gleaming eyes, with an invincible horror.

Visitors at the hotel had told her that the air of Cap Ferrino was relaxing—better suited to age than to youth, to sickness than to health. No doubt it was so. She was not so well as she had been at Walworth; but she told herself that she was suffering only from the pain of separation from the dear companion of her girlhood, the mother who had been nurse, sister, friend, flatterer, all things in this world to her. She had shed many tears over that parting, had spent many a melancholy hour on the marble terrace with yearning eyes looking westward, and with her heart's desire a thousand miles away.

She was sitting in her favorite spot, an angle at

the eastern end of the terrace, a quiet little nook sheltered by orange trees, when she heard a couple of Riviera habitués talking in the garden below. They were sitting on a bench against the terrace wall.

She had no idea of listening to their talk, till the sound of Lady Ducayne's name attracted her, and then she listened without any thought of wrong-doing. They were talking no secrets—just casually discussing a hotel acquaintance.

They were two elderly people whom Bella only knew by sight. An English clergyman who had wintered abroad for half his lifetime; a stout, comfortable, well-to-do spinster, whose chronic bronchitis obliged her to migrate annually.

"I have met her about Italy for the last ten years," said the lady, "but have never found out her real age."

"I put her down at a hundred—not a year less," replied the parson. "Her reminiscences all go back to the Regency. She was evidently then in her zenith; and I have heard her say things that showed she was in Parisian society when the First Empire was at its best—before Josephine was divorced."

"She doesn't talk much now."

"No, there's not much life left in her. She is wise in keeping herself secluded. I only wonder that wicked old quack, her Italian doctor, didn't finish her off years ago."

"I should think it must be the other way, and that he keeps her alive."

"My dear Miss Manders, do you think foreign quackery ever kept anybody alive?"

"Well, there she is—and she never goes anywhere without him. He certainly has an unpleasant countenance."

"Unpleasant," echoed the parson. "I don't believe the foul fiend himself can beat him in ugliness. I pity that poor young woman who has to live between old Lady Ducayne and Dr. Parravicini."

"But the old lady is very good to her companions."

"No doubt. She is very free with her cash; the servants call her good Lady Ducayne. She is a withered old female Croesus, and knows she'll never be able to get through her money, and doesn't relish the idea of other people enjoying it when she's in her coffin. People who live to be as old as she is become slavishly attached to life. I daresay she's generous to those poor girls—but she can't make them happy. They die in her service."

"Don't say 'they,' Mr. Carton; I know that one poor girl died at Mentone last spring."

"Yes, and another poor girl died in Rome three years ago. I was there at the time. Good Lady Ducayne left her there in an English family. The girl had every comfort. The old woman was very liberal to her—but she died. I tell you, Miss Manders, it is not good for any young woman to live with two such horrors as Lady Ducayne and Parravicini."

They talked of other things—but Bella hardly heard them. She sat motionless, and a cold wind seemed to come down upon her from the mountains and to creep up to her from the sea, till she shivered as she sat there in the sunshine, in the shelter of the orange trees in the midst of all that beauty and brightness.

Yes, they were uncanny, certainly, the pair of them—she so like an aristocratic witch in her withered old age; he of no particular age, with a face that was more like a waxen mask than any human countenance Bella had ever seen. What did it matter? Old age is venerable, and worthy of all reverence; and Lady Ducayne had been very kind to her. Dr. Parravicini was a harmless, inoffensive student, who seldom looked up from the book he was reading. He had his private sitting-room, where he made experiments in chemistry and natural science—perhaps in alchemy. What could it matter to Bella? He had always been polite to her, in his far-off way. She could not be more happily placed than she was—in this palatial hotel, with this rich old lady.

No doubt she missed the young English girl who had been so friendly, and it might be that she missed the girl's brother, for Mr. Stafford had talked to her a good deal—had interested himself in the books she was reading, and her manner of amusing herself when she was not on duty.

"You must come to our little salon when you

are 'off,' as the hospital nurses call it, and we can have some music. No doubt you play and sing?" Upon which Bella had to own with a blush of shame that she had forgotten how to play the piano ages ago.

"Mother and I used to sing duets sometimes between the lights, without accompaniment," she said, and the tears came into her eyes as she thought of the humble room, the half-hour's respite from work, the sewing machine standing where a piano ought to have been, and her mother's plaintive voice, so sweet, so true, so dear.

Sometimes she found herself wondering whether she would ever see that beloved mother again. Strange forebodings came into her mind. She was angry with herself for giving way to melancholy thoughts.

One day she questioned Lady Ducayne's French maid about those two companions who had died within three years.

"They were poor, feeble creatures," Francine told her. "They looked fresh and bright enough when they came to Miladi, but they ate too much, and they were lazy. They died of luxury and idleness. Miladi was too kind to them. They had nothing to do, and so they took to fancying things; fancying the air didn't suit them, that they couldn't sleep."

"I sleep well enough, but I have had a strange dream several times since I have been in Italy."

"Ah, you had better not begin to think about dreams, or you will be like those other girls. They were dreamers—and they dreamt themselves into the cemetery."

The dream troubled her a little, not because it was a ghastly or frightening dream, but on account of sensations which she had never felt before in sleep—a whirring of wheels that went round in her brain, a great noise like a whirlwind, but rhythmical like the ticking of a gigantic clock: and then in the midst of this uproar as of winds and waves she seemed to sink into a gulf of unconsciousness, out of sleep into far deeper sleep— total extinction. And then, after that black interval, there had come the sound of voices, and then again the whirr of wheels, louder and louder—and again

the black—and then she awoke, feeling languid and oppressed.

She told Dr. Parravicini of her dream one day, on the only occasion when she wanted his professional advice. She had suffered rather severely from the mosquitoes before Christmas—and had been almost frightened at finding a wound upon her arm which she could only attribute to the venomous sting of one of these torturers. Parravicini put on his glasses, and scrutinized the angry mark on the round, white arm, as Bella stood before him and Lady Ducayne with her sleeve rolled up above her elbow.

"Yes, that's rather more than a joke," he said. "He has caught you on the top of a vein. What a vampire! But there's no harm done, signorina, nothing that a little dressing of mine won't heal. You must always show me any bite of this nature. It might be dangerous if neglected. These creatures feed on poison and disseminate it."

"And to think that such tiny creatures can bite like this," said Bella. "My arm looks as if it had been cut by a knife."

"If I were to show you a mosquito's sting under my microscope you wouldn't be surprised at that," replied Parravicini.

Bella had to put up with the mosquito bites, even when they came on the top of a vein, and produced that ugly wound. The wound recurred now and then at longish intervals, and Bella found Dr. Parravicini's dressing a speedy cure. If he were the quack his enemies called him, he had at least a light hand and a delicate touch in performing this small operation.

Bella Rolleston to Mrs. Rolleston—April 14th.

*Ever Dearest,*

*Behold the check for my second quarter's salary—five and twenty pounds. There is no one to pinch off a whole tenner for a year's commission as there was last time, so it is all for you, mother, dear. I have plenty of pocket-money in hand from the cash I brought away with me, when you insisted on my keeping more than I wanted. It isn't possible to spend money here—except on occasional tips to servants, or sous to beggars and children—unless one had lots to spend, for everything one would like to buy—tortoise-shell, coral, lace—is so ridiculously dear that only a millionaire ought to look at it. Italy is a dream of beauty; but for shopping, give me Newington Causeway.*

*You ask me so earnestly if I am quite well that I fear my letters must have been very dull lately. Yes, dear, I am well—but I am not quite so strong as I was when I used to trudge to the West-end to buy half a pound of tea—just for a constitutional walk—or to Dulwich to look at the pictures. Italy is relaxing, and I feel what the people here call "slack." But I fancy I can see your dear face looking worried as you read this.Indeed, and indeed, I am not ill. I am only a little tired of this lovely scene—as I suppose one might get tired of looking at one of Turner's pictures if it hung on a wall that was always opposite one. I think of you every hour in every day—think of you and our homely little room—our dear little shabby parlor, with the armchairs from the wreck of your old home, and Dick singing in his cage over the sewing machine. Dear, shrill, maddening Dick, who, we flattered ourselves, was so passionately fond of us. Do tell me in your next letter that he is well.*

*My friend Lotta and her brother never came back after all. They went from Pisa to Rome. Happy mortals! And they are to be on the Italian lakes in May; which lake was not decided when Lotta last wrote to me. She has been a charming correspondent, and has confided all her little flirtations to me. We are all to go to Bellaggio next week—by Genoa and Milan. Isn't that lovely? Lady Ducayne travels by the easiest stages—except when she is bottled up in the train deluxe. We shall stop two days at Genoa and one at Milan. What a bore I shall be to you with my talk about Italy when I come home.*

*Love and love—and ever more love from your adoring,*

BELLA.

## IV

Herbert Stafford and his sister had often talked of the pretty English girl with her fresh complexion, which made such a pleasant touch of rosy color among all those sallow faces at the Grand Hotel. The young doctor thought of her with a compassionate tenderness—her utter loneliness in that great hotel where there were so many people, her bondage to that old, old woman, where everybody else was free to think of nothing but enjoying life. It was a hard fate, and the poor child was evidently devoted to her mother, and felt the pain of separation—"only two of them, and very poor, and all the world to each other," he thought.

Lotta told him one morning that they were to meet again at Bellaggio. "The old thing and her court are to be there before we are," she said. "I shall be charmed to have Bella again. She is so bright and gay—in spite of an occasional touch of homesickness. I never took to a girl on a short acquaintance as I did to her."

"I like her best when she is homesick," said Herbert, "for then I am sure she has a heart."

"What have you to do with hearts, except for dissection? Don't forget that Bella is an absolute pauper. She told me in confidence that her mother makes mantles for a West-end shop. You can hardly have a lower depth than that."

"I shouldn't think any less of her if her mother made matchboxes."

"Not in the abstract—of course not. Matchboxes are honest labor. But you couldn't marry a girl whose mother makes mantles."

"We haven't come to the consideration of that question yet," answered Herbert, who liked to provoke his sister.

In two years' hospital practice he had seen too much of the grim realities of life to retain any prejudices about rank. Cancer, phthisis, gangrene leave a man with little respect for the humanity. The kernel is always the same—fearfully and wonderfully made—a subject for pity and terror.

Mr. Stafford and his sister arrived at Bellaggio in a fair May evening. The sun was going down as the steamer approached the pier; and all that glory of purple bloom which curtains every wall at this season of the year flushed and deepened in the glowing light. A group of ladies were standing on the pier watching the arrivals, and among them Herbert saw a pale face that startled him out of his wonted composure.

"There she is," murmured Lotta, at his elbow, "but how dreadfully changed. She looks a wreck."

They were shaking hands with her a few minutes later, and a flush had lighted up her poor pinched face in the pleasure of meeting.

"I thought you might come this evening," she said. "We have been here a week."

She did not add that she had been there every evening to watch the boat in, and a good many times during the day. The Grand Bretagne was close by, and it had been easy for her to creep to the pier when the boat bell rang. She felt a joy in meeting these people again; a sense of being with friends; a confidence which Lady Ducayne's goodness had never inspired in her.

"Oh, you poor darling, how awfully ill you must have been," exclaimed Lotta, as the two girls embraced.

Bella tried to answer, but her voice was choked with tears.

"What has been the matter, dear? That horrid influenza, I suppose?"

"No, no, I have not been ill—I have only felt a little weaker than I used to be. I don't think the air of Cap Ferrino quite agreed with me."

"It must have disagreed with you abominably. I never saw such a change in anyone. Do let Herbert doctor you. He is fully qualified, you know. He prescribed for ever so many influenza patients at the Londres. They were glad to get advice from an English doctor in a friendly way."

"I am sure he must be very clever!" faltered Bella. "But there is really nothing the matter. I am not ill, and if I were ill, Lady Ducayne's physician—"

"That dreadful man with the yellow face? I would as soon one of the Borgias prescribed for me. I hope you haven't been taking any of his medicines."

"No, dear, I have taken nothing. I have never complained of being ill."

This was said while they were all three walking to the hotel. The Staffords' rooms had been secured in advance, pretty ground-floor rooms, opening into the garden. Lady Ducayne's statelier apartments were on the floor above.

"I believe these rooms are just under ours," said Bella.

"Then it will be all the easier for you to run down to us," replied Lotta, which was not really the case, as the grand staircase was in the center of the hotel.

"Oh, I shall find it easy enough," said Bella. "I'm afraid you'll have too much of my society. Lady Ducayne sleeps away half the day in this warm weather, so I have a good deal of idle time; and I get awfully moped thinking of mother and home."

Her voice broke upon the last word. She could not have thought of that poor lodging which went by the name of home more tenderly had it been the most beautiful that art and wealth ever created. She moped and pined in this lovely garden, with the sunlit lake and the romantic hills spreading out their beauty before her. She was homesick and she had dreams; or, rather, an occasional recurrence of that one bad dream with all its strange sensations—it was more like a hallucination than dreaming—the whirring of wheels, the sinking into an abyss, the struggling back to consciousness. She had the dream shortly before she left Cap Ferrino, but not since she had come to Bellaggio, and she began to hope the air in this lake district suited her better, and that those strange sensations would never return.

Mr. Stafford wrote a prescription and had it made up at the chemist's near the hotel. It was a powerful tonic, and after two bottles, and a row or two on the lake, and some rambling over the hills and in the meadows where the spring flowers made earth seem paradise, Bella's spirits and looks improved as if by magic.

"It is a wonderful tonic," she said, but perhaps in her heart of hearts she knew that the doctor's kind voice, and the friendly hand that helped her in and out of the boat, and the lake, had something to do with her cure.

"I hope you don't forget that her mother makes mantles," Lotta said warningly.

"Or matchboxes; it is just the same thing, so far as I am concerned."

"You mean that in no circumstances could you think of marrying her?"

"I mean that if ever I love a woman well enough to think of marrying her, riches or rank will count for nothing with me. But I fear—I fear your poor friend may not live to be any man's wife."

"Do you think her so very ill?"

He sighed, and left the question unanswered.

One day, while they were gathering wild hyacinths in an upland meadow, Bella told Mr. Stafford about her bad dream.

"It is curious only because it is hardly like a dream," she said. "I daresay you could find some commonsense reason for it. The position of my head on my pillow, or the atmosphere, or something."

And then she described her sensations: how in the midst of sleep there came a sudden sense of suffocation; and then those whirring wheels, so loud, so terrible; and then a blank; and then a coming back to waking consciousness.

"Have you ever had chloroform given you—by a dentist, for instance?"

"Never—Dr. Parravicini asked me that question one day."

"Lately?"

"No, long ago, when were were in the train deluxe."

"Has Dr. Parravicini prescribed for you since you began to feel weak and ill?"

"Oh, he has given me a tonic from time to time, but I hate medicine, and took very little of the stuff. And then I am not ill, only weaker than I used to be. I was ridiculously strong and well when I lived at Walworth, and used to take long walks every day. Mother made me take those tramps to Dulwich or Norwood, for fear I should suffer from too much sewing machine; sometimes—but very seldom—she went with me. She was generally toiling at home while I was enjoying fresh air and exercise. And she was very careful about our food—that, however plain it was, it should be always nourishing and ample. I owe it to her care that I grew up such a great, strong creature."

"You don't look great or strong now, you poor dear," said Lotta.

"I'm afraid Italy doesn't agree with me."

"Perhaps it is not Italy, but being cooped up with Lady Ducayne that has made you ill."

"But I am never cooped up. Lady Ducayne is absurdly kind, and lets me roam about or sit in the balcony all day if I like. I have read more novels since I have been with her than in all the rest of my life."

"Then she is very different from the average old lady, who is usually a slave driver," said Stafford. "I wonder why she carries a companion about with her if she has so little need of society."

"Oh, I am only part of her state. She is inordinately rich—and the salary she gives me doesn't count. Apropos of Dr. Parravicini, I know he is a clever doctor, for he cures my horrid mosquito bites."

"A little ammonia would do that, in the early stage of the mischief. But there are no mosquitoes to trouble you now."

"Oh, yes, there are; I had a bite just before we left Cap Ferrino." She pushed up her loose lawn sleeve, and exhibited a scar, which he scrutinized intently, with a surprised and puzzled look.

"This is no mosquito bite," he said.

"Oh, yes it is—unless there are snakes or adders at Cap Ferrino."

"It is not a bite at all. You are trifling with me. Miss Rolleston—you have allowed that wretched Italian quack to bleed you. They killed the greatest man in modern Europe that way, remember. How very foolish of you."

"I was never bled in my life, Mr. Stafford."

"Nonsense! Let me look at your other arm. Are there any more mosquito bites?"

"Yes; Dr. Parravicini says I have a bad skin for healing, and that the poison acts more virulently with me than with most people."

Stafford examined both her arms in the broad sunlight, scars new and old.

"You have been very badly bitten, Miss Rolleston," he said, "and if ever I find the mosquito I shall make him smart. But, now tell me, my dear girl, on your word of honor, tell me as you would tell a friend who is sincerely anxious for your health and happiness—as you would tell your mother if she were here to question you—have you no knowledge of any cause for these scars except mosquito bites—no suspicion even?"

"No, indeed! No, upon my honor! I have never seen a mosquito biting my arm. One never does see the horrid little fiends. But I have heard them trumpeting under the curtains and I know that I have often had one of the pestilent wretches buzzing about me."

Later in the day Bella and her friends were sitting at tea in the garden, while Lady Ducayne took her afternoon drive with her doctor.

"How long do you mean to stop with Lady Ducayne, Miss Rolleston?" Herbert Stafford asked, after a thoughtful silence, breaking suddenly upon the trivial talk of the two girls.

"As long as she will go on paying me twenty-five pounds a quarter."

"Even if you feel your health breaking down in her service?"

"It is not the service that has injured my health. You can see that I have really nothing to do—to read aloud for an hour or so once or twice a week; to write a letter once in a while to a London tradesman. I shall never have such an easy time with anybody. And nobody else would give me a hundred a year."

"Then you mean to go on till you break down; to die at your post?"

"Like the other two companions? No! If ever I feel seriously ill—really ill—I shall put myself in a train and go back to Walworth without stopping."

"What about the other two companions?"

"They both died. It was very unlucky for Lady Ducayne. That's why she engaged me; she chose me because I was ruddy and robust. She must feel rather disgusted at my having grown white and weak. By-the-bye, when I told her about the good your tonic had done me, she said she would like to see you and have a little talk with you about her own case."

"And I should like to see Lady Ducayne. When did she say this?"

"The day before yesterday."

"Will you ask her if she will see me this evening?"

"With pleasure! I wonder what you will think of her? She looks rather terrible to a stranger; but Dr. Parravicini says she was once a famous beauty."

It was nearly ten o'clock when Mr. Stafford was summoned by message from Lady Ducayne, whose courier came to conduct him to her ladyship's salon. Bella was reading aloud when the visitor was admitted; and he noticed the languor in the low, sweet tones, the evident effort.

"Shut up the book," said the querulous old voice. "You are beginning to drawl like Miss Blandy."

Stafford saw a small, bent figure crouching over the piled-up olive logs; a shrunken old figure in a gorgeous garment of black and crimson brocade, a skinny throat emerging from a mass of old Venetian lace, clasped with diamonds that flashed like fireflies as the trembling old head turned towards him.

The eyes that looked at him out of the face were almost as bright as the diamonds—the only living feature in that narrow parchment mask. He had seen terrible faces in the hospital—faces on which disease had set dreadful marks—but he had never seen a face that impressed him so painfully as this withered countenance, with its indescribable horror of death outlived, a face that should have been hidden under a coffin-lid years and years ago.

The Italian physician was standing on the other side of the fireplace, smoking a cigarette, and looking down at the little old woman brooding over the hearth as if he were proud of her.

"Good evening, Mr. Stafford; you can go to your room, Bella, and write your everlasting letter to your mother at Walworth," said Lady Ducayne. "I believe she writes a page about every wild flower she discovers in the woods and meadows. I don't know what else she can find to write about," she added, as Bella quietly withdrew to the pretty little bedroom opening out of Lady Ducayne's spacious apartment. Here, as at Cap Ferrino, she slept in a room adjoining the old lady's.

"You are a medical man, I understand, Mr. Stafford."

"I am a qualified practitioner, but I have not begun to practice."

"You have begun upon my companion, she tells me."

"I have prescribed for her, certainly, and I am happy to find my prescription has done her good, but I look upon that improvement as temporary. Her case will require more drastic treatment."

"Never mind her case. There is nothing the matter with the girl—absolutely nothing—except girlish nonsense; too much liberty and not enough work."

"I understand that two of your ladyship's previous companions died of the same disease," said Stafford, looking first at Lady Ducayne, who gave her tremulous old head an impatient jerk, and then at Parravicini, whose yellow complexion had paled a little under Stafford's scrutiny.

"Don't bother me about my companions, sir," said Lady Ducayne. "I sent for you to consult you about myself—not about a parcel of anemic girls. You are young, and medicine is a progressive science, the newspapers tell me. Where have you studied?"

"In Edinburgh—and in Paris."

"Two good schools. And know all the new-fangled theories, the modern discoveries—that remind one of the medieval witchcraft, of Albertus Magnus, and George Ripley; you have studied hypnotism—electricity?"

"And the transfusion of blood," said Stafford, very slowly, looking at Parravicini.

"Have you made any discovery that teaches you to prolong human life—any elixir—any mode of treatment? I want my life prolonged, young man. That man there has been my physician for thirty years. He does all he can to keep me alive—after his lights. He studies all the new theories of all the scientists—but he is old; he gets older every day—his brain-power is going—he is bigoted—prejudiced—can't receive new ideas—can't grap-

ple with new systems. He will let me die if I am not on my guard against him."

"You are of an unbelievable ingratitude, Ecclenza," said Parravicini.

"Oh, you needn't complain. I have paid you thousands to keep me alive. Every year of my life has swollen your hoards; you know there is nothing to come to you when I am gone. My whole fortune is left to endow a home for indigent women of quality who have reached their ninetieth year. Come, Mr. Stafford, I am a rich woman. Give me a few years more in the sunshine, a few years more above ground, and I will give you the price of a fashionable London practice—I will set you up at the West-end."

"How old are you, Lady Ducayne?"

"I was born the day Louis XVI was guillotined."

"Then I think you have had your share of the sunshine and the pleasures of the earth, and that you should spend your few remaining days in repenting your sins and trying to make atonement for the young lives that have been sacrificed to your love of life."

"What do you mean by that, sir?"

"Oh, Lady Ducayne, need I put your wickedness and your physician's still greater wickedness in plain words? The poor girl who is now in your employment has been reduced from robust health to a condition of absolute danger by Dr. Parravicini's experimental surgery; and I have no doubt those other two young women who broke down in your service were treated by him in the same manner. I could take upon myself to demonstrate—by most convincing evidence, to a jury of medical men—that Dr. Parravicini has been bleeding Miss Rolleston after putting her under chloroform, at intervals, ever since she has been in your service. The deterioration in the girl's health speaks for itself; the lancet marks upon the girl's arms are unmistakable; and her description of a series of sensations, which she calls a dream, points unmistakably to the administration of chloroform while she was sleeping. A practice so nefarious, so murderous, must, if exposed, result in a sentence only less severe than the punishment of murder."

"I laugh," said Parravicini, with an airy motion of his skinny fingers. "I laugh at once at your theories and at your threats. I, Parravicini Leopold, have no fear that the law can question anything I have done."

"Take the girl away, and let me hear no more of her," cried Lady Ducayne, in the thin, old voice, which so poorly matched the energy and fire of the wicked old brain that guided its utterances. "Let her go back to her mother—I want no more girls to die in my service. There are girls enough and to spare in the world, God knows."

"If you ever engage another companion—or take another English girl into your service, Lady Ducayne, I will make all England ring with the story of your wickedness."

"I want no more girls. I don't believe in his experiments. They have been full of danger for me as well as for the girl—an air bubble, and I should be gone. I'll have no more of his dangerous quackery. I'll find some new man—a better man than you, sir, a discoverer like Pasteur, or Virchow, a genius—to keep me alive. Take your girl away, young man. Marry her if you like. I'll write a check for a thousand pounds, and let her go and live on beef and beer, and get strong and plump again. I'll have no more such experiments. Do you hear, Parravicini?" she screamed, vindictively, the yellow, wrinkled face distorted with fury, the eyes glaring at him.

The Staffords carried Bella Rolleston off to Varese next day, she very loath to leave Lady Ducayne, whose liberal salary afforded such help for the dear mother. Herbert Stafford insisted, however, treating Bella as coolly as if he had been the family physician, and she had been given over wholly to his care.

"Do you suppose your mother would let you stop here to die?" he asked. "If Mrs. Rolleston knew how ill you are, she would come post haste to fetch you."

"I shall never be well again till I get back to Walworth," answered Bella, who was low-spirited and inclined to tears this morning, a reaction after her good spirits of yesterday.

"We'll try a week or two at Varese first," said Stafford. "When you can walk halfway up Monte Generoso without palpitation of the heart, you shall go back to Walworth."

"Poor mother, how glad she will be to see me, and how sorry that I've lost such a good place."

This conversation took place on the boat when they were leaving Bellaggio. Lotta had gone to her friend's room at seven o'clock that morning, long before Lady Ducayne's withered eyelids had opened to the daylight, before even Francine, the French maid, was astir, and had helped to pack a Gladstone bag with essentials, and hustled Bella downstairs and out of doors before she could make any strenuous resistance.

"It's all right," Lotta assured her. "Herbert had a good talk with Lady Ducayne last night, and it was settled for you to leave this morning. She doesn't like invalids, you see."

"No," sighed Bella, "she doesn't like invalids. It was very unlucky that I should break down, just like Miss Tomson and Miss Blandy."

"At any rate, you are not dead, like them," answered Lotta, "and my brother says you are not going to die."

It seemed rather a dreadful thing to be dismissed in that offhand way, without a word of farewell from her employer.

"I wonder what Miss Torpinter will say when I go to her for another situation," Bella speculated, ruefully, while she and her friends were breakfasting on board the steamer.

"Perhaps you may never want another situation," said Stafford.

"You mean that I may never be well enough to be useful to anybody?"

"No, I don't mean anything of the kind."

It was after dinner at Varese, when Bella had been induced to take a whole glass of Chianti, and quite sparkled after that unaccustomed stimulant, that Mr. Stafford produced a letter from his pocket.

"I forgot to give you Lady Ducayne's letter of adieu!" he said.

"What, did she write to me? I am so glad—I hated to leave her in such a cool way; for after all she was very kind to me, and if I didn't like her it was only because she was too dreadfully old."

She tore open the envelope. The letter was short and to the point:—

*Goodbye, child. Go and marry your doctor. I enclose a farewell gift for your trousseau.*
—ADELINE DUCAYNE

"A hundred pounds, a whole year's salary—no—why, it's for a— A check for a thousand!" cried Bella. "What a generous old soul! She really is the dearest old thing."

"She just missed being very dear to you, Bella," said Stafford.

He had dropped into the use of her Christian name while they were on board the boat. It seemed natural now that she was to be in his charge till they all three went back to England.

"I shall take upon myself the privileges of an elder brother till we land at Dover," he said. "After that—well, it must be as you please."

The question of their future relations must have been satisfactorily settled before they crossed the Channel, for Bella's next letter to her mother communicated three startling facts.

First, that the inclosed check for £1,000 was to be invested in debenture stock in Mrs. Rolleston's name, and was to be her very own, income and principal, for the rest of her life.

Next, that Bella was going home to Walworth immediately.

And last, that she was going to be married to Mr. Herbert Stafford in the following autumn.

"And I am sure you will adore him, mother, as much as I do," wrote Bella.

"It is all good Lady Ducayne's doing. I never could have married if I had not secured that little nest-egg for you. Herbert says we shall be able to add to it as the years go by, and that wherever we live there shall be always a room in our house for you. The word 'mother-in-law' has no terrors for him."

# THE LAST LORDS OF GARDONAL

# William Gilbert

William Gilbert (1804–90) was born in Bishopstoke, Hampshire, England, and moved to London when he was seven. He served as a midshipman for the East India Company and later was an assistant surgeon in the navy for several years. Such early novels as *Dives and Lazarus; or, the Adventures of an Obscure Medical Man in a Low Neighborhood* (1858) and *The Weaver's Family* (1860) illustrated the disparity between the lives of the rich and the poor; they were published anonymously. Other themes in Gilbert's work were his antipathy toward organized religion and the dangers of drink, which he wrote led to "crime, profligacy, suicide, homicide, brutality, cruelty, pauperism, idiocy and insanity." His forays into magical and supernatural realms proved to be his most popular works, notably *The Magic Mirror* (1865), about a looking glass that grants wishes, and *The Wizard of the Mountain* (1867), which collects stories that he wrote for *Argosy* magazine about an enigmatic wizard and astrologer called the Innominato (in English, "Nameless"), who tried to use his powers to help people in thirteenth-century Italy.

William Gilbert is perhaps most famous for being the father of W. S. Gilbert, the collaborator of Arthur Sullivan.

"The Last Lords of Gardonal" was first published in the July, August, and September 1867 issues of *Argosy* magazine; it was first published in book form in *The Wizard of the Mountain* (London: Strahan, 1867).

# The Last Lords of Gardonal

## WILLIAM GILBERT

### I

One of the most picturesque objects of the valley of the Engadin is the ruined castle of Gardonal, near the village of Madaline. In the feudal times it was the seat of a family of barons, who possessed as their patrimony the whole of the valley, which with the castle had descended from father to son for many generations. The two last of the race were brothers; handsome, well-made, fine-looking young men, but in nature they more resembled fiends than human beings—so cruel, rapacious, and tyrannical were they. During the earlier part of his life their father had been careful of his patrimony. He had also been unusually just to the serfs on his estates, and in consequence they had attained to such a condition of comfort and prosperity as was rarely met with among those in the power of the feudal lords of the country; most of whom were arbitrary and exacting in the extreme. For several years in the latter part of his life he had been subject to a severe illness, which had confined him to the castle, and the management of his possessions and the government of his serfs had thus fallen into the hands of his sons. Although the old baron had placed so much power in their hands, still he was far from resigning his own authority. He exacted a strict account from them of the manner in which they performed the different duties he had intrusted to them; and having a strong suspicion of their character, and the probability of their endeavouring to conceal their misdoings, he caused agents to watch them secretly, and to report to him as to the correctness of the statements they gave. These agents, possibly knowing that the old man had but a short time to live, invariably gave a most favourable description of the conduct of the two young nobles, which, it must be admitted, was not, during their father's lifetime, particularly reprehensible on the whole. Still, they frequently showed as much of the cloven foot as to prove to the tenants what they had to expect at no distant day.

At the old baron's death, Conrad, the elder, inherited as his portion the castle of Gardonal, and the whole valley of Engadin; while to Hermann, the younger, was assigned some immense estates belonging to his father in the Bresciano district; for even in those early days, there was considerable intercourse between the inhabitants of that northern portion of Italy and those of the valley of the Engadin. The old baron had also willed, that should either of his sons die without children his estates should go to the survivor.

Conrad accordingly now took possession of the castle and its territory, and Hermann of the estates on the southern side of the Alps; which, although much smaller than those left to his elder brother, were still of great value. Notwithstanding the disparity in the worth of the legacies bequeathed to the two brothers, a perfectly good feeling existed between them, which promised to continue, their tastes being the same, while the mountains which divided them tended to the continuance of peace.

Conrad had hardly been one single week feudal lord of the Engadin before the inhabitants found, to their sorrow, how great was the difference between him and the old baron. Instead of the score of armed retainers his father had kept, Conrad increased the number to three hundred men, none of whom were natives of the valley. They had been chosen with great care from a body of Bohemian, German, and Italian outlaws, who at that time infested the borders of the Grisons, or had found refuge in the fastnesses of the mountains—men capable of any atrocity and to whom pity was unknown. From these miscreants the baron especially chose for his body-guard those who were ignorant of the language spoken by the peasantry of the Engadin, as they would be less likely to be influenced by any supplications or excuses which might be made to them when in the performance of their duty. Although the keeping of so numerous a body of armed retainers might naturally be considered to have entailed great expense, such a conclusion would be most erroneous, at least as far as regarded the present baron, who was as avaricious as he was despotic. He contrived to support his soldiers by imposing a most onerous tax on his tenants, irrespective of his ordinary feudal imposts; and woe to the unfortunate villagers who from inability, or from a sense of the injustice inflicted on them, did not contribute to the uttermost farthing the amount levied on them. In such a case a party of soldiers was immediately sent off to the defaulting village to collect the tax, with permission to live at free quarters till the money was paid; and they knew their duty too well to return home till they had succeeded in their errand. In doing this they were frequently merciless in the extreme, exacting the money by torture or any other means they pleased; and when they had been successful in obtaining the baron's dues, by way of further punishment they generally robbed the poor peasantry of everything they had which was worth the trouble of carrying away, and not unfrequently, from a spirit of sheer mischief, they spoiled all that remained. Many were the complaints which reached the ears of the baron of the cruel behaviour of his retainers; but in no case did they receive any redress; the baron making it a portion of his policy that no crimes committed by those under his command should be invested, so long as those crimes took place when employed in collecting taxes which he had imposed, and which had remained unpaid.

But the depredations and cruelties of the Baron Conrad were not confined solely to the valley of the Engadin. Frequently in the summer-time when the snows had melted on the mountains, so as to make the road practicable for his soldiers and their plunder, he would make a raid on the Italian side of the Alps. There they would rob and commit every sort of atrocity with impunity; and when they had collected sufficient booty they returned with it to the castle. Loud indeed were the complaints which reached the authorities of Milan. With routine tardiness, the government never took any energetic steps to punish the offenders until the winter had set in; and to cross the mountains in that season would have been almost an impossibility, at all events for an army. When the spring returned, more prudential reasons prevailed, and the matter, gradually diminishing in interest, was at last allowed to die out without any active measures being taken. Again, the districts in which the atrocities had been committed were hardly looked upon by the Milanese government as being Italian. The people themselves were beginning to be infected by a heresy which approached closely to the Protestantism of the present day; nor was their language that of Italy, but a patois of their own. Thus the government began to consider it unadvisable to attempt to punish the baron, richly as he deserved it, on behalf of those who after all were little worthy of the protection they demanded. The only real step they took to chastise him was to get him excommunicated by the Pope; which, as the baron and his followers professed no religion at all, was treated by them with ridicule.

It happened that in one of his marauding expeditions in the Valteline, the baron, when near Bormio, saw a young girl of extraordinary beauty. He was only attended at the time by two followers, else it is more than probable he would have made her a prisoner and carried her off to Gardonal. As it was he would probably have made the attempt had she not been surrounded by a number of peasants, who were working in some fields belonging to her father. The baron was also aware that the militia of the town, who had been expecting his visit, were under arms, and on an alarm being given could be on the spot in a few minutes. Now as the baron combined with his despotism a considerable amount of cunning, he merely attempted to enter into conversation with the girl. Finding his advances coldly received, he contented himself with inquiring of one of the peasants the girl's name and place of abode. He received for reply that her name was Teresa Biffi, and that she was the daughter of a substantial farmer, who with his wife and four children (of whom Teresa was the eldest) lived in a house at the extremity of the land he occupied.

As soon as the baron had received this information, he left the spot, and proceeded to the farmer's house, which he inspected externally with great care. He found it was of considerable size, strongly built of stone, with iron bars to the lower windows, and a strong well-made oaken door which could be securely fastened from the inside. After having made the round of the house (which he did alone), he returned to his two men, whom, in order to avoid suspicion, he had placed at a short distance from the building, in a spot where they could not easily be seen.

"Ludovico," he said to one of them who was his lieutenant, and invariably accompanied him in all his expeditions, "mark well that house; for some day, or more probably night, you may have to pay it a visit."

Ludovico merely said in reply that he would be always ready and willing to perform any order his master might honour him with; and the baron, with his men, then left the spot.

The hold the beauty of Teresa Biffi had taken upon the imagination of the baron actually looked like enchantment. His love for her, instead of diminishing by time, seemed to increase daily. At last he resolved on making her his wife; and about a month after he had seen her, he commissioned his lieutenant Ludovico to carry to Biffi an offer of marriage with his daughter; not dreaming, at the moment, of the possibility of a refusal. Ludovico immediately started on his mission, and in due time arrived at the farmer's house and delivered the baron's message. To Ludovico's intense surprise, however, he received from Biffi a positive refusal. Not daring to take back so uncourteous a reply to his master, Ludovico went on to describe the great advantage which would accrue to the farmer and his family if the baron's proposal were accepted. Not only, he said, would Teresa be a lady of the highest rank, and in possession of enormous wealth both in gold and jewels, but that the other members of her family would also be ennobled, and each of them, as they grew up, would receive appointments under the baron, besides having large estates allotted to them in the Engadin Valley.

The farmer listened with patience to Ludovico, and when he had concluded, he replied—

"Tell your master I have received his message, and that I am ready to admit that great personal advantages might accrue to me and my family by accepting his offer. Say, that although I am neither noble nor rich, that yet at the same time I am not poor; but were I as poor as the blind mendicant whom you passed on the road in coming hither, I would spurn such an offer from so infamous a wretch as the baron. You say truly that he is well known for his power and his wealth; but the latter has been obtained by robbing both rich and poor, who had not the means to resist him, and his power has been greatly strengthened by engaging in his service a numerous band of robbers and cut-throats, who are ready and willing to murder any one at his bidding. You have my answer, and the sooner you quit this neighbourhood the better, for I can assure you that any one known to be in the service of the Baron Conrad is likely to meet with a most unfavourable reception from those who live around us."

"Then you positively refuse his offer?" said Ludovico.

"Positively, and without the slightest reservation," was the farmer's reply.

"And you wish me to give him the message in the terms you have made use of?"

"Without omitting a word," was the farmer's reply. "At the same time, you may add to it as many of the same description as you please."

"Take care," said Ludovico. "There is yet time for you to reconsider your decision. If you insist on my taking your message to the baron, I must of course do so; but in that case make your peace with heaven as soon as you can, for the baron is not a man to let such an insult pass. Follow my advice, and accept his offer ere it is too late."

"I have no other answer to give you," said Biffi.

"I am sorry for it," said Ludovico, heaving a deep sigh. "I have now no alternative," and mounting his horse he rode away.

Now it must not be imagined that the advice Ludovico gave the farmer, and the urgent requests and arguments he offered, were altogether the genuine effusions of his heart. On the contrary, Ludovico had easily perceived, on hearing the farmer's first refusal, that there was no chance of the proposal being accepted. He had therefore occupied his time during the remaining portion of the interview in carefully examining the premises, and mentally taking note of the manner in which they could be most easily entered, as he judged, rightly enough, that before long he might be sent to the house on a far less peaceable mission.

Nothing could exceed the rage of the baron when he heard the farmer's message.

"You cowardly villain!" he said to Ludovico. "Did you allow the wretch to live who could send such a message to your master?"

"So please you," said Ludovico. "What could I do?"

"You could have struck him to the heart with your dagger, could you not?" said the baron. "I have known you do such a thing to an old woman for half the provocation. Had it been Biffi's wife instead you might have shown more courage."

"Had I followed my own inclination," said Ludovico, "I would have killed the fellow on the spot; but then I could not have brought away the young lady with me, for there were too many persons about the house and in the fields at the time. So I thought, before acting further, I had better let you hear his answer. One favour I hope your excellency will grant me, that if the fellow is to be punished you will allow me to inflict it as a reward for the skill I showed in keeping my temper when I heard the message."

"Perhaps you have acted wisely, Ludovico," said the baron, after a few moments' silence. "At present my mind is too much ruffled by the villain's impertinence to think calmly on the subject. Tomorrow we will speak of it again."

Next day the baron sent for his lieutenant, and said to him—

"Ludovico, I have now a commission for you to execute which I think will be exactly to your taste. Take with you six men whom you can trust, and start this afternoon for Bormio. Sleep at some village on the road, but let not one word escape you as to your errand. Tomorrow morning leave the village—but separately—so that you may not be seen together, as it is better to avoid suspicion. Meet again near the farmer's house, and arrive there, if possible, before evening has set in, for in all probability you will have to make an attack upon the house, and you may thus become well acquainted with the locality before doing so; but keep yourselves concealed, otherwise you will spoil all. After you have done this, retire some distance, and remain concealed till midnight, as then all the family will be in their first sleep, and you will experience less difficulty than if you began later. I particularly wish you to enter the house without using force, but if you cannot do so, break into it in any way you consider best. Bring out the girl and do her no harm. If any resistance is made by her father, kill him; but not unless you are compelled, as I do not wish to enrage his daughter against me. However, let nothing prevent you from securing her. Burn the house down or anything you please, but bring her here. If you execute your mission promptly and to my satisfaction, I promise you and those with you a most liberal reward. Now go and get ready to depart as speedily as you can."

Ludovico promised to execute the baron's mission to the letter, and shortly afterwards left the castle accompanied by six of the greatest ruffians he could find among the men-at-arms.

Although on the spur of the moment Biffi had sent so defiant a message to the baron, he afterwards felt considerable uneasiness as to the manner in which it would be received. He did not repent having refused the proposal, but he knew that the baron was a man of the most cruel and vindictive disposition, and would in all probability seek some means to be avenged. The only defence he could adopt was to make the fastenings of his house as secure as possible, and to keep at least one of his labourers about him whom he could send as a messenger to Bormio for assistance, and to arouse the inhabitants in the immediate vicinity, in case of his being attacked. Without any hesitation all promised to aid Biffi in every way in their power, for he had acquired great renown among the inhabitants of the place for the courage he had shown in refusing so indignantly the baron's offer of marriage for his daughter.

About midnight, on the day after Ludovico's departure from the castle, Biffi was aroused by some one knocking at the door of his house, and demanding admission. It was Ludovico, for after attempting in vain to enter the house secretly, he had concealed his men, determining to try the effect of treachery before using force. On the inquiry being made as to who the stranger was, he replied that he was a poor traveller who had lost his way, and begged that he might be allowed a night's lodging, as he was so weary he could not go a step further.

"I am sorry for you," said Biffi, "but I cannot allow you to enter this house before daylight. As the night is fine and warm you can easily sleep on the straw under the windows, and in the morning I will let you in and give you a good breakfast."

Again and again did Ludovico plead to be admitted, but in vain; Biffi would not be moved from his resolution. At last, however, the bravo's patience got exhausted, and suddenly changing his manner he roared out in a threatening tone, "If you don't let me in, you villain, I will burn your house over your head. I have here, as you may see, plenty of men to help me to put my threat into execution," he continued, pointing to the men, who had now come up, "so you had better let me in at once."

In a moment Biffi comprehended the character of the person he had to deal with; so, instead of returning any answer, he retired from the window and alarmed the inmates of the house. He also told the labourer whom he had engaged to sleep there to drop from a window at the back and run as fast as he could to arouse the inhabitants in the vicinity, and tell them that his house was attacked by the baron and his men. He was to beg them to arm themselves and come to his aid as quickly as possible, and having done this, he was to go on to Bormio on the same errand. The poor fellow attempted to carry out his master's orders; but in dropping from the window he fell with such force on the ground that he could only move with difficulty, and in trying to crawl away he was observed by some of the baron's men, who immediately set on him and killed him.

Ludovico, finding that he could not enter the house either secretly or by threatenings, attempted to force open the door, but it was so firmly barricaded from within that he did not succeed; while in the meantime Biffi and his family employed themselves in placing wooden faggots and heavy articles of furniture against it, thus making it stronger than ever. Ludovico, finding he could not gain an entrance by the door, told his men to look around in search of a ladder, so that they might get to the windows on the first floor, as those on the ground floor were all small, high up, and well barricaded, as was common in Italian houses of the time; but in spite of all their efforts no ladder could be found. He now deliberated what step he should next take. As it was getting late, he saw that if they did not succeed in effecting an entrance quickly the dawn would break upon them, and the labourers going to their work would raise an alarm. At last one man suggested that as abundance of fuel could be obtained from the stacks at the back of the house they might place a quantity of it against the door and set fire to it; adding that the sight of the flames would soon make the occupants glad to effect their escape by the first-floor windows.

The suggestion was no sooner made than acted upon. A quantity of dry fuel was piled up against the house door to the height of many feet, and a light having been procured by striking a flint stone against the hilt of a sword over some dried leaves, fire was set to the pile. From the dry nature of the fuel, the whole mass was in a blaze in a few moments. But the scheme did not have the effect Ludovico had anticipated. True, the family rushed towards the windows in the front of the house, but when they saw the flames rising so fiercely they retreated in the utmost alarm. Meanwhile the screams from the women and children—who had now lost all self-control—mingled with the roar of the blazing element, which, besides having set fire to the faggots and furniture placed within the door, had now reached a quantity of fodder and Indian corn stored on the ground floor.

Ludovico soon perceived that the whole house was in flames, and that the case was becoming desperate. Not only was there the danger of the fire alarming the inhabitants in the vicinity by the light it shed around, but he also reflected what would be the rage of his master if the girl should perish in the flames, and the consequent punishment which would be inflicted on him and those under his command if he returned empty-handed. He now called out to Biffi and his family to throw themselves out of the window, and that he and his men would save them. It was some time before he was understood, but at last Biffi brought the two younger children to the window, and, lowering them as far as he could, he let them fall into the arms of Ludovico and his men, and they reached the ground in safety.

Biffi now returned for the others, and saw Teresa standing at a short distance behind him. He took her by the hand to bring her forward, and they had nearly reached the window, when she heard a scream from her mother, who being an incurable invalid was confined to her bed. Without a moment's hesitation, the girl turned back to assist her, and the men below, who thought that the prey they wanted was all but in their hands, and cared little about the fate of the rest of the family, were thus disappointed. Ludovico now anxiously awaited the reappearance of Teresa—but he waited in vain. The flames had gained entire mastery, and even the roof had taken fire. The screams of the inmates were now no longer heard, for if not stifled in the smoke they were lost in the roar of the fire; whilst the glare which arose from it illumined the landscape far and near.

It so happened that a peasant, who resided about a quarter of a mile from Biffi's house, had to go a long distance to his work, and having risen at an unusually early hour, he saw the flames, and aroused the inmates of the other cottages in the village, who immediately armed themselves and started off to the scene of the disaster, imagining, but too certainly, that it was the work of an incendiary. The alarm was also communicated to another village, and from thence to Bormio, and in a short time a strong band of armed men had collected, and proceeded together to assist in extinguishing the flames. On their arrival at the house, they found the place one immense heap of ashes—not a soul was to be seen, for Ludovico and his men had already decamped.

The dawn now broke, and the assembled peasantry made some attempt to account for the fire. At first they were induced to attribute it to accident, but on searching around they found the dead body of the murdered peasant, and afterwards the two children who had escaped, and who in their terror had rushed into a thick copse to conceal themselves. With great difficulty they gathered from them sufficient to show that the fire had been caused by a band of robbers who had come for the purpose of plundering the house; and their suspicion fell immediately on Baron Conrad, without any better proof than his infamous reputation.

As soon as Ludovico found that an alarm had been given, he and his men started off to find their horses, which they had hidden among some trees about a mile distant from Biffi's house. The daylight was just breaking, and objects around them began to be visible, but not so clearly as to allow them to see for any distance. Suddenly one of the men pointed to an indistinct figure in white some little way in advance of them. Ludovico halted for a moment to see what it might be, and, with his men, watched it attentively as it appeared to fly from them.

"It is the young girl herself," said one of the men. "She has escaped from the fire; and that was exactly as she appeared in her white dress with her father at the window. I saw her well, and am sure I am not mistaken."

"It is indeed the girl," said another. "I also saw her."

"I hope you are right," said Ludovico, "and if so, it will be fortunate indeed, for should we return without her we may receive but a rude reception from the baron."

They now quickened their pace, but, fast as they walked, the figure in white walked quite as rapidly. Ludovico, who of course began to suspect that it was Teresa attempting to escape from them, commanded his men to run as fast as they could in order to reach her. Although they tried their utmost, the figure, however, still kept the same distance before them. Another singularity about it was, that as daylight advanced the figure appeared to become less distinct, and ere they had reached their horses it seemed to have melted away.

## II

Before mounting their horses, Ludovico held a consultation with his men as to what course they had better adopt; whether they should depart at once or search the neighbourhood for the girl. Both suggestions seemed to be attended with danger. If they delayed their departure, they might be attacked by the peasantry, who by this time were doubtless in hot pursuit of them; and if they returned to the baron without Teresa, they were almost certain to receive a severe punishment for failing in their enterprise. At last the idea struck Ludovico that a good round lie might possibly succeed with the baron and do something to avert his anger, while there was little hope of its in the slightest manner availing with the enraged peasantry. He therefore gave the order for his men to mount their horses, resolving to tell the baron that Teresa had escaped from the flames, and had begged their assistance, but a number of armed inhabitants of Bormio chancing to approach, she had sought their protection. A great portion of this statement could be substantiated by his men, as they still fully believed that the figure in white which they had so indistinctly seen was the girl herself. Ludovico and his men during their homeward journey had great difficulty in crossing the mountains, in consequence of a heavy fall of snow (for it was now late in the autumn). Next day they arrived at the castle of Gardonal.

It would be difficult to describe the rage of the baron when he heard that his retainers had been unsuccessful in their mission. He ordered Ludovico to be thrown into a dungeon, where he remained for more than a month, and was only then liberated in consequence of the baron needing his services for some expedition requiring special skill and courage. The other men were also punished, though less severely than their leader, on whom, of course, they laid all the blame.

For some time after Ludovico's return, the baron occupied himself in concocting schemes, not only to secure the girl Teresa (for he fully believed the account Ludovico had given of her escape), but to revenge himself on the inhabitants of Bormio for the part they had taken in the affair; and it was to carry out these schemes that he liberated Ludovico from prison.

The winter had passed, and the spring sun was rapidly melting the snows on the mountains, when one morning three travel-stained men, having the appearance of respectable burghers, arrived at the Hospice, and requested to be allowed an interview with the Innominato. A messenger was despatched to the castle, who shortly afterwards returned, saying that his master desired the visitors should immediately be admitted into his presence. When they arrived at the castle they found him fully prepared to receive them, a handsome repast being spread out for their refreshment. At first the travellers seemed under some restraint; but this was soon dispelled by the friendly courtesy of the astrologer. After partaking of the viands which had been set before them, the Innominato inquired the object of their visit. One of them, who had been evidently chosen as spokesman, then rose from his chair, and addressed their host as follows:

"We have been sent to your excellency by the inhabitants of Bormio, as a deputation, to ask your advice and assistance in a strait we are in at present. Late in the autumn of last year, the Baron Conrad, feudal lord of the Engadin, was on some not very honest expedition in our neighbourhood, when by chance he saw a very beautiful girl, of the name of Teresa Biffi, whose father occupied a large farm about half a league from the town. The baron, it appears, became so deeply enamoured of the girl that he afterwards sent a messenger to her father with an offer of marriage for his daughter. Biffi, knowing full well the infamous reputation of the baron, unhesitatingly declined his proposal, and in such indignant terms as to arouse the tyrant's anger to the highest pitch. Determining not only to possess himself of the girl, but to avenge the insult he had received, he sent a body of armed retainers, who in the night attacked the farmer's house, and endeavoured to effect an entrance by breaking open the door.

Finding they could not succeed, and after murdering one of the servants who had been sent to a neighbouring village to give the alarm, they set fire to the house, and with the exception of two children who contrived to escape, the whole family, including the young girl herself, perished in the flames. It appears, however, that the baron (doubtless through his agents) received a false report that the young girl had escaped, and was taken under the protection of some of the inhabitants of Bormio. In consequence, he sent another body of armed men, who arrived in the night at the house of the podesta, and contrived to make his only son, a boy of about fifteen years old, a prisoner, bearing him off to the baron's castle. They left word, that unless Teresa Biffi was placed in their power before the first day of May, not only would the youth be put to death, but the baron would also wreak vengeance on the whole town. On the perpetration of this last atrocity, we again applied to the government of Milan for protection; but although our reception was most courteous, and we were promised assistance, we have too good reason to doubt our receiving it. Certainly up to the present time no steps have been taken in the matter, nor has a single soldier been sent, although the time named for the death of the child has nearly expired. The townsmen therefore, having heard of your great wisdom and power, your willingness to help those who are in distress, as well as to protect the weak and oppressed, have sent us to ask you to take them under your protection; as the baron is not a man to scruple at putting such a threat into execution."

The Innominato, who had listened to the delegate with great patience and attention, told him that he had no soldiers or retainers at his orders; while the baron, whose wicked life was known to him, had many.

"But your excellency has great wisdom, and from all we have heard, we feel certain that you could protect us."

"Your case," said the Innominato, "is a very sad one, I admit, and you certainly ought to be protected from the baron's machinations. I will not disguise from you that I have the power to help you. Tell the unhappy podesta that he need be under no alarm as to his son's safety, and that I will oblige the baron to release him. My art tells me that the boy is still alive, though confined in prison. As for your friends who sent you to me, tell them that the baron shall do them no harm. All you have to do is, to contrive some means by which the baron may hear that the girl Teresa Biffi has been placed by me where he will never find her without my permission."

"But Teresa Biffi," said the delegate, "perished with her father; and the baron will wreak his vengeance both on you and us, when he finds you cannot place the girl in his power."

"Fear nothing, but obey my orders," said the Innominato. "Do what I have told you, and I promise you shall have nothing to dread from him. The sooner you carry out my directions the better."

The deputation now returned to Bormio, and related all that had taken place at their interview with the Innominato. Although the result of their mission was scarcely considered satisfactory, they determined, after much consideration, to act on the astrologer's advice. But how to carry it out was a very difficult matter. This was, however, overcome by one of the chief inhabitants of the town— a man of most determined courage—offering himself as a delegate to the baron, to convey to him the Innominato's message. Without hesitation the offer was gratefully accepted, and the next day he started on his journey. No sooner had he arrived at the castle of Gardonal, and explained the object of his mission, than he was ushered into the presence of the baron, whom he found in the great hall, surrounded by a numerous body of armed men.

"Well," said the baron, as soon as the delegate had entered, "have your townspeople come to their senses at last, and sent me the girl Teresa?"

"No, they have not, baron," was the reply, "for she is not in their custody. All they can do is to inform you where you may possibly receive some information about her."

"And where may that be?"

"The only person who knows where she may be found is the celebrated astrologer who lives in a castle near Lecco."

"Ah now, you are trifling with me," said the baron sternly. "You must be a great fool or a very bold man to try such an experiment as that."

"I am neither the one nor the other, your excellency; nor am I trifling with you. What I have told you is the simple truth."

"And how did you learn it?"

"From the Innominato's own lips."

"Then you applied to him for assistance against me," said the baron, furiously.

"That is hardly correct, your excellency," said the delegate. "It is true we applied to him for advice as to the manner in which we should act in case you should attack us, and put your threat into execution respecting the son of the podesta."

"And what answer did he give you?"

"Just what I have told you—that he alone knows where Teresa Biffi is to be found, and that you could not remove her from the protection she is under without his permission."

"Did he send that message to me in defiance?" said the baron.

"I have no reason to believe so, your excellency."

The baron was silent for some time; he then inquired of the delegate how many armed retainers the Innominato kept.

"None, I believe," was the reply. "At any rate, there were none to be seen when the deputation from the town visited him."

The baron was again silent for some moments, and seemed deeply absorbed in thought. He would rather have met with any other opponent than the Innominato, whose reputation was well known to him, and whose learning he dreaded more than the power of any nobleman—no matter how many armed retainers he could bring against him.

"I very much suspect," he said at last, "that some deception is being practised on me. But should my suspicion be correct I shall exact terrible vengeance. I shall detain you," he continued, turning abruptly and fiercely on the delegate; "as a hostage while I visit the Innominato; and if I do not succeed with him, you shall die on the same scaffold as the son of your podesta."

It was in vain that the delegate protested against being detained as a prisoner, saying that it was against all rules of knightly usage; but the baron would not listen to reason, and the unfortunate man was immediately hurried out of the hall and imprisoned.

Although the baron by no means liked the idea of an interview with the Innominato, he immediately made preparations to visit him, and the day after the delegate's arrival he set out on his journey, attended by only four of his retainers. It should here be mentioned, that it is more than probable the baron would have avoided meeting the Innominato on any other occasion whatever, so great was the dislike he had to him. He seemed to be acting under some fatality; some power seemed to impel him in his endeavours to obtain Teresa which it was impossible to account for.

The road chosen by the baron to reach the castle of the Innominato was rather a circuitous one. In the first place, he did not consider it prudent to pass through the Valteline; and in the second, he thought that by visiting his brother on his way he might be able to obtain some particulars as to the character of the mysterious individual whom he was about to see, as his reputation would probably be better known among the inhabitants of the Bergamo district than by those in the valley of the Engadin.

The baron arrived safely at his brother's castle, where the reports which had hitherto indistinctly reached him of the wonderful power and skill of the astrologer were fully confirmed. After remaining a day with his brother, the baron started for Lecco. Under an assumed name he stayed here for two days, in order that he might receive the report of one of his men, whom he had sent forward to ascertain whether the Innominato had any armed men in his castle; for, being capable of any act of treachery himself, he naturally suspected treason in others. The man in due time returned, and reported that, although he had taken great pains to find out the truth, he was fully convinced that not only were there no soldiers in the castle, but that it did not, to the best of his belief, contain an arm of any kind—the Innominato relying solely on his occult power for his defence.

Perfectly assured that he had no danger to apprehend, the baron left Lecco, attended by his retainers, and in a few hours afterwards he arrived at the Hospice, where his wish for an interview was conveyed to the astrologer. After some delay a reply was sent that the Innominato was willing to receive the baron on condition that he came alone, as his retainers would not be allowed to enter the castle. The baron hesitated for some moments, not liking to place himself in the power of a man who, after all, might prove a very dangerous adversary, and who might even use treacherous means. His love for Teresa Biffi, however, urged him to accept the invitation, and he accompanied the messenger to the castle.

The Innominato received his guest with stern courtesy; and, without even asking him to be seated, requested to know the object of his visit.

"Perhaps I am not altogether unknown to you," said the baron. "I am lord of the Engadin."

"Frankly," said the Innominato, "your name and reputation are both well known to me. It would give me great satisfaction were they less so."

"I regret to hear you speak in that tone," said the baron, evidently making great efforts to repress his rising passion. "A person in my position is not likely to be without enemies, but it rather surprises me to find a man of your reputation so prejudiced against me without having investigated the accusations laid to my charge."

"You judge wrongly if you imagine that I am so," said the Innominato. "But once more, will you tell me the object of your visit?"

"I understood," said the baron, "by a message sent to me by the insolent inhabitants of Bormio, that you know the person with whom a young girl, named Teresa Biffi, is at present residing. Might I ask if that statement is correct?"

"I hardly sent it in those words," said the Innominato. "But admitting it to be so, I must first ask your reason for inquiring."

"I have not the slightest objection to inform you," said the baron. "I have nothing to conceal. I wish to make her my wife."

"On those terms I am willing to assist you," said the astrologer. "But only on the condition that you immediately release the messenger you have most unjustly confined in one of your dungeons, as well as the young son of the podesta, and that you grant them a safe escort back to Bormio, and further, that you promise to cease annoying the people of that district. Do all this, and I am willing to promise you that Teresa Biffi shall not only become your wife, but shall bring with her a dowry and wedding outfit sufficiently magnificent even for the exalted position to which you propose to raise her."

"I solemnly promise you," said the baron, "that the moment the wedding is over, the delegate from Bormio and the son of the podesta shall both leave my castle perfectly free and unhampered with any conditions; and moreover that I will send a strong escort with them to protect them on their road."

"I see you are already meditating treachery," said the Innominato. "But I will not, in any manner, alter my offer. The day week after their safe return to Bormio Teresa Biffi shall arrive at the castle of Gardonal for the wedding ceremony. Now you distinctly know my conditions, and I demand from you an unequivocal acceptance or refusal."

"What security shall I have that the bargain will be kept on your side?" said the baron.

"My word, and no other."

The baron remained silent for a moment, and then said—

"I accept your offer. But clearly understand me in my turn, sir astrologer. Fail to keep your promise, and had you ten times the power you have I will take my revenge on you; and I am not a man to threaten such a thing without doing it."

"All that I am ready to allow," said the Innominato, with great coolness, "that is to say, in case you have the power to carry out your threat, which in the present instance you have not. Do not imagine that because I am not surrounded by a band of armed cut-throats and miscreants I am not the stronger of the two. You little dream how powerless you are in my hands. You see this bird," he continued, taking down a common sparrow in a wooden cage from a nail in the wall on which it hung. "It is not more helpless in my hands than you are; nay more, I will now give the bird far greater power over you than I possess over it."

As he spoke he unfastened the door of the cage, and the sparrow darted from it through the window into the air, and in a moment afterwards was lost to sight.

"That bird," the astrologer went on to say, "will follow you till I deprive it of the power. I bear you no malice for doubting my veracity. Falsehood is too much a portion of your nature for you to disbelieve its existence in others. I will not seek to punish you for the treachery which I am perfectly sure you will soon be imagining against me without giving you fair warning; for, a traitor yourself, you naturally suspect treason in others. As soon as you entertain a thought of evading your promise to release your prisoners, or conceive any treason or ill feeling against me, that sparrow will appear to you. If you instantly abandon the thought no harm will follow; but if you do not a terrible punishment will soon fall upon you. In whatever position you may find yourself at the moment, the bird will be near you, and no skill of yours will be able to harm it."

The baron now left the Innominato, and returned with his men to Lecco, where he employed himself for the remainder of the day in making preparations for his homeward journey. To return by the circuitous route he had taken in going to Lecco would have occupied too much time, as he was anxious to arrive at his castle, that he might without delay release the prisoners and make preparations for his wedding with Teresa Biffi. To pass the Valteline openly with his retainers—which was by far the shortest road—would have exposed him to too much danger; he therefore resolved to divide his party and send three men back by his brother's castle, so that they could return the horses they had borrowed. Then he would disguise himself and the fourth man (a German who could not speak a word of Italian, and from whom he had nothing therefore to fear on the score of treachery) as two Tyrolese merchants returning to their own country. He also purchased two mules and some provisions for the journey, so that they need not be obliged to rest in any of the villages they passed through, where possibly they might be detected, and probably maltreated.

Next morning the baron and his servant, together with the two mules, went on board a large bark which was manned by six men, and which he had hired for the occasion, and in it they started for Colico. At the commencement of their voyage they kept along the eastern side of the lake, but after advancing a few miles the wind, which had hitherto been moderate, now became so strong as to cause much fatigue to the rowers, and the captain of the bark determined on crossing the lake, so as to be under the lee of the mountains on the other side. When half way across they came in view of the turrets of the castle of the Innominato. The sight of the castle brought to the baron's mind his interview with its owner, and the defiant manner in which he had been treated by him. The longer he gazed the stronger became his anger against the Innominato, and at last it rose to such a point that he exclaimed aloud, to the great surprise of the men in the boat, "Some day I will meet thee again, thou insolent villain, and I will then take signal vengeance on thee for the insult offered me yesterday."

The words had hardly been uttered when a sparrow, apparently driven from the shore by the wind, settled on the bark for a moment, and then flew away. The baron instantly remembered what the Innominato had said to him, and also the warning the bird was to give. With a sensation closely resembling fear, he tried to change the current of his thoughts, and was on the point of turning his head from the castle, when the rowers in the boat simultaneously set up a loud shout of warning, and the baron then perceived that a heavily-laden vessel, four times the size of his own, and with a huge sail set, was running before the wind with great velocity, threatening the next moment to strike his boat on the beam; in which case both he

and the men would undoubtedly be drowned. Fortunately, the captain of the strange bark had heard the cry of the rowers, and by rapidly putting down his helm, saved their lives; though the baron's boat was struck with so much violence on the quarter that she nearly sank.

The Baron Conrad had now received an earnest that the threat of the Innominato was not a vain one, and feeling that he was entirely in his power, resolved if possible not to offend him again. The boat continued on her voyage, and late in the evening arrived safely at Colico, where the baron, with his servant and the mules, disembarked, and without delay proceeded on their journey. They continued on their road till nightfall, when they began to consider how they should pass the night. They looked around them, but they could perceive no habitation or shelter of any kind, and it was now raining heavily. They continued their journey onwards, and had almost come to the conclusion that they should be obliged to pass the night in the open air, when a short distance before them they saw a low cottage, the door of which was open, showing the dim light of a fire burning within. The baron now determined to ask the owner of the cottage for permission to remain there for the night; but to be certain that no danger could arise, he sent forward his man to discover whether it was a house standing by itself, or one of a village; as in the latter case he would have to use great caution to avoid being detected. His servant accordingly left him to obey orders, and shortly afterwards returned with the news that the house was a solitary one, and that he could not distinguish a trace of any other in the neighbourhood. Satisfied with this information, the baron proceeded to the cottage door, and begged the inmates to afford him shelter for the night, assuring them that the next morning he would remunerate them handsomely. The peasant and his wife—a sickly-looking, emaciated old couple—gladly offered them all the accommodation the wretched cabin could afford. After fastening up the mules at the back of the house, and bringing in the baggage and some dry fodder to form a bed for the baron and his servant, they prepared some of the food their guests had brought with them for supper, and shortly afterwards the baron and his servant were fast asleep.

Next morning they rose early and continued on their journey. After they had been some hours on the road, the baron, who had before been conversing with his retainer, suddenly became silent and absorbed in thought. He rode on a few paces in advance of the man, thinking over the conditions made by the Innominato, when the idea struck him whether it would not be possible in some way to evade them. He had hardly entertained the thought, when the sparrow flew rapidly before his mule's head, and then instantly afterwards his servant, who had ridden up to him, touched him on the shoulder and pointed to a body of eight or ten armed men about a quarter of a mile distant, who were advancing towards them. The baron, fearing lest they might be some of the armed inhabitants of the neighbourhood who were banded together against him, and seeing that no time was to be lost, immediately plunged, with his servant, into a thick copse where, without being seen, he could command a view of the advancing soldiers as they passed. He perceived that when they came near the place where he was concealed they halted, and evidently set about examining the traces of the footsteps of the mules. They communed together for some time as if in doubt what course they should adopt, and finally, the leader giving the order, they continued their march onwards, and the baron shortly afterwards left his place of concealment.

Nothing further worthy of notice occurred that day; and late at night they passed through Bormio, fortunately without being observed. They afterwards arrived safely at the foot of the mountain pass, and at dawn began the ascent. The day was fine and calm, and the sun shone magnificently. The baron, who now calculated that the dangers of his journey were over, was in high spirits, and familiarly conversed with his retainer. When they had reached a considerable elevation, the path narrowed, so that the two could not ride abreast, and the baron went in advance. He now became very silent and thoughtful, all his thoughts being fixed on the approaching wedding, and in speculations as to how short a time it would take for the delegate and the youth to reach Bormio. Suddenly the thought occurred to him, whether the men whom he should send to escort the hostages back, could not, when they had completed their business, remain concealed in the immediate neighbourhood till after the celebration of the wedding, and then bring back with them some other hostage, and thus enable him to make further demands for compensation for the insult he considered had been offered him. Although the idea had only been vaguely formed, and possibly with but little intention of carrying it out, he had an immediate proof that the power of the astrologer was following him. A sparrow settled on the ground before him, and did not move until his mule was close to it, when it rose in the air right before his face. He continued to follow its course with his eyes, and as it rose higher he thought he perceived a tremulous movement in an immense mass of snow, which had accumulated at the base of one of the mountain peaks. All thought of treachery immediately vanished. He gave a cry of alarm to his servant, and they both hurried onwards, thus barely escaping being buried in an avalanche, which the moment afterwards overwhelmed the path they had crossed.

The baron was now more convinced than ever of the tremendous power of the Innominato, and so great was his fear of him, that he resolved for the future not to contemplate any treachery against him, or entertain any thoughts of revenge.

The day after the baron's arrival at the castle of Gardonal, he ordered the delegate and the podesta's son to be brought into his presence. Assuming a tone of much mildness and courtesy, he told them he much regretted the inconvenience they had been put to, but that the behaviour of the inhabitants of Bormio had left him no alternative. He was ready to admit that the delegate had told him the truth, although from the interview he had with the Innominato, he was by no means certain that the inhabitants of their town had acted in a friendly manner towards him, or were without blame in the matter. Still he did not wish to be harsh, and was willing for the future to be on friendly terms with them if they promised to cease insulting him—what possible affront they could have offered him it would be difficult to say. "At the same time, in justice to myself," he continued (his natural cupidity gaining the ascendant at the moment), "I hardly think I ought to allow you to return without the payment of some fair ransom."

He had scarcely uttered these words when a sparrow flew in at the window, and darting wildly two or three times across the hall, left by the same window through which it had entered. Those present who noticed the bird looked at it with an eye of indifference—but not so the baron. He knew perfectly well that it was a warning from the astrologer, and he tooked around him to see what accident might have befallen him had he continued the train of thought. Nothing of an extraordinary nature followed the disappearance of the bird. The baron now changed the conversation, and told his prisoners that they were at liberty to depart as soon as they pleased; and that to prevent any misfortune befalling them on the road, he would send four of his retainers to protect them. In this he kept his promise to the letter, and a few days afterwards the men returned, reporting that the delegate and the son of the podesta had both arrived safely at their destination.

## III

Immediately after the departure of his prisoners, the baron began to make preparations for his wedding, for although he detested the Innominato in his heart, he had still the fullest reliance on his fulfilling the promise he had made. His assurance was further confirmed by a messenger from the astrologer to inform him that on the next Wednesday the affianced bride would arrive with her suite, and that he (the Innominato) had given this notice, that all things might be in readiness for the ceremony.

Neither expense nor exertion was spared by the baron to make his nuptials imposing and magnificent. The chapel belonging to the castle, which had been allowed to fall into a most neglected con-dition, was put into order, the altar redecorated, and the walls hung with tapestry. Preparations were made in the inner hall for a banquet on the grandest scale, which was to be given after the ceremony; and on a dais in the main hall into which the bride was to be conducted on her arrival were placed two chairs of state, where the baron and his bride were to be seated.

When the day arrived for the wedding, everything was prepared for the reception of the bride. As no hour had been named for her arrival, all persons who were to be engaged in the ceremony were ready in the castle by break of day; and the baron, in a state of great excitement, mounted to the top of the watch-tower, that he might be able to give orders to the rest the moment her cavalcade appeared in sight. Hour after hour passed, but still Teresa did not make her appearance, and at last the baron began to feel considerable anxiety on the subject.

At last a mist, which had been over a part of the valley, cleared up, and all the anxiety of the baron was dispelled; for in the distance he perceived a group of travellers approaching the castle, some mounted on horseback and some on foot. In front rode the bride on a superb white palfrey, her face covered with a thick veil. On each side of her rode an esquire magnificently dressed. Behind her were a waiting woman on horseback and two men-servants; and in the rear were several led mules laden with packages. The baron now quitted his position in the tower and descended to the castle gates to receive his bride. When he arrived there, he found one of the esquires, who had ridden forward at the desire of his mistress, waiting to speak to him.

"I have been ordered," he said to the baron, "by the Lady Teresa, to request that you will be good enough to allow her to change her dress before she meets you."

The baron of course willingly assented, and then retired into the hall destined for the reception ceremony. Shortly afterwards Teresa arrived at the castle, and being helped from her palfrey, she proceeded with her lady in waiting and a female attendant (who had been engaged by the baron) into her private apartment, while two of the muleteers brought up a large trunk containing her wedding dress.

In less than an hour Teresa left her room to be introduced to the baron, and was conducted into his presence by one of the esquires. As soon as she entered the hall, a cry of admiration arose from all present—so extraordinary was her beauty. The baron, in a state of breathless emotion, advanced to meet her, but before he had reached her she bent on her knee, and remained in that position till he had raised her up. "Kneel not to me, thou lovely one," he said. "It is for all present to kneel to thee in adoration of thy wonderful beauty, rather than for thee to bend to any one." So saying, and holding her hand, he led her to one of the seats on the dais, and then, seating himself by her side, gave orders for the ceremony of introduction to begin. One by one the different persons to be presented were led up to her, all of whom she received with a grace and amiability which raised her very high in their estimation.

When the ceremony of introduction was over the baron ordered that the procession should be formed, and then, taking Teresa by the hand, he led her into the chapel, followed by the others. When all were arranged in their proper places the marriage ceremony was performed by the priest, and the newly-married couple, with the retainers and guests, entered into the banqueting hall. Splendid as was the repast which had been prepared for the company, their attention seemed for some time more drawn to the baron and his bride than to the duties of the feast. A handsomer couple it would have been impossible to find. The baron himself, as has been stated already, had no lack of manly beauty either in face or form; while the loveliness of his bride appeared almost more than mortal. Even their splendid attire seemed to attract little notice when compared with their personal beauty.

After the surprise and admiration had somewhat abated, the feast progressed most satisfactorily. All were in high spirits, and good humour and conviviality reigned throughout the hall. Even on the baron it seemed to produce a kindly effect, so that few who could have seen him at that mo-

ment would have imagined him to be the stern, cold-blooded tyrant he really was. His countenance was lighted up with good humour and friendliness. Much as his attention was occupied with his bride, he had still a little to bestow on his guests, and he rose many times from his seat to request the attention of the servants to their wants. At last he cast his eye over the tables as if searching for some person whom he could not see, and he then beckoned to the major domo, who, staff of office in hand, advanced to receive his orders.

"I do not see the esquires of the Lady Teresa in the room," said the baron.

"Your excellency," said the man, "they are not here."

"How is that?" said the baron, with some impatience. "You ought to have found room for them in the hall. Where are they?"

"Your excellency," said the major domo, who from the expression of the baron's countenance evidently expected a storm, "they are not here. The whole of the suite left the castle immediately after the mules were unladen and her ladyship had left her room. I was inspecting the places which I had prepared for them, when a servant came forward and told me that the esquires and attendants had left the castle. I at once hurried after them and begged they would return, as I was sure your excellency would feel hurt if they did not stay to the banquet. But they told me they had received express orders to leave the castle directly after they had seen the Lady Teresa lodged safely in it. I again entreated them to stay, but it was useless. They hurried on their way, and I returned by myself."

"The ill-bred hounds!" said the baron, in anger. "A sound scourging would have taught them better manners."

"Do not be angry with them," said Teresa, laying her hand gently on that of her husband's. "They did but obey their master's orders."

"Some day, I swear," said the baron, "I will be revenged on their master for this insult, miserable churl that he is!"

He had no sooner uttered these words than he looked round him for the sparrow, but the bird did not make its appearance. Possibly its absence alarmed him even more than its presence would have done, for he began to dread lest the vengeance of the astrologer was about to fall on him, without giving him the usual notice. Teresa, perceiving the expression of his countenance, did all in her power to calm him, but for some time she but partially succeeded. He continued to glance anxiously about him, to ascertain, if possible, from which side the blow might come. He was just on the point of raising a goblet to his lips, when the idea seized him that the wine might be poisoned. He declined to touch food for the same reason. The idea of being struck with death when at the height of his happiness seemed to overwhelm him. Thanks, however, to the kind soothing of Teresa, as well as the absence of any visible effects of the Innominato's anger, he at last became completely reassured, and the feast proceeded.

Long before the banquet had concluded the baron and his wife quitted the hall and retired through their private apartments to the terrace of the castle. The evening, which was now rapidly advancing, was warm and genial, and not a cloud was to be seen in the atmosphere. For some time they walked together up and down on the terrace; and afterwards they seated themselves on a bench. There, with his arm round her waist and her head leaning on his shoulder, they watched the sun in all his magnificence sinking behind the mountains. The sun had almost disappeared, when the baron took his wife's hand in his.

"How cold thou art, my dear!" he said to her. "Let us go in."

Teresa made no answer, but rising from her seat was conducted by her husband into the room which opened on to the terrace, and which was lighted by a large brass lamp which hung by a chain from the ceiling. When they were nearly under the lamp, whose light increased as the daylight declined, Conrad again cast his arm round his wife, and fondly pressed her head to his breast. They remained thus for some moments, entranced in their happiness.

"Dost thou really love me, Teresa?" asked the baron.

"Love you?" said Teresa, now burying her face in his bosom. "Love you? Yes, dearer than all the world. My very existence hangs on your life. When that ceases my existence ends."

When she had uttered these words, Conrad, in a state of intense happiness, said to her—

"Kiss me, my beloved."

Teresa still kept her face pressed on his bosom; and Conrad, to overcome her coyness, placed his hand on her head and gently pressed it backwards, so that he might kiss her.

He stood motionless, aghast with horror, for the light of the lamp above their heads showed him no longer the angelic features of Teresa, but the hideous face of a corpse that had remained some time in the tomb, and whose only sign of vitality was a horrible phosphoric light which shone in its eyes. Conrad now tried to rush from the room, and to scream for assistance—but in vain. With one arm she clasped him tightly round the waist, and raising the other, she placed her clammy hand upon his mouth, and threw him with great force upon the floor. Then seizing the side of his neck with her lips, she deliberately and slowly sucked from him his life's blood; while he, utterly incapable either of moving or crying, was yet perfectly conscious of the awful fate that was awaiting him.

In this manner Conrad remained for some hours in the arms of his vampire wife. At last faintness came over him, and he grew insensible. The sun had risen some hours before consciousness returned. He rose from the ground horror-stricken and pallid, and glanced fearfully around him to see if Teresa were still there; but he found himself alone in the room. For some minutes he remained undecided what step to take. At last he rose from his chair to leave the apartment, but he was so weak he could scarcely drag himself along. When he left the room he bent his steps towards the courtyard. Each person he met saluted him with the most profound respect, while on the countenance of each was visible an expression of intense surprise, so altered was he from the athletic young man they had seen him the day before. Presently he heard the merry laughter of a number of children, and immediately hastened to the spot from whence the noise came. To his surprise he found his wife Teresa, in full possession of her beauty, playing with several children, whose mothers had brought them to see her, and who stood delighted with the condescending kindness of the baroness towards their little ones.

Conrad remained motionless for some moments, gazing with intense surprise at his wife, and the idea occurred to him that the events of the last night must have been a terrible dream and nothing more. But he was at a loss how to account for his bodily weakness. Teresa, in the midst of her gambols with the children, accidentally raised her head and perceived her husband. She uttered a slight cry of pleasure when she saw him, and snatching up in her arms a beautiful child she had been playing with, she rushed towards him, exclaiming—

"Look, dear Conrad, what a little beauty this is! Is he not a little cherub?"

The baron gazed wildly at his wife for a few moments, but said nothing.

"My dearest husband, what ails you?" said Teresa. "Are you not well?"

Conrad made no answer, but turning suddenly round staggered hurriedly away, while Teresa, with an expression of alarm and anxiety on her face, followed him with her eyes as he went. He still hurried on till he reached the small sitting-room from which he was accustomed each morning to issue his orders to his dependants, and seated himself in a chair to recover if possible from the bewilderment he was in. Presently Ludovico, whose duty it was to attend on his master every morning for instructions, entered the room, and bowing respectfully to the baron, stood silently aside, waiting till he should be spoken to, but during the time marking the baron's altered appearance with the most intense curiosity. After some moments the baron asked him what he saw to make him stare in that manner.

"Pardon my boldness, your excellency," said Ludovico, "but I was afraid you might be ill. I trust I am in error."

"What should make you think I am unwell?" inquired the baron.

"Your highness's countenance is far paler than usual, and there is a small wound on the side of your throat. I hope you have not injured yourself."

The last remark of Ludovico decided the action that the events of the evening had been no hallucination. What stronger proof could be required than the marks of his vampire wife's teeth still upon him? He perceived that some course of action must be at once decided upon, and the urgency of his position aided him to concentrate his thoughts. He determined on visiting a celebrated anchorite who lived in the mountains about four leagues distant, and who was famous not only for the piety of his life, but for his power in exorcising evil spirits. Having come to this resolution, he desired Ludovico immediately to saddle for him a sure-footed mule, as the path to the anchorite's dwelling was not only difficult but dangerous.

Ludovico bowed, and after having been informed that there were no other orders, he left the room, wondering in his mind what could be the reason for his master's wishing a mule saddled, when he generally rode only the highest-spirited horses. The conclusion he came to was, that the baron must have been attacked with some serious illness, and was about to proceed to some skilful leech.

As soon as Ludovico had left the room, the baron called to one of the servants whom he saw passing, and ordered breakfast to be brought to him immediately, hoping that by a hearty meal he should recover sufficient strength for the journey he was about to undertake. To a certain extent he succeeded, though possibly it was from the quantity of wine he drank, rather than from any other cause, for he had no appetite and had eaten but little.

He now descended into the courtyard of the castle, cautiously avoiding his wife. Finding the mule in readiness, he mounted it and started on his journey. For some time he went along quietly and slowly, for he still felt weak and languid, but as he attained a higher elevation of the mountains, the cold breeze seemed to invigorate him. He now began to consider how he could rid himself of the horrible vampire he had married, and of whose real nature he had no longer any doubt. Speculations on this subject occupied him till he had entered on a path on the slope of an exceedingly high mountain. It was difficult to keep footing, and it required all his caution to prevent himself from falling. Of fear, however, the baron had none; and his thoughts continued to run on the possibility of separating himself from Teresa, and on what vengeance he would take on the Innominato for the treachery he had practised on him, as soon as he should be fairly freed. The more he dwelt on his revenge, the more excited he became, till at last he exclaimed aloud, "Infamous wretch! Let me be but once fairly released from the execrable fiend you have imposed upon me, and I swear I will burn thee alive in thy castle, as a fitting punishment for the sorcery thou hast practised."

Conrad had hardly uttered these words, when the pathway upon which he was riding gave way beneath him, and glided down the incline into a tremendous precipice below. He succeeded in throwing himself from his mule, which, with the *débris* of the rocks, was hurried over the precipice, while he clutched with the energy of despair at each object he saw likely to give him a moment's support. But everything he touched gave way, and he gradually sank and sank towards the verge of the precipice, his efforts to save himself becoming more violent the nearer he approached to what appeared certain death. Down he sank, till his legs actually hung over the precipice, when he succeeded in grasping a stone somewhat firmer than the others, thus retarding his fall for a moment. In horror he now glanced at the terrible chasm beneath him, when suddenly different objects came before his mind with fearful reality. There was an unhappy peasant, who had without permission killed a head of game, hanging from the branch of a tree, still struggling in the agonies of death, while his wife and children were in vain imploring the baron's clemency.

This vanished and he saw a boy with a knife in his hand, stabbing at his own mother for some slight offence she had given him.

This passed, and he found himself in a small village, the inhabitants of which were all dead within their houses; for at the approach of winter he had, in a fit of ill-temper, ordered his retainers to take from them all their provisions; and a snowstorm coming on immediately afterwards, they were blocked up in their dwellings, and all perished.

Again his thoughts reverted to the position he was in, and his eye glanced over the terrible precipice that yawned beneath him, when he saw, as if in a dream, the house of Biffi the farmer, with his wife and children around him, apparently contented and happy.

As soon as he had realized the idea, the stone which he had clutched began to give way, and all seemed lost to him, when a sparrow suddenly flew on the earth a short distance from him, and immediately afterwards darted away. "Save but my life," screamed the baron, "and I swear I will keep all secret!"

The words had hardly been uttered, when a goatherd with a long staff in his hand appeared on the incline above him. The man perceiving the imminent peril of the baron, with great caution, and yet with great activity, descended to assist him. He succeeded in reaching a ledge of rock a few feet above, and rather to the side of the baron, to whom he stretched forth the long mountain staff in his hand. The baron clutched it with such energy as would certainly have drawn the goatherd over with him, had it not been that the latter was a remarkably powerful man. With some difficulty the baron reached the ledge of the rock, and the goatherd then ascended to a higher position, and in like manner drew the baron on, till at last he had contrived to get him to a place of safety. As soon as Conrad found himself out of danger, he gazed wildly around him for a moment, then dizziness came over him, and he sank fainting on the ground.

When the baron had recovered his senses, he found himself so weak that it would have been impossible for him to have reached the castle that evening. He therefore willingly accompanied the goatherd to his hut in the mountains, where he proposed to pass the night. The man made what provision he could for his illustrious guest, and prepared him a supper of the best his hut afforded;

but had the latter been composed of the most exquisite delicacies, it would have been equally tasteless; for Conrad had not the slightest appetite. Evening was now rapidly approaching, and the goatherd prepared a bed of leaves, over which he threw a cloak, and the baron, utterly exhausted, reposed on it for the night, without anything occurring to disturb his rest.

Next morning he found himself somewhat refreshed by his night's rest, and he prepared to return to the castle, assisted by the goatherd, to whom he had promised a handsome reward. He had now given up all idea of visiting the anchorite, dreading that by so doing he might excite the animosity of the Innominato, of whose tremendous power he had lately received more than ample proof. In due time he reached home in safety, and the goatherd was dismissed after having received the promised reward. On entering the castle-yard the baron found his wife in a state of great alarm and sorrow, and surrounded by the retainers. No sooner did she perceive her husband, than, uttering a cry of delight and surprise, she rushed forward to clasp him in her arms; but the baron pushed her rudely away, and hurrying forwards, directed his steps to the room in which he was accustomed to issue his orders. Ludovico, having heard of the arrival of his master, immediately waited on him.

"Ludovico," said the baron, as soon as he saw him, "I want you to execute an order for me with great promptitude and secrecy. Go below, and prepare two good horses for a journey; one for you, the other for myself. See that we take with us provisions and equipments for two or three days. As soon as they are in readiness, leave the castle with them without speaking to any one, and wait for me about a league up the mountain, where in less than two hours I will join you. Now see that you faithfully carry out my orders, and if you do so, I assure you you will lose nothing by your obedience."

Ludovico left the baron's presence to execute his order, when immediately afterwards a servant came into the room, and inquired if the Lady Teresa might enter.

"Tell your mistress," said the baron, in a tone of great courtesy and kindness, "that I hope she will excuse me for the moment, as I am deeply engaged in affairs of importance; but I shall await her visit with great impatience in the afternoon."

The baron, now left to himself, began to draw out more fully the plan for his future operations. He resolved to visit his brother Hermann, and consult him as to what steps he ought to take in this horrible emergency; and in case no better means presented themselves, he determined on offering to give up to Hermann the castle of Gardonal and the whole valley of the Engadin, on condition of receiving from him an annuity sufficient to support him in the position he had always been accustomed to maintain. He then intended to retire to some distant country, where there would be no probability of his being followed by the horrible monster whom he had accepted as his wife. Of course he had no intention of receiving Teresa in the afternoon, and he had merely put off her visit for the purpose of allowing himself to escape with greater convenience from the castle.

About an hour after Ludovico had left him, the baron quitted the castle by a postern, with as much haste as his enfeebled strength would allow, and hurried after his retainer, whom he found awaiting him with the horses. The baron immediately mounted one, and followed by Ludovico, took the road to his brother's, where in three days he arrived in safety. Hermann received his brother with great pleasure, though much surprised at the alteration in his appearance.

"My dear Conrad," he said to him, "what can possibly have occurred to you? You look very pale, weak, and haggard. Have you been ill?"

"Worse, a thousand times worse," said Conrad. "Let us go where we may be by ourselves, and I will tell you all."

Hermann led his brother into a private room, where Conrad explained to him the terrible misfortune which had befallen him. Hermann listened attentively, and for some time could not help doubting whether his brother's mind was not affected; but Conrad explained everything in so circumstantial and lucid a manner as to dispel that idea. To the proposition which Conrad made, to make over the territory of the Engadin Valley for an annuity, Hermann promised to give full consideration. At the same time, before any further steps were taken in the matter, he advised Conrad to visit a villa he had, on the sea-shore, about ten miles distant from Genoa; where, in quiet and seclusion, he would be able to recover his energies.

Conrad thanked his brother for his advice, and willingly accepted the offer. Two days afterwards he started on the journey, and by the end of the week arrived safely, and without difficulty, at the villa.

On the evening of his arrival, Conrad, who had employed himself during the afternoon in visiting the different apartments as well as the grounds surrounding the villa, was seated at a window overlooking the sea. The evening was deliciously calm, and he felt such ease and security as he had not enjoyed for some time past. The sun was sinking in the ocean, and the moon began to appear, and the stars one by one to shine in the cloudless heavens. The thought crossed Conrad's mind that the sight of the sun sinking in the waters strongly resembled his own position when he fell over the precipice. The thought had hardly been conceived when some one touched him on the shoulder. He turned round, and saw standing before him, in the full majesty of her beauty—his wife Teresa!

"My dearest Conrad," she said, with much affection in her tone, "why have you treated me in this cruel manner? It was most unkind of you to leave me suddenly without giving the slightest hint of your intentions."

"Execrable fiend," said Conrad, springing from his chair, "leave me! Why do you haunt me in this manner?"

"Do not speak so harshly to me, my dear husband," said Teresa. "To oblige you I was taken from my grave, and on you now my very existence depends."

"Rather my death," said Conrad. "One night more such as we passed, and I should be a corpse."

"Nay, dear Conrad," said Teresa. "I have the power of indefinitely prolonging your life. Drink but of this," she continued, taking from the table behind her a silver goblet, "and tomorrow all ill effects will have passed away."

Conrad mechanically took the goblet from her hand, and was on the point of raising it to his lips when he suddenly stopped, and with a shudder replaced it again on the table.

"It is blood," he said.

"True, my dear husband," said Teresa. "What else could it be? My life is dependent on your life's blood, and when that ceases so does my life. Drink then, I implore you," she continued, again offering him the goblet. "Look, the sun has already sunk beneath the wave; a minute more and daylight will have gone. Drink, Conrad, I implore you, or this night will be your last."

Conrad again took the goblet from her hand to raise it to his lips; but it was impossible, and he placed it on the table. A ray of pure moonlight now penetrated the room, as if to prove that the light of day had fled. Teresa, again transformed into a horrible vampire, flew at her husband, and throwing him on the floor, fastened her teeth on the half-healed wound in his throat. The next morning, when the servants entered the room, they found the baron a corpse on the floor; but Teresa was nowhere to be seen, nor was she ever heard of afterwards.

Little more remains to be told. Hermann took possession of the castle of Gardonal and the valley of the Engadin, and treated his vassals with even more despotism than his brother had done before him. At last, driven to desperation, they rose against him and slew him; and the valley afterwards became absorbed into the Canton of the Grisons.

# A MYSTERY OF THE CAMPAGNA

# Anne Crawford

Anne Crawford, Baroness Von Rabe (1846–?) is the largely unknown sister of the once enormously popular American writer F. Marion Crawford. Since her brother spent much of his life in Italy, and Anne Crawford's most famous story was set there, it may be surmised that she, too, lived there.

The Campagna, incidentally, is the level country around Rome, which was a great favorite of nineteenth-century landscape painters.

"A Mystery of the Campagna" was first published under the pseudonym Von Degen in *The Witching Time: Unwin's Christmas Annual* (London: T. Fisher Unwin, 1887), edited by Sir Henry Norman. It was first published in book form as *A Mystery of the Campagna and A Shadow on a Wave* (London: T. Fisher Unwin, 1891) in the publisher's Pseudonym Library series, also under the name Von Degen.

# A Mystery of the Campagna

## ANNE CRAWFORD

### I

Marcello's voice is pleading with me now, perhaps because after years of separation I have met an old acquaintance who had a part in his strange story. I have a longing to tell it, and have asked Monsieur Sutton to help me. He noted down the circumstances at the time, and he is willing to join his share to mine, that Marcello may be remembered.

One day, it was in spring, he appeared in my little studio amongst the laurels and green alleys of the Villa Medici. "Come *mon enfant*," he said, "put up your paints," and he unceremoniously took my palette out of my hand. "I have a cab waiting outside, and we are going in search of a hermitage." He was already washing my brushes as he spoke, and this softened my heart, for I hate to do it myself. Then he pulled off my velvet jacket and took down my respectable coat from a nail on the wall. I let him dress me like a child. We always did his will, and he knew it, and in a moment we were sitting in the cab, driving through the Via Sistina on our way to the Porta San Giovanni, whither he had directed the coachman to go.

I must tell my story as I can, for though I have been told by my comrades, who cannot know very well, that I can speak good English, writing it is another thing. Monsieur Sutton has asked me to use his tongue, because he has so far forgotten mine that he will not trust himself in it, though he has promised to correct my mistakes, that what I have to tell you may not seem ridiculous, and make people laugh when they read of Marcello. I tell him I wish to write this for my countrymen, not his; but he reminds me that Marcello had many English friends who still live, and that the English do not forget as we do. It is of no use to reason with him, for neither do they yield as we do, and so I have consented to his wish. I think he has a reason which he does not tell me, but let it go. I will translate it all into my own language for my own people. Your English phrases seem to me to be always walking sideways, or trying to look around the corner or stand upon their heads, and they have as many little tails as a kite. I will try not

41

to have recourse to my own language, but he must pardon me if I forget myself. He may be sure I do not do it to offend him. Now that I have explained so much, let me go on.

When we had passed out of the Porta San Giovanni, the coachman drove as slowly as possible; but Marcello was never practical. How could he be, I ask you, with an opera in his head? So we crawled along, and he gazed dreamily before him. At last, when we had reached the part where the little villas and vineyards begin, he began to look about him.

You all know how it is out there; iron gates with rusty names or initials over them, and beyond them straight walks bordered with roses and lavender leading up to a forlorn little casino, with trees and a wilderness behind it sloping down to the Campagna, lonely enough to be murdered in and no one to hear you cry. We stopped at several of these gates and Marcello stood looking in, but none of the places were to his taste. He seemed not to doubt that he might have whatever pleased him, but nothing did so. He would jump out and run to the gate, and return saying, "The shape of those windows would disturb my inspiration," or, "That yellow paint would make me fail my duet in the second act"; and once he liked the air of the house well enough, but there were marigolds growing in the walk, and he hated them. So we drove on and on, until I thought we should find nothing more to reject. At last we came to one which suited him, though it was terribly lonely, and I should have fancied it very *agaçant* to live so far away from the world with nothing but those melancholy olives and green oaks—ilexes, you call them—for company.

"I shall live here and become famous!" he said, decidedly, as he pulled the iron rod which rang a great bell inside. We waited, and then he rang again very impatiently and stamped his foot.

"No one lives here, *mon vieux*! Come, it is getting late, and it is so damp out here, and you know that the damp for a tenor voice—" He stamped his foot again and interrupted me angrily.

"Why, then, have you got a tenor? You are stupid! A bass would be more sensible; nothing hurts it. But you have not got one, and you call yourself my friend! Go home without me." How could I, so far on foot? "Go and sing your lovesick songs to your lean English misses! They will thank you with a cup of abominable tea, and you will be in Paradise! This is *my* Paradise, and I shall stay until the angel comes to open it."

He was very cross and unreasonable, and those were just the times when one loved him most, so I waited and enveloped my throat in my pocket-handkerchief and sang a passage or two just to prevent my voice from becoming stiff in that damp air.

"Be still! Silence yourself!" he cried. "I cannot hear if anyone is coming."

Someone came at last, a rough-looking sort of keeper, or *guardiano* as they are called there, who looked at us as though he thought we were mad. One of us certainly was, but it was not I. Marcello spoke pretty good Italian, with a French accent, it is true, but the man understood him, especially as he held his purse in his hand. I heard him say a great many impetuously persuasive things all in one breath, then he slipped a gold piece into the *guardiano*'s horny hand, and the two turned towards the house, the man shrugging his shoulders in a resigned sort of way, and Marcello called out to me over his shoulder—

"Go home in the cab, or you will be late for your horrible English party! I am going to stay here tonight." *Ma foi!* I took his permission and left him; for a tenor voice is as tyrannical as a jealous woman. Besides, I was furious, and yet I laughed. His was the artist temperament, and appeared to us by turns absurd, sublime, and intensely irritating; but this last never for long, and we all felt that were we more like him our pictures would be worth more. I had not got as far as the city gate when my temper had cooled, and I began to reproach myself for leaving him in that lonely place with his purse full of money, for he was not poor at all, and tempting the dark *guardiano* to murder him. Nothing could be easier than to kill him in his sleep and bury him away somewhere under the olive trees or in some old vault of a ruined catacomb, so common on the borders of the Campagna. There were sure to be a hundred convenient places. I stopped the coachman and told him to turn back, but he shook his head and said something about having to be in the Piazza of St. Peter at eight o'clock. His horse began to go lame, as though he had understood his master and was his accomplice. What could I do? I said to myself that it was fate, and let him take me back to the Villa Medici, where I had to pay him a pretty sum for our crazy expedition, and then he rattled off, the horse not lame at all, leaving me bewildered at this strange afternoon.

I did not sleep well that night, though my tenor song had been applauded, and the English misses had caressed me much. I tried not to think of Marcello, and he did not trouble me much until I went to bed; but then I could not sleep, as I have told you.

I fancied him already murdered, and being buried in the darkness by the *guardiano*. I saw the man dragging his body, with the beautiful head thumping against the stones, down dark passages, and at last leaving it all bloody and covered with earth under a black arch in a recess, and coming back to count the gold pieces. But then again I fell asleep, and dreamed that Marcello was standing at the gate and stamping his foot; and then I slept no more, but got up as soon as the dawn came, and dressed myself and went to my studio at the end of the laurel walk. I took down my painting jacket, and remembered how he had pulled it off my shoulders. I took up the brushes he had washed for me; they were only half cleaned after all, and stiff with paint and soap. I felt glad to be angry with him, and *sacré*'d a little, for it made me sure that he was yet alive if I could scold at him. Then I pulled out my study of his head for my picture of Mucius Scaevola holding his hand in the flame, and then I forgave him; for who could look upon that face and not love it?

I worked with the fire of friendship in my brush, and did my best to endow the features with the expression of scorn and obstinacy I had seen at the gate. It could not have been more suitable to my subject! Had I seen it for the last time? You will ask me why I did not leave my work and go to see if anything had happened to him, but against this there were several reasons. Our yearly exhibition was not far off and my picture was barely painted in, and my comrades had sworn that it would not be ready. I was expecting a model for the King of the Etruscans; a man who cooked chestnuts in the Piazza Montanara, and who had consented to stoop to sit to me as a great favour; and then, to tell the truth, the morning was beginning to dispel my fancies. I had a good northern light to work by, with nothing sentimental about it, and I was not fanciful by nature; so when I sat down to my easel I told myself that I had been a fool, and that Marcello was perfectly safe: the smell of the paints helping me to feel practical again. Indeed, I thought every moment that he would come in, tired of his caprice already, and even was preparing and practising a little lecture for him. Some one knocked at my door, and I cried *"Entrez!"* thinking it was he at last, but no, it was Pierre Magnin.

"There is a curious man, a man of the country, who wants you," he said. "He has your address on a dirty piece of paper in Marcello's handwriting, and a letter for you, but he won't give it up. He says he must see 'Il Signor Martino.' He'd make a superb model for a murderer! Come and speak to him, and keep him while I get a sketch of his head."

I followed Magnin through the garden, and outside, for the porter had not allowed him to enter. I found the *guardiano* of yesterday. He showed his white teeth, and said, "Good day, signore," like a Christian; and here in Rome he did not look half so murderous, only a stupid, brown, country fellow. He had a rough peasant-cart waiting, and he had tied up his shaggy horse to a ring in the wall. I held out my hand for the letter and pretended to find it difficult to read, for I saw Magnin standing with his sketch-book in the shadow of the entrance hall. The note said this: I have it still and I will copy it. It was written in pencil on a leaf torn from his pocketbook.

*Mon vieux! I have passed a good night here, and the man will keep me as long as I like. Nothing will happen to me, except that I shall be divinely quiet, and I already have a famous motif in my head. Go to my lodgings and pack up some clothes and all my manuscripts, with plenty of music paper and a few bottles of Bordeaux, and give them to my messenger. Be quick about it!*

*Fame is preparing to descend upon me! If you care to see me, do not come before eight days. The gate will not be opened if you come sooner. The guardiano is my slave, and he has instructions to kill any intruder who in the guise of a friend tries to get in uninvited. He will do it, for he has confessed to me that he has murdered three men already.*

(Of course this was a joke. I knew Marcello's way.)

*When you come, go to the* poste restante *and fetch my letters. Here is my card to legitimate you. Don't forget pens and a bottle of ink! Your Marcello.*

There was nothing for it but to jump into the cart, tell Magnin, who had finished his sketch, to lock up my studio, and go bumping off to obey these commands. We drove to his lodgings in the Via del Governo Vecchio, and there I made a bundle of all that I could think of; the landlady hindering me by a thousand questions about when the Signore would return. He had paid for the rooms in advance, so she had no need to be anxious about her rent. When I told her where he was, she shook her head, and talked a great deal about the bad air out there, and said "Poor Signorino!" in a melancholy way, as though he were already buried, and looked mournfully after us from the window when we drove away. She irritated me, and made me feel superstitious. At the corner of the Via del Tritone I jumped down and gave the man a franc out of pure sentimentality, and cried after him, "Greet the Signore!" but he did not hear me, and jogged away stupidly whilst I was longing to be with him.

Marcello was a cross to us sometimes, but we loved him always.

The eight days went by sooner than I had thought they would, and Thursday came, bright and sunny, for my expedition. At one o'clock I descended into the Piazza di Spagna, and made a bargain with a man who had a well-fed horse, remembering how dearly Marcello's want of good sense had cost me a week ago, and we drove off at a good pace to the Vigna Marziali, as I was almost forgetting to say that it was called. My heart was beating, though I did not know why I should feel so much emotion. When we reached the iron gate the *guardiano* answered my ring directly, and I had no sooner set foot in the long flower-walk than I saw Marcello hastening to meet me.

"I knew you would come," he said, drawing my arm within his, and so we walked towards the little grey house, which had a sort of portico and several balconies, and a sun-dial on its front. There were grated windows down to the ground floor, and the place, to my relief, looked safe and habitable. He told me that the man did not sleep there, but in a little hut down towards the Campagna, and that he, Marcello, locked himself in safely every night, which I was also relieved to know.

"What do you get to eat?" said I.

"Oh, I have goat's flesh, and dried beans and polenta, with pecorino cheese, and there is plenty of black bread and sour wine," he answered smilingly. "You see I am not starved."

"Do not overwork yourself, *mon vieux*," I said. "You are worth more than your opera will ever be."

"Do I look overworked?" he said, turning his face to me in the broad, outdoor light. He seemed a little offended at my saying that about his opera, and I was foolish to do it.

I examined his face critically, and he looked at me half defiantly. "No, not yet," I answered rather unwillingly, for I could not say that he did; but there was a restless, inward look in his eyes, and an almost imperceptible shadow lay around them. It seemed to me as though the full temples had grown slightly hollow, and a sort of faint mist lay over his beauty, making it seem strange and far off. We were standing before the door, and he pushed it open, the *guardiano* following us with slow, loud-resounding steps.

"Here is my Paradise," said Marcello, and we entered the house, which was like all the others of its kind. A hall, with stucco bas-reliefs, and a stairway adorned with antique fragments, gave access to the upper rooms. Marcello ran up the steps lightly, and I heard him lock a door somewhere above and draw out the key, then he came and met me on the landing.

"This," he said, "is my workroom," and he threw open a low door. The key was in the lock, so this room could not be the one I heard him close. "Tell me I shall not write like an angel here!" he cried. I was so dazzled by the flood of bright sunshine after the dusk of the passage, that I blinked like an owl at first, and then I saw a large room, quite bare except for a rough table and chair, the chair covered with manuscript music.

"You are looking for the furniture," he said, laughing. "It is outside. Look here!" And he drew me to a rickety door of worm-eaten wood and coarse greenish glass, and flung it open on to a rusty iron balcony. He was right; the furniture was outside, that is to say, a divine view met my eyes. The Sabine Mountains, the Alban Hills, and broad Campagna, with its mediaeval towers and ruined aqueducts, and the open plain to the sea. All this glowing and yet calm in the sunlight. No wonder he could write there! The balcony ran round the corner of the house, and to the right I looked down upon an alley of ilexes, ending in a grove of tall laurel trees—very old, apparently. There were bits of sculpture and some ancient sarcophagi standing gleaming against them, and even from so high I could hear a little stream of water pouring from an antique mask into a long, rough trough. I saw the brown *guardiano* digging at his cabbages and onions, and I laughed to think that I could fancy him a murderer! He had a little bag of relics, which dangled to and fro over his sun-burned breast, and he looked very innocent when he sat down upon an old column to eat a piece of black bread with an onion which he had just pulled out of the ground, slic-

ing it with a knife not at all like a dagger. But I kept my thoughts to myself, for Marcello would have laughed at them. We were standing together, looking down at the man as he drank from his hands at the running fountain, and Marcello now leaned down over the balcony, and called out a long "Ohé!" The lazy *guardiano* looked up, nodded, and then got up slowly from the stone where he had been half-kneeling to reach the jet of water.

"We are going to dine," Marcello explained. "I have been waiting for you." Presently he heard the man's heavy tread upon the stairs, and he entered bearing a strange meal in a basket.

There came to light pecorino cheese made from ewe's milk, black bread of the consistency of a stone, a great bowl of salad apparently composed of weeds, and a sausage which filled the room with a strong smell of garlic. Then he disappeared and came back with a dish full of ragged-looking goat's flesh cooked together with a mass of smoking polenta, and I am not sure that there was not oil in it.

"I told you I lived well, and now you see!" said Marcello. It was a terrible meal, but I had to eat it, and was glad to have some rough, sour wine to help me, which tasted of earth and roots. When we had finished I said, "And your opera! How are you getting on?"

"Not a word about that!" he cried. "You see how I have written!" And he turned over a heap of manuscript. "But do not talk to me about it. I will not lose my ideas in words." This was not like Marcello, who loved to discuss his work, and I looked at him astonished.

"Come," he said, "we will go down into the garden, and you shall tell me about the comrades. What are they doing? Has Magnin found a model for his Clytemnestra?"

I humoured him, as I always did, and we sat upon a stone bench behind the house, looking towards the laurel grove, talking of the pictures and the students. I wanted to walk down the ilex alley, but he stopped me.

"If you are afraid of the damp, don't go down there," he said. "The place is like a vault. Let us stay here and be thankful for this heavenly view."

"Well, let us stay here," I answered, resigned

as ever. He lit a cigar and offered me one in silence. If he did not care to talk, I could be still too. From time to time he made some indifferent observation, and I answered it in the same tone. It almost seemed to me as though we, the old heart-comrades, had become strangers who had not known each other a week, or as though we had been so long apart that we had grown away from each other. There was something about him which escaped me. Yes, the days of solitude had indeed put years and a sort of shyness, or rather ceremony, between us! It did not seem natural to me now to clap him on the back, and make the old, harmless jokes at him. He must have felt the constraint too, for we were like children who had looked forward to a game, and did not know now what to play at.

At six o'clock I left him. It was not like parting with Marcello. I felt rather as though I should find my old friend in Rome that evening, and here only left a shadowy likeness of him. He accompanied me to the gate, and pressed my hand, and for a moment the true Marcello looked out of his eyes; but we called out no last word to each other as I drove away. I had only said, "Let me know when you want me," and he said, *"Merci!"* and all the way back to Rome I felt a chill upon me, his hand had been so cold, and I thought and thought what could be the matter with him.

That evening I spoke out my anxiety to Pierre Magnin, who shook his head and declared that malaria fever must be taking hold of him, and that people often begin to show it by being a little odd.

"He must not stay there! We must get him away as soon as possible," I cried.

"We both know Marcello, and that nothing can make him stir against his will," said Pierre. "Let him alone, and he will get tired of his whim. It will not kill him to have a touch of malaria, and some evening he will turn up amongst us as merry as ever."

But he did not. I worked hard at my picture and finished it, but for a few touches, and he had not yet appeared. Perhaps it was the extreme application, perhaps the sitting out in that damp place, for I insist upon tracing it to something more material than emotion. Well, whatever it was, I fell ill; more ill than I had ever been in my life. It was almost twilight when it overtook me, and I remember it distinctly, though I forget what happened afterwards, or, rather, I never knew, for I was found by Magnin quite unconscious, and he has told me that I remained so for some time, and then became delirious, and talked of nothing but Marcello. I have told you that it was very nearly twilight; but just at the moment when the sun is gone the colours show in their true value. Artists know this, and I was putting last touches here and there to my picture and especially to my head of Mucius Scaevola, or rather, Marcello.

The rest of the picture came out well enough; but that head, which should have been the principal one, seemed faded and sunk in. The face appeared to grow paler and paler, and to recede from me; a strange veil spread over it, and the eyes seemed to close. I am not easily frightened, and I know what tricks some peculiar methods of colour will play by certain lights, for the moment I spoke of had gone, and the twilight greyness had set in; so I stepped back to look at it. Just then the lips, which had become almost white, opened a little, and sighed! An illusion, of course. I must have been very ill and quite delirious already, for to my imagination it was a real sigh, or, rather, a sort of exhausted gasp. Then it was that I fainted, I suppose, and when I came to myself I was in my bed, with Magnin and Monsieur Sutton standing by me, and a Sœur de Charité moving softly about among medicine bottles, and speaking in whispers. I stretched out my hands, and they were thin and yellow, with long, pale nails; and I heard Magnin's voice, which sounded very far away, say, *"Dieu Merci!"* And now Monsieur Sutton will tell you what I did not know until long afterwards.

## II

### ROBERT SUTTON'S ACCOUNT OF WHAT HAPPENED AT THE VIGNA MARZIALI

I am attached to Detaille, and was very glad to be of use to him, but I never fully shared his admiration for Marcello Souvestre, though I appreciated his good points. He was certainly very promising— I must say that. But he was an odd, flighty sort of fellow, not of the kind which we English care to take the trouble to understand. It is my business to write stories, but not having need of such characters I have never particularly studied them. As I say, I was glad to be of use to Detaille, who is a thorough good fellow, and I willingly gave up my work to go and sit by his bedside. Magnin knew that I was a friend of his, and very properly came to me when he found that Detaille's illness was a serious one and likely to last for a long time. I found him perfectly delirious, and raving about Marcello.

"Tell me what the *motif* is! I know it is a *Marche Funèbr*!" And here he would sing a peculiar melody, which, as I have a knack at music, I noted down, it being like nothing I had heard before. The Sister of Charity looked at me with severe eyes; but how could she know that all is grist for our mill, and that observation becomes with us a mechanical habit? Poor Detaille kept repeating this curious melody over and over, and then would stop and seem to be looking at his picture, crying that it was fading away.

"Marcello! Marcello! You are fading too! Let me come to you!" He was as weak as a baby, and could not have moved from his bed unless in the strength of delirium.

"I cannot come!" he went on. "They have tied me down." And here he made as though he were trying to gnaw through a rope at his wrists, and then burst into tears. "Will no one go for me and bring me a word from you? Ah! if I could know that you are alive!"

Magnin looked at me. I knew what he was thinking. He would not leave his comrade, but I must go. I don't mind acknowledging that I did not undertake this unwillingly. To sit by Detaille's bedside and listen to his ravings enervated me, and what Magnin wanted struck me as troublesome but not uninteresting to one of my craft, so I agreed to go. I had heard all about Marcello's strange seclusion from Magnin and Detaille himself, who lamented over it openly in his simple way at supper at the Academy, where I was a frequent guest.

I knew that it would be useless to ring at the gate of the Vigna Marziali. Not only should I not be admitted, but I should arouse Marcello's anger and suspicion, for I did not for a moment believe that he was not alive, though I thought it very possible that he was becoming a little crazy, as his countrymen are so easily put off their balance. Now, odd people are oddest late in the day and at evening time. Their nerves lose the power of resistance then, and the real man gets the better of them. So I determined to try to discover something at night, reflecting also that I should be safer from detection then. I knew his liking for wandering about when he ought to be in his bed, and I did not doubt that I should get a glimpse of him, and that was really all I needed.

My first step was to take a long walk out of the Porta San Giovanni, and this I did in the early morning, tramping along steadily until I came to an iron gate on the right of the road, with "Vigna Marziali" over it; and then I walked straight on, never stopping until I had reached a little bushy lane running down towards the Campagna to the right. It was pebbly, and quite shut in by luxuriant ivy and elder bushes, and it bore deep traces of the last heavy rains. These had evidently been effaced by no footprints, so I concluded that it was little used. Down this path I made my way cautiously, looking behind and before me, from a habit contracted in my lonely wanderings in the Abruzzi. I had a capital revolver with me—an old friend— and I feared no man; but I began to feel a dramatic interest in my undertaking, and determined that it should not be crossed by any disagreeable surprises. The lane led me further down the plain that I had reckoned upon, for the bushy edge shut out the view; and when I had got to the bottom and faced round, the Vigna Marziali was lying quite far to my left. I saw at a glance that behind the grey casino an alley of ilexes ended in a laurel grove; then there were plantations of kitchen stuff, with a sort of thatched cabin in their midst, probably that of a gardener. I looked about for a kennel, but saw none, so there was no watchdog. At the end of this primitive kitchen garden was a broad patch of grass, bounded by a fence, which

I could take at a spring. Now, I knew my way, but I could not resist tracing it out a little further. It was well that I did so, for I found just within the fence a sunken stream; rather full at the time, in consequence of the rains, too deep to wade and too broad to jump. It struck me that it would be easy enough to take a board from the fence and lay it over for a bridge. I measured the breadth with my eye, and decided the board would span it; then I went back as I had come, and returned to find Detaille still raving.

As he could understand nothing it seemed to me rather a fool's errand to go off in search of comfort for him; but a conscious moment might come, and moreover, I began to be interested in my undertaking; and so I agreed with Magnin that I should go and take some food and rest and return to the Vigna that night. I told my landlady that I was going into the country and should return the next day, and I went to Nazarri's and laid in a stock of sandwiches and filled my flask with something they called sherry, for, though I was no great wine-drinker, I feared the night chill.

It was about seven o'clock when I started, and I retraced my morning's steps exactly. As I reached the lane, it occurred to me that it was still too light for me to pass unobserved over the stream, and I made a place for myself under the hedge and lay down, quite screened by the thick curtain of tangled overhanging ivy.

I must have been out of training, and tired by the morning's walk, for I fell asleep. When I awoke it was night; the stars were shining, a dank mist made its way down my throat, and I felt stiff and cold. I took a pull at my flask, finding it nasty stuff, but it warmed me. Then I rang my repeater, which struck a quarter to eleven, got up and shook myself free of the leaves and brambles, and went on down the lane. When I got to the fence I sat down and thought the thing over. What did I expect to discover? What *was* there to discover? Nothing! Nothing but that Marcello was alive; and that was no discovery at all for I felt sure of it. I was a fool, and had let myself be allured by the mere stage nonsense and mystery of the business, and a mouse would creep out of this mountain of precautions!

Well, at least I could turn it to account by describing my own absurd behaviour in some story yet to be written, and, as it was not enough for a chapter, I would add to it by further experience. "Come along!" I said to myself. "You're an ass, but it may prove instructive." I raised the top board from the fence noiselessly. There was a little stile there, and the boards were easily moved. I laid down my bridge with some difficulty, and stepped carefully across, and made my way to the laurel grove as quickly and noiselessly as possible.

There all was thick darkness, and my eyes only grew slowly accustomed to it. After all there was not much to see; some stone seats in a semicircle, and some fragments of columns set upright with antique busts upon them. Then a little to the right a sort of arch, with apparently some steps descending into the ground, probably the entrance to some discovered branch of a catacomb. In the midst of the enclosure, not a very large one, stood a stone table, deeply fixed in the earth. No one was there; of that I felt certain, and I sat down, having now got used to the gloom, and fell to eat my sandwiches, for I was desperately hungry.

now that I had come so far, was nothing to take place to repay me for my trouble? It suddenly struck me that it was absurd to expect Marcello to come out to meet me and perform any mad antics he might be meditating there before my eyes for my especial satisfaction. Why had I supposed that something would take place in the grove I do not know, except that this seemed a fit place for it. I would go and watch the house, and if I saw a light anywhere I might be sure he was within. Any fool might have thought of that, but a novelist lays the scene of his drama and expects his characters to slide about in the grooves like puppets. It is only when mine surprise me that I feel they are alive. When I reached the end of the ilex alley I saw the house before me. There were more cabbages and onions after I had left the trees, and I saw that in this open space I could easily be perceived by any one standing on the balcony above. As I drew back again under the ilexes, a window above, not the one on the balcony, was suddenly lighted up; but the light did not remain long, and presently a gleam shone through the glass oval over the door below.

I had just time to spring behind the thickest trunk near me when the door opened. I took advantage of its creaking to creep up the slanting tree like a cat, and lie out upon a projecting branch.

As I expected, Marcello came out. He was very pale, and moved mechanically like a sleepwalker. I was shocked to see how hollow his face had become as he held the candle still lighted in his hand, and it cast deep shadows on his sunken cheeks and fixed eyes, which burned wildly and seemed to see nothing. His lips were quite white, and so drawn that I could see his gleaming teeth. Then the candle fell from his hand, and he came slowly and with a curiously regular step on into the darkness of the ilexes, I watching him from above. But I scarcely think he would have noticed me had I been standing in his path. When he had passed I let myself down and followed him. I had taken off my shoes, and my tread was absolutely noiseless; moreover, I felt sure he would not turn around.

On he went with the same mechanical step until he reached the grove. There I knelt behind an old sarcophagus at the entrance, and waited. What would he do? He stood perfectly still, not looking about him, but as though the clockwork within him had suddenly stopped. I felt that he was becoming psychologically interesting, after all. Suddenly he threw up his arms as men do when they are mortally wounded on the battle-field, and I expected to see him fall at full length. Instead of this he made a step forward.

I looked in the same direction, and saw a woman, who must have concealed herself there while I was waiting before the house, come from out of the gloom, and as she slowly approached and laid her head upon his shoulder, the outstretched arms clasped themselves closely around her, so that her face was hidden upon his neck.

So this was the whole matter, and I had been sent off on a wild-goose chase to spy out a common love affair! His opera and his seclusion for

the sake of work, his tyrannical refusal to see Detaille unless he sent for him—all this was but a mask to a vulgar intrigue which, for reasons best known to himself, could not be indulged in in the city. I was thoroughly angry! If Marcello passed his time mooning about in that damp hole all night, no wonder that he looked so wretchedly ill, and seemed half mad! I knew very well that Marcello was no saint. Why should he be? But I had not taken him for a fool! He had had plenty of romantic episodes, and as he was discreet without being uselessly mysterious, no one had ever unduly pried into them, nor should we have done so now. I said to myself that that mixture of French and Italian blood was at the bottom of it; French flimsiness and light-headedness and Italian love of cunning! I looked back upon all the details of my mysterious expedition. I suppose at the root of my anger lay a certain dramatic disappointment at not finding him lying murdered, and I despised myself for all the trouble I had taken to this ridiculous end: just to see him holding a woman in his arms. I could not see her face, and her figure was enveloped from head to foot in something long and dark; but I could make out that she was tall and slender, and that a pair of white hands gleamed from her drapery. As I was looking intently, for all my indignation, the couple moved on, and still clinging to one another descended the steps. So even the solitude of the lonely laurel grove could not satisfy Marcello's insane love of secrecy! I kept still awhile; then I stole to where they had disappeared, and listened; but all was silent, and I cautiously struck a match and peered down. I could see the steps for a short distance below me, and then the darkness seemed to rise and swallow them. It must be a catacomb as I had imagined, or an old Roman bath, perhaps, which Marcello had made comfortable enough, no doubt, and as likely as not they were having a nice little cold supper there. My empty stomach told me that I could have forgiven him even then could I have shared it; I was in truth frightfully hungry as well as angry, and sat down on one of the stone benches to finish my sandwiches.

The thought of waiting to see this love-sick

pair return to upper earth never for a moment occurred to me. I had found out the whole thing, and a great humbug it was! Now I wanted to get back to Rome before my temper had cooled, and to tell Magnin on what a fool's errand he had sent me. If he liked to quarrel with me, all the better!

All the way home I composed cutting French speeches, but they suddenly cooled and petrified like a gust of lava from a volcano when I discovered that the gate was closed. I had never thought of getting a pass, and Magnin ought to have warned me. Another grievance against the fellow! I enjoyed my resentment, and it kept me warm as I patrolled up and down. There are houses, and even small eating-shops outside the gate, but no light was visible, and I did not care to attract attention by pounding at the doors in the middle of the night; so I crept behind a bit of wall. I was getting used to hiding by this time, and made myself as comfortable as I could with my ulster, took another pull at my flask, and waited. At last the gate was opened and I slipped through, trying not to look as though I had been out all night like a bandit. The guard looked at me narrowly, evidently wondering at my lack of luggage. Had I had a knapsack I might have been taken for some innocently mad English tourist indulging in the mistaken pleasure of trudging in from Frascati or Albano; but a man in an ulster, with his hands in his pockets, sauntering in at the gate of the city at break of day as though returning from a stroll, naturally puzzled the officials, who looked at me and shrugged their shoulders.

Luckily I found an early cab in the Piazza of the Lateran, for I was dead-beat, and was soon at my lodgings in the Via della Croce, where my landlady let me in very speedily. Then at last I had the comfort of throwing off my clothes, all damp with the night dew, and turning in. My wrath had cooled to a certain point, and I did not fear to lower its temperature too greatly by yielding to an overwhelming desire for sleep. An hour or two could make no great difference to Magnin—let him fancy me still hanging about the Vigna Marziali! Sleep I must have, no matter what he thought.

I slept long, and was awakened at last by my landlady, Sora Nanna, standing over me, and saying, "There is a Signore who wants you."

"It is I, Magnin!" said a voice behind her. "I could not wait for you to come!" He looked haggard with anxiety and watching.

"Detaille is raving still," he went on, "only worse than before. Speak, for Heaven's sake! Why don't you tell me something?" And he shook me by the arm as though he thought I was still asleep.

"Have you nothing to say? You must have seen something! Did you see Marcello?"

"Oh! Yes, I saw him."

"Well?"

"Well, he was very comfortable—quite alive. He had a woman's arms around him."

I heard my door violently slammed to, a ferocious *"Sacré gamin!"* and then steps springing down the stairs. I felt perfectly happy at having made such an impression, and turned and resumed my broken sleep with almost a kindly feeling towards Magnin, who was at that moment probably tearing up the Spanish Scalinata two steps at a time, and making himself horribly hot. It could not help Detaille, poor fellow! He could not understand my news. When I had slept long enough I got up, refreshed myself with a bath and something to eat, and went off to see Detaille. It was not his fault that I had been made a fool of, so I felt sorry for him.

I found him raving just as I had left him the day before, only worse, as Magnin said. He persisted in continually crying, "Marcello, take care! No one can save you!" in hoarse, weak tones, but with the regularity of a knell, keeping up a peculiar movement with his feet, as though he were weary with a long road, but must press forward to his goal. Then he would stop and break into childish sobs.

"My feet are so sore," he murmured piteously, "and I am so tired! But I will come! They are following me, but I am strong!" Then a violent struggle with his invisible pursuers, in which he would break off into that singing of his, alternating with the warning cry. The singing voice was quite another from the speaking one. He went on and on repeating the singular air which he had himself called "A Funeral March," and which had become intensely disagreeable to me. If it was one indeed, it surely was intended for no Christian burial. As he sang, the tears kept trickling down his cheeks, and Magnin sat wiping them away as tenderly as a woman. Between his song he would clasp his hands, feebly enough, for he was very weak when the delirium did not make him violent, and cry in heart-rending tones, "Marcello, I shall never see you again! Why did you leave us?" At last, when he stopped for a moment, Magnin left his side, beckoning the Sister to take it, and drew me into the other room, closing the door behind him.

"Now tell me exactly how you saw Marcello," said he; so I related my whole absurd experience—forgetting, however, my personal irritation, for he looked too wretched and worn for anybody to be angry with him. He made me repeat several times my description of Marcello's face and manner as he had come out of the house. That seemed to make more impression upon him than the love-business.

"Sick people have strange intuitions," he said gravely, "and I persist in thinking that Marcello is very ill and in danger. *Tenez!*" And here he broke off, went to the door, and called, "*Ma Sœur!*" under his breath. She understood, and after having drawn the bedclothes straight, and once more dried the trickling tears, she came noiselessly to where we stood, the wet handkerchief still in her hand. She was a singularly tall and strong-looking woman, with piercing black eyes and a self-controlled manner. Strange to say, she bore the adopted name of Claudius, instead of a more feminine one.

"*Ma Sœur,*" said Magnin, "at what o'clock was it that he sprang out of bed and we had to hold him for so long?"

"Half-past eleven and a few minutes," she answered promptly. Then he turned to me.

"At what time did Marcello come out into the garden?"

"Well, it might have been half-past eleven," I answered unwillingly. "I should say that three-quarters of an hour might possibly have passed since I rang my repeater. Mind you, I won't swear it!" I hate to have people try to prove mysterious coincidences, and this was just what they were attempting.

"Are you sure of the hour, *ma sœur?*" I asked, a little tartly.

She looked at me calmly with her great, black eyes, and said:

"I heard the Trinità de' Monti strike the half-hour just before it happened."

"Be so good as to tell Monsieur Sutton exactly what took place," said Magnin.

"One moment, monsieur," and she went swiftly and softly to Detaille, raised him on her strong arm, and held a glass to his lips, from which he drank mechanically. Then she came and stood where she could watch him through the open door.

"He hears nothing," she said, as she hung the handkerchief to dry over a chair, and then she went on: "It was half-past eleven, and my patient had been very uneasy—that is to say, more so even than before. It might have been four or five minutes after the clock had finished striking that he became suddenly quite still, and then began to tremble all over, so that the bed shook with him." She spoke admirable English, as many of the Sisters do, so I need not translate, but will give her own words.

"He went on trembling until I thought he was going to have a fit, and told Monsieur Magnin to be ready to go for the doctor, when just then the trembling stopped, he became perfectly stiff, his hair stood up upon his head, and his eyes seemed coming out of their sockets, though he could see nothing, for I passed the candle before them. All at once he sprang out of his bed and rushed to the door. I did not know he was so strong. Before he got there I had him in my arms, for he has become very light, and I carried him back to bed again, though he was struggling, like a child. Monsieur Magnin came in from the next room just as he was trying to get up again, and we held him down until it was past, but he screamed Monsieur Souvestre's name for a long time after that. Afterwards he was very cold and exhausted, of course, and I gave him some beef-tea, though it was not the hour for it."

"I think you had better tell the Sister all about it," said Magnin turning to me. "It is the best that the nurse should know everything."

"Very well," said I, "though I do not think it's much in her line." She answered me herself: "Everything which concerns our patients is our business. Nothing shocks me." Thereupon she sat down and thrust her hands into her long sleeves, prepared to listen. I repeated the whole affair as I had done to Magnin. She never took her brilliant eyes from off my face, and listened as coolly as though she had been a doctor hearing an account of a difficult case, though to me it seemed almost sacrilege to be describing the behaviour of a love-stricken youth to a Sister of Charity.

"What do you say to that, *ma sœur?*" asked Magnin, when I had done. "I say nothing, monsieur. It is sufficient that I know it," and she withdrew her hands from her sleeves, took up the handkerchief, which was dry by this time, and returned quietly to her place at the bedside.

"I wonder if I have shocked her, after all?" I said to Magnin.

"Oh, no," he answered. "They see many things, and a *sœur* is as abstract as a confessor; they do not allow themselves any personal feelings. I have seen Sœur Claudius listen perfectly unmoved to the most abominable ravings, only crossing herself beneath her cape at the most hideous blasphemies. It was late summer when poor Justin Revol died. You were not here." Magnin put his hand to his forehead.

"You are looking ill yourself," I said. "Go and try to sleep, and I will stay."

"Very well," he answered, "but I cannot rest unless you promise to remember everything he says, that I may hear it when I wake," and he threw himself down on the hard sofa like a sack, and was asleep in a moment; and I, who had felt so angry with him but a few hours ago, put a cushion under his head and made him comfortable.

I sat down in the next room and listened to Detaille's monotonous ravings, while Sœur Claudius read in her book of prayers. It was getting dusk, and several of the academicians stole in and stood over the sick man and shook their heads. They looked around for Magnin, but I pointed to the other room with my finger on my lips, and they nodded and went away on tiptoe.

It required no effort of memory to repeat Detaille's words to Magnin when he woke, for they were always the same. We had another Sister that night, and as Sœur Claudius was not to return till the next day at midday, I offered to share the watch with Magnin, who was getting very nervous and exhausted, and who seemed to think that some such attack might be expected as had occurred the night before. The new Sister was a gentle, delicate-looking little woman, with tears in her soft brown eyes as she bent over the sick man, and crossed herself from time to time, grasping the crucifix which hung from the beads at her waist. Nevertheless she was calm and useful, and as punctual as Sœur Claudius herself in giving the medicines.

The doctor had come in the evening, and prescribed a change in these. He would not say what he thought of his patient, but only declared that it was necessary to wait for a crisis. Magnin sent for some supper, and we sat over it together in the silence, neither of us hungry. He kept looking at his watch.

"If the same thing happens tonight, he will die!" said he, and laid his head on his arms.

"He will die in a most foolish cause, then," I said angrily, for I thought he was going to cry, as those Frenchmen have a way of doing, and I wanted to irritate him by way of a tonic; so I went on—

"It would be dying for a *vaurien* who is making an ass of himself in a ridiculous business which will be over in a week! Souvestre may get as much fever as he likes! Only don't ask me to come and nurse him."

"It is not the fever," said he slowly. "It is a horrible nameless dread that I have; I suppose it is listening to Detaille that makes me nervous. Hark!" he added. "It strikes eleven. We must watch!"

"If you really expect another attack you had better warn the Sister," I said; so he told her in a few words what might happen.

"Very well, monsieur," she answered, and sat down quietly near the bed, Magnin at the pillow and I near him. No sound was to be heard but De-taille's ceaseless lament.

And now, before I tell you more, I must stop to entreat you to believe me. It will be almost im-possible for you to do so, I know, for I have laughed myself at such tales, and no assurances would have made me credit them. But I, Robert Sutton, swear that this thing happened. More I cannot do. It is the truth.

We had been watching Detaille intently. He was lying with closed eyes, and had been very rest-less. Suddenly he became quite still, and then began to tremble, exactly as Sœur Claudius had described. It was a curious, uniform trembling, apparently in every fibre, and his iron bedstead shook as though strong hands were at its head and foot. Then came the absolute rigidity she had also described, and I do not exaggerate when I say that not only did his short-cropped hair seem to stand erect, but that it literally did so. A lamp cast the shadow of his profile against the wall to the left of his bed, and as I looked at the immovable outline which seemed painted on the wall, I saw the hair slowly rise until the line where it joined the fore-head was quite a different one—abrupt instead of a smooth sweep. His eyes opened wide and were frightfully fixed, then as frightfully strained, but they certainly did not see us.

We waited breathlessly for what might follow. The little Sister was standing close to him, her lips pressed together and a little pale, but very calm. "Do not be frightened, *ma sœur*," whispered Magnin, and she answered in a business-like tone, "No, monsieur," and drew still nearer to her pa-tient, and took his hands, which were stiff as those of a corpse, between her own to warm them. I laid mine upon his heart; it was beating so impercep-tibly that I almost thought it had stopped, and as I leaned my face to his lips I could feel no breath issue from them. It seemed as though the rigour would last for ever.

Suddenly, without any transition, he hurled himself with enormous force, and literally at one bound, almost into the middle of the room, scat-tering us aside like leaves in the wind. I was upon him in a moment, grappling with him with all my strength, to prevent him from reaching the door. Magnin had been thrown backwards against the table, and I heard the medicine bottles crash with his fall. He had flung back his hand to save him-self, and rushed to help me with blood dripping from a cut in his wrist. The little Sister sprang to us. Detaille had thrown her violently back upon her knees, and now, with a nurse's instinct, she tried to throw a shawl over his bare breast. We four must have made a strange group!

Four? *We were five!* Marcello Souvestre stood before us, just within the door! We all saw him, for he was there. His bloodless face was turned towards us unmoved; his hands hung by his side as white as his face; only his eyes had life in them; they were fixed on Detaille.

"Thank God you have come at last!" I cried. "Don't stand there like a fool! Help us, can't you?" But he never moved. I was furiously angry, and, leaving my hold, sprang upon him to drag him forwards. My outstretched hands struck hard against the door, and I felt a thing like a spider's web envelop me. It seemed to draw itself over my mouth and eyes, and to blind and choke me, and then to flutter and tear and float from me.

Marcello was gone!

Detaille had slipped from Magnin's hold, and lay in a heap upon the floor, as though his limbs were broken. The Sister was trembling violently as she knelt over him and tried to raise his head. We gazed at one another, stooped and lifted him in our arms, and carried him back to his bed, while Sœur Marie quietly collected the broken phials.

"You saw it, *ma sœur?*" I heard Magnin whis-per hoarsely.

"Yes, monsieur!" she only answered, in a trem-bling voice, holding on to her crucifix. Then she said in a professional tone—

"Will monsieur let me bind up his wrist?" And though her fingers trembled and his hand was shaking, the bandage was an irreproachable one.

Magnin went into the next room, and I heard him throw himself heavily into a chair. Detaille seemed to be sleeping. His breath came regularly; his eyes were closed with a look of peace about the lids, his hands lying in a natural way upon the quilt. He had not moved since we laid him there. I went softly to where Magnin was sitting in the dark. He did not move, but only said: "Marcello is dead!"

"He is either dead or dying," I answered, "and we must go to him."

"Yes," Magnin whispered, "we must go to him, but we shall not reach him."

"We will go as soon as it is light," I said, and then we were still again.

When the morning came at last he went and found a comrade to take his place, and only said to Sœur Marie, "It is not necessary to speak of this night," and at her quiet "You are right, monsieur," we felt we could trust her. Detaille was still sleeping. Was this the crisis the doctor had expected? Perhaps; but surely not in such fearful form. I insisted upon my companion having some breakfast before we started, and I breakfasted myself, but I cannot say I tasted what passed between my lips.

We engaged a closed carriage, for we did not know what we might bring home with us, though neither of us spoke out his thoughts. It was early morning still when we reached the Vigna Marziali, and we had not exchanged a word all the way. I rang at the bell, while the coachman looked on curiously. It was answered promptly by the *guardiano*, of whom Detaille has already told you.

"Where is the Signore?" I asked through the gate.

"*Chi lo sa?*" he answered. "He is here, of course; he has not left the Vigna. Shall I call him?"

"*Call him?*" I knew that no mortal voice could reach Marcello now, but I tried to fancy he was still alive.

"No," I said. "Let us in. We want to surprise him; he will be pleased."

The man hesitated, but he finally opened the gate, and we entered, leaving the carriage to wait outside. We went straight to the house; the door at the back was wide open. There had been a gale in the night, and it had torn some leaves and bits of twigs from the trees and blown them into the entrance hall. They lay scattered across the threshold, and were evidence that the door had remained

open ever since they had fallen. The *guardiano* left us, probably to escape Marcello's anger at having let us in, and we went up the stairs unhindered, Magnin foremost, for he knew the house better than I, from Detaille's description. He had told him about the corner room with the balcony, and we pretended that Marcello might be there, absorbed betimes in his work, but we did not call him.

He was not there. His papers were strewn over the table as though he had been writing, but the inkstand was dry and full of dust; he could not have used it for days. We went silently into the other chambers. Perhaps he was still asleep? But, no! We found his bed untouched, so he could not have lain in it that night. The rooms were all unlocked but one, and this closed door made our hearts beat. Marcello could scarcely be there, however, for there was no key in the lock; I saw the daylight shining through the key-hole. We called his name, but there came no answer. We knocked loudly; still no sign from within; so I put my shoulder to the door, which was old and cracked in several places, and succeeded in bursting it open.

Nothing was there but a sculptor's modelling-stand, with something upon it covered with a white cloth, and the modelling-tools on the floor. At the sight of the cloth, still damp, we drew a deep breath. It could have hung there for many hours, certainly not for twenty-four. We did not raise it. "He would be vexed," said Magnin, and I nodded, for it is accounted almost a crime in the artist's world to unveil a sculptor's work behind his back. We expressed no surprise at the fact of his modelling: a ban seemed to lie upon our tongues. The cloth hung tightly to the object beneath it, and showed us the outline of a woman's head and rounded-bust, and so veiled we left her. There was a little winding stair leading out of the passage, and we climbed it, to find ourselves in a sort of belvedere, commanding a superb view. It was a small, open terrace, on the roof of the house, and we saw at a glance that no one was there.

We had now been all over the casino, which was small and simply built, being evidently intended only for short summer use. As we stood leaning

54

over the balustrade we could look down into the garden. No one was there but the *guardiano,* lying amongst his cabbages with his arms behind his head, half asleep. The laurel grove had been in my mind from the beginning, only it had seemed more natural to go to the house first. Now we descended the stairs silently and directed our steps thither.

As we approached it, the *guardiano* came towards us lazily.

"Have you seen the Signore?" he asked, and his stupidly placid face showed me that he, at least, had no hand in his disappearance.

"No, not yet," I answered, "but we shall come across him somewhere, no doubt. Perhaps he has gone to take a walk, and we will wait for him. What is this?" I went on, trying to seem careless. We were standing now by the little arch of which you know.

"This?" said he. "I have never been down there, but they say it is something old. Do the Signori want to see it? I will fetch a lantern."

I nodded, and he went off to his cabin. I had a couple of candles in my pocket, for I had intended to explore the place, should we not find Marcello. It was there that he had disappeared that night, and my thoughts had been busy with it; but I kept my candles concealed, reflecting that they would give our search an air of premeditation which would excite curiosity.

"When did you see the Signore last?" I asked, when he had returned with the lantern.

"I brought him his supper yesterday evening."

"At what o'clock?"

"It was the Ave Maria, Signore," he replied. "He always sups then."

It would be useless to put any more questions. He was evidently utterly unobserving, and would lie to please us.

"Let me go first," said Magnin, taking the lantern. We set our feet upon the steps; a cold air seemed to fill our lungs and yet to choke us, and a thick darkness lay beneath. The steps, as I could see by the light of my candle, were modern, as well as the vaulting above them. A tablet was let into the wall, and in spite of my excitement I paused

to read it, perhaps because I was glad to delay whatever awaited us below. It ran thus:

"Questo antico sepolcro Romano scoprì il Conte Marziali nell' anno 1853, e piamente conservo." In plain English:

"Count Marziali discovered this ancient Roman sepulchre in the year 1853, and piously preserved it."

I read it more quickly than it has taken time to write here, and hurried after Magnin, whose footsteps sounded faintly below me. As I hastened, a draught of cold air extinguished my candle, and I was trying to make my way down by feeling along the wall, which was horribly dark and clammy, when my heart stood still at a cry from far beneath me—a cry of horror!

"Where are you?" I shouted; but Magnin was calling my name, and could not hear me. "I am here. I am in the dark!"

I was making haste as fast as I could, but there were several turnings.

"I have found him!" came up from below.

"Alive?" I shouted. No answer.

One last short flight brought me face to face with the gleam of the lantern. It came from a low doorway, and within stood Magnin peering into the darkness. I knew by his face, as he held the light high above him, that our fears were realized.

Yes; Marcello was there. He was lying stretched upon the floor, staring at the ceiling, dead, and already stiff, as I could see at a glance. We stood over him, saying not a word, then I knelt down and felt him, for mere form's sake, and said, as though I had not known it before, "He has been dead for some hours."

"Since yesterday evening," said Magnin in a horror-stricken voice, yet with a certain satisfaction in it, as though to say, "You see, I was right."

Marcello was lying with his head slightly thrown back, no contortions in his handsome features; rather the look of a person who has quietly died of exhaustion—who has slipped unconsciously from life to death. His collar was thrown open and a part of his breast, of a ghastly white, was visible. Just over the heart was a small spot.

"Give me the lantern," I whispered, as I stooped

over it. It was a very little spot, of a faint purplish-brown, and must have changed colour within the night.

I examined it intently, and should say that the blood had been sucked to the surface, and then a small prick or incision made. The slight subcutaneous effusion led me to this conclusion. One tiny drop of coagulated blood closed the almost imperceptible wound. I probed it with the end of one of Magnin's matches. It was scarcely more than skin deep, so it could not be the stab of a stiletto, however slender, or the track of a bullet. Still, it was strange, and with one impulse we turned to see if no one were concealed there, or if there were no second exit. It would be madness to suppose that the murderer, if there was one, would remain by his victim. Had Marcello been making love to a pretty *contadina*, and was this some jealous lover's vengeance? But it was not a stab. Had one drop of poison in the little wound done this deadly work?

We peered about the place, and I saw that Magnin's eyes wert blinded by tears and his face as pale as that upturned one on the floor, whose lids I had vainly tried to close. The chamber was low, and beautifully ornamented with stucco bas-reliefs, in the manner of the well-known one not far from there upon the same road. Winged genii, griffins, and arabesques, modelled with marvellous lightness, covered the walls and ceiling. There was no other door than the one we had entered by. In the centre stood a marble sarcophagus, with the usual subjects sculptured upon it, on the one side Hercules conducting a veiled figure, on the other a dance of nymphs and fauns. A space in the middle contained the following inscription, deeply cut in the stone, and still partially filled with red pigment:

D . M .

VESPERTILIAE•THC•AIMA-

ΤΟΠΩΤΙΔΟC • Q • FLAVIVS •

VIX•IPSE•SOSPES•MON•

POSVIT

"What is this?" whispered Magnin. It was only a pickaxe and a long crowbar, such as the country people use in hewing out their blocks of "tufa," and his foot had struck against them. Who could have brought them here? They must belong to the *guardiano* above, but he said that he had never come here, and I believed him, knowing the Italian horror of darkness and lonely places; but what had Marcello wanted with them? It did not occur to us that archaeological curiosity could have led him to attempt to open the sarcophagus, the lid of which had evidently never been raised, thus justifying the expression "piously preserved."

As I rose from examining the tools my eyes fell upon the line of mortar where the cover joined to the stone below, and I noticed that some of it had been removed, perhaps with the pickaxe which lay at my feet. I tried it with my nails and found that it was very crumbly. Without a word I took the tool in my hand, Magnin instinctively following my movements with the lantern. What impelled us I do not know. I had myself no thought, only an irresistible desire to see what was within. I saw that much of the mortar had been broken away, and lay in small fragments upon the ground, which I had not noticed before. It did not take long to complete the work. I snatched the lantern from Magnin's hand and set it upon the ground, where it shone full upon Marcello's dead face, and by its light I found a little break between the two masses of stone and managed to insert the end of my crowbar, driving it in with a blow of the pickaxe. The stone chipped and then cracked a little. Magnin was shivering.

"What are you going to do?" he said, looking around at where Marcello lay.

"Help me!" I cried, and we two bore with all our might upon the crowbar. I am a strong man, and I felt a sort of blind fury as the stone refused to yield. What if the bar should snap? With another blow I drove it in still further, then using it as a lever, we weighed upon it with our outstretched arms until every muscle was at its highest tension. The stone moved a little, and almost fainting we stopped to rest.

From the ceiling hung the rusty remnant of an iron chain which must once have held a lamp. To this, by scrambling upon the sarcophagus, I contrived to make fast the lantern.

"Now!" said I, and we heaved again at the lid. It rose, and we alternately heaved and pushed until it lost its balance and fell with a thundering crash upon the other side; such a crash that the walls seemed to shake, and I was for a moment utterly deafened, while little pieces of stucco rained upon us from the ceiling. When we had paused to recover from the shock we leaned over the sarcophagus and looked in.

The light shone full upon it, and we saw—how is it possible to tell? We saw lying there, amidst folds of mouldering rags, the body of a woman, perfect as in life, with faintly rosy face, soft crimson lips, and a breast of living pearl, which seemed to heave as though stirred by some delicious dream. The rotten stuff swathed about her was in ghastly contrast to this lovely form, fresh as the morning! Her hands lay stretched at her side, the pink palms were turned a little outwards, her eyes were closed as peacefully as those of a sleeping child, and her long hair, which shone red-gold in the dim light from above, was wound around her head in numberless finely plaited tresses, beneath which little locks escaped in rings upon her brow. I could have sworn that the blue veins on that divinely perfect bosom held living blood!

We were absolutely paralyzed, and Magnin leaned gasping over the edge as pale as death, paler by far than this living, almost smiling face to which his eyes were glued. I do not doubt that I was as pale as he at this inexplicable vision. As I looked the red lips seemed to grow redder. They *were* redder! The little pearly teeth showed between them. I had not seen them before, and now a clear ruby drop trickled down to her rounded chin and from there slipped sideways and fell upon her neck. Horror-struck I gazed upon the living corpse, till my eyes could not bear the sight any longer. As I looked away my glance fell once more upon the inscription, but now I could see—*and read*—it all. "To Vespertilia"—that was in Latin, and even the Latin name of the woman suggested a thing of evil flitting in the dusk. But the full horror of the nature of that thing had been veiled to Roman eyes under the Greek τηζαίματοπωίδοζ, "the blood-drinker, the vampire woman." And Flavius—her lover—*vix ipse sospes*, "himself hardly saved" from that deadly embrace, had buried her here, and set a seal upon her sepulchre, trusting to the weight of stone and the strength of clinging mortar to imprison for ever the beautiful monster he had loved.

"Infamous murderess!" I cried. "You have killed Marcello!" And a sudden, vengeful calm came over me.

"Give me the pickaxe," I said to Magnin; I can hear myself saying it still. He picked it up and handed it to me as in a dream; he seemed little better than an idiot, and the beads of sweat were shining on his forehead. I took my knife, and from the long wooden handle of the pickaxe I cut a fine, sharp stake. Then I clambered, scarcely feeling any repugnance, over the side of the sarcophagus, my feet amongst the folds of Vespertilia's decaying winding-sheet, which crushed like ashes beneath my boot.

I looked for one moment at that white breast, but only to choose the loveliest spot, where the network of azure veins shimmered like veiled turquoises, and then with one blow I drove the pointed stake deep down through the breathing snow and stamped it in with my heel.

An awful shriek, so ringing and horrible that I thought my ears must have burst; but even then I felt neither fear nor horror. There are times when these cannot touch us. I stopped and gazed once again at the face, now undergoing a fearful change—fearful and final!

"Foul vampire!" I said quietly in my concentrated rage. "You will do no more harm now!" And then, without looking back upon her cursed face, I clambered out of the horrible tomb.

We raised Marcello, and slowly carried him up the steep stairs—a difficult task, for the way was narrow and he was so stiff. I noticed that the steps were ancient up to the end of the second flight; above, the modern passage was somewhat broader. When we reached the top, the *guardiano* was lying upon one of the stone benches; he did not mean us to cheat him out of his fee. I gave him a couple of francs.

"You see that we have found the Signore," I tried to say in a natural voice. "He is very weak, and we will carry him to the carriage." I had thrown my handkerchief over Marcello's face, but the man knew as well as I did that he was dead. Those stiff feet told their own story, but Italians are timid of being involved in such affairs. They have a childish dread of the police, and he only answered, "Poor Signorino! He is very ill; it is better to take him to Rome," and kept cautiously clear of us as we went up to the ilex alley with our icy burden, and he did not go to the gate with us, not liking to be observed by the coachman who was dozing on his box. With difficulty we got Marcello's corpse into the carriage, the driver turning to look at us suspiciously. I explained we had found our friend very ill, and at the same time slipped a gold piece into his hand, telling him to drive to the Via del Governo Vecchio. He pocketed the money, and whipped his horses into a trot, while we sat supporting the stiff body, which swayed like a broken doll at every pebble in the road. When we reached the Via del Governo Vecchio at last, no one saw us carry him into the house. There was no step before the door, and we drew up so close to it that it was possible to screen our burden from sight. When we had brought him into his room and laid him upon his bed, we noticed that his eyes were closed; from the movement of the carriage, perhaps, though that was scarcely possible. The landlady behaved very much as I had expected her to do, for, as I told you, I know the Italians. She pretended, too, that the Signore was very ill, and made a pretence of offering to fetch a doctor, and when I thought it best to tell her that he was dead, declared that it must have happened that very moment, for she had seen him look at us and close his eyes again. She had always told him that he ate too little and that he would be ill. Yes, it was weakness and that bad air out there which had killed him; and then he worked too hard. When she had successfully established this fiction, which we were glad enough to agree to, for neither did we wish for the publicity of an inquest, she ran

out and fetched a gossip to come and keep her company.

So died Marcello Souvestre, and so died Vespertilia the blood-drinker at last.

There is not much more to tell. Marcello lay calm and beautiful upon his bed, and the students came and stood silently looking at him, then knelt down for a moment to say a prayer, crossed themselves, and left him for ever.

We hastened to the Villa Medici, where Detaille was sleeping, and Sister Claudius watching him with a satisfied look on her strong face. She rose noiselessly at our entrance, and came to us at the threshold.

"He will recover," said she, softly. She was right. When he awoke and opened his eyes he knew us directly, and Magnin breathed a devout "Thank God!"

"Have I been ill, Magnin?" he asked, very feebly.

"You have had a little fever," answered Magnin, promptly, "but it is over now. Here is Monsieur Sutton come to see you."

"Has Marcello been here?" was the next question. Magnin looked at him very steadily.

"No," he only said, letting his face tell the rest.

"Is he dead, then?" Magnin only bowed his head. "Poor friend!" Detaille murmured to himself, then closed his heavy eyes and slept again.

A few days after Marcello's funeral we went to the fatal Vigna Marziali to bring back the objects which had belonged to him. As I laid the manuscript score of the opera carefully together, my eye fell upon a passage which struck me as the identical one which Detaille had so constantly sung in his delirium, and which I noted down. Strange to say, when I reminded him of it later, it was perfectly new to him, and he declared that Marcello had not let him examine his manuscript. As for the veiled bust in the other room, we left it undisturbed, and to crumble away unseen.

## THE FATE OF MADAME CABANEL

# Eliza Lynn Linton

Eliza Lynn Linton (1822–98) was born in Keswick, England, the daughter of a clergyman. An independent-minded woman, she moved on her own to London in 1845 as the protégée of the poet William Savage Landor.

She wrote several novels without notable success and turned to journalism, joining the staff of the *Morning Chronicle* and Charles Dickens's *All the Year Round.* In 1858 she married W. J. Linton, a well-known poet and wood engraver, but separated after a decade, evidently on good terms, as she raised one of his daughters by a previous marriage. Her former husband moved to America and she returned to writing novels, this time achieving a wide readership with such titles as *The True History of Joshua Davidson* (1872) and *Christopher Kirkland* (1885), which is largely autobiographical, though in the voice of a man. She has been a source of confusion for scholars attempting to understand her politics because, although a strong woman with a powerful individual personality and lifestyle, she was violently opposed to the New Woman movement of feminism.

Her very leisurely and measured style has not meshed well with modern readers, and she is rarely read today.

"The Fate of Madame Cabanel" was first published in book form in *With a Silken Thread and Other Stories* (London: Chatto & Windus, 1880).

# The Fate of Madame Cabanel

## ELIZA LYNN LINTON

rogress had not invaded, science had not enlightened, the little hamlet of Pieuvrot, in Brittany. They were a simple, ignorant, superstitious set who lived there, and the luxuries of civilization were known to them as little as its learning. They toiled hard all the week on the ungrateful soil that yielded them but a bare subsistence in return; they went regularly to mass in the little rock-set chapel on Sundays and saints' days; believed implicitly all that monsieur le curé said to them, and many things which he did not say; and they took all the unknown, not as magnificent, but as diabolical.

The sole link between them and the outside world of mind and progress was Monsieur Jules Cabanel, the proprietor, par excellence, of the place: *maire, juge de paix*, and all the public functionaries rolled into one. And he sometimes went to Paris whence he returned with a cargo of novelties that excited envy, admiration, or fear, according to the degree of intelligence in those who beheld them.

Monsieur Jules Cabanel was not the most charming man of his class in appearance, but he was generally held to be a good fellow at bottom. A short, thickset, low-browed man, with blue-black hair cropped close like a mat, as was his blue-black beard, inclined to obesity and fond of good living, he had need have some virtues behind the bush to compensate for his want of personal charms. He was not bad, however; he was only common and unlovely.

Up to fifty years of age he had remained the unmarried prize of the surrounding country; but hitherto he had resisted all the overtures made by maternal fowlers, and had kept his liberty and his bachelorhood intact. Perhaps his handsome housekeeper, Adèle, had something to do with his persistent celibacy. They said she had, under their breath as it were, down at *la Veuve Prieur*'s; but no one dared to so much as hint the like to herself. She was a proud, reserved kind of woman; and had strange notions of her own dignity which no one cared to disturb. So, whatever the underhand gossip of the place might be, neither she nor her master got wind of it.

Presently and quite suddenly, Jules Cabanel, who had been for a longer time than usual in Paris, came home with a wife. Adèle had only twenty-four hours' notice to prepare for this strange homecoming; and the task seemed heavy. But she got through it in her old way of silent determination; arranged the rooms as she knew her master would wish them to be arranged; and even supplemented the usual nice adornments by a voluntary bunch of flowers on the salon table.

"Strange flowers for a bride," said to herself little Jeannette, the goose-girl who was sometimes brought into the house to work, as she noticed heliotrope—called in France *la fleur des veuves*—scarlet poppies, a bunch of belladonna, another of aconite—scarcely, as even ignorant little Jeannette said, flowers of bridal welcome or bridal significance. Nevertheless, they stood where Adèle had placed them; and if Monsieur Cabanel meant anything by the passionate expression of disgust with which he ordered them out of his sight, madame seemed to understand nothing, as she smiled with that vague, half-deprecating look of a person who is assisting at a scene of which the true bearing is not understood.

Madame Cabanel was a foreigner, and an Englishwoman: young, pretty, and fair as an angel.

"*La beauté du diable*," said the Pieuvrotines, with something between a sneer and a shudder; for the words meant with them more than they mean in ordinary use. Swarthy, ill-nourished, low of stature, and meagre in frame as they were themselves, they could not understand the plump form, tall figure, and fresh complexion of the Englishwoman. Unlike their own experience, it was therefore more likely to be evil than good. The feeling which had sprung up against her at first sight deepened when it was observed that, although she went to mass with praiseworthy punctuality, she did not know her missal and signed herself *à travers*. *La beauté du diable*, in faith!

"*Pouf!*" said Martin Briolic, the old gravedigger of the little cemetery. "With those red lips of hers, her rose cheeks, and her plump shoulders, she looks like a vampire and as if she lived on blood."

He said this one evening down at *la Veuve Prieur*'s; and he said it with an air of conviction that had its weight. For Martin Briolic was reputed the wisest man of the district, not even excepting monsieur le curé who was wise in his own way, which was not Martin's—nor Monsieur Cabanel who was wise in his, which was neither Mar-

tin's nor the curé's. He knew all about the weather and the stars, the wild herbs that grew on the plains, and the wild shy beasts that eat them, and he had the power of divination and could find where the hidden springs of water lay far down in the earth when he held the baguette in his hand. He knew too, where treasures could be had on Christmas Eve if only you were quick and brave enough to enter the cleft in the rock at the right moment and come out again before too late; and he had seen with his own eyes the White Ladies dancing in the moonlight; and the little imps, the Infins, playing their prankish gambols by the pit at the edge of the wood. And he had a shrewd suspicion as to who, among those black-hearted men of La Crèche-en-bois—the rival hamlet—was a loup-garou, if ever there was one on the face of the earth and no one had doubted that! He had other powers of a yet more mystic kind; so that Martin Briolic's bad word went for something, if, with the illogical injustice of ill-nature his good went for nothing.

Fanny Campbell, or, as she was now Madame Cabanel, would have excited no special attention in England, or indeed anywhere but at such a dead-alive, ignorant, and consequently gossiping place as Pieuvrot. She had no romantic secret as her background; and what history she had was commonplace enough, if sorrowful too in its own way. She was simply an orphan and a governess; very young and very poor; whose employers had quarrelled with her and left her stranded in Paris, alone and almost moneyless; and who had married Monsieur Jules Cabanel as the best thing she could do for herself. Loving no one else, she was not difficult to be won by the first man who showed her kindness in her hour of trouble and destitution; and she accepted her middle-aged suitor, who was fitter to be her father than her husband, with a clear conscience and a determination to do her duty cheerfully and faithfully—all without considering herself as a martyr or an interesting victim sacrificed to the cruelty of circumstances. She did not know however, of the handsome housekeeper Adèle, nor of the housekeeper's little nephew—to whom her master was so kind that he allowed him to live at the Maison Cabanel and had him well taught by the curé. Perhaps if she had she would have thought twice before she put herself under the same roof with a woman who for a bridal bouquet offered her poppies, heliotrope, and poison-flowers.

If one had to name the predominant characteristic of Madame Cabanel it would be easiness of temper. You saw it in the round, soft, indolent lines of her face and figure; in her mild blue eyes and placid, unvarying smile; which irritated the more petulant French temperament and especially disgusted Adèle. It seemed impossible to make madame angry or even to make her understand when she was insulted, the housekeeper used to say with profound disdain; and, to do the woman justice, she did not spare her endeavours to enlighten her. But madame accepted all Adèle's haughty reticence and defiant continuance of mistress-hood with unwearied sweetness; indeed, she expressed herself gratified that so much trouble was taken off her hands, and that Adèle so kindly took her duties on herself.

The consequences of this placid lazy life, where all her faculties were in a manner asleep, and where she was enjoying the reaction from her late years of privation and anxiety, was, as might be expected, an increase in physical beauty that made her freshness and good condition still more remarkable. Her lips were redder, her cheeks rosier, her shoulders plumper than ever; but as she waxed, the health of the little hamlet waned, and not the oldest inhabitant remembered so sickly a season, or so many deaths. The master too, suffered slightly; the little Adolphe desperately.

This failure of general health in undrained hamlets is not uncommon in France or in England; neither is the steady and pitiable decline of French children; but Adèle treated it as something out of all the lines of normal experience; and, breaking through her habits of reticence spoke to every one quite fiercely of the strange sickliness that had fallen on Pieuvrot and the Maison Cabanel; and how she believed it was something more than common; while as to her little nephew, she could give neither a name nor find a remedy for the mysterious disease that had attacked him. There were strange things among them, she used to say; and Pieuvrot had never done well since the old times were changed. Jeannette used to notice how she would sit gazing at the English lady, with such a deadly look on her handsome face when she turned from the foreigner's fresh complexion and grand physique to the pale face of the stunted, meagre, fading child. It was a look, she said afterwards, that used to make her flesh get like ice and creep like worms.

One night Adèle, as if she could bear it no longer, dashed down to where old Martin Briolic lived, to ask him to tell her how it had all come about—and the remedy.

"Hold, Ma'am Adèle," said Martin, as he shuffled his greasy tarot cards and laid them out in triplets on the table. "There is more in this than one sees. One sees only a poor little child become suddenly sick; that may be, is it not so? And no harm done by man? God sends sickness to us all and makes my trade profitable to me. But the little Adolphe has not been touched by the Good God. I see the will of a wicked woman in this. *Hein!*" Here he shuffled the cards and laid them out with a kind of eager distraction of manner, his withered hands trembling and his mouth uttering words that Adèle could not catch. "Saint Joseph and all the saints protect us!" he cried. "The foreigner—the Englishwoman—she whom they call Madame Cabanel—no rightful madame she!—Ah, misery!"

"Speak, Father Martin! What do you mean!" cried Adèle, grasping his arm. Her black eyes were wild; her arched nostrils dilated; her lips, thin, sinuous, flexible, were pressed tight over her small square teeth.

"Tell me in plain words what you would say!"

"Broucolaque!" said Martin in a low voice.

"It is what I believed!" cried Adèle. "It is what I knew. Ah, my Adolphe! Woe on the day when the master brought that fair-skinned devil home!"

"Those red lips don't come by nothing, Ma'am Adèle," cried Martin, nodding his head. "Look at them—they glisten with blood! I said so from the beginning; and the cards, they said so too. I drew 'blood' and a 'bad fair woman' on the evening when the master brought her home, and I said to myself, 'Ha, ha, Martin! You are on the track, my boy—on the track, Martin!'—and, Ma'am Adèle, I have never left it! Broucolaque! That's what the cards say, Ma'am Adèle. Vampire. Watch and see, watch and see, and you'll find that the cards have spoken true."

"And when we have found, Martin?" said Adèle in a hoarse whisper.

The old man shuffled his cards again. "When we have found, Ma'am Adèle?" he said slowly. "You know the old pit out there by the forest—the old pit where the lutins run in and out, and where the White Ladies wring the necks of those who come upon them in the moonlight? Perhaps the White Ladies will do as much for the English wife of Monsieur Cabanel; who knows?"

"They may," said Adèle, gloomily.

"Courage, brave woman!" said Martin. "They will."

The only really pretty place about Pieuvrot was the cemetery. To be sure there was the dark gloomy forest which was grand in its own mysterious way; and there was the broad wide plain where you might wander for a long summer's day and not come to the end of it; but these were scarcely places where a young woman would care to go by herself; and for the rest, the miserable little patches of cultivated ground, which the peasants had snatched from the surrounding waste and where they had raised poor crops, were not very lovely. So Madame Cabanel, who, for all the soft indolence that had invaded her, had the Englishwoman's inborn love for walking and fresh air, haunted the pretty little graveyard a good deal. She had no sentiment connected with it. Of all the dead who laid there in their narrow coffins, she knew none and cared for none; but she liked to see the pretty little flower-beds and the wreaths of immortelles, and the like; the distance too, from her own home was just enough for her; and the view over the plain to the dark belt of forest and the mountains beyond, was fine.

The Pieuvrotines did not understand this. It was inexplicable to them that any one, not out of her mind, should go continually to the cemetery—not on the day of the dead and not to adorn the grave of one she loved—only to sit there and wander among the tombs, looking out on to the plain and the mountains beyond when she was tired.

"It was just like—" The speaker, one Lesouëf, had got so far as this, when he stopped for a word.

He said this down at *la Veuve Prieur*'s where the hamlet collected nightly to discuss the day's small doings, and where the main theme, ever since she had come among them, three months ago now, had been Madame Cabanel and her foreign ways and her wicked ignorance of her mass-book and her wrong-doings of a mysterious kind generally, interspersed with jesting queries, banded from one to the other, of how Ma'am Adèle liked it?—and what would become of le petit Adolphe when the rightful heir appeared?—some adding that monsieur was a brave man to shut up two wild cats under the same roof together; and what would become of it in the end? Mischief of a surety.

"Wander about the tombs just like what, Jean Lesouëf?" said Martin Briolic. Rising, he added in a low but distinct voice, every word falling clear and clean: "I will tell you like what, Lesouëf—like a vampire! La femme Cabanel has red lips and red cheeks, and Ma'am Adèle's little nephew is perishing before your eyes. La femme Cabanel has red lips and red cheeks, and she sits for hours among the tombs. Can you read the riddle, my friends? For me it is as clear as the blessed sun."

"Ha, Father Martin, you have found the word—like a vampire!" said Lesouëf with a shudder.

"Like a vampire!" they all echoed with a groan.

"And I said vampire the first," said Martin Briolic. "Call to mind I said it from the first."

"Faith! And you did," they answered, "and you said true."

So now the unfriendly feeling that had met and accompanied the young Englishwoman ever since she came to Pieuvrot had drawn to a focus. The seed which Martin and Adèle had dropped so sedulously had at last taken root; and the Pieuvrotines would have been ready to accuse of atheism and immorality any one who had doubted their decision, and had declared that pretty Madame Cabanel was only a young woman with nothing special to do, a naturally fair complexion, superb health—and no vampire at all, sucking the blood of a living child or living among the tombs to make the newly buried her prey.

The little Adolphe grew paler and paler, thinner and thinner; the fierce summer sun told on the half-starved dwellers within those foul mud-huts surrounded by undrained marshes; and Monsieur Jules Cabanel's former solid health followed the law of the rest. The doctor, who lived at Crèche-en-bois, shook his head at the look of things, and said it was grave. When Adèle pressed him to tell her what was the matter with the child and with monsieur, he evaded the question, or gave her a word which she neither understood nor could pronounce. The truth was, he was a credulous and intensely suspicious man; a viewy man who made theories and then gave himself to the task of finding them true. He had made the theory that Fanny was secretly poisoning both her husband and the child; and though he would not give Adèle a hint of this, he would not set her mind at rest by a definite answer that went on any other line.

As for Monsieur Cabanel, he was a man without imagination and without suspicion; a man to take life easily and not distress himself too much for the fear of wounding others; a selfish man but not a cruel one; a man whose own pleasure was his supreme law and who could not imagine, still less brook, opposition or the want of love and respect for himself. Still, he loved his wife as he had never loved a woman before. Coarsely moulded, common-natured as he was, he loved her with what strength and passion of poetry nature had given him; and if the quantity was small, the quality was sincere. But that quality was sorely tried when—now Adèle, now the doctor—hinted mysteriously, the one at diabolical influences, the other at underhand proceedings of which it behoved him to be careful, especially careful what he ate and drank and how it was prepared and by whom; Adèle adding hints about the perfidiousness of Englishwomen and the share which the devil had in fair hair and brilliant complexions. Love his young wife as he might, this constant dropping of poison was not without some effect. It told much for his steadfastness and loyalty that it should have had only so small effect.

One evening however, when Adèle, in an agony, was kneeling at his feet—madame had gone out for her usual walk—crying: "Why did you leave me for such as she is?—I, who loved you, who was faithful to you, and she, who walks among the graves, who sucks your blood and our child's—she who has only the devil's beauty for her portion and who loves you not?"—something seemed suddenly to touch him with electric force.

"Miserable fool that I was!" he said, resting his head on Adèle's shoulders and weeping. Her heart leapt with joy. Was her reign to be renewed? Was her rival to be dispossessed?

From that evening Monsieur Cabanel's manner changed to his young wife but she was too easy-tempered and unsuspicious to notice anything, or if she did, there was too little depth in her own love for him—it was so much a matter of untroubled friendliness only—that she did not fret but accepted the coldness and brusqueness that had crept into his manner as good-naturedly as she accepted all things. It would have been wiser if she had cried and made a scene and come to an open fracas with Monsieur Cabanel. They would have understood each other better; and Frenchmen like the excitement of a quarrel and a reconciliation.

Naturally kind-hearted, Madame Cabanel went much about the village, offering help of various kinds to the sick. But no one among them all, not the very poorest—indeed, the very poorest the least—received her civilly or accepted her aid. If she attempted to touch one of the dying children, the mother, shuddering, withdrew it hastily to her own arms; if she spoke to the adult sick, the wan eyes would look at her with a strange horror and the feeble voice would mutter words in a patois she could not understand. But always came the same word, "broucolaque!"

"How these people hate the English!" she used

to think as she turned away, perhaps just a little depressed, but too phlegmatic to let herself be uncomfortable or troubled deeply.

It was the same at home. If she wanted to do any little act of kindness to the child, Adèle passionately refused her. Once she snatched him rudely from her arms, saying as she did so: "Infamous broucolaque! Before my very eyes?" And once, when Fanny was troubled about her husband and proposed to make him a cup of beef-tea à l'Anglaise, the doctor looked at her as if he would have looked through her; and Adèle upset the saucepan, saying insolently—but yet hot tears were in her eyes—"Is it not fast enough for you, madame? Not faster, unless you kill me first!"

To all of which Fanny replied nothing, thinking only that the doctor was very rude to stare so fixedly at her and that Adèle was horribly cross; and what an ill-tempered creature she was, and how unlike an English housekeeper!

But Monsieur Cabanel, when he was told of the little scene, called Fanny to him and said in a more caressing voice than he had used to her of late: "Thou wouldst not hurt me, little wife? It was love and kindness, not wrong, that thou wouldst do?"

"Wrong? What wrong could I do?" answered Fanny, opening her blue eyes wide. "What wrong should I do to my best and only friend?"

"And I am thy friend? Thy lover? Thy husband? Thou lovest me dear?" said Monsieur Cabanel.

"Dear Jules, who is so dear; who so near?" she said kissing him, while he said fervently:

"God bless thee!"

The next day Monsieur Cabanel was called away on urgent business. He might be absent for two days, he said, but he would try to lessen the time; and the young wife was left alone in the midst of her enemies, without even such slight guard as his presence might prove.

Adèle was out. It was a dark, hot summer's night, and the little Adolphe had been more feverish and restless than usual all the day. Towards evening he grew worse; and though Jeannette,

the goose-girl, had strict commands not to allow madame to touch him, she grew frightened at the condition of the boy; and when madame came into the small parlour to offer her assistance, Jeannette gladly abandoned a charge that was too heavy for her and let the lady take him from her arms.

Sitting there with the child in her lap, cooing to him, soothing him by a low, soft nursery song, the paroxysm of his pain seemed to her to pass and it was as if he slept. But in that paroxysm he had bitten both his lip and tongue; and the blood was now oozing from his mouth. He was a pretty boy; and his mortal sickness made him at this moment pathetically lovely. Fanny bent her head and kissed the pale still face—and the blood that was on his lips was transferred to hers.

While she still bent over him—her woman's heart touched with a mysterious force and prevision of her own future motherhood—Adèle, followed by old Martin and some others of the village, rushed into the room.

"Behold her!" she cried, seizing Fanny by the arm and forcing her face upwards by the chin—"behold her in the act! Friends, look at my child—dead, dead in her arms; and she with his blood on her lips! Do you want more proofs? Vampire that she is, can you deny the evidence of your own senses?"

"No! no!" roared the crowd hoarsely. "She is a vampire—a creature cursed by God and the enemy of man; away with her to the pit. She must die as she has made others to die!"

"Die, as she has made my boy to die!" said Adèle, and more than one who had lost a relative or child during the epidemic echoed her words, "Die, as she has made mine to die!"

"What is the meaning of all this?" said Madame Cabanel, rising and facing the crowd with the true courage of an Englishwoman. "What harm have I done to any of you that you should come about me, in the absence of my husband, with these angry looks and insolent words?"

"What harm hast thou done?" cried old Martin, coming close to her. "Sorceress as thou art, thou hast bewitched our good master; and vampire as thou art, thou nourishest thyself on our blood! Have we not proof of that at this very moment? Look at thy mouth—cursed broucolaque; and here lies thy victim, who accuses thee in his death!"

Fanny laughed scornfully. "I cannot condescend to answer such folly," she said, lifting her head. "Are you men or children?"

"We are men, madame," said Legros the miller, "and being men we must protect our weak ones. We have all had our doubts—and who more cause than I, with three little ones taken to heaven before their time?—and now we are convinced."

"Because I have nursed a dying child and done my best to soothe him!" said Madame Cabanel with unconscious pathos.

"No more words!" cried Adèle, dragging her by the arm from which she had never loosed her hold. "To the pit with her, my friends, if you would not see all your children die as mine has died—as our good Legros' have died!"

A kind of shudder shook the crowd, and a groan that sounded in itself a curse burst from them.

"To the pit!" they cried. "Let the demons take their own!"

Quick as thought Adèle pinioned the strong white arms whose shape and beauty had so often maddened her with jealous pain; and before the poor girl could utter more than one cry Legros had placed his brawny hand over her mouth. Though this destruction of a monster was not the murder of a human being in his mind, or in the mind of any there, still they did not care to have their nerves disturbed by cries that sounded so human as Madame Cabanel's. Silent then, and gloomy, that dreadful cortege took its way to the forest, carrying its living load; gagged and helpless as if it had been a corpse among them. Save with Adèle and old Martin, it was not so much personal animosity as the instinctive self-defence of fear that animated them. They were executioners, not enemies; and the executioners of a more righteous law than that allowed by the national code. But one by one they all dropped off, till their numbers were reduced to six; of whom Legros

was one, and Lesouëf, who had lost his only sister, was also one.

The pit was not more than an English mile from the Maison Cabanel. It was a dark and lonesome spot, where not the bravest man of all that assembly would have dared to go alone after nightfall, not even if the curé had been with him; but a multitude gives courage, said old Martin Briolic; and half a dozen stalwart men, led by such a woman as Adèle, were not afraid of even lutins or the White Ladies.

As swiftly as they could for the burden they bore, and all in utter silence, the cortège strode over the moor; one or two of them carrying rude torches; for the night was black and the way was not without its physical dangers. Nearer and nearer they came to the fatal bourn; and heavier grew the weight of their victim. She had long ceased to struggle; and now lay as if dead in the hands of her bearers. But no one spoke of this or of aught else. Not a word was exchanged between them; and more than one, even of those left, began to doubt whether they had done wisely, and whether they had not better have trusted to the law. Adèle and Martin alone remained firm to the task they had undertaken; and Legros too was sure; but he was weakly and humanly sorrowful for the thing he felt obliged to do. As for Adèle, the woman's jealousy, the mother's anguish, and the terror of superstition had all wrought in her so that she would not have raised a finger to have lightened her victim of one of her pains, or have found her a woman like herself and no vampire after all.

The way got darker; the distance between them and their place of execution shorter; and at last they reached the border of the pit where this fearful monster, this vampire—poor innocent Fanny Cabanel—was to be thrown. As they lowered her, the light of their torches fell on her face.

"Grand Dieu!" cried Legros, taking off his cap. "She is dead!"

"A vampire cannot die," said Adèle. "It is only an appearance. Ask Father Martin."

"A vampire cannot die unless the evil spirits take her, or she is buried with a stake thrust through her body," said Martin Briolic sententiously.

"I don't like the look of it," said Legros; and so said some others.

They had taken the bandage from the mouth of the poor girl; and as she lay in the flickering light, her blue eyes half open, and her pale face white with the whiteness of death, a little return of human feeling among them shook them as if the wind had passed over them.

Suddenly they heard the sound of horses' hoofs thundering across the plain. They counted two, four, six; and they were now only four unarmed men, with Martin and Adèle to make up the number. Between the vengeance of man and the power and malice of the wood-demons, their courage faded and their presence of mind deserted them. Legros rushed frantically into the vague darkness of the forest; Lesouëf followed him; the other two fled over the plain while the horsemen came nearer and nearer. Only Adèle held the torch high above her head, to show more clearly both herself in her swarthy passion and revenge and the dead body of her victim. She wanted no concealment; she had done her work, and she gloried in it. Then the horsemen came plunging to them—Jules Cabanel the first, followed by the doctor and four gardes champêtres.

"Wretches! murderers!" was all he said, as he flung himself from his horse and raised the pale face to his lips.

"Master," said Adèle, "she deserved to die. She is a vampire and she has killed our child."

"Fool!" cried Jules Cabanel, flinging off her hand. "Oh, my loved wife! Thou who did no harm to man or beast, to be murdered now by men who are worse than beasts!"

"She was killing thee," said Adèle. "Ask monsieur le docteur. What ailed the master, monsieur?"

"Do not bring me into this infamy," said the doctor looking up from the dead. "Whatever ailed monsieur, she ought not to be here. You have made yourself her judge and executioner, Adèle, and you must answer for it to the law."

"You say this too, master?" said Adèle.

"I say so too," returned Monsieur Cabanel. "To the law you must answer for the innocent life

you have so cruelly taken—you and all the fools and murderers you have joined to you."

"And is there to be no vengeance for our child?"

"Would you revenge yourself on God, woman?" said Monsieur Canabel sternly.

"And our past years of love, master?"

"Are memories of hate, Adèle," said Monsieur Cabanel, as he turned again to the pale face of his dead wife.

"Then my place is vacant," said Adèle, with a bitter cry. "Ah, my little Adolphe, it is well you went before!"

"Hold, Ma'am Adèle!" cried Martin.

But before a hand could be stretched out, with one bound, one shriek, she had flung herself into the pit where she had hoped to bury Madame Cabanel; and they heard her body strike the water at the bottom with a dull splash, as of something falling from a great distance.

"They can prove nothing against me, Jean," said old Martin to the garde who held him. "I neither bandaged her mouth nor carried her on my shoulders. I am the gravedigger of Pieuvrot, and, *ma foi*, you would all do badly, you poor creatures, when you die, without me! I shall have the honour of digging madame's grave, never doubt it; and, Jean," he whispered, "they may talk as they like, those rich aristos who know nothing. She is a vampire, and she shall have a slat through her body yet! Who knows better than I? If we do not tie her down like this, she will come out of her grave and suck our blood; it is a way these vampires have."

"Silence there!" said the garde, commanding the little escort. "To prison with the assassins; and keep their tongues from wagging."

"To prison with martyrs and the public benefactors," retorted old Martin. "So the world rewards its best!"

And in this faith he lived and died, as a forçat at Toulon, maintaining to the last that he had done the world a good service by ridding it of a monster who else would not have left one man in Pieuvrot to perpetuate his name and race. But Legros and also Lesouëf, his companion, doubted gravely of the righteousness of that act of theirs on that dark summer's night in the forest; and though they always maintained that they should not have been punished, because of their good motives, yet they grew in time to disbelieve old Martin Briolic and his wisdom, and to wish that they had let the law take its own course unhelped by them—reserving their strength for the grinding of the hamlet's flour and the mending of the hamlet's sabots—and the leading of a good life according to the teaching of monsieur le curé and the exhortations of their own wives.

## *LET LOOSE*

# Mary Cholmondeley

Mary Cholmondeley (1859–1925) was born in Shropshire, England, and spent the first half of her life tending her ill mother and eventually died without ever having been married. Although living a relatively quiet and isolated life, she and her family became acquainted with many literary figures of the day. Her uncle Reginald was a friend of Mark Twain's, and her niece, Stella Benson, also became a novelist.

Mary Cholmondeley wrote more than a dozen novels, including such well-regarded mystery novels as *The Danvers Jewels* (1887), *Sir Charles Danvers* (1889), *Diana Tempest* (1893), and *Prisoners* (1906); she also wrote mixed collections of short stories, including *The Lowest Rung* (1908) and *The Romance of His Life and Other Stories* (1921). Her best-known work was *Red Pottage* (1899), a satirical novel that was one of the more successful expressions of the New Woman movement of the 1880s and '90s in England, which advanced the notion of greater autonomy for women—a cultural movement that was roundly mocked by Bram Stoker in *Dracula*. Her name, incidentally, is pronounced "Chumley."

"Let Loose" was first published in the April 1890 issue of *Temple Bar: A London Magazine for Town and Country Readers* and collected in book form in the U.S. edition of *Moth and Rust* (New York: Dodd, Mead, 1902); it was omitted from the London edition published in the same year by John Murray.

# Let Loose

## MARY CHOLMONDELEY

*The dead abide with us! Though stark and cold
Earth seems to grip them, they are with us still.*

Some years ago I took up architecture, and made a tour through Holland, studying the buildings of that interesting country. I was not then aware that it is not enough to take up art. Art must take you up, too. I never doubted but that my passing enthusiasm for her would be returned. When I discovered that she was a stern mistress, who did not immediately respond to my attentions, I naturally transferred them to another shrine. There are other things in the world besides art. I am now a landscape gardener.

But at the time of which I write I was engaged in a violent flirtation with architecture. I had one companion on this expedition, who has since become one of the leading architects of the day. He was a thin, determined-looking man with a screwed-up face and heavy jaw, slow of speech, and absorbed in his work to a degree which I quickly found tiresome. He was possessed of a certain quiet power of overcoming obstacles which I have rarely seen equalled. He has since become my brother-in-law, so I ought to know; for my parents did not

like him much and opposed the marriage, and my sister did not like him at all, and refused him over and over again; but, nevertheless, he eventually married her.

I have thought since that one of his reasons for choosing me as his travelling companion on this occasion was because he was getting up steam for what he subsequently termed "an alliance with my family," but the idea never entered my head at the time. A more careless man as to dress I have rarely met, and yet, in all the heat of July in Holland, I noticed that he never appeared without a high, starched collar, which had not even fashion to commend it at that time.

I often chaffed him about his splendid collars, and asked him why he wore them, but without eliciting any response. One evening, as we were walking back to our lodgings in Middleberg, I attacked him for about the thirtieth time on the subject.

"Why on earth do you wear them?" I said.

"You have, I believe, asked me that question many times," he replied, in his slow, precise utterance, "but always on occasions when I was occupied. I am now at leisure, and I will tell you."

And he did.

I have put down what he said, as nearly in his own words as I can remember them.

Ten years ago, I was asked to read a paper on English Frescoes at the Institute of British Architects. I was determined to make the paper as good as I could, down to the slightest details, and I consulted many books on the subject, and studied every fresco I could find. My father, who had been an architect, had left me, at his death, all his papers and notebooks on the subject of architecture. I searched them diligently, and found in one of them a slight unfinished sketch of nearly fifty years ago that specially interested me. Underneath was noted, in his clear small hand—*Frescoed east wall of crypt. Parish Church. Wet Waste-on-the-Wolds, Yorkshire (via Pickering.)*

The sketch had such a fascination for me that I decided to go there and see the fresco for myself. I had only a very vague idea as to where Wet Waste-on-the-Wolds was, but I was ambitious for the success of my paper; it was hot in London, and I set off on my long journey not without a certain degree of pleasure, with my dog Brian, a large non-descript brindled creature, as my only companion.

I reached Pickering, in Yorkshire, in the course of the afternoon, and then began a series of experiments on local lines which ended, after several hours, in my finding myself deposited at a little out-of-the-world station within nine or ten miles of Wet Waste. As no conveyance of any kind was to be had, I shouldered my portmanteau, and set out on a long white road that stretched away into the distance over the bare, treeless wold. I must have walked for several hours, over a waste of moorland patched with heather, when a doctor passed me, and gave me a lift to within a mile of my destination. The mile was a long one, and it was quite dark by the time I saw the feeble glimmer of lights in front of me, and found that I had reached Wet Waste. I had considerable difficulty in getting anyone to take me in; but at last I persuaded the owner of the public-house to give me a bed, and quite tired out, I got into it as soon as possible, for fear he should change his mind, and fell asleep to the sound of a little stream below my window.

I was up early next morning, and inquired directly after breakfast the way to the clergyman's house, which I found was close at hand. At Wet Waste everything was close at hand. The whole village seemed composed of a straggling row of one-storied grey stone houses, the same colour as the stone walls that separated the few fields enclosed from the surrounding waste, and as the little bridges over the beck that ran down one side of the grey wide street. Everything was grey. The church, the low tower of which I could see at a little distance, seemed to have been built of the same stone; so was the parsonage when I came up to it, accompanied on my way by a mob of rough, uncouth children, who eyed me and Brian with half-defiant curiosity.

The clergyman was at home, and after a short delay I was admitted. Leaving Brian in charge of my drawing materials, I followed the servant into a low panelled room, in which, at a latticed window, a very old man was sitting. The morning light fell on his white head bent low over a litter of papers and books.

"Mr. er—?" he said, looking up slowly, with one finger keeping his place in a book.

"Blake."

"Blake," he repeated after me, and was silent.

I told him that I was an architect; that I had come to study a fresco in the crypt of his church, and asked for the keys.

"The crypt," he said, pushing up his spectacles and peering hard at me. "The crypt has been closed for thirty years. Ever since—" And he stopped short.

"I should be much obliged for the keys," I said again.

He shook his head.

"No," he said. "No one goes in there now."

"It is a pity," I remarked, "for I have come a long way with that one object," and I told him about the paper I had been asked to read, and the trouble I was taking with it.

He became interested. "Ah!" he said, laying down his pen, and removing his finger from the page before him. "I can understand that. I also was young once, and fired with ambition. The lines have fallen to me in somewhat lonely places, and for forty years I have held the cure of souls in this place, where, truly, I have seen but little of the world, though I myself may be not unknown in the paths of literature. Possibly you may have read a pamphlet, written by myself, on the Syrian version of the Three Authentic Epistles of Ignatius?"

"Sir," I said, "I am ashamed to confess that I have not time to read even the most celebrated books. My one object in life is my art. *Ars longa, vita brevis*, you know."

"You are right, my son," said the old man, evidently disappointed, but looking at me kindly. "There are diversities of gifts, and if the Lord has entrusted you with a talent, look to it. Lay it not up in a napkin."

I said I would not do so if he would lend me the keys of the crypt. He seemed startled by my recurrence to the subject and looked undecided.

"Why not?" he murmured to himself. "The youth appears a good youth. And superstition! What is it but distrust in God!"

He got up slowly, and taking a large bunch of keys out of his pocket, opened with one of them an oak cupboard in the corner of the room.

"They should be here," he muttered, peering in, "but the dust of many years deceives the eye. See, my son, if among these parchments there be two keys: one of iron and very large, and the other steel, and of a long and thin appearance."

I went eagerly to help him, and presently found in a back drawer two keys tied together, which he recognized at once.

"Those are they," he said. "The long one opens the first door at the bottom of the steps which go down against the outside wall of the church hard by the sword graven in the wall. The second opens (but it is hard of opening and of shutting) the iron door within the passage leading to the crypt itself. My son, is it necessary to your treatise that you should enter this crypt?"

I replied that it was absolutely necessary.

"Then take them," he said, "and in the evening you will bring them to me again."

I said I might want to go several days running, and asked if he would not allow me to keep them till I had finished my work; but on that point he was firm.

"Likewise," he added, "be careful that you lock the first door at the foot of the steps before you unlock the second, and lock the second also while you are within. Furthermore, when you come out lock the iron inner door as well as the wooden one."

I promised I would do so, and, after thanking him, hurried away, delighted at my success in obtaining the keys. Finding Brian and my sketching materials waiting for me in the porch, I eluded the vigilance of my escort of children by taking the narrow private path between the parsonage and the church which was close at hand, standing in a quadrangle of ancient yews.

The church itself was interesting, and I noticed that it must have arisen out of ruins of a previous building, judging from the number of fragments of stone caps and arches, bearing traces of very early carving, now built into the walls. There were incised crosses, too, in some places, and one especially caught my attention, being flanked by a large sword. It was in trying to get a nearer look at this that I stumbled, and, looking down, saw at my feet a flight of narrow stone steps green with moss and mildew. Evidently this was the entrance to the crypt. I at once descended the steps, taking care of my footing, for they were damp and slippery in the extreme. Brian accompanied me, as nothing would induce him to remain behind. By the time I had reached the bottom of the stairs, I found myself almost in darkness, and I had to strike a light before I could find the keyhole and the proper key to fit into it. The door, which was of wood, opened inwards fairly easily, although an accumulation of mould and rubbish on the ground outside showed it had not been used for many years. Having got through it, which was not altogether an easy matter, as nothing would induce it to open more than about eighteen inches, I carefully locked it behind me, although I should have preferred to leave it open, as there is to some minds an unpleasant feeling in being locked in anywhere, in case of sudden exit seeming advisable.

I kept my candle alight with some difficulty, and after groping my way down a low and of course exceedingly dank passage, came to another door. A toad was squatting against it, who looked as if he had been sitting there about a hundred years. As I lowered the candle to the floor, he gazed at the light with unblinking eyes, and then retreated slowly into a crevice in the wall, leaving against the door a small cavity in the dry mud which had gradually silted up round his person. I noticed that this door was of iron, and had a long bolt, which, however, was broken. Without delay, I fitted the second key into the lock, and pushing the door open after considerable difficulty, I felt the cold breath of the crypt upon my face. I must own I experienced a momentary regret at locking the second door again as soon as I was well inside, but I felt it my duty to do so. Then, leaving the key in the lock, I seized my candle and looked round. I was standing in a low vaulted chamber with groined roof, cut out of the solid rock. It was difficult to see where the crypt ended, as further light thrown on any point only showed other rough archways or openings, cut in the rock, which had probably served at one time for family vaults. A peculiarity of the Wet Waste crypt, which I had not noticed in other places of that description, was the tasteful arrangement of skulls and bones which were packed about four feet high on either side. The skulls were symmetrically built up to within a few inches of the top of the low archway on my left, and the shin bones were arranged in the same manner on my right. *But the fresco!* I looked round for it in vain. Perceiving at the further end of the crypt a very low and very massive archway, the entrance to which was not filled up with bones, I passed under it, and found myself in a second smaller chamber. Holding my candle above my head, the first object its light fell upon was—the fresco, and at a glance I saw that it was unique. Setting down some of my things with a trembling hand on a rough stone shelf hard by, which had evidently been a credence table, I examined the work more closely. It was a reredos over what had

probably been the altar at the time the priests were proscribed. The fresco belonged to the earliest part of the fifteenth century, and was so perfectly preserved that I could almost trace the limits of each day's work in the plaster, as the artist had dashed it on and smoothed it out with his trowel. The subject was the Ascension, gloriously treated. I can hardly describe my elation as I stood and looked at it, and reflected that this magnificent specimen of English fresco painting would be made known to the world by myself. Recollecting myself at last, I opened my sketching bag, and, lighting all the candles I had brought with me, set to work.

Brian walked about near me, and though I was not otherwise than glad of his company in my rather lonely position, I wished several times I had left him behind. He seemed restless, and even the sight of so many bones appeared to exercise no soothing effect upon him. At last, however, after repeated commands, he lay down, watchful but motionless, on the stone floor.

I must have worked for several hours, and I was pausing to rest my eyes and hands, when I noticed for the first time the intense stillness that surrounded me. No sound from *me* reached the outer world. The church clock which had clanged out so loud and ponderously as I went down the steps, had not since sent the faintest whisper of its iron tongue down to me below. All was silent as the grave. This *was* the grave. Those who had come here had indeed gone down into silence. I repeated the words to myself, or rather they repeated themselves to me.

Gone down into silence.

I was awakened from my reverie by a faint sound. I sat still and listened. Bats occasionally frequent vaults and underground places.

The sound continued, a faint, stealthy, rather unpleasant sound. I do not know what kinds of sounds bats make, whether pleasant or otherwise. Suddenly there was a noise as of something falling, a momentary pause—and then—an almost imperceptible but distinct jangle as of a key.

I had left the key in the lock after I had turned it, and I now regretted having done so. I got up, took one of the candles, and went back into the larger crypt—for though I trust I am not so effeminate as to be rendered nervous by hearing a noise for which I cannot instantly account; still, on occasions of this kind, I must honestly say I should prefer that they did not occur. As I came towards the iron door, there was another distinct (I had almost said hurried) sound. The impression on my mind was one of great haste. When I reached the door, and held the candle near the lock to take out the key, I perceived that the other one, which hung by a short string to its fellow, was vibrating slightly. I should have preferred not to find it vibrating, as there seemed no occasion for such a course; but I put them both into my pocket, and turned to go back to my work. As I turned, I saw on the ground what had occasioned the louder noise I had heard, namely a skull which had evidently just slipped from its place on the top of one of the walls of bones, and had rolled almost to my feet. There, disclosing a few more inches of the top of an archway behind was the place from which it had been dislodged. I stooped to pick it up, but fearing to displace any more skulls by meddling with the pile, and not liking to gather up its scattered teeth, I let it lie, and went back to my work, in which I was soon so completely absorbed that I was only roused at last by my candles beginning to burn low and go out one after another.

Then, with a sigh of regret, for I had not nearly finished, I turned to go. Poor Brian, who had never quite reconciled himself to the place, was beside himself with delight. As I opened the iron door he pushed past me, and a moment later I heard him whining and scratching, and I had almost added, beating, against the wooden one. I locked the iron door, and hurried down the passage as quickly as I could, and almost before I had got the other one ajar there seemed to be a rush past me into the open air, and Brian was bounding up the steps and out of sight. As I stopped to take out the key, I felt quite deserted and left behind. When I came out once more into the sunlight, there was a vague sensation all about me in the air of exultant freedom.

It was already late in the afternoon, and after I had sauntered back to the parsonage to give up the keys, I persuaded the people of the public-house to let me join in the family meal, which was spread out in the kitchen. The inhabitants of Wet Waste were primitive people, with the frank, unabashed manner that flourishes still in lonely places, especially in the wilds of Yorkshire; but I had no idea that in these days of penny posts and cheap newspapers such entire ignorance of the outer world could have existed in any corner, however remote, of Great Britain.

When I took one of the neighbour's children on my knee—a pretty little girl with the palest aureole of flaxen hair I had ever seen—and began to draw pictures for her of the birds and beasts of other countries, I was instantly surrounded by a crowd of children, and even grown-up people, while others came to their doorways and looked on from a distance, calling to each other in the strident unknown tongue which I have since discovered goes by the name of "Broad Yorkshire."

The following morning, as I came out of my room, I perceived that something was amiss in the village. A buzz of voices reached me as I passed the bar, and in the next house I could hear through the open window a high-pitched wail of lamentation.

The woman who brought me my breakfast was in tears, and in answer to my questions, told me that the neighbour's child, the little girl whom I had taken on my knee the evening before, had died in the night.

I felt sorry for the general grief that the little creature's death seemed to arouse, and the uncontrolled wailing of the poor mother took my appetite away.

I hurried off early to my work, calling on my way for the keys, and with Brian for my companion descended once more into the crypt and drew and measured with an absorption that gave me no time that day to listen for sounds real or fancied. Brian, too, on this occasion seemed quite content, and slept peacefully beside me on the stone floor. When I had worked as long as I could, I put away my books with regret that even then I had not quite finished, as I had hoped to do. It would be necessary to come again for a short time on the morrow. When I returned the keys late that afternoon, the old clergyman met me at the door, and asked me to come in and have tea with him.

"And has the work prospered?" he asked, as we sat down in the long, low room, into which I had just been ushered, and where he seemed to live entirely.

I told him it had, and showed it to him.

"You have seen the original, of course?" I said.

"Once," he replied, gazing fixedly at it. He evidently did not care to be communicative, so I turned the conversation to the age of the church.

"All here is old," he said. "When I was young, forty years ago, and came here because I had no means of mine own, and was much moved to marry at that time, I felt oppressed that all was so old; and that this place was so far removed from the world, for which I had at times longings grievous to be borne; but I had chosen my lot, and with it I was forced to be content. My son, marry not in youth, for love, which truly in that season is a mighty power, turns away the heart from study, and young children break the back of ambition. Neither marry in middle life, when a woman is seen to be but a woman and her talk a weariness, so you will not be burdened with a wife in your old age."

I had my own views on the subject of marriage, for I am of opinion that a well-chosen companion of domestic tastes and docile and devoted temperament may be of material assistance to a professional man. But, my opinions once formulated, it is not of moment to me to discuss them with others, so I changed the subject, and asked if the neighbouring villages were as antiquated as Wet Waste.

"Yes, all about here is old," he repeated. "The paved road leading to Dyke Fens is an ancient pack road, made even in the time of the Romans. Dyke Fens, which is very near here, a matter of but four or five miles, is likewise old, and forgotten by the world. The Reformation never reached it. It stopped here. And at Dyke Fens they still have a priest and a bell, and bow down before the saints. It is a damnable heresy, and weekly I expound it as such

to my people, showing them true doctrines; and I have heard that this same priest has so far yielded himself to the Evil One that he has preached against me as withholding gospel truths from my flock; but I take no heed of it, neither of his pamphlet touching the Clementine Homilies, in which he vainly contradicts that which I have plainly set forth and proven beyond doubt, concerning the word *Asaph*."

The old man was fairly off on his favourite subject, and it was some time before I could get away. As it was, he followed me to the door, and I only escaped because the old clerk hobbled up at that moment, and claimed his attention.

The following morning I went for the keys for the third and last time. I had decided to leave early the next day. I was tired of Wet Waste, and a certain gloom seemed to my fancy to be gathering over the place. There was a sensation of trouble in the air, as if, although the day was bright and clear, a storm were coming.

This morning, to my astonishment, the keys were refused to me when I asked for them. I did not, however, take the refusal as final—I make it a rule never to take a refusal as final—and after a short delay I was shown into the room where, as usual, the clergyman was sitting, or rather, on this occasion, was walking up and down.

"My son," he said with vehemence, "I know wherefore you have come, but it is of no avail. I cannot lend the keys again."

I replied that, on the contrary, I hoped he would give them to me at once.

"It is impossible," he repeated. "I did wrong, exceeding wrong. I will never part with them again."

"Why not?"

He hesitated, and then said slowly:

"The old clerk, Abraham Kelly, died last night." He paused, and then went on: "The doctor has just been here to tell me of that which is a mystery to him. I do not wish the people of the place to know it, and only to me has he mentioned it, but he has discovered plainly on the throat of the old man, and also, but more faintly on the child's, marks as of strangulation. None but he has observed it, and he is at a loss how to account for it. I, alas! can account for it but in one way, but in one way!"

I did not see what all this had to do with the crypt, but to humour the old man, I asked what that way was.

"It is a long story, and, haply, to a stranger it may appear but foolishness, but I will even tell it; for I perceive that unless I furnish a reason for withholding the keys, you will not cease to entreat me for them.

"I told you at first when you inquired of me concerning the crypt, that it had been closed these thirty years, and so it was. Thirty years ago a certain Sir Roger Despard departed this life, even the Lord of the manor of Wet Waste and Dyke Fens, the last of his family, which is now, thank the Lord, extinct. He was a man of a vile life, neither fearing God nor regarding man, nor having compassion on innocence, and the Lord appeared to have given him over to the tormentors even in this world, for he suffered many things of his vices, more especially from drunkenness, in which seasons, and they were many, he was as one possessed by seven devils, being an abomination to his household and a root of bitterness to all, both high and low.

"And, at last, the cup of his iniquity being full to the brim, he came to die, and I went to exhort him on his death-bed; for I heard that terror had come upon him, and that evil imaginations encompassed him so thick on every side, that few of them that were with him could abide in his presence. But when I saw him I perceived that there was no place of repentance left for him, and he scoffed at me and my superstition, even as he lay dying, and swore there was no God and no angel, and all were damned even as he was. And the next day, towards evening, the pains of death came upon him, and he raved the more exceedingly, inasmuch as he said he was being strangled by the Evil One. Now on his table was his hunting knife, and with his last strength he crept and laid hold upon it, no man withstanding him, and swore a great oath that if he went down to burn in hell, he would leave one of his hands behind on earth, and

that it would never rest until it had drawn blood from the throat of another and strangled him, even as he himself was being strangled. And he cut off his own right hand at the wrist, and no man dared go near him to stop him, and the blood went through the floor, even down to the ceiling of the room below, and thereupon he died.

"And they called me in the night, and told me of his oath, and I counselled that no man should speak of it, and I took the dead hand, which none had ventured to touch, and I laid it beside him in his coffin; for I thought it better he should take it with him, so that he might have it, if haply some day after much tribulation he should perchance be moved to stretch forth his hands towards God. But the story got spread about, and the people were affrighted, so, when he came to be buried in the place of his fathers, he being the last of his family, and the crypt likewise full, I had it closed, and kept the keys myself, and suffered no man to enter therein any more; for truly he was a man of an evil life, and the devil is not yet wholly overcome, nor cast chained into the lake of fire. So in time the story died out, for in thirty years much is forgotten. And when you came and asked me for the keys, I was at the first minded to withhold them; but I thought it was a vain superstition, and I perceived that you do but ask a second time for what is first refused; so I let you have them, seeing it was not an idle curiosity, but a desire to improve the talent committed to you, that led you to require them."

The old man stopped, and I remained silent, wondering what would be the best way to get them just once more.

"Surely, sir," I said at last, "one so cultivated and deeply read as yourself cannot be biased by an idle superstition."

"I trust not," he replied, "and yet—it is a strange thing that since the crypt was opened two people have died, and the mark is plain upon the throat of the old man and visible on the young child. No blood was drawn, but the second time the grip was stronger than the first. The third time, perchance—"

"Superstition such as that," I said with authority, "is an entire want of faith in God. You once said so yourself."

I took a high moral tone which is often efficacious with conscientious, humble-minded people.

He agreed, and accused himself of not having faith as a grain of mustard seed; but even when I had got him so far as that, I had a severe struggle for the keys. It was only when I finally explained to him that if any malign influence *had* been let loose the first day, at any rate, it was out now for good or evil, and no further going or coming of mine could make any difference, that I finally gained my point. I was young, and he was old; and, being much shaken by what had occurred, he gave way at last, and I wrested the keys from him.

I will not deny that I went down the steps that day with a vague, indefinable repugnance, which was only accentuated by the closing of the two doors behind me. I remembered then, for the first time, the faint jangling of the key and other sounds which I had noticed the first day, and how one of the skulls had fallen. I went to the place where it still lay. I have already said these walls of skulls were built up so high as to be within a few inches of the top of the low archways that led into more distant portions of the vault. The displacement of the skull in question had left a small hole just large enough for me to put my hand through. I noticed for the first time, over the archway above it, a carved coat-of-arms, and the name, now almost obliterated, of Despard. This, no doubt, was the Despard vault. I could not resist moving a few more skulls and looking in, holding my candle as near the aperture as I could. The vault was full. Piled high, one upon another, were old coffins, and remnants of coffins, and strewn bones. I attribute my present determination to be cremated to the painful impression produced on me by this spectacle. The coffin nearest the archway alone was intact, save for a large crack across the lid. I could not get a ray from my candle to fall on the brass plates, but I felt no doubt this was the coffin of the wicked Sir Roger. I put back the skulls,

including the one which had rolled down, and carefully finished my work. I was not there much more than an hour, but I was glad to get away.

If I could have left Wet Waste at once I should have done so, for I had a totally unreasonable longing to leave the place; but I found that only one train stopped during the day at the station from which I had come, and that it would not be possible to be in time for it that day.

Accordingly I submitted to the inevitable, and wandered about with Brian for the remainder of the afternoon and until late in the evening, sketching and smoking. The day was oppressively hot, and even after the sun had set across the burnt stretches of the wolds, it seemed to grow very little cooler. Not a breath stirred. In the evening, when I was tired of loitering in the lanes, I went up to my own room, and after contemplating afresh my finished study of the fresco, I suddenly set to work to write the part of my paper bearing upon it. As a rule, I write with difficulty, but that evening words came to me with winged speed, and with them a hovering impression that I must make haste, that I was much pressed for time. I wrote and wrote, until my candles guttered out and left me trying to finish by the moonlight, which, until I endeavoured to write by it, seemed as clear as day.

I had to put away my MS, and, feeling it was too early to go to bed, for the church clock was just counting out ten, I sat down by the open window and leaned out to try and catch a breath of air. It was a night of exceptional beauty; and as I looked out my nervous haste and hurry of mind were allayed. The moon, a perfect circle, was—if so poetic an expression be permissible—as it were, sailing across a calm sky. Every detail of the little village was as clearly illuminated by its beams as if it were broad day; so, also, was the adjacent church with its primeval yews, while even the wolds beyond were dimly indicated, as if through tracing paper.

I sat a long time leaning against the window-sill. The heat was still intense. I am not, as a rule, easily elated or readily cast down; but as I sat that night in the lonely village on the moors, with Brian's head against my knee, how, or why, I know not, a great depression gradually came upon me.

My mind went back to the crypt and the countless dead who had been laid there. The sight of the goal to which all human life, and strength, and beauty, travel in the end, had not affected me at the time, but now the very air about me seemed heavy with death.

What was the good, I asked myself, of working and toiling, and grinding down my heart and youth in the mill of long and strenuous effort, seeing that in the grave folly and talent, idleness and labour lie together, and are alike forgotten? Labour seemed to stretch before me till my heart ached to think of it, to stretch before me even to the end of life, and then came, as the recompense of my labour—the grave. Even if I succeeded, if, after wearing my life threadbare with toil, I succeeded, what remained to me in the end? The grave. A little sooner, while the hands and eyes were still strong to labour, or a little later, when all power and vision had been taken from them; sooner or later only—*the grave*.

I do not apologize for the excessively morbid tenor of these reflections, as I hold that they were caused by the lunar effects which I have endeavoured to transcribe. The moon in its various quarterings has always exerted a marked influence on what I may call the sub-dominant, namely, the poetic side of my nature.

I roused myself at last, when the moon came to look in upon me where I sat, and, leaving the window open, I pulled myself together and went to bed.

I fell asleep almost immediately, but I do not fancy I could have been alseep very long when I was wakened by Brian. He was growling in a low, muffled tone, as he sometimes did in his sleep, when his nose was buried in his rug. I called out to him to shut up; and as he did not do so, turned in bed to find my match box or something to throw at him. The moonlight was still in the room, and as I looked at him I saw him raise his head and evidently wake up. I admonished him, and was just on the point of falling asleep when he began to growl again in a low, savage manner that waked

me most effectually. Presently he shook himself and got up, and began prowling about the room. I sat up in bed and called to him, but he paid no attention. Suddenly I saw him stop short in the moonlight; he showed his teeth, and crouched down, his eyes following something in the air. I looked at him in horror. Was he going mad? His eyes were glaring, and his head moved slightly as if he were following the rapid movements of an enemy. Then, with a furious snarl, he suddenly sprang from the ground, and rushed in great leaps across the room towards me, dashing himself against the furniture, his eyes rolling, snatching and tearing wildly in the air with his teeth. I saw he had gone mad. I leaped out of bed, and rushing at him, caught him by the throat. The moon had gone behind a cloud; but in the darkness I felt him turn upon me, felt him rise up, and his teeth close in my throat. I was being strangled. With all the strength of despair, I kept my grip of his neck and, dragging him across the room, tried to crush in his head against the iron rail of my bedstead. It was my only chance. I felt the blood running down my neck. I was suffocating. After one moment of frightful struggle, I beat his head against the bar and heard his skull give way. I felt him give one strong shudder, a groan, and then I fainted away.

When I came to myself I was lying on the floor, surrounded by the people of the house, my reddened hands still clutching Brian's throat. Someone was holding a candle towards me, and the draught from the window made it flare and waver. I looked at Brian. He was stone dead. The blood from his battered head was trickling slowly over my hands. His great jaw was fixed in something that—in the uncertain light—I could not see.

They turned the light a little.

"Oh, God!" I shrieked. "There! Look! Look!"

"He's off his head," said someone, and I fainted again.

I was ill for about a fortnight without regaining consciousness, a waste of time which even now I cannot think without poignant regret. When I did recover consciousness, I found I was being carefully nursed by the old clergyman and the people of the house. I have often heard the unkindness of the world in general inveighed against, but for my part I can honestly say that I have received many more kindnesses than I have time to repay. Country people especially are remarkably attentive to strangers in illness.

I could not rest until I had seen the doctor who attended me, and had received his assurance that I should be equal to reading my paper on the appointed day. This pressing anxiety removed, I told him of what I had seen before I fainted the second time. He listened attentively and then assured me, in a manner that was intended to be soothing, that I was suffering from an hallucination, due, no doubt, to the shock of my dog's sudden madness.

"Did you see the dog after it was dead?" I asked.

He said he did. The whole jaw was covered with blood and foam; the teeth certainly seemed convulsively fixed, but the case being evidently one of extraordinarily virulent hydrophobia, owing to the intense heat, he had had the body buried immediately.

My companion stopped speaking as we reached our lodgings, and went upstairs. Then lighting a candle, he slowly turned down his collar.

"You see I have the marks still," he said, "but I have no fear of dying of hydrophobia. I am told such peculiar scars could not have been made by the teeth of a dog. If you look closely you see the pressure of five fingers. That is the reason why I wear high collars."

## THE VAMPIRE

# Vasile Alecsandri

Vasile Alecsandri (1821–90) was born in Bacău, Moldavia. He studied at an elite boarding school for boys, then moved to Paris to continue his studies in chemistry, medicine, and law, eventually giving them all up to pursue a career in literature. At only nineteen years of age, he became the director of the National Theatre of Iaşi, for which he wrote two plays. He also became an active collector of Romanian folk songs and folklore, which he published in two volumes.

He became a leader in the revolutionary movement to form a united Romania, joining Moldavia and Walachia. He wrote poetry, plays, essays, tracts, and stories for the first Romanian-language literary magazine and the first newspaper. When the unionist movement collapsed in 1848, he fled to Transylvania to avoid arrest. The revolutionaries soon sent him to Paris to inform France and the rest of Europe about the Romanian national cause. His widely read poems continued to advance the unification cause, one of them, written in 1856, serving as the hymn of the unionist movement. In 1881 he wrote "Long Live the King," which became the national anthem of the Kingdom of Romania until the abolition of the monarchy in 1947. His activities as a literary figure, politician, and diplomat were so significant, wide-ranging, and influential that he was known as the Victor Hugo of Eastern Europe.

"The Vampire" was first published in English in the November 1886 issue of the *English Illustrated Magazine*.

# The Vampire

## VASILE ALECSANDRI

Near the cliff's sharp edge, on high
Standing out against the sky,
Dost thou see a ruined cross
Weatherstained, o'ergrown by moss,
Gloomy, desolate, forsaken,
By unnumbered tempests shaken?

Not a blade of grass grows nigh it,
Not a peasant lingers by it.
E'en the sombre bird of night
Shuns it in her darksome flight,
Startled by the piteous groan
That arises from the stone.

All around, on starless nights,
Myriad hosts of livid lights
Flicker fretfully, revealing
At its foot a phantom, kneeling
Whilst it jabbers dismal plaints,
Cursing God and all the saints.

Tardy traveller, beware
Of that spectre gibbering there;
Close your eyes, and urge your steed
To the utmost of his speed;—
For beneath that cross, I ween,
Lies a Vampyre's corpse obscene!

Though the night is black and cold
Love's fond story, often told,
Floats in whispers through the air.
Stalwart youth and maiden fair
Seal sweet vows of ardent passion
With their lips, in lovers' fashion.

Restless, pale, a shape I see
Hov'ring nigh; what may it be?
'Tis a charger, white as snow,
Pacing slowly to and fro
Like a sentry. As he turns
Haughtily the sward he spurns.

"Leave me not, beloved, tonight!
Stay with me till morning's light!"
Weeping, thus besought the maid;
"Love, my soul is sore afraid!
Brave not the dread Vampyre's power,
Mightiest at this mystic hour!"

Not a word he spake, but prest
The sobbing maiden to his breast;
Kissed her lips and cheeks and eyes
Heedless of her tears and sighs;
Waved his hand, with gesture gay,
Mounted—smiled—and rode away.

Who rides across the dusky plain
Tearing along with might and main
Like some wild storm-fiend, in his flight
Nursed on the ebony breast of Night?
'Tis he, who left her in her need—
Her lover, on his milk-white steed!

The blast in all its savage force
Strives to o'erthrow the gallant horse
That snorts defiance to his foe
And struggles onward. See! below
The causeway, 'long the river-side
A thousand flutt'ring flamelets glide!

Now they approach and now recede,
Still followed by the panting steed;
He nears the ruined cross! A crash,
A piteous cry, a heavy splash,
And in the rocky river-bed
Rider and horse lie crushed and dead.

Then from those dismal depths arise
Blaspheming yells and strident cries
Re-echoing through the murky air.
And, like a serpent from its lair,
Brandishing high a blood-stained glaive
The Vampyre rises from his grave!

—TRANSLATED INTO ENGLISH BY
WILLIAM BEATTY-KINGSTON

# THE DEATH OF HALPIN FRAYSER

# Ambrose Bierce

Ambrose Gwinnett Bierce (1842–1914) was born in Meigs County, Ohio, and grew up in Indiana with his mother and eccentric father; he was the tenth of thirteen children, all of whose names began with the letter *A*. When the Civil War broke out, he volunteered and was soon commissioned a first lieutenant in the Union army, seeing action in the Battle of Shiloh.

It seems that every bit of his life and every word he wrote was dark and cynical, earning him the sobriquet Bitter Bierce. He became one of the most important and influential journalists in America, writing columns for William Randolph Hearst's *San Francisco Examiner*.

He is remembered today for his devastating *Devil's Dictionary*, in which he defined *saint* as "a sinner revised and edited," *befriend* as "to make an ingrate," and *birth* as "the first and direst of all tragedies."

His most famous story is "An Occurrence at Owl Creek Bridge," in which a condemned prisoner believes he has been reprieved—just before the rope snaps his neck. It was filmed three times and was twice made for television, once by Rod Serling and once by Alfred Hitchcock.

In 1913 he accompanied Pancho Villa's army as an observer. He wrote a letter to a friend dated December 26, 1913. He then vanished—one of the most famous disappearances in history.

"The Death of Halpin Frayser" was first published in book form in *Can Such Things Be?* (New York: Cassell, 1893).

# The Death of Halpin Frayser

## AMBROSE BIERCE

*For by death is wrought greater change than hath been shown. Whereas in general the spirit that removed cometh back upon occasion, and is sometimes seen of those in flesh (appearing in the form of the body it bore) yet it hath happened that the veritable body without the spirit hath walked. And it is attested of those encountering who have lived to speak thereon that a lich so raised up hath no natural affection, nor remembrance thereof, but only hate. Also, it is known that some spirits which in life were benign become by death evil altogether.*

—Hall

## 1

One dark night in midsummer a man waking from a dreamless sleep in a forest lifted his head from the earth, and staring a few moments into the blackness, said: "Catherine Larue." He said nothing more; no reason was known to him why he should have said so much.

The man was Halpin Frayser. He lived in St. Helena, but where he lives now is uncertain, for he is dead. One who practises sleeping in the woods with nothing under him but the dry leaves and the damp earth, and nothing over him but the branches from which the leaves have fallen and the sky from which the earth has fallen, cannot hope for great longevity, and Frayser had already attained the age of thirty-two. There are persons in this world, millions of persons, and far and away the best persons, who regard that as a very advanced age. They are the children. To those who view the voyage of life from the port of departure the bark that has accomplished any considerable distance appears already in close approach to the farther shore. However, it is not certain that Halpin Frayser came to his death by exposure.

He had been all day in the hills west of the Napa Valley, looking for doves and such small game as was in season. Late in the afternoon it had come on to be cloudy, and he had lost his bearings; and although he had only to go always downhill—everywhere the way to safety when one is lost—the absence of trails had so impeded him that he was overtaken by night while still in the forest. Unable in the darkness to penetrate the thickets of manzanita and other undergrowth, utterly bewildered and overcome with fatigue, he had lain down near the root of a large madrono and fallen into a dreamless sleep. It was hours later, in the very middle of the night, that one of God's mysterious messengers, gliding ahead of the incalculable host of his companions sweeping westward with the dawn line, pronounced the awakening word in the ear of the sleeper, who sat upright and spoke, he knew not why, a name, he knew not whose.

Halpin Frayser was not much of a philosopher, nor a scientist. The circumstance that, waking from a deep sleep at night in the midst of the forest, he had spoken aloud a name that he had not in memory and hardly had in mind did not arouse an enlightened curiosity to investigate the phenomenon. He thought it odd, and with a little perfunctory shiver, as if in deference to a seasonal presumption that the night was chill, he lay down again and went to sleep. But his sleep was no longer dreamless.

He thought he was walking along a dusty road that showed white in the gathering darkness of a summer night. Whence and whither it led, and why he travelled it, he did not know, though all seemed simple and natural, as is the way in dreams; for in the Land Beyond the Bed surprises cease from troubling and the judgement is at rest. Soon he came to a parting of the ways; leading from the highway was a road less travelled, having the appearance, indeed, of having been long abandoned, because, he thought, it led to something evil; yet he turned into it without hesitation, impelled by some imperious necessity.

As he pressed forward he became conscious that his way was haunted by invisible existences whom he could not definitely figure to his mind. From among the trees on either side he caught broken and incoherent whispers in a strange tongue which yet he partly understood. They seemed to him fragmentary utterances of a monstrous conspiracy against his body and soul.

It was now long after nightfall, yet the interminable forest through which he journeyed was lit with a wan glimmer having no point of diffusion, for in its mysterious lumination nothing cast a shadow. A shallow pool in the guttered depression of an old wheel rut, as from a recent rain, met his eye with a crimson gleam. He stooped and plunged his hand into it. It stained his fingers; it was blood! Blood, he then observed, was about him everywhere. The weeds growing rankly by the roadside, showed it in blots and splashes on their big, broad leaves. Patches of dry dust between the wheelways were pitted and spattered as with a red rain. Defiling the trunks of the trees were broad maculations of crimson, and blood dripped like dew from their foliage.

All this he observed with a terror which seemed not incompatible with the fulfilment of a natural expectation. It seemed to him that it was all in expiation of some crime which, though conscious of his guilt, he could not rightly remember. To the menaces and mysteries of his surroundings the consciousness was an added horror. Vainly he sought, by tracing life backward in memory, to reproduce the moment of his sin; scenes and incidents came crowding tumultuously into his mind, one picture effacing another, or commingling with it in confusion and obscurity, but nowhere could he catch a glimpse of what he sought. The failure augmented his terror; he felt as one who has murdered in the dark, not knowing whom or why. So frightful was the situation—the mysterious light burned with so silent and awful a menace; the noxious plants, the trees that by common consent are invested with a melancholy or baleful character, so openly in his sight conspired against his peace; from overhead and all about came so audible and startling whispers and the sighs of creatures so obviously not of earth—that he could endure it no longer, and with a great effort to break some malign spell that bound his faculties to silence and inaction, he shouted with the full strength of his lungs! His voice, broken, it seemed, into an infinite multitude of unfamiliar sounds, went babbling and stammering away into the distant reaches of the forest, died into silence, and all was as before. But he had made a beginning at resistance and was encouraged. He said:

"I will not submit unheard. There may be powers that are not malignant travelling this accursed road. I shall leave them a record and an appeal. I shall relate my wrongs, the persecutions that I endure—I, a helpless mortal, a penitent, an unoffending poet!" Halpin Frayser was a poet only as he was a penitent: in his dream.

Taking from his clothing a small red-leather pocket book, one half of which was leaved for memoranda, he discovered that he was without a pencil. He broke a twig from a bush, dipped it into a pool of blood, and wrote rapidly. He had hardly touched the paper with the point of his twig when a low, wild peal of laughter broke out at a measureless distance away, and growing ever louder, seemed approaching ever nearer; a soulless, heartless, and unjoyous laugh, like that of the loon, solitary by the lakeside at midnight; a laugh which culminated in an unearthly shout close at hand, then died away by slow gradations, as if the accursed being that uttered it had withdrawn over the verge of the world whence it had come. But the man felt that this was not so—that it was near by and had not moved.

A strange sensation began slowly to take possession of his body and his mind. He could not have said which, if any, of his senses was affected; he felt it rather as a consciousness—a mysterious mental assurance of some overpowering presence—some supernatural malevolence different in kind from the invisible existences that swarmed about him, and superior to them in power. He knew that it had uttered that hideous laugh. And now it seemed to be approaching him; from what direction he did not know—dared not conjecture. All his former fears were forgotten or merged in the gigantic terror that now held him in thrall. Apart from that, he had but one thought: to complete his written appeal to the benign powers who, traversing the haunted wood, might some time rescue him if he should be denied the blessing of annihilation. He wrote with terrible rapidity, the twig in his fingers rilling blood without renewal; but in the middle of a sentence his hands denied their service to his will, his arms fell to his sides, the book to the earth; and powerless to move or cry out, he found himself staring into the sharply drawn face and blank, dead eyes of his own mother, standing white and silent in the garments of the grave!

# 2

In his youth Halpin Frayser had lived with his parents in Nashville, Tennessee. The Fraysers were well-to-do, having a good position in such society as had survived the wreck wrought by civil war. Their children had the social and educational opportunities of their time and place, and had responded to good associations and instruction with agreeable manners and cultivated minds. Halpin being the youngest and not over robust was perhaps a trifle "spoiled." He had the double disadvantage of a mother's assiduity and a father's neglect. Frayser père was what no Southern man of means is not—a politician. His country, or rather his section and State, made demands upon his time and attention so exacting that to those of his family he was compelled to turn an ear partly deafened by the thunder of the political captains and the shouting, his own included.

Young Halpin was of a dreamy, indolent, and rather romantic turn, somewhat more addicted to literature than law, the profession to which he was bred. Among those of his relations who professed the modern faith of heredity it was well understood that in him the character of the late Myron Bayne, a maternal great-grandfather, had revisited the glimpses of the moon—by which orb Bayne had in his lifetime been sufficiently affected to be a poet of no small Colonial distinction. If not specially observed, it was observable that while a Frayser who was not the proud possessor of a sumptuous copy of the ancestral "poetical works" (printed at the family expense, and long ago withdrawn from an inhospitable market) was a rare Frayser indeed, there was an illogical indisposition to honour the great deceased in the person of his spiritual ancestor. Halpin was pretty generally deprecated as an intellectual black sheep who was likely at any moment to disgrace the flock by bleating in metre. The Tennessee Fraysers were a practical folk—not practical in the popular sense of devotion to sordid pursuits, but having a robust contempt for any qualities unfitting a man for the wholesome vocation of politics.

In justice to young Halpin it should be said that while in him were pretty faithfully reproduced most of the mental and moral characteristics ascribed by history and family tradition to the famous Colonial bard, his succession to the gift and faculty divine was purely inferential. Not only had he never been known to court the Muse, but in truth he could not have written correctly a line of verse to save himself from the Killer of the Wise. Still, there was no knowing when the dormant faculty might wake and smite the lyre.

In the meantime the young man was rather a loose fish, anyhow. Between him and his mother was the most perfect sympathy, for secretly the lady was herself a devout disciple of the late and great Myron Bayne, though with the tact so generally and justly admired in her sex (despite the hardy calumniators who insist that it is essentially the same thing as cunning) she had always taken care to conceal her weakness from all eyes but those of him who shared it. Their common guilt in respect of that was an added tie between them. If in Halpin's youth his mother had "spoiled" him he had assuredly done his part towards being spoiled. As he grew to such manhood as is attainable by a Southerner who does not care which way elections go, the attachment between him and his beautiful mother—whom from early childhood he had called Katy—became yearly stronger and more tender. In these romantic natures was manifest in a signal way that neglected phenomenon, the dominance of the sexual element in all the relations of life, strengthening, softening, and beautifying even those of consanguinity. The two were nearly inseparable, and by strangers observing their manners were not infrequently mistaken for lovers.

Entering his mother's boudoir one day Halpin Frayser kissed her upon the forehead, toyed for a moment with a lock of her dark hair which had escaped from its confining pins, and said, with an obvious effort at calmness:

"Would you greatly mind, Katy, if I were called away to California for a few weeks?"

It was hardly needful for Katy to answer with her lips a question to which her tell-tale cheeks had made instant reply. Evidently she would greatly mind; and the tears, too, sprang into her large brown eyes as corroborative testimony.

"Ah, my son," she said, looking up into his face with infinite tenderness, "I should have known that this was coming. Did I not lie awake a half of the night weeping because, during the other half, Grandfather Bayne had come to me in a dream, and standing by his portrait—young, too, as handsome as that—pointed to yours on the same wall? And when I looked it seemed that I could not see the features; you had been painted with a face cloth, such as we put upon the dead. Your father has laughed at me, but you and I, dear, know that such things are not for nothing. And I saw below the edge of the cloth the marks of hands on your throat—forgive me, but we have not been used to keeping such things from each other. Perhaps you have another interpretation. Perhaps it does not mean that you will go to California. Or maybe you will take me with you?"

It must be confessed that this ingenious interpretation of the dream in the light of newly discovered evidence did not wholly commend itself to the son's more logical mind; he had, for the moment at least, a conviction that it foreshadowed a more simple and immediate, if less tragic, disaster than a visit to the Pacific Coast. It was Halpin Frayser's impression that he was to be garroted on his native heath.

"Are there not medicinal springs in California?" Mrs. Frayser resumed before he had time to give her the true reading of the dream—"places where one recovers from rheumatism and neuralgia? Look—my fingers feel so stiff; and I am almost sure they have been giving me great pain while I slept."

She held out her hands for his inspection. What diagnosis of her case the young man may have thought it best to conceal with a smile, the historian is unable to state, but for himself he feels bound to say that fingers looking less stiff, and showing fewer evidences of even insensible pain, have seldom been submitted for medical inspection by even the fairest patient desiring a prescription of unfamiliar scenes.

The outcome of it was that of these two odd persons having equally odd notions of duty, the one went to California, as the interest of his client required, and the other remained at home in compliance with a wish that her husband was scarcely conscious of entertaining.

While in San Francisco Halpin Frayser was walking one dark night along the waterfront of the city, when, with a suddenness that surprised and disconcerted him, he became a sailor. He was in fact "shanghaied" aboard a gallant, gallant ship, and sailed for a far country. Nor did his misfortunes end with the voyage; for the ship was cast ashore on an island of the South Pacific, and it was six years afterward when the survivors were taken off by a venturesome trading schooner and brought back to San Francisco.

Though poor in purse, Frayser was no less proud in spirit than he had been in the years that seemed ages and ages ago. He would accept no assistance from strangers, and it was while living with a fellow survivor near the town of St. Helena, awaiting news and remittances from home, that he had gone gunning and dreaming.

**3**

The apparition confronting the dreamer in the haunted wood—the things so like, yet so unlike, his mother—was horrible! It stirred no love nor longing in his heart; it came unattended with pleasant memories of a golden past—inspired no sentiment of any kind; all the finer emotions were swallowed up in fear. He tried to turn and run from before it, but his legs were as lead; he was unable to lift his feet from the ground. His arms hung helpless at his sides; of his eyes only he retained control, and these he dared not remove from the lustreless orbs of the apparition, which he knew was not a soul without a body, but that most dreadful of all existences infesting that haunted wood—a body without a soul! In its blank stare was neither love, nor pity, nor intelligence—nothing to which to address an appeal for mercy. "An appeal will not lie," he thought, with an absurd reversion to professional slang, making the situation more horrible, as the fire of a cigar might light up a tomb.

For a time, which seemed so long that the world grew grey with age and sin, and the haunted forest, having fulfilled its purpose in this monstrous culmination of its terrors, vanished out of his consciousness with all its sights and sounds, the apparition stood within a pace, regarding him with the mindless malevolence of a wild brute; then thrust its hands forward and sprang upon him with appalling ferocity! The act released his physical energies without unfettering his will, his mind was still spellbound, but his powerful body and agile limbs, endowed with a blind insensate life of their own, resisted stoutly and well. For an instant he seemed to see this unnatural contest between a dead intelligence and a breathing mechanism only as a spectator—such fancies are in dreams; then he regained his identity almost as if by a leap forward into his body, and the straining automaton had a directing will as alert and fierce as that of its hideous antagonist.

But what mortal can cope with a creature of his dream? The imagination creating the enemy is already vanquished; the combat's result is the combat's cause. Despite his struggles—despite his strength and activity, which seemed wasted in a void, he felt the cold fingers close upon his throat. Borne backward to the earth, he saw above him the dead and drawn face within a hand's-breadth of his own, and then all was black. A sound as of the beating of distant drums—a murmur of swarming voices, a sharp, far cry signing all to silence, and Halpin Frayser dreamed that he was dead.

**4**

A warm, clear night had been followed by a morning of drenching fog. At about the middle of the afternoon of the preceding day a little whiff of light vapour—a mere thickening of the atmosphere, the ghost of a cloud—had been observed clinging to the western side of Mount St. Helena, away up along the barren altitudes near the summit. It was so thin, so diaphanous, so like a fancy made visible, that one would have said: "Look quickly! In a moment it will be gone."

In a moment it was visibly larger and denser. While with one edge it clung to the mountain, with the other it reached farther and farther out into the air above the lower slopes. At the same time it extended itself to north and south, joining small patches of mist that appeared to come out of the mountainside on exactly the same level, with an intelligent design to be absorbed. And so it grew and grew until the summit was shut out of view from the valley, and over the valley itself was an ever-extending canopy, opaque and grey. At Calistoga, which lies near the head of the valley and the foot of the mountain, there were a starless night and a sunless morning. The fog, sinking into the valley, had reached southward, swallowing up ranch after ranch, until it had blotted out the town of St. Helena, nine miles away. The dust in the road was laid; trees were adrip with moisture; birds silent in their coverts; the morning light was wan and ghastly, with neither colour nor fire.

Two men left the town of St. Helena at the first glimmer of dawn, and walked along the road northward up the valley towards Calistoga. They carried guns on their shoulders, yet no one having knowledge of such matters could have mistaken them for hunters of bird or beast. They were a deputy sheriff from Napa and a detective from San Francisco—Holker and Jaralson, respectively. Their business was manhunting.

"How far is it?" inquired Holker, as they strode along, their feet stirring white the dust beneath the damp surface of the road.

"The White Church? Only a half mile farther," the other answered. "By the way," he added, "it is neither white nor a church; it is an abandoned schoolhouse, grey with age and neglect. Religious services were once held in it—when it was white,

and there is a graveyard that would delight a poet. Can you guess why I sent for you, and told you to come armed?"

"Oh, I never have bothered you about things of that kind. I've always found you communicative when the time came. But if I may hazard a guess, you want me to help you arrest one of the corpses in the graveyard."

"You remember Branscom?" said Jaralson, treating his companion's wit with the inattention that it deserved.

"The chap who cut his wife's throat? I ought; I wasted a week's work on him and had my expenses for my trouble. There is a reward of five hundred dollars, but none of us ever got a sight of him. You don't mean to say—"

"Yes, I do. He has been under the noses of you fellows all the time. He comes by night to the old graveyard at the White Church."

"The devil! That's where they buried his wife."

"Well, you fellows might have had sense enough to suspect that he would return to her grave sometime?"

"The very last place that anyone would have expected him to return to."

"But you had exhausted all the other places. Learning your failure at them, I 'laid for him' there."

"And you found him?"

"Damn it! He found *me*. The rascal got the drop on me—regularly held me up and made me travel. It's God's mercy that he didn't go through me. Oh, he's a good one, and I fancy the half of that reward is enough for me if you're needy."

Holker laughed good-humouredly, and explained that his creditors were never more importunate.

"I wanted merely to show you the ground, and arrange a plan with you," the detective explained. "I thought it as well for us to be armed, even in daylight."

"The man must be insane," said the deputy sheriff. "The reward is for his capture and conviction. If he's mad he won't be convicted."

Mr. Holker was so profoundly affected by the possible failure of justice that he involuntarily stopped in the middle of the road, then resumed his walk with abated zeal.

"Well, he looks it," assented Jaralson. "I'm bound to admit that a more unshaven, unshorn, unkempt, and uneverything wretch I never saw outside the ancient and honourable order of tramps. But I've gone in for him, and can't make up my mind to let go. There's glory in it for us, anyhow. Not another soul knows that he is this side of the Mountains of the Moon."

"All right," Holker said, "we will go and view the ground," and he added, in the words of a once favourite inscription for tombstones: "'where you must shortly lie'—I mean if old Branscom ever gets tired of you and your impertinent intrusion. By the way, I heard the other day that 'Branscom' was not his real name."

"What is?"

"I can't recall it. I had lost all interest in the wretch, and it did not fix itself in my memory— something like Pardee. The woman whose throat he had the bad taste to cut was a widow when he met her. She had come to California to look up some relatives—there are persons who will do that sometimes. But you know all that."

"Naturally."

"But not knowing the right name, by what happy inspiration did you find the right grave? The man who told me what the name was said it had been cut on the headboard."

"I don't know the right grave." Jaralson was apparently a trifle reluctant to admit his ignorance of so important a point of his plan. "I have been watching about the place generally. A part of our work this morning will be to identify that grave. Here is the White Church."

For a long distance the road had been bordered by fields on both sides, but now on the left there was a forest of oaks, madronos, and gigantic spruces whose lower parts only could be seen, dim and ghostly in the fog. The undergrowth was, in places, thick, but nowhere impenetrable. For some moments Holker saw nothing of the building, but as they turned into the woods it revealed itself in faint grey outline through the fog, looking huge and far away. A few steps more, and it was within an arm's

length, distinct, dark with moisture, and insignificant in size. It had the usual country-schoolhouse form—belonged to the packing-box order of architecture; had an underpinning of stones, a moss-grown roof, and blank window spaces, whence both glass and sash had long departed. It was ruined, but not a ruin—a typical Californian substitute for what are known to the guide-bookers abroad as "monuments of the past." With scarcely a glance at this uninteresting structure Jaralson moved on into the dripping undergrowth beyond.

"I will show you where he held me up," he said. "This is the graveyard."

Here and there among the bushes were small enclosures containing graves, sometimes no more than one. They were recognized as graves by the discoloured stones or rotting boards at head and foot, leaning at all angles, some prostrate; by the ruined picket fences surrounding them; or, infrequently, by the mound itself showing its gravel through the fallen leaves. In many instances nothing marked the spot where lay the vestiges of some poor mortal—who, leaving "a large circle of sorrowing friends," had been left by them in turn— except a depression in the earth, more lasting than that in the spirits of the mourners. The paths, if any paths had been, were long obliterated; trees of a considerable size had been permitted to grow up from the graves and thrust aside with root or branch the enclosing fences. Over all was that air of abandonment and decay which seems nowhere so fit and significant as in a village of the forgotten dead.

As the two men, Jaralson leading, pushed their way through the growth of young trees, that enterprising man suddenly stopped and brought up his shotgun to the height of his breast, uttered a low note of warning, and stood motionless, his eyes fixed upon something ahead. As well as he could, obstructed by brush, his companion, though seeing nothing, imitated the posture and so stood, prepared for what might ensue. A moment later Jaralson moved cautiously forward, the other following.

Under the branches of an enormous spruce lay the dead body of a man. Standing silent above it they noted such particulars as first strike the attention—the face, the attitude, the clothing; whatever most promptly and plainly answers the unspoken question of a sympathetic curiosity.

The body lay upon its back, the legs wide apart. One arm was thrust upward, the other outward; but the latter was bent acutely, and the hand was near the throat. Both hands were tightly clenched. The whole attitude was that of desperate but ineffectual resistance to—what?

Nearby lay a shotgun and a game bag through the meshes of which was seen the plumage of shot birds. All about were evidences of a furious struggle; small sprouts of poison-oak were bent and denuded of leaf and bark; dead and rotting leaves had been pushed into heaps and ridges on both sides of the legs by the action of other feet than theirs; alongside the hips were unmistakable impressions of human knees.

The nature of the struggle was made clear by a glance at the dead man's throat and face. While breast and hands were white, those were purple—almost black. The shoulders lay upon a low mound, and the head was turned back at an angle otherwise impossible, the expanded eyes staring blankly backward in a direction opposite to that of the feet. From the froth filling the open mouth the tongue protruded, black and swollen. The throat showed horrible contusions; not mere finger-marks but bruises and lacerations wrought by two strong hands that must have buried themselves in the yielding flesh, maintaining their terrible grasp until long after death. Breast, throat, face, were wet; the clothing was saturated; drops of water, condensed from the fog, studded the hair and moustache.

All this the two men observed without speaking—almost at a glance. Then Holker said:

"Poor devil! He had a rough deal."

Jaralson was making a vigilant circumspection of the forest, his shotgun held in both hands and at full cock, his finger upon the trigger.

"The work of a maniac," he said, without withdrawing his eyes from the enclosing wood. "It was done by Branscom—Pardee."

Something half hidden by the disturbed leaves on the earth caught Holker's attention. It was a red-leather pocket book. He picked it up and opened it. It contained leaves of white paper for memoranda, and upon the first leaf was the name "Halpin Frayser." Written in red on several succeeding leaves—scrawled as if in haste and barely legible—were the following lines, which Holker read aloud, while his companion continued scanning the dim grey confines of their narrow world and hearing matter of apprehension in the drip of water from every burdened branch:

*Enthralled by some mysterious spell, I stood*
*In the lit gloom of an enchanted wood.*
*The cypress there and myrtle twined their*
*    boughs,*
*Significant, in baleful brotherhood.*

*The brooding willow whispered to the yew;*
*Beneath, the deadly nightshade and the rue,*
*With immortelles self-woven into strange,*
*Funeral shapes, and horrid nettles grew.*

*No song of bird nor any drone of bees,*
*Nor light leaf lifted by the wholesome breeze:*
*The air was stagnant all, and Silence was*
*A living thing that breathed among the trees.*

*Conspiring spirits whispered in the gloom,*
*Half-heard, the stilly secrets of the tomb.*
*With blood the trees were all adrip; the leaves*
*Shone in the witch-light with a ruddy bloom.*

*I cried aloud!—the spell, unbroken still,*
*Rested upon my spirit and my will.*
*Unsouled, unhearted, hopeless and forlorn,*
*I strove with monstrous presages of ill!*

*At last the viewless—*

Holker ceased reading; there was no more to read. The manuscript broke off in the middle of a line.

"That sounds like Bayne," said Jaralson, who was something of a scholar in his way. He had abated his vigilance and stood looking down at the body.

"Who's Bayne?" Holker asked rather incuriously.

"Myron Bayne, a chap who flourished in the early years of the nation—more than a century ago. Wrote mighty dismal stuff; I have his collected works. That poem is not among them, but it must have been omitted by mistake."

"It is cold," said Holker. "Let us leave here; we must have up the coroner from Napa."

Jaralson said nothing, but made a movement in compliance. Passing the end of the slight elevation of earth upon which the dead man's head and shoulders lay, his foot struck some hard substance under the rotting forest leaves, and he took the trouble to kick it into view. It was a fallen headboard, and painted on it were the hardly decipherable words, "Catherine Larue."

"Larue, Larue!" exclaimed Holker, with sudden animation. "Why, that is the real name of Branscom—not Pardee. And—bless my soul! how it all comes to me—the murdered woman's name had been Frayser!"

"There is some rascally mystery here," said Detective Jaralson. "I hate anything of that kind."

There came to them out of the fog—seemingly from a great distance—the sound of a laugh, a low, deliberate soulless laugh which had no more of joy than that of a hyena night-prowling in the desert; a laugh that rose by slow gradation, louder and louder, clearer, more distinct and terrible, until it seemed barely outside the narrow circle of their vision; a laugh so unnatural, so unhuman, so devilish, that it filled those hardy man-hunters with a sense of dread unspeakable! They did not move their weapons nor think of them; the menace of that horrible sound was not of the kind to be met with arms. As it had grown out of silence, so now it died away; from a culminating shout which had seemed almost in their ears, it drew itself away in the distance, until its failing notes, joyless and mechanical to the last, sank to silence at a measureless remove.

## KEN'S MYSTERY

# Julian Hawthorne

Julian Hawthorne (1846–1934) was born in Boston, the only son of Nathaniel Hawthorne. Because of his father's job as American consul in England, the family traveled extensively throughout Europe, and Julian displayed interest in drawing and philosophy, then studied civil engineering at Harvard. He was bored with this career, however, and against his family's wishes, decided to become a writer. What he lacked in genius he compensated for with perspicacity, producing a vast number of novels and short stories, many uncollected from their magazine appearances, much of which was in the mystery, horror, and supernatural genres.

His first story, "Love & Counter Love; or, Masquerading," was immediately accepted by *Harper's Weekly,* which paid the then-generous sum of fifty dollars for it, and he quickly sold more stories to *Scribner's* and *Lippincott's.* Working as a journalist, he covered the Indian famine for *Cosmopolitan* magazine in 1897 and the Spanish-American War for the *New York Journal* in 1898. Having lost his money in a farming venture in Jamaica, he entered a contest, reputedly writing *A Fool of Nature* in eighteen days under a pseudonym (published under his own name in 1896) and won a ten-thousand-dollar prize. He was caught in a silver mine stock fraud and served a year in prison.

"Ken's Mystery" was first published in the November 1883 issue of *Harper's New Monthly Magazine*; it was first published in book form in *David Poindexter's Disappearance and Other Tales* (New York: Appleton, 1888).

# Ken's Mystery

## JULIAN HAWTHORNE

One cool October evening—it was the last day of the month, and unusually cool for the time of year—I made up my mind to go and spend an hour or two with my friend Keningale. Keningale was an artist (as well as a musical amateur and poet), and had a very delightful studio built onto his house, in which he was wont to sit of an evening. The studio had a cavernous fire-place, designed in imitation of the old-fashioned fire-places of Elizabethan manor-houses, and in it, when the temperature out-doors warranted, he would build up a cheerful fire of dry logs. It would suit me particularly well, I thought, to go and have a quiet pipe and chat in front of that fire with my friend.

I had not had such a chat for a very long time—not, in fact, since Keningale (or Ken, as his friends called him) had returned from his visit to Europe the year before. He went abroad, as he affirmed at the time, "for purposes of study," whereat we all smiled, for Ken, so far as we knew him, was more likely to do anything else than to study. He was a young fellow of buoyant temperament, lively and social in his habits, of a brilliant and versatile mind, and possessing an income of twelve or fifteen thousand dollars a year; he could sing, play, scribble, and paint very cleverly, and some of his heads and figure-pieces were really well done, considering that he never had any regular training in art; but he was not a worker. Personally he was fine-looking, of good height and figure, active, healthy, and with a remarkably fine brow, and clear, full-gazing eye. Nobody was surprised at his going to Europe, nobody expected him to do anything there except amuse himself, and few anticipated that he would be soon again seen in New York. He was one of the sort that find Europe agrees with them. Off he went, therefore; and in the course of a few months the rumour reached us that he was engaged to a handsome and wealthy New York girl whom he had met in London. This was nearly all we did hear of him until, not very long afterward, he turned up again on Fifth Avenue, to every one's astonishment; made no satisfactory answer to those who wanted to know how he happened to tire so soon of the Old World; while, as to the reported engagement, he cut short all allusion to that in so peremptory a manner as to show that it was not a permissible topic of conversation with him. It was surmised that the lady had jilted him; but on the other hand, she herself returned home not a great while after, and, though she had plenty of opportunities, she has never married to this day.

Be the rights of that matter what they may, it was soon remarked that Ken was no longer the careless and merry fellow he used to be; on the contrary, he appeared grave, moody, averse from general society, and habitually taciturn and undemonstrative even in the company of his most intimate friends. Evidently something had happened to him, or he had done something. What? Had he committed a murder? Or joined the Nihilists? Or was his unsuccessful love affair at the bottom of it? Some declared that the cloud was only temporary, and would soon pass away. Nevertheless, up to the period of which I am writing, it had not passed away, but had rather gathered additional gloom, and threatened to become permanent.

Meanwhile I had met him twice or thrice at the club, at the opera, or in the street, but had as yet had no opportunity of regularly renewing my acquaintance with him. We had been on a footing of more than common intimacy in the old days, and I was not disposed to think that he would refuse to renew the former relations now. But what I had heard and myself seen of his changed condition imparted a stimulating tinge of suspense or curiosity to the pleasure with which I looked forward to the prospects of this evening. His house stood at a distance of two or three miles beyond the general range of habitations in New York at this time, and as I walked briskly along in the clear twilight air I had leisure to go over in my mind all that I had known of Ken and had divined of his character. After all, had there not always been something in his nature—deep down, and held in abeyance by the activity of his animal spirits—but something strange and separate, and capable of developing under suitable conditions into—into what? As I asked myself this question I arrived at his door; and it was with a feeling of relief that I felt the next moment the cordial grasp of his hand, and his voice bidding me welcome in a tone that indicated unaffected gratification at my presence. He drew me at once into the studio, relieved me of my hat and cane, and then put his hand on my shoulder.

"I am glad to see you," he repeated, with singular earnestness—"glad to see you and to feel you; and tonight of all nights in the year."

"Why tonight especially?"

"Oh, never mind. It's just as well, too, you didn't let me know beforehand you were coming; the unreadiness is all, to paraphrase the poet. Now, with you to help me, I can drink a glass of whisky and water and take a bit draw of the pipe. This would have been a grim night for me if I'd been left to myself."

"In such a lap of luxury as this, too!" said I, looking round at the glowing fire-place, the low, luxurious chairs, and all the rich and sumptuous fittings of the room. "I should have thought a condemned murderer might make himself comfortable here."

"Perhaps; but that's not exactly my category at present. But have you forgotten what night this is? This is November-eve, when, as tradition asserts, the dead arise and walk about, and fairies, goblins, and spiritual beings of all kinds have more freedom and power than on any other day of the year. One can see you've never been in Ireland."

"I wasn't aware till now that you had been there, either."

"Yes, I have been in Ireland. Yes—" He paused, sighed, and fell into a reverie, from which, however, he soon roused himself by an effort, and went to a cabinet in a corner of the room for the liquor and tobacco. While he was thus employed I sauntered about the studio, taking note of the various beauties, grotesquenesses, and curiosities that it contained. Many things were there to repay study and arouse admiration; for Ken was a good collector, having excellent taste as well as means to back it. But, upon the whole, nothing interested me more than some studies of a female head, roughly done in oils, and, judging from the sequestered positions in which I found them, not intended by the artist for exhibition or criticism. There were three or four of these studies, all of the same face, but in different poses and costumes. In one the head was enveloped in a dark hood, overshadowing and partly concealing the features; in another she seemed to be peering duskily through a latticed casement, lit by a faint moonlight; a third showed her splendidly attired in evening costume, and jewels in her hair and ears, and sparkling on her snowy bosom. The expressions were as various as the poses; now it was demure penetration, now a subtle inviting glance, now burning passion, and again a look of elfish and elusive mockery. In whatever phase, the countenance possessed a singular and poignant fascination, not of beauty merely, though that was very striking, but of character and quality likewise.

"Did you find this model abroad?" I inquired at length. "She has evidently inspired you, and I don't wonder at it."

Ken, who had been mixing the punch, and had not noticed my movements, now looked up, and said: "I didn't mean those to be seen. They don't satisfy me, and I am going to destroy them; but I couldn't rest till I'd made some attempts to reproduce— What was it you asked? Abroad? Yes—or no. They were all painted here within the last six weeks."

"Whether they satisfy you or not, they are by far the best things of yours I have ever seen."

"Well, let them alone, and tell me what you think of this beverage. To my thinking, it goes to the right spot. It owes its existence to your coming here. I can't drink alone, and those portraits are not company, though, for aught I know, she might have come out of the canvas tonight and sat down in that chair." Then, seeing my inquiring look, he added, with a hasty laugh, "It's November-eve, you know, when anything may happen, provided it's strange enough. Well, here's to ourselves."

We each swallowed a deep draught of the smoking and aromatic liquor, and set down our glasses with approval. The punch was excellent. Ken now opened a box of cigars, and we seated ourselves before the fire-place.

"All we need now," I remarked, after a short silence, "is a little music. By-the-by, Ken, have you still got the banjo I gave you before you went abroad?"

He paused so long before replying that I sup-posed he had not heard my question. "I have got it," he said, at length, "but it will never make any more music."

"Got broken, eh? Can't it be mended? It was a fine instrument."

"It's not broken, but it's past mending. You shall see for yourself."

He arose as he spoke, and going to another part of the studio, opened a black oak coffer, and took out of it a long object wrapped up in a piece of faded yellow silk. He handed it to me, and when I had unwrapped it, there appeared a thing that might once have been a banjo, but had little resemblance to one now. It bore every sign of extreme age. The wood of the handle was honey-combed with the gnawings of worms, and dusty with dry-rot. The parchment head was green with mould, and hung in shrivelled tatters. The hoop, which was of solid silver, was so blackened and tarnished that it looked like dilapidated iron. The strings were gone, and most of the tuning-screws had dropped out of their decayed sockets. Altogether it had the appearance of having been made before the Flood, and been forgotten in the fore-castle of Noah's Ark ever since.

"It is a curious relic, certainly," I said. "Where did you come across it? I had no idea that the banjo was invented so long ago as this. It certainly can't be less than two hundred years old, and may be much older than that."

Ken smiled gloomily. "You are quite right," he said. "It is at least two hundred years old, and yet it is the very same banjo that you gave me a year ago."

"Hardly," I returned, smiling in my turn, "since that was made to my order with a view to presenting it to you."

"I know that; but the two hundred years have passed since then. Yes; it is absurd and impossible, I know, but nothing is truer. That banjo, which was made last year, existed in the sixteenth century, and has been rotting ever since. Stay. Give it to me a moment, and I'll convince you. You recollect that your name and mine, with the date, were engraved on the silver hoop?"

"Yes; and there was a private mark of my own there, also."

"Very well," said Ken, who had been rubbing a place on the hoop with a corner of the yellow silk wrapper. "Look at that."

I took the decrepit instrument from him, and examined the spot which he had rubbed. It was incredible, sure enough; but there were the names and the date precisely as I had caused them to be engraved; and there, moreover, was my own private mark, which I had idly made with an old etching point not more than eighteen months before. After convincing myself that there was no mistake, I laid the banjo across my knees, and stared at my friend in bewilderment. He sat smoking with a kind of grim composure, his eyes fixed upon the blazing logs.

"I'm mystified, I confess," said I. "Come; what is the joke? What method have you discovered of producing the decay of centuries on this unfortunate banjo in a few months? And why did you do it? I have heard of an elixir to counteract the effects of time, but your recipe seems to work the other way—to make time rush forward at two hundred times his usual rate, in one place, while he jogs on at his usual gait elsewhere. Unfold your mystery, magician. Seriously, Ken, how on earth did the thing happen?"

"I know no more about it than you do," was his reply. "Either you and I and all the rest of the living world are insane, or else there has been wrought a miracle as strange as any in tradition. How can I explain it? It is a common saying—a common experience, if you will—that we may, on certain trying or tremendous occasions, live years in one moment. But that's a mental experience, not a physical one, and one that applies, at all events, only to human beings, not to senseless things of wood and metal. You imagine the thing is some trick or jugglery. If it be, I don't know the secret of it. There's no chemical appliance that I ever heard of that will get a piece of solid wood into that condition in a few months, or a few years. And it wasn't done in a few years, or a few months either. A year ago today at this very hour that banjo was as sound as when it left the maker's hands, and twenty-four hours afterward—I'm telling you the simple truth—it was as you see it now."

The gravity and earnestness with which Ken made this astounding statement were evidently not assumed. He believed every word that he uttered. I knew not what to think. Of course my friend might be insane, though he betrayed none of the ordinary symptoms of mania; but, however that might be, there was the banjo, a witness whose silent testimony there was no gainsaying. The more I meditated on the matter the more inconceivable did it appear. Two hundred years—twenty-four hours; these were the terms of the proposed equation. Ken and the banjo both affirmed that the equation had been made; all worldly knowledge and experience affirmed it to be impossible. What was the explanation? What is time? What is life? I felt myself beginning to doubt the reality of all things. And so this was the mystery which my friend had been brooding over since his return from abroad. No wonder it had changed him. More to be wondered at was it that it had not changed him more.

"Can you tell me the whole story?" I demanded at length.

Ken quaffed another draught from his glass of whisky and water and rubbed his hand through his thick brown beard. "I have never spoken to any one of it heretofore," he said, "and I had never meant to speak of it. But I'll try and give you some idea of what it was. You know me better than any one else; you'll understand the thing as far as it can ever be understood, and perhaps I may be relieved of some of the oppression it has caused me. For it is rather a ghastly memory to grapple with alone, I can tell you."

Hereupon, without further preface, Ken related the following tale. He was, I may observe in passing, a naturally fine narrator. There were deep, lingering tones in his voice, and he could strikingly enhance the comic or pathetic effect of a sentence by dwelling here and there upon some syllable. His features were equally susceptible of humorous and of solemn expressions, and his eyes were in form and hue wonderfully adapted to showing great varieties of emotion. Their mournful aspect was extremely earnest and affecting; and when Ken was giving utterance to some mysterious passage of the tale they had a doubtful, melancholy, exploring look which appealed irresistibly to the imagination. But the interest of his story was too pressing to allow of noticing these incidental embellishments at the time, though they doubtless had their influence upon me all the same.

"I left New York on an Inman Line steamer, you remember," began Ken, "and landed at Havre. I went the usual round of sight-seeing on the Continent, and got round to London in July, at the height of the season. I had good introductions, and met any number of agreeable and famous people. Among others was a young lady, a countrywoman of my own—you know whom I mean—who interested me very much, and before her family left London she and I were engaged. We parted there for the time, because she had the Continental trip still to make, while I wanted to take the opportunity to visit the north of England and Ireland. I landed at Dublin about the 1st of October, and, zigzagging about the country, I found myself in County Cork about two weeks later.

"There is in that region some of the most lovely scenery that human eyes ever rested on, and it seems to be less known to tourists than many places of infinitely less picturesque value. A lonely region too: during my rambles I met not a single stranger like myself, and few enough natives. It seems incredible that so beautiful a country should be so deserted. After walking a dozen Irish miles you come across a group of two or three one-roomed cottages, and, like as not, one or more of those will have the roof off and the walls in ruins. The few peasants whom one sees, however, are affable and hospitable, especially when they hear you are from that terrestrial heaven whither most of their friends and relatives have gone before them. They seem simple and primitive enough at first sight, and yet they are as strange and incomprehensible a race as any in the world. They are as superstitious, as credulous of marvels, fairies, magicians, and omens,

as the men whom St. Patrick preached to, and at the same time they are shrewd, sceptical, sensible, and bottomless liars. Upon the whole, I met with no nation on my travels whose company I enjoyed so much, or who inspired me with so much kindliness, curiosity, and repugnance.

"At length I got to a place on the sea-coast, which I will not further specify than to say that it is not many miles from Ballymacheen, on the south shore. I have seen Venice and Naples, I have driven along the Cornice Road, I have spent a month at our own Mount Desert, and I say that all of them together are not so beautiful as this glowing, deep-hued, soft-gleaming, silvery-lighted, ancient harbour and town, with the tall hills crowding round it and the black cliffs and headlands planting their iron feet in the blue, transparent sea. It is a very old place, and has had a history which it has outlived ages since. It may once have had two or three thousand inhabitants; it has scarce five or six hundred today. Half the houses are in ruins or have disappeared; many of the remainder are standing empty. All the people are poor, most of them abjectly so; they saunter about with bare feet and uncovered heads, the women in quaint black or dark-blue cloaks, the men in such anomalous attire as only an Irishman knows how to get together, the children half naked. The only comfortable-looking people are the monks and the priests, and the soldiers in the fort. For there is a fort there, constructed on the huge ruins of one which may have done duty in the reign of Edward the Black Prince, or earlier, in whose mossy embrasures are mounted a couple of cannon, which occasionally sent a practice-shot or two at the cliff on the other side of the harbour. The garrison consists of a dozen men and three or four officers and non-commissioned officers. I suppose they are relieved occasionally, but those I saw seemed to have become component parts of their surroundings.

"I put up at a wonderful little old inn, the only one in the place, and took my meals in a dining-saloon fifteen feet by nine, with a portrait of George I (a print varnished to preserve it) hanging over the mantelpiece. On the second evening after dinner a young gentleman came in—the dining-saloon being public property of course—and ordered some bread and cheese and a bottle of Dublin stout. We presently fell into talk; he turned out to be an officer from the fort, Lieutenant O'Connor, and a fine young specimen of the Irish soldier he was. After telling me all he knew about the town, the surrounding country, his friends, and himself, he intimated a readiness to sympathize with whatever tale I might choose to pour into his ear; and I had pleasure in trying to rival his own outspokenness. We became excellent friends; we had up a half-pint of Kinahan's whisky, and the lieutenant expressed himself in terms of high praise of my countrymen, my country, and my own particular cigars. When it became time for him to depart I accompanied him—for there was a splendid moon abroad—and bade him farewell at the fort entrance, having promised to come over the next day and make the acquaintance of the other fellows. 'And mind your eye, now, going back, my dear boy,' he called out, as I turned my face homeward. 'Faith, 'tis a spooky place, that graveyard, and you'll as likely meet the black woman there as anywhere else!'

"The graveyard was a forlorn and barren spot on the hill-side, just the hither side of the fort: thirty or forty rough head-stones, few of which retained any semblance of the perpendicular, while many were so shattered and decayed as to seem nothing more than irregular natural projections from the ground. Who the black woman might be I knew not, and did not stay to inquire. I had never been subject to ghostly apprehensions, and as a matter of fact, though the path I had to follow was in places very bad going, not to mention a haphazard scramble over a ruined bridge that covered a deep-lying brook, I reached my inn without any adventure whatever.

"The next day I kept my appointment at the fort, and found no reason to regret it; and my friendly sentiments were abundantly reciprocated, thanks more especially, perhaps, to the success of my banjo, which I carried with me, and which was as novel as it was popular with those who listened to it. The chief personages in the social circle besides my friend the lieutenant were Major Molloy, who was in command, a racy and juicy old campaigner, with a face like a sunset, and the surgeon, Dr. Dudeen, a long, dry, humorous genius, with a wealth of anecdotical and traditional lore at his command that I have never seen surpassed. We had a jolly time of it, and it was the precursor of many more like it. The remains of October slipped away rapidly, and I was obliged to remember that I was a traveller in Europe, and not a resident in Ireland. The major, the surgeon, and the lieutenant all protested cordially against my proposed departure, but, as there was no help for it, they arranged a farewell dinner to take place in the fort on All-halloween.

"I wish you could have been at that dinner with me! It was the essence of Irish good-fellowship. Dr. Dudeen was in great force; the major was better than the best of Lever's novels; the lieutenant was overflowing with hearty good-humour, merry chaff, and sentimental rhapsodies anent this or the other pretty girl of the neighbourhood. For my part I made the banjo ring as it had never rung before, and the others joined in the chorus with a mellow strength of lungs such as you don't often hear outside of Ireland. Among the stories that Dr. Dudeen regaled us with was one about the Kern of Querin and his wife, Ethelind Fionguala— which being interpreted signifies 'the white-shouldered.' The lady, it appears, was originally betrothed to one O'Connor (here the lieutenant smacked his lips), but was stolen away on the wedding night by a party of vampires, who, it would seem, were at that period a prominent feature among the troubles of Ireland. But as they were bearing her along—she being unconscious—to that supper where she was not to eat but to be eaten, the young Kern of Querin, who happened to be out duck-shooting, met the party, and emptied his gun at it. The vampires fled, and the Kern carried the fair lady, still in a state of insensibility, to his house. 'And by the same token, Mr. Keningale,' observed the doctor, knocking the ashes out of his pipe, 'ye're after passing that very house on your way here.

The one with the dark archway underneath it, and the big mullioned window at the corner, ye recollect, hanging over the street as I might say—'

"'Go 'long wid the house, Dr. Dudeen, dear,' interrupted the lieutenant. 'Sure can't you see we're all dying to know what happened to sweet Miss Fionguala, God be good to her, when I was after getting her safe upstairs—'

"'Faith, then, I can tell ye that myself, Mr. O'Connor,' exclaimed the major, imparting a rotary motion to the remnants of whisky in his tumbler. ' 'Tis a question to be solved on general principles, as Colonel O'Halloran said that time he was asked what he'd do if he'd been the Dook o' Wellington, and the Prussions hadn't come up in the nick o' time at Waterloo. "Faith," says the colonel, "I'll tell ye—"

"'Arrah, then, major, why would ye be interruptin' the doctor, and Mr. Keningale there lettin' his glass stay empty till he hears— The Lord save us! The bottle's empty!'

"In the excitement consequent upon this discovery, the thread of the doctor's story was lost; and before it could be recovered the evening had advanced so far that I felt obliged to withdraw. It took some time to make my proposition heard and comprehended; and a still longer time to put it in execution; so that it was fully midnight before I found myself standing in the cool pure air outside the fort, with the farewells of my boon companions ringing in my ears.

"Considering that it had been rather a wet evening indoors, I was in a remarkably good state of preservation, and I therefore ascribed it rather to the roughness of the road than to the smoothness of the liquor, when, after advancing a few rods, I stumbled and fell. As I picked myself up I fancied I had heard a laugh, and supposed that the lieutenant, who had accompanied me to the gate, was making merry over my mishap; but on looking round I saw that the gate was closed and no one was visible. The laugh, moreover, had seemed to be close at hand, and to be even pitched in a key that was rather feminine than masculine. Of course I must have been deceived; nobody was near me: my imagination had played me a trick, or else there

was more truth than poetry in the tradition that Halloween is the carnival-time of disembodied spirits. It did not occur to me at the time that a stumble is held by the superstitious Irish to be an evil omen, and had I remembered it it would only have been to laugh at it. At all events, I was physically none the worse for my fall, and I resumed my way immediately.

"But the path was singularly difficult to find, or rather the path I was following did not seem to be the right one. I did not recognize it; I could have sworn (except I knew the contrary) that I had never seen it before. The moon had risen, though her light was as yet obscured by clouds, but neither my immediate surroundings nor the general aspect of the region appeared familiar. Dark, silent hill-sides mounted up on either hand, and the road, for the most part, plunged downward, as if to conduct me into the bowels of the earth. The place was alive with strange echoes, so that at times I seemed to be walking through the midst of muttering voices and mysterious whispers, and a wild, faint sound of laughter seemed ever and anon to reverberate among the passes of the hills. Currents of colder air sighing up through narrow defiles and dark crevices touched my face as with airy fingers. A certain feeling of anxiety and insecurity began to take possession of me, though there was no definable cause for it, unless that I might be belated in getting home. With the perverse instinct of those who are lost I hastened my steps, but was impelled now and then to glance back over my shoulder, with a sensation of being pursued. But no living creature was in sight. The moon, however, had now risen higher, and the clouds that were drifting slowly across the sky flung into the naked valley dusky shadows, which occasionally assumed shapes that looked like the vague semblance of gigantic human forms.

"How long I had been hurrying onward I know not, when, with a kind of suddenness, I found myself approaching a graveyard. It was situated on the spur of a hill, and there was no fence around it, nor anything to protect it from the incursions of passers-by. There was something in the general appearance of this spot that made me half fancy I had seen it before; and I should have taken it to be the same that I had often noticed on my way to the fort, but that the latter was only a few hundred yards distant therefrom, whereas I must have traversed several miles at least. As I drew near, moreover, I observed that the head-stones did not appear so ancient and decayed as those of the other. But what chiefly attracted my attention was the figure that was leaning or half sitting upon one of the largest of the upright slabs near the road. It was a female figure draped in black, and a closer inspection—for I was soon within a few yards of her—showed that she wore the calla, or long hooded cloak, the most common as well as the most ancient garment of Irish women, and doubtless of Spanish origin.

"I was a trifle startled by this apparition, so unexpected as it was, and so strange did it seem that any human creature should be at that hour of the night in so desolate and sinister a place. Involuntarily I paused as I came opposite her, and gazed at her intently. But the moonlight fell behind her, and the deep hood of her cloak so completely shadowed her face that I was unable to discern anything but the sparkle of a pair of eyes, which appeared to be returning my gaze with much vivacity.

"'You seem to be at home here,' I said, at length. 'Can you tell me where I am?'

"Hereupon the mysterious personage broke into a light laugh, which, though in itself musical and agreeable, was of a timbre and intonation that caused my heart to beat rather faster than my late pedestrian exertions warranted; for it was the identical laugh (or so my imagination persuaded me) that had echoed in my ears as I arose from my tumble an hour or two ago. For the rest, it was the laugh of a young woman, and presumably of a pretty one; and yet it had a wild, airy, mocking quality, that seemed hardly human at all, or not, at any rate, characteristic of a being of affections and limitations like unto ours. But this impression of mine was fostered, no doubt, by the unusual and uncanny circumstances of the occasion.

"'Sure, sir,' said she, 'you're at the grave of Ethelind Fionguala.'

"As she spoke she rose to her feet, and pointed to the inscription on the stone. I bent forward, and was able, without much difficulty, to decipher the name, and a date which indicated that the occupant of the grave must have entered the disembodied state between two and three centuries ago.

"'And who are you?' was my next question.

"'I'm called Elsie,' she replied. 'But where would your honour be going November-eve?'

"I mentioned my destination, and asked her whether she could direct me thither.

"'Indeed, then, 'tis there I'm going myself,' Elsie replied, 'and if your honour'll follow me, and play me a tune on the pretty instrument, 'tisn't long we'll be on the road.'

"She pointed to the banjo which I carried wrapped up under my arm. How she knew that it was a musical instrument I could not imagine; possibly, I thought, she may have seen me playing on it as I strolled about the environs of the town. Be that as it may, I offered no opposition to the bargain, and further intimated that I would reward her more substantially on our arrival. At that she laughed again, and made a peculiar gesture with her hand above her head. I uncovered my banjo, swept my fingers across the strings, and struck into a fantastic dance-measure, to the music of which we proceeded along the path, Elsie slightly in advance, her feet keeping time to the airy measure. In fact, she trod so lightly, with an elastic, undulating movement, that with a little more it seemed as if she might float onward like a spirit. The extreme whiteness of her feet attracted my eye, and I was surprised to find that instead of being bare, as I had supposed, these were incased in white satin slippers quaintly embroidered with gold thread.

"'Elsie,' said I, lengthening my steps so as to come up with her, 'where do you live, and what do you do for a living?'

"'Sure, I live by myself,' she answered, 'and if you'd be after knowing how, you must come and see for yourself.'

"'Are you in the habit of walking over the hills at night in shoes like that?'

"'And why would I not?' she asked, in her turn.

'And where did your honour get the pretty gold ring on your finger?'

"The ring, which was of no great intrinsic value, had struck my eye in an old curiosity-shop in Cork. It was an antique of very old-fashioned design, and might have belonged (as the vendor assured me was the case) to one of the early kings or queens of Ireland.

" 'Do you like it?' said I.

" 'Will your honour be after making a present of it to Elsie?' she returned, with an insinuating tone and turn of the head.

" 'Maybe I will, Elsie, on one condition. I am an artist; I make pictures of people. If you will promise to come to my studio and let me paint your portrait, I'll give you the ring, and some money besides.'

" 'And will you give me the ring now?' said Elsie.

" 'Yes, if you'll promise.'

" 'And will you play the music to me?' she continued.

" 'As much as you like.'

" 'But maybe I'll not be handsome enough for ye,' said she, with a glance of her eyes beneath the dark hood.

" 'I'll take the risk of that,' I answered, laughing, 'though, all the same, I don't mind taking a peep beforehand to remember you by.' So saying I put forth a hand to draw back the concealing hood. But Elsie eluded me, I scarce know how, and laughed a third time, with the same airy, mocking cadence.

" 'Give me the ring first, and then you shall see me,' she said, coaxingly.

" 'Stretch out your hand, then,' returned I, removing the ring from my finger. 'When we are better acquainted, Elsie, you won't be so suspicious.'

"She held out a slender, delicate hand, on the forefinger of which I slipped the ring. As I did so, the folds of her cloak fell a little apart, affording me a glimpse of a white shoulder and of a dress that seemed in that deceptive semi-darkness to be wrought of rich and costly material; and I caught,

to, or so I fancied, the frosty sparkle of precious stones.

" 'Arrah, mind where ye tread!' said Elsie, in a sudden, sharp tone.

"I looked round, and became aware for the first time that we were standing near the middle of a ruined bridge which spanned a rapid stream that flowed at a considerable depth below. The parapet of the bridge on one side was broken down, and I must have been, in fact, in imminent danger of stepping over into empty air. I made my way cautiously across the decaying structure; but, when I turned to assist Elsie, she was nowhere to be seen.

"What had become of the girl? I called, but no answer came. I gazed about on every side, but no trace of her was visible. Unless she had plunged into the narrow abyss at my feet, there was no place where she could have concealed herself—none at least that I could discover. She had vanished, nevertheless; and since her disappearance must have been premeditated, I finally came to the conclusion that it was useless to attempt to find her. She would present herself again in her own good time, or not at all. She had given me the slip very cleverly, and I must make the best of it. The adventure was perhaps worth the ring.

"On resuming my way, I was not a little relieved to find that I once more knew where I was. The bridge that I had just crossed was none other than the one I mentioned some time back; I was within a mile of the town, and my way lay clear before me. The moon, moreover, had now quite dispersed the clouds, and shone down with exquisite brilliance. Whatever her other failings, Elsie had been a trustworthy guide; she had brought me out of the depth of elf-land into the material world again. It had been a singular adventure, certainly; and I mused over it with a sense of mysterious pleasure as I sauntered along, humming snatches of airs, and accompanying myself on the strings. Hark! What light step was that behind me? It sounded like Elsie's; but no, Elsie was not there. The same impression or hallucination, however, recurred several times before I reached the outskirts of the town—the tread of an airy foot behind or beside my own. The fancy did not make me nervous; on the contrary, I was pleased with the notion of being thus haunted, and gave myself up to a romantic and genial vein of reverie.

"After passing one or two roofless and moss-grown cottages, I entered the narrow and rambling street which leads through the town. This street a short distance down widens a little, as if to afford the wayfarer space to observe a remarkable old house that stands on the northern side. The house was built of stone, and in a noble style of architecture; it reminded me somewhat of certain palaces of the old Italian nobility that I had seen on the Continent, and it may very probably have been built by one of the Italian or Spanish immigrants of the sixteenth or seventeenth century. The moulding of the projecting windows and arched doorway was richly carved, and upon the front of the building was an escutcheon wrought in high relief, though I could not make out the purport of the device. The moonlight falling upon this picturesque pile enhanced all its beauties, and at the same time made it seem like a vision that might dissolve away when the light ceased to shine. I must often have seen the house before, and yet I retained no definite recollection of it; I had never until now examined it with my eyes open, so to speak. Leaning against the wall on the opposite side of the street, I contemplated it for a long while at my leisure. The window at the corner was really a very fine and massive affair. It projected over the pavement below, throwing a heavy shadow aslant; the frames of the diamond-paned lattices were heavily mullioned. How often in past ages had that lattice been pushed open by some fair hand, revealing to a lover waiting beneath in the moonlight the charming countenance of his high-born mistress! Those were brave days. They had passed away long since. The great house had stood empty for who could tell how many years; only bats and vermin were inhabitants. Where now were those who had built it? And who were they? Probably the very name of them was forgotten.

"As I continued to stare upward, however, a conjecture presented itself to my mind which rapidly ripened into a conviction. Was not this the house that Dr. Dudeen had described that very evening as having been formerly the abode of the Kern of Querin and his mysterious bride? There was the projecting window, the arched doorway. Yes, beyond a doubt this was the very house. I emitted a low exclamation of renewed interest and pleasure, and my speculations took a still more imaginative, but also a more definite turn.

"What had been the fate of that lovely lady after the Kern had brought her home insensible in his arms? Did she recover, and were they married and made happy ever after; or had the sequel been a tragic one? I remembered to have read that the victims of vampires generally became vampires themselves. Then my thoughts went back to that grave on the hill-side. Surely that was unconsecrated ground. Why had they buried her there? Ethelind of the white shoulder! Ah! Why had not I lived in those days; or why might not some magic cause them to live again for me? Then would I seek this street at midnight, and standing here beneath her window, I would lightly touch the strings of my bandore until the casement opened cautiously and she looked down. A sweet vision indeed! And what prevented my realizing it? Only a matter of a couple of centuries or so. And was time, then, at which poets and philosophers sneer, so rigid and real a matter that a little faith and imagination might not overcome it? At all events, I had my banjo, the bandore's legitimate and lineal descendant, and the memory of Fionguala should have the love-ditty.

"Hereupon, having retuned the instrument, I launched forth into an old Spanish love-song, which I had met with in some mouldy library during my travels, and had set to music of my own. I sang low, for the deserted street re-echoed the lightest sound, and what I sang must reach only my lady's ears. The words were warm with the fire of the ancient Spanish chivalry, and I threw into their expression all the passion of the lovers of romance. Surely Fionguala, the white-shouldered, would hear, and awaken from her sleep of centuries, and come to the latticed casement and look down! Hist! See yonder! What light—what shadow is that that seems to flit from room to room within the abandoned house, and now approaches the mullioned window? Are my eyes dazzled by the play of the moonlight, or does the casement move—does it open! Nay, this is no delusion; there is no error of the senses here. There is simply a woman, young, beautiful, and richly attired, bending forward from the window, and silently beckoning me to approach.

"Too much amazed to be conscious of amazement, I advanced until I stood directly beneath the casement, and the lady's face, as she stooped toward me, was not more than twice a man's height from my own. She smiled and kissed her fingertips; something white fluttered in her hand, then fell through the air to the ground at my feet. The next moment she had withdrawn, and I heard the lattice close.

"I picked up what she had let fall; it was a delicate lace handkerchief, tied to the handle of an elaborately wrought bronze key. It was evidently the key of the house, and invited me to enter. I loosened it from the handkerchief, which bore a faint, delicious perfume, like the aroma of flowers in an ancient garden, and turned to the arched doorway. I felt no misgiving, and scarcely any sense of strangeness. All was as I had wished it to be, and as it should be; the mediaeval age was alive once more, and as for myself, I almost felt the velvet cloak hanging from my shoulder and the long rapier dangling at my belt. Standing in front of the door I thrust the key into the lock, turned it, and felt the bolt yield. The next instant the door was opened, apparently from within; I stepped across the threshold, the door closed again, and I was alone in the house, and in darkness.

"Not alone, however! As I extended my hand to grope my way it was met by another hand, soft, slender, and cold, which insinuated itself gently into mine and drew me forward. Forward I went, nothing loath; the darkness was impenetrable, but I could hear the light rustle of a dress close to me, and the same delicious perfume that had emanated from the handkerchief enriched the air that I breathed, while the little hand that clasped and was clasped by my own alternately tightened and half relaxed the hold of its soft cold fingers. In this manner, and treading lightly, we traversed what I presumed to be a long, irregular passageway, and ascended a staircase. Then another corridor, until finally we paused, a door opened, emitting a flood of soft light, into which we entered, still hand in hand. The darkness and the doubt were at an end.

"The room was of imposing dimensions, and was furnished and decorated in a style of antique splendour. The walls were draped with mellow hues of tapestry; clusters of candles burned in polished silver sconces, and were reflected and multiplied in tall mirrors placed in the four corners of the room. The heavy beams of the dark oaken ceiling crossed each other in squares, and were laboriously carved; the curtains and the drapery of the chairs were of heavy-figured damask. At one end of the room was a broad ottoman, and in front of it a table, on which was set forth, in massive silver dishes, a sumptuous repast, with wines in crystal beakers. At the side was a vast and deep fire-place, with space enough on the broad hearth to burn whole trunks of trees. No fire, however, was there, but only a great heap of dead embers; and the room, for all its magnificence, was cold—cold as a tomb, or as my lady's hand—and it sent a subtle chill creeping to my heart.

"But my lady! How fair she was! I gave but a passing glance at the room; my eyes and my thoughts were all for her. She was dressed in white, like a bride; diamonds sparkled in her dark hair and on her snowy bosom; her lovely face and slender lips were pale, and all the paler for the dusky glow of her eyes. She gazed at me with a strange, elusive smile; and yet there was, in her aspect and bearing, something familiar in the midst of strangeness, like the burden of a song heard long ago and recalled among other conditions and surroundings. It seemed to me that something in me recognized her and knew her, had known her always. She was the woman of whom I had dreamed, whom I had beheld in visions, whose voice and face had haunted me from boyhood up. Whether we had ever met before, as human beings meet, I knew not; perhaps I had been blindly seeking her all over the world, and she had been awaiting me in this splendid room, sitting by those dead embers until all the warmth had gone out of her blood, only to be restored by the heat with which my love might supply her.

"'I thought you had forgotten me,' she said, nodding as if in answer to my thought. 'The night was so late—our one night of the year! How my heart rejoiced when I heard your dear voice singing the song I know so well! Kiss me—my lips are cold!'

"Cold indeed they were—cold as the lips of death. But the warmth of my own seemed to revive them. They were now tinged with a faint colour, and in her cheeks also appeared a delicate shade of pink. She drew fuller breath, as one who recovers from a long lethargy. Was it my life that was feeding her? I was ready to give her all. She drew me to the table and pointed to the viands and the wine.

"'Eat and drink,' she said. 'You have travelled far, and you need food.'

"'Will you eat and drink with me?' said I, pouring out the wine.

"'You are the only nourishment I want,' was her answer. 'This wine is thin and cold. Give me wine as red as your blood and as warm, and I will drain a goblet to the dregs.'

"At these words, I know not why, a slight shiver passed through me. She seemed to gain vitality and strength at every instant, but the chill of the great room struck into me more and more.

"She broke into a fantastic flow of spirits, clapping her hands, and dancing about me like a child. Who was she? And was I myself, or was she mocking me when she implied that we had belonged to each other of old? At length she stood still before me, crossing her hands over her breast. I saw upon the forefinger of her right hand the gleam of an antique ring.

"'Where did you get that ring?' I demanded.

"She shook her head and laughed. 'Have you been faithful?' she asked. 'It is my ring; it is the ring that unites us; it is the ring you gave me when you loved me first. It is the ring of the Kern—the fairy ring, and I am your Ethelind—Ethelind Fionguala.'

"'So be it,' I said, casting aside all doubt and fear, and yielding myself wholly to the spell of her inscrutable eyes and wooing lips. 'You are mine, and I am yours, and let us be happy while the hours last.'

"'You are mine, and I am yours,' she repeated, nodding her head with an elfish smile. 'Come and sit beside me, and sing that sweet song again that you sang to me so long ago. Ah, now I shall live a hundred years.'

"We seated ourselves on the ottoman, and while she nestled luxuriously among the cushions, I took my banjo and sang to her. The song and the music resounded through the lofty room, and came back in throbbing echoes. And before me as I sang I saw the face and form of Ethelind Fionguala, in her jewelled bridal dress, gazing at me with burning eyes. She was pale no longer, but ruddy and warm, and life was like a flame within her. It was I who had become cold and bloodless, yet with the last life that was in me I would have sung to her of love that can never die. But at length my eyes grew dim, the room seemed to darken, the form of Ethelind alternately brightened and waxed indistinct, like the last flickerings of a fire; I swayed toward her, and felt myself lapsing into unconsciousness, with my head resting on her white shoulder."

Here Keningale paused a few moments in his story, flung a fresh log upon the fire, and then continued:

"I awoke, I know not how long afterward. I was in a vast, empty room in a ruined building. Rotten shreds of drapery depended from the walls, and heavy festoons of spiders' webs gray with dust covered the windows, which were destitute of glass or sash; they had been boarded up with rough planks which had themselves become rotten with age, and admitted through their holes and crevices pallid rays of light and chilly draughts of air. A bat, disturbed by these rays or by my own movement, detached himself from his hold on a remnant of mouldy tapestry near me, and after circling dizzily around my head, wheeled the flickering noiselessness of his flight into a darker corner. As I arose unsteadily from the heap of miscellaneous rubbish on which I had been lying, something which had been resting across my knees fell to the floor with a rattle. I picked it up, and found it to be my banjo—as you see it now.

"Well, that is all I have to tell. My health was seriously impaired; all the blood seemed to have been drawn out of my veins; I was pale and haggard, and the chill— Ah, that chill," murmured Keningale, drawing nearer to the fire and spreading out his hands to catch the warmth— "I shall never get over it; I shall carry it to my grave."

# CARMILLA

# Sheridan Le Fanu

Joseph Sheridan Le Fanu (1814–73), generally regarded as the father of the modern ghost story, was born in Dublin to a well-to-do Huguenot family. Although he received a law degree, he never practiced, favoring a career in journalism. He joined the staff of the *Dublin University Magazine,* which published many of his early stories, and later was the full or partial owner of several newspapers. Although active politically, he did not permit contemporary affairs to enter his fictional works.

Several of his novels were among the most popular of their time, including the mysteries *Wylder's Hand* (1863) and *Uncle Silas* (1864), which was filmed as *The Inheritance* (1947), starring Jean Simmons and Derrick De Marney.

It is for his atmospheric ghost stories, however, that he is most remembered today, especially "Green Tea," in which a tiny monkey drives a minister to slash his own throat; "The Familiar," in which lethal demons pursue their victims; and the classic vampire story "Carmilla," which has been filmed numerous times, including as *Vampyr* (1932), *Blood and Roses* (1960), *Crypt of Horror* (1964), *The Vampire Lovers* (1970), and *Carmilla* (1999).

"Carmilla" was first published in the December 1871 and January–March 1872 issues of *The Dark Blue*; it was revised for its first book publication in *In a Glass Darkly* (London: Bentley, 1872).

# Carmilla

## SHERIDAN LE FANU

Upon a paper attached to the narrative which follows, Doctor Hesselius has written a rather elaborate note, which he accompanies with a reference to his Essay on the strange subject which the Manuscript illuminates.

This mysterious subject he treats, in that Essay, with his usual learning and acumen, and with remarkable directness and condensation. It will form but one volume of the series of that extraordinary man's collected papers.

As I publish the case, in this volume, simply to interest the "laity," I shall in no way forestall the intelligent lady who relates it; and, after due consideration, I have determined, therefore, to abstain from presenting any *précis* of the learned Doctor's reasoning, or extract from his statement on a subject which he describes as "involving, not improbably, some of the profoundest arcana of our dual existence, and its intermediates."

I was anxious, on discovering this paper, to reopen the correspondence commenced by Doctor Hesselius, so many years before, with a person so clever and careful as his informant seems to have been. Much to my regret, however, I found that she had died in the interval.

She, probably, could have added little to the Narrative which she communicates in the following pages, with, so far as I can pronounce, such a conscientious particularity.

## I. AN EARLY FRIGHT

Although we are by no means magnificent people, we inhabit a schloss, a castle in Styria. A small income, in that part of the world, goes a great way. Eight or nine hundred a year does wonders. Scantily enough ours would have answered among wealthy people at home. My father is English, and I bear an English name, although I never saw England. But here, in this lonely and primitive place, where everything is so marvelously cheap, I really don't see how ever so much more money would at all materially add to our comforts, or even luxuries.

My father was in the Austrian service, and retired upon a pension and his patrimony, and purchased this feudal residence, and the small estate on which it stands, a bargain.

Nothing can be more picturesque or solitary. It stands on a slight eminence in a forest. The road, very old and narrow, passes in front of its drawbridge, never raised in my time, and its moat, stocked with perch, and sailed over by many swans, and floating on its surface white fleets of water-lilies.

Over all this the schloss shows its many-windowed front, its towers, and its Gothic chapel.

The forest opens in an irregular and very picturesque glade before its gate, and at the right a steep Gothic bridge carries the road over a stream that winds in deep shadow through the wood.

I have said that this is a very lonely place. Judge whether I say truth. Looking from the hall door towards the road, the forest in which our castle stands extends fifteen miles to the right, and twelve to the left. The nearest inhabited village is about seven of your English miles to the left. The nearest inhabited schloss of any historic associations, is that of old General Spielsdorf, nearly twenty miles away to the right.

I have said "the nearest *inhabited* village," because there is, only three miles westward, that is to say in the direction of General Spielsdorf's schloss, a ruined village, with its quaint little church, now roofless, in the aisle of which are the moldering tombs of the proud family of Karnstein, now extinct, who once owned the equally-desolate château which, in the thick of the forest, overlooks the silent ruins of the town.

Respecting the cause of the desertion of this striking and melancholy spot, there is a legend which I shall relate to you another time.

I must tell you now, how very small is the party who constitute the inhabitants of our castle. I don't include servants or those dependents who occupy rooms in the buildings attached to the schloss. Listen, and wonder! My father, who is the kindest man on earth, but growing old; and I, at the date of my story, only nineteen. Eight years have passed since then. I and my father constituted the family at the schloss. My mother, a Styrian lady, died in my infancy, but I had a good-natured governess, who had been with me from, I might almost say, my infancy. I could not remember the time when her fat, benignant face was not a familiar picture in my memory. This was Madame Perrodon, a native of Berne, whose care and good nature in part supplied to me the loss of my mother, whom

I do not even remember, so early did I lose her. She made a third at our little dinner party. There was a fourth, Mademoiselle De Lafontaine, a lady such as you term, I believe, a "finishing governess." She spoke French and German, Madame Perrodon French and broken English, to which my father and I added English, which, partly from patriotic motives, we spoke every day. The consequence was a Babel, at which strangers used to laugh, and which I shall make no attempt to reproduce in this narrative. And there were two or three young lady friends besides, pretty nearly of my own age, who were occasional visitors, for longer or shorter terms; and these visits I sometimes returned.

These were our regular social resources; but of course there were chance visits from "neighbors" of only five or six leagues' distance. My life was, notwithstanding, rather a solitary one, I can assure you.

My elders had just so much control over me as you might conjecture such sage persons would have in the case of a rather spoiled girl, whose only parent allowed her pretty nearly her own way in everything.

The first occurrence in my existence, which produced a terrible impression upon my mind, which, in fact, never has been effaced, was one of the very earliest incidents of my life which I can recollect. Some people will think it so trifling that it should not be recorded here. You will see, however, by-and-by, why I mention it. The nursery, as it was called, though I had it all to myself, was a large room in the upper story of the castle, with a steep oak roof. I can't have been more than six years old, when one night I awoke, and looking round the room from my bed, failed to see the nursery-maid. Neither was my nurse there; and I thought myself alone. I was not frightened, for I was one of those happy children who are studiously kept in ignorance of ghost stories, of fairy tales, and of all such lore as makes us cover up our heads when the door creaks suddenly, or the flicker of an expiring candle makes the shadow of a bed-post dance upon the wall, nearer to our faces. I was vexed and insulted at finding myself, as I conceived, neglected, and I began to whimper, preparatory to a hearty bout of roaring; when to my surprise, I saw a solemn, but very pretty face looking at me from the side of the bed. It was that of a young lady who was kneeling, with her hands under the coverlet. I looked at her with a kind of pleased wonder, and ceased whimpering. She caressed me with her hands, and lay down beside me on the bed, and drew me towards her, smiling; I felt immediately delightfully soothed, and fell asleep again. I was wakened by a sensation as if two needles ran into my breast very deep at the same moment, and I cried loudly. The lady started back, with her eyes fixed on me, and then slipped down upon the floor, and, as I thought, hid herself under the bed.

I was now for the first time frightened, and I yelled with all my might and main. Nurse, nursery-maid, housekeeper, all came running in, and hearing my story, they made light of it, soothing me all they could meanwhile. But, child as I was, I could perceive that their faces were pale with an unwonted look of anxiety, and I saw them look under the bed, and about the room, and peep under tables and pluck open cupboards; and the housekeeper whispered to the nurse: "Lay your hand along that hollow in the bed; some one *did* lie there, so sure as you did not; the place is still warm."

I remember the nursery-maid petting me, and all three examining my chest, where I told them I felt the puncture, and pronouncing that there was no sign visible that any such thing had happened to me.

The housekeeper and the two other servants who were in charge of the nursery, remained sitting up all night; and from that time a servant always sat up in the nursery until I was about fourteen.

I was very nervous for a long time after this. A doctor was called in, he was pallid and elderly. How well I remember his long saturnine face, slightly pitted with smallpox, and his chestnut wig. For a good while, every second day, he came and gave me medicine, which of course I hated.

The morning after I saw this apparition I was in a state of terror, and could not bear to be left alone, daylight though it was, for a moment.

I remember my father coming up and standing at the bedside, and talking cheerfully, and asking the nurse a number of questions, and laughing very heartily at one of the answers; and patting me on the shoulder, and kissing me, and telling me not to be frightened, that it was nothing but a dream and could not hurt me.

But I was not comforted, for I knew the visit of the strange woman was *not* a dream; and I was *awfully* frightened.

I was a little consoled by the nursery-maid's assuring me that it was she who had come and looked at me, and lain down beside me in the bed, and that I must have been half-dreaming not to have known her face. But this, though supported by the nurse, did not quite satisfy me.

I remember, in the course of that day, a venerable old man, in a black cassock, coming into the room with the nurse and housekeeper, and talking a little to them, and very kindly to me; his face was very sweet and gentle, and he told me they were going to pray, and joined my hands together, and desired me to say, softly, while they were praying, "Lord, hear all good prayers for us, for Jesus' sake." I think these were the very words, for I often repeated them to myself, and my nurse used for years to make me say them in my prayers.

I remember so well the thoughtful sweet face of that white-haired old man, in his black cassock, as he stood in that rude, lofty, brown room, with the clumsy furniture of a fashion three hundred years old, about him, and the scanty light entering its shadowy atmosphere through the small lattice. He kneeled, and the three women with him, and he prayed aloud with an earnest quavering voice for, what appeared to me, a long time. I forget all my life preceding that event, and for some time after it is all obscure also; but the scenes I have just described stand out vivid as the isolated pictures of the phantasmagoria surrounded by darkness.

## II. A GUEST

I am now going to tell you something so strange that it will require all your faith in my veracity to believe my story. It is not only true, nevertheless, but truth of which I have been an eyewitness.

It was a sweet summer evening, and my father asked me, as he sometimes did, to take a little ramble with him along that beautiful forest vista which I have mentioned as lying in front of the schloss.

"General Spielsdorf cannot come to us so soon as I had hoped," said my father, as we pursued our walk.

He was to have paid us a visit of some weeks, and we had expected his arrival next day. He was to have brought with him a young lady, his niece and ward, Mademoiselle Rheinfeldt, whom I had never seen, but whom I had heard described as a very charming girl, and in whose society I had promised myself many happy days. I was more disappointed than a young lady living in a town, or a bustling neighborhood can possibly imagine. This visit, and the new acquaintance it promised, had furnished my day dream for many weeks.

"And how soon does he come?" I asked.

"Not till autumn. Not for two months, I dare say," he answered.

"And I am very glad now, dear, that you never knew Mademoiselle Rheinfeldt."

"And why?" I asked, both mortified and curious.

"Because the poor young lady is dead," he replied. "I quite forgot I had not told you, but you were not in the room when I received the General's letter this evening."

I was very much shocked. General Spielsdorf had mentioned in his first letter, six or seven weeks before, that she was not so well as he would wish her, but there was nothing to suggest the remotest suspicion of danger.

"Here is the General's letter," he said, handing it to me. "I am afraid he is in great affliction; the letter appears to me to have been written very nearly in distraction."

We sat down on a rude bench, under a group of magnificent lime trees. The sun was setting with all its melancholy splendor behind the sylvan horizon, and the stream that flows beside our home, and passes under the steep old bridge I have mentioned, wound through many a group of noble trees, almost at our feet, reflecting in its current the fading crimson of the sky. General Spielsdorf's letter was so extraordinary, so vehement, and in some places so self-contradictory, that I read it twice over—the second time aloud to my father—and was still unable to account for it, except by supposing that grief had unsettled his mind.

It said, "I have lost my darling daughter, for as such I loved her. During the last days of dear Bertha's illness I was not able to write to you. Before then I had no idea of her danger. I have lost her, and now learn *all*, too late. She died in the peace of innocence, and in the glorious hope of a blessed futurity. The fiend who betrayed our infatuated hospitality has done it all. I thought I was receiving into my house innocence, gaiety, a charming companion for my lost Bertha. Heavens! What a fool have I been! I thank God my child died without a suspicion of the cause of her sufferings. She is gone without so much as conjecturing the nature of her illness, and the accursed passion of the agent of all this misery. I devote my remaining days to tracking and extinguishing a monster. I am told I may hope to accomplish my righteous and merciful purpose. At present there is scarcely a gleam of light to guide me. I curse my conceited incredulity, my despicable affectation of superiority, my blindness, my obstinacy—all—too late. I cannot write or talk collectedly now. I am distracted. So soon as I shall have a little recovered, I mean to devote myself for a time to enquiry, which may possibly lead me as far as Vienna. Some time in the autumn, two months hence, or earlier if I live, I will see you—that is, if you permit me; I will then tell you all that I scarce dare put upon paper now. Farewell. Pray for me, dear friend."

In these terms ended this strange letter. Though I had never seen Bertha Rheinfeldt, my eyes filled with tears at the sudden intelligence; I was startled, as well as profoundly disappointed.

The sun had now set, and it was twilight by the time I had returned the General's letter to my father.

It was a soft clear evening, and we loitered, speculating upon the possible meanings of the violent and incoherent sentences which I had just been reading. We had nearly a mile to walk before reaching the road that passes the schloss in front, and by that time the moon was shining brilliantly. At the drawbridge we met Madame Perrodon and Mademoiselle De Lafontaine, who had come out, without their bonnets, to enjoy the exquisite moonlight.

We heard their voices gabbling in animated dialogue as we approached. We joined them at the drawbridge, and turned about to admire with them the beautiful scene.

The glade through which we had just walked lay before us. At our left the narrow road wound away under clumps of lordly trees, and was lost to sight amid the thickening forest. At the right the same road crosses the steep and picturesque bridge, near which stands a ruined tower, which once guarded that pass; and beyond the bridge an abrupt eminence rises, covered with trees, and showing in the shadow some grey ivy-clustered rocks.

Over the sward and low grounds, a thin film of mist was stealing like smoke, marking the distances with a transparent veil; and here and there we could see the river faintly flashing in the moonlight.

No softer, sweeter scene could be imagined. The news I had just heard made it melancholy; but nothing could disturb its character of profound serenity, and the enchanted glory and vagueness of the prospect.

My father, who enjoyed the picturesque, and I, stood looking in silence over the expanse beneath us. The two good governesses, standing a little way behind us, discoursed upon the scene, and were eloquent upon the moon.

Madame Perrodon was fat, middle-aged, and romantic, and talked and sighed poetically. Mademoiselle De Lafontaine—in right of her father, who was a German, assumed to be psychological, metaphysical, and something of a mystic—now

declared that when the moon shone with a light so intense it was well known that it indicated a special spiritual activity. The effect of the full moon in such a state of brilliancy was manifold. It acted on dreams, it acted on lunacy, it acted on nervous people; it had marvelous physical influences connected with life. Mademoiselle related that her cousin, who was mate of a merchant ship, having taken a nap on deck on such a night, lying on his back, with his face full in the light of the moon, had awakened, after a dream of an old woman clawing him by the cheek, with his features horribly drawn to one side; and his countenance had never quite recovered its equilibrium.

"The moon, this night," she said, "is full of odylic* and magnetic influence—and see, when you look behind you at the front of the schloss, how all its windows flash and twinkle with that silvery splendor, as if unseen hands had lighted up the rooms to receive fairy guests."

There are indolent states of the spirits in which, indisposed to talk ourselves, the talk of others is pleasant to our listless ears; and I gazed on, pleased with the tinkle of the ladies' conversation.

"I have got into one of my moping moods tonight," said my father, after a silence, and quoting Shakespeare, whom, by way of keeping up our English, he used to read aloud, he said:

> "'In truth I know not why I am so sad;
> It wearies me; you say it wearies you;
> But how I got it—came by it.'

"I forget the rest. But I feel as if some great misfortune were hanging over us. I suppose the poor General's afflicted letter has had something to do with it."

At this moment the unexpected sound of carriage wheels and many hoofs upon the road, arrested our attention.

They seemed to be approaching from the high ground overlooking the bridge, and very soon the

*Od was a term given to a mysterious vital force in nature. See The Odic Force by Karl von Reichenbach, University Books Inc., 1968.

equipage emerged from that point. Two horsemen first crossed the bridge, then came a carriage drawn by four horses, and two men rode behind.

It seemed to be the travelling carriage of a person of rank; and we were all immediately absorbed in watching that very unusual spectacle. It became, in a few moments, greatly more interesting, for just as the carriage had passed the summit of the steep bridge, one of the leaders, taking fright, communicated his panic to the rest, and, after a plunge or two, the whole team broke into a wild gallop together, and dashing between the horsemen who rode in front, came thundering along the road towards us with the speed of a hurricane.

The excitement of the scene was made more painful by the clear, long-drawn screams of a female voice from the carriage window.

We all advanced in curiosity and horror; my father in silence, the rest with various ejaculations of terror.

Our suspense did not last long. Just before you reach the castle drawbridge, on the route they were coming, there stands by the roadside a magnificent lime tree, on the other stands an ancient stone cross, at the sight of which the horses, now going at a pace that was perfectly frightful, swerved so as to bring the wheel over the projecting roots of the tree.

I knew what was coming. I covered my eyes, unable to see it out, and turned my head away; at the same moment I heard a cry from my ladyfriends, who had gone on a little.

Curiosity opened my eyes, and I saw a scene of utter confusion. Two of the horses were on the ground, the carriage lay upon its side, with two wheels in the air; the men were busy removing the traces, and a lady, with a commanding air and figure had got out, and stood with clasped hands, raising the handkerchief that was in them every now and then to her eyes. Through the carriage door was now lifted a young lady, who appeared to be lifeless. My dear old father was already beside the elder lady, with his hat in his hand, evidently tendering his aid and the resources of his schloss. The lady did not appear to hear him, or to have eyes for anything but the slender girl who was being placed against the slope of the bank.

I approached; the young lady was apparently stunned, but she was certainly not dead. My father, who prided himself on being something of a physician, had just had his fingers to her wrist and assured the lady, who declared herself her mother, that her pulse, though faint and irregular, was undoubtedly still distinguishable. The lady clasped her hands and looked upward, as if in a momentary transport of gratitude; but immediately she broke out again in that theatrical way which is, I believe, natural to some people.

She was what is called a fine-looking woman for her time of life, and must have been handsome; she was tall, but not thin, and dressed in black velvet, and looked rather pale, but with a proud and commanding countenance, though now agitated strangely.

"Was ever being so born to calamity?" I heard her say, with clasped hands, as I came up. "Here am I, on a journey of life and death, in prosecuting which to lose an hour is possibly to lose all. My child will not have recovered sufficiently to resume her route for who can say how long. I must leave her; I cannot, dare not, delay. How far on, sir, can you tell, is the nearest village? I must leave her there; and shall not see my darling, or even hear of her till my return, three months hence."

I plucked my father by the coat, and whispered earnestly in his ear, "Oh! Papa, pray ask her to let her stay with us—it would be so delightful. Do, pray."

"If Madame will entrust her child to the care of my daughter and of her good governess, Madame Perrodon, and permit her to remain as our guest, under my charge, until her return, it will confer a distinction and an obligation upon us, and we shall treat her with all the care and devotion which so sacred a trust deserves."

"I cannot do that, sir, it would be to task your kindness and chivalry too cruelly," said the lady, distractedly.

"It would, on the contrary, be to confer on us a very great kindness at the moment when we most need it. My daughter has just been disappointed by a cruel misfortune, in a visit from which she had long anticipated a great deal of happiness. If you confide this young lady to our care it will be her best consolation. The nearest village on your route is distant, and affords no such inn as you could think of placing your daughter at; you cannot allow her to continue her journey for any considerable distance without danger. If, as you say, you cannot suspend your journey, you must part with her tonight, and nowhere could you do so with more honest assurances of care and tenderness than here."

There was something in this lady's air and appearance so distinguished, and even imposing, and in her manner so engaging, as to impress one, quite apart from the dignity of her equipage, with a conviction that she was a person of consequence.

By this time the carriage was replaced in its upright position, and the horses, quite tractable, in the traces again.

The lady threw on her daughter a glance which I fancied was not quite so affectionate as one might have anticipated from the beginning of the scene; then she beckoned slightly to my father and withdrew two or three steps with him out of hearing; and talked to him with a fixed and stern countenance, not at all like that with which she had hitherto spoken.

I was filled with wonder that my father did not seem to perceive the change, and also unspeakably curious to learn what it could be that she was speaking, almost in his ear, with so much earnestness and rapidity.

Two or three minutes at most, I think, she remained thus employed, then she turned, and a few steps brought her to where her daughter lay, supported by Madame Perrodon. She kneeled beside her for a moment and whispered, as Madame supposed, a little benediction in her ear; then hastily kissing her, she stepped into her carriage, the door was closed, the footmen in stately liveries jumped up behind, the outriders spurred on, the postilions cracked their whips, the horses plunged and broke suddenly into a furious canter that threatened soon again to become a gallop, and the carriage whirled away, followed at the same rapid pace by the two horsemen in the rear.

## III. WE COMPARE NOTES

We followed the *cortège* with our eyes until it was swiftly lost to sight in the misty wood; and the very sound of the hoofs and wheels died away in the silent night air.

Nothing remained to assure us that the adventure had not been an illusion for a moment but the young lady, who just at that moment opened her eyes. I could not see, for her face was turned from me, but she raised her head, evidently looking about her, and I heard a very sweet voice ask complainingly, "Where is mamma?"

Our good Madame Perrodon answered tenderly, and added some comfortable assurances.

I then heard her ask:

"Where am I? What is this place?" and after that she said, "I don't see the carriage; and Matska, where is she?"

Madame answered all her questions in so far as she understood them; and gradually the young lady remembered how the misadventure came about, and was glad to hear that no one in, or in attendance on, the carriage was hurt; and on learning that her mamma had left her here, till her return in about three months, she wept.

I was going to add my consolations to those of Madame Perrodon when Mademoiselle De Lafontaine placed her hand upon my arm, saying:

"Don't approach, one at a time is as much as she can at present converse with; a very little excitement would possibly overpower her now."

As soon as she is comfortably in bed, I thought, I will run up to her room and see her.

My father in the meantime had sent a servant on horseback for the physician, who lived about two leagues away; and a bedroom was being prepared for the young lady's reception.

The stranger now rose, and leaning on Madame's arm, walked slowly over the drawbridge and into the castle gate.

In the hall the servants waited to receive her, and she was conducted forthwith to her room.

The room we usually sat in as our drawing-room is long, having four windows, that looked over the moat and drawbridge, upon the forest scene I have just described.

It is furnished in old carved oak, with large carved cabinets, and the chairs are cushioned with crimson Utrecht velvet. The walls are covered with tapestry, and surrounded with great gold frames, the figures being as large as life, in ancient and very curious costume, and the subjects represented are hunting, hawking, and generally festive. It is not too stately to be extremely comfortable; and here we had our tea, for with his usual patriotic leanings he insisted that the national beverage should make its appearance regularly with our coffee and chocolate.

We sat here this night, and with candles lighted, were talking over the adventure of the evening.

Madame Perrodon and Mademoiselle De Lafontaine were both of our party. The younger stranger had hardly lain down in her bed when she sank into a deep sleep; and those ladies had left her in the care of a servant.

"How do you like our guest?" I asked, as soon as Madame entered. "Tell me all about her."

"I like her extremely," answered Madame, "she is, I almost think, the prettiest creature I ever saw; about your age, and so gentle and nice."

"She is absolutely beautiful," threw in Mademoiselle, who had peeped for a moment into the stranger's room.

"And such a sweet voice!" added Madame Perrodon.

"Did you remark a woman in the carriage, after it was set up again, who did not get out," inquired Mademoiselle, "but only looked from the window?"

No, we had not seen her.

Then she described a hideous black woman, with a sort of colored turban on her head, who was gazing all the time from the carriage window, nodding and grinning derisively towards the ladies, with gleaming eyes and large white eyeballs, and her teeth set as if in fury.

"Did you remark what an ill-looking pack of men the servants were?" asked Madame.

"Yes," said my father, who had just come in, "ugly, hangdog looking fellows, as ever I beheld in my life. I hope they mayn't rob the poor lady in the forest. They are clever rogues, however; they got everything to rights in a minute."

"I dare say they are worn out with too long travelling," said Madame. "Besides looking wicked, their faces were so strangely lean, and dark, and sullen. I am very curious, I own; but I dare say the young lady will tell us all about it tomorrow, if she is sufficiently recovered."

"I don't think she will," said my father, with a mysterious smile, and a little nod of his head, as if he knew more about it than he cared to tell us.

This made me all the more inquisitive as to what had passed between him and the lady in the black velvet, in the brief but earnest interview that had immediately preceded her departure.

We were scarcely alone, when I entreated him to tell me. He did not need much pressing.

"There is no particular reason why I should not tell you. She expressed a reluctance to trouble us with the care of her daughter, saying she was in delicate health, and nervous, but not subject to any kind of seizure—she volunteered that—nor to any illusion; being, in fact, perfectly sane."

"How very odd to say all that!" I interpolated. "It was so unnecessary."

"At all events it *was* said," he laughed, "and as you wish to know all that passed, which was indeed very little, I tell you. She then said, 'I am making a long journey of *vital* importance'—she emphasized the word—'rapid and secret; I shall return for my child in three months; in the meantime, she will be silent as to who we are, whence we come, and whither we are travelling.' That is all she said. She spoke very pure French. When she said the word 'secret,' she paused for a few seconds, looking sternly, her eyes fixed on mine. I fancy she makes a great point of that. You saw how quickly she was gone. I hope I have not done a very foolish thing in taking charge of the young lady."

For my part, I was delighted. I was longing to see and talk to her; and only waiting till the doctor should give me leave. You who live in towns can have no idea how great an event the introduction of a new friend is, in such a solitude as surrounded us.

The doctor did not arrive till nearly one o'clock; but I could no more have gone to my bed and slept, than I could have overtaken, on foot, the carriage in which the princess in black velvet had driven away.

When the physician came down to the drawing-room, it was to report very favorably upon his patient. She was now sitting up, her pulse quite regular, apparently perfectly well. She had sustained no injury, and the little shock to her nerves had passed away quite harmlessly. There could be no harm certainly in my seeing her, if we both wished it; and, with this permission, I sent forthwith, to know whether she would allow me to visit her for a few minutes in her room.

The servant returned immediately to say that she desired nothing more.

You may be sure I was not long in availing myself of this permission.

Our visitor lay in one of the handsomest rooms in the schloss. It was, perhaps, a little stately. There was a somber piece of tapestry opposite the foot of the bed, representing Cleopatra with the asp to her bosom; and other solemn classic scenes were displaced, a little faded, upon the other walls. But there was gold carving, and rich and varied color enough in the other decorations of the room, to more than redeem the gloom of the old tapestry.

There were candles at the bed side. She was sitting up; her slender pretty figure enveloped in the soft silk dressing-gown, embroidered with flowers, and lined with thick quilted silk, which her mother had thrown over her feet as she lay upon the ground.

What was it that, as I reached the bedside and had just begun my little greeting, struck me dumb in a moment, and made me recoil a step or two from before her? I will tell you.

I saw the very face which had visited me in my childhood at night, which remained so fixed in my memory, and on which I had for so many years so often ruminated with horror, when no one suspected of what I was thinking.

It was pretty, even beautiful; and when I first beheld it, wore the same melancholy expression.

But this almost instantly lighted into a strange fixed smile of recognition.

There was a silence of fully a minute, and then at length *she* spoke; *I* could not.

"How wonderful!" she exclaimed. "Twelve years ago, I saw your face in a dream, and it has haunted me ever since."

"Wonderful indeed!" I repeated, overcoming with an effort the horror that had for a time suspended my utterances. "Twelve years ago, in vision or reality, *I* certainly saw you. I could not forget your face. It has remained before my eyes ever since."

Her smile had softened. Whatever I had fancied strange in it, was gone, and it and her dimpling cheeks were now delightfully pretty and intelligent.

I felt reassured, and continued more in the vein which hospitality indicated, to bid her welcome, and to tell her how much pleasure her accidental arrival had given us all, and especially what a happiness it was to me.

I took her hand as I spoke. I was a little shy, as lonely people are, but the situation made me eloquent, and even bold. She pressed my hand, she laid hers upon it, and her eyes glowed, as, looking hastily into mine, she smiled again, and blushed.

She answered my welcome very prettily. I sat down beside her, still wondering; and she said:

"I must tell you my vision about you; it is so very strange that you and I should have had, each of the other so vivid a dream, that each should have seen, I you and you me, looking as we do now, when of course we both were mere children. I was a child about six years old, and I awoke from a confused and troubled dream, and found myself in a room, unlike my nursery, wainscoted clumsily in some dark wood, and with cupboards and bedsteads, and chairs, and benches placed about it. The beds were, I thought, all empty, and the room itself without any one but myself in it; and I, after looking about me for some time, and admiring especially an iron candlestick, with two branches, which I should certainly know again, crept under one of the beds to reach the window; but as I got from under the bed, I heard someone crying; and looking up, while I was still upon my knees, I saw *you*—most assuredly you—as I see you now; a beautiful young lady, with golden hair and large blue eyes, and lips—your lips—you, as you are here. Your looks won me; I climbed on the bed and put my arms about you, and I think we both fell asleep. I was aroused by a scream; you were sitting up screaming. I was frightened, and slipped down upon the ground, and, it seemed to me, lost consciousness for a moment; and when I came to myself, I was again in my nursery at home. Your face I have never forgotten since. I could not be misled by mere resemblance. You *are* the lady whom I then saw."

It was now my turn to relate my corresponding vision, which I did, to the undisguised wonder of my new acquaintance.

"I don't know which should be most afraid of the other," she said, again smiling. "If you were less pretty I think I should be very much afraid of you, but being as you are, and you and I both so young, I feel only that I have made your acquaintance twelve years ago, and have already a right to your intimacy; at all events, it does seem as if we were destined, from our earliest childhood, to be friends. I wonder whether you feel as strangely drawn towards me as I do to you; I have never had a friend—shall I find one now?" She sighed, and her fine dark eyes gazed passionately on me.

Now the truth is, I felt rather unaccountably towards the beautiful stranger. I did feel, as she said, "drawn towards her," but there was also something of repulsion. In this ambiguous feeling, however, the sense of attraction immensely prevailed. She interested and won me; she was so beautiful and so indescribably engaging.

I perceived now something of languor and exhaustion stealing over her, and hastened to bid her goodnight.

"The doctor thinks," I added, "that you ought to have a maid to sit up with you tonight; one of ours is waiting, and you will find her a very useful and quiet creature."

"How kind of you, but I could not sleep, I never could with an attendant in the room. I shan't require any assistance—and, shall I confess my weakness, I am haunted with a terror of robbers. Our house was robbed once, and two servants murdered, so I always lock my door. It has become a habit—and you look so kind I know you will forgive me. I see there is a key in the lock."

She held me close in her pretty arms for a moment and whispered in my ear, "Goodnight, darling, it is very hard to part with you, but goodnight; tomorrow, but not early, I shall see you again."

She sank back on the pillow with a sigh, and her fine eyes followed me with a fond and melancholy gaze, and she murmured again, "Goodnight, dear friend."

Young people like, and even love, on impulse. I was flattered by the evident, though as yet undeserved, fondness she showed me. I liked the confidence with which she at once received me. She was determined that we should be very dear friends.

Next day came and we met again. I was delighted with my companion; that is to say, in many respects.

Her looks lost nothing in daylight—she was certainly the most beautiful creature I had ever seen, and the unpleasant remembrance of the face presented in my early dream, had lost the effect of the first unexpected recognition.

She confessed that she had experienced a similar shock on seeing me, and precisely the same faint antipathy that had mingled with my admiration of her. We now laughed together over our momentary horrors.

## IV. HER HABITS—A SAUNTER

I told you that I was charmed with her in most particulars.

There were some that did not please me so well.

She was above the middle height of women. I shall begin by describing her. She was slender, and wonderfully graceful. Except that her movements were languid—*very* languid—indeed, there was nothing in her appearance to indicate an invalid. Her complexion was rich and brilliant; her features were small and beautifully formed; her eyes large, dark, and lustrous; her hair was quite wonderful, I never saw hair so magnificently thick and long when it was down about her shoulders; I have often placed my hands under it, and laughed with wonder at its weight. It was exquisitely fine and soft, and in color a rich very dark brown, with something of gold. I loved to let it down, tumbling with its own weight, as, in her room, she lay back in her chair talking in her sweet low voice, I used to fold and braid it, and spread it out and play with it. Heavens! If I had but known all!

I said there were particulars which did not please me. I have told you that her confidence won me the first night I saw her; but I found that she exercised with respect to herself, her mother, her history, everything in fact connected with her life, plans, and people an ever-wakeful reserve. I dare say I was unreasonable, perhaps I was wrong; I dare say I ought to have respected the solemn injunction laid upon my father by the stately lady in black velvet. But curiosity is a restless and unscrupulous passion, and no one girl can endure, with patience, that hers should be baffled by another. What harm could it do anyone to tell me what I so ardently desired to know? Had she no trust in my good sense or honor? Why would she not believe me when I assured her, so solemnly, that I would not divulge one syllable of what she told me to any mortal breathing?

There was a coldness, it seemed to me, beyond her years, in her smiling melancholy persistent refusal to afford me the least ray of light.

I cannot say we quarreled upon this point, for she would not quarrel upon any. It was, of course, very unfair of me to press her, very ill-bred, but I really could not help it; and I might just as well have let it alone.

What she did tell me amounted, in my unconscionable estimation—to nothing.

It was all summed up in three very vague disclosures.

First.—Her name was Carmilla.

Second.—Her family was very ancient and noble.

Third.—Her home lay in the direction of the west.

She would not tell me the name of her family, nor their armorial bearings, nor the name of the estate, nor even that of the country they lived in.

You are not to suppose that I worried her incessantly on these subjects. I watched opportunity, and rather insinuated than urged my inquiries. Once or twice, indeed, I did attack more directly. But no matter what my tactics, utter failure was invariably the result. Reproaches and caresses were all lost upon her. But I must add this, that her evasion was conducted with so pretty a melancholy and deprecation, and so many, and even passionate declarations of her liking for me, and trust in my honor, and with so many promises, that I should at last know all, that I could not find it in my heart long to be offended with her.

She used to place her pretty arms about my neck, draw me to her, and laying her cheek to mine, murmur with her lips near my ear, "Dearest, your little heart is wounded; think me not cruel because I obey the irresistible law of my strength and weakness; if your dear heart is wounded, my wild heart bleeds with yours. In the rapture of my enormous humiliation I live in your warm life, and you shall die—die, sweetly die—into mine. I cannot help it; as I draw near to you, you, in your turn, will draw near to others, and learn the rapture of that cruelty, which yet is love; so, for a while, seek to know no more of me and mine, but trust me with all your loving spirit."

And when she had spoken such a rhapsody, she would press me more closely in her trembling embrace, and her lips in soft kisses gently glow upon my cheek.

Her agitations and her language were unintelligible to me.

From these foolish embraces, which were not of very frequent occurrence, I must allow, I used to wish to extricate myself; but my energies seemed to fail me. Her murmured words sounded like a lullaby in my ear, and soothed my resistance into a trance, from which I only seemed to recover myself when she withdrew her arms.

In these mysterious moods I did not like her.

I experienced a strange tumultuous excitement that was pleasurable, ever and anon, mingled with a vague sense of fear and disgust. I had no distinct thoughts about her while such scenes lasted, but I was conscious of a love growing into adoration, and also of abhorrence. This I know is paradox, but I can make no other attempt to explain the feeling.

I now write, after an interval of more than ten years, with a trembling hand, with a confused and horrible recollection of certain occurrences and situations, in the ordeal through which I was unconsciously passing; though with a vivid and very sharp remembrance of the main current of my story. But, I suspect, in all lives there are certain emotional scenes, those in which our passions have been most wildly and terribly roused, that are of all others the most vaguely and dimly remembered.

Sometimes after an hour of apathy, my strange and beautiful companion would take my hand and hold it with a fond pressure, renewed again and again; blushing softly, gazing in my face with languid and burning eyes, and breathing so fast that her dress rose and fell with the tumultuous respiration. It was like the ardor of a lover; it embarrassed me; it was hateful and yet overpowering; and with gloating eyes she drew me to her, and her hot lips travelled along my cheek in kisses; and she would whisper, almost in sobs, "You are mine, you *shall* be mine, and you and I are one for ever." Then she has thrown herself back in her chair, with her small hands over her eyes, leaving me trembling.

"Are we related?" I used to ask. "What can you mean by all this? I remind you perhaps of some one whom you love; but you must not, I hate it; I don't know you—I don't know myself when you look so and talk so."

She used to sigh at my vehemence, then turn away and drop my hand.

Respecting these very extraordinary manifestations I strove in vain to form any satisfactory theory—could not refer them to affectation or trick. It was unmistakably the momentary breaking out of suppressed instinct and emotion. Was she, notwithstanding her mother's volunteered denial, subject to brief visitations of insanity, or was there here a disguise and a romance? I had read in old story books of such things. What if a boyish lover had found his way into the house, and sought to make advances in masquerade, with the assistance of a clever old adventuress. But here were many things against this hypothesis, highly interesting as it was to my vanity.

I could boast of no little attentions such as masculine gallantry delights to offer. Between these passionate moments there were long intervals of commonplace, of gaiety, of brooding melancholy, during which, except that I detected her eyes so full of melancholy fire, following me, at times I might have been as nothing to her. Except in these brief periods of mysterious excitement her ways were girlish; and there was always a languor about her, quite incompatible with a masculine system in a state of health.

In some respects her habits were odd. Perhaps not so singular in the opinion of a town lady like you, as they appeared to us rustic people. She used to come down very late, generally not till one o'clock, she would then take a cup of chocolate, but eat nothing; we then went out for a walk, which was a mere saunter, and she seemed, almost immediately, exhausted, and either returned to the schloss or sat on one of the benches that were placed, here and there, among the trees. This was a bodily languor in which her mind did not sympathize. She was always an animated talker, and very intelligent.

She sometimes alluded for a moment to her own home, or mentioned an adventure or situation, or an early recollection, which indicated a people of strange manners, and described customs of which we knew nothing. I gathered from these chance hints that her native country was much more remote than I had at first fancied.

As we sat thus one afternoon under the trees, a funeral passed us by. It was that of a pretty young girl, whom I had often seen, the daughter of one of the rangers of the forest. The poor man was walking behind the coffin of his darling; she was his only child, and he looked quite heartbroken.

Peasants walking two-and-two came behind, they were singing a funeral hymn.

I rose to mark my respect as they passed, and joined in the hymn they were very sweetly singing.

My companion shook me a little roughly, and I turned surprised.

She said brusquely, "Don't you perceive how discordant that is?"

"I think it is very sweet, on the contrary," I answered, vexed at the interruption, and very uncomfortable, lest the people who composed the little procession should observe and resent what was passing.

I resumed, therefore, instantly, and was again interrupted. "You pierce my ears," said Carmilla, almost angrily, and stopping her ears with her tiny fingers. "Besides, how can you tell that your religion and mine are the same; your forms wound me, and I hate funerals. What a fuss! Why, *you* must die—*everyone* must die; and all are happier when they do. Come home."

"My father has gone on with the clergyman to the churchyard. I thought you knew she was to be buried today."

"*She?* I don't trouble my head about peasants. I don't know who she is," answered Carmilla, with a flash from her fine eyes.

"She is the poor girl who fancied she saw a ghost a fortnight ago, and has been dying ever since, till yesterday, when she expired."

"Tell me nothing about ghosts. I shan't sleep tonight if you do."

"I hope there is no plague or fever coming; all this looks very like it," I continued. "The swineherd's young wife died only a week ago, and she thought something seized her by the throat as she lay in her bed, and nearly strangled her. Papa says such horrible fancies do accompany some forms of fever. She was quite well the day before. She sank afterwards, and died before a week."

"Well, *her* funeral is over, I hope, and *her* hymn sung; and our ears shan't be tortured with that discord and jargon. It has made me nervous. Sit down here, beside me; sit close; hold my hand; press it hard—hard—harder."

We had moved a little back, and had come to another seat.

She sat down. Her face underwent a change that alarmed and even terrified me for a moment. It darkened, and became horribly livid; her teeth and hands were clenched, and she frowned and compressed her lips, while she stared down upon the ground at her feet, and trembled all over with a continued shudder as irrepressible as ague. All her energies seemed strained to suppress a fit, with which she was then breathlessly tugging; and at length a low convulsive cry of suffering broke from her, and gradually the hysteria subsided. "There! That comes of strangling people with hymns!" she said at last. "Hold me, hold me still. It is passing away."

And so gradually it did; and perhaps to dissipate the somber impression which the spectacle had left upon me, she became unusually animated and talkative; and so we got home.

This was the first time I had seen her exhibit any definable symptoms of that delicacy of health which her mother had spoken of. It was the first time, also, I had seen her exhibit anything like temper.

Both passed away like a summer cloud; and never but once afterwards did I witness on her part a momentary sign of anger. I will tell you how it happened.

She and I were looking out of one of the long drawing-room windows, when there entered the courtyard, over the drawbridge, a figure of a wanderer whom I knew very well. He used to visit the schloss generally twice a year.

It was the figure of a hunchback, with the sharp lean features that generally accompany deformity. He wore a pointed black beard, and he was smiling from ear to ear, showing his white fangs. He was dressed in buff, black, and scarlet, and crossed with more straps and belts than I could count, from which hung all manner of things. Behind, he carried a magic-lantern, and two boxes, which I well knew, in one of which was a salamander, and in the other a mandrake. These monsters used to make my father laugh. They were compounded of parts of monkeys, parrots, squirrels, fish, and hedgehogs, dried and stitched together with great neatness and startling effect. He had a fiddle, a box of conjuring apparatus, a pair of foils and masks attached to his belt, several other mysterious cases dangling about him, and a black staff with copper ferrules in his hand. His companion was a rough spare dog, that followed at his heels, but stopped short, suspiciously at the drawbridge, and in a little while began to howl dismally.

In the meantime, the mountebank, standing in the midst of the courtyard, raised his grotesque hat, and made us a very ceremonious bow, paying his compliments very volubly in execrable French, and German not much better. Then, disengaging his fiddle, he began to scrape a lively air, to which he sang with a merry discord, dancing with ludicrous airs and activity, that made me laugh, in spite of the dog's howling.

Then he advanced to the window with many smiles and salutations, and his hat in his left hand, his fiddle under his arm, and with a fluency that never took breath, he gabbled a long advertisement of all his accomplishments, and the resources of the various arts which he placed at our service, and the curiosities and entertainments which it was in his power, at our bidding to display.

"Will your ladyships be pleased to buy an amulet against the vampire, which is going like the wolf, I hear, through these woods," he said, dropping his hat on the pavement. "They are dying of it right and left, and here is a charm that never fails; only pinned to the pillow, and you may laugh in his face."

These charms consisted of oblong slips of vellum, with cabalistic ciphers and diagrams upon them.

Carmilla instantly purchased one, and so did I.

He was looking up, and we were smiling down upon him, amused; at least, I can answer for myself. His piercing black eye, as he looked up in our faces, seemed to detect something that fixed for a moment his curiosity.

In an instant he unrolled a leather case, full of all manner of odd little steel instruments.

"See here, my lady," he said, displaying it, and addressing me, "I profess, among other things less useful, the art of dentistry. Plague take the dog!" he interpolated. "Silence, beast! He howls so that your ladyships can scarcely hear a word. Your noble friend, the young lady at your right, has the sharpest tooth—long, thin, pointed, like an awl, like a needle; ha, ha! With my sharp and long sight, as I look up, I have seen it distinctly; now if it happens to hurt the young lady, and I think it must, here am I, here are my file, my punch, my nippers; I will make it round and blunt, if her ladyship pleases; no longer the tooth of a fish, but of a beautiful young lady as she is. Hey? Is the young lady displeased? Have I been too bold? Have I offended her?"

The young lady, indeed, looked very angry as she drew back from the window.

"How dares that mountebank insult us so? Where is your father? I shall demand redress from him. My father would have had the wretch tied up to the pump, and flogged with a cartwhip, and burnt to the bones with the castle brand!"

She retired from the window a step or two, and sat down, and hardly lost sight of the offender, when her wrath subsided as suddenly as it had risen, and she gradually recovered her usual tone, and seemed to forget the little hunchback and his follies.

My father was out of spirits that evening. On coming in he told us that there had been another case similar to the two fatal ones which had lately occurred. The sister of a young peasant on his estate, only a mile away, was very ill, had been, as she described it, attacked very nearly in the same way, and was now slowly but steadily sinking.

"All this," said my father, "is strictly referable to natural causes. These poor people infect one another with their superstitions, and so repeat in imagination the images of terror that have infested their neighbors."

"But that very circumstance frightens one horribly," said Carmilla.

"How so?" inquired my father.

"I am so afraid of fancying I see such things; I think it would be as bad as reality."

"We are in God's hands; nothing can happen without His permission, and all will end well for those who love Him. He is our faithful creator; He had made us all, and will take care of us."

"Creator! *Nature!*" said the young lady in answer to my gentle father. "And this disease that invades the country is natural. Nature. All things proceed from Nature—don't they? All things in the heaven, in the earth, and under the earth, act and live as Nature ordains? I think so."

"The doctor said he would come here today," said my father, after a silence. "I want to know what he thinks about it, and what he thinks we had better do."

"Doctors never did me any good," said Carmilla.

"Then you have been ill?" I asked.

"More ill than ever you were," she answered.

"Long ago?"

"Yes, a long time. I suffered from this very illness; but I forget all but my pain and weakness, and they were not so bad as are suffered in other diseases."

"You were very young then?"

"I dare say; let us talk no more of it. You would not wound a friend?" She looked languidly in my eyes, and passed her arm round my waist lovingly, and led me out of the room. My father was busy over some papers near the window.

"Why does your papa like to frighten us?" said the pretty girl, with a sigh and a little shudder.

"He doesn't, dear Carmilla, it is the very furthest thing from his mind."

"Are you afraid, dearest?"

"I should be very much if I fancied there was any real danger of my being attacked as those poor people were."

"You are afraid to die?"

"Yes, every one is."

"But to die as lovers may—to die together, so that they may live together. Girls are caterpillars while they live in the world, to be finally butterflies when the summer comes; but in the meantime there are grubs and larvae, don't you see—each with their peculiar propensities, necessities and structure. So says Monsieur Buffon, in his big book, in the next room."

Later in the day the doctor came, and was closeted with papa for some time. He was a skilful man, of sixty and upwards, he wore powder, and shaved his pale face as smooth as a pumpkin. He and papa emerged from the room together, and I heard papa laugh, and say as they came out:

"Well, I do wonder at a wise man like you. What do you say to hippogriffs and dragons?"

The doctor was smiling, and made answer, shaking his head—

"Nevertheless, life and death are mysterious states, and we know little of the resources of either."

And so they walked on, and I heard no more. I did not then know what the doctor had been suggesting, but I think I guess it now.

## V. A WONDERFUL LIKENESS

This evening there arrived from Gratz the grave, dark-faced son of the picture-cleaner, with a horse and cart laden with two large packing-cases, having many pictures in each. It was a journey of ten leagues, and whenever a messenger arrived at the schloss from our little capital of Gratz, we used to crowd about him in the hall, to hear the news.

This arrival created in our secluded quarters quite a sensation. The cases remained in the hall, and the messenger was taken charge of by the servants till he had eaten his supper. Then with assistants, and armed with hammer, ripping chisel, and turnscrew he met us in the hall, where we had assembled to witness the unpacking of the cases.

Carmilla sat looking listlessly on, while one after the other the old pictures, nearly all portraits, which had undergone the process of renovation, were brought to light. My mother was of an old Hungarian family, and most of these pictures, which were about to be restored to their places, had come to us through her.

My father had a list in his hand, from which he read, as the artist rummaged out the corresponding numbers. I don't know that the pictures were very good, but they were, undoubtedly, very old, and some of them very curious also. They had, for the most part, the merit of being now seen by me, I may say, for the first time; for the smoke and dust of time had all but obliterated them.

"There is a picture that I have not seen yet," said my father. "In one corner, at the top of it, is the name, as well as I could read, 'Marcia Karnstein,' and the date '1698'; and I am curious to see how it has turned out."

I remembered it; it was a small picture, about a foot and a half high, and nearly square, without a frame; but it was so blackened by age that I could not make it out.

The artist now produced it, with evident pride. It was quite beautiful; it was startling; it seemed to live. It was the likeness of Carmilla!

"Carmilla, dear, here is an absolute miracle. Here you are, living, smiling, ready to speak, in this picture. Isn't it beautiful, papa? And see, even the little mole on her throat."

My father laughed, and said, "Certainly it is a wonderful likeness," but he looked away, and to my surprise seemed but little struck by it, and went on talking to the picture-cleaner, who was also something of an artist, and discoursed with intelligence about the portraits of other works, which his art had just brought into light and color, while *I* was more and more lost in wonder the more I looked at the picture.

"Will you let me hang this picture in my room, papa?" I asked.

"Certainly dear," said he, smiling, "I'm very glad you think it so like. It must be prettier even than I thought it, if it is."

The young lady did not acknowledge this pretty speech, did not seem to hear it. She was leaning back in her seat, her fine eyes under their long lashes gazing on me in contemplation, and she smiled in a kind of rapture.

"And now you can read quite plainly the name that is written in the corner. It is not Marcia; it looks as if it was done in gold. The name is Mircalla, Countess Karnstein, and this is a little coronet over it, and underneath A.D. 1698. I am descended from the Karnsteins; that is, mamma was."

"Ah!" said the lady, languidly, "so am I, I think, a very long descent, very ancient. Are there any Karnsteins living now?"

"None who bear the name, I believe. The family were ruined, I believe, in some civil wars, long ago, but the ruins of the castle are only about three miles away."

"How interesting!" she said, languidly. "But see what beautiful moonlight!" She glanced through the hall door, which stood a little open. "Suppose you take a little ramble round the court and look down at the road and river."

"It is so like the night you came to us," I said.

She sighed, smiling.

She rose, and each with her arm about the other's waist, we walked out upon the pavement.

In silence, slowly we walked down to the draw-bridge, where the beautiful landscape opened before us.

"And so you were thinking of the night I came here?" she almost whispered. "Are you glad I came?"

"Delighted, dear Carmilla," I answered.

"And you asked for the picture you think like me, to hang in your room," she murmured with a sigh, as she drew her arm closer about my waist, and let her pretty head sink upon my shoulder.

"How romantic you are, Carmilla," I said. "Whenever you tell me your story, it will be made up chiefly of some one great romance."

She kissed me silently.

"I am sure, Carmilla, you have been in love; that there is, at this moment, an affair of the heart going on."

"I have been in love with no one, and never shall," she whispered, "unless it should be with you."

How beautiful she looked in the moonlight!

Shy and strange was the look with which she quickly hid her face in my neck and hair, with tumultuous sighs, that seemed to sob, and pressed in mine a hand that trembled.

Her soft cheek was glowing against mine. "Darling, darling," she murmured. "I live in you; and you would die for me, I love you so."

I started from her.

She was glazing on me with eyes from which all fire, all meaning had flown, and a face colorless and apathetic.

"Is there a chill in the air, dear?" she said drowsily. "I almost shiver; have I been dreaming? Let us come in. Come, come; come in."

"You look ill, Carmilla; a little faint. You certainly must take some wine," I said.

"Yes, I will. I'm better now. I shall be quite well in a few minutes. Yes, do give me a little wine," answered Carmilla, as we approached the door. "Let us look again for a moment; it is the last time, perhaps, I shall see the moonlight with you."

"How do you feel now, dear Carmilla? Are you really better?" I asked.

I was beginning to take alarm lest she should have been stricken with the strange epidemic that they said had invaded the country about us.

"Papa would be grieved beyond measure," I added, "if he thought you were ever so little ill, without immediately letting us know. We have a very skilful doctor near this, the physician who was with papa today."

"I'm sure he is. I know how kind you all are; but, dear child, I am quite well again. There is nothing ever wrong with me but a little weakness. People say I am languid; I am incapable of exertion; I can scarcely walk as far as a child of three years old; and every now and then the little strength I have falters, and I become as you have just seen me. But after all I am very easily set up again; in a moment I am perfectly myself. See how I have recovered."

So, indeed, she had; and she and I talked a great deal, and very animated she was; and the remainder of that evening passed without any recurrence of what I called her infatuations. I mean her crazy talk and looks, which embarrassed, and even frightened me.

But there occurred that night an event which gave my thoughts quite a new turn, and seemed to startle even Carmilla's languid nature into momentary energy.

## VI. A VERY STRANGE AGONY

When we got into the drawing-room, and had sat down to our coffee and chocolate, although Carmilla did not take any, she seemed quite herself again, and Madame and Mademoiselle De Lafontaine, joined us, and made a little card party, in the course of which papa came in for what he called his "dish of tea."

When the game was over he sat down beside Carmilla on the sofa, and asked her, a little anxiously, whether she had heard from her mother since her arrival.

She answered "No."

He then asked her whether she knew where a letter would reach her at present.

"I cannot tell," she answered, ambiguously, "but I have been thinking of leaving you; you have been already too hospitable and too kind to me. I have given you an infinity of trouble, and I should wish to take a carriage tomorrow and post in pursuit of her; I know where I shall ultimately find her, although I dare not yet tell you."

"But you must not dream of any such thing," exclaimed my father, to my great relief. "We can't afford to lose you so, and I won't consent to your leaving us, except under the care of your mother, who was so good as to consent to your remaining with us till she should herself return. I should be quite happy if I knew that you heard from her; but this evening the accounts of the progress of the mysterious disease that has invaded our neighborhood grow even more alarming; and my beautiful guest, I do feel the responsibility, unaided by advice from your mother, very much. But I shall do my best; and one thing is certain, that you must not think of leaving us without her distinct direction to that effect. We should suffer too much in parting from you to consent to it easily."

"Thank you, sir, a thousand times for your hospitality," she answered, smiling bashfully. "You have all been too kind to me; I have seldom been so happy in all my life before, as in your beautiful château, under your care, and in the society of your dear daughter."

So he gallantly, in his old-fashioned way, kissed her hand, smiling, and pleased at her little speech.

I accompanied Carmilla as usual to her room, and sat and chatted with her while she was preparing for bed.

"Do you think," I said, at length, "that you will ever confide fully in me?"

She turned round smiling, but made no answer, only continued to smile on me.

"You won't answer that?" I said. "You can't answer pleasantly; I ought not to have asked you."

"You were quite right to ask me that, or anything. You do not know how dear you are to me, or you could not think any confidence too great to look for. But I am under vows, no nun half so awfully, and I dare not tell my story yet, even to you. The time is very near when you shall know everything. You will think me cruel, very selfish, but love is always selfish; the more ardent the more selfish. How jealous I am you cannot know. You must come with me, loving me, to death; or else hate me, and still come with me, and *hating* me through death and after. There is no such word as indifference in my apathetic nature."

"Now, Carmilla, you are going to talk your wild nonsense again," I said hastily.

"Not I, silly little fool as I am, and full of whims and fancies; for your sake I'll talk like a sage. Were you ever at a ball?"

"No; how you do run on. What is it like? How charming it must be."

"I almost forget, it is years ago."

I laughed.

"You are not so old. Your first ball can hardly be forgotten yet."

"I remember everything about it—with an effort. I see it all, as divers see what is going on above them, through a medium, dense, rippling, but transparent. There occurred that night what has confused the picture, and made its colors faint. I was all but assassinated in my bed, wounded *here*," she touched her breast, "and never was the same since."

"Were you near dying?"

"Yes, very—a cruel love—strange love, that would have taken my life. Love will have its sacrifices. No sacrifice without blood. Let us go to sleep now; I feel so lazy. How can I get up just now and lock my door?"

She was lying with her tiny hands buried in her rich wavy hair, under her cheek, her little head upon the pillow, and her glittering eyes followed me wherever I moved, with a kind of shy smile that I could not decipher.

I bid her goodnight, and crept from the room with an uncomfortable sensation.

I often wondered whether our pretty guest ever said her prayers. *I* certainly had never seen her upon her knees. In the morning she never came down until long after our family prayers were over, and at night she never left the drawing-room to attend our brief evening prayers in the hall.

If it had not been that it had casually come out in one of our careless talks that she had been baptized, I should have doubted her being a Christian. Religion was a subject on which I had never heard her speak a word. If I had known the world better, this particular neglect or antipathy would not have so much surprised me.

The precautions of nervous people are infectious, and persons of a like temperament are pretty sure, after a time, to imitate them. I had adopted Carmilla's habit of locking her bedroom door, having taken into my head all her whimsical alarms about midnight invaders, and prowling assassins. I had also adopted her precaution of making a brief search through her room, to satisfy herself that no lurking assassin or robber was "ensconced."

These wise measures taken, I got into my bed and fell asleep. A light was burning in my room. This was an old habit, of very early date, and which nothing could have tempted me to dispense with.

Thus fortified I might take my rest in peace. But dreams come through stone walls, light up dark rooms, or darken light ones, and their persons make their exits and their entrances as they please, and laugh at locksmiths.

I had a dream that night that was the beginning of a very strange agony.

I cannot call it a nightmare, for I was quite conscious of being asleep. But I was equally conscious of being in my room, and lying in bed, precisely as I actually was. I saw, or fancied I saw, the room and its furniture just as I had seen it last, except that it was very dark, and I saw something moving round the foot of the bed, which at first I could not accurately distinguish. But I soon saw that it was a sooty-black animal that resembled a monstrous cat. It appeared to me about four or five feet long, for it measured fully the length of the hearth-rug as it passed over it; and it continued to-ing and fro-ing with the lithe sinister restlessness of a beast in a cage. I could not cry out, although as you may suppose, I was terrified. Its pace was growing faster, and the room rapidly darker and darker, and at length so dark that I could no longer see anything of it but its eyes. I felt it spring lightly on the bed. The two broad eyes approached my face, and suddenly I felt a stinging pain as if two large needles darted, an inch or two apart, deep into my breast. I awoke with a scream. The room was lighted by the candle that burnt there all through the night, and I saw a female figure standing at the foot of the bed, a little at the right side. It was in a dark loose dress, and its hair was down and covered its shoulders. A block of stone could not have been more still. There was not the slightest stir of respiration. As I stared at it, the figure appeared to have changed its place, and was now nearer the door; then, close to it, the door opened, and it passed out.

I was now relieved, and able to breathe and move. My first thought was that Carmilla had been playing me a trick, and that I had forgotten to secure my door. I hastened to it, and found it locked as usual on the inside. I was afraid to open it—I was horrified. I sprang into my bed and covered my head up in the bed-clothes, and lay there more dead than alive till morning.

## VII. DESCENDING

It would be vain my attempting to tell you the horror with which, even now, I recall the occurrence of that night. It was no such transitory terror as a dream leaves behind it. It seemed to deepen by time, and communicated itself to the room and the very furniture that had encompassed the apparition.

I could not bear next day to be alone for a moment. I should have told papa, but for two opposite reasons. At one time I thought he would laugh at my story, and I could not bear its being treated as a jest; and at another, I thought he might fancy that I had been attacked by the mysterious complaint which had invaded our neighborhood. I had myself no misgivings of the kind, and as he had been rather an invalid for some time, I was afraid of alarming him.

I was comfortable enough with my good-natured companions, Madame Perrodon, and the vivacious Mademoiselle Lafontaine. They both perceived that I was out of spirits and nervous and at length I told them what lay so heavy at my heart. Mademoiselle laughed, but I fancied that Madame Perrodon looked anxious.

"By-the-by," said Mademoiselle, laughing, "the long lime tree walk, behind Carmilla's bedroom window, is haunted!"

"Nonsense!" exclaimed Madame, who probably thought the theme rather inopportune, "and who tells that story, my dear?"

"Martin says that he came up twice, when the old yard-gate was being repaired before sunrise, and twice saw the same female figure walking down the lime tree avenue."

"So he well might, as long as there are cows to milk in the river fields," said Madame.

"I dare say; but Martin chooses to be frightened, and never did I see a fool *more* frightened."

"You must not say a word about it to Carmilla, because she can see down that walk from her room window," I interposed, "and she is, if possible, a greater coward than I."

Carmilla came down rather later than usual that day.

"I was so frightened last night," she said so soon as we were together, "and I am sure I should have seen something dreadful if it had not been for that charm I bought from the poor little hunchback whom I called such hard names. I had a dream of something black coming round my bed, and I awoke in a perfect horror, and I really thought, for some seconds, I saw a dark figure near the chimney piece, but I felt under my pillow for my charm, and the moment my fingers touched it, the figure disappeared, and I felt quite certain, only that I had it by me, that something frightful would have made its appearance, and perhaps, throttled me, as it did those poor people we heard of."

"Well, listen to me," I began, and recounted

my adventure, at the recital of which she appeared horrified.

"And had you the charm near you?" she asked, earnestly.

"No, I had dropped it into a china vase in the drawing-room, but I shall certainly take it with me tonight, as you have so much faith in it."

At this distance of time I cannot tell you, or even understand, how I overcame my horror so effectually as to lie alone in my room that night. I remember distinctly that I pinned the charm to my pillow. I fell asleep almost immediately, and slept even more soundly than usual all night.

Next night I passed as well. My sleep was delightfully deep and dreamless. But I wakened with a sense of lassitude and melancholy which, however, did not exceed a degree that was almost luxurious.

"Well, I told you so," said Carmilla, when I described my quiet sleep, "I had such delightful sleep myself last night; I pinned the charm to the breast of my nightdress. It was too far away the night before. I am quite sure it was all fancy except the dreams. I used to think that evil spirits made dreams, but our doctor told me it is no such thing. Only a fever passing by, or some other malady, as they often do, he said, knocks at the door, and not being able to get in, passes on, with that alarm."

"And what do you think the charm is?" said I.

"It has been fumigated or immersed in some drug, and is an antidote against the malaria," she answered.

"Then it acts only on the body?"

"Certainly; you don't suppose that evil spirits are frightened by bits of ribbon, or the perfumes of a druggist's shop? No, these complaints, wandering in the air, begin by trying the nerves, and so infect the brain; but before they can seize upon you, the antidote repels them. That I am sure is what the charm has done for us. It is nothing magical, it is simply natural."

I should have been happier if I could quite have agreed with Carmilla, but I did my best, and the impression was a little losing its force.

For some nights I slept profoundly; but still every morning I felt the same lassitude, and a languor weighed upon me all day. I felt myself a changed girl. A strange melancholy was stealing over me, a melancholy that I would not have interrupted. Dim thoughts of death began to open, and an idea that I was slowly sinking took gentle, and, somehow, not unwelcome possession of me. If it was sad, the tone of mind which this induced was also sweet. Whatever it might be, my soul acquiesced in it.

I would not admit that I was ill, I would not consent to tell my papa, or to have the doctor sent for.

Carmilla became more devoted to me than ever, and her strange paroxysms of languid adoration more frequent. She used to dote on me with increasing ardor the more my strength and spirits waned. This always shocked me like a momentary glare of insanity.

Without knowing it, I was now in a pretty advanced stage of the strangest illness under which mortal ever suffered. There was an unaccountable fascination in its earlier symptoms that more than reconciled me to the incapacitating effect of that stage of the malady. This fascination increased for a time, until it reached a certain point, when gradually a sense of the horrible mingled itself with it, deepening, as you shall hear, until it discolored and perverted the whole state of my life.

The first change I experienced was rather agreeable. It was very near the turning point from which began the descent of Avernus.

Certain vague and strange sensations visited me in my sleep. The prevailing one was of that pleasant, peculiar cold thrill which we feel in bathing, when we move against the current of a river. This was soon accompanied by dreams that seemed interminable, and were so vague that I could never recollect their scenery and persons, or any one connected portion of their action. But they left an awful impression, and a sense of exhaustion, as if I had passed through a long period of great mental exertion and danger. After all these dreams there remained on waking a remembrance of having been in a place very nearly dark, and of having spoken to people whom I could not see; and especially of one clear voice, of a female's, very deep, that spoke as if at a distance, slowly, and producing always the same sensation of indescribable solemnity and fear. Sometimes there came a sensation as if a hand was drawn softly along my cheek and neck. Sometimes it was as if warm lips kissed me, and longer and more lovingly as they reached my throat, but there the caress fixed itself. My heart beat faster, my breathing rose and fell rapidly and full drawn; a sobbing, that rose into a sense of strangulation, supervened, and turned into a dreadful convulsion, in which my senses left me, and I became unconscious.

It was now three weeks since the commencement of this unaccountable state. My sufferings had, during the last week, told upon my appearance. I had grown pale, my eyes were dilated and darkened underneath, and the languor which I had long felt began to display itself in my countenance.

My father asked me often whether I was ill; but, with an obstinacy which now seems to me unaccountable, I persisted in assuring him that I was quite well.

In a sense this was true, I had no pain, I could complain of no bodily derangement. My complaint seemed to be one of the imagination, or the nerves, and, horrible as my sufferings were, I kept them, with a morbid reserve, very nearly to myself.

It could not be that terrible complaint which the peasants call the vampire, for I had now been suffering for three weeks, and they were seldom ill for much more than three days, when death put an end to their miseries.

Carmilla complained of dreams and feverish sensations, but by no means of so alarming a kind as mine. I say that mine were extremely alarming. Had I been capable of comprehending my condition, I would have invoked aid and advice on my knees. The narcotic of an unsuspected influence was acting upon me, and my perceptions were benumbed.

I am going to tell you now of a dream that led immediately to an odd discovery.

One night, instead of the voice I was accustomed to hear in the dark, I heard one, sweet and tender, and at the same time terrible, which said, "Your mother warns you to beware of the assassin." At the same time a light unexpectedly sprang up, and I saw Carmilla, standing, near the foot of my bed, in her white nightdress, bathed, from her chin to her feet, in one great stain of blood.

I wakened with a shriek, possessed with the one idea that Carmilla was being murdered. I remember springing from my bed, and my next recollection is that of standing on the lobby, crying for help.

Madame and Mademoiselle came scurrying out of their rooms in alarm; a lamp burned always on the lobby, and seeing me, they soon learned the cause of my terror.

I insisted on our knocking at Carmilla's door. Our knocking was unanswered. It soon became a pounding and an uproar. We shrieked her name but all was vain.

We all grew frightened, for the door was locked. We hurried back, in panic, to my room. There we rang the bell long and furiously. If my father's room had been at that side of the house, we would have called him up at once to our aid. But, alas! he was quite out of hearing, and to reach him involved an excursion for which we none of us had courage.

Servants, however, soon came running up the stairs; I had got on my dressing-gown and slippers meanwhile, and my companions were already similarly furnished. Recognizing the voices of the servants on the lobby, we sallied out together; and having renewed, as fruitlessly, our summons at Carmilla's door, I ordered the men to force the lock. They did so, and we stood, holding our lights aloft, in the doorway, and so stared into the room.

We called her by name; but there was still no reply. We looked round the room. Everything was undisturbed. It was exactly in the state in which I left it on bidding her good night. But Carmilla was gone.

## VIII. SEARCH

At sight of the room, perfectly undisturbed except for our violent entrance, we began to cool a little, and soon recovered our senses sufficiently to dismiss the men. It had struck Mademoiselle that possibly Carmilla had been wakened by the uproar at her door, and in her first panic had jumped from her bed, and hid herself in a press, or behind a curtain, from which she could not, of course, emerge until the majordomo and his men had withdrawn. We now recommenced our search, and began to call her by name again.

It was all to no purpose. Our perplexity and agitation increased. We examined the windows, but they were secured. I implored of Carmilla, if she had concealed herself, to play this cruel trick no longer—to come out, and to end our anxieties. It was all useless. I was by this time convinced that she was not in the room, nor in the dressing-room, the door of which was still locked on this side. She could not have passed it. I was utterly puzzled. Had Carmilla discovered one of those secret passages which the old housekeeper said were known to exist in the schloss, although the tradition of their exact situation had been lost. A little time would, no doubt, explain all—utterly perplexed as, for the present, we were.

It was past four o'clock, and I preferred passing the remaining hours of darkness in Madame's room. Daylight brought no solution of the difficulty.

The whole household, with my father at its head, was in a state of agitation next morning. Every part of the château was searched. The grounds were explored. Not a trace of the missing lady could be discovered. The stream was about to be dragged; my father was in distraction; what a tale to have to tell the poor girl's mother on her return. I, too, was almost beside myself, though my grief was quite of a different kind.

The morning was passed in alarm and excitement. It was now one o'clock, and still no tidings. I ran up to Carmilla's room, and found her standing at her dressing-table! I was astounded. I could not believe my eyes. She beckoned me to her with her pretty finger, in silence. Her face expressed extreme fear.

I ran to her in an ecstasy of joy; I kissed and embraced her again and again. I ran to the bell and rang it vehemently, to bring others to the spot, who might at once relieve my father's anxiety.

"Dear Carmilla, what has become of you all this time? We have been in agonies of anxiety about you," I exclaimed. "Where have you been? How did you come back?"

"Last night has been a night of wonders," she said.

"For mercy's sake, explain all you can."

"It was past two last night," she said, "when I went to sleep as usual in my bed, with my doors locked, that of the dressing-room and that opening upon the gallery. My sleep was uninterrupted, and, so far as I know, dreamless; but I awoke just now on the sofa in the dressing-room there, and I found the door between the rooms open, and the other door forced. How could all this have happened without my being awakened? It must have been accompanied with a great deal of noise, and I am particularly easily wakened; and how could I have been carried out of my bed without my sleep having been interrupted, I whom the slightest stir startles?"

By this time, Madame, Mademoiselle, my father, and a number of the servants were in the room. Carmilla was, of course, overwhelmed with inquiries, congratulations, and welcomes. She had but one story to tell, and seemed the least able of all the party to suggest any way of accounting for what had happened.

My father took a turn up and down the room, thinking. I saw Carmilla's eye follow him for a moment with a sly, dark glance.

When my father had sent the servants away, Mademoiselle having gone in search of a little bottle of valerian and sal-volatile, and there being no one now in the room with Carmilla except my father, Madame, and myself, he came to her thoughtfully, took her hand very kindly, led her to the sofa, and sat down beside her.

"Will you forgive me, my dear, if I risk a conjecture, and ask a question?"

"Who can have a better right?" she said. "Ask what you please, and I will tell you everything. But my story is simply one of bewilderment and darkness. I know absolutely nothing. Put any question you please. But you know, of course, the limitations mamma has placed me under."

"Perfectly, my dear child. I need not approach the topics on which she desires our silence. Now, the marvel of last night consists in your having been removed from your bed and your room without being wakened, and this removal having occurred apparently while the windows were still secured, and the two doors locked upon the inside. I will tell you my theory, and first ask you a question."

Carmilla was leaning on her hand dejectedly; Madame and I were listening breathlessly.

"Now, my question is this. Have you ever been suspected of walking in your sleep?"

"Never since I was very young indeed."

"But you did walk in your sleep when you were young?"

"Yes; I know I did. I have been told so often by my old nurse."

My father smiled and nodded.

"Well, what has happened is this. You got up in your sleep, unlocked the door, not leaving the key, as usual, in the lock, but taking it out and locking it on the outside; you again took the key out, and carried it away with you to some one of the five-and-twenty rooms on this floor, or perhaps upstairs or downstairs. There are so many rooms and closets, so much heavy furniture, and such accumulations of lumber, that it would require a week to search this old house thoroughly. Do you see, now, what I mean?"

"I do, but not all," she answered.

"And how, papa, do you account for her finding herself on the sofa in the dressing-room, which we had searched so carefully?"

"She came there after you had searched it, still in her sleep, and at last awoke spontaneously, and was as much surprised to find herself where she was as anyone else. I wish all mysteries were as easily and innocently explained as yours, Carmilla," he said, laughing. "And so we may congratulate ourselves on the certainty that the most natural explanation of the occurrence is one that involves no drugging, no tampering with locks, no bur-glars, or poisoners, or witches—nothing that need alarm Carmilla, or any one else, for our safety."

Carmilla was looking charmingly. Nothing could be more beautiful than her tints. Her beauty was, I think enhanced by that graceful languor that was peculiar to her. I think my father was silently contrasting her looks with mine, for he said:

"I wish my poor Laura was looking more like herself"; and he sighed.

So our alarms were happily ended, and Carmilla restored to her friends.

## IX. THE DOCTOR

As Carmilla would not hear of an attendant sleeping in her room, my father arranged that a servant should sleep outside her door so that she could not attempt to make another such excursion without being arrested at her own door.

That night passed quietly; and next morning early, the doctor, whom my father had sent for without telling me a word about it, arrived to see me.

Madame accompanied me to the library; and there the grave little doctor, with white hair and spectacles, whom I mentioned before, was waiting to receive me.

I told him my story, and as I proceeded he grew graver and graver.

We were standing, he and I, in the recess of one of the windows, facing one another. When my statement was over, he leaned with his shoulders against the wall, and with his eyes fixed on me earnestly with an interest in which was a dash of horror.

After a minute's reflection, he asked Madame if he could see my father.

He was sent for accordingly, and as he entered, smiling, he said:

"I dare say, doctor, you are going to tell me that I am an old fool for having brought you here; I hope I am."

But his smile faded into shadow as the doctor, with a very grave face, beckoned him to him.

He and the doctor talked for some time in the same recess where I had just conferred with the physician. It seemed an earnest and argumentative conversation. The room is very large, and I and Madame stood together, burning with curiosity, at the further end. Not a word could we hear, however, for they spoke in a very low tone, and the deep recess of the window quite concealed the doctor from view, and very nearly my father, whose foot, arm, and shoulder only could we see; and the voices were, I suppose, all the less audible for the sort of closet which the thick wall and window formed.

After a time my father's face looked into the room; it was pale, thoughtful, and, I fancied, agitated.

"Laura, dear, come here for a moment. Madame, we shan't trouble you, the doctor says, at present."

Accordingly I approached, for the first time a little alarmed; for, although I felt very weak, I did not feel ill; and strength, one always fancies, is a thing that may be picked up when we please.

My father held out his hand to me as I drew near, but he was looking at the doctor, and he said:

"It certainly *is* very odd; I don't understand it quite. Laura, come here, dear; now attend to Doctor Spielsberg, and recollect yourself."

"You mentioned a sensation like that of two needles piercing the skin, somewhere about your neck, on the night when you experienced your first horrible dream. Is there still any soreness?"

"None at all," I answered.

"Can you indicate with your finger about the point at which you think this occurred?"

"Very little below my throat—*here,*" I answered.

I wore a morning dress, which covered the place I pointed to.

"Now you can satisfy yourself," said the doctor. "You won't mind your papa's lowering your dress a very little. It is necessary, to detect a symptom of the complaint under which you have been suffering."

I acquiesced. It was only an inch or two below the edge of my collar.

"God bless me!—so it is," exclaimed my father, growing pale.

"You see it now with your own eyes," said the doctor, with a gloomy triumph.

"What is it?" I exclaimed, beginning to be frightened.

"Nothing, my dear young lady, but a small blue spot, about the size of the tip of your little finger, and now," he continued, turning to papa, "the question is what is best to be done?"

"Is there any danger?" I urged, in great trepidation.

"I trust not, my dear," answered the doctor. "I don't see why you should not recover. I don't see why you should not begin *immediately* to get better. That is the point at which the sense of strangulation begins?"

"Yes," I answered.

"And—recollect as well as you can—the same point was a kind of center of that thrill which you described just now, like the current of a cold stream running against you?"

"It may have been; I think it was."

"Ay, you see?" he added, turning to my father. "Shall I say a word to Madame?"

"Certainly," said my father.

He called Madame to him, and said:

"I find my young friend here far from well. It won't be of any great consequence, I hope; but it will be necessary that some steps be taken, which I will explain by-and-by; but in the meantime, Madame, you will be so good as not to let Miss Laura be alone for one moment. That is the only direction I need give for the present. It is indispensable."

"We may rely upon your kindness, Madame, I know," added my father.

Madame satisfied him eagerly.

"And you, dear Laura, I know you will observe the doctor's direction."

"I shall have to ask your opinion upon another patient, whose symptoms slightly resemble those of my daughter, that have just been detailed to you—very much milder in degree, but I believe quite of the same sort. She is a young lady—our guest; but as you say you will be passing this way again this evening, you can't do better than take your supper here, and you can then see her. She does not come down till the afternoon."

"I thank you," said the doctor. "I shall be with you, then, at about seven this evening."

And then they repeated their directions to me and to Madame, and with this parting charge my father left us, and walked out with the doctor; and I saw them pacing together up and down between the road and the moat, on the grassy platform in front of the castle, evidently absorbed in earnest conversation.

The doctor did not return. I saw him mount his horse there, take his leave, and ride away eastward through the forest. Nearly at the same time I saw the man arrive from Dranfeld with the letters, and dismount and hand the bag to my father.

In the meantime, Madame and I were both busy, lost in conjecture as to the reasons of the singular and earnest direction which the doctor and my father concurred in imposing. Madame, as she afterwards told me, was afraid the doctor apprehended a sudden seizure, and that, without prompt assistance, I might either lose my life in a fit, or at least be seriously hurt.

This interpretation did not strike me; and I fancied perhaps luckily for my nerves, that the arrangement was prescribed simply to secure a companion, who would prevent my taking too much exercise, or eating unripe fruit, or doing any of the fifty foolish things to which young people are supposed to be prone.

About half-an-hour after, my father came in— he had a letter in his hand—and said:

"This letter had been delayed; it is from General Spielsdorf. He might have been here yesterday, he may not come till tomorrow, or he may be here today."

He put the open letter into my hand; but he did not look pleased, as he used to when a guest, especially one so much loved as the General, was coming. On the contrary, he looked as if he wished him at the bottom of the Red Sea. There was plainly something on his mind which he did not choose to divulge.

"Papa, darling, will you tell me this?" said I

suddenly laying my hand on his arm, and looking, I am sure, imploringly in his face.

"Perhaps," he answered, smoothing my hair caressingly over my eyes.

"Does the doctor think me very ill?"

"No, dear; he thinks, if right steps are taken, you will be quite well again, at least on the high road to a complete recovery, in a day or two," he answered, a little drily. "I wish our good friend, the General, had chosen any other time; that, is, I wish you had been perfectly well to receive him."

"But do tell me, papa," I insisted, "*what* does he think is the matter with me?"

"Nothing; you must not plague me with questions," he answered, with more irritation than I ever remember him to have displayed before; and seeing that I looked wounded, I suppose, he kissed me, and added, "You shall know all about it in a day or two; that is, all that *I* know. In the meantime, you are not to trouble your head about it."

He turned and left the room, but came back before I had done wondering and puzzling over the oddity of all this; it was merely to say that he was going to Karnstein and had ordered the carriage to be ready at twelve, and that I and Madame should accompany him; he was going to see the priest who lived near those picturesque grounds, upon business, and as Carmilla had never seen them, she could follow, when she came down, with Mademoiselle, who would bring materials for what you call a picnic, which might be laid for us in the ruined castle.

At twelve o'clock, accordingly, I was ready, and not long after, my father, Madame and I set out upon our projected drive. Passing the drawbridge we turn to the right, and follow the road over the steep Gothic bridge westward, to reach the deserted village and ruined castle of Karnstein.

No sylvan drive can be fancied prettier. The ground breaks into gentle hills and hollows, all clothed with beautiful wood, totally destitute of the comparative formality which artificial planting and early culture and pruning impart.

The irregularities of the ground often lead the road out of its course, and cause it to wind beautifully round the sides of broken hollows and the steeper sides of the hills, among varieties of ground almost inexhaustible.

Turning one of these points, we suddenly encountered our old friend, the General, riding towards us, attended by a mounted servant. His portmanteaus were following in a hired wagon, such as we term a cart.

The General dismounted as we pulled up, and, after the usual greetings, was easily persuaded to accept the vacant seat in the carriage, and send his horse on with his servant to the schloss.

## X. BEREAVED

It was about ten months since we had last seen him; but that time had sufficed to make an alteration of years in his appearance. He had grown thinner; something of gloom and anxiety had taken the place of that cordial serenity which used to characterize his features. His dark eyes, always penetrating, now gleamed with a sterner light from under his shaggy grey eyebrows. It was not such a change as grief alone usually induces, and angrier passions seemed to have had their share in bringing it about.

We had not long resumed our drive, when the General began to talk, with his usual soldierly directness, of the bereavement, as he termed it, which he had sustained in the death of his beloved niece and ward; and he then broke out in a tone of intense bitterness and fury, inveighing against the "hellish arts" to which she had fallen a victim, and expressing with more exasperation than piety, his wonder that Heaven should tolerate so monstrous an indulgence of the lusts and malignity of hell.

My father, who saw at once that something very extraordinary had befallen, asked him, if not too painful to him, to detail the circumstances which he thought justified the strong terms in which he expressed himself.

"I should tell you all with pleasure," said the General, "but you would not believe me."

"Why should I not?" he asked.

"Because," he answered testily, "you believe in nothing but what consists with your own prejudices and illusions. I remember when I was like you, but I have learned better."

"Try me," said my father; "I am not such a dogmatist as you suppose. Besides which, I very well know that you generally require proof for what you believe, and am, therefore, very strongly predisposed to respect your conclusions."

"You are right in supposing that I have not been led lightly into a belief in the marvelous—for what I have experienced is marvelous—and I have been forced by extraordinary evidence to credit that which ran counter, diametrically, to all my theories. I have been made the dupe of a preternatural conspiracy."

Notwithstanding his professions of confidence in the General's penetration, I saw my father, at this point, glance at the General, with, as I thought, a marked suspicion of his sanity.

The General did not see it, luckily. He was looking gloomily and curiously into the glades and vistas of the woods that were opening before us.

"You are going to the Ruins of Karnstein?" he said. "Yes, it is a lucky coincidence; do you know I was going to ask you to bring me there to inspect them. I have a special object in exploring. There is a ruined chapel, isn't there, with a great many tombs of that extinct family?"

"So there are—highly interesting," said my father. "I hope you are thinking of claiming the title and estates?"

My father said this gaily, but the General did not recollect the laugh, or even the smile, which courtesy exacts for a friend's joke; on the contrary, he looked grave and even fierce, ruminating on a matter that stirred his anger and horror.

"Something very different," he said, gruffly. "I mean to unearth some of those fine people. I hope, by God's blessing, to accomplish a pious sacrilege here, which will relieve our earth of certain monsters, and enable honest people to sleep in their beds without being assailed by murderers. I have strange things to tell you, my dear friend, such as I myself would have scouted as incredible a few months since."

My father looked at him again, but this time not with a glance of suspicion—with an eye, rather, of keen intelligence and alarm.

"The house of Karnstein," he said, "has been long extinct: a hundred years at least. My dear wife was maternally descended from the Karnsteins. But name and title have long ceased to exist. The castle is a ruin; the very village is deserted; it is fifty years since the smoke of a chimney was seen there; not a roof left."

"Quite true. I have heard a great deal about that since I last saw you; a great deal that will astonish you. But I had better relate everything in the order in which it occurred," said the General. "You saw my dear ward—my child, I may call her. No creature could have been more beautiful and only three months ago none more blooming."

"Yes, poor thing! When I saw her last she certainly was quite lovely," said my father. "I was grieved and shocked more than I can tell you, my dear friend; I knew what a blow it was to you."

He took the General's hand, and they exchanged a kind pressure. Tears gathered in the old soldier's eyes. He did not seek to conceal them. He said:

"We have been very old friends; I knew you would feel for me, childless as I am. She had become an object of very dear interest to me, and repaid my care by affection that cheered my home and made my life happy. That is all gone. The years that remain to me on earth may not be very long; but by God's mercy I hope to accomplish a service to mankind before I die, and to subserve the vengeance of Heaven upon the fiends who have murdered my poor child in the spring of her hopes and beauty!"

"You said, just now, that you intended relating everything as it occurred," said my father. "Pray do; I assure you that it is not mere curiosity that prompts me."

By this time we had reached the point at which the Drunstall road, by which the General had come, diverges from the road which we were travelling to Karnstein.

"How far is it to the ruins?" inquired the General, looking anxiously forward.

"About half a league," answered my father. "Pray let us hear the story you were so good as to promise."

## XI. THE STORY

"With all my heart," said the General, with an effort; and after a short pause in which to arrange his subject, he commenced one of the strangest narratives I ever heard.

"My dear child was looking forward with great pleasure to the visit you had been so good as to arrange for her to your charming daughter." Here he made me a gallant but melancholy bow.

"In the meantime we had an invitation to my old friend the Count Carlsfeld, whose schloss is about six leagues to the other side of Karnstein. It was to attend the series of fêtes which, you remember, were given by him in honor of his illustrious visitor, the Grand Duke Charles."

"Yes; and very splendid, I believe, they were," said my father.

"Princely! But then his hospitalities are quite regal. He has Aladdin's lamp. The night from which my sorrow dates was devoted to a magnificent masquerade. The grounds were thrown open, the trees hung with colored lamps. There was such a display of fireworks as Paris itself had never witnessed. And such music—music, you know, is my weakness—such ravishing music! The finest instrumental band, perhaps, in the world, and the finest singers who could be collected from all the great operas in Europe. As you wandered through these fantastically illuminated grounds, the moonlighted château throwing a rosy light from its long rows of windows, you would suddenly hear these ravishing voices stealing from the silence of some grove, or rising from boats upon the lake. I felt myself, as I looked and listened, carried back into the romance and poetry of my early youth.

"When the fireworks were ended, and the ball beginning, we returned to the noble suite of rooms that was thrown open to the dancers. A masked ball, you know, is a beautiful sight; but so brilliant a spectacle of the kind I never saw before.

"It was a very aristocratic assembly. I was myself almost the only 'nobody' present.

"My dear child was looking quite beautiful. She wore no mask. Her excitement and delight added an unspeakable charm to her features, always lovely. I remarked a young lady, dressed magnificently, but wearing a mask, who appeared to me to be observing my ward with extraordinary interest. I had seen her, earlier in the evening, in the great hall, and again, for a few minutes, walking near us, on the terrace under the castle windows, similarly employed. A lady, also masked, richly and gravely dressed, and with a stately air, like a person of rank, accompanied her as a chaperon. Had the young lady not worn a mask, I could, of course, have been much more certain upon the question whether she was really watching my poor darling. I am now well assured that she was.

"We were now in one of the *salons*. My poor dear child had been dancing, and was resting a little on one of the chairs near the door; I was standing near. The two ladies I have mentioned had approached, and the younger took the chair next my ward; while her companion stood beside me, and for a little time addressed herself, in a low tone, to her charge.

"Availing herself of the privilege of her mask she turned to me, and in the tone of an old friend, and calling me by my name, opened a conversation with me, which piqued my curiosity a good deal. She referred to many scenes where she had met me—at Court, and at distinguished houses. She alluded to little incidents which I had long ceased to think of, but which, I found, had only lain in abeyance in my memory, for they instantly started into life at her touch.

"I became more and more curious to ascertain who she was, every moment. She parried my attempts to discover very adroitly and pleasantly. The knowledge she showed of many passages in my life seemed to me all but unaccountable; and she appeared to take a not unnatural pleasure in foiling my curiosity, and in seeing me flounder, in my eager perplexity, from one conjecture to another.

"In the meantime the young lady, whom her mother called by the odd name of Millarca, when she once or twice addressed her, had, with the same ease and grace, got into conversation with my ward.

"She introduced herself by saying that her mother was a very old acquaintance of mine. She spoke of the agreeable audacity which a mask rendered practicable; she talked like a friend; she admired her dress, and insinuated very prettily her admiration of her beauty. She amused her with laughing criticisms upon the people who crowded the ballroom, and laughed at my poor child's fun. She was very witty and lively when she pleased, and after a time they had grown very good friends, and the young stranger lowered her mask, displaying a remarkably beautiful face. I had never seen it before, neither had my dear child. But though it was new to us, the features were so engaging, as well as lovely, that it was impossible not to feel the attraction powerfully. My poor girl did so. I never saw anyone more taken with another at first sight, unless indeed, it was the stranger herself, who seemed quite to have lost her heart to her.

"In the meantime, availing myself of the license of a masquerade, I put not a few questions to the elder lady.

"'You have puzzled me utterly,' I said laughing. 'Is that not enough? Won't you, now consent to stand on equal terms, and do me the kindness to remove your mask?'

"'Can any request be more unreasonable?' she replied. 'Ask a lady to yield an advantage! Besides, how do you know you should recognize me? Years make changes.'

"'As you see,' I said, with a bow, and, I suppose, a rather melancholy little laugh.

"'As philosophers tell us,' she said; 'and how do you know that a sight of my face would help you?'

"'I should take chance for that,' I answered.

'It is vain trying to make yourself out an old woman; your figure betrays you.'

"'Years, nevertheless, have passed since I saw you, rather since you saw me, for that is what I am considering. Millarca, there, is my daughter; I cannot then be young, even in the opinion of people whom time has taught to be indulgent, and I may not like to be compared with what you remember me. You have no mask to remove. You can offer me nothing in exchange.'

"'My petition is to your pity, to remove it.'

"'And mine to yours, to let it stay where it is,' she replied.

"'Well, then, at least you will tell me whether you are French or German; you speak both languages so perfectly.'

"'I don't think I shall tell you that, General; you intend a surprise, and are meditating the particular point of attack.'

"'At all events, you won't deny this,' I said, 'that being honored by your permission to converse, I ought to know how to address you. Shall I say Madame la Comtesse!'

"She laughed, and she would, no doubt, have met me with another evasion—if, indeed, I can treat any occurrence in an interview every circumstance of which was prearranged, as I now believe, with the profoundest cunning, as liable to be modified by accident.

"'As to that,' she began; but she was interrupted, almost as she opened her lips, by a gentleman, dressed in black, who looked particularly elegant and distinguished, with this drawback, that his face was the most deadly pale I ever saw, except in death. He was in no masquerade—in the plain evening dress of a gentleman; and he said, without a smile, but with a courtly and unusually low bow:

"'Will Madame la Comtesse permit me to say a very few words which may interest her?'

"The lady turned quickly to him, and touched her lip in token of silence; she then said to me, 'Keep my place for me, General; I shall return when I have said a few words.'

"And with this injunction, playfully given, she walked a little aside with the gentleman in black, and talked for some minutes, apparently very earnestly. They then walked away slowly together in the crowd, and I lost them for some minutes.

"I spent the interval in cudgelling my brains for conjecture as to the identity of the lady who seemed to remember me so kindly, and I was thinking of turning about and joining in the conversation between my pretty ward and the Countess's daughter, and trying whether, by the time she returned, I might not have a surprise in store for her, by having her name, title, château, and estates at my fingers' ends. But at this moment she returned, accompanied by the pale man in black, who said:

"'I shall return and inform Madame la Comtesse when her carriage is at the door.'

"He withdrew with a bow."

## XII. A PETITION

"'Then we are to lose Madame la Comtesse, but I hope only for a few hours,' I said, with a low bow.

"'It may be that only, or it may be a few weeks. It was very unlucky his speaking to me just now as he did. Do you now know me?'

"I assured her I did not.

"'You shall know me,' she said, 'but not at present. We are older and better friends than, perhaps, you suspect. I cannot yet declare myself. I shall in three weeks pass your beautiful schloss about which I have been making inquiries. I shall then look in upon you for an hour or two, and renew a friendship which I never think of without a thousand pleasant recollections. This moment a piece of news has reached me like a thunderbolt. I must set out now, and travel by a devious route, nearly a hundred miles, with all the dispatch I can possibly make. My perplexities multiply. I am only deterred by the compulsory reserve I practice as to my name from making a very singular request of you. My poor child has not quite recovered her strength. Her horse fell with her, at a hunt which she had ridden out to witness, her nerves have not yet recovered the shock, and our physician says that she must on no account exert herself for some time to come. We came here, in consequence, by very easy stages—hardly six leagues a day. I must now travel day and night on a mission of life and death—a mission the critical and momentous nature of which I shall be able to explain to you when we meet, as I hope we shall, in a few weeks, without the necessity of any concealment.'

"She went on to make her petition, and it was in the tone of a person from whom such a request amounted to conferring, rather than seeking a favor. This only in manner, and, as it seemed, quite unconsciously. Than the terms in which it was expressed, nothing could be more deprecatory. It was simply that I would consent to take charge of her daughter during her absence.

"This was, all things considered, a strange, not to say, an audacious request. She in some sort disarmed me, by stating and admitting everything that could be urged against it, and throwing herself entirely upon my chivalry. At the same moment, by a fatality that seems to have predetermined all that happened, my poor child came to my side, and, in an undertone, besought me to invite her new friend, Millarca, to pay us a visit. She had just been sounding her, and thought, if her mamma would allow her, she would like it extremely.

"At another time I should have told her to wait a little, until, at least, we knew who they were. But I had not a moment to think in. The two ladies assailed me together, and I must confess the refined and beautiful face of the young lady, about which there was something extremely engaging, as well as the elegance and fire of high birth, determined me; and quite overpowered, I submitted, and undertook, too easily, the care of the young lady, whom her mother called Millarca.

"The Countess beckoned to her daughter, who listened with grave attention while she told her, in general terms, how suddenly and peremptorily she had been summoned, and also of the arrangement she had made for her under my care, adding that I was one of her earliest and most valued friends.

"I made, of course, such speeches as the case seemed to call for, and found myself, on reflection, in a position which I did not half like.

"The gentleman in black returned, and very ceremoniously conducted the lady from the room.

"The demeanor of this gentleman was such as to impress me with the conviction that the Countess was a lady of very much more importance than her modest title alone might have led me to assume.

"Her last charge to me was that no attempt was to be made to learn more about her than I might have already guessed, until her return. Our distinguished host, whose guest she was, knew her reasons.

"'But here,' she said, 'neither I nor my daughter could safely remain for more than a day. I removed my mask imprudently for a moment, about an hour ago, and, too late, I fancied you saw me. So I resolved to seek an opportunity of talking a little to you. Had I found that you *had* seen me, I should have thrown myself on your high sense of honor to keep my secret for some weeks. As it is, I am satisfied that you did not see me; but if you now *suspect*, or, on reflection, *should* suspect, who I am, I commit myself, in like manner, entirely to your honor. My daughter will observe the same secrecy, and I well know that you will, from time to time, remind her, lest she should thoughtlessly disclose it.'

"She whispered a few words to her daughter, kissed her hurriedly twice, and went away, accompanied by the pale gentleman in black and disappeared in the crowd.

"'In the next room,' said Millarca, 'there is a window that looks upon the hall door. I should like to see the last of mamma, and to kiss my hand to her.'

"We assented, of course, and accompanied her to the window. We looked out, and saw a handsome old-fashioned carriage, with a troop of couriers and footmen. We saw the slim figure of the pale gentleman in black, as he held a thick velvet cloak, and placed it about her shoulders and threw the hood over her head. She nodded to him, and just touched his hand with hers. He bowed low repeatedly as the door closed, and the carriage began to move.

"'She is gone,' said Millarca, with a sigh.

" 'She is gone,' I repeated to myself, for the first time—in the hurried moments that had elapsed since my consent—reflecting upon the folly of my act.

" 'She did not look up,' said the young lady, plaintively.

" 'The Countess had taken off her mask, perhaps, and did not care to show her face,' I said: 'and she could not know that you were in the window.'

"She sighed and looked in my face. She was so beautiful that I relented. I was sorry I had for a moment repented of my hospitality, and I determined to make her amends for the unavowed churlishness of my reception.

"The young lady, replacing her mask, joined my ward in persuading me to return to the grounds, where the concert was soon to be renewed. We did so, and walked up and down the terrace that lies under the castle windows. Millarca became very intimate with us, and amused us with lively descriptions and stories of most of the great people whom we saw upon the terrace. I liked her more and more every minute. Her gossip, without being ill-natured, was extremely diverting to me, who had been so long out of the great world. I thought what life she would give to our sometimes lonely evenings at home.

"This ball was not over until the morning sun had almost reached the horizon. It pleased the Grand Duke to dance till then, so loyal people could not go away, or think of bed.

"We had just got through a crowded saloon, when my ward asked me what had become of Millarca. I thought she had been by my side, and she fancied she was by mine. The fact was, we had lost her.

"All my efforts to find her were vain. I feared that she had mistaken, in the confusion of momentary separation from us, other people for her new friends, and had, possibly, pursued and lost them in the extensive grounds which were thrown open to us.

"Now, in its full force, I recognized a new folly in my having undertaken the charge of a young lady without so much as knowing her full name;

and fettered as I was by promises, of the reasons for imposing which I knew nothing, I could not even point my inquiries by saying that the missing young lady was the daughter of the Countess who had taken her departure a few hours before.

"Morning broke. It was clear daylight before I gave up my search. It was not till near two o'clock next day that we heard anything of my missing charge.

"At about that time a servant knocked at my niece's door, to say that he had been earnestly requested by a young lady, who appeared to be in great distress, to make out where she could find the General Baron Spielsdorf and the young lady his daughter, in whose charge she had been left by her mother.

"There could be no doubt, notwithstanding the slight inaccuracy, that our young friend had turned up; and so she had. Would to Heaven we had lost her!

"She told my poor child a story to account for her having failed to recover us for so long. Very late, she said, she had got into the housekeeper's bedroom in despair of finding us, and had then fallen into a deep sleep which, long as it was, hardly sufficed to recruit her strength after the fatigues of the ball.

"That day Millarca came home with us. I was only too happy, after all, to have secured so charming a companion for my dear girl."

## XIII. THE WOODSMAN

"There soon, however, appeared some drawbacks. In the first place, Millarca complained of extreme languor—the weakness that remained after her late illness—and she never emerged from her room till the afternoon was pretty far advanced. In the next place, it was accidentally discovered, although she always locked her door on the inside, and never disturbed the key from its place, till she admitted the maid to assist at her toilet, that she was undoubtedly sometimes absent from her room in the very early morning, and at various times later in the day, before she wished it to be understood that she was stirring. She was repeatedly seen from the windows of the schloss, in the first faint grey of the morning, walking through the trees, in an easterly direction, and looking like a person in a trance. This convinced me that she walked in her sleep. But this hypothesis did not solve the puzzle. How did she pass out from her room, leaving the door locked on the inside? How did she escape from the house without unbarring door or window?

"In the midst of my perplexities, an anxiety of a far more urgent kind presented itself.

"My dear child began to lose her looks and health, and that in a manner so mysterious, and even horrible, that I became thoroughly frightened.

"She was at first visited by appalling dreams; then, as she fancied by a specter, something resembling Millarca, sometimes in the shape of a beast, indistinctly seen, walking round the foot of the bed, from side to side. Lastly came sensations. One not unpleasant, but very peculiar, she said, resembled the flow of an icy stream against her breast. At a later time, she felt something like a pair of large needles pierce her, a little below the throat with a very sharp pain. A few nights after, followed a gradual and convulsive sense of strangulation; then came unconsciousness."

I could hear distinctly every word the kind old General was saying, because by this time we were driving upon the short grass that spreads on either side of the road as you approach the roofless village which had not shown the smoke of a chimney for more than half a century.

You may guess how strangely I felt as I heard my own symptoms so exactly described in those which had been experienced by the poor girl who, but for the catastrophe which followed, would have been at that moment a visitor at my father's château. You may suppose, also, how I felt as I heard him detail habits and mysterious peculiarities which were, in fact, those of our beautiful guest, Carmilla!

A vista opened in the forest; we were on a sudden under the chimney and gables of the ruined village, and the towers and battlements of the dismantled castle, round which gigantic trees are grouped, overhung us from a slight eminence.

In a frightened dream I got down from the carriage, and in silence, for we had each abundant matters for thinking; we soon mounted the ascent, and were among the spacious chambers, winding stairs, and dark corridors of the castle.

"And this was once the palatial residence of the Karnsteins!" said the old General at length, as from a great window he looked out across the village, and saw the wide, undulating expanse of forest. "It was a bad family, and here its bloodstained annals were written," he continued. "It is hard that they should, after death, continue to plague the human race with their atrocious lusts. That is the chapel of the Karnsteins, down there."

He pointed down to the grey walls of the Gothic building, partly visible through the foliage, a little way down the steep. "And I hear the axe of a woodsman," he added, "busy among the trees that surround it; he possibly may give us the information of which I am in search, and point out the grave of Mircalla, Countess of Karnstein. These rustics preserve the local traditions of great families, whose stories die out among the rich and titled so soon as the families themselves become extinct."

"We have a portrait, at home, of Mircalla, the Countess Karnstein; should you like to see it?" asked my father.

"Time enough, dear friend," replied the General. "I believe that I have seen the original; and one motive which has led me to you earlier than I at first intended, was to explore the chapel which we are now approaching,"

"What! See the Countess Mircalla," exclaimed my father. "Why, she has been dead more than a century!"

"Not so dead as you fancy, I am told," answered the General.

"I confess, General, you puzzle me utterly," replied my father, looking at him, I fancied, for a moment with a return of the suspicion I detected before. But although there was anger and detestation, at times, in the old General's manner, there was nothing flighty.

"There remains to me," he said, as we passed under the heavy arch of the Gothic church—for its dimensions would have justified its being so styled—"but one object which can interest me during the few years that remain to me on earth, and that is to wreak on her the vengeance which, I thank God, may still be accomplished by a mortal arm."

"What vengeance can you mean?" asked my father, in increasing amazement.

"I mean, to decapitate the monster," he answered, with a fierce flush, and a stamp that echoed mournfully through the hollow ruin, and his clenched hand was at the same moment raised, as if it grasped the handle of an axe, while he shook it ferociously in the air.

"What!" exclaimed my father, more than ever bewildered.

"To strike her head off."

"Cut her head off!"

"Aye, with a hatchet, with a spade, or with anything that can cleave through her murderous throat. You shall hear," he answered, trembling with rage. And hurrying forward he said: "That beam will answer for a seat; your dead child is fatigued; let her be seated, and I will, in a few sentences, close my dreadful story."

The squared block of wood, which lay on the grass-grown pavement of the chapel, formed a bench on which I was very glad to seat myself, and in the meantime the General called to the woodsman, who had been removing some boughs which leaned upon the old walls; and, axe in hand, the hardy old fellow stood before us.

He could not tell us anything of these monuments; but there was an old man, he said, a ranger of this forest, at present sojourning in the house of the priest, about two miles away, who could point out every monument of the old Karnstein family and, for a trifle, he undertook to bring him back with him, if we would lend him one of our horses, in little more than half-an-hour.

"Have you been long employed about this forest?" asked my father of the old man.

"I have been a woodsman here," he answered in his dialect, "under the forester, all my days; so has my father before me, and so on, as many generations as I can count up. I could show you the very house in the village here, in which my ancestors lived."

"How came the village to be deserted?" asked the General.

"It was troubled by ghosts, sir; several were tracked to their graves, there detected by the usual tests, and extinguished in the usual way, by decapitation, by the stake, and by burning; but not until many of the villagers were killed.

"But after all these proceedings according to law," he continued—"so many graves opened, and so many vampires deprived of the horrible animation—the village was not relieved. But a Moravian nobleman, who happened to be travelling this way, heard how matters were, and being skilled—as many people are in his country—in such affairs, he offered to deliver the village from its tormentor. He did so thus: There being a bright moon that night, he ascended, shortly after sunset, the tower of the chapel here, from whence he could distinctly see the churchyard beneath him; you can see it from that window. From this point he watched until he saw the vampire come out of his grave, and place near it the linen clothes in which he had been folded, and glide away towards the village to plague its inhabitants.

"The stranger, having seen all this, came down from the steeple, took the linen wrappings of the vampire, and carried them up to the top of the tower, which he again mounted. When the vampire returned from his prowlings and missed his clothes, he cried furiously to the Moravian, whom he saw at the summit of the tower, and who, in reply beckoned him to ascend and take them. Whereupon the vampire, accepting his invitation, began to climb the steeple, and so soon as he had reached the battlements, the Moravian, with a stroke of his sword, split his skull in two, hurling him down to the churchyard, whither, descending by the winding stairs, the stranger followed and cut his head off, and next day delivered it and the body to the villagers, who duly impaled and burnt them.

"This Moravian nobleman had authority from the then head of the family to remove the tomb of Mircalla, Countess Karnstein, which he did effectually, so that in a little while its site was quite forgotten."

"Can you point out where it stood?" asked the General, eagerly.

The forester shook his head and smiled.

"Not a soul living could tell you that now," he said. "Besides they say her body was removed; but no one is sure of that either."

Having thus spoken, as time pressed, he dropped his axe and departed, leaving us to hear the remainder of the General's strange story.

## XIV. THE MEETING

"My beloved child," he resumed, "was now growing rapidly worse. The physician who attended her had failed to produce the slightest impression upon her disease, for such I then supposed it to be. He saw my alarm, and suggested a consultation. I called in an abler physician, from Gratz. Several days elapsed before he arrived. He was a good and pious, as well as a learned man. Having seen my poor ward together, they withdrew to my library to confer and discuss. I, from the adjoining room, where I awaited their summons, heard these two gentlemen's voices raised in something sharper than a strictly philosophical discussion. I knocked at the door and entered, I found the old physician from Gratz maintaining his theory. His rival was combating it with undisguised ridicule, accompanied with bursts of laughter. This unseemly manifestation subsided and the altercation ended on my entrance.

"'Sir,' said my first physician, 'my learned brother seems to think that you want a conjuror, and not a doctor.'

"'Pardon me,' said the old physician from Gratz, looking displeased. 'I shall state my own view of the case in my own way another time. I grieve, Monsieur le Général, that by my skill and science I can be of no use. Before I go I shall do myself the honor to suggest something to you.'

"He seemed thoughtful, and sat down at a table, and began to write. Profoundly disappointed, I made my bow, and as I turned to go, the other doc-

tor pointed over his shoulder to his companion who was writing, and then, with a shrug, significantly touched his forehead.

"This consultation, then, left me precisely where I was. I walked out into the grounds, all but distracted. The doctor from Gratz, in ten or fifteen minutes, overtook me. He apologized for having followed me, but said that he could not conscientiously take his leave without a few words more. He told me that he could not be mistaken; no natural disease exhibited the same symptoms; and that death was already very near. There remained, however, a day, or possibly two, of life. If the fatal seizure were at once arrested, with great care and skill her strength might possibly return. But all hung now upon the confines of the irrevocable. One more assault might extinguish the last spark of vitality which is, every moment, ready to die.

"'And what is the nature of the seizure you speak of?' I entreated.

"'I have stated all fully in this note, which I place in your hands, upon the distinct condition that you send for the nearest clergyman, and open my letter in his presence, and on no account read it till he is with you; you would despise it else, and it is a matter of life and death. Should the priest fail you, then, indeed, you may read it.'

"He asked me, before taking his leave finally, whether I would wish to see a man curiously learned upon the very subject, which after I had read his letter, would probably interest me above all others, and he urged me earnestly to invite him to visit him there; and so took his leave.

"The ecclesiastic was absent, and I read the letter by myself. At another time, or in another case, it might have excited my ridicule. But into what quackeries will not people rush for a last chance, where all accustomed means have failed, and the life of a beloved object is at stake?

"Nothing, you will say, could be more absurd than the learned man's letter. It was monstrous enough to have consigned him to a madhouse. He said that the patient was suffering from the visits of a vampire! The punctures which she described as having occurred near the throat, were, he insisted, the insertion of those two long, thin, and sharp teeth which, it is well known, are peculiar to vampires; and there could be no doubt, he added, as to the well-defined presence of the small livid mark which all concurred in describing as that induced by the demon's lips, and every symptom described by the sufferer was in exact conformity with those recorded in every case of a similar visitation.

"Being myself wholly skeptical as to the existence of any such portent as the vampire, the supernatural theory of the good doctor furnished, in my opinion, but another instance of learning and intelligence oddly associated with some hallucination. I was so miserable, however, that, rather than try nothing, I acted upon the instructions of the letter.

"I concealed myself in the dark dressing-room, that opened upon the poor patient's room, in which a candle was burning, and watched there till she was fast asleep. I stood at the door, peeping through the small crevice, my sword laid on the table beside me, as my directions prescribed, until, a little after one, I saw a large black object, very ill-defined, crawl, as it seemed to me, over the foot of the bed, and swiftly spread itself up to the poor girl's throat, where it swelled, in a moment, into a great, palpitating mass.

"For a few moments I had stood petrified. I now sprang forward, with my sword in my hand. The black creature suddenly contracted toward the foot of the bed, glided over it, and, standing on the floor about a yard below the foot of the bed, with a glare of skulking ferocity and horror fixed on me, I saw Millarca. Speculating I know not what, I struck at her instantly with my sword; but I saw her standing near the door, unscathed. Horrified, I pursued, and struck again. She was gone! And my sword flew to splinters against the door.

"I can't describe to you all that passed on that horrible night. The whole house was up and stirring. The specter Millarca was gone. But her victim was sinking fast, and before the morning dawned, she died."

The old General was agitated. We did not speak to him. My father walked to some little distance, and began reading the inscriptions on the tombstones; and thus occupied, he strolled into the door of a side chapel to pursue his researches. The General leaned against the wall, dried his eyes, and sighed heavily. I was relieved on hearing the voices of Carmilla and Madame, who were at that moment approaching. The voices died away.

In this solitude, having just listened to so strange a story, connected, as it was, with the great and titled dead, whose monuments were moldering amongst the dust and ivy round us, and every incident of which bore so awfully upon my own mysterious case—in this haunted spot, darkened by the towering foliage that rose on every side, dense and high above its noiseless walls—a horror began to steal over me, and my heart sank as I thought that my friends were, after all, not about to enter and disturb this sad and ominous scene.

The old General's eyes were fixed on the ground, as he leaned with his hand upon the basement of a shattered monument.

Under a narrow, arched doorway, surmounted by one of those demoniacal grotesques in which the cynical and ghastly fancy of old Gothic carving delights, I saw very gladly the beautiful face and figure of Carmilla enter the shadowy chapel.

I was just about to rise and speak, and nodded smiling, in answer to her peculiarly engaging smile; when, with a cry, the old man by my side caught up the woodsman's hatchet, and started forward. On seeing him a brutalized change came over her features. It was an instantaneous and horrible transformation, as she made a crouching step backwards. Before I could utter a scream, he struck at her with all his force, but she dived under his blow, and unscathed, caught him in her tiny grasp by the wrist. He struggled for a moment to release his arm, but his hand opened, the axe fell to the ground, and the girl was gone.

He staggered against the wall. His grey hair stood upon his head, and a moisture shone over his face, as if he were at the point of death.

The frightful scene had passed in a moment. The first thing I recollect after, is Madame standing before me, and impatiently repeating again and again, the question, "Where is Mademoiselle Carmilla?"

I answered at length, "I don't know—I can't tell—she went there," and I pointed to the door through which Madame had just entered, "only a minute or two since."

"But I have been standing there, in the passage, ever since Mademoiselle Carmilla entered; and she did not return."

She then began to call "Carmilla" through every door and passage and from the windows, but no answer came.

"She called herself Carmilla?" asked the General, still agitated.

"Carmilla, yes," I answered.

"Aye," he said, "that is Millarca. That is the same person who long ago was called Mircalla, Countess Karnstein. Depart from this accursed ground, my poor child, as quickly as you can. Drive to the clergyman's house, and stay there till we come. Begone! May you never behold Carmilla more; you will not find her here."

## XV. ORDEAL AND EXECUTION

As he spoke, one of the strangest-looking men I ever beheld entered the chapel at the door through which Carmilla had made her entrance and her exit. He was tall, narrow-chested, stooping, with high shoulders, and dressed in black. His face was brown and dried in with deep furrows; he wore an oddly-shaped hat with a broad leaf. His hair, long and grizzled, hung on his shoulders. He wore a pair of gold spectacles, and walked slowly, with an odd shambling gait, and his face sometimes turned up to the sky, and sometimes bowed down toward the ground, seemed to wear a perpetual smile; his long thin arms were swinging, and his lank hands, in old black gloves ever so much too wide for them, waving and gesticulating in utter abstraction.

"The very man!" exclaimed the General, advancing with manifest delight. "My dear Baron,

how happy I am to see you, I had no hope of meeting you so soon." He signed to my father, who had by this time returned, and leading the fantastic old gentleman, whom he called the Baron, to meet him. He introduced him formally, and they at once entered into earnest conversation. The stranger took a roll of paper from his pocket, and spread it on the worn surface of a tomb that stood by. He had a pencil case in his fingers, with which he traced imaginary lines from point to point on the paper, which from their often glancing from it, together, at certain points of the building, I concluded to be a plan of the chapel. He accompanied, what I may term his lecture, with occasional readings from a dirty little book, whose yellow leaves were closely written over.

They sauntered together down the side aisle, opposite to the spot where I was standing, conversing as they went; then they began measuring distances by paces, and finally they all stood together, facing a piece of the side-wall, which they began to examine with great minuteness; pulling off the ivy that clung over it, and rapping the plaster with the ends of their sticks, scraping here, and knocking there. At length they ascertained the existence of a broad marble tablet, with letters carved in relief upon it.

With the assistance of the woodsman, who soon returned, a monument inscription, and carved escutcheon, were disclosed. They proved to be those of the long lost monument of Mircalla, Countess Karnstein.

The old General, though not I fear given to the praying mood, raised his hand and eyes to heaven, in mute thanksgiving for some moments.

Then turning to the old man with the gold spectacles, whom I have described, he shook him warmly by both hands and said:

"Baron, how can I thank you? How can we all thank you? You will have delivered this region from a plague that has scourged its inhabitants for more than a century. The horrible enemy, thank God, is at last tracked."

My father led the stranger aside, and the General followed. I knew that he had led them out of hearing, that he might relate my case, and I saw them glance often quickly at me, as the discussion proceeded.

My father came to me, kissed me again and again, and leading me from the chapel, said:

"It is time to return, but before we go home, we must add to our party the good priest, who lives but a little way from this; and persuade him to accompany us to the schloss."

In this quest we were successful: and I was glad, being unspeakably fatigued when we reached home. But my satisfaction was changed to dismay, on discovering that there were no tidings of Carmilla. Of the scene that had occurred in the ruined chapel, no explanation was offered to me, and it was clear that it was a secret which my father for the present determined to keep from me.

The sinister absence of Carmilla made the remembrance of the scene more horrible to me. The arrangements for that night were singular. Two servants and Madame were to sit up in my room that night; and the ecclesiastic with my father kept watch in the adjoining dressing-room.

The priest had performed certain solemn rites that night, the purport of which I did not understand any more than I comprehended the reason of this extraordinary precaution taken for my safety during sleep.

I saw all clearly a few days later.

The disappearance of Carmilla was followed by the discontinuance of my nightly sufferings.

You have heard, no doubt, of the appalling superstition that prevails in Upper and Lower Styria, in Moravia, Silesia, in Turkish Serbia, in Poland, even in Russia; the superstition, so we must call it, of the vampire.

If human testimony, taken with every care and solemnity, judicially, before commissions innumerable, each consisting of many members, all chosen for integrity and intelligence, and constituting reports more voluminous perhaps than exist upon any one other class of cases, is worth anything, it is difficult to deny, or even to doubt the existence of such a phenomenon as the vampire.

For my part I have heard no theory by which to explain what I myself have witnessed and experienced other than that supplied by the ancient and well-attested belief of the country.

The next day the formal proceedings took place in the Chapel of Karnstein. The grave of the Countess Mircalla was opened; and the General and my father recognized each his perfidious and beautiful guest, in the face now disclosed to view. The features, though a hundred and fifty years had passed since her funeral, were tinted with the warmth of life. Her eyes were open; no cadaverous smell exhaled from the coffin. The two medical men, one officially present, the other on the part of the promoter of the inquiry, attested the marvelous fact, that there was a faint but appreciable respiration, and a corresponding action of the heart. The limbs were perfectly flexible, the flesh elastic; and the leaden coffin floated with blood, in which to a depth of seven inches, the body lay immersed. Here then, were all the admitted signs and proofs of vampirism. The body, therefore, in accordance with the ancient practice, was raised, and a sharp stake driven through the heart of the vampire, who uttered a piercing shriek at the moment, in all respects such as might escape from a living person in the last agony. Then the head was struck off, and a torrent of blood flowed from the severed neck. The body and head were next placed on a pile of wood, and reduced to ashes, which were thrown upon the river and borne away, and that territory has never since been plagued by the visits of a vampire.

My father has a copy of the report of the Imperial Commission with the signatures of all who were present at these proceedings attached in verification of the statement. It is from this official paper that I have summarized my account of this last shocking scene.

## XVI. CONCLUSION

I write all this you suppose with composure. But far from it; I cannot think of it without agitation. Nothing but your earnest desire so repeatedly expressed, could have induced me to sit down to a task that has unstrung my nerves for months to come, and it induced a shadow of the unspeakable horror which years after my deliverance continued to make my days and nights dreadful, and solitude insupportably terrific.

Let me add a word or two about that quaint Baron Vordenburg, to whose curious lore we were indebted for the discovery of the Countess Mircalla's grave.

He had taken up his abode in Gratz, where, living upon a mere pittance, which was all that remained to him of the once princely estates of his family, in Upper Styria, he devoted himself to the minute and laborious investigation of the marvelously authenticated tradition of vampirism. He had at his fingers' ends all the great and little works upon the subject. *Magia Posthuma, Phlegon de Mirabilibus, Augustinus de curâ pro Mortuis, Philosophicae et Christianae Cogitationes de Vampiris,* by John Christofer Herenberg; and a thousand others, among which I remember only a few of those which he lent to my father. He had a voluminous digest of all the judicial cases, from which he had extracted a system of principles that appear to govern—some always, and others occasionally only—the condition of the vampire. I may mention, in passing, that the deadly pallor attributed to that sort of *revenants,* is a mere melodramatic fiction. They present, in the grave, and when they show themselves in human society, the appearance of healthy life. When disclosed to light in their coffins, they exhibit all the symptoms that are enumerated as those which proved the vampire-life of the long-dead Countess Karnstein.

How they escape from their graves and return to them for certain hours every day, without displacing the clay or leaving any trace of disturbance in the state of the coffin or the cerements, has always been admitted to be utterly inexplicable. The amphibious existence of the vampire is sustained by daily renewed slumber in the grave. Its horrible lust for living blood supplies the vigor of its waking existence. The vampire is prone to be fascinated with an engrossing vehemence, resembling the passion of love, by particular persons. In pursuit of these it will exercise inexhaustible patience and stratagem, for access to a particular object may be obstructed in a hundred ways. It will never desist until it has satiated its passion, and drained the very life of its coveted victim. But it will, in these cases, husband and protract its murderous enjoyment with the refinement of an epicure, and heighten it by the gradual approaches of an artful courtship. In these cases it seems to yearn for something like sympathy and consent. In ordinary ones it goes direct to its object, overpowers with violence, and strangles and exhausts often at a single feast.

The vampire is, apparently, subject, in certain situations, to special conditions. In the particular instance of which I have given you a relation, Mircalla seemed to be limited to a name which, if not her real one, should at least reproduce, without the omission or addition of a single letter, those, as we say anagrammatically, which compose it. *Carmilla* did this; so did *Millarca.*

My father related to the Baron Vordenburg, who remained with us for two or three weeks after the expulsion of Carmilla, the story about the Moravian nobleman and the vampire at Karnstein churchyard, and then he asked the Baron how he had discovered the exact position of the long-concealed tomb of the Countess Millarca. The Baron's grotesque features puckered up into a mysterious smile; he looked down, still smiling on his worn spectacle-case and fumbled with it. Then looking up, he said:

"I have many journals, and other papers, written by that remarkable man; the most curious among them is one treating of the visit of which you speak, to Karnstein. The tradition, of course, discolors and distorts a little. He might have been termed a Moravian nobleman, for he had changed his bode to that territory, and was, beside, a noble. But he was, in truth, a native of Upper Styria. It is enough to say that in very early youth he had been a passionate and favored lover of the beautiful Mircalla, Countess Karnstein. Her early death plunged him into inconsolable grief. It is the nature of vampires to increase and multiply, but according to an ascertained and ghostly law.

"Assume, at starting, a territory perfectly free from that pest. How does it begin, and how does it multiply itself? I will tell you. A person, more or less wicked, puts an end to himself. A suicide, under certain circumstances, becomes a vampire. That specter visits living people in their slumbers; *they* die, and almost invariably, in the grave develop into vampires. This happened in the case of the beautiful Mircalla, who was haunted by one of those demons. My ancestor, Vordenburg, whose title I still bear, soon discovered this, and in the course of the studies to which he devoted himself, learned a great deal more.

"Among other things, he concluded that suspicion of vampirism would probably fall, sooner or later, upon the dead Countess, who in life had been his idol. He conceived a horror, be she what she might, of her remains being profaned by the outrage of a posthumous execution. He has left a curious paper to prove that the vampire, on its expulsion from its amphibious existence, is projected into a far more horrible life; and he resolved to save his once beloved Mircalla from this.

"He adopted the stratagem of a journey here, a pretended removal of her remains, and a real obliteration of her monument. When age had stolen upon him, and from the vale of years he looked back on the scenes he was leaving, he considered, in a different spirit, what he had done, and a horror took possession of him. He made the tracings and notes which have guided me to the very spot, and drew up a confession of the deception that he had practiced. If he had intended any further action in this matter, death prevented him; and the hand of a remote descendant has, too late for many, directed the pursuit to the lair of the beast."

We talked a little more, and among other things he said was this:

"One sign of the vampire is the power of the hand. The slender hand of Mircalla closed like a vise of steel on the General's wrist when he raised the hatchet to strike. But its power is not confined to its grasp; it leaves a numbness in the limb it seizes, which is slowly, if ever, recovered from."

The following Spring my father took me on a tour through Italy. We remained away for more than a year. It was long before the terror of recent events subsided; and to this hour the image of Carmilla returns to memory with ambiguous alternations—sometimes the playful, languid, beautiful girl; sometimes the writhing fiend I saw in the ruined church; and often from a reverie I have started, fancying I heard the light step of Carmilla at the drawing-room door.

## THE TOMB OF SARAH

# F. G. Loring

Frederick George Loring (1869–1951) was a British author about whom little is known, although he appears to have been involved with the English post office in the early years of transatlantic communication, holding the title of inspector of wireless telegraphy, as cited in *The History of Broadcasting in the United Kingdom* by Asa Briggs (1961).

A low-budget Spanish-American film, *La tumba de la isla maldita* (*Crypt of the Living Dead* in English) was filmed in Turkey and released in 1973. It was directed by Julio Salvador and Ray Danton, with story and screenplay by Ricardo Ferrer, and starring Andrew Prine, Patty Shepard, and Mark Damon. By all accounts a dull, slow-moving vampire story, it was largely based on "The Tomb of Sarah," which was not credited.

"The Tomb of Sarah" was originally published in the February 1900 issue of *Pall Mall Magazine*.

# The Tomb of Sarah

## F. G. LORING

My father was the head of a celebrated firm of church restorers and decorators about sixty years ago. He took a keen interest in his work, and made an especial study of any old legends or family histories that came under his observation. He was necessarily very well read and thoroughly well posted in all questions of folk-lore and medieval legend. As he kept a careful record of every case he investigated the manuscripts he left at his death have a special interest. From amongst them I have selected the following, as being a particularly weird and extraordinary experience. In presenting it to the public I feel it is superfluous to apologize for its supernatural character.

### MY FATHER'S DIARY

1841, *17th June*. Received a commission from my old friend, Peter Grant, to enlarge and restore the chancel of his church at Hagarstone, in the wilds of the west country.

*5th July*. Went down to Hagarstone with my head man, Somers. A very long and tiring journey.

*7th July*. Got the work well started. The old church is one of special interest to the antiquarian, and I shall endeavour while restoring it to alter the existing arrangements as little as possible. One large tomb, however, must be moved bodily ten feet at least to the southward. Curiously enough there is a somewhat forbidding inscription upon it in Latin, and I am sorry that this particular tomb should have to be moved. It stands amongst the graves of the Kenyons, an old family which has been extinct in these parts for centuries. The inscription on it runs thus:

SARAH
1630
FOR THE SAKE OF THE DEAD AND
THE WELFARE OF THE LIVING,
LET THIS SEPULCHRE REMAIN UNTOUCHED
AND ITS OCCUPANT UNDISTURBED UNTIL
THE COMING OF CHRIST.
IN THE NAME OF THE FATHER, THE SON
AND THE HOLY GHOST.

*8th July*. Took counsel with Grant concerning the "Sarah Tomb." We are both very loth to disturb it, but the ground has sunk so beneath it that the safety of the church is in danger; thus we have no choice. However, the work shall be done as reverently as possible under our own direction.

Grant says there is a legend in the neighborhood that it is the tomb of the last of the Kenyons, the evil Countess Sarah, who was murdered in 1630. She lived quite alone in the old castle, whose ruins still stand three miles from here on the road to Bristol. Her reputation was an evil one even for those days. She was a witch or were-woman, the only companion of her solitude being a familiar in the shape of a huge Asiatic wolf. This creature was reputed to seize upon children, or failing these, sheep and other small animals, and convey them to the castle, where the countess used to suck their blood. It was popularly supposed that she could never be killed. This, however, proved a fallacy, since she was strangled one day by a mad peasant woman who had lost two children, she declaring that they had both been seized and carried off by the countess's familiar. This is a very interesting story, since it points to a local superstition very similar to that of the vampire, existing in Slavonic and Hungarian Europe.

The tomb is built of black marble, surmounted by an enormous slab of the same material. On the slab is a magnificent group of figures. A young and handsome woman reclines upon a couch; round her neck is a piece of rope, the end of which she holds in her hand. At her side is a gigantic dog with bared fangs and lolling tongue. The face of the reclining figure is a cruel one; the corners of the mouth are curiously lifted, showing the sharp points of long canine or dog teeth. The whole group, though magnificently executed, leaves a most unpleasant sensation.

If we move the tomb it will have to be done in two pieces, the covering slab first and then the tomb proper. We have decided to remove the covering slab tomorrow.

*9th July.* 6 p.m. A very strange day.

By noon everything was ready for lifting off the covering stone, and after the men's dinner we started the jacks and pulleys. The slab lifted easily enough, though it fitted closely into its seat and was further secured by some sort of mortar or putty, which must have kept the interior perfectly airtight.

None of us was prepared for the horrible rush of foul, mouldy air that escaped as the cover lifted clear of its seating. And the contents that gradually came into view were more startling still. There lay the fully dressed body of a woman, wizened and shrunk and ghastly pale as if from starvation. Round her neck was a loose cord, and, judging by the scars still visible, the story of death by strangulation was true enough.

The most horrible part, however, was the extraordinary freshness of the body. Except for the appearance of starvation, life might have been only just extinct. The flesh was soft and white, the eyes were wide open and seemed to stare at us with a fearful understanding in them. The body itself lay on mould, without any pretence to coffin or shell.

For several moments we gazed with horrible curiosity, and then it became too much for my workmen, who implored us to replace the covering slab. That, of course, we would not do; but I set the carpenters to work at once to make a temporary cover while we moved the tomb to its new position. This is a long job, and will take two or three days at least.

9 p.m. Just at sunset we were startled by the howling of, seemingly, every dog in the village. It lasted for ten minutes or a quarter of an hour, and then ceased as suddenly as it began. This, and a curious mist that has risen round the church, makes me feel rather anxious about the "Sarah Tomb." According to the best established traditions of the vampire-haunted countries, the disturbance of dogs or wolves at sunset is supposed to indicate the presence of one of these fiends, and local fog is always considered to be a certain sign. The vampire has the power of producing it for the purpose of concealing its movements near its hiding-place at any time.

I dare not mention or even hint my fears to the rector, for he is, not unnaturally perhaps, a rank disbeliever in many things that I know, from experience, are not only possible but even probable.

I must work this out alone at first, and get his aid without his knowing in what direction he is helping me. I shall now watch till midnight at least.

10:15 p.m. As I feared and half expected. Just before ten there was another outburst of the hideous howling. It was commenced most distinctly by a particularly horrible and blood-curdling wail from the vicinity of the churchyard. The chorus lasted only a few minutes, however, and at the end of it I saw a large dark shape, like a huge dog, emerge from the fog and lope away at a rapid canter towards the open country. Assuming this to be what I fear, I shall see it return soon after midnight.

12:30 p.m. I was right. Almost as midnight struck I saw the beast returning. It stopped at the spot where the fog seemed to commence, and, lifting up its head, gave tongue to that particularly long-drawn wail that I had noticed as preceding the outburst earlier in the evening.

Tomorrow I shall tell the rector what I have seen; and if, as I expect, we hear of some neighbouring sheepfold having been raided, I shall get him to watch with me for this nocturnal marauder. I shall also examine the "Sarah Tomb" for something which he may notice without any previous hint from me.

*10th July.* I found the workmen this morning much disturbed in mind about the howling of the dogs. "We doan't like it, zur," one of them said to me—"we doan't like it; there was summat abroad last night that was unholy." They were still more uncomfortable when the news came round that a large dog had made a raid upon a flock of sheep, scattering them far and wide, and leaving three of them dead with torn throats in the field.

When I told the rector of what I had seen and what was being said in the village, he immediately decided that we must try and catch or at least identify the beast I had seen. "Of course," said he, "it is some dog lately imported into the neighbourhood, for I know of nothing about here nearly as large as the animal you describe, though its size may be due to the deceptive moonlight."

This afternoon I asked the rector, as a favour, to assist me in lifting the temporary cover that was on the tomb, giving as an excuse the reason that I wished to obtain a portion of the curious mortar with which it had been sealed. After a slight demur he consented, and we raised the lid. If the sight that met our eyes gave me a shock, at least it appalled Grant.

"Great God!" he exclaimed. "The woman is alive!"

And so it seemed for a moment. The corpse had lost much of its starved appearance and looked hideously fresh and alive. It was still wrinkled and shrunken, but the lips were firm, and of the rich red hue of health. The eyes, if possible, were more appalling than ever, though fixed and staring. At one corner of the mouth I thought I noticed a slight dark-coloured froth, but I said nothing about it then.

"Take your piece of mortar, Harry," gasped Grant, "and let us shut the tomb again. God help me! Parson though I am, such dead faces frighten me!"

Nor was I sorry to hide that terrible face again; but I got my bit of mortar, and I have advanced a step towards the solution of the mystery.

This afternoon the tomb was moved several feet towards its new position, but it will be two or three days yet before we shall be ready to replace the slab.

10:15 p.m. Again the same howling at sunset, the same fog enveloping the church, and at ten o'clock the same great beast slipping silently out into the open country. I must get the rector's help and watch for its return. But precautions we must take, for if things are as I believe, we take our lives in our hands when we venture out into the night to waylay the—vampire. Why not admit it at once? For that the beast I have seen is the vampire of that evil thing in the tomb I can have no reasonable doubt.

Not yet come to its full strength, thank Heaven! After the starvation of nearly two centuries, for the present it can only maraud as wolf apparently. But, in a day or two, when full power returns, that dreadful woman in new strength and beauty will be able to leave her refuge. Then it would not be sheep merely that would satisfy her disgusting lust for blood, but victims that would yield their lifeblood without a murmur to her caressing touch—victims that, dying of her foul embrace, themselves must become vampires in their turn to prey on others.

Mercifully my knowledge gives me a safeguard; for that little piece of mortar that I rescued today from the tomb contains a portion of the sacred host, and who holds it, humbly and firmly believing in its virtue, may pass safely through such an ordeal as I intended to submit myself and the rector to tonight.

12:30 p.m. Our adventure is over for the present, and were are back safe.

After writing the last entry recorded above, I went off to find Grant and tell him that the marauder was out on the prowl again. "But, Grant," I said, "before we start out tonight I must insist that you will let me prosecute this affair in my own way; you must promise to put yourself completely under my orders, without asking any questions as to the why and wherefore."

After a little demur, and some excusable chaff on his part at the serious view I was taking of what he called a "dog hunt," he gave me his promise. I then told him that we were to watch tonight and try and track the mysterious beast, but not to interfere with it in any way. I think, in spite of his jests, that I impressed him with the fact that there might be, after all, good reason for my precautions.

It was just after eleven when we stepped out into the still night.

Our first move was to try and penetrate the dense fog round the church, but there was something so chilly about it, and a faint smell so disgustingly rank and loathsome, that neither our nerves nor our stomachs were proof against it. Instead, we stationed ourselves in the dark shadow of a yew-tree that commanded a good view of the wicket entrance to the churchyard.

At midnight the howling of the dogs began again, and in a few minutes we saw a large grey shape, with green eyes shining like lamps, shamble swiftly down the path towards us.

The rector started forward, but I laid a firm hand upon his arm and whispered a warning: "Remember!" Then we both stood very still and watched as the great beast cantered swiftly by. It was real enough, for we could hear the clicking of its nails on the stone flags. It passed within a few yards of us, and seemed to be nothing more nor less than a great grey wolf, thin and gaunt, with bristling hair and dripping jaws. It stopped where the mist commenced, and turned around. It was truly a horrible sight, and made one's blood run cold. The eyes burnt like fires, the upper lip was snarling and raised, showing the great canine teeth, while round the mouth clung and dripped a dark-coloured froth.

It raised its head and gave tongue to its long wailing howl, which was answered from afar by the village dogs. After standing for a few moments it turned and disappeared into the thickest part of the fog.

Very shortly afterwards the atmosphere began to clear, and within ten minutes the mist was all gone, the dogs in the village were silent, and the night seemed to reassume its normal aspect. We examined the spot where the beast had been standing and found, plainly enough upon the stone flags, dark spots of froth and saliva.

"Well, rector," I said, "will you admit now, in view of the things you have seen today, in consideration of the legend, the woman in the tomb, the fog, the howling dogs, and, last but not least, the mysterious beast you have seen so close, that there is something not quite normal in it all? Will you put yourself unreservedly in my hands and help me, whatever I may do, first to make assurance doubly sure, and finally to take the necessary steps for putting an end to this horror of the night?" I saw that the uncanny influence of the night was strong upon him, and wished to impress it as much as possible.

"Needs must," he replied, "when the Devil drives: and in the face of what I have seen I must believe that some unholy forces are at work. Yet, how can they work in the sacred precincts of a church? Shall we not call rather upon Heaven to assist us in our needs?"

"Grant," I said solemnly, "that we must do, each in his own way. God helps those who help themselves, and by His help and the light of my knowledge we must fight this battle for Him and the poor lost soul within."

We then returned to the rectory and to our rooms, though I have sat up to write this account while the scene is fresh in my mind.

*11th July.* Found the workmen again very much disturbed in their minds, and full of a strange dog that had been seen during the night by several people, who had hunted it. Farmer Stotman, who had been watching his sheep (the same flock that had been raided the night before), had surprised it over a fresh carcass and tried to drive it off, but its size and fierceness so alarmed him that he had beaten a hasty retreat for a gun. When he returned the animal was gone, though he found that three more sheep from his flock were dead and torn.

The "Sarah Tomb" was moved today to its new position; but it was a long, heavy business, and there was not time to replace the covering slab. For this I was glad, as in the prosaic light of day the rector almost disbelieves the events of the night, and is prepared to think everything to have been magnified and distorted by our imagination.

As, however, I could not possibly proceed with my war of extermination against this foul thing without assistance, and as there is nobody else I can rely upon, I appealed to him for one more night—to convince him that it was no delusion, but a ghastly, horrible truth, which must be fought and conquered for our own sakes, as well as that of all those living in the neighbourhood.

"Put yourself in my hands, rector," I said, "for tonight at least. Let us take those precautions which my study of the subject tells me are the right ones. Tonight you and I must watch in the church; and I feel assured that tomorrow you will be as convinced as I am, and be equally prepared to take those awful steps which I know to be proper, and I must warn you that we shall find a more startling change in the body lying there than you noticed yesterday."

My words came true; for on raising the wooden cover once more the rank stench of a slaughterhouse arose, making us feel positively sick. There lay the vampire, but how changed from the starved and shrunken corpse we saw two days ago for the first time! The wrinkles had almost disappeared, the flesh was firm and full, the crimson lips grinned horribly over the long pointed teeth, and a distinct smear of blood had trickled down one corner of the mouth. We set our teeth, however, and hardened our hearts. Then we replaced the cover and put what we had collected into a safe place in the vestry. Yet even now Grant could not believe that there was any real or pressing danger concealed in that awful tomb, as he raised strenuous objections to any apparent desecration of the body without further proof. This he shall have tonight, God grant that I am not taking too much on myself! If there is any truth in old legends it would be easy enough to destroy the vampire now; but Grant will not have it.

I hope for the best of this night's work, but the danger in waiting is very great.

6 p.m. I have prepared everything: the sharp knives, the pointed stake, fresh garlic, and the wild dog-roses. All these I have taken and concealed in the vestry, where we can get at them when our solemn vigil commences.

If either or both of us die with our fearful task undone, let those reading my record see that this is done. I lay it upon them as a solemn obligation. "That the vampire be pierced through the heart with the stake, then let the burial service be read over the poor clay at last released from its doom. Thus shall the vampire cease to be, and a lost soul rest."

*12th July.* All is over. After the most terrible night of watching and horror, one vampire at least will trouble the world no more. But how thankful should we be to a merciful Providence that that awful tomb was not disturbed by anyone not having the knowledge necessary to deal with its dreadful occupant! I write this with no feelings of self-complacency, but simply with a great gratitude for the years of study I have been able to devote to this subject.

And now to my tale.

Just before sunset last night the rector and I

locked ourselves into the church, and took up our position in the pulpit. It was one of those pulpits, to be found in some churches, which is entered from the vestry, the preacher appearing at a good height through an arched opening in the wall. This gave us a sense of security (which we felt we needed), a good view of the interior, and direct access to the implements which I had concealed in the vestry.

The sun set and the twilight gradually deepened and faded. There was, so far, no signs of the usual fog, nor any howling of the dogs. At nine o'clock the moon rose, and her pale light gradually flooded the aisles, and still no sign of any kind from the "Sarah Tomb." The rector had asked me several times what he might expect, but I was determined that no words or thought of mine should influence him, and that he should be convinced by his own senses alone.

By half-past ten we were both getting very tired, and I began to think that perhaps after all we should see nothing that night. However, soon after eleven we observed a light mist rising from the "Sarah Tomb." It seemed to scintillate and sparkle as it rose, and curled in a sort of pillar or spiral.

I said nothing, but I heard the rector give a sort of gasp as he clutched my arm feverishly. "Great Heaven!" he whispered. "It is taking shape."

And, true enough, in a very few moments we saw standing erect by the tomb the ghastly figure of the Countess Sarah!

She looked thin and haggard still, and her face was deadly white; but the crimson lips looked like a hideous gash in the pale cheeks, and her eyes glared like red coals in the gloom of the church.

It was a fearful thing to watch as she stepped unsteadily down the aisle, staggering a little as if from weakness and exhaustion. This was perhaps natural, as her body must have suffered much physically from her long incarceration, in spite of the unholy forces which kept it fresh and well.

We watched her to the door, and wondered what would happen; but it appeared to present no difficulty, for she melted through it and disappeared.

"Now, Grant," I said, "do you believe?"

"Yes," he replied, "I must. Everything is in your hands, and I will obey your commands to the letter, if you can only instruct me how to rid my poor people of this unnameable terror."

"By God's help I will," said I, "but you shall be yet more convinced first, for we have a terrible work to do, and much to answer for in the future, before we leave the church again this morning. And now to work, for in its present weak state the vampire will not wander far, but may return at any time, and must not find us unprepared."

We stepped down from the pulpit, and taking dog-roses and garlic from the vestry, proceeded to the tomb. I arrived first and, throwing off the wooden cover, cried: "Look! it's empty!" There was nothing there! Nothing except the impress of the body in the loose damp mould!

I took the flowers and laid them in a circle round the tomb, for legend teaches us that vampires will not pass over these particular blossoms if they can avoid it.

Then, eight or ten feet away, I made a circle on the stone pavement, large enough for the rector and myself to stand in, and within the circle I placed the implements that I had brought into the church with me.

"Now," I said, "from this circle, which nothing unholy can step across, you shall see the vampire face to face, and see her afraid to cross that other circle of garlic and dog-roses to regain her unholy refuge. But on no account step beyond the holy place you stand in, for the vampire has a fearful strength not her own, and, like a snake, can draw her victim willingly to his own destruction."

Now so far my work was done, and, calling the rector, we stepped into the holy circle to await the vampire's return.

Nor was this long delayed. Presently a damp, cold odour seemed to pervade the church, which made our hair bristle and flesh creep. And then, down the aisle with noiseless feet, came That which we watched for.

I heard the rector mutter a prayer, and I held him tightly by the arm, for he was shivering violently.

Long before we could distinguish the features we saw the glowing eyes and the crimson sensual mouth. She went straight to her tomb, but stopped short when she encountered my flowers. She walked right round the tomb seeking a place to enter, and as she walked she saw us. A spasm of diabolical hate and fury passed over her face; but it quickly vanished, and a smile of love, more devilish still, took its place. She stretched out her arms towards us. Then we saw that round her mouth gathered a bloody froth and from under her lips long pointed teeth gleamed and champed.

She spoke: a soft soothing voice, a voice that carried a spell with it, and affected us both strangely, particularly the rector. I wished to test as far as possible, without endangering our lives, the vampire's power.

Her voice had a soporific effect, which I resisted easily enough, but which seemed to throw the rector into a sort of trance. More than this: it seemed to compel him to her in spite of his efforts to resist.

"Come!" she said—"Come! I give sleep and peace—sleep and peace—sleep and peace."

She advanced a little towards us; but not far, for I noted that the sacred circle seemed to keep her back like an iron hand.

My companion seemed to become demoralized and spell-bound. He tried to step forward and, finding me detain him, whispered: "Harry, let go! She is calling me! I must! I must! Oh, help me! help me!" And he began to struggle.

It was time to finish.

"Grant!" I cried, in a loud, firm voice. "In the name of all that you hold sacred, have done and play the man!" He shuddered violently and gasped: "Where am I?" Then he remembered, and clung to me convulsively for a moment.

At this a look of damnable hate changed the smiling face before us, and with a sort of shriek she staggered back.

"Back!" I cried. "Back to your unholy tomb! No longer shall you molest the suffering world! Your end is near!"

It was fear that now showed itself on her beautiful face (for it was beautiful in spite of its hor-

ror) as she shrank back, back and over the circlet of flowers, shivering as she did so. At last, with a low mournful cry, she appeared to melt back again into her tomb.

As she did so the first gleams of the rising sun lit up the world, and I knew all danger was over for the day.

Taking Grant by the arm, I drew him with me out of the circle and led him to the tomb. There lay the vampire once more, still in her living death as we had a moment before seen her in her devilish life. But in the eyes remained that awful expression of hate, and cringing, appalling fear.

Grant was pulling himself together.

"Now," I said, "will you dare the last terrible act and rid the world for ever of this horror?"

"By God!" he said solemnly. "I will. Tell me what to do."

"Help me to lift her out of her tomb. She can harm us no more," I replied.

With averted faces we set to our terrible task, and laid her out upon the flags.

"Now," I said, "read the burial service over the poor body, and let us give it its release from this living hell that holds it."

Reverently the rector read the beautiful words, and reverently I made the necessary responses. When it was over I took the stake and, without giving myself time to think, plunged it with all my strength through the heart.

As though really alive, the body for a moment writhed and kicked convulsively, and an awful heart-rending shriek woke the silent church; then all was still.

Then we lifted the poor body back; and, thank God! the consolation that legend tells is never denied to those who have to do such awful work as ours came at last. Over the face stole a great and solemn peace; the lips lost their crimson hue, the prominent sharp teeth sank back into the mouth, and for a moment we saw before us the calm, pale face of a most beautiful woman, who smiled as she slept. A few minutes more, and she faded away to dust before our eyes as we watched. We set to work and cleaned up every trace of our work, and then departed for the rectory. Most thankful were we to step out of the church, with its horrible associations, into the rosy warmth of the summer morning.

With the above end the notes in my father's diary, though a few days later this further entry occurs.

*15th July.* Since the 12th everything has been quiet and as usual. We replaced and sealed up the "Sarah Tomb" this morning. The workmen were surprised to find the body had disappeared, but took it to be the natural result of exposing it to the air.

One odd thing came to my ears today. It appears that the child of one of the villagers strayed from home the night of the 11th inst., and was found asleep in a coppice near the church, very pale and quite exhausted. There were two small marks on her throat, which have since disappeared.

What does this mean? I have, however, kept it to myself, as, now that the vampire is no more, no further danger either to that child or any other is to be apprehended. It is only those who die of the vampire's embrace that become vampires at death in their turn.

## LIGEIA

# Edgar Allan Poe

Edgar Allan Poe (1809–49) was born in Boston and orphaned at the age of two when both his parents died of tuberculosis. He was taken in by a wealthy merchant, John Allan, and his wife; although never legally adopted, Poe nonetheless took Allan for his name. He received a classical education in England from 1815 to 1820. After returning to the United States, he published his first book, *Tamerlane and Other Poems* (1827). It and his next two volumes of poetry were financial disasters.

He won a prize for "Ms. Found in a Bottle" and began a series of jobs as editor and critic of several periodicals, and while he dramatically increased their circulation, his alcoholism, strong views, and arrogance enraged his bosses, costing him one job after another. He married his thirteen-year-old cousin, Virginia, living in abject poverty for many years with her and her mother. Lack of money undoubtedly contributed to the death of Poe's wife at twenty-four.

Influenced by the English romantic poets, Poe was unrivaled by his contemporaries. The most brilliant literary critic of his time, the master of horror stories, the poet whose work remains familiar and beloved to the present day, and the inventor of the detective story died a pauper.

"Ligeia" was first published in the September 1838 issue of *American Museum*; it was first published in book form in *Tales of the Grotesque and Arabesque* (Philadelphia: Lea and Blanchard, 1840).

# Ligeia

## EDGAR ALLAN POE

*And the will therein lieth, which dieth not.
Who knoweth the mysteries of the will, with
its vigor? For God is but a great will pervading all things by nature of its intentness. Man
doth not yield himself to the angels, nor unto
death utterly, save only through the weakness
of his feeble will.*

JOSEPH GLANVILL

I cannot, for my soul, remember how, when, or even precisely where, I first became acquainted with the lady Ligeia. Long years have since elapsed, and my memory is feeble through much suffering. Or, perhaps, I cannot *now* bring these points to mind, because, in truth, the character of my beloved, her rare learning, her singular yet placid cast of beauty, and the thrilling and enthralling eloquence of her low musical language, made their way into my heart by paces so steadily and stealthily progressive, that they have been unnoticed and unknown. Yet I believe that I met her first and most frequently in some large, old, decaying city near the Rhine. Of her family—I have surely heard her speak. That it is of a remotely ancient date cannot be doubted. Ligeia! Ligeia! Buried in studies of a nature more than all else adapted to deaden impressions of the outward world, it is by that sweet word alone—by Ligeia—that I bring before mine eyes in fancy the image of her who is no more.

And now, while I write, a recollection flashes upon me that I have *never known* the paternal name of her who was my friend and my betrothed, and who became the partner of my studies, and finally the wife of my bosom. Was it a playful charge on the part of my Ligeia? Or was it a test of my strength of affection, that I should institute no inquiries upon this point? Or was it rather a caprice of my own—a wildly romantic offering on the shrine of the most passionate devotion? I but indistinctly recall the fact itself—what wonder that I have utterly forgotten the circumstances which originated or attended it? And, indeed, if ever that spirit which is entitled *Romance*—if ever she, the wan and the misty-winged *Ashtophet* of idolatrous Egypt, presided, as they tell, over marriages ill-omened, then most surely she presided over mine.

There is one dear topic, however, on which my memory fails me not. It is the *person* of Ligeia. In stature she was tall, somewhat slender, and, in her latter days, even emaciated. I would in vain attempt to portray the majesty, the quiet ease of her demeanor, or the incomprehensible lightness and elasticity of her footfall. She came and departed as a shadow. I was never made aware of her entrance into my closed study, save by the dear music of her low sweet voice, as she placed her marble hand upon my shoulder. In beauty of face no maiden ever equalled her. It was the radiance of an opium dream—an airy and spirit-lifting vision more wildly divine than the phantasies which hovered about the slumbering souls of the daughters of Delos. Yet her features were not of that regular mould which we have been falsely taught to worship in the classical labors of the heathen. "There is no exquisite beauty," says Bacon, Lord Verulam, speaking truly of all the forms and *genera* of beauty, "without some *strangeness* in the proportion." Yet, although I saw that the features of Ligeia were not of a classic regularity—although I perceived that her loveliness was indeed "exquisite" and felt that there was much of "strangeness" pervading it, yet I have tried in vain to detect the irregularity and to trace home my own perception of "the strange." I examined the contour of the lofty and pale forehead—it was faultless— how cold indeed that word when applied to a majesty so divine!—the skin rivalling the purest ivory, the commanding extent and repose, the gentle prominence of the regions above the temples; and then the raven-black, the glossy, the luxuriant, and naturally-curling tresses, setting forth the full force of the Homeric epithet, "hyacinthine!" I looked at the delicate outlines of the nose—and nowhere but in the graceful medallions of the Hebrews had I beheld a similar perfection. There were the same luxurious smoothness of surface, the same scarcely perceptible tendency to the aquiline, the same harmoniously curved nostrils speaking the free spirit. I regarded the sweet mouth. Here was indeed the triumph of all things heavenly—the magnificent turn of the short upper lip—the soft, voluptuous slumber of the under— the dimples which sported, and the color which spoke—the teeth glancing back, with a brilliancy almost startling, every ray of the holy light which fell upon them in her serene and placid yet most exultingly radiant of all smiles. I scrutinized the formation of the chin—and, here too, I found the gentleness of breadth, the softness and the majesty,

the fulness and the spirituality of the Greek—the contour which the god Apollo revealed but in a dream, to Cleomenes, the son of the Athenian. And then I peered into the large eyes of Ligeia.

For eyes we have no models in the remotely antique. It might have been, too, that in these eyes of my beloved lay the secret to which Lord Verulam alludes. They were, I must believe, far larger than the ordinary eyes of our own race. They were even fuller than the fullest of the gazelle eyes of the tribe of the valley of Nourjahad. Yet it was only at intervals—in moments of intense excitement— that this peculiarity became more than slightly noticeable in Ligeia. And at such moments was her beauty—in my heated fancy thus it appeared perhaps—the beauty of beings either above or apart from the earth—the beauty of the fabulous Houri of the Turk. The hue of the orbs was the most brilliant of black, and, far over them, hung jetty lashes of great length. The brows, slightly irregular in outline, had the same tint. The "strangeness," however, which I found in the eyes was of a nature distinct from the formation, or the color, or the brilliancy of the features, and must, after all, be referred to the *expression*. Ah, word of no meaning! Behind whose vast latitude of mere sound we intrench our ignorance of so much of the spiritual. The expression of the eyes of Ligeia! How for long hours have I pondered upon it! How have I, through the whole of a midsummer night, struggled to fathom it! What was it—that something more profound than the well of Democritus— which lay far within the pupils of my beloved? What *was* it? I was possessed with a passion to discover. Those eyes! Those large, those shining, those divine orbs! They became to me twin stars of Leda, and I to them devoutest of astrologers.

There is no point, among the many incomprehensible anomalies of the science of mind, more thrillingly exciting than the fact—never, I believe, noticed in the schools—that in our endeavors to recall to memory something long forgotten, we often find ourselves *upon the very verge* of remembrance, without being able, in the end, to remember. And thus how frequently, in my intense scrutiny of Ligeia's eyes, have I felt approaching the full knowledge of their expression—felt it approaching—yet not quite be mine—and so at length entirely depart! And (strange, oh, strangest mystery of all!) I found, in the commonest objects of the universe, a circle of analogies to that expression. I mean to say that, subsequently to the period when Ligeia's beauty passed into my spirit, there dwelling as in a shrine, I derived, from many existences in the material world, a sentiment such as I felt always around, within me, by her large and luminous orbs. Yet not the more could I define that sentiment, or analyze, or even steadily view it. I recognized it, let me repeat, sometimes in the survey of a rapidly growing vine—in the contemplation of a moth, a butterfly, a chrysalis, a stream of running water. I have felt it in the ocean—in the falling of a meteor. I have felt it in the glances of unusually aged people. And there are one or two stars in heaven (one especially, a star of the sixth magnitude, double and changeable, to be found near the large star in Lyra) in a telescopic scrutiny of which I have been made aware of the feeling. I have been filled with it by certain sounds from stringed instruments, and not unfrequently by passages from books. Among innumerable other instances, I well remember something in a volume of Joseph Glanvill, which (perhaps merely from its quaintness—who shall say?) never failed to inspire me with the sentiment; "And the will therein lieth, which dieth not. Who knoweth the mysteries of the will, with its vigor? For God is but a great will pervading all things by nature of its intentness. Man doth not yield himself to the angels, nor unto death utterly, save only through the weakness of his feeble will."

Length of years and subsequent reflection have enabled me to trace, indeed, some remote connection between this passage in the English moralist and a portion of the character of Ligeia. An *intensity* in thought, action, or speech was possibly, in her, a result or at least an index, of that gigantic volition which, during our long intercourse, failed to give other and more immediate evidence of its existence. Of all the women whom I have ever known, she, the outwardly calm, the ever-placid Ligeia, was the most violently a prey to the tumultuous vultures of stern passion. And of such passion I could form no estimate save by the miraculous expansion of those eyes which at once so delighted and appalled me,—by the almost magical melody, modulation, distinctness, and placidity of her very low voice,—and by the fierce energy (rendered doubly effective by contrast with her manner of utterance) of the wild words which she habitually uttered.

I have spoken of the learning of Ligeia: it was immense—such as I have never known in woman. In the classical tongues was she deeply proficient, and as far as my own acquaintance extended in regard to the modern dialects of Europe, I have never known her at fault. Indeed upon any theme of the most admired because simply the most abstruse of the boasted erudition of the Academy, have I *ever* found Ligeia at fault? How singularly—how thrillingly, this one point in the nature of my wife has forced itself, at this late period only, upon my attention! I said her knowledge was such as I have never known in woman—but where breathes the man who has traversed, and successfully, *all* the wide areas of moral, physical, and mathematical science? I saw not then what I now clearly perceive, that the acquisitions of Ligeia were gigantic, were astounding; yet I was sufficiently aware of her infinite supremacy to resign myself, with a child-like confidence, to her guidance through the chaotic world of metaphysical investigation at which I was most busily occupied during the earlier years of our marriage. With how vast a triumph—with how vivid a delight—with how much of all that is ethereal in hope did I *feel,* as she bent over me in studies but little sought—but less known—that delicious vista by slow degrees expanding before me, down whose long, gorgeous, and all untrodden path, I might at length pass onward to the goal of a wisdom too divinely precious not to be forbidden!

How poignant, then, must have been the grief with which, after some years, I beheld my well-grounded expectations take wings to themselves and fly away! Without Ligeia I was but as a child groping benighted. Her presence, her readings alone, rendered vividly luminous the many mysteries of the transcendentalism in which we were immersed. Wanting the radiant lustre of her eyes, letters, lambent and golden, grew duller than Saturnian lead. And now those eyes shone less and less frequently upon the pages over which I pored. Ligeia grew ill. The wild eyes blazed with a too— too glorious effulgence; the pale fingers became of the transparent waxen hue of the grave; and the blue veins upon the lofty forehead swelled and sank impetuously with the tides of the most gentle emotion. I saw that she must die—and I struggled desperately in spirit with the grim Azrael. And the struggles of the passionate wife were, to my astonishment, even more energetic than my own. There had been much in her stern nature to impress me with the belief that, to her, death would have come without its terrors; but not so. Words are impotent to convey any just idea of the fierceness of resistance with which she wrestled with the Shadow. I groaned in anguish at the pitiable spectacle. I would have soothed—I would have reasoned; but in the intensity of her wild desire for life—for life—*but* for life—solace and reason were alike the uttermost of folly. Yet not until the last instance, amid the most convulsive writhings of her fierce spirit, was shaken the external placidity of her demeanor. Her voice grew more gentle— grew more low—yet I would not wish to dwell upon the wild meaning of the quietly uttered words. My brain reeled as I hearkened, entranced to a melody more than mortal—to assumptions and aspirations which mortality had never before known.

That she loved me I should not have doubted; and I might have been easily aware that, in a bosom such as hers, love would have reigned no ordinary passion. But in death only was I fully impressed with the strength of her affection. For long hours, detaining my hand, would she pour out before me the overflowing of a heart whose more than passionate devotion amounted to idolatry. How had I deserved to be so blessed by such confessions?— how had I deserved to be so cursed with the removal of my beloved in the hour of her making them? But upon this subject I cannot bear to dilate. Let me say only, that in Ligeia's more than womanly abandonment to a love, alas! all unmerited, all unworthily bestowed, I at length recognized the principle of her longing, with so wildly earnest a desire, for the life which was now fleeing so rapidly away. It is this wild longing—it is this eager vehemence of desire for life—*but* for life—that I have no power to portray—no utterance capable of expressing.

At high noon of the night in which she departed, beckoning me, peremptorily, to her side, she bade me repeat certain verses composed by herself not many days before. I obeyed her. They were these:—

Lo! 'tis a gala night
    Within the lonesome latter years!
An angel throng, bewinged, bedight
    In veils, and drowned in tears,
Sit in a theatre, to see
    A play of hopes and fears,
While the orchestra breathes fitfully
    The music of the spheres.

Mimes, in the form of God on high,
    Mutter and mumble low,
And hither and thither fly;
    Mere puppets they, who come and go
At bidding of vast formless things
    That shift the scenery to and fro,
Flapping from out their condor wings
    Invisible Woe!

That motley drama!—oh, be sure
    It shall not be forgot!
With its Phantom chased for evermore,
    By a crowd that seize it not,
Through a circle that ever returneth in
    To the self-same spot;
And much of Madness, and more of Sin,
    And Horror, the soul of the plot!

But see, amid the mimic rout
    A crawling shape intrude!
A blood-red thing that writhes from out
    The scenic solitude!
It writhes!—it writhes!—with mortal pangs
    The mimes become its food,
And the seraphs sob at vermin fangs
    In human gore imbued.

*Out—out are the lights—out all!*
　*And over each quivering form,*
*The curtain, a funeral pall,*
　*Comes down with the rush of a storm—*
*And the angels, all pallid and wan,*
　*Uprising, unveiling, affirm*
*That the play is the tragedy, "Man,"*
　*And its hero, the conqueror Worm.*

"O God!" half shrieked Ligeia, leaping to her feet and extending her arms aloft with a spasmodic movement, as I made an end of these lines—"O God! O Divine Father!—shall these things be un-deviatingly so?—shall this conqueror be not once conquered? Are we not part and parcel in Thee? Who—who knoweth the mysteries of the will with its vigor? Man doth not yield him to the angels, *nor unto death utterly,* save only through the weak-ness of his feeble will."

And now, as if exhausted with emotion, she suffered her white arms to fall, and returned solemnly to her bed of death. And as she breathed her last sighs, there came mingled with them a low murmur from her lips. I bent to them my ear, and distinguished, again, the concluding words of the passage in Glanvill: "*Man doth not yield himself to the angels, nor unto death utterly, save only through the weakness of his feeble will.*"

She died: and I, crushed into the very dust with sorrow, could no longer endure the lonely deso-lation of my dwelling in the dim and decaying city by the Rhine. I had no lack of what the world calls wealth. Ligeia had brought me far more, very far more, than ordinarily falls to the lot of mortals. After a few months, therefore, of weary and aim-less wandering, I purchased and put in some re-pair, an abbey, which I shall not name, in one of the wildest and least frequented portions of fair England. The gloomy and dreary grandeur of the building, the almost savage aspect of the domain, the many melancholy and time-honored memo-ries connected with both, had much in unison with the feelings of utter abandonment which had driven me into that remote and unsocial region of the country. Yet although the external abbey, with its verdant decay hanging about it, suffered but lit-

tle alteration, I gave way, with a child-like perver-sity, and perchance with a faint hope of alleviat-ing my sorrows, to a display of more than regal magnificence within. For such follies, even in child-hood, I had imbibed a taste, and now they came back to me as if in the dotage of grief. Alas, I feel how much even of incipient madness might have been discovered in the gorgeous and fantastic draperies, in the solemn carvings of Egypt, in the wild cornices and furniture, in the Bedlam pat-terns of the carpets of tufted gold! I had become a bounden slave in the trammels of opium, and my labors and my orders had taken a coloring from my dreams. But these absurdities I must not pause to detail. Let me speak only of that one chamber, ever accursed, whither, in a moment of mental alienation, I led from the altar as my bride—as the successor of the unforgotten Ligeia—the fair-haired and blue-eyed Lady Rowena Trevanion, of Tremaine.

There is no individual portion of the architec-ture and decoration of that bridal chamber which is not now visibly before me. Where were the souls of the haughty family of the bride, when, through thirst of gold, they permitted to pass the thresh-old of an apartment *so* bedecked, a maiden and a daughter so beloved? I have said, that I minutely remember the details of the chamber—yet I am sadly forgetful on topics of deep moment; and here there was no system, no keeping, in the fantastic display, to take hold upon the memory. The room lay in a high turret of the castellated abbey, was pentagonal in shape, and of capacious size. Occu-pying the whole southern face of the pentagon was the sole window—an immense sheet of unbroken glass from Venice—a single pane, and tinted of a leaden hue, so that the rays of either the sun or moon passing through it, fell with a ghastly lus-tre on the objects within. Over the upper portion of this huge window, extended the trellis-work of an aged vine, which clambered up the massy walls of the turret. The ceiling, of gloomy-looking oak, was excessively lofty, vaulted, and elaborately fret-ted with the wildest and most grotesque speci-mens of a semi-Gothic, semi-Druidical device. From out the most central recess of this melan-choly vaulting, depended, by a single chain of gold with long links, a huge censer of the same metal, Saracenic in pattern, and with many perforations so contrived that there writhed in and out of them, as if endued with a serpent vitality, a continual succession of parti-colored fires.

Some few ottomans and golden candelabra, of Eastern figure, were in various stations about; and there was the couch, too—the bridal couch—of an Indian model, and low, and sculptured of solid ebony, with a pall-like canopy above. In each of the angles of the chamber stood on end a gigantic sarcophagus of black granite, from the tombs of the kings over against Luxor, with their aged lids full of immemorial sculpture. But in the draping of the apartment lay, alas! the chief phantasy of all: The lofty walls, gigantic in height—even unproportionably so—were hung from summit to foot, in vast folds, with a heavy and massive-looking tapestry—tapestry of a material which was found alike as a carpet on the floor, as a covering for the ottomans and the ebony bed, as a canopy for the bed and as the gorgeous volutes of the curtains which partially shaded the window. The material was the richest cloth of gold. It was spotted all over, at irregular intervals, with arabesque figures, about a foot in diameter, and wrought upon the cloth in patterns of the most jetty black. But these figures partook of the true character of the arabesque only when regarded from a single point of view. By a contrivance now common, and indeed traceable to a very remote period of antiquity, they were made changeable in aspect. To one entering the room, they bore the appearance of simple monstrosities; but upon a further advance, this appearance gradually departed; and, step by step, as the visitor moved his station in the chamber, he saw himself surrounded by an endless succession of the ghastly forms which belong to the superstition of the Norman, or arise in the guilty slumbers of the monk. The phantasmagoric effect was vastly heightened by the artificial introduction of a strong continual current of wind behind the draperies—giving a hideous and uneasy animation to the whole.

In halls such as these—in a bridal chamber such as this—I passed, with the Lady of Tremaine, the unhallowed hours of the first month of our marriage—passed them with but little disquietude. That my wife dreaded the fierce moodiness of my temper—that she shunned me, and loved me but little—I could not help perceiving; but it gave me rather pleasure than otherwise. I loathed her with a hatred belonging more to demon than to man. My memory flew back (oh, with what intensity of regret!) to Ligeia, the beloved, the august, the beautiful, the entombed. I revelled in recollections of her purity, of her wisdom, of her lofty—her ethereal nature, of her passionate, her idolatrous love. Now, then, did my spirit fully and freely burn with more than all the fires of her own. In the excitement of my opium dreams (for I was habitually fettered in the shackles of the drug), I would call aloud upon her name, during the silence of the night, or among the sheltered recesses of the glens by day, as if, through the wild eagerness, the solemn passion, the consuming ardor of my longing for the departed, I could restore her to the pathways she had abandoned—ah, *could* it be for ever?—upon the earth.

About the commencement of the second month of the marriage, the Lady Rowena was attacked with sudden illness, from which her recovery was slow. The fever which consumed her rendered her nights uneasy; and in her perturbed state of half-slumber, she spoke of sounds, and of motions, in and about the chamber of the turret, which I concluded had no origin save in the distemper of her fancy, or perhaps in the phantasmagoric influences of the chamber itself. She became at length convalescent—finally, well. Yet but a brief period elapsed, ere a second more violent disorder again threw her upon a bed of suffering; and from this attack her frame, at all times feeble, never altogether recovered. Her illnesses were, after this epoch, of alarming character, and of more alarming recurrence, defying alike the knowledge and the great exertions of her physicians. With the increase of the chronic disease, which had thus, apparently, taken too sure hold upon her constitution to be eradicated by human means, I could not fail to observe a similar increase in the nervous irritation of her temperament, and in her excitability by trivial causes of fear. She spoke again, and now more frequently and pertinaciously, of the sounds—of the slight sounds—and of the unusual motions among the tapestries, to which she had formerly alluded.

One night, near the closing in of September, she pressed this distressing subject with more than usual emphasis upon my attention. She had just awakened from an unquiet slumber, and I had been watching, with feelings half of anxiety, half of vague terror, the workings of her emaciated countenance. I sat by the side of her ebony bed, upon one of the ottomans of India. She partly arose, and spoke, in an earnest low whisper, of sounds which she *then* heard, but which I could not hear—of motions which she *then* saw, but which I could not perceive. The wind was rushing hurriedly behind the tapestries, and I wished to show her (what, let me confess it, I could not *all* believe) that those almost inarticulate breathings, and those very gentle variations of the figures upon the wall, were but the natural effects of that customary rushing of the wind. But a deadly pallor, overspreading her face, had proved to me that my exertions to reassure her would be fruitless. She appeared to be fainting, and no attendants were within call. I remembered where was deposited a decanter of light wine which had been ordered by her physicians, and hastened across the chamber to procure it. But, as I stepped beneath the light of the censer, two circumstances of a startling nature attracted my attention. I had felt that some palpable although invisible object had passed lightly by my person; and I saw that there lay upon the golden carpet, in the very middle of the rich lustre thrown from the censer, a shadow—a faint, indefinite shadow of angelic aspect—such as might be fancied for the shadow of a shade. But I was wild with the excitement of an immoderate dose of opium, and heeded these things but little, nor spoke of them to Rowena. Having found the wine, I recrossed the chamber, and poured out a gobletful, which I held to the lips of the fainting lady. She had now partially recovered, however, and took the vessel herself, while I sank upon an ottoman near me, with my eyes fastened upon her person. It was then that I became distinctly aware of a gentle foot-

fall upon the carpet, and near the couch; and in a second thereafter, as Rowena was in the act of raising the wine to her lips, I saw, or may have dreamed that I saw, fall within the goblet, as if from some invisible spring in the atmosphere of the room, three or four large drops of a brilliant and ruby-coloured fluid. If this I saw—not so Rowena. She swallowed the wine unhesitatingly, and I forbore to speak to her of a circumstance which must, after all, I considered, have been but the suggestion of a vivid imagination, rendered morbidly active by the terror of the lady, by the opium, and by the hour.

Yet I cannot conceal it from my own perception that, immediately subsequent to the fall of the ruby-drops, a rapid change for the worse took place in the disorder of my wife; so that, on the third subsequent night, the hands of her menials prepared her for the tomb, and on the fourth, I sat alone, with her shrouded body, in that fantastic chamber which had received her as my bride. Wild visions, opium-engendered, flitted, shadow-like, before me. I gazed with unquiet eye upon the sarcophagi in the angles of the room, upon the varying figures of the drapery, and upon the writhing of the parti-colored fires in the censer overhead. My eyes then fell, as I called to mind the circumstances of a former night, to the spot beneath the glare of the censer where I had seen the faint traces of the shadow. It was there, however, no longer; and breathing with greater freedom, I turned my glances to the pallid and rigid figure upon the bed. Then rushed upon me a thousand memories of Ligeia—and then came back upon my heart, with the turbulent violence of a flood, the whole of that unutterable woe with which I had regarded *her* thus enshrouded. The night waned; and still, with a bosom full of bitter thoughts of the one only and supremely beloved, I remained gazing upon the body of Rowena.

It might have been midnight, or perhaps earlier, or later, for I had taken no note of time, when a sob, low, gentle, but very distinct, startled me from my reverie. I *felt* that it came from the bed of ebony—the bed of death. I listened in an agony of superstitious terror—but there was no repetition of the sound. I strained my vision to detect any motion in the corpse—but there was not the slightest perceptible. Yet I could not have been deceived. I *had* heard the noise, however faint, and my soul was awakened within me. I resolutely and perseveringly kept my attention riveted upon the body. Many minutes elapsed before any circumstance occurred tending to throw light upon the mystery. At length it became evident that a slight, a very feeble, and barely noticeable tinge of color had flushed up within the cheeks, and along the sunken small veins of the eyelids. Through a species of unutterable horror and awe, for which the language of mortality has no sufficiently energetic expression, I felt my heart cease to beat, my limbs grow rigid where I sat. Yet a sense of duty finally operated to restore my self-possession. I could no longer doubt that we had been precipitate in our preparations—that Rowena still lived. It was necessary that some immediate exertion be made; yet the turret was altogether apart from the portion of the abbey tenanted by the servants—there were none within call—I had no means of summoning them to my aid without leaving the room for many minutes—and this I could not venture to do. I therefore struggled alone in my endeavors to call back the spirit still hovering. In a short period it was certain, however, that a relapse had taken place; the color disappeared from both eyelid and cheek, leaving a wanness even more than that of marble; the lips became doubly shrivelled and pinched up in the ghastly expression of death; a repulsive clamminess and coldness overspread rapidly the surface of the body; and all the usual rigorous stiffness immediately supervened. I fell back with a shudder upon the couch from which I had been so startlingly aroused, and again gave myself up to passionate waking visions of Ligeia. An hour thus elapsed, when (could it be possible?) I was a second time aware of some vague sound issuing from the region of the bed.

I listened—in extremity of horror. The sound came again—it was a sigh. Rushing to the corpse, I saw—distinctly saw—a tremor upon the lips. In a minute afterward they relaxed, disclosing a bright line of the pearly teeth. Amazement now strug-gled in my bosom with the profound awe which had hitherto reigned there alone. I felt that my vision grew dim, that my reason wandered; and it was only by a violent effort that I at length succeeded in nerving myself to the task which duty thus once more had pointed out. There was now a partial glow upon the forehead and upon the cheek and throat; a perceptible warmth pervaded the whole frame; there was even a slight pulsation at the heart. The lady *lived*; and with redoubled ardor I betook myself to the task of restoration. I chafed and bathed the temples and the hands, and used every exertion which experience, and no little medical reading, could suggest. But in vain. Suddenly, the color fled, the pulsation ceased, the lips resumed the expression of the dead, and, in an instant afterward, the whole body took upon itself the icy chilliness, the livid hue, the intense rigidity, the sunken outline, and all the loathsome peculiarities of that which has been, for many days, a tenant of the tomb.

And again I sank into visions of Ligeia—and again (what marvel that I shudder while I write?), *again* there reached my ears a low sob from the region of the ebony bed. But why shall I minutely detail the unspeakable horrors of that night? Why shall I pause to relate how, time after time, until near the period of the gray dawn, this hideous drama of revivification was repeated; how each terrific relapse was only into a sterner and apparently more irredeemable death; how each agony wore the aspect of a struggle with some invisible foe; and how each struggle was succeeded by I know not what of wild change in the personal appearance of the corpse? Let me hurry to a conclusion.

The greater part of the fearful night had worn away, and she who had been dead once again stirred—and now more vigorously than hitherto, although arousing from a dissolution more appalling in its utter hopelessness than any. I had long ceased to struggle or to move, and remained sitting rigidly upon the ottoman, a helpless prey to a whirl of violent emotions, of which extreme awe was perhaps the least terrible, the least consuming. The corpse, I repeat, stirred, and now more vigorously than before. The hues of life flushed up with unwonted energy into the countenance—the limbs relaxed—and, save that the eyelids were yet pressed heavily together, and that the bandages and draperies of the grave still imparted their charnel character to the figure, I might have dreamed that Rowena had indeed shaken off, utterly, the fetters of Death. But if this idea was not, even then, altogether adopted, I could at least doubt no longer, when, arising from the bed, tottering, with feeble steps, with closed eyes, and with the manner of one bewildered in a dream, the thing that was enshrouded advanced boldly and palpably into the middle of the apartment.

I trembled not—I stirred not—for a crowd of unutterable fancies connected with the air, the stature, the demeanor, of the figure, rushing hurriedly through my brain, had paralyzed—had chilled me into stone. I stirred not—but gazed upon the apparition. There was a mad disorder in my thoughts—a tumult unappeasable. Could it, indeed, be the *living* Rowena who confronted me? Could it, indeed, be Rowena *at all*—the fair-haired, the blue-eyed Lady Rowena Trevanion of Tremaine? Why, *why* should I doubt it? The bandage lay heavily about the mouth—but then might it not be the mouth of the breathing Lady of Tremaine? And the cheeks—there were the roses as in her noon of life—yes, these might indeed be the fair cheeks of the living Lady of Tremaine. And the chin, with its dimples, as in health, might it not be hers?—but *had she then grown taller since her malady?* What inexpressible madness seized me with that thought? One bound, and I had reached her feet! Shrinking from my touch, she let fall from her head, unloosened, the ghastly cerements which had confined it, and there streamed forth into the rushing atmosphere of the chamber huge masses of long and dishevelled hair; *it was blacker than the raven wings of midnight!* And now slowly opened *the eyes* of the figure which stood before me. "Here then, at least," I shrieked aloud, "can I never—can I never be mistaken—these are the full, and the black, and the wild eyes—of my lost love—of the lady—of the Lady Ligeia."

# THE OLD PORTRAIT AND THE VAMPIRE MAID

# Hume Nisbet

James Hume Nisbet (1849–1923) was born in Stirling, Scotland, but moved to Australia at the age of sixteen, traveling and studying for seven years before returning to Scotland, where he was an instructor of freehand drawing at Watt College. Although he had studied art with Sam Bough of the Royal Scottish Academy, he did not have much success in this field, his watercolors failing to generate much excitement, even though he was an associate of John Ruskin's and his work was exhibited at the RSA. He eventually separated from that august institution because he felt it unfair to young artists.

He turned to literature and had a prolific period, writing about forty novels between 1888 and 1905, most of which were mystery and adventure fiction and were published only in England. More than half were set in Australia and Pacific regions. He was vehemently outspoken on social issues, writing about perceived prejudices within the context of his popular novels. His writings on such controversial themes made his novels unpopular in Australia.

In addition to his forty-six novels, he produced four volumes of poetry, five books on art, travel books, and short-story collections; he is largely unread today.

"The Old Portrait" and "The Vampire Maid" were published in magazines in 1890; they were first collected in book form in *Stories Weird and Wonderful* (London: White, 1900).

# The Old Portrait

## HUME NISBET

Old-fashioned frames are a hobby of mine. I am always on the prowl amongst the framers and dealers in curiosities for something quaint and unique in picture frames. I don't care much for what is inside them, for being a painter it is my fancy to get the frames first and then paint a picture which I think suits their probable history and design. In this way I get some curious and I think also some original ideas.

One day in December, about a week before Christmas, I picked up a fine but delapidated specimen of wood-carving in a shop near Soho. The gilding had been worn nearly away, and three of the corners broken off; yet as there was one of the corners still left, I hoped to be able to repair the others from it. As for the canvas inside this frame, it was so smothered with dirt and time stains that I could only distinguish it had been a very badly painted likeness of some sort, of some commonplace person, daubed in by a poor pot-boiling painter to fill the secondhand frame which his patron may have picked up cheaply as I had done after him; but as the frame was alright I took the spoiled canvas along with it, thinking it might come in handy.

For the next few days my hands were full of work of one kind and another, so that it was only on Christmas Eve that I found myself at liberty to examine my purchase, which had been lying with its face to the wall since I had brought into my studio.

Having nothing to do on this night, and not in the mood to go out, I got my picture and frame from the corner, and laying them upon the table, with a sponge, basin of water, and some soap, I began to wash so that I might see them the better. They were in a terrible mess, and I think I used the best part of a packet of soap-powder and had to change the water about a dozen times before the pattern began to show up on the frame, and the portrait within it asserted its awful crudeness, vile drawing, and intense vulgarity. It was the bloated, piggish visage of a publican clearly, with a plentiful supply of jewellery displayed, as is usual with such masterpieces, where the features are not considered of so much importance as a strict fidelity in the, depicting of such articles as watchguard and seals, finger rings, and breast pins; these were all there, as natural and hard as reality.

The frame delighted me, and the picture satisfied me that I had not cheated the dealer with my price, and I was looking at the monstrosity as the gaslight beat full upon it, and wondering how the owner could be pleased with himself as thus depicted, when something about the background attracted my attention—a slight marking underneath the thin coating as if the portrait had been painted over some other subject.

It was not much certainly, yet enough to make me rush over to my cupboard, where I kept my spirits of wine and turpentine, with which, and a plentiful supply of rags, I began to demolish the publican ruthlessly in the vague hope that I might find something worth looking at underneath.

A slow process that was, as well as a delicate one, so that it was close upon midnight before the gold cable rings and vermilion visage disappeared and another picture loomed up before me; then giving it the final wash over, I wiped it dry, and set it in a good light on my easel, while I filled and lit my pipe, and then sat down to look at it.

What had I liberated from that vile prison of crude paint? For I did not require to set it up to know that this bungler of the brush had covered and defiled a work as far beyond his comprehension as the clouds are from the caterpillar.

The bust and head of a young woman of uncertain age, merged within a gloom of rich accessories painted as only a master hand can paint who is above asserting his knowledge, and who has learnt to cover his technique. It was as perfect and natural in its sombre yet quiet dignity as if it had come from the brush of Moroni.

A face and neck perfectly colourless in their pallid whiteness, with the shadows so artfully managed that they could not be seen, and for this quality would have delighted the strong-minded Queen Bess.

At first as I looked I saw in the centre of a vague darkness a dim patch of grey gloom that drifted into the shadow. Then the greyness appeared to grow lighter as I sat from it, and leaned back in my chair until the features stole out softly, and became clear and definite, while the figure stood out from the background as if tangible, although, having washed it, I knew that it had been smoothly painted.

An intent face, with delicate nose, well-shaped, although bloodless, lips, and eyes like dark caverns without a spark of light in them. The hair loosely about the head and oval cheeks, massive, silky-textured, jet black, and lustreless, which hid the upper portion of her brow, with the ears, and fell in straight indefinite waves over the left breast, leaving the right portion of the transparent neck exposed.

The dress and background were symphonies of ebony, yet full of subtle colouring and masterly feeling; a dress of rich brocaded velvet with a background that represented vast receding space, wondrously suggestive and awe-inspiring.

I noticed that the pallid lips were parted slightly, and showed a glimpse of the upper front teeth, which added to the intent expression of the face. A short upper lip, which, curled upward, with the underlip full and sensuous, or rather, if colour had been in it, would have been so.

It was an eerie looking face that I had resurrected on this midnight hour of Christmas Eve; in its passive pallidity it looked as if the blood had been drained from the body, and that I was gazing upon an open-eyed corpse.

The frame, also, I noticed for the first time, in its details appeared to have been designed with the intention of carrying out the idea of life in death; what had before looked like scroll-work of flowers and fruit were loathsome snake-like worms twined amongst charnel-house bones which they half covered in a decorative fashion; a hideous design in spite of its exquisite workmanship, that made me shudder and wish that I had left the cleaning to be done by daylight.

I am not at all of a nervous temperament, and would have laughed had anyone told me that I was afraid, and yet, as I sat here alone, with that portrait opposite to me in this solitary studio, away from all human contact; for none of the other studios were tenanted on this night, and the janitor had gone on his holiday; I wished that I had spent my evening in a more congenial manner, for in spite of a good fire in the stove and the brilliant gas, that intent face and those haunting eyes were exercising a strange influence upon me.

I heard the clocks from the different steeples chime out the last hour of the day, one after the other, like echoes taking up the refrain and dying away in the distance, and still I sat spellbound, looking at that weird picture, with my neglected pipe in my hand, and a strange lassitude creeping over me.

It was the eyes which fixed me now with the unfathomable depths and absorbing intensity. They gave out no light, but seemed to draw my soul into them, and with it my life and strength as I lay inert before them, until overpowered I lost consciousness and dreamt.

I thought that the frame was still on the easel with the canvas, but the woman had stepped from them and was approaching me with a floating motion, leaving behind her a vault filled with coffins, some of them shut down whilst others lay or stood upright and open, showing the grizzly contents in their decaying and stained cerements.

I could only see her head and shoulders with the sombre drapery of the upper portion and the inky wealth of hair hanging round.

She was with me now, that pallid face touching my face and those cold bloodless lips glued to mine with a close lingering kiss, while the soft black hair covered me like a cloud and thrilled me through and through with a delicious thrill that, whilst it made me grow faint, intoxicated me with delight.

As I breathed she seemed to absorb it quickly into herself, giving me back nothing, getting stronger as I was becoming weaker, while the warmth of my contact passed into her and made her palpitate with vitality.

And all at once the horror of approaching death seized upon me, and with a frantic effort I flung her from me and started up from my chair dazed for a moment and uncertain where I was, then consciousness returned and I looked round wildly.

The gas was still blazing brightly, while the fire burned ruddy in the stove. By the timepiece on the mantel I could see that it was half-past twelve.

The picture and frame were still on the easel, only as I looked at them the portrait had changed, a hectic flush was on the cheeks while the eyes glittered with life and the sensuous lips were red and ripe-looking with a drop of blood still upon the nether one. In a frenzy of horror I seized my scraping knife and slashed out the vampire picture, then tearing the mutilated fragments out I crammed them into my stove and watched them frizzle with savage delight.

I have that frame still, but I have not yet had courage to paint suitable subject for it.

# The Vampire Maid

## HUME NISBET

It was the exact kind of abode that I had been looking after for weeks, for I was in that condition of mind when absolute renunciation of society was a necessity. I had become diffident of myself, and wearied of my kind. A strange unrest was in my blood; a barren dearth in my brains. Familiar objects and faces had grown distasteful to me. I wanted to be alone.

This is the mood which comes upon every sensitive and artistic mind when the possessor has been overworked or living too long in one groove. It is Nature's hint for him to seek pastures new; the sign that a retreat has become needful.

If he does not yield, he breaks down and becomes whimsical and hypochondriacal, as well as hypercritical. It is always a bad sign when a man becomes over-critical and censorious about his own or other people's work, for it means that he is losing the vital portions of work, freshness and enthusiasm.

Before I arrived at the dismal stage of criticism I hastily packed up my knapsack, and taking the train to Westmorland I began my tramp in search of solitude, bracing air, and romantic surroundings.

Many places I came upon during that early summer wandering that appeared to have almost the required conditions, yet some petty drawback prevented me from deciding. Sometimes it was the scenery that I did not take kindly to. At other places I took sudden antipathies to the landlady or landlord, and felt I would abhor them before a week was spent under their charge. Other places which might have suited me I could not have, as they did not want a lodger. Fate was driving me to this Cottage on the Moor, and no one can resist destiny.

One day I found myself on a wide and pathless moor near the sea. I had slept the night before at a small hamlet, but that was already eight miles in my rear, and since I had turned my back upon it I had nor seen any signs of humanity; I was alone with a fair sky above me, a balmy ozone-filled wind blowing over the stony and heather-clad mounds, and nothing to disturb my meditations.

How far the moor stretched I had no knowledge; I only knew that by keeping in a straight line I would come to the ocean cliffs, then perhaps after a time arrive at some fishing village.

I had provisions in my knapsack, and being young did not fear a night under the stars. I was inhaling the delicious summer air and once more getting back the vigour and happiness I had lost; my city-dried brains were again becoming juicy.

Thus hour after hour slid past me, with the paces, until I had covered about fifteen miles since morning, when I saw before me in the distance a solitary stone-built cottage with roughly slated roof. "I'll camp there if possible," I said to myself as I quickened my steps towards it.

To one in search of a quiet, free life, nothing could have possibly been more suitable than this cottage. It stood on the edge of lofty cliffs, with its front door facing the moor and the back-yard wall overlooking the ocean. The sound of the dancing waves struck upon my ears like a lullaby as I drew near; how they would thunder when the autumn gales came on and the seabirds fled shrieking to the shelter of the sedges.

A small garden spread in front, surrounded by a dry-stone wall just high enough for one to lean lazily upon when inclined. This garden was a flame of colour, scarlet predominating, with those other soft shades that cultivated poppies take on in their blooming, for this was all that the garden grew.

As I approached, taking notice of this singular assortment of poppies, and the orderly cleanness of the windows, the front door opened and a woman appeared who impressed me at once favourably as she leisurely came along the pathway to the gate, and drew it back as if to welcome me.

She was of middle age, and when young must have been remarkably good-looking. She was tall and still shapely, with smooth clear skin, regular features and a calm expression that at once gave me a sensation of rest.

To my inquiries she said that she could give me both a sitting and bedroom, and invited me inside to see them. As I looked at her smooth black hair, and cool brown eyes, I felt that I would not be too particular about the accommodation. With such a landlady, I was sure to find what I was after here.

The rooms surpassed my expectation, dainty white curtains and bedding with the perfume of lavender about them, a sitting-room homely yet cosy without being crowded. With a sigh of infinite relief I flung down my knapsack and clinched the bargain.

She was a widow with one daughter, whom I did not see the first day, as she was unwell and confined to her own room, but on the next day she was somewhat better, and then we met.

The fare was simple, yet it suited me exactly for the time, delicious milk and butter with home-made scones, fresh eggs and bacon; after a hearty tea I went early to bed in a condition of perfect content with my quarters.

Yet happy and tired out as I was I had by no means a comfortable night. This I put down to the strange bed. I slept certainly, but my sleep was filled with dreams so that I woke late and unrefreshed; a good walk on the moor, however, restored me, and I returned with a fine appetite for breakfast.

Certain conditions of mind, with aggravating circumstances, are required before even a young man can fall in love at first sight, as Shakespeare has shown in his Romeo and Juliet. In the city, where many fair faces passed me every hour, I had remained like a stoic, yet no sooner did I enter the cottage after that morning walk than I succumbed instantly before the weird charms of my landlady's daughter, Ariadne Brunnell.

She was somewhat better this morning and able to meet me at breakfast, for we had our meals together while I was their lodger. Ariadne was not beautiful in the strictly classical sense, her complexion being too lividly white and her expression too set to be quite pleasant at first sight; yet, as her mother had informed me, she had been ill for some time, which accounted for that defect. Her features were not regular, her hair and eyes seemed too black with that strangely white skin, and her lips too red for any except the decadent harmonies of an Aubrey Beardsley.

Yet my fantastic dreams of the preceding night, with my morning walk, had prepared me to be enthralled by this modern poster-like invalid.

The loneliness of the moor, with the singing of the ocean, had gripped my heart with a wistful longing. The incongruity of those flaunting and evanescent poppy flowers, dashing their giddy tints in the face of that sober heath, touched me with a shiver as I approached the cottage, and lastly that weird embodiment of startling contrasts completed my subjugation.

She rose from her chair as her mother introduced her, and smiled while she held out her hand. I clasped that soft snowflake, and as I did so a faint thrill tingled over me and rested on my heart, stopping for the moment its beating.

This contact seemed also to have affected her as it did me; a clear flush, like a white flame, lighted up her face, so that it glowed as if an alabaster lamp had been lit; her black eyes became softer and more humid as our glances crossed, and her scarlet lips grew moist. She was a living woman now, while before she had seemed half a corpse.

She permitted her white slender hand to remain in mine longer than most people do at an introduction, and then she slowly withdrew it, still regarding me with steadfast eyes for a second or two afterwards.

Fathomless velvety eyes these were, yet before they were shifted from mine they appeared to have absorbed all my willpower and made me her abject slave. They looked like deep dark pools of clear water, yet they filled me with fire and deprived me of strength. I sank into my chair almost as languidly as I had risen from my bed that morning.

Yet I made a good breakfast, and although she hardly tasted anything, this strange girl rose much refreshed and with a slight glow of colour on her cheeks, which improved her so greatly that she appeared younger and almost beautiful.

I had come here seeking solitude, but since I had seen Ariadne it seemed as if I had come for her only. She was not very lively; indeed, thinking back, I cannot recall any spontaneous remark of hers; she answered my questions by monosyllables and left me to lead in words; yet she was insinuating and appeared to lead my thoughts in her direction and speak to me with her eyes. I cannot describe her minutely, I only know that from the first glance and touch she gave me I was bewitched and could think of nothing else.

It was a rapid, distracting, and devouring infatuation that possessed me; all day long I followed her about like a dog, every night I dreamed of that white glowing face, those steadfast black eyes, those moist scarlet lips, and each morning I rose more languid than I had been the day before. Sometimes I dreamt that she was kissing me with those red lips, while I shivered at the contact of her silky black tresses as they covered my throat; sometimes that we were floating in the air, her arms about me and her long hair enveloping us both like an inky cloud, while I lay supine and helpless.

She went with me after breakfast on that first day to the moor, and before we came back I had spoken my love and received her assent. I held her in my arms and had taken her kisses in answer to mine, nor did I think it strange that all this had happened so quickly. She was mine, or rather I was hers, without a pause. I told her it was fate that had sent me to her, for I had no doubts about my love, and she replied that I had restored her to life.

Acting upon Ariadne's advice, and also from a natural shyness, I did not inform her mother how quickly matters had progressed between us, yet although we both acted as circumspectly as possible, I had no doubt Mrs. Brunnell could see how engrossed we were in each other. Lovers are not unlike ostriches in their modes of concealment. I was not afraid of asking Mrs. Brunnell for her daughter, for she already showed her partiality towards me, and had bestowed upon me some confidences regarding her own position in life, and I therefore knew that, so far as social position was concerned, there could be no real objection to our marriage. They lived in this lonely spot for the sake of their health, and kept no servant because they could not get any to take service so far away from other humanity. My coming had been opportune and welcome to both mother and daughter.

For the sake of decorum, however, I resolved to delay my confession for a week or two and trust to some favourable opportunity of doing it discreetly.

Meantime Ariadne and I passed our time in a thoroughly idle and lotus-eating style. Each night I retired to bed meditating starting work next day, each morning I rose languid from those disturbing dreams with no thought for anything outside my love. She grew stronger every day, while I appeared to be taking her place as the invalid, yet I was more frantically in love than ever, and only happy when with her. She was my lode-star, my only joy—my life.

We did not go great distances, for I liked best to lie on the dry heath and watch her glowing face and intense eyes while I listened to the surging of the distant waves. It was love made me lazy, I thought, for unless a man has all he longs for beside him, he is apt to copy the domestic cat and bask in the sunshine.

I had been enchanted quickly. My disenchantment came as rapidly, although it was long before the poison left my blood.

One night, about a couple of weeks after my coming to the cottage, I had returned after a delicious moonlight walk with Ariadne. The night was warm and the moon at the full, therefore I left my bedroom window open to let in what little air there was.

I was more than usually fagged out, so that I had only strength enough to remove my boots and coat before I flung myself wearily on the coverlet and fell almost instantly asleep without tasting the nightcap draught that was constantly placed on the table, and which I had always drained thirstily.

I had a ghastly dream this night. I thought I saw a monster bat, with the face and tresses of Ariadne, fly into the open window and fasten its white teeth and scarlet lips on my arm. I tried to beat the horror away, but could not, for I seemed chained down and thralled also with drowsy delight as the beast sucked my blood with a gruesome rapture.

I looked out dreamily and saw a line of dead bodies of young men lying on the floor, each with a red mark on their arms, on the same part where the vampire was then sucking me, and I remembered having seen and wondered at such a mark on my own arm for the past fortnight. In a flash I understood the reason for my strange weakness, and at the same moment a sudden prick of pain roused me from my dreamy pleasure.

The vampire in her eagerness had bitten a little too deeply that night, unaware that I had not tasted the drugged draught. As I woke I saw her fully revealed by the midnight moon, with her black tresses flowing loosely, and with her red lips glued to my arm. With a shriek of horror I dashed her backwards, getting one last glimpse of her savage eyes, glowing white face, and blood-stained red lips; then I rushed out to the night, moved on by my fear and hatred, nor did I pause in my mad flight until I had left miles between me and that accursed Cottage on the Moor.

## THE SAD STORY OF A VAMPIRE

# Eric (Count) Stenbock

Stanislaus Eric (Count) Stenbock (1859–95) was born in Estonia but studied at Oxford University before being forced to leave in disgrace after publishing a volume of homoerotic poems, *Love, Sleep and Dreams* (1881). He spent most of his short, strange life in England, founding the Idiot's Club, which also had a branch in Estonia. He mixed Catholicism, Buddhism, and paganism in bizarre rituals, and his love for animals attained absurd levels that included bringing them to the dinner table. He was an abuser of opium and alcohol, leading to cirrhosis of the liver.

Stenbock is scarcely remembered today, with his three volumes of suicidally sad, languid, supernatural, and perverted poems surviving in only single copies of their original editions. His only short-story collection, *Studies of Death: Romantic Tales,* contained seven stories and had a cover designed by Stenbock himself, depicting a graveyard scene. His clear, straightforward narrative style has been compared to Guy de Maupassant's.

It was said that on the day he died in a drunken stupor, his face appeared at his uncle's window, echoing a similar incident in one of his poems.

"The Sad Story of a Vampire" was first published in book form in *Studies of Death: Romantic Tales* (London: Nutt, 1894).

# The Sad Story of a Vampire

## ERIC (COUNT) STENBOCK

**V**ampire stories are generally located in Styria; mine is also. Styria is by no means the romantic kind of place described by those who have certainly never been there. It is a flat, uninteresting country, only celebrated by its turkeys, its capons, and the stupidity of its inhabitants. Vampires generally arrive at night, in carriages drawn by two black horses.

Our Vampire arrived by the commonplace means of the railway train, and in the afternoon. You must think I am joking, or perhaps that by the word "Vampire" I mean a financial vampire. No, I am quite serious. The Vampire of whom I am speaking, who laid waste our hearth and home, was a *real* vampire.

Vampires are generally described as dark, sinister-looking, and singularly handsome. Our Vampire was, on the contrary, rather fair, and certainly was not at first sight sinister-looking, and though decidedly attractive in appearance, not what one would call singularly handsome.

Yes, he desolated our home, killed my brother—the one object of my adoration—also my dear father. Yet, at the same time, I must say that I myself came under the spell of his fascination, and, in spite of all, have no ill-will towards him now.

Doubtless you have read in the papers *passim* of "the Baroness and her beasts." It is to tell how I came to spend most of my useless wealth on an asylum for stray animals that I am writing this.

I am old now; what happened then was when I was a little girl of about thirteen. I will begin by describing our household. We were Poles; our name was Wronski: we lived in Styria, where we had a castle. Our household was very limited. It consisted, with the exclusion of domestics, of only my father, our governess—a worthy Belgian named Mademoiselle Vonnaert—my brother, and myself. Let me begin with my father: he was old, and both my brother and I were children of his old age. Of my mother I remember nothing: she died in giving birth to my brother, who is only one year, or not as much, younger than myself. Our father was studious, continually occupied in reading books, chiefly on recondite subjects and in all kinds of unknown languages. He had a long white beard, and wore habitually a black velvet skull-cap.

How kind he was to us! It was more than I could tell. Still it was not I who was the favorite. His whole heart went out to Gabriel—"Gabryel" as we spelled it in Polish. He was always called by the Russian abbreviation Gavril—I mean, of course, my brother, who had a resemblance to the only portrait of my mother, a slight chalk sketch which hung in my father's study. But I was by no means jealous: my brother was and has been the only love of my life. It is for his sake that I am now keeping in Westbourne Park a home for stray cats and dogs.

I was at that time, as I said before, a little girl; my name was Carmela. My long tangled hair was always all over the place, and never would be combed straight. I was not pretty—at least, looking at a photograph of me at that time, I do not think I could describe myself as such. Yet at the same time, when I look at the photograph, I think my expression may have been pleasing to some people: irregular features, large mouth, and large wild eyes.

I was by way of being naughty—not so naughty as Gabriel in the opinion of Mlle. Vonnaert. Mlle. Vonnaert, I may interpose, was a wholly excellent person, middle-aged, who really *did* speak good French, although she was a Belgian, and could also make herself understood in German, which, as you may or may not know, is the current language of Styria.

I find it difficult to describe my brother Gabriel; there was something about him strange and superhuman, or perhaps I should rather say praeterhuman, something between the animal and the divine. Perhaps the Greek idea of the Faun might illustrate what I mean; but that will not do either. He had large, wild, gazelle-like eyes: his hair, like mine, was in a perpetual tangle—that point he had in common with me, and indeed, as I afterwards heard, our mother having been of gypsy race, it will account for much of the innate wildness there was in our natures. I was wild enough, but Gabriel was much wilder. Nothing would induce him to put on shoes and socks, except on Sundays—when he also allowed his hair to be combed, but only by me. How shall I describe the grace of that lovely mouth, shaped verily "en arc d'amour." I always think of the text in the Psalm, "Grace is shed forth on thy lips, therefore has God blessed thee eternally"—lips that seemed to exhale the very breath of life. Then that beautiful, lithe, living, elastic form!

He could run faster than any deer: spring like a squirrel to the topmost branch of a tree: he might have stood for the sign and symbol of vitality itself. But seldom could he be induced by Mlle. Vonnaert to learn lessons; but when he did so, he learned with extraordinary quickness. He would play upon every conceivable instrument, holding a violin here, there, and everywhere except the right place: manufacturing instruments for himself out of reeds—even sticks. Mlle. Vonnaert made futile efforts to induce him to learn to play the piano. I suppose he was what was called spoiled, though merely in the superficial sense of the word. Our father allowed him to indulge in every caprice.

One of his peculiarities, when quite a little child, was horror at the sight of meat. Nothing on earth would induce him to taste it. Another thing which was particularly remarkable about him was his extraordinary power over animals. Everything seemed to come tame to his hand. Birds would sit on his shoulder. Then sometimes Mlle. Vonnaert and I would lose him in the woods—he would suddenly dart away. Then we would find him singing softly or whistling to himself, with all manner of woodland creatures around him—hedgehogs, little foxes, wild rabbits, marmots, squirrels, and such like. He would frequently bring these things home with him and insist on keeping them. This strange menagerie was the terror of poor Mlle. Vonnaert's heart. He chose to live in a little room at the top of a turret; but which, instead of going upstairs, he chose to reach by means of a very tall chestnut tree, through the window. But in contradiction to all this, it was his custom to serve every Sunday Mass in the parish church, with hair nicely combed and with white surplice and red cassock. He looked as demure and tamed as possible. Then came the element of the divine. What an expression of ecstasy there was in those glorious eyes!

Thus far I have not been speaking about the Vampire. However, let me begin with my narrative at last. One day my father had to go to the neighboring town—as he frequently had. This time he returned accompanied by a guest. The gentleman, he said, had missed his train, through the late arrival of another at our station, which was a junction, and he would therefore, as trains were not frequent in our parts, have had to wait there all night. He had joined in conversation with my father in the too-late-arriving train from the town: and had consequently accepted my father's invitation to stay the night at our house. But of course, you know, in those out-of-the-way parts we are almost patriarchal in our hospitality.

He was announced under the name of Count Vardalek—the name being Hungarian. But he spoke German well enough: not with the monotonous accentuation of Hungarians, but rather, if anything, with a slight Slavonic intonation. His voice was peculiarly soft and insinuating. We soon afterwards found out he could talk Polish, and Mlle. Vonnaert vouched for his good French. Indeed he seemed to know all languages. But let me give my first impressions. He was rather tall, with fair wavy hair, rather long, which accentuated a certain effeminacy about his smooth face. His figure had something—I cannot say what—serpentine about it. The features were refined; and he had long, slender, subtle, magnetic-looking hands, a somewhat long sinuous nose, a graceful mouth, and an attractive smile, which belied the intense sadness of the expression of the eyes. When he arrived his eyes were half closed—indeed they were habitually so—so that I could not decide their color. He looked worn and wearied. I could not possibly guess his age.

Suddenly Gabriel burst into the room: a yellow butterfly was clinging to his hair. He was carrying in his arms a little squirrel. Of course he was bare-legged as usual. The stranger looked up at his approach; then I noticed his eyes. They were green: they seemed to dilate and grow larger. Gabriel stood stock-still, with a startled look, like that of a bird fascinated by a serpent. But nevertheless he held out his hand to the newcomer. Vardalek, taking his hand—I don't know why I noticed this trivial thing—pressed the pulse with his forefinger. Suddenly Gabriel darted from the room and rushed upstairs, going to his turret-room this time by the staircase instead of the tree. I was in terror what the Count might think of him. Great was my relief when he came down in his velvet

Sunday suit, and shoes and stockings. I combed his hair, and set him generally right.

When the stranger came down to dinner his appearance had somewhat altered; he looked much younger. There was an elasticity of the skin, combined with a delicate complexion, rarely to be found in a man. Before, he had struck me as being very pale.

Well, at dinner we were all charmed with him, especially my father. He seemed to be thoroughly acquainted with all my father's particular hobbies. Once, when my father was relating some of his military experiences, he said something about a drummer-boy who was wounded in battle. His eyes opened completely again and dilated: this time with a particularly disagreeable expression, dull and dead, yet at the same time animated by some horrible excitement. But this was only momentary.

The chief subject of his conversation with my father was about certain curious mystical books which my father had just lately picked up, and which he could not make out, but Vardalek seemed completely to understand. At dessert-time my father asked him if he were in a great hurry to reach his destination: if not, would he not stay with us a little while: though our place was out of the way, he would find much that would interest him in his library.

He answered, "I am in no hurry. I have no particular reason for going to that place at all, and if I can be of service to you in deciphering these books, I shall be only too glad." He added with a smile which was bitter, very very bitter:

"You see I am a cosmopolitan, a wanderer on the face of the earth."

After dinner my father asked him if he played the piano. He said, "Yes, I can a little," and he sat down at the piano. Then he played a Hungarian csardas—wild, rhapsodic, wonderful.

That is the music which makes men mad. He went on in the same strain.

Gabriel stood stock-still by the piano, his eyes dilated and fixed, his form quivering. At last he said very slowly, at one particular motive—for want of a better word you may call it the *relâche* of a csardas, by which I mean that point where the original quasi-slow movement begins again—"Yes, I think I could play that."

Then he quickly fetched his fiddle and self-made xylophone, and did actually, alternating the instruments, render the same very well indeed.

Vardalek looked at him, and said in a very sad voice, "Poor child! You have the soul of music within you."

I could not understand why he should seem to commiserate instead of congratulate Gabriel on what certainly showed an extraordinary talent.

Gabriel was shy even as the wild animals who were tame to him. Never before had he taken to a stranger. Indeed, as a rule, if any stranger came to the house by any chance, he would hide himself, and I had to bring him up his food to the turret chamber. You may imagine what was my surprise when I saw him walking about hand in hand with Vardalek the next morning, in the garden, talking livelily with him, and showing his collection of pet animals, which he had gathered from the woods, and for which we had had to fit up a regular zoological gardens. He seemed utterly under the domination of Vardalek. What surprised us was (for otherwise we liked the stranger, especially for being kind to him) that he seemed, though not noticeably at first—except perhaps to me, who noticed everything with regard to him—to be gradually losing his general health and vitality. He did not become pale as yet; but there was a certain languor about his movements which certainly there was by no means before.

My father got more and more devoted to Count Vardalek. He helped him in his studies: and my father would hardly allow him to go away, which he did sometimes—to Trieste, he said: he always came back, bringing us presents of strange Oriental jewelry or textures.

I knew all kinds of people came to Trieste, Orientals included. Still, there was a strangeness and magnificence about these things which I was sure even then could not possibly have come from such a place as Trieste, memorable to me chiefly for its necktie shops.

When Vardalek was away, Gabriel was continually asking for him and talking about him. Then at the same time he seemed to regain his old vitality and spirits. Vardalek always returned looking much older, wan, and weary. Gabriel would rush to meet him, and kiss him on the mouth. Then he gave a slight shiver: and after a little while began to look quite young again.

Things continued like this for some time. My father would not hear of Vardalek's going away permanently. He came to be an inmate of our house. I indeed, and Mlle. Vonnaert also, could not help noticing what a difference there was altogether about Gabriel. But my father seemed totally blind to it.

One night I had gone downstairs to fetch something which I had left in the drawing-room. As I was going up again I passed Vardalek's room. He was playing on a piano, which had been specially put there for him, one of Chopin's nocturnes, very beautifully: I stopped, leaning on the banisters to listen.

Something white appeared on the dark staircase. We believed in ghosts in our part. I was transfixed with terror, and clung to the banisters. What was my astonishment to see Gabriel walking slowly down the staircase, his eyes fixed as though in a trance! This terrified me even more than a ghost would. Could I believe my senses? Could that be Gabriel?

I simply could not move. Gabriel, clad in his long white nightshirt, came downstairs and opened the door. He left it open. Vardalek still continued playing, but talked as he played.

He said—this time speaking in Polish—*Nie umiem wyrazic jak ciehie kocham*—"My darling, I fain would spare thee; but thy life is my life, and I must live, I who would rather die. Will God not have *any* mercy on me? Oh! oh! life; oh the torture of life!" Here he struck one agonized and strange chord, then continued playing softly, "O Gabriel, my beloved! My life, yes *life*—oh, why life? I am sure this is but a little that I demand of thee. Surely thy superabundance of life can spare a little to one who is already dead. No, stay," he said now almost harshly, "what must be, must be!"

Gabriel stood there quite still, with the same fixed vacant expression, in the room. He was evidently walking in his sleep. Vardalek played on: then said, "Ah!" with a sigh of terrible agony. Then very gently, "Go now, Gabriel; it is enough." And Gabriel went out of the room and ascended the staircase at the same slow pace, with the same unconscious stare. Vardalek struck the piano, and although he did not play loudly, it seemed as though the strings would break. You never heard music so strange and so heart-rending!

I only know I was found by Mlle. Vonnaert in the morning, in an unconscious state, at the foot of the stairs. Was it a dream after all? I am sure now that it was not. I thought then it might be, and said nothing to any one about it. Indeed, what could I say?

Well, to let me cut a long story short, Gabriel, who had never known a moment's sickness in his life, grew ill: and we had to send to Gratz for a doctor, who could give no explanation of Gabriel's strange illness. Gradual wasting away, he said: absolutely no organic complaint. What could this mean?

My father at last became conscious of the fact that Gabriel was ill. His anxiety was fearful. The last trace of grey faded from his hair, and it became quite white. We sent to Vienna for doctors. But all with the same result.

Gabriel was generally unconscious, and when conscious, only seemed to recognize Vardalek, who sat continually by his bedside, nursing him with the utmost tenderness.

One day I was alone in the room: and Vardalek cried suddenly, almost fiercely, "Send for a priest at once, at once," he repeated. "It is now almost too late!"

Gabriel stretched out his arms spasmodically, and put them round Vardalek's neck. This was the only movement he had made for some time. Vardalek bent down and kissed him on the lips. I rushed downstairs: and the priest was sent for. When I came back Vardalek was not there. The priest administered extreme unction. I think Gabriel was already dead, although we did not think so at the time.

Vardalek had utterly disappeared; and when we looked for him he was nowhere to be found; nor have I seen or heard of him since.

My father died very soon afterwards: suddenly aged, and bent down with grief. And so the whole of the Wronski property came into my sole possession. And here I am, an old woman, generally laughed at for keeping, in memory of Gabriel, an asylum for stray animals—and—people do not, as a rule, believe in Vampires!

# A CASE OF ALLEGED VAMPIRISM

# Luigi Capuana

Luigi Capuana (1839–1915) was born in Mineo in the province of Catania in Sicily, the son of wealthy landowners. After graduating from the Royal College of Bronte, Catania, he attended the Faculty of Law at Catania from 1857 to 1860, resigning to become the secretary of the Secret Committee of Insurrection, later becoming chancellor of the civic council. He moved to Florence in 1864 to begin a serious literary career, although he had already released the highly important drama *Garibaldi* (1861) in three cantos. It was in Florence where he became acquainted with the most respected Italian authors of the era, wrote critical essays for the *Italian Review*, became a theater critic for *Nation*, and wrote his first novella, *Dr. Cymbalus*, which was published serially in a daily newspaper. He returned to Sicily in 1868.

His novels and other works were among the first Italian examples of naturalism in literature. They had profound pathological and occult tendencies as well as serious psychological themes, though they often were denounced for being merely pseudoscientific. He had been influenced by the novels of Émile Zola and the idealistic philosophy of Georg Wilhelm Friedrich Hegel, and in turn influenced Giovanni Verga and Luigi Pirandello. He also wrote fairy tales for children.

"A Case of Alleged Vampirism" was first published in Rome by Enrico Voghera in 1907 and titled "The Vampire."

# A Case of Alleged Vampirism

## LUIGI CAPUANA

It's no laughing matter!" said Lelio Giorgi. "Why shouldn't I laugh?" replied Mongeri. "*I* don't believe in ghosts."

"Neither did I, once . . . and I'd still rather not," went on Giorgi. 'That's why I've come to see you. You might be able to explain whatever it is that's making my life a misery and wrecking my marriage."

"*Whatever it is?* You mean whatever you *imagine* it is. You're not well. It's true that a hallucination is itself a fact, but what it represents has no reality outside yourself. Or, to put it better, it's the externalization of a sensation, a sort of projection of yourself, so that the eye sees what it in fact does not see, and the ear hears sounds that were never made. Previous impressions, often stored up unconsciously, project themselves rather like events in dreams. We still don't know how or why. We dream, and that's the right word, with our eyes wide open. But one has to distinguish between split-second hallucinations which don't necessarily indicate any organic or psychic disturbance, and those of a more persistent nature. . . . But of course that's not the case with you."

"But it *is*, with me *and* my wife."

"You don't understand. What we scientists call persistent hallucinations are those experienced by the insane. I don't have to give you an example. . . . The fact that you both suffer the same hallucinations is just a case of simple induction. You probably must have influenced your wife's nervous system."

"No. She was the first."

"Then you mean that your nervous system, having a greater receptivity, was the one to be influenced. And don't turn up your poetical nose at what you please to call my scientific jargon. It has its uses."

"If you would just let me get a word in edgeways . . ."

"Some things are best let well alone. Do you want a scientific explanation? Well, the answer is that for the moment you wouldn't get anything of the sort. We are in the realm of hypotheses. One today, a different one tomorrow, and a different one the day after. You are a curious lot, you artists! When you feel like it you make fun of Science, you undervalue the whole business of experiment, research, and hypothesis that makes it progress; then when a case comes along that interests you personally you want a clear, precise, and categorical answer. And there are scientists who play the game, out of conviction or vanity. But I'm not one of them. You want the plain truth? Science is the greatest proof of our own ignorance. To calm you down I can talk of hallucinations, of induction, receptivity. Words! Words! The more I study the more I despair of ever knowing anything for certain. It seems to happen on purpose; no sooner do scientists get a kick out of some new law they've discovered than along comes some new fact, some discovery, that upsets the lot. You need to take it easy, just let life flow by; what's happened to you and your wife has happened to so many others. It will pass. Why must you try and find out how and why it happened? Are you scared of dreams?"

"If you'd just let me tell you . . ."

"Go on then, tell me, if you want to get it off your chest. But I warn you, it can only make matters worse. The only way to get over it, is to busy yourself with other things, get away from it. Find a new devil to drive out the old—it's a good saying."

"We did all that. It wasn't any good. The first signs . . . the first manifestations, happened in the country, in our villa at Foscolara. We ran away from it, but the very night that we came back to town . . ."

"It's natural. What distraction could you find in your own house? You ought to travel, stay in hotels, one day here, another day there; spend the whole day sightseeing, looking at churches, museums, go to the theatre, come back late at night, tired out. . . ."

"We did all that too, but . . ."

"Just the two of you, on your own. You should have been with a friend, a party. . . ."

"But we were; it wasn't any good."

"It all depends on the party!"

"But they were a lively crowd. . . ."

"Selfish, you mean, and there you were, isolated, I know. . . ."

"But we were lively too, when we were with them. But you can hardly expect them to have come and slept with us. . . ."

"Then you *were* asleep? Really I don't know what you mean any more, dreams or hallucinations. . . ."

"To hell with your dreams and hallucinations. We were wide awake and completely sound in

mind and body, just as I am now, if you would only let me get a word in edgeways. . . ."

"As you wish."

"Well, you could at least let me give you the facts."

"I know. I can imagine it all. The books are full of them. There could be small differences in detail . . . but they don't count. The essentials are the same."

"Can't I even have the satisfaction of . . ."

"You can. Hundreds of them. You are one of those who seem to want to lay up troubles for themselves, even make them worse. . . . I'm sorry, that's stupid! But if it would please you . . ."

"Quite frankly, you seem to me to be scared."

"Scared of what? A nice idea!"

"Scared of having to change your mind. You've just said, 'I do not believe in ghosts.' And what if I force you to believe in them?"

"All right then. It would be a blow. What do you expect? We scientists are like that, we're men after all. When our way of seeing things, of judging them, takes a knock, the intellect refuses to follow the senses. Even intelligence is a matter of habit. But now you have me with my back to the wall. All right then. Let's hear your precious facts."

*W*ell," said Lelio Giorgi with a sigh, "you know already the unhappy background to my years in America. Luisa's parents were against our marrying—and they may well have been right, they were thinking above all of the economic situation of their future son-in-law—they had no faith in my abilities, and were doubtful about my future as a poet. That slim volume of early verse was my worst enemy. I haven't even written, let alone published, any more from that day to this, yet even now you called me 'poetical.' The label stuck. Oh well."

"Just like you writers to go right back to the remote beginning."

"Don't get impatient. Listen. I had no news of Luisa for the three years I was in Buenos Aires. Then came that rich uncle's will, after he had nothing to do with me while he was alive. I came back to Europe, hurried to London, and flew here with £200,000 in my pocket, only to find that Luisa had been married for six months! And I was as much in love with her as ever. The poor girl must have given in to family pressure. At that time I might have done anything. . . . All these details are important. . . . I was stupid enough, however, to write her a letter full of violent reproaches. I never thought that it could have fallen into the hands of her husband. The next day he turned up at my house, having realized the folly of my behaviour, and determined to persuade me to calm down. He was calm himself.

"'I have come to give you your letter back,' he said. 'I opened it by mistake, not out of inquisitiveness; and it's just as well I did. I am assured that you are a gentleman. I have every respect for your distress, but I do trust you have no intention of needlessly disturbing the peace of a family. If you can bring yourself to think things over you will realize that nobody wished to harm you intentionally. It was pure misfortune. You must see now where your duty lies, and I can tell you quite plainly that I am determined to defend my domestic happiness at all costs.'

"He was pale as he spoke, and his voice trembled.

"'I must apologize for my indiscretion,' I replied, 'and to reassure you I can add that tomorrow I shall be leaving for Paris.' I must have been even paler than him, the words would hardly come. I held out my hand, he shook it. And I kept my word. Six months later I received a telegram from Luisa: 'I am a widow. I still love you. And you?' Her husband had been dead for two months."

"Such is life; it's an ill wind. . . ."

"And that's what I somewhat selfishly thought; but it isn't always true. I had never been so happy in my life as I was on my wedding night and during the following months. We both of us avoided any mention of *him*. Luisa had destroyed every trace. Not out of ingratitude, for he had done everything to make her happy, but because she was afraid that even the slightest memory would have upset me. And she was right. Sometimes the thought that someone else, however legitimately, had once

possessed her, made me tremble from head to foot. I could scarcely hide it from her. Often she must have sensed this, and her lovely eyes were clouded with tears. But how radiant she looked on the day she felt sure enough to tell me of the expected arrival of a child. I remember it clearly, we were drinking coffee, I was standing and she was sitting down, with a look of touching weariness. And that was the first time she had ever made any reference to the past: 'How glad I am that this didn't happen *then*!' she exclaimed.

"A loud crash was heard at the door, as if someone had struck it a blow with their fist. We leapt up. I rushed out to see what had happened, imagining it was one of the servants, but the adjoining room was empty."

"It could have been one of the beams in the house shrinking in the heat."

"That was how I explained it to Luisa, seeing how upset she was, but I was not convinced myself. I felt somehow disturbed. We waited some minutes, nothing happened. But from then onwards I noticed that Luisa avoided being left on her own; she was still upset, though she would not admit it and I dared not question her."

"And now I see how you were both influencing each other, without realizing it."

"Not at all. A few days later I was laughing at the whole episode, and thought that Luisa's agitated state of mind was due to her condition. Then even she seemed to calm down. Eventually the child was born. After a few months, however, I noticed that the old feeling of fear and terror had returned. At night, all of a sudden, she would cling to me, cold and trembling. 'What is it? Are you ill?' I would ask anxiously. 'I'm frightened, didn't you hear?' 'No.' 'Don't you hear?' she insisted the following night. 'No.' Though this time I had heard the sound of footsteps in the room, pacing up and down, by the bed: I said 'no' so as not to frighten her anymore. I raised my head and looked around, 'It must be a mouse in the room. . . .' 'I'm afraid! . . . I'm afraid! . . .' And for several nights, at the same time, the same shuffling, the same uncanny coming and going, up and down, by the bed. We lay and waited for it!"

"And your jangling nerves did the rest."

"You know me; I'm not the sort to get worked up easily. I put up a brave show, because of Luisa; I tried to explain things: echoes of distant sounds, accidental resonances in the structure of the villa. . . . We went back to town. But that very night the phenomena turned up again worse than before. Twice the bedstead was shaken violently. I peered out. 'It's he! It's he!' stammered Luisa, huddled under the bedclothes."

"If you don't mind my saying so," interrupted Mongeri, "*I* wouldn't marry a widow for all the gold in the world! Something of the dead husband always remains with her, in spite of everything. Your wife wasn't seeing his ghost. 'It's *he*' is the 'he' of the sensations he left behind him, purely physiological."

"Well, maybe so," replied Lelio Giorgi. "But in that case where do *I* come in?"

"Suggestion. Now it seems perfectly plain."

"Suggestion only at specified times in the middle of the night?"

"Just waiting for it to happen would be enough."

"Well then, how can the phenomena vary every time when my imagination isn't working at all?"

"That's what you think; the Unconscious at work."

"Do let me go on. Keep your explanations until I've finished. Just note that the following morning we were able to discuss the matter with relative calm. Luisa described her impressions and I told her of mine, in such a way that I was convinced that it could not have been an unpleasant trick played on us by our over-excited imaginations; the same blow on the bedstead, the same tugging at the sheets in the same circumstances, when I was trying to comfort her with a kiss and prevent her from crying, as if this itself had provoked the malice of the invisible person. Then one night Luisa flung her arms round my neck and whispered in my ear in a voice that made me shudder: 'He spoke!' 'What did he say?' 'I couldn't hear. Now! He said: You're mine!' And as I held her closer I felt her being dragged violently away from me by two powerful hands, and I had to give way in spite of her resistance."

"What resistance could she offer to what must have been her own behaviour?"

"All right. . . . But I felt it too, a something trying to stop her coming into contact with me. . . . I saw her flung back with a jolt . . . then she tried to get to her feet, to go to the child, who was sleeping in the cot at the foot of the bed. Then we heard the cot wheels squeaking and saw it tossed across the room, blankets flying in all directions; that wasn't a hallucination. We picked things up, made up the cot, and soon they were flying through the air again and the child was whimpering with fear. Three nights later it was even worse. Luisa seemed drawn completely under *his* evil spell. She seemed unaware of me when I spoke to her, as if I were no longer there. She seemed to be talking to *him* and I could tell from her replies what he was saying to her. 'But can it be his fault that you are dead?' 'No, no, no, how could you think so? *I*, poison you? That's monstrous!' 'And what can the child have done to harm you?' 'But why are you unhappy? I have prayed for you . . . .' 'Why don't you want my prayers? You want *me*, but how can you, you're dead!' I tried without success to shake her from the trance. Then she came to. 'Did you hear that?' she said. 'He says I poisoned him. *You* wouldn't believe that of me. . . . O God! What about the child? He'll kill him. Did you hear?' I heard nothing, but I was well aware that Luisa was not raving. She wept, clutching the child to her. 'What shall we do? What shall we do?' "

"But the child was all right. That must have reassured her."

"What can you expect? This sort of thing would upset even the most strong-minded. I myself am not superstitious; but I'm not a free-thinker either. I just don't have much time for religion. But in a case like this, and with my wife saying, 'I'll pray for you,' I naturally thought of calling in a priest."

"You had him exorcize it?"

"No, but I had a blessing said in the house, with a fine sprinkling of holy water . . . as much to influence poor Luisa, if it really were a case of nerves, as anything. Luisa is a religious person. You can laugh; I'd like to have seen what you would have done in my place."

"What about the holy water?"

"Useless. No effect at all."

"Not a bad idea, though. Some nervous diseases can be cured that way. We had a case of a man who thought his nose was being stretched. The doctor went through all the motions of an operation, without actually doing anything, and the man was cured."

"But the holy water in fact made things worse. The next night . . . My God! I can't bear to think of it. This time *he* seemed to be taking everything out on the child. . . . It was awful. When Luisa saw . . ."

"Or thought she saw . . ."

"Saw, man, saw . . . And *I* saw too, almost. She couldn't get near the cot, something was holding her back. There she was, stretching out her hands to the child, while that *thing*—she described it to me—bent over the baby and did something horrible, its lips pressed to his mouth, sucking his blood. . . . For three nights this ghastly process has been repeated, and the poor little thing . . . you wouldn't recognize him. . . . He used to be so plump and rosy, and now . . . in only three nights . . . he's wasted away. This can't be imagination. Come and see for yourself."

"So it could really be? . . ."

Mongeri thought for a few minutes, frowning. The sarcastic and somewhat pitying smile with which he had listened to Lelio Giorgi had vanished all of a sudden. Then he looked up and said:

"So it could really be? . . . Listen. I can't explain anything because I'm convinced there is no explanation. One can't be more skeptical than that. But I could give you some advice, which might make you laugh, coming from me. . . . Anyway, that's up to you."

"I'll do as you suggest, at once."

"You would need several days for what you have to do. I'll help you to cut it as short as possible. I don't doubt the facts you've put before me. And I ought to add that since Science has come to examine this kind of problem, it, too, has been less skeptical. It has now become a question of trying to see this sort of thing as a natural phenomenon; but a physical problem, not a spiritual one. That's not our province; we leave that to priests or spiritualists. We are concerned with the flesh, blood, and bone that go to make an individual and disintegrate into their original elements when he dies. But then the question arises, does this disintegration, this cessation of organic function end instantaneously with death, annulling all individuality, or does this persist, in some cases, for any amount of time after death? One is beginning to suspect that this could be the case. And Science is on the verge of coming round to popular beliefs. I have been studying for three years now the empirical remedies of 'old wives' and witches and I am coming to the conclusion that they are in fact the remnants of the ancient secret sciences and also, even more likely, of the instincts we can still observe in animals. When man was closer to animals he knew instinctively the medicinal value of certain herbs, but as he evolved away from them he lost this primitive use of certain faculties, and the tradition died out. Only the honest peasant women, in whom it was more deeply rooted, preserved some of these natural medicines; and I think that Science should study them, for every superstition contains something more than mere popular error. I'm sorry about this digression. . . . What scientists now admit, that the existence of an individual does not cease at death, but only when actual decomposition of the body has taken place, popular superstition has already acknowledged through the belief in vampires, and has even offered a remedy. Vampires are individuals, rare but not unheard of, who persist after death. You may look surprised, but this is a case, and not the only one, where science and popular superstition, or rather, primitive intuition, find themselves at one. And what is the only defense against this evil thing, this disembodied individual sucking the blood and life-force from healthy individuals? The complete destruction of its former body. Where vampires have been known to occur the victims have run to the grave, dug up the body, and burned it; then the vampire really does die, and the visitations cease. Now you were saying that your child . . ."

"Come and see him, you wouldn't recognize him. Luisa is going crazy. And I'm not far off myself. I keep saying to myself that it can't be true, it couldn't possibly happen; I even think: 'Well, if she did poison him, it was for my sake, it shows how much she loves me. . . . ' But it won't work, the thought repels me, *she* repels me even . . . all *his* doing! And the reproaches go on, I can tell by her replies. 'What? Poison you? . . . How can you believe such a thing?' Life has become impossible, for months now we have gone on like this. You are the first person I have dared to confide in. I'm desperate, I need help. . . . And we would have put up with everything if it weren't for the child."

"As a friend and as a scientist, I give you this advice: Have the body cremated. Your wife will easily get permission, and I will help you to speed up the formalities. And Science herself would not be ashamed to have recourse to somewhat empirical methods, trying out a remedy which might well be a superstition in appearance only, seeking out the truth by unconventional methods. Cremate the body. Seriously," he added, seeing from the look in his friend's eye that he feared he was being treated like one of the ignorant populace.

"But what about the child?" cried Lelio Giorgi, wringing his hands. "One night I lost my temper and threw myself at him yelling, 'Get out! For God's sake get out!' But I was stopped dead in my tracks, unable to move, mumbling, with the words drying up in my throat. You can't imagine. . . ."

"Would you allow me to accompany you tonight?"

"I hardly dared to ask you such a favour. . . . But perhaps it would upset him even more; would you leave it until tomorrow?"

But the next day he returned in such shattered state that Mongeri really wondered if he had gone out of his mind.

"He knows!" stammered Lelio Giorgi. "God, what a night! He swore he would do the most terrible things if we dared to . . ."

"All the more reason for daring," replied Mongeri.

"If you had seen the cot tossed about! I don't know how the poor child survived! Luisa had to get down on her knees to him, weeping. 'I will be yours, all yours, only please don't hurt the child!' And I felt at that moment that every link with her was broken, that she belonged to him again and not to me."

"Calm down! We shall get rid of him. Let me come round tonight."

Mongeri went, thinking, convinced that his presence would keep the vampire away. "It's always the case, a neutral, indifferent force will counteract the unknown thing. We don't yet know how or why, but continued observation and study will show."

And in the early hours of the night this seemed to be the case. Luisa looked anxiously around but nothing happened. The child slept untroubled in his cot, pale and wan. Lelio Giorgi did his best to conceal his worry, but kept glancing fearfully from his wife to the complacent Mongeri. They kept up a conversation on various topics. Mongeri was describing some highly amusing incident on one of his holidays; he was a good talker, without any of his professional pomposity, and he hoped to distract the attention of both of them, so that if the phenomenon did occur he could observe it uninterrupted, when suddenly, as he glanced at the cot, he noticed a slight movement, which could not have been caused by either of the parents, since they were sitting at the other side of the room. He stopped, and they leapt to their feet. By the time they had followed his gaze to the cot it was rocking with some violence. Luisa cried "O heavens, my poor child!" and rushed towards the cot, but was stopped short and sank back onto the couch. Pale as death, she rolled her eyes in terror and muttered something unintelligible, on the point of suffocating.

"It's nothing!" said Mongeri, rising himself, and grasping the hand of Lelio, who was shaken with terror. Then Luisa, with a violent shudder, returned to her normal self though with her attention fixed on some invisible person, listening to words they could not hear but at which they could guess from the sense of her replies.

"Why do you say that I keep on wanting to hurt you? . . . But I've prayed for you. . . . No, I can't do anything about it, you're dead. . . . But how can you say I've poisoned you if you are not dead? . . . That I was plotting it with him? . . . That he sent me the poison? . . . But how can you? I kept my promise! . . . I did! It's absurd! . . . All right, I won't say you are dead any more . . . no, no more. . . ."

"This is a case of spontaneous trance!" said Mongeri. "Leave it to me."

He took Luisa by the wrists and said in a loud voice: "Come now!" At the sound of the robust, angry, and masculine voice with which she replied Mongeri was taken aback. She had drawn herself up with such a hard, truculent expression that she seemed another person. Her gentle, timid beauty had completely vanished.

"What do you want? Why must you interfere?"

Mongeri pulled himself together. The habitual reserve of the scientist might have made him fear that he too had come under the influence of an overheated imagination, but for the sight of the cot rocking to and fro and this sudden uncanny phenomenon of the personification of the fantasma. He drew himself up, angry for having been startled by the harsh masculine voice, and said sharply: "Stop that! Stop it at once!"

There was such a note of command in his voice, enough to dominate, as he thought, the young woman's mind, that he was surprised at the sardonic laugh with which she replied.

"Stop that! At once!" he replied in stronger tones.

"Aha! Another poisoner! You were in on this too?"

"That's a damned lie!"

Mongeri could not prevent himself from replying as if to a living person. His mind, already troubled, in spite of his efforts to remain calm and impartial, received another shock when he felt himself struck twice on the shoulder by an invisible fist, and turning towards the lamp, saw silhouetted against the light a greyish, wasted hand that seemed almost like smoke from the candle.

"You see? You see?" cried Giorgi with a sob in his voice.

Suddenly everything stopped. Luisa came out of her trance and looked around her as if waking from a natural sleep, questioning her husband and Mongeri with a pathetic movement of the head. They too were amazed and gazed around, speechless, overcome by the sense of peace and serenity. No one dared to break the silence. Only a slight sound of moaning from the cot made them turn in that direction. The baby whimpered and struggled under the pressure that was forcing something against his mouth. . . . Then without warning that, too, stopped, and nothing more happened.

The next morning, on his way home, Mongeri was thinking not only about the folly of scientists who fail to examine cases which coincide with popular superstition, but also of what he had said to his friend two days previously: *I wouldn't marry a widow for all the gold in the world.* As a scientist he had acquitted himself well, carrying out the experiment to its logical conclusion, without considering the humiliating consequences of failure if the experiment (the cremation of the body of Luisa's first husband) had failed. But notwithstanding the fact that the experiment had confirmed a popular superstition, and that from the day of the cremation the visitations had stopped completely, to the great relief of the good Lelio Giorgi and his Luisa, in his report, not yet published, he did not write with complete sincerity. He could not say, "The facts are such, and such is the result of the remedy: popular superstition has triumphed over the narrow-mindedness of science; the vampire died as soon as the body was cremated." No, he restricted his narrative with so many "if's" and "but's" and confused it with so many "hallucinations," "suggestions," and "inductions," simply to confirm what he had already admitted: that even intelligence is a matter of habit, and that having to change his mind had shaken him.

And what is even more curious, his own life

became somewhat incoherent, for he who had once sworn that he would not marry a widow for all the gold in the world, married one for far less, a pension of a mere £7,000! And when his friend Lelio Giorgi ingenuously remarked, "What? You!" he replied, "But her husband has been dead for the past seven years, not a scrap of him remains," without realizing that in so saying, he was contradicting the author of that learned paper, "A Case of Alleged Vampirism," namely, himself.

# AN AUTHENTICATED VAMPIRE STORY

# Franz Hartmann

Franz Hartmann (1838–1912) was born in Bavaria. After serving in an artillery regiment, he studied medicine and immigrated to America in 1865, serving as a doctor and coroner in Colorado during its boomtown mining era.

He became interested in spiritualism and the occult, studying with a medium in Denver and visiting several American Indian tribes to study their belief systems. In Texas he married and lived on his wife's ranch, but she died within months and he moved to San Francisco. Becoming more and more interested in theosophy, he worked with Helena Blavatsky, who regarded him as "a bad lot" because of his personal hygiene and shabby appearance. He was described by a contemporary as "perhaps the most terrifying-looking scientist in the annals of medicine—a maniacal, staring fellow with cavernous rings under his eyes who looks like he just escaped from an asylum for the criminally insane."

Nonetheless, he was a prolific writer, often on such esoteric subjects as alchemy and the Rosicrucians, and produced biographies of Jakob Böhme and Paracelsus, and translated the Bhagavad Gita into German. His works were despised by the Nazis and burned, some failing to have survived in even a single copy.

"An Authenticated Vampire Story" was first published in the September 1909 issue of *The Occult Review*.

# An Authenticated Vampire Story

## FRANZ HARTMANN

O
n June 10, 1909, there appeared in a prominent Vienna paper (the *Neues Wiener Journal*) a notice (which I herewith enclose) saying that the castle of B—— had been burned by the populace, because there was a great mortality among the peasant children, and it was generally believed that this was due to the invasion of a vampire, supposed to be the last Count B——, who died and acquired that reputation. The castle was situated in a wild and desolate part of the Carpathian Mountains and was formerly a fortification against the Turks. It was not inhabited owing to its being believed to be in the possession of ghosts, only a wing of it was used as a dwelling for the caretaker and his wife.

Now it so happened that when I read the above notice, I was sitting in a coffee-house at Vienna in company with an old friend of mine who is an experienced occultist and editor of a well known journal and who had spent several months in the neighborhood of the castle. From him I obtained the following account and it appears that the vampire in question was probably not the old Count, but his beautiful daughter, the Countess Elga, whose photograph, taken from the original painting, I obtained. My friend said:—

"Two years ago I was living at Hermannstadt, and being engaged in engineering a road through the hills, I often came within the vicinity of the old castle, where I made the acquaintance of the old castellan, or caretaker, and his wife, who occupied a part of the wing of the house, almost separate from the main body of the building. They were a quiet old couple and rather reticent in giving information or expressing an opinion in regard to the strange noises which were often heard at night in the deserted halls, or of the apparitions which the Wallachian peasants claimed to have seen when they loitered in the surroundings after dark. All I could gather was that the old Count was a widower and had a beautiful daughter, who was one day killed by a fall from her horse, and that soon after the old man died in some mysterious manner, and the bodies were buried in a solitary graveyard belonging to a neighboring village. Not long after their death an unusual mortality was noticed among the inhabitants of the village: several children and even some grown people died without any apparent illness; they merely wasted away; and thus a rumor was started that the old Count had become a vampire after his death. There is no doubt that he was not a saint, as he was addicted to drinking, and some shocking tales were in circulation about his conduct and that of his daughter; but whether or not there was any truth in them, I am not in a position to say.

"Afterwards the property came into possession of ——, a distant relative of the family, who is a young man and officer in a cavalry regiment at Vienna. It appears that the heir enjoyed his life at the capital and did not trouble himself much about the old castle in the wilderness; he did not even come to look at it, but gave his direction by letter to the old janitor, telling him merely to keep things in order and to attend to repairs, if any were necessary. Thus the castellan was actually master of the house and offered its hospitality to me and my friends.

"One evening myself and my two assistants, Dr. E——, a young lawyer, and Mr. W——, a literary man, went to inspect the premises. First we went to the stables. There were no horses, as they had been sold; but what attracted our special attention was an old queer-fashioned coach with gilded ornaments and bearing the emblems of the family. We then inspected the rooms, passing through some halls and gloomy corridors, such as may be found in any old castle. There was nothing remarkable about the furniture; but in one of the halls there hung in a frame an oil-painting, a portrait, representing a lady with a large hat and wearing a fur coat. We all were involuntarily startled on beholding this picture; not so much on account of the beauty of the lady, but on account of the uncanny expression of her eyes, and Dr. E——, after looking at the picture for a short time, suddenly exclaimed—

"'How strange! The picture closes its eyes and opens them again, and now begins to smile!'

"Now Dr. E—— is a very sensitive person and has more than once had some experience in spiritism, and we made up our minds to form a circle for the purpose of investigating this phenomenon. Accordingly, on the same evening we sat around a table in an adjoining room, forming a magnetic chain with our hands. Soon the table began to move and the name *"Elga"* was spelled.

We asked who this Elga was, and the answer was rapped out 'The lady, whose picture you have seen.'

"'Is the lady living?' asked Mr. W——. This question was not answered; but instead it was rapped out: 'If W—— desires it, I will appear to him bodily tonight at two o'clock.' W—— consented, and now the table seemed to be endowed with life and manifested a great affection for W——; it rose on two legs and pressed against his breast, as if it intended to embrace him.

"We inquired of the castellan whom the picture represented; but to our surpise he did not know. He said that it was the copy of a picture painted by the celebrated painter Hans Markart of Vienna, and had been bought by the old Count because its demoniacal look pleased him so much.

"We left the castle, and W—— retired to his room at an inn, a half-hour's journey distant from that place. He was of a somewhat skeptical turn of mind, being neither a firm believer in ghosts and apparitions nor ready to deny their possibility. He was not afraid, but anxious to see what would come out of his agreement, and for the purpose of keeping himself awake he sat down and began to write an article for a journal.

"Towards two o'clock he heard steps on the stairs and the door of the hall opened, there was a rustling of a silk dress and the sound of the feet of a lady walking to and fro in the corridor.

"It may be imagined that he was somewhat startled; but taking courage, he said to himself: 'If this is Elga, let her come in.' Then the door of his room opened and Elga entered. She was most elegantly dressed and appeared still more youthful and seductive than the picture. There was a lounge on the other side of the table where W—— was writing, and there she silently posed herself. She did not speak, but her looks and gestures left no doubt in regard to her desires and intentions.

"Mr. W—— resisted the temptation and remained firm. It is not known whether he did so out of principle or timidity or fear. Be this as it may, he kept on writing, looking from time to time at his visitor and silently wishing that she would leave. At last, after half an hour, which seemed to him much longer, the lady departed in the same manner in which she came.

"This adventure left W—— no peace, and we consequently arranged several sittings at the old castle, where a variety of uncanny phenomena took place. Thus, for instance, once the servant-girl was about to light a fire in the stove, when the door of the apartment opened and Elga stood there. The girl, frightened out of her wits, rushed out of the room, tumbling down the stairs in terror with the petroleum lamp in her hand, which broke and came very near to setting her clothes on fire. Lighted lamps and candles went out when brought near the picture, and many other 'manifestations' took place, which it would be tedious to describe; but the following incident ought not to be omitted.

"Mr. W—— was at that time desirous of obtaining the position as co-editor of a certain journal, and a few days after the above-narrated adventure he received a letter in which a noble lady of high position offered him her patronage for that purpose. The writer requested him to come to a certain place the same evening, where he would meet a gentleman who would give him further particulars. He went and was met by an unknown stranger, who told him that he was requested by the Countess Elga to invite Mr. W—— to a carriage drive and that she would await him at midnight at a certain crossing of two roads, not far from the village. The stranger then suddenly disappeared.

"Now it seems that Mr. W—— had some misgivings about the meeting and drive and he hired a policeman as detective to go at midnight to the appointed place, to see what would happen. The policeman went and reported next morning that he had seen nothing but the well-known, old-fashioned carriage from the castle with two black horses attached to it standing there as if waiting for somebody, and that he had no occasion to interfere and merely waited until the carriage moved on. When the castellan of the castle was asked, he swore that the carriage had not been out that night, and in fact it could not have been out, as there were no horses to draw it.

"But this is not all, for on the following day I met a friend who is a great skeptic and disbeliever in ghosts and always used to laugh at such things. Now, however, he seemed to be very serious and said: 'Last night something very strange happened to me. At about one o'clock this morning I returned from a late visit and as I happened to pass the graveyard of the village, I saw a carriage with gilded ornaments standing at the entrance. I wondered about this taking place at such an unusual hour, and being curious to see what would happen, I waited. Two elegantly dressed ladies issued from the carriage. One of these was young and pretty, but threw at me a devilish and scornful look as they both passed by and entered the cemetery. There they were met by a well-dressed man, who saluted the ladies and spoke to the younger one, saying: "Why, Miss Elga! Are you returned so soon?" Such a queer feeling came over me that I abruptly left and hurried home.'

"This matter has not been explained; but certain experiments which we subsequently made with the picture of Elga brought out some curious facts.

"To look at the picture for a certain time caused me to feel a very disagreeable sensation in the region of the solar plexus. I began to dislike the portrait and proposed to destroy it. We held a sitting in the adjoining room; the table manifested a great aversion against my presence. It was rapped out that I should leave the circle, and that the picture must not be destroyed. I ordered a Bible to be brought in and read the beginning of the first chapter of St. John, whereupon the above-mentioned Mr. E—— (the medium) and another man present claimed that they saw the picture distorting its face. I turned the frame and pricked the back of the picture with my penknife in different places, and Mr. E——, as well as the other man, felt all the pricks, although they had retired to the corridor.

"I made the sign of the pentagram over the picture, and again the two gentlemen claimed that the picture was horribly distorting its face.

"Soon afterwards we were called away and left that country. Of Elga I heard nothing more."

Thus far goes the account of my friend the editor. There are several points in it which call for an explanation. Perhaps the sages of the S.P.R. will find it by investigating the laws of nature ruling the astral plane, unless they prefer to take the easier route, by proclaiming it all to be humbug and fraud.

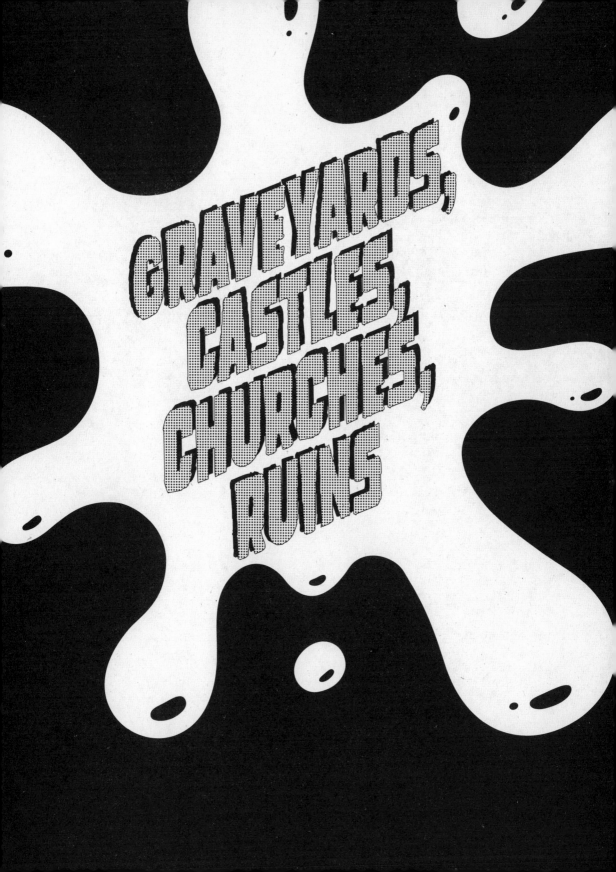

# REVELATIONS IN BLACK

# Carl Jacobi

Carl Richard Jacobi (1909–97) was born in Minneapolis and attended the University of Minnesota, where he studied writing and geology. He was the editor of two magazines, *Midwest Media* and the university's *Minnesota Quarterly*.

His writing career began when he won a short-story contest sponsored by the university; the story, "Mive," was subsequently sold to the prestigious *Weird Tales* magazine, for which he wrote many additional stories. He was also published in *Short Stories, MacLean's, Thrilling Mystery,* and other science-fiction, fantasy, and horror magazines, both in America and overseas. Jacobi was also a regular contributor to the original anthologies published by Arkham House.

"Revelations in Black" may well be Jacobi's masterpiece, becoming the titular story in his first published book, a 1947 Arkham House publication. Originally rejected by Farnsworth Wright, the editor of *Weird Tales,* the story stayed in his mind and he eventually wrote the author, asking to see it again. Such details as the secret handmade books of prose poetry in the fabulous library of the insane Larla are both original and haunting.

Other short-story collections by Jacobi include *Portraits in Moonlight* (1964) and *Disclosures in Scarlet* (1972).

"Revelations in Black" was first published in the April 1933 issue of *Weird Tales*.

# Revelations in Black

## CARL JACOBI

It was a dreary, forlorn establishment way down on Harbor Street. An old sign announced the legend: "Giovanni Larla— Antiques," and a dingy window revealed a display half masked in dust.

Even as I crossed the threshold that cheerless September afternoon, driven from the sidewalk by a gust of rain and perhaps a fascination for all antiques, the gloominess fell upon me like a material pall. Inside was half darkness, piled boxes and a monstrous tapestry, frayed with the warp showing in worn places. An Italian Renaissance wine cabinet shrank despondently in its corner and seemed to frown at me as I passed.

"Good afternoon, *Signor*. There is something you wish to buy? A picture, a ring, a vase perhaps?"

I peered at the squat, pudgy bulk of the Italian proprietor there in the shadows and hesitated.

"Just looking around," I said, turning my eyes to the jumble about me. "Nothing in particular . . ."

The man's oily face moved in a smile as though he had heard the remark a thousand times before. He sighed, stood there in thought a moment, the rain drumming and swishing against the outer pane. Then very deliberately he stepped to the shelves and glanced up and down them consider-

ing. I moved to his side, letting my eyes sweep across the stacked array of ancient oddities. At length he drew forth an object which I perceived to be a painted chalice.

"An authentic sixteenth century Tandart," he murmured. "A work of art, *Signor*."

I shook my head. "No pottery," I said. "Books perhaps, but no pottery."

He frowned slowly. "I have books too," he replied, "rare books which nobody sells but me, Giovanni Larla. But you must look at my other treasures too."

There was, I found, no hurrying the man. A quarter of an hour passed, during which I had to see a Glycon cameo brooch, a carved chair of some indeterminate style and period, and a muddle of yellowed statuettes, small oils, and one or two dreary Portland vases. Several times I glanced at my watch impatiently, wondering how I might break away from this Italian and his gloomy shop. Already the fascination of its dust and shadows had begun to wear off, and I was anxious to reach the street.

But when he had conducted me well towards the rear of the shop, something caught my fancy. I drew then from the shelf the first book of horror. If I had but known the terrible events that were to follow, if I could only have had a foresight into the future that September day, I swear I would have avoided the book like a leprous thing, would have shunned that wretched antique store and the very street it stood on like places accursed. A thousand times I have wished my eyes had never rested on that cover in black. What writhings of the soul, what terrors, what unrest, what madness would have been spared me!

But never dreaming the hideous secret of its pages I fondled it casually and remarked:

"An unusual book. What is it?"

Larla glanced up and scowled.

"That is not for sale," he said quietly. "I don't know how it got on these shelves. It was my poor brother's."

The volume in my hand was indeed unusual in appearance. Measuring but four inches across and five inches in length and bound in black velvet with each outside corner protected with a triangle of ivory, it was the most beautiful piece of bookbinding I had ever seen. In the centre of the cover was mounted a tiny piece of ivory intricately cut in the shape of a skull. But it was the title of the book that excited my interest. Embroidered in gold braid, the title read:

*"Five Unicorns and a Pearl."*

I looked at Larla. "How much?" I asked and reached for my wallet.

He shook his head. "No, it is not for sale. It is . . . it is the last work of my brother. He wrote it just before he died in the institution."

"The institution?" I queried.

Larla made no reply but stood staring at the book, his mind obviously drifting away in deep thought. A moment of silence dragged by. There was a strange gleam in his eyes when finally he spoke. And I thought I saw his fingers tremble slightly.

"My brother, Alessandro, was a fine man before he wrote that book," he said slowly. "He wrote beautifully, *Signor,* and he was strong and healthy. For hours I could sit while he read to me his poems. He was a dreamer, Alessandro; he loved everything beautiful, and the two of us were very happy.

"All . . . until that terrible night. Then he . . . but no . . . a year has passed now. It is best to forget." He passed his hand before his eyes and drew in his breath sharply.

"What happened?" I asked sympathetically, his words arousing my curiosity.

"Happened, *Signor*? I do not really know. It was all so confusing. He became suddenly ill, ill without reason. The flush of sunny Italy, which was always on his cheek, faded, and he grew white and drawn. His strength left him day by day. Doctors prescribed, gave medicines, but nothing helped. He grew steadily weaker until . . . until that night."

I looked at him curiously, impressed by his perturbation.

"And then?" I urged.

Hands opening and closing, Larla seemed to sway unsteadily; his liquid eyes opened wide to the brows, and his voice was strained and tense as he continued:

"And then . . . oh, if I could but forget! It was horrible. Poor Alessandro came home screaming, sobbing, tearing his hair. He was . . . he was stark, raving mad!

"They took him to the institution for the insane and said he needed a complete rest, that he had suffered from some terrific mental shock. He . . . died three weeks later with the crucifix on his lips."

For a moment I stood there in silence, staring out at the falling rain. Then I said:

"He wrote this book while confined to the institution?"

Larla nodded absently.

"Three books," he replied. "Two others exactly like the one you have in your hand. The bindings he made, of course, when he was quite well. It was his original intention, I believe, to pen in them by hand the verses of Marini. He was very clever at such work. But the wanderings of his mind which filled the pages now, I have never read. Nor do I intend to. I want to keep with me the memory of him when he was happy. This book has come on these shelves by mistake. I shall put it with his other possessions."

My desire to read the few pages bound in velvet increased a thousandfold when I found they were unobtainable. I have always had an interest in abnormal psychology and have gone through a number of books on the subject. Here was the work of a man confined in the asylum for the insane. Here was the unexpurgated writing of an educated brain gone mad. And unless my intuition failed me, here was a suggestion of some deep mystery. My mind was made up. I must have it.

I turned to Larla and chose my words carefully.

"I can well appreciate your wish to keep the book," I said, "and since you refuse to sell, may I ask if you would consider lending it to me for just one night? If I promised to return it in the morning? . . ."

The Italian hesitated. He toyed undecidedly with a heavy gold watch chain.

"No, I am sorry. . ."

"Ten dollars and back tomorrow unharmed." Larla studied his shoe.

"Very well, *Signor*, I will trust you. But please, I ask you, please be sure and return it."

That night in the quiet of my apartment I opened the book. Immediately my attention was drawn to three lines scrawled in a feminine hand across the inside of the front cover, lines written in a faded red solution that looked more like blood than ink. They read:

*"Revelations meant to destroy but only binding without the stake. Read, fool, and enter my field, for we are chained to the spot. Oh, woe unto Larla!"*

I mused over these undecipherable sentences for some time without solving their meaning. At last, shrugging my shoulders, I turned to the first page and began the last work of Alessandro Larla, the strangest story I had ever, in my years of browsing through old books, come upon.

*"On the evening of the fifteenth of October I turned my steps into the cold and walked until I was tired. The roar of the present was in the distance when I came to twenty-six blue-jays silently contemplating the ruins. Passing in the midst of them I wandered by the skeleton trees and seated myself where I could*

*watch the leering fish. A child worshipped. Glass threw the moon at me. Grass sang a litany at my feet. And the pointed shadow moved slowly to the left.*

*"I walked along the silver gravel until I came to five unicorns galloping beside water of the past. Here I found a pearl, a magnificent pearl, a pearl beautiful but black. Like a flower it carried a rich perfume, and once I thought the odour was but a mask; but why should such a perfect creation need a mask?*

*"I sat between the leering fish and the five galloping unicorns, and I fell madly in love with the pearl. The past lost itself in drabness and—"*

I laid the book down and sat watching the smoke-curls from my pipe eddy ceilingward. There was much more, but I could make no sense to any of it. All was in that strange style and completely incomprehensible. And yet it seemed the story was more than the mere wanderings of a madman. Behind it all seemed to lie a narrative cloaked in symbolism.

Something about the few sentences—just what I cannot say—had cast an immediate spell of depression over me. The vague lines weighed upon my mind, hung before my eyes like a design, and I felt myself slowly seized by a deep feeling of uneasiness.

The air of the room grew heavy and close. The open casement and the out-of-doors seemed to beckon to me. I walked to the window, thrust the curtain aside, stood there, smoking furiously. Let me say that regular habits have long been a part of my make-up. I am not addicted to nocturnal strolls or late meanderings before seeking my bed; yet now, curiously enough, with the pages of the book still in my mind I suddenly experienced an indefinable urge to leave my apartment and walk the darkened streets.

I paced the room nervously, irritated that the sensation did not pass. The clock on the mantel pushed its ticks slowly through the quiet. And at length with a shrug I threw my pipe to the table, reached for my hat and coat and made for the door.

Ridiculous as it may sound, upon reaching the street I found that urge had increased to a distinct attraction: felt that under no circumstances must

I turn any direction but northward, and although this way led into a district quite unknown to me, I was in a moment pacing forward, choosing streets deliberately and heading without knowing why towards the outskirts of the city. It was a brilliant moonlight night in September. Summer had passed and already there was the smell of frosted vegetation in the air. The great chimes in Capitol tower were sounding midnight, and the buildings and shops and later the private houses were dark and silent as I passed.

Try as I would to erase from my memory the queer book which I had just read, the mystery of its pages hammered at me, arousing my curiosity, dampening my spirits. "Five Unicorns and a Pearl!" What did it all mean?

More and more I realized as I went on that a power other than my own will was leading my steps. It was absurd, and I tried to resist, to turn back. Yet once I did momentarily come to a halt that attraction swept upon me as inexorably as the desire for a narcotic.

It was far out on Easterly Street that I came upon a high stone wall flanking the sidewalk. Over its ornamented top I could see the shadows of a dark building set well back in the grounds. A wrought-iron gate in the wall opened upon a view of wild desertion and neglect. Swathed in the light of the moon, an old courtyard strewn with fountains, stone benches and statues lay tangled in rank weeds and undergrowth. The windows of the building, which evidently had once been a private dwelling, were boarded up, all except those on a little tower or cupola rising to a point in the front. And here the glass caught the blue-grey light and refracted it into the shadows.

Before that gate my feet stopped like dead things. The psychic power which had been leading me had now become a reality. Directly from the courtyard it emanated, drawing me towards it with an intensity that smothered all reluctance.

Strangely enough, the gate was unlocked; and feeling like a man in a trance I swung the creaking hinges and entered, making my way along a grass-grown path to one of the benches. It seemed that once inside the court the distant sounds of the city died away, leaving a hollow silence broken only by the wind rustling through the tall dead weeds. Rearing up before me, the building with its dark wings, cupola and façade oddly resembled a colossal hound, crouched and ready to spring.

There were several fountains, weather-beaten and ornamented with curious figures, to which at the time I paid only casual attention. Farther on, half hidden by the underbrush, was the life-size statue of a little child kneeling in position of prayer. Erosion on the soft stone had disfigured the face, and in the half-light the carved features presented an expression strangely grotesque and repelling.

How long I sat there in the quiet, I don't know. The surroundings under the moonlight blended harmoniously with my mood. But more than that I seemed physically unable to rouse myself and pass on.

It was with a suddenness that brought me electrified to my feet that I became aware of the real significance of the objects about me. Held motionless, I stood there running my eyes wildly from place to place, refusing to believe. Surely I must be dreaming. In the name of all that was unusual this . . . this absolutely couldn't be. And yet—

It was the fountain at my side that had caught my attention first. Across the top of the water basin were *five stone unicorns,* all identically carved, each seeming to follow the other in galloping procession. Looking farther, prompted now by a madly rising recollection, I saw that the cupola, towering high above the house, eclipsed the rays of the moon and threw *a long pointed shadow* across the ground *at my left.* The other fountain some distance away was ornamented with the figure of a stone fish, *a fish* whose empty eye-sockets *were leering* straight in my direction. And the climax of it all—the wall! At intervals of every three feet on top of the street expanse were mounted crude carven stone shapes of birds. And counting them I saw *that those birds were twenty-six blue-jays.*

Unquestionably—startling and impossible as it seemed—I was in the same setting as described in Larla's book! It was a staggering revelation, and my mind reeled at the thought of it. How strange, how odd that I should be drawn to a portion of the city I had never before frequented and thrown into the midst of a narrative written almost a year before!

I saw now that Alessandro Larla, writing as a patient in the institution for the insane, had seized isolated details but neglected to explain them. Here was a problem for the psychologist, the mad, the symbolic, the incredible story of the dead Italian. I was bewildered, confused, and I pondered for an answer.

As if to soothe my perturbation there stole into the court then a faint odour of perfume. Pleasantly it touched my nostrils, seemed to blend with the moonlight. I breathed it in deeply as I stood there by the curious fountain. But slowly that odour became more noticeable, grew stronger, a sickish sweet smell that began to creep down my lungs like smoke. And absently I recognized it. Heliotrope! The honeyed aroma blanketed the garden, thickened the air, seemed to fall upon me like a drug.

And then came my second surprise of the evening. Looking about to discover the source of the irritating fragrance I saw opposite me, seated on another stone bench, a woman. She was dressed entirely in black, and her face was hidden by a veil. She seemed unaware of my presence. Her head was slightly bowed, and her whole position suggested a person deep in contemplation.

I noticed also the thing that crouched by her side. It was a dog, a tremendous brute with a head strangely out of proportion and eyes as large as the ends of big spoons. For several moments I stood staring at the two of them. Although the air was quite chilly, the woman wore no over-jacket, only the black dress relieved solely by the whiteness of her throat.

With a sigh of regret at having my pleasant solitude thus disturbed I moved across the court until I stood at side. Still she showed no recognition of my presence, and clearing my throat I said hesitatingly:

"I suppose you are the owner here. I . . . I really didn't know the place was occupied, and the gate . . . well, the gate was unlocked. I'm sorry I trespassed."

She made no reply to that, and the dog merely gazed at me in dumb silence. No graceful words of polite departure came to my lips, and I moved hesitatingly towards the gate.

"Please don't go," she said suddenly, looking up. "I'm lonely. Oh, if you but knew how lonely I am!" She moved to one side of the bench and motioned that I sit beside her. The dog continued to examine me with its big eyes.

Whether it was the nearness of that odour of heliotrope, the suddenness of it all, or perhaps the moonlight, I did not know, but at her words a thrill of pleasure ran through me, and I accepted the proffered seat.

There followed an interval of silence, during which I puzzled my brain for a means to start conversation. But abruptly she turned to the beast and said in German:

*"Fort mit dir, Johann!"*

The dog rose obediently to its feet and stole slowly off into the shadows. I watched it for a moment until it disappeared in the direction of the house. Then the woman said to me in English which was slightly stilted and marked with an accent:

"It has been ages since I have spoken to anyone . . . We are strangers. I do not know you, and you do not know me. Yet . . . strangers sometimes find in each other a bond of interest. Supposing . . . supposing we forget customs and formality of introduction? Shall we?"

For some reason I felt my pulse quicken as she said that. "Please do," I replied. "A spot like this is enough introduction in itself. Tell me, do you live here?"

She made no answer for a moment, and I began to fear I had taken her suggestion too quickly. Then she began slowly:

"My name is Perle von Mauren, and I am really a stranger to your country, though I have been here now more than a year. My home is in Austria near what is now the Czechoslovakian frontier. You see, it was to find my only brother that I came to the United States. During the war he was a lieutenant under General Makensen,* but in 1916, in April I believe it was, he . . . he was reported missing.

"War is a cruel thing. It took our money; it took our castle on the Danube, and then—my brother. Those following years were horrible. We lived always in doubt, hoping against hope that he was still living.

"Then after the Armistice a fellow officer claimed to have served next to him on grave-digging detail at a French prison camp near Monpré. And later came a thin rumour that he was in the United States. I gathered together as much money as I could and came here in search of him."

Her voice dwindled off, and she sat in silence staring at the brown weeds. When she resumed, her voice was low and wavering.

"I . . . found him . . . but would to God I hadn't! He . . . he was no longer living."

I stared at her. "Dead?" I asked.

The veil trembled as though moved by a shudder, as though her thoughts had exhumed some terrible event of the past. Unconscious of my interruption she went on:

"Tonight I came here—I don't know why—merely because the gate was unlocked, and there was a place of quiet within. Now have I bored you with my confidences and personal history?"

"Not at all," I replied. "I came here by chance myself. Probably the beauty of the place attracted me. I dabble in amateur photography occasionally and react strongly to unusual scenes. Tonight I went for a midnight stroll to relieve my mind from the bad effect of a book I was reading."

She made a strange reply to that, a reply away from our line of thought and which seemed an interjection that escaped her involuntarily.

"Books," she said, "are powerful things. They can fetter one more than the walls of a prison."

She caught my puzzled stare at the remark and added hastily: "It is odd that we should meet here."

*Properly Field-Marshal August von Makensen of the famous Death's Head Hussars in World War I. He served under the Kaiser and the Führer with distinction.

For a moment I didn't answer. I was thinking of her heliotrope perfume, which for a woman of her apparent culture was applied in far too great a quantity to manifest good taste. The impression stole upon me that the perfume cloaked some secret, that if it were removed I should find . . . but what? It was ridiculous, and I tried to cast the feeling aside.

The hours passed, and still we sat there talking, enjoying each other's companionship. She did not remove her veil, and though I was burning with a desire to see her features, I had not dared ask her to. A strange nervousness had slowly seized me. The woman was a charming conversationalist, but there was about her an indefinable something which produced in me a distinct feeling of unease.

It was, I should judge, but a few moments before the first streaks of dawn when it happened. As I look back now, even with mundane objects and thoughts on every side, it is not difficult to realize the dire significance, the absolute baseness of that vision. But at the time my brain was too much in a whirl to understand.

A thin shadow moving across the garden attracted my gaze once again into the night about me. I looked up over the spire of the deserted house and started as if struck by a blow. For a moment I thought I had seen a curious cloud formation racing low directly above me, a cloud black and impenetrable with two winglike ends strangely in the shape of a monstrous flying bat.

I blinked my eyes hard and looked again.

"That cloud!" I exclaimed. "That strange cloud! . . . Did you see—"

I stopped and stared dumbly.

The bench at my side was empty. The woman had disappeared.

During the next day I went about my professional duties in the law office with only half interest, and my business partner looked at me queerly several times when he came upon me mumbling to myself. The incidents of the evening before were rushing through my mind in grand turmoil. Questions unanswerable hammered at me. That I should have come upon the very details described by mad Larla in his strange book: the leering fish, the praying child, the twenty-six blue-jays, the pointed shadow of the cupola—it was unexplainable; it was weird.

*Five Unicorns and a Pearl.* The unicorns were the stone statues ornamenting the old fountain, yes—but the pearl? With a start I suddenly recalled the name of the woman in black: *Perle* von Mauren. The revelation climaxed my train of thought. What did it all mean?

Dinner had little attraction for me that evening. Earlier I had gone to the antique-dealer and begged him to loan me the sequel, the second volume of his brother Alessandro. When he had refused, objected because I had not yet returned the first book, my nerves had suddenly jumped on edge. I felt like a narcotic fiend faced with the realization that he could not procure the desired drug. In desperation, yet hardly knowing why, I offered the man money, more money, until at length I had come away, my powers of persuasion and my pocket book successful.

The second volume was identical in outward respects to its predecessor except that it bore no title. But if I was expecting more disclosures in symbolism I was doomed to disappointment. Vague as *Five Unicorns and a Pearl* had been, the text of the sequel was even more wandering and was obviously only the ramblings of a mad brain. By watching the sentences closely I did gather that Alessandro Larla had made a second trip to his court of the twenty-six blue-jays and met there again his "pearl."

*"Can it possibly be? I pray that it is not. And yet I have seen it and heard it snarl. Oh, the loathsome creature! I will not, I will not believe it."*

I closed the book with a snap and tried to divert my attention elsewhere by polishing the lens of my newest portable camera. But again, as before, that same urge stole upon me, that same desire to visit the garden. I confess that I had watched the intervening hours until I would meet the woman in black again; for strangely enough, in spite of her abrupt exit before, I never doubted but that she would be there waiting for me. I wanted her to lift the veil. I wanted to talk with her. I wanted

to throw myself once again into the narrative of Larla's book.

Yet the whole thing seemed preposterous, and I fought the sensation with every ounce of willpower I could call to mind. Then it suddenly occured to me what a remarkable picture she would make, sitting there on the stone bench, clothed in black, with the classic background of the old courtyard. If I could but catch the scene on a photographic plate . . .

I halted my polishing and mused a moment. With a new electric flash-lamp, that handy invention which has supplanted the old mussy flash-powder, I could illuminate the garden and snap the picture with ease. And if the result were satisfactory it would make a worthy contribution to the international Camera Contest at Geneva next month.

The idea appealed to me, and gathering together the necessary equipment I drew on an ulster (for it was a wet, chilly night) and slipped out of my rooms and headed northward. Mad, unseeing fool that I was! If only I had stopped then and there, returned the book to the antique dealer and closed the incident! But the strange magnetic attraction had gripped me in earnest, and I rushed headlong into the horror. A fall rain was drumming the pavement, and the streets were deserted. Off to the east, however, the heavy blanket of clouds glowed with a soft radiance where the moon was trying to break through, and a strong wind from the south gave promise of clearing the skies before long. With my collar turned well up at the throat I passed once again into the older section of the town and down forgotten Easterly Street. I found the gate to the grounds unlocked as before, and the garden a dripping place masked in shadow.

The woman was not there. Still the hour was early, and I did not for a moment doubt that she would appear later. Gripped now with the enthusiasm of my plan, I set the camera carefully on the stone fountain, training the lens as well as I could on the bench where we had sat the previous evening. The flash-lamp with its battery handle I laid within easy reach.

Scarcely had I finished my arrangements when

the crunch of gravel on the path caused me to turn. She was approaching the stone bench, heavily veiled as before and with the same sweeping black dress.

"You have come again," she said as I took my place beside her.

"Yes," I replied. "I could not stay away."

Our conversation that night gradually centred about her dead brother, although I thought several times that the woman tried to avoid the subject. He had been, it seemed, the black sheep of the family, had led more or less of a dissolute life and had been expelled from the University of Vienna not only because of his lack of respect for the pedagogues of the various sciences but also because of his queer unorthodox papers on philosophy. His sufferings in the war prison camp must have been intense. With a kind of grim delight she dwelt on his horrible experiences in the grave-digging detail which had been related to her by the fellow officer. But of the manner in which he had met his death she would say absolutely nothing.

Stronger than on the night before was the sweet smell of heliotrope. And again as the fumes crept nauseatingly down my lungs there came that same sense of nervousness, that same feeling that the perfume was hiding something I should know. The desire to see beneath the veil had become maddening by this time, but still I lacked the boldness to ask her to lift it.

Towards midnight the heavens cleared and the moon in splendid contrast shone high in the sky. The time had come for my picture.

"Sit where you are," I said. "I'll be back in a moment."

Stepping quickly to the fountain I grasped the flash–lamp, held it aloft for an instant and placed my finger on the shutter lever of the camera. The woman remained motionless on the bench, evidently puzzled as to the meaning of my movements. The range was perfect. A click, and a dazzling white light enveloped the courtyard about us. For a brief second she was outlined there against the old wall. Then the blue moonlight returned, and I was smiling in satisfaction.

"It ought to make a beautiful picture," I said. She leaped to her feet.

"Fool!" she cried hoarsely. "Blundering fool! What have you done?"

Even though the veil was there to hide her face I got the instant impression that her eyes were glaring at me, smouldering with hatred. I gazed at her curiously as she stood erect, head thrown back, body apparently taut as wire, and a slow shudder crept down my spine. Then without warning she gathered up her dress and ran down the path towards the deserted house. A moment later she had disappeared somewhere in the shadows of the giant bushes.

I stood there by the fountain, staring after her in a daze. Suddenly, off in the umbra of the house's façade there rose a low animal snarl.

And then before I could move, a huge grey shape came hurtling through the long weeds, bounding in great leaps straight towards me. It was the woman's dog, which I had seen with her the night before. But no longer was it a beast passive and silent. Its face was contorted in diabolic fury, and its jaws were dripping slaver. Even in that moment of terror as I stood frozen before it, the sight of those white nostrils and those black hyalescent eyes emblazoned itself on my mind, never to be forgotten.

Then with a lunge it was upon me. I had only time to thrust the flash–lamp upward in half protection and throw my weight to the side. My arm jumped in recoil. The bulb exploded, and I could feel those teeth clamp down hard on the handle. Backwards I fell, a scream gurgling to my lips, a terrific heaviness surging upon my body.

I struck out frantically, beat my fists into that growling face. My fingers groped blindly for its throat, sank deep into the hairy flesh. I could feel its breath mingling with my own now, but desperately I hung on.

The pressure of my hands told. The dog coughed and fell back. And seizing that instant I struggled to my feet, jumped forward and planted a terrific kick straight into the brute's middle.

*"Fort mit dir, Johann!"* I cried, remembering the woman's German command.

It leaped back and, fangs bared, glared at me motionless for a moment. Then abruptly it turned and slunk off through the weeds.

Weak and trembling, I drew myself together, picked up my camera, and passed through the gate towards home.

Three days passed. Those endless hours I spent confined to my apartment suffering the tortures of the damned.

On the day following the night of my terrible experience with the dog I realized I was in no condition to go to work. I drank two cups of strong black coffee and then forced myself to sit quietly in a chair, hoping to soothe my nerves. But the sight of the camera there on the table excited me to action. Five minutes later I was in the dark room arranged as my studio, developing the picture I had taken the night before. I worked feverishly, urged on by the thought of what an unusual contribution it would make for the amateur contest next month at Geneva, should the result be successful.

An exclamation burst from my lips as I stared at the still-wet print. There was the old garden clear and sharp with the bushes, the statue of the child, the fountain and the wall in the background, but the bench—the stone bench was empty. There was no sign, not even a blur of the woman in black.

My brain in a whirl, I rushed the negative through a saturated solution of mercuric chloride in water, then treated it with ferrous oxalate. But even after this intensifying process the second print was like the first, focused in every detail, the bench standing in the foreground in sharp relief, but no trace of the woman.

I stared incredulously. She had been in plain view when I snapped the shutter. Of that I was positive. And my camera was in perfect condition. What then was wrong? Not until I had looked at the print hard in the daylight would I believe my eyes. No explanation offered itself, none at all; at length, confused unto weakness, I returned to my bed and fell into a heavy sleep.

Straight through the day I slept. Hours later I seemed to wake from a vague nightmare, and had not strength to rise from my pillow. A great phys-ical faintness had overwhelmed me. My arms, my legs, lay like dead things. My heart was fluttering weakly. All was quiet, so still that the clock on my bureau ticked distinctly each passing second. The curtain billowed in the night breeze, though I was positive I had closed the casement when I entered the room.

And then suddenly I threw back my head and screamed from the bottomest depths of my soul! For slowly, slowly creeping down my lungs was that detestable odour of heliotrope.

Morning, and I found all was not a dream. My head was ringing, my hands trembling, and I was so weak I could hardly stand. The doctor I called in looked grave as he felt my pulse.

"You are on the verge of a complete collapse," he said. "If you do not allow yourself a rest it may permanently affect your mind. Take things easy for a while. And if you don't mind I'll cauterize those two little cuts on your neck. They're rather raw wounds. What caused them?"

I moved my fingers to my throat and drew them away again tipped with blood.

"I . . . I don't know," I faltered.

He busied himself with his medicines, and a few minutes later reached for his hat.

"I advise that you don't leave your bed for a week at least," he said. "I'll give you a thorough examination then and see if there are any signs of anaemia." But as he went out the door I thought I saw a puzzled look on his face.

Those subsequent hours allowed my thoughts to run wild once more. I vowed I would forget it all, go back to my work and never look upon the books again. But I knew I could not. The woman in black persisted in my mind, and each minute away from her became a torture. But more than that, if there had been a decided urge to continue my reading in the second book, the desire to see the third book, the last of the trilogy, was slowly increasing to an obsession. It gripped me, etched itself deep into my thoughts.

At length I could stand it no longer, and on the morning of the third day I took a cab to the antique store and tried to persuade Larla to give me the third volume of his brother. But the Italian was firm. I had already taken two books, neither of which I had returned. Until I brought them back he would not listen. Vainly I tried to explain that one was of no value without the sequel and that I wanted to read the entire narrative as a unit. He merely shrugged his shoulders and toyed with his watch chain.

Cold perspiration broke out on my forehead as I heard my desire disregarded. Like the blows of a bludgeon the thought beat upon me that I must have that book. I argued. I pleaded. But to no avail.

At length when Larla had turned the other way I gave in to desperation, seized the third book as I saw it lying on the shelf, slid it into my pocket, and walked guiltily out. I make no apologies for my action. In the light of what developed later it may be considered a temptation inspired, for my will at the time was a conquered thing blanketed by that strange lure.

Back in my apartment I dropped into a chair and hastened to open the velvet cover. Here was the last chronicle of that strange series of events which had so completely become a part of my life during the last five days. Larla's volume three. Would all be explained in its pages? If so, what secret would be revealed?

With the light from a reading lamp glaring full over my shoulder I opened the book, thumbed through it slowly, marvelling at the exquisite hand-printing. It seemed then as I saw there that an almost palpable cloud of intense quiet settled over me, a mental miasma muffling the distant sounds of the street. I was vaguely aware of an atmosphere, heavy and dense, in which objects other than the book lost their focus and became blurred in proportion.

For a moment I hesitated. Something psychic, something indefinable seemed to forbid me to read farther. Conscience, curiosity, that queer urge told me to go on. Slowly, like a man in a hypnotic trance wavering between two wills, I began to turn the pages, one at a time, from back to front.

Symbolism again. Vague wanderings with no sane meaning.

But suddenly my fingers stopped! My eyes had caught sight of the last paragraph on the last page, the final pennings of Alessandro Larla. I started downwards as a terrific shock ripped through me from head to foot. I read, re-read, and read again those words, those blasphemous words. I brought the book closer. I traced each word in the lamp-light, slowly, carefully, letter for letter. I opened and closed my eyes. Then the horror of it burst like a bomb within me.

In blood-red ink the lines read:

*"What shall I do? She has drained my blood and rotted my soul. My pearl is black, black as all evil. The curse be upon her brother, for it is he who made her thus. I pray the truth in these pages will destroy them for ever.*

*"But my brain is hammering itself apart. Heaven help me, Perle von Mauren and her brother, Johann, are vampires!"*

With a scream I leaped to my feet.

"Vampires!" I shrieked. "Vampires! Oh, my God!"

I clutched at the edge of the table and stood there swaying, the realization of it surging upon me like the blast of a furnace. Vampires! Those horrible creatures with a lust for human blood, fiends of hell, taking the shape of men, of bats, of dogs. I saw it all now, and my brain reeled at the horror of it.

Oh, why had I been such a fool? Why had I not looked beneath the surface, taken away the veil, gone farther than the perfume? That damnable heliotrope was a mask, a mask hiding all the unspeakable foulness of the grave.

My emotions burst out of control then. With a cry I swept the water-glass, the books, the vase from the table, smote my fist down upon the flat surface again and again until a thousand little pains were stabbing the flesh.

"Vampires!" I screamed. "No, no—oh God, it isn't true!"

But I knew that it was. The events of the past few days rose before me in all their horror now, and I could see the black significance of every detail.

The brother, Johann—some time since the war

he had become a vampire. When the woman sought him out years later he had forced this terrible existence upon her too. Yes, that was it.

With the garden as their lair the two of them had entangled poor Alessandro Larla in their serpentine coils a year before. He had loved the woman, had worshipped her madly And then he had found the truth, the awful truth that had sent him stumbling home, stark, raving mad.

Mad, yes, but not mad enough to keep him from writing the facts in his three velvet-bound books for the world to see. He had hoped the disclosures would dispatch the woman and her brother for ever. But it was not enough.

Following my thoughts, I whipped the first book from the table stand and opened the front cover. There again I saw those scratched lines which had meant nothing to me before.

*"Revelations meant to destroy but only binding without the stake. Read, fool, and enter my field, for we are chained to the spot. Oh, woe unto Larla!"*

Perle von Mauren had written that. Fool that I was, unseeing fool! The books had not put an end to the evil of her or her brother. No, only one thing could do that. Yet the exposures had not been written in vain. They were recorded for mortal posterity to see.

Those books bound the two vampires, Perle von Mauren and her brother, Johann, to the old garden, kept them from roaming the night streets in search of victims. Only he who had once passed through the gate could they pursue and attack.

It was the old metaphysical law: evil shrinking in the face of truth.

Yet if the books had bound their power in chains they had also opened a new avenue for their attacks. Once immersed in the pages of the trilogy, the reader fell helplessly into their clutches. Those printed lines had become the outer reaches of their web. They were an entrapping net within which the power of the vampires always crouched.

That was why my life had blended so strangely with the story of Larla. The moment I had cast my eyes on the opening paragraph I had fallen into their coils to do with as they had done with Larla a year before. I had been lured, drawn relentlessly into the tentacles of the woman in black. Once I was past the garden gate the binding spell of the books was gone, and they were free to pursue me and to—

A giddy sensation rose within me. Now I saw why the scientific doctor had been puzzled. Now I saw the reason for my physical weakness. Oh, the foulness of it! She had been—feasting on my blood!

With a sobbing cry I flung the book to a far corner, turned and began madly pacing up and down the room. Cold perspiration oozed from every pore. My heart pounded like a runner's. My brain ran wild.

Was I to end as Larla had ended, another victim of this loathsome being's power? Was she to gorge herself further on my life and live on? Were others to be preyed upon and go down into the pits of despair? No, and again no! If Larla had been ignorant of the one and only way in which to dispose of such a creature, I was not. I had not vacationed in southern Europe without learning something of these ancient evils.

Frantically I looked about the room, took in the objects about me. A chair, a table, a taboret, one of my cameras with its long tripod. I stared at the latter as in my terror-stricken mind a plan leaped into action. With a lunge I was across the floor, had seized one of the wooden legs of the tripod in my hands. I snapped it across my knee. Then, grasping the two broken pieces, both now with sharp splintered ends, I rushed hatless out of the door to the street.

A moment later I was racing northward in a cab bound for Easterly Street.

"Hurry!" I cried to the driver as I glanced at the westering sun. "Faster, do you hear?"

We shot along the cross-streets, into the old suburbs and towards the outskirts of town. Every traffic halt found me fuming at the delay. But at length we drew up before the wall of the garden.

Tossing the driver a bill, I swung the wrought-iron gate open and with the wooden pieces of the tripod still under my arm, rushed in. The courtyard was a place of reality in the daylight, but the mouldering masonry and tangled weeds were steeped in silence as before.

Straight for the house I made, climbing the rotten steps to the front entrance. The door was boarded up and locked. Smothering an impulse to scream, I retraced my steps at a run and began to circle the south wall of the building. It was this direction I had seen the woman take when she had fled after I had tried to snap her picture. The twenty-six blue-jays on the wall leered at me like a flock of harpies.

Well towards the rear of the building I reached a small half-open door leading to the cellar. For a moment I hesistated there, sick with the dread of what I knew lay before me. Then, clenching hard the two wooden tripod stakes, I entered.

Inside, cloaked in gloom, a narrow corridor stretched before me. The floor was littered with rubble and fallen masonry, the ceiling interlaced with a thousand cobwebs.

I stumbled forward, my eyes quickly accustoming themselves to the half-light from the almost opaque windows. A maddening urge to leave it all and flee back to the sunlight was welling up within me now. I fought it back. Failure would mean a continuation of the horrors—a lingering death—would leave the gate open for others.

At the end of the corridor a second door barred my passage. I thrust it open—and stood swaying there on the sill staring inward. A great loathing crept over me, a stifling sense of utter repulsion. Hot blood rushed to my head. The air seemed to move upward in palpable swirls.

Beyond was a small room, barely ten feet square, with a low-raftered ceiling. And by the light of the open door I saw side by side in the centre of the floor—two white wood coffins.

How long I stood there leaning weakly against the stone wall I don't know. There was a silence so profound the beating of my heart pulsed through the passage like the blows of a mallet. And there was a slow penetrating odour drifting from out of that chamber that entered my nostrils and claimed instant recognition. Heliotrope! But heliotrope defiled by the rotting smell of an ancient grave.

Then suddenly with a determination born of despair I leaped forward, rushed to the nearest coffin, seized its cover, and ripped it open.

Would to heaven I could forget the sight that met my eyes. There lay Perle von Mauren, the woman in black—unveiled.

That face—how can I describe it? It was divinely beautiful, the hair black as sable, the cheeks a classic white. But the lips—oh God! Those lips! I grew suddenly sick as I looked upon them. They were scarlet, crimson . . . and sticky with human blood.

I moved like an automaton then. With a low sob I reached for one of the tripod stakes, seized a flagstone from the floor and with the pointed end of the wood resting directly over the woman's heart, struck a crashing blow. The stake jumped downward. A sickening crunch—and a violent contortion shook the coffin. Up to my face rushed a warm, nauseating breath of rot and decay.

I wheeled and hurled open the lid of her brother's coffin. With only a flashing glance at the young masculine Teutonic face I raised the other stake high in the air and brought it stabbing down with all the strength in my right arm. Red blood suddenly began to form a thick pool on the floor.

For an instant I stood rooted to the spot, the utter obscenity of it all searing its way into my brain like a hot sword. Even in that moment of stark horror I realized that not even the most subtle erasures of Time would be able to remove that blasphemous sight from my inner eye.

It was a scene so abysmally corrupt—I pray heaven my dreams will never find it and re-vision its unholy tableau. There before me, focused in the shaft of light that filtered through the open door like the miasma from a fever swamp, lay the two white caskets.

And within them now, staring up at me from eyeless sockets—two grey and mouldering skeletons, each with its hideous leering head of death.

The rest is but a vague dream. I seem to remember rushing madly outside, along the path to the gate and down the street, down Easterly, away from that accursed garden of the jays.

At length, utterly exhausted, I reached my

apartment, burst open the door, and staggered in. Those mundane surroundings that confronted me were like balm to my burning eyes. But as if in mocking irony there centred into my gaze three objects lying where I had left them, the three volumes of Larla.

I moved across to them, picked them up, and stared down vacantly upon their black sides. These were the hellish works that had caused it all. These were the pages that were responsible . . .

With a low cry I turned to the grate on the other side of the room and flung the three of them on to the still glowing coals.

There was an instant hiss, and a line of yellow flame streaked upward and began eating into the velvet. I watched the fire grow higher . . . higher . . . and diminish slowly.

And as the last glowing spark died into a blackened ash there swept over me a mighty feeling of quiet and relief.

# THE MASTER OF RAMPLING GATE

# Anne Rice

Howard Allen O'Brien (1941– ) was born in New Orleans and took the first name Anne as a child. She married the poet Stan Rice in 1961 and took his last name; they were married for forty-one years, until his death in 2002. They had two children: Michele, in 1966, who died of leukemia less than six years later, and Christopher, in 1978, who has gone on to be a novelist.

Anne Rice's first novel, *Interview with the Vampire,* was completed in 1973, published in 1976, and went on to become an enormous bestseller. Although she has written many other books, those in the Vampire Chronicles series, continuing with *The Vampire Lestat* (1985) and *The Queen of the Damned* (1988), have been the greatest successes. She wrote the screenplay for the 1994 film *Interview with the Vampire,* which starred Tom Cruise as Lestat, Brad Pitt, and Kirsten Dunst. An unsuccessful sequel, *The Queen of the Damned,* combined muddled plot elements of the second and third books in the series.

Rice has also written two novels as Anne Rampling, *Exit to Eden* (1985) and *Belinda* (1986), and three erotic novels as A. N. Roquelaure. In recent years she has been writing religious novels based on the life of Jesus Christ.

"The Master of Rampling Gate," one of only two short stories by Anne Rice, was first published in the February 1984 issue of *Redbook* magazine.

# The Master of Rampling Gate

## ANNE RICE

Rampling Gate: It was so real to us in those old pictures, rising like a fairy-tale castle out of its own dark wood. A wilderness of gables and chimneys between those two immense towers, grey stone walls mantled in ivy, mullioned windows reflecting the drifting clouds.

But why had Father never gone there? Why had he never taken us? And why on his deathbed, in those grim months after Mother's passing, did he tell my brother, Richard, that Rampling Gate must be torn down stone by stone? Rampling Gate that had always belonged to Ramplings, Rampling Gate which had stood for over four hundred years.

We were in awe of the task that lay before us, and painfully confused. Richard had just finished four years at Oxford. Two whirlwind social seasons in London had proven me something of a shy success. I still preferred scribbling poems and stories in the quiet of my room to dancing the night away, but I'd kept that a good secret, and though we were not spoilt children, we had enjoyed the best of everything our parents could give. But now the carefree years were ended. We had to be careful and wise.

And our hearts ached as, sitting together in Fa-ther's book-lined study, we looked at the old pictures of Rampling Gate before the small coal fire. "Destroy it, Richard, as soon as I am gone," Fa-ther had said.

"I just don't understand it, Julie," Richard confessed, as he filled the little crystal glass in my hand with sherry. "It's the genuine article, that old place, a real fourteenth-century manor house in excellent repair. A Mrs. Blessington, born and reared in the village of Rampling, has apparently man-aged it all these years. She was there when Uncle Baxter died, and he was the last Rampling to live under that roof."

"Do you remember," I asked, "the year that Father took all these pictures down and put them away?"

"I shall never forget that," Richard said. "How could I? It was so peculiar, and so unlike Father, too." He sat back, drawing slowly on his pipe. "There had been that bizarre incident in Victoria Station, when he had seen that young man."

"Yes, exactly," I said, snuggling back into the velvet chair and looking into the tiny dancing flames in the grate. "You remember how upset Father was?"

Yet it was simple incident. In fact nothing

really happened at all. We couldn't have been more than six and eight at the time and we had gone to the station with Father to say farewell to friends. Through the window of a train Father saw a young man who startled and upset him. I could remember the face clearly to this day. Remarkably handsome, with a narrow nose and well drawn eyebrows, and a mop of lustrous brown hair. The large black eyes had regarded Father with the saddest expression as Father had drawn us back and hurried us away.

"And the argument that night, between Father and Mother," Richard said thoughtfully. "I remember that we listened on the landing and we were so afraid."

"And Father said *he* wasn't content to be master of Rampling Gate anymore; *he* had come to London and revealed himself. An unspeakable horror, that is what he called it, that *he* should be so bold."

"Yes, exactly, and when Mother tried to quiet him, when she suggested that he was imagining things, he went into a perfect rage."

"But who could it have been, the master of Rampling Gate, if Father wasn't the master? Uncle Baxter was long dead by then."

"I just don't know what to make of it," Richard murmured. "And there's nothing in Father's papers to explain any of it at all." He examined the most recent of the pictures, a lovely tinted engraving that showed the house perfectly reflected in the azure water of its lake. "But I tell you, the worst part of it, Julie," he said shaking his head, "is that we've never even seen the house ourselves."

I glanced at him and our eyes met in a moment of confusion that quickly passed to something else. I leant forward:

"He did not say we couldn't go there, did he, Richard?" I demanded. "That we couldn't visit the house before it was destroyed."

"No, of course he didn't!" Richard said. The smile broke over his face easily. "After all, don't we owe it to the others, Julie? Uncle Baxter who spent the last of his fortune restoring the house,

even this old Mrs. Blessington that has kept it all these years?"

"And what about the village itself?" I added quickly. "What will it mean to these people to see Rampling Gate destroyed? Of course we must go and see the place ourselves."

"Then it's settled. I'll write to Mrs. Blessington immediately. I'll tell her we're coming and that we can not say how long we will stay."

"Oh, Richard, that would be too marvelous!" I couldn't keep from hugging him, though it flustered him and he pulled on his pipe just exactly the way Father would have done. "Make it at least a fortnight," I said. "I want so to know the place, especially if . . ."

But it was too sad to think of Father's admonition. And much more fun to think of the journey itself. I'd pack my manuscripts, for who knew, maybe in that melancholy and exquisite setting I'd find exactly the inspiration I required. It was almost a wicked exhilaration I felt, breaking the gloom that had hung over us since the day that Father was laid to rest.

"It is the right thing to do, isn't it, Richard?" I asked uncertainly, a little disconcerted by how much I wanted to go. There was some illicit pleasure in it, going to Rampling Gate at last.

"'Unspeakable horror,'" I repeated Father's words with a little grimace. What did it all mean? I thought again of the strange, almost exquisite young man I'd glimpsed in that railway carriage, gazing at us all with that wistful expression on his lean face. He had worn a black greatcoat with a red woollen cravat, and I could remember how pale he had been against that dash of red. Like bone china his complexion had been. Strange to remember it so vividly, even to the tilt of his head, and that long luxuriant brown hair. But he had been a blaze against that window. And I realized now that, in those few remarkable moments, he had created for me an ideal of masculine beauty which I had never questioned since. But Father had been so angry in those moments . . . I felt an unmistakable pang of guilt.

"Of course it's the right thing, Julie," Richard

answered. He at the desk, already writing the letters, and I was at a loss to understand the full measure of my thoughts.

It was late afternoon when the wretched old trap carried us up the gentle slope from the little railway station, and we had at last our first real look at that magnificent house. I think I was holding my breath. The sky had paled to a deep rose hue beyond a bank of softly gilded clouds, and the last rays of the sun struck the uppermost panes of the leaded windows and filled them with solid gold.

"Oh, but it's too majestic," I whispered, "too like a great cathedral, and to think that it belongs to us." Richard gave me the smallest kiss on the cheek. I felt mad suddenly and eager somehow to be laid waste by it, through fear or enchantment I could not say, perhaps a sublime mingling of both.

I wanted with all my heart to jump down and draw near on foot, letting those towers grow larger and larger above me, but our old horse had picked up speed. And the little line of stiff starched servants had broken to come forward, the old withered housekeeper with her arms out, the men to take down the boxes and the trunks.

Richard and I were spirited into the great hall by the tiny, nimble figure of Mrs. Blessington, our footfalls echoing loudly on the marble tile, our eyes dazzled by the dusty shafts of light that fell on the long oak table and its heavily carved chairs, the sombre, heavy tapestries that stirred ever so slightly against the soaring walls.

"It is an enchanted place," I cried, unable to contain myself. "Oh, Richard, we are home!" Mrs. Blessington laughed gaily, her dry hand closing tightly on mine.

Her small blue eyes regarded me with the most curiously vacant expression despite her smile. "Ramplings at Rampling Gate again, I can not tell you what a joyful day this is for me. And yes, my dear," she said as if reading my mind that very second, "I am, and have been for many years, quite blind. But if you spy a thing out of place in this house, you're to tell me at once, for it would be the exception, I assure you, and not the rule." And such warmth emanated from her wrinkled little face that I adored her at once.

We found our bedchambers, the very finest in the house, well aired with snow white linen and fires blazing cozily to dry out the damp that never left the thick walls. The small diamond pane windows opened on a glorious view of the water and the oaks that enclosed it and the few scattered lights that marked the village beyond.

That night, we laughed like children as we supped at the great oak table, our candles giving only a feeble light. And afterwards, it was a fierce battle of pocket billiards in the game room which had been Uncle Baxter's last renovation, and a little too much brandy, I fear.

It was just before I went to bed that I asked Mrs. Blessington if there had been anyone in this house since Uncle Baxter died. That had been the year 1838, almost fifty years ago, and she was already housekeeper then.

"No, my dear," she said quickly, fluffing the feather pillows. "Your father came that year as you know, but he stayed for no more than a month or two and then went on home."

"There was never a young man after that . . ." I pushed, but in truth I had little appetite for anything to disturb the happiness I felt. How I loved the Spartan cleanliness of this bedchamber, the stone walls bare of paper or ornament, the high luster of the walnut-paneled bed.

"A young man?" She gave an easy, almost hearty laugh as with unerring certainty of her surroundings. She lifted the poker and stirred the fire. "What a strange thing for you to ask."

I sat silent for a moment looking in the mirror, as I took the last of the pins from my hair. It fell down heavy and warm around my shoulders. It felt good, like a cloak under which I could hide. But she turned as if sensing some uneasiness in me, and drew near.

"Why do you say a young man, Miss?" she asked. Slowly, tentatively, fingers examined the long tresses that lay over my shoulders. She took the brush from my hands.

I felt perfectly foolish telling her the story, but I managed a simplified version, somehow, our meeting unexpectedly a devilishly handsome young man whom my Father in anger had later called the master of Rampling Gate.

"Handsome, was he?" she asked as she brushed out the tangles in my hair gently. It seemed she hung upon every word as I described him again.

"There were no intruders in this house, then, Mrs. Blessington?" I asked. "No mysteries to be solved . . ."

She gave the sweetest laugh.

"Oh, no, darling, this house is the safest place in the world," she said quickly. "It is a happy house. No intruder would dare to trouble Rampling Gate!"

Nothing, in fact, troubled the serenity of the days that followed. The smoke and noise of London, and our Father's dying words, became a dream. What was real were our long walks together through the overgrown gardens, our trips in the little skiff to and fro across the lake. We had tea under the hot glass of the empty conservatory. And early evening found us on our way upstairs with the best of the books from Uncle Baxter's library to read by candlelight in the privacy of our rooms.

And all our discreet inquiries in the village met with more or less the same reply: the villagers loved the house and carried no old or disquieting tales. Repeatedly, in fact, we were told that Rampling was the most contented hamlet in all England, that no one dared—Mrs. Blessington's very words—to make trouble here.

"It's our guardian angel, that old house," said the old woman at the bookshop where Richard stopped for the London papers. "Was there ever the town of Rampling without the house called Rampling Gate?"

How were we going to tell them of Father's edict? How were we going to remind ourselves? But we spoke not one word about the proposed disaster, and Richard wrote to his firm to say that we should not be back in London till fall.

He was finding a wealth of classical material in the old volumes that had belonged to Uncle Baxter, and I had set up my writing in the little study that opened off the library which I had all to myself.

Never had I known such peace and quiet. It seemed the atmosphere of Rampling Gate permeated my simplest written descriptions and wove its way richly into the plots and characters I created. The Monday after our arrival I had finished my first short story and went off to the village on foot to boldly post it to editors of *Blackwood's Magazine*.

It was a glorious morning, and I took my time as I came back on foot.

What had disturbed our father so about this lovely corner of England, I wondered? What had so darkened his last hours that he laid upon this spot his curse?

My heart opened to this unearthly stillness, to an undeniable grandeur that caused me utterly to forget myself. There were times here when I felt I was a disembodied intellect drifting through a fathomless silence, up and down garden paths and stone corridors that had witnessed too much to take cognizance of one small and fragile young woman who in random moments actually talked aloud to the suits of armour around her, to the broken statues in the garden, the fountain cherubs who had had not water to pour from their conches for years and years.

But was there in this loveliness some malignant force that was eluding us still, some untold story to explain all? Unspeakable horror . . . In my mind's eye I saw that young man, and the strangest sensation crept over me, that some enrichment of the picture had taken place in my memory or imagination in the recent past. Perhaps in dream I had reinvented him, given a ruddy glow to his lips and his cheeks. Perhaps in my re-creation for Mrs. Blessington, I had allowed him to raise his hand to that red cravat and had seen the fingers long and delicate and suggestive of a musician's hand.

It was all very much on my mind when I entered the house again, soundlessly, and saw Richard in his favorite leather wing chair by the fire.

The air was warm coming through the open

garden doors, and yet the blaze was cheerful, made the vast room with its towering shelves of leather-bound volumes appear inviting and almost small.

"Sit down," Richard said gravely, scarcely giving me a glance. "I want to read you something right now." He held a long narrow ledger in his hands. "This was Uncle Baxter's," he said, "and at first I thought it was only an account book he kept during the renovations, but I've found some actual diary entries made in the last weeks of his life. They're hasty, almost indecipherable, but I've managed to make them out."

"Well, do read them to me," I said, but I felt a little tug of fear. I didn't want to know anything terrible about this place. If we could have remained here forever . . . but that was out of the question, to be to be sure.

"Now listen to this," Richard said, turning the page carefully. " 'Fifth of May, 1838: He is here, I am sure of it. He is come back again.' And days later: 'He thinks this is his house, he does, and he would drink my wine and smoke my cigars if only he could. He reads my books and my papers and I will not stand for it. I have given orders that everything is to be locked.' And finally, the last entry written the morning before he died: 'Weary, weary, unto death and he is no small cause of my weariness. Last night I beheld him with my own eyes. He stood in this very room. He moves and speaks exactly as a mortal man, and dares tell me his secrets, and he a demon wretch with the face of a seraph and I a mere mortal, how am I to bear with him!' "

"Good Lord," I whispered slowly. I rose from the chair where I had settled, and standing behind him, read the page for myself. It was scrawl, the writing, the very last notation in the book. I knew that Uncle Baxter's heart had given out. He had not died by violence, but peacefully enough in this very room with his prayer book in his hand.

"Could it be the very same person Father spoke of that night?" Richard asked.

In spite of the sun pouring through the open doors, I experienced a violent chill. For the first time I felt wary of this house, wary of our boldness in coming here, heedful of our Father's words.

"But that was years before, Richard . . ." I said. "And what could this mean, this talk of a supernatural being! Surely the man was mad! It was no spirit I saw in that railway carriage!"

I sank down into the chair opposite and tried to quiet the beating of my heart.

"Julie," Richard said gently, shutting the ledger. "Mrs. Blessington has lived here contentedly for years. There are six servants asleep every night in the north wing. Surely there is nothing to all of this."

"It isn't very much fun, though, is it?" I said timidly. "Not at all like swapping ghost stories the way we used to do, and peopling the dark with imaginary beings, and laughing at friends at school who were afraid."

"All my life," he said, his eyes fixing me steadily, "I've heard tales of spooks and spirits, some imagined, some supposedly true, and almost invariably there is some mention of the house in question feeling haunted, of having an atmosphere to it that fills one with foreboding, some sense of menace or alarm . . ."

"Yes, I know, and there is no such poisonous atmosphere here at all."

"On the contrary, I've never been more at ease in my life." He shoved his hand into his pocket to extract the inevitable match to light his pipe which had gone out. "As a matter of fact, Julie, I don't know how in the world I'm going to comply with Father's last wish to tear down this place."

I nodded sympathetically. The very same thing had been on my mind since we'd arrived. Even now, I felt so comfortable, natural, quite safe.

I was wishing suddenly, irrationally, that he had not found the entries in Uncle Baxter's book.

"I should talk to Mrs. Blessington again!" I said almost crossly. "I mean quite seriously . . ."

"But I have, Julie," he said. "I asked her about it all this morning when I first made the discovery, and she only laughed. She swears she's never seen anything unusual here, and that there's no one left alive in the village who can tell tales of this place. She said again how glad she was that we'd come home to Rampling Gate. I don't think she has an inkling we mean to destroy the house. Oh, it would destroy her heart if she did."

"Never seen anything unusual?" I asked. "That is what she said? But what strange words for her to use, Richard, when she can not see at all."

But he had not heard me. He had laid the ledger aside and risen slowly, almost sluggishly, and he was wandering out of the double doors into the little garden and was looking over the high hedge at the oaks that bent their heavy elbowed limbs almost to the surface of the lake. There wasn't a sound at this early hour of the day, save the soft rustle of the leaves in the moving air, the cry now and then of a distant bird.

"Maybe it's gone, Julie," Richard said, over his shoulder, his voice carrying clearly in the quiet, "if it was ever here. Maybe there is nothing any longer to frighten anyone at all. You don't suppose you could endure the winter in this house, do you? I suppose you'd want to be in London again by then." He seemed quite small against the towering trees, the sky broken into small gleaming fragments by the canopy of foliage that gently filtered the light.

Rampling Gate had him. And I understood perfectly, because it also had me. I could very well endure the winter here, no matter how bleak or cold. I never wanted to go home.

And the immediacy of the mystery only dimmed my sense of everything and every place else.

After a long moment, I rose and went out into the garden, and placed my hand gently on Richard's arm.

"I know this much, Julie," he said just as if we had been talking to each other all the while. "I swore to Father that I would do as he asked, and it is tearing me apart. Either way, it will be on my conscience forever, obliterating this house or going against my own father and the charge he laid down to me with his dying breath."

"We must seek help, Richard. The advice of our lawyers, the advice of our lawyers, the advice of Father's clergymen. You must write to them

and explain the whole thing. Father was feverish when he gave the order. If we could lay it out before them, they would help us decide."

It was three o'clock when I opened my eyes. But I had been awake for a long time. I had heard the dim chimes of the clock below hour by hour. And I felt not fear lying here alone in the dark but something else. Some vague and relentless agitation, some sense of emptiness and need that caused me finally to rise from my bed. What was required to dissolve this tension, I wondered. I stared at the simplest things in the shadows. The little arras that hung over the fireplace with its slim princes and princesses lost in fading fiber and thread. The portrait of an Elizabethan ancestor gazing with one almond-shaped eye from his small frame.

What was this house, really? Merely a place or a state of mind? What was it doing to my soul? Why didn't the entries in Uncle Baxter's book send us flying back to London? Why had we stayed so late in the great hall together after supper, speaking not a single word?

I felt overwhelmed suddenly, and yet shut out of some great and dazzling secret, and wasn't that the very word that Uncle Baxter had used?

Conscious only of an unbearable restlessness, I pulled on my woollen wrapper, buttoning the lace collar and tying the sash. And putting on my slippers, I went out into the hall.

The moon fell full on the oak stairway, and on the deeply recessed door to Richard's room. On tiptoe I approached and, peering in, saw the bed was empty, the covers completely undisturbed.

So he was off on his own tonight the same as I. Oh, if only he had come to me, asked me to go with him.

I turned and made my way soundlessly down the long stairs.

The great hall gaped like a cavern before me, the moonlight here and there touching upon a pair of crossed swords, or a mounted shield. But far beyond the great hall, in the alcove just outside the library, I saw unmistakably a flickering light. And a breeze moved briskly through the room, carrying with it the sound and the scent of a wood fire.

I shuddered with relief. Richard was there. We could talk. Or perhaps we could go exploring together, guarding our fragile candle flames behind cupped fingers as we went from room to room? A sense of well-being pervaded me and quieted me, and yet the dark distance between us seemed endless, and I was desperate to cross it, hurrying suddenly past the long supper table with its massive candlesticks, and finally into the alcove before the library doors.

Yes, Richard was there. He sat with his eyes closed, dozing against the inside of the leather wing chair, the breeze from the garden blowing the fragile flames of the candles on the stone mantel and on the table at his side.

I was about to go to him, about to shut the doors, and kiss him gently and ask did he not want to go up to bed, when quite abruptly I saw in the corner of my eye that there was someone else in the room.

In the far left corner at the desk stood another figure, looking down at the clutter of Richard's papers, his pale hands resting on the wood.

I knew that it could not be so. I knew that I must be dreaming, that nothing in this room, least of all this figure, could be real. For it was the same young man I had seen fifteen years ago in the railway carriage and not a single aspect of that taut young face had been changed. There was the very same hair, thick and lustrous and only carelessly combed as it hung to the thick collar of his black coat, and the skin so pale it was almost luminous in the shadows, and those dark eyes looking up suddenly and fixing me with the most curious expression as I almost screamed.

We stared at one another across the dark vista of that room, I stranded in the doorway, he visibly and undeniably shaken that I had caught him unawares. My heart stopped.

And in a split second he moved towards me, closed the gap between us, towering over me, those slender white fingers gently closing on my arms.

"Julie!" he whispered, in a voice so low it seemed my own thoughts speaking to me. But this was no dream. He was real. He was holding to me and the scream had broken loose from me, deafening, uncontrollable and echoing from the four walls.

I saw Richard rising from the chair. I was alone. Clutching to the door frame, I staggered forward, and then again in a moment of perfect clarity I saw the young intruder, saw him standing in the garden, looking back over his shoulder, and then he was gone.

I could not stop screaming. I could not stop even as Richard held me and pleaded with me, and sat me down in the chair.

And I was still crying when Mrs. Blessington finally came.

She got a glass of cordial for me at once, as Richard begged me once more to tell what I had seen.

"But you know who it was!" I said to Richard almost hysterically. "It was he, the young man from the train. Only he wore a frockcoat years out of fashion and his silk tie was open at his throat. Richard, he was reading your papers, turning them over, reading them in the pitch dark."

"All right," Richard said, gesturing with his hand up for calm. "He was standing at the desk. And there was no light there so you could not see him well."

"Richard, it was he! Don't you understand? He touched me, he held my arms." I looked imploringly to Mrs. Blessington, who was shaking her head, her little eyes like blue beads in the light. "He called me Julie," I whispered. "He knows my name!"

I rose, snatching up the candle, and all but pushing Richard out of the way went to the desk. "Oh, dear God," I said. "Don't you see what's happened? It's your letters to Dr. Partridge, and Mrs. Sellers, about tearing down the house!"

Mrs. Blessington gave a little cry and put her hand to her cheek. She looked like a withered child in her nightcap as she collapsed into the straight-backed chair by the door.

"Surely you don't believe it was the same man, Julie, after all these years . . ."

"But he had not changed, Richard, not in the

smallest detail. There is no mistake, Richard, it was he, I tell you, the very same."

"Oh, dear, dear . . ." Mrs. Blessington whispered. "What will he do if you try to tear it down? What will he do now?"

"What will who do?" Richard asked carefully, narrowing his eyes. He took the candle from me and approached her. I was staring at her, only half realizing what I had heard.

"So you know who he is!" I whispered.

"Julie, stop it!" Richard said.

But her face had tightened, gone blank, and her eyes had become distant and small.

"You knew he was here!" I insisted. "You must tell us at once!"

With an effort she climbed to her feet. "There is nothing in this house to hurt *you*," she said, "nor any of us." She turned, spurning Richard as he tried to help her, and wandered into the dark hallway alone. "You've no need of me here any longer," she said softly, "and if you should tear down this house built by your forefathers, then you should do it without need of me."

"Oh, but we don't mean to do it, Mrs. Blessington!" I insisted. But she was making her way through the gallery back towards the north wing. "Go after her, Richard. You heard what she said. She knows who he is."

"I've had quite enough of this tonight," Richard said almost angrily. "Both of us should go up to bed. By the light of day we will dissect this entire matter and search this house. Now come."

"But he should be told, shouldn't he?" I demanded.

"Told what? Of whom do you speak!"

"Told that we will not tear down this house!" I said clearly, loudly, listening to the echo of my own voice.

The next day was indeed the most trying since we had come. It took the better part of the morning to convince Mrs. Blessington that we had no intention of tearing down Rampling Gate. Richard posted his letters and resolved that we should do nothing until help came.

And together we commenced a search of the house. But darkness found us only half finished, having covered the south tower and the south wing, and the main portion of house itself. There remained still the north tower, in a dreadful state of disrepair, and some rooms beneath the ground which in former times might have served as dungeons and were now sealed off. And there were closets and private stairways everywhere that we had scarce looked into, and at times we lost all track of where precisely we had been.

But it was also quite clear by supper time that Richard was in a state of strain and exasperation, and that he did not believe that I had seen anyone in the study at all.

He was further convinced that Uncle Baxter had been mad before he died, or else his ravings were a code for some mundane happening that had him extraordinarily overwrought.

But I knew what I had seen. And as the day progressed, I became ever more quiet and withdrawn. A silence had fallen between me and Mrs. Blessington. And I understood only too well the anger I'd heard in my father's voice on that long ago night when we had come home from Victoria Station and my mother had accused him of imagining things.

Yet what obsessed me more than anything else was the gentle countenance of the mysterious man I had glimpsed, the dark almost innocent eyes that had fixed on me for one moment before I had screamed.

"Strange that Mrs. Blessington is not afraid of him," I said in a low distracted voice, no longer caring if Richard heard me. "And that no one here seems in fear of him at all . . ." The strangest fancies were coming to me. The careless words of the villagers were running through my head. "You would be wise to do one very important thing before you retire," I said. "Leave out in writing a note to the effect that you do not intend to tear down the house."

"Julie, you have created an impossible dilemma," Richard demanded. "You insist we reassure this apparition that the house will not be destroyed, when in fact you verify the existence of the very creature that drove our father to say what he did."

"Oh, I wish I had never come here!" I burst out suddenly.

"Then we should go, both of us, and decide this matter at home."

"No, that's just it. I could never go without knowing . . . 'his secrets' . . . 'the demon wretch.' I could never go on living without knowing now!"

Anger must be an excellent antidote to fear, for surely something worked to alleviate my natural alarm. I did not undress that night, nor even take off my shoes, but rather sat in that dark hollow bedroom gazing at the small square of diamond-paned window until I heard all of the house fall quiet. Richard's door at last closed. There came those distant echoing booms that meant other bolts had been put in place.

And when the grandfather clock in the great hall chimed the hour of eleven, Rampling Gate was as usual fast asleep.

I listened for my brother's step in the hall. And when I did not hear him stir from his room, I wondered at it, that curiosity would not impel him to come to me, to say that we must go together to discover the truth.

It was just as well. I did not want him to be with me. And I felt a dark exultation as I imagined myself going out of the room and down the stairs as I had the night before. I should wait one more hour, however, to be certain. I should let the night reach its pitch. Twelve, the witching hour. My heart was beating too fast at the thought of it, and dreamily I recollected the face I had seen, the voice that had said my name.

Ah, why did it seem in retrospect so intimate, that we had known each other, spoken together, that it was someone I recognized in the pit of my soul?

"What is your name?" I believe I whispered aloud. And then a spasm of fear startled me. Would I have the courage to go in search of him, to open the door to him? Was I losing my mind? Closing my eyes, I rested my head against the high back of the damask chair.

What was more empty than this rural night? What was more sweet?

I opened my eyes. I had been half dreaming or talking to myself, trying to explain to Father why it was necessary that we comprehend the reason ourselves. And I realized, quite fully realized—I think before I was even awake—that *he* was standing by the bed.

The door was open. And he was standing there, dressed exactly as he had been the night before, and his dark eyes were riveted on me with that same obvious curiosity, his mouth just a little slack like that of a schoolboy, and he was holding to the bedpost almost idly with his right hand. Why, he was lost in contemplating me. He did not seem to know that I was looking at him.

But when I sat forward, he raised his finger as if to quiet me, and gave a little nod of his head.

"Ah, it is you!" I whispered.

"Yes," he said in the softest, most unobtrusive voice.

But we had been talking to each other, hadn't we? I had been asking him questions, no, telling him things. And I felt suddenly I was losing my equilibrium or slipping back into a dream.

No. Rather I had all but caught the fragment of some dream from the past. That rush of atmosphere that can engulf one at any moment of the day following when something evokes the universe that absorbed one utterly in sleep. I mean I heard our voices for an instant, almost in argument, and I saw Father in his top hat and black overcoat rushing alone through the streets of the West End, peering into one door after another, and then, rising from the marble-top table in the dim smoky music hall you . . . your face.

"Yes . . ."

*Go back, Julie!* It was Father's voice.

". . . to penetrate the soul of it," I insisted, picking up the lost thread. But did my lips move? "To understand what it is that frightened him, enraged him. He said, 'Tear it down!'"

". . . you must never, never, can't do that." His face was stricken, like that of a schoolboy about to cry.

"No, absolutely, we don't want to, either of us, you know it . . . and you are not a spirit!" I looked at his mud-spattered boots, the faintest smear of dust on that perfect white cheek.

"A spirit?" he asked almost mournfully, almost bitterly. "Would that I were."

Mesmerized I watched him come towards me and the room darkened, and I felt his cool silken hands on my face. I had risen. I was standing before him, and I looked up into his eyes.

I heard my own heartbeat. I heard it as I had the night before, right at the moment I had screamed. Dear God, I was talking to him! He was in my room and I was talking to him! And I was in his arms.

"Real, absolutely real!" I whispered, and a low zinging sensation coursed through me so that I had to steady myself against the bed.

He was peering at me as if trying to comprehend something terribly important to him, and he didn't respond. His lips did have a ruddy look to them, a soft look for all his handsomeness, as if he had never been kissed. And a slight dizziness had come over me, a slight confusion in which I was not at all sure that he was even there.

"Oh, but I am," he said softly. I felt his breath against my cheek, and it was almost sweet. "I am here, and you are with me, Julie . . ."

"Yes . . ."

My eyes were closing. Uncle Baxter sat hunched over his desk and I could hear the furious scratch of his pen. "Demon wretch!" he said to the night air coming in the open doors.

"No!" I said. Father turned in the door of the music hall and cried my name.

"Love me, Julie," came that voice in my ear. I felt his lips against my neck. "Only a little kiss, Julie, no harm . . ." And the core of my being, that secret place where all desires and all commandments are nurtured, opened to him without a struggle or a sound. I would have fallen if he had not held me. My arms closed about him, my hands slipping into the soft silken mass of his hair.

I was floating, and there was as there had always been at Rampling Gate an endless peace. It was Rampling Gate I felt around me, it was that timeless and impenetrable soul that had opened itself at last . . . A power within me of enormous ken . . . To see as a god sees, and take the depth of things as nimbly as the outward eyes can size and shape pervade . . . Yes, I whispered aloud, those words from Keats, those words . . To cease upon the midnight without pain . . .

No. In a violent instant we had parted, he drawing back as surely as I.

I went reeling across the bedroom floor and caught hold of the frame of the window, and rested my forehead against the stone wall.

For a long moment I stood with my eyes closed. There was a tingling pain in my throat that was almost pleasurable where his lips had touched me, a delicious throbbing that would not stop.

Then I turned, and I saw all the room clearly, the bed, the fireplace, the chair. And he stood still exactly as I'd left him and there was the most appalling distress in his face.

"What have they done to me?" he whispered. "Have they played the cruelest trick of all?"

"Something of menace, unspeakable menace," I whispered.

"Something ancient, Julie, something that defies understanding, something that can and will go on."

"But why, what are you?" I touched that pulsing pain with the tips of my fingers and, looking down at them, gasped. "And you suffer so, and you are so seemingly innocent, and it is as if you can love!"

His face was rent as if by a violent conflict within. And he turned to go. With my whole will, I stood fast not to follow him, not to beg him to turn back. But he did turn, bewildered, struggling and then bent upon his purpose as he reached for my hand. "Come with me," he said.

He drew me to him ever so gently, and slipping his arm around me guided me to the door.

Through the long upstairs corridor we passed hurriedly, and through a small wooden doorway to a screw stairs that I had never seen before.

I soon realized we were ascending the north

tower of the house, the ruined portion of the structure that Richard and I had not investigated before.

Through one tiny window after another I saw the gently rolling landscape moving out from the forest that surrounded us, and the small cluster of dim lights that marked the village of Rampling and the pale streak of white that was the London road.

Up and up we climbed until we had reached the topmost chamber, and this he opened with an iron key. He held back the door for me to enter and I found myself in a spacious room whose high narrow windows contained no glass. A flood of moonlight revealed the most curious mixture of furnishings and objects, the clutter that suggests an attic and a sort of den. There was a writing table, a great shelf of books, soft leather chairs and scores of old yellowed and curling maps and framed pictures affixed to the walls. Candles were everywhere stuck in the bare stone niches or to the tables and the shelves. Here and there a barrel served as a table, right alongside the finest old Elizabethan chair. Wax had dripped over everything, it seemed, and in the very midst of the clutter lay rumpled copies of the most recent papers, the *Mercure de Paris*; the London *Times*.

There was no place for sleeping in this room.

And when I thought of that, where he must lie when he went to rest, a shudder passed over me and I felt, quite vividly, his lips touching my throat again, and I felt the sudden urge to cry.

But he was holding me in his arms, he was kissing my cheeks and my lips again ever so softly, and then he guided me to a chair. He lighted the candles about us one by one.

I shuddered, my eyes watering slightly in the light. I saw more unusual objects: telescopes and magnifying glasses and a violin in its open case, and a handful of gleaming and exquisitely shaped sea shells. There were jewels lying about, and a black silk top hat and a walking stick, and a bouquet of withered flowers, dry as straw, and daguerreotypes and tintypes in their little velvet cases, and opened books.

But I was too distracted now by the sight of him in the light, the gloss of his large black eyes, and the gleam of his hair. Not even in the railway station had I seen him so clearly as I did now amid the radiance of the candles. He broke my heart.

And yet he looked at me as though I were the feast for his eyes, and he said my name again and I felt the blood rush to my face. But there seemed a great break suddenly in the passage of time. I had been thinking, yes, what are you, how long have you existed . . . And I felt dizzy again.

I realized that I had risen and I was standing beside him at the window and he was turning me to look down and the countryside below had unaccountably changed. The lights of Rampling had been subtracted from the darkness that lay like a vapor over the land. A great wood, far older and denser than the forest of Rampling Gate, shrouded the hills, and I was afraid suddenly, as if I were slipping into a maelstrom from which I could never, of my own will, return.

There was that sense of us talking together, talking and talking in low agitated voices and I was saying that I should not give in.

"Bear witness, that is all I ask of you . . ."

And there was in me some dim certainty that by knowledge alone I should be fatally changed. It was the reading of a forbidden book, the chanting of a forbidden charm.

"No, only what was," he whispered.

And then even the shape of the land itself eluded me. And the very room had lost its substance, as if a soundless wind of terrific force had entered this place and was blowing it apart.

We were riding in a carriage through the night. We had long long ago left the tower, and it was late afternoon and the sky was the color of blood. And we rode into a forest whose trees were so high and so thick that scarcely any sun at all broke to the soft leafstrewn ground.

We had no time to linger in this magical place. We had come to the open country, to the small patches of tilled earth that surrounded the ancient village of Knorwood with its gabled roofs and its tiny crooked streets. We saw the walls of the monastery of Knorwood and the little church with the bell chiming Vespers under the lowering sky.

A great bustling life resided in Knorwood, a thousand hearts beat in Knorwood, a thousand voices gave forth their common prayer.

But far beyond the village on the rise above the forest stood the rounded tower of a truly ancient castle, and to that ruined castle, no more than a shell of itself anymore, as darkness fell in earnest, we rode. Through its empty chambers we roamed, impetuous children, the horse and the road quite forgotten, and to the Lord of the Castle, a gaunt and white-skinned creature standing before the roaring fire of the roofless hall, we came. He turned and fixed us with his narrow and glittering eyes. A dead thing he was, I understood, but he carried within himself a priceless magic. And my young companion, my innocent young man passed by me into the Lord's arms. I saw the kiss. I saw the young man grow pale and struggle to turn away. It was as I had done this very night, beyond this dream, in my own bedchamber; and from the Lord he retreated, clutching to the sharp pain in his throat.

I understood. I knew. But the castle was dissolving as surely as anything in this dream might dissolve, and we were in some damp and close place.

The stench was unbearable to me, it was that most terrible of all stenches, the stench of death. And I heard my steps on the cobblestones and I reached to steady myself against the wall. The tiny square was deserted; the doors and windows gaped open to the vagrant wind. Up one side and down the other of the crooked street I saw the marks on the houses. And I knew what the marks meant. The Black Death had come to the village of Knorwood. The Black Death had laid it waste. And in a moment of suffocating horror I realized that no one, not a single person, was left alive.

But this was not quite right. There was someone walking in fits and starts up the narrow alleyway. Staggering he was, almost falling, as he pushed in one door after another, and at last came to a hot, stinking place where a child screamed on the floor. Mother and Father lay dead in the bed. And the great fat cat of the household, unharmed, played with the screaming infant, whose eyes bulged from its tiny sunken face.

"Stop it," I heard myself gasp. I knew that I was holding my head with both hands. "Stop it, stop it please!" I was screaming and my screams would surely pierce the vision and this small crude little room should collapse around me, and I should rouse the household of Rampling Gate to me, but I did not. The young man turned and stared at me, and in the close stinking room, I could not see his face.

But I knew it was he, my companion, and I could smell his fever and his sickness and the stink of the dying infant, and see the sleek, gleaming body of the cat as it pawed at the child's outstretched hand.

"Stop it, you've lost control of it!" I screamed surely with all my strength, but the infant screamed louder. "Make it stop!"

"I can not . . ." he whispered. "It goes on forever! It will never stop!"

And with a great piercing shriek I kicked at the cat and sent it flying out of the filthy room, overturning the milk pail as it went, jetting like a witch's familiar over the stones.

Blanched and feverish, the sweat soaking his crude jerkin, my companion took me by the hand. He forced me back out of the house and away from the crying child and into the street.

Death in the parlour, death in the bedroom, death in the cloister, death before the high altar, death in the open fields. It seemed the Judgment of God that a thousand souls had died in the village of Knorwood—I was sobbing, begging to be released—it seemed the very end of Creation itself.

And at last night came down over the dead village and he was alive still, stumbling up the slopes, through the forest, towards that rounded tower where the Lord stood with his hand on the stone frame of the broken window waiting for him to come.

"Don't go!" I begged him. I ran alongside him crying, but he didn't hear. Try as I might, I could not affect these things.

The Lord stood over him smiling almost sadly as he watched him fall, watched the chest heave with its last breaths. Finally the lips moved, calling out for salvation when it was damnation the Lord offered, when it was damnation that the Lord would give.

"Yes, damned then, but living, breathing!" the young man cried, rising in a last spasmodic movement. And the Lord, who had remained still until that instant, bent to drink.

The kiss again, the lethal kiss, the blood drawn out of the dying body, and then the Lord lifting the heavy head of the young man to take the blood back again from the body of the Lord himself.

I was screaming again, *Do not, do not drink.* He turned and looked at me. His face was now so perfectly the visage of death that I couldn't believe there was animation left in him, yet he asked: What would you do? Would you go back to Knorwood, would you open those doors one after another, would you ring the bell in the empty church, and if you did would the dead rise?

He didn't wait for my answer. And I had none now to give. He had turned again to the Lord who waited for him, locked his innocent mouth to that vein that pulsed with every semblance of life beneath the Lord's cold and translucent flesh. And the blood jetted into the young body, vanquishing in one great burst the fever and the sickness that had wracked it, driving it out with the mortal life.

He stood now in the hall of the Lord alone. Immortality was his and the blood thirst he would need to sustain it, and that thirst I could feel with my whole soul. He stared at the broken walls around him, at the fire licking the blackened stones of the giant fireplace, at the night sky over the broken roof, throwing out its endless net of stars.

And each and every thing was transfigured in his vision, and in my vision—the vision he gave now to me—to the exquisite essence of itself. A wordless and eternal voice spoke from the starry veil of heaven; it sang in the wind that rushed through the broken timbers; it sighed in the flames that ate the sooted stones of the hearth.

It was the fathomless rhythm of the universe that played beneath every surface, as the last living creature—that tiny child—fell silent in the village below.

A soft wind sifted and scattered the soil from the new-turned furrows in the empty fields. The rain fell from the black and endless sky.

Years and years passed. And all that had been Knorwood melted into the very earth. The forest sent out its silent sentinels, and mighty trunks rose where there had been huts and houses, where there had been monastery walls.

Finally nothing of Knorwood remained: not the little cemetery, not the little church, not even the name of Knorwood lived still in the world. And it seemed the horror beyond all horrors that no one anymore should know of a thousand souls who had lived and died in that small and insignificant village, that not anywhere in the great archives in which all history is recorded should a mention of that town remain.

Yet one being remained who knew, one being who had witnessed, and stood now looking down upon the very spot where his mortal life had ended, he who had scrambled up on his hands and knees from the pit of Hell that had been that disaster; it was the young man who stood beside me, the master of Rampling Gate.

And all through the walls of his old house were the stones of the ruined castle, and all through the ceilings and floors the branches of those ancient trees.

What was solid and majestic here, and safe within the minds of those who slept tonight in the village of Rampling, was only the most fragile citadel against horror, the house to which he clung now.

A great sorrow swept over me. Somewhere in the drift of images I had relinquished myself, lost all sense of the point in space from which I saw. And in a great rush of lights and noise I was enlivened now and made whole as I had been when we rode together through the forest, only it was into the world of now, this hour, that we passed. We were flying it seemed through the rural darkness along the railway towards London, where the nighttime city burst like an enormous bubble in a shower of laughter, and motion, and glaring light. He was walking with me under the gas lamps, his face all but shimmering with that same dark innocence, that same irresistible warmth. And it seemed we were holding tight to one another in the very midst of a crowd. And the crowd was a living thing, a writhing thing, and everywhere there came a dark rich aroma from it, the aroma of fresh blood. Women in white fur and gentlemen in opera capes swept into the brightly lighted doors of the theatre; the blare of the music hall inundated us, then faded away. Only a thin soprano voice was left, singing a high, plaintive song. I was in his arms, and his lips were covering mine, and there came that dull zinging sensation again, that great uncontrollable opening within myself. Thirst, and the promise of satiation measured only by the intensity of that thirst. Up stairs we fled together, into high-ceilinged bedrooms papered in red damask where the loveliest women reclined on brass bedsteads, and the aroma was so strong now I could not bear it, and before me they offered themselves, they opened their arms. "Drink," he whispered, yes, drink. And I felt the warmth filling me, charging me, blurring my vision, until we broke again, free and light and invisible it seemed as we moved over the rooftops and down again through rain-drenched streets. But the rain did not touch us; the falling snow did not chill us; we had within ourselves a great and indissoluble heat. And together in the carriage, we talked to each other in low, exuberant rushes of language; we were lovers; we were constant; we were immortal. We were as enduring as Rampling Gate.

I tried to speak; I tried to end the spell. I felt his arms around me and I knew we were in the tower room together, and some terrible miscalculation had been made.

"Do not leave me," he whispered. "Don't you understand what I am offering you? I have told you everything; and all the rest is but the weariness, the fever and the fret, those old words from the poem. Kiss me, Julie, open to me. Against your will I will not take you . . ." Again I heard my own scream. My hands were on his cool white skin, his lips were gentle yet hungry, his eyes yielding and ever young. Father turned in the rain-drenched

London street and cried out: "Julie!" I saw Richard lost in the crowd as if searching for someone, his hat shadowing his dark eyes, his face haggard, old. Old!

I moved away. I was free. And I was crying softly and we were in this strange and cluttered tower room. He stood against the backdrop of the window, against the distant drift of pale clouds. The candle-light glimmered in his eyes. Immense and sad and wise they seemed, and oh, yes, innocent as I have said again and again. "I revealed myself to them," he said. "Yes, I told my secret. In rage or bitterness, I know not which, I made them my dark co-conspirators and always I won. They could not move against me, and neither will you. But they would triumph still. For they torment me now with their fairest flower. Don't turn away from me, Julie. You are mine, Julie, as Rampling Gate is mine. Let me gather the flower to my heart."

nights of argument. But finally Richard had come round. He would sign over to me his share of Rampling Gate, and I should absolutely refuse to allow the place torn down. There would be nothing he could do then to obey Father's command. I had given him the legal impediment he needed, and of course I should leave the house to him and his children. It should always be in Rampling hands.

A clever solution, it seemed to me, as Father had not told *me* to destroy the place, and I had no scruples in the matter now at all.

And what remained was for him to take me to the little train station and see me off for London, and not worry about me going home to Mayfair on my own.

"You stay here as long as you wish, and do not worry," I said. I felt more tenderly towards him than I could ever express. "You knew as soon as you set foot in the place that Father was all wrong. Uncle Baxter put it in his mind, undoubtedly, and Mrs. Blessington has always been right. There is nothing to harm there, Richard. Stay, and work or study as you please."

ANNE RICE

The great black engine was roaring past us, the carriages slowing to a stop. "Must go now, darling, kiss me," I said.

"But what came over you, Julie, what convinced you so quickly . . . ?"

"We've been through it all, Richard," I said. "What matters is that we are all happy, my dear." And we held each other close.

I waved until I couldn't see him anymore. The flickering lamps of the town were lost in the deep lavender light of the early evening, and the dark hulk of Rampling Gate appeared for one uncertain moment like the ghost of itself on the nearby rise.

I sat back and closed my eyes. Then I opened them slowly, savouring this moment for which I had waited too long.

He was smiling, seated there as he had been all along, in the far corner of the leather seat opposite, and now he rose with a swift, almost delicate movement and sat beside me and enfolded me in his arms.

"It's five hours to London," he whispered in my ear.

"I can wait," I said, feeling the thirst like a fever as I held tight to him, feeling his lips against my eyelids and my hair. "I want to hunt the London streets tonight," I confessed, a little shyly, but I saw only approbation in his eyes.

"Beautiful Julie, my Julie . . ." he whispered.

"You'll love the house in Mayfair," I said.

"Yes . . ." he said.

"And when Richard finally tires of Rampling Gate, we shall go home."

228

# THE VAMPIRE OF KALDENSTEIN

# Frederick Cowles

Frederick Ignatius Cowles (1900–48) was born in Cambridge, England, and graduated from Emmanuel College, Cambridge. He worked for a time at the library of Trinity College but then moved in 1927 to become chief librarian at Swinton and Pendlebury in Lancashire, a position he held until the end of his life. There he edited the library *Bulletin*, for which he wrote occasional ghost stories.

The fact that his grandmother was a gypsy may help account for his many wanderings throughout the British Isles as he researched a series of travel books, including *Dust of Years: Pilgrimages in Search of the Ancient Shrines of England* (1933), *'Neath English Skies* (1933), *The Magic of Cornwall* (1934), *Not Far from the Smoke* (1935), and *Vagabond Pilgrimages* (1948), all of which were illustrated by his talented wife, Doris. He also wrote children's books, including *The Magic Map* (1934) and one for his son, *Michael in Bookland* (1936).

When World War II erupted, he was commissioned a captain. Although unable to join the armed forces because of health problems, he traveled extensively to lecture the troops, further damaging his health; severe kidney problems were responsible for his death, but not before he was able to publish his most famous book, *This Is England* (1946).

"The Vampire of Kaldenstein" was originally published in *The Night Wind Howls* (London: Muller, 1938).

# The Vampire of Kaldenstein

## FREDERICK COWLES

### I

Since I was a lad, I have been accustomed to spending my vacations wandering about the more remote parts of Europe. I have had some pleasant times in Italy, Spain, Norway, and southern France, but of all the countries I have explored in this fashion, Germany is my favorite. It is an ideal vacationland for the lover of open-air life whose means are small and tastes simple, for the people are always so friendly and the inns are good and cheap. I have had many excellent vacations in Germany, but one will always stand out in my memory because of a very strange and remarkable experience which befell me.

It was in the summer of 1933, and I had practically made up my mind to go on a cruise to the Canaries with Donald Young. Then he caught a very childish complaint—the measles, in fact—and I was left to make my own arrangements. The idea of joining an organized cruise without a companion did not appeal to me. I am not a particularly sociable kind of person, and these cruises seem to be one round of dances, cocktail parties, and bridge drives. I was afraid of feeling like a fish out of water, so I decided to forgo the cruise. Instead I got out my maps of Germany and began to plan a walking tour.

Half the fun of a vacation is in the planning of it, and I suppose I decided on a particular part of the country and changed my mind half a dozen times. At first I liked the Moselle Valley, then it was the Lahn. I toyed with the idea of the Black Forest, swung over to the Harz Mountains, and then thought it might be fun to re-visit Saxony. Finally, I fixed upon southern Bavaria, because I had never been there and it seemed better to break fresh ground.

Two days of third-class travel is tiring even for a hardened globe-trotter, and I arrived at Munich feeling thoroughly weary and sore. By some good chance I discovered the Inn of the Golden Apple, near the Hofgarten, where Peter Schmidt sells both good wine and good food, and has a few rooms for the accommodation of guests. Peter, who lived in Canada for ten years and speaks excellent English, knew exactly how I was feeling. He gave me a comfortable room for one mark a night, served me with hot coffee and rolls, and advised me to go to bed and stay there until I was completely rested. I took his advice, slept soundly for twelve hours, and awakened feeling as fresh as a daisy. A dish of roast pork and two glasses of lager beer completed the cure, and I sallied forth to see something of Munich.

The city is the fourth largest in Germany and has much of interest to show the visitor. The day was well advanced, but I managed to inspect the Frauen-Kirche with its fine stained glass, the old Rathaus, and the fourteenth-century church of St. Peter, near the Marien-Platz. I looked in at the Regina-Palast, where a tea dance was in progress, and then went back to the Golden Apple for dinner. Afterward, I attended a performance of *Die Meistersinger* at the National Theater. It was past midnight when I retired to bed, and by then I had decided to stay in Munich for another day.

I won't bore you with a description of the things I saw and did on that second day. It was just the usual round of sights with nothing out of the ordinary.

After dinner Peter helped me to plan my tour. He revealed a very intimate knowledge of the Bavarian villages, and gave me a list of inns which eventually proved invaluable. It was he who suggested I should take a train to Rosenheim and begin my walk from there. We mapped out a route covering about two hundred miles and bringing me back to Munich at the end of fifteen days.

Well, to cut a long story short, I caught the early morning train to Rosenheim, and a deadly slow journey it was. It took nearly three hours to cover a distance of forty-six miles. The town itself is quite a cheerful place of the small industrial type, with a fifteenth-century church and a good museum of Bavarian paintings housed in an old chapel.

I did not linger there, but started off along the road to Traunstein—a pleasant road curving around the Chiem-See, the largest lake in Bavaria.

I spent the night at Traunstein and the next day pushed on to the old walled town of Mühldorf. From there I planned to make for Vilshofen by way of Pfarrkirchen. But I took a wrong turning and found myself in a small place called Gangkofen. The local innkeeper tried to be helpful and directed me to a field path which he said would prove a short cut to Pfarrkirchen. Evidently I misunder-

stood his instructions, for evening came and I was hopelessly lost in the heart of a range of low hills which were not marked on my map. Darkness was falling when I came upon a small village huddled under the shadow of a high cliff upon which stood a gray, stone castle.

Fortunately, the village possessed an inn—a primitive place but moderately comfortable. The landlord was an intelligent kind of chap and friendly enough, although he informed me that visitors were seldom seen in the district. The name of the hamlet was Kaldenstein.

I was served with a simple meal of goat's-milk cheese, salad, coarse bread, and a bottle of thin red wine, and, having done justice to the spread, went for a short stroll.

The moon had risen and the castle stood out against a cloudless sky like some magic castle in a fairy tale. It was only a small building—square, with four turrets—but it was the most romantic-looking fortress I had ever seen. A light twinkled in one of the windows, so I knew the place was inhabited. A steep path and a flight of steps cut in the rock led up to it, and I half considered paying the Lord of Kaldenstein a late visit. Instead I returned to the inn and joined the few men who were drinking in the public room.

The company was mainly composed of folk of the laboring class, and although they were polite they had little of that friendly spirit one is accustomed to meet with in German villages. They seemed morose and unresponsive and I had the impression that they shared some dread secret. I did my best to engage them in conversation without success. Then, to get one of them to speak, I asked, "Tell me, my friends, who lives in the castle on the hillside?"

The effect of the harmless question upon them was startling. Those who were drinking placed their beer mugs on the table and gazed at me with consternation on their faces. Some made the sign of the cross, and one old chap hoarsely whispered, "Silence, stranger. God forbid that he should hear."

My inquiry seemed to have upset them altogether, and within ten minutes they all left in a group. I apologized to the landlord for any indiscretion I had been guilty of, and hoped my presence had not robbed him of custom.

He waved aside my excuses and assured me that the men would not have stayed long in any case.

"They are terrified of any mention of the castle," he said, "and consider it unlucky to even glance at the building after nightfall."

"But why?" I inquired. "Who lives there?"

"It is the home of Count Ludwig von Kaldenstein."

"And how long has he lived up there?" I asked.

The man moved over to the door and carefully shut and barred it before he replied. Then he came over to my chair and whispered, "He has been up there for nearly three hundred years."

"Nonsense," I exclaimed laughing. "How can any man, be he count or peasant, live for three hundred years. I suppose you mean that his family has held the castle for that length of time?"

"I mean exactly what I say, young man," answered the old fellow earnestly. "The Count's family has held the castle for ten centuries, and the Count himself has dwelt in Burg Kaldenstein for nearly three hundred years."

"But how can that be possible?"

"He is a vampire. Deep down in the castle rock are great vaults and in one of these the Count sleeps during the day so that the sunlight may not touch him. Only at night does he walk outside."

This was too fantastic for anything. I am afraid I smiled in a skeptical manner, but the poor landlord was obviously very serious, and I hesitated to make another remark that might wound his feelings. I finished my beer and got up to go to bed. As I was mounting the stairs my host called me back, and, grasping my arm, said, "Please, sir, let me beg you to keep your window closed. The night air of Kaldenstein is not healthy."

On reaching my room I found the window already tightly shut, although the atmosphere was like that of an oven. Of course, I opened it at once and leaned out to fill my lungs with fresh air. The window looked directly upon the castle and, in the clear light of the full moon, the building appeared more than ever like some dream of fairyland.

I was just drawing back into the room when I thought I saw a black figure silhouetted against the sky on the summit of one of the turrets. Even as I watched, it flapped enormous wings and soared into the night. It seemed too large for an eagle, but the moonlight has an odd trick of distorting shapes. I watched until it was only a tiny, black speck in the far distance. Just then, from far away, a dog howled weirdly and mournfully.

Within a few moments I was ready for bed, and disregarding the innkeeper's warning, I left the window open. I took my electric flashlight from my rucksack and placed it on the small bedside table—a table above which hung a wooden crucifix.

I am usually asleep as soon as my head touches the pillow, but on this particular night I found it difficult to settle. The moonlight disturbed me and I tossed about, vainly trying to get comfortable. I counted sheep until I was heartily sick of imagining the silly creatures passing through a gap in a hedge, but still sleep eluded me.

A clock in the house chimed the hour of midnight, and suddenly I had the unpleasant feeling that I was no longer alone. For a moment I felt frightened and then, overcoming my fear, I turned over. There, by the window and black against the moonlight, was the figure of a tall man. I started up in bed and groped for my flashlight. In doing so I knocked something from the wall. It was the little crucifix and my fingers closed over it almost as soon as it touched the table. From the direction of the window came a muttered curse, and I saw the figure poise itself on the sill and spring out into the night. In that brief moment I noticed one other thing—the man, whoever he was, cast no shadow. The moonlight seemed to stream right through him.

It must have been almost half an hour before I dared get out of bed and close the window. After that, I fell asleep immediately and slept soundly until the maid called me at eight o'clock.

In the broad daylight the events of the night

seemed too ridiculous to be true, and I decided that I had been the victim of some fantastic nightmare. In answer to the landlord's polite inquiry, I vowed I had spent a most comfortable night, although I am afraid my looks must have belied the statement.

## II

After breakfast, I went out to explore the village. It was rather larger than it had appeared on the previous evening, with some of the houses lying in a valley at the side of the road.

There was even a small church, Romanesque in type and sadly in need of repair. I entered the building and was inspecting its gaudy high altar when a priest came in through a side door. He was a lean, ascetic-looking man, and at once gave me a friendly greeting. I returned his salutation and told him I was from England. He apologized for the obvious poverty of the building, pointed out some good fifteenth-century glass, a carved font of the same period, and a very pleasing statue of the Madonna.

Later, as I stood at the church door with him, I looked toward the castle and said, "I wonder, Father, if the Lord of Kaldenstein will give me a welcome as friendly as the one I have received from you?"

"The Lord of Kaldenstein," repeated the priest with a tremor in his voice. "Surely you are not proposing to visit the castle?"

"That is my intention," I replied. "It looks a very interesting place and I should be sorry to leave this part of the world without seeing it."

"Let me implore you not to attempt to enter that accursed place," he pleaded. "Visitors are not welcomed at Kaldenstein Castle. Besides that," he went on with a change in his voice, "there is nothing to see in the building."

"What about the wonderful vaults in the cliff and the man who has lived in them for three hundred years?" I laughed.

The priest's face visibly blanched. "Then you know of the vampire," he said. "Do not laugh at evil, my son. May God preserve us all from the living dead." He made the sign of the Cross.

"But Father," I cried, "surely you do not believe in such a medieval superstition?"

"Every man believes what he knows to be true, and we of Kaldenstein can prove that no burial has taken place in the castle since 1645, when Count Feodor died and his cousin Ludwig from Hungary inherited the estate."

"Such a tale is too absurd," I remonstrated. "There must be some reasonable explanation of the mystery. It is unthinkable that a man who came to this place in 1645 can still be alive."

"Much is possible to those who serve the Devil," answered the priest. "Always throughout the history of the world, evil has warred with good, and often triumphed. Kaldenstein Castle is the haunt of terrible, unnatural wickedness, and I urge you to keep as far away from it as you can."

He bade me a courteous farewell, lifted his hand in a gentle benediction, and re-entered the church.

Now I must confess that the priest's words gave me a most uncomfortable feeling and made me think of my nightmare. Had it been a dream after all? Or could it have been the vampire himself seeking to make me one of his victims, and only being frustrated in his plan by my accidental gripping of the crucifix? These thoughts passed through my mind and I almost abandoned my resolve to seek admittance to the castle. Then I looked up again at the gray old walls gleaming in the morning sunshine, and laughed at my fears. No mythical monster from the Middle Ages was going to frighten me away. The priest was just as superstitious as his ignorant parishioners.

Whistling a popular song, I made my way up the village street and was soon climbing the narrow path which led to the castle. As the ascent became steeper, the path gave place to a flight of steps which brought me onto a small plateau before the main door of the building. There was no sign of life about the place, but a ponderous bell hung before the entrance. I pulled a rusty chain and set the cracked thing jangling. The sound disturbed a colony of rooks in one of the turrets and started them chattering, but no human being appeared to answer my summons. Again, I set the bell ringing. This time the echoes had hardly died away when I heard bolts being withdrawn. The great door creaked on its hinges, and an old man stood blinking in the sunlight.

"Who comes to Castle Kaldenstein?" he asked in a curious high-pitched voice, and I could see that he was half-blind.

"I am an English visitor," I answered, "and would like to see the Count."

"His Excellency does not receive visitors," was the reply, and the man made to close the door in my face.

"But is it not permitted that I should see over the castle?" I asked hurriedly. "I am interested in medieval fortresses and should be sorry to leave Kaldenstein without inspecting this splendid building."

The old fellow peered out at me, and in a hesitant voice said, "There is little to see, sir, and I am afraid you would only be wasting your time."

"Yet, I should appreciate the privilege of a brief visit," I argued, "and I am sure the Count would not object. I do assure you I shall not be a nuisance and I have no desire to disturb His Excellency's privacy."

"What is the hour?" asked the man.

I informed him that it was barely eleven o'clock. He muttered something about it being "safe while the sun is in the sky," and motioned me to enter. I found myself in a bare hall, hung with rotting tapestry and smelling of damp and decay. At the end of the room was a canopied dais surmounted by a coat of arms.

"This is the main hall of the castle," mumbled my guide, "and it has witnessed many great historic scenes in the days of the great lords of Kaldenstein. Here Frederic, the sixth Count, put out the eyes of twelve Italian hostages, and afterward had them driven over the edge of the cliff. Here Count August is said to have poisoned a prince of Wurttemburg, and then sat at a feast with the dead body."

He went on with his tales of foul and treacherous deeds, and it was evident that the counts of Kaldenstein must have been a very unsavory lot. From the main hall he conducted me into a number of smaller rooms filled with moldering furniture. His own quarters were in the north turret, but although he showed me over the whole building I saw no room in which his master could be. The old fellow opened every door without hesitation and it seemed that, except for himself, the castle was untenanted.

"But where is the Count's room?" I inquired as we returned to the main hall.

He looked confused for a moment, and then replied, "We have certain underground apartments, and His Excellency uses one as his bedchamber. You see he can rest there undisturbed."

I thought that any room in the building would give him the quietness he required, without having to seek peace in the bowels of the earth.

"And have you no private chapel?" I asked.

"The chapel is also below."

I intimated that I was interested in chapels, and should very much like to see an example of an underground place of worship. The old man made several excuses, but at last consented to show me the crypt. Taking an old-fashioned lantern from a shelf, he lit the candle in it, and, lifting a portion of the tapestry from the wall, opened a hidden door. A sickly odor of damp corruption swept up at us. Muttering to himself, he led the way down a flight of stone steps and along a passage hollowed in the rock. At the end of this was another door which admitted us to a large cavern furnished like a church. The place stank like a charnel house, and the feeble light of the lantern only intensified the gloom. My guide led me toward the chancel and, lifting the light, pointed out a particularly revolting painting of Lazarus rising from the dead which hung above the altar. I moved forward to examine it more closely, and found myself near another door.

"And what is beyond this?"

"Speak softly, sir," he implored. "It is the vault

in which rest the mortal remains of the lords of Kaldenstein."

And while he was speaking, I heard a sound from beyond that barrier—a sigh, and the kind of noise that might be made by a person turning in his sleep.

I think the old servitor also heard it, for he grasped me with a trembling hand and led me out of the chapel. His flickering light went before me as I mounted the stairs, and I laughed sharply with relief as we stepped into the castle hall again. He gave me a quick look and said, "That is all, sir. You see there is little of interest in this old building."

I tried to press a five-mark piece into his hand, but he refused to accept it.

"Money is of no use to me, sir," he whispered. "I have nothing to spend it on, for I live with the dead. Give the coin to the priest in the village and ask him to say a mass for me if you will."

I promised it should be done as he desired and then, in some mad spirit of bravado, asked, "And when does the Count receive visitors?"

"My master never receives visitors," was the reply.

"But surely he is sometimes in the castle itself? He doesn't spend all his time in the vaults," I urged.

"Usually after nightfall he sits in the hall for an hour or so, and sometimes walks on the battlements."

"Then I shall be back tonight," I cried. "I owe it to His Excellency to pay my respects to him."

The old man turned in the act of unfastening the door, and fixing his dim eyes upon my face said, "Come not to Kaldenstein after the sun has set lest you find that which shall fill your heart with fear."

"Don't try to frighten me with any of your hobgoblins," I rudely replied. Then, raising my voice, I cried, "Tonight I shall wait upon the Count von Kaldenstein."

The servant flung the door wide and the sunlight streamed into the moldering building.

"If you come, he will be ready to receive you," he said, "and remember that if you enter the castle again, you do so of your own free will."

## III

By the time evening came, my courage had quite evaporated and I wished I had taken the priest's advice and left Kaldenstein. But there is a streak of obstinacy in my makeup and, having vowed to visit the castle again, nothing could turn me from my purpose. I waited until dusk had fallen, and, saying nothing to the innkeeper of my intentions, made my way up the steep path to the fortress. The moon had not yet risen and I had to use my flashlight on the steps. I rang the cracked bell and the door opened almost immediately. There stood the old servant bowing a welcome.

"His Excellency will see you, sir," he cried. "Enter Kaldenstein Castle—enter of your own free will."

For one second I hesitated. Something seemed to warn me to retreat while there was still time. Then I plucked up courage and stepped over the threshold.

A log fire was burning in the enormous grate and gave a more cheerful atmosphere to the gloomy apartment. Candles gleamed in the silver candelabra, and I saw that a man was sitting at the table on the dais. As I advanced, he came down to greet me.

How shall I describe the Count of Kaldenstein? He was unusually tall, with a face of unnatural pallor. His hair was intensely black, and his hands delicately shaped, but with very pointed fingers and long nails. His eyes impressed me most. As he crossed the room they seemed to glow with a red light, just as if the pupils were ringed with flame. However, his greeting was conventional enough.

"Welcome to my humble home, sir," he said, bowing very low. "I regret my inability to offer you a more hospitable welcome, but we live very frugally. It is seldom we entertain guests, and I am honored that you should take the trouble to call upon me."

I murmured some polite word of thanks, and he conducted me to a seat at the long table upon which stood a decanter and one glass.

"You will take wine?" he invited, and filled the glass to the brim. It was a rare old vintage, but I felt a little uncomfortable at having to drink alone.

"I trust you will excuse me for not joining you," he said, evidently noticing my hesitant manner. "I never drink wine." He smiled, and I saw that his front teeth were long and sharply pointed.

"And now tell me," he went on. "What are you doing in this part of the world? Kaldenstein is rather off the beaten track and we seldom see strangers."

I explained that I was on a walking tour and had missed my way to Pfarrkirchen. The Count laughed softly, and again showed his fanglike teeth.

"And so you came to Kaldenstein and of your own free will you have come to visit me."

I began to dislike these references to my free will. The expression seemed to be a kind of formula. The servant had used it when I was leaving after my morning visit, and again when he had admitted me that evening, and now the Count was making use of it.

"How else should I come but of my own free will?" I asked sharply.

"In the bad old days of the past, many have been brought to this castle by force. The only guests we welcome today are those who come willingly."

All this time a queer sensation was gradually coming over me; I felt as if all my energy was being sapped from me, and a deadly nausea was overpowering my senses. The Count went on uttering commonplaces, but his voice came from far away. I was conscious of his peculiar eyes gazing into mine. They grew larger and larger, and it seemed that I was looking into two wells of fire. And then, with a clumsy movement, I knocked my wine glass over. The frail thing shattered to fragments, and the noise restored me to my senses. A splinter pierced my hand and a tiny pool of blood formed on the table. I sought for a handkerchief, but before I could produce it I was terrified by an unearthly howl which echoed through the vaulted hall. The cry came from the lips of the Count, and in a moment he was bending over the blood on the table, licking it up with obvious relish. A more disgusting sight I have never witnessed, and, struggling to my feet, I made for the door.

But terror weakened my limbs, and the Count had overtaken me before I had covered many yards. His white hands grasped my arms and led me back to the chair I had vacated.

"My dear sir," he said. "I must beg you to excuse me for my discourtesy. The members of my family have always been peculiarly affected by the sight of blood. Call it an idiosyncrasy if you like, but it does at times make us behave like wild animals. I am grieved to have so far forgotten my manners as to behave in such a strange way before a guest. I assure you that I have sought to conquer this failing, and for that reason I keep away from my fellow men."

The explanation seemed plausible enough, but it filled me with horror and loathing—more especially as I could see a tiny globule of blood clinging to his mouth.

"I fear I am keeping Your Excellency from bed," I suggested, "and in any case I think it is time I got back to the inn."

"Ah, no, my friend," he replied. "The night hours are the ones I enjoy best, and I shall be very grateful if you will remain with me until morning. The castle is a lonely place and your company will be a pleasant change. There is a room prepared for you in the south turret and tomorrow, who knows, there may be other guests to cheer us."

A deadly fear gripped my heart and I staggered to my feet stammering, "Let me go . . . Let me go. I must return to the village at once."

"You cannot return tonight, for a storm is brewing and the cliff path will be unsafe."

As he uttered these words he crossed to a window, and, flinging it open, raised one arm toward the sky. As if in obedience to his gesture, a flash of vivid lightning split the clouds, and a clap of thunder seemed to shake the castle. Then the rain came in a terrible deluge and a great wind howled across the mountains. The Count closed the casement and returned to the table.

"You see, my friend," he chuckled, "the very elements are against your return to the village. You must be satisfied with such poor hospitality as we can offer you, for tonight at any rate."

The red-rimmed eyes met mine, and again I felt my will being sapped from my body. His voice was no more than a whisper, and seemed to come from far away.

"Follow me, and I will conduct you to your room. You are my guest for tonight."

He took a candle from the table and, like a man in a trance, I followed him up a winding staircase, along an empty corridor, and into a cheerless room furnished with an ancient four-poster bed.

"Sleep well," he said with a wicked leer. "Tomorrow night you shall have other company."

The heavy door slammed behind him as he left me alone, and I heard a bolt being shot on the other side. Summoning what little strength was left in my body, I hurled myself against the door. It was securely fastened and I was a prisoner.

Through the keyhole came the Count's purring voice.

"Yes, you shall have other company tomorrow night. The Lords of Kaldenstein shall give you a hearty welcome to their ancestral home."

A burst of mocking laughter died away in the distance as I fell to the floor in a dead faint.

## IV

I must have recovered somewhat after a time and dragged myself to the bed and again sunk into unconsciousness, for when I came around, daylight was streaming through the barred window of the room. I looked at my wristwatch. It was half-past three and, by the sun, it was afternoon, so the greater part of the day had passed.

I still felt weak, but struggled over to the window. It looked out upon the craggy slopes of the mountain, and there was no human habitation in sight. With a moan, I returned to the bed and tried to pray. I watched the patch of sunlight on the floor grow fainter and fainter until it had faded altogether. Then the shadows gathered and

at last, only the dim outline of the window remained.

The darkness filled my soul with a new terror, and I lay on the bed in a cold, clammy sweat. Then I heard footsteps approaching, the door was flung open, and the Count entered bearing a candle.

"You must pardon me for what may seem a shocking lack of manners on my part," he exclaimed, "but necessity compels me to keep to my chamber during the day. Now, however, I am able to offer you some entertainment."

I tried to rise, but my limbs refused to function. With a mirthless laugh he placed one arm around my waist and lifted me with as little effort as if I were a baby. In this fashion he carried me across the corridor and down the stairs into the hall.

Only three candles burned on the table, and I could see little of the room for some moments after he had dumped me into a chair. Then, as my eyes became accustomed to the gloom, I realized that there were two other guests at that board. The feeble light flickered on their faces, and I almost screamed with terror. I looked upon the ghastly countenances of dead men, every feature stamped with evil, and their eyes glowed with the same hellish light that shone in the Count's eyes.

"Allow me to introduce my uncle and my cousin," said my jailer. "August von Kaldenstein and Feodor von Kaldenstein."

"But," I blurted out, "I was told that Count Feodor died in 1645."

The three terrible creatures laughed heartily, as if I had recounted a good joke. Then August leaned over the table and pinched the fleshy part of my arm.

"He is full of good blood," he chuckled. "This feast has been long promised, Ludwig, but I think it has been worth waiting for."

I must have fainted at that, and when I came to myself I was lying on the table, and the three were bending over me. Their voices came in sibilant whispers.

"The throat must be mine," said the Count. "I claim the throat as my privilege."

"It should be mine," muttered August. "I am

the eldest and it is long since I fed. Yet, I am content to have the breast."

"The legs are mine," croaked the third monster. "Legs are always full of rich, red blood."

Their lips were drawn back like the lips of animals, and their white fangs gleamed in the candlelight. Suddenly, a clanging sound disturbed the silence of the night. It was the castle bell. The creatures darted to the back of the dais and I could hear them muttering. Then the bell gave a more persistent peal.

"We are powerless against it," the Count cried. "Back to your retreat."

His two companions vanished through the small door which led to the underground chapel, and the Count of Kaldenstein stood alone in the center of the room. I raised myself into a sitting posture, and, as I did so, I heard a strong voice calling beyond the main door.

"Open in the Name of God," it thundered. "Open by the power of the ever Blessed Sacrament of the altar."

As if drawn by some overwhelming force, the Count approached the door and loosened the bolts. It was immediately flung open, and there stood the tall figure of the parish priest, bearing aloft something in a silver box like a watch. With him was the innkeeper, and I could see the poor fellow was terrified. The two advanced into the hall, and the Count retreated before them.

"Thrice in ten years have I frustrated you by the power of God," cried the priest. "Thrice has the Holy Sacrament been carried into this house of sin. Be warned in time, accursed man. Back to your foul tomb, creature of Satan. Back, I command you."

With a strange whimpering cry, the Count vanished through the small door, and the priest came over and assisted me from the table. The innkeeper produced a flask and forced some brandy between my lips, and I made an effort to stand.

"Foolish boy," said the priest. "You would not take my warning, and see what your folly has brought you to."

They helped me out of the castle and down the steps, but I collapsed before we reached the inn.

I have a vague recollection of being helped into bed, and remember nothing more until I awakened in the morning.

The priest and the innkeeper were awaiting me in the dining room and we breakfasted together.

"What is the meaning of it all, Father?" I asked after the meal had been served.

"It is exactly as I told you," was the reply. "The Count of Kaldenstein is a vampire—he keeps the semblance of life in his evil body by drinking human blood. Eight years ago a headstrong youth, like yourself, determined to visit the castle. He did not return within reasonable time, and I had to save him from the clutches of the monster. Only by carrying with me the Body of Christ was I able to effect an entrance, and I was just in time. Then, two years later, a woman who professed to believe in neither God nor the Devil made up her mind to see the Count. Again, I was forced to bear the Blessed Sacrament into the castle, and, by its power, overcame the forces of Satan. Two days since I watched you climb the cliff and saw, with relief, that you returned safely. But yesterday morning, Heinrich came to inform me that your bed had not been slept in, and he was afraid the Count had got you. We waited until nightfall and then made our way up to the castle. The rest you know."

"I can never thank you both sufficiently for the manner in which you saved me from those creatures," I said.

"Creatures," repeated the priest in a surprised voice. "Surely there is only the Count? The servant does not share his master's blood-lust."

"No, I did not see the servant after he had admitted me. But there were two others—August and Feodor."

"August and Feodor," he murmured. "Then it is worse than we have ever dreamed. August died in 1572, and Feodor in 1645. Both were monsters of iniquity, but I did not suspect they were numbered among the living dead."

"Father," quavered the innkeeper. "We are not safe in our beds. Can we not call upon the government to rid us of these vampires?"

"The government would laugh at us," was the reply. "We must take the law into our own hands."

"What is to be done?" I asked.

"I wonder if you have the courage to see this ghastly business through, and to witness a sight that will seem incredible?"

I assured him I was willing to do anything to help; for I considered I owed my life to him.

"Then," he said, "I will return to the church for a few things and we will go up to the castle. Will you come with us, Heinrich?"

The innkeeper hesitated just a moment, but it was evident that he had the greatest confidence in the priest, and he answered, "Of course I will, Father."

It was almost midday when we set off on our mysterious mission. The castle door stood wide open exactly as we had left it on the previous night, and the hall was deserted. We soon discovered the door under the tapestry, and the priest, with a powerful electric flashlight in his hand, led the way down the damp steps. At the chapel door, he paused and from his robes drew three crucifixes and a vessel of holy water. To each of us he handed one of the crosses, and sprinkled the door with the water. Then he opened it, and we entered the cavern.

With hardly a glance at the altar and its gruesome painting, he made his way to the entrance of the vault. It was locked, but he burst the catch with a powerful kick. A wave of fetid air leaped out at us and we staggered back. Then, lifting his crucifix before him and crying, "In the Name of the Father, the Son, and the Holy Ghost," the priest led us into the tomb. I do not know what I expected to see, but I gave a gasp of horror as the light revealed the interior of the place. In the center, resting on a wooden bier, was the sleeping body of the Count of Kaldenstein. His red lips were parted in a smile, and his wicked eyes were half-open.

Around the vault, niches contained coffins, and the priest examined each in turn. Then he directed us to lift two of them to the floor. I noticed that one bore the name of August von Kaldenstein and the other that of Feodor. It took all our united strength to move the caskets, but at last we had them down. And all the time the eyes of the Count seemed to be watching us, although he never moved.

"Now," whispered the priest, "the most ghastly part of the business begins."

Producing a large screwdriver, he began to prise off the lid of the first coffin. Soon it was loose, and he motioned us to raise it. Inside was Count August looking exactly as I had seen him the previous night. His red-rimmed eyes were wide open and gleamed wickedly, and the stench of corruption hung about him. The priest set to work on the second casket, and soon revealed the body of Count Feodor, with his matted hair hanging about his white face.

Then began a strange ceremony. Taking the crucifixes from us, the priest laid them upon the breasts of the two bodies, and, producing his Breviary, recited some Latin prayers. Finally he stood back and flung holy water into the coffins. As the drops touched the leering corpses, they appeared to writhe in agony, to swell as though they were about to burst, and then, before our eyes, they crumbled into dust. Silently, we replaced the lids on the coffins and restored them to their niches.

"And now," said the priest, "we are powerless. Ludwig von Kaldenstein by evil arts has conquered death—for the time being at any rate—and we cannot treat him as we have treated these creatures whose vitality was only a semblance of life. We can but pray that God will curb the activities of this monster of sin."

So saying, he laid the third cross upon the Count's breast and, sprinkling him with holy water, uttered a Latin prayer. With that, we left the vault; but, as the door clanged behind us, something fell to the ground inside the place. It must have been the crucifix falling from the Count's breast.

We made our way up into the castle and never did God's good air taste sweeter. All this time, we had seen no sign of the old servant, and I suggested we should try to discover him. His quarters, I remembered, were in the north turret. There we found his crooked, old body hanging by the neck from a beam in the roof. He had been dead for at least twenty-four hours, and the priest said that nothing could be done other than to notify his death to the proper quarter and arrange for the funeral to take place.

I am still puzzled about the mystery of Kaldenstein Castle. The fact that Count August and Count Feodor had become vampires after death, although it sounds fantastic enough, is more easily understandable than Count Ludwig's seeming immunity from death. The priest could not explain the matter, and appeared to think that the Count might go on living and troubling the neighborhood for an indefinite period.

One thing I do know. On that last night at Kaldenstein, I opened my window before retiring to bed and looked out upon the castle. At the top of one of the turrets, clear in the bright moonlight, stood a black figure—the shadowy form of the Count of Kaldenstein.

Little more remains to be told. Of course, my stay in the village threw all my plans out, and by the time I arrived back at Munich my tour had taken nearly twenty days. Peter Schmidt laughed at me and wondered what blue-eyed maiden had caused me to linger in some Bavarian village. I didn't tell him that the real causes of the delay had been two dead men, and a third who, by all natural laws, should have been dead long ago.

# AN EPISODE OF CATHEDRAL HISTORY

# M. R. James

Montague Rhodes James (1862–1936) was born in Kent, moving to Suffolk at the age of three, where he lived at the rectory in Great Livermere for many years and set several of his ghost stories there. He studied at Cambridge University, living there as an undergraduate, then as a don and provost at King's College, also setting several stories there.

While remembered today mainly as arguably the greatest writer of ghost stories who ever lived, he was also a medieval scholar of prodigious knowledge and productivity, having cataloged many of the libraries of Cambridge and Oxford and being responsible, after the discovery of a manuscript fragment, for rediscovering the graves of several twelfth-century abbots. Among his scholarly publications are several about the Apocrypha.

His greatest macabre stories are generally regarded to have been published in his first two collections, *Ghost Stories of an Antiquary* (1904) and *More Ghost Stories of an Antiquary* (1911). Also published in his lifetime were *A Thin Ghost and Others* (1919), *A Warning to the Curious and Other Ghost Stories* (1925), *Wailing Well* (1928), and *The Collected Ghost Stories of M. R. James* (1931). For more on M. R. James, see the introductory notes to "Count Magnus."

"An Episode of Cathedral History" was first published in the June 10, 1914, issue of *Cambridge Review*. It was first published in book form in *A Thin Ghost* (London: Edward Arnold, 1919).

# An Episode of Cathedral History

## M. R. JAMES

There was once a learned gentleman who was deputed to examine and report upon the archives of the Cathedral of Southminster. The examination of these records demanded a very considerable expenditure of time: hence it became advisable for him to engage lodgings in the city: for though the Cathedral body were profuse in their offers of hospitality, Mr. Lake felt that he would prefer to be master of his day. This was recognised as reasonable. The Dean eventually wrote advising Mr. Lake, if he were not already suited, to communicate with Mr. Worby, the principal Verger, who occupied a house convenient to the church and was prepared to take in a quiet lodger for three or four weeks. Such an arrangement was precisely what Mr. Lake desired. Terms were easily agreed upon, and early in December, like another Mr. Datchery (as he remarked to himself), the investigator found himself in the occupation of a very comfortable room in an ancient and "cathedraly" house.

One so familiar with the customs of Cathedral churches, and treated with such obvious consideration by the Dean and Chapter of this Cathedral in particular, could not fail to command the respect of the Head Verger. Mr. Worby even acquiesced in certain modifications of statements he had been accustomed to offer for years to parties of visitors. Mr. Lake, on his part, found the Verger a very cheery companion, and took advantage of any occasion that presented itself for enjoying his conversation when the day's work was over.

One evening, about nine o'clock, Mr. Worby knocked at his lodger's door. "I've occasion," he said, "to go across to the Cathedral, Mr. Lake, and I think I made you a promise when I did so next I would give you the opportunity to see what it looked like at night time. It's quite fine and dry outside, if you care to come."

"To be sure I will; very much obliged to you, Mr. Worby, for thinking of it, but let me get my coat."

"Here it is, sir, and I've another lantern here that you'll find advisable for the steps, as there's no moon."

"Anyone might think we were Jasper and Durdles, over again, mightn't they?" said Lake, as they crossed the close, for he had ascertained that the Verger had read *Edwin Drood*.

"Well, so they might," said Mr. Worby, with a short laugh, "though I don't know whether we ought to take it as a compliment. Odd ways, I often think, they had at that Cathedral, don't it seem so to you, sir? Full choral matins at seven o'clock in the morning all the year round. Wouldn't suit our boys' voices nowadays, and I think there's one or two of the men would be applying for a rise if the Chapter was to bring it in—particular the altos."

They were now at the south-west door. As Mr. Worby was unlocking it, Lake said, "Did you ever find anybody locked in here by accident?"

"Twice I did. One was a drunk sailor; however he got in I don't know. I s'pose he went to sleep in the service, but by the time I got to him he was praying fit to bring the roof in. Lor'! What a noise that man did make! Said it was the first time he'd been inside a church for ten years, and blest if ever he'd try it again. The other was an old sheep: them boys it was, up to their games. That was the last time they tried it on, though. There, sir, now you see what we look like; our late Dean used now and again to bring parties in, but he preferred a moon-lit night, and there was a piece of verse he'd say to 'em, relating to a Scotch cathedral, I understand; but I don't know; I almost think the effect's better when it's all dark-like. Seems to add to the size and height. Now if you won't mind stopping somewhere in the nave while I go up into the choir where my business lays, you'll see what I mean."

Accordingly Lake waited, leaning against a pillar, and watched the light wavering along the length of the church, and up the steps into the choir, until it was intercepted by some screen or other furniture, which only allowed the reflection to be seen on the piers and roof. Not many minutes had passed before Worby reappeared at the door of the choir and by waving his lantern signalled to Lake to rejoin him.

"I suppose it *is* Worby, and not a substitute," thought Lake to himself, as he walked up the nave. There was, in fact, nothing untoward. Worby showed him the papers which he had come to fetch out of the Dean's stall, and asked him what he thought of the spectacle: Lake agreed that it was well worth seeing. "I suppose," he said, as they walked towards the altar-steps together, "that you're too much used to going about here at night to feel nervous—but you must get a start every

now and then, don't you, when a book falls down or a door swings to?"

"No, Mr. Lake, I can't say I think much about noises, not nowadays: I'm much more afraid of finding an escape of gas or a burst in the stove pipes than anything else. Still there have been times, years ago. Did you notice that plain altar-tomb there—fifteenth century we say it is, I don't know if you agree to that? Well, if you didn't look at it, just come back and give it a glance, if you'd be so good." It was on the north side of the choir, and rather awkwardly placed: only about three feet from the enclosing stone screen. Quite plain, as the Verger had said, but for some ordinary stone panelling. A metal cross of some size on the northern side (that next to the screen) was the solitary feature of any interest.

Lake agreed that it was not earlier than the Perpendicular period: "But," he said, "unless it's the tomb of some remarkable person, you'll forgive me for saying that I don't think it's particularly noteworthy."

"Well, I can't say as it is the tomb of anybody noted in 'istory," said Worby, who had a dry smile on his face, "for we don't own any record whatsoever of who it was put up to. For all that, if you've half an hour to spare, sir, when we get back to the house, Mr. Lake, I could tell you a tale about that tomb. I won't begin on it now; it strikes cold here, and we don't want to be dawdling about all night."

"Of course I should like to hear it immensely."

"Very well, sir, you shall. Now if I might put a question to you," he went on, as they passed down the choir aisle, "in our little local guide—and not only there, but in the little book on our Cathedral in the series—you'll find it stated that this portion of the building was erected previous to the twelfth century. Now of course I should be glad enough to take that view, but—mind the step, sir—but, I put it to you—does the lay of the stone 'ere in this portion of the wall"—which he tapped with his key—"does it to your eye carry the flavour of what you might call Saxon masonry? No, I thought not; no more it does to me: now, if you'll believe me, I've said as much to those men—one's the librarian of our Free Library here, and the other came down from London on purpose—fifty times, if I have once, but I might just as well have talked to that bit of stonework. But there it is, I suppose everyone's got their opinions."

The discussion of this peculiar trait of human nature occupied Mr. Worby almost up to the moment when he and Lake re-entered the former's house. The condition of the fire in Lake's sitting-room led to a suggestion from Mr. Worby that they should finish the evening in his own parlour. We find them accordingly settled there some short time afterwards.

Mr. Worby made his story a long one, and I will not undertake to tell it wholly in his own words, or in his own order. Lake committed the substance of it to paper immediately after hearing it, together with some few passages of the narrative which had fixed themselves *verbatim* in his mind; I shall probably find it expedient to condense Lake's record to some extent.

Mr. Worby was born, it appeared, about the year 1828. His father before him had been connected with the Cathedral, and likewise his grandfather. One or both had been choristers, and in later life both had done work as mason and carpenter respectively about the fabric. Worby himself, though possessed, as he frankly acknowledged, of an indifferent voice, had been drafted into the choir at about ten years of age.

It was in 1840 that the wave of the Gothic revival smote the Cathedral of Southminster. "There was a lot of lovely stuff went then, sir," said Worby, with a sigh. "My father couldn't hardly believe it when he got his orders to clear out the choir. There was a new dean just come in—Dean Burscough it was—and my father had been 'prenticed to a good firm of joiners in the city, and knew what good work was when he saw it. Crool it was, he used to say: all that beautiful wainscot oak, as good as the day it was put up, and garlands-like of foliage and fruit, and lovely old gilding work on the coats of arms and the organ pipes. All went to the timber yard—every bit except some little pieces worked up in the Lady Chapel, and 'ere in this overmantel. Well—I may be mistook, but I say our choir never looked as well since. Still there

was a lot found out about the history of the church, and no doubt but what it did stand in need of repair. There was very few winters passed but what we'd lose a pinnicle." Mr. Lake expressed his concurrence with Worby's views of restoration, but owned to a fear about this point lest the story proper should never be reached. Possibly this was perceptible in his manner.

Worby hastened to reassure him, "Not but what I could carry on about that topic for hours at a time, and do so when I see my opportunity. But Dean Burscough he was very set on the Gothic period, and nothing would serve him but everything must be made agreeable to that. And one morning after service he appointed for my father to meet him in the choir, and he came back after he'd taken off his robes in the vestry, and he'd got a roll of paper with him, and the verger that was then brought in a table, and they begun spreading it out on the table with prayer books to keep it down, and my father helped 'em, and he saw it was a picture of the inside of a choir in a Cathedral; and the Dean—he was a quick-spoken gentleman—he says, 'Well, Worby, what do you think of that?' 'Why,' says my father, 'I don't think I 'ave the pleasure of knowing that view. Would that be Hereford Cathedral, Mr. Dean?' 'No, Worby,' says the Dean, 'that's Southminster Cathedral as we hope to see it before many years.' 'Indeed, sir,' says my father, and that was all he did say—leastways to the Dean—but he used to tell me he felt really faint in himself when he looked round our choir as I can remember it, all comfortable and furnished-like, and then see this nasty little dry picter, as he called it, drawn out by some London architect. Well, there I am again. But you'll see what I mean if you look at this old view."

Worby reached down a framed print from the wall. "Well, the long and the short of it was that the Dean he handed over to my father a copy of an order of the Chapter that he was to clear out every bit of the choir—make a clean sweep—ready for the new work that was being designed up in town, and he was to put it in hand as soon as ever he could get the breakers together. Now then, sir, if you look at that view, you'll see where the pulpit used to stand: that's what I want you to notice, if you please." It was, indeed, easily seen; an unusually large structure of timber with a domed sounding-board, standing at the east end of the stalls on the north side of the choir, facing the bishop's throne. Worby proceeded to explain that during the alterations, services were held in the nave, the members of the choir being thereby disappointed of an anticipated holiday, and the organist in particular incurring the suspicion of having wilfully damaged the mechanism of the temporary organ that was hired at considerable expense from London.

The work of demolition began with the choir screens and organ loft, and proceeded gradually eastwards, disclosing, as Worby said, many interesting features of older work. While this was going on the members of the Chapter were, naturally, in and about the choir a great deal, and it soon became apparent to the elder Worby—who could not help overhearing some of their talk—that, on the part of the senior Canons especially, there must have been a good deal of disagreement before the policy now being carried out had been adopted. Some were of opinion that they should catch their deaths of cold in the return-stalls, unprotected by a screen from the draughts in the nave: others objected to being exposed to the view of persons in the choir aisles, especially, they said, during the sermons, when they found it helpful to listen in a posture which was liable to misconstruction. The strongest opposition, however, came from the oldest of the body, who up to the last moment objected to the removal of the pulpit. "You ought not to touch it, Mr. Dean," he said with great emphasis one morning, when the two were standing before it. "You don't know what mischief you may do." "Mischief? It's not a work of any particular merit, Canon." "Don't call me Canon," said the old man with great asperity, "that is, for thirty years I've been known as Dr. Ayloff, and I shall be obliged, Mr. Dean, if you would kindly humour me in that matter. And as to the pulpit (which I've preached from for thirty years, though I don't insist on that), all I'll say is, I *know* you're doing wrong in moving it." "But what sense could there

be, my dear Doctor, in leaving it where it is, when we're fitting up the rest of the choir in a totally different *style*? What reason could be given—apart from the look of the thing?" "Reason! Reason!" said old Dr. Ayloff. "If you young men—if I may say so without any disrespect, Mr. Dean—if you'd only listen to reason a little, and not be always asking for it, we should get on better. But there, I've said my say." The old gentleman hobbled off, and as it proved, never entered the Cathedral again. The season—it was a hot summer—turned sickly on a sudden. Dr. Ayloff was one of the first to go, with some affection of the muscles of the thorax, which took him painfully at night. And at many services the number of choirmen and boys was very thin.

Meanwhile the pulpit had been done away with. In fact, the sounding-board (part of which still exists as a table in a summer-house in the palace garden) was taken down within an hour or two of Dr. Ayloff's protest. The removal of the base—not effected without considerable trouble—disclosed to view, greatly to the exultation of the restoring party, an altar-tomb—the tomb, of course, to which Worby had attracted Lake's attention that same evening. Much fruitless research was expended in attempts to identify the occupant; from that day to this he has never had a name put to him. The structure had been most carefully boxed in under the pulpit-base, so that such slight ornament as it possessed was not defaced; only on the north side of it there was what looked like an injury; a gap between two of the slabs composing the side. It might be two or three inches across. Palmer, the mason, was directed to fill it up in a week's time, when he came to do some other small jobs near that part of the choir.

The season was undoubtedly a very trying one. Whether the church was built on a site that had once been a marsh, as was suggested, or for whatever reason, the residents in its immediate neighbourhood had, many of them, but little enjoyment of the exquisite sunny days and the calm nights of August and September. To several of the older people—Dr. Ayloff, among others, as we have seen—the summer proved downright fatal, but

# M. R. JAMES

even among the younger, few escaped either a sojourn in bed for a matter of weeks, or at the least, a brooding sense of oppression, accompanied by hateful nightmares. Gradually there formulated itself a suspicion—which grew into a conviction—that the alterations in the Cathedral had something to say in the matter. The widow of a former old verger, a pensioner of the Chapter of Southminster, was visited by dreams, which she retailed to her friends, of a shape that slipped out of the little door of the south transept as the dark fell in, and flitted—taking a fresh direction every night—about the Close, disappearing for a while in house after house, and finally emerging again when the night sky was paling. She could see nothing of it, she said, but that it was a moving form: only she had an impression that when it returned to the church, as it seemed to do in the end of the dream, it turned its head: and then, she could not tell why, but she thought it had red eyes. Worby remembered hearing the old lady tell this dream at a tea-party in the house of the chapter clerk. Its recurrence might, perhaps, he said, be taken as a symptom of approaching illness; at any rate before the end of September the old lady was in her grave.

The interest excited by the restoration of this great church was not confined to its own county. One day that summer an F.S.A., of some celebrity, visited the place. His business was to write an account of the discoveries that had been made, for the Society of Antiquaries, and his wife, who accompanied him, was to make a series of illustrative drawings for his report. In the morning she employed herself in making a general sketch of the choir; in the afternoon she devoted herself to details. She first drew the newly-exposed altar-tomb, and when that was finished, she called her husband's attention to a beautiful piece of diaper-ornament on the screen just behind it, which had, like the tomb itself, been completely concealed by the pulpit. Of course, he said, an illustration of that must be made; so she seated herself on the tomb and began a careful drawing which occupied her till dusk.

Her husband had by this time finished his work of measuring and description, and they agreed that it was time to be getting back to their hotel. "You may as well brush my skirt, Frank," said the lady, "it must have got covered with dust, I'm sure." He obeyed dutifully; but, after a moment, he said, "I don't know whether you value this dress particularly, my dear, but I'm inclined to think it's seen its best days. There's a great bit of it gone." "Gone? Where?" said she. "I don't know where it's gone, but it's off at the bottom edge behind here." She pulled it hastily into sight, and was horrified to find a jagged tear extending some way into the substance of the stuff; very much, she said, as if a dog had rent it away. The dress was, in any case, hopelessly spoilt, to her great vexation, and though they looked everywhere, the missing piece could not be found. There were many ways, they concluded, in which the injury might have come about, for the choir was full of old bits of woodwork with nails sticking out of them. Finally, they could only suppose that one of these had caused the mischief, and that the workmen, who had been about all day, had carried off that particular piece with the fragment of dress still attached to it.

It was about this time, Worby thought, that his little dog began to wear an anxious expression when the hour for it to be put into the shed in the back yard approached. (For his mother had ordained that it must not sleep in the house.) One evening, he said, when he was just going to pick it up and carry it out, it looked at him "like a Christian, and waved its 'and, and, I was going to say—well, you know 'ow they do carry on sometimes, and the end of it was I put it under my coat, and 'uddled it upstairs—and I'm afraid I as good as deceived my poor mother on the subject. After that the dog acted very artful with 'iding itself under the bed for half an hour or more before bedtime came, and we worked it so as my mother never found out what we'd done." Of course Worby was glad of its company anyhow, but more particularly when the nuisance that is still remembered in Southminster as "the crying" set in.

"Night after night," said Worby, "that dog seemed to know it was coming; he'd creep out, he

246

would, and snuggle into the bed and cuddle right up to me shivering, and when the crying come he'd be like a wild thing, shoving his head under my arm, and I was fully near as bad. Six or seven times we'd hear it, not more, and when he'd dror out his 'ed again I'd know it was over for that night. What was it like, sir? Well, I never heard but one thing that seemed to hit it off. I happened to be playing about in the Close, and there was two of the Canons met and said 'Good morning' one to another. 'Sleep well last night?' says one—it was Mr. Henslow that one, and Mr. Lyall was the other. 'Can't say I did,' says Mr. Lyall, 'rather too much of Isaiah xxxiv.14 for me,' 'xxxiv.14,' says Mr. Henslow, 'what's that?' 'You call yourself a Bible reader!' says Mr. Lyall. (Mr. Henslow, you must know, he was one of what used to be termed Simeon's lot—pretty much what we should call the Evangelical party.) 'You go and look it up.' I wanted to know what he was getting at myself, and so off I ran home and got out my own Bible, and there it was: 'the satyr shall cry to his fellow.' Well, I thought, is that what we've been listening to these past nights? And I tell you it made me look over my shoulder a time or two. Of course I'd asked my father and mother about what it could be before that, but they both said it was most likely cats: but they spoke very short, and I could see they was troubled. My word! that was a noise— 'ungry-like, as if it was calling after someone that wouldn't come. If ever you felt you wanted company, it would be when you was waiting for it to begin again. I believe two or three nights there was men put on to watch in different parts of the Close; but they all used to get together in one corner, the nearest they could to the High Street, and nothing came of it.

"Well, the next thing was this. Me and another of the boys—he's in business in the city now as a grocer, like his father before him—we'd gone up in the choir after morning service was over, and we heard old Palmer the mason bellowing to some of his men. So we went up nearer, because we knew he was a rusty old chap and there might be some fun going. It appears Palmer'd told this man to stop up the chink in that old tomb. Well, there was this man keeping on saying he'd done it the best he could, and there was Palmer carrying on like all possessed about it. 'Call that making a job of it?' he says. 'If you had your rights you'd get the sack for this. What do you suppose I pay you your wages for? What do you suppose I'm going to say to the Dean and Chapter when they come round, as come they may do any time, and see where you've been bungling about covering the 'ole place with mess and plaster and Lord knows what?' 'Well, master, I done the best I could,' says the man; 'I don't know no more than what you do 'ow it come to fall out this way. I tamped it right in the 'ole,' he says, 'and now it's fell out,' he says, 'I never see.'

" 'Fell out!' says old Palmer. 'Why it's nowhere near the place. Blowed out, you mean'; and he picked up a bit of plaster, and so did I, that was laying up against the screen, three or four feet off, and not dry yet; and old Palmer he looked at it curious-like, and then he turned round on me and he says, 'Now then, you boys, have you been up to some of your games here?' 'No,' I says, 'I haven't, Mr. Palmer; there's none of us been about here till just this minute'; and while I was talking the other boy, Evans, he got looking in through the chink, and I heard him draw in his breath, and he came away sharp and up to us, and says he, 'I believe there's something in there. I saw something shiny.' 'What! I dare say!' says old Palmer. 'Well, I ain't got time to stop about there. You, William, you go off and get some more stuff and make a job of it this time; if not, there'll be trouble in my yard,' he says.

"So the man he went off, and Palmer too, and us boys stopped behind, and I says to Evans, 'Did you really see anything in there?' 'Yes,' he says, 'I did indeed.' So then I says, 'Let's shove something in and stir it up.' And we tried several of the bits of wood that was laying about, but they were all too big. Then Evans he had a sheet of music he'd brought with him, an anthem or a service, I forget which it is now, and he rolled it up small and shoved it in the chink; two or three times he did it, and nothing happened. 'Give it to me, boy,' I said, and I had a try. No, nothing happened.

Then, I don't know why I thought of it, I'm sure, but I stooped down just opposite the chink and put my two fingers in my mouth and whistled—you know the way—and at that I seemed to think I heard something stirring, and I says to Evans, 'Come away,' I says; 'I don't like this.' 'Oh, rot,' he says, 'give me that roll,' and he took it and shoved it in. And I don't think ever I see anyone go so pale as he did. 'I say, Worby,' he says, 'it's caught, or else someone's got hold of it.' 'Pull it out or leave it,' I says. 'Come and let's get off.' So he gave a good pull, and it came away. Leastways most of it did, but the end was gone. Torn off it was, and Evans looked at it for a second and then he gave a sort of a croak and let it drop, and we both made off out of there as quick as ever we could. When we got outside Evans says to me, 'Did you see the end of that paper?' 'No,' I says, 'only it was torn.' 'Yes, it was,' he says, 'but it was wet too, and black!' Well, partly because of the fright we had, and partly because that music was wanted in a day or two, and we knew there'd be a set-out about it with the organist, we didn't say nothing to anyone else, and I suppose the workmen they swept up the bit that was left along with the rest of the rubbish. But Evans, if you were to ask him this very day about it, he'd stick to it he saw that paper wet and black at the end where it was torn."

After that the boys gave the choir a wide berth, so that Worby was not sure what was the result of the mason's renewed mending of the tomb. Only he made out from fragments of conversation dropped by the workmen passing through the choir that some difficulty had been met with, and that the governor—Mr. Palmer to wit—had tried his own hand at the job. A little later, he happened to see Mr. Palmer himself knocking at the door of the Deanery and being admitted by the butler. A day or so after that, he gathered from a remark his father let fall at breakfast, that something a little out of the common was to be done in the Cathedral after morning service on the morrow. "And I'd just as soon it was today," his father added. "I don't see the use of running risks." "'Father,' I says, 'what are you going to do in the Cathedral tomorrow?' And he turned on me as savage as I ever see him—he was a wonderful good-tempered man as a general thing, my poor father was. 'My lad,' he says, 'I'll trouble you not to go picking up your elders' and betters' talk: it's not manners and it's not straight. What I'm going to do or not going to do in the Cathedral tomorrow is none of your business: and if I catch sight of you hanging about the place tomorrow after your work's done, I'll send you home with a flea in your ear. Now you mind that.' Of course I said I was very sorry and that, and equally of course I went off and laid my plans with Evans. We knew there was a stair up in the corner of the transept which you can get up to the triforium, and in them days the door to it was pretty well always open, and even if it wasn't we knew the key usually laid under a bit of matting hard by. So we made up our minds we'd be putting away music and that, next morning while the rest of the boys was clearing off, and then slip up the stairs and watch from the triforium if there was any signs of work going on.

"Well, that same night I dropped off asleep as sound as a boy does, and all of a sudden the dog woke me up, coming into the bed, and thought I, now we're going to get it sharp, for he seemed more frightened than usual. After about five minutes sure enough came this cry. I can't give you no idea what it was like; and so near too—nearer than I'd heard it yet—and a funny thing, Mr. Lake, you know what a place this Close is for an echo, and particular if you stand this side of it. Well, this crying never made no sign of an echo at all. But, as I said, it was dreadful near this night; and on the top of the start I got with hearing it, I got another fright; for I heard something rustling outside in the passage. Now to be sure I thought I was done; but I noticed the dog seemed to perk up a bit, and next there was someone whispered outside the door, and I very near laughed out loud, for I knew it was my father and mother that had got out of bed with the noise. 'Whatever is it?' says my mother. 'Hush! I don't know,' says my father, excited-like, 'don't disturb the boy. I hope he didn't hear nothing.'

"So, me knowing they were just outside, it made me bolder, and I slipped out of bed across to my little window—giving on the Close—but the dog he bored right down to the bottom of the bed—and I looked out. First go off I couldn't see anything. Then right down in the shadow under a buttress I made out what I shall always say was two spots of red—a dull red it was—nothing like a lamp or a fire, but just so as you could pick 'em out of the black shadow. I hadn't but just sighted 'em when it seemed we wasn't the only people that had been disturbed, because I see a window in a house on the left-hand side become lighted up, and the light moving. I just turned my head to make sure of it, and then looked back into the shadow for those two red things, and they were gone, and for all I peered about and stared, there was not a sign more of them. Then come my last fright that night—something come against my bare leg—but that was all right: that was my little dog had come out of bed, and prancing about making a great to-do, only holding his tongue, and me seeing he was quite in spirits again, I took him back to bed and we slept the night out!

"Next morning I made out to tell my mother I'd had the dog in my room, and I was surprised, after all she'd said about it before, how quiet she took it. 'Did you?' she says. 'Well, by good rights you ought to go without your breakfast for doing such a thing behind my back: but I don't know as there's any great harm done, only another time you ask my permission, do you hear?' A bit after that I said something to my father about having heard cats again. *'Cats,'* he says; and he looked over at my poor mother, and she coughed and he says, 'Oh! Ah! Yes, cats. I believe I heard 'em myself.'

"That was a funny morning altogether: nothing seemed to go right. The organist he stopped in bed, and the minor Canon he forgot it was the 19th day and waited for the *Venite;* and after a bit the deputy set off playing the chant for evensong, which was a minor; and then the Decani boys were laughing so much they couldn't sing, and when it came to the anthem the solo boy he got took with the giggles, and made out his nose was bleeding, and shoved the book at me what hadn't practised the verse and wasn't much of a singer if I had

known it. Well, things was rougher, you see, fifty years ago, and I got a nip from the counter-tenor behind me that I remembered.

"So we got through somehow, and neither the men nor the boys weren't by way of waiting to see whether the Canon in residence—Mr. Henslow it was—would come to the vestries and fine 'em, but I don't believe he did: for one thing I fancy he'd read the wrong lesson for the first time in his life, and knew it. Anyhow, Evans and me didn't find no difficulty in slipping up the stairs as I told you, and when we got up we laid ourselves down flat on our stomachs where we could just stretch our heads out over the old tomb, and we hadn't but just done so when we heard the verger that was then, first shutting the iron porch-gates and locking the south-west door, and then the transept door, so we knew there was something up, and they meant to keep the public out for a bit.

"Next thing was, the Dean and the Canon come in by their door on the north and then I see my father, and old Palmer, and a couple of their best men, and Palmer stood a'talking for a bit with the Dean in the middle of the choir. He had a coil of rope and the men had crows. All of 'em looked a bit nervous. So there they stood talking, and at last I heard the Dean say, 'Well, I've no time to waste, Palmer. If you think this'll satisfy Southminster people, I'll permit it to be done; but I must say this, that never in the whole course of my life have I heard such arrant nonsense from a practical man as I have from you. Don't you agree with me, Henslow?' As far as I could hear Mr. Henslow said something like 'Oh well! We're told, aren't we, Mr. Dean, not to judge others?' And the Dean he gave a kind of sniff, and walked straight up to the tomb, and took his stand behind it with his back to the screen, and the others they come edging up rather gingerly. Henslow, he stopped on the south side and scratched on his chin, he did. Then the Dean spoke up: 'Palmer,' he says, 'which can you do easiest, get the slab off the top, or shift one of the side slabs?'

"Old Palmer and his men they pottered about a bit looking round the edge of the top slab and sounding the sides on the south and east and west and everywhere but the north. Henslow said something about it being better to have a try at the south side, because there was more light and more room to move about in. Then my father, who'd been a'watching of them, went round to the north side, and knelt down and felt the slab by the chink, and he got up and dusted his knees and says to the Dean: 'Beg pardon, Mr. Dean, but I think if Mr. Palmer'll try this here slab he'll find it'll come out easy enough. Seems to me one of the men could prise it out with his crow by means of this chink.' 'Ah! Thank you, Worby,' says the Dean. 'That's a good suggestion. Palmer, let one of your men do that, will you?'

"So the man come round, and put his bar in and bore on it, and just that minute when they were all bending over, and we boys got our heads well over the edge of the triforium, there came a most fearful crash down at the west end of the choir, as if a whole stack of big timber had fallen down a flight of stairs. Well, you can't expect me to tell you everything that happened all in a minute. Of course there was a terrible commotion. I heard the slab fall out, and the crowbar on the floor, and I heard the Dean say, 'Good God!'

"When I looked down again I saw the Dean tumbled over on the floor, the men was making off down the choir, Henslow was just going to help the Dean up, Palmer was going to stop the men (as he said afterwards), and my father was sitting on the altar step with his face in his hands. The Dean he was very cross. 'I wish to goodness you'd look where you're coming to, Henslow,' he says. 'Why you should all take to your heels when a stick of wood tumbles down I cannot imagine'; and all Henslow could do, explaining he was right away on the other side of the tomb, would not satisfy him.

"Then Palmer came back and reported there was nothing to account for this noise and nothing seemingly fallen down, and when the Dean finished feeling of himself they gathered round—except my father, he sat where he was—and someone lighted up a bit of candle and they looked into the tomb. 'Nothing there,' says the Dean. 'What did I tell you? Stay! Here's something. What's this?'

A bit of music paper, and a piece of torn stuff—part of a dress it looks like. Both quite modern—no interest whatever. Another time perhaps you'll take the advice of an educated man'—or something like that, and off he went, limping a bit, and out through the north door, only as he went he called back angry to Palmer for leaving the door standing open. Palmer called out, 'Very sorry, sir,' but he shrugged his shoulders, and Henslow says, 'I fancy Mr. Dean's mistaken. I closed the door behind me, but he's a little upset.' Then Palmer says, 'Why, where's Worby?' and they saw him sitting on the step and went up to him. He was recovering himself, it seemed, and wiping his forehead, and Palmer helped him up on to his legs, as I was glad to see.

"They were too far off for me to hear what they said, but my father pointed to the north door in the aisle, and Palmer and Henslow both of them looked very surprised and scared. After a bit, my father and Henslow went out of the church, and the others made what haste they could to put the slab back and plaster it in. And about as the clock struck twelve the Cathedral was opened again and us boys made the best of our way home.

"I was in a great taking to know what it was had given my poor father such a turn, and when I got in and found him sitting in his chair taking a glass of spirits, and my mother standing looking anxious at him, I couldn't keep from bursting out and making confession where I'd been. But he didn't seem to take on, not in the way of losing his temper. 'You was there, was you? Well, did you see it?' 'I saw everything, father,' I said, 'except when the noise came.' 'Did you see what it was knocked the Dean over?' he says. 'That what come out of the monument? You didn't? Well, that's a mercy.' 'Why, what was it, father?' I said. 'Come, you must have seen it,' he says. '*Didn't* you see? A thing like a man, all over hair, and two great eyes to it?'

"Well, that was all I could get out of him that time, and later on he seemed as if he was ashamed of being so frightened, and he used to put me off when I asked him about it. But years after when I was got to be a grown man, we had more talk now and again on the matter, and he always said the same thing. 'Black it was,' he'd say, 'and a mass of hair, and two legs, and the light caught on its eyes.'

"Well, that's the tale of that tomb, Mr. Lake; it's one we don't tell to our visitors, and I should be obliged to you not to make any use of it till I'm out of the way. I doubt Mr. Evans'll feel the same as I do, if you ask him."

This proved to be the case. But over twenty years have passed by, and the grass is growing over both Worby and Evans; so Mr. Lake felt no difficulty about communicating his notes—taken in 1890—to me. He accompanied them with a sketch of the tomb and a copy of the short inscription on the metal cross which was affixed at the expense of Dr. Lyall to the centre of the northern side. It was from the Vulgate of Isaiah xxiv, and consisted merely of the three words—

IBI CUBAVIT LAMIA.

# SCHLOSS WAPPENBURG

# D. Scott-Moncrieff

D. Scott-Moncrieff appears to be the mystery man of the horror and supernatural fiction world. None of the standard reference works (and some not so standard), nor a thorough search of the Internet, has revealed any biographical information.

Hyphenated names tend to be British, and as all the works attributed to him were first published in Great Britain, his nationality may be deduced.

In addition to the present story, the only other horror, fantasy, or science-fiction work for which a reference could be found is "Count Szolnok's Robots," a weird tale about a brilliant engineer and his mysterious plantation, deep in the Amazon basin, which is staffed entirely by a team of robots. The earliest discovered publication is in the author's 1948 short-story collection, *Not for the Squeamish*.

It is likely that D. Scott-Moncrieff was also an expert on automobiles, since the following three books bear that unusual name as a byline: *Veteran and Edwardian Motor Cars* (London: B.T. Batsford, 1955), *Three-Pointed Star: The Story of Mercedes-Benz* (London and New York: Cassell and Norton, 1955), and *Classic Cars 1930-40* (London: Bentley, 1963).

"Schloss Wappenburg" was first published in *Not for the Squeamish* (London: Background Books, 1948).

# Schloss Wappenburg

## D. SCOTT-MONCRIEFF

I suppose we should really think Uncle Ian pretty prehistoric because he fought in the Boer War. But he casts as good a fly as any of us and although he says his sight isn't what it was he's still a magnificent shot. He insists that as a concession to old age he had sold his big super-charged Mercédès and bought a Healy. We take this with a grain of salt because when he goes to Edinburgh he does the two hundred and fifty odd miles from his house in Rosshire ten minutes quicker than he ever did in the Mercédès. In fact his sixty-seven years sit very lightly on him indeed. His nephews, that's us, can't help thinking of him as one of our own generation, although he was born into a world as different from our own as that of Henry the Eighth. An invitation from him is a coveted possession. It's not even a proper invitation. It's just a few words on a postcard nearly an eighth of an inch thick to say that Collum will meet the London train at Inverness with the Period Piece. He always assumes we will be there and he's always right.

Collum and the Period Piece are quite an adventure in themselves. Collum, who is Uncle Ian's chauffeur, has a long, patriarchal white beard and looks old enough to be twice Uncle Ian's age, although in point of fact he is nearly fifteen years younger. This is accentuated by his not having a single tooth in his head which, coupled with the fact that he has nothing but the Gaelic and most surprisingly some German, makes him extremely hard to understand. He drives as well and nearly as fast as Uncle Ian. The Period Piece is an Alpine Eagle Rolls that Uncle Ian bought new in nineteen thirteen. It's a pretty impressive sight with acres of polished brass that fairly winks and a sort of waggonette body built of teak all copper fastened by the local boat yard.

When we left the train at Inverness it was snowing really hard, but in spite of this, Collum and the Period Piece were waiting for us in the station yard. We all piled ourselves and luggage into the capacious waggonette and set off for the eighty-mile drive to Uncle Ian's. Collum is an old hand at snow driving and he's been driving the Rolls for over thirty years, but even then it wasn't an easy assignment as we took a good four hours. By the time we arrived it was dark and the gaslight shone golden through the driving snow.

"Lucky you made it tonight," Uncle Ian greeted us. "You could never have got through tomorrow. With this wind the snow will drift and it will be days before the ploughs clear it everywhere."

Thawed out by the hottest of hot baths we dressed for dinner. Uncle Ian always dresses for dinner and, in his highland fastness, seems little troubled by austerity. We had onion soup, lobster, pheasant, and a savory omelette. It wasn't till old Cameron, the butler, brought in the port and the long Alvarez Lopez Coronas Grandes that the talk veered round to being frightened. Cameron, as he had done every night that we could remember since we were children, turned out the gas and lit tall candles in the eighteenth century candlesticks on the table.

"I think," said Uncle Ian, "much the most frightening kind of fright is not fear of bodily pain or even death, or worse of being crippled, but the fear one experiences when one comes up against something that cannot be physically explained, the supernatural in fact."

We scented a story. "Do tell us," we chorused. The setting was perfect. Outside the storm lashed itself to fresh fury and great dollops of snow thudded against the windows. Through the thick walls we could hear McRimmon piping a lament in the servants' hall. McRimmon is a ghillie, blinded in the first world war, who lives, like his blind ancestor in Skye, for his pipes.

The candle-light glinted on the silver buttons of Uncle Ian's velvet doublet and made the lovely old lace ruffles at his throat look even yellower than they are after two hundred years of use. He raised his glass of port and held it up to the candle-light.

"The year this wine was being laid down in Douro, it's '04 by the way, I bought my first Mercédès. I had them over thirty years, I suppose I would have one now if they still made them. It all started with the death of my great uncle Henry, almost the last of the old type of sporting parson, he hunted his own pack of hounds two days a week for nearly half a century and in his youth considered it quite normal to stand up to fourteen rounds with professional bare fist fighters. As a matter of fact he left most of his large fortune in trust for the relief of needy punch-drunk pugs who could no longer earn a living in the ring. But he forgot none of his relations in the eccentric codicils. To me he left eight hundred sovereigns 'to pay his bookie, or to spend on any other damned foolishness he may please.' About this time I was staying with friends in Ireland and saw Jenatzy win the Gordon-Bennet race. I decided at once nothing would satisfy me but one of the new sixty-horse-power Mercédès like Jenatzy's. My twenty-horse-power Darracq had what you boys call nowadays 'plenty of urge,' but it couldn't of course compare to this king among cars. Besides I could not but feel that this was exactly the sort of 'damned foolishness' of which my great uncle Henry would heartily approve.

"Archie Prendegast and I went out to the works near Stuttgart to take delivery of the car. We had conceived a grandiose and magnificent idea. Archie's brother was attaché at the Embassy to Austria-Hungary and was very keen for us to come on to Vienna and stay with him. Why shouldn't we motor from Stuttgart to Vienna? We had never heard of it being done, but there appeared to be no valid reason why we should not, if adequate supplies of tires and petrol could be maintained. It's difficult for you boys to realize what things were like then. Few people with cars, and there were not a lot of them anyway, went far away from their home towns and on a long journey—petrol and tires had to be sent ahead by rail or horse carrier. Filling stations were of course non-existent and garages only in the largest towns. 'Rough surgery' could be performed by country blacksmiths. The two great banes of motoring in those days are hard for you to comprehend. One was the frequency and absolute inevitability, unbelievable by modern standards, of tire trouble, the other the dust. We were not unduly worried about mechanical trouble because I had arranged with the Daimler Company to provide me with an engineer for a year. As a matter of fact he stayed for nearly ten years, and that's how Collum who has no English, but the Gaelic, learnt his German. He was a big slow-speaking Bavarian, a wheelwright's son, called Bauer. He was two years out of his seven years' apprenticeship and Jellineck the manager, who recommended him, said he was an absolutely reliable lad, who had grown up with the cars and knew them inside out. He certainly justified their faith in him.

"Towards the end of June we took delivery of both car and engineer. The former was equipped with a light, roomy, Roi des Belges four-seater body. It had, most up-to-date, a windscreen and a cape cart hood. We felt this to be the height of luxury, for my Darracq had an apology for a hood and no windscreen at all. As the car was to be used for extended touring, two stepney rims with tires were mounted on either side of the tonneau and two spare tires slung, like a bustle, behind. Even better, the acetylene generator for the big army type searchlights really worked, and worked with unfailing regularity. On my Darracq it almost always petered out and I could only rely on the feeble glimmer of the oil lamps. The performance judged even by comparatively modern cars was terrific. But what secretly pleased me the most, remember I was only twenty-four, was a small brass lever on the steering column. This operated an absolutely ear splitting exhaust whistle!

"The journey to Vienna was relatively uneventful although by the time we got there not a single spare tire was fit for use. Vienna forty years ago was terrific and every night we danced till dawn. There had been a good many bets laid as to whether our journey would succeed and we were 'lionized' more than a little. The ambasssador presented us to old Francis Joseph. He was rather a stern old man and questioned me for over an hour about the Boer War without troubling to conceal the fact that he thought we had given the Boers a pretty raw deal. Towards the end of the audience he thawed a bit and offered us use of riding horses from the Royal Stables during our stay. We accepted with delight, they were lovely beasts, Irish horses bred in Hungary. As you know, Austria-Hungary in those days stretched right down the Adriatic and included the port of Trieste. We planned to motor south through Styria to Trieste, put the car and ourselves on a boat, and make the long sea voyage home. This would get us home at the end of July, or at latest during the first week in August.

"We got a new lot of tires and Bauer the engineer declared that he had done everything that was necessary and that the car was absolutely ready for the trip. So, quite frankly, were we, after a fortnight of Viennese hospitality which included almost everything except sleep. The first day was a short run. Rudi Fürstenberg accompanied us in his forty-horse-power Fiat to one of his country estates directly on the road south from Vienna. We stopped the night with him and pressed on alone.

"The country was getting very wild although the road surface was not at all bad. There were, we were told, certain obligations about keeping up the old post road. Of course the road was unmetalled and the dust appalling. South of Gratz, villages were ever fewer and further apart and the mountains were covered with endless pine forests, stretching thirty or forty miles at a time. These trees come right up to the edges of the narrow road, darkening it and producing a shut in, somehow sinister effect even on the brightest summer day. But, in spite of this we bowled merrily along in a cloud of dust with not the faintest inkling of the horrible experience that was to befall us. We passed through a large pleasant village with an old stone bridge over a river and a Church with an onion dome. We stopped here for a glass of wine and the whole village turned out to see us. We were, they said, the first car that had ever come through the village although some people had seen them in Gratz. They told us that the road ahead was very lonely and desolate. And so it was; we drove for nearly an hour through the interminable forests, mounting steadily without seeing a soul or a sign of human habitation.

"We entered a deep narrow gorge, the rocky walls so steep and high that they seemed to almost meet a hundred feet up. This defile ended as abruptly as it had begun, but the deep pine forests appeared to go on forever. As we were coming out of it, Archie was saying to me, 'What a place for defense. A handful of men could hold an army here indefinitely.' Then it happened. There was an ominous rumbling under the floorboards, then a terrific metallic crack and grinding. It was obviously something pretty serious. Archie and I set out to take stock of our position while Bauer surveyed the damage to the car. The first thing that became apparent was that we had stopped a hundred yards short of a deserted village, the only sign of any building we had seen for thirty miles or more. The few houses were in ruins and their roofs had fallen in. The one building retaining its roof was a little Chapel and even that had all its windows broken and was completely overgrown with creeper. All this was a sight we had never seen before in the prosperous hard-working Austrian Empire, nor had we thought it possible.

"We walked back to the car speculating on the reason for this profoundly gloomy spectacle rendered even more so by the surroundings. Bauer reported that a metal coupling in the transmission had fractured, but luckily the short prop shaft did not appear to be bent nor was any other damage apparent. So it might have been a lot worse. Bauer declared that if he could find a blacksmith with a turning lathe he could easily make a replacement. The prospects in this cheerless place seemed pretty grim. We knew there was nothing for thirty miles back, and according to our reckoning, the little town of Grosskreutz where we had intended to spend the night lay at least twenty miles ahead. Bauer was busy detaching the broken part. 'If we could only get a horse,' said Archie. 'It's seven o'clock now, a hefty farm horse could tow us into Grosskreutz by morning.'

"'What a hope,' I answered, then suddenly I remembered. 'The only thing we passed on the way, a man in a light gig with a stocky little cob. Far too light a horse to tow of course, but he must be going somewhere.' When an hour later he did catch up with us he proved a surly independent chap, most reluctant to stop for all our halloings.

"His patois was so thick and outlandish that even Bauer couldn't understand half of what he said. There was, however, one thing that he repeated continually and seemed uppermost in his mind. This place was called Schloss Wappenburg and he couldn't care less what happened to our motorcar, or us, for that matter, so long as he got out of it quickly. He had, it appeared, bought the horse and gig in the village thirty miles back and been delayed in starting and the one thing in which he was really interested was to be out of Schloss Wappenburg and well on the way to Grosskreutz before it got dark. Finally for a couple of kroner he agreed reluctantly to take Bauer into town. Yes there was a blacksmith with a well-equipped workshop who would work all night and Bauer could be back with the coupling in the morning. It was obviously impossible for the light cob to take us as well on the long journey, and it seemed much less of a hardship to sleep out on a warm summer night than walk twenty miles. As Bauer climbed into the gig Achie asked, 'Schloss Wappenburg, where's your Schloss?' The surly horse dealer pointed ahead with his whip and said, repressing a shudder, 'If you go on beyond the village you'll see it all right.' And off he went at as smart a trot as he could summon from his tired beast.

"Apart from our gloomy and depressing surroundings we had little to worry about for we had not only our goatskin coats and plenty of rugs, but a hamper that Rudi Fürstenberg had insisted on us taking in case of emergencies. We opened this and found among other things half a ham, a brace of cold chickens, more peaches than we could possibly eat, and several bottles of Rudi's family Badaczon and Tokay. He had certainly given us credit for a pretty considerable thirst.

"We decided that before we supped we would kill time by strolling up to the village, exploring the Church and then strolling on to look at the ruined Schloss, for we never imagined for a moment that it would be inhabited. Entry was none too easy. The Church door although not locked was so overgrown with creeper that we had to force it. It was obviously the burial place of some great family, although the painted hatchments on the walls were so disfigured with mildew and decay as to be quite indistinguishable. What must once have been silken banners hung limp among the cobwebs, but when we tried to unfold them to see what proud arms they bore, they just crumbled into dust. Everything was covered with filth and fungus and in the aisle grew huge yellow puff balls that burst under our feet with the most unpleasant odor.

"Only one place on the walls was free from growth of some sort. This was a memorial plaque exquisitely carved in the French manner from marble, in the form of a draped urn. It seemed to be the last and latest. The old fashioned lettering was quite easy to read: 'Sophia Gräfin Wappenburg, 1778.' We were rather glad to leave this sad decaying little Church, dating from the look of it from the time of the Crusades, and left to moulder when the last of the Wappenburgs was laid to rest in 1778. Although it was a warm summer evening we both felt quite chill.

"I don't know where the man came from, he was just there standing beside us and handing me a note. He was so old that his yellow parchment skin seemed to be mummified and he wore his grey hair in a short queue and his black threadbare livery must have seen service for generations for it was of a cut the like of which I had only seen in old engravings. The note was not in an envelope but folded over and sealed. The spidery writing was in French with the *s*'s written long *f*'s. It was either very bad or very archaic French; I suspected the latter. It offered us dinner and bets at Schloss Wappenburg. But the signature caused my heart to miss a beat, it was like a message from the tomb; it read: 'Sophia Gräfin Wappenburg.'

"We followed the old servant up a narrow path darkened by pine trees overhead. Our feet on the thick carpet of pine needles made hardly a sound and neither Archie nor I felt like speaking. The castle came in view, standing on a crag, black against the evening sky. I have never seen anything more sinister or desolate. Much of it was ruined. But the keep although blackened by fire was evidently inhabited and approached by a drawbridge long rusted with disuse. One tall watch tower stood silhouetted, the evening light showing through its empty window holes, roof and floor had long since fallen away, and we saw what looked in the distance like a very large bat flying into it.

"Another ancient servant pulled the great nail-studded door ajar and our footsteps rang on the flags of a large courtyard, worn hollow long ago by the tramp of mailed feet and the grounding of pikes.

"The Gräfin received us in a hall, dusty but furnished with lovely seventeenth century mahogany. She moved with jerky movements like a marionette on wires. Her face was a skull with ill-fitting false teeth and the parchment skin drawn tight over it was crudely made up. Her clothes like those of the footmen were of a bygone age and even her wig was dressed in a fashion of long ago. But her manners were those of a great lady, and her English although guttural and occasionally halting for lack of practice was excellent. But when I shook hands with her, her hand was not like human flesh; it was dry yet clammy like a toad's belly.

"She led us to another room, smaller, but with more dim oil paintings of long dead and gone Wappenburgs on the walls, where in spite of the summer evening a fire blazed in the great hearth. Then the girl came in, fresh and unbelievably lovely in her bright peasant dirndl. She couldn't have been more than nineteen or twenty. She was like a nosegay of spring flowers in a mausoleum. The ancient lady presented her great niece. 'She also is Countess Sophia,' she told us.

"Drinks were brought in, in lovely Bohemian glasses, and we chatted on high backed chairs round the fire. The two Gräfins were enchantingly frank about the plight into which the once magnificent Wappenburg family had fallen. They, the sole survivors of the noble line, lived on the family estate which was self-supporting but provided no money and a Wappenburg, now dead, had gambled away the family fortunes. They were too poor to go to Vienna and the young Countess had not even been to Gratz, too proud to sell a single picture and too proud to leave the castle except in the magnificence which tradition demanded that they should travel. The wardrobes full of clothes belonging to more fortunate days clothed them. 'And even my wig,' cackled the old countess, 'was made in Paris in the year 1770.'

"The two ladies dressed for dinner, the old Countess with a glorious taffeta pompadour hooped dress hanging loose on her shrivelled form and the young Sophia a vision in a long white satin evening dress that she told us had been made in Vienna when Congress danced and Prince Metternich called the tune. We four dined at a small refectory table, an island of candle-light in a hall so vast that we could only guess its size. Suits of armor were faintly distinguishable in the darkness and from the high vaulted roof, banners were hung almost out of range of our little pool of light. It was a simple enough meal and although the old lady had a certain charm and considerable wit and Archie was clearly losing his heart to the young Countess, I could not shake off the feeling of being thoroughly scared, of what I had not the first idea. This feeling had been with me ever since I pushed against the door of the ruined Chapel in the valley and grew hourly.

"The candles stood in the most lovely candelabra, Venetian work of the seventeenth century I guessed, and round the bases ran a frieze of little satyrs playing ball. Each had his ball except the one nearest me. It had been broken away leaving his cupped hands empty. We were served with hare and on cutting mine up I found a large, old-fashioned lead shot. The Countess and I made some joke about the satyr putting the weight and I put it into the dainty little creature's cupped hands. We all laughed at this silly joke and I noticed that when the young Sophia laughed she showed the one flaw to her peerless beauty—very long pointed eye-teeth.

"Pleading our need for an early start on the morrow we retired to bed early. An old servant conducted us to our rooms along a maze of stone corridors, our candles, as we passed, revealing tapestry of heroic dimensions. These candles, when we reached our adjacent rooms, were quite unnecessary for the full moon had risen flooding the huge bed chambers with silvery light as clear and bright as daylight. Archie declared he had never felt sleepier, but I was exactly the reverse. Although the big fourposter in which I found myself was the last word in deep comfort, hour after hour sleep completely eluded me. I tried drawing the heavy brocade curtains to shut out the moonlight but they started to tear away at the top so I desisted before further damage occurred. Just before midnight, in desperation, I got up and walked

about. I looked out of the window and saw mile after mile of treetops black against the silver moonlight. Several bats were flying about and by some curious trick of perspective, they looked as big as humans.

"I threw myself on my bed again and there was a whirring and grinding of ancient machinery and a clock in some turret struck midnight. Soon afterwards I had an idea. I would smoke a cigar, perhaps that would calm my wretched nerves. Never in my life had I felt so wretchedly apprehensive of I didn't know what.

"I searched my pockets and found my cigar case, but no matches—what a curse. If, I thought, I tip-toed into Archie's room and rifled his pockets I would find a box for sure and probably get in and out without waking him. No sooner said than done, although the uncanny sense of fear of something unknown almost prevented me from opening the door of my bedroom. But there was nothing in the passage. I tip-toed to Archie's door and opened it as softly as I could. The curtains were drawn and the tall windows wide open and the room was as brilliantly moonlit as my own.

"At first I thought Archie had had a nightmare and pulled the sable curtains of his fourposter down on top of him. Then I realized that the curtains were intact and that something like a great sheet of dark colored leather was folded over him and hanging down almost to the floor on either side of the bed. *It looked like a great pair of wings— it was a pair of wings, and whatever grew between them, bulbous, horrid, covered with close fur like a seal, was alive, for I could see it breathing.*

"Terrified as I was, although even then the ghastly truth had not fully dawned on me, I rushed forward to drag the nameless horror off my friend. Instinct made me rash for I knew subconsciously that if I didn't act at once it would be too late. I grabbed it by a bony protuberance near where its neck should have been and jerked with all my might. The creature clung and then came away suddenly like a rubber sucker off glass, catching me as it did a wicked buffet backhanded, like an enraged swan, with its wing. I was sent spinning right across the room and momentarily lost consciousness feeling that every bone in my body must be broken. I cannot have been knocked out for more than a second, but when I opened my eyes the room was almost dark, for it was standing in the embrasure of the great windows, its wing spread blocking out the moonlight. It was agony, but I dragged myself to a sitting position. My senses reeled at the sight, for there was still enough light for me to see quite distinctly. The figure between the wings was human. *It stood with arms outstretched, holding up the wings, white graceful arms as far as the wrists but from below the wrists instead of hands the flesh grew into the leathern bony wings and became part of them.* The arms came from a pair of pretty white dimpled shoulders revealed by a low cut white evening dress. It was the Countess Sophia! She stood there balanced on the window ledge, her monstrous sable wings spread open, her lovely face aglow with excitement, and her silky colored hair tousled. *Her lips were parted showing the long pointed eye-teeth and smeared all over her chin and round her mouth was blood, like a child that had been eating chocolate. Blood, Archie's blood, had dripped all down the white satin frock moulded tightly round her superb young figure.* Near where I had fallen there was an old-fashioned mahogany commode. Gripping this to steady myself, I raised myself up and as I did so my hand closed round a heavy pewter candlestick. Summoning every ounce of strength I hurled it at her face.

"It caught her full between the eyes with a sickening thud, and would surely have spattered out the brains of a mortal. With a hideous shriek she fell backwards from the window, but, before she reached the tops of the pine trees far below, a stroke or two of her powerful wings arrested her fall and she went gliding down in the direction of the ruined chapel. There was little doubt that in the year 1778 the Gräfin Wappenburg had not died but joined the terrible ranks of the undead.

"With slow, painful movements I dragged myself to the bed. As far as I could feel, that crippling blow I had been dealt had not actually broken anything, although I might have a strain or two.

"Archie, thank God, was still alive although unconscious from the loss of blood. There were deep lacerations on his chest and in his throat, two neat punctures. I don't know to this day, battered as I was, how I managed to get him into his clothes and half drag, half carry him out of that dreadful place, peopled by the undead. Down the endless stone corridors, out of the great door, over the drawbridge, and down the rough mountain path. We were allowed to leave the castle without being molested or even seeing anything. High up, I could see in the moonlight, horrible things like great bats swooping and wheeling round the tops of the ruined towers, but they never came near us. Our slow painful trek must have taken several hours for dawn was breaking before we reached the ruined chapel of the tombs. I was devotedly thankful, for nothing would have induced me to approach it during the hours of darkness. I reached the car, slumped Archie into the tonneau, and then I must have fainted.

"The next thing I knew was the warmth of the morning sun on my face. Archie had come round and although very pale and weak was forcing peach brandy into my mouth from his silver pocket flask. I felt as if I had been dropped from the top of a high building. Bauer and a carrier with a light gig who had brought him from Grosskreutz were fussing round in a great state of perturbation.

"The first thing I asked Archie was what he remembered of the previous night. Archie remembered nothing between dreaming that the lovely Sophia bent over him and kissed him tenderly on the throat and waking up white and shaking and terribly weak in the tonneau of the Mercédès.

"The carrier ridiculed the theory that we spent the night with the Wappenburgs in the Schloss. There had been no Wappenburgs for over a hundred years he said and no one had set foot in the castle within the memory of the grandparents of any living man. The place is doubly accursed he said, it must have bewitched you in some terrible dream.

"Archie and I decided to drag our aching limbs up to the castle while Bauer replaced the re-made coupling. We tugged on the rusty iron bell-pull and somewhere far away we heard a faint clanging, but there were no answering footsteps. We put our shoulders against the postern door and a bolt almost rusted through gave way. The Schloss and all the rooms we entered were exactly as we had seen them the previous night except that the dust lay almost a quarter of an inch thick everywhere; there were no footprints and no indications that it had been disturbed by human tread for upwards of a century.

"Archie was beginning to propound a theory that we had slept in the car, both had the same fantastic nightmare and had attacked each other in our sleep. When we entered the great dining hall everything here was deep in the undisturbed dust of a century. The candles in the Venetian candelabras were heavy with mildew and spiders' webs ran from them to the backs of chairs. But round the base the little satyrs played ball and the one nearest where I had been sitting held in his graceful cupped hands, not a gilt ball but a large oldfashioned leaden shot.

"I can't begin to explain it, but I know that during the last twelve hours I was more frightened than I have ever been before or since. And I know, too, that I was never more glad in my life as when descending the path through the pines to hear the tickety-phonk of the Mercédès engine ticking over, and to be driven away from that accursed Schloss Wappenburg at a spanking forty miles an hour with Bauer at the wheel."

# THE HOUND

# H. P. Lovecraft

Howard Phillips Lovecraft (1890–1937) was born in Providence, Rhode Island, where he lived virtually all his life. Always frail, he was reclusive and had little formal education, but he read extensively, with particular emphasis on the sciences. He wrote monthly articles on astronomy for the *Providence Tribune* at the age of sixteen, then attempted fiction; his first published story was "The Alchemist," written in 1908 but not published until 1916. He wrote fiction for other small magazines, living in near poverty, earning his living by ghostwriting and editing the work of others, until he finally sold "Dagon" to the top fantasy pulp magazine in America, *Weird Tales*, in 1923. He became a regular contributor to that magazine until his death, with only a handful of his modest sixty stories appearing in other pulps.

He was neglected as a serious writer throughout his life, with only one volume being published while he was alive: *The Shadow over Innsmouth* (1936). After his early death, two friends, August Derleth and Donald Wandrei, attempted to sell his work to commercial publishers. When they were unsuccessful, they created their own firm, Arkham House, for the sole purpose of collecting and publishing Lovecraft's stories, poems, and letters, beginning with the cornerstone work *The Outsider and Others* (1939) and continuing with *Beyond the Wall of Sleep* (1939). Arkham House remains active as the leading specialty publisher of horror fiction.

"The Hound" was originally published in the February 1924 issue of *Weird Tales*.

# The Hound

## H. P. LOVECRAFT

In my tortured ears there sounds unceasingly a nightmare whirring and flapping, and a faint, distant baying as of some gigantic hound. It is not dream—it is not, I fear, even madness—for too much has already happened to give me these merciful doubts.

St. John is a mangled corpse; I alone know why, and such is my knowledge that I am about to blow out my brains for fear I shall be mangled in the same way. Down unlit and illimitable corridors of eldritch phantasy sweeps the black, shapeless Nemesis that drives me to self-annihilation.

May heaven forgive the folly and morbidity which led us both to so monstrous a fate! Wearied with the commonplaces of a prosaic world, where even the joys of romance and adventure soon grow stale, St. John and I had followed enthusiastically every aesthetic and intellectual movement which promised respite from our devastating ennui. The enigmas of the symbolists and the ecstasies of the pre-Raphaelites all were ours in their time, but each new moon was drained too soon of its diverting novelty and appeal.

Only the sombre philosophy of the decadents could help us, and this we found potent only by increasing gradually the depth and diabolism of our penetrations. Baudelaire and Huysmans were soon exhausted of thrills, till finally there remained for us only the more direct stimuli of unnatural personal experiences and adventures. It was this frightful emotional need which led us eventually to that detestable course which even in my present fear I mention with shame and timidity—that hideous extremity of human outrage, and abhorred practice of grave-robbing.

I cannot reveal the details of our shocking expedition, or catalogue even partly the worst of the trophies adorning the nameless museum we prepared in the great stone house where we jointly dwelt, alone and servantless. Our museum was a blasphemous, unthinkable place, where with the satanic taste of neurotic virtuosi we had assembled a universe of terror and decay to excite our jaded sensibilities. It was a secret room, far, far, underground; where huge winged daemons carven of basalt and onyx vomited from wide grinning mouths weird green and orange light, and hidden pneumatic pipes ruffled into kaleidoscopic dances of death the lines of red charnel things hand in hand woven in voluminous black hangings. Through these pipes came at will the odours our moods most craved; sometimes the scent of pale funereal lilies, sometimes the narcotic incense of imagined Eastern shrines of the kingly dead, and

sometimes—how I shudder to recall it!—the frightful, soul-upheaving stenches of the uncovered
grave.

Around the walls of this repellent chamber were
cases of antique mummies alternating with comely,
lifelike bodies perfectly stuffed and cured by the
taxidermist's art, and with head-stones snatched
from the oldest churchyards of the world. Niches
here and there contained skulls of all shapes, and
heads preserved in various stages of dissolution.
There one might find the rotting bald pates of famous noblemen, and the fresh and radiantly golden
heads of new-buried children.

Statues and paintings there were, all of fiendish
subjects and some executed by St. John and myself. A locked portfolio, bound in tanned human
skin, held certain unknown and unnameable drawings which it was rumoured Goya had perpetrated
but dared not acknowledge. There were nauseous
musical instruments, stringed, brass, and wood-
wind, on which St. John and I sometimes produced dissonances of exquisite morbidity and
cacodaemoniacal ghastliness; whilst in a multitude of inlaid ebony cabinets reposed the most incredible and unimaginable variety of tomb-loot
ever assembled by human madness and perver-
sity. It is of this loot in particular that I must not
speak—thank God I had the courage to destroy it
long before I thought of destroying myself!

The predatory excursions on which we collected our unmentionable treasures were always
artistically memorable events. We were no vulgar
ghouls, but worked only under certain conditions
of mood, landscape, environment, weather, season, and moonlight. These pastimes were to us
the most exquisite form of aesthetic expression,
and we gave their details a fastidious technical care.
An inappropriate hour, a jarring lighting effect,
or a clumsy manipulation of the damp sod, would
almost totally destroy for us that titillation which
followed the exhumation of some ominous, grinning secret of the earth. Our quest for novel scenes
and piquant conditions was feverish and insatiate—
St. John was always the leader, and he it was who
led the way to that mocking, accursed spot which
brought us our hideous and inevitable doom.

By what malign fatality were we lured to that
terrible Holland churchyard? I think it was the
dark rumour and legendry, the tales of one buried
for five centuries, who had himself been a ghoul
in his time and had stolen a potent thing from a
mighty sepulchre. I can recall the scene in these
final moments—the pale autumnal moon over the
graves, casting long horrible shadows; the grotesque
trees, dropping sullenly to meet the neglected grass
and the crumbling slabs; the vast legions of strangely
colossal bats that flew against the moon; the antique ivied church pointing a huge spectral finger
at the livid sky; the phosphorescent insects that
danced like death-fires under the yews in a distant corner—the odours of mould, vegetation, and
less explicable things that mingled feebly with the
night wind from over far swamps and seas; and,
worst of all, the faint deep-toned baying of some
gigantic hound which we could neither see nor
definitely place. As we heard this suggestion of
baying we shuddered, remembering the tales of
the peasantry; for he whom we sought had centuries before been found in this self-same spot,
torn and mangled by the claws and teeth of some
unspeakable beast.

I remember how we delved in the ghoul's grave
with our spades, and how we thrilled at the picture of ourselves, the grave, the pale watching
moon, the horrible shadows, the grotesque trees,
the titanic bats, the antique church, the dancing
death-fires, the sickening odours, the gentle moaning night wind, and the strange, half-heard directionless baying of whose objective existence we
could scarcely be sure.

Then we struck a substance harder than the
damp mould, and beheld a rotting oblong box
crusted with mineral deposits from the long undisturbed ground. It was incredibly tough and thick,
but so old that we finally pried it open and feasted
our eyes on what it held.

Much—amazingly much—was left of the object despite the lapse of five hundred years. The
skeleton, though crushed in places by the jaws of
the thing that had killed it, held together with surprising firmness, and we gloated over the clean
white skull and its long, firm teeth and its eyeless

sockets that once had glowed with a charnel fever like our own. In the coffin lay an amulet of curious and exotic design, which had apparently been worn around the sleeper's neck. It was the oddly conventionalized figure of a crouching winged hound, or sphinx with a semi-canine face, and was exquisitely carved in antique Oriental fashion from a small piece of green jade. The expression of its features was repellent in the extreme, savouring at once of death, bestiality, and malevolence. Around the base was an inscription in characters which neither St. John nor I could identify; and on the bottom, like a maker's seal, was given a grotesque and formidable skull.

Immediately upon beholding this amulet we knew that we must possess it; that this treasure alone was our logical pelt from the centuried grave. Even had its outlines been unfamiliar we would have desired it, but as we looked more closely we saw that it was not wholly unfamiliar. Alien it indeed was to all art and literature which sane and balanced readers know, but we recognized it as the thing hinted at in the forbidden *Necronomican* of the mad Arab Abdul Alhazred; the ghastly soul-symbol of the corpse-eating cult of inaccessible Leng, in Central Asia. All too well did we trace the sinister lineaments described by the old Arab daemonologist; lineaments, he wrote, drawn from some obscure supernatural manifestation of the souls of those who vexed and gnawed at the dead.

Seizing the green jade object, we gave a last glance at the bleached and cavern-eyed face of its owner and closed up the grave as we found it. As we hastened from the abhorrent spot, the stolen amulet in St. John's pocket, we thought we saw the bats descend in a body to the earth we had so lately rifled, as if seeking for some cursed and unholy nourishment. But the autumn moon shone weak and pale, and we could not be sure.

So, too, as we sailed the next day away from Holland to our home, we thought we heard the faint distant baying of some gigantic hound in the background. But the autumn wind moaned sad and wan, and we could not be sure.

Less than a week after our return to England, strange things began to happen. We lived as recluses; devoid of friends, alone, and without servants in a few rooms of an ancient manorhouse on a bleak and unfrequented moor; so that our doors were seldom disturbed by the knock of the visitor.

Now, however, we were troubled by what seemed to be a frequent fumbling in the night, not only around the doors but around the windows also, upper as well as lower. Once we fancied that a large opaque body darkened the library window when the moon was shining against it, and another time we thought we heard a whirring or flapping sound not far off. On each occasion investigation revealed nothing, and we began to ascribe the occurrences to imagination which still prolonged in our ears the faint far baying we thought we had heard in the Holland churchyard. The jade amulet now reposed in a niche in our museum, and sometimes we burned a strangely scented candle before it. We read much in Alhazred's *Necronomicon* about its properties, and about the relation of ghosts' souls to the objects it symbolized; and were disturbed by what we read.

Then terror came.

On the night of 24 September 19——, I heard a knock at my chamber door. Fancying it St. John's, I bade the knocker enter, but was answered only by a shrill laugh. There was no one in the corridor. When I aroused St. John from his sleep, he professed entire ignorance of the event, and became as worried as I. It was the night that the faint, distant baying over the moor became to us a certain and dreaded reality.

Four days later, whilst we were both in the hidden museum, there came a low, cautious scratching at the single door which led to the secret library staircase. Our alarm was now divided, for, besides our fear of the unknown, we had always entertained a dread that our grisly collection might be discovered. Extinguishing all lights, we proceeded to the door and threw it suddenly open; whereupon we felt an unaccountable rush of air, and heard, as if receding far away, a queer combination of rustling, tittering, and inarticulate chatter. Whether we were mad, dreaming, or in our senses, we did not try to determine. We only realized, with the blackest of apprehensions, that the apparently disembodied chatter was beyond a doubt in the Dutch language.

After that we lived in growing horror and fascination. Mostly we held to the theory that we were jointly going mad from our life of unnatural excitements, but sometimes it pleased us more to dramatize ourselves as the victims of some creeping and appalling doom. Bizarre manifestations were now too frequent to count. Our lonely house was seemingly alive with the presence of some malign being whose nature we could not guess, and every night that daemoniac baying rolled over the windswept moor, always louder and louder. On 29 October we found in the soft earth underneath the library window a series of footprints utterly impossible to describe. They were as baffling as the hordes of great bats which haunted the old manorhouse in unprecedented and increasing numbers.

The horror reached a culmination on 18 November, when St. John, walking home after dark from the dismal railway station, was seized by some frightful carnivorous thing and torn to ribbons. His screams had reached the house, and I had hastened to the terrible scene in time to hear a whirr of wings and see a vague black cloudy thing silhouetted against the rising moon.

My friend was dying when I spoke to him, and he could not answer coherently. All he could do was to whisper, "The amulet—that damned thing—"

Then he collapsed, an inert mass of mangled flesh.

I buried him the next midnight in one of our neglected gardens, and mumbled over his body one of the devilish rituals he had loved in life. And as I pronounced the last daemoniac sentence I heard afar on the moor the faint baying of some gigantic hound. The moon was up, but I dared not look at it. And when I saw on the dim-lighted moor a wide nebulous shadow sweeping from mound to mound, I shut my eyes and threw myself face down upon the ground. When I arose, trembling, I know not how much later, I staggered into the house and made shocking obeisances before the enshrined amulet of green jade.

Being now afraid to live alone in the ancient house on the moor, I departed on the following day for London, taking with me the amulet after destroying by fire and burial the rest of the impious collection in the museum. But after three nights I heard the baying again, and before a week was over felt strange eyes upon me whenever it was dark. One evening as I strolled on Victoria Embankment for some needed air, I saw a black shape obscure one of the reflections of the lamps in the water. A wind, stronger than the night wind, rushed by, and I knew that what had befallen St. John must soon befall me.

The next day I carefully wrapped the green jade amulet and sailed for Holland. What mercy I might gain by returning the thing to its silent, sleeping owner I knew not; but I felt that I must try any step conceivably logical. What the hound was, and why it had pursued me, were questions still vague; but I had first heard the baying in that ancient churchyard, and every subsequent event including St. John's dying whisper had served to connect the curse with the stealing of the amulet. Accordingly I sank into the nethermost abysses of despair when, at an inn in Rotterdam, I discovered that thieves had despoiled me of this sole means of salvation.

The baying was loud that evening, and in the morning I read of a nameless deed in the vilest quarter of the city. The rabble were in terror, for upon an evil tenement had fallen a red death beyond the foulest previous crime of the neighbourhood. In a squalid thieves' den an entire family had been torn to shreds by an unknown thing which left no trace, and those around had heard all night a faint, deep insistent note as of a gigantic hound.

So at last I stood again in the unwholesome churchyard where a pale winter moon cast hideous shadows, and leafless trees dropped sullenly to meet the withered, frosty grass and cracking slabs, and the ivied church pointed a jeering finger at the unfriendly sky, and the night wind howled maniacally from over frozen swamps and frigid seas. The baying was very faint now, and it ceased altogether as I approached the ancient grave I had once violated, and frightened away an abnormally large horde of bats which had been hovering curiously around it.

I know not why I went thither unless to pray, or gibber out insane pleas and apologies to the calm white thing that lay within; but, whatever my reason, I attacked the half-frozen sod with a desperation partly mine and partly that of a dominating will outside myself. Excavation was much easier than I expected, though at one point I encountered a queer interruption; when a lean vulture darted down out of the cold sky and pecked frantically at the grave-earth until I killed him with a blow of my spade. Finally I reached the rotting oblong box and removed the damp nitrous cover. This is the last rational act I ever performed.

For crouched within that centuried coffin, embraced by a close-packed nightmare retinue of high, sinewy, sleeping bats, was the bony thing my friend and I had robbed; not clean and placid as we had seen it then, but covered with caked blood and shreds of alien flesh and hair, and leering sentiently at me with phosphorescent sockets and sharp ensanguined fangs yawning twistedly in mockery of my inevitable doom. And when it gave from those grinning jaws a deep, sardonic bay as of some gigantic hound, and I saw that it held in its gory filthy claw the lost and fateful amulet of green jade, I merely screamed and ran away idiotically, my screams soon dissolving into peals of hysterical laughter.

Madness rides the star-wind . . . claws and teeth sharpened on centuries of corpses . . . dripping death astride a bacchanal of bats from night-black ruins of buried temples of Belial . . . Now, as the baying of that dead fleshless monstrosity grows louder and louder, and the stealthy whirring and flapping of those accursed web-wings circles closer and closer, I shall seek with my revolver the oblivion which is my only refuge from the unnamed and unnameable.

# BITE-ME-NOT OR, FLEUR DE FUR

# Tanith Lee

Tanith Lee (1947– ) was born in London, the daughter of Hylda and Bernard Lee (a ballroom dancer, not the actor who played M in the James Bond films). After her education was completed (including one year at an art institute), she worked as a file clerk, assistant librarian, shop assistant, and waitress before becoming a full-time writer.

Her first short story, "Eustace," was published in 1968; while working as a librarian, she sold a children's novel, *The Dragon Hoard,* in 1971. Since then, she has published more than fifty novels and nearly two hundred short stories in a variety of genres, including both children's and adult fantasy, horror, science-fiction, gothic romances, and historical novels. Her breakout book was *The Birthgrave* (1975). Lee has won or been nominated for numerous awards throughout her career, including the World Fantasy Award, the August Derleth Award, and the Nebula Award, and has been the guest of honor at several science-fiction conventions, including the British National Science Fiction Convention and Orbital, both in 2008. Aficionados of her work have generally regarded *The Silver Metal Lover* (1981) as her finest novel, although her much loved Unicorn series *(Black Unicorn,* 1991; *Gold Unicorn,* 1994; and *Red Unicorn,* 1997) has its devotees.

"Bite-Me-Not or, Fleur de Fur" (usually spelled "Fleur de Feu," but the author preferred the present form) was first published in the October 1984 issue of *Isaac Asimov's Science Fiction Magazine.*

# Bite-Me-Not or, Fleur De Fur

## TANITH LEE

### CHAPTER I

In the tradition of young girls and windows, the young girl looks out of this one. It is difficult to see anything. The panes of the window are heavily leaded, and secured by a lattice of iron. The stained glass of lizard-green and storm-purple is several inches thick. There is no red glass in the window. The colour red is forbidden in the castle. Even the sun, behind the glass, is a storm sun, a green-lizard sun.

The young girl wishes she had a gown of palest pastel rose—the nearest affinity to red which is never allowed. Already she has long dark beautiful eyes, a long white neck. Her long dark hair is however hidden in a dusty scarf and she wears rags. She is a scullery maid. As she scours dishes and mops stone floors, she imagines she is a princess floating through the upper corridors, gliding to the dais in the Duke's hall. The Cursed Duke. She is sorry for him. If he had been her father, she would have sympathized and consoled him. His own daughter is dead, as his wife is dead, but these things, being to do with the cursing, are never spoken of. Except, sometimes, obliquely.

"*Rohise!*" dim voices cry now, full of dim scolding soon to be actualized.

The scullery maid turns from the window and runs to have her ears boxed and a broom thrust into her hands.

Meanwhile, the Cursed Duke is prowling his chamber, high in the East Turret carved with swans and gargoyles. The room is lined with books, swords, lutes, scrolls, and has two eerie portraits, the larger of which represents his wife, and the smaller his daughter. Both ladies look much the same with their pale, egg-shaped faces, polished eyes, clasped hands. They do not really look like his wife or daughter, nor really remind him of them.

There are no windows at all in the turret, they were long ago bricked up and covered with hangings. Candles burn steadily. It is always night in the turret. Save, of course, by night there are particular *sounds* all about it, to which the Duke is accustomed, but which he does not care for. By night, like most of his court, the Cursed Duke closes his ears with softened tallow. However, if he sleeps, he dreams, and hears in the dream the beating of wings. . . . Often, the court holds loud revel all night long.

The Duke does not know Rohise the scullery maid has been thinking of him. Perhaps he does not even know that a scullery maid is capable of thinking at all.

**268**

Soon the Duke descends from the turret and goes down, by various stairs and curving passages, into a large, walled garden on the east side of the castle.

It is a very pretty garden, mannered and manicured, which the gardeners keep in perfect order. Over the tops of the high, high walls, where delicate blooms bell the vines, it is just possible to glimpse the tips of sun-baked mountains. But by day the mountains are blue and spiritual to look at, and seem scarcely real. They might only be inked on the sky.

A portion of the Duke's court is wandering about in the garden, playing games or musical instruments, or admiring painted sculptures, or the flora, none of which is red. But the Cursed Duke's court seems vitiated this noon. Nights of revel take their toll.

As the Duke passes down the garden, his courtiers acknowledge him deferentially. He sees them, old and young alike, all doomed as he is, and the weight of his burden increases.

At the furthest, most eastern end of the garden, there is another garden, sunken and rather curious, beyond a wall with an iron door. Only the Duke possesses the key to this door. Now he unlocks it and goes through. His courtiers laugh and play and pretend not to see. He shuts the door behind him.

The sunken garden, which no gardener ever tends, is maintained by other, spontaneous, means. It is small and square, lacking the hedges and the paths of the other, the sundials and statues and little pools. All the sunken garden contains is a broad paved border, and at its center a small plot of humid earth. Growing in the earth is a slender bush with slender velvet leaves.

The Duke stands and looks at the bush only a short while.

He visits it every day. He has visited it every day for years. He is waiting for the bush to flower. Everyone is waiting for this. Even Rohise, the scullery maid, is waiting, though she does not, being only sixteen, born in the castle and uneducated, properly understand why.

The light in the little garden is dull and strange, for the whole of it is roofed over by a dome of thick smoky glass. It makes the atmosphere somewhat depressing, although the bush itself gives off a pleasant smell, rather resembling vanilla.

Something is cut into the stone rim of the earth-plot where the bush grows. The Duke reads it for perhaps the thousandth time. *0, fleur de feu—*

When the Duke returns from the little garden into the large garden, locking the door behind him, no one seems truly to notice. But their obeisances now are circumspect.

One day, he will perhaps emerge from the sunken garden leaving the door wide, crying out in a great voice. But not yet. Not today.

The ladies bend to the bright fish in the pools, the knights pluck for them blossoms, challenge each other to combat at chess, or wrestling, discuss the menagerie lions; the minstrels sing of unrequited love. The pleasure garden is full of one long and weary sigh.

"Oh flurda fur

"Pourma souffrance—"

Sings Rohise as she scrubs the flags of the pantry floor.

"Ned ormey par,

"May say day mwar—"

"What are you singing, you slut?" someone shouts, and kicks over her bucket.

Rohise does not weep. She tidies her bucket and soaks up the spilled water with her cloths. She does not know what the song, because of which she seems, apparently, to have been chastised, means. She does not understand the words that somehow, somewhere—perhaps from her own dead mother—she learned by rote.

In the hour before sunset, the Duke's hall is lit by flambeaux. In the high windows, the casements of oil-blue and lavender glass and glass like storms and lizards, are fastened tight. The huge window by the dais was long ago obliterated, shut up, and a tapestry hung of gold and silver tissue with all the rubies pulled out and emeralds substituted. It describes the subjugation of a fearsome unicorn by a maiden, and huntsmen.

The court drifts in with its clothes of rainbow from which only the color red is missing.

Music for dancing plays. The lean pale dogs pace about, alert for tidbits as dish on dish comes in. Roast birds in all their plumage glitter and die a second time under the eager knives. Pastry castles fall. Pink and amber fruits, and green fruits and black, glow beside the goblets of fine yellow wine.

The Cursed Duke eats with care and attention, not with enjoyment. Only the very young of the castle still eat in that way, and there are not so many of those.

The murky sun slides through the stained glass. The musicians strike up more wildly. The dances become boisterous. Once the day goes out, the hall will ring to *chanson,* to drum and viol and pipe. The dogs will bark, no language will be uttered except in a bellow. The lions will roar from the menagerie. On some nights the cannons are set off from the battlements, which are now all of them roofed in, fired out through narrow mouths just wide enough to accommodate them, the charge crashing away in thunder down the darkness.

By the time the moon comes up and the castle rocks to its own cacophony, exhausted Rohise has fallen fast asleep in her cupboard bed in the attic. For years, from sunset to rise, nothing has woken her. Once, as a child, when she had been especially badly beaten, the pain woke her and she heard a strange silken scratching, somewhere over her head. But she thought it a rat, or a bird. Yes, a bird, for later it seemed to her there were also wings. . . . But she forgot all this half a decade ago. Now she sleeps deeply and dreams of being a princess, forgetting, too, how the Duke's daughter died. Such a terrible death, it is better to forget.

"The sun shall not smite thee by day, neither the moon by night," intones the priest, eyes rolling, his voice like a bell behind the Duke's shoulder.

"Ne moi mords pas," whispers Rohise in her deep sleep. "Ne mwar mor par, ne par mor mwar. . . ."

And under its impenetrable dome, the slender bush has closed its fur leaves also to sleep. O flower of fire, oh fleur de fur. Its blooms, though it has not bloomed yet, bear the ancient name *Nona Mordica.* In light parlance they call it Bite-Me-Not. There is a reason for that.

## CHAPTER II

He is the Prince of a proud and savage people. The pride they acknowledge, perhaps they do not consider themselves to be savages, or at least believe that savagery is the proper order of things.

Feroluce, that is his name. It is one of the customary names his kind give their lords. It has connotations with diabolic royalty and, too, with a royal flower of long petals curved like scimitars. Also the name might be the partial anagram of another name. The bearer of that name was also winged.

For Feroluce and his people are winged beings. They are more like a nest of dark eagles than anything, mounted high among the rocky pilasters and pinnacles of the mountain. Cruel and magnificent, like eagles, the somber sentries motionless as statuary on the ledge-edges, their sable wings folded about them.

They are very alike in appearance (less a race or tribe, more a flock, an unkindness of ravens). Feroluce also, black-winged, black-haired, aquiline of feature, standing on the brink of star-dashed space, his eyes burning through the night like all the eyes along the rocks, depthless red as claret.

They have their own traditions of art and science. They do not make or read books, fashion garments, discuss God or metaphysics or men. Their cries are mostly wordless and always mysterious, flung out like ribbons over the air as they wheel and swoop and hang in wicked cruciform, between the peaks. But they sing, long hours, for whole nights at a time, music that has a language only they know. All their wisdom and theosophy, and all their grasp of beauty, truth, or love, is in the singing.

They look unloving enough, and so they are. Pitiless fallen angels. A traveling people, they roam after sustenance. Their sustenance is blood. Finding a castle, they accepted it, every bastion and wall, as their prey. They have preyed on it and tried to prey on it for years.

In the beginning, their calls, their songs, could lure victims to the feast. In this way, the tribe or unkindness of Feroluce took the Duke's wife, somnambulist, from a midnight balcony. But the Duke's daughter, the first victim, they found seventeen years ago, benighted on the mountain side. Her escort and herself they left to the sunrise, marble figures, the life drunk away.

Now the castle is shut, bolted and barred. They are even more attracted by its recalcitrance (a woman who says "No"). They do not intend to go away until the castle falls to them.

By night, they fly like huge black moths round and round the carved turrets, the dull-lit leaded windows, their wings invoking a cloudy tindery wind, pushing thunder against thundery glass.

They sense they are attributed to some sin, reckoned a punishing curse, a penance, and this amuses them at the level whereon they understand it.

They also sense something of the flower, the *Nona Mordica*. Vampires have their own legends.

But tonight Feroluce launches himself into the air, speeds down the sky on the black sails of his wings, calling, a call like laughter or derision. This morning, in the tween-time before the light began and the sun-to-be drove him away to his shadowed eyrie in the mountain-guts, he saw a chink in the armour of the beloved refusing-woman-prey. A window, high in an old neglected tower, a window with a small eyelet which was cracked.

Feroluce soon reaches the eyelet and breathes on it, as if he would melt it. (His breath is sweet. Vampires do not eat raw flesh, only blood, which is a perfect food and digests perfectly, while their teeth are sound of necessity.) The way the glass mists at breath intrigues Feroluce. But presently he taps at the cranky pane, taps, then claws. A piece breaks away, and now he sees how it should be done.

Over the rims and upthrusts of the castle, which is only really another mountain with caves to Feroluce, the rumble of the Duke's revel drones on.

Feroluce pays no heed. He does not need to reason, he merely knows, *that* noise masks *this*— as he smashes in the window. Its panes were all faulted and the lattice rusty. It is, of course, more than that. The magic of Purpose has protected the castle, and, as in all balances, there must be, or come to be, some balancing contradiction, some flaw. . . .

The people of Feroluce do not notice what he is at. In a way, the dance with their prey has debased to a ritual. They have lived almost two decades on the blood of local mountain beasts, and bird-creatures like themselves brought down on the wing. Patience is not, with them, a virtue. It is a sort of foreplay, and can go on, in pleasure, a long, long while.

Feroluce intrudes himself through the slender window. Muscularly slender himself, and agile, it is no feat. But the wings catch, are a trouble. They follow him because they must, like two separate entities. They have been cut a little on the glass, and bleed.

He stands in a stony small room, shaking bloody feathers from him, snarling, but without sound.

Then he finds the stairway and goes down.

There are dusty landings and neglected chambers. They have no smell of life. But then there comes to be a smell. It is the scent of a nest, a colony of things, wild creatures, in constant proximity. He recognizes it. The light of his crimson eyes precedes him, deciphering blackness. And then other eyes, amber, green, and gold, spring out like stars all across his path.

Somewhere an old torch is burning out. To the human eye, only mounds and glows would be visible, but to Feroluce, the Prince of the vampires, all is suddenly revealed. There is a great stone area, barred with bronze and iron, and things stride and growl behind the bars, or chatter and flee, or only stare. And there, without bars, though bound by ropes of brass to rings of brass, three brazen beasts.

Feroluce, on the steps of the menagerie, looks into the gaze of the Duke's lions. Feroluce smiles, and the lions roar. One is the king, its mane like war-plumes. Feroluce recognizes the king and the king's right to challenge, for this is the lions' domain, their territory.

Feroluce comes down the stair and meets the lion as it leaps the length of its chain. To Feroluce, the chain means nothing, and since he has come close enough, very little either to the lion.

To the vampire Prince the fight is wonderful, exhilarating and meaningful, intellectual even, for it is colored by nuance, yet powerful as sex.

He holds fast with his talons, his strong limbs wrapping the beast which is almost stronger than he, just as its limbs wrap him in turn. He sinks his teeth in the lion's shoulder, and in fierce rage and bliss begins to draw out the nourishment. The lion kicks and claws at him in turn. Feroluce feels the gouges like fire along his shoulders, thighs, and hugs the lion more nearly as he throttles and drinks from it, loving it, jealous of it, killing it. Gradually the mighty feline body relaxes, still clinging to him, its cat teeth bedded in one beautiful swan-like wing, forgotten by both.

In a welter of feathers, stripped skin, spilled blood, the lion and the angel lie in embrace on the menagerie floor. The lion lifts its head, kisses the assassin, shudders, lets go.

Feroluce glides out from under the magnificent deadweight of the cat. He stands. And pain assaults him. His lover has severely wounded him.

Across the menagerie floor, the two lionesses are crouched. Beyond them, a man stands gaping in simple terror, behind the guttering torch. He had come to feed the beasts, and seen another feeding, and now is paralyzed. He is deaf, the menagerie-keeper, previously an advantage saving him the horror of nocturnal vampire noises.

Feroluce starts toward the human animal swifter than a serpent, and checks. Agony envelops Feroluce and the stone room spins. Involuntarily, confused, he spreads his wings for flight, there in the confined chamber. But only one wing will open. The other, damaged and partly broken, hangs like a snapped fan. Feroluce cries out, a beautiful singing note of despair and anger. He drops fainting at the menagerie-keeper's feet.

The man does not wait for more. He runs away through the castle, sreaming invective and prayer, and reaches the Duke's hall and makes the whole hall listen.

All this while, Feroluce lies in the ocean of almost-death that is sleep or swoon, while the smaller beasts in the cages discuss him, or seem to.

And when he is raised, Feroluce does not wake. Only the great drooping bloody wings quiver and are still. Those who carry him are more than ever revolted and frightened, for they have seldom seen blood. Even the food for the menagerie is cooked almost black. Two years ago, a gardener slashed his palm on a thorn. He was banished from the court for a week.

But Feroluce, the center of so much attention, does not rouse. Not until the dregs of the night are stealing out through the walls. Then some nervous instinct invests him. The sun is coming and this is an open place, he struggles through unconsciousness and hurt, through the deepest most bladed waters, to awareness.

And finds himself in a huge bronze cage, the cage of some animal appropriated for the occasion. Bars, bars all about him, and not to be got rid of, for he reaches to tear them away and cannot. Beyond the bars, the Duke's hall, which is only a pointless cold glitter to him in the maze of pain and dying lights. Not an open place, in fact, but too open for his kind. Through the window-spaces of thick glass, muddy sunglare must come in. To Feroluce it will be like swords, acids, and burning fire—

Far off he hears wings beat and voices soaring. His people search for him, call and wheel, and find nothing.

Feroluce cries out, a gravel shriek now, and the persons in the hall rush back from him, calling on God. But Feroluce does not see. He has tried to answer his own. Now he sinks down again under the coverlet of his broken wings, and the wine-red stars of his eyes go out.

### CHAPTER III

"And the Angel of Death," the priest intones, "shall surely pass over, but yet like the shadow, not substance—"

The smashed window in the old turret above the menagerie tower has been sealed with mortar and brick. It is a terrible thing that it was for so long overlooked. A miracle that only one of the creatures found and entered by it. God, the Protector, guarded the Cursed Duke and his court. And the magic that surrounds the castle, that too held fast. For from the possibility of a disaster was born a bloom of great value: Now one of the monsters is in their possession. A prize beyond price.

Caged and helpless, the fiend is at their mercy. It is also weak from its battle with the noble lion, which gave its life for the castle's safety (and will be buried with honour in an ornamented grave at the foot of the Ducal family tomb). Just before the dawn came, the Duke's advisers advised him, and the bronze cage was wheeled away into the darkest area of the hall, close by the dais where once the huge window was but is no more. A barricade of great screens was brought, and set around the cage, and the top of it covered. No sunlight now can drip into the prison to harm the specimen. Only the Duke's ladies and gentlemen steal in around the screens and see, by the light of a candlebranch, the demon still lying in its trance of pain and bloodloss. The Duke's alchemist sits on a stool nearby, dictating many notes to a nervous apprentice. The alchemist, and the apothecary for that matter, are convinced the vampire, having drunk the lion almost dry, will recover from its wounds. Even the wings will mend.

The Duke's court painter also came. He was ashamed presently, and went away. The beauty of the demon affected him, making him wish to paint it, not as something wonderfully disgusting, but as a kind of superlative man, vital and innocent, or as Lucifer himself, stricken in the sorrow of his colossal Fall. And all that has caused the painter to pity the fallen one, mere artisan that the painter is, so he slunk away. He knows, since the alchemist and the apothecary told him, what is to be done.

Of course much of the castle knows. Though scarcely anyone has slept or sought sleep, the whole place rings with excitement and vivacity. The Duke has decreed, too, that everyone who wishes shall be a witness. So he is having a progress through the castle, seeking every nook and cranny, while,

let it be said, his architect takes the opportunity to check no other windowpane has cracked.

From room to room the Duke and his entourage pass, through corridors, along stairs, through dusty attics and musty storerooms he has never seen, or if seen has forgotten. Here and there some retainer is come on. Some elderly women are discovered spinning like spiders up under the eaves, half-blind and complacent. They curtsy to the Duke from a vague recollection of old habit. The Duke tells them the good news, or rather, his messenger, walking before, announces it. The ancient women sigh and whisper, are left, probably forget. Then again, in a narrow courtyard, a simple boy, who looks after a dovecote, is magnificently told. He has a fit from alarm, grasping nothing; and the doves who love and understand him (by not trying to) fly down and cover him with their soft wings as the Duke goes away. The boy comes to under the doves as if in a heap of warm snow, comforted.

It is on one of the dark staircases above the kitchen that the gleaming entourage sweeps round a bend and comes on Rohise the scullery maid, scrubbing. In these days, when there are so few children and young servants, labor is scarce, and the scullerers are not confined to the scullery.

Rohise stands up, pale with shock, and for a wild instant thinks that, for some heinous crime she has committed in ignorance, the Duke has come in person to behead her.

"Hear then, by the Duke's will," cries the messenger. "One of Satan's night-demons, which do torment us, has been captured and lies penned in the Duke's hall. At sunrise tomorrow, this thing will be taken to that sacred spot where grows the bush of the Flower of the Fire, and here its foul blood shall be shed. Who then can doubt the bush will blossom, and save us all, by the Grace of God."

"And the Angel of Death," intones the priest, on no account to be omitted, "shall surely—"

"Wait," says the Duke. He is as white as Rohise. "Who is this?" he asks. "Is it a ghost?"

The court stare at Rohise, who nearly sinks in dread, her scrubbing rag in her hand.

Gradually, despite the rag, the rags, the rough hands, the court too begins to see.

"Why, it is a marvel."

The Duke moves forward. He looks down at Rohise and starts to cry. Rohise thinks he weeps in compassion at the awful sentence he is here to visit on her, and drops back on her knees.

"No, no," says the Duke tenderly. "Get up. Rise. You are so like my child, my daughter—"

Then Rohise, who knows few prayers, begins in panic to sing her little song as an orison:

"*Oh fleur de feu*

"*Pour ma souffrance—*"

"Ah!" says the Duke. "Where did you learn that song?"

"From my mother," says Rohise. And, all instinct now, she sings again:

"O flurda fur,

"Pourma souffrance

"Ned ormey par

"May say day mwar—"

It is the song of the fire-flower bush, the *Nona Mordica*, called Bite-Me-Not. It begins, and continues: *O flower of fire, For my misery's sake, Do not sleep but aid me; wake!* The Duke's daughter sang it very often. In those days the shrub was not needed, being just a rarity of the castle. Invoked as an amulet, on a mountain road, the rhyme itself had besides proved useless.

The Duke takes the dirty scarf from Rohise's hair. She is very, very like his lost daughter, the same pale smooth oval face, the long white neck and long dark polished eyes, and the long dark hair. (Or is it that she is very, very like the painting?)

The Duke gives instructions and Rohise is borne away.

In a beautiful chamber, the door of which has for seventeen years been locked, Rohise is bathed and her hair is washed. Oils and scents are rubbed into her skin. She is dressed in a gown of palest most pastel rose, with a girdle sewn with pearls. Her hair is combed, and on it is set a chaplet of stars and little golden leaves. "Oh, your poor hands," say the maids, as they trim her nails. Rohise has realized she is not to be executed. She has

realized the Duke has seen her and wants to love her like his dead daughter. Slowly, an uneasy stir of something, not quite happiness, moves through Rohise. Now she will wear her pink gown, now she will sympathize with and console the Duke. Her daze lifts suddenly.

The dream has come true. She dreamed of it so often it seems quite normal. The scullery was the thing which never seemed real.

She glides down through the castle and the ladies are astonished by her grace. The carriage of her head under the starry coronet is exquisite. Her voice is quiet and clear and musical, and the foreign tone of her mother, long unremembered, is quite gone from it. Only the roughened hands give her away, but smoothed by unguents, soon they will be soft and white.

"Can it be she is truly the princess returned to flesh?"

"Her life was taken so early—yes, as they believe in the Spice-Lands, by some holy dispensation, she might return."

"She would be about the age to have been conceived the very night the Duke's daughter d— That is, the very night the bane began—"

Theosophical discussion ensues. Songs are composed.

Rohise sits for a while with her adoptive father in the East Turret, and he tells her about the books and swords and lutes and scrolls, but not about the two portraits. Then they walk out together, in the lovely garden in the sunlight. They sit under a peach tree, and discuss many things, or the Duke discusses them. That Rohise is ignorant and uneducated does not matter at this point. She can always be trained. She has the basic requirements: docility, sweetness. There are many royal maidens in many places who know as little as she.

The Duke falls asleep under the peach tree. Rohise listens to the lovesongs her own (her very own) courtiers bring her.

When the monster in the cage is mentioned, she nods as if she knows what they mean. She supposes it is something hideous, a scaring treat to be shown at dinner time, when the sun has gone down.

When the sun moves towards the western line

of mountains just visible over the high walls, the court streams into the castle and all the doors are bolted and barred. There is an eagerness tonight in the concourse.

As the light dies out behind the colored windows that have no red in them, covers and screens are dragged away from a bronze cage. It is wheeled out into the center of the great hall.

Cannons begin almost at once to blast and bang from the roof-holes. The cannoneers have had strict instructions to keep up the barrage all night without a second's pause.

Drums pound in the hall. The dogs start to bark. Rohise is not surprised by the noise, for she has often heard it from far up, in her attic, like a sea-wave breaking over and over through the lower house.

She looks at the cage cautiously, wondering what she will see. But she sees only a heap of blackness like ravens, and then a tawny dazzle, torchlight on something like human skin. "You must not go down to look," says the Duke protectively, as his court pours about the cage. Someone pokes between the bars with a gemmed cane, trying to rouse the nightmare which lies quiescent there. But Rohise must be spared this.

So the Duke calls his actors, and a slight, pretty play is put on throughout dinner, before the dais, shutting off from the sight of Rohise the rest of the hall, where the barbaric gloating and goading of the court, unchecked, increases.

## CHAPTER IV

The Prince Feroluce becomes aware between one second and the next. It is the sound—heard beyond all others—of the wings of his people beating at the stones of the castle. It is the wings which speak to him, more than their wild orchestral voices. Beside these sensations, the anguish of healing and the sadism of humankind are not much.

Feroluce opens his eyes. His human audience, pleased, but afraid and squeamish, backs away, and asks each other for the two thousandth time if the cage is quite secure. In the torchlight the eyes of Feroluce are more black than red. He stares about. He is, though captive, imperious. If he were a lion or a bull, they would admire this "nobility." But the fact is, he is too much like a man, which serves to point up his supernatural differences unbearably.

Obviously, Feroluce understands the gist of his plight. Enemies have him penned. He is a show for now, but ultimately to be killed, for with the intuition of the raptor he divines everything. He had thought the sunlight would kill him, but that is a distant matter, now. And beyond all, the voices and the voices of the wings of his kindred beat the air outside this room-caved mountain of stone.

And so, Feroluce commences to sing, or at least, this is how it seems to the rabid court and all the people gathered in the hall. It seems he sings. It is the great communing call of his kind, the art and science and religion of the winged vampires, his means of telling them, or attempting to tell them, what they must be told before he dies. So the sire of Feroluce sang, and the grandsire, and each of his ancestors. Generally they died in flight, falling angels spun down the gulches and enormous stairs of distant peaks, singing. Feroluce, immured, believes that his cry is somehow audible.

To the crowd in the Duke's hall the song is merely that, a song, but how glorious. The dark silver voice, turning to bronze or gold, whitening in the higher registers. There seem to be words, but in some other tongue. This is how the planets sing, surely, or mysterious creatures of the sea.

Everyone is bemused. They listen, astonished.

No one now remonstrates with Rohise when she rises and steals down from the dais. There is an enchantment which prevents movement and coherent thought. Of all the roomful, only she is drawn forward. So she comes close, unhindered, and between the bars of the cage, she sees the vampire for the first time.

She has no notion what he can be. She imagined it was a monster or a monstrous beast. But it is neither. Rohise, starved for so long of beauty and always dreaming of it, recognizes Feroluce inevitably as part of the dream-come-true. She loves him instantly. Because she loves him, she is not afraid of him.

She attends while he goes on and on with his glorious song. He does not see her at all, or any of them. They are only things, like mist, or pain. They have no character or personality or worth; abstracts.

Finally, Feroluce stops singing. Beyond the stone and the thick glass of the siege, the wing-beats, too, eddy into silence.

Finding itself mesmerized, silent by night, the court comes to with a terrible joint start, shrilling and shouting, bursting, exploding into a compensation of sound. Music flares again. And the cannons in the roof, which have also fallen quiet, resume with a tremendous roar.

Feroluce shuts his eyes and seems to sleep. It is his preparation for death.

Hands grasp Rohise. "Lady—step back, come away. So close! It may harm you—"

The Duke clasps her in a father's embrace. Rohise, unused to this sort of physical expression, is unmoved. She pats him absently.

"My lord, what will be done?"

"Hush, child. Best you do not know."

Rohise persists.

The Duke persists in not saying.

But she remembers the words of the herald on the stair, and knows they mean to butcher the winged man. She attends thereafter more carefully to snatches of the bizarre talk about the hall, and learns all she needs. At earliest sunrise, as soon as the enemy retreat from the walls, their captive will be taken to the lovely garden with the peach trees. And so to the sunken garden of the magic bush, the fire-flower. And there they will hang him up in the sun through the dome of smoky glass, which will be slow murder to him, but they will cut him, too, so his blood, the stolen blood of the vampire, runs down to water the roots of the fleur de feu. And who can doubt that, from such nourishment, the bush will bloom? The blooms are salvation. Wherever they grow it is a safe place. Whoever wears them is safe from the draining bite of demons. Bite-Me-Not, they call it; vampire-repellent.

Rohise sits the rest of the night on her cushions, with folded hands, resembling the portrait of the princess, which is not like her.

Eventually the sky outside alters. Silence comes down beyond the wall, and so within the wall, and the court lifts its head, a corporate animal scenting day.

At the intimation of sunrise the black plague has lifted and gone away, and might never have been. The Duke, and almost all his castle full of men, women, children, emerge from the doors. The sky is measureless and bluely grey, with one cherry rift in the east that the court refers to as "mauve," since dawns and sunsets are never any sort of red here.

They move through the dimly lightening garden as the last stars melt. The cage is dragged in their midst.

They are too tired, too concentrated now, the Duke's people, to continue baiting their captive. They have had all the long night to do that, and to drink and opine, and now their stamina is sharpened for the final act.

Reaching the sunken garden, the Duke unlocks the iron door. There is no room for everyone within, so mostly they must stand outside, crammed in the gate, or teetering on erections of benches that have been placed around, and peering in over the walls through the glass of the dome. The places in the doorway are the best, of course; no one else will get so good a view. The servants and lower persons must stand back under the trees and only imagine what goes on. But they are used to that.

Into the sunken garden itself there are allowed to go the alchemist and the apothecary, and the priest, and certain sturdy soldiers attendant on the Duke, and the Duke. And Feroluce in the cage.

The east is all "mauve" now. The alchemist has prepared sorcerous safeguards which are being put into operation, and the priest, never to be left out, intones prayers. The bulge-thewed soldiers open the cage and seize the monster before it can stir. But drugged smoke has already been wafted into the prison, and besides, the monster has prepared itself for hopeless death and makes no demur.

Feroluce hangs in the arms of his loathing

guards, dimly aware the sun is near. But death is nearer, and already one may hear the alchemist's apprentice sharpening the knife an ultimate time.

The leaves of the *Nona Mordica* are trembling, too, at the commencement of the light, and beginning to unfurl. Although this happens every dawn, the court points to it with optimistic cries. Rohise, who has claimed a position in the doorway, watches it too, but only for an instant. Though she has sung of the fleur de fur since childhood, she had never known what the song was all about. And in just this way, though she has dreamed of being the Duke's daughter most of her life, such an event was never really comprehended either, and so means very little.

As the guards haul the demon forward to the plot of humid earth where the bush is growing, Rohise darts into the sunken garden, and lightning leaps in her hands. Women scream and well they might. Rohise has stolen one of the swords from the East Turret, and now she flourishes it, and now she has swung it and a soldier falls, bleeding red, red, *red,* before them all.

Chaos enters, as in yesterday's play, shaking its tattered sleeves. The men who hold the demon rear back in horror at the dashing blade and the blasphemous gore, and the mad girl in her princess's gown. The Duke makes a pitiful bleating noise, but no one pays him any attention.

The east glows in and like the liquid on the ground.

Meanwhile, the ironically combined sense of impending day and spilled hot blood have penetrated the stunned brain of the vampire. His eyes open and he sees the girl wielding her sword in a spray of crimson as the last guard lets go. Then the girl has run to Feroluce. Though, or because, her face is insane, it communicates her purpose, as she thrusts the sword's hilt into his hands.

No one has dared approach either the demon or the girl. Now they look on in horror and in horror grasp what Feroluce has grasped.

In that moment the vampire springs, and the great swanlike wings are reborn at his back, healed and whole. As the doctors predicted, he has mended perfectly, and prodigiously fast. He takes to the air like an arrow, unhindered, as if gravity does not any more exist. As he does so, the girl grips him about the waist, and slender and light, she is drawn upward too. He does not glance at her. He veers towards the gateway, and tears through it, the sword, his talons, his wings, his very shadow beating men and bricks from his path.

And now he is in the sky above them, a black star which has not been put out. They see the wings flare and beat, and the swirling of a girl's dress and unbound hair, and then the image dives and is gone into the shade under the mountains, as the sun rises.

## CHAPTER V

It is fortunate, the mountain shade in the sunrise. Lion's blood and enforced quiescence have worked wonders, but the sun could undo it all. Luckily the shadow, deep and cold as a pool, envelops the vampire, and in it there is a cave, deeper and colder. Here he alights and sinks down, sloughing the girl, whom he has almost forgotten. Certainly he fears no harm from her. She is like a pet animal, maybe, like the hunting dogs or wolves or lammergeyers that occasionally the unkindness of vampires have kept by them for a while. That she helped him is all he needs to know. She will help again. So when, stumbling in the blackness, she brings him in her cupped hands water from a cascade at the pool-cave's back, he is not surprised. He drinks the water, which is the only other substance his kind imbibe. Then he smooths her hair, absently, as he would pat or stroke the pet she seems to have become. He is not grateful, as he is not suspicious. The complexities of his intellect are reserved for other things. Since he is exhausted he falls asleep, and since Rohise is exhausted she falls asleep beside him, pressed to his warmth in the freezing dark. Like those of Feroluce, as it turns out, her thoughts are simple. She is sorry for distressing the Cursed Duke. But she has no regrets, for she could no more have left Feroluce to die than she could have refused to leave the scullery for the court.

The day, which had only just begun, passes swiftly in sleep.

Feroluce wakes as the sun sets, without seeing anything of it. He unfolds himself and goes to the cave's entrance, which now looks out on a whole sky of stars above a landscape of mountains. The castle is far below, and to the eyes of Rohise as she follows him, invisible. She does not even look for it, for there is something else to be seen.

The great dark shapes of angels are wheeling against the peaks, the stars. And their song begins, up in the starlit spaces. It is a lament, their mourning, pitiless and strong, for Feroluce, who has died in the stone heart of the thing they prey upon.

The tribe of Feroluce do not laugh, but, like a bird or wild beast, they have a kind of equivalent to laughter. This Feroluce now utters, and like a flung lance he launches himself into the air.

Rohise at the cave mouth, abandoned, forgotten, unnoted even by the mass of vampires, watches the winged man as he flies towards his people. She supposes for a moment that she may be able to climb down the tortuous ways of the mountain, undetected. Where then should she go? She does not spend much time on these ideas. They do not interest or involve her. She watches Feroluce and, because she learned long ago the uselessness of weeping, she does not shed tears, though her heart begins to break.

As Feroluce glides, body held motionless, wings outspread on a downdraught, into the midst of the storm of black wings, the red stars of eyes ignite all about him. The great lament dies. The air is very still.

Feroluce waits then. He waits, for the aura of his people is not as he has always known it. It is as if he had come among emptiness. From the silence, therefore, and from nothing else, he learns it all. In the stone he lay and he sang of his death, as the Prince must, dying. And the ritual was completed, and now there is the threnody, the grief, and thereafter the choosing of a new Prince. And none of this is alterable. He is dead. Dead. It cannot and will not be changed.

There is a moment of protest, then, from Feroluce. Perhaps his brief sojourn among men has taught him some of their futility. But as the cry leaves him, all about the huge wings are raised like swords. Talons and teeth and eyes burn against the stars. To protest is to be torn in shreds. He is not of their people now. They can attack and slaughter him as they would any other intruding thing. *Go,* the talons and the teeth and the eyes say to him. *Go far off.*

He is dead. There is nothing left him but to die.

Feroluce retreats. He soars. Bewildered, he feels the power and energy of his strength and the joy of flight, and cannot understand how this is, if he is dead. Yet he *is* dead. He knows it now.

So he closes his eyelids, and his wings. Spear swift he falls. And something shrieks, interrupting the reverie of nihilism. Disturbed, he opens his wings, shudders, turns like a swimmer, finds a ledge against his side and two hands outstretched, holding him by one shoulder, and by his hair.

"No," says Rohise. (The vampire cloud, wheeling away, have not heard her; she does not think of them.) His eyes stay shut. Holding him, she kisses these eyelids, his forehead, his lips, gently, as she drives her nails into his skin to hold him. The black wings beat, tearing to be free and fall and die. "No," say Rohise. "I love you," she says. "My life is your life." These are the words of the court and of courtly love songs. No matter, she means them. And though he cannot understand her language or her sentiments, yet her passion, purely that, communicates itself, strong and burning as the passions of his kind, who generally love only one thing, which is scarlet. For a second her intensity fills the void which now contains him. But then he dashes himself away from the ledge, to fall again, to seek death again.

Like a ribbon, clinging to him still, Rohise is drawn from the rock and falls with him.

Afraid, she buries her head against his breast, in the shadow of wings and hair. She no longer asks him to reconsider. This is how it must be. *Love* she thinks again, in the instant before they strike the earth. Then that instant comes, and is gone.

Astonished, she finds herself still alive, still in

the air. Touching so close feathers have been left on the rocks. Feroluce has swerved away, and upward. Now, conversely, they are whirling towards the very stars. The world seems miles below. Perhaps they will fly into space itself. Perhaps he means to break their bones instead on the cold face of the moon.

He does not attempt to dislodge her, he does not attempt any more to fall and die. But as he flies, he suddenly cries out, terrible lost lunatic cries.

They do not hit the moon. They do not pass through the stars like static rain.

But when the air grows thin and pure there is a peak like a dagger standing in their path. Here, he alights. As Rohise lets go of him, he turns away. He stations himself, sentry-fashion, in the manner of his tribe, at the edge of the pinnacle. But watching for nothing. He has not been able to choose death. His strength and the strong will of another, these have hampered him. His brain has become formless darkness. His eyes glare, seeing nothing.

Rohise, gasping a little in the thin atmosphere, sits at his back, watching for him, in case any harm may come near him.

At last, harm does come. There is a lightening in the east. The frozen, choppy sea of the mountains below and all about, grows visible. It is a marvelous sight, but holds no marvel for Rohise. She averts her eyes from the exquisitely penciled shapes, looking thin and translucent as paper, the rivers of mist between, the glimmer of nacreous ice. She searches for a blind hole to hide in.

There is a pale yellow wound in the sky when she returns. She grasps Feroluce by the wrist and tugs at him. "Come," she says. He looks at her vaguely, as if seeing her from the shore of another country. "The sun," she says. "Quickly."

The edge of the light runs along his body like a razor. He moves by instinct now, following her down the slippery dagger of the peak, and so eventually into a shallow cave. It is so small it holds him like a coffin. Rohise closes the entrance with her own body. It is the best she can do. She sits facing the sun as it rises, as if prepared to fight.

She hates the sun for his sake. Even as the light warms her chilled body, she curses it. Till light and cold and breathlessness fade together.

When she wakes, she looks up into twilight and endless stars, two of which are red. She is lying on the rock by the cave. Feroluce leans over her, and behind Feroluce his quiescent wings fill the sky.

She has never properly understood his nature: Vampire. Yet her own nature, which tells her so much, tells her some vital part of herself is needful to him, and that he is danger, and death. But she loves him, and is not afraid. She would have fallen to die with him. To help him by her death does not seem wrong to her. Thus, she lies still, and smiles at him to reassure him she will not struggle. From lassitude, not fear, she closes her eyes. Presently she feels the soft weight of hair brush by her cheek, and then his cool mouth rests against her throat. But nothing more happens. For some while, they continue in this fashion, she yielding, he kneeling over her, his lips on her skin. Then he moves a little away. He sits, regarding her. She, knowing the unknown act has not been completed, sits up in turn. She beckons to him mutely, telling him with her gestures and her expression *I consent. Whatever is necessary.* But he does not stir. His eyes blaze, but even of these she has no fear. In the end he looks away from her, out across the spaces of the darkness.

He himself does not understand. It is permissible to drink from the body of a pet, the wolf, the eagle. Even to kill the pet, if need demands. Can it be, outlawed from his people, he has lost their composite soul? Therefore, is he soulless now? It does not seem to him he is. Weakened and famished though he is, the vampire is aware of a wild tingling of life. When he stares at the creature which is his food, he finds he sees her differently. He has borne her through the sky, he has avoided death, by some intuitive process, for her sake, and she has led him to safety, guarded him from the blade of the sun. In the beginning it was she who rescued him from the human things which had taken him. She cannot be human, then. Not pet, and not prey. For no, he could not drain her of blood, as he would not seize upon his own kind, even in combat, to drink and feed. He starts to see her as beautiful, not in the way a man beholds a woman, certainly, but as his kind revere the sheen of water in dusk, or flight, or song. There are no words for this. But the life goes on tingling through him. Though he is dead, life.

In the end, the moon does rise, and across the open face of it something wheels by. Feroluce is less swift than was his wont, yet he starts in pursuit, and catches and brings down, killing on the wing, a great night bird. Turning in the air, Feroluce absorbs its liquors. The heat of life now, as well as its assertion, courses through him. He returns to the rock perch, the glorious flaccid bird dangling from his hand. Carefully, he tears the glory of the bird in pieces, plucks the feathers, splits the bones. He wakes the companion (asleep again from weakness) who is not pet or prey, and feeds her morsels of flesh. At first she is unwilling. But her hunger is so enormous and her nature so untamed that quite soon she accepts the slivers of raw fowl.

Strengthened by blood, Feroluce lifts Rohise and bears her gliding down the moon-slit quill-backed land of the mountains, until there is a rocky cistern full of cold, old rains. Here they drink together. Pale white primroses grow in the fissures where the black moss drips. Rohise makes a garland and throws it about the head of her beloved when he does not expect it. Bewildered but disdainful, he touches at the wreath of primroses to see if it is likely to threaten or hamper him. When it does not, he leaves it in place.

Long before dawn this time, they have found a crevice. Because it is so cold, he folds his wings about her. She speaks of her love to him, but he does not hear, only the murmur of her voice, which is musical and does not displease him. And later, she sings him sleepily the little song of the fleur de fur.

### CHAPTER VI

There comes a time then, brief, undated, chartless time, when they are together, these two creatures. Not together in any accepted sense, of course, but together in the strange feeling or emotion, instinct or ritual, that can burst to life in an instant or flow to life gradually across half a century, and which men call *Love*.

They are not alike. No, not at all. Their differences are legion and should be unpalatable. He is a supernatural thing and she a human thing, he was a lord and she a scullery sloven. He can fly, she cannot fly. And he is male, she female. What other items are required to make them enemies? Yet they are bound, not merely by love, they are bound by all they are, the very stumbling blocks. Bound, too, because they are doomed. Because the stumbling blocks have doomed them; everything has. Each has been exiled out of their own kind. Together, they cannot even communicate with each other, save by looks, touches, sometimes by sounds, and by songs neither understands, but which each comes to value since the other appears to value them, and since they give expression to that other. Nevertheless, the binding of the doom, the greatest binding, grows, as it holds them fast to each other, mightier and stronger.

Although they do not know it, or not fully, it is the awareness of doom that keeps them there, among the platforms and steps up and down, and the inner cups, of the mountains.

Here it is possible to pursue the airborne hunt, and Feroluce may now and then bring down a bird to sustain them both. But birds are scarce. The richer lower slopes, pastured with goats, wild sheep, and men—they lie far off and far down from this place as a deep of the sea. And Feroluce does not conduct her there, nor does Rohise ask that he should, or try to lead the way, or even dream of such a plan.

But yes, birds are scarce, and the pastures far away, and winter is coming. There are only two seasons in these mountains. High summer, which dies, and the high cold which already treads over the tips of the air and the rock, numbing the sky, making all brittle, as though the whole landscape might snap in pieces, shatter.

How beautiful it is to wake with the dusk, when the silver webs of night begin to form, frost and ice, on everything. Even the ragged dress—once that of a princess—is tinseled and shining with this magic substance, even the mighty wings—once those of a prince—each feather is drawn glittering with thin rime. And oh, the sky, thick as a daisy-field with the white stars. Up there, when they have fed and have strength, they fly, or, Feroluce flies and Rohise flies in his arms, carried by his wings. Up there in the biting chill like a pane of ghostly vitreous, they have become lovers, true blind lovers, embraced and linked, their bodies a bow, coupling on the wing. By the hour that this first happened the girl had forgotten all she had been, and he had forgotten too that she was anything but the essential mate. Sometimes, borne in this way, by wings and by fire, she cries out as she hangs in the ether. These sounds, transmitted through the flawless silence and amplification of the peaks, scatter over tiny half-buried villages countless miles away, where they are heard in fright and taken for the shrieks of malign invisible devils, tiny as bats, and armed with the barbed stings of scorpions. There are always misunderstandings.

After a while, the icy prologues and the stunning starry fields of winter nights give way to the main argument of winter.

The liquid of the pool, where the flowers made garlands, has clouded and closed to stone. Even the volatile waterfalls are stilled, broken cascades of glass. The wind tears through the skin and hair to gnaw the bones. To weep with cold earns no compassion of the cold.

There is no means to make fire. Besides, the one who was Rohise is an animal now, or a bird, and beasts and birds do not make fire, save for the phoenix in the Duke's bestiary. Also, the sun is fire, and the sun is a foe. Eschew fire.

There begin the calendar months of hibernation. The demon lovers too must prepare for just such a measureless winter sleep, that gives no hunger, asks no action. There is a deep cave they have lined with feathers and withered grass. But there are no more flying things to feed them. Long, long ago, the last warm frugal feast, long, long ago the last flight, joining, ecstasy and song. So, they

turn to their cave, to stasis, to sleep. Which each understands, wordlessly, thoughtlessly, is death.

What else? He might drain her of blood, he could persist some while on that, might even escape the mountains, the doom. Or she herself might leave him, attempt to make her way to the places below, and perhaps she could reach them, even now. Others, lost here, have done so. But neither considers these alternatives. The moment for all that is past. Even the death-lament does not need to be voiced again.

Installed, they curl together in their bloodless, icy nest, murmuring a little to each other, but finally still.

Outside, the snow begins to come down. It falls like a curtain. Then the winds take it. Then the night is full of the lashing of whips, and when the sun rises it is white as the snow itself, its flames very distant, giving nothing. The cave mouth is blocked up with snow. In the winter, it seems possible that never again will there be a summer in the world.

Behind the modest door of snow, hidden and secret, sleep is quiet as stars, dense as hardening resin. Feroluce and Rohise turn pure and pale in the amber, in the frigid nest, and the great wings lie like a curious articulated machinery that will not move. And the withered grass and the flowers are crystallized, until the snows shall melt.

At length, the sun deigns to come closer to the earth, and the miracle occurs. The snow shifts, crumbles, crashes off the mountains in rage. The waters hurry after the snow, the air is wrung and racked by splittings and splinterings, by rushes and booms. It is half a year, or it might be a hundred years, later.

Open now, the entry to the cave. Nothing emerges. Then, a flutter, a whisper. Something does emerge. One black feather, and caught in it, the petal of a flower, crumbling like dark charcoal and white, drifting away into the voids below. Gone. Vanished. It might never have been.

But there comes another time (half a year, a hundred years), when an adventurous traveler comes down from the mountains to the pocketed villages the other side of them. He is a swarthy cheerful fellow, you would not take him for herbalist or mystic, but he has in a pot a plant he found high up in the staring crags, which might after all contain anything or nothing. And he shows the plant, which is an unusual one, having slender, dark, and velvety leaves, and giving off a pleasant smell like vanilla. "See, the *Nona Mordica*," he says. "The Bite-Me-Not. The flower that repels vampires."

Then the villagers tell him an odd story, about a castle in another country, besieged by a huge flock, a menace of winged vampires, and how the Duke waited in vain for the magic bush that was in his garden, the Bite-Me-Not, to flower and save them all. But it seems there was a curse on this Duke, who on the very night his daughter was lost, had raped a serving woman, as he had raped others before. But this woman conceived. And bearing the fruit, or flower, of this rape, damaged her, so she lived only a year or two after it. The child grew up unknowing, and in the end betrayed her own father by running away to the vampires, leaving the Duke demoralized. And soon

after he went mad, and himself stole out one night, and let the winged fiends into his castle, so all there perished.

"Now if only the bush had flowered in time, as your bush flowers, all would have been well," the villagers cry.

The traveler smiles. He in turn does not tell them of the heap of peculiar bones, like parts of eagles mingled with those of a woman and a man. Out of the bones, from the heart of them, the bush was rising, but the traveler untangled the roots of it with care; it looks sound enough now in its sturdy pot, all of it twining together. It seems as if two separate plants are growing from a single stem, one with blooms almost black, and one pink-flowered, like a young sunset.

"Flur de fur," says the traveler, beaming at the marvel, and his luck.

Fleur de feu. Oh flower of fire. That fire is not hate or fear, which makes flowers come, not terror or anger or lust, it is love that is the fire of the Bite-Me-Not, love which cannot abandon, love which cannot harm. Love which never dies.

# THE HORROR AT CHILTON CASTLE

# Joseph Payne Brennan

Joseph Payne Brennan (1918–90) was born in Bridgeport, Connecticut, moving to New Haven at an early age and living and working (at the Yale library) there his entire life.

His first published work was a poem sold to the *Christian Science Monitor Home Forum* in 1940, and he continued to write poetry until his death a half century later. Several volumes of his verse, much of it macabre, were published during his lifetime. He edited two limited-circulation magazines, *Macabre* (1957 to 1976), which published prose and poetry in the weird and supernatural genre, and *Essence*, a semiannual poetry journal (1950 to 1977).

Brennan's fame rests with his works of horror fiction, most of which originally appeared in *Weird Tales* magazine and which Stephen King has acknowledged as a significant influence. His most anthologized story, "Slime," clearly inspired King's novella *Raft*, as well as Dean Koontz's novel *Phantoms*, all of which feature a large, water-dwelling, bloblike organism.

Brennan's best-known character, the occult detective Lucius Leffing, appeared in more than twenty stories that were collected in *The Casebook of Lucius Leffing* (1973), *The Chronicles of Lucius Leffing* (1977), and *The Adventures of Lucius Leffing* (1990). He also compiled *H. P. Lovecraft: A Bibliography* (1953) and wrote *H. P. Lovecraft: An Evaluation* (1955).

"The Horror at Chilton Castle" was originally published in *Screams at Midnight* (New Haven, CT: Macabre House, 1963).

# The Horror at Chilton Castle

## JOSEPH PAYNE BRENNAN

I had decided to spend a leisurely summer in Europe, concentrating, if at all, on genealogical research. I went first to Ireland, journeying to Kilkenny, where I unearthed a mine of legend and authentic lore concerning my remote Irish ancestors, the O'Braonains, chiefs of Ui Duach in the ancient kingdom of Ossory. The Brennans (as the name was later spelled) lost their estates in the British confiscation under Thomas Wentworth, Earl of Strafford. The thieving Earl, I am happy to report, was subsequently beheaded in the Tower.

From Kilkenny, I traveled to London and then to Chesterfield in search of maternal ancestors: the Holborns, Wilkersons, Searles, etc. Incomplete and fragmentary records left many great gaps, but my efforts were moderately successful, and at length, I decided to go farther north and visit the vicinity of Chilton Castle, seat of Robert Chilton-Payne, the Twelfth Earl of Chilton. My relationship to the Chilton-Paynes was a most distant one, and yet there existed a tenuous thread of past connection, and I thought it would amuse me to glimpse the castle.

Arriving in Wexwold, the tiny village near the castle, late in the afternoon, I engaged a room at the Inn of the Red Goose—the only one there was—unpacked, and went down for a simple meal consisting of a small loaf, cheese, and ale.

By the time I finished this stark and yet satisfying repast, darkness had set in, and with it came wind and rain.

I resigned myself to an evening at the inn. There was ale enough and I was in no hurry to go anywhere.

After writing a few letters, I went down and ordered a pint of ale. The taproom was almost deserted; the bartender, a stout gentleman who seemed forever on the point of falling asleep, was pleasant but taciturn, and at length I fell to musing on the strange and frightening legend of Chilton Castle.

There were variations of the legend, and without doubt the original tale had been embroidered down through the centuries, but the essential outline of the story concerned a secret room somewhere in the castle. It was said that this room contained a terrifying spectacle which the Chilton-Paynes were obliged to keep hidden from the world.

Only three persons were ever permitted to enter the room: the residing Earl of Chilton, the Earl's male heir, and one other person designated by the

284

Earl. Ordinarily, this person was the Factor of Chilton Castle. The room was entered only once in a generation; within three days after the male heir came of age, he was conducted to the secret room by the Earl and the Factor. The room was then sealed and never opened again until the heir conducted his own son to the grisly chamber.

According to the legend, the heir was never the same person again after entering the room. Invariably he would become somber and withdrawn; his countenance would acquire a brooding, apprehensive expression which nothing could long dispel. One of the earlier earls of Chilton had gone completely mad and hurled himself from the turrets of the castle.

Speculation about the contents of the secret room had continued for centuries. One version of the tale described the panic-stricken flight of the Gowers, with armed enemies hot on their flagging heels. Although there had been bad blood between the Chilton-Paynes and the Gowers, in their desperation the Gowers begged for refuge at Chilton Castle. The Earl gave them entry, conducted them to the hidden room, and left with a promise that they would be shielded from their pursuers. The Earl kept his promise; the Gowers' enemies were turned away from the castle, their murderous plans unconsummated. The Earl, however, simply left the Gowers in the locked room to starve to death. The chamber was not opened until thirty years later, when the Earl's son finally broke the seal. A fearful sight met his eyes. The Gowers had starved to death slowly, and at the last, judging by the appearance of the mingled skeletons, had turned to cannibalism.

Another version of the legend indicated that the secret room had been used by medieval earls as a torture chamber. It was said that the ingenious instruments of pain were yet in the room and that these lethal apparatuses still clutched the pitiful remains of their final victims, twisted fearfully in their last agonies.

A third version mentioned one of the female ancestors of the Chilton-Paynes, Lady Susan Glanville, who had reputedly made a pact with the Devil. She had been condemned as a witch, but had somehow managed to escape the stake. The date and even the manner of her death were unknown, but in some vague way the secret room was supposed to be connected with it.

As I speculated on these different versions of the gruesome legend, the storm increased in intensity. Rain drummed steadily against the leaded windows of the inn, and now I could occasionally hear the distant mutter of thunder.

Glancing at the rain-streaked panes, I shrugged and ordered another pint of ale.

I had the fresh tankard halfway to my lips when the taproom door burst open, letting in a blast of wind and rain. The door was shut and a tall figure, muffled to the ears in a dripping greatcoat, moved to the bar. Removing his cap, he ordered brandy.

Having nothing better to do, I observed him closely. He looked about seventy, grizzled and weather-worn, but wiry, with an appearance of toughness and determination. He was frowning, as if absorbed in thinking through some unpleasant problem, yet his cold, blue eyes inspected me keenly for a brief but deliberate interval.

I could not place him in a tidy niche. He might be a local farmer, and yet I did not think that he was. He had a vague aura of authority, and though his clothes were certainly plain, they were, I thought, somewhat better in cut and quality than those of the local countrymen I had observed.

A trivial incident opened a conversation between us. An unusually sharp crack of thunder made him turn toward the window. As he did so, he accidentally brushed his wet cap onto the floor. I retrieved it for him; he thanked me; and then we exchanged commonplace remarks about the weather.

I had an intuitive feeling that although he was normally a reticent individual, he was presently wrestling with some severe problem which made him want to hear a human voice. Realizing there was always the possibility that my intuition might, for once, have failed me, I nevertheless babbled on about my trip, about my genealogical researches in Kilkenny, London, and Chesterfield, and finally about my distant relationship to the Chilton-Paynes and my desire to get a good look at Chilton Castle.

Suddenly, I found that he was gazing at me with an expression which, if not fierce, was disturbingly intense. An awkward silence ensued. I coughed, wondering uneasily what I had said to make those cold, blue eyes stare at me so fixedly.

At length, he became aware of my growing embarrassment. "You must excuse me for staring," he apologized, "but something you said . . ." He hesitated. "Could we perhaps take that table?" He nodded toward a small table which sat half in shadow in the far corner of the room.

I agreed, mystified but curious, and we took our drinks to the secluded table.

He sat frowning for a minute, as if uncertain how to begin. Finally he introduced himself as William Cowath. I gave him my name and still he hesitated. At length he took a swallow of brandy and then looked straight at me. "I am," he stated, "the Factor at Chilton Castle."

I surveyed him with surprise and renewed interest. "What an agreeable coincidence!" I exclaimed. "Then perhaps tomorrow you could arrange for me to have a look at the castle?"

He seemed scarcely to hear me. "Yes, yes, of course," he replied absently.

Puzzled and a bit irritated by his air of detachment, I remained silent.

He took a deep breath and then spoke rapidly, running some of his words together. "Robert Chilton-Payne, the Twelfth Earl of Chilton, was buried in the family vaults one week ago. Frederick, the young heir and now Thirteenth Earl, came of age just three days ago. Tonight it is imperative that he be conducted to the secret chamber!"

I gaped at him in incredulous amazement. For a moment I had an idea that he had somehow heard of my interest in Chilton Castle and was merely "pulling my leg" for amusement, in the belief that I was the greenest of gullible tourists.

But there could be no mistaking his deadly seriousness. There was not the faintest suspicion of humor in his eyes.

I groped for words. "It seems so strange—so unbelievable! Just before you arrived, I had been thinking about the various legends connected with the secret room."

His cold eyes held my own. "It is not legend that confronts us; it is fact."

A thrill of fear and excitement ran through me. "You are going there tonight?"

He nodded. "Tonight. Myself, the young Earl—and one other."

I stared at him.

"Ordinarily," he continued, "the Earl himself would accompany us. That is the custom. But he is dead. Shortly before he passed away, he instructed me to select someone to go with the young Earl and myself. That person must be male—and preferably of the blood."

I took a deep drink of ale and said not a word.

He continued. "Besides the young Earl, there is no one at the castle save his elderly mother, Lady Beatrice Chilton, and an ailing aunt."

"Who could the Earl have had in mind?" I enquired cautiously.

The Factor frowned. "There are some distant male cousins residing in the country. I have an idea he thought at least one of them might appear for the obsequies. But not one of them did."

"That was most unfortunate!" I observed.

"Extremely unfortunate. And I am therefore asking you, as one of the blood, to accompany the young Earl and myself to the secret room tonight!"

I gulped like a bumpkin. Lightning flashed against the windows and I could hear rain swishing along the stones outside. When feathers of ice stopped fluttering in my stomach, I managed a reply.

"But I . . . that is . . . my relationship is so very remote! I am 'of the blood' by courtesy only, you might say. The strain in me is so very diluted."

He shrugged. "You bear the name. And you possess at least a few drops of the Payne blood. Under the present urgent circumstances, no more is necessary. I am sure that the old Earl would agree with me, could he still speak. You will come?"

There was no escaping the intensity, the pressure, of those cold, blue eyes. They seemed to follow my mind about as it groped for further excuses.

Finally, inevitably it seemed, I agreed. A feeling grew in me that the meeting had been preordained, that somehow I had always been destined to visit the secret chamber in Chilton Castle.

We finished our drinks and I went up to my room for rainwear. When I descended, suitably attired for the storm, the obese bartender was snoring on his stool, in spite of savage crashes of thunder which had now become almost incessant. I envied him as I left the cozy room with William Cowath.

Once outside, my guide informed me that we would have to go on foot to the castle. He had purposely walked down to the inn, he explained, in order that he might have time and solitude to straighten out in his own mind the things which he would have to do.

The sheets of heavy rain, the strong wind, and the roar of thunder made conversation difficult. I walked steps behind the Factor, who took enormous strides and appeared to know every inch of the way in spite of the darkness.

We walked only a short distance down the village street and then struck into a side road, which very soon dwindled to a footpath made slippery and treacherous by the driving rain.

Abruptly, the path began to ascend; the footing became more precarious. It was at once necessary to concentrate all one's attention on one's feet. Fortunately, the flashes of lightning were frequent.

It seemed to me that we had been walking for an hour—actually, I suppose, it was only a few minutes—when the Factor finally stopped.

I found myself standing beside him on a flat, rocky plateau. He pointed up an incline which rose before us. "Chilton Castle," he said.

For a moment I saw nothing in the unrelieved darkness. Then the lightning flashed.

Beyond high battlemented walls, fissured with age, I glimpsed a great, square Norman castle with four rectangular corner towers pierced by narrow window apertures which looked like evil slitted eyes. The huge, weathered pile was half-covered by a mantle of ivy which appeared more black than green.

"It looks incredibly old!" I commented.

William Cowath nodded. "It was begun in 1122 by Henry de Montargis." Without another word, he started up the incline.

As we approached the castle wall, the storm grew worse. The slanting rain and powerful wind now made speech all but impossible. We bent our heads and staggered upward.

When the wall finally loomed in front of us, I was amazed at its height and thickness. It had been constructed, obviously, to withstand the best siege guns and battering rams which its early enemies could bring to bear on it.

As we crossed a massive, timbered drawbridge, I peered down into the black ditch of a moat but I could not be sure whether there was water in it. A low, arched gateway gave access through the wall to an inner, cobblestoned courtyard. This courtyard was entirely empty, save for rivulets of rushing water.

Crossing the cobblestones with swift strides, the Factor led me to another arched gateway in yet another wall. Inside was a second, smaller yard and beyond spread the ivy-clutched base of the ancient keep itself.

Traversing a darkened, stone-flagged passage, we found ourselves facing a ponderous door, age-blackened oak reinforced with pitted bands of iron. The Factor flung open this door, and there before us was the great hall of the castle.

Four long, hand-hewn tables with their accompanying benches stretched almost the entire length of the hall. Metal torch brackets, stained with age, were affixed to sculptured stone columns which supported the roof. Ranged around the walls were suits of armor, heraldic shields, halberds, pikes, and banners—the accumulated trophies and prizes of bloody centuries when each castle was almost a kingdom unto itself. In flickering candlelight, which appeared to be the only illumination, the grim array was eerily impressive.

William Cowath waved a hand, "The holders of Chilton lived by the sword for many centuries."

Walking the length of the great hall, he entered another dim passageway. I followed silently.

As we strode along, he spoke in a subdued voice, "Frederick, the young heir, does not enjoy robust health. The shock of his father's death was severe—and he dreads tonight's ordeal, which he knows must come."

Stopping before a wooden door embellished with carved fleurs-de-lis and metal scrollwork, he gave me a shadowed, enigmatic glance and then knocked.

Someone enquired who was there and he identified himself. Presently a heavy bolt was lifted and the door opened.

If the Chilton-Paynes had been stubborn fighters in their day, the warrior blood appeared to have become considerably diluted in the veins of Frederick, the young heir and now Thirteenth Earl. I saw before me a thin, pale-complexioned young man whose dark, sunken eyes looked haunted and fearful. His dress was both theatrical and anachronistic: a dark-green velvet coat and trousers, a green satin waistband, flounces of white lace at neck and wrists.

He beckoned us in as if with reluctance and closed the door. The walls of the small room were entirely covered with tapestries depicting the hunt or medieval battle scenes. A draft of air from a window or other aperture made them undulate constantly; they seemed to have a disturbing life of their own. In one corner of the room there was an antique canopy bed; in another, a large writing-table with an agate lamp.

After a brief introduction which included an explanation of how I came to be accompanying them, the Factor enquired if his Lordship was ready to visit the chamber.

Although he was wan in any case, Frederick's face now lost every last trace of color. He nodded, however, and preceded us into the passage.

William Cowath led the way; the young Earl followed him, and I brought up the rear.

At the far end of the passage, the Factor opened the door of a cobwebbed supply room. Here he secured candles, chisels, a pick, and a sledgehammer. After packing these into a leather bag which he slung over one shoulder, he picked up a faggot torch which lay on one of the shelves in the room. He lit this, then waited while it flared into a steady flame. Satisfied with this illumination, he closed the room and beckoned for us to continue after him.

Nearby was a descending spiral of stone steps. Lifting his torch, the Factor started down. We trailed after him wordlessly.

There must have been fifty steps in that long, downward spiral. As we descended, the stones became wet and cold; the air, too, grew colder, but the cold was not of the type that refreshes. It was too laden with the smell of mold and dampness.

At the bottom of the steps, we faced a tunnel, pitch-black and silent.

The Factor raised his torch. "Chilton Castle is Norman, but is said to have been reared over a Saxon ruin. It is believed that the passageways in these depths were constructed by the Saxons." He peered, frowning into the tunnel. "Or by some still earlier folk."

He hesitated briefly, and I thought he was listening. Then, glancing around at us, he proceeded down the passage.

I walked after the Earl, shivering. The dead, icy air seemed to pierce to the pith of my bones. The stones underfoot grew slippery with a film of slime. I longed for more light, but there was none save that cast by the flickering, bobbing torch of the Factor.

Partway down the passage he paused, and again I sensed that he was listening. The silence seemed absolute, however, and we went on.

The end of the passage brought us to more descending steps. We went down some fifteen and entered another tunnel which appeared to have been cut out of the solid rock on which the castle had been reared. White-crusted niter clung to the walls. The reek of mold was intense, the icy air was fetid with some other odor which I found peculiarly repellent, though I could not name it.

At last the Factor stopped, lifted his torch, and slid the leather bag from his shoulder.

I saw that we stood before a wall made of some kind of building stone. Though damp and stained with niter, it was obviously of much more recent construction than anything we had previously encountered.

Glancing around at us, William Cowath handed me the torch. "Keep good hold on it, if you please. I have candles, but. . ."

Leaving the sentence unfinished, he drew the pick from his sling bag, and began an assault on the wall. The barrier was solid enough, but after he had worked a hole in it, he took up the sledgehammer and quicker progress was made. Once I offered to take up the hammer while he held the torch, but he only shook his head and went on with his work of demolition.

All this time the young Earl had not spoken a word. As I looked at his tense white face, I felt sorry for him, in spite of my own mounting trepidation.

Abruptly, there was silence as the Factor lowered the sledgehammer. I saw that a good two feet of the lower wall remained.

William Cowath bent to inspect it. "Strong enough," he commented cryptically. "I will leave that to build on. We can step over it."

For a full minute he stood looking silently into the blackness beyond. Finally, shouldering his bag, he took the torch from my hand and stepped over the ragged base of the wall. We followed suit.

As I entered that chamber, the fetid odor which I had noticed in the passage seemed to overwhelm us. It washed around us in a nauseating wave and we all gasped for breath.

The Factor spoke between coughs. "It will subside in a minute or two. Stand near the aperture."

Although the reek remained repellently strong, we could at length breathe more freely.

William Cowath lifted his torch and peered into the black depths of the chamber. Fearfully, I gazed around his shoulder.

There was no sound and at first I could see nothing but niter-encrusted walls and wet stone floor. Presently, however in a far corner, just beyond the flickering halo of the faggot torch, I saw two tiny, fiery spots of red. I tried to convince myself that they were two red jewels, two rubies, shining in the torchlight.

But I knew at once—I *felt* at once—what they were. They were two red eyes and they were watching us with a fierce, unwavering stare.

The Factor spoke softly. "Wait here."

He crossed toward the corner, stopped halfway, and held out his torch at arm's length. For a moment he was silent. Finally he emitted a long, shuddering sigh.

When he spoke again, his voice had changed. It was only a sepulchral whisper. "Come forward," he told us in that strange, hollow voice.

I followed Frederick until we stood at either side of the Factor.

When I saw what crouched on a stone bench in that far corner, I felt sure that I would faint. My heart literally stopped beating for perceptible seconds. The blood left my extremities; I reeled with dizziness. I might have cried out, but my throat would not open.

The entity which rested on that stone bench was like something that had crawled up out of hell. Piercing, malignant red eyes proclaimed that it had a terrible life, and yet that life sustained itself in a black, shrunken, half-mummified body which resembled a disinterred corpse. A few moldy rags clung to the cadaverlike frame. Wisps of white hair sprouted out of its ghastly gray-white skull. A red smear or blotch of some sort covered the wizened slit which served it as a mouth.

It surveyed us with a malignancy which was beyond anything merely human. It was impossible to stare back into those monstrous red eyes. They were so inexpressibly evil, one felt that one's soul would be consumed in the fires of their malevolence.

Glancing aside, I saw that the Factor was now supporting Frederick. The young heir had sagged against him, staring fixedly at the fearful apparition with terror-glazed eyes. In spite of my own sense of horror, I pitied him.

The Factor sighed again, and then he spoke once more in that low, sepulchral voice.

"You see before you," he told us, "Lady Susan Glanville. She was carried into this chamber and then fettered to the wall in 1473."

A thrill of horror coursed through me; I felt that we were in the presence of malign forces from the Pit itself.

To me the hideous thing had appeared sexless, but at the sound of its name, the ghastly mockery of a grin contorted the puckered, red-smeared mouth.

I noticed now for the first time that the monster actually was secured to the wall. The great double shackles were so blackened with age, I had not noticed them before.

The Factor went on, as if he spoke by rote. "Lady Glanville was a maternal ancestor of the Chilton-Paynes. She had commerce with the Devil. She was condemned as a witch but escaped the stake. Finally her own people forcibly overcame her. She was brought in here, fettered, and left to die."

He was silent a moment and then continued. "It was too late. She had already made a pact with the Powers of Darkness. It was an unspeakably evil thing and it has condemned her issue to a life of torment and nightmare, a lifetime of terror and dread."

He swung his torch toward the blackened, red-eyed thing. "She was a beauty once. She hated death. She feared death. And so she finally bartered her own immortal soul—and the bodies of her issue—for eternal, earthly life."

I heard his voice as in a nightmare; it seemed to be coming from an infinite distance.

He went on. "The consequences of breaking the pact are too terrible to describe. No descendant of hers has ever dared to do so, once the forfeit is known. And so she has bided here for these nearly five hundred years."

I had thought he was finished, but he resumed. Glancing upward, he lifted his torch toward the roof of that accursed chamber. "This room," he said, "lies directly underneath the family vaults. Upon the death of the Earl, the body is ostensibly left in the vaults. When the mourners have gone, however, the false bottom of the vault is thrust aside and the body of the Earl is lowered into this room."

Looking up, I saw the square rectangle of a trapdoor above.

The Factor's voice now became barely audible. "Once every generation Lady Glanville feeds—on the corpse of the deceased Earl. It is a provision of that unspeakable pact which cannot be broken."

I knew now—with a sense of horror utterly beyond description—whence came that red smear on the repulsive mouth of the creature before us.

As if to confirm his words, the Factor lowered his torch until its flame illuminated the floor at the foot of the stone bench where the vampiric monster was fettered.

Strewn around the floor were the scattered bones and skull of an adult male, red with fresh blood. And at some distance were other human bones, brown, and crumbling with age.

At this point, Frederick began to scream. His shrill, hysterical cries filled the chamber. Although the Factor shook him roughly, his terrible shrieks continued, terror-filled, nerve-shaking.

For moments, the corpselike thing on the bench watched him with its frightful red eyes. It uttered sound finally, a kind of animal squeal which might have been intended as laughter.

Abruptly then, and without any warning, it slid from the bench and lunged toward the young Earl. The blackened shackles which fettered it to the wall permitted it to advance only a yard or two. It was pulled back sharply; yet it lunged again and again, squealing with a kind of hellish glee which stirred the hair on my head.

William Cowath thrust his torch toward the monster, but it continued to lunge at the end of its fetters. The nightmare room resounded with the Earl's screams and the creature's horrible squeals of bestial laughter. I felt that my own mind would give way unless I escaped from that anteroom of hell.

For the first time during an ordeal which would have sent any lesser man fleeing for his life and sanity, the iron control of the Factor appeared to be shaken. He looked beyond the wild lunging thing toward the wall where the fetters were fastened.

I sensed what was in his mind. Would those fastenings hold, after all these centuries of rust and dampness?

On a sudden resolve, he reached into an inner pocket and drew out something which glittered in the torchlight. It was a silver crucifix. Striding forward, he thrust it almost into the twisted face of the leaping monstrosity which had once been the ravishing Lady Susan Glanville.

The creature reeled back with an agonized scream which drowned out the cries of the Earl. It cowered on the bench, abruptly silent and motionless, only the pulsating of its wizened mouth and the fires of hatred in its red eyes giving evidence that it still lived.

William Cowath addressed it grimly. "Creature of hell! If ye leave that bench ere we quit this room and seal it once again, I swear that I shall hold this cross against ye!"

The thing's red eyes watched the Factor with an expression of abysmal hatred which no combination of mere letters could convey. They actually appeared to glow with fire. And yet I read in them something else—fear.

I suddenly became aware that silence had descended on that room of the damned. It lasted only a few moments. The Earl had finally stopped screaming, but now came something worse. He began to laugh.

It was only a low chuckle, but it was somehow worse than all his screams. It went on and on, softly, mindlessly.

The Factor turned, beckoning me toward the partially demolished wall. Crossing the room, I climbed out. Behind me, the Factor led the young Earl, who shuffled like an old man, chuckling to himself.

There was then what seemed an interminable interval, during which the Factor carried back a sack of mortar and a keg of water which he had previously left somewhere in the tunnel. Working by torchlight, he prepared the cement and proceeded to seal up the chamber, using the same stones which he had displaced.

While the Factor labored, the young Earl sat motionless in the tunnel, chuckling softly.

There was silence from within. Once, only, I heard the thing's fetters clank against the stone.

At last, the Factor finished and led us back through those niter-stained passageways and up the icy stairs. The Earl could scarcely ascend; with difficulty, the Factor supported him from step to step.

Back in his tapestry-paneled chamber, Frederick sat on his canopy bed and stared at the floor, laughing quietly. With horror, I noticed that the black hair had actually turned gray. After persuading him to drink a glass of liquid which I had no doubt contained a heavy dose of sedative, the Factor managed to get him stretched out on the bed.

William Cowath then led me to a nearby bedchamber. My impulse was to rush from that hellish pile without delay, but the storm still raged and I was by no means sure I could find my way back to the village without a guide.

The Factor shook his head sadly. "I fear his Lordship is doomed to an early death. He was never strong and tonight's events may have deranged his mind . . . may have weakened him beyond hope of recovery."

I expressed my sympathy and horror. The Factor's cold, blue eyes held my own. "It may be," he said, "that in the event of the young Earl's death, you yourself might be considered . . ." He hesitated. "Might be considered," he finally concluded, "as one somewhat in the line of succession."

I wanted to hear no more. I gave him a curt goodnight, bolted the door after him, and tried—quite unsuccessfully—to salvage a few minutes' sleep.

But sleep would not come. I had feverish visions of that red-eyed thing in the sealed chamber escaping its fetters, breaking through the wall, and crawling up those icy, slime-covered stairs. . . .

Even before dawn, I softly unbolted my door and, like a marauding thief, crept shivering through the cold passageways and the great deserted hall of the castle. Crossing the cobbled courtyards and the black moat, I scrambled down the incline toward the village.

Long before noon I was well on my way to London. Luck was with me; the next day, I was on a boat bound for the Atlantic run.

I shall never return to England. I intend always to keep Chilton Castle and its permanent occupant at least an ocean away.

# THE SINGULAR DEATH OF MORTON

# Algernon Blackwood

Algernon Blackwood (1869–1951) was born in Southeast London and educated at Wellington College, the Moravian Brotherhood, and the University of Edinburgh, studying mainly Oriental religions and occult subjects. He lived in Canada and New York for sixteen years, working as a farmer, model, bartender, editor, private secretary, businessman, and violin teacher before returning to England full-time at the age of thirty-six.

Although he wrote sixteen full-length novels, beginning with *Jimbo* in 1909 and concluding with *The Fruit Stoners* in 1934, Blackwood is most remembered today for the numerous short stories that filled more than thirty volumes (although later collections were primarily rearranged reprints from earlier works).

His finest work is in the areas of supernatural and macabre stories, notably the frequently anthologized "The Willows" (1907), regarded by the noted horror-fiction writer H. P. Lovecraft as Blackwood's greatest work; "The Wendigo" (1910), which is based on a cannibalistic monster from Algonquin folklore; and the excellent series about a psychic detective whose exploits were collected in *John Silence* (1908).

"The Singular Death of Morton" was first published in the December 1910 issue of *The Tramp* magazine.

# The Singular Death of Morton

## ALGERNON BLACKWOOD

**D**usk was melting into darkness as the two men slowly made their way through the dense forest of spruce and fir that clothed the flanks of the mountain. They were weary with the long climb, for neither was in his first youth, and the July day had been a hot one. Their little inn lay further in the valley among the orchards that separated the forest from the vineyards.

Neither of them talked much. The big man led the way, carrying the knapsack, and his companion, older, shorter, evidently the more fatigued of the two, followed with small footsteps. From time to time he stumbled among the loose rocks. An exceptionally observant mind would possibly have divined that his stumbling was not entirely due to fatigue, but to an absorption of spirit that made him careless how he walked.

"All right behind?" the big man would call from time to time, half glancing back.

"Eh? What?" the other would reply, startled out of a reverie.

"Pace too fast?"

"Not a bit. I'm coming." And once he added: "You might hurry on and see to supper, if you feel like it. I shan't be long behind you."

But his big friend did not adopt the suggestion.

He kept the same distance between them. He called out the same question at intervals, Once or twice *he* stopped and looked back too.

In this way they came at length to the skirts of the wood. A deep hush covered all the valley; the limestone ridges they had climbed gleamed down white and ghostly upon them from the fading sky. Midway in its journeys, the evening wind dropped suddenly to watch the beauty of the moonlight— to hold the branches still so that the light might slip between and weave its silver pattern on the moss below.

And, as they stood a moment to take it in, a step sounded behind them on the soft pine-needles, and the older man, still a little in the rear, turned with a start as though he had been suddenly called by name.

"There's that girl—again!" he said, and his voice expressed a curious mingling of pleasure, surprise, and—apprehension.

Into a patch of moonlight passed the figure of a young girl, looked at them as though about to stop yet thinking better of it, smiled softly, and moved on out of sight into the surrounding darkness. The moon just caught her eyes and teeth, so that they shone; the rest of her body stood in shadow; the effect was striking—almost as though head and shoulders hung alone in mid air, watching them with this shining smile, then fading away.

"Come on, for heaven's sake," the big man cried. There was impatience in his manner, not unkindness. The other lingered a moment, peering closely into the gloom where the girl had vanished. His friend repeated his injunction, and a moment later the two had emerged upon the high road with the village lights in sight beyond, and the forest left behind them like a vast mantle that held the night within its folds.

For some minutes neither of them spoke; then the big man waited for his friend to draw up alongside.

"About all this valley of the Jura," he said presently, "there seems to me something—rather weird." He shifted the knapsack vigorously on his back. It was a gesture of unconscious protest. "Something uncanny," he added, as he set a good pace.

"But extraordinarily beautiful—"

"It attracts you more than it does me, I think," was the short reply.

"The picturesque superstitions still survive here," observed the older man. "They touch the imagination in spite of oneself."

A pause followed during which the other tried to increase the pace. The subject evidently made him impatient for some reason.

"Perhaps," he said presently. "Though I think myself it's due to the curious loneliness of the place. I mean, we're in the middle of tourist-Europe here, yet so utterly remote. It's such a neglected little corner of the world. The contradiction bewilders. Then, being so near the frontier, too, with the clock changing an hour a mile from the village, makes one think of time as unreal and imaginary." He laughed. He produced several other reasons as well. His friend admitted their value, and agreed half-heartedly. He still turned occasionally to look back. The mountain ridge where they had climbed was clearly visible in the moonlight.

"Odd," he said, "but I don't see that farmhouse where we got the milk anywhere. It ought to be easily visible from here."

"Hardly—in this light. It was a queer place rather, I thought," he added. He did not deny the curiously suggestive atmosphere of the region, he merely wanted to find satisfactory explanations. "A case in point, I mean. I didn't like it quite— that farmhouse—yet I'm hanged if I know why. It made me feel uncomfortable. That girl appeared so suddenly, although the place seemed deserted. And her silence was so odd. Why in the world couldn't she answer a single question? I'm glad I didn't take the milk. I spat it out. I'd like to know where she got it from, for there was no sign of a cow or a goat to be seen anywhere!"

"I swallowed mine—in spite of the taste," said the other, half smiling at his companion's sudden volubility.

Very abruptly, then, the big man turned and faced his friend. Was it merely an effect of the moonlight, or had his skin really turned pale beneath the sunburn?

"I say, old man," he said, his face grave and serious. "What do you think she was? What made her seem like that, and why the devil do you think she followed us?"

"I think," was the slow reply, "it was *me* she was following."

The words, and particularly the tone of conviction in which they were spoken, clearly were displeasing to the big man, who already regretted having spoken so frankly what was in his mind. With a companion so imaginative, so impressionable, so nervous, it had been foolish and unwise. He led the way home at a pace that made the other arrive five minutes in his rear, panting, limping, and perspiring as if he had been running.

"I'm rather for going on into Switzerland tomorrow, or the next day," he ventured that night in the darkness of their two-bedded room. "I think we've had enough of this place. Eh? What do you think?"

But there was no answer from the bed across the room, for its occupant was sound asleep and snoring.

"Dead tired, I suppose!" he muttered to himself, and then turned over to follow his friend's example. But for a long time sleep refused him.

Queer, unwelcome thoughts and feelings kept him awake—of a kind he rarely knew, and thoroughly disliked. It was rubbish, yet it made him uncomfortable, so that his nerves tingled. He tossed about in the bed. "I'm overtired," he persuaded himself, "that's all."

The strange feelings that kept him thus awake were not easy to analyse, perhaps, but their origin was beyond all question: they grouped themselves about the picture of that deserted, tumble-down châlet on the mountain ridge where they had stopped for refreshment a few hours before. It was a farmhouse, dilapidated and dirty, and the name stood in big black letters against a blue background on the wall above the door: "La Chenille." Yet not a living soul was to be seen anywhere about it; the doors were fastened, windows shuttered; chimneys smokeless; dirt, neglect, and decay everywhere in evidence.

Then, suddenly, as they had turned to go, after much vain shouting and knocking at the door, a face appeared for an instant at a window, the shutter of which was half open. His friend saw it first, and called aloud. The face nodded in reply, and presently a young girl came round the corner of the house, apparently by a back door, and stood staring at them both from a little distance.

And from that very instant, so far as he could remember, these queer feelings had entered his heart—fear, distrust, misgiving. The thought of it now, as he lay in bed in the darkness, made his hair rise. There was something about that girl that struck cold into the soul. Yet she was a mere slip of a thing, very pretty, seductive even, with a certain serpent-like fascination about her eyes and movements; and although she only replied to their questions as to refreshment with a smile, uttering no single word, she managed to convey the impression that she was a managing little person who might make herself very disagreeable if she chose. In spite of her undeniable charm there was about her an atmosphere of something sinister. He himself did most of the questioning, but it was his older friend who had the benefit of her smile. Her eyes hardly ever left his face, and once she had slipped quite close to him and touched his arm.

The strange part of it now seemed to him that he could not remember in the least how she was dressed, or what was the colouring of her eyes and hair. It was almost as though he had *felt*, rather than seen, her presence.

The milk—she produced a jug and two wooden bowls after a brief disappearance round the corner of the house—was—well, it tasted so odd that he had been unable to swallow it, and had spat it out. His friend, on the other hand, savage with thirst, had drunk his bowl to the last drop too quickly to taste it even, and, while he drank, had kept his eyes fixed on those of the girl, who stood close in front of him.

And from that moment his friend had somehow changed. On the way down he said things that were unusual, talking chiefly about the "Chenille," and the girl, and the delicious, delicate flavour of the milk, yet all phrased in such a way that it sounded singular, unfamiliar, unpleasant even. Now that he tried to recall the sentences the actual words evaded him; but the memory of the uneasiness and apprehension they caused him to feel remained. And night ever italicizes such memories!

Then, to cap it all, the girl had followed them. It was wholly foolish and absurd to feel the things he did feel, yet there the feelings were, and what was the good of arguing? That girl frightened him; the change in his friend was in some way or other a danger signal. More than this he could not tell. An explanation might come later, but for the present his chief desire was to get away from the place and to get his friend away, too.

And on this thought sleep overtook him—heavily.

The windows were wide open; outside was a garden with a rather high enclosing wall, and at the far end a gate that was kept locked because it led into private fields and so, by a back way, to the cemetery and the little church. When it was open the guests of the inn made use of it and got lost in the network of fields and vines, for there was no proper route that way to the road or the mountains. They usually ended up prematurely in the cemetery, and got back to the village by passing through the church, which was always open; or by knocking at the kitchen doors of the other houses and explaining their position. Hence the gate was locked now to save trouble.

After several hours of hot, unrefreshing sleep the big man turned in his bed and woke. He tried to stretch, but couldn't; then sat up panting with a sense of suffocation. And by the faint starlight of the summer night, he saw next that his friend was up and moving about the room. Remembering that sometimes he walked in his sleep, he called to him gently:

"Morton, old chap," he said in a low voice, with a touch of authority in it, "go back to bed! You've walked enough for one day!"

And the figure, obeying as sleep-walkers often will, passed across the room and disappeared among the shadows over his bed. The other plunged and burrowed himself into a comfortable position again for sleep, but the heat of the room, the shortness of the bed, and this tiresome interruption of his slumbers made it difficult to lose consciousness. He forced his eyes to keep shut, and his body to cease from fidgeting, but there was something nibbling at his mind like a spirit mouse that never permitted him to cross the frontier into actual oblivion. He slept with one eye open, as the saying is. Odours of hay and flowers and baked ground stole in through the open window; with them, too, came from time to time sounds—little sounds that disturbed him without being ever loud enough to claim definite attention.

Perhaps, after all, he did lose consciousness for a moment—when, suddenly, a thought came with a sharp rush into his mind and galvanized him once more into utter wakefulness. It amazed him that he had not grasped it before. It was this: the figure he had seen was *not the figure of his friend*.

Alarm gripped him at once before he could think or argue, and a cold perspiration broke out all over his body. He fumbled for matches, couldn't find them; then, remembering there was electric light, he scraped the wall with his fingers—and turned on the little white switch. In the sudden glare that filled the room he saw instantly that his friend's bed was no longer occupied. And his mind,

then acting instinctively, without process of conscious reasoning, flew like a flash to their walk of the day—to the tumble-down "Chenille," the glass of milk, the odd behaviour of his friend, and—to the girl.

At the same second he noticed that the odour in the room which hitherto he had taken to be the composite odour of fields, flowers, and night was really something else: it was the odour of freshly turned earth. Immediately on the top of this discovery came another. Those slight sounds he had heard outside the window were not ordinary night-sounds, the murmur of wind and insects: they were footsteps moving softly, stealthily down the little paths of crushed granite.

He was dressed in wonderful short order, noticing as he did so that his friend's night-garments lay upon the bed, and that he, too, had therefore dressed; further—that the door had been unlocked and stood half an inch ajar. There was now no question that he *had* slept again: between the present and the moment when he had seen the figure there had been a considerable interval. A couple of minutes later he had made his way cautiously downstairs and was standing on the garden path in the moonlight. And as he stood there, his mind filled with the stories the proprietor had told a few days before of the superstitions that still lived in the popular imagination and haunted this little, remote pine-clad valley. The thought of that girl sickened him. The odour of newly-turned earth remained in his nostrils and made his gorge rise. Utterly and vigorously he rejected the monstrous fictions he had heard, yet for all that, could not prevent their touching his imagination as he stood there in the early hours of the morning, alone with night and silence. The spell was undeniable; only a mind without sensibility could have ignored it.

He searched the little garden from end to end. Empty! Opposite the high gate he stopped, peering through the iron bars, wet with dew to his hands. Far across the intervening fields he fancied something moved. A second later he was sure of it. Something down there to the right beyond the trees was astir. It was in the cemetery.

And this definite discovery sent a shudder of

terror and disgust through him from head to foot. He framed the name of his friend with his lips, yet the sound did not come forth. Some deeper instinct warned him to hold it back. Instead, after incredible efforts, he climbed that iron gate and dropped down into the soaking grass upon the other side. Then, taking advantage of all the cover he could find, he ran, swiftly and stealthily, towards the cemetery. On the way, without quite knowing why he did so, he picked up a heavy stick; and a moment later he stood beside the low wall that separated the fields from the churchyard—stood and stared.

There, beside the tombstones, with their hideous metal wreaths and crowns of faded flowers, he made out the figure of his friend; he was stooping, crouched down upon the ground; behind him rose a couple of bushy yew trees, against the dark of which his form was easily visible. He was not alone; in front of him, bending close over him it seemed, was another figure—a slight, shadowy, slim figure.

This time the big man found his voice and called aloud:

"Morton, Morton!" he cried. "What, in the name of heaven, are you doing? What's the matter—?"

And the instant his deep voice broke the stillness of the night with its clamour, the little figure, half hiding his friend, turned about and faced him. He saw a white face with shining eyes and teeth as the form rose; the moonlight painted it with its own strange pallor; it was weird, unreal, horrible; and across the mouth, downwards from the lips to the chin, ran a deep stain of crimson.

The next moment the figure slid with a queer, gliding motion towards the trees, and disappeared among the yews and tombstones in the direction of the church. The heavy stick, hurled whirling after it, fell harmlessly half way, knocking a metal cross from its perch upon an upright grave; and the man who had thrown it raced full speed towards the huddled up figure of his friend, hardly noticing the thin, wailing cry that rose trembling through the night air from the vanished form. Nor did he notice more particularly that several of the graves, newly made, showed signs of recent disturbance, and that the odour of turned earth he had noticed in the room grew stronger. All his attention was concentrated upon the figure at his feet.

"Morton, man, get up! Wake for God's sake! You've been walking in—"

Then the words died upon his lips. The unnatural attitude of his friend's shoulders, and the way the head dropped back to show the neck, struck him like a blow in the face. There was no sign of movement. He lifted the body up and carried it, all limp and unresisting, by ways he never remembered afterwards, back to the inn.

It was all a dreadful nightmare—a nightmare that carried over its ghastly horror into waking life. He knew that the proprietor and his wife moved busily to and fro about the bed, and that in due course the village doctor was upon the scene, and that he was giving a muddled and feverish description of all he knew, telling how his friend was a confirmed sleep-walker and all the rest. But he did not realize the truth until he saw the face of the doctor as he straightened up from the long examination.

"Will you wake him?" he heard himself asking, "or let him sleep it out till morning?" And the doctor's expression, even before the reply came to confirm it, told him the truth. "Ah, monsieur, your friend will not ever wake again, I fear! It is the heart, you see; *hélas*, it is sudden failure of the heart!"

The final scenes in the little tragedy which thus brought his holiday to so abrupt and terrible a close need no description, being in no way essential to this strange story. There were one or two curious details, however, that came to light afterwards. One was, that for some weeks before there had been signs of disturbance among newly-made graves in the cemetery, which the authorities had been trying to trace to the nightly wanderings of the village madman—in vain; and another, that the morning after the death a trail of blood had been found across the church floor, as though someone had passed through from the back entrance to the front. A special service was held that very week to cleanse the holy building from the evil of that stain; for the villagers, deep in their superstitions, declared that nothing human had left that trail; nothing could have made those marks but a vampire disturbed at midnight in its awful occupation among the dead.

Apart from such idle rumours, however, the bereaved carried with him to this day certain other remarkable details which cannot be so easily dismissed. For he had a brief conversation with the doctor, it appears, that impressed him profoundly. And the doctor, an intelligent man, prosaic as granite into the bargain, had questioned him rather closely as to the recent life and habits of his dead friend. The account of their climb to the "Chenille" he heard with an amazement he could not conceal.

"But no such châlet exists," he said. "There is no 'Chenille.' A long time ago, fifty years or more, there was such a place, but it was destroyed by the authorities on account of the evil reputation of the people who lived there. They burnt it. Nothing remains today but a few bits of broken wall and foundation."

"Evil reputation—?"

The doctor shrugged his shoulders "Travellers, even peasants, disappeared," he said. "An old woman lived there with her daughter, and poisoned milk was supposed to be used. But the neighbourhood accused them of worse than ordinary murder—"

"In what way?"

"Said the girl was a vampire," answered the doctor shortly.

And, after a moment's hesitation, he added, turning his face away as he spoke:

"It was a curious thing, though, that tiny hole in your friend's throat, small as a pin-prick, yet so deep. And the heart—did I tell you?—was almost completely drained of blood."

## THE DEATH OF ILALOTHA

# Clark Ashton Smith

Clark Ashton Smith (1893–1961) was born in Long Valley, California, a few miles south of Auburn, where he grew up. He spent little time in school, preferring to self-educate by reading through the *Encyclopædia Britannica* and an unabridged dictionary several times, also teaching himself French and Spanish in the same way.

He was still a teenager when his early stories were published in *Overland Monthly* and *Black Cat,* but he quickly turned his focus to poetry, achieving astonishing success when *The Star-Treader and Other Poems* was published in 1912. Reviewers hailed him as "the Keats of the Pacific Coast" and "the boy genius of the Sierras," though a few voices found him "sinister" and "ghoulish." He continued to write poetry for another fifteen years, though his early fame and accolades vanished quickly and completely, forcing him to self-publish his next two volumes.

He and H. P. Lovecraft started a correspondence in 1922. The great writer of macabre fiction suggested that Smith try his hand at dark fantasy, and his first weird story, "The Abominations of Yondo," ran in *Overland Monthly* in 1926. Needing to earn a living, he began to write fiction in earnest and became a regular contributor to *Weird Tales,* producing more than a story per month from 1929 to 1937, assuring his reputation as one of the greatest writers of pulp horror fiction of all time.

"The Death of Ilalotha" was first published in the September 1937 issue of *Weird Tales.*

# The Death of Ilalotha

## CLARK ASHTON SMITH

*Black Lord of bale and fear, master of all*
    *confusion!*
*By thee, thy prophet saith,*
*New power is given to wizards after death,*
*And witches in corruption draw forbidden*
    *breath,*
*And weave such wild enchantment and illusion*
*As none but lamiae may use;*
*And through thy grace the charnelled corpses*
    *lose*
*Their horror, and nefandous loves are lighted*
*In noisome vaults long nighted*
*And vampires make their sacrifice to thee—*
*Disgorging blood as if great urns had poured*
*Their bright vermilion hoard*
*About the washed and weltering sarcophagi.*
—LUDAR'S LITANY TO THASAIDON

A ccording to the custom in old Tasuun, the obsequies of Ilalotha, lady-in-waiting to the self-widowed Queen Xantlicha, had formed an occasion of much merry-making and prolonged festivity. For three days, on a bier of diverse-coloured silks from the Orient, under a rose-hued canopy that might well have domed some nuptial couch, she had lain clad with gala garments amid the great feasting hall of the royal palace in Miraab. About her, from morning dusk to sunset, from cool even to torridly glaring dawn, the feverish tide of the funeral orgies had surged and eddied without slackening. Nobles, court officials, guardsmen, scullions, astrologers, eunuchs, and all the high ladies, waiting women, and female slaves of Xantlicha had taken part in that prodigal debauchery which was believed to honour most fitly the deceased. Mad songs and obscene ditties were sung, and dancers whirled in vertiginous frenzy to the lascivious pleading of untirable lutes. Wines and liquors were poured torrentially from monstrous amphoras; the tables fumed with spicy meats piled in huge hummocks and forever replenished. The drinkers offered libation to Ilalotha, till the fabrics of her bier were stained to darker hues by the spilt vintages. On all sides around her, in attitudes of disorder or prone abandonment, lay those who had yielded to amorous licence or the fullness of their potations. With half-shut eyes and lips slightly parted, in the rosy shadow cast by the catafalque, she bore no aspect of death but seemed a sleeping empress who ruled impartially over the living and the dead. This appearance, together with a strange heightening of her natural beauty, was remarked by many: and some said that she seemed to await a lover's kiss rather than the kisses of the worm.

On the third evening, when the many-tongued brazen lamps were lit and the rites drew to their end, there returned to court the Lord Thulos, acknowledged lover of Queen Xantlicha, who had gone a week previous to visit his domain on the western border and had heard nothing of Ilalotha's death. Still unaware, he came into the hall at that hour when the saturnalia began to flag and the fallen revellers to outnumber those who still moved and drank and made riot.

He viewed the disordered hall with little surprise, for such scenes were familiar to him from childhood. Then, approaching the bier, he recognized its occupant with a certain startlement. Among the numerous ladies of Miraab who had drawn his libertine affections, Ilalotha had held sway longer than most; and, it was said, she had grieved more passionately over his defection than any other. She had been superseded a month before by Xantlicha, who had shown favour to Thulos in no ambiguous manner; and Thulos, perhaps, had abandoned her not without regret: for the role of lover to the queen, though advantageous and not wholly disagreeable, was somewhat precarious. Xantlicha, it was universally believed, had rid herself of the late King Archain by means of a tomb-discovered vial of poison that owed its peculiar subtlety and virulence to the art of ancient sorcerers. Following this act of disposal, she had taken many lovers, and those who failed to please her came invariably to ends no less violent than that of Archain. She was exigent, exorbitant, demanding a strict fidelity somewhat irksome to Thulos; who, pleading urgent affairs on his remote estate, had been glad enough of a week away from court.

Now, as he stood beside the dead woman, Thulos forgot the queen and bethought him of certain summer nights that had been honeyed by the fragrance of jasmine and the jasmine-white beauty of Ilalotha. Even less than the others could he believe her dead: for her present aspect differed in no wise from that which she had often assumed during their old intercourse. To please his whim

she had feigned the inertness and complaisance of slumber or death; and at such times he had loved her with an ardour undismayed by the pantherine vehemence with which, at other whiles, she was wont to reciprocate or invite his caresses.

Moment by moment, as if through the working of some powerful necromancy, there grew upon him a curious hallucination, and it seemed that he was again the lover of those lost nights, and had entered that bower in the palace gardens where Ilalotha awaited him on a couch strewn with overblown petals, lying with bosom quiet as her face and hands. No longer was he aware of the crowded hall: the highflaring lights, the wine-flushed faces had become a moon-bright parterre of drowsily nodding blossoms, and the voices of the courtiers were no more than a faint suspiration of wind amid cypress and jasmine. The warm, aphrodisiac perfumes of the June night welled about him; and again, as of old, it seemed that they arose from the person of Ilalotha no less than from the flowers. Prompted by intense desire, he stooped over and felt her cool arm stir involuntarily beneath his kiss.

Then, with the bewilderment of a sleepwalker awakened rudely, he heard a voice that hissed in his ear with soft venom. "Hast forgotten thyself, my Lord Thulos? Indeed, I wonder little, for many of my bawcocks deem that she is fairer in death than in life." And, turning from Ilalotha, while the weird spell dissolved from his senses, he found Xantlicha at his side. Her garments were disarrayed, her hair was unbound and dishevelled, and she reeled slightly, clutching him by the shoulder with sharp-nailed fingers. Her full, poppy-crimson lips were curled by a vixenish fury, and in her long-lidded yellow eyes there blazed the jealousy of an amorous cat.

Thulos, overwhelmed by a strange confusion, remembered but partially the enchantment to which he had succumbed; and he was unsure whether or not he had actually kissed Ilalotha and had felt her flesh quiver to his mouth. Verily, he thought, this thing could not have been, and a waking dream had momentarily seized him. But he was troubled by the words of Xantlicha and her anger, and by the half-furtive drunken laughters and ribald whispers that he heard passing among the people about the hall.

"Beware, my Thulos," the queen murmured, her strange anger seeming to subside, "for men say that she was a witch . . ."

"How did she die?" queried Thulos.

"From no other fever than that of love, it is rumoured."

"Then, surely, she was no witch," Thulos argued with a lightness that was far from his thoughts and feelings, "for true sorcery should have found the cure."

"It was from love of thee," said Xantlicha darkly, "and, as all women know, thy heart is blacker and harder than black adamant. No witchcraft, however potent, could prevail thereon." Her mood, as she spoke, appeared to soften suddenly. "Thy absence has been over-long, my lord. Come to me at midnight: I will wait for thee in the south pavilion." Then, eyeing him sultrily for an instant from under drooped lids, and pinching his arm in such manner that her nails pierced through cloth and skin like a cat's talons, she turned from Thulos to hail certain of the harem eunuchs.

Thulos, when the queen's attention was disengaged from him, ventured to look again at Ilalotha; pondering, meanwhile, the curious remarks of Xantlicha. He knew that Ilalotha, like many of the court ladies, had dabbled in spells and philtres; but her witchcraft had never concerned him, since he felt no interest in other charms or enchantments than those with which nature had endowed the bodies of women. And it was quite impossible for him to believe that Ilalotha had died from a fatal passion: since, in his experience, passion was never fatal.

Indeed, as he regarded her with confused emotions, he was again beset by the impression that she had not died at all. There was no repetition of the weird, half-remembered hallucination of other time and place; but it seemed to him that she had stirred from her former position on the wine-stained bier, turning her face towards him a little, as a woman turns to an expected lover; that the arm he had kissed (either in dream or reality) was outstretched a little farther from her side.

Thulos bent nearer, fascinated by the mystery and drawn by a stronger attraction that he could not have named. Again, surely, he had dreamt or had been mistaken. But even as the doubt grew, it seemed that the bosom of Ilalotha stirred in faint respiration and he heard an almost inaudible but thrilling whisper: "Come to me at midnight. I will wait for thee . . . in the tomb."

At this instant there appeared beside the catafalque certain people in the sober and rusty raiment of sextons, who had entered the hall silently, unperceived by Thulos or by any of the company. They carried among them a thin-walled sarcophagus of newly welded and burnished bronze. It was their office to remove the dead woman and bear her to the sepulchral vaults of her family, which were situated in the old necropolis lying somewhat to northward of the palace gardens.

Thulos would have cried out to restrain them from their purpose; but his tongue clove tightly; nor could he move any of his members. Not knowing whether he slept or woke, he watched the people of the cemetery as they placed Ilalotha in the sarcophagus and bore her quickly from the hall, unfollowed and still unheeded by the drowsy bacchanalians. Only when the sombre cortège had departed was he able to stir from his position by the empty bier. His thoughts were sluggish, and full of darkness and indecision. Smitten by an immense fatigue that was not unnatural after his day-long journey, he withdrew to his apartments and fell instantly into death-deep slumber.

Freeing itself gradually from the cypress-boughs, as if from the long, stretched fingers of witches, a waning and misshapen moon glared horizontally through the eastern window when Thulos awoke. By this token, he knew that the hour drew towards midnight, and recalled the assignation which Queen Xantlicha had made with him: an assignation which he could hardly break without incurring the queen's deadly displeasure. Also, with singular clearness, he recalled another rendezvous . . . at the same time but in a different place. Those incidents and impressions of Ilalotha's funeral, which, at the time, had seemed so dubitable and dreamlike, returned to him with a profound conviction of reality, as if etched on his mind by some mordant chemistry of sleep . . . or the strengthening of some sorcerous charm. He felt that Ilalotha had indeed stirred on her bier and spoken to him; that the sextons had borne her still living to the tomb. Perhaps her supposed demise had been merely a sort of catalepsy; or else she had deliberately feigned death in a last effort to revive his passion. These thoughts awoke within him a raging fever of curiosity and desire; and he saw before him her pale, inert, luxurious beauty, presented as if by enchantment.

Direly distraught, he went down by the lampless stairs and hallways to the moonlit labyrinth of the gardens. He cursed the untimely exigence of Xantlicha. However, as he told himself, it was more than likely that the queen, continuing to imbibe the liquors of Tasuun, had long since reached a condition in which she would neither keep nor recall her appointment. This thought reassured him: in his queerly bemused mind, it soon became a certainty; and he did not hasten towards the south pavilion but strolled vaguely amid the wan and sombre boscage.

More and more it seemed unlikely that any but himself was abroad: for the long unlit wings of the palace sprawled as in vacant stupor; and in the gardens there were only dead shadows, and pools of still fragrance in which the winds had drowned. And over all, like a pale, monstrous poppy, the moon distilled her death-white slumber.

Thulos, no longer mindful of his rendezvous with Xantlicha, yielded without further reluctation to the urgence that drove him towards another goal. Truly, it was no less than obligatory that he should visit the vaults and learn whether or not he had been deceived in his belief concerning Ilalotha. Perhaps, if he did not go, she would stifle in the shut sarcophagus, and her pretended death would quickly become an actuality. Again, as if spoken in the moonlight before him, he heard the words she had whispered, or seemed to whisper, from the bier. "Come to me at midnight . . . I will wait for thee . . . in the tomb."

With the quickening steps and pulses of one who fares to the warm, petal-sweet couch of an adored mistress, he left the palace grounds by an unguarded northern postern and crossed the weedy common between the royal gardens and the old cemetery. Unchilled and undismayed, he entered those always-open portals of death, where ghoul-headed monsters of black marble, glaring with hideously pitted eyes, maintained their charnel postures before the crumbling pylons.

The very stillness of the low-bosomed graves, the rigour and pallor of the tall shafts, the deepness of bedded cypress shadows, the inviolacy of death by which all things were invested, served to heighten the singular excitement that had fired Thulos' blood. It was as if he had drunk a philtre spiced with mummia. All around him the mortuary silence seemed to burn and quiver with a thousand memories of Ilalotha, together with those expectations to which he had given as yet no formal image . . .

Once, with Ilalotha, he had visited the subterranean tomb of her ancestors; and recalling its situation clearly, he came without indirection to the low-arched and cedar-darkened entrance. Rank nettles and fetid fumitories, growing thickly about the seldom-used adit, were crushed down by the tread of those who had entered there before Thulos; and the rusty, iron-wrought door sagged heavily inward on its loose hinges. At his feet there lay an extinguished flambeau, dropped, no doubt, by one of the departing sextons. Seeing it, he realized that he had brought with him neither candle nor lanthorn for the exploration of the vaults, and found in that providential torch an auspicious omen.

Bearing the lit flambeau, he began his investigation. He gave no heed to the piled and dusty sarcophagi in the first reaches of the subterrane: for during their past visit, Ilalotha had shown to him a niche at the innermost extreme, where, in due time, she herself would find sepulture among the members of that decaying line. Strangely, insidiously, like the breath of some vernal garden, the languid and luscious odour of jasmine swam to meet him through the musty air, amid the tiered presence of the dead; and it drew him to the sarcophagus that stood open between others tightly lidded. There he beheld Ilalotha, lying in the gay garments of her funeral, with half-shut eyes and half-parted lips; and upon her was the same weird and radiant beauty, the same voluptuous pallor and stillness, that had drawn Thulos with a necromantic charm.

"I knew that thou wouldst come, O Thulos," she murmured, stirring a little, as if involuntarily, beneath the deepening ardour of his kisses that passed quickly from throat to bosom . . .

The torch that had fallen from Thulos' hand expired in the thick dust . . .

Xantlicha, retiring to her chamber betimes, had slept illy. Perhaps she had drunk too much or too little of the dark ardent vintages; perhaps her blood was fevered by the return of Thulos, and her jealousy still troubled by the hot kiss which he had laid on Ilalotha's arm during the obsequies. A restlessness was upon her; and she rose well before the hour of her meeting with Thulos, and stood at her chamber window seeking such coolness as the night air might afford.

The air, however, seemed heated as by the burning of hidden furnaces; her heart appeared to swell in her bosom and stifle her; and her unrest and agitation were increased rather than diminished by the spectacle of the moon-lulled gardens. She would have hurried forth to the tryst in the pavilion; but despite her impatience, she thought it well to keep Thulos waiting. Leaning thus from her sill, she beheld Thulos when he passed amid the parterres and arbors below. She was struck by the unusual haste and intentness of his steps; and she wondered at their direction, which could only bring him to places remote from the rendezvous she had named. He disappeared from her sight in the cypress-lined alley that led to the north garden gate; and her wonderment was soon mingled with alarm and anger when he did not return.

It was incomprehensible to Xantlicha that Thulos, or any man, would dare to forget the tryst in his normal senses; and seeking an explanation, she surmised that the working of some baleful

and potent sorcery was probably involved. Nor, in the light of certain incidents that she had observed, and much else that had been rumoured, was it hard for her to identify the sorceress. Ilalotha, the queen knew, had loved Thulos to the point of frenzy, and had grieved inconsolably after his desertion for her. People said that she had wrought various ineffectual spells to bring him back; that she had vainly invoked demons and sacrificed to them, and had made futile invultuations and death-charms against Xantlicha. In the end, she had died of sheer chagrin and despair, or perhaps had slain herself with some undetected poison . . . But, as was commonly believed in Tasuun, a witch dying thus, with unslaked desires and frustrate cantrips, could turn herself into a lamia or vampire and procure thereby the consummation of all her sorceries . . .

The queen shuddered, remembering these things; and remembering also the hideous and malign transformation that was said to accompany the achievement of such ends: for those who used in this manner the power of hell must take on the very character and the actual semblance of infernal beings. Too well she surmised the destination of Thulos, and the danger to which he had gone forth if her suspicions were true. And, knowing that she might face an equal danger, Xantlicha determined to follow him.

She made little preparation, for there was no time to waste; but took from beneath her silken bedcushions a small, straight-bladed dagger that she kept always within reach. The dagger had been anointed from point to hilt with such venom as was believed efficacious against either the living or the dead. Bearing it in her right hand, and carrying in the other a slot-eyed lanthorn that she might require later, Xantlicha stole swiftly from the palace.

The last lees of the evening's wine ebbed wholly from her brain, and dim, ghastly fears awoke, warning her like the voices of ancestral phantoms. But, firm in her determination, she followed the path taken by Thulos; the path taken earlier by those sextons who had borne Ilalotha to her place of sepulture. Hovering from tree to tree, the moon accompanied her like a worm-hollowed visage. The soft, quick patter of her cothurns, breaking the white silence, seemed to tear the filmy cobweb pall that withheld from her a world of spectral abominations. And more and more she recalled of those legendries that concerned such beings as Ilalotha; and her heart was shaken within her: for she knew that she would meet no mortal woman but a thing raised up and inspirited by the seventh hell. But amid the chill of these horrors, the thought of Thulos in the lamia's arms was like a red brand that seared her bosom.

Now the necropolis yawned before Xantlicha, and her path entered the cavernous gloom of far-vaulted funeral trees, as if passing into monstrous and shadowy mouths that were tusked with white monuments. The air grew dank and noisome, as if filled with the breathings of open crypts. Here the queen faltered, for it seemed that black, unseen cacodemons rose all about her from the graveyard ground, towering higher than the shafts and boles, and standing in readiness to assail her if she went farther. Nevertheless, she came anon to the dark adit that she sought. Tremulously she lit the wick of the slot-eyed lanthorn; and, piercing the gross underground darkness before her with its bladed beam, she passed with ill-subdued terror and repugnance into that abode of the dead . . . and perchance of the Undead.

However, as she followed the first turnings of the catacomb, it seemed that she was to encounter nothing more abhorrent than charnel mould and century-sifted dust; nothing more formidable than the serried sarcophagi that lined the deeply hewn shelves of stone: sarcophagi that had stood silent and undisturbed ever since the time of their deposition. Here, surely, the slumber of all the dead was unbroken, and the nullity of death was inviolate.

Almost the queen doubted that Thulos had preceded her there; till, turning her light on the ground, she discerned the print of his poulaines, long-tipped and slender in the deep dust amid those footmarks left by the rudely shod sextons. And she saw that the footprints of Thulos pointed only in one direction, while those of the others plainly went and returned.

Then, at an undetermined distance in the shadows ahead, Xantlicha heard a sound in which the sick moaning of some amorous woman was blent with a snarling as of jackals over the meat. Her blood returned frozen upon her heart as she went onward step by slow step, clutching her dagger in a hand drawn sharply back, and holding the light high in advance. The sound grew louder and more distinct; and there came to her now a perfume as of flowers in some warm June night; but, as she still advanced, the perfume was mixed with more and more of a smothering foulness such as she had never heretofore known, and was touched with the hot reeking of blood.

A few paces more, and Xantlicha stood as if a demon's arm had arrested her: for her lanthorn's light had found the inverted face and upper body of Thulos, hanging from the end of a burnished, new-wrought sarcophagus that occupied a scant interval between others green with rust. One of Thulos' hands clutched rigidly the rim of the sarcophagus, while the other hand, moving feebly, seemed to caress a dim shape that leaned above him with arms showing jasmine-white in the narrow beam, and dark fingers plunging into his bosom. His head and body seemed but an empty hull, and his hand hung skeleton-thin on the bronze rim, and his whole aspect was vein-drawn, as if he had lost more blood than was evident on his torn throat and face, and in his sodden raiment and dripping hair.

From the thing stooping above Thulos, there came ceaselessly that sound which was half moan and half snarl. And as Xantlicha stood in petrific fear and loathing, she seemed to hear from Thulos' lips an indistinct murmur, more of ecstasy than pain. The murmur ceased, and his head hung slacklier than before, so that the queen deemed him verily dead. At this she found such wrathful courage as enabled her to step nearer and raise the lanthorn higher: for, even amid her extreme panic, it came to her that by means of the wizard-poisoned dagger she might still haply slay the thing that had slain Thulos.

Waveringly the light crept aloft, disclosing inch by inch that infamy which Thulos had caressed in the darkness.

. . . It crept even to the crimson-smeared wattles, and the fanged and ruddled orifice that was half mouth and half beak . . . till Xantlicha knew why the body of Thulos was a mere shrunken hull . . . In what the queen saw, there remained nothing of Ilalotha except the white, voluptuous arms, and a vague outline of human breasts melting momently into breasts that were not human, like clay moulded by a demon sculptor. The arms too began to change and darken; and, as they changed, the dying hand of Thulos stirred again and fumbled with a caressing movement towards the horror. And the thing seemed to heed him not but withdrew its fingers from his bosom, and reached across him with members stretching enormously, as if to claw the queen or fondle her with its dribbling talons.

It was then that Xantlicha let fall the lanthorn and the dagger, and ran with shrill, endless shriekings and laughters of immitigable madness from the vault.

## THE BRIDE OF CORINTH

# Johann Wolfgang von Goethe

Johann Wolfgang von Goethe (1749–1832) was born in Frankfurt and studied law but went on to become a poet, dramatist, novelist, philosopher, statesman, and scientist. His work of a lifetime, *Faust*, completed the year before his death, is cosmic in its significance, ranging from the romantic egocentrism of part I to the altruistic idealism of part II. It epitomizes Western intellectual history in the eighteenth and nineteenth centuries, and, combined with his vast body of work in several genres, raised his reputation beyond that of a literary figure to wise old man of Europe. He is ranked with Virgil, Shakespeare, and Dante as one of the few manifestations of transcendent literary genius.

His poem "Die Braut von Korinth" ("The Bride of Corinth") may not have been the beginning of the vampire legend in Germany, but it brought it into sharp focus. It was inspired by "Philinnium" by Phlegon of Tralles, in which a young Athenian who visits his father's old friend to whose daughter he has been betrothed receives at midnight the vampire body of the girl whom death has prevented from becoming his bride.

Goethe produced it as part of a friendly contest with Friedrich Schiller in the art of ballad writing.

"The Bride of Corinth" was first published in Schiller's journal, *Die Horen*, in 1797. It was first published in English in 1835 in a translation by John Anster.

# The Bride of Corinth

## JOHANN WOLFGANG VON GOETHE

Once a stranger youth to Corinth came,
Who in Athens lived, but hoped that he
From a certain townsman there might claim,
As his father's friend, kind courtesy.
Son and daughter, they
Had been wont to say
Should thereafter bride and bridegroom be.
But can he that boon so highly prized,
Save 'tis dearly bought, now hope to get?
They are Christians and have been baptized,
He and all of his are heathens yet.
For a newborn creed,
Like some loathsome weed,
Love and truth to root out oft will threat.
Father, daughter, all had gone to rest,
And the mother only watches late;
She receives with courtesy the guest,
And conducts him to the room of state.
Wine and food are brought,
Ere by him besought;
Bidding him good night, she leaves him straight.
But he feels no relish now, in truth,
For the dainties so profusely spread;
Meat and drink forgets the wearied youth,
And, still dress'd, he lays him on the bed.
Scarce are closed his eyes,
When a form in-hies

Through the open door with silent tread.
By his glimmering lamp discerns he now
How, in veil and garment white array'd,
With a black and gold band round her brow,
Glides into the room a bashful maid.
But she, at his sight,
Lifts her hand so white,
And appears as though full sore afraid.
"Am I," cries she, "such a stranger here,
That the guest's approach they could not name?
Ah, they keep me in my cloister drear,
Well nigh feel I vanquish'd by my shame.
On thy soft couch now
Slumber calmly thou!
I'll return as swiftly as I came."
"Stay, thou fairest maiden!" cries the boy,
Starting from his couch with eager haste:
"Here are Ceres', Bacchus' gifts of joy;
Amor bringest thou, with beauty grac'd!
Thou art pale with fear!
Loved one let us here
Prove the raptures the Immortals taste."
"Draw not nigh, O Youth! afar remain!
Rapture now can never smile on me;
For the fatal step, alas! is ta'en,
Through my mother's sick-bed phantasy.
Cured, she made this oath:

'Youth and nature both
Shall henceforth to Heav'n devoted be.'
From the house, so silent now, are driven
All the gods who reign'd supreme of yore;
One Invisible now rules in heaven,
On the cross a Saviour they adore.
Victims slay they here,
Neither lamb nor steer,
But the altars reek with human gore."
And he lists, and ev'ry word he weighs,
While his eager soul drinks in each sound:
"Can it be that now before my gaze
Stands my loved one on this silent ground?
Pledge to me thy troth!
Through our fathers' oath:
With Heav'ns blessing will our love be crown'd."
"Kindly youth, I never can be thine!
'Tis my sister they intend for thee.
When I in the silent cloister pine,
Ah, within her arms remember me!
Thee alone I love,
While love's pangs I prove;
Soon the earth will veil my misery."
"No! for by this glowing flame I swear,
Hymen hath himself propitious shown:
Let us to my father's house repair,
And thoult find that joy is not yet flown,
Sweetest, here then stay,
And without delay
Hold we now our wedding feast alone!"
Then exchange they tokens of their truth;
She gives him a golden chain to wear,
And a silver chalice would the youth
Give her in return of beauty rare.
"That is not for me;
Yet I beg of thee,
One lock only give me of thy hair."
Now the ghostly hour of midnight knell'd,
And she seem'd right joyous at the sign;
To her pallid lips the cup she held,
But she drank of nought but blood-red wine.
For to taste the bread
There before them spread,
Nought he spoke could make the maid incline.
To the youth the goblet then she brought,—
He too quaff'd with eager joy the bowl.

Love to crown the silent feast he sought,
Ah! full love-sick was the stripling's soul.
From his prayer she shrinks,
Till at length he sinks
On the bed and weeps without control.
And she comes, and lays her near the boy:
"How I grieve to see thee sorrowing so!
If thou think'st to clasp my form with joy,
Thou must learn this secret sad to know;
Yes! the maid, whom thou
Call'st thy loved one now,
Is as cold as ice, though white as snow."
Then he clasps her madly in his arm,
While love's youthful might pervades his frame:
"Thou might'st hope, when with me, to grow warm,
E'en if from the grave thy spirit came!
Breath for breath, and kiss!
Overflow of bliss!
Dost not thou, like me, feel passion's flame?"
Love still closer rivets now their lips,
Tears they mingle with their rapture blest,
From his mouth the flame she wildly sips,
Each is with the other's thought possess'd.
His hot ardour's flood
Warms her chilly blood,
But no heart is beating in her breast.
In her care to see that nought went wrong,
Now the mother happen'd to draw near;
At the door long hearkens she, full long,
Wond'ring at the sounds that greet her ear.
Tones of joy and sadness,
And love's blissful madness,
As of bride and bridegroom they appear,
From the door she will not now remove
'Till she gains full certainty of this;
And with anger hears she vows of love,
Soft caressing words of mutual bliss.
"Hush! the cock's loud strain!
But thoult come again,
When the night returns!"—then kiss on kiss.
Then her wrath the mother cannot hold,
But unfastens straight the lock with ease.
"In this house are girls become so bold,
As to seek e'en strangers' lusts to please?"
By her lamp's clear glow
Looks she in,—and oh!

Sight of horror!—'tis her child she sees.
Fain the youth would, in his first alarm,
With the veil that o'er her had been spread,
With the carpet, shield his love from harm;
But she casts them from her, void of dread,
And with spirit's strength,
In its spectre length,
Lifts her figure slowly from the bed.
"Mother! mother!"—Thus her wan lips say:
"May not I one night of rapture share?
From the warm couch am I chased away?
Do I waken only to despair?
It contents not thee
To have driven me
An untimely shroud of death to wear?
But from out my coffin's prison-bounds
By a wond'rous fate I'm forced to rove,
While the blessings and the chaunting sounds
That your priests delight in, useless prove.
Water, salt, are vain
Fervent youth to chain,
Ah, e'en Earth can never cool down love!
When that infant vow of love was spoken,
Venus' radiant temple smiled on both.
Mother! thou that promise since hast broken,

Fetter'd by a strange, deceitful oath.
Gods, though, hearken ne'er,
Should a mother swear
To deny her daughter's plighted troth.
From my grave to wander I am forc'd,
Still to seek The Good's long-sever'd link,
Still to love the bridegroom I have lost,
And the life-blood of his heart to drink;
When his race is run,
I must hasten on,
And the young must 'neath my vengeance sink,
Beauteous youth! no longer mayst thou live;
Here must shrivel up thy form so fair;
Did not I to thee a token give,
Taking in return this lock of hair?
View it to thy sorrow!
Grey thoult be to-morrow,
Only to grow brown again when there.
Mother, to this final prayer give ear!
Let a funeral pile be straightway dress'd;
Open then my cell so sad and drear,
That the flames may give the lovers rest!
When ascends the fire
From the glowing pyre,
To the gods of old we'll hasten, blest."

# THE GIAOUR

# Lord Byron

George Gordon (Lord) Byron (1788–1824) was born in London and attended Harrow and then Trinity College at Cambridge. Although born with a clubfoot, he was very handsome, attracting both male and female admirers. As early as his university days, he was involved in bisexual affairs and gambling, accumulating large debts. From 1809 to 1811 he toured the Mediterranean, during which time he first became acquainted with the vampire legend and wrote the first two cantos of *Childe Harold's Pilgrimage,* which, when published, made him famous. He then wrote the final two cantos, along with four popular Oriental tales, including "The Giaour."

One of the great figures of the Romantic period, Byron was a great friend of Percy Bysshe Shelley and John Polidori. Byron lived with Shelley when he was essentially exiled from England because of his shocking behavior, which flouted most social mores of the time, and John Polidori based his aristocratic vampire, Lord Ruthven, on him. To his irritation, Byron was even rumored to have written Polidori's *The Vampyre* (1819). Among his many great poetic works, his masterpiece is generally thought to be the very long *Don Juan,* left incomplete at his death, which occurred at Missolonghi, Greece, when he was attempting to help the Greeks free themselves from the oppression of the Ottoman Empire.

"The Giaour: A Fragment of a Turkish Tale" was first published in London by John Murray in 1813.

# The Giaour

## LORD BYRON

# A FRAGMENT OF A TURKISH TALE

A turban carved in coarsest stone,
A pillar with rank weeds o'ergrown,
Whereon can now be scarcely read
The Koran verse that mourns the dead,
Point out the spot where Hassan fell
A victim in that lonely dell.
There sleeps as true an Osmanlie
As e'er at Mecca bent the knee;
As ever scorn'd forbidden wine,
Or pray'd with face towards the shrine,
In orisons resumed anew
At solemn sound of "Alla Hu!"
Yet died he by a stranger's hand,
And stranger in his native land;
Yet died he as in arms he stood,
And unavenged, at least in blood.
But him the maids of Paradise
Impatient to their halls invite,
And the dark Heaven of Houris' eyes
On him shall glance for ever bright;
They come—their kerchiefs green they wave,
And welcome with a kiss the brave!
Who falls in battle 'gainst a Giaour
Is worthiest an immortal bower.

But thou, false Infidel! shall writhe
Beneath avenging Monkir's scythe;

And from its torments 'scape alone
To wander round lost Eblis' throne;
And fire unquench'd, unquenchable,
Around, within, thy heart shall dwell;
Nor ear can hear nor tongue can tell
The tortures of that inward hell!
But first, on earth as Vampire sent,
Thy corse shall from its tomb be rent:
Then ghastly haunt thy native place,
And suck the blood of all thy race;
There from thy daughter, sister, wife,
At midnight drain the stream of life;
Yet loathe the banquet which perforce
Must feed thy livid living corse:
Thy victims ere they yet expire
Shall know the demon for their sire,
As cursing thee, thou cursing them,
Thy flowers are withered on the stem.
But one that for thy crime must fall,
The youngest, most beloved of all,
Shall bless thee with a father's name—
That word shall wrap thy heart in flame!
Yet must thou end thy task, and mark
Her cheek's last tinge, her eye's last spark,
And the last glassy glance must view
Which freezes o'er its lifeless blue;
Then with unhallow'd hand shalt tear

316

The tresses of her yellow hair,
Of which in life a lock when shorn
Affection's fondest pledge was worn,
But now is borne away by thee,
Memorial of thine agony!
Wet with thine own best blood shall drip

Thy gnashing tooth and haggard lip;
Then stalking to thy sullen grave,
Go—and with Gouls and Afrits rave;
Till these in horror shrink away
From Spectre more accursed than they!

## LA BELLE DAME SANS MERCI

# John Keats

John Keats (1795–1821) was born in Moorfields, London, the son of a stable manager. He was apprenticed to a surgeon in Edmonton, and although he passed his examinations at the Court of Apothecaries in 1816, he was most deeply involved with writing poetry. He was sixteen when he translated the *Aeneid* and twenty when his first important poem, "On First Looking into Chapman's Homer," was published by Leigh Hunt. His first book, *Poems* (1817), soon followed, but it did not receive good reviews. Nor did his next book, the long narrative poem *Endymion* (1818), with its often-quoted first line, "A thing of beauty is a joy forever."

In the summer of 1818 he went on a walking tour of Scotland with a friend and is believed to have contracted tuberculosis there, though it is also possible he had caught it as a child from his mother or later from his brother. He moved to Hampstead, where he fell deeply in love with a seventeen-year-old girl, Fanny Brawne, which seems to have given him little joy yet inspired the most creative period of his life. Within a year he had written "The Eve of St. Agnes," "La Belle Dame Sans Merci," and the famous odes "To a Nightingale," "On a Grecian Urn," "To Psyche," and "On Melancholy." His tuberculosis worsened and he moved to Rome to escape the cold English winters, but he died soon thereafter, not having reached his twenty-sixth birthday.

"La Belle Dame Sans Merci: A Ballad" was first published in the May 10, 1820, issue of *The Indicator*.

# La Belle Dame Sans Merci

## JOHN KEATS

## A BALLAD

O what can ail thee, knight at arms,
Alone and palely loitering?
The sedge has wither'd from the lake,
And no birds sing.

O what can ail thee, knight at arms,
So haggard and so woe-begone?
The squirrel's granary is full,
And the harvest's done.

I see a lily on thy brow
With anguish moist and fever dew,
And on thy cheeks a fading rose
Fast withereth too.

I met a lady in the meads,
Full beautiful, a fairy's child;
Her hair was long; her foot was light,
And her eyes were wild.

I made a garland for her head,
And bracelets too, and fragrant zone;
She look'd at me as she did love,
And made sweet moan.

I set her on my pacing steed,
And nothing else saw all day long,
For sidelong would she bend, and sing
A fairy's song.

She found me roots of relish sweet,
And honey wild, and manna dew,
And sure in language strange she said—
I love thee true.

She took me to her elfin grot,
And there she wept, and sigh'd full sore,
And there I shut her wild wild eyes
With kisses four.

And there she lulled me asleep,
And there I dream'd—Ah! woe betide!
The latest dream I ever dream'd
On the cold hill's side.

I saw pale kings, and princes too,
Pale warriors, death pale were they all;
They cried—"La belle dame sans merci
Hath thee in thrall!"

I saw their starv'd lips in the gloom
With horrid warning gaped wide,
And I awoke and found me here
On the cold hill's side.

And this is why I sojourn here,
Alone and palely loitering,
Though the sedge is wither'd from the lake,
And no birds sing.

## *PLACE OF MEETING*

# Charles Beaumont

Charles Beaumont (1929–67) was born in Chicago as Charles Leroy Nutt. His mother was abusive, forcing him to wear girls' clothing and even killing a pet as punishment. He contracted meningitis as a child, which may have contributed to his early death, once diagnosed as due to Alzheimer's or Pitt's disease. Dropping out of high school in the tenth grade to join the army, he went on to work as an illustrator, disc jockey, usher, and dishwasher before selling his first story to *Amazing* in 1950. Four years later he wrote "Black Country," which was published in the September 1954 issue of *Playboy*—the first piece of original fiction it had ever published.

Beaumont also began writing for television at this time and was both prolific and critically successful, writing twenty-two episodes of *The Twilight Zone* and becoming a favorite of Alfred Hitchcock's, producing scripts for both *Alfred Hitchcock Presents* and *The Alfred Hitchcock Hour*. He also wrote scripts for *Alcoa Presents; Have Gun, Will Travel; Richard Diamond, Private Eye; Naked City;* and *Journey to the Unknown.*

Mainly known as a short-story writer—his first collection, *The Hunger and Other Stories* (1957), is a high spot of fantastic fiction—he wrote one solo novel, *The Intruder* (1959), for which he wrote the screenplay for Roger Corman's production, which starred William Shatner in the title role. He also co-authored *Run from the Hunter* (1957) as Keith Grantland.

"Place of Meeting" was originally published in *Orbit* no. 2 in 1953.

# Place of Meeting

## CHARLES BEAUMONT

It swept down from the mountains, a loose, crystal-smelling wind, an autumn chill of moving wetness. Down from the mountains and into the town, where it set the dead trees hissing and the signboards creaking. And it even went into the church, because the bell was ringing and there was no one to ring the bell.

The people in the yard stopped their talk and listened to the rusty music.

Big Jim Kroner listened too. Then he cleared his throat and clapped his hands—thick hands, callused and work-dirtied.

"All right," he said loudly. "All right, let's us settle down now." He walked out from the group and turned. "Who's got the list?"

"Got it right here, Jim," a woman said, coming forward with a loose-leaf folder.

"All present?"

"Everybody except that there German, Mr. Grunin—Grunger—"

Kroner smiled; he made a megaphone of his hands. "Grüninger—Barthold Grüninger?"

A small man with a mustache called out excitedly, "Ja, ja! . . . S'war schwer den Friedhof zu finden."

"All right. That's all we wanted to know, whether you was here or not." Kroner studied the pages carefully. Then he reached into the back pocket of his overalls and withdrew a stub of pencil and put the tip to his mouth.

"Now, before we start off," he said to the group, "I want to know is there anybody here that's got a question or anything to ask?" He looked over the crowd of silent faces. "Anybody don't know who I am? No?"

It came another wind then, mountain-scattered and fast: it billowed dresses, set damp hair moving; it pushed over pewter vases, and smashed dead roses and hydrangeas to swirling dust against the gritty tombstones. Its clean rain smell was gone now, though, for it had passed over the fields with the odors of rotting life.

Kroner made a check mark in the notebook. "Anderson," he shouted. "Edward L."

A man in overalls like Kroner's stepped forward.

"Andy, you covered Skagit valley, Snohomish and King counties, as well as Seattle and the rest?"

"Yes, sir."

"What you got to report?"

"They're all dead," Anderson said.

"You looked everywhere? You was real careful?"

"Yes, sir. Ain't nobody alive in the whole state."

Kroner nodded and made another check mark. "That's all, Andy. Next: Avakian, Katina."

A woman in a wool skirt and gray blouse walked up from the back, waving her arms. She started to speak.

Kroner tapped his stick. "Listen here for a second, folks," he said. "For those that don't know how to talk English, you know what this is all about—so when I ask my question, you just nod up-and-down for yes (like this) and sideways (like this) for no. Makes it a lot easier for those of us as don't remember too good. All right?"

There were murmurings and whispered consultations and for a little while the yard was full of noise. The woman called Avakian kept nodding.

"Fine," Kroner said. "Now, Miss Avakian. You covered what? . . . Iran, Iraq, Turkey, Syria. Did you—find—an-ybody a-live?"

The woman stopped nodding. "No," she said. "No, no."

Kroner checked the name. "Let's see here. Boleslavsky, Peter. You go on back, Miss Avakian."

A man in bright city clothes walked briskly to the tree clearing. "Yes, sir," he said.

"What have you got for us?"

The man shrugged. "Well, I tell you; I went over New York with a fine-tooth comb. Then I hit Brooklyn and Jersey. Nothin', man. Nothin' nowhere."

"He is right," a dark-faced woman said in a tremulous voice. "I was there too. Only the dead in the streets, all over, all over the city; in the cars I looked even, in the *offices*. Everywhere is people dead."

"Chavez, Pietro. Baja California."

"All dead, señor chief."

"Ciodo, Ruggiero. Capri."

The man from Capri shook his head violently.

"Denman, Charlotte. Southern United States."

"Dead as doornails . . ."

"Elgar, David S. . . . "

"Ferrazio, Ignatz . . . "

"Goldfarb, Bernard . . . "

"Halpern . . . "

"Ives . . . Kranek . . . O'Brian . . . "

The names exploded in the pale evening air like deep gunshots; there was much head-shaking, many people saying, "No. No."

At last Kroner stopped marking. He closed the notebook and spread his big workman's hands. He saw the round eyes, the trembling mouths, the young faces; he saw all the frightened people.

A girl began to cry. She sank to the damp ground, and covered her face and made these crying sounds. An elderly man put his hand on her head. The elderly man looked sad. But not afraid. Only the young ones seemed afraid.

"Settle down now," Kroner said firmly. "Settle on down. Now, listen to me. I'm going to ask you all the same question one more time, because we got to be sure." He waited for them to grow quiet. "All right. This here is all of us, every one. We've covered all the spots. Did anybody here find one single solitary sign of life?"

The people were silent. The wind had died again, so there was no sound at all. Across the corroded wire fence the gray meadows lay strewn with the carcasses of cows and horses and, in one of the fields, sheep. No flies buzzed near the dead animals; there were no maggots burrowing. No vultures; the sky was clean of birds. And in all the untended rolling hills of grass and weeds which had once sung and pulsed with a million voices, in all the land there was only this immense stillness now, still as years, still as the unheard motion of the stars.

Kroner watched the people. The young woman in the gay print dress; the tall African with his bright paint and cultivated scars; the fierce-looking Swede looking not so fierce now in this graying twilight. He watched all the tall and short and old and young people from all over the world, pressed together now, a vast silent polyglot in this country meeting place, this always lonely and long-deserted spot—deserted even before the gas bombs and the disease and the flying pestilences that had covered the earth in three days and three nights. Deserted. Forgotten.

"Talk to us, Jim," the woman who had handed him the notebook said. She was new.

Kroner put the list inside his big overalls pocket.

"Tell us," someone else said. "How shall we be nourished? What will we do?"

"The world's all dead," a child moaned. "Dead as dead, the whole world . . ."

"Todo el mund—"

"Monsieur Kroner, Monsieur Kroner, what will we do?"

Kroner smiled. "Do?" He looked up through the still-hanging poison cloud, the dun blanket, up to where the moon was now risen in full coldness. His voice was steady, but it lacked life. "What some of us have done before," he said. "We'll go back and wait. It ain't the first time. It ain't the last."

A little fat bald man with old eyes sighed and began to waver in the October dusk. The outline of his form wavered and disappeared in the shadows under the trees where the moonlight did not reach. Others followed him as Kroner talked.

"Same thing we'll do again and likely keep on doing. We'll go back and—sleep. And we'll wait. Then it'll start all over again and folks'll build their cities—new folks with new blood—and then we'll wake up. Maybe a long time yet. But it ain't so bad; it's quiet, and time passes." He lifted a small girl of fifteen or sixteen with pale cheeks and red lips. "Come on, now! Why, just think of the appetite you'll have all built up!"

The girl smiled. Kroner faced the crowd and waved his hands, large hands, rough from the stone of midnight pyramids and the feel of muskets, boil-speckled from night hours in packing plants and trucking lines; broken by the impact of a tomahawk and a machine-gun bullet; but white where the dirt was not caked, and bloodless. Old hands, old beyond years.

As he waved, the wind came limping back from the mountains. It blew the heavy iron bell high in the steepled white barn, and set the signboards creaking, and lifted ancient dusts and hissed again through the dead trees.

Kroner watched the air turn black. He listened to it fill with the flappings and the flutterings and the squeakings. He waited; then he stopped waving and sighed and began to walk.

He walked to a place of vines and heavy brush. Here he paused for a moment and looked out at the silent place of high dark grass, of hidden huddled tombs, of scrolls and stone-frozen children stained silver in the night's wet darkness; at the crosses he did not look. The people were gone; the place was empty.

Kroner kicked away the foliage. Then he got into the coffin and closed the lid.

Soon he was asleep.

# *DUTY*

# Ed Gorman

Edward Gorman (1941– ) was born in Cedar Rapids, Iowa, and attended Coe College in his home state. After twenty years in advertising, working as a copywriter and freelance writer, he became a full-time fiction writer in 1989. In addition, he has been the executive editor of a fan magazine for many years and has edited numerous anthologies, mainly in the mystery and horror genres, including the distinguished *Big Book of Noir* (1998).

Working in several genres, Gorman has built a good following in the mystery field, most notably with his six-book series about Jack Dwyer, an ex-cop in Cedar Rapids, beginning with *Rough Cut* (1985). He also produced four novels in four years about a bounty hunter in the West, Leo Guild, beginning with *Guild* in 1987. Other series characters are Dev Mallory, a Secret Service agent who appears in *Bad Money* (2005) and *Fast Track* (2006); Robert Payne, an ex–FBI profiler in four novels; and Sam McCain, an attorney in Black River Falls, Iowa, who has been in six novels. The Western Writers of America gave him a Spur Award for Best Short Fiction in 1992 for "The Face," and he has been nominated for Bram Stoker Awards from the Horror Writers Association for two collections: *Cages* (1995) and *The Dark Fantastic* (2001).

"Duty" was first published in *Under the Fang,* edited by Robert R. McCammon (New York: Pocket Books, 1991).

# Duty

## ED GORMAN

Earlier this morning, just as the sun had begun to burn the dew off the farm fields, Keller got out his old Schwinn and set off. In less than a minute, he'd left behind the tar-paper shack where he lived with a goat, three chickens he'd never had the heart to eat, four cats, and a hamster. The hamster had been Timmy's.

Today he traveled the old two-lane highway. The sun hot on his back, he thought of how it used to be on this stretch of asphalt, the bright red convertibles with the bright pink blondes in them and the sound of rock and roll waving like a banner in the wind. Or the green John Deere tractors moving snail-slow, trailing infuriated city drivers behind.

The old days. Before the change. He used to sit in a chair in front of his shack and talk to his wife, Martha, and his son, Timmy, till Timmy went to sleep in Martha's lap. Then Keller would take the boy inside and lay him gently in bed and kiss the boy-moist brow good night. The Kellers had always been referred to locally, and not unkindly, as "that hippie family." Keller had worn the tag as a badge of honor. In a world obsessed with money and power, he'd wanted to spend his

days discovering again and again the simple pleasures of starry nights, of clear quick country streams, of mountain music strummed on an old six-string and accompanied by owls and kitties and crocuses. Somehow back in time he'd managed to get himself an advanced degree in business and finance. But after meeting Martha, the happiest and most contented person he'd ever known, he'd followed her out here and he never once yearned for the treacherous world he'd deserted.

He thought of these things as he angled the Schwinn down the center of the highway, his golden collie, Andy, running alongside, appreciative of the exercise. Across Keller's shoulder was strapped his ancient backpack, the one he'd carried twenty years ago in college. You could see faintly where the word *Adidas* had been.

He rode on. The Schwinn's chain was loose and banged noisily sometimes, and so on a particularly hard bump the front fender sometimes rubbed the tire. He fixed the bike methodically, patiently, at least once a week, but the Schwinn was like a wild boy and would never quite be tamed. Timmy had been that way.

The trip took two hours. By that time, Andy was tired of running, his pink tongue lolling out of his mouth, exhausted, and Keller was tired of pedaling.

The farmhouse was up a high sloping hill, east of the highway.

From his backpack Keller took his binoculars. He spent ten minutes scanning the place. He had no idea what he was looking for. He just wanted to reassure himself that the couple who'd sent the message with Conroy—a pig farmer ten miles to the west of Keller's—were who and what they claimed to be.

He saw a stout woman in a faded housedress hanging laundry on a backyard clothesline. He saw a sun-reddened man in blue overalls moving among a waving carpet of white hungry chickens, throwing them golden kernels of corn. He saw a windmill turning with rusty dignity in the southern wind.

After returning his binoculars to his backpack, he mounted the Schwinn again, patted Andy on the head, and set off up the steep gravel hill.

The woman saw Keller first. He had come around the edge of the big two-story frame house when she was just finishing with her laundry.

She looked almost angry when she saw who he was.

She didn't speak to him; instead, she called out in a weary voice for her husband. Somehow, the man managed to hear her above the squawking chickens. He set down the tin pan that held the kernels of corn then walked over and stood by his wife.

"You're a little early," the farmer said. His name was Dodds, Alcie Dodds, and his wife was Myrna. Keller used to see them at the potluck dinners the community held back before the change.

"I wasn't sure how long it would take. Guess I left a little before I needed to."

"You enjoy what you do, Mr. Keller? Does it give you pleasure?" Myrna Dodds said.

"Now, Myrna, don't be—"

"I just want him to answer the question. I just want him to answer honestly."

By now, Keller was used to being treated this way. It was, he knew, a natural reaction.

Alcie Dodds said, "She hasn't had much sleep the last couple of nights, Keller. You know what I'm saying."

Keller nodded.

"You want a cup of coffee?" Alcie Dodds said.

"I'd appreciate it."

Suddenly the woman started crying. She put her hands to her face and simply began wailing, her fleshy body shaking beneath the loose fitting housedress.

Keller saw such grief everywhere he went. He wished there was something he could do about it.

Dodds went over and slid his arm around his wife. "Why don't you go in and see Beth, honey?"

Mention of the name only caused the woman to begin sobbing even more uncontrollably.

She took her hands from her face and glared at Keller. "I hope you rot in hell, Mr. Keller. I hope you rot in hell."

Shadows cooled the kitchen. The air smelled of the stew bubbling on the stove, of beef and tomatoes and onions and paprika.

The two men sat at a small kitchen table beneath a funeral home calendar that had a picture of Jesus as a young and very handsome bearded man. By now, they were on their second cup of coffee.

"Sorry about the missus."

"I understand. I'd feel the same way."

"We always assume it won't happen to us."

"Ordinarily, they don't get out this far. It isn't worth it for them. They stick to cities, or at least areas where the population is heavy."

"But they do get out here," Dodds said. "More often than people like to admit."

Keller sighed. He stared down into his coffee cup. "I guess that's true."

"I hear it happened to you."

"Yes."

"Your boy."

"Right."

"The fucking bastards. The fucking bastards."
Dodds made a large fist and brought it down thunderously on the table that smelled of the red-and-white checkered oilcloth. In the window above the sink the sky was very blue and the blooming trees very green.

After a time, Dodds said, "You ever seen one? In person, I mean?"

"No."

"We did once. We were in Chicago. We were supposed to get back to our hotel room before dusk, before they came out into the streets but we got lost. Anybody ever tell you about their smell?"

"Yes."

"It's like rotting meat. You can't believe it. Especially when a lot of them are in one place at the same time. And they've got these sores all over them. Like leprosy. We made it back to the hotel all right, but before we did we saw these two young children—they'd turned already—they found this old lady and they started chasing her, having a good time with her, really prolonging it, and then she tripped in the street and one of them knelt beside her and went to work. You heard about how they puke afterward?"

"Yes. The shock to their digestive systems. All the blood."

"Never saw anybody puke like this. And the noise they made when they were puking. Sickening. Then the old lady got up and let out this cry. I've never heard anything even close to it. Just this loud animal noise. She was already starting to turn."

Keller finished his coffee.

"You want more?"

"No, thanks, Mr. Dodds."

"You want a Pepsi? Got a six-pack we save for special occasions." He shrugged. "I'm not much of a liquor drinker."

"No, thanks, Mr. Dodds."

Dodds drained his own coffee. "Can I ask you something?"

"Sure."

It was time to get it over with. Dodds was stalling. Keller didn't blame him.

"You ever find that you're wrong?"

"How so, Mr. Dodds?"

"You know, that you think they've turned but they really haven't?"

Keller knew what Dodds was trying to say, of course. He was trying to say—to whatever God existed—please let it be a mistake. Please let it not be what it seems to be.

"Not so far, I haven't, Mr. Dodds. I'm sorry."

"You know how it's going to be on her, don't you, on my wife?"

"Yes, I'm afraid I do, Mr. Dodds."

"She won't ever be the same."

"No, I don't suppose she will."

Dodds stared down at his hands and turned them into fists again. Under his breath, he said, "Fucking bastards."

"Maybe we'd better go have a look, Mr. Dodds."

"You sure you don't want another cup of coffee?"

"No, thanks, Mr. Dodds. I appreciate the offer, though."

Dodds led them through the cool, shadowy house. The place was old. You could tell that by all the mahogany trim and the height of the ceilings and the curve of the time-swollen floor. But even given its age it was a pleasant and comfortable place, a nook of sweet shade on a hot day.

Down the hall Keller could hear Mrs. Dodds singing, humming really, soft noises rather than words.

"Forgive her if she acts up again, Mr. Keller."

Keller nodded.

And it was then the rock came sailing through the window in the front room. The smashing glass had an almost musical quality to it on the hot silent afternoon.

"What the hell was that?" Dodds wondered.

He turned around and ran back down the pink wallpapered hall and right out the front door, almost slamming the screen door in Keller's face.

There were ten of them on the lawn, in the shade of the elm, six men, four women. Two of the men held carbines.

"There he is," one of the men said.

"That sonofabitch Keller," another man said.

"You people get out of here, and now," Dodds said, coming down off the porch steps. "This is my land."

"You really gonna let him do it, Alcie?" a man said.

"That's my business," Dodds said, pawing at the front of his coveralls.

A pretty woman leaned forward. "I'm sorry we came, Alcie. The men just wouldn't have it any other way. Us women just came along to make sure there wasn't no violence."

"Speak for yourself, honey," a plump woman in a man's checkered shirt and jeans said. "Personally, I'd like to cut Keller's balls off and feed 'em to my pigs."

Two of the men laughed at her. She'd said it to impress them and she'd achieved her end.

"Go on, now, before somethin' is said or done that can't be unsaid or undone," Dodds said.

"Your wife want this done?" the man with the second carbine said. He answered his own question: "Bet she don't. Bet she fought you on it all the way."

A soft breeze came. It was an afternoon for drinking lemonade and watching monarch butterflies and seeing the foals in the pasture running up and down the summer green hills. It was not an afternoon for angry men with carbines.

"You heard me now," Dodds said.

"How 'bout you, chickenshit? You got anything to say for yoruself, Keller?"

"Goddamnit, Davey—" Dodds started to say.

"Won't use my gun, Alcie. Don't need it."

And with that the man named Davey tossed his carbine to one of the other men and then stepped up near the steps where Dodds and Keller stood.

Keller recognized Davey. He ran the feed and grain in town and was a legendary tavern bully.

God forbid you should ever beat him at snooker. He had freckles like a pox and fists like anvils.

"You hear what I asked you, chickenshit?"

"Davey—" Dodds started to say again.

Keller stepped down off the steps. He was close enough to smell the afternoon beer on Davey's breath.

"This wasn't easy for Mr. Dodds, Davey," Keller said. He spoke so softly Davey's friends had to lean forward to hear. "But it's his decision to make. His and his wife's."

"You enjoy it, don't you, chickenshit?" Davey said. "You're some kind of pervert who gets his kicks that way, aren't you?"

Behind him, his friends started cursing Keller, and that only emboldened Davey all the more.

He threw a big roundhouse right and got Keller right in the mouth.

Keller started to drop to the ground, black spots alternating with yellow spots before his eyes, and then Davey raised his right foot and kicked Keller square in the chest.

"Kill that fucker, Davey! Kill that fucker!" one of the men with the carbines shouted.

And then, on the sinking afternoon, the shotgun was fired.

The bird shot got so close to Davey that it tore tiny holes in his right sleeve, like something that had been gnawed on by a puppy.

"You heard my husband," Mrs. Dodds said, standing on the porch with a sawed-off double barrel that looked to be one mean and serious weapon. "You get off our land."

Davey said, "We was only tryin' to help you, missus. We knew you didn't want—"

But she silenced him. "I was wrong about Keller here. If he didn't care about them, he couldn't do it. He had to do it to his own wife and son, or are you forgetting that?"

Davey said, "But—"

And Mrs. Dodds leveled the shotgun right at his chest. "You think I won't kill you, Davey, you're wrong."

Davey's wife took him by the sleeve. "C'mon, honey; you can't see she's serious."

But Davey had one last thing to say. "It ain't right what he does. Don't you know that, Mrs. Dodds? It ain't right!"

But Mrs. Dodds could only sadly shake her head. "You know what'd become of 'em if he didn't do it, don't you? Go into the city sometime and watch 'em. Then tell me you'd want one of your own to be that way."

Davey's wife tugged on his sleeve again. Then she looked up at Mrs. Dodds and said, "I'm sorry for this, Mrs. Dodds. I really am. The boys here just had too much to drink and—" She shook her head. "I'm sorry."

And in ones and twos they started drifting back to the pickup trucks they'd parked on the downslope side of the gravel drive.

It's a nice room," Keller said twenty minutes later. And it was. The wallpaper was blue. Teddy bears and unicorns cavorted across it. There was a tiny table and chairs and a globe and a set of junior encyclopedias, things she would grow up to use someday. Or would have, anyway.

In the corner was the baby's bed. Mrs. Keller stood in front of it, protecting it. "I'm sorry how I treated you when you first came."

"I know."

"And I'm sorry Davey hit you."

"Not your fault."

By now he realized that she was not only stalling. She was also doing something else—pleading. "You look at little Beth and you be sure."

"I will."

"I've heard tales of how sometimes you think they've turned but it's just some other illness with the same symptoms."

"I'll be very careful."

Mr. Dodds said, "You want us to leave the room?"

"It'd be better for your wife."

And then she spun around and looked down into the baby's bed where her seven-month-old daughter lay discolored and breathing as if she could not catch her breath, both primary symptoms of the turning.

She picked the infant up and clutched it to her chest. And began sobbing so loudly, all Keller could do was put his head down.

It fell to Mr. Dodds to pry the baby from his wife's grip and to lead Mrs. Dodds from the baby's room.

On his way out, starting to cry a man's hard embarrassed tears, Mr. Dodds looked straight at Keller and said, "Just be sure, Mr. Keller. Just be sure."

Keller nodded that he'd be sure.

The room smelled of sunlight and shade and baby powder.

The bed had the sort of slatted sides you could pull up or down. He put it down and leaned over to the baby. She was very pretty, chunky, blond, with a cute little mouth. She wore diapers. They looked very white compared to the blue, asphyxiated color of her skin.

His examination was simple. The Dodds could easily have done it themselves, but of course they didn't want to. It would only have confirmed their worst fears.

He opened her mouth. She started to cry. He first examined her gums and then her teeth. The tissue on the former had started to harden and scab; the latter had started to elongate.

The seven-month-old child was in the process of turning.

Sometimes they roamed out here from the cities and took what they could find. One of them had broken into the Dodds' two weeks ago and had stumbled on the baby's room.

He worked quickly, as he always did, as he'd done with his wife and son when they'd been ambushed in the woods one day and had then started to turn.

All that was left of civilization was in the outlands such as these. Even though you loved them, you could not let them turn because the life ahead for them was so unimaginably terrible. The endless hunt for new bodies, the feeding frenzies, the constant illness that was a part of the condition and the condition was forever—

No, if you loved them, you had only one choice.

In this farming community, no one but Keller

could bring himself to do what was necessary. They always deluded themselves that their loved ones hadn't really been infected, hadn't really begun turning—

And so it fell to Keller.

He rummaged quickly through his Adidas backpack now, finding hammer and wooden stake.

He returned to the bed and leaned over and kissed the little girl on the forehead. "You'll be with God, honey," he said. "You'll be with God."

He stood up straight, took the stake in his left hand and set it against her heart, and then with great sad weariness raised the hammer.

He killed her as he killed them all, clean and quick, hot infected blood splattering his face and shirt, her final cry one more wound in his soul.

On the porch, Mrs. Dodds inside in her bedroom, Mr. Dodds put his hand on Keller's shoulder and said, "I'll pray for you, Mr. Keller."

"I'll be needing your prayers, Mr. Dodds," Keller said, and then nodded good-bye and left.

In half an hour, he was well down the highway again, Andy getting another good run for the day, pink tongue lolling.

In his backpack he could feel the sticky hammer and stake, the same tools he used over and over again as the sickness of the cities spread constantly outward.

In a while it began to rain. He was still thinking of the little Dodds girl, of her innocent eyes there at the very last.

He did not seem to notice the rain, or the soft quick darkness.

He rode on, the bicycle chain clattering, the front wheel wobbling from the twisted fender, and Andy stopping every quarter mile or so to shake the rain off.

*The fucking sonsofbitches,* he thought.
*The fucking sonsofbitches.*

## *A WEEK IN THE UNLIFE*

# David J. Schow

David (James) Schow (1955– ) was born in Marburg, Germany, of American parents. After writing film and book criticism, he turned to fiction at the age of twenty-three, publishing his first story in *Galileo* magazine. He became a prolific short-story writer, winning a Dimension Award from *Rod Serling's Twilight Zone Magazine* for most popular short story in 1985 and a World Fantasy Award for Best Short Story in 1987. He also won a Bram Stoker Award in 1987 for "Pamela's Get" for Best Long Fiction. His first short-story collection was *Seeing Red* (1990), followed by a half-dozen others. His first novel was *Kill Riff* (1988); his most recent is *Gun Work* (2008).

Schow's greatest success has come as a screenwriter, beginning with uncredited dialogue polish on *A Nightmare on Elm Street 5: The Dream Child* (1989), which was immediately followed by the "Safe Sex" episode of the television series *Freddie's Nightmares* (1989) and the feature film *Leatherface: Texas Chainsaw Massacre III* (1989). He has also written the screenplays for *Critters 3* (1991), *Critters 4* (1993), *The Crow* (1994), and *The Texas Chainsaw Massacre: The Beginning* (2006).

He is given credit for having invented the terms *stalk-and-slash films*, later shortened to *slasher films*, in 1977, and *splatterpunk* in 1986.

"A Week in the Unlife" was first published in *A Whisper of Blood*, edited by Ellen Datlow (New York: Morrow, 1991).

# A Week in the Unlife

## DAVID J. SCHOW

## I

When you stake a bloodsucker, the heartblood pumps out thick and black, the consistency of honey. I saw it make bubbles as it glurped out. The creature thrashed and squirmed and tried out pull out the stake—they always do, if you leave on their arms for the kill—but by the third whack it was, as Stoker might say, dispatched well and duly.

I lost count a long time ago. Doesn't matter. I no longer think of them as being even *former* human beings, and feel no anthropomorphic sympathy. In their eyes I see no tragedy, no romance, no seductive pulp appeal. Merely lust, rage at being outfoxed, and debased appetite, focused and sanguine.

People usually commit journals as legacy. So be it. Call me sentry, vigilante if you like. When they sleep their comatose sleep, I stalk and terminate them. When they walk, I hide. Better than they do.

They're really not as smart as popular fiction and films would lead you to believe. They do have cunning, an animalistic savvy. But I'm an experienced tracker; I know their spoor, the traces they leave, the way their presence charges the air. Things invisible or ephemeral to ordinary citizens, blackly obvious to me.

The journal is so you'll know, just in case my luck runs out. Sundown. Nap time.

## II

Naturally the police think of me as some sort of homicidal crackpot. That's a given; always has been for my predecessors. More watchers to evade. Caution comes reflexively to me these days. Police are slow and rational; they deal in the minutiae of a day-to-day world, deadly enough without the inclusion of bloodsuckers.

The police love to stop and search people. Fortunately for me, mallets and stakes and crosses and such are not yet illegal in this country. Lots of raised eyebrows and jokes and nudging but no actual arrests. When the time comes for them to recognize the plague that has descended upon their city, they will remember me, perhaps with grace.

My lot is friendless, solo. I know and expect such. It's okay.

City by city. I'm good at ferreting out the nests. To me, their kill-patterns are like a flashing red

335

light. The police only see presumed loonies, draw no linkages; they bust and imprison mortals and never see the light.

I am not foolhardy enough to leave bloodsuckers lying. Even though the mean corpus usually dissolves, the stakes might be discovered. Sometimes there is other residue. City dumpsters and sewers provide adequate and fitting disposal for the leftovers of my mission.

The enemy casualties.

I wish I could advise the authorities, work hand-in-hand with them. Too complicated. Too many variables. Not a good control situation. Bloodsuckers have a maddening knack for vanishing into crevices, even hairline splits in logic.

Rule: Trust no one.

# III

A female one, today. Funny. There aren't as many of them as you might suppose.

She had courted a human lover, so she claimed, like Romeo and Juliet—she could only visit him at night, and only after feeding, because bloodsuckers too can get carried away by passion.

I think she was intimating that she was a physical lover of otherworldly skill; I think she was fighting hard to tempt me not to eliminate her by saying so.

She did not use her mouth to seduce mortal men. I drove the stake into her brain, through the mouth. She was of recent vintage and did not melt or vaporize. When I fucked her remains, I was surprised to find her warm inside, not cold, like a cadaver. Warm.

With some of them, the human warmth is longer in leaving. But it always goes.

# IV

I never met one before that gave up its existence without a struggle, but today I did, one that acted like he had been expecting me to wander along and relieve him of the burden of unlife. He did not deny what he was, nor attempt to trick me. He asked if he could talk a bit, before.

In a third-floor loft, the windows of which had been spray-painted flat black, he talked. Said he had always hated the taste of blood; said he preferred pineapple juice, or even coffee. He actually brewed a pot of coffee while we talked.

I allowed him to finish his cup before I put the ashwood length to his chest and drove deep and let his blackness gush. It dribbled, thinned by the coffee he had consumed.

# V

Was thinking this afternoon perhaps I should start packing a Polaroid or somesuch, to keep a visual body count, just in case this journal becomes public record someday. It'd be good to have illustrations, proof. I was thinking of that line you hear overused in the movies. I'm sure you know it: *"But there's no such THING as a vampire!"* What a howler; ranks right up there alongside *"It's crazy—but it just might work!"* and *"We can't stop now for a lot of silly native superstitions!"*

Right; shoot cozy little memory snaps, in case they whizz to mist or drop apart to smoking goo. That bull about how you're not supposed to be able to record their images is from the movies, too. There's so much misleading information running loose that the bloodsuckers—the real ones—have no trouble at all moving through any urban center, *with impunity,* as they say on cop shows.

Maybe it would be a good idea to tape record the sounds they make when they die. Videotape them begging not to be exterminated. That would bug the eyes of all those monster movie fans, you bet.

# VI

So many of them beleaguering this city, it's easy to feel outnumbered. Like I said, I've lost count.

Tonight might be a good window for moving on. Like them, I become vulnerable if I remain too long, and it's prudent operating procedure not to leave patterns or become predictable.

It's easy. I don't own much. Most of what I carry, I carry inside.

## VII

They pulled me over on Highway Ten, outbound, for a broken left tail-light. A datafax photo of me was clipped to the visor in the Highway Patrol car. The journal book itself has been taken as evidence, so for now it's a felt-tip and high school notebook paper, which notes I hope to append to the journal proper later.

I have a cell with four bunks all to myself. The door is solid gray, with a food slot, unlike the barred cage of the bullpen. On the way back I noticed they had caught themselves a bloodsucker. Probably an accident; they probably don't even know what they have. There is no sunrise or sunset in the block, so if he gets out at night, they'll never know what happened. But I already know. Right now I will not say anything. I am exposed and at a disadvantage. The one I let slip today I can eliminate tenfold, next week.

## VIII

New week. And I am vindicated at last.

I relaxed as soon as they showed me the pho-tographs. How they managed documentation on the last few bloodsuckers I trapped, I have no idea. But I was relieved. Now I don't have to explain the journal—which, as you can see, they returned to me immediately. They had thousands of questions. They needed to know about the mallets, the stakes, the preferred method of killstrike. I cautioned them not to attempt a sweep and clear at night, when the enemy is stronger.

They paid serious attention this time, which made me feel much better. Now the fight can be mounted en masse.

They also let me know I wouldn't have to stay in the cell. Just some paperwork to clear, and I'm out among them again. One of the officials—not a cop, but a doctor—congratulated me on a stout job well done. He shook my hand, on behalf of all of them, he said, and mentioned writing a book on my work. This is exciting!

As per my request, the bloodsucker in the adjacent solitary cell was moved. I told them that to be really sure, they should use one of my stakes. It was simple vanity, really, on my part. I turn my stakes out of ashwood on a lathe. I made sure they knew I'd permit my stakes to be used as working models for the proper manufacture of all they would soon need.

When the guards come back I really must ask how they managed such crisp 8×10s of so many bloodsuckers. All those names and dates. First class documentation.

I'm afraid I may be a bit envious.

## FOUR WOODEN STAKES

# Victor Roman

Victor Roman appears to be a mystery figure, with no information about him available. He is listed on one Web site as an African American author, but there is no evidence to either support or refute this. There is no listing of any other works by him, though this story has been reprinted on numerous occasions and has deservedly risen to the status of a classic in the genre.

"Four Wooden Stakes" was apparently first published in the February 1925 issue of *Weird Tales;* it was first published in Great Britain in the first volume of the highly successful Not at Night series, edited by Christine Campbell Thompson (London: Selwyn & Blount, 1925).

# Four Wooden Stakes

## VICTOR ROMAN

There it lay on the desk in front of me, that missive so simple in wording, yet so perplexing, so urgent in tone.

*Jack, Come at once for old time's sake. Am all alone. Will explain upon arrival. Remson.*

Having spent the past three weeks in bringing to a successful termination a case that had puzzled the police and two of the best detective agencies in the city, I decided that I was entitled to a rest, so I ordered two suitcases packed and went in search of a timetable. It was several years since I had seen Remson Holroyd; in fact I had not seen him since we had matriculated from college together. I was curious to know how he was getting along, to say nothing of the little diversion he promised me in the way of a mystery.

The following afternoon found me standing on the platform of the little town of Charing, a village of about fifteen hundred souls. Remson's place was about ten miles from there so I stepped forward to the driver of a shay and asked if he would kindly take me to the Holroyd estate. He clasped his hands in what seemed a silent prayer, shuddered slightly, then looked at me with an air of wonder, mingled with suspicion.

"I don't know what ye wants to go out there for, stranger, but if ye'll take the advice o' a God-fearing man, ye'll turn back whence ye come from. There be some mighty fearful tales concernin' that place floatin' around, and more'n one tramp's been found near there so weak from loss of blood and fear he could hardly crawl. They's somethin' there. Be it man or beast I don't know, but as for me, I wouldn't drive ye out there for a hundred dollars cash."

This was not at all encouraging, but I was not to be influenced by the talk of a superstitious old gossip, so I cast about for a less impressionable rustic who would undertake the trip to earn the ample reward I promised at the end of my ride. To my chagrin, they all acted like the first; some crossed themselves fervently, while others gave me one wild look and ran, as if I were in alliance with the devil.

By now my curiosity was thoroughly aroused, and I was determined to see the thing through to a finish if it cost me my life. So, casting a last, contemptuous look upon those poor souls, I stepped

342

out briskly in the direction pointed out to me. However, I had gone but a scant two miles when the weight of the suitcases began to tell, and I slackened pace considerably.

The sun was just disappearing beneath the tree-tops when I caught my first glimpse of the old homestead, now deserted but for its one occupant. Time and the elements had laid heavy hands upon it, for there was hardly a window that could boast its full quota of panes, while the shutters banged and creaked with a noise dismal enough to daunt even the strong of heart.

About one hundred yards back I discerned a small building of grey stone, pieces of which seemed to be lying all around it, partly covered by the dense growth of vegetation that overran the entire countryside. On closer observation I realized that the building was a crypt, while what I had taken to be pieces of the material scattered around were really tombstones. Evidently this was the family burying ground. But why had certain members been interred in a mausoleum while the remainder of the family had been buried in the ground in the usual manner?

Having observed thus much, I turned my steps towards the house, for I had no intention of spending the night with naught but the dead for company. Indeed, I began to realize just why those simple country folk had refused to aid me, and a hesitant doubt began to assert itself as to the expedience of my being here, when I might have been at the shore or at the country club enjoying life to the full.

By now the sun had completely slid from view, and in the semi-darkness the place presented an even drearier aspect than before. With a great display of bravado I stepped upon the veranda, slammed my suitcases upon a seat very much the worse for wear, and pulled lustily at the knob.

Peal after peal reverberated through the house, echoing and reechoing from room to room, till the whole structure rang. Then all was still once more, save for the sighing of the wind and the creaking of the shutters.

A few minutes passed, and the sound of footsteps approaching the door reached my ears. Another interval, and the door was cautiously opened a few inches, while a head, shrouded by the darkness, scrutinized me closely. Then the door was flung wide, and Remson (I hardly knew him, so changed was he) rushed forward and throwing his arms around me thanked me again and again for heeding his plea, till I thought he would go into hysterics.

I begged him to brace up, and the sound of my voice seemed to help him, for he apologized rather shamefacedly for his discourtesy and led the way along the wide hall. There was a fire blazing merrily away in the sitting room, and after partaking generously of a repast, for I was famished after my long walk, I was seated in front of it, facing Remson and waiting to hear his story.

"Jack," he began, "I'll start at the beginning and try and give you the facts in their proper sequence. Five years ago my family circle consisted of five persons; my grandfather, my father, two brothers, and myself, the baby of the family. My mother died, you know when I was a few weeks old. Now . . ."

His voice broke and for a moment he was unable to continue.

"There's only myself left," he went on, "and so help me God, I'm going too, unless you can solve this damnable mystery that hovers over this house, and put an end to that something which took my kin and is gradually taking me.

"Grandad was the first to go. He spent the last few years of his life in South America. Just before leaving there he was attacked while asleep by one of those huge bats. Next morning he was so weak that he couldn't walk. That awful thing had sucked his life blood away. He arrived here, but was sickly until his death a few weeks later. The doctors couldn't agree as to the cause of death, so they laid it to old age and let it go at that. But I knew better. It was his experience in the south that had done for him. In his will he asked that a crypt be built immediately and his body interred therein. His wish was carried out, and his remains lie in that little grey vault that you may have noticed if you cut around behind the house. Then my dad began failing and just pined away until he died. What puzzled the doctors was the fact that right up until the end he consumed enough food to sustain three men, yet he was so weak he lacked the strength to drag his legs over the floor. He was buried, or rather interred, with Grandad. The same symptoms were in evidence in the cases of George and Fred. They are both lying in the vault. And now, Jack, I'm going, too, for of late my appetite has increased to alarming proportions, yet I am as weak as a kitten."

"Nonsense!" I chided. "We'll just leave this place for a while and take a trip somewhere, and when you return you'll laugh at your fears. It's all a case of overwrought nerves, and there is certainly nothing strange about the deaths you speak of. Probably due to some hereditary disease. More than one family has passed out in a hurry just on that account."

"Jack, I only wish I could think so, but somehow I know better. And as for leaving here, I just can't. Understand, I hate the place; I loathe it, but I can't get away. There is a morbid fascination about the place which holds me. If you want to be a real friend, just stay with me for a couple of days and if you don't find anything, I'm sure the sight of you and the sound of your voice will do wonders for me."

I agreed to do my best, although I was hard put to it to keep from smiling at his fears, so apparently groundless were they. We talked on other subjects for several hours, then I proposed bed, saying that I was very tired after my journey and subsequent walk. Remson showed me to my room, and after seeing that everything was as comfortable as possible, he bade me good night.

As he turned to leave the room the flickering light from the lamp fell on his neck and I noticed two small punctures in the skin. I questioned him regarding them, but he replied that he must have beheaded a pimple and that he hadn't noticed them before. He again said good night and left the room.

I undressed and tumbled into bed. During the night I was conscious of an overpowering feeling of suffocation—as if some great burden was lying on my chest which I could not dislodge; and in the morning when I awoke, I experienced a curious sensation of weakness. I arose, not without an effort, and began divesting myself of my sleeping suit.

As I folded the jacket, I noticed a thin line of blood on the collar. I felt my neck, a terrible fear overwhelming me. It pained slightly at the touch. I rushed to examine it in the mirror. Two tiny dots rimmed with blood—my blood—and on my neck! No longer did I chuckle at Remson's fears, for it, the thing, had attacked me as I slept!

I dressed as quickly as my condition would permit and went downstairs, thinking to find my friend there. He was not about, so I looked outside, but he was not in evidence. There was but one answer to the question. He had not yet risen. It was nine o'clock, so I resolved to awaken him.

Not knowing which room he occupied, I entered one after another in a fruitless search. They were all in various stages of disorder, and the thick coating of dust on the furniture showed that they had been untenanted for some time. At last, in a bedroom on the north side of the third floor, I found him.

He was lying spread-eagle fashion across the bed, still in his pajamas, and as I leaned forward to shake him, my eyes fell on two drops of blood, splattered on the coverlet. I crushed back a wild desire to scream and shook Remson rather roughly. His head rolled to one side, and the hellish perforations on his throat showed up vividly. They looked fresh and raw, and had increased to much greater dimensions. I shook him with increased vigor, and at last he opened his eyes stupidly and looked around. Then, seeing me, he said in a voice loaded with anguish, resignation, and despair:

"It's been here again, Jack. I can't hold out much longer. May God take my soul when I go."

So saying, he fell back again from sheer weakness. I left him and went about preparing myself some breakfast. I thought it best not to destroy his faith in me by telling him that I, too, had suffered at the hands of his persecutor.

A walk brought me some peace of mind if not a solution, and when I returned about noon to the big house, Remson was up and about. Together we prepared a really excellent meal. I was hungry and did justice to my share; but after I had finished, my friend continued eating until I thought he must either disgorge or burst. Then after putting things to rights, we strolled about the long hall, looking at the oil paintings, many of which were very valuable.

At one end of the hall I discovered a portrait of an old gentleman, evidently a dandy of his day. He wore his hair in the long, flowing fashion adopted by the old school and sported a carefully trimmed moustache and Vandyke beard. Remson noticed my interest in the painting and came forward.

"I don't wonder that picture holds your interest, Jack. It has a great fascination for me, also. At times I sit for hours, studying the expression on that face. I sometimes think that he has something to tell me, but of course that's all tommy rot. But I beg your pardon, I haven't introduced the old gent yet, have I? This is my grandad. He was a great old boy in his day, and he might be living yet but for that cursed bloodsucker. Perhaps it is such a creature that is doing for me; what do you think?"

"I wouldn't like to venture an opinion, Remson, but unless I'm badly mistaken we must dig deeper for an explanation. We'll know tonight, however. You retire as usual and I'll keep a close watch and we'll solve the riddle or die in the attempt."

Remson said not a word but silently extended his hand. I clasped it in a firm embrace and in each other's eyes we read complete understanding. To change the trend of thought I questioned him on the servant problem.

"I've tried time and again to get servants that would stay," he replied, "but about the third day they would begin acting queer, and the first thing I'd know, they'd have skipped, bag and baggage."

That night I accompanied my friend to his room and remained until he had disrobed and was ready to retire. Several of the window panes were cracked and one was entirely missing. I suggested boarding up the aperture, but he declined, saying that he rather enjoyed the night air, so I dropped the matter.

As it was still early, I sat by the fire in the sitting room and read for an hour or two. I confess that there were many times when my mind wandered from the printed page before me and chills raced up and down my spine as some new sound was borne to my ears. The wind had risen, and was whistling through the trees with a peculiar whining sound. The creaking of the shutters tended to further the eerie effect, and in the distance could be heard the hooting of numerous owls, mingled with the cries of miscellaneous night fowl and other nocturnal creatures.

As I ascended the two flights of steps, the candle in my hand casting grotesque shadows on the walls and ceiling, I had little liking for my job. Many times in the course of duty I had been called upon to display courage, but it took more than mere courage to keep me going now.

I extinguished the candle and crept forward to Remson's room, the door of which was closed. Being careful to make no noise I knelt and looked in at the keyhole. It afforded me a clear view of the bed and two of the windows in the opposite wall. Gradually my eye became accustomed to the darkness and I noticed a faint reddish glow outside one of the windows. It apparently emanated from nowhere. Hundreds of little specks danced and whirled in the spot of light, and as I watched them, fascinated, they seemed to take on the form of a human face. The features were masculine, as was also the arrangement of the hair. Then the mysterious glow disappeared.

So great had the strain been on me that I was wet from perspiration, although the night was quite cool. For a moment I was undecided whether to enter the room or to stay where I was and use the keyhole as a means of observation. I concluded that to remain where I was would be the better plan, so I once more placed my eye to the hole.

Immediately my attention was drawn to something moving where the light had been. At first, owing to the poor light, I was unable to distinguish the general outline and form of the thing; then I saw. It was a man's head.

I will swear it was the exact reproduction of that picture I had seen in the hall that very morning. But, oh, the difference in expression! The lips were drawn back in a snarl, disclosing two sets of pearly white teeth, the canines overdeveloped and remarkably sharp. The eyes, an emerald green in color, stared in a look of consuming hate. The hair was sadly disarranged while on the beard was a large clot of what seemed to be congealed blood.

I noticed thus much, then the head melted from my sight and I transferred my attention to a great bat that circled round and round, his huge wings beating a tattoo on the glass. Finally he circled round the broken pane and flew straight through the hole made by the missing glass. For a few moments he was shut off from my view, then he reappeared and began circling round my friend, who lay sound asleep, blissfully ignorant of all that was occurring. Nearer and nearer it drew, then swooped down and fastened itself on Remson's throat, just over the jugular vein.

At this I rushed into the room and made a wild dash for the thing that had come night after night to gorge itself on my friend, but to no avail. It flew out of the window and away, and I turned my attention to the sleeper.

"Remson, old man, get up."

He sat up like a shot. "What's the matter, Jack? Has it been here?"

"Never mind just now," I replied. "Just dress as hurriedly as possible. We have a little work before us this evening."

He glanced questioningly towards me, but followed my command without argument. I turned and cast my eye about the room for a suitable weapon. There was a stout stick lying in the corner and I made toward it.

"Jack!"

I wheeled about.

"What is it? Damn it, haven't you any sense, almost scaring a man to death?"

He pointed a shaking finger towards the window.

"There! I swear I saw him. It was my grandad, but oh, how disfigured!"

He threw himself upon the bed and began sobbing. The shock had completely unnerved him.

"Forgive me, old man," I pleaded, "I was too quick. Pull yourself together and we may get to the bottom of things tonight, yet."

I handed him my flask. He took a generous swallow and squared up. When he had finished dressing we left the house. There was no moon out, and it was pitch dark.

I led the way, and soon we came to within ten yards of the little grey crypt. I stationed Remson behind a tree with instructions to just use his eyes, and I took up my stand on the other side of the vault, after making sure that the door into it was closed and locked. For the greater part of an hour we waited without results, and I was about ready to call it off when I perceived a white figure flitting between the trees about fifty yards off.

Slowly it advanced, straight towards us, and as it drew closer I looked not *at* it, but *through* it. The wind was blowing strongly, yet not a fold in the long shroud quivered. Just outside the vault it paused and looked around. Even knowing as I did about what to expect, it came as a decided shock when I looked into the eyes of the old Holroyd, deceased these past five years. I heard a gasp and knew that Remson had seen, too, and had recognized. Then the spirit, ghost, or whatever it was, passed into the crypt through the crack between the door and the jamb, a space not one-sixteenth of an inch wide.

As it disappeared, Remson came running forward, his face wholly drawn of color.

"What was it, Jack? What was it? I know it resembled Grandad, but it couldn't have been he. He's been dead five years."

"Let's go back to the house," I answered, "and I'll do my best to explain things to the best of my ability. I may be wrong, of course, but it won't hurt to try my remedy. Remson, what we are up against is a vampire. Not the female species usually spoken of today, but the real thing. I noticed you had an old edition of the Encyclopedia on your shelf. If you'll bring me volume XXIV I'll be able to explain more fully the meaning of the word."

He left the room and returned, carrying the desired book. Turning to page 52, I read—

*Vampire.* A term apparently of Serbian origin originally applied in Eastern Europe to blood-sucking ghosts, but in modern usage transferred to one or more species of blood-sucking bats inhabiting South America . . . In the first-mentioned meaning a vampire is usually supposed to be the soul of a dead man which quits the buried body by night to suck the blood of living persons. Hence, when the vampire's grave is opened his corpse is found to be fresh and rosy from the blood thus absorbed . . . They are accredited with the power of assuming any form they may so desire, and often fly about as specks of dust, pieces of down or straw, etc. . . . To put an end to his ravages, a stake is driven through him, or his head cut off, or his heart torn out, or boiling water and vinegar poured over the grave . . . The persons who turn vampires are wizards, witches, suicides, and those who have come to a violent end. Also, the death of anyone resulting from these vampires will cause that person to join their hellish throng . . . See Calumet's "Dissertation on the Vampires of Hungary."

I looked at Remson. He was staring straight into the fire. I knew that he realized the task before us and was steeling himself to it. Then he turned to me.

"Jack, we'll wait till morning."

That was all. I understood and he knew. There we sat, each struggling with his own thoughts, until the first faint glimmers of light came struggling through the trees and warned us of approaching dawn.

Remson left to fetch a sledge-hammer and a large knife with its edge honed to a razorlike keenness. I busied myself making four wooden stakes, shaped like wedges. He returned, bearing the horrible tools, and we struck out towards the crypt.

We walked rapidly, for had either of us hesitated an instant I verily believe both would have fled. However, our duty lay clearly before us. Remson unlocked the door and swung it outwards. With a prayer on our lips we entered.

As if by mutual understanding, we both turned to the coffin on our left. It belonged to the grandfather. We unplaced the lid, and there lay the old Holroyd. He appeared to be sleeping. His face was full of color, and he had none of the stiffness of death. The hair was matted, the moustache untrimmed, and on the beard were matted stains of a dull brownish hue.

But it was his eyes that attracted me. They were greenish, and they glowed with an expression of fiendish malevolence such as I had never seen before. The look of baffled rage on the face might well have adorned the features of the devil in his hell.

Remson swayed and would have fallen, but I forced some whisky down his throat and he took a grip on himself. He placed one of the stakes directly over its heart, then shut his eyes and prayed that the good God above take this soul that was to be delivered to Him.

I took a step backward, aimed carefully, and swung the sledge-hammer with all my strength. It hit the wedge squarely, and a terrible scream filled the place, while the blood gushed out of the open wound, up and over us, staining the walls and our clothes. Without hesitating, I swung again, and again, and again, while it struggled vainly to rid itself of that awful instrument of death. Another swing and the stake was driven through.

The thing squirmed about in the narrow confines of the coffin, much after the manner of a dismembered worm, and Remson proceeded to sever the head from the body, making a rather crude but effectual job of it. As the final stroke of the knife cut the connection a scream issued from the mouth; and the whole corpse fell away into dust, leaving nothing but a wooden stake lying in a bed of bones.

This finished, we despatched the remaining three. Simultaneously as if struck by the same thought, we felt our throats. The slight pain was gone from mine, and the wounds had entirely disappeared from my friend's, leaving not even a scar.

I wished to place before the world the whole facts contingent upon the mystery and the solution, but Remson prevailed upon me to hold my peace.

Some years later Remson died a Christian death and with him went the only confirmation of my tale. However, ten miles from the little town of Charing there sits an old house, forgotten these many years, and near it is a little grey crypt. Within are four coffins; and in each lies a wooden stake, stained a brownish hue, and bearing the fingerprints of the deceased Remson Holroyd.

# THE ROOM IN THE TOWER
## AND
## MRS. AMWORTH

# E. F. Benson

Edward Frederic Benson (1867–1940) was born in Wokingham, Berkshire, England, and had early success with a society novel, *Dodo* (1893), which remained in print for more than eighty years. It enabled him to devote himself full-time to writing, and he produced a prodigious amount of work in social satire, notably the series about Emmeline "Lucia" Lucas and Elizabeth Mapp, which was adapted for TV by London Weekend Television as *Lucia and Mapp*, in 1985–86. He also wrote highly regarded biographies, including the standard one at the time for Charlotte Brontë. Benson wrote more than seventy books in all.

While most of his fiction is now predictably dated, his frequent forays into the realm of supernatural and horror fiction remain high points in the literature. Among his novels in the genre are *The Judgement Books* (1895), *The Angel of Pain* (1905), *Across the Stream* (1919), *Colin: A Novel* (1923), *Colin II* (1925), *The Inheritor* (1930), and *Raven's Brood* (1934).

Even more cherished than the novels are the short stories, of which the unquestioned masterpieces are "The Room in the Tower," "Mrs. Amworth," and "Caterpillars."

"The Room in the Tower" was first published in *The Room in the Tower and Other Stories* (London: Mills & Boon, 1912); "Mrs. Amworth" was first collected in book form in *Visible and Invisible* (London: Hutchinson, 1923).

# The Room in the Tower

## E. F. BENSON

It is probable that everybody who is at all a constant dreamer has had at least one experience of an event or a sequence of circumstances which have come to his mind in sleep being subsequently realized in the material world. But, in my opinion, so far from this being a strange thing, it would be far odder if this fulfilment did not occasionally happen, since our dreams are, as a rule, concerned with people whom we know and places with which we are familiar, such as might very naturally occur in the awake and daylit world. True, these dreams are often broken into by some absurd and fantastic incident, which puts them out of court in regard to their subsequent fulfilment, but on the mere calculation of chances, it does not appear in the least unlikely that a dream imagined by anyone who dreams constantly should occasionally come true. Not long ago, for instance, I experienced such a fulfilment of a dream which seems to me in no way remarkable and to have no kind of psychical significance. The manner of it was as follows.

A certain friend of mine, living abroad, is amiable enough to write to me about once in a fortnight. Thus, when fourteen days or thereabouts have elapsed since I last heard from him, my mind, probably, either consciously or subconsciously, is expectant of a letter from him. One night last week I dreamed that as I was going upstairs to dress for dinner I heard, as I often heard, the sound of the postman's knock on my front door, and diverted my direction downstairs instead. There, among other correspondence, was a letter from him. Thereafter the fantastic entered, for on opening it I found inside the ace of diamonds, and scribbled across it in his well-known handwriting, "I am sending you this for safe custody, as you know it is running an unreasonable risk to keep aces in Italy." The next evening I was just preparing to go upstairs to dress when I heard the postman's knock, and did precisely as I had done in my dream. There, among other letters, was one from my friend. Only it did not contain the ace of diamonds. Had it done so, I should have attached more weight to the matter, which, as it stands, seems to me a perfectly ordinary coincidence. No doubt I consciously or subconsciously expected a letter from him, and this suggested to me my dream. Similarly, the fact that my friend had not written to me for a fortnight suggested to him that he should do so. But occasionally it is not so easy to find such an explanation, and for the following story I can find no explanation at all. It came out of the dark, and into the dark it has gone again.

All my life I have been a habitual dreamer: the nights are few, that is to say, when I do not find on awaking in the morning that some mental experience has been mine, and sometimes, all night long, apparently, a series of the most dazzling adventures befall me. Almost without exception these adventures are pleasant, though often merely trivial. It is of an exception that I am going to speak.

It was when I was about sixteen that a certain dream first came to me, and this is how it befell. It opened with my being set down at the door of a big red-brick house, where, I understood, I was going to stay. The servant who opened the door told me that tea was being served in the garden, and led me through a low dark-panelled hall, with a large open fireplace, on to a cheerful green lawn set round with flower beds. There were grouped about the tea-table a small party of people, but they were all strangers to me except one, who was a school-fellow called Jack Stone, clearly the son of the house, and he introduced me to his mother and father and a couple of sisters. I was, I remember, somewhat astonished to find myself here, for the boy in question was scarcely known to me, and I rather disliked what I knew of him; moreover, he had left school nearly a year before. The afternoon was very hot, and an intolerable oppression reigned. On the far side of the lawn ran a red-brick wall, with an iron gate in its center, outside which stood a walnut tree. We sat in the shadow of the house opposite a row of long windows, inside which I could see a table with cloth laid, glimmering with glass and silver. This garden front of the house was very long, and at one end of it stood a tower of three stories, which looked to me much older than the rest of the building.

Before long, Mrs. Stone, who, like the rest of the party, had sat in absolute silence, said to me, "Jack will show you your room: I have given you the room in the tower."

Quite inexplicably my heart sank at her words. I felt as if I had known that I should have the room in the tower, and that it contained something dreadful and significant. Jack instantly got up and I understood that I had to follow him. In silence we passed through the hall, and mounted a great oak staircase with many corners, and arrived at a small landing with two doors set in it. He pushed one of these open for me to enter, and without coming in himself, closed it after me. Then I knew that my conjecture had been right: there was something awful in the room, and with the terror of nightmare growing swiftly and enveloping me, I awoke in a spasm of terror.

Now that dream or variations on it occurred to me intermittently for fifteen years. Most often it came in exactly this form, the arrival, the tea laid out on the lawn, the deadly silence succeeded by that one deadly sentence, the mounting with Jack Stone up to the room in the tower where horror dwelt, and it always came to a close in the nightmare of terror at that which was in the room, though I never saw what it was. At other times I experienced variations on this same theme. Occasionally, for instance, we would be sitting at dinner in the dining-room, into the windows of which I had looked on the first night when the dream of this house visited me, but wherever we were, there was the same silence, the same sense of dreadful oppression and foreboding. And the silence I knew would always be broken by Mrs. Stone saying to me, "Jack will show you your room: I have given you the room in the tower." Upon which (this was invariable) I had to follow him up the oak staircase with many corners, and enter the place that I dreaded more and more each time that I visited it in sleep. Or, again, I would find myself playing cards still in silence in a drawing-room lit with immense chandeliers, that gave a blinding illumination. What the game was I have no idea; what I remember, with a sense of miserable anticipation, was that soon Mrs. Stone would get up and say to me, "Jack will show you your room: I have given you the room in the tower." This drawing-room where we played cards was next to the dining-room, and, as I have said, was always brilliantly illuminated, whereas the rest of the house was full of dusk and shadows. And yet, how often, in spite of those bouquets of lights, have I not pored over the cards that were dealt me, scarcely able for some reason to see them. Their designs, too, were strange: there were no red suits, but all were black, and among them there were certain cards which were black all over. I hated and dreaded those.

As this dream continued to recur, I got to know the greater part of the house. There was a smoking-room beyond the drawing-room, at the end of a passage with a green baize door. It was always very dark there, and as often as I went there I passed somebody whom I could not see in the doorway coming out. Curious developments, too, took place in the characters that peopled the dream as might happen to living persons. Mrs. Stone, for instance, who, when I first saw her, had been black-haired, became gray, and instead of rising briskly, as she had done at first when she said, "Jack will show you your room: I have given you the room in the tower," got up very feebly, as if the strength was leaving her limbs. Jack also grew up, and became a rather ill-looking young man, with a brown moustache, while one of the sisters ceased to appear, and I understood she was married.

Then it so happened that I was not visited by this dream for six months or more, and I began to hope, in such inexplicable dread did I hold it, that it had passed away for good. But one night after this interval I again found myself being shown out onto the lawn for tea, and Mrs. Stone was not there, while the others were all dressed in black. At once I guessed the reason, and my heart leaped at the thought that perhaps this time I should not have to sleep in the room in the tower, and though we usually all sat in silence, on this occasion the sense of relief made me talk and laugh as I had never yet done. But even then matters were not altogether comfortable, for no one else spoke, but they all looked secretly at each other. And soon the foolish stream of my talk ran dry, and gradually an apprehension worse than anything I had previously known gained on me as the light slowly faded.

Suddenly a voice which I knew well broke the stillness, the voice of Mrs. Stone, saying, "Jack will show you your room: I have given you the room in the tower." It seemed to come from near the gate in the red-brick wall that bounded the lawn, and looking up, I saw that the grass outside was sown thick with gravestones. A curious greyish light shone from them, and I could read the lettering on the grave nearest me, and it was, "In evil memory of Julia Stone." And as usual Jack got up, and again I followed him through the hall and up the staircase with many corners. On this occasion it was darker than usual, and when I passed into the room in the tower I could only just see the furniture, the position of which was already familiar to me. Also there was a dreadful odor of decay in the room, and I woke screaming.

The dream, with such variations and developments as I have mentioned, went on at intervals for fifteen years. Sometimes I would dream it two or three nights in succession; once, as I have said, there was an intermission of six months, but taking a reasonable average, I should say that I dreamed it quite as often as once in a month. It had, as is plain, something of nightmare about it, since it always ended in the same appalling terror, which so far from getting less, seemed to me to gather fresh fear every time that I experienced it. There was, too, a strange and dreadful consistency about it. The characters in it, as I have mentioned, got regularly older, death and marriage visited this silent family, and I never in the dream, after Mrs. Stone had died, set eyes on her again. But it was always her voice that told me that the room in the tower was prepared for me, and whether we had tea out on the lawn, or the scene was laid in one of the rooms overlooking it, I could always see her gravestone standing just outside the iron gate. It was the same, too, with the married daughter; usually she was not present, but once or twice she returned again, in company with a man, whom I took to be her husband. He, too, like the rest of them, was always silent. But, owing to the constant repetition of the dream, I had ceased to attach, in my waking hours, any significance to it. I never met

Jack Stone again during all those years, nor did I ever see a house that resembled this dark house of my dream. And then something happened.

I had been in London in this year, up till the end of July, and during the first week in August went down to stay with a friend in a house he had taken for the summer months, in the Ashdown Forest district of Sussex. I left London early, for John Clinton was to meet me at Forest Row Station, and we were going to spend the day golfing, and go to his house in the evening. He had his motor with him, and we set off, about five of the afternoon, after a thoroughly delightful day, for the drive, the distance being some ten miles. As it was still so early we did not have tea at the club house, but waited till we should get home. As we drove, the weather, which up till then had been, though hot, deliciously fresh, seemed to me to alter in quality, and become very stagnant and oppressive, and I felt that indefinable sense of ominous apprehension that I am accustomed to before thunder. John, however, did not share my views, attributing my loss of lightness to the fact that I had lost both my matches. Events proved, however, that I was right, though I do not think that the thunderstorm that broke that night was the sole cause of my depression.

Our way lay through deep high-banked lanes, and before we had gone very far I fell asleep, and was only awakened by the stopping of the motor. And with a sudden thrill, partly of fear but chiefly of curiosity, I found myself standing in the doorway of my house of dream. We went, I half wondering whether or not I was dreaming still, through a low oak-panelled hall, and out onto the lawn, where tea was laid in the shadow of the house. It was set in flower beds, a red-brick wall, with a gate in it, bounded one side, and out beyond that was a space of rough grass with a walnut tree. The façade of the house was very long, and at one end stood a three-storied tower, markedly older than the rest.

Here for the moment all resemblance to the repeated dream ceased. There was no silent and somehow terrible family, but a large assembly of exceedingly cheerful persons, all of whom were known to me. And in spite of the horror with which the dream itself had always filled me, I felt nothing of it now that the scene of it was thus reproduced before me. But I felt intensest curiosity as to what was going to happen.

Tea pursued its cheerful course, and before long Mrs. Clinton got up. And at that moment I think I knew what she was going to say. She spoke to me, and what she said was:

"Jack will show you your room: I have given you the room in the tower."

At that, for half a second, the horror of the dream took hold of me again. But it quickly passed, and again I felt nothing more than the most intense curiosity. It was not very long before it was amply satisfied.

John turned to me.

"Right up at the top of the house," he said, "but I think you'll be comfortable. We're absolutely full up. Would you like to go and see it now? By Jove, I believe that you are right, and that we are going to have a thunderstorm. How dark it has become."

I got up and followed him. We passed through the hall, and up the perfectly familiar staircase. Then he opened the door, and I went in. And at that moment sheer unreasoning terror again possessed me. I did not know for certain what I feared: I simply feared. Then like a sudden recollection, when one remembers a name which has long escaped the memory, I knew what I feared. I feared Mrs. Stone, whose grave with the sinister inscription, "In evil memory," I had so often seen in my dream, just beyond the lawn which lay below my window. And then once more the fear passed so completely that I wondered what there was to fear, and I found myself, sober and quiet and sane, in the room in the tower, the name of which I had so often heard in my dream, and the scene of which was so familiar.

I looked round it with a certain sense of proprietorship, and found that nothing had been changed from the dreaming nights in which I knew it so well. Just to the left of the door was the bed, lengthways along the wall, with the head of it in the angle. In a line with it was the fireplace and a small bookcase; opposite the door the outer wall was pierced by two lattice-paned windows, between which stood the dressing-table, while ranged along the fourth wall was the washing-stand and a big cupboard. My luggage had already been unpacked, for the furniture of dressing and undressing lay orderly on the wash-stand and toilet-table, while my dinner clothes were spread out on the coverlet of the bed. And then, with a sudden start of unexplained dismay, I saw that there were two rather conspicuous objects which I had not seen before in my dreams: one a life-sized oil painting of Mrs. Stone, the other a black-and-white sketch of Jack Stone, representing him as he had appeared to me only a week before in the last of the series of these repeated dreams, a rather secret and evil-looking man of about thirty. His picture hung between the windows, looking straight across the room to the other portrait, which hung at the side of the bed. At that I looked next, and as I looked I felt once more the horror of nightmare seize me.

It represented Mrs. Stone as I had seen her last in my dreams: old and withered and white-haired. But in spite of the evident feebleness of body, a dreadful exuberance and vitality shone through the envelope of flesh, an exuberance wholly malign, a vitality that foamed and frothed with unimaginable evil. Evil beamed from the narrow, leering eyes; it laughed in the demon-like mouth. The whole face was instinct with some secret and appalling mirth; the hands, clasped together on the knee, seemed shaking with suppressed and nameless glee. Then I saw also that it was signed in the left-hand bottom corner, and wondering who the artist could be, I looked more closely, and read the inscription, "Julia Stone by Julia Stone."

There came a tap at the door, and John Clinton entered. "Got everything you want?" he asked.

"Rather more than I want," said I, pointing to the picture.

He laughed.

"Hard-featured old lady," he said. "By herself, too, I remember. Anyhow she can't have flattered herself much."

"But don't you see?" said I. "It's scarcely a human face at all. It's the face of some witch, of some devil."

He looked at it more closely.

"Yes; it isn't very pleasant," he said. "Scarcely a bedside manner, eh? Yes; I can imagine getting the nightmare if I went to sleep with that close by my bed. I'll have it taken down if you like."

"I really wish you would," I said. He rang the bell, and with the help of a servant we detached the picture and carried it out onto the landing, and put it with its face to the wall.

"By Jove, the old lady is a weight," said John, mopping his forehead. "I wonder if she had something on her mind."

The extraordinary weight of the picture had struck me too. I was about to reply, when I caught sight of my own hand. There was blood on it, in considerable quantities, covering the whole palm.

"I've cut myself somehow," said I.

John gave a little startled exclamation.

"Why, I have too," he said.

Simultaneously the footman took out his handkerchief and wiped his hand with it. I saw that there was blood also on his handkerchief.

John and I went back into the tower room and washed the blood off; but neither on his hand nor on mine was there the slightest trace of a scratch or cut. It seemed to me that, having ascertained this, we both, by a sort of tacit consent, did not allude to it again. Something in my case had dimly occurred to me that I did not wish to think about. It was but a conjecture, but I fancied that I knew the same thing had occurred to him.

The heat and oppression of the air, for the storm we had expected was still undischarged, increased very much after dinner, and for some time most of the party, among whom were John Clinton and myself, sat outside on the path bounding the lawn, where we had had tea. The night was absolutely dark, and no twinkle of star or moon ray could penetrate the pall of cloud that overset the sky. By degrees our assembly thinned, the women went up to bed, men dispersed to the smoking or billiard room, and by eleven o'clock my host and I were the only two left. All the evening I thought that he had something on his mind, and as soon as we were alone he spoke.

"The man who helped us with the picture had blood on his hand, too, did you notice?" he said.

"I asked him just now if he had cut himself, and he said he supposed he had, but that he could find no mark of it. Now where did that blood come from?"

By dint of telling myself that I was not going to think about it, I had succeeded in not doing so, and I did not want, especially just at bedtime, to be reminded of it.

"I don't know," said I, "and I don't really care so long as the picture of Mrs. Stone is not by my bed."

He got up.

"But it's odd," he said. "Ha! Now you'll see another odd thing."

A dog of his, an Irish terrier by breed, had come out of the house as we talked. The door behind us into the hall was open, and a bright oblong of light shone across the lawn to the iron gate which led on to the rough grass outside, where the walnut tree stood. I saw that the dog had all his hackles up, bristling with rage and fright; his lips were curled back from his teeth, as if he was ready to spring at something, and he was growling to himself. He took not the slightest notice of his master or me, but stiffly and tensely walked across the grass to the iron gate. There he stood for a moment, looking through the bars and still growling. Then of a sudden his courage seemed to desert him: he gave one long howl, and scuttled back to the house with a curious crouching sort of movement.

"He does that half a dozen times a day," said John. "He sees something which he both hates and fears."

I walked to the gate and looked over it. Something was moving on the grass outside, and soon a sound which I could not instantly identify came to my ears. Then I remembered what it was: it was the purring of a cat. I lit a match, and saw the purrer, a big blue Persian, walking round and round in a little circle just outside the gate, stepping high and ecstatically, with tail carried aloft like a banner. Its eyes were bright and shining, and every now and then it put its head down and sniffed at the grass.

I laughed.

"The end of that mystery, I am afraid," I said. "Here's a large cat having Walpurgis night all alone."

"Yes, that's Darius," said John. "He spends half the day and all night there. But that's not the end of the dog mystery, for Toby and he are the best of friends, but the beginning of the cat mystery. What's the cat doing there? And why is Darius pleased, while Toby is terror-stricken?"

At that moment I remembered the rather horrible detail of my dreams when I saw through the gate, just where the cat was now, the white tombstone with the sinister inscription. But before I could answer the rain began, as suddenly and heavily as if a tap had been turned on, and simultaneously the big cat squeezed through the bars of the gate, and came leaping across the lawn to the house for shelter. Then it sat in the doorway, looking out eagerly into the dark. It spat and struck at John with its paw, as he pushed it in, in order to close the door.

Somehow, with the portrait of Julia Stone in the passage outside, the room in the tower had absolutely no alarm for me, and as I went to bed, feeling very sleepy and heavy, I had nothing more than interest for the curious incident about our bleeding hands, and the conduct of the cat and dog. The last thing I looked at before I put out my light was the square empty space by my bed where the portrait had been. Here the paper was of its original full tint of dark red: over the rest of the walls it had faded. Then I blew out my candle and instantly fell asleep.

My awaking was equally instantaneous, and I sat bolt upright in bed under the impression that some bright light had been flashed in my face, though it was now absolutely pitch dark. I knew exactly where I was, in the room which I had dreaded in dreams, but no horror that I ever felt when asleep approached the fear that now invaded and froze my brain. Immediately after a peal of thunder crackled just above the house, but the probability that it was only a flash of lightning which awoke me gave no reassurance to my galloping heart. Something I knew was in the room with me, and instinctively I put out my right hand, which was nearest the wall, to keep it away. And my hand touched the edge of a picture-frame hanging close to me.

I sprang out of bed, upsetting the small table that stood by it, and I heard my watch, candle, and matches clatter onto the floor. But for the moment there was no need of light, for a blinding flash leaped out of the clouds, and showed me that by my bed again hung the picture of Mrs. Stone. And instantly the room went into blackness again. But in that flash I saw another thing also, namely a figure that leaned over the end of my bed, watching me. It was dressed in some close-clinging white garment, spotted and stained with mold, and the face was that of the portrait.

Overhead the thunder cracked and roared, and when it ceased and the deathly stillness succeeded, I heard the rustle of movement coming nearer me, and, more horrible yet, perceived an odor of corruption and decay. And then a hand was laid on the side of my neck, and close beside my ear I heard quick-taken, eager breathing. Yet I knew that this thing, though it could be perceived by touch, by smell, by eye and by ear, was still not of this earth, but something that had passed out of the body and had power to make itself manifest. Then a voice, already familiar to me, spoke.

"I knew you would come to the room in the tower," it said. "I have been long waiting for you. At last you have come. Tonight I shall feast; before long we will feast together."

And the quick breathing came closer to me; I could feel it on my neck.

At that the terror, which I think had paralyzed me for the moment, gave way to the wild instinct of self-preservation. I hit wildly with both arms, kicking out at the same moment, and heard a little animal-squeal, and something soft dropped with a thud beside me. I took a couple of steps forward, nearly tripping up over whatever it was that lay there, and by the merest good-luck found the handle of the door. In another second I ran out on the landing, and had banged the door behind me. Almost at the same moment I heard a door open somewhere below, and John Clinton, candle in hand, came running upstairs.

"What is it?" he said. "I sleep just below you, and heard a noise as if— Good heavens, there's blood on your shoulder."

I stood there, so he told me afterwards, swaying from side to side, white as a sheet, with the mark on my shoulder as if a hand covered with blood had been laid there.

"It's in there," I said, pointing. "She, you know. The portrait is in there, too, hanging up on the place we took it from."

At that he laughed.

"My dear fellow, this is mere nightmare," he said.

He pushed by me, and opened the door, I standing there simply inert with terror, unable to stop him, unable to move.

"Phew! What an awful smell," he said.

Then there was silence; he had passed out of my sight behind the open door. Next moment he came out again, as white as myself, and instantly shut it.

"Yes, the portrait's there," he said, "and on the floor is a thing—a thing spotted with earth, like what they bury people in. Come away, quick, come away."

How I got downstairs I hardly know. An awful shuddering and nausea of the spirit rather than of the flesh had seized me, and more than once he had to place my feet upon the steps, while every now and then he cast glances of terror and apprehension up the stairs. But in time we came to his dressing-room on the floor below, and there I told him what I have here described.

The sequel can be made short; indeed, some of my readers have perhaps already guessed what it was, if they remember that inexplicable affair of the churchyard at West Fawley, some eight years ago, where an attempt was made three times to bury the body of a certain woman who had committed suicide. On each occasion the coffin was found in the course of a few days again protruding from the ground. After the third attempt, in order that the thing should not be talked about, the body was buried elsewhere in unconsecrated ground. Where it was buried was just outside the iron gate of the garden belonging to the house where this woman had lived. She had committed suicide in a room at the top of the tower in that house. Her name was Julia Stone.

Subsequently the body was again secretly dug up, and the coffin was found to be full of blood.

# Mrs. Amworth

## E. F. BENSON

The village of Maxley, where last summer and autumn, these strange events took place, lies on a heathery and pine-clad upland of Sussex. In all England you could not find a sweeter and saner situation. Should the wind blow from the south, it comes laden with the spices of the sea; to the east high downs protect it from the inclemencies of March; and from the west and north the breezes which reach it travel over miles of aromatic forest and heather. The village itself is insignificant enough in point of population, but rich in amenities and beauty. Half-way down the single street, with its road and spacious areas of grass on each side, stands the little Norman Church and the antique graveyard long disused: for the rest there are a dozen small, sedate Georgian houses, red-bricked and long-windowed, each with a square of flower-garden in front, and an ampler strip behind; a score of shops, and a couple of score of thatched cottages belonging to laborers on neighboring estates, complete the entire cluster of its peaceful habitations. The general peace, however, is sadly broken on Saturdays and Sundays, for we lie on one of the main roads between London and Brighton and our quiet street becomes a racecourse for flying motor-cars and bicycles. A notice just outside the village begging them to go slowly only seems to encourage them to accelerate their speed, for the road lies open and straight, and there is really no reason why they should do otherwise. By way of protest, therefore, the ladies of Maxley cover their noses and mouths with their handkerchiefs as they see a motor-car approaching, though, as the street is asphalted, they need not really take these precautions against dust. But late on Sunday night the horde of scorchers has passed, and we settle down again to five days of cheerful and leisurely seclusion. Railway strikes which agitate the country so much leave us undisturbed because most of the inhabitants of Maxley never leave it at all.

I am the fortunate possessor of one of these small Georgian houses, and consider myself no less fortunate in having so interesting and stimulating a neighbor as Francis Urcombe, who, the most confirmed of Maxleyites, has not slept away from his house, which stands just opposite to mine in the village street, for nearly two years, at which date, though still in middle life, he resigned his Physiological Professorship at Cambridge University and devoted himself to the study of those occult and curious phenomena which seem equally to concern the physical and the psychical sides of human nature. Indeed his retirement was not un-connected with his passion for the strange un-charted places that lie on the confines and borders of science, the existence of which is so stoutly de-nied by the more materialistic minds, for he ad-vocated that all medical students should be obliged to pass some sort of examination in mesmerism, and that one of the tripos papers should be de-signed to test their knowledge in such subjects as appearances at time of death, haunted houses, vampirism, automatic writing, and possession.

"Of course they wouldn't listen to me," ran his account of the matter, "for there is nothing that these seats of learning are so frightened of as knowl-edge, and the road to knowledge lies in the study of things like these. The functions of the human frame are, broadly speaking, known. They are a country, anyhow, that has been charted and mapped out. But outside that lie huge tracts of undiscov-ered country, which certainly exist, and the real pioneers of knowledge are those who, at the cost of being derided as credulous and superstitious, want to push on into those misty and probably perilous places. I felt that I could be of more use by setting out without compass or knapsack into the mists than by sitting in a cage like a canary and chirping about what was known. Besides, teach-ing is very bad for a man who knows himself only to be a learner; you only need to be a self-conceited ass to teach."

Here, then, in Francis Urcombe, was a delight-ful neighbor to one who, like myself, has an un-easy and burning curiosity about what he called the "misty and perilous places"; and this last spring we had a further and most welcome addition to our pleasant little community, in the person of Mrs. Amworth, widow of an Indian civil servant. Her husband had been a judge in the North-West Provinces, and after his death at Peshawar she came back to England, and after a year in London found herself starving for the ampler air and sun-shine of the country to take the place of the fogs and griminess of town. She had, too, a special rea-son for settling in Maxley, since her ancestors up till a hundred years ago had long been native to the place, and in the old churchyard, now disused,

are many gravestones bearing her maiden name of Chaston. Big and energetic, her vigorous and genial personality speedily woke Maxley up to a higher degree of sociality than it had ever known. Most of us were bachelors or spinsters or elderly folk not much inclined to exert ourselves in the expense and effort of hospitality, and hitherto the gaiety of a small tea-party, with bridge afterwards and galoshes (when it was wet) to trip home in again for a solitary dinner, was about the climax of our festivities. But Mrs. Amworth showed us a more gregarious way, and set an example of lun-cheon parties and little dinners, which we began to follow. On other nights when no such hospital-ity was on foot, a lone man like myself found it pleasant to know that a call on the telephone to Mrs. Amworth's house not a hundred yards off, and an inquiry as to whether I might come over after dinner for a game of piquet before bedtime, would probably evoke a response of welcome. There she would be, with a comrade-like eager-ness for companionship, and there was a glass of port and cup of coffee and a cigarette and game of piquet. She played the piano, too, in a free and ex-uberant manner, and had a charming voice and sang to her own accompaniment; and as the days grew long and the light lingered late, we played our game in her garden, which in the course of a few months she had turned from being a nursery for slugs and snails into a glowing patch of luxu-riant blossoming. She was always cheery and jolly; she was interested in everything, and in music, in gardening, in games of all sorts was a competent performer. Everybody (with one exception) liked her, everybody felt her to bring with her the tonic of a sunny day. That one exception was Francis Urcombe; he, though he confessed he did not like her, acknowledged that he was vastly interested in her. This always seemed strange to me, for pleas-ant and jovial as she was, I could see nothing in her that could call forth conjecture or intrigued surmise, so healthy and unmysterious a figure did she present. But of the genuineness of Urcombe's interest there could be no doubt; one could see him watching and scrutinizing her. In matter of age, she frankly volunteered the information that she was forty-five; but her briskness, her activity, her unravaged skin, her coal-black hair, made it difficult to believe that she was not adopting an unusual device, and adding ten years on to her age instead of subtracting them.

Often, also, as our quite unsentimental friendship ripened, Mrs. Amworth would ring me up and propose her advent. If I was busy writing, I was to give her, so we definitely bargained, a frank negative, and in answer I could hear her jolly laugh and her wishes for a successful evening of work. Sometimes, before her proposal arrived, Urcombe would already have stepped across from his house opposite for a smoke and a chat, and he, hearing who my intending visitor was, always urged me to beg her to come. She and I should play our piquet, said he, and he would look on, if we did not object, and learn something of the game. But I doubt whether he paid much attention to it, for nothing could be clearer than that, under that penthouse of forehead and thick eyebrows, his attention was fixed not on the cards, but on one of the players. But he seemed to enjoy an hour spent thus, and often, until one particular evening in July, he would watch her with the air of a man who has some deep problem in front of him. She, enthusiastically keen about our game, seemed not to notice his scrutiny. Then came that evening, when, as I see in the light of subsequent events, began the first twitching of the veil that hid the secret horror from my eyes. I did not know it then, though I noticed that thereafter, if she rang up to propose coming round, she always asked not only if I was at leisure, but whether Mr. Urcombe was with me. If so, she said, she would not spoil the chat of two old bachelors, and laughingly wished me good night.

Urcombe, on this occasion, had been with me for some half-hour before Mrs. Amworth's appearance, and had been talking to me about the medieval beliefs concerning vampirism, one of those borderland subjects which he declared had not been sufficiently studied before it had been consigned by the medical profession to the dust-heap of exploded superstitions. There he sat, grim

and eager, tracing, with that pellucid clearness which had made him in his Cambridge days so admirable a lecturer, the history of those mysterious visitations. In them all there were the same general features; one of those ghoulish spirits took up its abode in a living man or woman, conferring supernatural powers of bat-like flight and glutting itself with nocturnal blood-feasts. When its host died it continued to dwell in the corpse, which remained undecayed. By day it rested, by night it left the grave and went on its awful errands. No European country in the Middle Ages seemed to have escaped them; earlier yet, parallels were to be found, in Roman and Greek and in Jewish history.

"It's a large order to set all that evidence aside as being moonshine," he said. "Hundreds of totally independent witnesses in many ages have testified to the occurrence of these phenomena, and there's no explanation known to me which covers all the facts. And if you feel inclined to say 'Why, then, if these are facts, do we not come across them now?' there are two answers I can make you. One is that there were diseases known in the Middle Ages, such as the black death, which were certainly existent then and which have become extinct since, but for that reason we do not assert that such diseases never existed. Just as the black death visited England and decimated the population of Norfolk, so here in this very district about three hundred years ago there was certainly an outbreak of vampirism, and Maxley was the center of it. My second answer is even more convincing, for I tell you that vampirism is by no means extinct now. An outbreak of it certainly occurred in India a year or two ago."

At that moment I heard my knocker plied in the cheerful and peremptory manner in which Mrs. Amworth is accustomed to announce her arrival, and I went to the door to open it.

"Come in at once," I said, "and save me from having my blood curdled. Mr. Urcombe has been trying to alarm me."

Instantly her vital, voluminous presence seemed to fill the room.

"Ah, but how lovely!" she said. "I delight in having my blood curdled. Go on with your ghost story, Mr. Urcombe. I adore ghost stories."

I saw that, as his habit was, he was intently observing her.

"It wasn't a ghost story exactly," said he. "I was only telling our host how vampirism was not extinct yet. I was saying that there was an outbreak of it in India only a few years ago."

There was a more than perceptible pause, and I saw that, if Urcombe was observing her, she on her side was observing him with fixed eye and parted mouth. Then her jolly laugh invaded that rather tense silence.

"Oh, what a shame!" she said. "You're not going to curdle my blood at all. Where did you pick up such a tale, Mr. Urcombe? I have lived for years in India and never heard a rumor of such a thing. Some storyteller in the bazaars must have invented it: they are famous at that."

I could see that Urcombe was on the point of saying something further, but checked himself.

"Ah! Very likely that was it," he said.

But something had disturbed our usual peaceful sociability that night, and something had damped Mrs. Amworth's usual high spirits. She had no gusto for her piquet, and left after a couple of games. Urcombe had been silent too, indeed he hardly spoke again till she departed.

"That was unfortunate," he said, "for the outbreak of—of a very mysterious disease, let us call it, took place at Peshawar where she and her husband were. And—"

"Well?" I asked.

"He was one of the victims of it," said he. "Naturally I had quite forgotten that when I spoke."

The summer was unreasonably hot and rainless, and Maxley suffered much from drought, and also from a plague of big black night-flying gnats, the bite of which was very irritating and virulent. They came sailing in of an evening, settling on one's skin so quietly that one perceived nothing till the sharp stab announced that one had been bitten. They did not bite the hands or face, but chose always the neck and throat for their feeding-ground, and most of us, as the poison spread, assumed a temporary goitre. Then about the middle of August appeared the first of those mysterious cases of illness which our local doctor attributed to the long-continued heat coupled with the bite of these venomous insects. The patient was a boy of sixteen or seventeen, the son of Mrs. Amworth's gardener, and the symptoms were an anemic pallor and a languid prostration, accompanied by great drowsiness and an abnormal appetite. He had, too, on his throat two small punctures where, so Dr. Ross conjectured, one of these great gnats had bitten him. But the odd thing was that there was no swelling or inflammation round the place where he had been bitten. The heat at this time had begun to abate, but the cooler weather failed to restore him, and the boy, in spite of the quantity of good food which he so ravenously swallowed, wasted away to a skin-clad skeleton.

I met Dr. Ross in the street one afternoon about this time, and in answer to my inquiries about his patient he said that he was afraid the boy was dying. The case, he confessed, completely puzzled him: some obscure form of pernicious anemia was all he could suggest. But he wondered whether Mr. Urcombe would consent to see the boy, on the chance of his being able to throw some new light on the case, and since Urcombe was dining with me that night, I proposed to Dr. Ross to join us. He could not do this, but said he would look in later. When he came, Urcombe at once consented to put his skill at the other's disposal, and together they went off at once. Being thus shorn of my sociable evening, I telephoned to Mrs. Amworth to know if I might inflict myself on her for an hour. Her answer was a welcoming affirmative, and between piquet and music the hour lengthened itself into two. She spoke of the boy who was lying so desperately and mysteriously ill, and told me that she had often been to see him, taking him nourishing and delicate food. But today—and her kind eyes moistened as she spoke—she was afraid she had paid her last visit. Knowing the antipathy between her and Urcombe, I did not tell her that he had been called into consultation; and when I returned home she accompanied me to my door, for the sake of a breath of night air, and in order to borrow a magazine which contained an article on gardening which she wished to read.

"Ah, this delicious night air," she said, luxuriously sniffing in the coolness. "Night air and gardening are the great tonics. There is nothing so stimulating as bare contact with rich mother earth. You are never so fresh as when you have been grubbing in the soil—black hands, black nails, and boots covered with mud." She gave her great jovial laugh.

"I'm a glutton for air and earth," she said. "Positively I look forward to death, for then I shall be buried and have the kind earth all round me. No leaden caskets for me—I have given explicit directions. But what shall I do about air? Well, I suppose one can't have everything. The magazine? A thousand thanks, I will faithfully return it. Good night; garden and keep your windows open, and you won't have anemia."

"I always sleep with my windows open," said I. I went straight up to my bedroom, of which one of the windows looks out over the street, and as I undressed I thought I heard voices talking outside not far away. But I paid no particular attention, put out my lights, and falling asleep plunged into the depths of a most horrible dream, distortedly suggested no doubt, by my last words with Mrs. Amworth. I dreamed that I woke, and found that both my bedroom windows were shut. Half-suffocating I dreamed that I sprang out of bed, and went across to open them. The blind over the first was drawn down, and pulling it up I saw, with the indescribable horror of incipient nightmare, Mrs. Amworth's face suspended close to the pane in the darkness outside, nodding and smiling at me. Pulling down the blind again to keep that terror out, I rushed to the second window on the other side of the room, and there again was Mrs. Amworth's face. Then the panic came upon me in full blast; here was I suffocating in the airless room, and whichever window I opened Mrs. Amworth's face would float in, like those noiseless black gnats that bit before one was aware. The nightmare rose to screaming point, and with stran-

gled yells I awoke to find my room cool and quiet with both windows open and blinds up and a half-moon high in its course, casting an oblong of tranquil light on the floor. But even when I was awake the horror persisted, and I lay tossing and turning. I must have slept long before the nightmare seized me, for now it was nearly day, and soon in the east the drowsy eyelids of morning began to lift.

I was scarcely downstairs next morning—for after the dawn I slept late—when Urcombe rang up to know if he might see me immediately. He came in, grim and preoccupied, and I noticed that he was pulling on a pipe that was not even filled.

"I want your help," he said, "and so I must tell you first of all what happened last night. I went round with the little doctor to see his patient, and found him just alive, but scarely more. I instantly diagnosed in my own mind what this anemia, unaccountable by any other explanation, meant. The boy is the prey of a vampire."

He put his empty pipe on the breakfast-table, by which I had just sat down, and folded his arms, looking at me steadily from under his overhanging brows.

"Now about last night," he said. "I insisted that he should be moved from his father's cottage into my house. As we were carrying him on a stretcher, whom should we meet but Mrs. Amworth? She expressed shocked surprise that we were moving him. Now why do you think she did that?"

With a start of horror, as I remembered my dream that night before, I felt an idea come into my mind so preposterous and unthinkable that I instantly turned it out again.

"I haven't the smallest idea," I said.

"Then listen, while I tell you about what happened later. I put out all light in the room where the boy lay, and watched. One window was a little open, for I had forgotten to close it, and about midnight I heard something outside, trying apparently to push it farther open. I guessed who it was—yes, it was full twenty feet from the ground—and I peeped round the corner of the blind. Just outside was the face of Mrs. Amworth and her hand was on the frame of the window. Very softly I crept close, and then banged the window down, and I think I just caught the tip of one of her fingers."

"But it's impossible," I cried. "How could she be floating in the air like that? And what had she come for? Don't tell me such—"

Once more, with closer grip, the remembrance of my nightmare seized me.

"I am telling you what I saw," said he. "And all night long, until it was nearly day, she was fluttering outside, like some terrible bat, trying to gain admittance. Now put together various things I have told you."

He began checking them off on his fingers.

"Number one," he said, "there was an outbreak of disease similar to that which this boy is suffering from at Peshawar, and her husband died of it. Number two: Mrs. Amworth protested against my moving the boy to my house. Number three: she, or the demon that inhabits her body, a creature powerful and deadly, tries to gain admittance. And add this, too: in medieval times there was an epidemic of vampirism here at Maxley. The vampire, so the accounts run, was found to be Elizabeth Chaston . . . I see you remember Mrs. Amworth's maiden name. Finally, the boy is stronger this morning. He would certainly not have been alive if he had been visited again. And what do you make of it?"

There was a long silence, during which I found this incredible horror assuming the hues of reality.

"I have something to add," I said, "which may or may not bear on it. You say that the—the specter went away shortly before dawn."

"Yes."

I told him of my dream, and he smiled grimly.

"Yes, you did well to awake," he said. "That warning came from your subconscious self, which never wholly slumbers, and cried out to you of deadly danger. For two reasons, then, you must help me: one to save others, the second to save yourself."

"What do you want me to do?" I asked.

"I want you first of all to help me in watching this boy, and ensuring that she does not come near him. Eventually I want you to help me in tracking the thing down, in exposing and destroying it. It is not human: it is an incarnate fiend. What steps we shall have to take I don't yet know."

It was now eleven of the forenoon, and presently I went across to his house for a twelve-hour vigil while he slept, to come on duty again that night, so that for the next twenty-four hours either Urcombe or myself was always in the room where the boy, now getting stronger every hour, was lying. The day following was Saturday and a morning of brilliant, pellucid weather, and already when I went across to his house to resume my duty the stream of motors down to Brighton had begun. Simultaneously I saw Urcombe with a cheerful face, which boded good news of his patient, coming out of his house, and Mrs. Amworth, with a gesture of salutation to me and a basket in her hand, walking up the broad strip of grass which bordered the road. There we all three met. I noticed (and saw that Urcombe noticed it too) that one finger of her left hand was bandaged.

"Good morning to you both," said she. "And I hear your patient is doing well, Mr. Urcombe. I have come to bring him a bowl of jelly, and to sit with him for an hour. He and I are great friends. I am overjoyed at his recovery."

Urcombe paused a moment, as if making up his mind, and then shot out a pointing finger at her.

"I forbid that," he said. "You shall not sit with him or see him. And you know the reason as well as I do."

I have never seen so horrible a change pass over a human face as that which now blanched hers to the color of a grey mist. She put up her hands as if to shield herself from that pointing finger, which drew the sign of the cross in the air, and shrank back cowering onto the road. There was a wild hoot from a horn, a grinding of brakes, a shout—too late—from a passing car, and one long scream suddenly cut short. Her body rebounded from the roadway after the first wheel had gone over it, and the second followed. It lay there, quivering and twitching, and was still.

She was buried three days afterwards in the cemetery outside Maxley, in accordance with the wishes she had told me that she had devised about her interment, and the shock which her sudden and awful death had caused to the little community began by degrees to pass off. To two people only, Urcombe and myself, the horror of it was mitigated from the first by the nature of the relief that her death brought; but, naturally enough, we kept our own counsel, and no hint of what greater horror had been thus averted was ever let slip. But, oddly enough, so it seemed to me, he was still not satisfied about something in connection with her, and would give no answer to my questions on the subject. Then as the days of a tranquil mellow September and the October that followed began to drop away like the leaves of the yellowing trees, uneasiness relaxed. But before the entry of November the seeming tranquillity broke into hurricane.

I had been dining one night at the far end of the village, and about eleven o'clock was walking home again. The moon was of an unusual brilliance, rendering all that it shone on as distinct as in some etching. I had just come opposite the house which Mrs. Amworth had occupied, where there was a board up telling that it was to let, when I heard the click of her front gate, and next moment I saw, with a sudden chill and quaking of my very spirit, that she stood there. Her profile, vividly illuminated, was turned to me, and I could not be mistaken in my identification of her. She appeared not to see me (indeed the shadow of the yew hedge in front of her garden enveloped me in its blackness) and she went swiftly across the road, and entered the gate of the house directly opposite. There I lost sight of her completely.

My breath was coming in short pants as if I had been running—and now indeed I ran, with fearful backward glances, along the hundred yards that separated me from my house and Urcombe's. It was to his that my flying steps took me, and next minute I was within.

"What have you come to tell me?" he asked. "Or shall I guess?"

"You can't guess," said I.

"No; it's no guess. She has come back and you

have seen her. Tell me about it." I gave him my story.

"That's Major Pearsall's house," he said. "Come back with me there at once."

"But what can we do?" I asked.

"I've no idea. That's what we have got to find out."

A minute later, we were opposite the house. When I had passed it before, it was all dark; now lights gleamed from a couple of windows upstairs. Even as we faced it, the front door opened, and next moment Major Pearsall emerged from the gate. He saw us and stopped.

"I'm on my way to Dr. Ross," he said quickly. "My wife has been taken suddenly ill. She had been in bed an hour when I came upstairs, and I found her white as a ghost and utterly exhausted. She had been to sleep, it seemed—but you will excuse me."

"One moment, Major," said Urcombe. "Was there any mark on her throat?"

"How did you guess that?" said he. "There was: one of those beastly gnats must have bitten her twice there. She was streaming with blood."

"And there's someone with her?" asked Urcombe.

"Yes, I roused her maid." He went off, and Urcombe turned to me. "I know now what we have to do," he said. "Change your clothes, and I'll join you at your house."

"What is it?" I asked.

"I'll tell you on our way. We're going to the cemetery."

He carried a pick, a shovel, and a screwdriver when he rejoined me and wore round his shoulders a long coil of rope. As we walked, he gave me the outlines of the ghastly hour that lay before us.

"What I have to tell you," he said, "will seem to you now too fantastic for credence, but before dawn we shall see whether it outstrips reality. By a most fortunate happening, you saw the specter, the astral body, whatever you choose to call it, of

Mrs. Amworth, going on its grisly business, and therefore, beyond doubt, the vampire spirit which abode in her during life animates her again in death. That is not exceptional—indeed, all these weeks since her death I have been expecting it. If I am right, we shall find her body undecayed and untouched by corruption."

"But she has been dead nearly two months," said I.

"If she had been dead two years it would still be so, if the vampire has possession of her. So remember, whatever you see done, it will be done not to her, who in the natural course would now be feeding the grasses above her grave, but to a spirit of untold evil and malignancy, which gives a phantom life to her body."

"But what shall I see done?" said I.

"I will tell you. We know that now, at this moment, the vampire clad in her mortal semblance is out; dining out. But it must get back before dawn, and it will pass into the material form that lies in her grave. We must wait for that, and then with your help I shall dig up her body. If I am right, you will look on her as she was in life, with the full vigor of the dreadful nutriment she has received pulsing in her veins. And then, when dawn has come, and the vampire cannot leave the lair of her body, I shall strike her with this"—and he pointed to his pick—"through the heart, and she, who comes to life again only with animation the fiend gives her, she and her hellish partner will be dead indeed. Then we must bury her again, delivered at last."

We had come to the cemetery, and in the brightness of the moonshine there was no difficulty in identifying her grave. It lay some twenty yards from the small chapel, in the porch of which, obscured by shadow, we concealed ourselves. From there we had a clear and open sight of the grave, and now we must wait till its infernal visitor returned home. The night was warm and windless, yet even if a freezing wind had been raging I think I should have felt nothing of it, so intense was my preoccupation as to what the night and dawn would bring. There was a bell in the turret of the chapel, that struck the quarters of the hour, and it amazed me to find how swiftly the chimes succeeded one another.

The moon had long set, but a twilight of stars shone in a clear sky, when five o'clock of the morning sounded from the turret. A few minutes more passed, and then I felt Urcombe's hand softly nudging me; and looking out in the direction of his pointing finger, I saw that the form of a woman, tall and large in build, was approaching from the right. Noiselessly, with a motion more of gliding and floating than walking, she moved across the cemetery to the grave which was the center of our observation. She moved round it as if to be certain of its identity, and for a moment stood directly facing us. In the greyness to which now my eyes had grown accustomed, I could easily see her face, and recognize its features.

She drew her hand across her mouth as if wiping it, and broke into a chuckle of such laughter as made my hair stir on my head. Then she leaped onto the grave, holding her hands high above her head, and inch by inch disappeared into the earth. Urcombe's hand was laid on my arm, in an injunction to keep still, but now he removed it.

"Come," he said.

With pick and shovel and rope we went to the grave. The earth was light and sandy, and soon after six struck we had delved down to the coffin lid. With his pick he loosened the earth round it, and, adjusting the rope through the handles by which it had been lowered, we tried to raise it. This was a long and laborious business, and the light had begun to herald day in the east before we had it out, and lying by the side of the grave. With his screwdriver he loosened the fastenings of the lid, and slid it aside, and standing there we looked on the face of Mrs. Amworth. The eyes, once closed in death, were open, the cheeks were flushed with color, the red, full-lipped mouth seemed to smile.

"One blow and it is all over," he said. "You need not look."

Even as he spoke he took up the pick again,

and, laying the point of it on her left breast, measured his distance. And though I knew what was coming I could not look away. . . .

He grasped the pick in both hands, raised it an inch or two for the taking of his aim, and then with full force brought it down on her breast. A fountain of blood, though she had been dead so long, spouted high in the air, falling with the thud of a heavy splash over the shroud, and simultaneously from those red lips came one long, appalling cry, swelling up like some hooting siren, and dying away again. With that, instantaneous as a lightning flash, came the touch of corruption on her face, the color of it faded to ash, the plump cheeks fell in, the mouth dropped.

"Thank God, that's over," said he, and without pause slipped the coffin lid back into its place.

Day was coming fast now, and, working like men possessed, we lowered the coffin into its place again, and shovelled the earth over it. . . . The birds were busy with their earliest pipings as we went back to Maxley.

# DOCTOR PORTHOS

# Basil Copper

Basil Copper (1924– ) was born in London and had a long career as a journalist and newspaper editor. His first work of fiction was published in 1938. Although a prolific author of supernatural and horror fiction, Copper did not publish work in this genre until 1964 when "The Spider" saw print in *The Fifth Pan Book of Horror Stories*.

Copper has written a great deal of mystery fiction, including eight short-story collections and a novel about Solar Pons, the Sherlock Holmes–like detective created by August Derleth, and more than fifty novels about a Los Angeles–based private detective, Mike Faraday, produced at the rate of at least two volumes a year between 1966 and 1988. This series has the predictable shortcomings to be expected of an author who never visited the United States.

It is in the horror field that Copper has had his greatest success, with such works as *Not After Nightfall* (1967), *From Evil's Pillow* (1973), *The Curse of the Fleers* (1976), *Necropolis* (1977), and *Here Be Daemons* (1978). Many of his stories have been adapted for radio and television productions. He wrote a highly praised television script based on M. R. James's classic horror story "Count Magnus." He has also written two significant works of nonfiction: *The Vampire: In Legend, Fact and Art* (1973) and *The Werewolf: In Legend, Fact and Art* (1977).

"Doctor Porthos" was first published in *The Midnight People*, edited by Peter Haining (London: Leslie Frewin, 1968).

# Doctor Porthos

## BASIL COPPER

### I

Nervous debility, the doctor says. And yet Angelina has never been ill in her life. Nervous debility! Something far more powerful is involved here; I am left wondering if I should not call in specialist advice. Yet we are so remote and Dr. Porthos is well spoken of by the local people. Why on earth did we ever come to this house? Angelina was perfectly well until then. It is extraordinary to think that two months can have wrought such a change in my wife.

In the town she was lively and vivacious; yet now I can hardly bear to look at her without profound emotion. Her cheeks are sunken and pale, her eyes dark and tired, her bloom quite gone at twenty-five. Could it be something in the air of the house? It seems barely possible. But in that case Dr. Porthos' ministrations should have proved effective. But so far all his skills have been powerless to produce any change for the better. If it had not been for the terms of my uncle's will we would never have come at all.

Friends may call it cupidity, the world may think what it chooses, but the plain truth is that I needed the money. My own health is far from ro-

bust and long hours in the family business—ours is an honoured and well-established counting house—had made it perfectly clear to me that I must seek some other mode of life. And yet I could not afford to retire; the terms of my uncle's will, as retailed to me by the family solicitor, afforded the perfect solution.

An annuity—a handsome annuity to put it bluntly—but with the proviso that my wife and I should reside in the old man's house for a period of not less than five years from the date the terms of the will became effective. I hestitated long; both my wife and I were fond of town life and my uncle's estate was in a remote area, where living for the country people was primitive and amenities few. As I had understood it from the solicitor, the house itself had not even the benefit of gas-lighting; in summer it was not so bad but the long months of winter would be melancholy indeed with only the glimmer of candles and the pale sheen of oil lamps to relieve the gloom of the lonely old place.

I debated with Angelina and then set off one week-end alone for a tour of the estate. I had cabled ahead and after a long and cold railway journey which itself occupied most of the day, I was met at my destination by a horse and chaise. The next part of my pilgrimage occupied nearly four hours and I was dismayed on seeing into what a wild and remote region my uncle had chosen to penetrate in order to select a dwelling.

The night was dark but the moon occasionally burst its veiling of cloud to reveal in feeble detail the contours of rock and hill and tree; the chaise jolted and lurched over an unmade road, which was deeply rutted by the wheels of the few vehicles which had torn up the surface in their passing over many months. My solicitor had wired an old friend, Dr. Porthos, to whose good offices I owed my mode of transport, and he had promised to greet me on arrival at the village nearest the estate.

Sure enough, he came out from under the great porch of the timbered hostelry as our carriage grated into the inn-yard. He was a tall, spare man, with square pince-nez which sat firmly on his thin nose; he wore a many-pleated cape like an ostler and the green top hat, worn rakishly over one eye gave him a somewhat dissipated look. He greeted me effusively but there was something about the man which did not endear him to me.

There was nothing that one could isolate. It was just his general manner; perhaps the coldness of his hand which struck my palm with the clamminess of a fish. Then too, his eyes had a most disconcerting way of looking over the tops of his glasses; they were a filmy grey and their piercing glance seemed to root one to the spot. To my dismay I learned that I was not yet at my destination. The estate was still some way off, said the doctor, and we would have to stay the night at the inn. My ill-temper at his remarks was soon dispelled by the roaring fire and the good food with which he plied me; there were few travellers at this time of year and we were the only ones taking dinner in the vast oak-panelled dining room.

The doctor had been my uncle's medical attendant and though it was many years since I had seen my relative I was curious to know what sort of person he had been.

"The Baron was a great man in these parts," said Porthos. His genial manner emboldened me to ask a question to which I had long been awaiting an answer.

"Of what did my uncle die?" I asked.

Firelight flickered through the gleaming redness of Dr. Porthos' wineglass and tinged his face with amber as he replied simply, "Of a lacking of richness in the blood. A fatal quality in his immediate line, I might say."

I pondered for a moment. "Why do you think he chose me as his heir?" I added.

Dr. Porthos' answer was straight and clear and given without hesitation.

"You were a different branch of the family," he said. "New blood, my dear sir. The Baron was most particular on that account. He wanted to carry on the great tradition."

He cut off any further questions by rising abruptly. "Those were the Baron's own words as he lay dying. And now we must retire as we still have a fair journey before us in the morning."

## II

Dr. Porthos' words come back to me in my present trouble. "Blood, new blood . . ." What if this be concerned with those dark legends the local people tell about the house? One hardly knows what to think in this atmosphere. My inspection of the house with Dr. Porthos confirmed my worst fears; sagging lintels, mouldering cornices, worm-eaten panelling. The only servitors a middle-aged couple, husband and wife, who have been caretakers here since the Baron's death; the local people sullen and unco-operative, so Porthos says. Certainly, the small hamlet a mile or so from the mansion had every door and window shut as we clattered past and not a soul was stirring. The house has a Gothic beauty, I suppose, viewed from a distance; it is of no great age, being largely rebuilt on the remains of an older pile destroyed by fire. The restorer—whether he be my uncle or some older resident I have not bothered to discover—had the fancy of adding turrets, a drawbridge with castellated towers, and a moated surround. Our footsteps echoed mournfully over this as we turned to inspect the grounds.

I was surprised to see marble statuary and worn

obelisks, all tumbled and awry, as though the uneasy dead were bursting from the soil, protruding over an ancient moss-grown wall adjoining the courtyard of the house.

Dr. Porthos smiled sardonically.

"The old family burial ground," he explained. "Your uncle is interred here. He said he likes to be near the house."

## III

Well, it is done; we came not two months since and then began the profound and melancholy change of which I have already spoken. Not just the atmosphere—though the very stones of the house seem steeped in evil whispers—but the surroundings, the dark, unmoving trees, even the furniture, seem to exude something inimical to life as we knew it; as it is still known to those fortunate enough to dwell in towns.

A poisonous mist rises from the moat at dusk; it seems to doubly emphasize our isolation. The presence of Angelina's own maid and a handyman who was in my father's employ before me, does little to dispel the ambiance of this place. Even their sturdy matter of factness seems affected by a miasma that wells from the pores of the building. It has become so manifest of late that I even welcome the daily visits of Dr. Porthos, despite the fact that I suspect him to be the author of our troubles.

They began a week after our arrival when Angelina failed to awake by my side as usual; I shook her to arouse her and my screams must have awakened the maid. I think I fainted then and came to myself in the great morning room; the bed had been awash with blood, which stained the sheets and pillows around my dear wife's head; Porthos' curious grey eyes had a steely look in them which I had never seen before. He administered a powerful medicine and had then turned to attend to me.

Whatever had attacked Angelina had teeth like the sharpest canine, Porthos said; he had found two distinct punctures in Angelina's throat, sufficient to account for the quantities of blood. Indeed, there had been so much of it that my own

hands and linen were stained with it where I had touched her; I think it was this which had made me cry so violently. Porthos had announced that he would sit up by the patient that night.

Angelina was still asleep, as I discovered when I tiptoed in later. Porthos had administered a sleeping draught and had advised me to take the same, to settle my nerves, but I declined. I said I would wait up with him. The doctor had some theory about rats or other nocturnal creatures and sat long in the library looking through some of the Baron's old books on natural history. The man's attitude puzzles me; what sort of creature would attack Angelina in her own bedroom? Looking at Porthos' strange eyes, my old fears are beginning to return, bringing with them new ones.

## IV

There have been three more attacks, extending over a fortnight. My darling grows visibly weaker, though Porthos had been to the nearest town for more powerful drugs and other remedies. I am in purgatory; I have not known such dark hours in my life until now. Yet Angelina herself insists that we should stay to see this grotesque nightmare through. The first evening of our vigil both Porthos and I slept; and in the morning the result was as the night before. Considerable emissions of blood and the bandage covering the wound had been removed to allow the creature access to the punctures. I hardly dare conjecture what manner of beast could have done this.

I was quite worn out and on the evening of the next day I agreed to Porthos' suggestion that I should take a sleeping draught. Nothing happened for several nights and Angelina began to recover; then the terror struck again. And so it will go on, my reeling senses tell me. I daren't trust Porthos and on the other hand I cannot accuse him before the members of my household. We are isolated here and any mistake I make might be fatal.

On the last occasion I almost had him. I woke at dawn and found Porthos stretched on the bed, his long, dark form quivering, his hands at Angelina's throat. I struck at him, for I did not know who it was, being half asleep, and he turned, his grey eyes glowing in the dim room. He had a hypodermic syringe half full of blood in his hand. I am afraid I dashed it to the floor and shattered it beneath my heel.

In my own heart I am convinced I have caught this creature which has been plaguing us, but how to prove it? Dr. Porthos is staying in the house now; I dare not sleep and continually refuse the potions he urgently presses upon me. How long before he destroys me as well as Angelina? Was man ever in such an appalling situation since the world began?

I sit and watch Porthos, who stares at me sideways with those curious eyes, his inexpressive face seeming to hint that he can afford to watch and wait and that his time is coming; my pale wife, in her few intervals of consciousness sits and fearfully watches both of us. Yet I cannot even confide in her for she would think me mad. I try to calm my racing brain. Sometimes I think I shall go insane altogether, the nights are so long. God help me.

## V

It is over. The crisis has come and gone. I have laid the mad demon which has us in thrall. I caught him at it. Porthos writhed as I got my hands at his throat. I would have killed him at his foul work, the syringe glinted in his hand. Now he has slipped aside, eluded me for the moment. My cries brought in the servants who have my express instructions to hunt him down. He shall not escape me this time. I pace the corridors of this worm-eaten mansion and when I have cornered him I shall destroy him. Angelina shall live! And my hands will perform the healing work of his destruction . . . But now I must rest. Already it is dawn again. I will sit in this chair by the pillar, where I can watch the hall. I sleep.

## VI

Later. I awake to pain and cold. I am lying on earth. Something slippery trickles over my hand. I open my eyes. I draw my hand across my mouth. It comes away scarlet. I can see more clearly now. Angelina is here too. She looks terrified but somehow sad and composed. She is holding the arm of Dr. Porthos.

He is poised above me, his face looking satanic in the dim light of the crypt beneath the house. He whirls a mallet while shriek after shriek disturbs the silence of this place. Dear Christ, the stake is against MY BREAST!

# FOR THE BLOOD IS THE LIFE

# F. Marion Crawford

Francis Marion Crawford (1854–1909) was born in Bagni di Lucca, Italy, the son of American parents and the nephew of the famous poet Julia Ward Howe. He studied at Cambridge, Heidelberg, and Rome. When he was twenty-five, he went to India to study Sanskrit and continued its study at Harvard. His first novel, *Mr. Isaacs* (1882), was an immediately popular sketch of Anglo-Indian life. He returned to Italy the following year, making it his permanent residence.

One of the most commercially successful authors of his day, Crawford wrote more than forty books, mostly in the romantic tradition, frequently using supernatural and mystical themes, notably in his first novel, *Khaled: A Tale of Arabia* (1891), and the horror tale *The Witch of Prague* (1891). *Corleone* (1897) was the first novel to feature the Mafia and also the first to use the plot device of a priest unable to testify about criminal activity because of the strictures of confession. Mario Puzo used the now-familiar Corleone name for the primary family in *The Godfather* (1969). In spite of their once-great popularity, Crawford's novels are seldom read today, his name kept alive only through a handful of first-rate short stories.

"For the Blood Is the Life" was first published in the December 16, 1905, issue of *Collier's* magazine; it was first collected in book form in *Wandering Ghosts* (New York: Macmillan, 1911), which was published two weeks earlier in London as *Uncanny Tales* (Unwin, 1911).

# For the Blood Is the Life

## F. MARION CRAWFORD

he had dined at sunset on the broad roof of the old tower, because it was cooler there during the great heat of summer. Besides, the little kitchen was built at one corner of the great square platform, which made it more convenient than if the dishes had to be carried down the steep stone steps, broken in places and everywhere worn with age. The tower was one of those built all down the west coast of Calabria by the Emperor Charles V early in the sixteenth century, to keep off the Barbary pirates, when the unbelievers were allied with Francis I against the Emperor and the Church. They have gone to ruin, a few still stand intact, and mine is one of the largest. How it came into my possession ten years ago, and why I spend a part of each year in it, are matters which do not concern this tale. The tower stands in one of the loneliest spots in Southern Italy, at the extremity of a curving rocky promontory, which forms a small but safe natural harbor at the southern extremity of the Gulf of Policastro, and just north of Cape Scalea, the birthplace of Judas Iscariot, according to the old local legend. The tower stands alone on this hooked spur of the rock, and there is not a house to be seen within three miles of it. When I go there I take a couple of sailors, one

of whom is a fair cook, and when I am away it is in charge of a gnome-like little being who was once a miner and who attached himself to me long ago.

My friend, who sometimes visits me in my summer solitude, is an artist by profession, a Scandinavian by birth, and a cosmopolitan by force of circumstances. We had dined at sunset; the sunset glow had reddened and faded again, and the evening purple steeped the vast chain of the mountains that embrace the deep gulf to eastward and rear themselves higher and higher toward the south. It was hot, and we sat at the landward corner of the platform, waiting for the night breeze to come down from the lower hills. The color sank out of the air, there was a little interval of deep-grey twilight, and a lamp sent a yellow streak from the open door of the kitchen, where the men were getting their supper.

Then the moon rose suddenly above crest of the promontory, flooding the platform and lighting up every little spur of rock and knoll of grass below us, down to the edge of the motionless water. My friend lighted his pipe and sat looking at a spot on the hillside. I knew that he was looking at it, and for a long time past I had wondered whether he would ever see anything there that would fix his attention. I knew that spot well. It was clear that he was interested at last, though it was a long time before he spoke. Like most painters, he trusts to his own eyesight, as a lion trusts his strength and a stag his speed, and he is always disturbed when he cannot reconcile what he sees with what he believes that he ought to see.

"It's strange," he said. "Do you see that little mound just on this side of the boulder?"

"Yes," I said, and I guessed what was coming.

"It looks like a grave," observed Holger.

"Very true. It does look like a grave."

"Yes," continued my friend, his eyes still fixed on the spot. "But the strange thing is that I see the body lying on the top of it. Of course," continued Holger, turning his head on one side as artists do, "it must be an effect of light. In the first place, it is not a grave at all. Secondly, if it were, the body would be inside and not outside. Therefore, it's an effect of the moonlight. Don't you see it?"

"Perfectly; I always see it on moonlit nights."

"It doesn't seem to interest you much," said Holger.

"On the contrary, it does interest me, though I am used to it. You're not so far wrong, either. The mound is really a grave."

"Nonsense!" cried Holger, incredulously. "I suppose you'll tell me what I see lying on it is really a corpse!"

"No," I answered, "it's not. I know, because I have taken the trouble to go down and see."

"Then what is it?" asked Holger.

"It's nothing."

"You mean that it's an effect of light, I suppose?"

"Perhaps it is. But the inexplicable part of the matter is that it makes no difference whether the moon is rising or setting, or waxing or waning. If there's any moonlight at all, from east or west or overhead, so long as it shines on the grave you can see the outline of the body on top."

Holger stirred up his pipe with the point of his knife, and then used his finger for a stopper. When the tobacco burned well he rose from his chair.

"If you don't mind," he said, "I'll go down and take a look at it."

He left me, crossed the roof, and disappeared down the dark steps. I did not move, but sat looking down until he came out of the tower below. I heard him humming an old Danish song as he crossed the open space in the bright moonlight, going straight to the mysterious mound. When he was ten paces from it, Holger stopped short, made two steps forward, and then three or four backward, and then stopped again. I know what that meant. He had reached the spot where the Thing ceased to be visible—where, as he would have said, the effect of light changed.

Then he went on till he reached the mound and stood upon it. I could see the Thing still, but it was no longer lying down; it was on its knees now, winding its white arms round Holger's body and looking up into his face. A cool breeze stirred my hair at that moment, as the night wind began to come down from the hills, but it felt like a breath from another world.

The Thing seemed to be trying to climb to its feet, helping itself up by Holger's body while he stood upright, quite unconscious of it and apparently looking toward the tower, which is very picturesque when the moonlight falls upon it on that side.

"Come along!" I shouted. "Don't stay there all night!"

It seemed to me that he moved reluctantly as he stepped from the mound, or else with difficulty. That was it. The Thing's arms were still round his waist, but its feet could not leave the grave. As he came slowly forward it was drawn and lengthened like a wreath of mist, thin and white, till I saw distinctly that Holger shook himself, as a man does who feels a chill. At the same instant a little wail of pain came to me on the breeze—it might have been the cry of the small owl that lives among the rocks—and the misty presence floated swiftly back from Holger's advancing figure and lay once more at its length upon the mound.

Again I felt the cool breeze in my hair, and this time an icy thrill of dread ran down my spine. I remembered very well that I had once gone down there alone in the moonlight; that presently, being near, I had seen nothing; that, like Holger, I had gone and had stood upon the mound; and I remembered how, when I came back, sure that there was nothing there, I had felt the sudden conviction that there was something after all if I would only look behind me. I remembered the strong temptation to look back, a temptation I had resisted as unworthy of a man of sense, until, to get rid of it, I had shaken myself just as Holger did.

And now I knew that those white, misty arms had been round me too; I knew it in a flash, and I shuddered as I remembered that I had heard the night owl then too. But it had not been the night owl. It was the cry of the Thing.

I refilled my pipe and poured out a cup of strong southern wine; in less than a minute Holger was seated beside me again.

"Of course there's nothing there," he said, "but it's creepy, all the same. Do you know, when I was coming back I was so sure that there was something behind me that I wanted to turn round and look? It was an effort not to."

He laughed a little, knocked the ashes out of his pipe, and poured himself out some wine. For a while neither of us spoke, and the moon rose higher, and we both looked at the Thing that lay on the mound.

"You might make a story about that," said Holger after a long time.

"There is one," I answered. "If you're not sleepy, I'll tell it to you."

"Go ahead," said Holger, who liked stories.

Old Alario was dying up there in the village behind the hill. You remember him, I have no doubt. They say that he made his money by selling sham jewelry in South America, and escaped with his gains when he was found out. Like all those fellows, if they bring anything back with them, he at once set to work to enlarge his house, and as there are no masons here, he sent all the way to Paola for two workmen. They were a rough-looking pair of scoundrels—a Neapolitan who had lost one eye and a Sicilian with an old scar half an inch deep across his left cheek. I often saw them, for on Sundays they used to come down here and fish off the rocks. When Alario caught the fever

that killed him, the masons were still at work. As he had agreed that part of their pay should be their board and lodging, he made them sleep in the house. His wife was dead, and he had an only son called Angelo, who was a much better sort than himself. Angelo was to marry the daughter of the richest man in the village, and, strange to say, though the marriage was arranged by their parents, the young people were said to be in love with each other.

For that matter, the whole village was in love with Angelo, and among the rest a wild, goodlooking creature called Cristina, who was more like a gypsy than any girl I ever saw about here. She had very red lips and very black eyes, she was built like a greyhound, and had the tongue of the devil. But Angelo did not care a straw for her. He was rather a simpleminded fellow, quite different from his old scoundrel of a father, and under what I should call normal circumstances I really believe that he would never have looked at any girl except the nice plump little creature, with a fat dowry, whom his father meant him to marry. But things turned up which were neither normal nor natural.

On the other hand, a very handsome young shepherd from the hills above Maratea was in love with Cristina, who seems to have been quite indifferent to him. Cristina had no regular means of subsistence, but she was a good girl and willing to do any work or go on errands to any distance for the sake of a loaf of bread or a mess of beans, and permission to sleep under cover. She was especially glad when she could get something to do about the house of Angelo's father. There is no doctor in the village, and when the neighbors saw that old Alario was dying they sent Cristina to Scalea to fetch one. That was late in the afternoon, and if they had waited so long, it was because the dying miser refused to allow any such extravagance while he was able to speak. But while Cristina was gone matters grew rapidly worse, the priest was brought to the bedside, and when he had done what he could he gave it as his opinion to the bystanders that the old man was dead, and left the house.

You know these people. They have a physical

horror of death. Until the priest spoke, the room had been full of people. The words were hardly out of his mouth before it was empty. It was night now. They hurried down the dark steps and out into the street.

Angelo, as I have said, was away, Cristina had not come back—the simple woman-servant who had nursed the sick man fled with the rest, and the body was left alone in the flickering light of the earthen oil lamp.

Five minutes later two men looked in cautiously and crept forward toward the bed. They were the one-eyed Neapolitan mason and his Sicilian companion. They knew what they wanted. In a moment they had dragged from under the bed a small but heavy iron-bound box, and long before any one thought of coming back to the dead man they had left the house and the village under cover of the darkness. It was easy enough, for Alario's house is the last toward the gorge which leads down here, and the thieves merely went out by the back door, got over the stone wall, and had nothing to risk after that except the possibility of meeting some belated countryman, which was very small indeed, since few of the people use that path. They had a mattock and shovel, and they made their way here without accident.

I am telling you this story as it must have happened, for, of course, there were no witnesses to this part of it. The men brought the box down by the gorge, intending to bury it until they should be able to come back and take it away in a boat. They must have been clever enough to guess that some of the money would be in paper notes, for they would otherwise have buried it on the beach in the wet sand, where it would have been much safer. But the paper would have rotted if they had been obliged to leave it there long, so they dug their hole down there, close to that boulder. Yes, just where the mound is now.

Cristina did not find the doctor in Scalea, for he had been sent for from a place up the valley, halfway to San Domenico. If she had found him, he would have come on his mule by the upper road, which is smoother but much longer. But Cristina took the short cut by the rocks, which

passes about fifty feet above the mound, and goes round that corner. The men were digging when she passed, and she heard them at work. It would not have been like her to go by without finding out what the noise was, for she was never afraid of anything in her life, and, besides, the fishermen sometimes come ashore here at night to get a stone for an anchor or to gather sticks to make a little fire. The night was dark, and Cristina probably came close to the two men before she could see what they were doing. She knew them, of course, and they knew her, and understood instantly that they were in her power. There was only one thing to be done for their safety, and they did it. They knocked her on the head, they dug the hole deep, and they buried her quickly with the iron-bound chest. They must have understood that their only chance of escaping suspicion lay in getting back to the village before their absence was noticed, for they returned immediately, and were found half an hour later gossiping quietly with the man who was making Alario's coffin. He was a crony of theirs, and had been working at the repairs in the old man's house. So far as I have been able to make out, the only persons who were supposed to know where Alario kept his treasure were Angelo and the one woman-servant I have mentioned. Angelo was away; it was the woman who discovered the theft.

It is easy enough to understand why no one else knew where the money was. The old man kept his door locked and the key in his pocket when he was out, and did not let the woman enter to clean the place unless he was there himself. The whole village knew that he had money somewhere, however, and the masons had probably discovered the whereabouts of the chest by climbing in at the window in his absence. If the old man had not been delirious until he lost consciousness, he would have been in frightful agony of mind for his riches. The faithful woman-servant forgot their existence only for a few moments when she fled with the rest, overcome by the horror of death. Twenty minutes had not passed before she returned with the two hideous old hags who are always called in to prepare the dead for burial. Even then she had not at first the courage to go near the bed with them, but she made a pretense of dropping something, went down on her knees as if to find it, and looked under the bedstead. The walls of the room were newly whitewashed down to the floor, and she saw at a glance that the chest was gone. It had been there in the afternoon; it had therefore been stolen in the short interval since she had left the room.

There are no carabineers stationed in the village; there is not so much as a municipal watchman, for there is no municipality. There never was such a place, I believe. Scalea is supposed to look after it in some mysterious way, and it takes a couple of hours to get anybody from there. As the old woman had lived in the village all her life, it did not even occur to her to apply to any civil authority for help. She simply set up a howl and ran through the village in the dark, screaming out that her dead master's house had been robbed. Many of the people looked out, but at first no one seemed inclined to help her. Most of them, judging her by themselves, whispered to each other that she had probably stolen the money herself. The first man to move was the father of the girl whom Angelo was to marry; having collected his household, all of whom felt a personal interest in the wealth which was to have come into the family, he declared it to be his opinion that the chest had been stolen by the two journeyman masons who lodged in the house. He headed a search for them, which naturally began in Alario's house and ended in the carpenter's workshop, where the thieves were found discussing a measure of wine with the carpenter over the half-finished coffin, by the light of one earthen lamp filled with oil and tallow. The search party at once accused the delinquents of the crime, and threatened to lock them up in the cellar till the carabineers could be fetched from Scalea. The two men looked at each other for one moment, and then without the slightest hesitation they put out the single light, seized the unfinished coffin between them, and using it as a sort of battering ram, dashed upon their assailants in the dark. In a few moments they were beyond pursuit.

That is the end of the first part of the story. The treasure had disappeared, and as no trace of it could be found the people naturally supposed that the thieves had succeeded in carrying it off. The old man was buried, and when Angelo came back at last he had to borrow money to pay for the miserable funeral, and had some difficulty in doing so. He hardly needed to be told that in losing his inheritance he had lost his bride. In this part of the world marriages are made on strictly business principles, and if the promised cash is not forthcoming on the appointed day the bride or the bridegroom whose parents have failed to produce it may as well take themselves off, for there will be no wedding. Poor Angelo knew that well enough. His father had been possessed of hardly any land, and now that the hard cash which he had brought from South America was gone, there was nothing left but debts for the building materials that were to have been used for enlarging and improving the old house. Angelo was beggared, and the nice plump little creature who was to have been his turned up her nose at him in the most approved fashion. As for Cristina, it was several days before she was missed, for no one remembered that she had been sent to Scalea for the doctor, who had never come. She often disappeared in the same way for days together, when she could find a little work here and there at the distant farms among the hills. But when she did not come back at all, people began to wonder, and at last made up their minds that she had connived with the masons and had escaped with them.

*I paused and emptied my glass.*

*"That sort of thing could not happen anywhere else," observed Holger, filling his everlasting pipe again. "It is wonderful what a natural charm there is about murder and sudden death in a romantic country like this. Deeds that would be simply brutal and disgusting anywhere else become dramatic and mysterious because this is Italy and we are living in a genuine tower of Charles V built against genuine Barbary pirates."*

*"There's something in that," I admitted. Holger is the most romantic man in the world inside of him-*

self, but he always thinks it necessary to explain why he feels anything.

"I suppose they found the poor girl's body with the box," he said presently.

"As it seems to interest you," I answered, "I'll tell you the rest of the story."

The moon had risen high by this time; the outline of the Thing on the mound was clearer to our eyes than before.

The village very soon settled down to its small, dull life. No one missed old Alario, who had been away so much on his voyages to South America that he had never been a familiar figure in his native place. Angelo lived in the half-finished house, and because he had no money to pay the old woman-servant she would not stay with him, but once in a long time she would come and wash a shirt for him for old acquaintance's sake. Besides the house, he had inherited a small patch of ground at some distance from the village; he tried to cultivate it, but he had no heart in the work, for he knew he could never pay the taxes on it and on the house, which would certainly be confiscated by the Government, or seized for the debt of the building material, which the man who had supplied it refused to take back.

Angelo was very unhappy. So long as his father had been alive and rich, every girl in the village had been in love with him; but that was all changed now. It had been pleasant to be admired and courted, and invited to drink wine by fathers who had girls to marry. It was hard to be stared at coldly, and sometimes laughed at because he had been robbed of his inheritance. He cooked his miserable meals for himself, and from being sad became melancholy and morose.

At twilight, when the day's work was done, instead of hanging about in the open space before the church with young fellows of his own age, he took to wandering in lonely places on the outskirts of the village till it was quite dark. Then he slunk home and went to bed to save the expense of a light. But in those lonely twilight hours he began to have strange waking dreams. He was not always alone, for often when he sat on the stump of a tree, where the narrow path turns down the gorge, he was sure that a woman came up noiselessly over the rough stones, as if her feet were bare; and she stood under a clump of chestnut trees only half a dozen yards down the path, and beckoned to him without speaking. Though she was in the shadow he knew that her lips were red, and that when they parted a little and smiled at him she showed two small sharp teeth. He knew this at first rather than saw it, and he knew that it was Cristina, and that she was dead. Yet he was not afraid; he only wondered whether it was a dream, for he thought that if he had been awake he should have been frightened.

Besides, the dead woman had red lips, and that could only happen in a dream. Whenever he went near the gorge after sunset she was already there waiting for him, or else she very soon appeared, and he began to be sure that she came a little nearer to him every day. At first he had only been sure of her blood-red mouth, but now each feature grew distinct, and the pale face looked at him with deep and hungry eyes.

It was the eyes that grew dim. Little by little he came to know that some day the dream would not end when he turned away to go home, but would lead him down the gorge out of which the vision rose. She was nearer now when she beckoned to him. Her cheeks were not livid like those of the dead, but pale with starvation, with the furious and unappeased physical hunger of her eyes that devoured him. They feasted on his soul and cast a spell over him, and at last they were close to his own and held him. He could not tell whether her breath was as hot as fire or as cold as ice; he could not tell whether her red lips burned his or froze them, or whether her five fingers on his wrists seared scorching scars or bit his flesh like frost; he could not tell whether he was awake or asleep, whether she was alive or dead, but he knew that she loved him, she alone of all creatures, earthly or unearthly, and her spell had power over him.

When the moon rose high that night the shadow of that Thing was not alone down there upon the mound.

Angelo awoke in the cool dawn, drenched with

dew and chilled through flesh, and blood, and bone. He opened his eyes to the faint grey light, and saw the stars still shining overhead. He was very weak, and his heart was beating so slowly that he was almost like a man fainting. Slowly he turned his head on the mound, as on a pillow, but the other face was not there. Fear seized him suddenly, a fear unspeakable and unknown; he sprang to his feet and fled up the gorge, and he never looked behind him until he reached the door of the house on the outskirts of the village. Drearily he went to his work that day, and wearily the hours dragged themselves after the sun, till at last it touched the sea and sank, and the great sharp hills above Maratea turned purple against the dove-colored eastern sky.

Angelo shouldered his heavy hoe and left the field. He felt less tired now than in the morning when he had begun to work, but he promised himself that he would go home without lingering by the gorge, and eat the best supper he could get himself, and sleep all night in his bed like a Christian man. Not again would he be tempted down the narrow way by a shadow with red lips and icy breath; not again would he dream that dream of terror and delight. He was near the village now; it was half an hour since the sun had set, and the cracked church bell sent little discordant echoes across the rocks and ravines to tell all good people that the day was done. Angelo stood still a moment where the path forked, where it led toward the village on the left, and down to the gorge on the right, where a clump of chestnut trees overhung the narrow way. He stood still a minute, lifting his battered hat from his head and gazing at the fast-fading sea westward, and his lips moved as he silently repeated the familiar evening prayer. His lips moved, but the words that followed them in his brain lost their meaning and turned into others and ended in a name that he spoke aloud— Cristina! With the name, the tension of his will relaxed suddenly, reality went out, and the dream took him again, and bore him on swiftly and surely like a man walking in his sleep, down, down, by the steep path in the gathering darkness. And as she glided beside him, Cristina whispered strange,

sweet things in his ear, which somehow, if he had been awake, he knew that he could not quite have understood; but now they were the most wonderful words he had ever heard in his life. And she kissed him also, but not upon his mouth. He felt her sharp kisses upon his white throat, and he knew that her lips were red. So the wild dream sped on through twilight and darkness and moonrise, and all the glory of the summer's night. But in the chilly dawn he lay as one half dead upon the mound down there, recalling and not recalling, drained of his blood, yet strangely longing to give those red lips more. Then came the fear, the awful nameless panic, the mortal horror that guards the confines of the world we see not, neither know of as we know of other things, but which we feel when its icy chill freezes our bones and stirs our hair with the touch of a ghostly hand. Once more Angelo sprang from the mound and fled up the gorge in the breaking day, but his step was less sure this time, and he panted for breath as he ran; and when he came to the bright spring of water that rises halfway up the hillside, he dropped upon his knees and hands and plunged his whole face in and drank as he had never drunk before—for it was the thirst of the wounded man who has lain bleeding all night long upon the battle-field.

She had him fast now, and he could not escape her, but would come to her every evening at dusk until she had drained him of his last drop of blood. It was in vain that when the day was done he tried to take another turning and to go home by a path that did not lead near the gorge. It was in vain that he made promises to himself each morning at dawn when he climbed the lonely way up from the shore to the village. It was all in vain, for when the sun sank burning into the sea, and the coolness of the evening stole out as from a hiding-place to delight the weary world, his feet turned toward the old way, and she was waiting for him in the shadow under the chestnut trees; and then all happened as before and she fell to kissing his white throat even as she flitted lightly down the way, winding one arm about him. And as his blood failed, she grew more hungry and more thirsty every day, and every day when he awoke in the early dawn it was harder to rouse himself to the effort of climbing the steep path to the village; and when he went to his work his feet dragged painfully, and there was hardly strength in his arms to wield the heavy hoe. He scarcely spoke to anyone now but the people said he was "consuming himself" for the love of the girl he was to have married when he lost his inheritance; and they laughed heartily at the thought, for this is not a very romantic country. At this time, Antonio, the man who stays here to look after the tower, returned from a visit to his people, who live near Salerno. He had been away all the time since before Alario's death and knew nothing of what had happened. He has told me that he came back late in the afternoon and shut himself up in the tower to eat and sleep, for he was very tired. It was past midnight when he awoke, and when he looked out the waning moon was rising over the shoulder of the hill. He looked out toward the mound, and he saw something, and he did not sleep again that night. When he went out again in the morning it was broad daylight, and there was nothing to be seen on the mound but loose stones and driven sand. Yet he did not go very near it; he went straight up the path to the village and directly to the house of the old priest.

"I have seen an evil thing this night," he said. "I have seen how the dead drink the blood of the living. And the blood is the life."

"Tell me what you have seen," said the priest in reply.

Antonio told him everything he had seen.

"You must bring your book and your holy water tonight," he added. "I will be here before sunset to go down with you, and if it pleases your reverence to sup with me while we wait, I will make ready."

"I will come," the priest answered, "for I have read in old books of these strange beings which are neither quick nor dead, and which lie ever fresh in their graves, stealing out in the dusk to taste life and blood."

Antonio cannot read, but he was glad to see that the priest understood the business; for, of course, the books must have instructed him as to the best means of quieting the half-living Thing forever.

So Antonio went away to his work, which consists largely in sitting on the shady side of the tower, when he is not perched upon a rock with a fishing-line catching nothing. But on that day he went twice to look at the mound in the bright sunlight, and he searched round and round it for some hole through which the being might get in and out; but he found none. When the sun began to sink and the air was cooler in the shadows, he went up to fetch the old priest, carrying a little wicker basket with him; and in this they placed a bottle of holy water, and the basin, and sprinkler, and the stole which the priest would need; and they came down and waited in the door of the tower till it should be dark. But while the light still lingered very grey and faint, they saw something moving, just there, two figures, a man's that walked, and a woman's that flitted beside him, and while her head lay on his shoulder she kissed his throat. The priest has told me that, too, and that his teeth chattered and he grasped Antonio's arm. The vision passed and disappeared into the shadow. Then Antonio got the leathern flask of strong liquor, which he kept for great occasions, and poured such a draught as made the old man feel almost young again; and he got the lantern, and his pick and shovel, and gave the priest his stole to put on and the holy water to carry, and they went out together toward the spot where the work was to be done. Antonio says that in spite of the rum his own knees shook together, and the priest stumbled over his Latin. For when they were yet a few yards from the mound the flickering light of the lantern fell upon Angelo's white face, unconscious as if in sleep, and on his upturned throat, over which a very thin red line of blood trickled down into his collar; and the flickering light of the lantern played upon another face that looked up from the feast— upon two deep, dead eyes that saw in spite of death—upon parted lips redder than life itself— upon two gleaming teeth on which glistened a rosy drop. Then the priest, good old man, shut his eyes tight and showered holy water before him, and his cracked voice rose almost to a scream; and then Antonio, who is no coward after all, raised his pick in one hand and the lantern in the other, as he sprang forward, not knowing what the end should be; and then he swears that he heard a woman's cry, and the Thing was gone, and Angelo lay alone on the mound unconscious, with the red line on his throat and the beads of deadly sweat on his cold forehead. They lifted him, half-dead as he was, and laid him on the ground close by; then Antonio went to work, and the priest helped him, though he was old and could not do much; and they dug deep, and at last Antonio, standing in the grave, stooped down with his lantern to see what he might see.

His hair used to be dark brown, with grizzled streaks about the temples; in less than a month from that day he was as grey as a badger. He was a miner when he was young, and most of these fellows have seen ugly sights now and then, when accidents have happened, but he had never seen what he saw that night—that Thing that will abide neither above ground nor in the grave. Antonio had brought something with him which the priest had not noticed. He had made it that afternoon— a sharp stake shaped from a piece of tough old driftwood. He had it with him now, and he had his heavy pick, and he had taken the lantern down into the grave. I don't think any power on earth could make him speak of what happened then, and the old priest was too frightened to look in. He says he heard Antonio breathing like a wild beast, and moving as if he were fighting with something almost as strong as himself; and he heard an evil sound also, with blows, as of something violently driven through flesh and bone; and then the most awful sound of all—a woman's shriek, the unearthly scream of a woman neither dead nor alive, but buried deep for many days. And he, the poor old priest, could only rock himself as he knelt there in the sand, crying aloud his prayers and exorcisms to drown these dreadful sounds. Then suddenly a small iron-bound chest was thrown up and rolled over against the old man's knee, and in a moment more Antonio was beside him, his face as white as tallow in the flickering light of the lantern, shovelling the sand and pebbles into the grave with furious haste, and looking over the edge till the pit was half full; and the priest said that there was much fresh blood on Antonio's hands and on his clothes.

*I had come to the end of my story. Holger finished his wine and leaned back in his chair.*

"So Angelo got his own again," he said. "Did he marry the prim and plump young person to whom he had been betrothed?"

"No; he had been badly frightened. He went to South America, and has not been heard of since."

"And that poor thing's body is there still, I suppose," said Holger. "Is it quite dead yet, I wonder?"

*I wonder, too. But whether it be dead or alive, I should hardly care to see it, even in broad daylight. Antonio is as grey as a badger, and he has never been quite the same man since that night.*

## COUNT MAGNUS

# M. R. James

Montague Rhodes James (1862–1936) was born in Kent and became provost of King's College, Cambridge (1905–18), and Eton College (1918–36), gaining a worldwide reputation as a scholar. It is for his supernatural and macabre fiction that he is most remembered today, notably the ghost stories that he wrote and read to friends (distinguishing himself as a fine actor) as Christmas Eve entertainments. The BBC took the idea and filmed famed horror actor Christopher Lee reading the stories in a candlelit room in King's College.

James's atmospheric ghost stories have a classic structure requiring certain elements: an old abbey, cathedral, university, or estate, usually in a remote village or seaside town; a quiet and naive gentleman-scholar; an old book or other antiquarian object that calls down the wrath of a supernatural creature, usually from beyond the grave. For James, the ghost cannot be friendly or playful; it must be evil. He once wrote, "The ghost must be malevolent or odious: amiable and helpful apparitions are all very well in fairy tales or in local legends, but I have no use for them in a fictitious ghost story."

James's famous story "Casting the Runes" was filmed by Jacques Tourneur as *Night of the Demon* (U.S. title *Curse of the Demon*) in 1957, a high point of British horror movies.

"Count Magnus" was first published in *Ghost Stories of an Antiquary* (London: Edward Arnold, 1904).

# Count Magnus

## M. R. JAMES

By what means the papers out of which I have made a connected story came into my hands is the last point which the reader will learn from these pages. But it is necessary to prefix to my extracts from them a statement of the form in which I possess them.

They consist, then, partly of a series of collections for a book of travels, such a volume as was a common product of the forties and fifties. Horace Marryat's *Journal of a Residence in Jutland and the Danish Isles* is a fair specimen of the class to which I allude. These books usually treated of some unfamiliar district on the Continent. They were illustrated with woodcuts or steel plates. They gave details of hotel accommodations, and of means of communication, such as we now expect to find in any well-regulated guidebook, and they dealt largely in reported conversations with intelligent foreigners, racy inn keepers, and garrulous peasants. In a word, they were chatty.

Begun with the idea of furnishing material for such a book, my papers as they progressed assumed the character of a record of one single personal experience, and this record was continued up to the very eve, almost, of its termination.

The writer was a Mr. Wraxall. For my knowledge of him I have to depend entirely on the evidence his writings afford, and from these I deduce that he was a man past middle age, possessed of some private means, and very much alone in the world. He had, it seems no settled abode in England, but was a denizen of hotels and boarding houses. It is probable that he entertained the idea of settling down at some future time which never came; and I think it also likely that the Pantechnicon fire in the early seventies must have destroyed a great deal that would have thrown light on his antecedents, for he refers once or twice to property of his that was warehoused at that establishment.

It is further apparent that Mr. Wraxall had published a book, and that it treated of a holiday he had once taken in Brittany. More than this I cannot say about his work, because a diligent search in bibliographical works has convinced me that it must have appeared either anonymously or under a pseudonym.

As to his character, it is not difficult to form some superficial opinion. He must have been an intelligent and cultivated man. It seems that he was near being a Fellow of his college at Oxford—Brasenose, as I judge from the Calendar. His besetting fault was pretty clearly that of over-inquisitiveness, possibly a good fault in a traveler, certainly a fault for which this traveler paid dearly enough in the end.

On what proved to be his last expedition, he was plotting another book. Scandinavia, a region not widely known to Englishmen forty years ago, had struck him as an interesting field. He must have lighted on some old books of Swedish history or memoirs, and the idea had struck him that there was room for a book descriptive of travel in Sweden, interspersed with episodes from the history of some of the great Swedish families. He procured letters of introduction, therefore, to some persons of quality in Sweden, and set out thither in the early summer of 1863.

Of his travels in the north there is no need to speak, nor of his residence of some weeks in Stockholm. I need only mention that some savant resident there put him on the track of an important collection of family papers belonging to the proprietors of an ancient manor house in Vestergothland, and obtained for him permission to examine them.

The manor house, or herrgård, in question is to be called Råbäck (pronounced something like Roebeck), though that is not its name. It is one of the best buildings of its kind in all the country, and the picture of it in Dahlenberg's *Suecia antique et moderna*, engraved in 1694, shows it very much as the tourist may see it today. It was built soon after 1600, and is, roughly speaking, very much like an English house of that period in respect of material—red brick with stone facings—and style. The man who built it was a scion of the great house of De la Gardie, and his descendants possess it still. De la Gardie is the name by which I will designate them when mention of them becomes necessary.

They received Mr. Wraxall with great kindness and courtesy, and pressed him to stay in the house as long as his researches lasted. But, preferring to be independent, and mistrusting his powers of conversing in Swedish, he settled himself at the village inn, which turned out quite sufficiently comfortable, at any rate during the summer months. This arrangement would entail a short walk daily to and from the manor house of something under a mile. The house itself stood in a park, and was protected—we should say grown up—with large old timber. Near it you found the walled garden, and then entered a close wood fringing one of the small lakes with which the whole country is pitted. Then came the wall of the demesne and you climbed a steep knoll—a knob of rock lightly covered with soil—and on the top of this stood the church, fenced in with tall dark trees. It was a curious building to English eyes. The nave and aisles were low, and filled with pews and galleries. In the western gallery stood the handsome old organ, gaily painted, and with silver pipes. The ceiling was flat, and had been adorned by a seventeenth-century artist with a strange and hideous "Last Judgment," full of lurid flames, falling cities, burning ships, crying souls, and brown and smiling demons. Handsome brass coronae hung from the roof; the pulpit was like a doll's house, covered with little painted wooden cherubs and saints; a stand with three hour glasses was hinged to the preacher's desk. Such sights as these may be seen in many a church in Sweden now, but what distinguished this one was an addition to the original building. At the eastern end of the north aisle the builder of the manor house had erected a mausoleum for himself and his family. It was a largish eight-sided building, lighted by a series of oval windows, and it had a domed roof, topped by a kind of pumpkin-shaped object rising into a spire, a form in which Swedish architects greatly delighted. The roof was of copper externally, and was painted black, while the walls, in common with those of the church, were staringly white. To this mausoleum there was no access from the church. It had a portal and steps of its own on the northern side.

Past the churchyard the path to the village goes, and not more than three or four minutes bring you to the inn door.

On the first day of his stay at Råbäck Mr. Wraxall found the church door open, and made those notes of the interior which I have epitomized. Into the mausoleum, however, he could not make his way. He could by looking through the keyhole just descry that there were fine marble effigies and sarcophagi of copper, and a wealth of armorial ornament, which made him very anxious to spend some time in investigation.

The papers he had come to examine at the manor house proved to be of just the kind he wanted for his book. There were family correspondence, journals, and account books of the earliest owners of the estate, very carefully kept and clearly written, full of amusing and picturesque detail. The first De la Gardie appeared in them as a strong and capable man. Shortly after the building of the mansion there had been a period of distress in the district, and the peasants had risen and attacked several chateaux and done some damage. The owner of Råbäck took a leading part in suppressing the trouble, and there was reference to executions of ringleaders and severe punishments inflicted with no sparing hand.

The portrait of this Magnus de la Gardie was one of the best in the house, and Mr. Wraxall studied it with no little interest after his day's work. He gives no detailed description of it, but I gather that the face impressed him rather by its strength than by its beauty or goodness; in fact, he writes that Count Magnus was an almost phenomenally ugly man.

On this day Mr. Wraxall took his supper with the family, and walked back in the late but still bright evening.

"I must remember," he writes, "to ask the sexton if he can let me into the mausoleum at the church. He evidently has access to it himself, for I saw him tonight standing on the steps, and, as I thought, locking or unlocking the door."

I find that early on the following day Mr. Wraxall had some conversation with his landlord. His setting it down at such length as he does surprised me at first; but I soon realized that the papers I was reading were, at least in their beginning, the materials for the book he was meditating, and that it was to have been one of those quasi-journalistic productions which admit of the introduction of an admixture of conversational matter.

His object, he says, was to find out whether any traditions of Count Magnus de la Gardie lingered on in the scenes of that gentleman's activity, and whether the popular estimate of him were favorable or not. He found that the Count was decidedly not a favorite. If his tenants came late to their work on the days which they owed to him as lord of the manor, they were set on the wooden horse, or flogged and branded in the manor-house yard. One or two cases there were of men who had occupied lands which encroached on the lord's domain, and whose houses had been mysteriously burnt on a winter's night, with the whole family inside. But what seemed to dwell on the innkeeper's mind most—for he returned to the subject more than once—was that the Count had been on the Black Pilgrimage, and had brought something or someone back with him.

You will naturally inquire, as Mr. Wraxall did, what the Black Pilgrimage may have been. But your curiosity on the point must remain unsatisfied for the time being, just as his did. The landlord was evidently unwilling to give a full answer, or indeed any answer, on the point, and, being called out for a moment, trotted off with obvious alacrity, only putting his head in at the door a few minutes afterwards to say that he was called away to Skara, and should not be back till evening.

So Mr. Wraxall had to go unsatisfied to his day's work at the manor house. The papers on which he was just then engaged soon put his thoughts into another channel, for he had to occupy himself with glancing over the correspondence between Sophia Albertina in Stockholm and her married cousin Ulrica Leonora at Råbäck in the years 1705–1710. The letters were of exceptional interest from the light they threw upon the culture of that period in Sweden, as anyone can testify who has read the full edition of them in the publications of the Swedish Historical Manuscripts Commission.

In the afternoon he had done with these, and after returning the boxes in which they were kept to their places on the shelf, he proceeded, very naturally, to take down some of the volumes nearest to them, in order to determine which of them had best be his principal subject of investigation next day. The shelf he had hit upon was occupied mostly by a collection of account books in the writing of the first Count Magnus. But one among them was not an account book, but a book of alchemical and other tracts in another sixteenth-century hand. Not being very familiar with alchemical literature, Mr. Wraxall spends much space which he might have spared in setting out the names and beginnings of the various treatises: The book of the Phoenix, book of the Thirty Words, book of the Toad, book of Miriam, Turba philosophorum, and so forth; and then he announces with a good deal of circumstance his delight at finding, on a leaf originally left blank near the middle of the book, some writing of Count Magnus himself headed "Liber nigrae peregrinationis." It is true that only a few lines were written, but there was quite enough to show that the landlord had that morning been referring to a belief at least as old as the time of Count Magnus, and probably shared by him. This is the English of what was written:

"If any man desires to obtain a long life, if he would obtain a faithful messenger and see the blood of his enemies, it is necessary that he should first go into the city of Chorazin, and there salute the prince. . . ." Here there was an erasure of one word, not very thoroughly done, so that Mr. Wraxall felt pretty sure that he was right in reading it as aëris ("of the air"). But there was no more of the text copied, only a line in Latin: "Quaere reliqua hujus materiei inter secretiora" (See the rest of this matter among the more private things).

It could not be denied that this threw a rather lurid light upon the tastes and beliefs of the Count; but to Mr. Wraxall, separated from him by nearly three centuries, the thought that he might have added to his general forcefulness alchemy, and to alchemy something like magic, only made him a more picturesque figure; and when, after a rather prolonged contemplation of his picture in the hall, Mr. Wraxall set out on his homeward way, his mind was full of the thought of Count Magnus. He had no eyes for his surroundings, no perception of the evening scents of the woods or the evening light on the lake; and when all of a sudden he pulled up short, he was astonished to find himself already at the gate of the churchyard, and within a few minutes of his dinner. His eyes fell on the mausoleum.

"Ah," he said, "Count Magus, there you are. I should dearly like to see you."

"Like many solitary men," he writes, "I have a habit of talking to myself aloud; and, unlike some of the Greek and Latin particles, I do not expect an answer. Certainly, and perhaps fortunately in this case, there was neither voice nor any that regarded: only the woman who, I suppose, was cleaning up the church, dropped some metallic object on the floor, whose clang startled me. Count Magnus, I think, sleeps sound enough."

That same evening the landlord of the inn, who had heard Mr. Wraxall say that he wished to see the clerk or deacon (as he would be called in Sweden) of the parish, introduced him to that official in the inn parlor. A visit to the De la Gardie tomb house was soon arranged for the next day, and a little general conversation ensued.

Mr. Wraxall, remembering that one function of Scandinavian deacons is to teach candidates for Confirmation, thought he would refresh his own memory on a Biblical point.

"Can you tell me," he said, "anything about Chorazin?"

The deacon seemed startled, but readily reminded him how that village had once been denounced.

"To be sure," said Mr. Wraxall. "It is, I suppose, quite a ruin now?"

"So I expect," replied the deacon. "I have heard some of our old priests say that Antichrist is to be born there; and there are tales—"

"Ah! What tales are those?" Mr. Wraxall put in.

"Tales, I was going to say, which I have forgotten," said the deacon; and soon after that he said good night.

The landlord was now alone, and at Mr. Wraxall's mercy; and that inquirer was not inclined to spare him.

"Herr Nielsen," he said, "I have found out something about the Black Pilgrimage. You may as well tell me what you know. What did the Count bring back with him?"

Swedes are habitually slow, perhaps, in answering, or perhaps the landlord was an exception. I am not sure; but Mr. Wraxall notes that the landlord spent at least one minute in looking at him before he said anything at all. Then he came close up to his guest, and with a good deal of effort he spoke:

"Mr. Wraxall, I can tell you this one little tale, and no more—not any more. You must not ask anything when I have done. In my grandfather's time—that is, ninety-two years ago—there were two men who said: 'The Count is dead; we do not care for him. We will go tonight and have a free hunt in his wood'—the long wood on the hill that you have seen behind Råbäck. Well, those that heard them say this, they said: 'No, do not go; we are sure you will meet with persons walking who should not be walking. They should be resting, not walking.' These men laughed. There were no forest men to keep the wood, because no one wished to hunt there. The family were not here at the house. These men could do what they wished.

"Very well, they go to the wood that night. My grandfather was sitting here in this room. It was the summer, and a light night. With the window open, he could see out to the wood, and hear.

"So he sat there, and two or three men with him, and they listened. At first they hear nothing at all; then they hear someone—you know how far away it is—they hear someone scream, just as if the most inside part of his soul was twisted out of him. All of them in the room caught hold of each other, and they sat so for three-quarters of an hour. Then they hear someone else, only about three hundred ells off. They hear him laugh out loud: it was not one of those two men that laughed, and indeed, they have all of them said that it was not any man at all. After that they hear a great door shut.

"Then, when it was just light with the sun, they all went to the priest. They said to him:

"'Father, put on your gown and your ruff, and come to bury these men, Anders Bjornsen and Hans Thorbjorn.'

"You understand that they were sure these men were dead. So they went to the wood—my grandfather never forgot this. He said they were all like so many dead men themselves. The priest, too, he was in a white fear. He said when they came to him:

"'I heard one cry in the night, and I heard one laugh afterwards. If I cannot forget that, I shall not be able to sleep again.'

"So they went to the wood, and they found these men on the edge of the wood. Hans Thorbjorn was standing with his back against a tree, and all the time he was pushing with his hands—pushing something away from him which was not there. So he was not dead. And they led him away, and took him to the house at Nykjoping, and he died before the winter; but he went on pushing with his hands. Also Anders Bjornsen was there; but he was dead. And I tell you this about Anders Bjornsen, that he was once a beautiful man, but now his face was not there, because the flesh of it was sucked away off the bones. You understand that? My grandfather did not forget that. And they laid him on the bier which they brought, and they put a cloth over his head, and the priest walked before; and they began to sing the psalm for the dead as well as they could. So, as they were singing the end of the first verse, one fell down, who was carrying the head of the bier, and the others looked back, and they saw that the cloth had fallen off, and the eyes of Anders Bjornsen were looking up, because there was nothing to close over them. And this they could not bear. Therefore the priest laid the cloth upon him, and sent for a spade, and they buried him in that place."

The next day Mr. Wraxall records that the deacon called for him soon after his breakfast, and took him to the church and mausoleum. He noticed that the key of the latter was hung on a nail just by the pulpit, and it occurred to him that, as the church door seemed to be left unlocked as a rule, it would not be difficult for him to pay a second and more private visit to the monuments if there proved to be more of interest among them than could be digested at first. The building, when he entered it, he found not unimposing. The monuments, mostly large erections of the seventeenth and eighteenth centuries, were dignified if luxuriant, and the epitaphs and heraldry were copious. The central space of the dome room was occupied by three copper sarcophagi, covered with finely engraved ornament. Two of them had, as is commonly the case in Denmark and Sweden, a large metal crucifix on the lid. The third, that of Count Magnus, as it appeared, had, instead of that, a full-length effigy engraved upon it, and round the edge were several bands of similar ornament representing various scenes. One was a battle, with cannon belching out smoke, and walled towns, and troops of pike-men. Another showed an execution. In a third, among trees, was a man running at full speed, with flying hair and outstretched hands. After him followed a strange form; it would be hard to say whether the artist had intended it for a man, and was unable to give the requisite similitude, or whether it was intentionally made as monstrous as it looked. In view of the skill with which the rest of the drawing was done, Mr. Wraxall felt inclined to adopt the latter idea. The figure was unduly short, and was for the most part muffled in a hooded garment which swept the ground. The only part of the form which projected from that shelter was not shaped like any hand or arm. Mr. Wraxall compares it to the tentacle of a devil fish, and continues: "On seeing this, I said to myself, 'This, then, which is evidently an allegorical representation of some kind—a fiend pursuing a hunted soul—may be the origin of the story of Count Magnus and his mysterious companion. Let us see how the huntsman is pictured: doubtless it will be a demon blowing his horn.'" But, as it turned out, there was no such sensational figure, only the semblance of a cloaked man on a hillock, who stood leaning on a stick, and watching the hunt with an interest which the engraver had tried to express in his attitude.

Mr. Wraxall noted the finely-worked and massive steel padlocks—three in number—which secured the sarcophagus. One of them, he saw, was detached, and lay on the pavement. And then, unwilling to delay the deacon longer or to waste his own working time, he made his way onward to the manor house.

"It is curious," he notes, "how on retracing a familiar path one's thoughts engross one to the absolute exclusion of surrounding objects. Tonight, for the second time, I had entirely failed to notice where I was going (I had planned a private visit to the tomb house to copy the epitaphs), when I suddenly, as it were, awoke to consciousness, and found myself (as before) turning in at the churchyard gate, and, I believe, singing or chanting some such words as, 'Are you awake, Count Magnus? Are you asleep, Count Magnus?' and then something more which I have failed to recollect. It seemed to me that I must have been behaving in this nonsensical way for some time."

He found the key of the mausoleum where he had expected to find it, and copied the greater part of what he wanted; in fact, he stayed until the light began to fail him.

"I must have been wrong," he writes, "in saying that one of the padlocks of my Count's sarcophagus was unfastened; I see tonight that two are loose. I picked both up, and laid them carefully on the window ledge, after trying unsuccessfully to close them. The remaining one is still firm, and, though I take it to be a spring lock, I cannot guess how it is opened. Had I succeeded in undoing it, I am almost afraid I should have taken the liberty of opening the sarcophagus. It is strange, the interest I feel in the personality of this, I fear, somewhat ferocious and grim old noble."

The day following was, as it turned out, the last of Mr. Wraxall's stay at Råbäck. He received letters connected with certain investments which made it desirable that he should return to England; his work among the papers was practically done, and traveling was slow. He decided, therefore, to make his farewells, put some finishing touches to his notes, and be off.

These finishing touches and farewells, as it turned out, took more time than he had expected. The hospitable family insisted on his staying to dine with them—they dined at three—and it was verging on half-past six before he was outside the iron gates of Råbäck. He dwelt on every step of his walk by the lake, determined to saturate himself, now that he trod it for the last time, in the sentiment of the place and hour. And when he reached the summit of the churchyard knoll, he lingered for many minutes, gazing at the limitless prospect of woods near and distant, all dark beneath a sky of liquid green. When at last he turned to go, the thought struck him that surely he must bid farewell to Count Magnus as well as the rest of the De la Gardies. The church was but twenty yards away, and he knew where the key of the mausoleum hung. It was not long before he was standing over the great copper coffin, and, as usual, talking to himself aloud. "You may have been a bit of a rascal in your time, Magnus," he was saying, "but for all that I should like to see you, or, rather—"

"Just at that instant," he says, "I felt a blow on my foot. Hastily enough I drew it back, and something fell on the pavement with a clash. It was the third, the last of the three padlocks which had fastened the sarcophagus. I stooped to pick it up, and—Heaven is my witness that I am writing only the bare truth—before I had raised myself there was a sound of metal hinges creaking, and I distinctly saw the lid shifting upwards. I may have behaved like a coward, but I could not for my life stay for one moment. I was outside that dreadful building in less time than I can write—almost as quickly as I could have said the words; and what frightens me yet more, I could not turn the key in the lock. As I sit here in my room noting these facts, I ask myself (it was not twenty minutes ago) whether that noise of creaking metal continued, and I cannot tell whether it did or not. I only know that there was something more than I have written that alarmed me, but whether it was sound or sight I am not able to remember. What is this that I have done?"

Poor Mr. Wraxall! He set out on his journey to England on the next day, as he had planned, and he reached England in safety; and yet, as I gather from his changed hand and inconsequent jottings, a broken man. One of several small notebooks that have come to me with his papers gives, not a key to, but a kind of inkling of, his experiences. Much of his journey was made by canal boat, and I find not less than six painful attempts to enumerate and describe his fellow passengers. The entries are of this kind:

"24. Pastor of village in Swåne. Usual black coat and soft black hat.

"25. Commercial traveler from Stockholm going to Trollhättan. Black cloak, brown hat.

"26. Man in long black cloak, broad-leafed hat, very old-fashioned."

This entry is lined out, and a note added: "Perhaps identical with No. 13. Have not yet seen his face." On referring to No. 13, I find that he is a Roman priest in a cassock.

The net result of the reckoning is always the same. Twenty-eight people appear in the enumeration, one being always a man in a long black cloak and broad hat, and the other a "short figure in a dark cloak and hood." On the other hand, it is always noted that only twenty-six passengers appear at meals, and that the man in the cloak is perhaps absent, and the short figure is certainly absent.

On reaching England, it appears that Mr. Wraxall landed at Harwich, and that he resolved at once to put himself out of the reach of some person or persons whom he never specifies, but whom he had evidently come to regard as his pursuers. Accordingly he took a vehicle—it was a closed fly—not trusting the railway, and drove across country to the village of Belchamp St. Paul. It was about nine o'clock on a moonlight August night when he neared the place. He was sitting forward, and looking out the window at the fields and thickets—there was little else to be seen—racing past him. Suddenly he came to a crossroad. At the corner two figures were standing motionless; both were in dark cloaks; the taller one wore a hat, the shorter a hood. He had no time to see their faces, nor did they make any motion that he could discern. Yet the horse shied violently and broke into a gallop, and Mr. Wraxall sank back into his seat in something like desperation. He had seen them before.

Arrived at Belchamp St. Paul, he was fortunate enough to find a decent furnished lodging, and for the next twenty-four hours he lived, comparatively speaking, in peace. His last notes were written on this day. They are too disjointed and ejaculatory to be given here in full, but the substance of them is clear enough. He is expecting a visit from his pursuers—how or when he knows not—and his constant cry is "What has he done?" and "Is there no hope?" Doctors, he knows, would call him mad, policemen would laugh at him. The parson is away. What can he do but lock his door and cry to God?

People still remembered last year at Belchamp St. Paul how a strange gentleman came one evening in August years back; and how the next morning but one he was found dead, and there was an inquest; and the jury that viewed the body fainted, seven of 'em did, and none of 'em wouldn't speak of what they see, and the verdict was visitation of God; and how the people as kep' 'ouse moved out that same week, and went away from that part. But they do not, I think, know that any glimmer of light has even been thrown, or could be thrown, on the mystery. It so happened that last year the little house came into my hands as part of a legacy. It had stood empty since 1863, and there seemed no prospect of letting it; so I had it pulled down, and the papers of which I have given you an abstract were found in a forgotten cupboard under the window in the best bedroom.

# WHEN IT WAS MOONLIGHT

# Manly Wade Wellman

Manly Wade Wellman moved to North Carolina in 1955 and remained there for the rest of his life, becoming an expert in mountain music, the Civil War, and the historic regions and peoples of the old South, and writing numerous nonfiction books on those subjects, including *Dead and Gone: Classic Crimes of North Carolina* (1954), which won the Edgar Allan Poe Award from the Mystery Writers of America for Best Fact Crime Book, *They Took Their Stand: The Founders of the Confederacy* (1959), and *The Rebel Songster: Songs the Confederates Sang* (1959). He also wrote fourteen children's books.

Wellman's short story "A Star for a Warrior" won the Best Story of the Year award from *Ellery Queen's Mystery Magazine* in 1946, beating out William Faulkner, who wrote an angry letter of protest. Other major honors include Lifetime Achievement awards from the World Fantasy Convention (1980) and the British Fantasy Society (1986), and the World Fantasy Award for Best Collection for *Worse Things Waiting* (1975).

Several of Wellman's stories have been adapted for television, including "The Valley Was Still" for *The Twilight Zone* (1961), "The Devil Is Not Mocked" for *Night Gallery* (1971), and "Larroes Catch Meddlers" (1951) and "School for the Unspeakable" (1952) for *Lights Out*.

"When It Was Moonlight" was originally published in the February 1940 issue of *Unknown Worlds*.

# Ꮤhen It Ꮤas Ꮇoonlight

## *MANLY WADE WELLMAN*

*Let my heart be still a moment, and this mystery explore.*

　　　　　　　　　—*The Raven*

**h**is hand, as slim as a white claw, dipped a quillful of ink and wrote in one corner of the page the date—3 March 1842. Then:

### THE PREMATURE BURIAL
by Edgar A. Poe.

He hated his middle name, the name of his miserly and spiteful stepfather. For a moment he considered crossing out even the initial; then he told himself that be was only wool-gathering, putting off the drudgery of writing. And write he must, or starve—the Philadelphia *Dollar Newspaper* was clamouring for the story he had promised. Well, today he had heard a tag of gossip—his mother-in-law had it from a neighbour—that revived in his mind a subject always fascinating.

He began rapidly to write, in a fine copperplate hand:

There are certain themes of which the interest is all-absorbing, but which are entirely too horrible for the purposes of legitimate fiction . . .

This would really be an essay, not a tale, and he could do it justice. Often he thought of the whole world as a vast fat cemetery, close set with tombs in which not all the occupants were at rest—too many struggled unavailingly against their smothering shrouds, their locked and weighted coffin lids. What were his own literary labours, he mused, but a struggle against being shut down and throttled by a society as heavy and grim and senseless as clods heaped by a sexton's spade?

He paused, and went to the slate mantelshelf for a candle. His kerosene lamp had long ago been pawned, and it was dark for mid-afternoon, even in March. Elsewhere in the house his mother-in-law swept busily, and in the room next to his sounded the quiet breathing of his invalid wife. Poor Virginia slept, and for the moment knew no pain. Returning with his light, he dipped more ink and continued down the sheet:

To be buried while alive is, beyond question, the most terrific of these extremes which has ever fallen to the lot of mere mortality. That it has frequently, very frequently, fallen will scarcely be denied . . .

Again his dark imagination savoured the tale he had heard that day. It had happened here in Philadelphia, in this very quarter, less than a month ago. A widower had gone, after weeks of mourning, to his wife's tomb, with flowers. Stooping to place them on the marble slab, he had heard noise beneath. At once joyful and aghast, he fetched men and crowbars, and recovered the body, all untouched by decay. At home that night, the woman returned to consciousness.

So said the gossip, perhaps exaggerated, perhaps not. And the house was only six blocks away from Spring Garden Street, where he sat.

Poe fetched out his notebooks and began to marshal bits of narrative for his composition—a gloomy tale of resurrection in Baltimore, another from France, a genuinely creepy citation from the *Chirurgical Journal* of Leipzig; a sworn case of revival, by electrical impulses, of a dead man in London. Then he added an experience of his own, romantically embellished, a dream adventure of his boyhood in Virginia. Just as he thought to make an end, he had a new inspiration.

Why not learn more about that reputed Philadelphia burial and the one who rose from seeming death? It would point up his piece, give it a timely local climax, ensure acceptance—he could hardly risk a rejection. Too, it would satisfy his own curiosity. Laying down the pen, Poe got up. From a peg he took his wide black hat, his old military cloak that he had worn since his ill-fated cadet days at West Point. Huddling it round his slim little body, he opened the front door and went out.

March had come in like a lion and, lion-like, roared and rampaged over Philadelphia. Dry, cold dust blew up into Poe's full grey eyes, and he hardened his mouth under the gay dark moustache. His shins felt goosefleshy; his striped trousers were unseasonably thin and his shoes badly needed mending. Which way lay his journey?

He remembered the name of the street, and something about a ruined garden. Eventually he came to the place, or what must be the place—the garden was certainly ruined, full of dry, hardy weeds that still stood in great ragged clumps after the hard winter. Poe forced open the creaky gate, went up the rough-flagged path to the stoop. He saw a bronzed nameplate—"Gauber," it said. Yes, that was the name he had heard. He swung the knocker loudly, and thought he caught a whisper of movement inside. But the door did not open.

"Nobody lives there, Mr. Poe," said someone from the street. It was a grocery boy, with a heavy basket on his arm. Poe left the doorstep. He knew the lad; indeed he owed the grocer eleven dollars.

"Are you sure?" Poe prompted.

"Well"—and the boy shifted the weight of his burden—"if anybody lived there, they'd buy from our shop, wouldn't they? And I'd deliver, wouldn't I? But I've had this job for six months, and never set foot inside that door."

Poe thanked him and walked down the street, but did not take the turn that would lead home. Instead he sought the shop of one Pemberton, a printer and friend, to pass the time of day and ask for a loan.

Pemberton could not lend even one dollar—times were hard—but offered a drink of Monongahela whiskey, which Poe forced himself to refuse; then a supper of crackers, cheese, and garlic sausage, which Poe thankfully shared. At home, unless his mother-in-law had begged or borrowed from the neighbors, would be only bread and molasses. It was past sundown when the writer shook hands with Pemberton, thanked him with warm courtesy for his hospitality, and ventured into the evening.

Thank Heaven, it did not rain. Poe was saddened by storms. The wind abated and the March sky was clear save for a tiny fluff of scudding cloud and a banked dark line at the horizon, while up rose a full moon the colour of frozen cream. Poe squinted from under his hat brim at the shadow-pattern on the disc. Might he not write another story of a lunar voyage—like the one about Hans Pfaal, but dead serious this time? Musing thus, he walked along the dusk-filling street until he came again opposite the ruined garden, the creaky gate, and the house with the doorplate marked: "Gauber."

Hello, the grocery boy had been wrong. There was light inside the front window, water-blue light—or was there? Anyway, motion—yes, a figure stooped there, as if to peer out at him.

Poe turned in at the gate, and knocked at the door once again.

Four or five moments of silence; then he heard the old lock grating. The door moved inwards, slowly and noisily. Poe fancied that he had been wrong about the blue light; for he saw only darkness inside. A voice spoke:

"Well, sir."

The two words came huskily but softly, as though the door-opener scarcely breathed. Poe swept off his broad black hat and made one of his graceful bows.

"If you will pardon me . . ." He paused, not knowing whether he addressed man or woman. "This is the Gauber residence?"

"It is," was the reply, soft, hoarse, and sexless. "Your business, sir?"

Poe spoke with official crispness; he had been a sergeant-major of artillery before he was twenty-one, and knew how to inject the proper note. "I am here on public duty," he announced. "I am a journalist, tracing a strange report."

"Journalist?" repeated his interrogator. "Strange report? Come in, sir."

Poe complied, and the door closed abruptly behind him, with a rusty snick of the lock. He remembered being in jail once, and how the door of his cell had slammed just so. It was not a pleasant memory. But he saw more clearly, now he was inside—his eyes got used to the tiny trickle of moonlight.

He stood in a dark hallway, all panelled in wood, with no furniture, drapes, or pictures. With him was a woman, in full skirt and down-drawn lace cap, a woman as tall as he and with intent eyes that glowed as from within. She neither moved nor spoke, but waited for him to tell her more of his errand.

Poe did so, giving his name and, stretching a point, claiming to be a sub-editor of the *Dollar Newspaper*, definitely assigned to the interview. "And now, madam, concerning this story that is rife concerning a premature burial . . ."

She had moved very close, but as his face turned towards her she drew back. Poe fancied that his breath had blown her away like a feather; then, remembering Pemberton's garlic sausage, he was chagrined. To confirm his new thought, the woman was offering him wine—to sweeten his breath.

"Would you take a glass of canary, Mr. Poe," she invited, and opened a side door. He followed her into a room papered in pale blue. Moonglow, drenching it, reflected from that paper and seemed an artificial light. That was what he had seen from outside. From an undraped table his hostess lifted a bottle, poured wine into a metal goblet, and offered it.

Poe wanted that wine, but he had recently promised his sick wife, solemnly and honestly, to abstain from even a sip of the drink that so easily upset him. Through thirsty lips he said: "I thank you kindly, but I am a temperance man."

"Oh," and she smiled. Poe saw white teeth. Then: "I am Elva Gauber—Mrs. John Gauber. The matter of which you ask I cannot explain clearly, but it is true. My husband was buried, in the Eastern Lutheran Churchyard . . ."

"I had heard, Mrs. Gauber, that the burial concerned a woman."

"No, my husband. He had been ill. He felt cold and quiet. A physician, a Dr. Mechem, pronounced him dead, and he was interred beneath a marble slab in his family vault." She sounded weary, but her voice was calm. "This happened shortly after the New Year. On Valentine's Day, I brought flowers. Beneath his slab he stirred and struggled. I had him brought forth. And he lives—after a fashion—today."

"Lives today?" repeated Poe. "In this house?"

"Would you care to see him? Interview him?"

Poe's heart raced, his spine chilled. It was his peculiarity that such sensations gave him pleasure. "I would like nothing better," he assured her, and she went to another door, an inner one.

Opening it, she paused on the threshold, as though summoning her resolution for a plunge into cold, swift water. Then she started down a flight of steps.

Poe followed, unconsciously drawing the door shut behind him.

The gloom of midnight, of prison—yes, of the tomb—fell at once upon those stairs. He heard Elva Gauber gasp:

"No—the moonlight—let it in . . ." And then she fell, heavily and limply, rolling downstairs.

Aghast, Poe quickly groped his way after her. She lay against a door at the foot of the flight, wedged against the panel. He touched her—she was cold and rigid, without motion or elasticity of life. His thin hand groped for and found the knob of the lower door, flung it open. More dim reflected moonlight, and he made shift to drag the woman into it.

Almost at once she sighed heavily, lifted her head, and rose. "How stupid of me," she apologized hoarsely.

"The fault was mine," protested Poe. "Your nerves, your health, have naturally suffered. The sudden dark—the closeness—overcame you." He fumbled in his pocket for a tinderbox. "Suffer me to strike a light."

But she held out a hand to stop him. "No, no. The moon is sufficient." She walked to a small oblong pane set in the wall. Her hands, thin as Poe's own, with long grubby nails, hooked on the sill. Her face, bathed in the full light of the moon, strengthened and grew calm. She breathed deeply, almost voluptuously. "I am quite recovered," she said. "Do not fear for me. You need not stand so near, sir."

He had forgotten that garlic odour, and drew back contritely. She must be as sensitive to the smell as . . . as . . . what was it that was sickened and driven by garlic? Poe could not remember, and he took time to note that they were in a base-ment, stone-walled and with a floor of dirt. In one corner water seemed to drip, forming a dank pool of mud. Close to this, set into the wall, showed a latched trapdoor of planks, thick and wide, cleated crosswise, as though to cover a window. But no window would be set so low. Everything smelt earthy and close, as though fresh air had been shut out for decades.

"Your husband is here?" he inquired.

"Yes." She walked to the shutter-like trap, unlatched it, and drew it open.

The recess beyond was black as ink, and from it came a feeble mutter. Poe followed Elva Gauber, and strained his eyes. In a little stone-flagged nook a bed had been made up. Upon it lay a man, stripped almost naked. His skin was as white as dead bone, and only his eyes, now opening, had life. He gazed at Elva Gauber and past her at Poe.

"Go away," he mumbled.

"Sir," ventured Poe formally, "I have come to hear of how you came to life in the grave . . ."

"It's a lie," broke in the man on the pallet. He writhed halfway to a sitting posture, labouring upwards as against a crushing weight. The wash of moonlight showed how wasted and fragile he was. His face stared and snarled bare-toothed, like a skull. "A lie, I say!" he cried, with a sudden strength that might well have been his last. "Told by this monster who is not—my wife . . ."

The shutter-trap slammed upon his cries. Elva Gauber faced Poe, withdrawing a pace to avoid his garlic breath.

"You have seen my husband," she said. "Was it a pretty sight, sir?"

He did not answer, and she moved across the dirt to the stair doorway. "Will you go up first?" she asked. "At the top, hold the door open, that I may have"—she said "life," or, perhaps, "light." Poe could not be sure which.

Plainly she, who had almost welcomed his intrusion at first, now sought to lead him away. Her eyes, compelling as shouted commands, were fixed upon him. He felt their power, and bowed to it.

Obediently he mounted the stairs, and stood with the upper door wide open. Elva Gauber came up after him. At the top her eyes seized his. Suddenly Poe knew more than ever before about the mesmeric impulses he loved to write about. "I hope," she said measuredly, "that you have not found your mission fruitless. I live here alone— seeing nobody, caring for the poor thing that was once my husband, John Gauber. My mind is not clear. Perhaps my manners are not good. Forgive me, and goodnight."

Poe found himself ushered from the house and outside the wind was howling again. The front door closed behind him, and the lock grated.

The fresh air, the whip of gale in his face, and the absence of Elva Gauber's impelling gaze suddenly brought him back, as though from sleep, to a realization of what had happened—or what had not happened.

He had come out, on this uncomfortable March evening, to investigate the report of a premature burial. He had seen a ghastly thing, that had called the gossip a lie. Somehow, then, he had been drawn abruptly away—stopped from full study of what might be one of the strangest adventures it was ever a writer's good fortune to know. Why was he letting things drop at this stage?

He decided not to let them drop. That would be worse than staying away altogether.

He made up his mind, formed quickly a plan. Leaving the doorstep, he turned from the gate, slipped quickly around the house. He knelt by the foundation at the side, just where a small oblong pane was set flush with the ground.

Bending his head, he found that he could see plainly inside, by reason of the flood of moonlight— a phenomenon, he realized, for generally an apartment was disclosed only by light within. The open doorway to the stairs, the swamp mess of mud in the corner, the out-flung trapdoor, were discernible. And something stood or huddled at the exposed niche—something that bent itself upon and above the frail white body of John Gauber.

Full skirt, white cap—it was Elva Gauber. She bent herself down, her face was touching the face or shoulder of her husband.

Poe's heart, never the healthiest of organs, began to drum and race. He pressed closer to the pane, for a better glimpse of what went on in the cellar. His shadow cut away some of the light. Elva Gauber turned to look.

Her face was as pale as the moon itself. Like the moon, it was shadowed in irregular patches. She came quickly, almost running, towards the pane where Poe crouched. He saw her, plainly and at close hand.

Dark, wet, sticky stains lay upon her mouth and cheeks. Her tongue roved out, licking at the stains—

Blood!

Poe sprang up and ran to the front of the house. He forced his thin, trembling fingers to seize the knocker, to swing it heavily again and again. When there was no answer, he pushed heavily against the door itself—it did not give. He moved to a window, rapped on it, pried at the sill, lifted his fist to smash the glass.

A silhouette moved beyond the pane, and threw it up. Something shot out at him like a pale snake striking—before he could move back, fingers had twisted in the front of his coat. Elva Gauber's eyes glared into his.

Her cap was off, her dark hair fallen in disorder. Blood still smeared and dewed her mouth and jowls.

"You have pried too far," she said, in a voice as measured and cold as the drip from icicles. "I was going to spare you, because of the odour about you that repelled me—the garlic. I showed you a little, enough to warn any wise person, and let you go. Now . . ."

Poe struggled to free himself. Her grip was immovable, like the clutch of a steel trap. She grimaced in triumph, yet she could not quite face him—the garlic still clung to his breath.

"Look in my eyes," she bade him. "Look—you cannot refuse, you cannot escape. You will die, with John—and the two of you, dying, shall rise again like me. I'll have two fountains of life while you remain—two companions after you die."

"Woman," said Poe, fighting against her stabbing gaze, "you are mad."

She snickered gustily. "I am sane, and so are you. We both know that I speak the truth. We both know the futility of your struggle." Her voice rose a little. "Through a chink in the tomb, as I lay dead, a ray of moonlight streamed and struck my eyes. I woke. I struggled. I was set free. Now at night, when the moon shines—Ugh! Don't breathe that herb in my face!"

She turned her head away. At that instant it seemed to Poe that a curtain of utter darkness fell and with it sank down the form of Elva Gauber.

He peered into the sudden gloom. She was collapsed across the window sill, like a discarded puppet in its booth. Her hand still twisted in the bosom of his coat, and he pried himself loose from it, finger by steely, cold finger. Then he turned to flee from this place of shadowed peril to body and soul.

As he turned, he saw whence had come the dark. A cloud had come up from its place on the horizon—the fat, sooty bank he had noted there at sundown—and now it obscured the moon. Poe paused, in mid-retreat, gazing.

His thoughtful eye gauged the speed and size of the cloud. It curtained the moon, would continue to curtain it for—well, ten minutes. And for that ten minutes Elva Gauber would lie motionless, lifeless. She had told the truth about the moon giving her life. Hadn't she fallen like one slain on the stairs when they were darkened? Poe began grimly to string the evidence together.

It was Elva Gauber, not her husband, who had died and gone to the family vault. She had come back to life, or a mockery of life, by touch of the moon's rays. Such light was an unpredictable force—it made dogs howl, it flogged madmen to violence, it brought fear, or black sorrow, or ecstasy. Old legends said that it was the birth of fairies, the transformation of werewolves, the motive power of broom-riding witches. It was surely the source of the strength and evil animating what had been the corpse of Elva Gauber—and he, Poe, must not stand there dreaming.

He summoned all the courage that was his, and scrambled in at the window through which clumped the woman's form. He groped across the room to the cellar door, opened it, and went down the stairs, through the door at the bottom, and into the stone-walled basement.

It was dark, moonless still. Poe paused only to bring forth his tinderbox, strike a light, and kindle the end of a tightly twisted linen rag. It gave a feeble steady light, and he found his way to the shutter, opened it, and touched the naked, wasted shoulder of John Gauber.

"Get up," he said. "I've come to save you."

The skull-face feebly shifted its position to meet his gaze. The man managed to speak, moaningly:

"Useless. I can't move—unless she lets me. Her eyes keep me here—half-alive. I'd have died long ago, but somehow . . ."

Poe thought of a wretched spider, paralysed by the sting of a mud-wasp, lying helpless in its captive's close den until the hour of feeding comes. He bent down, holding his blazing tinder close. He could see Gauber's neck, and it was a mass of tiny puncture wounds, some of them still beaded with blood drops fresh or dried. He winced but bode firm in his purpose.

"Let me guess the truth," he said quickly. "Your wife was brought home from the grave, came back to a seeming of life. She put a spell on you, or played a trick—made you a helpless prisoner. That isn't contrary to nature, that last. I've studied mesmerism."

"It's true," John Gauber mumbled.

"And nightly she comes to drink your blood?"

Gauber weakly nodded. "Yes. She was beginning just now, but ran upstairs. She will be coming back."

"Good," said Poe bleakly. "Perhaps she will come back to more than she expects. Have you ever heard of vampires? Probably not, but I have studied them, too. I began to guess, I think, when first she was so repelled by the odour of garlic. Vampires lie motionless by day and walk and feed at night. They are creatures of the moon—their food is blood. Come."

Poe broke off, put out his light, and lifted the man in his arms. Gauber was as light as a child. The writer carried him to the slanting shelter of the closed-in staircase, and there set him against the wall stones. The poor fellow would be well hidden.

Next Poe flung off his coat, waistcoat, and shirt. Heaping his clothing in a deeper shadow of the stairway, he stood up, stripped to the waist. His skin was almost as bloodlessly pale as Gauber's, his chest and arms almost as gaunt. He dared believe that he might pass momentarily for the unfortunate man.

The cellar sprang full of light again. The cloud must be passing from the moon. Poe listened. There was a dragging sound above, then footsteps.

Elva Gauber, the blood drinker by night, had revived.

Now for it. Poe hurried to the niche, thrust himself in, and pulled the trapdoor shut after him.

He grinned, sharing a horrid paradox with the blackness around him. He had heard all the fabled ways of destroying vampires—transfixing stakes, holy water, prayer, fire. But he, Edgar Allan Poe, had evolved a new way. Myriads of tales whispered frighteningly of fiends lying in wait for normal men, but who had ever heard of a normal man lying in wait for a fiend? Well, he had never considered himself normal, in spirit, or brain, or taste.

He stretched out, feet together, hands crossed on his bare midriff. Thus it would be in the tomb, he found himself thinking. To his mind came a snatch of poetry by a man named Bryant, published long ago in a New England review—"Breathless darkness, and the narrow house." It was breathless and dark enough in this hole, Heaven knew, and narrow as well. He rejected, almost hysterically, the implication of being buried. To break the ugly spell that daunted him where thought of Elva Gauber failed, he turned sideways to face the wall, his naked arm lying across his cheek and temple.

As his ear touched the musty bedding, it brought to him once again the echo of footsteps, footsteps descending the stairs. They were rhythmic, confident. They were eager.

Elva Gauber was coming to seek again her interrupted repast.

Now she was crossing the floor. She did not pause or turn aside—she had not noticed her husband, lying under the cadet cloak in the shadow of the stairs. The noise came straight to the trapdoor, and he heard her fumbling for the latch.

Light, blue as skimmed milk, poured into his nook. A shadow fell in the midst of it, full upon him. His imagination, ever out-stripping reality, whispered that the shadow had weight, like lead—oppressive, baleful.

"John," said the voice of Elva Gauber in his ear, "I've come back. You know why—you know what for." Her voice sounded greedy, as though it came through loose, trembling lips. "You're my only source of strength now. I thought tonight, that a stranger—but he got away. He had a cursed odour about him, anyway."

Her hand touched the skin of his neck. She was prodding him, like a butcher fingering a doomed beast.

"Don't hold yourself away from me, John," she was commanding, in a voice of harsh mockery. "You know it won't do any good. This is the night of the full moon, and I have power for anything, anything!" She was trying to drag his arm away from his face. "You won't gain by—" She broke off, aghast. Then, in a wild dry-throated scream:

"You're not John!"

Poe whipped over on his back, and his bird-claw hands shot out and seized her—one hand clinching upon her snaky disorder of dark hair, the other digging its fingertips into the chill flesh of her arm.

The scream quivered away into a horrible breathless rattle. Poe dragged his captive violently inwards, throwing all his collected strength into the effort. Her feet were jerked from the floor and she flew into the recess, hurtling above and beyond Poe's recumbent body. She struck the inner stones with a crashing force that might break bones, and would have collapsed upon Poe; but, at the same moment, he had released her and slid swiftly out upon the floor of the cellar.

With frantic haste he seized the edge of the back-flung trapdoor. Elva Gauber struggled upon hands and knees, among the tumbled bedclothes in the niche; then Poe had slammed the panel shut.

She threw herself against it from within, yammering and wailing like an animal in a trap. She was almost as strong as he, and for a moment he thought that she would burst out of the niche. But, sweating and wheezing, he bore against the planks with his shoulder, bracing his feet against the earth. His fingers found the latch, lifted it, forced it into place.

"Dark," moaned Elva Gauber from inside. "Dark—no moon—" Her voice trailed off.

Poe went to the muddy pool in the corner, thrust in his hands. The mud was slimy but workable. He pushed a double handful of it against the trapdoor, sealing cracks and edges. Another handful, another. Using his palms like trowels, he coated the boards with thick mud.

"Gauber," he said breathlessly, "how are you?"

"All right—I think." The voice was strangely strong and clear. Looking over his shoulder, Poe saw that Gauber had come upright of himself, still pale but apparently steady. "What are you doing?" Gauber asked.

"Walling her up," jerked out Poe, scooping still more mud. "Walling her up forever, with her evil."

He had a momentary flash of inspiration, a symbolic germ of a story; in it a man sealed a woman into such a nook of the wall, and with her an embodiment of active evil—perhaps in the form of a black cat.

Pausing at last to breathe deeply, he smiled to himself. Even in the direst of danger, the most heart-breaking moment of toil and fear, he must ever be coining up new plots for stories.

"I cannot thank you enough," Gauber was say-

ing to him. "I feel that all will be well—if only she stays there."

Poe put his ear to the wall. "Not a whisper of motion, sir. She's shut off from moonlight—from life and power. Can you help me with my clothes? I feel terribly chilled."

His mother-in-law met him on the threshold when he returned to the house in Spring Garden Street. Under the white widow's cap, her strong-boned face was drawn with worry.

"Eddie, are you ill?" She was really asking if he had been drinking. A look reassured her. "No," she answered herself, "but you've been away from home so long. And you're dirty, Eddie—filthy. You must wash."

He let her lead him in, pour hot water into a basin. As he scrubbed himself, he formed excuses, a banal lie about a long walk for inspiration, a moment of dizzy weariness, a stumble into a mud puddle.

"I'll make you some nice hot coffee, Eddie," his mother-in-law offered.

"Please," he responded and went back to his own room with the slate mantelpiece. Again he lighted the candle, sat down, and took up his pen.

His mind was embellishing the story inspiration that had come to him at such a black moment, in the cellar of the Gauber house. He'd work on that tomorrow. The *United States Saturday Post* would take it, he hoped. Title? He would call it simply "The Black Cat."

But to finish the present task! He dipped his pen in ink. How to begin? How to end? How, after writing and publishing such an account, to defend himself against the growing whisper of his insanity?

He decided to forget it, if he could—at least to seek healthy company, comfort, quiet—perhaps even to write some light verse, some humorous articles and stories. For the first time in his life, he had had enough of the macabre.

Quickly he wrote a final paragraph:

There are moments when, even to the sober eye of Reason, the world of our sad Human-

ity may assume the semblance of a Hell—
but the imagination of man is no Carathis, to
explore with impunity its every cavern. Alas!
The grim legion of sepulchral terrors cannot
be regarded as altogether fanciful—but, like
the Demons in whose company Afrasiab made
his voyage down the Oxus, they must sleep, or they will devour us—they must be suffered to slumber, or we will perish.

That would do for the public, decided Edgar
Allan Poe. In any case, it would do for the Philadelphia *Dollar Newspaper*. His mother-in-law brought
in the coffee.

# THE DRIFTING SNOW

# August Derleth

August William Derleth (1909–71) was born in Sauk City, Wisconsin, where he remained his entire life. He received an M.A. from the University of Wisconsin in 1930, by which time he had already begun to sell horror stories to *Weird Tales* (the first appearing in 1926) and other pulp magazines, sometimes in collaboration with his boyhood friend Mark Schorer but more frequently by himself. During his lifetime he wrote more than three thousand stories and articles and published more than a hundred books, including detective stories (featuring Judge Peck and an American Sherlock Holmes clone, Solar Pons), supernatural stories, and what he regarded as his serious fiction: a very lengthy series of books, stories, poems, journals, etc., about life in his small town, which he renamed Sac Prairie.

Derleth was almost single-handedly responsible for recognizing and celebrating the work of H. P. Lovecraft, who had enjoyed little success in his lifetime. Derleth took his Cthulhu mythos, dominated by the evil Old Ones, and expanded it to include the benevolent Elder Gods, featuring them in numerous pulp stories. Later, in what may have been his most important contribution to the horror-fiction genre, he founded Arkham House with Donald Wandrei, publishing many volumes of Lovecraft's work while also publishing the first work of such future giants of the genre as Robert Bloch, Fritz Leiber, Ray Bradbury, and Joseph Payne Brennan.

"The Drifting Snow" was first published in the February 1939 issue of *Weird Tales*.

# The Drifting Snow

## AUGUST DERLETH

Aunt Mary's advancing footsteps halted suddenly, short of the table, and Clodetta turned to see what was keeping her. She was standing very rigidly, her eyes fixed upon the French windows just opposite the door through which she had entered, her cane held stiffly before her.

Clodetta shot a quick glance across the table toward her husband, whose attention had also been drawn to his aunt; his face vouchsafed her nothing. She turned again to find that the old lady had transferred her gaze to her, regarding her stonily and in silence. Clodetta felt uncomfortable.

"Who withdrew the curtains from the west windows?"

Clodetta flushed, remembering. "I did, Aunt. I'm sorry. I forgot about your not wanting them drawn away."

The old lady made an odd, grunting sound, shifting her gaze once again to the French windows. She made a barely perceptible movement, and Lisa ran forward from the shadow of the hall, where she had been regarding the two at table with stern disapproval. The servant went directly to the west windows and drew the curtains.

Aunt Mary came slowly to the table and took her place at its head. She put her cane against the side of her chair, pulled at the chain around her neck so that her lorgnette lay in her lap, and looked from Clodetta to her nephew, Ernest.

Then she fixed her gaze on the empty chair at the foot of the table, and spoke without seeming to see the two beside her.

"I told both of you that none of the curtains over the west windows was to be withdrawn after sundown, and you must have noticed that none of those windows has been for one instant uncovered at night. I took especial care to put you in rooms facing east, and the sitting room is also in the east."

"I'm sure Clodetta didn't mean to go against your wishes, Aunt Mary," said Ernest abruptly.

"No, of course not, Aunt."

The old lady raised her eyebrows, and went on impassively. "I didn't think it wise to explain why I made such a request. I'm not going to explain. But I do want to say that there is a very definite danger in drawing away the curtains. Ernest has heard that before, but you, Clodetta, have not."

Clodetta shot a startled glance at her husband. The old lady caught it, and said, "It's all very well to believe that my mind's wandering or that I'm getting eccentric, but I shouldn't advise you to be satisfied with that."

A young man came suddenly into the room and made for the seat at the foot of the table, into which he flung himself with an almost inaudible greeting to the other three.

"Late again, Henry," said the old lady.

Henry mumbled something and began hurriedly to eat. The old lady sighed, and began presently to eat also, whereupon Clodetta and Ernest did likewise. The old servant, who had continued to linger behind Aunt Mary's chair, now withdrew, not without a scornful glance at Henry.

Clodetta looked up after a while and ventured to speak. "You aren't as isolated as I thought you might be up here, Aunt Mary."

"We aren't, my dear, what with telephones and cars and all. But only twenty years ago it was quite a different thing, I can tell you." She smiled reminiscently and looked at Ernest. "Your grandfather was living then, and many's the time he was snowbound with no way to let anybody know."

"Down in Chicago, when they speak of 'up north' or the 'Wisconsin woods' it seems very far away," said Clodetta.

"Well, it *is* far away," put in Henry, abruptly. "And, Aunt, I hope you've made some provision in case we're locked in here for a day or two. It looks like snow outside, and the radio says a blizzard's coming."

The old lady grunted and looked at him. "Ha, Henry—you're overly concerned, it seems to me. I'm afraid you've been regretting this trip ever since you set foot in my house. If you're worrying about a snowstorm, I can have Sam drive you down to Wausau, and you can be in Chicago tomorrow."

"Of course not."

Silence fell, and presently the old lady called gently, "Lisa," and the servant came into the room to help her from her chair, though, as Clodetta had previously said to her husband, "She didn't need help."

From the doorway, Aunt Mary bade them all goodnight, looking impressively formidable with her cane in one hand and her unopened lorgnette in the other, and vanished into the dusk of the hall, from which her receding footsteps sounded together with those of the servant, who was seldom seen away from her. These two were alone in the house most of the time, and only very brief periods when the old lady had up her nephew Ernest, "dear John's boy," or Henry, of whose father the old lady never spoke, helped to relieve the pleasant somnolence of their quiet lives. Sam, who usually slept in the garage, did not count.

Clodetta looked nervously at her husband, but it was Henry who said what was uppermost in their thoughts.

"I think she's losing her mind," he declared matter-of-factly. Cutting off Clodetta's protest on her lips, he got up and went into the sitting room, from which came presently the strains of music from the radio.

Clodetta fingered her spoon idly and finally said, "I do think she is a little queer, Ernest."

Ernest smiled tolerantly. "No, I don't think so. I've an idea why she keeps the west windows covered. My grandfather died out there—he was overcome by the cold one night, and froze on the slope of the hill. I don't rightly know how it happened— I was away at the time. I suppose she doesn't like to be reminded of it."

"But where's the danger she spoke of, then?"

He shrugged. "Perhaps it lies in her—she might be affected and affect us in turn." He paused for an instant, and finally added, "I suppose she *does* seem a little strange to you—but she was like that as long as I can remember; next time you come, you'll be used to it."

Clodetta looked at her husband for a moment before replying. At last she said, "I don't think I like the house, Ernest."

"Oh, nonsense, darling." He started to get up, but Clodetta stopped him.

"Listen, Ernest. I remembered perfectly well Aunt Mary's not wanting those curtains drawn away—but I just felt I had to do it. I didn't want to, but—*something made me do it*." Her voice was unsteady.

"Why, Clodetta," he said, faintly alarmed. "Why didn't you tell me before?"

She shrugged. "Aunt Mary might have thought I'd gone wool-gathering."

"Well, it's nothing serious, but you've let it

bother you a little and that isn't good for you. Forget it; think of something else. Come and listen to the radio."

They rose and moved toward the sitting room together. At the door Henry met them. He stepped aside a little, saying, "I might have known we'd be marooned up here," and adding, as Clodetta began to protest, "We're going to be all right. There's a wind coming up and it's beginning to snow, and I know what that means." He passed them and went into the deserted dining room, where he stood a moment looking at the too-long table. Then he turned aside and went over to the French windows, from which he drew away the curtains and stood there peering out into the darkness. Ernest saw him standing at the window, and protested from the sitting room.

"Aunt Mary doesn't like those windows uncovered, Henry."

Henry half turned and replied, "Well, *she* may think it's dangerous, but I can risk it."

Clodetta, who had been staring beyond Henry into the night through the French windows, said suddenly, "Why, there's someone out there!"

Henry looked quickly through the glass and replied, "No, that's the snow; it's coming down heavily, and the wind's drifting it this way and that." He dropped the curtains and came away from the windows.

Clodetta said uncertainly, "Why, I could have sworn I saw someone out there, walking past the window."

"I suppose it does look that way from here," offered Henry, who had come back into the sitting room. "But personally, I think you've let Aunt Mary's eccentricities impress you too much."

Ernest made an impatient gesture at this, and Clodetta did not answer. Henry sat down before the radio and began to move the dial slowly. Ernest had found himself a book, and was becoming interested, but Clodetta continued to sit with her eyes fixed upon the still slowly-moving curtains cutting off the French windows. Presently she got up and left the room, going down the long hall into the east wing, where she tapped gently upon Aunt Mary's door.

"Come in," called the old lady.

Clodetta opened the door and stepped into the room where Aunt Mary sat in her dressing robe, her dignity, in the shape of her lorgnette and cane, resting respectively on her bureau and in the corner. She looked surprisingly benign, as Clodetta at once confessed.

"Ha, thought I was an ogre in disguise, did you?" said the old lady, smiling in spite of herself. "I'm really not, you see, but I am a sort of bogey about the west windows, as you have seen."

"I wanted to tell you something about those windows, Aunt Mary," said Clodetta. She stopped suddenly. The expression on the old lady's face had given way to a curiously dismaying one. It was not anger, not distaste—it was a lurking suspense. Why, the old lady was afraid!

"What?" she asked Clodetta shortly.

"I was looking out—just for a moment or so—and I thought I saw someone out there."

"Of course, you didn't, Clodetta. Your imagination, perhaps, or the drifting snow."

"My imagination? Maybe. But there was no wind to drift the snow, though one has come up since."

"I've often been fooled that way, my dear. Sometimes I've gone out in the morning to look for footprints—there weren't any, ever. We're pretty far away from civilization in a snowstorm, despite our telephones and radios. Our nearest neighbor is at the foot of the long, sloping rise—over three miles away—and all wooded land between. There's no highway nearer than that."

"It was so clear, I could have sworn to it."

"Do you want to go out in the morning and look?" asked the old lady shortly.

"Of course not."

"Then you didn't see anything."

It was half-question, half-demand. Clodetta said, "Oh, Aunt Mary, you're making an issue of it now."

"Did you or didn't you in your own mind see anything, Clodetta?"

"I guess I didn't, Aunt Mary."

"Very well. And now do you think we might talk about something more pleasant?"

"Why, I'm sure—I'm sorry, Aunt. I didn't know that Ernest's grandfather had died out there."

"Ha, he's told you that, has he? Well?"

"Yes, he said that was why you didn't like the slope after sunset—that you didn't like to be reminded of his death."

The old lady looked at Clodetta impassively.

"Perhaps he'll never know how nearly right he was."

"What do you mean, Aunt Mary?"

"Nothing for you to know, my dear." She smiled again, her sternness dropping from her. "And now I think you'd better go, Clodetta; I'm tired."

Clodetta rose obediently and made for the door, where the old lady stopped her. "How's the weather?"

"It's snowing—hard, Henry says—and blowing."

The old lady's face showed her distaste at the news. "I don't like to hear that, not at all. Suppose someone should look down that slope tonight?" She was speaking to herself, having forgotten Clodetta at the door. Seeing her again abruptly, she said, "But you don't know, Clodetta. Goodnight."

Clodetta stood with her back against the closed door, wondering what the old lady could have meant. *But you don't know, Clodetta.* That was curious. For a moment or two the old lady had completely forgotten her.

She moved away from the door, and came upon Ernest just turning into the east wing.

"Oh, there you are," he said. "I wondered where you had gone."

"I was talking a bit with Aunt Mary."

"Henry's been at the west windows again—and now *he* thinks there's someone out there."

Clodetta stopped short. "Does he really think so?"

Ernest nodded gravely. "But the snow's drifting frightfully, and I can imagine how that suggestion of yours worked on his mind."

Clodetta turned and went back along the hall. "I'm going to tell Aunt Mary."

He started to protest, but to no avail, for she was already tapping on the old lady's door, and indeed opening the door and entering the room before he could frame an adequate protest.

"Aunt Mary," she said, "I didn't want to disturb you again, but Henry's been at the French windows in the dining room, and he says he's seen someone out there."

The effect on the old lady was magical. "He's seen them!" she exclaimed. Then she was on her feet, coming rapidly over to Clodetta. "How long ago?" she demanded, seizing her almost roughly by the arms. "Tell me, quickly. How long ago did he see them?"

Clodetta's amazement kept her silent for a moment, but at last she spoke, feeling the old lady's keen eyes staring at her. "It was some time ago, Aunt Mary, after supper."

The old lady's hands relaxed, and with it her tension. "Oh," she said, and turned and went back slowly to her chair, taking her cane from the corner where she had put it for the night.

"Then there *is* someone out there?" challenged Clodetta, when the old lady had reached her chair.

For a long time, it seemed to Clodetta, there was no answer. Then presently, the old lady began to nod gently, and a barely audible "yes" escaped her lips.

"Then we had better take them in, Aunt Mary."

The old lady looked at Clodetta earnestly for a moment; then she replied, her voice firm and low, her eyes fixed upon the wall beyond. "We can't take them in, Clodetta—because they're not alive."

At once Henry's words came flashing into Clodetta's memory—"She's losing her mind"—and her involuntary start betrayed her thought.

"I'm afraid I'm not mad, my dear—I hoped at first I might be, but I wasn't. I'm not, now. There was only one of them out there at first—the girl; Father is the other. Quite long ago, when I was young, my father did something which he regretted all his days. He had a too strong temper, and it maddened him. One night, he found out that one of my brothers—Henry's father—had been very familiar with one of the servants, a very pretty girl, older than I was. He thought she was to blame, though she wasn't, and he didn't find it out until too late. He drove her from the house, then and there. Winter had not yet set in, but it was quite cold, and she had some five miles to go to her home. We begged Father not to send her away—though we didn't know what was wrong then—but he paid no attention to us. The girl had to go.

"Not long after she had gone, a biting wind came up, and close upon it a fierce storm. Father had already repented his hasty action, and sent some of the men to look for the girl. They didn't find her, but in the morning she was found frozen to death on the long slope of the hill to the west."

The old lady sighed, paused a moment, and went on. "Years later—she came back. She came in a snowstorm, as she went; but she had become a vampire. We all saw her. We were at supper table, and Father saw her first. The boys had already gone upstairs, and Father and the two of us girls, my sister and I, did not recognize her. She was just a dim shape floundering around in the drifting snow beyond the French windows. Father ran out to her, calling to us to send the boys after him. We never saw him alive again. In the morning we found him in the same spot where years before the girl had been found. He, too, had died of exposure.

"Then, a few years after—she returned with the snow, and she brought him along; he, too, had become a vampire. They stayed until the last snow, always trying to lure someone out there. After that, I knew, and had the windows covered during the winter nights, from sunset to dawn, because they never went beyond the west slope.

"Now you know, Clodetta."

Whatever Clodetta was going to say was cut short by running footsteps in the hall, a hasty rap, and Ernest's head appearing suddenly in the open doorway.

"Come on, you two," he said, almost gaily, "there *are* people out on the west slope—a girl and an old man—and Henry's gone out to fetch them in!"

Then, triumphant, he was off. Clodetta came to her feet, but the old lady was before her, passing her and almost running down the hall, calling loudly for Lisa, who presently appeared in nightcap and gown from her room.

"Call Sam, Lisa," said the old lady, "and send him to me in the dining room."

She ran on into the dining room, Clodetta close on her heels. The French windows were open, and Ernest stood on the snow-covered terrace beyond, calling his cousin. The old lady went directly over to him, even striding into the snow to his side, though the wind drove the snow against her with great force. The wooded western slope was lost in a snow-fog; the nearest trees were barely discernible.

"Where could they have gone?" Ernest said, turning to the old lady, whom he had thought to be Clodetta. Then, seeing that it was the old lady, he said, "Why, Aunt Mary—and so little on, too! You'll catch your death of cold."

"Never mind, Ernest," said the old lady. "I'm all right. I've had Sam get up to help you look for Henry—but I'm afraid you won't find him."

"He can't be far; he just now went out."

"He went before you saw where; he's far enough gone."

Sam came running into the blowing snow from the dining room, muffled in a greatcoat. He was considerably older than Ernest, almost the old lady's age. He shot a questioning glance at her and asked, "Have they come again?"

Aunt Mary nodded. "You'll have to look for Henry. Ernest will help you. And remember, don't separate. And don't go far from the house."

Clodetta came with Ernest's overcoat, and together the two women stood there, watching them until they were swallowed up in the wall of driven snow. Then they turned slowly, and went back into the house.

The old lady sank into a chair facing the windows. She was pale and drawn, and looked, as Clodetta said afterward, "as if she'd fallen together." For a long time she said nothing. Then, with a gentle little sigh, she turned to Clodetta and spoke.

"Now there'll be three of them out there."

Then, so suddenly that no one knew how it happened, Ernest and Sam appeared beyond the windows, and between them they dragged Henry. The old lady flew to open the windows, and the three of them, cloaked in snow, came into the room.

"We found him—but the cold's hit him pretty hard, I'm afraid," said Ernest.

The old lady sent Lisa for cold water, and Ernest ran to get himself other clothes. Clodetta went with him, and in their rooms told him what the old lady had related to her.

Ernest laughed. "I think you believed that, didn't you, Clodetta? Sam and Lisa do, I know, because Sam told me the story long ago. I think the shock of Grandfather's death was too much for all three of them."

"But the story of the girl, and then—"

"That part's true, I'm afraid. A nasty story, but it did happen."

"But those people Henry and I saw!" protested Clodetta weakly.

Ernest stood without movement. "That's so," he said, "I saw them, too. Then they're out there yet, and we'll have to find them!" He took up his overcoat again, and went from the room, Clodetta protesting in a shrill unnatural voice. The old lady met him at the door of the dining room, having overheard Clodetta pleading with him.

"No, Ernest—you can't go out there again," she said. "There's no one there."

He pushed gently into the room and called to Sam. "Coming, Sam? There's still two of them out there—we almost forgot them."

Sam looked at him strangely. "What do you mean?" he demanded roughly. He looked challengingly at the old lady, who shook her head.

"The girl and the old man, Sam. We've got to get them, too."

"Oh, *them*," said Sam. "They're dead!"

"Then I'll go out alone," said Ernest.

Henry came to his feet suddenly, looking dazed. He walked forward a few steps, his eyes travelling from one to the other of them, yet apparently not seeing them. He began to speak abruptly, in an unnatural, childlike voice.

"*The snow,*" he murmured, "*the snow—the beautiful hands, so little, so lovely—her beautiful hands—and the snow, the beautiful, lovely snow, drifting and falling around her . . .*"

He turned slowly and looked toward the French windows, the others following his gaze. Beyond was a wall of white, where the snow was drifting against the house. For a moment Henry stood quietly watching, then suddenly a white figure came forward from the snow—a young girl, cloaked in long snow-whips, her glistening eyes strangely fascinating.

The old lady flung herself forward, her arms outstretched to cling to Henry, but she was too late. Henry had run toward the windows, had opened them, and even as Clodetta cried out, had vanished into the wall of snow beyond.

Then Ernest ran forward, but the old lady threw her arms around him and held him tightly, murmuring, "You shall not go! Henry is gone beyond our help!"

Clodetta came to help her, and Sam stood menacingly at the French windows, now closed against the wind and the sinister snow. So they held him, and would not let him go.

"And tomorrow," said the old lady in a harsh whisper, "we must go to their graves and stake them down. We should have gone before."

In the morning they found Henry's body crouched against the bole of an ancient oak, where the two others had been found years before. There were almost obliterated marks of where something had dragged him, a long, uneven swath in the snow, and yet no footprints, only strange, hollowed places along the way, as if the wind had whirled the snow away, and only the wind.

But on his skin were signs of the snow vampire—the delicate small prints of a young girl's hands.

## AYLMER VANCE AND THE VAMPIRE

# Alice and Claude Askew

Alice Jane de Courcey (1874–1917) was born in St. Pancras, London. Claude Arthur Cary Askew (1866–1917) was born in Notting Hill, London, and was educated at Eton and on the Continent. They were married in 1900 and began a stunningly prolific writing collaboration that produced numerous newspaper serials, short stories, and more than ninety novels published between 1904 and a few years after their deaths, the result of a World War I submarine attack on their ship in the Mediterranean.

Their first book, *The Shulamite* (1904), was dramatized for the London stage by Claude Askew and Edward Knoblauch; it was later made into silent films in 1915 and again in 1921 under the title *Under the Lash*. Other films based on their work were *John Heriot's Wife* (1909, filmed in 1920), *Testimony* (1909, filmed in 1926), *Poison* (1913, filmed as *The Pleydell Mystery*, 1916), and *God's Clay* (1913, filmed in 1919).

Although most of their novels and short stories were mystery and detective fiction, they also wrote romances, adventure novels—indeed, every type of popular fiction, including one supernatural series about a psychic detective, or ghost hunter, which was not collected until *Aylmer Vance: Ghost-Seer* was published by Ash-Tree Press in 1998.

"Aylmer Vance and the Vampire" was first published in *The Weekly Tale-Teller* (July 1914).

# Aylmer Vance and the Vampire

## ALICE AND CLAUDE ASKEW

ylmer Vance had rooms in Dover Street, Piccadilly, and now that I had decided to follow in his footsteps and to accept him as my instructor in matters psychic, I found it convenient to lodge in the same house. Aylmer and I quickly became close friends, and he showed me how to develop that faculty of clairvoyance which I had possessed without being aware of it. And I may say at once that this particular faculty of mine proved of service on several important occasions.

At the same time I made myself useful to Vance in other ways, not the least of which was that of acting as recorder of his many strange adventures. For himself, he never cared much about publicity, and it was some time before I could persuade him, in the interests of science, to allow me to give any detailed account of his experiences to the world.

The incidents which I will now narrate occurred very soon after we had taken up our residence together, and while I was still, so to speak, a novice.

It was about ten o'clock in the morning that a visitor was announced. He sent up a card which bore upon it the name of Paul Davenant.

The name was familiar to me, and I wondered if this could be the same Mr. Davenant who was so well known for his polo playing and for his success as an amateur rider, especially over the hurdles. He was a young man of wealth and position, and I recollected that he had married, about a year ago, a girl who was reckoned the greatest beauty of the season. All the illustrated papers had given their portraits at the time, and I remember thinking what a remarkably handsome couple they made.

Mr. Davenant was ushered in, and at first I was uncertain as to whether this could be the individual whom I had in mind, so wan and pale and ill did he appear. A finely-built, upstanding man at the time of his marriage, he had now acquired a languid droop of the shoulders and a shuffling gait, while his face, especially about the lips, was bloodless to an alarming degree.

And yet it was the same man, for behind all this I could recognize the shadow of the good looks that had once distinguished Paul Davenant.

He took the chair which Aylmer offered him—after the usual preliminary civilities had been exchanged—and then glanced doubtfully in my direction. "I wish to consult you privately, Mr. Vance," he said. "The matter is of considerable importance to myself, and, if I may say so, of a somewhat delicate nature."

Of course I rose immediately to withdraw from the room, but Vance laid his hand upon my arm.

"If the matter is connected with research in my particular line, Mr. Davenant," he said, "if there is any investigation you wish me to take up on your behalf, I shall be glad if you will include Mr. Dexter in your confidence. Mr. Dexter assists me in my work. But, of course—"

"Oh, no," interrupted the other, "if that is the case, pray let Mr. Dexter remain. I think," he added, glancing at me with a friendly smile, "that you are an Oxford man, are you not, Mr. Dexter? It was before my time, but I have heard of your name in connection with the river. You rowed at Henley, unless I am very much mistaken."

I admitted the fact, with a pleasurable sensation of pride. I was very keen upon rowing in those days, and a man's prowess at school and college always remains dear to his heart.

After this we quickly became on friendly terms, and Paul Davenant proceeded to take Aylmer and myself into his confidence.

He began by calling attention to his personal appearance. "You would hardly recognize me for the same man I was a year ago," he said. "I've been losing flesh steadily for the last six months. I came up from Scotland about a week ago, to consult a London doctor. I've seen two—in fact, they've held a sort of consultation over me—but the result, I may say, is far from satisfactory. They don't seem to know what is really the matter with me."

"Anaemia—heart," suggested Vance. He was scrutinizing his visitor keenly, and yet without any particular appearance of doing so. "I believe it not infrequently happens that you athletes overdo yourselves—put too much strain upon the heart—"

"My heart is quite sound," responded Davenant. "Physically it is in perfect condition. The trouble seems to be that it hasn't enough blood to pump into my veins. The doctors wanted to know if I had met with an accident involving a great loss of blood—but I haven't. I've had no accident at all, and as for anaemia, well, I don't seem to show the ordinary symptoms of it. The inexplicable thing is that I've lost blood without knowing it,

and apparently this has been going on for some time, for I've been getting steadily worse. It was almost imperceptible at first—not a sudden collapse, you understand, but a gradual failure of health."

"I wonder," remarked Vance slowly, "what induced you to consult me? For you know, of course, the direction in which I pursue my investigations. May I ask if you have reason to consider that your state of health is due to some cause which we may describe as super-physical?"

A slight colour came to Davenant's white cheeks.

"There are curious circumstances," he said in a low and earnest tone of voice. "I've been turning them over in my mind, trying to see light through them. I daresay it's all the sheerest folly—and I must tell you that I'm not in the least a superstitious sort of man. I don't mean to say that I'm absolutely incredulous, but I've never given thought to such things—I've led too active a life. But, as I have said, there are curious circumstances about my case, and that is why I decided upon consulting you."

"Will you tell me everything without reserve?" said Vance. I could see that he was interested. He was sitting up in his chair, his feet supported on a stool, his elbows on his knees, his chin in his hands—a favourite attitude of his. "Have you," he suggested, slowly, "any mark upon your body, anything that you might associate, however remotely, with your present weakness and ill-health?"

"It's a curious thing that you should ask me that question," returned Davenant, "because I have got a curious mark, a sort of scar, that I can't account for. But I showed it to the doctors, and they assured me that it could have nothing whatever to do with my condition. In any case, if it had, it was something altogether outside their experience. I think they imagined it to be nothing more than a birthmark, a sort of mole, for they asked me if I'd had it all my life. But that I can swear I haven't. I only noticed it for the first time about six months ago, when my health began to fail. But you can see for yourself."

He loosened his collar and bared his throat. Vance rose and made a careful scrutiny of the suspicious mark. It was situated a very little to the left of the central line, just above the clavicle, and, as Vance pointed out, directly over the big vessels of the throat. My friend called to me so that I might examine it, too. Whatever the opinion of the doctors may have been, Aylmer was obviously deeply interested.

And yet there was very little to show. The skin was quite intact, and there was no sign of inflammation. There were two red marks, about an inch apart, each of which was inclined to be crescent in shape. They were more visible than they might otherwise have been owing to the peculiar whiteness of Davenant's skin.

"It can't be anything of importance," said Davenant, with a slightly uneasy laugh. "I'm inclined to think the marks are dying away."

"Have you ever noticed them more inflamed than they are at present?" inquired Vance. "If so, was it at any special time?"

Davenant reflected. "Yes," he replied slowly, "there have been times, usually, I think perhaps invariably, when I wake up in the morning, that I've noticed them larger and more angry looking. And I've felt a slight sensation of pain—a tingling—oh, very slight, and I've never worried about it. Only now you suggest it to my mind, I believe that those same mornings I have felt particularly tired and done up—a sensation of lassitude absolutely unusual to me. And once, Mr. Vance, I remember quite distinctly that there was a stain of blood close to the mark. I didn't think anything of it at the time, and just wiped it away."

"I see." Aylmer Vance resumed his seat and invited his visitor to do the same. "And now," he resumed, "you said, Mr. Davenant, that there are certain peculiar circumstances you wish to acquaint me with. Will you do so?"

And so Davenant readjusted his collar and proceeded to tell his story. I will tell it as far as I can, without any reference to the occasional interruptions of Vance and myself.

Paul Davenant, as I have said, was a man of wealth and position, and so, in every sense of the word, he was a suitable husband for Miss Jessica MacThane, the young lady who eventually be-

came his wife. Before coming to the incidents attending his loss of health, he had a great deal to recount about Miss MacThane and her family history.

She was of Scottish descent, and although she had certain characteristic features of her race, she was not really Scotch in appearance. Hers was the beauty of the far South rather than that of the Highlands from which she had her origin. Names are not always suited to their owners, and Miss MacThane's was peculiarly inappropriate. She had, in fact, been christened Jessica in a sort of pathetic effort to counteract her obvious departure from normal type. There was a reason for this which we were soon to learn.

Miss MacThane was especially remarkable for her wonderful red hair, hair such as one hardly ever sees outside of Italy—not the Celtic red—and it was so long that it reached to her feet, and it had an extraordinary gloss upon it so that it seemed almost to have individual life of its own. Then she had just the complexion that one would expect with such hair, the purest ivory white, and not in the least marred by freckles, as is so often the case with red-haired girls. Her beauty was derived from an ancestress who had been brought to Scotland from some foreign shore—no one knew exactly whence.

Davenant fell in love with her almost at once and he had every reason to believe, in spite of her many admirers, that his love was returned. At this time he knew very little about her personal history. He was aware only that she was very wealthy in her own right, an orphan, and the last representative of a race that had once been famous in the annals of history—or rather infamous, for the MacThanes had distinguished themselves more by cruelty and lust of blood than by deeds of chivalry. A clan of turbulent robbers in the past, they had helped to add many a blood-stained page to the history of their country.

Jessica had lived with her father, who owned a house in London, until his death when she was about fifteen years of age. Her mother had died in Scotland when Jessica was still a tiny child. Mr. MacThane had been so affected by his wife's death that, with his little daughter, he had abandoned his Scotch estate altogether—or so it was believed—leaving it to the management of a bailiff—though, indeed, there was but little work for the bailiff to do, since there were practically no tenants left. Blackwick Castle had borne for many years a most unenviable reputation.

After the death of her father, Miss MacThane had gone to live with a certain Mrs. Meredith, who was a connection of her mother's—on her father's side she had not a single relation left. Jessica was absolutely the last of a clan once so extensive that intermarriage had been a tradition of the family, but for which the last two hundred years had been gradually dwindling to extinction.

Mrs. Meredith took Jessica into Society—which would never have been her privilege had Mr. MacThane lived, for he was a moody, self-absorbed man, and prematurely old—one who seemed worn down by the weight of a great grief.

Well, I have said that Paul Davenant quickly fell in love with Jessica, and it was not long before he proposed for her hand. To his great surprise, for he had good reason to believe that she cared for him, he met with a refusal; nor would she give any explanation, though she burst into a flood of pitiful tears.

Bewildered and bitterly disappointed, he consulted Mrs. Meredith, with whom he happened to be on friendly terms, and from her he learnt that Jessica had already had several proposals, all from quite desirable men, but that one after another had been rejected.

Paul consoled himself with the reflection that perhaps Jessica did not love them, whereas he was quite sure that she cared for himself. Under these circumstances he determined to try again.

He did so, and with better result. Jessica admitted her love, but at the same time she repeated that she would not marry him. Love and marriage were not for her. Then, to his utter amazement, she declared that she had been born under a curse—a curse which, sooner or later was bound to show itself in her, and which, moreover, must react cruelly, perhaps fatally, upon anyone with whom she linked her life. How could she allow a man she

loved to take such a risk? Above all, since the evil was hereditary, there was one point upon which she had quite made up her mind: no child should ever call her mother—she must be the last of her race indeed.

Of course, Davenant was amazed and inclined to think that Jessica had got some absurd idea into her head which a little reasoning on his part would dispel. There was only one other possible explanation. Was it lunacy she was afraid of?

But Jessica shook her head. She did not know of any lunacy in her family. The ill was deeper, more subtle than that. And then she told him all that she knew.

The curse—she made use of that word for want of a better—was attached to the ancient race from which she had her origin. Her father had suffered from it, and his father and grandfather before him. All three had taken to themselves young wives who had died mysteriously, of some wasting disease, within a few years. Had they observed the ancient family tradition of intermarriage this might possibly not have happened, but in their case, since the family was so near extinction, this had not been possible.

For the curse—or whatever it was—did not kill those who bore the name of MacThane. It only rendered them a danger to others. It was as if they absorbed from the blood-soaked walls of their fatal castle a deadly taint which reacted terribly upon those with whom they were brought into contact, especially their nearest and dearest.

"Do you know what my father said we have it in us to become?" said Jessica with a shudder. "He used the word vampires. Paul, think of it—vampires—preying upon the life blood of others."

And then, when Davenant was inclined to laugh, she checked him. "No," she cried out, "it is not impossible. Think. We are a decadent race. From the earliest times our history has been marked by bloodshed and cruelty. The walls of Blackwick Castle are impregnated with evil—every stone could tell its tale of violence, pain, lust, and murder. What can one expect of those who have spent their lifetime between its walls?"

"But you have not done so," exclaimed Paul.

"You have been spared that, Jessica. You were taken away after your mother died, and you have no recollection of Blackwick Castle, none at all. And you need never set foot in it again."

"I'm afraid the evil is in my blood," she replied sadly, "although I am unconscious of it now. And as for not returning to Blackwick—I'm not sure I can help myself. At least, that is what my father warned me of. He said there is something there, some compelling force, that will call me to it in spite of myself. But, oh, I don't know—I don't know, and that is what makes it so difficult. If I could only believe that all this is nothing but an idle superstition, I might be happy again, for I have it in me to enjoy life, and I'm young, very young, but my father told me these things when he was on his death-bed." She added the last words in a low, awe-stricken tone.

Paul pressed her to tell him all that she knew, and eventually she revealed another fragment of family history which seemed to have some bearing upon the case. It dealt with her own astonishing likeness to that ancestress of a couple of hundred years ago, whose existence seemed to have presaged the gradual downfall of the clan of the Mac-Thanes.

A certain Robert MacThane, departing from the traditions of his family, which demanded that he should not marry outside his clan, brought home a wife from foreign shores, a woman of wonderful beauty, who was possessed of glowing masses of red hair and a complexion of ivory whiteness—such as had more or less distinguished since then every female of the race born in the direct line.

It was not long before this woman came to be regarded in the neighbourhood as a witch. Queer stories were circulated abroad as to her doings, and the reputation of Blackwick Castle became worse than ever before.

And then one day she disappeared. Robert Mac-Thane had been absent upon some business for twenty-four hours, and it was upon his return that he found her gone. The neighbourhood was searched, but without avail, and then Robert, who was a violent man and who had adored his foreign wife, called together certain of his tenants whom he suspected, rightly or wrongly, of foul play, and had them murdered in cold blood. Murder was easy in those days, yet such an outcry was raised that Robert had to take to flight, leaving his two children in the care of their nurse, and for a long while Blackwick Castle was without a master.

But its evil reputation persisted. It was said that Zaida, the witch, though dead, still made her presence felt. Many children of the tenantry and young people of the neighbourhood sickened and died—possibly of quite natural causes; but this did not prevent a mantle of terror settling upon the countryside, for it was said that Zaida had been seen—a pale woman clad in white—flitting about the cottages at night, and where she passed sickness and death were sure to supervene.

And from that time the fortune of the family gradually declined. Heir succeeded heir, but no sooner was he installed at Blackwick Castle than his nature, whatever it may previously have been, seemed to undergo a change. It was as if he absorbed into himself all the weight of evil that had stained his family name—as if he did, indeed, become a vampire, bringing blight upon any not directly connected with his own house.

And so, by degrees, Blackwick was deserted of its tenantry. The land around it was left uncultivated—the farms stood empty. This had persisted to the present day, for the superstitious peasantry still told their tales of the mysterious white woman who hovered about the neighbourhood, and whose appearance betokened death—and possibly worse than death.

And yet it seemed that the last representatives of the MacThanes could not desert their ancestral home. Riches they had, sufficient to live happily upon elsewhere, but, drawn by some power they could not contend against, they had preferred to spend their lives in the solitude of the now half-ruined castle, shunned by their neighbours, feared and execrated by the few tenants that still clung to their soil.

So it had been with Jessica's grandfather and great-grandfather. Each of them had married a young wife, and in each case their love story had been all too brief. The vampire spirit was still abroad, expressing itself—or so it seemed—through the living representatives of bygone generations of evil, and young blood had been demanded as the sacrifice.

And to them had succeeded Jessica's father. He had not profited by their example, but had followed directly in their footsteps. And the same fate had befallen the wife whom he passionately adored. She had died of pernicious anaemia—so the doctors said—but he had regarded himself as her murderer.

But, unlike his predecessors, he had torn himself away from Blackwick—and this for the sake of his child. Unknown to her, however, he had returned year after year, for there were times when the passionate longing for the gloomy, mysterious halls and corridors of the old castle, for the wild stretches of moorland, and the dark pinewoods, would come upon him too strongly to be resisted. And so he knew that for his daughter, as for himself, there was no escape, and he warned her, when the relief of death was at last granted to him, of what her fate must be.

This was the tale that Jessica told the man who wished to make her his wife, and he made light of it, as such a man would, regarding it all as foolish superstition, the delusion of a mind overwrought. And at last—perhaps it was not very difficult, for she loved him with all her heart and soul—he succeeded in inducing Jessica to think as he did, to banish morbid ideas, as he called them, from her brain, and to consent to marry him at an early date.

"I'll take any risk you like," he declared. "I'll even go and live at Blackwick if you should desire it. To think of you, my lovely Jessica, a vampire! Why, I never heard such nonsense in my life."

"Father said I'm very like Zaida, the witch," she protested, but he silenced her with a kiss.

And so they were married and spent their honeymoon abroad, and in the autumn Paul accepted an invitation to a house party in Scotland for the grouse shooting, a sport to which he was absolutely devoted, and Jessica agreed with him that there was no reason why he should forgo his pleasure.

Perhaps it was an unwise thing to do, to venture to Scotland, but by this time the young cou-

ple, more deeply in love with each other than ever, had got quite over their fears. Jessica was redolent with health and spirits, and more than once she declared that if they should be anywhere in the neighbourhood of Blackwick she would like to see the old castle out of curiosity, and just to show how absolutely she had got over the foolish terrors that used to assail her.

This seemed to Paul to be quite a wise plan, and so one day, since they were actually staying at no great distance, they motored over to Blackwick, and finding the bailiff, got him to show them over the castle.

It was a great castellated pile, grey with age, and in places falling into ruin. It stood on a steep hillside, with the rock of which it seemed to form part, and on one side of it there was a precipitous drop to a mountain stream a hundred feet below. The robber MacThanes of the old days could not have desired a better stronghold.

At the back, climbing up the mountainside were dark pinewoods, from which, here and there, rugged crags protruded, and these were fantastically shaped, some like gigantic and misshapen human forms, which stood up as if they mounted guard over the castle and the narrow gorge, by which alone it could be approached.

This gorge was always full of weird, uncanny sounds. It might have been a storehouse for the wind, which, even on calm days, rushed up and down as if seeking an escape, and it moaned among the pines and whistled in the crags and shouted derisive laughter as it was tossed from side to side of the rocky heights. It was like the plaint of lost souls—that is the expression Davenant made use of—the plaint of lost souls.

The road, little more than a track now, passed through this gorge, and then, after skirting a small but deep lake, which hardly knew the light of the sun so shut in was it by overhanging trees, climbed the hill to the castle.

And the castle! Davenant used but a few words to describe it, yet somehow I could see the gloomy edifice in my mind's eye, and something of the lurking horror that it contained communicated itself to my brain. Perhaps my clairvoyant sense assisted me, for when he spoke of them I seemed already acquainted with the great stone halls, the long corridors, gloomy and cold even on the brightest and warmest of days, the dark, oak-panelled rooms, and the broad central staircase up which one of the early MacThanes had once led a dozen men on horseback in pursuit of a stag which had taken refuge within the precincts of the castle. There was the keep, too, its walls so thick that the ravages of time had made no impression upon them, and beneath the keep were dungeons which could tell terrible tales of ancient wrong and lingering pain.

Well, Mr. and Mrs. Davenant visited as much as the bailiff could show them of this ill-omened edifice, and Paul, for his part, thought pleasantly of his own Derbyshire home, the fine Georgian mansion, replete with every modern comfort, where he proposed to settle with his wife. And so he received something of a shock when, as they drove away, she slipped her hand into his and whispered:

"Paul, you promised, didn't you, that you would refuse me nothing?"

She had been strangely silent till she spoke those words. Paul, slightly apprehensive, assured her that she only had to ask—but the speech did not come from his heart, for he guessed vaguely what she desired.

She wanted to go and live at the castle—oh, only for a little while, for she was sure she would soon tire of it. But the bailiff had told her that there were papers, documents, which she ought to examine, since the property was now hers—and, besides, she was interested in this home of her ancestors, and wanted to explore it more thoroughly. Oh, no, she wasn't in the least influenced by the old superstition—that wasn't the attraction—she had quite got over those silly ideas. Paul had cured her, and since he himself was so convinced that they were without foundation he ought not to mind granting her her whim.

This was a plausible argument, not easy to controvert. In the end Paul yielded, though it was not without a struggle. He suggested amendments. Let him at least have the place done up for her—

that would take time; or let them postpone their visit till next year—in the summer—not move in just as the winter was upon them.

But Jessica did not want to delay longer than she could help, and she hated the idea of redecoration. Why, it would spoil the illusion of the old place, and, besides, it would be a waste of money since she only wished to remain there for a week or two. The Derbyshire house was not quite ready yet; they must allow time for the paper to dry on the walls.

And so, a week later, when their stay with their friends was concluded, they went to Blackwick, the bailiff having engaged a few raw servants and generally made things as comfortable for them as possible. Paul was worried and apprehensive, but he could not admit this to his wife after having so loudly proclaimed his theories on the subject of superstition.

They had been married three months at this time—nine had passed since then, and they had never left Blackwick for more than a few hours—till now Paul had come to London—alone.

"Over and over again," he declared, "my wife has begged me to go. With tears in her eyes, almost upon her knees, she has entreated me to leave her, but I have steadily refused unless she will accompany me. But that is the trouble, Mr. Vance, she cannot; there is something, some mysterious horror, that holds her there as surely as if she were bound with fetters. It holds her more strongly even than it held her father—we found out that he used to spend six months at least of every year at Blackwick—months when he pretended that he was travelling abroad. You see the spell—or whatever the accursed thing may be—never really relaxed its grip of him."

"Did you never attempt to take your wife away?" asked Vance.

"Yes, several times; but it was hopeless. She would become so ill as soon as we were beyond the limit of the estate that I invariably had to take her back. Once we got as far as Dorekirk—that is the nearest town, you know—and I thought I should be successful if only I could get through the night. But she escaped me; she climbed out of a window—she meant to go back on foot, at night, all those long miles. Then I have had doctors down; but it is I who wanted the doctors, not she. They have ordered me away, but I have refused to obey them till now."

"Is your wife changed at all—physically?" interrupted Vance.

Davenant reflected. "Changed," he said, "yes, but so subtly that I hardly know how to describe it. She is more beautiful than ever—and yet it isn't the same beauty, if you can understand me. I have spoken of her white complexion, well, one is more than ever conscious of it now, because her lips have become so red—they are almost like a splash of blood upon her face. And the upper one has a peculiar curve that I don't think it had before, and when she laughs she doesn't smile—do you know what I mean? Then her hair—it has lost its wonderful gloss. Of course, I know she is fretting about me; but that is so peculiar, too, for at times, as I have told you, she will implore me to go and leave her, and then perhaps only a few minutes later, she will wreathe her arms round my neck and say she cannot live without me. And I feel that there is a struggle going on within her, that she is only yielding slowly to the horrible influence—whatever it is—that she is herself when she begs me to go, but when she entreats me to stay—and it is then that her fascination is most intense—oh, I can't help remembering what she told me before we were married, and that word"—he lowered his voice—"the word 'vampire'—"

He passed his hand over his brow that was wet with perspiration. "But that's absurd, ridiculous," he muttered. "These fantastic beliefs have been exploded years ago. We live in the twentieth century."

A pause ensued, then Vance said quietly, "Mr. Davenant, since you have taken me into your confidence, since you have found doctors of no avail, will you let me try to help you? I think I may be of some use—if it is not already too late. Should you agree, Mr. Dexter and I will accompany you, as you have suggested, to Blackwick Castle as early as possible—by tonight's mail North. Under ordinary circumstances I should tell you as you value your life, not to return—"

Davenant shook his head. "That is advice which I should never take," he declared. "I had already decided, under any circumstances, to travel North tonight. I am glad that you both will accompany me."

And so it was decided. We settled to meet at the station, and presently Paul Davenant took his departure. Any other details that remained to be told he would put us in possession of during the course of the journey.

"A curious and most interesting case," remarked Vance when we were alone. "What do you make of it, Dexter?"

"I suppose," I replied cautiously, "that there is such a thing as vampirism even in these days of advanced civilization? I can understand the evil influence that a very old person may have upon a young one if they happen to be in constant intercourse—the worn-out tissue sapping healthy vitality for their own support. And there are certain people—I could think of several myself—who seem to depress one and undermine one's energies, quite unconsciously, of course, but one feels somehow that vitality has passed from oneself to them. And in this case, when the force is centuries old, expressing itself, in some mysterious way, through Davenant's wife, is it not feasible to believe that he may be physically affected by it, even though the whole thing is sheerly mental?"

"You think, then," demanded Vance, "that it is sheerly mental? Tell me, if that is so, how do you account for the marks on Davenant's throat?"

This was a question to which I found no reply, and though I pressed him for his views, Vance would not commit himself further just then.

Of our long journey to Scotland I need say nothing. We did not reach Blackwick Castle till late in the afternoon of the following day. The place was just as I had conceived it—as I have already described it. And a sense of gloom settled upon me as our car jolted us over the rough road that led through the Gorge of the Winds—a gloom that deepened when we penetrated into the vast cold hall of the castle.

Mrs. Davenant, who had been informed by telegram of our arrival, received us cordially. She knew nothing of our actual mission, regarding us merely as friends of her husband's. She was most solicitous on his behalf, but there was something strained about her tone, and it made me me feel vaguely uneasy. The impression that I got was that the woman was impelled to everything that she said or did by some force outside herself—but, of course, this was a conclusion that the circumstances I was aware of might easily have conduced to. In every other aspect she was charming, and she had an extraordinary fascination of appearance and manner that made me readily understand the force of a remark made by Davenant during our journey.

"I want to live for Jessica's sake. Get her away from Blackwick, Vance, and I feel that all will be well. I'd go through hell to have her restored to me—as she was."

And now that I had seen Mrs. Davenant I realized what he meant by those last words. Her fascination was stronger than ever, but it was not a natural fascination—not that of a normal woman, such as she had been. It was the fascination of a Circe, of a witch, of an enchantress—and as such was irresistible.

We had a strong proof of the evil within her soon after our arrival. It was a test that Vance had quietly prepared. Davenant had mentioned that no flowers grew at Blackwick, and Vance declared that we must take some with us as a present for the lady of the house. He purchased a bouquet of pure white roses at the little town where we left the train, for the motorcar had been sent to meet us.

Soon after our arrival he presented these to Mrs. Davenant. She took them it seemed to me nervously, and hardly had her hand touched them before they fell to pieces, in a shower of crumpled petals, to the floor.

"We must act at once," said Vance to me when we were descending to dinner that night. "There must be no delay."

"What are you afraid of?" I whispered.

"Davenant has been absent a week," he replied grimly. "He is stronger than when he went away, but not strong enough to survive the loss of more blood. He must be protected. There is danger tonight."

"You mean from his wife?" I shuddered at the ghastliness of the suggestion.

"That is what time will show." Vance turned to me and added a few words with intense earnestness. "Mrs. Davenant, Dexter, is at present hovering between two conditions. The evil thing has not yet completely mastered her—you remember what Davenant said, how she would beg him to go away and the next moment entreat him to stay? She has made a struggle, but she is gradually succumbing; and this last week, spent here alone, has strengthened the evil. And that is what I have got to fight, Dexter—it is to be a contest of will, a contest that will go on silently till one or the other obtains the mastery. If you watch, you may see. Should a change show itself in Mrs. Davenant you will know that I have won."

Thus I knew the direction in which my friend proposed to act. It was to be a war of his will against the mysterious power that had laid its curse upon the house of MacThane. Mrs. Davenant must be released from the fatal charm that held her.

And I, knowing what was going on, was able to watch and understand. I realized that the silent contest had begun even while we ate dinner. Mrs. Davenant ate practically nothing and seemed ill at ease; she fidgeted in her chair, talked a great deal, and laughed—it was the laugh without a smile, as Davenant had described it. And as soon as she was able to she withdrew.

Later, as we sat in the drawing-room, I could feel the clash of wills. The air in the room felt electric and heavy, charged with tremendous but invisible forces. And outside, round the castle, the wind whistled and shrieked and moaned—it was as if all the dead and gone MacThanes, a grim army, had collected to fight the battle of their race.

And all this while we four in the drawing-room were sitting and talking the ordinary commonplaces of after-dinner conversation! That was the extraordinary part of it—Paul Davenant suspected nothing, and I, who knew, had to play my part. But I hardly took my eyes from Jessica's face. When would the change come, or was it, indeed, too late!

At last Davenant rose and remarked that he was tired and would go to bed. There was no need for Jessica to hurry. He would sleep that night in his dressing-room and did not want to be disturbed.

And it was at that moment, as his lips met hers in a goodnight kiss, as she wreathed her enchantress arms about him, careless of our presence, her eyes gleaming hungrily, that the change came.

It came with a fierce and threatening shriek of wind, and a rattling of the casement, as if the horde of ghosts without was about to break in upon us. A long, quivering sigh escaped from Jessica's lips, her arms fell from her husband's shoulders, and she drew back, swaying a little from side to side.

"Paul," she cried, and somehow the whole timbre of her voice was changed, "what a wretch I've been to bring you back to Blackwick, ill as you are! But we'll go away, dear; yes, I'll go, too. Oh, will you take me away—take me away tomorrow?" She spoke with an intense earnestness—unconscious all the time of what had been happening to her. Long shudders were convulsing her frame. "I don't know why I've wanted to stay here," she kept repeating. "I hate the place, really—it's evil—evil."

Having heard these words I exulted, for surely Vance's success was assured. But I was to learn that the danger was not yet past.

Husband and wife separated, each going to their own room. I noticed the grateful, if mystified glance that Davenant threw at Vance, vaguely aware, as he must have been, that my friend was somehow responsible for what had happened. It was settled that plans for departure were to be discussed on the morrow.

"I have succeeded," Vance said hurriedly, when we were alone, "but the change may be a transitory one. I must keep watch tonight. Go you to bed, Dexter, there is nothing that you can do."

I obeyed—though I would sooner have kept watch, too—watch against a danger of which I had no understanding. I went to my room, a gloomy and sparsely furnished apartment, but I knew that it was quite impossible for me to think of sleeping. And so, dressed as I was, I went and sat by the open window, for now the wind that had raged round the castle had died down to a low moaning in the pinetrees—a whimpering of time-worn agony.

And it was as I sat thus that I became aware of a white figure that stole out from the castle by a door that I could not see, and, with hands clasped, ran swiftly across the terrace to the wood. I had but a momentary glance, but I felt convinced that the figure was that of Jessica Davenant.

And instinctively I knew that some great danger was imminent. It was, I think, the suggestion of despair conveyed by those clasped hands. At any rate, I did not hesitate. My window was some height from the ground, but the wall below was ivy-clad and afforded good foothold. The descent was quite easy. I achieved it, and was just in time to take up the pursuit in the right direction, which was into the thickness of the wood that clung to the slope of the hill.

I shall never forget that wild chase. There was just sufficient room to enable me to follow the rough path, which, luckily, since I had now lost sight of my quarry, was the only possible way that she could have taken; there were no intersecting tracks, and the wood was too thick on either side to permit of deviation.

And the wood seemed full of dreadful sounds—moaning and wailing and hideous laughter. The wind, of course, and the screaming of night birds—once I felt the fluttering of wings in close proximity to my face. But I could not rid myself of the thought that I, in my turn, was being pursued, that the forces of hell were combined against me.

The path came to an abrupt end on the border of the sombre lake that I have already mentioned. And now I realized that I was indeed only just in time, for before me, plunging knee deep in the water, I recognized the white-clad figure of the woman I had been pursuing. Hearing my footsteps, she turned her head, and then threw up her arms and screamed. Her red hair fell in heavy masses about her shoulders, and her face, as I saw it in that moment, was hardly human for the agony of remorse that it depicted.

YLMER VANCE AND THE VAMPIRE

"Go!" she screamed. "For God's sake let me die!"

But I was by her side almost as she spoke. She struggled with me—sought vainly to tear herself from my clasp—implored me, with panting breath, to let her drown.

"It's the only way to save him!" she gasped. "Don't you understand that I am a thing accursed? For it is I—I—who have sapped his life blood! I know it now, the truth has been revealed to me tonight! I am a vampire, without hope in this world or the next, so for his sake—for the sake of his unborn child—let me die—let me die!"

Was ever so terrible an appeal made? Yet I—what could I do? Gently I overcame her resistance and drew her back to shore. By the time I reached it she was lying a dead weight upon my arm. I laid her down upon a mossy bank, and, kneeling by her side, gazed intently into her face.

And then I knew that I had done well. For the face I looked upon was not that of Jessica the vampire, as I had seen it that afternoon, it was the face of Jessica, the woman whom Paul Davenant had loved.

And later Aylmer Vance had his tale to tell. "I waited," he said, "until I knew that Davenant was asleep, and then I stole into his room to watch by his bedside. And presently she came, as I guessed she would, the vampire, the accursed thing that has preyed upon the souls of her kin, making them like to herself when they too have passed into Shadowland, and gathering sustenance for her horrid task from the blood of those who are alien to her race. Paul's body and Jessica's soul—it is for one and the other, Dexter, that we have fought."

"You mean," I hesitated, "Zaida the witch?"

"Even so," he agreed. "Hers is the evil spirit that has fallen like a blight upon the house of Mac-Thane. But now I think she may be exorcised for ever."

"Tell me."

"She came to Paul Davenant last night, as she must have done before, in the guise of his wife. You know that Jessica bears a strong resemblance to her ancestress. He opened his arms, but she was foiled of her prey, for I had taken my precautions; I had placed that upon Davenant's breast while he slept which robbed the vampire of her power of ill. She sped wailing from the room—a shadow—she who a minute before had looked at him with Jessica's eyes and spoken to him with Jessica's voice. Her red lips were Jessica's lips, and they were close to his when his eyes were opened and he saw her as she was—a hideous phantom of the corruption of the ages. And so the spell was removed, and she fled away to the place whence she had come—"

He paused. "And now?" I inquired.

"Blackwick Castle must be razed to the ground," he replied. "That is the only way. Every stone of it, every brick, must be ground to powder and burnt with fire, for therein is the cause of all the evil. Davenant has consented."

"And Mrs. Davenant?"

"I think," Vance answered cautiously, "that all may be well with her. The curse will be removed with the destruction of the castle. She has not—thanks to you—perished under its influence. She was less guilty than she imagined—herself preyed upon rather than preying. But can't you understand her remorse when she realized, as she was bound to realize, the part she had played? And the knowledge of the child to come—its fatal inheritance—"

"I understand," I muttered with a shudder. And then, under my breath, I whispered, "Thank God!"

## DRACULA'S GUEST

# Bram Stoker

Bram (Abraham) Stoker (1847–1912) was born in a seaside suburb of Dublin. He was extremely sickly as a child, his long bedridden hours made bearable by his mother's stories of horror: fictional, folklore, and real-life, including grisly tales of the 1832 cholera epidemic in Sligo. His health improved when he went to school at seven, becoming a star athlete at Trinity College in Dublin. He began writing short fiction as well as theater reviews for the *Dublin Mail*, which was partly owned by the famous writer of horror and supernatural fiction Sheridan Le Fanu, then took the job of manager to Henry Irving, the most popular and acclaimed actor of his generation, a position Stoker held for twenty-six years of eighteen-hour working days.

In spite of the debilitating schedule, Stoker was able to write more than a dozen novels and other works during his years managing Irving, including the most famous horror novel of the nineteenth century, *Dracula* (1897). *Dracula* became both a critical and popular success, reprinted countless times. Freudian elements may have been at work in Stoker's subconscious, as he named the tireless vampire hunter Abraham Van Helsing, using his own first name, while Irving had the attributes of a "psychic" vampire, draining the life of the author with the relentless workload.

"Dracula's Guest" was written as a chapter in *Dracula* that was never used. It was published for the first time in the posthumous *Dracula's Guest and Other Stories* (London: Routledge, 1914).

# Dracula's Guest

## BRAM STOKER

When we started for our drive the sun was shining brightly on Munich, and the air was full of the joyousness of early summer. Just as we were about to depart, Herr Delbrück (the maître d'hôtel of the Quatre Saisons, where I was staying) came down, bareheaded, to the carriage and, after wishing me a pleasant drive, said to the coachman, still holding his hand on the handle of the carriage door:

"Remember you are back by nightfall. The sky looks bright but there is a shiver in the north wind that says there may be a sudden storm. But I am sure you will not be late." Here he smiled, and added, "For you know what night it is."

Johann answered with an emphatic, "Ja, mein Herr," and, touching his hat, drove off quickly. When we had cleared the town, I said, after signalling to him to stop:

"Tell me, Johann, what is tonight?"

He crossed himself, as he answered laconically: "Walpurgisnacht." Then he took out his watch, a great, old-fashioned German silver thing as big as a turnip, and looked at it, with his eyebrows gathered together and a little impatient shrug of his shoulders. I realized that this was his way of respectfully protesting against the unnecessary delay, and sank back in the carriage, merely motioning him to proceed. He started off rapidly, as if to make up for lost time. Every now and then the horses seemed to throw up their heads and sniffed the air suspiciously. On such occasions I often looked round in alarm. The road was pretty bleak, for we were traversing a sort of high, windswept plateau. As we drove, I saw a road that looked but little used, and which seemed to dip through a little, winding valley. It looked so inviting that, even at the risk of offending him, I called Johann to stop—and when he had pulled up, I told him I would like to drive down that road. He made all sorts of excuses, and frequently crossed himself as he spoke. This somewhat piqued my curiosity, so I asked him various questions. He answered fencingly, and repeatedly looked at his watch in protest. Finally I said:

"Well, Johann, I want to go down this road. I shall not ask you to come unless you like; but tell me why you do not like to go, that is all I ask." For answer he seemed to throw himself off the box, so quickly did he reach the ground. Then he stretched out his hands appealingly to me, and implored me not to go. There was just enough of English mixed with the German for me to understand the drift of his talk. He seemed always just about to tell me something—the very idea of which evidently frightened him; but each time he pulled himself up, saying, as he crossed himself: "Walpurgisnacht!"

I tried to argue with him, but it was difficult to argue with a man when I did not know his language. The advantage certainly rested with him, for although he began to speak in English, of a very crude and broken kind, he always got excited and broke into his native tongue—and every time he did so, he looked at his watch. Then the horses became restless and sniffed the air. At this he grew very pale, and, looking around in a frightened way, he suddenly jumped forward, took them by the bridles, and led them on some twenty feet. I followed, and asked why he had done this. For answer he crossed himself, pointed to the spot we had left and drew his carriage in the direction of the other road, indicating a cross, and said, first in German, then in English: "Buried him—him what killed themselves."

I remembered the old custom of burying suicides at cross-roads: "Ah! I see, a suicide. How interesting!" But for the life of me I could not make out why the horses were frightened.

While we were talking, we heard a sort of sound between a yelp and a bark. It was far away; but the horses got very restless, and it took Johann all his time to quiet them. He was pale, and said: "It sounds like a wolf—but yet there are no wolves here now."

"No?" I said, questioning him. "Isn't it long since the wolves were so near the city?"

"Long, long," he answered, "in the spring and summer; but with the snow the wolves have been here not so long."

While he was petting the horses and trying to quiet them, dark clouds drifted rapidly across the sky. The sunshine passed away, and a breath of cold wind seemed to drift past us. It was only a breath, however, and more in the nature of a warning than a fact, for the sun came out brightly again. Johann looked under his lifted hand at the horizon and said:

"The storm of snow, he comes before long time." Then he looked at his watch again, and, straightway holding his reins firmly—for the horses

were still pawing the ground restlessly and shaking their heads—he climbed to his box as though the time had come for proceeding on our journey.

I felt a little obstinate and did not at once get into the carriage.

"Tell me," I said, "about this place where the road leads," and I pointed down.

Again he crossed himself and mumbled a prayer, before he answered: "It is unholy."

"What is unholy?" I enquired.

"The village."

"Then there is a village?"

"No, no. No one lives there hundreds of years."

My curiosity was piqued: "But you said there was a village."

"There was."

"Where is it now?"

Whereupon he burst out into a long story in German and English, so mixed up that I could not quite understand exactly what he said, but roughly I gathered that long ago, hundreds of years, men had died there and been buried in their graves; and sounds were heard under the clay, and when the graves were opened, men and women were found rosy with life, and their mouths red with blood. And so, in haste to save their lives (aye, and their souls!—and here he crossed himself) those who were left fled away to other places, where the living died, and the dead were dead and not—not something. He was evidently afraid to speak the last words. As he proceeded with his narration, he grew more and more excited. It seemed as if his imagination had got hold of him, and he ended in a perfect paroxysm of fear—white-faced, perspiring, trembling, and looking round him, as if expecting that some dreadful presence would manifest itself there in the bright sunshine on the open plain. Finally, in an agony of desperation, he cried:

"Walpurgisnacht!" and pointed to the carriage for me to get in. All my English blood rose at this, and, standing back, I said:

"You are afraid, Johann—you are afraid. Go home; I shall return alone; the walk will do me good." The carriage door was open. I took from the seat my oak walking stick—which I always carry on my holiday excursions—and closed the door, pointing back to Munich, and said, "Go home, Johann—Walpurgisnacht doesn't concern Englishmen."

The horses were now more restive than ever, and Johann was trying to hold them in while excitedly imploring me not to do anything so foolish. I pitied the poor fellow, he was so deeply in earnest; but all the same I could not help laughing. His English was quite gone now. In his anxiety he had forgotten that his only means of making me understand was to talk my language, so he jabbered away in his native German. It began to be a little tedious. After giving the direction, "Home!" I turned to go down the cross-road into the valley.

With a despairing gesture, Johann turned his horses towards Munich. I leaned on my stick and looked after him. He went slowly along the road for a while; then there came over the crest of the hill a man tall and thin. I could see so much in the distance. When he drew near the horses, they began to jump and kick about, then to scream with terror. Johann could not hold them in; they bolted down the road, running away madly. I watched them out of sight, then looked for the stranger, but I found that he, too, was gone.

With a light heart I turned down the side road through the deepening valley to which Johann had objected. There was not the slightest reason, that I could see, for his objection; and I daresay I tramped for a couple of hours without thinking of time or distance, and certainly without seeing a person or a house. So far as the place was concerned, it was desolation itself. But I did not notice this particularly till, on turning a bend in the road, I came upon a scattered fringe of wood; then I recognized that I had been impressed unconsciously by the desolation of the region through which I had passed.

I sat down to rest myself, and began to look around. It struck me that it was considerably colder than it had been at the commencement of my walk—a sort of sighing sound seemed to be around me, with, now and then, high overhead, a sort of muffled roar. Looking upwards I noticed that great thick clouds were drifting rapidly across the sky from North to South at a great height. There were

signs of a coming storm in some lofty stratum of the air. I was a little chilly, and, thinking that it was the sitting still after the exercise of walking, I resumed my journey.

The ground I passed over was now much more picturesque. There were no striking objects that the eye might single out; but in all there was a charm of beauty. I took little heed of time and it was only when the deepening twilight forced itself upon me that I began to think of how I should find my way home. The brightness of the day had gone. The air was cold, and the drifting of clouds high overhead was more marked. They were accompanied by a sort of far-away rushing sound, through which seemed to come at intervals that mysterious cry which the driver had said came from a wolf. For a while I hesitated. I had said I would see the deserted village, so on I went, and presently came on a wide stretch of open country, shut in by hills all around. Their sides were covered with trees which spread down to the plain, dotting, in clumps, the gentler slopes and hollows which showed here and there. I followed with my eye the winding of the road, and saw that it curved close to one of the densest of these clumps and was lost behind it.

As I looked there came a cold shiver in the air, and the snow began to fall. I thought of the miles and miles of bleak country I had passed, and then hurried on to seek the shelter of the wood in front. Darker and darker grew the sky, and faster and heavier fell the snow, till the earth before and around me was a glistening white carpet the further edge of which was lost in misty vagueness. The road was here but crude, and when on the level its boundaries were not so marked, as when it passed through the cuttings; and in a little while I found that I must have strayed from it, for I missed underfoot the hard surface, and my feet sank deeper in the grass and moss. Then the wind grew stronger and blew with ever increasing force, till I was fain to run before it. The air became icy cold, and in spite of my exercise I began to suffer. The snow was now falling so thickly and whirling around me in such rapid eddies that I could hardly keep my eyes open. Every now and then the heavens were torn asunder by vivid lightning, and in the flashes I could see ahead of me a great mass of trees, chiefly yew and cypress all heavily coated with snow.

I was soon amongst the shelter of the trees, and there in comparative silence, I could hear the rush of the wind high overhead. Presently the blackness of the storm had become merged in the darkness of the night. By-and-by the storm seemed to be passing away: it now only came in fierce puffs and blasts. At such moments the weird sound of the wolf appeared to be echoed by many similar sounds around me.

Now and again, through the black mass of drifting cloud, came a straggling ray of moonlight, which lit up the expanse, and showed me that I was at the edge of a dense mass of cypress and yew trees. As the snow had ceased to fall, I walked out from the shelter and began to investigate more closely. It appeared to me that, amongst so many old foundations as I had passed, there might be still standing a house in which, though in ruins, I could find some sort of shelter for a while. As I skirted the edge of the copse, I found that a low wall encircled it, and following this I presently found an opening. Here the cypresses formed an alley leading up to a square mass of some kind of building. Just as I caught sight of this, however, the drifting clouds obscured the moon, and I passed up the path in darkness. The wind must have grown colder, for I felt myself shiver as I walked; but there was hope of shelter, and I groped my way blindly on.

I stopped, for there was a sudden stillness. The storm had passed; and, perhaps in sympathy with nature's silence, my heart seemed to cease to beat. But this was only momentarily; for suddenly the moonlight broke through the clouds, showing me that I was in a graveyard, and that the square object before me was a great massive tomb of marble, as white as the snow that lay on and all around it. With the moonlight there came a fierce sigh of the storm, which appeared to resume its course with a long, low howl, as of many dogs or wolves. I was awed and shocked, and felt the cold percep-

tibly grow upon me till it seemed to grip me by the heart. Then while the flood of moonlight still fell on the marble tomb, the storm gave further evidence of renewing, as though it was returning on its track. Impelled by some sort of fascination, I approached the sepulchre to see what it was, and why such a thing stood alone in such a place. I walked around it, and read, over the Doric door, in German—

## COUNTESS DOLINGEN OF GRATZ

### IN STYRIA
#### SOUGHT AND FOUND DEATH,
#### 1801

On the top of the tomb, seemingly driven through the solid marble—for the structure was composed of a few vast blocks of stone—was a great iron spike or stake. On going to the back I saw, graven in great Russian letters:

### THE DEAD TRAVEL FAST

There was something so weird and uncanny about the whole thing that it gave me a turn and made me feel quite faint. I began to wish, for the first time, that I had taken Johann's advice. Here a thought struck me, which came under almost mysterious circumstances and with a terrible shock. This was Walpurgis Night!

Walpurgis Night, when, according to the belief of millions of people, the devil was abroad—when the graves were opened and the dead came forth and walked. When all evil things of earth and air and water held revel. This very place the driver had specially shunned. This was the depopulated village of centuries ago. This was where the suicide lay; and this was the place where I was alone—unmanned, shivering with cold in a shroud of snow with a wild storm gathering again upon me! It took all my philosophy, all the religion I had been taught, all my courage, not to collapse in a paroxysm of fright.

And now a perfect tornado burst upon me. The

ground shook as though thousands of horses thundered across it; and this time the storm bore on its icy wings, not snow, but great hailstones which drove with such violence that they might have come from the thongs of Balearic slingers—hailstones that beat down leaf and branch and made the shelter of the cypresses of no more avail than though their stems were standing corn. At the first I had rushed to the nearest tree; but I was soon fain to leave it and seek the only spot that seemed to afford refuge, the deep Doric doorway of the marble tomb. There, crouching against the massive bronze door, I gained a certain amount of protection from the beating of the hailstones, for now they only drove against me as they ricocheted from the ground and the side of the marble.

As I leaned against the door, it moved slightly and opened inwards. The shelter of even a tomb was welcome in that pitiless tempest, and I was about to enter it when there came a flash of forked lightning that lit up the whole expanse of the heavens. In the instant, as I am a living man, I saw, as my eyes were turned into the darkness of the tomb, a beautiful woman, with rounded cheeks and red lips, seemingly sleeping on a bier. As the thunder broke overhead, I was grasped as by the hand of a giant and hurled out into the storm. The whole thing was so sudden that, before I could realize the shock, moral as well as physical, I found the hailstones beating me down. At the same time I had a strange, dominating feeling that I was not alone. I looked towards the tomb. Just then there came another blinding flash, which seemed to strike the iron stake that surmounted the tomb and to pour through to the earth, blasting and crumbling the marble, as in a burst of flame. The dead woman rose for a moment of agony, while she was lapped in the flame, and her bitter scream of pain was drowned in the thundercrash. The last thing I heard was this mingling of dreadful sound, as again I was seized in the giant grasp and dragged away, while the hailstones beat on me, and the air around seemed reverberant with the howling of wolves. The last sight that I remembered was a vague, white, moving mass, as if all the graves around me had sent out the phantoms of their sheeted dead, and that they were closing in on me through the white cloudiness of the driving hail.

Gradually there came a sort of vague beginning of consciousness; then a sense of weariness that was dreadful. For a time I remembered nothing; but slowly my senses returned. My feet seemed positively racked with pain, yet I could not move them. They seemed to be numbed. There was an icy feeling at the back of my neck and all down my spine, and my ears, like my feet, were dead, yet in torment; but there was in my breast a sense of warmth which was, by comparison, delicious. It was as a nightmare, if one may use such an expression; for some heavy weight on my chest made it difficult for me to breathe.

This period of semi-lethargy seemed to remain a long time, and as it faded away I must have slept or swooned. Then came a sort of loathing, like the first stage of sea-sickness, and a wild desire to be free from something—I knew not what. A vast stillness enveloped me, as though all the world were asleep or dead—only broken by the low panting as of some animal close to me. I felt a warm rasping at my throat, then came a consciousness of the awful truth, which chilled me to the heart and sent the blood surging up through my brain. Some great animal was lying on me and now licking my throat. I feared to stir, for some instinct of prudence bade me lie still; but the brute seemed to realize that there was now some change in me, for it raised its head. Through my eyelashes I saw above me the two great flaming eyes of a gigantic wolf. Its sharp white teeth gleamed in the gaping red mouth, and I could feel its hot breath fierce and acrid upon me.

For another spell of time I remembered no more. Then I became conscious of a low growl, followed by a yelp, renewed again and again. Then, seemingly very far away, I heard a "Holloa! Holloa!" as of many voices calling in unison. Cautiously I raised my head and looked in the direction whence the sound came; but the cemetery blocked my view. The wolf still continued to yelp in a strange way, and a red glare began to move round the grove of cypresses, as though following the sound. As the voices drew closer, the wolf yelped faster and louder. I feared to make either sound or motion. Nearer came the red glow, over the white pall which stretched into the darkness around me. Then all at once from beyond the trees there came at a trot a troop of horsemen bearing torches. The wolf rose from my breast and made for the cemetery. I saw one of the horsemen (soldiers by their caps and their long military cloaks) raise his carbine and take aim. A companion knocked up his arm, and I heard the ball whizz over my head. He had evidently taken my body for that of the wolf. Another sighted the animal as it slunk away, and a shot followed. Then, at a gallop, the troop rode forward—some towards me, others following the wolf as it disappeared amongst the snow-clad cypresses.

As they drew nearer I tried to move, but was powerless, although I could see and hear all that went on around me. Two or three of the soldiers jumped from their horses and knelt beside me. One of them raised my head, and placed his hand over my heart.

"Good news, comrades!" he cried. "His heart still beats!"

Then some brandy was poured down my throat; it put vigor into me, and I was able to open my eyes fully and look around. Lights and shadows were moving among the trees, and I heard men call to one another. They drew together, uttering frightened exclamations; and the lights flashed as the others came pouring out of the cemetery pell-mell, like men possessed. When the further ones came close to us, those who were around me asked them eagerly:

"Well, have you found him?"

The reply rang out hurriedly:

"No! No! Come away quick—quick! This is no place to stay, and on this of all nights!"

"What was it?" was the question, asked in all manner of keys. The answer came variously and all indefinitely as though the men were moved by some common impulse to speak, yet were restrained by some common fear from giving their thoughts.

"It—it—indeed!" gibbered one, whose wits had plainly given out for the moment.

"A wolf—and yet not a wolf!" another put in shudderingly.

"No use trying for him without the sacred bullet," a third remarked in a more ordinary manner.

"Serve us right for coming out on this night! Truly we have earned our thousand marks!" were the ejaculations of a fourth.

"There was blood on the broken marble," another said after a pause—"the lightning never brought that there. And for him—is he safe? Look at his throat! See, comrades, the wolf has been lying on him and keeping his blood warm."

The officer looked at my throat and replied:

"He is all right; the skin is not pierced. What does it all mean? We should never have found him but for the yelping of the wolf."

"What became of it?" asked the man who was holding up my head, and who seemed the least panic-stricken of the party, for his hands were steady and without tremor. On his sleeve was the chevron of a petty officer.

"It went to its home," answered the man, whose long face was pallid, and who actually shook with terror as he glanced around him fearfully. "There are graves enough there in which it may lie. Come, comrades—come quickly! Let us leave this cursed spot."

The officer raised me to a sitting posture, as he uttered a word of command; then several men placed me upon a horse. He sprang to the saddle behind me, took me in his arms, gave the word to advance; and, turning our faces away from the cypresses, we rode away in swift, military order.

As yet my tongue refused its office, and I was perforce silent. I must have fallen asleep; for the next thing I remembered was finding myself standing up, supported by a soldier on each side of me. It was almost broad daylight, and to the north a red streak of sunlight was reflected, like a path of blood, over the waste of snow. The officer was telling the men to say nothing of what they had seen, except that they found an English stranger, guarded by a large dog.

"Dog! That was no dog," cut in the man who had exhibited such fear. "I think I know a wolf when I see one."

The young officer answered calmly: "I said a dog."

"Dog!" reiterated the other ironically. It was evident that his courage was rising with the sun; and, pointing to me, he said, "Look at his throat. Is that the work of a dog, master?"

Instinctively I raised my hand to my throat, and as I touched it I cried out in pain. The men crowded round to look, some stooping down from their saddles; and again there came the calm voice of the young officer:

"A dog, as I said. If aught else were said we should only be laughed at."

I was then mounted behind a trooper, and we rode on into the suburbs of Munich. Here we came across a stray carriage, into which I was lifted, and it was driven off to the Quatre Saisons—the young officer accompanying me, while a trooper followed with his horse, and the others rode off to their barracks.

When we arrived, Herr Delbrück rushed so quickly down the steps to meet me, that it was apparent he had been watching within. Taking me by both hands he solicitously led me in. The officer saluted me and was turning to withdraw, when I recognized his purpose, and insisted that he should come to my rooms. Over a glass of wine I warmly thanked him and his brave comrades for saving me. He replied simply that he was more than glad, and that Herr Delbrück had at the first taken steps to make all the searching party pleased; at which ambiguous utterance the maître d'hôtel smiled, while the officer pleaded duty and withdrew.

"But Herr Delbrück," I inquired, "how and why was it that the soldiers searched for me?"

He shrugged his shoulders, as if in depreciation of his own deed, as he replied:

"I was so fortunate as to obtain leave from the commander of the regiment in which I served, to ask for volunteers."

"But how did you know I was lost?" I asked.

"The driver came hither with the remains of his carriage, which had been upset when the horses ran away."

"But surely you would not send a search-party of soldiers merely on this account?"

"Oh, no!" he answered. "But even before the coachman arrived, I had this telegram from the Boyar whose guest you are," and he took from his pocket a telegram which he handed to me, and I read:

*Bistritz*

*Be careful of my guest—his safety is most precious to me. Should aught happen to him, or if he be missed, spare nothing to find him and ensure his safety. He is English and therefore adventurous. There are often dangers from snow and wolves and night. Lose not a moment if you suspect harm to him. I answer your zeal with my fortune.*

DRACULA

As I held the telegram in my hand, the room seemed to whirl around me; and, if the attentive maître d'hôtel had not caught me, I think I should have fallen. There was something so strange in all this, something so weird and impossible to imagine, that there grew on me a sense of my being in some way the sport of opposite forces—the mere vague idea of which seemed in a way to paralyze me. I was certainly under some form of mysterious protection. From a distant country had come, in the very nick of time, a message that took me out of the danger of the snow-sleep and the jaws of the wolf.

# THE TRANSFER

# Algernon Blackwood

Algernon Blackwood (1869–1951) was born in southeast London and was educated at Wellington College, the Moravian Brotherhood, and the University of Edinburgh, studying Oriental religions and the occult and joining several occult societies. He moved to Canada at the age of twenty and worked on a farm, then ran a hotel before moving to New York as a newspaper reporter for the *New York Sun* and the *New York Times*. He returned in England at the age of thirty-six to become a full-time writer.

He was a prolific author of supernatural short stories, producing more than a dozen collections, plus sixteen novels. He is probably best known for his many stories about a psychic detective, some of which were collected in *John Silence* (1908). These tales had originally been submitted to his publisher as essays recounting his own true-life experiences, but he was persuaded to turn them into fictional works. Silence is a stand-in for the author, then, which contributes to the intensity of the suspense.

His most famous non-Silence stories are the often-anthologized "The Willows" (1907) and "Wendigo" (1910). He also wrote an autobiography of his early years, *Episodes Before Thirty* (1923).

"The Transfer" was first published in book form in *Pan's Garden* (London: Macmillan, 1912).

# The Transfer

## ALGERNON BLACKWOOD

The child began to cry in the early afternoon—about three o'clock, to be exact. I remember the hour, because I had been listening with secret relief to the sound of the departing carriage. Those wheels fading into the distance down the gravel drive with Mrs. Frene, and her daughter Gladys to whom I was governess, meant for me some hours' welcome rest, and the June day was oppressively hot. Moreover, there was this excitement in the little country household that had told upon us all, but especially upon myself. This excitement, running delicately behind all the events of the morning, was due to some mystery, and the mystery was of course kept concealed from the governess. I had exhausted myself with guessing and keeping on the watch. For some deep and unexplained anxiety possessed me, so that I kept thinking of my sister's dictum that I was really much too sensitive to make a good governess, and that I should have done far better as a professional clairvoyante.

Mr. Frene, senior, "Uncle Frank," was expected for an unusual visit from town about teatime. That I knew. I also knew that his visit was concerned somehow with the future welfare of little Jamie, Gladys' seven-year-old brother. More

than this, indeed, I never knew, and this missing link makes my story in a fashion incoherent—an important bit of the strange puzzle left out. I only gathered that the visit of Uncle Frank was of a condescending nature, that Jamie was told he must be upon his very best behavior to make a good impression, and that Jamie, who had never seen his uncle, dreaded him horribly already in advance. Then, trailing thinly through the dying crunch of the carriage wheels this sultry afternoon, I heard the curious little wail of the child's crying, with the effect, wholly unaccountable, that every nerve in my body shot its bolt electrically, bringing me to my feet with a tingling of unequivocal alarm. Positively, the water ran into my eyes. I recalled his white distress that morning when told that Uncle Frank was motoring down for tea and that he was to be "very nice indeed" to him. It had gone into me like a knife. All through the day, indeed, had run this nightmare quality of terror and vision.

"The man with the 'normous face?" he had asked in a little voice of awe, and then gone speechless from the room in tears that no amount of soothing management could calm. That was all I saw; and what he meant by "the 'normous face" gave me only a sense of vague presentiment. But it came as anticlimax somehow—a sudden revelation of the mystery and excitement that pulsed beneath the quiet of the stifling summer day. I feared for him. For of all that commonplace household I loved Jamie best, though professionally I had nothing to do with him. He was a high-strung, ultrasensitive child, and it seemed to me that no one understood him, least of all his honest, tenderhearted parents; so that his little wailing voice brought me from my bed to the window in a moment like a call for help.

The haze of June lay over that big garden like a blanket; the wonderful flowers, which were Mr. Frene's delight, hung motionless; the lawns, so soft and thick, cushioned all other sounds; only the limes and huge clumps of guelder roses hummed with bees. Through this muted atmosphere of heat and haze the sound of the child's crying floated faintly to my ears—from a distance. Indeed, I wonder now that I heard it at all, for the next moment I saw him down beyond the garden, standing in his white sailor suit alone, two hundred yards away. He was down by the ugly patch where nothing grew—the Forbidden Corner. A faintness then came over me at once, a faintness as of death, when I saw him *there* of all places—where he never was allowed to go, and where, moreover, he was usually too terrified to go. To see him standing solitary in that singular spot, above all to hear him crying there, bereft me momentarily of the power to act. Then, before I could recover my composure sufficiently to call him in, Mr. Frene came round the corner from the Lower Farm with the dogs, and, seeing his son, performed that office for me. In his loud, good-natured, hearty voice he called him, and Jamie turned and ran as though some spell had broken just in time—ran into the open arms of his fond but uncomprehending father, who carried him indoors on his shoulder, while asking "what all this hubbub was about?" And, at their heels, the tailless sheep-dogs followed, barking loudly, and performing what Jamie called their "Gravel Dance," because they ploughed up the moist, rolled gravel with their feet.

I stepped back swiftly from the window lest I

should be seen. Had I witnessed the saving of the child from fire or drowning the relief could hardly have been greater. Only Mr. Frene, I felt sure, would not say and do the right thing quite. He would protect the boy from his own vain imaginings, yet not with the explanation that could really heal. They disappeared behind the rose trees, making for the house. I saw no more till later, when Mr. Frene, senior, arrived.

To describe the ugly patch as "singular" is hard to justify, perhaps, yet some such word is what the entire family sought, though never—oh, never!—used. To Jamie and myself, though equally we never mentioned it, that treeless, flowerless spot was more than singular. It stood at the far end of the magnificent rose garden, a bald, sore place, where the black earth showed uglily in winter, almost like a piece of dangerous bog, and in summer baked and cracked with fissures where green lizards shot their fire in passing. In contrast to the rich luxuriance of death amid life, a center of disease that cried for healing lest it spread. But it never did spread. Behind it stood the thick wood of silver birches and, glimmering beyond, the orchard meadow, where the lambs played.

The gardeners had a very simple explanation of its barrenness—that the water all drained off it owing to the lie of the slopes immediately about it, holding no remnant to keep the soil alive. I cannot say. It was Jamie—Jamie who felt its spell and haunted it, who spent whole hours there, even while afraid, and for whom it was finally labelled "strictly out of bounds" because it stimulated his already big imagination, not wisely but too darkly—it was Jamie who buried ogres there and heard it crying in an earthy voice, swore that it shook its surface sometimes while he watched it, and secretly gave it food in the form of birds or mice or rabbits he found dead upon his wanderings. And it was Jamie who put so extraordinarily into words the *feeling* that the horrid spot had given me from the moment I first saw it.

"It's bad, Miss Gould," he told me.

"But, Jamie, nothing in Nature is bad—exactly; only different from the rest sometimes."

"Miss Gould, if you please, then it's empty. It's not fed. It's dying because it can't get the food it wants."

And when I stared into the little pale face where the eyes shone so dark and wonderful, seeking within myself for the right thing to say to him, he added, with an emphasis and conviction that made me suddenly turn cold: "Miss Gould"—he always used my name like this in all his sentences—"it's hungry, don't you see? But *I* know what would make it feel all right."

Only the conviction of an earnest child, perhaps, could have made so outrageous a suggestion worth listening to for an instant; but for me, who felt that things an imaginative child believed were important, it came with a vast disquieting shock of reality. Jamie, in this exaggerated way, had caught at the edge of a shocking fact—a hint of dark, undiscovered truth had leaped into that sensitive imagination. Why there lay horror in the words I cannot say, but I think some power of darkness trooped across the suggestion of that sentence at the end, "I know what would make it feel all right." I remember that I shrank from asking explanation. Small groups of other words, veiled fortunately by his silence, gave life to an unspeakable possibility that hitherto had lain at the back of my own consciousness. The way it sprang to life proves, I think, that my mind already contained it. The blood rushed from my heart as I listened. I remember that my knees shook. Jamie's idea was—had been all along—my own as well.

And now, as I lay down on my bed and thought about it all, I understood why the coming of his uncle involved somehow an experience that wrapped terror at its heart. With a sense of nightmare certainty that left me too weak to resist the preposterous idea, too shocked, indeed, to argue or reason it away, this certainty came with its full, black blast of conviction; and the only way I can put it into words, since nightmare horror really is not properly tellable at all, seems this: that there *was* something missing in that dying patch of garden; something lacking that it ever searched for; something, once found and taken, that would turn it rich and living as the rest; more—that there *was* some living person who could do this for it. Mr. Frene, senior, in a word, "Uncle Frank," was this person who out of his abundant life could supply the lack—unwittingly.

For this connection between the dying, empty patch and the person of this vigorous, wealthy, and successful man had already lodged itself in my subconsciousness before I was aware of it. Clearly it must have lain there all along, though hidden. Jamie's words, his sudden pallor, his vibrating emotion of fearful anticipation had developed the plate, but it was his weeping alone there in the Forbidden Corner that had printed it. The photograph shone framed before me in the air. I hid my eyes. But for the redness—the charm of my face goes to pieces unless my eyes are clear—I could have cried. Jamie's words that morning about the "'normous face" came back upon me like a battering-ram.

Mr. Frene, senior, had been so frequently the subject of conversation in the family since I came, I had so often heard him discussed, and had then read so much about him in the papers—his energy, his philanthropy, his success with everything he laid his hand to—that a picture of the man had grown complete within me. I knew him as he was—within; or, as my sister would have said—clairvoyantly. And the only time I saw him (when I took Gladys to a meeting where he was chairman, and later *felt* his atmosphere and presence while for a moment he patronizingly spoke with her) had justified the portrait I had drawn. The rest, you may say, was a woman's wild imagining; but I think rather it was that kind of divining intuition which women share with children. If souls could be made visible, I would stake my life upon the truth and accuracy of my portrait.

For this Mr. Frene was a man who drooped alone, but grew vital in a crowd—because he used their vitality. He was a supreme, unconscious artist in the science of taking the fruits of others' work and living—for his own advantage. He vampired, unknowingly no doubt, every one with whom he came in contact; left them exhausted, tired, listless. Others fed him, so that while in a full room he shone, alone by himself and with no life to draw upon he languished and declined. In the man's immediate neighborhood you felt his presence draining you; he took your ideas, your strength, your very words, and later used them for his own benefit and aggrandizement. Not evilly, of course; the man was good enough; but you felt that he was dangerous owing to the facile way he absorbed into himself all loose vitality that was to be had. His eyes and voice and presence devitalized you. Life, it seemed, not highly organized enough to resist, must shrink from his too near approach and hide away for fear of being appropriated, for fear, that is, of—death.

Jamie, unknowingly, put in the finishing touch to my unconscious portrait. The man carried about with him some silent, compelling trick of drawing out all your reserves—then swiftly pocketing them. At first you would be conscious of taut resistance; this would slowly shade off into weariness; the will would become flaccid; then you either moved away or yielded—agreed to all he said with a sense of weakness pressing ever closer upon the edges of collapse. With a male antagonist it might be different, but even then the effort of resistance would generate force that *he* absorbed and not the other. He never gave out. Some instinct taught him how to protect himself from that. To human beings, I mean, he never gave out. This time it was a very different matter. He had no more chance than a fly before the wheels of a huge—what Jamie used to call—"attraction" engine.

So this was how I saw him—a great human sponge, crammed and soaked with the life, or proceeds of life, absorbed from others—stolen. My idea of a human vampire was satisfied. He went about carrying these accumulations of the life of others. In this sense his "life" was not really his own. For the same reason, I think, it was not so fully under his control as he imagined.

And in another hour this man would be here.

I went to the window. My eye wandered to the empty patch, dull black there amid the rich luxuriance of the garden flowers. It struck me as a hideous bit of emptiness yawning to be filled and nourished. The idea of Jamie playing round its bare edge was loathsome. I watched the big summer clouds above, the stillness of the afternoon, the haze. The silence of the overheated garden was oppressive. I had never felt a day so stifling, motionless. It lay there waiting. The household, too, was waiting—waiting for the coming of Mr. Frene from London in his big motor-car.

And I shall never forget the sensation of icy shrinking and distress with which I heard the rumble of the car. He had arrived. Tea was all ready on the lawn beneath the lime trees, and Mrs. Frene and Gladys, back from their drive, were sitting in wicker chairs. Mr. Frene, junior, was in the hall to meet his brother, but Jamie, as I learned afterwards, had shown such hysterical alarm, offered such bold resistance, that it had been deemed wiser to keep him in his room. Perhaps, after all, his presence might not be necessary. The visit clearly had to do with something on the uglier side of life—money, settlements, or what not; I never knew exactly; only that his parents were anxious, and that Uncle Frank had to be propitiated. It does not matter. That has nothing to do with the affair. What has to do with it—or I should not be telling the story—is that Mrs. Frene sent for me to come down "in my nice white dress, if I didn't mind," and that I was terrified, yet pleased, because it meant that a pretty face would be considered a welcome addition to the visitor's landscape. Also, most odd it was, I felt my presence was somehow inevitable, that in some way it was intended that I should witness what I did witness. And the instant I came upon the lawn—I hesitate to set it down, it sounds so foolish, disconnected—I could have sworn, as my eyes met his, that a kind of sudden darkness came, taking the summer brilliance out of everything, and that it was caused by troops of small black horses that raced about us from his person—to attack.

After a first momentary approving glance he

took no further notice of me. The tea and talk went smoothly; I helped to pass the plates and cups, filling in pauses with little under-talk to Gladys. Jamie was never mentioned. Outwardly all seemed well, but inwardly everything was awful—skirting the edge of things unspeakable, and so charged with danger that I could not keep my voice from trembling when I spoke.

I watched his hard, bleak face; I noticed how thin he was, and the curious, oily brightness of his steady eyes. They did not glitter, but they drew you with a sort of soft, creamy shine like Eastern eyes. And everything he said or did announced what I may dare to call the *suction* of his presence. His nature achieved this result automatically. He dominated us all, yet so gently that until it was accomplished no one noticed it.

Before five minutes had passed, however, I was aware of one thing only. My mind focussed exclusively upon it, and so vividly that I marvelled the others did not scream, or run, or do something violent to prevent it. And it was this; that, separated merely by some dozen yards or so, this man, vibrating with the acquired vitality of others, stood within easy reach of that spot of yawning emptiness, waiting and eager to be filled. Earth scented her prey.

These two active "centers" were within fighting distance; he so thin, so hard, so keen, yet really spreading large with the loose "surround" of others' life he had appropriated, so practiced and triumphant; that other so patient, deep, with so mighty a draw of the whole earth behind it, and—ugh!—so obviously aware that its opportunity at last had come.

I saw it all as plainly as though I watched two great animals prepare for battle, both unconsciously; yet in some inexplicable way I saw it, of course, within me, and not externally. The conflict would be hideously unequal. Each side had already sent out emissaries, how long before I could not tell, for the first evidence *he* gave that something was going wrong with him was when his voice grew suddenly confused, he missed his words, and his lips trembled a moment and turned flabby. The next second his face betrayed that singular and horrid change, growing somehow loose about the bones of the cheek, and larger, so that I remembered Jamie's miserable phrase. The emissaries of the two kingdoms, the human and the vegetable, had met, I make it out, in that very second. For the first time in his long career of battening on others, Mr. Frene found himself pitted against a vaster kingdom than he knew and, so finding, shook inwardly in that little part that was his definite actual self. He felt the huge disaster coming.

"Yes, John," he was saying, in his drawling, self-congratulating voice, "Sir George gave me that car—gave it to me as a present. Wasn't it char—?" and then broke off abruptly, stammered, drew breath, stood up, and looked uneasily about him. For a second there was a gaping pause. It was like the click which starts some huge machinery moving—that instant's pause before it actually starts. The whole thing, indeed, then went with the rapidity of machinery running down and beyond control. I thought of a giant dynamo working silently and invisible.

"What's that?" he cried, in a soft voice charged with alarm. "What's that horrid place? And someone's crying there—who is it?"

He pointed to the empty patch. Then, before anyone could answer, he started across the lawn towards it, going every minute faster. Before anyone could move he stood upon the edge. He leaned over—peering down into it.

It seemed a few hours passed, but really they were seconds, for time is measured by the quality and not the quantity of sensations it contains. I saw it all with merciless, photographic detail, sharply etched amid the general confusion. Each side was intensely active, but only one side, the human, exerted *all* its force—in resistance. The other merely stretched out a feeler, as it were, from its vast, potential strength; no more was necessary. It was such a soft and easy victory. Oh, it was rather pitiful! There was no bluster or great effort, on one side at least. Close by his side I witnessed it, for I, it seemed, alone had moved and followed him. No one else stirred, though Mrs.

Frene clattered noisily with the cups, making some sudden impulsive gesture with her hands, and Gladys, I remember, gave a cry—it was like a little scream—"Oh, mother, it's the heat, isn't it?" Mr. Frene, her father, was speechless, pale as ashes.

But the instant I reached his side, it became clear what had drawn me there thus instinctively. Upon the other side, among the silver birches, stood little Jamie. He was watching. I experienced—for him—one of those moments that shake the heart; a liquid fear ran all over me, the more effective because unintelligible really. Yet I felt that if I could know all, and what lay actually behind, my fear would be more than justified; that the thing *was* awful, full of awe.

And then it happened—a truly wicked sight— like watching a universe in action, yet all contained within a small square foot of space. I think he understood vaguely that if someone could only take his place he might be saved, and that was why, discerning instinctively the easiest substitute within reach, he saw the child and called aloud to him across the empty patch, "James, my boy, come here!"

His voice was like a thin report, but somehow flat and lifeless, as when a rifle misses fire, sharp, yet weak; it had no "crack" in it. It was really supplication. And, with amazement, I heard my own ring out imperious and strong, though I was not conscious of saying it, "Jamie, don't move. Stay where you are!" But Jamie, the little child, obeyed neither of us. Moving up nearer to the edge, he stood there—laughing! I heard that laughter, but could have sworn it did not come from him. The empty, yawning patch gave out that sound.

Mr. Frene turned sideways, throwing up his arms. I saw his hard, bleak face grow somehow wider, spread through the air, and downwards. A similar thing, I saw, was happening at the same time to his entire person, for it drew out into the atmosphere in a stream of movement. The face for a second made me think of those toys of green india rubber that children pull. It grew enormous. But this was an external impression only. What actually happened, I clearly understood, was that all this vitality and life he had transferred from

others to himself for years was now in turn being taken from him and transferred—elsewhere.

One moment on the edge he wobbled horribly, then with that queer sideways motion, rapid yet ungainly, he stepped forward into the middle of the patch and fell heavily upon his face. His eyes, as he dropped, faded shockingly, and across the countenance was written plainly what I can only call an expression of destruction. He looked utterly destroyed. I caught a sound—from Jamie?— but this time not of laughter. It was like a gulp; it was deep and muffled and it dipped away into the earth. Again I thought of a troop of small black horses galloping away down a subterranean passage beneath my feet—plunging into the depths— their tramping growing fainter and fainter into buried distance. In my nostrils was a pungent smell of earth.

And then—all passed. I came back into myself. Mr. Frene, junior, was lifting his brother's head from the lawn where he had fallen from the heat, close beside the tea-table. He had never really moved from there. And Jamie, I learned afterwards, had been the whole time asleep upon his bed upstairs, worn out with his crying and unreasoning alarm. Gladys came running out with cold water, sponge and towel, brandy too—all kinds of things. "Mother, it *was* the heat, wasn't it?" I heard her whisper, but I did not catch Mrs. Frene's reply. From her face it struck me that she was bordering on collapse herself. Then the butler followed, and they just picked him up and carried him into the house. He recovered even before the doctor came.

But the queer thing to me is that I was convinced the others all had seen what I saw, only that no one said a word about it; and to this day no one *has* said a word. And that was, perhaps, the most horrid part of all.

From that day to this I have scarcely heard a mention of Mr. Frene, senior. It seemed as if he dropped suddenly out of life. The papers never mentioned him. His activities ceased, as it were. His after-life, at any rate, became singularly ineffective. Certainly he achieved nothing worth public mention. But it may be only that, having left the employ of Mrs. Frene, there was no particular occasion for me to hear anything.

The after-life of that empty patch of garden, however, was quite otherwise. Nothing, so far as I know, was done to it by gardeners, or in the way of draining it or bringing in new earth, but even before I left in the following summer it had changed. It lay untouched, full of great, luscious, driving weeds and creepers, very strong, full-fed, and bursting thick with life.

# THE STONE CHAMBER

# H. B. Marriott Watson

Henry Brereton Marriott Watson (1863–1921) was born in Caulfield, Melbourne, Australia, and moved to New Zealand at the age of ten, when his Anglican minister father was made incumbent at St. John's in Christchurch. He was educated there, then moved to England permanently in 1883, becoming a journalist (he was the assistant editor of *Black and White* and the *Pall Mall Gazette*) and fiction writer under the tutelage of W. E. Henley. He became a prolific novelist and short-story writer, mainly of swashbuckling adventure tales and historical romances, and was one of the most successful writers of this type of fiction in the late nineteenth and early twentieth centuries. Silent films of his work are *A Conspiracy Against the King* (1911), *Her Face* (1912), *Stanton's Last Fling* (1913), *On the Isle of Same* (1914), and *Romance at Random* (1916).

Although they were never married, Watson had a long partnership with the decadent poet who took his name, Rosamund Marriott Watson, until her death from cancer in 1911. Their only son was killed in World War I.

Not known as a writer of supernatural fiction, Watson nonetheless produced numerous short stories in this genre, two of which, the present story and "The Devil of the Marsh," have become classics.

"The Stone Chamber" was first published in book form in *The Heart of Miranda* (London: John Lane, 1899).

# The Stone Chamber

## H. B. MARRIOTT WATSON

It was not until early summer that Warrington took possession of Marvyn Abbey. He had bought the property in the preceding autumn, but the place had so fallen into decay through the disorders of time that more than six months elapsed ere it was inhabitable. The delay, however, fell out conveniently for Warrington; for the Bosanquets spent the winter abroad, and nothing must suit but he must spend it with them. There was never a man who pursued his passion with such ardour. He was ever at Miss Bosanquet's skirts, and bade fair to make her as steadfast a husband as he was attached a lover. Thus it was not until after his return from that prolonged exile that he had the opportunity of inspecting the repairs discharged by his architect. He was nothing out of the common in character, but was full of kindly impulses and a fellow of impetuous blood. When he called upon me in my chambers he spoke with some excitement of his Abbey, as also of his approaching marriage; and finally, breaking into an exhibition of genuine affection, declared that we had been so long and so continuously intimate that I, and none other, must help him warm his house and marry his bride. It had indeed been always understood between us that I should serve him at the cere-

mony, but now it appeared that I must start my duties even earlier. The prospect of a summer holiday in Utterbourne pleased me. It was a charming village, set upon the slope of a wooded hill and within call of the sea. I had a slight knowledge of the district from a riding excursion taken through that part of Devonshire; and years before, and ere Warrington had come into his money, had viewed the Abbey ruins from a distance with the polite curiosity of a passing tourist.

I examined them now with new eyes as we drove up the avenue. The face which the ancient building presented to the valley was of magnificent design, but now much worn and battered. Part of it, the right wing, I judged to be long past the uses of a dwelling, for the walls had crumbled away, huge gaps opened in the foundations, and the roof was quite dismantled. Warrington had very wisely left this portion to its own sinister decay; it was the left wing which had been restored, and which we were to inhabit. The entrance, I will confess, was a little mean, for the large doorway had been bricked up and an ordinary modern door gave upon the spacious terrace and the winding gardens. But apart from this, the work of restoration had been undertaken with skill and piety, and the interior had retained its native dignity, while re-

437

suming an air of proper comfort. The old oak had been repaired congruous with the original designs, and the great rooms had been as little altered as was requisite to adapt them for daily use.

Warrington passed quickly from chamber to chamber in evident delight, directing my attention upon this and upon that, and eagerly requiring my congratulations and approval. My comments must have satisfied him, for the place attracted me vastly. The only criticism I ventured was to remark upon the size of the rooms and to question if they might dwarf the insignificant human figures they were to entertain.

He laughed. "Not a bit," said he. "Roaring fires in winter in those fine old fireplaces; and as for summer, the more space the better. We shall be jolly."

I followed him along the noble hall, and we stopped before a small door of very black oak.

"The bedrooms," he explained, as he turned the key, "are all upstairs, but mine is not ready yet. And besides, I am reserving it; I won't sleep in it till—you understand," he concluded, with a smiling suggestion of embarrassment.

I understood very well. He threw the door open.

"I am going to use this in the meantime," he continued. "Queer little room, isn't it? It used to be a sort of library. How do you think it looks."

We had entered as he spoke, and stood, distributing our glances in that vague and general way in which a room is surveyed. It was a chamber of much smaller proportions than the rest, and was dimly lighted by two long narrow windows sunk in the great walls. The bed and the modern fittings looked strangely out of keeping with its ancient privacy. The walls were rudely distempered with barbaric frescos dating, I conjectured, from the fourteenth century; and the floor was of stone, worn into grooves and hollows with the feet of many generations. As I was taking in these facts, there came over me a sudden curiosity as to those dead Marvyns who had held the Abbey for so long. This silent chamber seemed to suggest questions of their history; it spoke eloquently of past ages and past deeds, fallen now into oblivion. Here,

within these thick walls, no echo from the outer world might carry, no sound would ring within its solitary seclusion. Even the silence seemed to confer with one upon the ancient transactions of that extinct House.

Warrington stirred, and turned suddenly to me. "I hope it's not damp," said he, with a slight shiver. "It looks rather solemn. I thought furniture would brighten it up."

"I should think it would be very comfortable," said I. "You will never be disturbed by any sounds at any rate."

"No," he answered, hesitatingly; and then, quickly, on one of his impulses: "Hang it, Heywood, there's too much silence here for me." Then he laughed. "Oh, I shall do very well for a month or two." And with that appeared to return to his former placid cheerfulness.

The train of thought started in that sombre chamber served to entertain me several times that day. I questioned Warrington at dinner, which we took in one of the smaller rooms, commanding a lovely prospect of dale and sea. He shook his head. Archæological lore, as indeed anything else out of the borders of actual life, held very little interest for him.

"The Marvyns died out in 1714, I believe," he said, indifferently. "Someone told me that—the man I bought it from, I think. They might just as well have kept the place up since; but I think it has been only occupied twice between then and now, and the last time was forty years ago. It would have rotted to pieces if I hadn't taken it. Perhaps Mrs. Batty could tell you. She's lived in these parts almost all her life."

To humour me, and affected, I doubt not, by a certain pride in his new possession, he put the query to his housekeeper upon her appearance subsequently; but it seemed that her knowledge was little fuller than his own, though she had gathered some vague traditions of the countryside. The Marvyns had not left a reputable name, if rumour spoke truly; theirs was a family to which black deeds had been credited. They were ill-starred also in their fortunes, and had become extinct suddenly; but for the rest, the events had fallen too many generations ago to be current now between the memories of the village.

Warrington, who was more eager to discuss the future than to recall the past, was vastly excited by his anticipations. St. Pharamond, Sir William Bosanquet's house, lay across the valley, barely five miles away; and as the family had now returned, it was easy to forgive Warrington's elation.

"What do you think?" he said, late that evening; and clapping me upon the shoulder. "You have seen Marion, here is the house. Am I not lucky? Damn it, Heywood, I'm not pious, but I am disposed to thank God! I'm not a bad fellow, but I'm no saint; it's fortunate that it's not only the virtuous that are rewarded. In fact, it's usually contrariwise. I owe this to—Lord, I don't know what I owe it to. Is it my money? Of course, Marion doesn't care a rap for that; but then, you see, I mightn't have known her without it. Of course, there's the house, too. I'm thankful I have money. At any rate, here's my new life. Just look about and take it in, old fellow. If you knew how a man may be ashamed of himself! But there, I've done. You know I'm decent at heart—you must count my life from today." And with this outbreak he lifted the glass between fingers that trembled with the warmth of his emotions, and tossed off his wine.

He did himself but justice when he claimed to be a good fellow; and, in truth, I was myself somewhat moved by his obvious feeling. I remember that we shook hands very affectionately, and my sympathy was the prelude to a long and confidential talk, which lasted until quite a late hour.

At the foot of the staircase, where we parted, he detained me.

"This is the last of my wayward days," he said, with a smile. "Late hours—liquor—all go. You shall see. Goodnight. You know your room. I shall be up long before you." And with that he vanished briskly into the darkness that hung about the lower parts of the passage.

I watched him go, and it struck me quite vaguely what a slight impression his candle made upon that channel of opaque gloom. It seemed merely as a thread of light that illumined nothing. Warrington himself was rapt into the prevalent blackness; but long afterwards, and even when his footsteps had died away upon the heavy carpet, the tiny beam was visible, advancing and flickering in the distance.

My window, which was modern, opened upon a little balcony, where, as the night was warm and I was indisposed for sleep, I spent half an hour enjoying the air. I was in a sentimental mood, and my thoughts turned upon the suggestions which Warrington's conversation had induced. It was not until I was in bed, and had blown out the light, that they settled upon the square, dark chamber in which my host was to pass the night. As I have said, I was wakeful, owing, no doubt, to the high pitch of the emotions which we had encouraged; but presently my fancies became inarticulate and incoherent, and then I was overtaken by profound sleep.

Warrington was up before me, as he had predicted, and met me in the breakfast-room.

"What a beggar you are to sleep!" he said, with a smile. "I've hammered at your door for half an hour."

I apologized for myself, alleging the rich country air in my defence, and mentioned that I had had some difficulty in getting to sleep.

"So had I," he remarked, as we sat down to the table. "We got very excited, I suppose. Just see what you have there, Heywood. Eggs? Oh, damn it, one can have too much of eggs!" He frowned, and lifted a third cover. "Why in the name of common sense can't Mrs. Batty give us more variety?" he asked, impatiently.

I deprecated his displeasure, suggesting that we should do very well; indeed, his discontent seemed to me quite unnecessary. But I supposed Warrington had been rather spoiled by many years of club life.

He settled himself without replying, and began to pick over his plate in a gingerly manner.

"There's one thing I will have here, Heywood," he observed. "I will have things well appointed.

I'm not going to let life in the country mean an uncomfortable life. A man can't change the habits of a lifetime."

In contrast with his exhilarated professions of the previous evening, this struck me with a sense of amusement at the moment; and the incongruity may have occurred to him, for he went on: "Marion's not over strong, you know, and must have things *comme il faut*. She shan't decline upon a lower level. The worst of these rustics is that they have no imagination." He held up a piece of bacon on his fork, and surveyed it with disgust. "Now, look at that! Why the devil don't they take tips from civilized people like the French?"

It was so unlike him to exhibit this petulance that I put it down to a bad night, and without discovering the connection of my thoughts, asked him how he liked his bedroom.

"Oh, pretty well, pretty well," he said, indifferently. "It's not so cold as I thought. But I slept badly. I always do in a strange bed," and pushing aside his plate, he lit a cigarette. "When you've finished that garbage, Heywood, we'll have a stroll round the Abbey," he said.

His good temper returned during our walk, and he indicated to me various improvements which he contemplated, with something of his old ardour. The left wing of the house, as I have said, was entire, but a little apart were the ruins of a chapel. Surrounded by a low moss-grown wall, it was full of picturesque charm; the roofless chancel was spread with ivy, but the aisles were intact. Grass grew between the stones and the floor, and many creepers had strayed through chinks in the wall into those sacred precincts. The solemn quietude of the ruin, maintained under the spell of death, awed me a little, but upon Warrington apparently it made no impression. He was only zealous that I should properly appreciate the distinction of such a property. I stooped and drew the weeds away from one of the slabs in the aisle, and was able to trace upon it the relics of lettering, well-nigh obliterated under the corrosion of time.

"There are tombs," said I.

"Oh, yes," he answered, with a certain relish. "I understand the Marvyns used it as a mausoleum.

They are all buried here. Some good brasses, I am told."

The associations of the place engaged me; the aspect of the Abbey faced the past; it seemed to refuse communion with the present; and somehow the thought of those two decent humdrum lives which should be spent within its shelter savoured of the incongruous. The white-capped maids and the emblazoned butlers that should tread these halls offered a ridiculous appearance beside my fancies of the ancient building. For all that, I envied Warrington his home, and so I told him, with a humorous hint that I was fitter to appreciate its glories than himself.

He laughed. "Oh, I don't know," said he. "I like the old-world look as much as you do. I have always had a notion of something venerable. It seems to serve you for ancestors." And he was undoubtedly delighted with my enthusiasm.

But at lunch again he chopped round to his previous irritation, only now quite another matter provoked his anger. He had received a letter by the second post from Miss Bosanquet, which, if I may judge from his perplexity, must have been unusually confused. He read and re-read it, his brow lowering.

"What the deuce does she mean?" he asked, testily. "She first makes an arrangement for us to ride over today, and now I can't make out whether we are to go to St. Pharamond, or they are coming to us. Just look at it, will you, Heywood?"

I glanced through the note, but could offer no final solution, whereupon he broke out again:

"That's just like women—they never can say anything straightforwardly. Why, in the name of goodness, couldn't she leave things as they were? You see," he observed, rather in answer, as I fancied, to my silence, "we don't know what to do now; if we stay here they mayn't come, and if we go probably we shall cross them." And he snapped his fingers in annoyance.

I was cheerful enough, perhaps because the responsibility was not mine, and ventured to suggest that we might ride over, and return if we missed them. But he dismissed the subject sharply by saying:

"No, I'll stay. I'm not going on a fool's errand," and drew my attention to some point in the decoration of the room.

The Bosanquets did not arrive during the afternoon, and Warrington's ill-humour increased. His love-sick state pleaded in excuse of him, but he was certainly not a pleasant companion. He was sour and snappish, and one could introduce no statement to which he would not find a contradiction. So unamiable did he grow that at last I discovered a pretext to leave him, and rambled to the back of the Abbey into the precincts of the old chapel. The day was falling, and the summer sun flared through the western windows upon the bare aisle. The creepers rustled upon the gaping walls, and the tall grasses waved in shadows over the bodies of the forgotten dead. As I stood contemplating the effect, and meditating greatly upon the anterior fortunes of the Abbey, my attention fell upon a huge slab of marble, upon which the yellow light struck sharply. The faded lettering rose into greater definition before *my* eyes and I read slowly:

*"Here lyeth the body of Sir Rupert Marvyn."*

Beyond a date, very difficult to decipher, there was nothing more; of eulogy, of style, of record, of pious considerations such as were usual to the period, not a word. I read the numerals variously as 1723 and 1745; but however they ran it was probable that the stone covered the resting-place of the last Marvyn. The history of this futile house interested me not a little, partly for Warrington's sake, and in part from a natural bent towards ancient records; and I made a mental note of the name and date.

When I returned Warrington's surliness had entirely vanished, and had given place to an effusion of boisterous spirits. He apologized jovially for his bad temper.

"It was the disappointment of not seeing Marion," he said. "You will understand that some day, old fellow. But, anyhow, we'll go over tomorrow," and forthwith proceeded to enliven the dinner with an ostentation of good-fellowship I had seldom witnessed in him. I began to suspect that he had heard again from St. Pharamond, though he

chose to conceal the fact from me. The wine was admirable; though Warrington himself was no great judge, he had entrusted the selection to a good palate. We had a merry meal, drank a little more than was prudent, and smoked our cigars upon the terrace in the fresh air. Warrington was restless. He pushed his glass from him. "I'll tell you what, old chap," he broke out, "I'll give you a game of billiards. I've got a decent table."

I demurred. The air was too delicious, and I was in no humour for a sharp use of my wits. He laughed, though he seemed rather disappointed.

"It's almost sacrilege to play billiards in an Abbey," I said, whimsically. "What would the ghosts of the old Marvyns think?"

"Oh, hang the Marvyns!" he rejoined, crossly. "You're always talking of them."

He rose and entered the house, returning presently with a flagon of whisky and some glasses.

"Try this," he said. "We've had no liqueurs." And pouring out some spirit he swallowed it raw.

I stared, for Warrington rarely took spirits, being more of a wine drinker; moreover, he must have taken nearly the quarter of a tumbler. But he did not notice my surprise, and, seating himself, lit another cigar.

"I don't mean to have things quiet here," he observed, reflectively. "I don't believe in your stagnant rustic life. What I intend to do is to keep the place warm—plenty of house parties, things going on all the year. I shall expect you down for the shooting, Ned. The coverts promise well this year."

I assented willingly enough, and he rambled on again.

"I don't know that I shall use the Abbey so much. I think I'll live in town a good deal. It's brighter there. I don't know though. I like the place. Hang it, it's a rattling good shop, there's no mistake about it. Look here," he broke off, abruptly, "bring your glass in, and I'll show you something."

I was little inclined to move, but he was so peremptory that I followed him with a sigh. We entered one of the smaller rooms which overlooked the terrace, and had been diverted into a comfortable library. He flung back the windows.

"There's air for you," he cried. "Now, sit down,"

and walking to a cupboard produced a second flagon of whisky. "Irish!" he ejaculated, clumping it on the table. "Take your choice," and turning again to the cupboard, presently sat down with his hands under the table. "Now, then, Ned," he said, with a short laugh. "Fill up, and we'll have some fun," with which he suddenly threw a pack of cards upon the board.

I opened my eyes, for I do not suppose Warrington had touched cards since his college days; but, interpreting my look in his own way, he cried:

"Oh, I'm not married yet. Warrington's his own man still. Poker? Eh?"

"Anything you like," said I, with resignation.

A peculiar expression of delight gleamed in his eyes, and he shuffled the cards feverishly.

"Cut," said he, and helped himself to more whisky.

It was shameful to be playing there with that beautiful night without, but there seemed no help for it. Warrington had a run of luck, though he played with little skill; and his excitement grew as he won.

"Let us make it ten shillings," he suggested.

I shook my head. "You forget I'm not a millionaire," I replied.

"Bah!" he cried. "I like a game worth the victory. Well, fire away."

His eyes gloated upon the cards, and he fingered them with unctuous affection. The behaviour of the man amazed me. I began to win.

Warrington's face slowly assumed a dull, lowering expression; he played eagerly, avariciously; he disputed my points, and was querulous.

"Oh, we've had enough!" I cried in distaste.

"By Jove, you don't!" he exclaimed, jumping to his feet. "You're the winner, Heywood, and I'll see you damned before I let you off my revenge!"

The words startled me no less than the fury which rang in his accents. I gazed at him in stupefaction. The whites of his eyes showed wildly, and a sullen, angry look determined his face. Suddenly I was arrested by the suspicion of something upon his neck.

"What's that?" I asked. "You've cut yourself."

He put his hand to his face. "Nonsense," he replied, in a surly fashion.

I looked closer, and then I saw my mistake. It was a round, faint red mark, the size of a florin, upon the column of his throat, and I set it down to the accidental pressure of some button.

"Come on!" he insisted, impatiently.

"Bah! Warrington," I said, for I imagined that he had been over-excited by the whisky he had taken. "It's only a matter of a few pounds. Why make a fuss? Tomorrow will serve."

After a moment his eyes fell, and he gave an awkward laugh. "Oh, well, that'll do," said he. "But I got so infernally excited."

"Whisky," said I, sententiously.

He glanced at the bottle. "How many glasses have I had?" and he whistled. "By Jove, Ned, this won't do! I must turn over a new leaf. Come on; let's look at the night."

I was only too glad to get away from the table, and we were soon upon the terrace again. Warrington was silent, and his gaze went constantly across the valley, where the moon was rising, and in the direction in which, as he had indicated to me, St. Pharamond lay. When he said goodnight he was still pre-occupied.

"I hope you will sleep better," he said.

"And you, too," I added.

He smiled. "I don't suppose I shall wake the whole night through," he said; and then, as I was turning to go, he caught me quickly by the arm.

"Ned," he said, impulsively and very earnestly, "don't let me make a fool of myself again. I know it's the excitement of everything. But I want to be as good as I can for her."

I pressed his hand. "All right, old fellow," I said; and we parted.

I think I have never enjoyed sounder slumber than that night. The first thing I was aware of was the singing of thrushes outside my window. I rose and looked forth, and the sun was hanging high in the eastern sky, the grass and the young green of the trees were shining with dew. With an uncomfortable feeling that I was very late I hastily dressed and went downstairs. Warrington was waiting for me in the breakfast-room, as upon the previous morning, and when he turned from the window at my approach, the sight of his face startled me. It was drawn and haggard, and his eyes were shot with blood; it was a face broken and savage with dissipation. He made no answer to my questioning, but seated himself with a morose air.

"Now you have come," he said, sullenly, "we may as well begin. But it's not my fault if the coffee's cold."

I examined him critically, and passed some comment upon his appearance.

"You don't look up to much," I said. "Another bad night?"

"No; I slept well enough," he responded, ungraciously; and then, after a pause: "I'll tell you what, Heywood. You shall give me my revenge after breakfast."

"Nonsense," I said, after a momentary silence. "You're going over to St. Pharamond."

"Hang it!" was his retort. "One can't be always bothering about women. You seem mightily indisposed to meet me again."

"I certainly won't this morning," I answered, rather sharply, for the man's manner grated upon me. "This evening, if you like; and then the silly business shall end."

He said something in an undertone of grumble, and the rest of the meal passed in silence. But I entertained an uneasy suspicion of him, and after all he was my friend, with whom I was under obligations not to quarrel; and so when we rose, I approached him.

"Look here, Warrington," I said. "What's the matter with you? Have you been drinking? Remember what you asked me last night."

"Hold your damned row!" was all the answer he vouchsafed, as he whirled away from me, but with an embarrassed display of shame.

But I was not to be put off in that way, and I spoke somewhat more sharply.

"We're going to have this out, Warrington," I said. "If you are ill, let us understand that; but I'm not going to stay here with you in this cantankerous spirit."

"I'm not ill," he replied testily.

"Look at yourself," I cried, and turned him about to the mirror over the mantelpiece.

He started a little, and a frown of perplexity gathered on his forehead.

"Good Lord! I'm not like that, Ned," he said, in a different voice. "I must have been drunk last night." And with a sort of groan, he directed a piteous look at me.

"Come," I was constrained to answer, "pull yourself together. The ride will do you good. And no more whisky."

"No, by Heaven, no!" he cried vehemently, and seemed to shiver; but then, suddenly taking my arm, he walked out of the room.

The morning lay still and golden. Warrington's eyes went forth across the valley.

"Come round to the stables, Ned," he said, impulsively. "You shall choose your own nag."

I shook my head. "I'll choose yours," said I, "but I am not going with you." He looked surprised. "No, ride by yourself. You don't want a companion on such an errand. I'll stay here, and pursue my investigations into the Marvyns."

A scowl crossed his face, but only for an instant, and then he answered: "All right, old chap; do as you like. Anyway, I'm off at once." And presently, when his horse was brought, he was laughing merrily.

"You'll have a dull day, Ned; but it's your own fault, you duffer. You'll have to lunch by yourself, as I shan't be back till late." And, gaily flourishing his whip, trotted down the drive.

It was some relief for me to be rid of him, for, in truth, his moods had worn my nerves, and I had not looked for a holiday of this disquieting nature. When he returned, I had no doubt it would be with quite another face, and meanwhile I was excellent company for myself. After lunch I amused myself for half an hour with idle tricks upon the billiard-table, and, tiring of my pastime, fell upon the housekeeper as I returned along the corridor. She was a woman nearer to sixty than fifty, with a comfortable, portly figure, and an amiable expression. Her eyes invited me ever so respectfully to conversation, and stopping, I entered into talk. She inquired if I liked my room and how I slept.

"'Tis a nice look-out you have, Sir," said she. "That was where old Lady Martin slept."

It appeared that she had served as kitchen-maid to the previous tenants of the Abbey, nearly fifty years before.

"Oh, I know the old house in and out," she asserted, "and I arranged the rooms with Mr. Warrington."

We were standing opposite the low doorway which gave entrance to Warrington's bedroom, and my eyes unconsciously shot in that direction. Mrs. Batty followed my glance.

"I didn't want him to have that," she said, "but he was set upon it. It's smallish for a bedroom, and in my opinion isn't fit for more than a lumber-room. That's what Sir William used it for."

I pushed open the door and stepped over the threshold, and the housekeeper followed me.

"No," she said, glancing round, "and it's in my mind that it's damp, Sir."

Again I had a curious feeling that the silence was speaking in my ear; the atmosphere was thick and heavy, and a musty smell, as of faded draperies, penetrated my nostrils. The whole room looked indescribably dingy, despite the new hangings. I went over to the narrow window and peered through the diamond panes. Outside, but seen dimly through that ancient and discoloured glass, the ruins of the chapel confronted me, bare and stark, in the yellow sunlight. I turned.

"There are no ghosts in the Abbey, I suppose, Mrs. Batty?" I asked, whimsically.

But she took my inquiry very gravely. "I have never heard tell of one, Sir," she protested, "and if there was such a thing I should have known it."

As I was rejoining her a strange low whirring was audible, and looking up I saw in a corner of the high-arched roof a horrible face watching me out of black narrow eyes. I confess that I was very much startled at the apparition, but the next moment realized what it was. The creature hung with its ugly fleshy wings extended over a grotesque stone head that leered down upon me, its evil-looking snout projecting into the room; it lay perfectly still, returning me glance for glance, until moved by the repulsion of its presence I clapped my hands, and cried loudly; then, slowly flitting in a circle round the roof, it vanished with a flapping of wings into some darker corner of the rafters. Mrs. Batty was astounded, and expressed surprise that it had managed to conceal itself for so long.

"Oh, bats live in holes," I answered. "Probably there is some small access through the masonry." But the incident had sent an uncomfortable shiver through me all the same.

Later that day I began to recognize that, short of an abrupt return to town, my time was not likely to be spent very pleasantly. But it was the personal problem so far as it concerned Warrington himself that distressed me even more. He came back from St. Pharamond in a morose and ugly temper, quite alien to his kindly nature. It seems that he had quarrelled bitterly with Miss Bosanquet, but upon what I could not determine, nor did I press him for an explanation. But the fumes of his anger were still rising when we met, and our dinner was a most depressing meal. He was in a degree of irritation which rendered it impossible to address him, and I soon withdrew into my thoughts. I saw, however, that he was drinking far too much, as, indeed, was plain subsequently when he invited me into the library. Once more he produced the hateful cards, and I was compelled to play, as he reminded me somewhat churlishly that I had promised him his revenge.

"Understand, Warrington," I said, firmly, "I play tonight, but never again, whatever the result. In fact, I am in half the mind to return to town tomorrow."

He gave me a look as he sat down, but said nothing, and the game began. He lost heavily from the first, and as nothing would content him but we must constantly raise the stakes, in a short time I had won several hundred pounds. He bore the reverses very ill, breaking out from time to time into some angry exclamation, now petulantly questioning my playing, and muttering oaths under his breath. But I was resolved that he should have no cause of complaint against me for this one night, and disregarding his insane fits of temper, I played steadily and silently. As the tally of my gains mounted he changed colour slowly, his face assuming a ghastly expression, and his eyes suspiciously denoting my actions. At length he rose, and throwing himself quickly across the table, seized my hand ferociously as I dealt a couple of cards.

"Damn you! I see your tricks," he cried, in frenzied passion. "Drop that hand, do you hear? Drop that hand, or by—"

But he got no further, for, rising myself, I wrenched my hand from his grasp, and turned upon him, in almost as great a passion as himself. But suddenly, and even as I opened my mouth to speak, I stopped short with a cry of horror. His face was livid to the lips, his eyes were cast with blood, and upon the dirty white of his flesh, right in the centre of his throat, the round red scar, flaming and ugly as a wound, stared upon me.

"Warrington!" I cried. "What is this? What have you—" And pointed in alarm to the spot.

"Mind your own business," he said, with a sneer. "It is well to try and draw off attention from your knavery. But that trick won't answer with me."

Without another word I flung the IOU's upon the table, and turning on my heel, left the room. I was furious with him, and fully resolved to leave the Abbey in the morning. I made my way upstairs to my room, and then, seating myself upon the balcony, endeavoured to recover my self-possession.

The more I considered, the more unaccountable was Warrington's behaviour. He had always been a perfectly courteous man, with a great lump of kindness in his nature; whereas these last few days he had been nothing other than a savage. It seemed certain that he must be ill or going mad; and as I reflected upon this the conjecture struck me with a sense of pity. If it was that he was losing his senses, how horrible was the tragedy in face of the new and lovely prospects opening in his life. Stimulated by this growing conviction, I resolved to go down and see him, more particularly as I now recalled his pleading voice that I should help him, on the previous evening. Was it not possible that

this pathetic appeal derived from the instinct of the insane to protect themselves?

I found him still in the library; his head had fallen upon the table, and the state of the whisky bottle by his arm showed only too clearly his condition. I shook him vigorously, and he opened his eyes.

"Warrington, you must go to bed," I said.

He smiled, and greeted me quite affectionately. Obviously he was not so drunk as I had supposed.

"What is the time, Ned?" he asked.

I told him it was one o'clock, at which he rose briskly.

"Lord, I've been asleep," he said. "Help me, Ned. I don't think I'm sober. Where have you been?"

I assisted him to his room, and he undressed slowly, and with an effort. Somehow, as I stood watching him, I yielded to an unknown impulse and said, suddenly:

"Warrington, don't sleep here. Come and share my room."

"My dear fellow," he replied, with a foolish laugh, "yours is not the only room in the house. I can use a half-a-dozen if I like."

"Well, use one of them," I answered.

He shook his head. "I'm going to sleep here," he returned, obstinately.

I made no further effort to influence him, for, after all, now that the words were out, I had absolutely no reason to give him or myself for my proposition. And so I left him. When I had closed the door, and was turning to go along the passage, I heard very clearly, as it seemed to me, a plaintive cry, muffled and faint, but very disturbing, which sounded from the room. Instantly I opened the door again. Warrington was in bed, and the heavy sound of his breathing told me that he was asleep. It was impossible that he could have uttered the cry. A night-light was burning by his bedside, shedding a strong illumination over the immediate vicinity, and throwing antic shadows on the walls. As I turned to go, there was a whirring of wings, a brief flap behind me, and the room was plunged in darkness. The obscene creature that lived in the recesses of the roof must have knocked out the tiny light with its wings. Then Warrington's breathing ceased, and there was no sound at all. And then once more the silence seemed to gather round me slowly and heavily, and whisper to me. I had a vague sense of being prevailed upon, of being enticed and lured by something in the surrounding air; a sort of horror circumscribed me, and I broke from the invisible ring and rushed from the room. The door clanged behind me, and as I hastened along the hall, once more there seemed to ring in my ears the faint and melancholy cry.

I awoke, in the sombre twilight that precedes the dawn, from a sleep troubled and encumbered with evil dreams. The birds had not yet begun their day, and a vast silence brooded over the Abbey gardens. Looking out of my window, I caught sight of a dark figure stealing cautiously round the corner of the ruined chapel. The furtive gait, as well as the appearance of a man at that early hour, struck me with surprise; and hastily throwing on some clothes, I ran downstairs, and, opening the hall-door, went out. When I reached the porch which gave entrance to the aisle I stopped suddenly, for there before me, with his head to the ground, and peering among the tall grasses, was the object of my pursuit. Then I stepped quickly forward and laid a hand upon his shoulder. It was Warrington.

"What are you doing here?" I asked.

He turned and looked at me in bewilderment. His eyes wore a dazed expression, and he blinked in perplexity before he replied.

"It's you, is it?" he said weakly. "I thought—" and then paused. "What is it?" he asked.

"I followed you here," I explained. "I only saw your figure, and thought it might be some intruder."

He avoided my eyes. "I thought I heard a cry out here," he answered.

"Warrington," I said, with some earnestness, "come back to bed."

He made no answer, and slipping my arm in his, I led him away. On the doorstep he stopped, and lifted his face to me.

"Do you think it's possible—" he began, as if to inquire of me, and then again paused. With a slight shiver he proceeded to his room, while I followed him. He sat down upon his bed, and his eyes strayed to the barred window absently. The black shadow of the chapel was visible through the panes.

"Don't say anything about this," he said, suddenly. "Don't let Marion know."

I laughed, but it was an awkward laugh.

"Why, that you were alarmed by a cry for help, and went in search like a gentleman?" I asked, jestingly.

"You heard it, then?" he said, eagerly.

I shook my head, for I was not going to encourage his fancies. "You had better go to sleep," I replied, "and get rid of these nightmares."

He sighed and lay back upon his pillow, dressed as he was. Ere I left him he had fallen into a profound slumber.

If I had expected a surly mood in him at breakfast I was much mistaken. There was not a trace of his nocturnal dissipations; he did not seem even to remember them, and he made no allusion whatever to our adventure in the dawn. He perused a letter carefully, and threw it over to me with a grin.

"Lor', what queer sheep women are!" he exclaimed, with rather a coarse laugh.

I glanced at the letter without thinking, but ere I had read half of it I put it aside. It was certainly not meant for my eyes, and I marvelled at Warrington's indelicacy in making public, as it were, that very private matter. The note was from Miss Bosanquet, and was clearly designed for his own heart, couched as it was in the terms of warm and fond affection. No man should see such letters save he for whom they are written.

"You see, they're coming over to dine," he remarked, carelessly. "Trust a girl to make it up if you let her alone long enough."

I made no answer; but though Warrington's grossness irritated me, I reflected with satisfaction upon his return to good humour, which I attributed to the reconciliation.

When I moved out upon the terrace the maid had entered to remove the breakfast things. I was conscious of a slight exclamation behind me, and Warrington joined me presently, with a loud guffaw.

"That's a damned pretty girl!" he said, with unction. "I'm glad Mrs. Batty got her. I like to have good-looking servants."

I suddenly interpreted the incident, and shrugged my shoulders.

"You're a perfect boot this morning, Warrington," I exclaimed, irritably.

He only laughed. "You're a dull dog of a saint, Heywood," he retorted. "Come along," and dragged me out in no amiable spirit.

I had forgotten how perfect a host Warrington could be, but that evening he was displayed at his best. The Bosanquets arrived early. Sir William was an easy-going man, fond of books and of wine, and I now guessed at the taste which had decided Warrington's cellar. Miss Bosanquet was as charming as I remembered her to be; and if any objection might be taken to Warrington himself by my anxious eyes it was merely that he seemed a trifle excited, a fault which, in the circumstances, I was able to condone. Sir William hung about the table, sipping his wine. Warrington, who had been very abstemious, grew restless, and, finally apologizing in his graceful way, left me to keep the baronet company. I was the less disinclined to do so as I was anxious not to intrude upon the lovers, and Sir William was discussing the history of the Abbey. He had an old volume somewhere in his library which related to it, and, seeing that I was interested, invited me to look it up.

We sat long, and it was not until later that the horrible affair which I must narrate occurred. The evening was close and oppressive, owing to the thunder, which already rumbled far away in the south. When we rose we found that Warrington and Miss Bosanquet were in the garden, and thither we followed. As at first we did not find them, Sir William, who had noted the approaching storm with some uneasiness, left me to make arrangements for his return; and I strolled along the paths by myself, enjoying a cigarette. I had reached the shrubbery upon the further side of the chapel, when I heard the sound of voices—a man's rough and rasping, a woman's pleading and informed

with fear. A sharp cry ensued, and without hesitation I plunged through the thicket in the direction of the speakers. The sight that met me appalled me for the moment. Darkness was falling, lit with ominous flashes; and the two figures stood out distinctly in the bushes, in an attitude of struggle. I could not mistake the voices now. I heard Warrington's, brusque with anger, and almost savage in its tones, crying, "You shall!" and there followed a murmur from the girl, a little sob, and then a piercing cry. I sprang forward and seized Warrington by the arm; when, to my horror, I perceived that he had taken her wrist in both hands and was roughly twisting it, after the cruel habit of schoolboys. The malevolent cruelty of the action so astounded me that for an instant I remained motionless; I almost heard the bones in the frail wrist cracking; and then, in a second, I had seized Warrington's hands in a grip of iron, and flung him violently to the ground. The girl fell with him, and as I picked her up he rose too, and, clenching his fists, made as though to come at me, but instead turned and went sullenly, and with a ferocious look of hate upon his face, out of the thicket.

Miss Bosanquet came to very shortly, and though the agony of the pain must have been considerable to a delicate girl, I believe it was rather the incredible horror of the act under which she swooned. For my part I had nothing to say: not one word relative to the incident dared pass my lips. I inquired if she was better, and then, putting her arm in mine, led her gently towards the house. Her heart beat hard against me, and she breathed heavily, leaning on me for support. At the chapel I stopped, feeling suddenly that I dare not let her be seen in this condition, and bewildered greatly by the whole atrocious business.

"Come and rest in here," I suggested, and we entered the chapel.

I set her on a slab of marble, and stood waiting by her side. I talked fluently about anything; for lack of a subject, upon the state of the chapel and the curious tomb I had discovered. Recovering a little, she joined presently in my remarks. It was plain that she was putting a severe restraint upon herself. I moved aside the grasses, and read aloud the inscription on Sir Rupert's grave-piece, and turning to the next, which was rankly overgrown, feigned to search further. As I was bending there, suddenly, and by what thread of thought I know not, I identified the spot with that upon which I had found Warrington stooping that morning. With a sweep of my hand I brushed back the weeds, uprooting some with my fingers, and kneeling in the twilight, pored over the monument. Suddenly a wild flare of light streamed down the sky, and a great crash of thunder followed. Miss Bosanquet started to her feet and I to mine. The heaven was lit up, as it were, with sunlight, and, as I turned, my eyes fell upon the now uncovered stone. Plainly the lettering flashed in my eyes:

*"Priscilla, Lady Marvyn."*

Then the clouds opened, and the rain fell in spouts, shouting and dancing upon the ancient roof overhead.

We were under a very precarious shelter, and I was uneasy that Miss Bosanquet should run the risk of that flimsy, ravaged edifice; and so in a momentary lull I managed to get her to the house. I found Sir William in a restless state of nerves. He was a timorous man, and the thunder had upset him, more particularly as he and his daughter were now storm-bound for some time. There was no possibility of venturing into those rude elements for an hour or more. Warrington was not inside, and no one had seen him. In the light Miss Bosanquet's face frightened me; her eyes were large and scared, and her colour very dead white. Clearly she was very near a breakdown. I found Mrs. Batty, and told her that the young lady had been severely shaken by the storm, suggesting that she had better lie down for a little. Returning with me, the housekeeper led off the unfortunate girl, and Sir William and I were left together. He paced the room impatiently, and constantly inquired if there were any signs of improvement in the weather. He also asked for Warrington, irritably. The burden of the whole dreadful night seemed fallen upon me. Passing through the hall I met Mrs. Batty again. Her usually placid features were disturbed and aghast.

"What is the matter?" I asked. "Is Miss Bosanquet—"

"No, Sir; I think she's sleeping," she replied. "She's in—she is in Mr. Warrington's room."

I started. "Are there no other rooms?" I asked, abruptly.

"There are none ready, Sir, except yours," she answered, "and I thought—"

"You should have taken her there," I said, sharply. The woman looked at me and opened her mouth. "Good heavens!" I said, irritably. "What is the matter? Everyone is mad tonight."

"Alice is gone, Sir," she blurted forth.

Alice, I remembered, was the name of one of her maids.

"What do you mean?" I asked, for her air of panic betokened something graver than her words. The thunder broke over the house and drowned her voice.

"She can't be out in this storm—she must have taken refuge somewhere," I said.

At that the strings of her tongue loosened, and she burst forth with her tale. It was an abominable narrative.

"Where is Mr. Warrington?" I asked; but she shook her head.

There was a moment's silence between us, and we eyed each other aghast. "She will be all right," I said at last, as if dismissing the subject.

The housekeeper wrung her hands. "I never would have thought it!" she repeated dismally. "I never would have thought it!"

"There is some mistake," I said; but, somehow, I knew better. Indeed, I felt now that I had almost been prepared for it.

"She ran towards the village," whispered Mrs. Batty. "God knows where she was going! The river lies that way."

"Pooh!" I exclaimed. "Don't talk nonsense. It is all a mistake. Come, have you any brandy?"

Brought back to the material round of her duties she bustled away with a sort of briskness, and returned with a flagon and glasses. I took a strong nip, and went back to Sir William. He was feverish, and declaimed against the weather unceasingly. I had to listen to the string of misfortunes which he recounted in the season's crops. It seemed all so futile, with his daughter involved in her horrid tragedy in a neighbouring room. He was better after some brandy, and grew more cheerful, but assiduously wondered about Warrington.

"Oh, he's been caught in the storm and taken refuge somewhere," I explained, vainly. I wondered if the next day would ever dawn.

By degrees that thunder rolled slowly into the northern parts of the sky, and only fitful flashes seamed the heavens. It had lasted now more than two hours. Sir William declared his intention of starting, and asked for his daughter. I rang for Mrs. Batty, and sent her to rouse Miss Bosanquet. Almost immediately there was a knock upon the door, and the housekeeper was in the doorway, with an agitated expression, demanding to see me. Sir William was looking out of the window, and fortunately did not see her.

"Please come to Miss Bosanquet, Sir," she cried, very scared. "Please come at once."

In alarm I hastily ran down the corridor and entered Warrington's room. The girl was lying upon the bed, her hair flowing upon the pillow; her eyes, wide open and filled with terror, stared at the ceiling, and her hands clutched and twined in the coverlet as if in an agony of pain. A gasping sound issued from her, as though she were struggling for breath under suffocation. Her whole appearance was as of one in the murderous grasp of an assailant.

I bent over. "Throw the light, quick," I called to Mrs. Batty; and as I put my hand on her shoulder to lift her, the creature that lived in the chamber rose suddenly from the shadow upon the further side of the bed, and sailed with a flapping noise up to the cornice. With an exclamation of horror I pulled the girl's head forward, and the candlelight glowed on her pallid face. Upon the soft flesh of the slender throat was a round red mark, the size of a florin.

At the sight I almost let her fall upon the pillow again; but, commanding my nerves, I put my arms round her, and, lifting her bodily from the bed, carried her from the room. Mrs. Batty followed.

"What shall we do?" she asked, in a low voice.

"Take her away from this damned chamber!" I cried. "Anywhere—the hall, the kitchen rather."

I laid my burden upon a sofa in the dining-room, and despatching Mrs. Batty for the brandy, gave Miss Bosanquet a draught. Slowly the horror faded from her eyes; they closed, and then she looked at me.

"What have you—where am I?" she asked.

"You have been unwell," I said. "Pray don't disturb yourself yet."

She shuddered, and closed her eyes again.

Very little more was said. Sir William pressed for his horses, and as the sky was clearing I made no attempt to detain him, more particularly as the sooner Miss Bosanquet left the Abbey the better for herself. In half an hour she recovered sufficiently to go, and I helped her into the carriage. She never referred to her seizure, but thanked me for my kindness. That was all. No one asked after Warrington—not even Sir William. He had forgotten everything, save his anxiety to get back. As the carriage turned from the steps I saw the mark upon the girl's throat, now grown fainter.

I waited up till late into the morning, but there was no sign of Warrington when I went to bed. Nor had he made his appearance when I descended to breakfast. A letter in his handwriting, however, and with the London postmark, awaited me. It was a pitiful scrawl, in the very penmanship of which one might trace the desperate emotions by which he was torn. He implored my forgiveness. *"Am I a devil?"* he asked. *"Am I mad? It was not I! It was not I!"* he repeated, underlining the sentence with impetuous dashes. *"You know,"* he wrote, *"and you know, therefore, that everything is at an end for me. I am going abroad today. I shall never see the Abbey again."*

It was well that he had gone, as I hardly think that I could have faced him; and yet I was loth myself to leave the matter in this horrible tangle. I felt that it was enjoined upon me to meet the problems, and I endeavoured to do so as best I might.

Mrs. Batty gave me news of the girl Alice. It was bad enough, though not so bad as both of us had feared. I was able to make arrangements on the instant, which I hoped might bury that lamentable affair for the time. There remained Miss Bosanquet; but that difficulty seemed beyond me. I could see no avenue out of the tragedy. I heard nothing save that she was ill—an illness attributed upon all hands to the shock of exposure to the thunderstorm. Only I knew better, and a vague disinclination to fly from the responsibilities of the position kept me hanging on at Utterbourne.

It was in those days before my visit to St. Pharamond that I turned my attention more particularly to the thing which had forced itself relentlessly upon me. I was never a superstitious man; the gossip of old wives interested me merely as a curious and unsympathetic observer. And yet I was vaguely discomfited by the transaction in the Abbey, and it was with some reluctance that I decided to make a further test of Warrington's bedroom. Mrs. Batty received my determination to change my room easily enough, but with a protest as to the dampness of the Stone Chamber. It was plain that her suspicions had not marched with mine. On the second night after Warrington's departure I occupied the room for the first time.

I lay awake for a couple of hours, with a reading lamp by my bed, and a volume of travels in my hand, and then, feeling very tired, put out the light and went to sleep. Nothing distracted me that night; indeed, I slept more soundly and peaceably than before in that house. I rose, too, experiencing quite an exhilaration, and it was not until I was dressing before the glass that I remembered the circumstances of my mission; but then I was at once pulled up, startled swiftly out of my cheerful temper. Faintly visible upon my throat was the same round mark which I had already seen stamped upon Warrington and Miss Bosanquet. With that, all my former doubts returned in force, augmented and militant. My mind recurred to the bat, and tales of bloodsucking by those evil creatures revived in my memory. But when I had remembered that these were of foreign beasts, and that I was in England, I dismissed them lightly enough. Still,

the impress of that mark remained, and alarmed me. It could not come by accident; to suppose so manifold a coincidence was absurd. The puzzle dwelt with me, unsolved, and the fingers of dread slowly crept over me.

Yet I slept again in the room. Having but myself for company, and being somewhat bored and dull, I fear I took more spirit than was my custom, and the result was that I again slept profoundly. I awoke about three in the morning, and was surprised to find the lamp still burning. I had forgotten it in my stupid state of somnolence. As I turned to put it out, the bat swept by me and circled for an instant above my head. So overpowered with torpor was I that I scarcely noticed it, and my head was no sooner at rest than I was once more unconscious. The red mark was stronger next morning, though, as on the previous day, it wore off with the fall of evening. But I merely observed the fact without any concern; indeed, now the matter of my investigation seemed to have drawn very remote. I was growing indifferent, I supposed, through familiarity. But the solitude was palling upon me, and I spent a very restless day. A sharp ride I took in the afternoon was the one agreeable experience of the day. I reflected that if this burden were to continue I must hasten up to town. I had no desire to tie myself to Warrington's apron, in his interest. So dreary was the evening, that after I had strolled round the grounds and into the chapel by moonlight, I returned to the library and endeavoured to pass the time with Warrington's cards. But it was poor fun with no antagonist to pit myself against; and I was throwing down the pack in disgust when one of the manservants entered with the whisky.

It was not until long afterwards that I fully realized the course of my action; but even at the time I was aware of a curious sub-feeling of shamefacedness. I am sure that the thing fell naturally, and that there was no awkwardness in my approaching him. Nor, after the first surprise, did he offer any objection. Later he was hardly expected to do so, seeing that he was winning very quickly. The reason of that I guessed afterwards, but during the play I was amazed to note at intervals how strangely my irritation was aroused. Finally, I swept the cards to the floor, and rose, the man, with a smile in which triumph blended with uneasiness, rose also.

"Damn you, get away!" I said, angrily.

True to his traditions to the close, he answered me with respect, and obeyed; and I sat staring at the table. With a sudden flush, the grotesque folly of the night's business came to me, and my eyes fell on the whisky bottle. It was nearly empty. Then I went to bed.

Voices cried all night in that chamber—soft, pleading voices. There was nothing to alarm in them; they seemed in a manner to coo me to sleep. But presently a sharper cry roused me from my semi-slumber; and getting up, I flung open the window. The wind rushed round the Abbey, sweeping with noises against the corners and gables. The black chapel lay still in the moonlight, and drew my eyes. But, resisting a strange, unaccountable impulse to go further, I went back to bed.

The events of the following day are better related without comment.

At breakfast I found a letter from Sir William Bosanquet, inviting me to come over to St. Pharamond. I was at once conscious of an eager desire to do so: it seemed somehow as though I had been waiting for this. The visit assumed preposterous proportions, and I was impatient for the afternoon.

Sir William was polite, but not, as I thought, cordial. He never alluded to Warrington, from which I guessed that he had been informed of the breach, and I conjectured also that the invitation extended to me was rather an act of courtesy to a solitary stranger than due to a desire for my company. Nevertheless, when he presently suggested that I should stay to dinner, I accepted promptly. For, to say the truth, I had not yet seen Miss Bosanquet, and I experienced a strange curiosity to do so. When at last she made her appearance, I was struck, almost for the first time, by her beauty. She was certainly a handsome girl, though she had a delicate air of ill-health.

After dinner Sir William remembered by accident the book on the Abbey which he had promised to show me, and after a brief hunt in the library

we found it. Shortly afterwards he was called away, and with an apology left me. With a curious eagerness I turned the pages of the volume and settled down to read.

It was published early in the century, and purported to relate the history of the Abbey and its owners. But it was one chapter which specially drew my interest—that which recounted the fate of the last Marvyn. The family had become extinct through a bloody tragedy; that fact held me. The bare narrative, long since passed from the memory of tradition, was here set forth in the baldest statements. The names of Sir Rupert Marvyn and Priscilla, Lady Marvyn, shook me strangely, but particularly the latter. Some links of connection with those gravestones lying in the Abbey chapel constrained me intimately. The history of that evil race was stained and discoloured with blood, and the end was in fitting harmony—a lurid holocaust of crime. There had been two brothers, but it was hard to choose between the foulness of their lives. If either, the younger, William, was the worse; so at least the narrative would have it. The details of his excesses had not survived, but it was abundantly plain that they were both notorious gamblers. The story of their deaths was wrapt in doubt, the theme of conjecture only, and probability; for none was by to observe save the three veritable actors—who were at once involved together in a bloody dissolution. Priscilla, the wife of Sir Rupert, was suspected of an intrigue with her brother-in-law. She would seem to have been tainted with the corruption of the family into which she had married. But according to a second rumour, chronicled by the author, there was some doubt if the woman were not the worst of the three. Nothing was known of her parentage; she had returned with the passionate Sir Rupert to the Abbey after one of his prolonged absences, and was accepted as his legal wife. This was the woman whose infamous beauty had brought a terrible sin between the brothers.

Upon the night which witnessed the extinction of this miserable family, the two brothers had been gambling together. It was known from the high voices that they had quarrelled, and it is supposed that, heated with wine and with the lust of play, the younger had thrown some taunt at Sir Rupert in respect to his wife. Whereupon—but this is all conjecture—the elder stabbed him to death. At least, it was understood that at this point the sounds of a struggle were heard, and a bitter cry. The report of the servants ran that upon this noise Lady Marvyn rushed into the room and locked the door behind her. Fright was busy with those servants, long used to the savage manners of the house. According to witnesses, no further sound was heard subsequently to Lady Marvyn's entrance; yet when the doors were at last broken open by the authorities, the three bodies were discovered upon the floor.

How Sir Rupert and his wife met their deaths there was no record. "This tragedy," proceeded the scribe, "took place in the Stone Chamber underneath the stairway."

I had got so far when the entrance of Miss Bosanquet disturbed me. I remember rising in a dazed condition—the room swung about me. A conviction, hitherto resisted and stealthily entertained upon compulsion, now overpowered me.

"I thought my father was here," explained Miss Bosanquet, with a quick glance round the room.

I explained the circumstances, and she hesitated in my neighbourhood with a slight air of embarrassment.

"I have not thanked you properly, Mr. Heywood," she said presently, in a low voice, scarcely articulate. "You have been very considerate and kind. Let me thank you now." And ended with a tiny spasmodic sob.

Somehow, an impulse overmastered my tongue. Fresh from the perusal of that chapter, queer possibilities crowded in my mind, odd considerations urged me.

"Miss Bosanquet," said I, abruptly, "let me speak of that a little. I will not touch on details."

"Please," she cried, with a shrinking notion as of one that would retreat in very alarm.

"Nay," said I, eagerly. "Hear me. It is no wantonness that would press the memory upon you. You have been a witness to distressful acts; you have seen a man under the influence of temporary madness. Nay, even yourself, you have been a victim to the same unaccountable phenomena."

"What do you mean?" she cried, tensely.

"I will say no more," said I. "I should incur your laughter. No, you would not laugh, but my dim suspicions would leave you still incredulous. But if this were so, and if these were the phenomena of a brief madness, surely you would make your memory a grave to bury the past."

"I cannot do that," she said, in low tones.

"What!" I asked. "Would you turn from your lover, aye, even from a friend, because he was smitten with disease? Consider; if your dearest upon earth tossed in a fever upon his bed, and denied you in his ravings, using you despitefully, it would not be he that entreated you so. When he was quit of his madness and returned to his proper person, would you not forget—would you not rather recall his insanity with the pity of affection?"

"I do not understand you," she whispered.

"You read your Bible," said I. "You have wondered at the evil spirits that possessed poor victims. Why should you decide that these things have ceased? We are too dogmatic in our modern world. Who can say under what malign influence a soul may pass, and out of its own custody?"

She looked at me earnestly, searching my eyes.

"You hint at strange things," said she, very low.

But somehow, even as I met her eyes, the spirit of my mission failed me. My gaze, I felt, devoured her ruthlessly. The light shone on her pale and comely features; they burned me with an irresistible attraction. I put forth my hand and took hers gently. It was passive to my touch, as though in acknowledgment of my kindly offices. All the while I experienced a sense of fierce elation. In my blood ran, as it had been fire, a horrible incentive, and I knew that I was holding her hand very tightly. She herself seemed to grow conscious of this, for she made an effort to withdraw her fingers, at which, the passion rushing through my body, I clutched them closer, laughing aloud. I saw a wondering look dawn in her eyes, and her bosom thinly veiled, heaved with a tiny tremor. I was aware that I was drawing her steadily to me. Suddenly her bewildered eyes, dropping from my face, lit with a flare of terror, and, wrenching her hand away, she fell back with a cry, her gaze riveted upon my throat.

"That accursed mark! What is it? What is it?—" she cried, shivering from head to foot.

In an instant, the wild blood singing in my head, I sprang towards her. What would have followed I know not, but at that moment the door opened and Sir William returned. He regarded us with consternation; but Miss Bosanquet had fainted, and the next moment he was at her side. I stood near, watching her come to with a certain nameless fury, as of a beast cheated of its prey. Sir William turned to me, and in his most courteous manner begged me to excuse the untoward scene. His daughter, he said, was not at all strong, and he ended by suggesting that I should leave them for a time.

Reluctantly I obeyed, but when I was out of the house, I took a sudden panic. The demoniac possession lifted, and in a craven state of trembling I saddled my horse, and rode for the Abbey as if my life depended upon my speed.

I arrived at about ten o'clock, and immediately gave orders to have my bed prepared in my old room. In my shaken condition the sinister influences of that stone chamber terrified me, and it was not until I had drunk deeply that I regained my composure.

But I was destined to get little sleep. I had steadily resolved to keep my thoughts off the matter until the morning, but the spell of the chamber was strong upon me. I awoke after midnight with an irresistible feeling drawing me to the room. I was conscious of the impulse, and combated it, but in the end succumbed; and throwing on my clothes, took a light and went downstairs. I flung wide the door of the room and peered in, listening, as though for some voice of welcome. It was as silent as a sepulchre; but directly I crossed the threshold voices seemed to surround and coax me. I stood wavering, with a curious fascination upon me. I knew I could not return to my own room, and I now had no desire to do so. As I stood, my candle flaring solemnly against the darkness, I noticed upon the floor in an alcove bare of carpet, a

large black mark, which appeared to be a stain. Bending down, I examined it, passing my fingers over the stone. It moved to my touch. Setting the candle upon the floor, I put my fingertips to the edges, and pulled hard. As I did so the sounds that were ringing in my ears died instantaneously; the next moment the slab turned with a crash, and I discovered a gaping hole of impenetrable blackness.

The patch of chasm thus opened to my eyes was near a yard square. The candle held to it shed a dim light upon a stone step a foot or two below, and it was clear to me that a stairway communicated with the depths. Whether it had been used as a cellar in times gone by I could not divine, but I was soon to determine this doubt; for, stirred by a strange eagerness, I slipped my legs through the hole, and let myself cautiously down with the light in my hand. There were a dozen steps to descend ere I reached the floor and what turned out to be a narrow passage. The vault ran forward straight as an arrow before my eyes, and slowly I moved on. Dank and chill was the air in those close confines, and the sound of my feet returned from those walls dull and sullen. But I kept on, and, with infinite care, must have penetrated quite a hundred yards along that musty corridor ere I came out upon an ampler chamber. Here the air was freer, and I could perceive with the aid of my light that the dimensions of the place were lofty. Above, a solitary ray of moonlight, sliding through a crack, informed me that I was not far from the level of the earth. It fell upon a block of stone which rose in the middle of the vault, and which I now inspected with interest. As the candle threw its flickering beams upon this I realized where I was. I scarcely needed the rude lettering upon the coffins to acquaint me that here was the family vault of the Marvyns. And now I began to perceive upon all sides whereon my feeble light fell the crumbling relics of the forgotten dead—coffins fallen into decay, bones and grinning skulls resting in corners, disposed by the hand of chance and time. This formidable array of the mortal remains of that poor family moved me to a shudder. I turned from those ugly memorials once more to the central altar where the two coffins rested in this sombre silence. The lid had fallen from the one, disclosing to my sight the grisly skeleton of a man, that mocked and leered at me. It seemed in a manner to my fascinated eyes to challenge my mortality, inviting me too to the rude and grotesque sleep of death. I knew, as by an instinct, that I was standing by the bones of Sir Rupert Marvyn, the protagonist in that terrible crime which had locked three souls in eternal ruin. The consideration of this miserable spectacle held me motionless for some moments, and then I moved a step closer and cast my light upon the second coffin.

As I did so I was aware of a change within myself. The grave and melancholy thoughts which I had entertained, the sober bent of my solemn reflections, gave place instantly to a strange exultation, an unholy sense of elation. My pulse swung feverishly, and, while my eyes were riveted upon the tarnished silver of the plate, I stretched forth a tremulously eager hand and touched the lid. It rattled gently under my fingers. Disturbed by the noise, I hastily withdrew them; but whether it was the impetus offered by my touch, or through some horrible and nameless circumstance—God knows—slowly and softly a gap opened between the lid and the body of the coffin! Before my startled eyes the awful thing happened, and yet I was conscious of no terror, merely of surprise and—it seems terrible to admit—of a feeling of eager expectancy. The lid rose slowly on the one side, and as it lifted the dark space between it and the coffin grew gently charged with light. At that moment my feeble candle, which had been gradually diminishing, guttered and flickered. I seemed to catch a glimpse of something, as it were, of white and shining raiment inside the coffin; and then came a rush of wings and a whirring sound within the vault. I gave a cry, and stepping back missed my foothold; the guttering candle was jerked from my grasp, and I fell prone to the floor in darkness. The next moment a sheet of flame flashed in the chamber and lit up the grotesque skeletons about me; and at the same time a piercing cry rang forth. Jumping to my feet, I gave a dazed glance at the conflagration. The whole vault was in flames. Dazed and horror-struck, I rushed blindly to the entrance; but as I did so the horrible cry pierced my ears again, and I saw the bat swoop round and circle swiftly into the flames. Then, finding the exit, I dashed with all the speed of terror down the passage, groping my way along the walls, and striking myself a dozen times in my terrified flight.

Arrived in my room, I pushed over the stone and listened. Not a sound was audible. With a white face and a body torn and bleeding I rushed from the room, and locking the door behind me, made my way upstairs to my bedroom. Here I poured myself out a stiff glass of brandy.

It was six months later ere Warrington returned. In the meantime he had sold the Abbey. It was inevitable that he should do so; and yet the new owner, I believe, has found no drawback in his property, and the Stone Chamber is still used for a bedroom upon occasions, being considered very old-fashioned. But there are some facts against which no appeal is possible, and so it was in his case. In my relation of the tragedy I have made no attempt at explanation, hardly even to myself; and it appears now for the first time in print, of course with suppositious names.

## THE VAMPIRE

# Jan Neruda

Jan Nepomuk Neruda (1834–91) was born in Prague, Bohemia, in a part of the city noted for its steep, narrow, crooked streets, old houses, and staid citizens who were later satirized in his stories. He was educated in Germany, then in the Czech Academic Gymnasium, where he acquired his nationalism. He became a journalist, producing feuilletons, criticism, and sketches of his European travels. His active love life, which included affairs with well-known women, some of whom were married, was severely criticized by a shocked and conservative public.

Neruda, a prolific poet and short-story writer, is regarded as a major Czech writer, though little of his work has been translated into English. A notable exception is *Tales of the Little Quarter* (1877), rendered into English by the famous mystery novelist Ellis Peters in 1957.

He was a member of the May school that dominated Czech literature in the 1860s and '70s; it took its name from "May," Karel Macha's epic poem, which expressed a desire to break away from provincialism and nationalism, and to emphasize general human themes.

The Chilean Nobel Prize–winning poet Neftali Ricardo Reyes Basoalto took the pseudonym Pablo Neruda in tribute to Jan Neruda.

"The Vampire" was first published in English in *Czechoslovakian Stories* (New York: Duffield, 1920); it was translated by Sarka B. Tirbkova.

# The Vampire

## JAN NERUDA

The excursion steamer brought us from Constantinople to the shore of the island of Prinkipo and we disembarked. The number of passengers was not large. There was one Polish family, a father, a mother, a daughter and her bridegroom, and then we two. Oh, yes, I must not forget that when we were already on the wooden bridge which crosses the Golden Horn to Constantinople, a Greek, a rather youthful man, joined us. He was probably an artist, judging by the portfolio he carried under his arm. Long black locks floated to his shoulders, his face was pale, and his black eyes were deeply set in their sockets. From the first moment he interested me, especially for his obligingness and for his knowledge of local conditions. But he talked too much, and I then turned away from him.

All the more agreeable was the Polish family. The father and mother were good-natured, fine people, the lover a handsome young fellow, of direct and refined manners. They had come to Prinkipo to spend the summer months for the sake of the daughter, who was slightly ailing. The beautiful pale girl was either just recovering from a severe illness or else a serious disease was just fastening its hold upon her. She leaned upon her lover when she walked and very often sat down to rest, while a frequent dry little cough interrupted her whispers. Whenever she coughed, her escort would considerately pause in their walk. He always cast upon her a glance of sympathetic suffering and she would look back at him as if she would say: "It is nothing. I am happy!" They believed in health and happiness.

On the recommendation of the Greek, who departed from us immediately at the pier, the family secured quarters in the hotel on the hill. The hotel-keeper was a Frenchman and his entire building was equipped comfortably and artistically, according to the French style.

We breakfasted together and when the noon heat had abated somewhat we all betook ourselves to the heights, where in the grove of Siberian stone-pines we could refresh ourselves with the view. Hardly had we found a suitable spot and settled ourselves when the Greek appeared again. He greeted us lightly, looked about, and seated himself only a few steps from us. He opened his portfolio and began to sketch.

"I think he purposely sits with his back to the rocks so that we can't look at his sketch," I said.

456

"We don't have to," said the young Pole. "We have enough before us to look at." After a while he added, "It seems to me he's sketching us in as a sort of background. Well—let him!"

We truly did have enough to gaze at. There is not a more beautiful or more happy corner in the world than that very Prinkipo! The political martyr, Irene, contemporary of Charles the Great, lived there for a month as an exile. If I could live a month of my life there I would be happy for the memory of it for the rest of my days! I shall never forget even that one day spent at Prinkipo.

The air was as clear as a diamond, so soft, so caressing, that one's whole soul swung out upon it into the distance. At the right beyond the sea projected the brown Asiatic summits; to the left in the distance purpled the steep coasts of Europe. The neighboring Chalki, one of the nine islands of the "Prince's Archipelago," rose with its cypress forests into the peaceful heights like a sorrowful dream, crowned by a great structure—an asylum for those whose minds are sick.

The Sea of Marmora was but slightly ruffled and played in all colors like a sparkling opal. In the distance the sea was as white as milk, then rosy, between the two islands a glowing orange and below us it was beautifully greenish blue, like a transparent sapphire. It was resplendent in its own beauty. Nowhere were there any large ships—only two small craft flying the English flag sped along the shore. One was a steamboat as big as a watchman's booth, the second had about twelve oarsmen, and when their oars rose simultaneously molten silver dripped from them. Trustful dolphins darted in and out among them and dove with long, arching flights above the surface of the water. Through the blue heavens now and then calm eagles winged their way, measuring the space between two continents.

The entire slope below us was covered with blossoming roses whose fragrance filled the air. From the coffee-house near the sea music was carried up to us through the clear air, hushed somewhat by the distance.

The effect was enchanting. We all sat silent and steeped our souls completely in the picture of paradise. The young Polish girl lay on the grass with her head supported on the bosom of her lover. The pale oval of her delicate face was slightly tinged with soft color, and from her blue eyes tears suddenly gushed forth. The lover understood, bent down, and kissed tear after tear. Her mother also was moved to tears, and I—even I—felt a strange twinge.

"Here mind and body both must get well," whispered the girl. "How happy a land this is!"

"God knows I haven't any enemies, but if I had I would forgive them here!" said the father in a trembling voice.

And again we became silent. We were all in such a wonderful mood—so unspeakably sweet it all was! Each felt for himself a whole world of happiness and each one would have shared his happiness with the whole world. All felt the same—and so no one disturbed another. We had scarcely even noticed the Greek, after an hour or so, had arisen, folded his portfolio, and with a slight nod had taken his departure. We remained.

Finally after several hours, when the distance was becoming overspread with a darker violet, so magically beautiful in the south, the mother reminded us it was time to depart. We arose and walked down towards the hotel with the easy, elastic steps that characterize carefree children. We sat down in the hotel under the handsome veranda.

Hardly had we been seated when we heard below the sounds of quarreling and oaths. Our Greek was wrangling with the hotel-keeper, and for the entertainment of it we listened.

The amusement did not last long. "If I didn't have other guests," growled the hotel-keeper, and ascended the steps towards us.

"I beg you to tell me, sir," asked the young Pole of the approaching hotel-keeper, "who is that gentleman? What's his name?"

"Eh—who knows what the fellow's name is?" grumbled the hotel-keeper, and he gazed venomously downwards. "We call him the Vampire."

"An artist?"

"Fine trade! He sketches only corpses. Just as

soon as someone in Constantinople or here in the neighborhood dies, that very day he has a picture of the dead one completed. That fellow paints them beforehand—and he never makes a mistake—just like a vulture!"

The old Polish woman shrieked affrightedly. In her arms lay her daughter pale as chalk. She had fainted.

In one bound the lover had leaped down the steps. With one hand he seized the Greek and with the other reached for the portfolio.

We ran down after him. Both men were rolling in the sand. The contents of the portfolio were scattered all about. On one sheet, sketched with a crayon, was the head of the young Polish girl, her eyes closed and a wreath of myrtle on her brow.

## THE END OF THE STORY

# Clark Ashton Smith

After a successful early career as a poet, Clark Ashton Smith began to write horror and bizarre fantasy stories, strongly influenced by his friend H. P. Lovecraft. His youthful reading of Edgar Allan Poe and *The Arabian Nights* provided him with the background and tone to write the tales of grisly death upon which his reputation rests. Along with Lovecraft and Robert E. Howard, he is now regarded as one of the three greatest writers for *Weird Tales,* the most prestigious of the fantasy and supernatural pulp magazines of the 1920s and '30s. He was also a frequent contributor to such excellent Hugo Gernsback pulps as *Amazing Stories* and *Strange Stories.*

After a great deal of productivity, Smith became depressed in the 1930s owing to the death of his mother in 1935, his friend Howard in 1936, and both his father and Lovecraft in 1937. For the remaining twenty-five years of his life, he wrote almost nothing.

When younger, he had begun to draw and paint, becoming proficient, though he was unpolished as a self-taught artist. When the flow of prose slowed to a trickle, he began to sculpt in soft stone, such as lava, sandstone, talc, and soapstone. The subjects were usually grotesque, as were those of his paintings, and brought him only trifling income. Later in life, his works began to be collected in hardcover books by Arkham House, which produced five volumes of his fiction, including *Out of Space and Time* (1942) and *Lost Worlds* (1944), and two collections of verse.

"The End of the Story" was first published in the May 1930 issue of *Weird Tales.*

# The End of the Story

## CLARK ASHTON SMITH

The following narrative was found among the papers of Christophe Morand, a young law student of Tours, after his unaccountable disappearance during a visit at his father's home near Moulins, in November, 1789:

A sinister brownish-purple autumn twilight, made premature by the imminence of a sudden thunderstorm, had filled the forest of Averoigne. The trees along my road were already blurred to ebon masses, and the road itself, pale and spectral before me in the thickening gloom, seemed to waver and quiver slightly, as with the tremor of some mysterious earthquake. I spurred my horse, who was woefully tired with a journey begun at dawn, and had fallen hours ago to a protesting and reluctant trot, and we galloped adown the darkening road between enormous oaks that seemed to lean towards us with boughs like clutching fingers as we passed.

With dreadful rapidity, the night was upon us, the blackness became a tangible clinging veil; a nightmare confusion and desperation drove me to spur my mount again with a more cruel rigour; and now, as we went, the first far-off mutter of the storm mingled with the clatter of my horse's hoofs,

and the first lightning flashes illumed our way, which to my amazement (since I believed myself on the main highway through Averoigne), had inexplicably narrowed to a well-trodden footpath. Feeling sure that I had gone astray, but not caring to retrace my steps in the teeth of darkness and the towering clouds of the tempest, I hurried on, hoping, as seemed reasonable, that a path so plainly worn would lead eventually to some house or château where I could find refuge for the night. My hope was well-founded, for within a few minutes I descried a glimmering light through the forest-boughs, and came suddenly to an open glade, where, on a gentle eminence, a large building loomed, with several litten windows in the lower storey, and a top that was well-nigh indistinguishable against the bulks of driven cloud.

"Doubtless a monastery," I thought, as I drew rein, and descending from my exhausted mount, lifted the heavy brazen knocker in the form of a dog's head and let it fall on the oaken door. The sound was unexpectedly loud and sonorous, with a reverberation almost sepulchral, and I shivered involuntarily, with a sense of startlement, of unwonted dismay. This, a moment later, was wholly dissipated when the door was thrown open and a tall, ruddy-featured monk stood before me in the cheerful glow of the cressets that illumed a capacious hallway.

"I bid you welcome to the abbey of Perigon," he said, in a suave rumble, and even as he spoke, another robed and hooded figure appeared and took my horse in charge. As I murmured my thanks and acknowledgements, the storm broke and tremendous gusts of rain, accompanied by ever-nearing peals of thunder, drove with demoniac fury on the door that closed behind me.

"It is fortunate that you found us when you did," observed my host. "'Twere ill for man and beast to be abroad in such a hell-brew."

Divining without question that I was hungry as well as tired, he led me to the refectory and set before me a bountiful meal of mutton, brown bread, lentils, and a strong excellent red wine.

He sat opposite me at the refectory table while I ate, and, with my hunger a little mollified, I took occasion to scan him more attentively. He was both tall and stoutly built, and his features, where the brow was no less broad than the powerful jaw, betokened intellect as well as a love for good living. A certain delicacy and refinement, an air of scholarship, of good taste and good breeding, emanated from him, and I thought to myself: "This monk is probably a connoisseur of books as well as of wines." Doubtless my expression betrayed the quickening of my curiosity, for he said, as if in answer:

"I am Hilaire, the abbot of Perigon. We are a Benedictine order, who live in amity with God and with all men, and we do not hold that the spirit is to be enriched by the mortification or impoverishment of the body. We have in our butteries an abundance of wholesome fare, in our cellars the best and oldest vintage of the district of Averoigne. And, if such things interest you, as mayhap they do, we have a library that is stocked with rare tomes, with precious manuscripts, with the finest works of heathendom and christendom, even to certain unique writings that survived the holocaust of Alexandria."

"I appreciate your hospitality," I said bowing.

"I am Christophe Morand, a law student, on my way home from Tours to my father's estate near Moulins. I, too, am a lover of books, and nothing would delight me more than the privilege of inspecting a library so rich and curious as the one whereof you speak."

Forthwith, while I finished my meal, we fell to discussing the classics, and to quoting and capping passages from Latin, Greek, or Christian authors. My host, I soon discovered, was a scholar of uncommon attainments, with an erudition, a ready familiarity with both ancient and modern literature that made my own seem as that of the merest beginner by comparison. He, on his part, was so good as to commend my far from perfect Latin, and by the time I had emptied my bottle of red wine we were chatting familiarly like old friends.

All my fatigue had now flown, to be succeeded by a rare sense of well-being, of physical comfort combined with mental alertness and keenness. So, when the abbot suggested that we pay a visit to the library, I assented with alacrity.

He led me down a long corridor, on each side of which were cells belonging to the brothers of the order, and unlocked, with a large brazen key that depended from his girdle, the door of a great room with lofty ceiling and several deepset windows. Truly, he had not exaggerated the resources of the library, for the long shelves were overcrowded with books, and many volumes were piled high on the tables or stacked in corners. There were rolls of papyrus, or parchment, of vellum; there were strange Byzantine and Coptic bibles; there were old Arabic and Persian manuscripts with floriated or jewel-studded covers; there were scores of incunabula from the first printing presses; there were innumerable monkish copies of antique authors, bound in wood or ivory, with rich illuminations and lettering that was often in itself a work of art.

With a care that was both loving and meticulous, the abbot Hilaire brought out volume after volume for my inspection. Many of them I had never seen before; some were unknown to me even by fame or rumour. My excited interest, my unfeigned enthusiasm, evidently pleased him, for at length he pressed a hidden spring in one of the library tables and drew out a long drawer, in which, he told me, were certain treasures that he did not care to bring forth for the edification or delectation of many, and whose very existence was undreamed of by the monks.

"Here," he continued, "are three odes by Catullus which you will not find in any published edition of his works. Here, also, is an original manuscript of Sappho—a complete copy of a poem otherwise extant only in brief fragments; here are two of the lost tales of Miletus, a letter of Pericles to Aspasia, an unknown dialogue of Plato, and an old Arabian work on astronomy, by some anonymous author, in which the theories of Copernicus are anticipated. And, lastly, here is the somewhat infamous *Histoire d'Amour,* by Bernard de Vaillant-coeur, which was destroyed immediately on publication, and of which only one other copy is known to exist."

As I gazed with mingled awe and curiosity on the unique, unheard-of treasures he displayed, I saw in one corner of the drawer what appeared to be a thin volume with plain untitled binding of dark leather. I ventured to pick it up, and found that it contained a few sheets of closely written manuscript in old French.

"And this?" I queried, turning to look at Hilaire, whose face, to my amazement, had suddenly assumed a melancholy and troubled expression.

"It were better not to ask, my son." He crossed himself as he spoke, and his voice was no longer mellow, but harsh, agitated, full of sorrowful perturbation. "There is a curse on the pages that you hold in your hand: an evil spell, a malign power is attached to them, and he who would venture to peruse them is henceforward in dire peril both of body and soul." He took the little volume from me as he spoke, and returned it to the drawer, again crossing himself as he did so.

"But father," I dared to expostulate, "how can such things be? How can there be danger in a few written sheets of parchment?"

"Christophe, there are things beyond your un-derstanding, things that it were not well for you to know. The might of Satan is manifestable in devious modes, in diverse manners; there are other temptations than those of the world and the flesh, there are evils no less subtle than irresistible, there are hidden heresies, and necromancies other than those which sorcerers practise."

"With what, then, are these pages concerned, that such occult peril, such unholy power, lurks within them?"

"I forbid you to ask." His tone was one of great rigour, with a finality that dissuaded me from further questioning.

"For you, my son," he went on, "the danger would be doubly great, because you are young, ardent, full of desires and curiosities. Believe me, it is better to forget that you have even seen this man-uscript." He closed the hidden drawer, and as he did so, the melancholy troubled look was replaced by his former benignity.

"Now," he said, as he turned to one of the book-shelves, "I will show you the copy of Ovid that was owned by the poet Petrarch." He was again the mellow scholar, the kindly, jovial host, and it was evident that the mysterious manuscript was not to be referred to again. But his odd perturbation, the dark and awful hints he had let fall, the vague terrific terms of his proscription, had all served to awaken my wildest curiosity, and, though I felt the obsession to be unreasonable, I was quite unable to think of anything else for the rest of the evening. All manner of speculations, fantastic, absurd, outrageous, ludicrous, terrible, defiled through my brain as I duly admired the incunabula which Hilaire took down so tenderly from the shelves for my delectation.

At last, towards midnight, he led me to my room—a room especially reserved for visitors, and with more of comfort, of actual luxury in its hangings, carpets, and deeply quilted bed than was allowable in the cells of the monks or of the abbot himself. Even when Hilaire had withdrawn, and I had proved for my satisfaction the softness of the bed allotted me, my brain still whirled with questions concerning the forbidden manuscript.

Though the storm had now ceased, it was long before I fell asleep; but slumber, when it finally came, was dreamless and profound.

When I awoke, a river of sunshine clear as molten gold was pouring through my window. The storm had wholly vanished, and no lightest tatter of cloud was visible anywhere in the pale-blue October heavens. I ran to the window and peered out on a world of autumnal forest and fields all a-sparkle with the diamonds of rain. All was beautiful, all was idyllic to a degree that could be fully appreciated only by one who had lived for a long time, as I had, within the walls of a city, with towered buildings in lieu of trees and cobbled pavements where grass should be. But, charming as it was, the foreground held my gaze only for a few moments; then, beyond the tops of the trees, I saw a hill, not more than a mile distant, on whose summit there stood the ruins of some old château, the crumbling, broken-down condition of whose walls and towers was plainly visible. It drew my gaze irresistibly, with an overpowering sense of romantic attraction which somehow seemed so natural, so inevitable, that I did not pause to analyse or wonder; and once having seen it, I could not take my eyes away, but lingered at the window for how long I knew not, scrutinizing as closely as I could the details of each time-shaken turret and bastion. Some undefinable fascination was inherent in the very form, the extent, the disposition of the pile— some fascination not dissimilar to that exerted by a strain of music, by a magical combination of words in poetry, by the features of a beloved face. Gazing, I lost myself in reveries that I could not recall afterwards, but which left behind them the same tantalizing sense of innominable delight which forgotten nocturnal dreams may sometimes leave.

I was recalled to the actualities of life by a gentle knock at my door, and realized that I had forgotten to dress myself. It was the abbot, who came to inquire how I had passed the night, and to tell me that breakfast was ready whenever I should care to arise. For some reason, I felt a little embarrassed, even shamefaced, to have been caught day-dreaming; and, though this was doubtless unnecessary, I apologized for my dilatoriness. Hilaire, I thought, gave me a keen, inquiring look, which was quickly withdrawn, as, with the suave courtesy of a good host, he assured me that there was nothing whatever for which I need apologize.

When I had breakfasted, I told Hilaire, with many expressions of gratitude for his hospitality, that it was time for me to resume my journey. But his regret at the announcement of my departure was so unfeigned, his invitation to tarry for at least another night was so genuinely hearty, so sincerely urgent, that I consented to remain. In truth, I required no great amount of solicitation, for, apart from the real liking I had taken to Hilaire, the mystery of the forbidden manuscript had entirely enslaved my imagination, and I was loth to leave without having learned more concerning it. Also, for a youth with scholastic leanings, the freedom of the abbot's library was a rare privilege, a precious opportunity not to be passed over.

"I should like," I said, "to pursue certain studies while I am here, with the aid of your incomparable collection."

"My son, you are more than welcome to remain for any length of time, and you can have access to my books whenever it suits your need or inclination." So saying, Hilaire detached the key of the library from his girdle and gave it to me. "There are duties," he went on, "which will call me away from the monastery for a few hours today, and doubtless you will desire to study in my absence."

A little later, he excused himself and departed. With inward felicitations on the longed-for opportunity that had fallen so readily into my hands, I hastened to the library, with no thought save to read the proscribed manuscript. Giving scarcely a glance at the laden shelves, I sought the table with the secret drawer, and fumbled for the spring. After a little anxious delay, I pressed the proper spot and drew forth the drawer. An impulsion that had become a veritable obsession, a fever of curiosity that bordered upon actual madness, drove me, and if the safety of my soul had really depended upon it, I could not have denied the desire which forced me to take from the drawer the thin volume with plain unlettered binding.

Seating myself in a chair near one of the windows, I began to peruse the pages, which were only six in number. The writing was peculiar, with letter-forms of a fantasticality I had never met before, and the French was not only old but wellnigh barbarous in its quaint singularity. Notwithstanding the difficulty I found in deciphering them, a mad, unaccountable thrill ran through me at the first words, and I read on with all the sensations of a man who has been bewitched or who has drunken a philtre of bewildering potency.

There was no title, no date, and the writing was a narrative which began almost as abruptly as it ended. It concerned one Gérard, Comte de Venteillon, who, on the eve of his marriage to the renowned and beautiful demoiselle, Eleanor des Lys, had met in the forest near his château a strange, half-human creature with hoofs and horns. Now Gérard, as the narrative explained, was a knightly youth of indisputably proven valour, as well as a true Christian; so, in the name of our Saviour, Jesus Christ, he bade the creature stand and give an account of itself.

Laughing wildly in the twilight, the bizarre being capered before him, and cried:

"I am a satyr, and your Christ is less to me than the weeds that grow on your kitchen-middens."

Appalled by such blasphemy, Gérard would have drawn his sword to slay the creature, but again it cried, saying:

"Stay, Gérard de Venteillon, and I will tell you a secret, knowing which, you will forget the worship of Christ, and forget your beautiful bride of tomorrow, and turn your back on the world and on the very sun itself with no reluctance and no regret."

Now, albeit unwillingly, Gérard lent the satyr an ear and it came closer and whispered to him. And that which it whispered is not known; but before it vanished amid the blackening shadows of the forest, the satyr spoke aloud once more, and said:

"The power of Christ has prevailed like a black frost on all the woods, the fields, the rivers, the mountains, where abode in their felicity the glad, immortal goddesses and nymphs of yore. But still, in the cryptic caverns of earth, in places far underground, like the hell your priests have fabled, there dwells the pagan loveliness, there cry pagan ecstasies." And with the last words, the creature laughed again its wild unhuman laugh, and disappeared among the darkening boles of the twilight trees.

From that moment, a change was upon Gérard de Venteillon. He returned to his château with downcast mien, speaking no cheery or kindly word to his retainers, as was his wont, but sitting or pacing always in silence, and scarcely heeding the food that was set before him. Nor did he go that evening to visit his betrothed, as he had promised, but, towards midnight, when a waning moon had arisen red as from a bath of blood, he went forth clandestinely by the postern door of the château, and following an old, half-obliterated trail through the woods, found his way to the ruins of the Château des Faussesflammes, which stands on a hill opposite the Benedictine abbey of Perigon.

Now these ruins (said the manuscript) are very old, and have long been avoided by the people of the district; for a legendry of immemorial evil clings about them, and it is said that they are the dwelling-place of foul spirits, the rendezvous of sorcerers and succubi. But Gérard, as if oblivious or fearless of their ill-renown, plunged like one who is devil-driven into the shadow of the crumbling walls, and went, with the careful groping of a man who follows some given direction, to the northern end of the courtyard. There, directly between and below the two centremost windows, which, it may be, looked forth from the chamber of forgotten chatelaines, he pressed with his right foot on a flagstone differing from those about it in being of a triangular form. And the flagstone moved and tilted beneath his foot revealing a flight of granite steps that went down into the earth.

Then, lighting a taper he had brought with him, Gérard descended the steps, and the flagstone swung into place behind him.

On the morrow, his betrothed, Eleanor des Lys, and all her bridal train, waited vainly for him at the cathedral of Vyones, the principal town of Averoigne, where the wedding had been set. And from that time his face was beheld by no man, and no vaguest rumour of Gérard de Venteillon or of the fate that befell him has ever passed among the living . . .

Such was the substance of the forbidden manuscript, and thus it ended. As I have said before, there was no date, nor was there anything to indicate by whom it had been written or how the knowledge of the happenings related had come into the writer's possession. But, oddly enough, it did not occur to me to doubt their veridity for a moment; and the curiosity I had felt concerning the contents of all the manuscript was now replaced by a burning desire, a thousandfold more powerful, more obsessive, to know the ending of the story and to learn what Gérard de Venteillon had found when he descended the hidden steps.

In reading the tale, it had of course occurred to me that the ruins of the Château des Faussesflammes, described therein, were the very same ruins I had seen that morning from my chamber window; and pondering this, I became more and more possessed by an insane fever, by a frenetic, unholy excitement. Returning the manuscript to the secret drawer, I left the library and wandered for awhile in an aimless fashion about the corridors of the monastery. Chancing to meet there the same monk who had taken my horse in charge the previous evening, I ventured to question him, as discreetly as I could, regarding the ruins which were visible from the abbey windows.

He crossed himself, and a frightened look came over his broad, placid face at my query.

"The ruins are those of the Château des Faussesflammes," he replied. "For untold years, men say, they have been the haunt of unholy spirits, of witches and demons; and festivals not to be described or even named are held within their walls. No weapon known to man, no exorcism or holy water, has ever prevailed against these demons; many brave cavaliers and monks have disappeared amid the shadows of Faussesflammes, never to return; and once, it is told, an abbot of Perigon went thither to make war on the powers of evil; but what befell him at the hands of the succubi is not known or conjectured. Some say that the demons are abominable hags whose bodies terminate in serpentine coils; others, that they are women of more than mortal beauty, whose kisses are diabolic delight that consumes the flesh of men with the fierceness of hell-fire . . . As for me, I know not whether such tales are true; but I should not care to venture within the walls of Faussesflammes."

Before he had finished speaking, a resolve had sprung to life full-born in my mind; I felt that I must go to the Château des Faussesflammes and learn for myself, if possible, all that could be learned. The impulse was immediate, overwhelming, ineluctable; and even if I had so desired, I could no more have fought against it than if I had been the victim of some sorcerer's invultuation. The proscription of the abbot Hilaire, the strange unfinished tale in the old manuscript, the evil legendry at which the monk had now hinted—all these, it would seem, should have served to frighten and deter me from such a resolve; but, on the contrary, by some bizarre inversion of thought, they seemed to conceal some delectable mystery, to denote a hidden world of ineffable things, of vague undreamable pleasures that set my brain on fire and made my pulses throb deliriously. I did not know, I could not conceive, of what these pleasures would consist; but in some mystical manner I was as sure of their ultimate reality as the abbot Hilaire was sure of heaven.

I determined to go that very afternoon, in the absence of Hilaire, who, I felt instinctively, might be suspicious of any such intention on my part and would surely be inimical towards its fulfilment.

My preparations were very simple: I put in my pockets a small taper from my room and the heel of a loaf of bread from the refectory; and making sure that a little dagger which I always carried was in its sheath, I left the monastery forthwith. Meeting two of the brothers in the courtyard, I told them I was going for a short walk in the neighbouring woods. They gave me a jovial "*pax vobis-*

*cum"* and went upon their way in the spirit of their words.

Heading as directly as I could for Fausses-flammes, whose turrets were often lost behind the high and interlacing boughs, I entered the forest. There were no paths, and often I was compelled to brief detours and divagations by the thickness of the underbrush. In my feverous hurry to reach the ruins, it seemed hours before I came to the top of the hill which Fausses-flammes surmounted, but probably it was little more than thirty minutes. Climbing the last declivity of the boulderstrewn slope, I came suddenly within view of the château, standing close at hand in the centre of the level table which formed the summit. Trees had taken root in its broken-down walls, and the ruinous gateway that gave on the courtyard was half-choked by bushes, brambles and nettle-plants. Forcing my way through, not without difficulty, and with clothing that had suffered from the bramble-thorns, I went, like Gérard de Venteillon in the old manuscript, to the northern end of the court. Enormous evil-looking weeds were rooted between the flagstones, rearing their thick and fleshy leaves that had turned to dull sinister maroons and purples with the onset of autumn. But I soon found the triangular flagstone indicated in the tale, and without the slightest delay or hesitation I pressed upon it with my right foot.

A mad shiver, a thrill of adventurous triumph that was mingled with something of trepidation, leaped through me when the great flagstone tilted easily beneath my foot, disclosing dark steps of granite, even as in the story. Now, for a moment, the vaguely hinted horrors of the monkish legends became imminently real in my imagination, and I paused before the black opening that was to engulf me, wondering if some satanic spell had not drawn me thither to perils of unknown terror and inconceivable gravity.

Only for a few instants, however, did I hesitate. Then the sense of peril faded, the monkish horrors became a fantastic dream, and the charm of things unformulable, but ever closer at hand, always more readily attainable, tightened about me like the embrace of amorous arms. I lit my taper, I descended the stair, and even as behind Gérard de Venteillon, the triangular block of stone silently resumed its place in the paving of the court above me. Doubtless it was moved by some mechanism operable by a man's weight on one of the steps; but I did not pause to consider its *modus operandi*, or to wonder if there were any way by which it could be worked from beneath to permit my return.

There were perhaps a dozen steps, terminating in a low, narrow, musty vault that was void of anything more substantial than ancient, dust-encumbered cobwebs. At the end, a small doorway admitted me to a second vault that differed from the first only in being larger and dustier. I passed through several such vaults, and then found myself in a long passage or tunnel, half blocked in places by boulders or heaps of rubble that had fallen from the crumbling sides. It was very damp, and full of the noisome odour of stagnant waters and subterranean mould. My feet splashed more than once in little pools, and drops fell upon me from above, fetid and foul as if they had oozed from a charnel. Beyond the wavering circle of light that my taper maintained, it seemed to me that the coils of dim and shadowy serpents slithered away in the darkness at my approach; but I could not be sure whether they really were serpents, or only the troubled and retreating shadows, seen by an eye that was still unaccustomed to the gloom of the vaults.

Rounding a sudden turn in the passage, I saw the last thing I had dreamt of seeing—the gleam of sunlight at what was apparently the tunnel's end. I scarcely know what I had expected to find, but such an eventuation was somehow altogether unanticipated. I hurried on, in some confusion of thought, and stumbled through the opening, to find myself blinking in the full rays of the sun.

Even before I had sufficiently recovered my wits and my eyesight to take note of the landscape before me, I was struck by a strange circumstance. Though it had been early afternoon when I entered the vaults, and though my passage through them could have been a matter of no more than a few minutes, the sun was now nearing the horizon. There was also a difference in its light, which was both brighter and mellower than the sun I had seen above Averoigne; and the sky itself was intensely blue, with no hint of autumnal pallor.

Now, with ever-increasing stupefaction, I stared about me and could find nothing familiar or even credible in the scene upon which I had emerged. Contrary to all reasonable expectation, there was no semblance of the hill upon which Faussesflammes stood, or of the adjoining country; but around me was a placid land of rolling meadows, through which a golden-gleaming river meandered towards a sea of deepest azure that was visible beyond the tops of laurel-trees . . . But there are no laurel-trees in Averoigne, and the sea is hundreds of miles away: judge, then, my complete confusion and dumbfoundment.

It was a scene of such loveliness as I have never before beheld. The meadow-grass at my feet was softer and more lustrous than emerald velvet, and was full of violets and many-coloured asphodels. The dark green of ilex-trees was mirrored in the golden river, and far away I saw the pale gleam of a marble acropolis on a low summit above the plain. All things bore the aspect of a mild and clement spring that was verging upon an opulent summer. I felt as if I had stepped into a land of classic myth, of Grecian legend; and moment by moment, all surprise, all wonder as to how I could have come there, was drowned in a sense of ever-growing ecstasy before the utter, ineffable beauty of the landscape.

Near by, in a laurel-grove, a white roof shone in the late rays of the sun. I was drawn towards it by the same allurement, only far more potent and urgent, which I had felt on seeing the forbidden manuscript and the ruins of Faussesflammes. Here, I knew with an esoteric certainty, was the culmination of my quest, the reward of all my mad and perhaps impious curiosity.

As I entered the grove, I heard laughter among the trees, blending harmoniously with the low murmur of their leaves in a soft, balmy wind. I thought I saw vague forms that melted among the boles at my approach; and once a shaggy, goat-like creature with human head and body ran across my path, as if in pursuit of a flying nymph.

In the heart of the grove, I found a marble palace with a portico of Doric columns. As I neared it, I was greeted by two women in the costume of ancient slaves; and though my Greek is of the meagrest, I found no difficulty whatever in comprehending their speech, which was of Attic purity.

"Our mistress, Nycea, awaits you," they told me. I could no longer marvel at anything, but accepted my situation without question or surmise, like one who resigns himself to the progress of some delightful dream. Probably, I thought, it was a dream, and I was still lying in my bed at the monastery; but never before had I been favoured by nocturnal visions of such clarity and surpassing loveliness.

The interior of the palace was full of a luxury that verged upon the barbaric, and which evidently belonged to the period of Greek decadence, with its intermingling of Oriental influences. I was led through a hallway gleaming with onyx and polished prophyry, into an opulently furnished room, where, on a couch of gorgeous fabrics, there reclined a woman of goddess-like beauty.

At sight of her, I trembled from head to foot with the violence of a strange emotion. I had heard of the sudden mad loves by which men are seized on beholding for the first time a certain face and form; but never before had I experienced a passion of such intensity, such all-consuming ardour, as the one I conceived immediately for this woman. Indeed, it seemed as if I had loved her for a long time, without knowing that it was she whom I loved, and without being able to identify the nature of my emotion or to orient the feeling in any manner.

She was not tall, but was formed with exquisite voluptuous purity of line and contour. Her eyes were of a dark sapphire blue, with molten depths into which the soul was fain to plunge as into the soft abysses of a summer ocean. The curve of her lips was enigmatic, a little mournful, and gravely tender as the lips of an antique Venus. Her hair, brownish rather than blonde, fell over her neck and ears and forehead in delicious ripples confined by a plain fillet of silver. In her expression, there was a mixture of pride and voluptuousness, of regal imperiousness and feminine yielding. Her movements were all as effortless and graceful as those of a serpent.

"I knew you would come," she murmured in the same soft-vowelled Greek I had heard from the lips of her servants. "I have waited for you long; but when you sought refuge from the storm in the abbey of Perigon, and saw the manuscript in the secret drawer, I knew that the hour of your arrival was at hand. Ah! You did not dream that the spell which drew you so irresistibly, with such unaccountable potency, was the spell of my beauty, the magical allurement of my love!"

"Who are you?" I queried. I spoke readily in Greek, which would have surprised me greatly an hour before. But now, I was prepared to accept anything whatever, no matter how fantastic or preposterous, as part of the miraculous fortune, the unbelievable adventure which had befallen me.

"I am Nycea," she replied to my question. "I love you, and the hospitality of my palace and of my arms is at your disposal. Need you know anything more?"

The slaves had disappeared. I flung myself beside the couch and kissed the hand she offered me, pouring out protestations that were no doubt incoherent, but were nevertheless full of an ardour that made her smile tenderly.

Her hand was cool to my lips, but the touch of it fired my passion. I ventured to seat myself beside her on the couch, and she did not deny my familiarity. While a soft purple twilight began to fill the corners of the chamber, we conversed happily, saying over and over again all the sweet absurd litanies, all the felicitous nothings that come instinctively to the lips of lovers. She was incredibly soft in my arms, and it seemed almost as if the completeness of her yielding was unhindered by the presence of bones in her lovely body.

The servants entered noiselessly, lighting rich lamps of intricately carven gold, and setting before us a meal of spicy meats, of unknown savorous fruits and potent wines. But I could eat little, and while I drank, I thirsted for the sweeter wine of Nycea's mouth.

I do not know when we fell asleep; but the evening had flown like an enchanted moment. Heavy with felicity, I drifted off on a silken tide of drowsiness, and the golden lamps and the face of Nycea blurred in a blissful mist and were seen no more.

Suddenly, from the depths of a slumber beyond all dreams, I found myself compelled into full wakefulness. For an instant, I did not even realize where I was, still less what had aroused me. Then I heard a footfall in the open doorway of the room, and peering across the sleeping head of Nycea, saw in the lamplight the abbot Hilaire, who had paused on the threshold. A look of absolute horror was imprinted upon his face, and as he caught sight of me, he began to gibber in Latin, in tones where something of fear was blended with fanatical abhorrence and hatred. I saw that he carried in his hands a large bottle and an aspergillum. I felt sure that the bottle was full of holy water, and of course divined the use for which it was intended.

Looking at Nycea, I saw that she too was awake, and knew that she was aware of the abbot's presence. She gave me a strange smile, in which I read an affectionate pity, mingled with the reassurance that a woman offers a frightened child.

"Do not fear for me," she whispered.

"Foul vampire! Accursed Lamia! She-serpent of hell!" thundered the abbot suddenly, as he crossed the threshold of the room, raising the aspergillum aloft. At the same moment, Nycea glided from the couch, with an unbelievable swiftness of motion, and vanished through an outer door that gave upon the forest of laurels. Her voice hovered in my ear, seeming to come from an immense distance.

"Farewell for awhile, Christophe. But have no fear. You shall find me again if you are brave and patient."

As the words ended, the holy water from the aspergillum fell on the floor of the chamber and on the couch where Nycea had lain beside me. There was a crash as of many thunders, and the golden lamps went out in a darkness that seemed full of falling dust, of raining fragments. I lost all consciousness, and when I recovered, I found myself lying on a heap of rubble in one of the vaults I had traversed earlier in the day. With a taper in his hand, and an expression of great solicitude, of infinite pity upon his face, Hilaire was stooping over me. Beside him lay the bottle and the dripping aspergillum.

"I thank God, my son, that I found you in good time," he said. "When I returned to the abbey this evening and learned that you were gone, I surmised all that had happened. I knew you had read the accursed manuscript in my absence, and had fallen under its baleful spell, as have so many others, even to a certain reverend abbot, one of my predecessors. All of them, alas! beginning hundreds of years ago with Gérard de Venteillon, have fallen victims to the lamia who dwells in these vaults."

"The lamia?" I questioned, hardly comprehending his words.

"Yes, my son, the beautiful Nycea who lay in your arms this night is a lamia, an ancient vampire, who maintains in these noisome vaults her palace of beatific illusions. How she came to take up her abode at Faussesflammes is not known, for her coming antedates the memory of men. She is as old as paganism: the Greeks knew her; she was exorcised by Apollonius of Tyana; and if you could behold her as she really is, you would see, in lieu of her voluptuous body, the folds of a foul and monstrous serpent. All those whom she loves and admits to her hospitality, she devours in the end, after she has drained them of life and vigour with the diabolic delight of her kisses. The laurel-wooded plain you saw, the ilex-bordered river, the marble palace and all the luxury therein, were no more than a satanic delusion, a lovely bubble that arose from the dust and mould of immemorial death, of ancient corruption. They crumbled at the kiss of the holy water I brought with me when I followed you. But Nycea, alas! has escaped, and I fear she will still survive, to build again her palace of demoniacal enchantments, to commit again and again the unspeakable abomination of her sins."

Still in a sort of stupor at the ruin of my new-found happiness, at the singular revelations made by the abbot, I followed him obediently as he led the way through the vaults of Faussesflammes. He mounted the stairway by which I had descended, and as he neared the top and was forced to stoop a little, the great flagstone swung upward, letting in a stream of chill moonlight. We emerged, and I permitted him to take me back to the monastery.

As my brain began to clear, and the confusion into which I had been thrown resolved itself, a feeling of resentment grew apace—a keen anger at the interference of Hilaire. Unheedful whether or not he had rescued me from dire physical and spiritual perils, I lamented the beautiful dream of which he had deprived me. The kisses of Nycea burned softly in my memory, and I knew that whatever she was, woman or demon or serpent, there was no one in all the world who could ever arouse in me the same love and the same delight. I took care, however, to conceal my feelings from Hilaire, realizing that a betrayal of such emotions would merely lead him to look upon me as a soul that was lost beyond redemption.

On the morrow, pleading the urgency of my return home, I departed from Perigon. Now, in the library of my father's house near Moulins, I write this account of my adventures. The memory of Nycea is magically clear, ineffably dear as if she were still beside me, and still I see the rich draperies of a midnight chamber illumed by lamps of curiously carven gold, and still I hear the words of her farewell:

"Have no fear. You shall find me again if you are brave and patient."

Soon I shall return, to visit again the ruins of the Château des Faussesflammes, and redescend into the vault below the triangular flatstone. But, in spite of the nearness of Perigon to Faussesflammes, in spite of my esteem for the abbot, my gratitude for his hospitality, and my admiration for his incomparable library, I shall not care to revisit my friend Hilaire.

## THE LOVELY LADY

# D. H. Lawrence

David Herbert Lawrence (1885–1930) was born in the coal-mining town of East-wood, Nottinghamshire, the son of a coal miner and a schoolteacher. After attending Nottingham University, he became a teacher. When his mother took ill in 1910, he helped her die by giving her an overdose of sleeping pills. He was engaged to (and eventually married) a German woman, Frieda von Richtofen, and while living on the Cornish coast, he was accused of spying for the Germans at the outset of World War I. Expelled from his home in 1917, he left England in 1919 and traveled extensively thereafter, living as an expatriate for most of his life, mainly in Italy, America, and France, where he died.

Lawrence was a prolific poet (with nearly eight hundred poems), critic, short-story writer, playwright, essayist, travel writer, translator, and novelist, much of his work being controversial. Feminists have found his fiction misogynistic, and the forthright sexuality of several of his works, most famously *Lady Chatterley's Lover* (1928), was regarded as pornographic. His other novels now regarded as important works of modern literature include *The White Peacock* (1911), *Sons and Lovers* (1913), *The Rainbow* (1915), and *Women in Love* (1920).

"The Lovely Lady" was first published in *The Black Cap,* edited by Cynthia Asquith (London: Hutchinson, 1927).

# The Lovely Lady

## D. H. LAWRENCE

At seventy-two, Pauline Attenborough could still sometimes be mistaken, in the half-light, for thirty. She really was a wonderfully-preserved woman, of perfect *chic*. Of course it helps a great deal to have the right frame. She would be an exquisite skeleton, and her skull would be an exquisite skull, like that of some Etruscan woman with feminine charm still in the swerve of the bone and the pretty, naïve teeth.

Mrs. Attenborough's face was of the perfect oval and slightly flat type that wears best. There is no flesh to sag. Her nose rode serenely, in its finely-bridged curve. Only the big grey eyes were a tiny bit prominent, on the surface of her face, and they gave her away most. The bluish lids were heavy, as if they ached sometimes with the strain of keeping the eyes beneath them arch and bright; and at the corners of the eyes were fine little wrinkles which would slacken into haggardness, then be pulled up tense again to that bright, gay look like a Leonardo woman who really could laugh outright.

Her niece Cecilia was perhaps the only person in the world who was aware of the invisible little wire which connected Pauline's eye-wrinkles with Pauline's willpower. Only Cecilia consciously watched the eyes go haggard and old and tired, and remain so, for hours; until Robert came home. Then ping!—the mysterious little wire that worked between Pauline's will and her face went taut, the weary, haggard, prominent eyes suddenly began to gleam, the eyelids arched, the queer, curved eyebrows which floated in such frail arches on Pauline's forehead began to gather a mocking significance, and you had the *real* lovely lady, in all her charm.

She really had the secret of everlasting youth: that is to say, she could don her youth again like an eagle. But she was sparing of it. She was wise enough not to try being young for too many people. Her son Robert, in the evenings, and Sir Wilfrid Knipe sometimes in the afternoon to tea; then occasional visitors on Sunday, when Robert was home—for these she was her lovely and changeless self, that age could not wither, nor custom stale; so bright and kindly and yet subtly mocking, like Mona Lisa, who knew a thing or two. But Pauline knew more, so she needn't be smug at all. She could laugh that lovely, mocking Bacchante laugh of hers, which was at the same time never malicious, always good-naturedly tolerant, both of virtues and vices—the former, of course, taking much more tolerating. So she suggested, roguishly.

Only with her niece Cecilia she did not trouble to keep up the glamour. Ciss was not very observant, anyhow; and, more than that, she was plain; more still, she was in love with Robert; and most of all, she was thirty, and dependent on her aunt Pauline. Oh, Cecilia—why make music for her?

Cecilia, called by her aunt and by her cousin Robert just Ciss, like a cat spitting, was a big, dark-complexioned, pug-faced young woman who very rarely spoke, and when she did couldn't get it out. She was the daughter of a poor Congregational clergyman who had been, while he lived, brother to Ronald, Aunt Pauline's husband. Ronald and the Congregational minister were both well dead, and Aunt Pauline had had charge of Ciss for the last five years.

They lived all together in a quite exquisite though rather small Queen Anne house some twenty-five miles out of town, secluded in a little dale, and surrounded by small but very quaint and pleasant grounds. It was an ideal place and an ideal life for Aunt Pauline, at the age of seventy-two. When the kingfishers flashed up the little stream in her garden, going under the alders, something still flashed in her heart. She was that kind of woman.

Robert, who was two years older than Ciss, went every day to town, to his chambers in one of the Inns. He was a barrister, and, to his secret but very deep mortification, he earned about a hundred pounds a year. He simply *couldn't* get above that figure, though it was rather easy to get below it. Of course, it didn't matter. Pauline had money. But then, what was Pauline's was Pauline's, and though she could give almost lavishly, still, one was always aware of having a *lovely* and *undeserved* present made to one. Presents are so much nicer when they're undeserved, Aunt Pauline would say.

Robert, too, was plain, and almost speechless. He was medium sized, rather broad and stout, though not fat. Only his creamy, clean-shaven face was rather fat, and sometimes suggestive of an Italian priest, in its silence and its secrecy. But he had grey eyes like his mother, but very shy and uneasy, not bold like hers. Perhaps Ciss was the only person who fathomed his awful shyness and *malaise,* his habitual feeling that he was in the wrong place: almost like a soul that has got into a wrong body. But he never did anything about it. He went up to Chambers, and read law. It was, however, all the weird old processes that interested him. He had, unknown to everybody but his mother, a quite extraordinary collection of old Mexican legal documents—reports of processes and trials, pleas, accusations: the weird and awful mixture of ecclesiastical law and common law in seventeenth-century Mexico. He had started a study in this direction through coming across the report of a trial of two English sailors, for murder, in Mexico, in 1620, and he had gone on, when the next document was an accusation against a Don Miguel Estrada by seducing one of the nuns of the Sacred Heart Convent in Qaxaca in 1680.

Pauline and her son Robert had wonderful evenings with these old papers. The lovely lady knew a little Spanish. She even looked a trifle Spanish herself, with a high comb and a marvellous dark-brown shawl embroidered in thick silvery silk embroidery. So she would sit at the perfect old table, soft as velvet in its deep brown surface, a high comb in her hair, ear-rings with dropping pendants in her ears, her arms bare and still beautiful, a few strings of pearls round her throat, a puce velvet dress on and this or another beautiful shawl, and by candlelight she looked, yes, a Spanish high-bred beauty of thirty-two or -three. She set the candles to give her face just the chiaroscuro she knew suited her; her high chair that rose behind her face was done in old green brocade, against which her face emerged like a Christmas rose.

They were always three at table, and they always drank a bottle of champagne: Pauline two glasses, Ciss two glasses, Robert the rest. The lovely lady sparkled and was radiant. Ciss, her black hair bobbed, her broad shoulders in a very nice and becoming dress that Aunt Pauline had helped her to make, stared from her aunt to her cousin and back again, with rather confused, mute hazel eyes, and played the part of an audience suitably impressed. She *was* impressed, somewhere, all the time. And even rendered speechless by Pauline's brilliancy, even after five years. But at the bottom of her consciousness was the *data* of as weird a document as Robert ever studied: all the things she knew about her aunt and her cousin.

Robert was always a gentleman, with an old-fashioned, punctilious courtesy that covered his shyness quite completely. He was, and Ciss knew it, more confused than shy. He was worse than she was. Cecilia's own confusion dated from only five years back. Robert's must have started before he was born. In the lovely lady's womb he must have felt *very* confused.

He paid all his attention to his mother, drawn to her as a humble flower to the sun. And yet, priest-like, he was all the time aware, with the tail of his consciousness, that Ciss was there, and that she was a bit shut out of it, and that something wasn't right. He was aware of the third consciousness in the room. Whereas to Pauline, her niece Cecilia was an appropriate part of her own setting, rather than a distinct consciousness.

Robert took coffee with his mother and Ciss in the warm drawing-room, where all the furniture was so lovely, all collectors' pieces—Mrs. Attenborough had made her own money, dealing privately in pictures and furniture and rare things from barbaric countries—and the three talked desultorily till about eight or half-past. It was very pleasant, very cosy, very homely even; Pauline made a real home cosiness out of so much elegant material. The chat was simple, and nearly always bright. Pauline was her *real* self, emanating a friendly mockery and an odd, ironic gaiety—till there came a little pause.

At which Ciss always rose and said good-night, and carried out the coffee-tray, to prevent Burnett from intruding any more.

And then! Ah, then, the lovely, glowing intimacy of the evening, between mother and son, when they deciphered manuscripts and discussed points, Pauline with that eagerness of a girl for which she was famous. And it was quite genuine. In some mysterious way she had saved up her power for being thrilled, in connection with a man. Robert, solid, rather quiet and subdued, seemed like the elder of the two—almost like a priest with a young girl pupil. And that was rather how he felt.

Ciss had a flat for herself just across the courtyard, over the old coach-house and stables. There were no horses. Robert kept his car in the coach-house. Ciss had three very nice rooms up there, stretching along in a row one after the other, and she had got used to the ticking of the stable clock.

But sometimes she did not go to her rooms. In the summer she would sit on the lawn, and from the open window of the drawing-room upstairs she would hear Pauline's wonderful, heart-searching laugh. And in winter the young woman would put on a thick coat and walk slowly to the little balustraded bridge over the stream, and then look back at the three lighted windows of that drawing-room where mother and son were so happy together.

Ciss loved Robert, and she believed that Pauline intended the two of them to marry—when she was dead. But poor Robert, he was so convulsed with shyness already, with man or woman. What would he be when his mother was dead?—in a dozen more years. He would be just a shell, the shell of a man who had never lived.

The strange, unspoken sympathy of the young with one another, when they are overshadowed by the old, was one of the bonds between Robert and Ciss. But another bond, which Ciss did not know how to draw tight, was the bond of passion. Poor Robert was by nature a passionate man. His silence and his agonised, though hidden, shyness were both the result of a secret physical passionateness. And how Pauline could play on this! Ah, Ciss was not blind to the eyes which he fixed on his mother—eyes fascinated yet humiliated, full of shame. He was ashamed that he was not a man. And he did not love his mother. He was fascinated by her. Completely fascinated. And for the rest, paralysed in a life-long confusion.

Ciss stayed in the garden till the lights leapt up in Pauline's bedroom—about ten o'clock. The lovely lady had retired. Robert would now stay another hour or so, alone. Then he, too, would retire. Ciss, in the dark outside, sometimes wished she could creep up to him and say: "Oh, Robert! It's all wrong!" But Aunt Pauline would hear. And, anyhow, Ciss couldn't do it. She went off to her own rooms, once more, once more, and so for ever.

In the morning coffee was brought up on a tray to each of the rooms of the three relatives. Ciss had to be at Sir Wilfrid Knipe's at nine o'clock, to give two hours' lessons to his little grand-daughter. It was her sole serious occupation, except that she played the piano for the love of it. Robert set off to town about nine. And as a rule, Aunt Pauline appeared to lunch, though sometimes not till tea-time. When she appeared, she looked fresh and young. But she was inclined to fade rather rapidly, like a flower without water, in the daytime. Her hour was the candle hour.

So she always rested in the afternoon. When the sun shone, if possible she took a sun-bath. This was one of her secrets. Her lunch was very light; she could take her sun-and-air-bath before noon or after, as it pleased her. Often it was in the afternoon, when the sun shone very warmly into a queer little yew-walled square just behind the stables. Here Ciss stretched out the lying-chair and rugs, and put the light parasol handy in the silent little enclosure of thick dark yew-hedges beyond the old red walls of the unused stables. And hither came the lovely lady with her book. Ciss then had to be on guard in one of her own rooms, should her aunt, who was very keen-eared, hear a footstep.

One afternoon it occurred to Cecilia that she herself might while away this rather long afternoon hour by taking a sun-bath. She was growing restive. The thought of the flat roof of the stable buildings, to which she could climb from a loft at the end, started her on a new adventure. She often went on to the roof; she had to, to wind up the stable clock, which was a job she had assumed to herself. Now she took a rug, climbed out under the heavens, looked at the sky and the great elm-tops, looked at the sun, then took off her things and lay down perfectly securely, in a corner of the roof under the parapet, full in the sun.

It was rather lovely, to bask all one's length like this in warm sun and air. Yes, it was very lovely! It even seemed to melt some of the hard bitterness of her heart, some of that core of unspoken resentment which never dissolved. Luxuriously, she spread herself, so that the sun should touch her limbs fully, fully. If she had no other lover, she should have the sun! She rolled over voluptuously.

And suddenly her heart stood still in her body, and her hair almost rose on end as a voice said very softly, musingly, in her ear:

"No, Henry dear! It was not my fault you died instead of marrying that Claudia. No, darling. I was quite, quite willing for you to marry her, unsuitable though she was."

Cecilia sank down on her rug, powerless and perspiring with dread. That awful voice, so soft, so musing, yet so unnatural. Not a human voice at all. Yet there must, there *must* be someone on the roof! Oh, how unspeakably awful!

She lifted her weak head and peeped across the sloping leads. Nobody! The chimneys were too narrow to shelter anybody. There was nobody on the roof. Then it must be someone in the trees, in the elms. Either that, or—terror unspeakable—a bodiless voice! She reared her head a little higher.

And as she did so, came the voice again:

"No, darling! I told you you would tire of her in six months. And you see it was true, dear. It was true, true, true! I wanted to spare you that. So it wasn't I who made you feel weak and disabled, wanting that very silly Claudia—poor thing, she looked so woebegone afterwards!—wanting her and not wanting her. You got yourself into that perplexity, my dear. I only warned you. What else could I do? And you lost your spirit and died without ever knowing me again. It was bitter, bitter—"

The voice faded away. Cecilia subsided weakly on her rug, after the anguished tension of listening. Oh, it was awful. The sun shone, the sky was blue, all seemed so lovely and afternoony and summery. And yet, oh, horror!—she was going to be forced to believe in the supernatural! And she loathed the supernatural, ghosts and voices and rappings and all the rest.

But that awful, creepy, bodiless voice, with its rusty sort of whispers of an overtone! It had something so fearfully familiar in it, too! And yet was so utterly uncanny. Poor Cecilia could only lie there unclothed, and so all the more agonisingly helpless, inert, collapsed in sheer dread.

And then she heard the thing sigh!—a deep sigh that seemed weirdly familiar, yet was not human. "Ah well, ah well! The heart must bleed. Better it should bleed than break. It is grief, grief! But it wasn't my fault, dear. And Robert could marry our poor, dull Ciss tomorrow, if he wanted her. But he doesn't care about it, so why force him into anything?" The sounds were very uneven, sometimes only a husky sort of whisper. Listen! Listen!

Cecilia was about to give vent to loud and piercing screams of hysteria, when the last two sentences arrested her. All her caution and her cunning sprang alert. It was Aunt Pauline! It *must* be Aunt Pauline, practising ventriloquism, or something like that. What a devil she was!

Where was she? She must be lying down there, right below where Cecilia herself was lying. And it was either some fiend's trick of ventriloquism, or else thought-transference. The sounds were very uneven; sometimes quite inaudible, sometimes only a brushing sort of noise. Ciss listened intently. No, it could not be ventriloquism. It was worse: some form of thought-transference that conveyed itself like sound. Some horror of that sort! Cecilia still lay weak and inert, too terrified to move; but she was growing calmer with suspicion. It was some diabolic trick of that unnatural woman.

But *what* a devil of a woman! She even knew that she, Cecilia, had mentally accused her of killing her son Henry. Poor Henry was Robert's elder brother, twelve years older than Robert. He had died suddenly when he was twenty-two, after an awful struggle with himself, because he was passionately in love with a young and very good-looking actress, and his mother had humorously despised him for the attachment. So he had caught some sudden ordinary disease, but the poison had gone to his brain and killed him before he ever regained consciousness. Ciss knew the few facts from her own father. And lately she had been thinking that Pauline was going to kill Robert as she had killed Henry. It was clear murder: a mother murdering her sensitive sons, who were fascinated by her: the Circe!

"I suppose I may as well get up," murmured the dim, unbreathing voice. "Too much sun is as bad as too little. Enough sun, enough love-thrill, enough proper food, and not too much of any of them, and a woman might live for ever. I verily believe, for ever. If she absorbs as much vitality as she expends. Or perhaps a trifle more!"

It was certainly Aunt Pauline! How—how terrible! She, Ciss, was hearing Aunt Pauline's thoughts. Oh, how ghastly! Aunt Pauline was sending out her thoughts in a sort of radio, and she, Ciss, had to *hear* what her aunt was thinking. How ghastly! How insufferable! One of them would surely have to die.

She twisted and lay inert and crumpled, staring vacantly in front of her. Vacantly! Vacantly! And her eyes were staring almost into a hole. She was staring in it unseeing, a hole going down in the corner, from the lead gutter. It meant nothing to her. Only it frightened her a little more.

When suddenly, out of the hole came a sigh and a last whisper: "Ah well! Pauline! Get up, it's enough for to-day." Good God! Out of the hole of the rain-pipe! The rain-pipe was acting as a speaking-tube! Impossible! No, quite possible. She had read of it even in some book. And Aunt Pauline, like the old and guilty woman she was, talked aloud to herself. That was it!

A sullen exultance sprang in Ciss's breast. *That* was why she would never have anybody, not even Robert, in her bedroom. That was why she never dozed in a chair, never sat absent-minded anywhere, but went to her room, and kept to her room, except when she roused herself to be alert. When she slackened off she talked to herself! She talked in a soft little crazy voice to herself. But she was not crazy. It was only her thoughts murmuring themselves aloud.

So she had qualms about poor Henry! Well she might have! Ciss believed that Aunt Pauline had loved her big, handsome, brilliant first-born much more than she loved Robert, and that his death had been a terrible blow and a chagrin to her. Poor Robert had been only ten years old when Henry died. Since then he had been the substitute.

Ah, how awful!

But Aunt Pauline was a strange woman. She had left her husband when Henry was a small child, some years even before Robert was born. There was no quarrel. Sometimes she saw her husband again, quite amiably, but a little mockingly. And she even gave him money.

For Pauline earned all her own. Her father had been a Consul in the East and in Naples, and a devoted collector of beautiful exotic things. When he died, soon after his grandson Henry was born, he left his collection of treasures to his daughter. And Pauline, who had really a passion and a genius for loveliness, whether in texture or form or colour, had laid the basis of her fortune on her father's collection. She had gone on collecting, buying where she could, and selling to collectors or to museums. She was one of the first to sell old, weird, African figures to the museums, and ivory carvings from New Guinea. She bought Renoir as soon as she saw his pictures. But not Rousseau. And all by herself she made a fortune.

After her husband died she had not married again. She was not even *known* to have had lovers. If she did have lovers, it was not among the men who admired her most and paid her devout and open attendance. To these she was a "friend."

Cecilia slipped on her clothes and caught up her rug, hastening carefully down the ladder to the loft. As she descended she heard the ringing, musical call: "All right, Ciss"—which meant that the lovely lady was finished, and returning to the house. Even her voice was wonderfully young and sonorous, beautifully balanced and self-possessed.

So different from the little voice in which she talked to herself. *That* was much more the voice of an old woman.

Ciss hastened round to the yew enclosure, where lay the comfortable *chaise longue* with the various delicate rugs. Everything Pauline had was choice, to the fine straw mat on the floor. The great yew walls were beginning to cast long shadows. Only in the corner where the rugs tumbled their delicate colours was there hot, still sunshine.

The rugs folded up, the chair lifted away, Cecilia stooped to look at the mouth of the rain-pipe. There it was, in the corner, under a little hood of masonry and just projecting from the thick leaves of the creeper on the wall. If Pauline, lying there, turned her face towards the wall, she would speak into the very mouth of the tube. Cecilia was reassured. She had heard her aunt's thoughts indeed, but by no uncanny agency.

That evening, as if aware of something, Pauline was a little quieter than usual, though she looked her own serene, rather mysterious self. And after coffee she said to Robert and Ciss:

"I'm so sleepy. The sun has made me so sleepy. I feel full of sunshine like a bee. I shall go to bed, if you don't mind. You two sit and have a talk."

Cecilia looked quickly at her cousin.

"Perhaps you'd rather be alone?" she said to him.

"No—no," he replied. "Do keep me company for a while, if it doesn't bore you."

The windows were open, the scent of honeysuckle wafted in, with the sound of an owl. Robert smoked in silence. There was a sort of despair in his motionless, rather squat body. He looked like a caryatid bearing a weight.

"Do you remember Cousin Henry?" Cecilia asked him suddenly.

He looked up in surprise.

"Yes. Very well," he said.

"What did he look like?" she said, glancing into her cousin's big, secret-troubled eyes, in which there was so much frustration.

"Oh, he was handsome: tall, and fresh-coloured, with mother's soft brown hair." As a matter of fact, Pauline's hair was grey. "The ladies admired him very much: he was at all the dances."

"And what kind of character had he?"

"Oh, very good-natured and jolly. He liked to be amused. He was rather quick and clever, like mother, and very good company."

"And did he love your mother?"

"Very much. She loved him too—better than she does me, as a matter of fact. He was so much more nearly her idea of a man."

"Why was he more her idea of a man?"

"Tall—handsome—attractive, and very good company—and would, I believe, have been very successful at law. I'm afraid I am merely negative in all those respects."

Ciss looked at him attentively, with her slow-thinking hazel eyes. Under his impassive mask she knew he suffered.

"Do you think you are so much more negative than he?" she said.

He did not lift his face. But after a few moments he replied:

"My life, certainly, is a negative affair."

She hesitated before she dared ask him:

"And do you mind?"

He did not answer her at all. Her heart sank.

"You see, I'm afraid my life is as negative as yours is," she said. "And I'm beginning to mind bitterly. I'm thirty."

She saw his creamy, well-bred hand tremble.

"I suppose," he said, without looking at her, "one will rebel when it is too late."

That was queer, from him.

"Robert!" she said. "Do you like me at all?"

She saw his dusky-creamy face, so changeless in its folds, go pale.

"I am very fond of you," he murmured.

"Won't you kiss me? Nobody ever kisses me," she said pathetically.

He looked at her, his eyes strange with fear and a certain haughtiness. Then he rose, and came softly over to her, and kissed her gently on the cheek.

"It's an awful shame, Ciss!" he said softly.

She caught his hand and pressed it to her breast.

"And sit with me sometimes in the garden," she said, murmuring with difficulty. "Won't you?"

He looked at her anxiously and searchingly.

"What about mother?"

Ciss smiled a funny little smile, and looked into his eyes. He suddenly flushed crimson, turning aside his face. It was a painful sight.

"I know," he said. "I am no lover of women."

He spoke with sarcastic stoicism, against himself, but even she did not know the shame it was to him.

"You never try to be," she said.

Again his eyes changed uncannily.

"Does one have to try?" he said.

"Why, yes. One never does anything if one doesn't try."

He went pale again.

"Perhaps you are right," he said.

In a few minutes she left him, and went to her rooms. At least she had tried to take off the everlasting lid from things.

The weather continued sunny, Pauline continued her sun-baths, and Ciss lay on the roof eavesdropping, in the literal sense of the word. But Pauline was not to be heard. No sound came up the pipe. She must be lying with her face away into the open. Ciss listened with all her might. She could just detect the faintest, faintest murmur away below, but no audible syllable.

And at night, under the stars, Cecilia sat and waited in silence, on the seat which kept in view the drawing-room windows and the side door into the garden. She saw the light go up in her aunt's room. She saw the lights at last go out in the drawing-room. And she waited. But he did not come. She stayed on in the darkness half the night, while the owl hooted. But she stayed alone.

Two days she heard nothing; her aunt's thoughts were not revealed; and at evening nothing happened. Then, the second night, as she sat with heavy, helpless persistence in the garden, suddenly she started. He had come out. She rose and went softly over the grass to him.

"Don't speak!" he murmured.

And in silence, in the dark, they walked down

the garden and over the little bridge to the paddock, where the hay, cut very late, was in cock. There they stood disconsolate under the stars.

"You see," he said, "how can I ask for love, if I don't feel any love in myself? You know I have a real regard for you—"

"How *can* you feel any love, when you never feel anything?" she said.

"That is true," he replied.

And she waited for what next.

"And how can I marry?" he said. "I am a failure even at making money. I can't ask my mother for money."

She sighed deeply.

"Then don't bother yet about marrying," she said. "Only love me a little. Won't you?"

He gave a short laugh.

"It sounds so atrocious, to say it is hard to begin," he said.

She sighed again. He was so stiff to move.

"Shall we sit down a minute?" she said. And then, as they sat on the hay, she added: "May I touch you? Do you mind?"

"Yes, I mind. But do as you wish," he replied, with that mixture of shyness and queer candour which made him a little ridiculous, as he knew quite well. But in his heart there was almost murder.

She touched his black, always tidy, hair with her fingers.

"I suppose I shall rebel one day," he said again suddenly.

They sat some time, till it grew chilly. And he held her hand fast, but he never put his arms round her. At last she rose, and went indoors, saying good-night.

The next day, as Cecilia lay stunned and angry on the roof, taking her sun-bath, and becoming hot and fierce with sunshine, suddenly she started. A terror seized her in spite of herself. It was the voice.

"Caro, caro, tu non l'hai visto!" it was murmuring away; in a language Cecilia did not understand. She lay and writhed her limbs in the sun, listening intently to words she could not follow.

Softly, whisperingly, with infinite caressiveness and yet with that subtle, insidious arrogance under its velvet, came the voice, murmuring in Italian: "Bravo, sì, molto bravo, poverino, ma uomo come te non sarà mai, mai, mai!" Oh, especially in Italian Cecilia heard the poisonous charm of the voice, so caressive, so soft and flexible, yet so utterly egoistic. She hated it with intensity as it sighed and whispered out of nowhere. Why, why should it be so delicate, so subtle and flexible and beautifully controlled, when she herself was so clumsy? Oh, poor Cecilia, she writhed in the afternoon sun, knowing her own clownish clumsiness and lack of suavity, in comparison.

"No, Robert dear, you will never be the man your father was, though you have some of his looks. He was a marvellous lover, soft as a flower yet piercing as a humming-bird. Cara, cara mia bellissima, ti hoaspettato come l'agonissante aspetta la morte, morte deliziosa, quasi quasi troppo deliziosa per una mera anima humana. He gave himself to a woman as he gave himself to God. Mauro! Mauro! How you loved me! How you loved me!"

The voice ceased in reverie, and Cecilia knew what she had guessed before—that Robert was not the son of her Uncle Ronald, but of some Italian.

"I am disappointed in you, Robert. There is no poignancy in you. Your father was a Jesuit, but he was the most perfect and poignant lover in the world. You are a Jesuit like a fish in a tank. And that Ciss of yours is the cat fishing for you. It is less edifying even than poor Henry."

Cecilia suddenly bent her mouth down to the tube, and said in a deep voice:

"Leave Robert alone! Don't kill him as well."

There was dead silence in the hot July afternoon that was lowering for thunder. Cecilia lay prostrate, her heart beating in great thumps. She was listening as if her whole soul were an ear. At last she caught the whisper:

"Did someone speak?"

She leaned again to the mouth of the tube:

"Don't kill Robert as you killed me," she said, with slow enunciation, and a deep but small voice.

"Ah!" came the sharp little cry. "Who is that speaking?"

"Henry," said the deep voice.

There was dead silence. Poor Cecilia lay with all the use gone out of her. And there was dead silence. Till at last came the whisper:

"I didn't kill Henry. No, no! No, no! Henry, surely you can't blame me! I loved you, dearest; I only wanted to help you."

"You killed me!" came the deep, artificial, accusing voice. "Now let Robert live. Let him go! Let him marry!"

There was a pause.

"How very, very awful!" mused the whispering voice. "Is it possible, Henry, you are a spirit, and you condemn me?"

"Yes, I condemn you!"

Cecilia felt all the pent-up rage going down that rain-pipe. At the same time, she almost laughed. It was awful.

She lay and listened and listened. No sound! As if time had ceased, she lay inert in the weakening sun, till she heard a far-off rumble of thunder. She sat up. The sky was yellowing. Quickly she dressed herself, went down, and out to the corner of the stables.

"Aunt Pauline!" she called discreetly. "Did you hear thunder?"

"Yes. I am going in. Don't wait," came the feeble voice.

Cecilia retired, and from the loft watched, spying, as the figure of the lovely lady, wrapped in a lovely wrap of old blue silk, went rather totteringly to the house.

The sky gradually darkened. Cecilia hastened in with the rugs. Then the storm broke. Aunt Pauline did not appear to tea. She found the thunder trying. Robert also did not arrive till after tea, in the pouring rain. Cecilia went down the covered passage to her own house, and dressed carefully for dinner, putting some white columbines at her breast.

The drawing-room was lit with a softly-shaded lamp. Robert, dressed, was waiting, listening to the rain. He too seemed strangely crackling and on edge. Cecilia came in, with the white flowers nodding at her dusky breast. Robert was watching her curiously, a new look on his face. Cecilia went to the bookshelves near the door, and was peering for something, listening acutely. She heard a rustle, then the door softly opening. And as it opened, Ciss suddenly switched on the strong electric light by the door.

Her aunt, in a dress of black lace over ivory colour, stood in the doorway. Her face was made up, but haggard with a look of unspeakable irritability, as if years of suppressed exasperation and dislike of her fellow-men had suddenly crumpled her into an old witch.

"Oh, aunt!" cried Cecilia.

"Why, mother, you're a little old lady!" came the astounded voice of Robert—like an astonished boy as if it were a joke.

"Have you only just found it out?" snapped the old woman venomously.

"Yes! Why, I thought—" his voice tailed out in misgiving.

The haggard, old Pauline, in a frenzy of exasperation, said:

"Aren't we going down?"

She had not even noticed the excess of light, a thing she shunned. And she went downstairs almost tottering.

At table she sat with her face like a crumpled mask of unspeakable irritability. She looked old, very old, and like a witch. Robert and Cecilia fetched furtive glances at her. And Ciss, watching Robert, saw that he was so astonished and repelled by his mother's looks that he was another man.

"What kind of a drive home did you have?" snapped Pauline, with an almost gibbering irritability.

"It rained, of course," he said.

"How clever of you to have found that out!" said his mother, with the grisly grin of malice that had succeeded her arch smile.

"I don't understand," he said, with quiet suavity.

"It's apparent," said his mother, rapidly and sloppily eating her food.

She rushed through the meal like a crazy dog, to the utter consternation of the servant. And the moment it was over she darted in a queer, crab-like way upstairs. Robert and Cecilia followed her, thunderstruck, like two conspirators.

"You pour the coffee. I loathe it! I'm going. Good-night!" said the old woman, in a succession of sharp shots. And she scrambled out of the room.

There was a dead silence. At last he said:

"I'm afraid mother isn't well. I must persuade her to see a doctor."

"Yes," said Cecilia.

The evening passed in silence. Robert and Ciss stayed on in the drawing-room, having lit a fire. Outside was cold rain. Each pretended to read. They did not want to separate. The evening passed with ominous mysteriousness, yet quickly.

At about ten o'clock the door suddenly opened, and Pauline appeared, in a blue wrap. She shut the door behind her, and came to the fire. Then she looked at the two young people in hate, real hate.

"You two had better get married quickly," she said, in an ugly voice. "It would look more decent; such a passionate pair of lovers!"

Robert looked up at her quietly.

"I thought you believed that cousins should not marry, mother," he said.

"I do. But you're not cousins. Your father was an Italian priest." Pauline held her daintily-slippered foot to the fire, in an old coquettish gesture. Her body tried to repeat all the old graceful gestures. But the nerve had snapped, so it was a rather dreadful caricature.

"Is that really true, mother?" he asked.

"True! What do you think? He was a distinguished man, or he wouldn't have been my lover. He was far too distinguished a man to have had you for a son. But that joy fell to me."

"How unfortunate all round," he said slowly.

"Unfortunate for you? *You* were lucky. It was *my* misfortune," she said acidly to him.

She was really a dreadful sight, like a piece of lovely Venetian glass that has been dropped and gathered up again in horrible, sharp-edged fragments.

Suddenly she left the room again.

For a week it went on. She did not recover. It was as if every nerve in her body had suddenly started screaming in an insanity of discordance. The doctor came, and gave her sedatives, for she never slept. Without drugs she never slept at all, only paced back and forth in her room, looking hideous and evil, reeking with malevolence. She could not bear to see either her son or her niece. Only when either of them came she asked, in pure malice:

"Well! When's the wedding? Have you celebrated the nuptials yet?"

At first Cecilia was stunned by what she had done. She realised vaguely that her aunt, once a definite thrust of condemnation had penetrated her beautiful armour, had just collapsed, squirming, inside her shell. It was too terrible. Ciss was almost terrified into repentance. Then she thought: "This is what she always was. Now let her live the rest of her days in her true colours."

But Pauline would not live long. She was literally shrivelling away. She kept to her room, and saw no one. She had her mirrors taken away.

Robert and Cecilia sat a good deal together. The jeering of the mad Pauline had not driven them apart, as she had hoped. But Cecilia dared not confess to him what she had done.

"Do you think your mother ever loved anybody?" Ciss asked him tentatively, rather wistfully, one evening.

He looked at her fixedly.

"Herself!" he said at last.

"She didn't even *love* herself," said Ciss. "It was something else. What was it?" She lifted a troubled, utterly puzzled face to him.

"Power," he said curtly.

"But what power?" she asked. "I don't understand."

"Power to feed on other lives," he said bitterly. "She was beautiful, and she fed on life. She had fed on me as she fed on Henry. She put a sucker into one's soul, and sucked up one's essential life."

"And don't you forgive her?"

"No."

"Poor Aunt Pauline!"

But even Ciss did not mean it. She was only aghast.

"I *know* I've got a heart," he said, passionately striking his breast. "But it's almost sucked dry. I *know* I've got a soul, somewhere. But it's gnawed bare. I *hate* people who want power over others."

Ciss was silent. What was there to say?

And two days later Pauline was found dead in her bed, having taken too much veronal, for her heart was weakened. From the grave even she hit back at her son and her niece. She left Robert the noble sum of one thousand pounds, and Ciss one hundred. All the rest, with the nucleus of her valuable antiques, went to form the "Pauline Attenborough Museum."

# THE PARASITE

# Arthur Conan Doyle

Sir Arthur Ignatius Conan Doyle (1859–1930) was born in Edinburgh, Scotland, of an aristocratic Irish Catholic family. He received his medical degrees from the University of Edinburgh and established a medical practice in 1885, by which time he had already sold several short stories. A very small list of patients allowed him the time to continue writing, though some stories and such novels as *The Firm of Girdlestone* and *Micah Clarke* failed to sell for several years. In 1887 he sold the first Sherlock Holmes story, *A Study in Scarlet*, for publication in *Beeton's Christmas Annual* for 1887.

Although Doyle is mainly known today for the Holmes canon, his science-fiction novels featuring Professor Challenger, especially *The Lost World* (1912) and *The Poison Belt* (1913), remain popular today, the former having been the basis for five motion pictures and the inspiration for numerous others. Doyle was also a prolific author of supernatural and horror stories. Perhaps his own fervid belief in spiritualism brought an aura of verisimilitude to some of these adventures that would not have existed in a more secular nature.

"The Parasite" is an early and exceptionally compelling story of psychic vampirism, the vampire just as dominant as if she were drawing blood from her victim's throat every night.

"The Parasite" was first published as a slim volume in the Acme Library (London: Constable, 1894).

# The Parasite

## ARTHUR CONAN DOYLE

### I

March 24. The spring is fairly with us now. Outside my laboratory window the great chestnut-tree is all covered with the big, glutinous, gummy buds, some of which have already begun to break into little green shuttlecocks. As you walk down the lanes you are conscious of the rich, silent forces of nature working all around you. The wet earth smells fruitful and luscious. Green shoots are peeping out everywhere. The twigs are stiff with their sap; and the moist, heavy English air is laden with a faintly resinous perfume. Buds in the hedges, lambs beneath them—everywhere the work of reproduction going forward!

I can see it without, and I can feel it within. We also have our spring when the little arterioles dilate, the lymph flows in a brisker stream, the glands work harder, winnowing and straining. Every year nature readjusts the whole machine. I can feel the ferment in my blood at this very moment, and as the cool sunshine pours through my window I could dance about in it like a gnat. So I should, only that Charles Sadler would rush upstairs to know what was the matter. Besides, I must remember that I am Professor Gilroy. An old professor may afford to be natural, but when fortune has given one of the first chairs in the university to a man of four-and-thirty he must try and act the part consistently.

What a fellow Wilson is! If I could only throw the same enthusiasm into physiology that he does into psychology, I should become a Claude Bernard at the least. His whole life and soul and energy work to one end. He drops to sleep collating his results of the past day, and he wakes to plan his researches for the coming one. And yet, outside the narrow circle who follow his proceedings, he gets so little credit for it. Physiology is a recognized science. If I add even a brick to the edifice, every one sees and applauds it. But Wilson is trying to dig the foundations for a science of the future. His work is underground and does not show. Yet he goes on uncomplainingly, corresponding with a hundred semi-maniacs in the hope of finding one reliable witness, sifting a hundred lies on the chance of gaining one little speck of truth, collating old books, devouring new ones, experimenting, lecturing, trying to light up in others the fiery interest which is consuming him. I am filled with wonder and admiration when I think of him, and yet, when he asks me to associate myself with his researches, I am compelled to tell him that, in their present state, they offer little attraction to a man who is devoted to exact science. If he could show me something positive and objective, I might then be tempted to approach the question from its physiological side. So long as half his subjects are tainted with charlatanry and the other half with hysteria we physiologists must content ourselves with the body and leave the mind to our descendants.

No doubt I am a materialist. Agatha says that I am a rank one. I tell her that is an excellent reason for shortening our engagement, since I am in such urgent need of her spirituality. And yet I may claim to be a curious example of the effect of education upon temperament, for by nature I am, unless I deceive myself, a highly psychic man. I was a nervous, sensitive boy, a dreamer, a somnambulist, full of impressions and intuitions. My black hair, my dark eyes, my thin, olive face, my tapering fingers, are all characteristic of my real temperament, and cause experts like Wilson to claim me as their own. But my brain is soaked with exact knowledge. I have trained myself to deal only with fact and with proof. Surmise and fancy have no place in my scheme of thought. Show me what I can see, with my microscope, cut with my scalpel, weigh in my balance, and I will devote a lifetime to its investigation. But when you ask me to study feelings, impressions, suggestions, you ask me to do what is distasteful and even demoralizing. A departure from pure reason affects me like an evil smell or a musical discord.

Which is very sufficient reason why I am a little loath to go to Professor Wilson's tonight. Still I feel that I could hardly get out of the invitation without positive rudeness, and, now that Mrs. Marden and Agatha are going, of course I would not if I could. But I had rather meet them anywhere else. I know that Wilson would draw me into this nebulous semi-science of his if he could. In his enthusiasm he is perfectly impervious to hints or remonstrances. Nothing short of a positive quarrel will make him realize my aversion to the whole business. I have no doubt that he has some new mesmerist or clairvoyant or medium or trickster of some sort whom he is going to exhibit

to us, for even his entertainments bear upon his hobby. Well, it will be a treat for Agatha, at any rate. She is interested in it, as woman usually is in whatever is vague and mystical and indefinite.

10:50 p.m. This diary-keeping of mine is, I fancy, the outcome of that scientific habit of mind about which I wrote this morning. I like to register impressions while they are fresh. Once a day at least endeavour to define my own mental position. It is a useful piece of self-analysis, and has, I fancy, a steadying effect upon the character. Frankly, I must confess that my own needs what stiffening I can give it. I fear that, after all, much of my neurotic temperament survives, and that I am far from that cool, calm precision which characterizes Murdoch or Pratt-Haldane. Otherwise, why should the tomfoolery which I have witnessed this evening have set my nerves thrilling so that even now I am all unstrung? My only comfort is that neither Wilson nor Miss Penelosa nor even Agatha could have possibly known my weakness.

And what in the world was there to excite me? Nothing, or so little that it will seem ludicrous when I set it down.

The Mardens got to Wilson's before me. In fact, I was one of the last to arrive and found the room crowded. I had hardly time to say a word to Mrs. Marden and to Agatha, who was looking charming in white and pink, with glittering wheat-ears in her hair, when Wilson came twitching at my sleeve.

"You want something positive, Gilroy," said he, drawing me apart into a corner. "My dear fellow, I have a phenomenon—a phenomenon!"

I should have been more impressed had I not heard the same before. His sanguine spirit turns every fire-fly into a star.

"No possible question about the *bona fides* this time," said he, in answer, perhaps, to some little gleam of amusement in my eyes. "My wife has known her for many years. They both come from Trinidad, you know. Miss Penelosa has only been in England a month of two and knows no one outside the university circle, but I assure you that the things she has told us suffice in themselves to establish clairvoyance upon an absolutely scientific basis. There is nothing like her, amateur or professional. Come and be introduced!"

I like none of these mystery-mongers, but the amateur least of all. With the paid performer you may pounce upon him and expose him the instant that you have seen through his trick. He is there to deceive you, and you are there to find him out. But what are you to do with the friend of your host's wife? Are you to turn on a light suddenly and expose her slapping a surreptitious banjo? Or are you to hurl cochineal over her evening frock when she steals round with her phosphorus bottle and her supernatural platitude? There would be a scene, and you would be looked upon as a brute. So you have your choice of being that or a dupe. I was in no very good humour as I followed Wilson to the lady.

Any one less like my idea of a West Indian could not be imagined. She was a small, frail creature, well over forty, I should say, with a pale, peaky face, and hair of a very light shade of chestnut. Her presence was insignificant and her manner retiring. In any group of ten women she would have been the last whom one would have picked out. Her eyes were perhaps her most remarkable, and also, I am compelled to say, her least pleasant, feature. They were grey in colour—grey with a shade of green—and their expression struck me as being decidedly furtive. I wonder if furtive is the word, or should I have said fierce? On second thoughts, feline would have expressed it better. A crutch leaning against the wall told me what was painfully evident when she rose: that one of her legs was crippled.

So I was introduced to Miss Penelosa, and it did not escape me that as my name was mentioned she glanced across at Agatha. Wilson had evidently been talking. And presently, no doubt, thought I, she will inform me by occult means that I am engaged to a young lady with wheat-ears in her hair. I wondered how much more Wilson had been telling her about me.

"Professor Gilroy is a terrible sceptic," said he. "I hope, Miss Penelosa, that you will be able to convert him."

She looked keenly up at me.

"Professor Gilroy is quite right to be sceptical if he has not seen anything convincing," said she. "I should have thought," she added, "that you would yourself have been an excellent subject."

"For what, may I ask?" said I.

"Well, for mesmerism, for example."

"My experience has been that mesmerists go for their subjects to those who are mentally unsound. All their results are vitiated, as it seems to me, by the fact that they are dealing with abnormal organisms."

"Which of these ladies would you say possessed a normal organism?" she asked. "I should like you to select the one who seems to you to have the best balanced mind. Should we say the girl in pink and white?—Miss Agatha Marden, I think the name is?"

"Yes, I should attach weight to any results from her."

"I have never tried how far she is impressionable. Of course some people respond much more rapidly than others. May I ask how far your scepticism extends? I suppose that you admit the mesmeric sleep and the power of suggestion."

"I admit nothing, Miss Penelosa."

"Dear me, I thought science had got further than that. Of course I know nothing about the scientific side of it. I only know what I can do. You see the girl in red, for example, over near the Japanese jar. I shall will that she come across to us."

She bent forward as she spoke and dropped her fan upon the floor. The girl whisked round and came straight toward us, with an enquiring look upon her face, as if some one had called her.

"What do you think of that, Gilroy?" cried Wilson, in a kind of ecstacy.

I did not dare to tell him what I thought of it. To me it was the most barefaced, shameless piece of imposture that I had ever witnessed. The collusion and the signal had really been too obvious.

"Professor Gilroy is not satisfied," said she, glancing up at me with her strange little eyes. "My poor fan is to get the credit of that experiment. Well, we must try something else. Miss Marden, would you have any objection to my putting you off?"

"Oh, I should love it!" cried Agatha.

By this time all the company had gathered round us in a circle, the shirt-fronted men, and the white-throated women, some awed, some critical, as though it were something between a religious ceremony and a conjurer's entertainment. A red velvet armchair had been pushed into the centre, and Agatha lay back in it, a little flushed and trembling slightly from excitement. I could see it from the vibration of the wheat-ears. Miss Penelosa rose from her seat and stood over her, leaning upon her crutch.

And there was a change in the woman. She no longer seemed small or insignificant. Twenty years were gone from her age. Her eyes were shining, a tinge of colour had come into her sallow cheeks, her whole figure had expanded. So I have seen a dull-eyed, listless lad change in an instant into briskness and life when given a task of which he felt himself master. She looked down at Agatha with an expression which I resented from the bottom of my soul—the expression with which a Roman empress might have looked at her kneeling slave. Then with a quick, commanding gesture she tossed up her arms and swept them slowly down in front of her.

I was watching Agatha narrowly. During three passes she seemed to be simply amused. At the fourth I observed a slight glazing of her eyes, accompanied by some dilation of her pupils. At the sixth there was a momentary rigor. At the seventh her lids began to droop. At the tenth her eyes were closed, and her breathing was slower and fuller than usual. I tried as I watched to preserve my scientific calm, but a foolish, causeless agitation convulsed me. I trust that I hid it, but I felt as a child feels in the dark. I could not have believed that I was still open to such weakness.

"She is in the trance," said Miss Penelosa.

"She is sleeping!" I cried.

"Wake her, then!"

I pulled her by the arm and shouted in her ear. She might have been dead for all the impression that I could make. Her body was there on the velvet chair. Her organs were acting—her heart, her lungs. But her soul! It had slipped from beyond our ken. Whither had it gone? What power had dispossessed it? I was puzzled and disconcerted.

"So much for the mesmeric sleep," said Miss Penelosa. "As regards suggestion, whatever I may suggest Miss Marden will infallibly do, whether it be now or after she has awakened from her trance. Do you demand proof of it?"

"Certainly," said I.

"You shall have it." I saw a smile pass over her face, as though an amusing thought had struck her. She stooped and whispered earnestly into her subject's ear. Agatha, who had been so deaf to me, nodded her head as she listened.

"Awake!" cried Miss Penelosa, with a sharp tap of her crutch upon the floor. The eyes opened, the glazing cleared slowly away, and the soul looked out once more after its strange eclipse.

We went away early. Agatha was none the worse for her strange excursion, but I was nervous and unstrung, unable to listen to or answer the stream of comments which Wilson was pouring out for my benefit. As I bade her goodnight Miss Penelosa slipped a piece of paper into my hand.

"Pray forgive me," said she, "if I take means to overcome your scepticism. Open this note at ten o'clock tomorrow morning. It is a little private test."

I can't imagine what she means, but there is the note, and it shall be opened as she directs. My head is aching, and I have written enough for tonight. Tomorrow I dare say that what seems so inexplicable will take quite another complexion. I shall not surrender my convictions without a struggle.

March 25. I am amazed, confounded. It is clear that I must reconsider my opinion upon this matter. But first let me place on record what has occurred.

I had finished breakfast, and was looking over some diagrams with which my lecture is to be illustrated, when my housekeeper entered to tell me that Agatha was in my study and wished to see me immediately. I glanced at the clock and saw with surprise that it was only half-past nine.

When I entered the room, she was standing on the hearth-rug facing me. Something in her pose chilled me and checked the words which were rising to my lips. Her veil was half down, but I could see that she was pale and that her expression was constrained.

"Austin," she said, "I have come to tell you that our engagement is at an end."

I staggered. I believe that I literally did stagger. I know that I found myself leaning against the bookcase for support.

"But—but—" I stammered. "This is very sudden, Agatha."

"Yes, Austin, I have come here to tell you that our engagement is at an end."

"But surely," I cried, "you will give me some reason! This is unlike you, Agatha. Tell me how I have been unfortunate enough to offend you."

"It is all over, Austin."

"But why? You must be under some delusion, Agatha. Perhaps you have been told some falsehood about me. Or you may have misunderstood something that I have said to you. Only let me know what it is, and a word may set it all right."

"We must consider it all at an end."

"But you left me last night without a hint at any disagreement. What could have occurred in the interval to change you so? It must have been something that happened last night. You have been thinking it over and you have disapproved of my conduct. Was it the mesmerism? Did you blame me for letting that woman exercise her power over you? You know that at the least sign I should have interfered."

"It is useless, Austin. All is over."

Her voice was cold and measured; her manner strangely formal and hard. It seemed to me that she was absolutely resolved not to be drawn into any argument or explanation. As for me, I was shaking with agitation, and I turned my face aside, so ashamed was I that she should see my want of control.

"You must know what this means to me!" I cried. "It is the blasting of all my hopes and the ruin of my life! You surely will not inflict such a punishment upon me unheard. You will let me know what is the matter. Consider how impossible it would be for me, under any circumstances, to treat you so. For God's sake, Agatha, let me know what I have done!"

She walked past me without a word and opened the door.

"It is quite useless, Austin," said she. "You must consider our engagement at an end." An instant later she was gone, and, before I could recover myself sufficiently to follow her, I heard the hall door close behind her.

I rushed into my room to change my coat, with the idea of hurrying round to Mrs. Marden's to learn from her what the cause of my misfortune might be. So shaken was I that I could hardly lace my boots. Never shall I forget those horrible ten minutes. I had just pulled on my overcoat when the clock upon the mantel-piece struck ten.

Ten! I associated the idea with Miss Penelosa's note. It was lying before me on the table, and I tore it open. It was scribbled in pencil in a peculiarly angular handwriting.

*My dear Professor Gilroy* [it said]: *Pray excuse the personal nature of the test which I am giving you. Professor Wilson happened to mention the relations between you and my subject of this evening, and it struck me that nothing could be more convincing to you than if I were to suggest to Miss Marden that she should call upon you at half-past nine tomorrow morning and suspend your engagement for half an hour or so. Science is so exacting that it is difficult to give a satisfying test, but I am convinced that this at least will be an action which she would be most unlikely to do of her own free will. Forget anything that she may have said, as she has really nothing whatever to do with it, and will certainly not recollect anything about it. I write this note to shorten your anxiety, and to beg you to forgive me for the momentary unhappiness which my suggestion must have caused you.*

YOURS FAITHFULLY,
HELEN PENELOSA

Really, when I had read the note, I was too relieved to be angry. It was a liberty. Certainly it was a very great liberty indeed on the part of a lady whom I had only met once. But, after all, I had challenged her by my scepticism. It may have been, as she said, a little difficult to devise a test which would satisfy me.

And she had done that. There could be no question at all upon the point. For me hypnotic suggestion was finally established. It took its place from now onward as one of the facts of life. That Agatha, who of all women of my acquaintance has the best balanced mind, had been reduced to a condition of automatism appeared to be certain. A person at a distance had worked her as an engineer on the shore might guide a Brennan torpedo. A second soul had stepped in, as it were, had pushed her own aside, and had seized her nervous mechanism, saying: "I will work this for half an hour." And Agatha must have been unconscious as she came and as she returned. Could she make her way in safety through the streets in such a state? I put on my hat and hurried round to see if all was well with her.

Yes. She was at home. I was shown into the drawing-room and found her sitting with a book upon her lap.

"You are an early visitor, Austin," said she, smiling. "And you have been an even earlier one," I answered.

She looked puzzled. "What do you mean?" she asked. "You have not been out today?"

"No, certainly not."

"Agatha," said I seriously, "would you mind telling me exactly what you have done this morning?"

She laughed at my earnestness.

"You've got on your professional look, Austin. See what becomes of being engaged to a man of science. However, I will tell you, though can't imagine what you want to know for. I got up at eight. I breakfasted at half-past. I came into this room at ten minutes past nine and began to read the 'Memoirs of Mme de Remusat.' In a few minutes I did the French lady the bad compliment of dropping to sleep over her pages, and

I did you, sir, the very flattering one of dreaming about you. It is only a few minutes since I woke up."

"And found yourself where you had been before?"

"Why, where else should I find myself?"

"Would you mind telling me, Agatha, what it was that you dreamed about me? It really is not mere curiosity on my part."

"I merely had a vague impression that you came into it. I cannot recall anything definite."

"If you have not been out today, Agatha, how is it that your shoes are dusty?"

A pained look came over her face.

"Really, Austin, I do not know what is the matter with you this morning. One would almost think that you doubted my word. If my boots are dusty, it must be, of course, that I have put on a pair which the maid has not cleaned."

It was perfectly evident that she knew nothing whatever about the matter, and I reflected that, after all, perhaps it was better that I should not enlighten her. It might frighten her, and could serve no good purpose that I could see. I said no more about it, therefore, and left shortly afterward to give my lecture.

But I am immensely impressed. My horizon of scientific possibilities has suddenly been enormously extended. I no longer wonder at Wilson's demonic energy and enthusiasm. Who would not work hard who had a vast virgin field ready to his hand? Why, I have known the novel shape of a nucleolus, or a trifling peculiarity of striped muscular fibre seen under a 300 diameter lens, fill me with exultation. How petty do such researches seem when compared with this one which strikes at the very roots of life and the nature of the soul! I had always looked upon spirit as a product of matter. The brain, I thought, secreted the mind, as the liver does the bile. But how can this be when I see mind working from a distance and playing upon matter as a musician might upon a violin? The body does not give rise to the soul, then, but is rather the rough instrument by which the spirit manifests itself. The windmill does not give rise to the wind, but only indicates it. It was opposed to my whole habit of thought, and yet it was undeniably possible and worthy of investigation.

And why should I not investigate it? I see that under yesterday's date I said: "If I could see something positive and objective, I might be tempted to approach it from the physiological aspect." Well, I have got my test. I shall be as good as my word. The investigation would, I am sure, be of immense interest. Some of my colleagues might look askance at it, for science is full of unreasoning prejudices, but if Wilson has the the courage of his convictions, I can afford to have it also. I shall go to him tomorrow morning—to him and to Miss Penelosa. If she can show us so much, it is probable that she can show us more.

## II

March 26. Wilson was, as I had anticipated, very exultant over my conversion, and Miss Penelosa was also demurely pleased at the result of her experiment. Strange what a silent, colourless creature she is save only when she exercises her power! Even talking about it gives her colour and life. She seems to take a singular interest in me. I cannot help observing how her eyes follow me about the room.

We had the most interesting conversation about her own powers. It is just as well to put her views on record, though they cannot, of course, claim any scientific weight.

"You are on the very fringe of the subject," said she, when I had expressed wonder at the remarkable instance of suggestion which she had shown me. "I had no direct influence upon Miss Marden when she came round to you. I was not even thinking of her that morning. What I did was to set her mind as I might set the alarm of a clock so that at the hour named it would go off of its own accord. If six months instead of twelve hours had been suggested, it would have been the same."

"And if the suggestion had been to assassinate me?"

"She would most inevitably have done so."

"But this is a terrible power!" I cried.

"It is, as you say, a terrible power," she answered gravely, "and the more you know of it the more terrible will it seem to you."

"May I ask," said I, "what you meant when you said that this matter of suggestion is only at the fringe of it? What do you consider the essential?"

"I had rather not tell you."

I was surprised at the decision of her answer.

"You understand," said I, "that it is not out of curiosity I ask, but in the hope that I may find some scientific explanation for the facts with which you furnish me."

"Frankly, Professor Gilroy," said she, "I am not at all interested in science, nor do I care whether it can or cannot classify these powers."

"But I was hoping—"

"Ah, that is quite another thing. If you make it a personal matter," said she, with the pleasantest of smiles, "I shall be only too happy to tell you anything you wish to know. Let me see; what was it you asked me? Oh, about the further powers. Professor Wilson won't believe in them, but they are quite true all the same. For example, it is possible for an operator to gain complete command over his subject—presuming that the latter is a good one. Without any previous suggestion he may make him do whatever he likes."

"Without the subject's knowledge?"

"That depends. If the force were strongly exerted, he would know no more about it than Miss Marden did when she came round and frightened you so. Or, if the influence was less powerful, he might be conscious of what he was doing, but be quite unable to prevent himself from doing it."

"Would he have lost his own will power, then?"

"It would be over-ridden by another stronger one."

"Have you ever exercised this power yourself?"

"Several times."

"Is your own will so strong, then?"

"Well, it does not entirely depend upon that. Many have strong wills which are not detachable from themselves. The thing is to have the gift of projecting it into another person and superseding his own. I find that the power varies with my own strength and health."

"Practically, you send your soul into another person's body."

"Well, you might put it that way."

"And what does your own body do?"

"It merely feels lethargic."

"Well, but is there no danger to your own health?" I asked.

"There might be a little. You have to be careful never to let your own consciousness absolutely go; otherwise, you might experience some difficulty in finding your way back again. You must always preserve the connection, as it were. I am afraid I express myself very badly, Professor Gilroy, but of course I don't know how to put these things in a scientific way. I am just giving you my own experiences and my own explanations."

Well, I read this over now at my leisure, and I marvel at myself! Is this Austin Gilroy, the man who has won his way to the front by his hard reasoning power and by his devotion to fact? Here I am gravely retailing the gossip of a woman who tells me how her soul may be projected from her body, and how, while she lies in a lethargy, she can control the actions of people at a distance. Do I accept it? Certainly not. She must prove and reprove before I yield a point. But if I am still a sceptic, I have at least ceased to be a scoffer. We are to have a sitting this evening, and she is to try if she can produce any mesmeric effect upon me. If she can, it will make an excellent starting point for our investigation. No one can accuse *me*, at any rate, of complicity. If she cannot, we must try and find some subject who will be like Caesar's wife. Wilson is perfectly impervious.

10 p.m. I believe that I am on the threshold of an epoch-making investigation. To have the power of examining these phenomena from inside—to have an organism which will respond, and at the same time a brain which will appreciate and criticize—that is surely a unique advantage. I am quite sure that Wilson would give five years of his life to be as susceptible as I have proved myself to be.

There was no one present except Wilson and his wife. I was seated with my head leaning back, and Miss Penelosa, standing in front and a little to the left, used the same long, sweeping strokes as with Agatha. At each of them a warm current of air seemed to strike me, and to suffuse a thrill and glow all through me from head to foot. My eyes were fixed upon Miss Penelosa's face, but as I gazed the features seemed to blur and to fade away. I was conscious only of her own eyes looking down at me, grey, deep, inscrutable. Larger they grew and larger, until they changed suddenly into two mountain lakes toward which I seemed to be falling with horrible rapidity. I shuddered, and as I did so some deeper stratum of thought told me that the shudder represented the rigor which I had observed in Agatha. An instant later I struck the surface of the lakes, now jointed into one and down I went beneath the water with a fullness in my head and a buzzing in my ears. Down I went, down, down, and then with a swoop up again until I could see the light streaming brightly through the green water. I was almost at the surface when the word "Awake!" rang through my head, and, with a start, I found myself back in the armchair, with Miss Penelosa leaning on her crutch, and Wilson, his notebook in his hand, peeping over her shoulder. No heaviness or weariness was left behind. On the contrary, though it is only an hour or so since the experiment, I feel so wakeful that I am more inclined for my study than my bedroom. I see quite a vista of interesting experiments extending before us, and am all impatience to begin upon them.

March 27. A blank day, as Miss Penelosa goes with Wilson and his wife to the Suttons'. Have begun Binet and Ferre's "Animal Magnetism." What strange, deep waters these are! Results, results, results—and the cause an absolute mystery. It is stimulating to the imagination, but I must be on my guard against that. Let us have no inferences nor deductions, and nothing but solid facts. I *know* that the mesmeric trance is true; I *know* that mesmeric suggestion is true; I *know* that I am myself sensitive to this force. That is my present position. I have a large new notebook which shall be devoted entirely to scientific detail.

Long talk with Agatha and Mrs. Marden in the evening about our marriage. We think that the summer vac. (the beginning of it) would be the best time for the wedding. Why should we delay? I grudge even those few months. Still, as Mrs. Marden says, there are a good many things to be arranged.

March 28. Mesmerized again by Miss Penelosa. Experience much the same as before, save that insensibility came on more quickly. See Notebook A for temperature of room, barometric pressure, pulse, and respiration as taken by Professor Wilson.

March 29. Mesmerized again. Details in Notebook A.

March 30. Sunday, and a blank day. I grudge any interruption of our experiments. At present they merely embrace the physical signs which go with slight, with complete, and with extreme insensibility. Afterwards we hope to pass on to the phenomena of suggestion and of lucidity. Professors have demonstrated these things upon women at Nancy and at the Salpetriere. It will be more convincing when a woman demonstrates it upon a professor, with a second professor as a witness. And that I should be the subject—I, the sceptic, the materialist! At least, I have shown that my devotion to science is greater than to my own personal consistency. The eating of our own words is the greatest sacrifice which truth ever requires of us.

My neighbour, Charles Sadler, the handsome young demonstrator of anatomy, came in this evening to return a volume of Virchow's "Archives" which I had lent him. I call him young, but, as a matter of fact, he is a year older than I am.

"I understand, Gilroy," said he, "that you are being experimented upon by Miss Penelosa."

"Well," he went on, when I had acknowledged it, "if I were you, I should not let it go any further. You will think me very impertinent, no doubt, but, none the less, I feel it to be my duty to advise you to have no more to do with her."

Of course I asked him why.

"I am so placed that I cannot enter into particulars as freely as I could wish," said he. "Miss Penelosa is the friend of my friend, and my position is a delicate one. I can only say this: that I have myself been the subject of some of the woman's

experiments, and that they have left a most unpleasant impression upon my mind."

He could hardly expect me to be satisfied with that, and I tried hard to get something more definite out of him, but without success. Is it conceivable that he could be jealous at my having superseded him? Or is he one of those men of science who feel personally injured when facts run counter to their preconceived opinions? He cannot seriously suppose that because he has some vague grievance I am, therefore, to abandon a series of experiments which promise to be so fruitful of results. He appeared to be annoyed at the light way in which I treated his shadowy warnings, and we parted with some little coldness on both sides.

March 31. Mesmerized by Miss P.

April 1. Mesmerized by Miss P. (Notebook A.)

April 2. Mesmerized by Miss P. (Sphygmographic chart taken by Professor Wilson.)

April 3. It is possible that this course of mesmerism may be a little trying to the general constitution. Agatha says that I am thinner and darker under the eyes. I am conscious of a nervous irritability, which I had not observed in myself before. The least noise, for example, makes me start, and the stupidity of a student causes me exasperation instead of amusement. Agatha wishes me to stop, but I tell her that every course of study is trying, and that one can never attain a result without paying some price for it. When she sees the sensation which my forthcoming paper on "The Relation between Mind and Matter" may make, she will understand that it is worth a little nervous wear and tear. I should not be surprised if I got my F.R.S. over it.

Mesmerized again in the evening. The effect is produced more rapidly now, and the subjective visions are less marked. I keep full notes of each sitting. Wilson is leaving for town for a week or ten days, but we shall not interrupt the experiments, which depend for their value as much upon my sensations as on his observations.

April 4. I must be carefully on my guard. A complication has crept into our experiments which I had not reckoned upon. In my eagerness for scientific facts I have been foolishly blind to the human relations between Miss Penelosa and myself. I can write here what I would not breathe to a living soul. The unhappy woman appears to have formed an attachment for me.

I should not say such a thing, even in the privacy of my own intimate journal, if it had not come to such a pass that it is impossible to ignore it. For some time—that is, for the last week—there have been signs which I have brushed aside and refused to think of. Her brightness when I come, her dejection when I go, her eagerness that I should come often, the expression of her eyes, the tone of her voice—I tried to think that they meant nothing, and were, perhaps, only her ardent West Indian manner. But last night, as I awoke from the mesmeric sleep, I put out my hand, unconsciously, involuntarily, and clasped hers. When I came fully to myself, we were sitting with them locked, she looking up at me with an expectant smile. And the horrible thing was that I felt impelled to say what she expected me to say. What a false wretch I should have been! How I should have loathed myself today had I yielded to the temptation of that moment! But, thank God, I was strong enough to spring up and hurry from the room. I was rude, I fear, but I could not, no, I *could* not, trust myself another moment. I, a gentleman, a man of honour, engaged to one of the sweetest girls in England—and yet in a moment of reasonless passion I nearly professed love for this woman whom I hardly know. She is far older than myself and a cripple. It is monstrous, odious; and yet the impulse was so strong that, had I stayed another minute in her presence, I should have committed myself. What was it? I have to teach others the workings of our organism, and what do I know of it myself? Was it the sudden upcropping of some lower stratum in my nature—a brutal primitive instinct suddenly asserting itself? I could almost believe the tales of obsession by evil spirits, so overmastering was the feeling.

Well, the incident places me in a most unfortunate position. On the one hand, I am very loath to abandon a series of experiments which have already gone so far, and which promise such brilliant results. On the other, if this unhappy woman has conceived a passion for me—But surely even now I must have made some hideous mistake. She, with her age and her deformity! It is impossible. And then she knew about Agatha. She understood how I was placed. She only smiled out of amusement, perhaps, when in my dazed state I seized her hand. It was my half-mesmerized brain which gave it a meaning, and sprang with such bestial swiftness to meet it. I wish I could persuade myself that it was indeed so. On the whole, perhaps, my wisest plan would be to postpone our other experiments until Wilson's return. I have written a note to Miss Penelosa, therefore, making no allusion to last night, but saying that a press of work would cause me to interrupt our sittings for a few days. She has answered, formally enough, to say that if I should change my mind I should find her at home at the usual hour.

10 p.m. Well, well, what a thing of straw I am! I am coming to know myself better of late, and the more I know the lower I fall in my own estimation. Surely I was not always so weak as this. At four o'clock I should have smiled had anyone told me that I should go to Miss Penelosa's tonight, and yet, at eight, I was at Wilson's door as usual. I don't know how it occurred. The influence of habit, I suppose. Perhaps there is a mesmeric craze as there is an opium craze, and I am a victim to it. I only know that as I worked in my study I became more and more uneasy. I fidgeted. I worried. I could not concentrate my mind upon the papers in front of me. And then, at last, almost before I knew what I was doing, I seized my hat and hurried round to keep my usual appointment.

We had an interesting evening. Mrs. Wilson was present during most of the time, which prevented the embarrassment which one at least of us must have felt. Miss Penelosa's manner was quite the same as usual, and she expressed no surprise at my having come in spite of my note. There was nothing in her bearing to show that yesterday's incident had made any impression upon her, and so I am inclined to hope that I overrated it.

April 6 (evening). No, no, no, I did not overrate it. I can no longer attempt to conceal from myself that this woman has conceived a passion for me. It is monstrous, but it is true. Again, tonight, I awoke from the mesmeric trance to find my hand in hers, and to suffer that odious feeling which urges me to throw away my honour, my career, everything, for the sake of this creature who, as I can plainly see when I am away from her influence, possesses no single charm upon earth. But when I am near her, I do not feel this. She rouses something in me, something evil, something I had rather not think of. She paralyzes my better nature, too, at the moment when she stimulates my worse. Decidedly it is not good for me to be near her.

Last night was worse than before. Instead of flying I actually sat for sometime with my hand in hers talking over the most intimate subjects with her. We spoke of Agatha, among other things. What could I have been dreaming of? Miss Penelosa said that she was conventional, and I agreed with her. She spoke once or twice in a disparaging way of her, and I did not protest. What a creature I have been!

Weak as I have proved myself to be, I am still strong enough to bring this sort of thing to an end. It shall not happen again. I have sense enough to fly when I cannot fight. From this Sunday night onward I shall never sit with Miss Penelosa again. Never! Let the experiments go, let the research come to an end; anything is better than facing this monstrous temptation which drags me so low. I have said nothing to Miss Penelosa, but I shall simply stay away. She can tell the reason without any words of mine.

April 7. Have stayed away, as I said. It is a pity to ruin such an interesting investigation, but it would be a greater pity still to ruin my life, and I *know* that I cannot trust myself with that woman.

11 p.m. God help me! What is the matter with me? Am I going mad? Let me try and be calm and reason with myself. First of all I shall set down exactly what occurred.

It was nearly eight when I wrote the lines with which this day begins. Feeling strangely restless and uneasy, I left my rooms and walked round to spend the evening with Agatha and her mother. They both remarked that I was pale and haggard.

About nine Professor Pratt-Haldane came in, and we played a game of whist. I tried hard to concentrate my attention upon the cards, but the feeling of restlessness grew and grew until I found it impossible to struggle against it. I simply *could* not sit still at the table. At last, in the very middle of a hand, I threw my cards down and, with some sort of incoherent apology about having an appointment, I rushed from the room. As if in a dream I have a vague recollection of tearing through the hall, snatching my hat from the stand, and slamming the door behind me. As if in a dream, too, I have the impression of the double line of gas-lamps, and my bespattered boots tell me that I must have run down the middle of the road. It was all misty and strange and unnatural. I came to Wilson's house; I saw Mrs. Wilson and I saw Miss Penelosa. I hardly recall what we talked about, but I do remember that Miss P. shook the head of her crutch at me in a playful way, and accused me of being late and of losing interest in our experiments. There was no mesmerism, but I stayed some time and have only just returned.

My brain is quite clear again now, and I can think over what has occurred. It is absurd to suppose that it is merely weakness and force of habit. I tried to explain it in that way the other night, but it will no longer suffice. It is something much deeper and more terrible than that. Why, when I was at the Mardens' whist-table, I was dragged away as if the noose of a rope had been cast round me. I can no longer disguise it from myself. The woman has her grip upon me. I am in her clutch. But I must keep my head and reason it out and see what is best to be done.

But what a blind fool I have been! In my enthusiasm over my research I have walked straight into the pit, although it lay gaping before me. Did she not herself warn me? Did she not tell me, as I can read in my own journal, that when she has acquired power over a subject she can make him do her will? And she has acquired that power over me. I am for the moment at the beck and call of this creature with the crutch. I must come when she wills it. I must do as she wills. Worst of all, I must feel as she wills. I loathe her and fear her, yet, while I am under the spell, she can doubtless make me love her.

There is some consolation in the thought, then, that those odioius impulses for which I have blamed myself do not really come from me all. They are all transferred from her, little as I could have guessed it at the time. I feel cleaner and lighter for the thought.

April 8. Yes, now, in broad daylight, writing coolly and with time for reflection, I am compelled to confirm everything which I wrote in my journal last night. I am in a horrible position, but, above all, I must not lose my head. I must pit my intellect against her powers. After all, I am no silly puppet, to dance at the end of a string. I have energy, brains, courage. For all her devil's tricks I may beat her yet. May! I *must*, or what is to become of me?

Let me try to reason it out! This woman, by her own explanation, can dominate my nervous organism. She can project herself into my body and take command of it. She has a parasite soul; yes, she is a parasite, a monstrous parasite. She creeps into my frame as the hermit crab does into the whelk's shell. I am powerless. What can I do? I am dealing with forces of which I know nothing. And I can tell no one of my trouble. They would set me down as a madman. Certainly, if it got noised abroad, the university would say that they had no need of a devil-ridden professor. And Agatha! No, no, I must face it alone.

# III

I read over my notes of what the woman said when she spoke about her powers. There is one point which fills me with dismay. She implies that when the influence is slight the subject knows what he is doing, but cannot control himself, whereas when it is strongly exerted he is absolutely unconscious. Now, I have always known what I did, though less so last night than on the previous occasions. That seems to mean that she has never yet exerted her full powers upon me. Was ever a man so placed before?

Yes, perhaps there was, and very near me, too. Charles Sadler must know something of this! His vague words of warning take a meaning now. Oh, if I had only listened to him then, before I helped by these repeated sittings to forge the links of the chain which binds me! But I will see him today. I will apologize to him for having treated his warning so lightly. I will see if he can advise me.

4 p.m. No, he cannot. I have talked with him, and he showed such surprise at the first words in which I tried to express my unspeakable secret that I went no further. As far as I can gather (by hints and inferences rather than by any statement), his own experience was limited to some words or looks such as I have myself endured. His abandonment of Miss Penelosa is in itself a sign that he was never really in her toils. Oh, if he only knew his escape! He has to thank his phlegmatic Saxon temperament for it. I am dark and Celtic, and this hag's clutch is deep in my nerves. Shall I ever get it out? Shall I ever be the same man that I was just one short fortnight ago?

Let me consider what I had better do. I cannot leave the university in the middle of the term. If I were free, my course would be obvious. I should start at once and travel in Persia. But would she allow me to start? And could her influence not reach me in Persia, and bring me back to within touch of her crutch? I can only find out the limits of this hellish power by my own bitter experience. I will fight and fight and fight—and what can I do more?

I know very well that about eight o'clock tonight that craving for her society, that irresistible restlessness, will come upon me. How shall I overcome it? What shall I do? I must make it impossible for me to leave the room. I shall lock the door and throw the key out of the window. But, then, what am I to do in the morning? Never mind about the morning. I must at all costs break this chain which holds me.

April 9. Victory! I have done splendidly! At seven o'clock last night I took a hasty dinner, and then locked myself up in my bedroom and dropped the key into the garden. I chose a cheery novel, and lay in bed for three hours trying to read it, but really in a horrible state of trepidation, expecting every instant that I should become conscious of the impulse. Nothing of the sort occurred, however, and I awoke this morning with the feeling that a black nightmare had been lifted off me. Perhaps the creature realized what I had done, and understood that it was useless to try to influence me. At any rate, I have beaten her once, and if I can do it once, I can do it again.

It was most awkward about the key in the morning. Luckily, there was an under-gardener below, and I asked him to throw it up. No doubt he thought I had just dropped it. I will have doors and windows screwed up and six stout men to hold me down in my bed before I will surrender myself to be hag-ridden in this way.

I had a note from Mrs. Marden this afternoon asking me to go round and see her. I intended to do so in any case, but had not expected to find bad news waiting for me. It seems that the Armstrongs, from whom Agatha has expectations, are due home from Adelaide in the *Aurora,* and that they have written to Mrs. Marden and her to meet them in town. They will probably be away for a month or six weeks, and, as the *Aurora* is due on Wednesday, they must go at once—tomorrow, if they are ready in time. My consolation is that when we meet again there will be no more parting between Agatha and me.

"I want you to do one thing, Agatha," said I, when we were alone together. "If you should happen to meet Miss Penelosa, either in town or here, you must promise me never again to allow her to mesmerize you."

Agatha opened her eyes.

"Why, it was only the other day that you were saying how interesting it all was, and how determined you were to finish your experiments."

"I know, but I have changed my mind since then."

"And you won't have it any more?"

"No."

"I am so glad, Austin. You can't think how pale and worn you have been lately. It was really our principal objection to going to London now that we did not wish to leave you when you were so

pulled down. And your manner has been so strange occasionally—especially that night when you left poor Professor Pratt-Haldane to play dummy. I am convinced that these experiments are very bad for your nerves."

"I think so, too, dear."

"And for Miss Penelosa's nerves as well. You have heard that she is ill?"

"No."

"Mrs. Wilson told us so last night. She described it as a nervous fever. Professor Wilson is coming back this week, and of course Mrs. Wilson is very anxious that Miss Penelosa should be well again then, for he has quite a programme of experiments which he is anxious to carry out."

I was glad to have Agatha's promise, for it was enough that this woman should have one of us in her clutch. On the other hand, I was disturbed to hear about Miss Penelosa's illness. It rather discounts the victory which I appeared to win last night. I remember that she said that loss of health interfered with her power. That may be why I was able to hold my own so easily. Well, well, I must take the same precautions tonight and see what comes of it. I am childishly frightened when I think of her.

April 10. All went well last night. I was amused at the gardener's face when I had again to hail him this morning and to ask him to throw up my key. I shall get a name among the servants if this sort of thing goes on. But the great point is that I stayed in my room without the slightest inclination to leave it. I do believe that I am shaking myself clear of this incredible bond—or is it only that the woman's power is in abeyance until she recovers her strength? I can but pray for the best.

The Mardens left this morning, and the brightness seems to have gone out of the spring sunshine. And yet it is very beautiful also as it gleams on the green chestnuts opposite my windows, and gives a touch of gaiety to the heavy, lichen-mottled walls of the old colleges. How sweet and gentle and soothing is Nature! Who would think that lurked in her also such vile forces, such odious possibilities! For of course I understand that this dreadful thing which has sprung out at me is neither supernatural nor even preternatural. No, it is a natural force which this woman can use and society is ignorant of. The mere fact that it ebbs with her strength shows how entirely it is subject to physical laws. If I had time, I might probe it to the bottom and lay my hands upon its antidote. But you cannot tame the tiger when you are beneath his claws. You can but try to writhe away from him. Ah, when I look in the glass and see my own dark eyes and clear-cut Spanish face, I long for a vitriol splash or a bout of the smallpox. One or the other might have saved me from this calamity.

I am inclined to think that I may have trouble tonight. There are two things which make me fear so. One is that I met Mrs. Wilson in the street, and she tells me that Miss Penelosa is better, though still weak. I find myself wishing in my heart that the illness had been her last. The other is that Professor Wilson comes back in a day or two, and his presence would act as a constraint upon her. I should not fear our interviews if a third person were present. For both these reasons I have a presentiment of trouble tonight, and I shall take the same precautions as before.

April 10. No, thank God, all went well last night. I really could not face the gardener again. I locked my door and thrust the key underneath it, so that I had to ask the maid to let me out in the morning. But the precaution was really not needed, for I never had any inclination to go out at all. Three evenings in succession at home! I am surely near the end of my troubles, for Wilson will be home again either today or tomorrow. Shall I tell him of what I have gone through or not? I am convinced that I should not have the slightest sympathy from him. He would look upon me as an interesting case, and read a paper about me at the next meeting of the Psychical Society, in which he would gravely discuss the possibility of my being a deliberate liar, and weigh it against the chances of my being in an early stage of lunacy. No, I shall get no comfort out of Wilson.

I am feeling wonderfully fit and well. I don't think I ever lectured with greater spirit. Oh, if I could only get this shadow off my life, how happy I should be! Young, fairly wealthy, in the front rank of my profession, engaged to a beautiful and charming girl—have I not everything which a man could ask for? Only one thing to trouble me, but what a thing it is!

Midnight. I shall go mad. Yes, that will be the end of it. I shall go mad. I am not far from it now. My head throbs as I rest it on my hot hand. I am quivering all over like a scared horse. Oh, what a night I have had! And yet I have some cause to be satisfied also.

At the risk of becoming the laughing-stock of my own servant, I again slipped my key under the door, imprisoning myself for the night. Then, finding it too early to go to bed, I lay down with my clothes on and began to read one of Dumas's novels. Suddenly I was gripped—gripped and dragged from the couch. It is only thus that I can describe the overpowering nature of the force which pounced upon me. I clawed at the coverlet. I clung to the wood-work. I believe that I screamed out in my frenzy. It was all useless, hopeless, I must go. There is no way out of it. It was only at the outset that I resisted. The force soon became too overmastering for that. I thank goodness that there were no watchers there to interfere with me. I could not have answered for myself if there had been. And, besides the determination to get out, there came to me also, the keenest and coolest judgment in choosing means. I lit a candle and endeavoured, kneeling in front of the door, the key through with the feather-end of a quill pen. It was just short and pushed it further away: Then with quiet persistence I got a paper-knife out of one of the drawers, and with that I managed to draw the key back. I opened the door, stepped into my study, took a photograph of myself from the bureau, wrote something across it, placed it in the inside pocket of my coat, and then started off for Wilson's.

It was all wonderfully clear, and yet disassociated from the rest of my life, as the incidents of even the most vivid dream might be. A peculiar double consciousness possessed me. There was the predominant alien will, which was bent upon drawing me to the side of its owner, and there was the feebler protesting personality, which I recognized as being myself, tugging feebly at the overmastering impulse as a led terrier might at its chain. I can remember recognizing these two conflicting forces, but I recall nothing of my walk, nor of how I was admitted to the house.

Very vivid, however, is my recollection of how I met Miss Penelosa. She was reclining on the sofa in the little boudoir in which our experiments had usually been carried out. Her head was rested on her hand, and a tiger-skin rug had been partly drawn over her. She looked up expectantly as I entered, and, as the lamp-light fell upon her face, I could see that she was very pale and thin, with dark hollows under her eyes. She smiled at me, and pointed to a stool beside her. It was with her left hand that she pointed, and I, running eagerly forward, seized it—I loathe myself as I think of it—and pressed it passionately to my lips. Then, seating myself upon the stool, and still retaining her hand, I gave her the photograph which I had brought with me, and talked and talked and talked— of my love for her, of my grief over her illness, of my joy at her recovery, of the misery it was to be absent a single evening from her side. She lay quietly looking down at me with imperious eyes and her provocative smile. Once I remember that she passed her hand over my hair as one caresses a dog; and it gave me pleasure—the caress. I thrilled under it. I was her slave, body and soul, for the moment I rejoiced in my slavery.

And then came the blessed change. Never tell me that there is not a Providence! I was on the brink of perdition. My feet were on the edge. Was it a coincidence that at that very instant help should come? No, no, no; there is a Providence, and its hand has drawn me back. There is something in the universe stronger than this devil woman with her tricks. Ah, what a balm to my heart it is to think so!

As I looked up at her I was conscious of a change in her. Her face, which had been pale before, was now ghastly. Her eyes were dull, and the lids dropped heavily over them. Above all, the look of serene confidence had gone from her features. Her mouth had weakened. Her forehead had puckered. She was frightened and undecided. And as I watched the change my own spirit fluttered and struggled, trying hard to tear itself from the grip which held it—a grip which, from moment to moment, grew less secure.

"Austin," she whispered, "I have tried to do too much. I was not strong enough. I have not recovered yet from my illness. But I could not live longer without seeing you. You won't leave me, Austin? This is only a passing weakness. If you will only give me five minutes, I shall be myself again. Give me the small decanter from the table in the window."

But I had regained my soul. With her waning strength the influence had cleared away from me and left me free. And I was aggressive—bitterly, fiercely aggressive. For once at least I could make this woman understand what my real feelings toward her were. My soul was filled with a hatred as bestial as the love against which it was a reaction. It was the savage, murderous passion of the revolted serf. I could have taken the crutch from her side and beaten her face in with it. She threw her hands up, as if to avoid a blow, and cowered away from me into the corner of the settee.

"The brandy!" she gasped. "The brandy!"

I took the decanter and poured it over the roots of a palm in the window. Then I snatched the photograph from her hand and tore it into a hundred pieces.

"You vile woman," I said, "if I did my duty to society, you would never leave this room alive!"

"I love you, Austin; I love you!" she wailed.

"Yes," I cried, "and Charles Sadler before. And how many others before that?"

"Charles Sadler!" she gasped. "He has spoken to you? So, Charles Sadler, Charles Sadler!" Her voice came through her white lips like a snake's hiss.

"Yes, I know you, and others shall know you, too. You shameless creature! You knew how I stood. And yet you used your vile power to bring me to your side. You may, perhaps, do so again, but at least you will remember that you have heard me say that I love Miss Marden from the bottom of my soul, and that I loathe you, abhor you! The very sight of you and the sound of your voice fill me with horror and disgust. The thought of you is repulsive. That is how I feel toward you, and if it pleases you by your tricks to draw me again to your side as you have done tonight, you will at least, I should think, have little satisfaction in trying to make a lover out of a man who has told you his real opinion of you. You may put what words you will into my mouth, but you cannot help remembering—"

I stopped, for the woman's head had fallen back, and she had fainted. She could not bear to hear what I had to say to her! What a glow of satisfaction it gives me to think that, come what may, in the future she can never misunderstand my true feelings toward her. But what will occur in the future? What will she do next? I dare not think of it. Oh, if only I could hope that she will leave me alone! But when I think of what I said to her— Never mind; I have been stronger than she for once.

April 11. I hardly slept last night, and found myself in the morning so unstrung and feverish that I was compelled to ask Pratt-Haldane to do my lecture for me. It is the first that I have ever missed. I rose at midday, but my head is aching, my hands quivering, and my nerves in a pitiable state.

Who should come round this evening but Wilson. He has just come back from London, where he has lectured, read papers, convened meetings, exposed a medium, conducted a series of experiments on thought transference, entertained Professor Richet of Paris, spent hours gazing into a crystal, and obtained some evidence as to the passage of matter through matter. All this he poured into my ears in a single gust.

"But you!" he cried at last. "You are not looking well. And Miss Penelosa is quite prostrated today. How about the experiments?"

"I have abandoned them."

"Tut, tut! Why?"

"The subject seems to me a dangerous one."

Out came his big brown notebook.

"This is of great interest," said he. "What are your grounds for saying that it is a dangerous one? Please give your facts in chronological order, with approximate dates and names of reliable witnesses with their permanent addresses."

"First of all," I asked, "would you tell me whether you have collected any cases where the mesmerist has gained a command over the subject and has used it for evil purposes?"

"Dozens!" he cried exultantly. "Crime by suggestion—"

"I don't mean suggestion. I mean where a sudden impulse comes from a person at a distance— an uncontrollable impulse."

"Obsession!" he shrieked, in an ecstasy of delight. "It is the rarest condition. We have eight cases, five well attested. You don't mean to say—" His exultation made him hardly articulate.

"No, I don't," I said. "Good-evening! You will excuse me, but I am not very well tonight." And so at last I got rid of him, still brandishing his pencil and his notebook. My troubles may be bad to bear, but at least it is better to hug them to myself than to have myself exhibited by Wilson, like a freak at a fair. He has lost sight of human beings. Everything to him is a case and a phenomenon. I will die before I speak to him again upon the matter.

April 12. Yesterday was a blessed day of quiet, and I enjoyed an uneventful night. Wilson's presence is a great consolation. What can the woman do now? Surely, when she has heard me say what I have said, she will conceive the same disgust for me which I have for her. She could not, no, she *could* not, desire to have a lover who had insulted her so. No, I believe I am free from her love—but how about her hate? Might she not use these powers of hers for revenge? Tut! Why should I frighten myself over shadows? She will forget about me, and I shall forget about her, and all will be well.

April 13. My nerves have quite recovered their tone. I really believe that I have conquered the creature. But I must confess to living in some suspense. She is well again, for I hear that she was driving with Mrs. Wilson in the High Street in the afternoon.

April 14. I do wish I could get away from the place altogether. I shall fly to Agatha's side the very day that the term closes. I suppose it is pitiably weak of me, but this woman gets upon my nerves most terribly. I have seen her again, and I have spoken with her.

It was just after lunch, and I was smoking a cigarette in my study, when I heard the step of my servant Murray in the passage. I was languidly conscious that a second step was audible behind, and had hardly troubled myself to speculate who it might be, when suddenly a slight noise brought me out of my chair with my skin creeping with apprehension. I had never particularly observed before what sort of sound the tapping of a crutch was, but my quivering nerves told me that I heard it now in the sharp wooden clack which alternated with the muffled thud of the foot-fall. Another instant and my servant had shown her in.

I did not attempt the usual conventions of society, nor did she. I simply stood with the smouldering cigarette in my hand, and gazed at her. She in turn looked silently at me, and at her look I remembered how in these very pages I had tried to define the expression of her eyes, whether they were furtive or fierce. Today they were fierce— coldly and inexorably so.

"Well," she said, at last, "are you still of the same mind as when I saw you last?"

"I have always been of the same mind."

"Let us understand each other, Professor Gilroy," said she slowly. "I am not a very safe person to trifle with, as you should realize by now. It was you who asked me to enter into a series of experiments with you, it was you who won my affections, it was you who professed your love for me, it was you who brought me your own photograph with words of affection upon it, and, finally, it was you who on the very same evening thought it fit to insult me most outrageously, addressing me as no man has ever dared to speak to me yet. Tell me that those words came from you in a moment of passion and I am prepared to forget and forgive them. You did not mean what you said, Austin? You do not really hate me?"

I might have pitied this deformed woman— such a longing for love broke suddenly through the menace of her eyes. But then I thought of what I had gone through, and my heart set like flint.

"If ever you heard me speak of love," said I, "you know very well that it was your own voice which spoke, and not mine. The only words of truth which I have ever been able to say to you are those which you heard when last we met."

"I know. Someone has set you against me. It was he!" She tapped with her crutch upon the floor. "Well, you know very well that I could bring you this minute crouching like a spaniel to my feet. You will not find me again in my hour of weakness, when you can insult me with impunity. Have a care what you are doing, Professor Gilroy. You stand in a terrible position. You have not yet realized the hold which I have upon you."

I shrugged my shoulders and turned away.

"Well," said she, after a pause, "if you despise my love, I must see what can be done with fear. You smile, but the day will come when you will come screaming to me for pardon. Yes, you will grovel on the ground before me, proud as you are, and you will curse the day that ever you turned me from your best friend into your most bitter enemy. Have a care, Professor Gilroy!" I saw a white hand shaking in the air, and a face which was scarcely human, so convulsed was it with passion. An instant later she was gone, and I heard the quick hobble and tap receding down the passage.

But she has left a weight upon my heart. Vague presentiments of coming misfortune lie heavy upon me. I try in vain to persuade myself that these are only words of empty anger. I can remember those relentless eyes too clearly to think so. What shall I do—ah, what shall I do? I am no longer master of my own soul. At any moment this loathsome parasite may creep into me, and then—? I must tell someone my hideous secret—I must tell it or go mad. If I had someone to sympathize and advise! Wilson is out of the question. Charles Sadler would understand me only so far as his own experience carries him. Pratt-Haldane! He is a well-balanced man, a man of great common sense and resource. I will go to him. I will tell him everything. God grant that he may be able to advise me!

# IV

6:45 p.m. No, it is useless. There is no human help for me; I must fight this out single-handed. Two courses lie before me. I might become this woman's lover. Or I must endure such persecutions as she can inflict upon me. Even if none come, I shall live in a well of apprehension. But she may torture me, she may drive me mad, she may kill me: I will never, never, never give in. What can she inflict which would be worse that the loss of Agatha, and the knowledge that I am a perjured liar, and have forfeited the name of gentleman?

Pratt-Haldane was most amiable, and listened with all politeness to my story. But when I looked at his heavy-set features, his slow eyes, and the ponderous study furniture which surrounded him, I could hardly tell him what I had come to say. It was all so substantial, so material. And, besides, what would I myself have said a short month ago if one of my colleagues had come to me with a story of demonic possession? Perhaps I should have been less patient than he was. As it was, he took notes of my statement, asked me how much tea I drank, how many hours I slept, whether I had been over-working much, had I had sudden pains in the head, evil dreams, singing in the ears, flashing before the eyes—all questions which pointed to his belief that brain congestion was at the bottom of my trouble. Finally he dismissed me with a great many platitudes about open-air exercise, and avoidance of nervous excitement. His prescription, which was for chloral and bromide, I rolled up and threw into the gutter.

No, I can look for no help from any human being. If I consult any more, they may put their heads together and I may find myself in an asylum. I can but grip my courage with both hands, and pray that an honest man may not be abandoned.

April 15. It is the sweetest spring within the memory of man. So green, so mild, so beautiful! Ah, what a contrast between nature without and my own soul so torn with doubt and terror! It has been an uneventful day, but I know that I am on the edge of an abyss. I know it, and yet I go on with the routine of my life. The one bright spot is that Agatha is happy and well and out of all danger. If this creature had a hand on each of us, what might she not do?

April 16. The woman is ingenious in her torments. She knows how fond I am of my work, and how highly my lectures are thought of. So it is from that point that she now attacks me. It will end, I can see, in my losing my professorship, but I will fight to the finish. She shall not drive me out of it without a struggle.

I was not conscious of any change during my lecture this morning save that for a minute or two I had a dizziness and swimminess which rapidly passed away. On the contrary, I congratulated myself upon having made my subject (the functions of the red corpuscles) both interesting and clear. I was surprised, therefore, when a student came into my laboratory immediately after the lecture, and complained of being puzzled by the discrepancy between my statements and those in the textbooks. He showed me his notebook, in which I was reported as having in one portion of the lecture championed the most outrageous and unscientific heresies. Of course I denied it, and declared that he had misunderstood me, but on comparing his notes with those of his companions, it became clear that he was right, and that I really had made some most preposterous statements. Of course I shall explain it away as being the result of a moment of aberration, but I feel only too sure that it will be the first of a series. It is but a month now to the end the session, and I pray that I may be able to hold out until then.

April 26. Ten days have elapsed since I have had the heart to make any entry in my journal. Why should I record my own humiliation and degradation? I had vowed never to open it again. And yet the force of habit is strong, and here I find myself taking up once more the record of my own dreadful experiences—in much the same spirit in which a suicide has been known to take notes of the effects of the poison which killed him.

Well, the crash which I had foreseen has come—and that no further back than yesterday. The university authorities have taken my lectureship away from me. It has been done in the most delicate way, purporting to be a temporary measure to relieve me from the effects of overwork, and to give me the opportunity of recovering my health. None the less, it has been done, and I am no longer Professor Gilroy. The laboratory is still in my charge, but I have little doubt that that also will soon go.

The fact is that my lectures had become the laughing-stock of the university. My class was crowded with students who came to see and hear what the eccentric professor would do or say next. I cannot go into the detail of my humiliation. Oh, that devilish woman! There is no depth of buffoonery and imbecility to which she has not forced me. I would begin my lecture clearly and well, but always with the sense of a coming eclipse. Then as I felt the influence I would struggle against it, striving with clenched hands and beads of sweat upon my brow to get the better of it, while the students, hearing my incoherent words and watching my contortions, would roar with laughter at the antics of their professor. And then, when she had once fairly mastered me, out would come the most outrageous things—silly jokes, sentiments as though I were proposing a toast, snatches of ballads, personal abuse even against some member of my class. And then in a moment my brain would clear again, and my lecture would proceed decorously to the end. No wonder that my conduct has been the talk of the colleges. No wonder that the University Senate has been compelled to take official notice of such a scandal. Oh, that devilish woman!

And the most dreadful part of it all is my own loneliness. Here I sit in a commonplace English bow-window, looking out upon a commonplace English street with its garish buses and its lounging policeman, and behind me there hangs a shadow which is out of all keeping with the age and place.

In the home of knowledge I am weighed down and tortured by a power of which science knows nothing. No magistrate would listen to me. No paper would discuss my case. No doctor would believe my symptoms. My own most intimate friends would only look upon it as a sign of brain derangement. I am out of all touch with my kind. Oh, that devilish woman! Let her have a care! She may push me too far. When the law cannot help a man, he may make a law for himself.

She met me in the High Street yesterday evening and spoke to me. It was as well for her, perhaps, that it was not between the hedges of a lonely country road. She asked me with her cold smile whether I had been chastened yet. I did not deign to answer her. "We must try another turn of the screw," said she. Have a care, my lady, have a care! I had her at my mercy once. Perhaps another chance may come.

April 28. The suspension of my lectureship has had the effect also of taking away her means of annoying me, and so I have enjoyed two blessed days of peace. After all, there is no reason to despair. Sympathy pours in to me from all sides, and everyone agrees that it is my devotion to science and the arduous nature of my researches which have shaken my nervous system. I have had the kindest message from the council advising me to travel abroad, and expressing the confident hope that I may be able to resume all my duties by the beginning of the summer term. Nothing could be more flattering than their allusions to my career and to my services to the university. It is only in misfortune that one can test one's own popularity. This creature may weary of tormenting me, and then all may yet be well. May God grant it!

April 29. Our sleepy little town has had a small sensation. The only knowledge of crime which we ever have is when a rowdy undergraduate breaks a few lamps or comes to blows with a policeman. Last night, however, there was an attempt made to break into the branch of the Bank of England, and we are all in a flutter in consequence.

Parkinson, the manager, is an intimate friend of mine, and I found him very much excited when I walked round there after breakfast. Had the thieves broken into the counting-house, they would still have had the safes to reckon with, so that the defence was considerably stronger than the attack. Indeed, the latter does not appear to have ever been very formidable. Two of the lower windows have marks as if a chisel or some such instrument had been pushed under them to force them open. The police should have a good clue, for the woodwork had been done with green paint only the day before, and from the smears it is evident that some of it has found its way on to the criminal's hands or clothes.

4:30 p.m. Ah, that accursed woman! That thrice accursed woman! Never mind! She shall not beat me! No, she shall not! But, oh, the she-devil! She has taken my professorship. Now she would take my honour. Is there nothing I can do against her, nothing save—Ah, but, hard pushed as I am, I cannot bring myself to think of that!

It was about an hour ago that I went into my bedroom, and was brushing my hair before the glass, when suddenly my eyes lit upon something which left me so sick and cold that I sat down upon the edge of the bed and began to cry. It is many a long year since I shed tears, but all my nerve was gone, and I could but sob and sob in impotent grief and anger. There was my house jacket, the coat I usually wear after dinner, hanging on its peg by the wardrobe, with the right sleeve thickly crusted from wrist to elbow with daubs of green paint.

So this was what she meant by another turn of the screw! She had made a public imbecile of me. Now she would brand me as a criminal. This time she has failed. But how about the next? I dare not think of it—and of Agatha and my poor old mother! I wish that I were dead!

Yes, this is the other turn of the screw. And this is also what she meant, no doubt, when she said that I had not realized yet the power she has over me. I look back at my account of my conversation with her, and I see how she declares that with a slight exertion of her will her subject would be conscious, and with a stronger one unconscious. Last night I was unconscious. I could have sworn that I slept soundly in my bed without so much as a dream. And yet those stains tell me that I dressed, made my way out, attempted to open the bank windows, and returned. Was I observed? Is it possible that someone saw me do it and followed me home? Ah, what a hell my life has become! I have no peace, no rest. But my patience is nearing its end.

10 p.m. I have cleaned my coat with turpentine. I do not think that anyone could have seen me. It was with my screwdriver that I made the marks. I found it all crusted with paint, and I have cleaned it. My head aches as if it would burst, and I have taken five grains of antipyrine. If it were not for Agatha, I should have taken fifty and had an end of it.

May 3. Three quiet days. This hell-fiend is like a cat with a mouse. She lets me loose only to pounce upon me again. I am never so frightened as when everything is still. My physical state is deplorable—perpetual hiccough and ptosis of the left eyelid.

I have heard from the Mardens that they will be back the day after tomorrow. I do not know whether I am glad or sorry. They were safe in London. Once here they may be drawn into the miserable network in which I am myself struggling. And I must tell them of it. I cannot marry Agatha so long as I know that I am not responsible for my own actions. Yes, I must tell them, even if it brings everything to an end between us.

Tonight is the university ball, and I must go. God knows I never felt less in the humour for festivity, but I must not have it said that I am unfit to appear in public. If I am seen there, and have speech with some of the elders of the university it will go a long way toward showing them that it would be unjust to take my chair away from me.

11:30 p.m. I have been to the ball. Charles Sadler and I went together, but I have come away before him. I shall wait up for him, however, for, indeed, I fear to go to sleep these nights. He is a cheery, practical fellow, and a chat with him will steady my nerves. On the whole, the evening was a great success. I talked to everyone who has influence, and I think that I made them realize that my chair is not vacant quite yet. The creature was at the ball—unable to dance, of course, but sitting with Mrs. Wilson. Again and again her eyes rested upon me. They were almost the last things I saw before I left the room. Once, as I sat sideways to her, I watched her, and saw that her gaze was following someone else. It was Sadler, who was dancing at the time with the second Miss Thurston. To judge by her expression, it is well for him that he is not in her grip as I am. He does not know the escape he has had. I think I hear his step in the street now, and I will go down and let him in. If he will—

May 4. Why did I break off in this way last night? I never went downstairs after all—at least, I have no recollection of doing so. But, on the other hand, I cannot remember going to bed. One of my hands is greatly swollen this morning, and yet I have no remembrance of injuring it yesterday. Otherwise, I am feeling all the better for last night's festivity. But I cannot understand how it is that I did not meet Charles Sadler when I so fully intended to do so. Is it possible—My God, it is only too probable! Has she been leading me in some devil's dance again? I will go down to Sadler and ask him.

Midday. The thing has come to a crisis. My life is not worth living. But, if I am to die, then she shall come also. I will not leave her behind, to drive some other man mad as she has me. No, I have come to the limit of my endurance. She has made me as desperate and dangerous a man as walks the earth. God knows I have never had the heart to hurt a fly, and yet, if I had my hands now upon that woman, she should never leave this room alive. I shall see her this very day, and she shall learn what she has to expect of me.

I went to Sadler and found him, to my surprise, in bed. As I entered he sat up and turned a face toward me which sickened me as I looked at it.

"Why, Sadler, what has happened?" I cried, but my heart turned cold as I said it.

"Gilroy," he answered, mumbling with his swollen lips, "I have for some weeks been under the impression that you are a madman. Now I know it, and that you are a dangerous one as well. If it were not that I am unwilling to make a scandal in the college, you would now be in the hands of the police."

"Do you mean—" I cried.

"I mean that as I opened the door last night you rushed out upon me, struck me with both your fists in the face, knocked me down, kicked me furiously in the side, and left me lying almost unconscious in the street. Look at your own hand bearing witness against you."

Yes, there it was, puffed up, with sponge-like knuckles, as after some terrific blow. What could I do? Though he put me down as a madman, I must tell him all. I sat by his bed and went over all my troubles from the beginning. I poured them out with quivering hands and burning words which might have carried conviction to the most sceptical. "She hates you and she hates me!" I cried. "She revenged herself last night on both of us at once. She saw me leave the ball, and she must have seen you also. She knew how long it would take you to reach home. Then she had but to use her wicked will. Ah, your bruised face is a small thing beside my bruised soul!"

He was struck by my story. That was evident. "Yes, yes, she watched me out of the room," he muttered. "She is capable of it. But is it possible that she has really reduced you to this? What do you intend to do?"

"To stop it!" I cried. "I am perfectly desperate; I shall give her fair warning today, and the next time will be the last."

"Do nothing rash," said he.

"Rash!" I cried. "The only rash thing is that I should postpone it another hour." With that I rushed to my room, and here I am on the eve of what may be the great crisis of my life. I shall start at once. I have gained one thing today, for I have made one man, at least, realize the truth of this monstrous experience of mine. And, if the worst should happen, this diary remains as a proof of the goad that has driven me.

Evening. When I came to Wilson's, I was shown up, and found that he was sitting with Miss Penelosa. For half an hour I had to endure his fussy talk about his recent research into the exact nature of the spiritualistic rap, while the creature and I sat in silence looking across the room at each other. I read a sinister amusement in her eyes, and she must have seen hatred and menace in mine. I had almost despaired of having speech with her when he was called from the room, and we were left for a few moments together.

"Well, Professor Gilroy—or is it Mr. Gilroy?" said she, with that bitter smile of hers. "How is your friend Mr. Charles Sadler after the ball?"

"You fiend!" I cried. "You have come to the end of your tricks now. I will have no more of them. Listen to what I say." I strode across and shook her roughly by the shoulder. "As sure as there is a God in heaven, I swear that if you try another of your devilries upon me, I will have your life for it. Come what may, I will have your life. I have come to the end of what a man can endure."

"Accounts are not quite settled between us," said she, with a passion that equalled my own. "I can love, and I can hate. You had your choice. You chose to spurn the first; now you must test the other. It will take a little more to break your spirit, I see, but broken it shall be. Miss Marden comes back tomorrow as I understand."

"What has that to do with you?" I cried. "It is a pollution that you should dare even to think of her. If I thought that you would harm her—"

She was frightened, I could see, though she tried to brazen it out. She read the black thought in my mind, and cowered away from me.

"She is fortunate in having such a champion," said she. "He actually dares to threaten a lonely woman. I must really congratulate Miss Marden upon her protector."

The words were bitter, but the voice and manner were more acid still.

"There is no use talking," said I. "I only came here to tell you—and to tell you most solemnly— that your next outrage upon me will be your last." With that, as I heard Wilson's step upon the stair, I walked from the room. Ay, she may look venomous and deadly, but, for all that, she is beginning to see now that she has as much to fear from me as I can have from her. Murder! It has an ugly sound. But you don't talk of murdering a snake or of murdering a tiger. Let her have a care now.

May 5. I met Agatha and her mother at the station at eleven o'clock. She is looking so bright, so happy, so beautiful. And she was so overjoyed to see me. What have I done to deserve such love? I went back home with them, and we lunched together. All the troubles seem in a moment to have been shredded back from my life. She tells me that I am looking pale and worried and ill. The dear child puts it down to my loneliness and the perfunctory attention of a housekeeper. I pray that she may never know the truth! May the shadow, if shadow there must be, lie ever black across my life and leave hers in the sunshine. I have just come back from them, feeling a new man. With her by my side I think that I could show a bold face to anything which life might send.

5 p.m. Now, let me try to be accurate. Let me try to say exactly how it occurred. It is fresh in my mind, and I can set it down correctly, though it is not likely that the time will ever come when I shall forget the doings of today.

I had returned from the Mardens' after lunch, and was cutting some microscopic sections in my freezing microtome, when in an instant I lost consciousness in the sudden hateful fashion which has become only too familiar to me of late.

When my senses came back to me I was sitting in a small chamber, very different from the one in which I had been working. It was cosy and bright, with chintz-covered settees, coloured hangings, and a thousand pretty little trifles upon the wall. A small ornamental clock ticked in front of me, and the hands pointed to half-past three. It was all quite familiar to me, and yet I stared about for a moment in a half-dazed way until my eyes fell upon a cabinet photograph of myself upon the top of the piano. On the other side stood one of Mrs. Marden. Then, of course, I remembered where I was. It was Agatha's boudoir.

But how came I there, and what did I want? A horrible sinking came to my heart. Had I been sent there on some devilish errand? Had that errand already been done? Surely it must; otherwise, why should I be allowed to come back to consciousness? Oh, the agony of that moment! What had I done? I sprang to my feet in my despair, and as I did so a small glass bottle fell from my knees onto the carpet.

It was unbroken, and I picked it up. Outside

was written "Sulphuric Acid. Fort." When I drew the round glass stopper, a thick fume rose slowly up, and a pungent, choking smell pervaded the room. I recognized it as one which I kept for chemical testing in my chambers. But why had I brought a bottle of vitriol into Agatha's chamber? Was it not this thick, reeking liquid with which jealous women had been known to mar the beauty of their rivals? My heart stood still as I held the bottle to the light. Thank God, it was full! No mischief had been done as yet. But had Agatha come in a minute sooner, was it not certain that the hellish parasite within me would have dashed the stuff into her— Ah, it will not bear to be thought of! But it must have been for that. Why else should I have brought it? At the thought of what I might have done my worn nerves broke down, and I sat shivering and twitching, the pitiable wreck of a man.

It was the sound of Agatha's voice and the rustle of her dress which restored me. I looked up, and saw her blue eyes, so full of tenderness and pity, gazing down at me.

"We must take you away to the country, Austin," she said. "You want rest and quiet. You look wretchedly ill."

"Oh, it is nothing!" said I, trying to smile. "It was only a momentary weakness. I am all right again now."

"I am so sorry to keep you waiting. Poor boy, you must have been here quite half an hour! The vicar was in the drawing-room, and, as I knew that you did not care for him, I thought it better that Jane should show you up here. I thought the man would never go!"

"Thank God he stayed! Thank God he stayed!" I cried hysterically.

"Why, what is the matter with you, Austin?" she asked, holding my arm as I staggered up from the chair. "Why are you glad that the vicar stayed? And what is this little bottle in your hand?"

"Nothing," I cried, thrusting it into my pocket. "But I must go. I have something important to do."

"How stern you look, Austin! I have never seen your face like that. You are angry?"

"Yes, I am angry."

"But not with me?"

"No, no, my darling! You would not understand."

"But you have not told me why you came."

"I came to ask you whether you would always love me—no matter what I did, or what shadow might fall on my name. Would you believe in me and trust me however black appearances might be against me?"

"You know that I would, Austin."

"Yes. I know that you would. What I do I shall do for you. I am driven to it. There is no other way out, my darling!" I kissed her and rushed from the room.

The time for indecision was at an end. As long as the creature threatened my own prospects and my honour there might be a question as to what I should do. But now, when Agatha—my innocent Agatha—was endangered, my duty lay before me like a turnpike road. I had no weapon, but I never paused for that. What weapon should I need, when I felt every muscle quivering with the strength of a frenzied man? I ran through the streets, so set upon what I had to do that I was only dimly conscious also that Professor Wilson met me, running with equal precipitance in the opposite direction. Breathless but resolute I reached the house and rang the bell. A white-cheeked maid opened the door, and turned whiter yet when she saw the face that looked in at her.

"Show me up at once to Miss Penelosa," I demanded.

"Sir," she gasped, "Miss Penelosa died this afternoon at half-past three!"

# LONELY WOMEN ARE THE VESSELS OF TIME

# Harlan Ellison

Harlan Jay Ellison (1934– ) was born in Cleveland, Ohio. After taking jobs in widely diverse fields in various parts of the country (performer in minstrel shows, tuna fisherman, crop picker, short-order cook, dynamite-truck driver, taxi driver, lithographer, book salesman, department store floor walker, door-to-door brush salesman, stand-up comedian, and actor), he settled in New York to pursue a writing career.

In addition to being a prodigiously prolific short-story writer, essayist, critic, novelist, and screenplay and teleplay writer, he is perhaps the most honored author of speculative fiction who ever lived. He has won ten Hugo Awards (for best science-fiction or fantasy work); four Nebula Awards, including the Grand Master for lifetime achievement (presented by the Science Fiction and Fantasy Writers of America); five Bram Stoker Awards, including one for lifetime achievement (given by the Horror Writers Association); eighteen Locus Awards (presented by the preeminent fan magazine in the speculative fiction field); and two Edgar Allan Poe Awards from the Mystery Writers of America. He is the only writer ever to win the Writers Guild of America award for Most Outstanding Teleplay four times.

"Lonely Women Are the Vessels of Time" was first published in *MidAmerican Program Book,* edited by Tom Reamy, in 1976; it was first published in book form in *Strange Wine* (New York: Harper & Row, 1978).

# Lonely Women Are the Vessels of Time

## HARLAN ELLISON

After the funeral, Mitch went to Dynamite's. It was a singles' bar. Vernon, the day-shift bartender, had Mitch's stool reserved, waiting for him. "I figured you'd be in," he said, mixing up a Tia Maria Cooler and passing it across the bar. "Sorry about Anne." Mitch nodded and sipped off the top of the drink. He looked around Dynamite's; it was too early in the day, even for a Friday; there wasn't much action. A few dudes getting the best corners at the inlaid-tile and stained-glass bar, couples in the plush back booths stealing a few minutes before going home to their wives and husbands. It was only three o'clock and the secretaries didn't start coming in till five thirty. Later, Dynamite's would be pulsing with the chatter and occasional shriek of laughter, the chatting-up and the smell of hot bodies circling each other for the kill. The traditional mating ritual of the singles' bar scene.

He saw one girl at a tiny deuce, way at the rear, beside the glass-fronted booth where the DJ played his disco rock all night, every night. But she was swathed in shadow, and he wasn't up to hustling anybody at the moment, anyhow. But he marked her in his mind for later.

He sipped at the Cooler, just thinking about Anne, until a space salesman from the *Enquirer*, whom he knew by first name but not by last, plopped himself onto the next stool and started laying a commiseration trip on him about Anne. He wanted to turn to the guy and simply say, "Look, fuck off, will you; she was just a Friday night pickup who hung on a little longer than most of them; so stop busting my chops and get lost." But he didn't. He listened to the bullshit as long as he could, then he excused himself and took what was left of the Cooler, and a double Cutty-&-water, and trudged back to a booth. He sat there in the semidarkness trying to figure out why Anne had killed herself, and couldn't get a handle on the question.

He tried to remember *exactly* what she had looked like, but all he could bring into focus was the honey-colored hair and her height. The special smile was gone. The tilt of the head and the hand movement when she was annoyed . . . gone. The exact timbre of her voice . . . gone. All of it was gone, and he knew he should be upset about it, but he wasn't.

He hadn't loved her; had, in fact, been ready to dump her for that BOAC hostess. But she had left a note pledging her undying love, and he knew he ought to feel some deep responsibility for her death.

But he didn't.

What it was all about, dammit, was not being lonely. It was all about getting as much as one could, as best as one could, from as many different places as one could, without having to be alone, without having to be unhappy, without having them sink their fangs in too deeply.

*That*, dammit, was what it was all about.

He thought about the crap a libber had laid on him in this very bar only a week ago. He had been chatting up a girl who worked for a surety underwriters firm, letting her bore him with a lot of crap about contract bonds, probate, temporary restraining orders and suchlike nonsense, but never dropping his gaze from those incredible green eyes, when Anne had gotten pissed-off and come over to suggest they leave.

He had been abrupt with her. Rude, if he wanted to honest with himself, and had told her to go back and sit down till he was ready. The libber on the next stool had laid into him, whipping endless jingoism on him, telling him what a shithead he was.

"Lady, if you don't like the way the system works, why not go find a good clinic where they'll graft a dork on you, and then you won't have to bother people who're minding their own business."

The bar had given him a standing ovation.

The Cutty tasted like sawdust. The air in the bar smelled like mildew. His body didn't fit. He turned this way and that, trying to find a comfortable position. Why the hell did he feel lousy? Anne, that was why. But he wasn't responsible. She'd known it was frolic, nothing more than frolic. She'd known that from the moment they'd met. She hadn't been fresh to these bars, she was a swinger, what was all the *sturm und drang* about! But he felt like shit, and that was the bottom line.

"Can I buy you a drink?" the girl said.

Mitch looked up. It seemed to be the girl from the deuce in the rear.

She was incredible. Cheekbones like cut crystal; a full lower lip. Honey hair . . . again. Tall, willowy, with a good chest and fine legs. "Sure. Sit down."

She sat and pushed a double Cutty-&-water at him. "The bartender told me what you were drinking."

Four hours later—and he still hadn't learned her name—she got around to suggesting they go back to her place. He followed her out of the bar, and she hailed a cab. In the back seat he looked at her, lights flickering on and off in her blue eyes as the street lamps whizzed past, and he said, "It's nice to meet a girl who doesn't waste time."

"I gather you've been picked up before," she replied. 'But then, you're a very nice-looking man."

"Why, thank you."

At her apartment in the East Fifties, they had a few more drinks; the usual preparatory ritual. Mitch was starting to feel it, getting a little wobbly. He refused a refill. He wanted to be able to perform. He knew the rules. Get it up or get the hell out.

So they went into the bedroom.

He stopped and stared at the set-up. She had it hung with white, sheer hangings, tulle perhaps, some kind of very fine netting. White walls, white ceiling, white carpet so thick and deep he lost his ankles in it. And an enormous circular bed covered with white fur.

"Polar bear," he said, laughing a little drunkenly.

"The color of loneliness," she said.

"What?"

"Nothing, forget it," she said, and began to undress him.

She helped him lie down, and he stared at her as she took off her clothes. Her body was pale and filled with light; she was an ice maiden from a far magical land. He felt himself getting hard.

Then she came to him.

**W**hen he awoke, she was standing at the other side of the room, watching him. Her eyes were no longer a lovely blue. They were dark and filled with smoke. He felt . . .

He felt . . . awful. Uncomfortable, filled with vague terrors and a limitless desperation. He felt . . . lonely.

"You don't hold nearly as much as I thought," she said.

He sat up, tried to get out of the bed, the sea of white, and could not. He lay back and watched her.

Finally, after a time of silence, she said, "Get up and get dressed and get out of here."

He did it, with difficulty, and as he dressed, sluggishly and with the loneliness in him growing, choking his mind and physically causing him to tremble, she told him things he did not want to know.

About the loneliness of people that makes them do things they hate the next day. About the sickness to which people are heir, the sickness of being without anyone who truly cares. About the predators who smell out such victims and use them and, when they go, leave them emptier than when they first picked up the scent. And about herself, the vessel that contained the loneliness like smoke, waiting only for other containers such as Michah to decant a little of the poison,

waiting only to return some of the pain for pain given.

What she was, where she came from, what dark land had given her birth, he did not know and would not ask. But when he stumbled to the door, and she opened it for him, the smile on her lips frightened him more than anything in his life.

"Don't feel neglected, baby," she said. "There are others like you. You'll run into them. Maybe you can start a club."

He didn't know what to say; he wanted to run, but he knew she had spread fog across his soul and he knew if he walked out the door he was never going to reclaim his feeling of self-satisfaction. He had to make one last attempt . . .

"Help me . . . please, I feel so—so—"

"I know how you feel, baby," she said, moving him through the door. "Now you know how they feel."

And she closed the door behind him. Very softly.

Very firmly.

## *BLOOD*

# Fredric Brown

Fredric William Brown (1906–72) was born in Cincinnati, Ohio, and attended the University of Cincinnati at night and then spent a year at Hanover College, Indiana. He was an office worker for a dozen years before becoming a proofreader for the *Milwaukee Journal* for a decade. He was not able to devote himself full-time to writing fiction until 1949, although he had for several years been a prolific writer of short stories and, in the form that he mastered and for which he is much loved today, the short-short story, generally one to three pages long.

He claimed he wrote mysteries for the money but science fiction for fun, though he is revered equally in both genres. Although he was never financially secure, which forced him to write at a prodigious pace, he seemed to be having fun in spite of the workload. Many of his stories and novels are imbued with humor, including a devotion to puns and wordplay. A writer's writer, he was highly regarded by his colleagues, including Mickey Spillane, who called him his favorite writer of all time; Robert Heinlein, who made him a dedicatee of *Stranger in a Strange Land;* and Ayn Rand, who in *The Romantic Manifesto* regarded him as ingenious. After more than three hundred short stories, he wrote his first novel, *The Fabulous Clipjoint* (1947), for which he won an Edgar Award.

"Blood" was first published in the February 1954 issue of *The Magazine of Fantasy & Science Fiction.*

# Blood

## FREDRIC BROWN

In their time machine, Vron and Dreena, last two survivors of the race of vampires, fled into the future to escape annihilation. They held hands and consoled one another in their terror and their hunger.

In the twenty-second century mankind had found them out, had discovered that the legend of vampires living secretly among humans was not a legend at all, but fact. There had been a pogrom that had found and killed every vampire but these two, who had already been working on a time machine and who had finished in time to escape in it. Into the future, far enough into the future that the very word *vampire* would be forgotten so they could again live unsuspected—and from their loins regenerate their race.

"I'm hungry, Vron. Awfully hungry."

"I too, Dreena dear. We'll stop again soon."

They had stopped four times already and had narrowly escaped dying each time. They had *not* been forgotten. The last stop, half a million years back, had shown them a world gone to the dogs—quite literally: human beings were extinct and dogs had become civilized and manlike. Still they had

been recognized for what they were. They'd managed to feed once, on the blood of a tender young bitch, but then they'd been hounded back to their time machine and into flight again.

"Thanks for stopping," Dreena said. She sighed.

"Don't thank me," said Vron grimly. "This is the end of the line. We're out of fuel and we'll find none here—by now all radioactives will have turned to lead. We live here—or else."

They went out to scout. "Look," said Dreena excitedly, pointing to something walking toward them. "A new creature! The dogs are gone and something else has taken over. And surely we're forgotten."

The approaching creature was telepathic. "I have heard your thoughts," said a voice inside their brains. "You wonder whether we know 'vampires,' whatever they are. We do not."

Dreena clutched Vron's arm in ecstasy. "Freedom!" she murmured hungrily. "And *food*!"

"You also wonder," said the voice, "about my origin and evolution. All life today is vegetable. I—" He bowed low to them. "I, a member of the dominant race, was once what you called a turnip."

# POPSY

# Stephen King

Stephen Edwin King (1947– ) was born in Portland, Maine, and graduated from the University of Maine with a B.A. in English. Unable to find a position as a high school teacher, he sold some stories to various publications, including *Playboy*. Heavily influenced by H. P. Lovecraft and the macabre stories published by EC Comics, he directed his energies to horror and supernatural fiction. His first book, *Carrie* (1973), about a girl with psychic powers, was thrown into a wastebasket and famously rescued by his wife, Tabitha, who encouraged him to polish and submit it. It received a very modest advance but had great success as a paperback, and a career was launched—a career of such spectacular magnitude that King was the most consistently successful writer in America for two decades.

In addition to writing novels and short stories, King has written screenplays and nonfiction, proving himself an expert in macabre fiction and film. More than one hundred films and television programs have been made from his work, most notably *Carrie* (1976), *The Shining* (1980), *Stand by Me* (1986, based on the novella *Body*), *The Shawshank Redemption* (1994, based on the short story "Rita Hayworth and the Shawshank Redemption"), and *The Green Mile* (1999).

"Popsy" was originally published in *Masques II: All-New Stories of Horror & the Supernatural*, edited by J. N. Williamson (Baltimore, MD: Maclay, 1987). It was adapted for a short film (twenty-four minutes) in 2006 by Brian Haynes, who also directed.

# Popsy

## STEPHEN KING

Sheridan was cruising slowly down the long blank length of the shopping mall when he saw the little kid push out through the main doors under the lighted sign which read COUSINTOWN. It was a boy-child, perhaps a big three and surely no more than five. On his face was an expression to which Sheridan had become exquisitely attuned. He was trying not to cry but soon would.

Sheridan paused for a moment, feeling the familiar soft wave of self-disgust . . . though every time he took a child, that feeling grew a little less urgent. The first time he hadn't slept for a week. He kept thinking about that big greasy Turk who called himself Mr. Wizard, kept wondering what he did with the children.

"They go on a boat-ride, Mr. Sheridan," the Turk told him, only it came out *Dey goo on a bot-rahd, Messtair Shurdunn.* The Turk smiled. *And if you know what's good for you, you won't ask any more about it,* that smile said, and it said it loud and clear, without an accent.

Sheridan *hadn't* asked any more, but that didn't mean he hadn't kept wondering. Especially afterward. Tossing and turning, wishing he had the whole thing to do over again so he could turn it around, so he could walk away from temptation. The second time had been almost as bad . . . the third time a little less . . . and by the fourth time he had almost stopped wondering about the bot-rahd, and what might be at the end of it for the little kids.

Sheridan pulled his van into one of the handicap parking spaces right in front of the mall. He had one of the special license plates the state gave to crips on the back of his van. That plate was worth its weight in gold, because it kept any mall security cop from getting suspicious, and those spaces were so convenient and almost always empty.

*You always pretend you're not going out looking, but you always lift a crip plate a day or two before.*

Never mind all that bullshit; he was in a jam and that kid over there could solve some very big problems.

He got out and walked toward the kid, who was looking around with increasing panic. Yes, Sheridan thought, he was five all right, maybe even six—just very frail. In the harsh fluorescent glare thrown through the glass doors the boy looked parchment-white, not just scared but perhaps

518

physically ill. Sheridan reckoned it was just big fear, however. Sheridan usually recognized that look when he saw it, because he'd seen a lot of big fear in his own mirror over the last year and a half or so.

The kid looked up hopefully at the people passing around him, people going into the mall eager to buy, coming out laden with packages, their faces dazed, almost drugged, with something they probably thought was satisfaction.

The kid, dressed in Tuffskin jeans and a Pittsburgh Penguins tee-shirt, looked for help, looked for somebody to look at him and see something was wrong, looked for someone to ask the right question—*You get separated from your dad, son?* would do—looking for a friend.

*Here I am,* Sheridan thought, approaching. *Here I am, sonny—I'll be your friend.*

He had almost reached the kid when he saw a mall rent-a-cop ambling slowly up the concourse toward the doors. He was reaching in his pocket, probably for a pack of cigarettes. He would come out, see the boy, and, there would go Sheridan's sure thing.

*Shit,* he thought, but at least he wouldn't be seen talking to the kid when the cop came out. That would have been worse.

Sheridan drew back a little and made a business of feeling in his own pockets, as if to make sure he still had his keys. His glance flicked from the boy to the security cop and back to the boy. The boy had started to cry. Not all-out bawling, not yet, but great big tears that looked pinkish in the reflected glow of the red COUSINTOWN sign as they tracked down his smooth cheeks.

The girl in the information booth flagged down the cop and said something to him. She was pretty, dark-haired, about twenty-five; he was sandy-blond with a moustache. As the cop leaned on his elbows, smiling at her, Sheridan thought they looked like the cigarette ads you saw on the backs of magazines. Salem Spirit. Light My Lucky. He was dying out here and they were in there making chit-chat—whatcha doin after work, ya wanna go and get a drink at that new place, and blah-blah-

blah. Now she was also batting her eyes at him. How cute.

Sheridan abruptly decided to take the chance. The kid's chest was hitching, and as soon as he started to bawl out loud, someone would notice him. Sheridan didn't like moving in with a cop less than sixty feet away, but if he didn't cover his markers at Mr. Reggie's within the next twenty-four hours, he thought a couple of very large men would pay him a visit and perform impromptu surgery on his arms, adding several elbow-bends to each.

He walked up to the kid, a big man dressed in an ordinary Van Heusen shirt and khaki pants, a man with a broad, ordinary face that looked kind at first glance. He bent over the little boy, hands on his legs just above the knees, and the boy turned his pale, scared face up to Sheridan's. His eyes were as green as emeralds, their color accentuated by the light-reflecting tears that washed them.

"You get separated from your dad, son?" Sheridan asked.

"My *Popsy,*" the kid said, wiping his eyes. "I . . . I can't find my P-P-Popsy!"

Now the kid *did* begin to sob, and a woman headed in glanced around with some vague concern.

"It's all right," Sheridan said to her, and she went on. Sheridan put a comforting arm around the boy's shoulders and drew him a little to the right . . . in the direction of the van. Then he looked back inside.

The rent-a-cop had his face right down next to the information girl's now. Looked like maybe more than that little girl's Lucky was going to get lit tonight. Sheridan relaxed. At this point there could be a stick-up going on at the bank just up the concourse and the cop wouldn't notice a thing. This was starting to look like a cinch.

"I want my Popsy!" the boy wept.

"Sure you do, of course you do," Sheridan said. "And we're going to find him. Don't you worry."

He drew him a little more to the right.

The boy looked up at him, suddenly hopeful.

"Can you? Can you, mister?"

"Sure!" Sheridan said, and grinned heartily. "Finding lost Popsys . . . well, you might say it's kind of a specialty of mine."

"It is?" The kid actually smiled a little, although his eyes were still leaking.

"It sure is," Sheridan said, glancing inside again to make sure the cop, whom he could now barely see (and who would barely be able to see Sheridan and the boy, should he happen to look up), was still enthralled. He was. "What was your Popsy wearing, son?"

"He was wearing his suit," the boy said. "He almost always wears his suit. I only saw him once in jeans." He spoke as if Sheridan should know all these things about his Popsy.

"I bet it was a black suit," Sheridan said.

The boy's eyes lit up. "You *saw* him! Where?"

He started eagerly back toward the doors, tears forgotten, and Sheridan had to restrain himself from grabbing the pale-faced little brat right then and there. That type of thing was no good. Couldn't cause a scene. Couldn't do anything people would remember later. Had to get him in the van. The van had sun-filter glass everywhere except in the windshield; it was almost impossible to see inside unless you had your face smashed right up against it.

Had to get him in the van first.

He touched the boy on the arm. "I didn't see him inside, son. I saw him right over there."

He pointed across the huge parking lot with its endless platoons of cars. There was an access road at the far end of it, and beyond that were the double yellow arches of McDonald's.

"Why would Popsy go over *there?*" the boy asked, as if either Sheridan or Popsy—or maybe both of them—had gone utterly mad.

"I don't know," Sheridan said. His mind was working fast, clicking along like an express train as it always did when it got right down to the point where you had to stop shitting and either do it up right or fuck it up righteously. Popsy. Not Dad or Daddy but Popsy. The kid had corrected him on it. Maybe Popsy meant Granddad, Sheridan decided. "But I'm pretty sure that was him. Older guy in a black suit. White hair . . . green tie . . ."

"Popsy had his blue tie on," the boy said. "He knows I like it the best."

"Yeah, it could have been blue," Sheridan said. "Under these lights, who can tell? Come on, hop in the van, I'll run you over there to him."

"Are you *sure* it was Popsy? Because I don't know why he'd go to a place where they—"

Sheridan shrugged. "Look, kid, if you're sure that wasn't him, maybe you better look for him on your own. You might even find him." And he started brusquely away, heading back toward the van.

The kid wasn't biting. He thought about going back, trying again, but it had already gone on too long—you either kept observable contact to a minimum or you were asking for twenty years in Hammerton Bay. He'd better go on to another mall. Scoterville, maybe. Or—

"Wait, mister!" It was the kid, with panic in his voice. There was the light thud of running sneakers. "Wait up! I told him I was thirsty, he must have thought he had to go way over there to get me a drink. Wait!"

Sheridan turned around, smiling. "I wasn't really going to leave you anyway, son."

He led the boy to the van, which was four years old, and painted a nondescript blue. He opened the door and smiled at the kid, who looked up at him doubtfully, his green eyes swimming in that pallid little face, as huge as the eyes of a waif in a velvet painting, the kind advertised in the cheap weekly tabloids like *The National Enquirer* and *Inside View.*

"Step into my parlor, little buddy," Sheridan said, and produced a grin which looked almost entirely natural. It was really sort of creepy, how good he'd gotten at this.

The kid did, and although he didn't know it, his ass belonged to Briggs Sheridan the minute the passenger door swung shut.

There was only one problem in his life. It wasn't broads, although he liked to hear the swish of a skirt or feel the smooth smoke of silken hose as well as any man, and it wasn't booze, although he had been known to take a drink or three of an evening. Sheridan's problem—his fatal flaw, you might even say—was cards. Any kind of cards, as long as it was the kind of game where wagers were allowed. He had lost jobs, credit cards, the home his mother had left him. He had never, at least so far, been in jail, but the first time he got in trouble with Mr. Reggie, he'd thought jail would be a rest-cure by comparison.

He had gone a little crazy that night. It was better, he had found, when you lost right away. When you lost right away you got discouraged, went home, watched Letterman on the tube, and then went to sleep. When you won a little bit at first, you chased. Sheridan had chased that night and had ended up owing seventeen thousand dollars. He could hardly believe it; he went home dazed, almost elated, by the enormity of it. He kept telling himself in the car on the way home that he owed Mr. Reggie not seven hundred, not seven *thousand*, but *seventeen thousand* iron men. Every time he tried to think about it he giggled and turned up the volume on the radio.

But he wasn't giggling the next night when the two gorillas—the ones who would make sure his arms bent in all sorts of new and interesting ways if he didn't pay up—brought him into Mr. Reggie's office.

"I'll pay," Sheridan began babbling at once. "I'll pay, listen, it's no problem, couple of days, a week at the most, two weeks at the outside—"

"You bore me, Sheridan," Mr. Reggie said.

"I—"

"Shut up. If I give you a week, don't you think I know what you'll do? You'll tap a friend for a couple of hundred if you've got a friend left to tap. If you can't find a friend, you'll hit a liquor store . . . if you've got the guts. I doubt if you do, but anything is possible." Mr. Reggie leaned forward, propped his chin on his hands, and smiled. He smelled of Ted Lapidus cologne. "And if you do come up with two hundred dollars, what will you do with it?"

"Give it to you," Sheridan had babbled. By then he was very close to tears. "I'll give it to you, right away!"

"No you won't," Mr. Reggie said. "You'll take it to the track and try to make it grow. What you'll give me is a bunch of shiny excuses. You're in over your head this time, my friend. Way over your head."

Sheridan could hold back the tears no longer; he began to blubber.

"These guys could put you in the hospital for a long time," Mr. Reggie said reflectively. "You would have a tube in each arm and another one coming out of your nose."

Sheridan began to blubber louder.

"I'll give you this much," Mr. Reggie said, and pushed a folded sheet of paper across his desk to Sheridan. "You might get along with this guy. He calls himself Mr. Wizard, but he's a shitbag just like you. Now get out of here. I'm gonna have you back in here in a week, though, and I'll have your markers on this desk. You either buy them back or I'm going to have my friends tool up on you. And like Booker T. says, once they start, they do it until they're satisfied."

The Turk's real name was written on the folded sheet of paper. Sheridan went to see him, and heard about the kids and the botrahds. Mr. Wizard also named a figure which was a fairish bit larger than the markers Mr. Reggie was holding. That was when Sheridan started cruising the malls.

h e pulled out of the Cousintown Mall's main parking lot, looked for traffic, then drove across the access road and into the McDonald's in-lane. The kid was sitting all the way forward on the passenger seat, hands on the knees of his Tuffskins, eyes agonizingly alert. Sheridan drove toward the building, swung wide to avoid the drive-thru lane, and kept on going.

"Why are you going around the back?" the kid asked.

"You have to go around to the other doors," Sheridan said. "Keep your shirt on, kid. I think I saw him in there."

"You did? You really did?"

"I'm pretty sure, yeah."

Sublime relief washed over the kid's face, and

for a moment Sheridan felt sorry for him—hell, he wasn't a monster or a maniac, for Christ's sake. But his markers had gotten a little deeper each time, and that bastard Mr. Reggie had no compunctions at all about letting him hang himself. It wasn't seventeen thousand this time, or twenty thousand, or even twenty-five thousand. This time it was thirty-five grand, a whole damn marching battalion of iron men, if he didn't want a few new sets of elbows by next Saturday.

He stopped in the back by the trash-compactor. Nobody was parked back here. Good. There was an elasticized pouch on the side of the door for maps and things. Sheridan reached into it with his left hand and brought out a pair of blued-steel Kreig handcuffs. The loop-jaws were open.

"Why are we stopping here, mister?" the kid asked. The fear was back in his voice, but the quality of it had changed; he had suddenly realized that maybe getting separated from good old Popsy in the busy mall wasn't the worst thing that could happen to him, after all.

"We're not, not really," Sheridan said easily. He had learned the second time he'd done this that you didn't want to underestimate even a six-year-old once he had his wind up. The second kid had kicked him in the balls and had damn near gotten away. "I just remembered I forgot to put my glasses on when I started driving. I could lose my license. They're in that glasses-case on the floor there. They slid over to your side. Hand 'em to me, would you?"

The kid bent over to get the glasses-case, which was empty. Sheridan leaned over and snapped one of the cuffs on the kid's reaching hand as neat as you please. And then the trouble started. Hadn't he just been thinking it was a bad mistake to underestimate even a six-year-old? The brat fought like a timberwolf pup, twisting with a powerful muscularity Sheridan would not have credited had he not been experiencing it. He bucked and fought and lunged for the door, panting and uttering weird birdlike cries. He got the handle. The door swung open, but no domelight came on—Sheridan had broken it after that second outing.

Sheridan got the kid by the round collar of his Penguins tee-shirt and hauled him back in. He tried to clamp the other cuff on the special strut beside the passenger seat and missed. The kid bit his hand twice, bringing blood. God, his teeth were like razors. The pain went deep and sent a steely ache all the way up his arm. He punched the kid in the mouth. The kid fell back into the seat, dazed, Sheridan's blood on his lips and chin and dripping onto the ribbed neck of the tee-shirt. Sheridan locked the other cuff onto the strut and then fell back into his own seat, sucking the back of his right hand.

The pain was really bad. He pulled his hand away from his mouth and looked at it in the weak glow of the dashlights. Two shallow, ragged tears, each maybe two inches long, ran up toward his wrist from just above the knuckles. Blood pulsed in weak little rills. Still, he felt no urge to pop the kid again, and that had nothing to do with damaging the Turk's merchandise, in spite of the almost fussy way the Turk had warned him against that—*demmege the goots end you demmege the velue,* the Turk had said in his greasy accent.

No, he didn't blame the kid for fighting—he would have done the same. He would have to disinfect the wound as soon as he could, though, might even have to have a shot; he had read somewhere that human bites were the worst kind. Still, he couldn't help but admire the kid's guts.

He dropped the transmission into drive and pulled around the hamburger stand, past the drive-thru window, and back onto the access road. He turned left. The Turk had a big ranch-style house in Taluda Heights, on the edge of the city. Sheridan would go there by secondary roads, just to be safe. Thirty miles. Maybe forty-five minutes, maybe an hour.

He passed a sign which read THANK YOU FOR SHOPPING THE BEAUTIFUL COUSINTOWN MALL, turned left, and let the van creep up to a perfectly legal forty miles an hour. He fished a handkerchief out of his back pocket, folded it over the back of his right hand, and concentrated on following his headlights to the forty grand the Turk had promised for a boy-child.

You'll be sorry," the kid said.

Sheridan looked impatiently around at him, pulled from a dream in which he had just won twenty straight hands and had Mr. Reggie grovelling at *his* feet for a change, sweating bullets and begging him to stop, what did he want to do, break him?

The kid was crying again, and his tears still had that odd pinkish cast, even though they were now well away from the bright lights of the mall. Sheridan wondered for the first time if the kid might have some sort of communicable disease. He supposed it was a little late to start worrying about such things, so he put it out of his mind.

"When my *Popsy* finds you you'll be sorry," the kid elaborated.

"Yeah," Sheridan said, and lit a cigarette. He turned off State Road 28 and onto an unmarked stretch of two-lane blacktop. There was a long marshy area on the left, unbroken woods on the right.

The kid pulled at the handcuffs and made a sobbing noise.

"Quit it. Won't do you any good."

Nevertheless, the kid pulled again. And this time there was a groaning, protesting sound Sheridan didn't like at *all*. He looked around and was amazed to see that the metal strut on the side of the seat—a strut he had welded in place himself—was twisted out of shape. *Shit!* he thought. *He's got teeth like razors and now I find out he's also strong as a fucking ox. If this is what he's like when he's sick, God forbid I should have grabbed him on a day when he was feeling well.*

He pulled over onto the soft shoulder and said, "Stop it!"

"I *won't!*"

The kid yanked at the handcuff again, and Sheridan saw the metal strut bend a little more. Christ, how could *any* kid do that?

*It's panic,* he answered himself. *That's how he can do it.*

But none of the others had been able to do it, and many of them had been a lot more terrified than this kid by this stage of the game.

He opened the glove compartment in the center of the dash. He brought out a hypodermic needle. The Turk had given it to him, and cautioned him not to use it unless he absolutely had to. Drugs, the Turk said (pronouncing it *drocks*), could demmege the merchandise.

"See this?"

The kid gave the hypo a glimmering sideways glance and nodded.

"You want me to use it?"

The kid shook his head at once. Strong or not, he had any kid's instant terror of the needle, Sheridan was happy to see.

"That's very smart. It would put out your lights." He paused. He didn't want to say it—hell, he was a nice guy, really, when he didn't have his ass in a sling—but he had to. "Might even kill you."

The kid stared at him, lips trembling, cheeks papery with fear.

"You stop yanking the cuff, I put away the needle. Deal?"

"Deal," the kid whispered.

"You promise?"

"Yes." The kid lifted his lip, showing white teeth. One of them was spotted with Sheridan's blood.

"You promise on your mother's name?"

"I never had a mother."

"Shit," Sheridan said, disgusted, and got the van rolling again. He moved a little faster now, and not only because he was finally off the main road. The kid was a spook. Sheridan wanted to turn him over to the Turk, get his money, and split.

"My Popsy's really strong, mister."

"Yeah?" Sheridan asked and thought: *I bet he is, kid. Only guy in the old folks' home who can bench-press his own truss, right?*

"He'll find me."

"Uh-huh."

"He can smell me."

Sheridan believed it. *He* could smell the kid. That fear had an odor was something he had learned on his previous expeditions, but this was unreal—the kid smelled like a mixture of sweat, mud, and slowly cooking battery acid. Sheridan was becoming more and more sure that something was seriously wrong with the kid . . . but soon that would be Mr. Wizard's problem, not his, and *caveat emptor,* as those old fellows in the togas used to say, *caveat* fucking *emptor.*

Sheridan cracked his window. On the left, the marsh went on and on. Broken slivers of moonlight glimmered in the stagnant water.

"Popsy can fly."

"Yeah," Sheridan said, "after a couple of bottles of Night Train, I bet he flies like a sonofabitchin eagle."

"Popsy—"

"Enough of the Popsy shit, kid—okay?"

The kid shut up.

Four miles farther on, the marsh on the left broadened into a wide empty pond. Sheridan made a turn onto a stretch of hardpan dirt that skirted the pond's north side. Five miles west of here he would turn right onto Highway 41, and from there it would be a straight shot into Taluda Heights.

He glanced toward the pond, a flat silver sheet in the moonlight . . . and then the moonlight was gone. Blotted out.

Overhead there was a flapping sound like big sheets on a clothesline.

"Popsy!" the kid cried.

"Shut up. It was only a bird."

But suddenly he was spooked, very spooked. He looked at the kid. The kid's lip was drawn back from his teeth again. His teeth were very white, very big.

No . . . not big. Big wasn't the right word. *Long* was the right word. Especially the two at the top at each side. The . . . what did you call them? The canines.

His mind suddenly started to fly again, clicking along as if he were on speed.

*I told him I was thirsty.*

*Why would Popsy go to a place where they—*

*(?eat was he going to say eat?)*

*He'll find me.*

*He can smell me.*

*Popsy can fly.*

Something landed on the roof of the van with a heavy clumsy thump.

"Popsy!" the kid screamed again, almost delirious with delight, and suddenly Sheridan could not see the road anymore—a huge membranous wing, pulsing with veins, covered the windshield from side to side.

*Popsy can fly.*

Sheridan screamed and jumped on the brake, hoping to tumble the thing on the roof off the front. There was that groaning, protesting sound of metal under stress from his right again, this time followed by a short bitter snap. A moment later the kid's fingers were clawing into his face, pulling open his cheek.

*"He stole me, Popsy!"* the kid was screeching at the roof of the van in that birdlike voice. *"He stole me, he stole me, the bad man stole me!"*

*You don't understand, kid,* Sheridan thought. He groped for the hypo and found it. *I'm not a bad guy, I just got in a jam.*

Then a hand, more like a talon than a real hand, smashed through the side window and ripped the hypo from Sheridan's grasp—along with two of his fingers. A moment later Popsy peeled the entire driver's-side door out of its frame, the hinges now bright twists of meaningless metal. Sheridan saw a billowing cape, black on the outside, lined with red silk on the inside, and the creature's tie . . . and although it was actually a cravat, it was blue all right—just as the boy had said.

Popsy yanked Sheridan out of the car, talons sinking through his jacket and shirt and deep into the meat of his shoulders; Popsy's green eyes suddenly turned as red as blood-roses.

"We came to the mall because my grandson wanted some Ninja Turtle figures," Popsy whispered, and his breath was like flyblown meat. "The ones they show on TV. All the children want them. You should have left him alone. You should have left *us* alone."

Sheridan was shaken like a rag doll. He shrieked and was shaken again. He heard Popsy asking solicitously if the kid was still thirsty; heard the kid saying yes, very, the bad man had scared him and his throat was *so* dry. He saw Popsy's thumbnail for just a second before it disappeared under the shelf of his chin, the nail ragged and thick. His throat was cut with that nail before he realized what was happening, and the last things he saw before his sight dimmed to black were the kid, cupping his hands to catch the flow the way Sheridan himself had cupped his hands under the back-yard faucet for a drink on a hot summer day when he was a kid, and Popsy, stroking the boy's hair gently, with grandfatherly love.

## THE WEREWOLF AND THE VAMPIRE

# R. Chetwynd-Hayes

Ronald Henry Glynn Chetwynd-Hayes (1919–2001) was born in Isleworth, West London. He left school at the age of fourteen and worked in a variety of menial jobs, including as an extra in crowd scenes in British war films. He served in the army in World War II.

Known in the United Kingdom as Britain's Prince of Chill, he began his writing career with a science-fiction novel, *The Man from the Bomb* (1959), then sold a supernatural romance, *The Dark Man* (1964), which has had several film options. He sold his first horror story, "The Thing," to Herbert van Thal for *The Seventh Pan Book of Horror Stories* (1966). Having noticed a great number of horror titles on the shelves of a bookseller, he wrote his own collection of horror stories and submitted it to two publishers simultaneously, embarrassing himself when they both accepted it. He became a highly prolific writer of short stories in the genre and was given the Lifetime Achievement Award in 1989 by both the Horror Writers of America and the British Fantasy Society. His stories were adapted for the films *From Beyond the Grave* (1973) and *The Monster Club* (1980). His story "Housebound" was the basis for an episode of *Rod Serling's Night Gallery* titled "Something in the Woodwork" (1973).

"The Werewolf and the Vampire" was first published in *The Monster Club* (London: New English Library, 1975).

# The Werewolf and the Vampire

## R. CHETWYND-HAYES

George Hardcastle's downfall undoubtedly originated in his love for dogs. He could not pass one without stopping and patting its head. A flea-bitten mongrel had only to turn the corner of the street and he was whistling, calling out: "Come on, boy. Come on then," and behaving in the altogether outrageous fashion that is peculiar to the devoted animal lover.

Tragedy may still have been averted had he not decided to spend a day in the Greensand Hills. Here in the region of Clandon Down, where dwarf oaks, pale birches, and dark firs spread up in a long sweep to the northern heights, was a vast hiding place where many forms of often invisible life lurked in the dense undergrowth. But George, like many before him, knew nothing about this, and tramped happily up the slope, aware only that the air was fresh, the silence absolute, and he was young.

The howl of what he supposed to be a dog brought him to an immediate standstill and for a while he listened, trying to determine from which direction the sound came. Afterwards he had reason to remember that none of the conditions laid down by legend and superstition prevailed. It was midafternoon and in consequence there was not, so far as he was aware, a full moon. The sun was sending golden spears of light through the thick foliage and all around was a warm, almost overpowering atmosphere, tainted with the aroma of decaying undergrowth. The setting was so commonplace and he was such an ordinary young man—not very bright perhaps, but gifted with good health and clean boyish good looks, the kind of Saxon comeliness that goes with clear skin and blond hair.

The howl rang out again, a long, drawn-out cry of canine anguish, and now it was easily located. Way over to his left, somewhere in the midst of, or just beyond a curtain of, saplings and low, thick bushes. Without thought of danger, George turned off the beaten track and plunged into the dim twilight that held perpetual domain during the summer months under the interlocked higher branches. Imagination supplied a mental picture of a gin-trap and a tortured animal that was lost in a maze of pain. Pity lent speed to his feet and made him ignore the stinging offshoots that whipped at his face and hands, while brambles tore his trousers and coiled round his ankles. The howl came again, now a little to his right, but this time it was fol-

527

lowed by a deep-throated growl, and if George had not been the person he was, he might have paid heed to this warning note of danger.

For some fifteen minutes, he ran first in one direction, then another, finally coming to rest under a giant oak which stood in a small clearing. For the first time fear came to him in the surrounding gloom. It did not seem possible that one could get lost in an English wood, but here, in the semilight, he conceived the ridiculous notion that night left its guardians in the wood during the day, which would at any moment move in and smother him with shadows.

He moved away from the protection of the oak tree and began to walk in the direction he thought he had come, when the growl erupted from a few yards to his left. Pity fled like a leaf before a raging wind, and stark terror fired his brain with blind, unreasoning panic. He ran, fell, got up, and ran again, and from behind came the sound of a heavy body crashing through undergrowth, the rasp of laboured breathing, the bestial growl of some enraged being. Reason had gone, coherent thought had been replaced by an animal instinct for survival; he knew that whatever ran behind him was closing the gap.

Soon, and he dare not turn his head, it was but a few feet away. There was snuffling, whining, terribly eager growling, and suddenly he shrieked as a fierce, burning pain seared his right thigh. Then he was down on the ground and the agony rose up to become a scarlet flame, until it was blotted out by a merciful darkness.

An hour passed, perhaps more, before George Hardcastle returned to consciousness. He lay quite still and tried to remember why he should be lying on the ground in a dense wood, while a dull ache held mastery over his right leg. Then memory sent its first cold tentacles shuddering across his brain and he dared to sit up and face reality.

The light had faded: night was slowly reinforcing its advance guard, but he was still able to see the dead man who lay but a few feet away. He shrank back with a little muffled cry and tried to dispel this vision of a purple face and bulging eyes,

by the simple act of closing his own. But this was not a wise action for the image of that awful countenance was etched upon his brain, and the memory was even more macabre than the reality. He opened his eyes again, and there it was: a man in late middle life, with grey, close-cropped hair, a long moustache, and yellow teeth, that were bared in a death grin. The purple face suggested he had died of a sudden heart attack.

The next hour was a dimly remembered nightmare. George dragged himself through the undergrowth and by sheer good fortune emerged out on to one of the main paths.

He was found next morning by a team of boy scouts.

Police and an army of enthusiastic volunteers scoured the woods, but no trace of a ferocious wild beast was found. But they did find the dead man, and he proved to be a farm worker who had a reputation locally of being a person of solitary habits. An autopsy revealed he had died of a heart attack, and it was assumed that this had been the result of his efforts in trying to assist the injured boy.

The entire episode assumed the proportions of a nine-day wonder, and then was forgotten.

**M**rs. Hardcastle prided herself on being a mother who, while combating illness, did not pamper it. She had George back on his feet within three weeks and despatched him on prolonged walks. Being an obedient youth he followed these instructions to the letter, and so, on one overcast day, found himself at Hampton Court. As the first drops of rain were caressing his face, he decided to make a long-desired tour of the staterooms. He wandered from room to room, examined pictures, admired four-poster beds, then listened to a guide who was explaining the finer points to a crowd of tourists. By the time he had reached the Queen's Audience Room, he felt tired, so seated himself on one of the convenient window-seats. For some while he sat looking out at the rain-drenched gardens, then with a yawn, he turned and gave a quick glance along the long corridor that ran through a series of open doorways.

Suddenly his attention was captured by a figure approaching over the long carpet. It was that of a girl in a black dress; she was a beautiful study in black and white. Black hair, white face and hands, black dress. Not that there was anything sinister about her, for as she drew nearer he could see the look of indescribable sadness in the large, black eyes, and the almost timid way she looked round each room. Her appearance was outstanding, so vivid, like a black-and-white photograph that had come to life.

She entered the Queen's Audience Room and now he could hear the light tread of her feet, the whisper of her dress, and even those small sounds seemed unreal. She walked round the room, looking earnestly at the pictures, then as though arrested by a sudden sound, she stopped. Suddenly the lovely eyes came round and stared straight at George.

They held an expression of alarmed surprise, that gradually changed to one of dawning wonderment. For a moment George could only suppose she recognised him, although how he had come to forget her, was beyond his comprehension. She glided towards him, and as she came a small smile parted her lips. She sank down on the far end of the seat and watched him with those dark, wondering eyes.

She said: "Hullo. I'm Carola."

No girl had made such an obvious advance towards George before, and shyness, not to mention shock, robbed him of speech. Carola seemed to be reassured by his reticence, for her smile deepened and when she spoke her voice held a gentle bantering tone.

"What's the matter? Cat got your tongue?"

This impertinent probe succeeded in freeing him from the chains of shyness and he ventured to make a similar retort.

"I can speak when I want to."

"That's better. I recognised the link at once. We have certain family connections, really. Don't you think so?"

This question was enough to dry up his powers of communication for some time, but presently he was able to breathe one word. "Family!"

"Yes." She nodded and her hair trembled like black silk in sunlight. "We must be at least distantly related in the allegorical sense. But don't let's talk about that. I am so pleased to be able to walk about in daylight. It is so dreary at night, and besides, I'm not really myself then."

George came to the conclusion that this beautiful creature was at least slightly mad, and therefore made a mundane, but what he thought must be a safe remark.

"Isn't it awful weather?"

She frowned slightly and he got the impression he had committed a breach of good taste.

"Don't be so silly. You know it's lovely weather. Lots of beautiful clouds."

He decided this must be a joke. There could be no other interpretation. He capped it by another.

"Yes, and soon the awful sun will come out."

She flinched as though he had hit her, and there was the threat of tears in the lovely eyes.

"You beast. How could you say a dreadful thing like that? There won't be any sun, the weather forecast said so. I thought you were nice, but all you want to do is frighten me."

And she dabbed her eyes with a black lace handkerchief, while George tried to find his way out of a mental labyrinth where every word seemed to have a double meaning.

"I am sorry. But I didn't mean . . ."

She stifled a tiny sob. "How would you like it if I said—silver bullets?"

He scratched his head, wrinkled his brow, and then made a wry grimace.

"I wouldn't know what you meant, but I wouldn't mind."

She replaced the lace handkerchief in a small handbag, then got up and walked quickly away. George watched her retreating figure until it disappeared round the corner in the direction of the long gallery. He muttered: "Potty. Stark raving potty."

On reflection he decided it was a great pity that her behaviour was so erratic, because he would have dearly liked to have known her better. In fact, when he remembered the black hair and white face, he was aware of a deep disappointment, a sense of loss, and he had to subdue an urge to run after her. He remained seated in the window bay and when he looked out on to the gardens, he saw the rain had ceased, but thick cloud banks were billowing across the sky. He smiled gently and murmured, "Lovely clouds—horrible sunshine."

George was half way across Anne Boleyn's courtyard when a light touch on his shoulder made him turn, and there was Carola of the white face and black hair, with a sad smile parting her lips.

"Look," she said, "I'm sorry I got into a huff back there, but I can't bear to be teased about— well, you know what. But you are one of us, and we mustn't quarrel. All forgiven?"

George said, "Yes, I'm sorry I offended you. But I didn't mean to." And at that moment he was so happy, so ridiculously elated, he was prepared to apologise for breathing.

"Good." She sighed and took hold of his arm as though it were the most natural action in the world. "We'll forget all about it. But, please, don't joke about such things again."

"No. Absolutely not." George had not the slightest idea what it was he must not joke about, but made a mental note to avoid mention of the weather and silver bullets.

"You must come and meet my parents," Carola insisted, "they'll be awfully pleased to see you. I bet they won't believe their noses."

This remark was in the nature of a setback, but George's newly found happiness enabled him to ignore it—pretend it must be a slip of the tongue.

"That's very kind of you, but won't it be a bit sudden? I mean, are you sure it will be convenient?"

She laughed, a lovely little silver sound and, if possible, his happiness increased.

"You are a funny boy. They'll be tickled pink, and so they should be. For the first time for years,

we won't have to be careful of what we say in front of a visitor."

George had a little mental conference and came to the conclusion that this was meant to be a compliment. So he said cheerfully, "I don't mind what people say. I like them to be natural."

Carola thought that was a very funny remark and tightened her grip on his arm, while laughing in a most enchanting fashion.

"You have a most wonderful sense of humour. Wait until I tell Daddy that one. 'I like them to be natural . . .'"

And she collapsed into a fit of helpless laughter in which George joined, although he was rather at a loss to know what he had said that was so funny. Suddenly the laugh was cut short, was killed by a gasp of alarm, and Carola was staring at the western sky where the clouds had taken on a brighter hue. The words came out as a strangled whisper.

"The sun! O Lucifer, the sun is coming out."

"Is it?" George looked up and examined the sky with assumed interest. "I wouldn't be surprised if you're not right . . ." Then he stopped and looked down at his lovely companion with concern. "I'm sorry, you . . . you don't like the sun, do you?"

Her face was a mask of terror and she gave a terrible little cry of anguish. George's former suspicion of insanity returned, but she was still appealing—still a flawless pearl on black velvet. He put his arm round the slim shoulders, and she hid her eyes against his coat. The muffled, tremulous whisper came to him.

"Please take me home. Quickly."

He felt great joy in the fact that he was able to bring comfort.

"There's no sign of sunlight. Look, it was only a temporary break in the clouds."

Slowly the dark head was raised, and the eyes, so bright with unshed tears, again looked up at the western sky. Now, George was rewarded, for her lips parted, the skin round her eyes crinkled, and her entire face was transformed by a wonderful, glorious smile.

"Oh, how beautiful! Lovely, lovely, *lovely*

clouds. The wind is up there, you know. A big, fat wind-god, who blows out great bellows of mist, so that we may not be destroyed by demon-sun. And sometimes he shrieks his rage across the sky; at others he whispers soft comforting words and tells us to have faith. The bleak night of loneliness is not without end."

George was acutely embarrassed, not knowing what to make of this allegorical outburst. But the love and compassion he had so far extended to dogs was now enlarged and channelled towards the lovely, if strange, young girl by his side.

"Come," he said, "let me take you home."

George pulled open a trellis iron gate and allowed Carola to precede him up a crazy-paved path, which led to a house that gleamed with new paint and well-cleaned windows. Such a house could have been found in any one of a thousand streets in the London suburbs, and brashly proclaimed that here lived a woman who took pride in the crisp whiteness of her curtains, and a man who was no novice in the art of wielding a paint brush. They had barely entered the tiny porch, where the red tiles shone like a pool at sunset, when the door was flung open and a plump, grey-haired woman clasped Carola in her arms.

"Ee, love, me and yer dad were that worried. We thought you'd got caught in a sun-storm."

Carola kissed her mother gently, on what George noted was another dead-white cheek, then turned and looked back at him with shining eyes.

"Mummy, this . . ." She giggled and shook her head. "It's silly, but I don't know your name."

"George. George Hardcastle."

To say Carola's mother looked alarmed is a gross understatement. For a moment she appeared to be terrified, and clutched her daughter as though they were confronted by a man-eating tiger. Then Carola laughed softly and whispered into her mother's ear. George watched the elder woman's expression change to one of incredulity and dawning pleasure.

"You don't say so, love? Where on earth did you find him?"

"In the Palace," Carola announced proudly. "He was sitting in the Queen's Audience Room."

Mummy almost ran forward and, after clasping the startled George with both hands, kissed him soundly on either cheek. Then she stood back and examined him with obvious pleasure.

"I ought to have known," she said, nodding her head as though with sincere conviction. "Been out of touch for too long. But what will you think of me manners? Come in, love. Father will be that pleased. It's not much of a death for him, with just us two women around."

Again George was aware of a strange slip of the tongue, which he could only assume was a family failing. So he beamed with the affability that is expected from a stranger who is the recipient of sudden hospitality, and allowed himself to be pulled into a newly decorated hall, and relieved of his coat. Then Mummy opened a door and ordered in a shouted whisper: "Father, put yer tie on, we've got company." There was a startled snort, as though someone had been awakened from a fireside sleep, and Mummy turned a bright smile on George.

"Would you like to go upstairs and wash yer hands, like? Make yourself comfy, if you get my meaning."

"No, thank you. Very kind, I'm sure."

"Well then, you'd best come into parlour."

The "parlour" had a very nice paper on the walls, bright pink lamps, a well stuffed sofa and matching armchairs, a large television set, a low, imitation walnut table, a record player, some awful coloured prints, and an artificial log electric fire. A stout man with thinning grey hair struggled up from the sofa, while he completed the adjustment of a tie that was more eye-catching than tasteful.

"Father," Mummy looked quickly round the room as though to seek reassurance that nothing was out of place, "this is George. A young man that Carola has brought home, like." Then she added in an undertone, "He's all right. No need to worry."

Father advanced with outstretched hand and announced in a loud, very hearty voice: "Ee, I'm pleased to meet ye, lad. I've always said it's about time the lass found herself a young spark. But the reet sort is 'ard to come by, and that's a fact."

Father's hand was unpleasantly cold and flabby, but he radiated such an air of goodwill, George was inclined to overlook it.

"Now, Father, you're embarrassing our Carola," Mummy said. And indeed the girl did appear to be somewhat disconcerted, only her cheeks instead of blushing, had assumed a greyish tinge. "Now, George, don't stand around, lad. Sit yerself down and make yerself at 'ome. We don't stand on ceremony here."

George found himself on the sofa next to Father, who would insist on winking, whenever their glances met. In the meanwhile Mummy expressed solicitous anxiety regarding his well-being.

"Have you supped lately? I know you young doggies don't 'ave to watch yer diet like we do, so just say what you fancy. I've a nice piece of 'am in t' fridge, and I can fry that with eggs, in no time at all."

George knew that somewhere in that kindly invitation there had been another slip of the tongue, but he resolutely did not think about it.

"That's very kind of you, but really . . ."

"Let 'er do a bit of cooking, lad," Father pleaded. "She don't get much opportunity, if I can speak without dotting me *i*'s and crossing me *t*'s."

"If you are sure it will be no trouble."

Mummy made a strange neighing sound. "Trouble! 'Ow you carry on. It's time for us to have a glass of something rich, anyway."

Mother and daughter departed for the kitchen and George was left alone with Father, who was watching him with an embarrassing interest.

"Been on 'olidays yet, lad?" he enquired.

"No, it's a bit late now . . ."

Father sighed with the satisfaction of a man who is recalling a pleasant memory. "We 'ad smashing time in Clacton. Ee, the weather was summat greet. Two weeks of thick fog—couldn't see 'and in front of face."

George said, "Oh, dear," then lapsed into silence while he digested this piece of information. Presently he was aware of an elbow nudging his ribs.

"I know it's delicate question, lad, so don't answer if you'd rather not. But—'ow often do you change?"

George thought it was a very delicate question, and could only think of a very indelicate reason why it had been asked. But his conception of politeness demanded he answer.

"Well . . . every Friday actually. After I've had a bath."

Father gasped with astonishment. "As often as that! I'm surprised. The last lad I knew in your condition only changed when the moon was full."

George said, "Goodness gracious!" and then tried to ask a very pertinent question. "Why, do I . . ."

Father nodded. "There's a goodish pong. But don't let it worry you. We can smell it, because we've the reet kind of noses."

An extremely miserable, not to say self-conscious, young man was presently led across the hall and into the dining-room, where one place was set with knife, fork, and spoon, and three with glass and drinking straw. He was too dejected to pay particular heed to this strange and unequal arrangement, and neither was he able to really enjoy the plate of fried eggs and ham that Mummy put down before him, with the remark: "Here you are, lad, get wrapped round that, and you'll not starve."

The family shared the contents of a glass jug between them, and as this was thick and red, George could only suppose it to be tomato juice. They all sucked through straws; Carola, as was to be expected, daintily, Mummy with some anxiety, and Father greedily. When he had emptied his glass, he presented it for a refill and said: "You know, Mother, that's as fine a jug of AB as you've ever served up."

Mummy sighed. "It's not so bad. Mind you, youngsters don't get what I call top-grade nourishment, these days. There's nothing like getting yer teeth stuck into the real thing. This stuff 'as lost the natural goodness."

Father belched and made a disgusting noise with his straw.

"We must be thankful, Mother. There's many who 'asn't a drop to wet their lips, and be pleased to sup from tin."

George could not subdue a natural curiosity and the question slipped out before he had time to really think about it.

"Excuse me, but don't you ever eat anything?"

The shocked silence which followed told him he had committed a well nigh unforgivable sin. Father dropped his glass and Carola said, "Oh, George," in a very reproachful voice, while Mummy creased her brow into a very deep frown.

"George, haven't you ever been taught manners?"

It was easy to see she spoke more in sorrow than anger, and although the exact nature of his transgression was not quite clear to George, he instantly apologised.

"I am very sorry, but . . ."

"I should think so, indeed." Mummy continued to speak gently but firmly. "I never expected to hear a question like that at my table. After all, you wouldn't like it if I were to ask who or what you chewed up on one of your moonlight strolls. Well, I've said me piece, and now we'll forget that certain words were ever said. Have some chocolate pudding."

Even while George smarted under this rebuke, he was aware that once again, not so much a slip of the tongue, as a sentence that demanded thought had been inserted between an admonishment and a pardon. There was also a growing feeling of resentment. It seemed that whatever he said to this remarkable family gave offence, and his supply of apologies was running low. He waited until Mummy had served him with a generous helping of chocolate pudding, and then replenished the three glasses from the jug, before he relieved his mind.

"I don't chew anyone."

Mummy gave Father an eloquent glance, and he cleared his throat.

"Listen, lad, there are some things you don't mention in front of ladies. What you do in change

period is between you and black man. So let's change subject."

Like all peace-loving people George sometimes reached a point where war, or to be more precise, attack seemed to be the only course of action. Father's little tirade brought him to such a point. He flung down his knife and fork and voiced his complaints.

"Look here, I'm fed up. If I mention the weather, I'm ticked off. If I ask why you never eat, I'm in trouble. I've been asked when I change, told that I stink. Now, after being accused of chewing people, I'm told I mustn't mention it. Now, I'll tell you something. I think you're all round the bend."

Carola burst into tears and ran from the room. Father swore, or rather he said, "Satan's necktie," which was presumably the same thing, and Mummy looked very concerned.

"Just a minute, son." She raised a white, rather wrinkled forefinger. "You're trying to tell us you don't know the score?"

"I haven't the slightest idea what you're talking about," George retorted.

Mummy and Father looked at each other for some little while, then as though prompted by a single thought, they both spoke in unison.

"He's a just bittener."

"Someone should tell 'im," Mummy stated, after she had watched the, by now, very frightened George for an entire minute. "It should come from a man."

"If 'e 'ad gumption he were born with, 'e'd know," Father said, his face becoming quite grey with embarrassment. "Hell's bells, my dad didn't 'ave to tell me I were vampire."

"Yes, but you can see he's none too bright," Mummy pointed out. "We can't all 'ave your brains. No doubt the lad has 'eart, and I say 'eart is better than brains any day. Been bitten lately, lad?"

George could only nod and look longingly at the door.

"Big long thing, with a wet snout, I wouldn't be surprised. It's a werewolf you are, son. You can't deceive the noses of we vamps: yer glands are beginning to play up—give out a bit of smell, see? I should think . . . What's the state of the moon, Father?"

"Seven eights."

Mummy nodded with grim relish. "I should think you're due for a change round about Friday night. Got any open space round your way?"

"There's . . ." George took a deep breath. "There's Clapham Common."

"Well, I should go for a run round there. Make sure you cover your face up. Normal people go all funny like when they first lays eyes on a werewolf. Start yelling their 'eads off, mostly."

George was on his feet and edging his way towards the door. He was praying for the priceless gift of disbelief. Mummy was again displaying signs of annoyance.

"Now there's no need to carry on like that. You must 'ave known we were all vampires—what did you think we were drinking? Raspberry juice? And let me tell you this. We're the best friends you've got. No one else will want to know you, once full moon is peeping over barn door. So don't get all lawn tennis with us . . ."

But George was gone. Running across the hall, out of the front door, down the crazy-paving path, and finally along the pavement. People turned their heads as he shouted: "They're mad . . . mad . . . mad . . ."

T here came to George—as the moon waxed full—a strange restlessness. It began with insomnia, which rocketed him out of a deep sleep into a strange, instant wakefulness. He became aware of an urge to go for long moonlit walks; and when he had surrendered to this temptation, an overwhelming need to run, leap, roll over and over down a grassy bank, anything that would enable him to break down the hated walls of human convention—and express. A great joy—greater than he had ever known—came to him when he leaped and danced on the common, and could only be released by a shrill, doglike howl that rose up from the sleeping suburbs and went out, swift as a beam of light, to the face of mother-moon.

This joy had to be paid for. When the sun sent its first enquiring rays in through George's window, sanity returned and demanded a reckoning. He examined his face and hands with fearful expectancy. So far as he was aware there had been no terrible change, as yet. But these were early days—or was it nights? Sometimes he would fling himself down on his bed and cry out his great desire for disbelief.

"It can't happen. Mad people are sending me mad."

The growing strangeness of his behaviour could not go undetected. He was becoming withdrawn, apt to start at every sound, and betrayed a certain distrust of strangers by an eerie widening of his eyes, and later, the baring of his teeth in a mirthless grin. His mother commented on these peculiarities in forcible language.

"I think you're going up the pole. Honest I do. The milkman told me yesterday, he saw you snarling at Mrs. Redfem's dog."

"It jumped out at me," George explained. "You might have done the same."

Mrs. Hardcastle shook her head. "No. I can honestly say I've never snarled at a dog in my life. You never inherited snarling from me."

"I'm all right." George pleaded for reassurance. "I'm not turning into—anything."

"Well, you should know." George could not help thinking that his mother was regarding him with academic interest; rather than concern. "Do you go out at nights after I'm asleep?"

He found it impossible to lie convincingly, so he countered one question with another. "Why should I do that?"

"Don't ask me. But some nut has been seen prancing round the common at three o'clock in the morning. I just wondered."

The physical change came gradually. One night he woke with a severe pain in his right hand and lay still for a while, not daring to examine it. Then he switched on the bedside lamp with his left hand and, after further hesitation, brought its right counterpart out from the sheets. A thick down had spread over the entire palm and he found the fingers would not straighten. They had curved and the nails were thicker and longer than he remembered. After a while the fear—the loathing—went away, and it seemed most natural for him to have claws for fingers and hair-covered hands. Next morning his right hand was as normal as his left, and at that period he was still able to dismiss, even if with little conviction, the episode as a bad dream.

But one night there was a dream—a nightmare of the blackest kind, where fantasy blended with fact and George was unable to distinguish one from the other. He was running over the common, bounding with long, graceful leaps, and there was a wonderful joy in his heart and a limitless freedom in his head. He was in a black-and-white world. Black grass, white-tinted trees, grey sky, white moon. But with all the joy, all the freedom, there was a subtle, ever-present knowledge, that this was an unnatural experience, that he should be utilising all his senses to dispel. Once his brain— that part which was still unoccupied territory— screamed: "Wake up," but he was awake, for did not the black grass crunch beneath his feet, and the night breeze ruffle his fur? A large cat was running in front, trying to escape—up trees—across the roofs—round bushes—he finally trapped it in a hole. Shrieks—scratching claws—warm blood— tearing teeth . . . It was good. He was fulfilled.

Next morning when he awoke in his own bed, it could have been dismissed as a mad dream, were it not for the scratches on his face and hands and the blood in his hair. He thought of psychiatrists, asylums, priests, religion, and at last came to the only possible conclusion. There was, so far as he knew, only one set of people on earth who could explain and understand.

**M**ummy let George in. Father shook him firmly by the hand. Carola kissed him gently and put an arm round his shoulders when he started to cry.

"We don't ask to be what we are," she whispered. "We keep more horror than we give away."

"We all 'ave our place in the great graveyard,"

Father said. "You hunt, we sup, ghouls tear, shaddies lick, mocks blow, and fortunately shadmocks can only whistle."

"Will I always be—what I am?" George asked.

They all nodded. Mummy grimly, Father knowingly, Carola sadly. "Until the moon leaves the sky," they all chanted.

"Or you are struck in the heart by a silver bullet," Carola whispered, "fired by one who has only thought about sin. Or maybe when you are very, very old, the heart may give out after a transformation . . . "

"Don't be morbid," Mummy ordered. "Poor lad's got enough on plate without you adding to it. Make him a nice cup of tea. And you can mix us a jug of something rich while you're about it. Don't be too 'eavy-handed on the O group."

They sat round the artificial log fire, drinking tea, absorbing nourishment, three giving, one receiving advice, and there was a measure of cosiness.

"All 'M's' should keep away from churches, parsons, and boy scouts," Father said.

"Run from a cross and fly from a prayer," intoned Mummy.

"Two can run better than one," Carola observed shyly.

Next day George told his mother he intended to leave home and set up house for himself. Mrs. Hardcastle did not argue as strongly as she might have had a few weeks earlier. What with one thing and another, there was a distinct feeling that the George, who was standing so grim and white-faced in the kitchen doorway, was not the one she had started out with. She said, "Right, then. I'd say it's about time," and helped him to pack.

Father, who knew someone in the building line, found George a four-roomed cottage that was situated on the edge of a churchyard, and this he furnished with a few odds and ends that the family were willing to part with. The end product was by no means as elegant or deceptive as the house at Hampton Court, but it was somewhere for George to come back to after his midnight run.

He found the old legends had been embellished, for he experienced no urge to rend or even bite. There was no reason why he should; the body was well fed and the animal kingdom only hunts when goaded by hunger. It was sufficient for him to run, leap, chase his tail by moonlight, and sometimes howl with the pure joy of living. And it is pleasant to record that his joy grew day by day.

For obvious reasons the wedding took place in a registry office, and it seemed that the dark gods smiled down upon the union, for there was a thick fog that lasted from dawn to sunset. The wedding-supper and the reception which followed were, of necessity, simple affairs. There was a wedding cake for those that could eat it: a beautiful, three-tier structure, covered with pink icing, and studded with what George hoped were glace cherries. He of course had invited no guests, for there was much that might have alarmed or embarrassed the uninitiated. Three ghouls in starched, white shrouds sat gnawing something that was best left undescribed. The bride and her family sipped a basic beverage from red goblets, and as the bridegroom was due for a turn, he snarled when asked to pass the salt. Then there was Uncle Deitmark, a vampire of the old school, who kept demanding a trussed-up victim, so that he could take his nourishment direct from the neck.

But finally the happy couple were allowed to depart, and Mummy and Father wept as they threw the traditional coffin nails after the departing hearse. "Ee, it were champion," Father exclaimed, wiping his eyes on the back of his hand. "Best blood-up I've seen for many a day. You did 'em proud, Mother."

"I believe in giving the young 'uns a good send-off," Mummy said. "Now they must open their own vein, as the saying goes."

Carola and George watched the moon come up over the church steeple, which was a little dangerous for it threw the cross into strong relief, but on that one night they would have defied the very Pope of Rome himself.

"We are no longer alone," Carola whispered. "We love and are loved, and that surely has transformed us from monsters into gods."

"If happiness can transform a tumbledown cottage into paradise," George said, running his as yet uncurved fingers through her hair, "then I guess we are gods."

But he forgot that every paradise must have its snake, and their particular serpent was disguised in the rotund shape of the Reverend John Cole. This worthy cleric had an allegorical nose for smelling out hypothetical evil, and it was not long before he was considering the inhabitants of the house by the churchyard with a speculative eye.

He called when George was out and invited Carola to join the young wives' altar dressing committee. She turned grey and begged to be excused. Mr. Cole then suggested she partake in a brief reading from holy scripture, and Carola shrank from the proffered Bible, even as a rabbit recoils from a hooded cobra. Then the Reverend John Cole accidentally dropped his crucifix on to her lap, and she screamed like one who is in great pain, before falling to the floor in a deathlike faint. And the holy minister departed with the great joy that comes to the sadist who knows he is only doing his duty.

Next day George met the Reverend Cole, who was hastening to the death bed of a sinful woman, and laid a not too gentle hand on the flabby arm.

"I understand you frightened my wife, when I was out yesterday."

The clergyman bared his teeth and, although George was now in the shape with which he had been born, they resembled two dogs preparing to fight.

"I'm wondering," the Reverend Cole said, "what kind of woman recoils from the good book and screams when the crucifix touches her."

"Well, it's like this," George tightened his grip on the black-clad arm, "we are both allergic to Bibles, crosses, and nosy parsons. I am apt to burn one, break two, and pulverise three. Am I getting through?"

"And I have a duty before God and man," John Cole said, looking at the retaining hand with marked distaste, "and that is to stamp evil whenever it be found. And may I add, with whatever means are at my disposal."

They parted in mutual hate, and George in his

innocence decided to use fear as an offensive weapon, not realising that its wounds strengthen resistance more often than they weaken. One night, when the moon was full, turning the graveyard into a gothic wonderland, the Reverend John Cole met something that robbed him of speech for nigh on twelve hours. It walked on bent hindlegs, and had two very long arms which terminated in talons that seemed hungry for the ecclesiastical throat, and a nightmare face whose predominant feature was a long, slavering snout.

At the same time, Mrs. Cole, a very timid lady who had yet to learn of the protective virtues of two pieces of crossed wood, was trying so hard not to scream as a white-faced young woman advanced across the bedroom. The reaction of husband and wife was typical of their individual characters. The Reverend John Cole, after the initial cry, did not stop running until he was safely barricaded in the church with a processional cross jammed across the doorway. Mrs. Cole, being unable to scream, promptly fainted, and hence fared worse than her fleetfooted spouse. John Cole, after his run, was a little short of breath: Mary Cole, when she returned to consciousness, was a little short of blood.

Mr. Cole was an erratic man who often preached sermons guaranteed to raise the scalps of the most urbane congregation, if that is to say they took the trouble to listen. The tirade which was poured out from the puplit on the Sunday after Mrs. Cole's loss and Mr. Cole's fright woke three slumbering worshippers, and caused a choirboy to swallow his chewing-gum.

"The devil has planted his emissaries in our midst," the vicar proclaimed. "Aye, do they dwell in the church precincts and do appear to the God-fearing in their bestial form."

The chewing-gum-bereft choirboy giggled, and Mr. Cole's wrath rose and erupted into admonishing words.

"Laugh not. I say to you of little faith, laugh not. For did I not come face to face—aye, but a few yards from where you now sit—with a fearsome beast that did drool and nuzzle, and I feared that my windpipe might soon lie upon my shirt-front. But, and this be the truth, which did turn my bowels to water, there was the certain knowledge that I was in the presence of a creature that is without precedence in Satan's hierarchy—the one—the only—the black angel of hell—the dreaded werewolf."

At least ten people in the congregation thought their vicar had at last turned the corner and become stark raving mad. Twenty more did not understand what he was talking about, and one old lady assumed she was listening to a brilliant interpretation of Revelation, chapter XIII, verses 1 to 3. The remainder of the congregation had not been listening, but noted the vicar was in fine fettle, roaring and pounding the pulpit with his customary gusto. His next disclosure suffered roughly the same reception.

"My dear wife—my helpmeet, who has walked by my side these past twenty years—was visited in her chamber by a female of the species . . ." Mr. Cole nodded bitterly. "A vampire, an unclean thing that has crept from its foul grave, and did take from my dear one, that which she could ill afford to lose . . ."

Ignorance, inattention, Mr. Cole's words fell on very stony ground and no one believed—save Willie Mitcham. Willie did believe in vampires, werewolves, and, in fact, also accepted the existence of banshees, demons, poltergeists, ghosts of every description, monsters of every shape and form, and the long wriggly thing, which as everyone knows, has yet to be named. As Willie was only twelve years of age, he naturally revelled in his belief, and moreover made himself an expert on demonology. To his father's secret delectation and his mother's openly expressed horror, he had an entire cupboard filled with literature that dwelt on every aspect of the subject. He knew, for example, that the only sure way of getting a banshee off your back is to spit three times into an open grave, bow three times to the moon, then chant in a loud voice.

*Go to the north, go to the south,*
*Go to the devil, but shut your mouth.*
*Scream not by day, or howl by night,*
*But gibber alone by candlelight.*

He also knew, for had not the facts been advertised by printed page, television set, and cinema screen, that the only sure way of killing a vampire is to drive a sharp pointed object through its heart between the hours of sunrise and sunset. He was also joyfully aware of the fatal consequences that attend the arrival of a silver bullet in a werewolf's hairy chest. So it was that Willie listened to the Reverend John Cole with ears that heard and understood, and he wanted so desperately to shout out the simple and time-honoured cures, the withal, the ways and means, the full, glorious, and gory details. But his mother nudged him in the ribs and told him to stop fidgeting, so he could only sit and seethe with well-nigh uncontrollable impatience.

One bright morning in early March the total population of the graveyard cottage was increased by one. The newly risen sun peeped in through the neatly curtained windows and gazed down upon what, it is to be hoped, was the first baby werevamp. It was like all newly born infants, small, wrinkled, extremely ugly, and favoured its mother in so far as it had been born with two prominent eye-teeth. Instead of crying, it made a harsh hissing sound, not unlike that of an infant king-cobra, and was apt to bite anything that moved.

"Isn't he sweet?" Carola sighed, then waved a finger at her offspring, who promptly curled back an upper lip and made a hissing snarl. "Yes he is . . . he's a sweet 'ickle diddums . . . he's Mummy's 'ickle diddums . . ."

"I think he's going to be awfully clever," George stated after a while. "What with that broad forehead and those dark eyes, one can see there is a great potential for intelligence. He's got your mouth, darling."

"Not yet he hasn't," Carola retorted, "but he soon will have, if I'm not careful. I suppose he's in his humvamp period now; but when the moon is full, he'll have sweet little hairy talons, and a dinky-winky little tail."

Events proved her to be absolutely correct.

The Reverend John Cole allowed several weeks to pass before he made an official call on the young parents. During this time he reinforced his courage, of which it must be confessed he had an abundance; sought advice from his superiors, who were not at all helpful; and tried to convince anyone who would listen of the danger in their midst. His congregation shrank, people crossed the road whenever he came into view, and he was constantly badgered by a wretched little boy, who poured out a torrent of nauseating information. But at last the vicar was as ready for the fatal encounter as he ever would be, and so, armed with a crucifix, faith, and a small bottle of whisky, he went forth to do battle. From his bedroom window that overlooked the vicarage, Willie Mitcham watched the black figure as it trudged along the road. He flung the window open and shouted: "Yer daft coot. It's a full moon."

No one answered Mr. Cole's thunderous assault on the front door. This was not surprising, as Carola was paying Mrs. Cole another visit, and George was chasing a very disturbed sheep across a stretch of open moorland. Baby had not yet reached the age when answering doors would be numbered among his accomplishments. At last the reverend gentleman opened the door and, after crossing himself with great fervour, entered the cottage.

He found himself in the living-room, a cosy little den with whitewashed walls, two ancient chairs, a folding table, and some very nice rugs on the floor. There was also a banked-up fire, and a beautiful old ceiling oil-lamp that George had cleverly adapted for electricity. Mr. Cole called out: "Anyone there?" and, receiving no answer, sank down into one of the chairs to wait. Presently, the chair being comfortable, the room warm, the clergyman felt his caution dissolve into a hazy atmosphere of well-being. His head nodded, his eyelids flickered, his mouth fell open and, in no time at all, a series of gentle snores filled the room with their even cadence.

It is right to say Mr. Cole fell asleep reluctantly, and while he slept he displayed a certain amount of dignity. But he awoke with a shriek and began to thresh about in a most undignified manner. There was a searing pain in his right ankle, and when he moved something soft and rather heavy flopped over his right foot and at the same time made a strange hissing sound. The vicar screamed again and kicked out with all his strength, and that which clung to his ankle went hurling across the room and landed on a rug near the window. It hissed, yelped; then turning over, began to crawl back towards the near prostrate clergyman. He tried to close his eyes, but they insisted on remaining open and so permitted him to see something that a person with a depraved sense of humour might have called a baby. A tiny, little white—oh, so white—face, which had two microscopic fangs jutting out over the lower lip. But for the rest it was very hairy; had two wee claws, and a proudly erect, minute tail, that was, at this particular moment in time lashing angrily from side to side. Its little hind legs acted as projectors and enabled the hair-covered torso to leap along at quite an amazing speed. There was also a smear of Mr. Cole's blood round the mouth; and the eyes held an expression that suggested the ecclesiastical fluid was appealing to the taste-buds, and their owner could hardly wait to get back to the fount of nourishment.

Mr. Cole released three long, drawn-out screams, then, remembering that legs have a decided and basic purpose, leaped for the door. It was truly an awe-inspiring sight to see a portly clergyman, who had more than reached the years of discretion, running between graves, leaping over tombstones, and sprinting along paths. Baby-werevamp on his hind legs and looked as wistfully as his visage permitted the swiftly retreating cleric. After a while baby set up a prolonged howl, and thumped the floor with clenched claws. His distress was understandable. He had just seen a well-filled feeding bottle go running out of the door.

**W**illie Mitcham had at last got through. One of the stupid, blind, not to mention thick-headed adults had been finally shocked into seeing the light. When Willie found the Reverend John Cole entangled in a hawthorn bush, he also stumbled on a man who was willing to listen to advice from any source. He had also retreated from the frontiers of sanity, and was therefore in a position to be driven, rather than to command.

"I saw 'im." Willie was possibly the happiest boy in the world at that moment. "I saw 'im with his 'orrible fangs and he went leaping towards the moors."

Mr. Cole said, "Ah!" and began to count his fingers.

"And I saw 'er," Willie went on. "She went to your house and drifted up to the main bedroom window. Just like in the film *Mark of the Vampire*."

"Destroy all evil," the Reverend Cole shouted. "Root it out. Cut into . . ."

"Its 'eart," Willie breathed. "The way to kill a vampire is drive a stake through its 'eart. And a werewolf must be shot with a silver bullet fired by 'im who had only thought about sin."

"From what authority do you quote this information?" the vicar demanded.

"Me 'orror comics," Willie explained. "They give all the details, and if you go and see the *Vampire of 'Ackney Wick*, you'll see a 'oly father cut off the vampire's 'ead and put a sprig of garlic in its mouth."

"Where are these documents?" the clergyman enquired.

Mr. and Mrs. Mitcham were surprised and perhaps a little alarmed when their small son conducted the vicar through the kitchen and, after a perfunctory "It's all right, Mum, parson wants to see me 'orror comics," led the frozen-faced clergyman upstairs to the attic.

It was there that Mr. Cole's education was completed. Assisted by lurid pictures and sensational text, he learned of the conception, habits, hobbies, and disposal procedures of vampires, werewolves, and other breathing or non-breathing creatures that had attended the same school.

"Where do we get . . . ?" he began.

"A tent peg and Mum's coal 'ammer will do fine." Willie was quick to give expert advice.

"But a silver bullet." The vicar shook his head. "I cannot believe there is a great demand . . ."

"Two of Grandad's silver collar studs melted down with a soldering iron, and a cartridge from Dad's old .22 rifle. Mr. Cole, please say we can do it. I promise never to miss Sunday school again, if you'll say we can do it."

The Reverend John Cole did not consider the problem very long. A bite from a baby werevamp is a great decision maker.

"Yes," he nodded, "we have been chosen. Let us gird up our loins, gather the sinews of battle, and go forth to destroy the evil ones."

"Cool." Willie nodded vigorously. "All that blood. Can I cut 'er 'ead off?"

If anyone had been taking the air at two o'clock next morning, they might have seen an interesting sight. A large clergyman, armed with a crucifix and a coal hammer, was creeping across the churchyard, followed by a small boy with a tent peg in one hand and a light hunting rifle in the other.

They came to the cottage and Mr. Cole first turned the handle, then pushed the door open with his crucifix. The room beyond was warm and cosy; firelight painted a dancing pattern on the ceiling, brass lamp twinkled and glittered like a suspended star, and it was as though a brightly designed nest had been carved out of the surrounding darkness. John Cole strode into the room like a black marble angel of doom and, raising his crucifix, bellowed, "I have come to drive out the iniquity, burn out the sin. For, thus saith the Lord, cursed be you who hanker after darkness."

There was a sigh, a whimper—maybe a hissing whimper. Carola was crouched in one corner, her face whiter than a slab of snow in moonlight, her eyes dark pools of terror, her lips deep, deep red, as they had been brought to life by a million, blood-tinted kisses, and her hands were pale ghost-moths, beating out their life against the wall of intolerance. The vicar lowered his cross and the whimper grew up and became a cry of despair.

"Why?"

"Where is the foul babe that did bite my ankle?"

Carola's staring eyes never left the crucifix towering over her. "I took him . . . took him . . . to his grandmother."

"There is more of your kind? Are you legion? Has the devil's spawn been hatched?"

"We are on the verge of extinction."

The soul of the Reverend John Cole rejoiced when he saw the deep terror in the lovely eyes, and he tasted the fruits of true happiness when she shrieked. He bunched the front of her dress up between trembling fingers and jerked her first upright, then down across the table. She made a little hissing sound; an instinctive token of defiance, and for a moment the delicate ivory fangs were bared and nipped the clergyman's hand, but that was all. There was no savage fight for existence, no calling on the dark gods; just a token resistance, the shedding of a tiny dribble of blood, then complete surrender. She lay back across the table, her long, black hair brushing the floor, as though this were the inevitable conclusion from which she had been too long withheld. The vicar placed the tip of the tent peg over her heart, and taking the coal hammer from the overjoyed Willie, shouted the traditional words.

"Get thee to hell. Burn for ever and a day. May thy foul carcase be food for jackals, and thy blood drink for pariah dogs."

The first blow sent the tent peg in three or four inches, and the sound of a snapping rib grated on the clergyman's ear, so that for a moment he turned his head aside in revulsion. Then, as though alarmed lest his resolve weaken, he struck again, and the blood rose up in a scarlet fountain; a cascade of dancing rubies, each one reflecting the room with its starlike lamp, and the dripping, drenched face of a man with a raised coal hammer. The hammer, like the mailed hand of fate, fell again, and the ruby fountain sank low, then collapsed into a weakly gushing pool. Carola released her life in one long, drawn-out sigh, then became a black and white study in still life.

"You gotta cut 'er 'ead off," Willie screamed.

"Ain't no good, unless you cut 'er 'ead off and put a sprig of garlic in 'er mouth."

But Mr. Cole had, at least temporarily, had a surfeit of blood. It matted his hair, clogged his eyes, salted his mouth, drenched his clothes from neck to waist, and transformed his hands into scarlet claws.

Willie was fumbling in his jacket pocket.

"I've got me mum's bread knife here, somewhere. Should go through 'er neck a treat."

The reverend gentleman wiped a film of red from his eyes and then daintily shook his fingers.

"Truly is it said a little child shall lead them. Had I been more mindful of the Lord's business, I would have brought me a tenon saw."

He was not more than half way through his appointed task, when the door was flung back and George entered. He was on the turn. He was either about to "become," or return to "as was." His silhouette filled the moonlit doorway, and he became still; a black menace that was no less dangerous because it did not move. Then he glided across the room, round the table and the Reverend John Cole retreated before him.

George gathered up the mutilated remains of his beloved, then raised agony-filled eyes.

"We loved—she and I. Surely, that should have forgiven us much. Death we would have welcomed—for what is death, but a glorious reward for having to live. But this . . ."

He pointed to the jutting tent peg, the half-severed head, then looked up questioningly at the clergyman. Then the Reverend John Cole took up his cross and, holding it before him, he called out in a voice that had been made harsh by the dust of centuries.

"I am Alpha and Omega, saith the Lord, and into the pit which in before the beginning and after the end shall ye be cast. For you and your kind are a stench and an abomination, and whatever evil is done unto you shall be deemed good in my sight."

The face of George Hardcastle became like an effigy carved from rock. Then it seemed to shimmer, the lines dissolved and ran one into the other; the hairline advanced, while the eyes retreated into deep sockets, and the jaw and nose merged and slithered into a long, pointed snout. The werewolf dropped the mangled remains of its mate and advanced upon her killer.

"Satanus Avaunt."

The Reverend Cole thrust his crucifix forward as though it were a weapon of offence, only to have it wrenched from his grasp and broken by a quick jerk of hair-covered wrists. The werewolf tossed the pieces to one side, then with a howl leaped forward and buried his long fangs into the vicar's shoulder.

The two locked figures—one representing good, the other evil—swayed back and forth in the lamplight, and there was no room in either hate-fear-filled brain for the image of one small boy, armed with a rifle. The sharp little cracking sound could barely be heard above the grunting, snarling battle that was being raged near the hanging brass lamp, but the result was soon apparent. The werewolf shrieked, before twisting round and staring at the exuberant Willie, as though in dumb reproach. Then it crashed to the floor. When the clergyman had recovered to look down, he saw the dead face of George Hardcastle, and had he been a little to the right of the sanity frontier, there might well have been terrible doubts.

"Are you going to finish cutting off 'er head?" Willie enquired.

They put the Reverend John Cole in a quiet house surrounded by a beautiful garden. Willie Mitcham they placed in a home, as a juvenile court decided, in its wisdom, that he was in need of care and protection. The remains of George and Carola they buried in the churchyard and said some beautiful words over their graves.

It is a great pity they did not listen to Willie, who after all knew what he was talking about when it came to a certain subject.

One evening, when the moon was full, two gentlemen who were employed in the house surrounded by the beautiful garden, opened the door, behind which resided all that remained of the Reverend John Cole. They both entered the room and prepared to talk. They never did. One dropped dead from pure, cold terror, and the other achieved a state of insanity which had so far not been reached by one of his patients.

The Reverend John Cole had been bitten by a baby werevamp, nipped by a female vampire, and clawed and bitten by a full-blooded buck werewolf.

Only the good Lord above, and the bad one below, knew what he was.

# DRINK MY RED BLOOD

# Richard Matheson

Richard Burton Matheson (1926– ) was born in Allendale, New Jersey, then moved to Brooklyn, New York. He joined the army in World War II, serving in the infantry. He received a B.A. in journalism from the University of Missouri and then moved to California, where he became a prolific writer of short stories, novels, and screenplays.

His work has spawned a surprisingly large and diverse number of dramatic works for television and theatrically released films, including *Duel* (1971), Stephen Spielberg's first film, a made-for-TV movie about a sadistic trucker who terrorizes an innocent driver; *The Night Stalker* (1973), which won an Edgar Award from the Mystery Writers of America for Best Teleplay; and episodes of numerous series, including *Have Gun, Will Travel, The Alfred Hitchcock Hour, Night Gallery*, and some of *The Twilight Zone*'s most memorable programs.

Matheson works that were made into feature films include his own screenplay for *The Shrinking Man* (1956, filmed as *The Incredible Shrinking Man* in 1957), *Hell House* (1971, filmed as *The Legend of Hell House* in 1971), several screenplays for Roger Corman motion pictures loosely based on stories by Edgar Allan Poe, and, most famously, *I Am Legend* (1954, filmed as *The Last Man on Earth* in 1964, *The Omega Man* in 1971, and *I Am Legend* in 2007, and the basis for George A. Romero's *Night of the Living Dead* in 1968).

"Drink My Red Blood" was first published in the April 1951 issue of *Imagination*.

# Drink My Red Blood

## RICHARD MATHESON

The people on the block decided definitely that Jules was crazy when they heard about his composition. There had been suspicions for a long time. He made people shiver with his blank stare. His coarse, guttural tongue sounded unnatural in his frail body. The paleness of his skin upset many children. It seemed to hang loose around his flesh. He hated sunlight.

And, his ideas were a little out of place for the people who lived on the block.

Jules wanted to be a vampire.

People declared it common knowledge that he was born on a night when winds uprooted trees. They said he was born with three teeth. They said he'd used them to fasten himself on his mother's breast, drawing blood with the milk.

They said he used to cackle and bark in his crib after dark. They said he walked at two months and sat staring at the moon whenever it shone.

Those were things that people said.

His parents were always worried about him. An only child, they noticed his flaws quickly.

They thought he was blind until the doctor told them it was just a vacuous stare. He told them that

Jules, with his large head, might be a genius or an idot. It turned out he was an idiot.

He never spoke a word until he was five. Then one night, coming up to supper, he sat down at the table and said, "Death."

His parents were torn between delight and disgust. They finally settled for a place in-between the two feelings. They decided that Jules couldn't have realized what the word meant.

But Jules did.

From that night on, he built up such a large vocabulary that everyone who knew him was astonished. He not only acquired every word spoken to him, words from signs, magazines, books; he made up his own words.

Like, nighttouch. Or, killove. They were really several words that melted into each other. They said things Jules felt but couldn't explain with other words.

He used to sit on the porch while the other children played hopscotch, stickball, and other games. He sat there and stared at the sidewalk, and made up words.

Until he was twelve, Jules kept pretty much out of trouble. Of course, there was the time they found him undressing Olive Jones in an alley. And

544

another time he was discovered dissecting a kitten on his bed.

But there were many years in-between. Those scandals were forgotten.

In general, he went through childhood merely disgusting people.

He went to school, but never studied. He spent about two or three years in each grade. The teachers all knew him by his first name. In some subjects, like reading and writing, he was almost brilliant.

In others, he was hopeless.

One Saturday when he was twelve, Jules went to the movies. He saw *Dracula*.

When the show was over he walked, a throbbing nerve mass, through the little-girl and -boy ranks.

He went home and locked himself in the bathroom for two hours.

His parents pounded on the door and threatened but he wouldn't come out.

Finally, he unlocked the door and sat down at the supper table. He had a bandage on his thumb and a satisfied look on his face.

The morning after, he went to the library. It was Sunday. He sat on the steps all day, waiting for it to open. Finally he went home.

The next day he came back instead of going to school.

He found *Dracula* on the shelves. He couldn't borrow it because he wasn't a member and to be a member, he had to bring in one of his parents.

So he stuck the book down his pants and left the library and never brought it back.

He went to the park and sat down and read the book through. It was late evening before he finished.

He started at the beginning again, reading as he ran from streetlight to streetlight, all the way home.

He didn't hear a word of the scolding he got for missing lunch and supper. He ate, went in his room, and read the book to the finish. They asked him where he got the book. He said he found it.

As the days passed, Jules read the story over and over. He never went to school.

Late at night, when he had fallen into an exhausted slumber, his mother used to take the book into the living room and show it to her husband.

One night they noticed that Jules had underlined certain sentences with dark, shaky pencil lines.

Like: "The lips were crimson with fresh blood and the stream had trickled over her chin and stained the purity of her lawn death-robe."

Or: "When the blood began to spurt out, he took my hands in one of his, holding them tight and, with the other seized my neck and pressed my mouth to the wound. . . ."

When his mother saw this, she threw the book down the garbage chute.

The next morning when Jules found the book missing he screamed and twisted his mother's arm until she told him where the book was.

Then he ran down to the basement and dug in the piles of garbage until he found the book.

Coffee grounds and egg yolk on his hands and wrists, he went to the park and read it again.

For a month, he read the book avidly. Then he knew it so well he threw it away and just thought about it.

Absence notes were coming from school. His mother yelled. Jules decided to go back for a while.

He wanted to write a composition.

One day he wrote it in class. When everyone was finished writing, the teacher asked if anyone wanted to read their composition to the class.

Jules raised his hand.

The teacher was surprised. But she felt charity. She wanted to encourage him. She drew in her tiny jab of a chin and smiled.

"Alright," she said, "pay attention, children. Jules is going to read us his composition."

Jules stood up. He was excited. The paper shook in his hands.

"My Ambition, by . . ."

"Come to the front of the class, Jules, dear."

Jules went to the front of the class. The teacher smiled lovingly. Jules started again.

"My Ambition, by Jules Dracula."

The smile sagged.

"When I grow up, I want to be a vampire."

The teacher's smiling lips jerked down and out. Her eyes popped wide.

"I want to live forever and get even with everybody and make all the girls vampires. I want to smell of death."

"Jules!"

"I want to have a foul breath that stinks of dead earth crypts and sweet coffins."

The teacher shuddered. Her hands twitched on her green blotter. She couldn't believe her ears. She looked at the children. They were gaping. Some of them were giggling. But not the girls.

"I want to be all cold and have rotten flesh with stolen blood in the veins."

"That will . . . hrrumph!"

The teacher cleared her throat mightily.

"That will be all, Jules," she said.

Jules talked louder and desperately.

"I want to sink my terrible white teeth in my victims' necks. I want them to . . ."

"Jules! Go to your seat this instant!"

"I want them to slide like razors in the flesh and into the veins," read Jules ferociously.

The teacher jolted to her feet. Children were shivering. None of them were giggling.

"Then I want to draw my teeth out and let the blood flow easy in my mouth and run hot in my throat and . . ."

The teacher grabbed his arm. Jules tore away and ran to a corner. Barricaded behind a stool, he yelled:

"And drip off my tongue and run out of my lips down my victims' throats! I want to drink girls' blood!"

The teacher lunged for him. She dragged him out of the corner. He clawed at her and screamed all the way to the door and the principal's office.

"That is my ambition! That is my ambition! That is my ambition!"

It was grim.

Jules was locked in his room. The teacher and the principal sat with Jules' parents. They were talking in sepulchral voices.

They were recounting the scene.

All along the block, parents were discussing it. Most of them didn't believe it at first. They thought their children made it up.

Then they thought what horrible children they'd raised if the children could make up such things.

So they believed it.

After that, everyone watched Jules like a hawk. People avoided his touch and look. Parents pulled their children off the street when he approached. Everyone whispered tales of him.

There were more absence notes.

Jules told his mother he wasn't going to school any more. Nothing would change his mind. He never went again.

When an attendance officer came to the apartment, Jules would run over the roofs until he was far away from there.

A year wasted by.

Jules wandered the streets searching for something; he didn't know what. He looked in alleys. He looked in garbage cans. He looked in lots. He looked on the east side and the west side and in the middle.

He couldn't find what he wanted.

He rarely slept. He never spoke. He stared down all the time. He forgot his special words.

Then.

One day in the park, Jules strolled through the zoo.

An electric shock passed through him when he saw the vampire bat.

His eyes grew wide and his discolored teeth shone dully in a wide smile.

From that day on, Jules went daily to the zoo and looked at the bat. He spoke to it and called it the Count. He felt in his heart it was really a man who had changed.

A rebirth of culture struck him.

He stole another book from the library. It told all about wildlife.

He found the page on the vampire bat. He tore it out and threw the book away.

He learned the section by heart.

He knew how the bat made its wound. How it lapped up the blood like a kitten drinking cream.

How it walked on folded wing stalks and hind legs like a black furry spider. Why it took no nourishment but blood.

Month after month, Jules stared at the bat and talked to it. It became the one comfort in his life. The one symbol of dreams come true.

One day Jules noticed that the bottom of the wire covering the cage had become loose.

He looked around, his black eyes shifting. He didn't see anyone looking. It was a cloudy day. Not many people were there.

Jules tugged at the wire.

It moved a little.

Then he saw a man come out of the monkey house. So he pulled back his hand and strolled away, whistling a song he had just made up.

Late at night, when he was supposed to be asleep, he would walk barefoot past his parents' room. He would hear his father and mother snoring. He would hurry out, put on his shoes, and run to the zoo.

Every time the watchman was not around, Jules would tug at the wiring.

He kept on pulling it loose.

When he had finished and had to run home, he pushed the wire in again. Then no one could tell.

All day Jules would stand in front of the cage and look at the Count and chuckle and tell him he'd soon be free again.

He told the Count all the things he knew. He told the Count he was going to practice climbing down walls headfirst.

He told the Count not to worry. He'd soon be out. Then, together, they could go all around and drink girls' blood. One night Jules pulled the wire out and crawled under it into the cage.

It was very dark.

He crept on his knees to the little wooden house. He listened to see if he could hear the Count squeaking.

He stuck his arm in the black doorway. He kept whispering.

He jumped when he felt a needle jab in his finger.

With a look of great pleasure on his thin face, Jules drew the fluttering hairy bat to him.

He climbed down from the cage with it and ran out of the zoo; out of the park. He ran down the silent streets.

It was getting late in the morning. Light touched the dark skies with gray. He couldn't go home. He had to have a place.

He went down an alley and climbed over a fence. He held tight to the bat. It lapped at the dribble of blood from his finger.

He went across a yard into a little deserted shack.

It was dark inside and damp. It was full of rubble and tin cans and soggy cardboard and excrement.

Jules made sure there was no way the bat could escape. Then he pulled the door tight and put a stick through the metal loop.

He felt his heart beating hard and his limbs trembling.

He let go of the bat. It flew to a dark corner and hung on the wood.

Jules feverishly tore off his shirt. His lips shook. He smiled a crazy smile.

He reached down into his pants' pocket and took out a little pocketknife he had stolen from his mother.

He opened it and ran a finger over the blade. It sliced through the flesh.

With shaking fingers he jabbed at his throat. He hacked. The blood ran through his fingers.

"Count! Count!" he cried in frenzied joy. "Drink my red blood! Drink me! Drink me!"

He stumbled over the tin cans and slipped and felt for the bat. It sprang from the wood and soared across the shack and fastened itself on the outer side.

Tears ran down Jules' cheeks.

He gritted his teeth. The blood ran across his shoulders and across his thin, hairless chest.

His body shook in fever. He staggered back toward the other side. He tripped and felt his side torn open on the sharp edge of a tin can.

His hands went out. They clutched the bat. He placed it against his throat. He sank on his back on the cool wet earth. He sighed.

He started to moan and clutch at his chest. His

stomach heaved. The black bat on his neck silently lapped his blood.

Jules felt his life seeping away.

He thought of all the years past. The waiting. His parents. School. Dracula. Dreams. For this. This sudden glory.

Jules' eyes flickered open.

The side of the reeking shack swam around him.

It was hard to breathe. He opened his mouth to gasp in the air. He sucked it in. It was foul. It made him cough. His skinny body lurched on the cold ground.

Mists crept away in his brain.

One by one like drawn veils.

Suddenly his mind was filled with terrible clarity.

He knew he was lying half-naked on garbage and letting a flying bat drink his blood.

With a strangled cry, he reached up and tore away the furry throbbing bat. He flung it away from him. It came back, fanning his face with its vibrating wings.

Jules staggered to his feet.

He felt for the door. He could hardly see. He tried to stop his throat from bleeding so.

He managed to get the door open.

Then, lurching into the dark yard, he fell on his face in the long grass blades.

He tried to call out for help.

But no sounds, save a bubbling mockery of words, came from his lips.

He heard the fluttering wings.

Then, suddenly, they were gone.

Strong fingers lifted him gently. Through dying eyes, Jules saw a tall, dark, man whose eyes shone like rubies.

"My son," the man said.

## DAYBLOOD

# Roger Zelazny

Roger Joseph Zelazny (1937–95) was born in Euclid, Ohio, and received his B.A. in English from Western Reserve University and his M.A. in Elizabethan and Jacobean drama from Columbia University. While working days for the Social Security Administration in Cleveland and Baltimore, he spent his nights writing short stories, progressing to novelettes, novellas, and, eventually, novels. In 1969 he resigned in order to become a full-time writer.

His first sale was the short fantasy story "Mr. Fuller's Revolt," published in *Literary Cavalcade* in 1954. His first novel was *This Immortal* (also titled . . . *and Call Me Conrad*, 1966), which was the cowinner of the Hugo Award with Frank Herbert's *Dune*, followed by *The Dream Master* (1966), *Lord of Light* (1967), another Hugo winner, *Creatures of Light and Darkness* (1969), *Isle of the Dead* (1969), and *Damnation Alley* (1969), which was made with a wildly different plot into a 1977 film of the same title, starring George Peppard, Jan-Michael Vincent, and Paul Winfield. It was planned as a blockbuster but was overshadowed by the second science-fiction film released by 20th Century Fox in the same year, *Star Wars*. Zelazny was one of the most significant members of the New Wave movement in the science fiction of the 1960s, which moved away from hardware into psychological areas. In all, he won six Hugo Awards from the World Science Fiction Society, as well as two Nebula Awards from the Science Fiction and Fantasy Writers of America.

"Dayblood" was originally published in the May/June 1985 issue of *Rod Serling's Twilight Zone Magazine*.

# Dayblood

## ROGER ZELAZNY

I crouched in the corner of the collapsed shed behind the ruined church. The dampness soaked through the knees of my jeans, but I knew that my wait was just about ended. Picturesquely, a few tendrils of mist rose from the soaked ground, to be stirred feebly by predawn breezes. How Hollywood of the weather. . . .

I cast my gaze around the lightening sky, guessing correctly as to the direction of arrival. Within a minute I saw them flapping their way back—a big, dark one and a smaller, pale one. Predictably, they entered the church through the opening where a section of the roof had years before fallen in. I suppressed a yawn as I checked my watch. Fifteen minutes from now they should be settled and dozing as the sun spills morning all over the east. Possibly a little sooner, but give them a bit of leeway. No hurry yet.

I stretched and cracked my knuckles. I'd rather be home in bed. Nights are for sleeping, not for playing nursemaid to a couple of stupid vampires.

Yes, Virginia, there really are vampires. Nothing to get excited about, though. Odds are you'll never meet one. There just aren't that many around. In fact, they're damn near an endangered species—which is entirely understandable, considering the general level of intelligence I've encountered among them.

Take this guy Brodsky as an example. He lives—pardon me resides—near a town containing several thousand people. He could have visited a different person each night without even repeating himself, leaving his caterers (I understand that's their in-term these days) with little more than a slight sore throat, a touch of temporary anaemia, and a couple of soon-to-be-forgotten scratches on the neck.

But no. He took a fancy to a local beauty—one Elaine Wilson, ex-majorette. Kept going back for more. Pretty soon she entered the customary coma and underwent the *nosferatu* transformation. All right, I know I said there aren't that many of them around—and personally I do feel that the world could use a few more vampires. But it's not a population-pressure thing with Brodsky, just stupidity and greed. No real finesse, no planning. While I applaud the creation of another member of the Un-Dead, I am sufficiently appalled by the carelessness of his methods to consider serious action. He left a trail that just about anybody could trace here; he also managed to display so many of the traditional signs and leave such a multitude of clues that even in these modern times a reasonable person could become convinced of what was going on.

Poor old Brodsky—still living in the Middle Ages and behaving just as he did in the days of their population boom. It apparently never occurred to him to consider the mathematics of that sort of thing. He drains a few people he becomes particularly attracted to and they become *nosferatu*. If they feel and behave the same way they go out and recruit a few more of their caterers. And so on. It's like a chain letter. After a time, everyone would be *nosferatu* and there wouldn't be any caterers left. Then what? Fortunately, nature has ways of dealing with population explosions, even at this level. Still, a sudden rash of recruits in this mass-media age could really mess up the underground ecosystem.

So much for philosophy. Time to get inside and beat the crowd.

I picked up my plastic bag and worked my way out of the shed, cursing softly when I bumped against a post and brought a shower down over me. I made my way through the field then, and up to the side door of the old building. It was secured by a rusty padlock which I snapped and threw into the distant cemetery.

Inside, I perched myself on the sagging railing of the choir section and opened my bag. I withdrew my sketchbook and the pencil I'd brought along. Light leaked in through the broken window to the rear. What it fell upon was mostly trash. Not a particularly inspiring scene. Whatever . . . I began sketching it. It's always good to have a hobby that can serve as an excuse for odd actions, as an ice-breaker. . . .

Ten minutes, I guessed. At most.

Six minutes later, I heard their voices. They weren't particularly noisy, but I have exceptionally acute hearing. There were three of them, as I'd guessed there would be.

They entered through the side door also, slinking, jumpy—looking all around and seeing nothing. At first they didn't even notice me creating art where childish voices had filled Sunday mornings with off-key praise in years gone by.

There was old Dr. Morgan, several wooden stakes protruding from his black bag (I'll bet there was a hammer in there, too—I guess the Hippocratic Oath doesn't extend to the Un-Dead—*primum, non nocere*, etc.); and Father O'Brien, clutching his Bible like a shield, crucifix in his other hand; and young Ben Kelman (Elaine's fiancé), with a shovel over his shoulder and a bag from which I suspected the sudden odor of garlic to have its origin.

I cleared my throat and all three of them stopped, turned, bumped into each other.

"Hi, Doc," I said. "Hi, Father. Ben . . ."

"Wayne!" Doc said. "What are you doing here?"

"Sketching," I said. "I'm into old buildings these days."

"The hell you are!" Ben said. "Excuse me, Father. . . . You're just after a story for your damned newspaper!"

I shook my head.

"Really I'm not."

"Well, Gus'd never let you print anything about this and you know it."

"Honest," I said. "I'm not here for a story. But I know why you're here, and you're right—even if I wrote it up it would never appear. You really believe in vampires?"

Doc fixed me with a steady gaze.

"Not until recently," he said. "But son, if you'd seen what we've seen, you'd believe."

I nodded my head and closed my sketchpad.

"All right," I replied, "I'll tell you. I'm here because I'm curious. I wanted to see it for myself, but I don't want to go down there alone. Take me with you."

They exchanged glances.

"I don't know . . ." Ben said.

"It won't be anything for the squeamish," Doc told me.

Father O'Brien just nodded.

"I don't know about having anyone else in on this," Ben added.

"How many more know about it?" I asked.

"It's just us, really," Ben explained. "We're the only ones who actually saw him in action."

"A good newspaperman knows when to keep

his mouth shut," I said, "but he's also a very curious creature. Let me come along."

Ben shrugged and Doc nodded. After a moment Father O'Brien nodded too.

I replaced my pad and pencil in the bag and got down from the railing.

I followed them across the church, out into a short hallway, and up into an open, sagging door. Doc flicked on a flashlight and played it upon a rickety flight of stairs leading down into darkness. Slowly then, he began to descend. Father O'Brien followed him. The stairs groaned and seemed to move. Ben and I waited till they had reached the bottom. Then Ben stuffed his bag of pungent groceries inside his jacket and withdrew a flashlight from his pocket. He turned it on and stepped down. I was right behind him.

I halted when we reached the foot of the stair. In the beams from their lights I beheld the two caskets set up on sawhorses, a thing on the wall above the larger one.

"Father, what is that?" I pointed.

Someone obligingly played a beam of light upon it.

"It looks like a sprig of mistletoe tied to the figure of a little stone deer," he said.

"Probably has something to do with black magic," I offered. He crossed himself, went over to it, and removed it.

"Probably so," he said, crushing the mistletoe and throwing it across the room, shattering the figure on the floor and kicking the pieces away.

I smiled, I moved forward then.

"Let's get things open and have a look," Doc said.

I lent them a hand.

When the caskets were open I ignored the comments about paleness, preservation, and bloody mouths. Brodsky looked the same as he always did—dark hair, heavy dark eyebrows, sagging jowls, a bit of a paunch. The girl was lovely, though. Taller than I'd thought, however, with a very faint pulsation at the throat and an almost bluish cast to her skin.

Father O'Brien opened his Bible and began reading, holding the flashlight above it with a trembling hand. Doc placed his bag upon the floor and fumbled around inside it.

Ben turned away, tears in his eyes. I reached out then and broke his neck quietly while the others were occupied. I lowered him to the floor and stepped up beside Doc.

"What—?" he began, and that was his last word.

Father O'Brien stopped reading. He stared at me across his Bible.

"You work for *them?*" he said hoarsely, darting a glance at the caskets.

"Hardly," I said, "but I need them. They're my life's blood."

"I don't understand. . . ."

"Everything is prey to something else, and we do what we must. That's ecology. Sorry, Father."

I used Ben's shovel to bury the three of them beneath an earthen section of the floor toward the rear—garlic, stakes, and all. Then I closed the caskets and carried them up the stairs.

I checked around as I hiked across a field and back up the road after the pickup truck. It was still relatively early and there was no one around.

I loaded them both in back and covered them with a tarp. It was a thirty-mile drive to another ruined church I knew of.

Later, when I had installed them safely in their new quarters, I penned a note and placed it in Brodsky's hand:

*Dear B,*
  *Let this be a lesson to you. You are going to have to stop acting like Bela Lugosi. You lack his class. You are lucky to be waking up at all this night. In the future be more circumspect in your activities or I may retire you myself. After all, I'm not here to serve you.*
                        YOURS TRULY,
                              W
  *P.S. The mistletoe and the statue of Cernunnos don't work anymore. Why did you suddenly get superstitious?*

I glanced at my watch as I left the place. It was eleven fifteen. I stopped at a 7-11 a little later and used their outside phone.

"Hi Kiela," I said when I heard her voice. "It's me."

"Werdeth," she said. "It's been a while."

"I know. I've been busy."

"With what?"

"Do you know where the old Church of the Apostles out off Route 6 is?"

"Of course. It's on my backup list, too."

"Meet me there at twelve thirty and I'll tell you about it over lunch."

# REPLACEMENTS

# Lisa Tuttle

Lisa Tuttle (1952– ) was born in Houston, Texas, and received her B.A. in English literature from Syracuse University. She has lived in the United Kingdom since 1980, currently living in Scotland with her husband. When still quite young, she joined the Turkey City Writer's Workshop in Austin, Texas, and was the cowinner of the John W. Campbell Award for Best New Writer in 1974.

Her first novel, *Windhaven* (1981), was written with George R. R. Martin after they collaborated on a short story, "The Storms of Windhaven," which won a Hugo Award in 1975; she wrote a young-adult fantasy novel illustrated by Una Woodruff *(Catwitch,* 1983) and coauthored a novel with Michael Johnson (*Angela's Rainbow,* 1983). She has written ten novels on her own, including *Familiar Spirit* (1983), *Gabriel* (1987), *Lost Futures* (1992), and *The Silver Bough* (2006).

In 1981, as the guest of honor at Microcon, she was awarded the Nebula Award for Best Short Story but turned it down. In 1989 she won the BSFA Award for short fiction, which she accepted. Beyond the fantasy and horror genres, she wrote *Encyclopedia of Feminism* (1986).

"Replacements" was originally published in her short-story collection *Memories of the Body: Tales of Desire and Transformation* (London: Grafton/Collins, 1992). It served very loosely as the basis for an episode of the television series *The Hunger* in 1999.

# Replacements

## LISA TUTTLE

**W**alking through gray north London to the tube station, feeling guilty that he hadn't let Jenny drive him to work and yet relieved to have escaped another pointless argument, Stuart Holder glanced down at a pavement covered in a leaf-fall of fast-food cartons and white paper bags and saw, amid the dog turds, beer cans, and dead cigarettes, something horrible.

It was about the size of a cat, naked-looking, with leathery, hairless skin and thin, spiky limbs that seemed too frail to support the bulbous, ill-proportioned body. The face, with tiny bright eyes and a wet slit of a mouth, was like an evil monkey's. It saw him and moved in a crippled, spasmodic way. Reaching up, it made a clotted, strangled noise. The sound touched a nerve, like metal between the teeth, and the sight of it, mewling and choking and scrabbling, scaly claws flexing and wriggling, made him feel sick and terrified. He had no phobias, he found insects fascinating, not frightening, and regularly removed, unharmed, the spiders, wasps, and mayflies which made Jenny squeal or shudder helplessly.

But this was different. This wasn't some rare species of wingless bat escaped from a zoo, it wasn't something he would find pictured in any reference book. It was something that should not exist, a mistake, something alien. It did not belong in his world.

A little snarl escaped him and he took a step forward and brought his foot down hard.

The small, shrill scream lanced through him as he crushed it beneath his shoe and ground it into the road.

Afterward, as he scraped the sole of his shoe against the curb to clean it, nausea overwhelmed him. He leaned over and vomited helplessly into a red-and-white-striped box of chicken bones and crumpled paper.

He straightened up, shaking, and wiped his mouth again and again with his pocket handkerchief. He wondered if anyone had seen, and had a furtive look around. Cars passed at a steady crawl. Across the road a cluster of schoolgirls dawdled near a man smoking in front of a newsagent's, but on this side of the road the fried chicken franchise and bathroom suppliers had yet to open for the day and the nearest pedestrians were more than a hundred yards away.

Until that moment, Stuart had never killed

anything in his life. Mosquitoes and flies of course, other insects probably, a nest of hornets once, that was all. He had never liked the idea of hunting, never lived in the country. He remembered his father putting out poisoned bait for rats, and he remembered shying bricks at those same vermin on a bit of waste ground where he had played as a boy. But rats weren't like other animals; they elicited no sympathy. Some things had to be killed if they would not be driven away.

He made himself look to make sure the thing was not still alive. Nothing should be left to suffer. But his heel had crushed the thing's face out of recognition, and it was unmistakably dead. He felt a cool tide of relief and satisfaction, followed at once, as he walked away, by a nagging uncertainty, the imminence of guilt. Was he right to have killed it, to have acted on violent, irrational impulse? He didn't even know what it was. It might have been somebody's pet.

He went hot and cold with shame and self-disgust. At the corner he stopped with five or six others waiting to cross the road and because he didn't want to look at them he looked down.

And there it was, alive again.

He stifled a scream. No, of course it was not the same one, but another. His leg twitched; he felt frantic with the desire to kill it, and the terror of his desire. The thin wet mouth was moving as if it wanted to speak.

As the crossing-signal began its nagging blare he tore his eyes away from the creature squirming at his feet. Everyone else had started to cross the street, their eyes, like their thoughts, directed ahead. All except one. A woman in a smart business suit was standing still on the pavement, looking down, a sick fascination on her face. As he looked at her looking at it, the idea crossed his mind that he should kill it for her, as a chivalric, protective act. But she wouldn't see it that way. She would be repulsed by his violence. He didn't want her to think he was a monster. He didn't want to be the monster who had exulted in the crunch of fragile bones, the flesh and viscera merging pulpily beneath his shoe.

He forced himself to look away, to cross the road, to spare the alien life. But he wondered, as he did so, if he had been right to spare it.

Stuart Holder worked as an editor for a publishing company with offices an easy walk from St. Paul's. Jenny had worked there, too, as a secretary, when they met five years ago. Now, though, she had quite a senior position with another publishing house, south of the river, and recently they had given her a car. He had been supportive of her ambitions, supportive of her learning to drive, and proud of her on all fronts when she succeeded, yet he was aware, although he never spoke of it, that something about her success made him uneasy. One small, niggling, insecure part of himself was afraid that one day she would realize she didn't need him anymore. That was why he picked at her, and second-guessed her decisions when she was behind the wheel and he was in the passenger seat. He recognized this as he walked briskly through more crowded streets toward his office, and he told himself he would do better. He would have to. If anything drove them apart it was more likely to be his behavior than her career. He wished he had accepted her offer of a ride today. Better any amount of petty irritation between husband and wife than to be haunted by the memory of that tiny face, distorted in the death he had inflicted. Entering the building, he surreptitiously scraped the sole of his shoe against the carpet.

Upstairs two editors and one of the publicity girls were in a huddle around his secretary's desk; they turned on him the guilty-defensive faces of women who have been discussing secrets men aren't supposed to know.

He felt his own defensiveness rising to meet theirs as he smiled. "Can I get any of you chaps a cup of coffee?"

"I'm sorry, Stuart, did you want . . . ?" As the others faded away, his secretary removed a stiff white paper bag with the NEXT logo, printed on it from her desktop.

"Joke, Frankie, joke." He always got his own coffee because he liked the excuse to wander, and he was always having to reassure her that she was not failing in her secretarial duties. He wondered if Next sold sexy underwear, decided it would be unkind to tease her further.

He felt a strong urge to call Jenny and tell her what had happened, although he knew he wouldn't be able to explain, especially not over the phone. Just hearing her voice, the sound of sanity, would be a comfort, but he restrained himself until just after noon, when he made the call he made every day.

Her secretary told him she was in a meeting. "Tell her Stuart rang," he said, knowing she would call him back as always.

But that day she didn't. Finally, at five minutes to five, Stuart rang his wife's office and was told she had left for the day.

It was unthinkable for Jenny to leave work early, as unthinkable as for her not to return his call. He wondered if she was ill. Although he usually stayed in the office until well after six, now he shoved a manuscript in his briefcase and went out to brave the rush hour.

He wondered if she was mad at him. But Jenny didn't sulk. If she was angry she said so. They didn't lie or play those sorts of games with each other, pretending not to be in, "forgetting" to return calls.

As he emerged from his local underground station Stuart felt apprehensive. His eyes scanned the pavement and the gutters, and once or twice the flutter of paper made him jump, but of the creatures he had seen that morning there were no signs. The body of the one he had killed was gone, perhaps eaten by a passing dog, perhaps returned to whatever strange dimension had spawned it. He noticed, before he turned off the high street, that other pedestrians were also taking a keener than usual interest in the pavement and the edge of the road, and that made him feel vindicated somehow.

London traffic being what it was, he was home before Jenny. While he waited for the sound of her key in the lock he made himself a cup of tea, cursed, poured it down the sink, and had a stiff whiskey instead. He had just finished it and was feeling much better when he heard the street door open.

"Oh!" The look on her face reminded him unpleasantly of those women in the office this morning, making him feel like an intruder in his own place. Now Jenny smiled, but it was too late. "I didn't expect you to be here so early."

"Nor me. I tried to call you, but they said you'd left already. I wondered if you were feeling all right."

"I'm fine!"

"You look fine." The familiar sight of her melted away his irritation. He loved the way she looked: her slender, boyish figure, her close-cropped, curly hair, her pale complexion and bright blue eyes.

Her cheeks now had a slight hectic flush. She caught her bottom lip between her teeth and gave him an assessing look before coming straight out with it. "How would you feel about keeping a pet?"

Stuart felt a horrible conviction that she was not talking about a dog or a cat. He wondered if it was the whiskey on an empty stomach which made him feel dizzy.

"It was under my car. If I hadn't happened to notice something moving down there I could have run over it." She lifted her shoulders in a delicate shudder.

"Oh, God, Jenny, you haven't brought it home!"

She looked indignant. "Well, of course I did! I couldn't just leave it in the street—somebody else might have run it over."

Or stepped on it, he thought, realizing now that he could never tell Jenny what he had done. That made him feel even worse, but maybe he was wrong. Maybe it was just a cat she'd rescued. "What is it?"

She gave a strange, excited laugh. "I don't know. Something very rare, I think. Here, look." She slipped the large, woven bag off her shoulder, opening it, holding it out to him. "Look. Isn't it the sweetest thing?"

How could two people who were so close, so

alike in so many ways, see something so differently? He only wanted to kill it, even now, while she had obviously fallen in love. He kept his face carefully neutral although he couldn't help flinching from her description. *"Sweet?"*

It gave him a pang to see how she pulled back, holding the bag protectively close as she said, "Well, I know it's not pretty, but so what? I thought it was horrible, too, at first sight. . . ." Her face clouded, as if she found her first impression difficult to remember, or to credit, and her voice faltered a little. "But then, then I realized how *helpless* it was. It needed me. It can't help how it looks. Anyway, doesn't it kind of remind you of the Psammead?"

"The what?"

"Psammead. You know, *The Five Children and It?*"

He recognized the title but her passion for old-fashioned children's books was something he didn't share. He shook his head impatiently. "That thing didn't come out of a book, Jen. You found it in the street and you don't know what it is or where it came from. It could be dangerous, it could be diseased."

"Dangerous," she said in a withering tone.

"You don't know."

"I've been with him all day and he hasn't hurt me, or anybody else at the office, he's perfectly happy being held, and he likes being scratched behind the ears."

He did not miss the pronoun shift. "It might have rabies."

"Don't be silly."

"Don't *you* be silly; it's not exactly native, is it? It might be carrying all sorts of foul parasites from South America or Africa or wherever."

"Now you're being racist. I'm not going to listen to you. *And* you've been drinking." She flounced out of the room.

If he'd been holding his glass still he might have thrown it. He closed his eyes and concentrated on breathing in and out slowly. This was worse than any argument they'd ever had, the only crucial disagreement of their marriage. Jenny had stronger views about many things than he did, so her wishes usually prevailed. He didn't mind that. But this was different. He wasn't having that creature in his home. He had to make her agree.

Necessity cooled his blood. He had his temper under control when his wife returned. "I'm sorry," he said, although she was the one who should have apologized. Still looking prickly, she shrugged and would not meet his eyes. "Want to go out to dinner tonight?"

She shook her head. "I'd rather not. I've got some work to do."

"Can I get you something to drink? I'm only one whiskey ahead of you, honest."

Her shoulders relaxed. "I'm sorry. Low blow. Yeah, pour me one. And one for yourself." She sat down on the couch, her bag by her feet. Leaning over, reaching inside, she cooed, "Who's my little sweetheart, then?"

Normally he would have taken a seat beside her. Now, though, he eyed the pale, misshapen bundle on her lap and, after handing her a glass, retreated across the room. "Don't get mad, but isn't having a pet one of those things we discuss and agree on beforehand?"

He saw the tension come back into her shoulders, but she went on stroking the thing, keeping herself calm. "Normally, yes. But this is special. I didn't plan it. It happened, and now I've got a responsibility to him. Or her." She giggled. "We don't even know what sex you are, do we, my precious?"

He said carefully, "I can see that you had to do something when you found it, but keeping it might not be the best thing."

"I'm not going to put it out in the street."

"No, no, but . . . don't you think it would make sense to let a professional have a look at it? Take it to a vet, get it checked out . . . maybe it needs shots or something."

She gave him a withering look and for a moment he faltered, but then he rallied. "Come on, Jenny, be reasonable! You can't just drag some strange animal in off the street and keep it, just like that. You don't even know what it eats."

"I gave it some fruit at lunch. It ate that. Well, it sucked out the juice. I don't think it can chew."

"But you don't know, do you? Maybe the fruit juice was just an aperitif, maybe it needs half its weight in live insects every day, or a couple of small, live mammals. Do you really think you could cope with feeding it mice or rabbits fresh from the pet shop every week?"

"Oh, Stuart."

"Well? Will you just take it to a vet? Make sure it's healthy? Will you do that much?"

"And then I can keep it? If the vet says there's nothing wrong with it, and it doesn't need to eat anything too impossible?"

"Then we can talk about it. Hey, don't pout at me; I'm not your father, I'm not telling you what to do. We're partners, and partners don't make unilateral decisions about things that affect them both; partners discuss things and reach compromises and. . ."

"There can't be any compromise about this."

He felt as if she'd doused him with ice water. "What?"

"Either I win and I keep him or you win and I give him up. Where's the compromise?"

This was why wars were fought, thought Stuart, but he didn't say it. He was the picture of sweet reason, explaining as if he meant it, "The compromise is that we each try to see the other person's point. You get the animal checked out, make sure it's healthy and I, I'll keep an open mind about having a pet, and see if I might start liking . . . him. Does he have a name yet?"

Her eyes flickered. "No . . . we can choose one later, together. If we keep him."

He still felt cold and, although he could think of no reason for it, he was certain she was lying to him.

In bed that night as he groped for sleep Stuart kept seeing the tiny, hideous face of the thing screaming as his foot came down on it. That moment of blind, killing rage was not like him. He couldn't deny he had done it, or how he had felt, but now, as Jenny slept innocently beside him, as

the creature she had rescued, a twin to his victim, crouched alive in the bathroom, he tried to remember it differently.

In fantasy, he stopped his foot, he controlled his rage, and, staring at the memory of the alien animal, he struggled to see past his anger and his fear, to see through those fiercer masculine emotions and find his way to Jenny's feminine pity. Maybe his intuition had been wrong and hers was right. Maybe, if he had waited a little longer, instead of lashing out, he would have seen how unnecessary his fear was.

Poor little thing, poor little thing. It's helpless, it needs me, it's harmless so I won't harm it.

Slowly, in imagination, he worked toward that feeling, *her* feeling, and then, suddenly, he was there, through the anger, through the fear, through the hate to . . . not love, he couldn't say that, but compassion. Glowing and warm, compassion filled his heart and flooded his veins, melting the ice there and washing him out into the sea of sleep, and dreams where Jenny smiled and loved him and there was no space between them for misunderstanding.

He woke in the middle of the night with a desperate urge to pee. He was out of bed in the dark hallway when he remembered what was waiting in the bathroom. He couldn't go back to bed with the need unsatisfied, but he stood outside the bathroom door, hand hovering over the light switch on this side, afraid to turn it on, open the door, go in.

It wasn't, he realized, that he was afraid of a creature no bigger than a football and less likely to hurt him; rather, he was afraid that he might hurt it. It was a stronger variant of that reckless vertigo he had felt sometimes in high places, the fear, not of falling, but of throwing oneself off, of losing control and giving in to self-destructive urges. He didn't *want* to kill the thing—had his own feelings not undergone a sea change, Jenny's love for it would have been enough to stop him—but something, some dark urge stronger than himself, might make him.

Finally he went down to the end of the hall and outside to the weedy, muddy little area which passed for the communal front garden and in which the rubbish bins, of necessity, were kept, and, shivering in his thin cotton pajamas in the damp, chilly air, he watered the sickly forsythia, or whatever it was, that Jenny had planted so optimistically last winter.

When he went back inside, more uncomfortable than when he had gone out, he saw the light was on in the bathroom, and as he approached the half-open door, he heard Jenny's voice, low and soothing. "There, there. Nobody's going to hurt you, I promise. You're safe here. Go to sleep now. Go to sleep."

He went past without pausing, knowing he would be viewed as an intruder, and got back into bed. He fell asleep, lulled by the meaningless murmur of her voice, still waiting for her to join him.

S tuart was not used to doubting Jenny, but when she told him she had visited a veterinarian who had given her new pet a clean bill of health, he did not believe her.

In a neutral tone he asked, "Did he say what kind of animal it was?"

"He didn't know."

"He didn't know what it was, but he was sure it was perfectly healthy."

"God, Stuart, what do you want? It's obvious to everybody but you that my little friend is healthy and happy. What do you want, a birth certificate?"

He looked at her "friend," held close against her side, looking squashed and miserable. "What do you mean, 'everybody'?"

She shrugged. "Everybody at work. They're all jealous as anything." She planted a kiss on the thing's pointy head. Then she looked at him, and he realized that she had not kissed him, as she usually did, when he came in. She'd been clutching that thing the whole time. "I'm going to keep him," she said quietly. "If you don't like it, then . . ." Her pause seemed to pile up in solid, transparent blocks between them. "Then, I'm sorry, but that's how it is."

So much for an equal relationship, he thought.

So much for sharing. Mortally wounded, he decided to pretend it hadn't happened.

"Want to go out for Indian tonight?"

She shook her head, turning away. "I want to stay in. There's something on telly. You go on. You could bring me something back, if you wouldn't mind. A spinach bahjee and a couple of nans would do me."

"And what about . . . something for your little friend?"

She smiled a private smile. "He's all right. I've fed him already."

Then she raised her eyes to his and acknowledged his effort. "Thanks."

He went out and got take-away for them both, and stopped at the off-license for the Mexican beer Jenny favored. A radio in the off-license was playing a sentimental song about love that Stuart remembered from his earliest childhood: his mother used to sing it. He was shocked to realize he had tears in his eyes.

That night Jenny made up the sofa bed in the spare room, explaining, "He can't stay in the bathroom; it's just not satisfactory, you know it's not."

"He needs the bed?"

"I do. He's confused, everything is new and different, I'm the one thing he can count on. I have to stay with him. He needs me."

"He needs you? What about me?"

"Oh, Stuart," she said impatiently. "You're a grown man. You can sleep by yourself for a night or two."

"And that thing can't?"

"Don't call him a thing."

"What am I supposed to call it? Look, you're not its mother—it doesn't need you as much as you'd like to think. It was perfectly all right in the bathroom last night—it'll be fine in here on its own."

"Oh? And what do you know about it? You'd like to kill him, wouldn't you? Admit it."

"No," he said, terrified that she had guessed the truth. If she knew how he had killed one of those things she would never forgive him. "It's not true, I don't—I couldn't hurt it any more than I could hurt you."

Her face softened. She believed him. It didn't matter how he felt about the creature. Hurting it, knowing how she felt, would be like committing an act of violence against her, and they both knew he wouldn't do that. "Just for a few nights, Stuart. Just until he settles in."

He had to accept that. All he could do was hang on, hope that she still loved him and that this wouldn't be forever.

The days passed. Jenny no longer offered to drive him to work. When he asked her, she said it was out of her way and with traffic so bad a detour would make her late. She said it was silly to take him the short distance to the station, especially as there was nowhere she could safely stop to let him out, and anyway, the walk would do him good. They were all good reasons, which he had used in the old days himself, but her excuses struck him painfully when he remembered how eager she had once been for his company, how ready to make any detour for his sake. Her new pet accompanied her everywhere, even to work, snug in the little nest she had made for it in a woven carrier bag.

"Of course things are different now. But I haven't stopped loving you," she said when he tried to talk to her about the breakdown of their marriage. "It's not like I've found another man. This is something completely different. It doesn't threaten you; you're still my husband."

But it was obvious to him that a husband was no longer something she particularly valued. He began to have fantasies about killing it. Not, this time, in a blind rage, but as part of a carefully thought-out plan. He might poison it, or spirit it away somehow and pretend it had run away. Once it was gone he hoped Jenny would forget it and be his again.

But he never had a chance. Jenny was quite obsessive about the thing, as if it were too valuable to be left unguarded for a single minute. Even when she took a bath, or went to the toilet, the creature was with her, behind the locked door of the bathroom. When he offered to look after it for her for a few minutes she just smiled, as if the idea was manifestly ridiculous, and he didn't dare insist.

So he went to work, and went out for drinks with colleagues, and spent what time he could with Jenny, although they were never alone. He didn't argue with her, although he wasn't above trying to move her to pity if he could. He made seemingly casual comments designed to convince her of his change of heart so that eventually, weeks or months from now, she would trust him and leave the creature with him—and then, later, perhaps, they could put their marriage back together.

One afternoon, after an extended lunch break, Stuart returned to the office to find one of the senior editors crouched on the floor beside his secretary's empty desk, whispering and chuckling to herself.

He cleared his throat nervously. "Linda?"

She lurched back on her heels and got up awkwardly. She blushed and ducked her head as she turned, looking very unlike her usual high-powered self. "Oh, uh, Stuart, I was just—"

Frankie came in with a pile of photocopying. "Uh-huh," she said loudly.

Linda's face got even redder. "Just going," she mumbled, and fled.

Before he could ask, Stuart saw the creature, another crippled bat-without-wings, on the floor beside the open bottom drawer of Frankie's desk. It looked up at him, opened its slit of a mouth and gave a sad little hiss. Around one matchstick-thin leg it wore a fine golden chain which was fastened at the other end to the drawer.

"Some people would steal anything that's not chained down," said Frankie darkly. "People you wouldn't suspect."

He stared at her, letting her see his disapproval, his annoyance, disgust, even. "Animals in the office aren't part of the contract, Frankie."

"It's not an animal."

"What is it, then?"

"I don't know. You tell me."

"It doesn't matter what it is, you can't have it here."

"I can't leave it at home."

"Why not?"

She turned away from him, busying herself with her stacks of paper. "I can't leave it alone. It might get hurt. It might escape."

"Chance would be a fine thing."

She shot him a look, and he was certain she knew he wasn't talking about *her* pet. He said, "What does your boyfriend think about it?"

"I don't have a boyfriend." She sounded angry but then, abruptly, the anger dissipated, and she smirked. "I don't have to have one, do I?"

"You can't have that animal here. Whatever it is. You'll have to take it home."

She raised her fuzzy eyebrows. "Right now?"

He was tempted to say yes, but thought of the manuscripts that wouldn't be sent out, the letters that wouldn't be typed, the delays and confusions, and he sighed. "Just don't bring it back again. All right?"

"Yowza."

He felt very tired. He could tell her what to do but she would no more obey than would his wife. She would bring it back the next day and keep bringing it back, maybe keeping it hidden, maybe not, until he either gave in or was forced into firing her. He went into his office, closed the door, and put his head down on his desk.

That evening he walked in on his wife feeding the creature with her blood.

It was immediately obvious that it was that way round. The creature might be a vampire—it obviously was—but his wife was no helpless victim. She was wide-awake and in control, holding the creature firmly, letting it feed from a vein in her arm.

She flinched as if anticipating a shout, but he couldn't speak. He watched what was happening without attempting to interfere and gradually she relaxed again, as if he wasn't there.

When the creature, sated, fell off, she kept it cradled on her lap and reached with her other hand for the surgical spirit and cotton wool on the table, moistened a piece of cotton wool and tamped it to the tiny wound. Then, finally, she met her husband's eyes.

"He has to eat," she said reasonably. "He can't chew. He needs blood. Not very much, but . . ."

"And he needs it from you? You can't . . . ?"

"I can't hold down some poor scared rabbit or dog for him, no." She made a shuddering face. "Well, really, think about it. You know how squeamish I am. This is so much easier. It doesn't hurt."

*It hurts me,* he thought, but couldn't say it. "Jenny . . ."

"Oh, don't start," she said crossly. "I'm not going to get any disease from it, and he doesn't take enough to make any difference. Actually, I like it. We both do."

"Jenny, please don't. Please. For me. Give it up."

"No." She held the scraggy, ugly thing close and gazed at Stuart like a dispassionate executioner. "I'm sorry, Stuart, I really am, but this is nonnegotiable. If you can't accept that you'd better leave."

This was the showdown he had been avoiding, the end of it all. He tried to rally his arguments and then he realized he had none. She had said it. She had made her choice, and it was nonnegotiable. And he realized, looking at her now, that although she reminded him of the woman he loved, he didn't want to live with what she had become.

He could have refused to leave. After all, he had done nothing wrong. Why should he give up his home, this flat which was half his? But he could not force Jenny out onto the streets with nowhere to go; he still felt responsible for her.

"I'll pack a bag, and make a few phone calls," he said quietly. He knew someone from work who was looking for a lodger, and if all else failed, his brother had a spare room. Already, in his thoughts, he had left.

He ended up, once they'd sorted out their finances and formally separated, in a flat just off the Holloway Road, near Archway. It was not too far to walk if Jenny cared to visit, which she never did. Sometimes he called on her, but it was painful to feel himself an unwelcome visitor in the home they once had shared.

He never had to fire Frankie; she handed in her notice a week later, telling him she'd been offered an editorial job at The Women's Press. He wondered if pets in the office were part of the contract over there.

He never learned if the creatures had names. He never knew where they had come from, or how many there were. Had they fallen only in Islington? (Frankie had a flat somewhere off Upper Street.) He never saw anything on the news about them, or read any official confirmation of their existence, but he was aware of occasional oblique references to them in other contexts, occasional glimpses.

One evening, coming home on the tube, he found himself looking at the woman sitting opposite. She was about his own age, probably in her early thirties, with strawberry-blond hair, greenish eyes, and an almost translucent complexion. She was strikingly dressed in high, soft-leather boots, a long black woolen skirt, and an enveloping cashmere cloak of cranberry red. High on the cloak, below and to the right of the fastening at the neck, was a simple, gold circle brooch. Attached to it he noticed a very fine golden chain which vanished inside the cloak, like the end of a watch fob.

He looked at it idly, certain he had seen something like it before, on other women, knowing it reminded him of something. The train arrived at Archway, and as he rose to leave the train, so did the attractive woman. Her stride matched his. They might well leave the station together. He tried to think of something to say to her, some pretext for striking up a conversation. He was, after all, a single man again now, and she might be a single woman. He had forgotten how single people in London contrived to meet.

He looked at her again, sidelong, hoping she would turn her head and look at him. With one slender hand she toyed with her gold chain. Her cloak fell open slightly as she walked, and he caught a glimpse of the creature she carried beneath it, close to her body, attached by a slender golden chain.

He stopped walking and let her get away from him. He had to rest for a little while before he felt able to climb the stairs to the street.

By then he was wondering if he had really seen what he thought he had seen. The glimpse had been so brief. But he had been deeply shaken by what he saw or imagined, and he turned the wrong way outside the station. When he finally realized, he was at the corner of Jenny's road, which had once also been his. Rather than retrace his steps, he decided to take the turning and walk past her house.

Lights were on in the front room, the curtains drawn against the early winter dark. His footsteps slowed as he drew nearer. He felt such a longing to be inside, back home, belonging. He wondered if she would be pleased at all to see him. He wondered if she ever felt lonely, as he did.

Then he saw the tiny, dark figure between the curtains and the window. It was spread-eagled against the glass, scrabbling uselessly; inside, longing to be out.

As he stared, feeling its pain as his own, the curtains swayed and opened slightly as a human figure moved between them. He saw the woman reach out and pull the creature away from the glass, back into the warm, lighted room with her, and the curtains fell again, shutting him out.

## PRINCESS OF DARKNESS

# Frederick Cowles

Frederick Ignatius Cowles was a British author who became a member of The Royal Society of Literature and was an honorary member of the Institut Littéraire et Artistique de France, which awarded him its Silver Laureate Medal in 1936.

Two collections of Cowles's supernatural stories were published during his lifetime, *The Horror of Abbot's Grange* (London: Muller, 1936), which contained his first published story, "The Headless Leper," and *The Night Wind Howls* (London: Muller, 1938).

His work, while much admired, is generally regarded as derivative of the work of other authors in the horror genre, most notably M. R. James. Cowles was evidently also influenced by the filmed version of Bram Stoker's *Dracula,* as his best-known story, "The Vampire of Kaldenstein," actually steals the line made so famous by Bela Lugosi in the movie: "I don't drink . . . wine."

A third collection of stories, *Fear Walks the Night,* remained unpublished during his lifetime, but the efforts of horror editor and scholar Hugh Lamb brought his work back into print, most importantly this collection (London: Ghost Story Press, 1993) and *The Night Wind Howls: The Complete Supernatural Stories* (Ashcroft: B.C., Ash-Tree Press, 1999).

"Princess of Darkness" was first published in *Fear Walks the Night* (London: Ghost Story Press, 1993).

# Princess of Darkness

## FREDERICK COWLES

### I

In the spring of 1938 I was sent to Budapest on a rather delicate mission. For some years diplomatic circles, in at least five European countries, had been somewhat puzzled about a certain Princess Bessenyei who made sporadic appearances in the Hungarian capital, and was vaguely suspected of being involved in international espionage. The lady first attracted notice early in 1925 when she suddenly appeared in Budapest and just as suddenly departed after dazzling her admirers for little more than two months. Nearly a year passed before she was again seen in public and thereafter, at varying intervals, she was back in the capital for periods of from six weeks to three months at a time.

Lots of ugly rumours were whispered about the Princess. It was said that her departures from the city always coincided with the mysterious deaths of men who were reputed to have been her lovers. There were those who even asserted the woman, strangely like the Princess, had been closely associated with Bela Kun, the notorious Communist leader, and had inspired many of the bloody orgies perpetrated by his regime. This suggestion was treated as idle gossip, for who could credit a story which linked such a proud aristocrat with the lowest of the vile criminals who, for a brief time, held in their incompetent hands the reins of government in Hungary?

No one could speak with any certainty of encountering the lady prior to 1925. The only facts one could accept with any degree of certainty were that the Princess was a member of a very ancient Hungarian family and that she appeared to have unlimited wealth at her disposal. Her claim to possess an estate on the borders of Transylvania was unquestioned as a place called Bessenyei appeared on the map. The story that she was a spy was difficult to believe as, so far as could be ascertained, Budapest was the only city she favoured with her presence. Yet the suggestion was taken seriously in certain quarters and my journey to Hungary must have been backed by some definite information. My task was simply to become acquainted with the Princess and to discover, if possible, something of her background.

Budapest, in the years between wars, was a favourite rendezvous for crooks of all types, as well as a very popular tourist resort. It was a lovable and romantic city and I remember, with nostalgic pleasure, the twinkling lights along the Danube, the great flood-lit statue of St. Gellert, and the eternal Gypsy music throbbing through the night.

Istvan Zichy was one of our agents in those days and we had become fairly close friends during my many visits to his country. He was an attractive young man and, being a Count, moved in the best society. His greeting was very warm when he met me at the *Nyugati Pályaudvar,* and he chattered of trifling things as we drove to the *Dunapalota* where accommodation had been reserved for me. He became more serious in the privacy of my suite and I was surprised to find that he regarded my mission with some uneasiness.

"I don't like it, my friend," he said. "There is something uncanny about the woman, but it is all nonsense to suggest she is a spy. For myself I am of the opinion that she is thoroughly evil and a worshipper of the devil." He made a quick sign of the Cross and, catching an involuntary smile on my face, continued. "Ah! You laugh at me and think that Istvan grows superstitious. I am a Hungarian and I know that in this country the old beliefs die hard. What do we know of this Princess Bessenyei? For a few months she stays with us in Budapest and then back she goes to her castle near Arad—a castle which no one has ever visited and which, to my certain knowledge, is little more than a ruin. She leaves the city and immediately some young man who has enjoyed her favours dies in a strange fashion. Wait until you have seen the lady. I think you will find that cold shivers will go down your spine."

"But," I protested, "I have been led to believe that the Princess is very beautiful."

"Certainly she is lovely," he replied. "But I do not like her kind of beauty. A snake is a splendid thing—to those who like snakes. There is another queer point to which I must draw your attention. Why has this Princess no relatives to show? Often she speaks of her father but he never comes with her to Budapest, nor have I known of any person who has ever met him."

"Relations can be an awful nuisance at times,"

I laughed. "Perhaps the lady prefers to keep hers in the background."

"Possibly she prefers to keep a lot of other things in the background," he replied. "Well, my friend, I will help you all I can, but I do not envy you the job. Everything is arranged for you to meet the Princess tomorrow night and you can form your own conclusions. For myself I think that if she is a spy, the government for which she works is ruled over by a gentleman with horns on his head."

## II

The following evening, at the *Astoria,* I was presented to the Princess. Istvan had carefully paved the way for the encounter and I had been spoken of as a wealthy English nobleman visiting Hungary on my way to Constantinople.

It is not easy to describe the Princess nor to set down my first impression of her. She was a slim woman of medium height, with auburn hair and piercing green eyes. She appeared to be about thirty years of age, and her face and hands were so pale that they seemed quite bloodless, although her lips were unnaturally red. I noticed that the hand she extended for me to kiss was intensely cold and, when she smiled, sharp fang-like teeth were revealed. As the night advanced and I was able to examine the woman more closely, I became more and more uncertain about her. Although, when animated, her face was that of a young woman, in repose there was an indefinable air of age about it. Not a single wrinkle marred its loveliness and yet, in those odd moments, it was old in the way that a flawless piece of ivory may have been carved centuries ago. Then, whilst her eyes were definitely green when the light reflected upon them, in the shadow they appeared almost black.

For most of the time she kept up a lively flow of conversation, discussing all manner of topics from the international situation to the play then running at the *Nemzeti Szinház.* She ate nothing but a couple of peaches and drank only aerated water. This, I afterwards discovered, was her invariable practice, and no one had ever seen her eat a more substantial meal. The leader of the Gypsy orchestra seemed to avoid her as much as possible and, in his perambulations of the tables, seldom paused by our party. When he did he was careful to stand behind the Princess. Once she snapped a remark at him and I am sure I saw fear in the man's eyes.

During the next few days I encountered the Princess on several occasions and she always seemed pleased to see me. Within a week or so we were on fairly intimate terms and, to tell the truth, I found her very fascinating although, in some unaccountable way, I was afraid of her. One night we had been dancing at the *Hungaria* and I was taking her back to the flat she rented in one of the old palaces in Buda. We had just crossed the *Széchenyi Lánchid* when the taxi lurched and threw her against me. I put out my arm to steady her and she pressed herself against me, lifting her face with such obvious invitation in her eyes that I bent over and kissed her red lips. Her mouth opened and I felt her sharp teeth pierce my lower lip. It all happened in a moment and, just as quickly, she drew away from me with a long, satisfied sigh. Then she laughed softly. It was an unpleasant sound with no humour in it, and I felt that she was secretly gloating over gaining some purpose of her own. This impression was confirmed when we were parting and she said very quietly, "Now you are mine for ever. I think you will dream of me tonight."

I did dream about her and it was not a nice experience. As is my usual practice I read for about half an hour and then switched off the light and settled down to sleep. I suppose I must have dozed off for what followed could only have been a dream in spite of its seeming reality. I thought a ray of dull green light suddenly shone through the window and upon it, floating into the room, came the Princess Bessenyei. She was dressed in a long white robe, her teeth appeared abnormally long, and her eyes blazed like cold emeralds. I was powerless to stir or to utter one word, although I knew that those teeth would soon be fixed upon my throat. Closer she came, her mouth dripping with saliva

in a most repulsive manner. She lifted the bed-clothes and then, like a snake darting upon its victim, she bent down to my neck. There was a sudden jar of metal upon bone, and I realized her teeth had struck the little silver crucifix which I always wear about my neck. With a bitter, frustrated cry she stood erect and I saw her pale face change in a most horrible manner. The cheeks sunk inwards, the eyes became hollow sockets, the mouth a gaping hole—I was gazing upon the ghastly head of a corpse. From this nightmare I awakened in a cold perspiration to find the window wide open and the curtains billowing in the breeze. I did not get to sleep again that night.

The following evening Istvan and I attended a gala performance at the Opera. The Princess was there with a party from the German Embassy. During the interval we went to the box to pay our respects and the first thing I noticed was that her mouth was disfigured by a thin white scar—a mark which might have been made by a thin piece of hot metal. She observed my glance and, with a forced laugh, said something about being careless with a cigarette.

Nearly a week passed before we met again and then it was an accidental encounter in the *Allatkert*—the Budapest Zoological Garden. The park was almost deserted, for it was a chilly day, and I came upon the Princess by the house in which the Siberian wolves are kept. She had climbed inside the barrier and was stroking the animals through the bars of the cage. I was amazed to see the ferocious beasts behaving like huge dogs—grovelling at her touch and licking her hands.

"Be careful," I exclaimed as I approached. "Surely it is hardly safe to tempt them with such dainty morsels."

"They will not hurt me," she replied. "I am used to wolves and know when they are dangerous."

She swung herself through the rail and came to my side. For a few moments we stood looking at the animals and then I invited her to take some refreshment with me in the restaurant. She excused herself, saying she never ate between meals, but suggested she should sit with me whilst I drank a coffee. We went into the almost empty café and, sitting at a table against the wall, talked trivialities for a time. Suddenly she said, "Tell me, are you a Catholic?" I admitted the fact and she went on, "Then perhaps you have such a thing as a small cross or holy medal you would give me for a keepsake. Tomorrow I must go away and we may never meet again."

"I have a little crucifix which I always wear," I replied. "But it has a sentimental value and I would not care to part with it. Let us go into the city and I will buy you a small souvenir of our friendship."

"No," she exclaimed rather pettishly. "I want something that has a real personal association— something you wear. You see I have a fondness for you and would wish to remember these happy days."

I surprised a hard gleam in those green eyes and knew that she was anxious to obtain possession of my cross and that nothing else would satisfy her. I also realized that the crucifix was my shield against some unknown danger and, without it, I should be at the mercy of a power I did not understand. As casually as possible I changed the subject and we chatted amiably for another ten or fifteen minutes. Then I escorted her to the gates where she called a taxi and held out her hand in farewell. As I kissed the cold fingers she whispered, "You have refused my request, but the cross will not save you. You are mine for ever and I can afford to wait." The red lips parted in a mirthless smile as she gave a sharp instruction to the driver and was borne away.

I was sufficiently disturbed by the events of the morning to seek out Istvan and recount them to him. He listened without comment as I told of the Princess's familiarity with the wolves and of her desire to possess my little crucifix. I also gave him a brief account of my unpleasant dream.

"It all confirms my suspicions," he said when I had finished. "This apparently attractive woman is not what she seems. If I were to tell you exactly what I believe her to be I am afraid it would tax your credulity. I am, however, convinced that, in your own interest, some immediate action must be taken to put a stop to something that is devilish. Will you do me the favour of telling your experiences to my friend Professor Otto Nemetz?"

"Do you mean the famous psychical investigator and the author of so many learned books and monographs on occult subjects?" I enquired.

"The very same. The Professor is very interested in our friend the Princess and may feel disposed to give you some surprising information regarding the lady."

"I shall be delighted to meet Nemetz," I replied. "I have read many of his works and, if the man is only half as interesting as his writings, he should be a remarkable individual."

"I promise that you will not be disappointed," said Istvan.

## III

My friend took me along to Otto Nemetz's apartment and, having performed the necessary introductions, pleaded another engagement and left me alone with my host. The Professor was utterly unlike what I had pictured him to be. Instead of the tall, scholarly man with a slightly sinister air which I had imagined, I found a small, rotund individual with merry twinkling eyes. When Istvan had departed Nemetz drew me over to the wide window and enthused about the wonderful vista of the Danube. It was certainly a marvellous scene from that fourth floor balcony—the silver ribbon of the stream far below, the Royal Palace and the Coronation church beyond, and, to the north, the blue heights of the encircling mountains.

Suddenly the Professor pulled me back into the room, closed the window, and said, "Now let us get down to business." He piloted me to a chair and, taking a bunch of keys from his pocket, unlocked a drawer in his desk. Carefully withdrawing a parcel wrapped in green baize, he removed the covering and placed a small oil-painting in my hands. It was a portrait of the Princess Bessenyei and the artist had caught, with uncanny skill, the wicked gleam of the green eyes and the bitter curl of the red lips.

"It is a remarkable likeness," I exclaimed. "Who is the artist?"

"You mean who *was* the artist. It was painted by Nicholas Erdösi and he, it may surprise you to know, died in 1502."

"But that is impossible," I protested somewhat feebly. "It is certainly a portrait of the Princess Bessenyei but, according to your statement, it is over four hundred years old."

"Exactly," replied the Professor drawing his chair closer to mine and speaking in a low tone. "That, in my opinion, is the age of the Princess. I believe that this woman has troubled the world for over four hundred years. Don't think me mad. Listen to what I have to say before you decide to dismiss my theories as fantastic dreams."

He passed me the cigarettes and lit his own pipe before he continued.

"In parts of Hungary, more especially in the Transylvanian district, a belief in vampires still exists. Throughout the centuries it has been held that certain persons can, by evil arts, retain a semblance of life within the tomb. I need only refer you to Johann Christofer Herenberg's *Philosophicae et Christianae Cogitationes de Vampiris* as proof of the fact that this belief has been seriously studied by learned men. The unholy dead nourish their bodies upon the blood of living men and women and, when this sustenance is available, can walk the world and behave like normal people. Time and distance mean nothing to the vampire and, after a period of quiet rest in the grave, it is capable of living like a human being for as long as six months at a time. In its lust for living blood it is inspired by a passion which often resembles love, and its victims are frequently wooed by an artful courtship. Usually the vampire does not care to be away from its home for a long period and, in fact, it cannot manage this unless it obtains the nourishment it requires. Yet, in the grave, it can retain the appearance of healthy life for hundreds of years providing it rises, from time to time, to drink human blood.

"It is a recognized fact that certain families in this part of Europe were, in the Middle Ages, brought under the vampire curse through their own criminal activities. The Bessenyeis were one of these. In the fifteenth century certain members of this family dabbled in the black arts and Prince Lóránd was the worst of them all. He undoubtedly sold his soul to the Evil One and initiated his daughter, the Princess Gizella, in all the foul rites of Satanism. She became the terror of the countryside—an avowed murderess who was eventually executed for her misdeeds in 1506. Unfortunately, having regard for her rank, her body was interred in the chapel of Bessenyei Castle. If it had been burned much trouble would have been saved, for I am convinced, that she and her father have been as active from the tomb as they were in life. At different times throughout the centuries this woman has appeared in the world, and she is the person you know as the Princess Bessenyei."

"But surely such a tale is ridiculous," I interrupted. "I am prepared to swear that the Princess is a woman of flesh and blood, and I cannot believe that your theory will bear scientific investigation. After all this is the twentieth century."

"She is certainly a creature of flesh and blood," replied Nemetz. "But that flesh and blood is over four centuries old. I know it all sounds like a medieval fantasy and yet I believe it to be true. I am so convinced that I am determined to prove my contention and, in doing so, to rid the world of a devilish evil. Hungarians are naturally superstitious and I should find it difficult to persuade any person in this country to give me the assistance I require. You are an Englishman and can help me if you will."

"How is that possible?" I asked in some trepidation for, remembering the strange incidents connected with my short acquaintance with the Princess, I felt myself becoming convinced against my will.

"Come with me to the Castle of Bessenyei," suggested the little Professor. "I can guarantee you protection against the undead, but I do not promise that the sights I may reveal will be pleasant. You are, I take it, a man with good nerves and are not afraid of things which may live in your memory for ever."

"I am not afraid of anything I can understand,

but this is quite beyond me," I replied. "I have to find out all I can about the woman and, for this reason if for no other, I am prepared to help you even to the extent of accompanying you to Bessenyei."

"Good," cried Nemetz. "No time must be wasted and we will start at nine o'clock in the morning. Meanwhile it may be as well for us to visit the *Országos Levéltár*—the department of State Archives—to see if we can obtain any information about the home of the Bessenyeis."

He seized his hat and stick and presently we were hurrying along the *Horthy Miklos Ut*. By the bridge the Professor signalled a taxi which carried us across the river to Buda, by the Coronation church, to the modern building in the *Bécsikapu Tér* where all documents of the Hungarian State are housed. Soon we were closeted with a courteous official who, in the pleasant fashion of the country, produced a bottle of wine before he dealt with our enquiry.

"Yes," he said. "I have heard of the castle but, so far as I can recollect, it is situated in disputed territory. I will, however, let you have all the information that is available." He rang a bell and instructed the subordinate, who answered the summons, to bring certain documents and maps. When these were before him he gave us the startling intelligence that the Bessenyei family, at least that branch of it which owned the castle, had become extinct in 1723.

"But," I said, "there is certainly a Princess Bessenyei who is well known in Budapest society."

"She probably comes from another branch of the family," he replied. "Bessenyei Castle, with its estates, seems to have become State property about the middle of the last century. The building can be little more than a picturesque ruin and I see from our records that a caretaker was maintained there until the outbreak of the last war. Since the Treaty of Trianon we have had no official connection with the estate which appears to be in territory still the subject of litigation. If you wish to visit the place you will encounter no difficulties, although I think it most unlikely that any custodian is on the premises. Certainly we have met no charges for maintenance during the past twenty or thirty years."

Thanking him for his assistance we parted with mutual expressions of goodwill, and Nemetz and I returned to Pest.

## IV

Punctually at nine o'clock the following day the professor was at my hotel. He came up to my suite and, spreading a map on the table, pointed out the road we had to follow.

"The actual distance," he said, "is little more than a hundred English miles. But I am afraid the latter part of the journey will be by bad roads and we cannot expect to arrive at our destination before late evening. It may be helpful if we can spend the night in the castle. Do you think you can face such an ordeal?"

"Having undertaken this adventure," I replied, "I am in your hands. If you think we should spend the night in the building I am quite agreeable."

"Excellent! One more thing before we start. Are you wearing the crucifix about your neck?"

I showed him the cross on its thin silver chain and he gave a grunt of approval. He led me out to the waiting car which he was driving himself. I noticed two travelling cases in the back seat, also a small crowbar.

On the whole it was a pleasant drive with brief stops at Kecskemét and Szeged. At the latter place we had a meal and inspected the splendid votive church. From Makó the roads were little more than dusty tracks through cornfields and vineyards. At last we came to a gloomy forest and, upon the edge of it, was a Gypsy encampment. Nemetz pulled up and called out to one of the men, asking if he could direct us to the castle. The fellow came over to the car and appeared to be afraid to answer the question. On the Professor repeating his request the Gypsy burst into a torrent of words accompanied by urgent gestures. So far as I could make out the castle was in the forest, but it was only a deserted ruin. It was an evil place and we would be well advised to give it a wide berth.

Nemetz laughed and said something about calling on the Princess. This remark served to increase the man's agitation and his incoherent warnings rang in our ears as we drove away.

"You see," said my companion, "even the Gypsies are afraid of the castle and know it to be the home of evil things."

It was so dark under the trees that we had to switch on the headlights to enable us to see the way. After about a couple of miles there was a break in the trees and a pair of ruined columns, one still surmounted by a heraldic device, indicated the approach to a large house. In the distance we could see the outline of a tower, but the drive was overgrown and hardly distinguishable from the surrounding fields. Dusk was falling as we turned into the entrance and suddenly there was a blood-curdling howl and a gaunt grey wolf leaped from the shadows and bounded along at the side of the car. Nemetz applied the brakes, pulled out a revolver, and fired three rounds at the animal. At such short range he could hardly have failed to hit it. But, with a howl of rage, it reared up on its hind legs and then ran off among the trees. Then, from all over the forest, came the answering cries of a pack of wolves howling in anger.

Beyond the shattered gates the track led through a wilderness which must have originally been parkland. A few stunted trees hung above a reedy lake into which flowed the waters of a dark moat, which we crossed by a crumbling bridge.

As we neared the castle I could see that it was little more than a shell, with a round tower on the western side and, beyond it, a detached building which looked like a chapel. Drawing up before the main doorway the Professor handed me a powerful electric torch and, carrying a bag each, we climbed the broken steps.

"There is just a chance that there may be a caretaker in the place," said Nemetz, "although I think it most unlikely." He pulled a chain which hung from a pillar and, far away inside the building, a bell tolled with a hollow sound. As its echoes died we heard the sound of shuffling footsteps and the heavy door swung open. On the threshold stood a tall man dressed in the dark costume of an old-fashioned retainer. He held a lighted candle in his hand and the light fell upon a bearded face in which the eyes glowed with a curious red glow. I confess that I was afraid and wished myself back in the pleasant comfort of the *Dunapalota*. But the Professor did not appear unduly alarmed.

"You are the custodian I presume?" he asked. The man gave a barely perceptible nod and Nemetz went on. "We are two travellers who desire shelter for the night. Can it be arranged?"

"The accommodation is poor," was the reply in a thin, fluting voice. "But you are welcome to such as it is. Enter, gentlemen. Enter of your own free will and become the guests of Castle Bessenyei."

He stood aside, holding the candle high, and we entered the building. The hall, which appeared to be in a tolerable state of repair, stank of damp and decay. A ragged tapestry fluttered on one wall, but the others were green with mildew. Our guide gave us little chance to examine our surroundings for, after slamming the door, he led the way up a wide staircase, along a narrow corridor on the first floor, and ushered us into a room at the end of it. It was apparently a large apartment and the feeble light of the candle revealed a bare floor, a heavy table, two chairs, and an oak settle.

"This is the best we can offer," said the strange custodian. "I trust you have food with you, for there is none in the castle. You will, I hope, find this better than a night spent in the forest." With a soft chuckle he added, "It is many years since last we entertained guests in Castle Bessenyei."

"Can you light a fire?" demanded the Professor. "The room is as cold as a tomb."

"I regret there is no fuel in the castle," was the reply. "This is all we can provide—a roof over your heads and chairs in which you can await the dawn. Even a tomb is not so cold as the living believe." As he spoke, the howl of a wolf sounded from under the windows. With a muttered word of apology he grabbed the candle and hurried from the room, leaving us in the semi-darkness.

The door had hardly closed when Nemetz quietly opened it again and, beckoning me to follow, led the way along the passage to the head of the stairs. The old man was descending and his candle cast queer shadows on the damp walls. Moving with a strange gliding motion he hurried over to the heavy door and flung it open. At once a long grey shape bounded over the threshold and I started back in fear. But immediately, before our eyes, the wolf changed into a woman. It was the Princess Bessenyei. We heard the muttering of low conversation and then the woman raised her eyes and looked to where we were standing. The Professor pulled me back into the deeper shadow and we watched as the two figures below moved towards a door near the foot of the stairs and vanished through it. We waited a few moments and then silently crept back to our room.

"Now we know exactly where we stand," said the Professor, driving home the rusty bolt on the door. "The Princess is here and it is obvious that the custodian is not what he pretends to be. We must prepare ourselves for the night."

From the first case he unpacked a portable electric lamp which was powerful enough to illuminate the sombre chamber. We saw that the dust of years covered the floor and the barred windows were festooned with cobwebs. A coat of arms was carved above the wide stone fireplace and this was repeated over each of the two windows. Nemetz then produced handfuls of garlic and spread the herb on the threshold of the rooms and on the window-sills. On the table he placed a pair of brass candle-sticks containing long yellow tapers which he lighted.

"We are now safe from direct attack," he explained. "For some reason the undead loathe the smell of garlic and it has always been considered a sure protection against their spells. The candles were blessed by the archbishop last Candlemas Day and, to make things doubly sure, I shall now sprinkle the room with holy water."

He took a flask from his pocket and, reciting the prayer of the *Asperges,* sprayed drops of the blessed water into every corner of the apartment. We then drew the chairs up to the table and ate a light meal of sandwiches washed down with a bottle of seltzer water.

"It will be safe enough to sleep," said the little man when we had finished our repast. "But on no account must you attempt to leave the room or to open the door or windows."

For a while we chatted of ordinary things which seemed ridiculously unreal in those sinister surroundings. But I was very tired and could feel my lids growing heavier. After a time I saw that my companion was finding it difficult to remain awake. Suddenly he slumped over the table and settled his head on his arm. I also must have fallen asleep and yet it seemed that I never closed my eyes. I became aware of a reddish glow which appeared to come from the fireplace and eventually resolved itself into minute particles of gleaming dust which danced in the light of the electric lamp. Gradually they took shape, misty at first and then more clearly defined until the Princess Bessenyei stood before me. Her green eyes were tender and inviting, and she beckoned me to follow her. I knew that I must remove the crucifix from my neck before I could rise from the chair. But I found it impossible to lift my hands—I was chained to the spot and could not move. The woman's face changed as she watched my fruitless efforts to obey her unspoken command. Angry frustration blazed from her eyes, her mouth twisted into a horrible dribbling leer, and she bared the white fangs of her teeth. Then the figure became blurred and a cloud of red dust hung in the light of the lamp before it faded away. The hungry cry of a wolf, echoing through the ruined castle, awakened me. Nemetz was already on his feet and he put his finger to his lips to enjoin silence. From beyond the door came the sibilant whisper of voices and then the wolf's howl rang out again.

"There is nothing to fear," the Professor assured me. He went on to explain that the vampire frequently assumes the shape of a wolf and, in this guise, is able to satisfy its lust for blood. I suppose the even murmur of his voice must have lulled me off to sleep again. When I awakened next time it was morning and the sun blazed through the dirty windows. The little man was bending over a primus stove and the warm, friendly aroma of coffee pervaded the apartment.

## V

We made a good breakfast, for Nemetz had brought a liberal supply of food. I noticed, however, that no meat was provided and this was explained when the Professor remarked that, in dealing with the occult, it was best to avoid flesh-meat. After the meal we packed everything back into the cases in readiness to carry them out to the car.

"The real business of our visit remains to be performed," said my companion. "The task we have set ourselves is to rid the world of this evil creature and we shall require all our courage if we are to succeed. God grant we do not fail."

He opened the door and we were carrying our things into the passage when I stopped with a sudden exclamation. Just over the threshold, written in the dust on the floor, were the words, "You are mine for ever." Nothing I had experienced during my association with the Princess had affected me as did that strange message. I literally trembled with fear and it took all Nemetz's assurances to restore some of my self-control. Even then I would have backed out of the business if I could have done so honourably.

There was no sign of the old man we had seen on the previous evening and, in the cold light of day, the castle looked an utterly abandoned ruin. We peeped into some of the rooms on the ground floor and, apart from a few broken articles of antique furniture, they were quite empty. In what had evidently been the dining hall some of the carved panelling had been roughly ripped from the walls and birds were nesting in the crevices.

Before we packed the bags into the car Nemetz removed certain articles and placed them in his capacious pockets. These included a wooden crucifix, a wicked-looking dagger, a handful of garlic, and the bottle of holy water. Taking the crowbar in his hand he led the way towards the chapel.

The little building probably dated from the early fourteenth century and was graceful in design. The door opened to our touch and a wave of cold, dank air greeted us. The interior was filthy and littered with fallen masonry. A few fragments of coloured glass remained in the windows and there was a stone altar at the east end. The Professor mounted the steps and examined the slab. It was covered with the droppings of birds and, scraping some of the dirt away, he pointed to dark brown patches which stained the centre of the table. He also showed me that the five consecration crosses had been roughly obliterated and the receptacle for relics was empty.

"Here are the marks of unholy sacrifices," he said, "and proofs that this altar has been used for the wicked blasphemy of the Black Mass."

At the back of the altar we found a flight of narrow steps leading down into the depths of the earth. At the bottom was a small door marked with the same coat of arms we had seen in the castle.

"Now comes the real test," said Nemetz. "This is the burial vault of the Bessenyei family and here we shall find the evidence we seek. Let us pray for strength to enable us to finish this awful business."

Beside the desecrated altar we knelt and asked heaven to bless our efforts and to shield us from evil. Then the Professor led the way down the steps and tried the door of the vault. It was apparently secured, but the rusty lock soon gave way before the crowbar and the door swung inwards. With a wild shriek which froze the blood in our veins, something flapped out of the darkness and soared towards the roof of the chapel. It was only a great white owl but our nerves, keyed almost to breaking point, were badly shaken. Speaking for myself I would, at that moment, gladly have abandoned the task we had set ourselves. But the Professor soon recovered himself and, with a self-conscious laugh, directed the beam of his torch into the vault. A ghastly sight met our eyes. Coffins of all shapes and sizes were ranged in niches around the walls and most of them had been broken open. Here and there bones protruded and the floor was coveted with fragments of human bodies, some of them with dried scraps of flesh still adhering. In the centre of the place two great leaden coffins stood side by side.

"These are the ones we want," said the Professor advancing into the vault. "The others are of no importance for we can see that their inmates have suffered the normal course of corruption."

He placed the torch in my hands and motioned me to hold it so that the light fell upon the first of the two coffins. Then, with the crowbar, he prised the lid and found that it was not sealed in any way. He moved it a little so that he could get a grip on the edges. Evidently it was not so weighty as he had anticipated, for he lifted it off with comparative ease. There, before us in the leaden casket, was the body of the man we had taken to be the caretaker of the castle. He appeared to be sleeping and, in repose, the cruel lines of his mouth were set in an evil grin.

"Just as I suspected," muttered Nemetz. "This is Prince Lorand who is supposed to have died in the fifteenth century. You see for yourself how he lives in the grave and can arise when occasion demands. Now let us look at the other."

We turned to the second coffin and, without any difficulty, the two of us lifted the lid and placed it on the floor. I was more or less prepared for the sight that met our gaze but, even so, it gave me a nasty shock. The light of the torch showed us the Princess Bessenyei to all intents and purposes resting quietly in the tomb. She could hardly be described as sleeping, for her wicked eyes were wide open and gleamed with mocking scorn. Looking upon that beautiful face it was hard to believe that this woman had roamed the earth for over four centuries and that the source of her immunity from death was the blood of the innocent people who became her victims. Yet I was convinced at last.

We turned back to the first coffin and the Professor drew his dagger. Whispering to me to hold the torch steady he raised his arm and plunged the weapon deep into the heart of the thing in the casket. An unearthly scream of agony came from the twisted lips, the body writhed in grotesque fashion for a few moments and then, before our eyes, it turned to dust. Nemetz, who seemed quite unmoved, put a few bulbs of garlic into the coffin and sprinkled it with holy water. We were bending to lift the lid when I dropped the torch and plunged the vault into darkness. Before I could retrieve it a burst of harsh laughter rang out. We both sprang round and there, framed in the narrow doorway and wrapped in a pale, phosphorescent glow, was the Princess with her green eyes blazing with hellish anger. In a second the Professor had drawn his revolver and emptied it into the figure. He might have spared himself the trouble for the shots had no effect at all.

Lifting her hand in a commanding gesture which seemed to paralyse us into immobility, the Princess addressed us.

"You, Professor Nemetz," she said, "have taken my father from me and, for this, you shall pay the penalty. You have failed to destroy me and nothing can save you from my vengeance when the hour comes, for the undead do not forget." Then turning to me she smiled a slow mysterious smile. "There is no need for me to tell you again that you will be mine in the end. Your lips have touched mine and, although years may pass and seas may divide us, I shall come for you in my own good time."

With these words she vanished from our sight. Power was suddenly restored to our limbs and we rushed up the steps into the chapel. There was no sign of the Princess but, with a hoot of derision and a flapping of wings, the great white owl swooped down and flew back into the vault.

The Professor seemed very badly shaken. "Too late," he groaned. "Too late. I should have realized that she is too skilled in her evil arts to allow herself to be destroyed by the usual methods."

We made our way back to the car and were soon driving through the forest. Nemetz hardly spoke a word. He drove as if trying desperately to escape from a pursuing terror and we were back in Budapest by the late afternoon. I gave him a stiff brandy in my room, but all life seemed to have gone out of him.

"I must again seriously warn you of the danger in which you stand," he said before we parted. "This creature has a passion for you which resembles, to some degree, the passion of violent love.

It will never be content until you have become its victim—even if it has to wait many years. I can only urge you to protect yourself by every means in your power. I fear for you and I also fear for myself. The Princess has promised to have her revenge and I am convinced it will not be long before the attack comes. God be with you, my friend. If all is well I will call upon you in the morning."

I never saw Professor Nemetz alive again. That same night he was killed in most brutal fashion. The authorities decided that some wild animal had gained access to the poor man's apartment, though how it was impossible to determine, for he was literally savaged to death. But I know how and why he died. I saw the glazed terror in his dead eyes and remembered the gaunt grey wolf of Bessenyei.

My turn will come. I feel safe with the little cross around my neck, but she will find some way of overcoming its power. I write down this story so that the truth may be known and perhaps, in God's good time, someone will be brave enough to again attempt the destruction of the undead. I leave this city with fear in my heart, for I know she will follow me to the ends of the earth.

### POSTSCRIPT BY DR. REGINALD STAINES, MEDICAL OFFICER IN CHARGE OF EASTDOWN MENTAL HOME, DEVON.

The foregoing manuscript was written by Harvey Gorton, a former member of the Diplomatic Service, who was admitted to this institution on 10th November 1939. His was a case of psychosis, the chief feature of which was a fixed delusion that he was being hunted by the woman he called the Princess Bessenyei. Apart from this he was apparently normal and never caused any trouble. I found him a most cultured man and we often chatted together about the international situation. He was very perturbed about the war and seemed particularly anxious that Hungary, for which country he had a great affection, should not be drawn into the conflict. In the ordinary course of events I think

we should have effected a complete cure within a few months.

On 2nd December, after a light fall of snow, he was walking in the grounds when he stumbled over the root of a tree and fell some five or six feet down an embankment, injuring his left shoulder. He was evidently in great pain and an x-ray revealed a fracture in a bad position at the upper end of the humerus. It was decided to give an anaesthetic for reduction. Gorton always wore a little crucifix at his neck and I noticed that, when the surgeon lifted it aside to enable him to examine the shoulder more carefully, the man became unduly agitated and protested that the cross must on no account be removed. We injected pentolthal into a vein in the arm and, as Gorton was becoming unconscious, the nurse, by some clumsy movement, broke the chain on which the cross was suspended and it fell to the floor. The patient was only out for about forty seconds and, when he was taken back to his room, the crucifix was apparently forgotten. Later he became very anxious about the loss and worked himself up into such a state that I gave instructions for it to be restored to him. Unfortunately the operating theatre had been swept and, although the cross had been found, it had been locked up in the desk of the Matron. She had gone off duty and it was impossible for us to secure the thing until she returned.

I tried to soothe Gorton, but he made a terrible fuss about the business and demanded that the desk should be broken open. As he seemed likely to become violent I gave him a strong sleeping draught as the best way out of the difficulty.

Later in the evening, having ascertained that the patient was sleeping soundly, I went over to the vicarage for an hour to discuss with the vicar's wife the formation of some First Aid classes. I had hardly settled down when the telephone rang and I was recalled to the Home.

The whole place was in confusion. My deputy, Doctor Snell, reported that, about five minutes after I had left, a woman, speaking with a foreign accent, had called at the Home and asked to see

Gorton. She was shown into a waiting room whilst the nurse went to inform Snell of the request. He naturally said it was quite impossible for Gorton to be seen and the nurse, returning to inform the visitor, found the waiting-room empty. At that moment she heard a terrified scream and members of the staff, rushing upstairs, discovered the door of Gorton's room wide open. The poor wretch was lying half in and half out of bed and was already dead. When I came to examine the corpse I found that it was almost entirely drained of blood—a most difficult condition to describe or explain. The only wound on the body was a tiny double puncture in the throat.

## THE SILVER COLLAR

# Garry Kilworth

Garry Kilworth (1941– ) was born in York, England, but traveled extensively in his early years, since his father was a pilot in the Royal Air Force, as he himself would be for seventeen years. He attended the University of London, graduating with a degree in English with honors.

In 1974 he won a short-story competition sponsored by Gollancz and *The Sunday Times* with "Let's Go to Golgotha"; he subsequently wrote more than a hundred fantasy, science-fiction, historical, and general fiction stories, as well as more than sixty novels in the same categories; in 1980 he began to write children's books, also on science fiction, fantasy, and supernatural themes, winning numerous awards for them.

His fiction has received four nominations for World Fantasy Awards. In 1985 he was nominated for Best Collection for *The Songbirds of Pain;* in 1988 his nomination was in the Best Short Story category for "Hogfoot Right and Bird-Hands"; in 1992 *Ragfoot*, written in collaboration with Robert Holdstock, was the winner for Best Novella; and in 1994 he was nominated for Best Collection again for *Hogfoot Right and Bird-Hand*.

Kilworth has said he loves writing. "If it were outlawed tomorrow," he wrote, "I would be a criminal."

"The Silver Collar" was first published in *Blood Is Not Enough*, edited by Ellen Datlow (New York: Morrow, 1989).

# The Silver Collar

## GARRY KILWORTH

The remote Scottish island came into view just as the sun was setting. Outside the natural harbor, the sea was kicking a little in its traces and tossing its white manes in the dying light. My small outboard motor struggled against the ebbing tide, sometimes whining as it raced in the air as a particularly low trough left it without water to push against the blades of its propeller. By the time I reached the jetty, the moon was up and casting its chill light upon the shore and purple-heather hills beyond. There was a smothered atmosphere to this lonely place of rock and thin soil, as if the coarse grass and hardy plants had descended as a complete layer to wrap the ruggedness in a faded cover, hiding the nakedness from mean, inquisitive eyes.

As the agents had promised, he was waiting on the quay, his tall, emaciated figure stark against the gentle upward slope of the hinterland: a splinter of granite from the rock on which he made his home.

"I've brought the provisions," I called, as he took the line and secured it.

"Good. Will you come up to the croft? There's a peat fire going—it's warm, and I have some

scotch. Nothing like a dram before an open fire, with the smell of burning peat filling the room."

"I could just make it out with the tide," I said. "Perhaps I should go now." It was not that I was reluctant to accept the invitation from this eremite, this strange recluse—on the contrary, he interested me—but I had to be sure to get back to the mainland that night, since I was to crew a fishing vessel the next day.

"You have time for a dram," his voice drifted away on the cold wind that had sprung up within minutes, like a breath from the mouth of the icy north. I had to admit to myself that a whisky, by the fire, would set me on my toes for the return trip, and his tone had a faintly insistent quality about it which made the offer difficult to refuse.

"Just a minute then—and thanks. You lead the way."

I followed his lean, lithe figure up through the heather, which scratched at my ankles through my seasocks. The path was obviously not well used and I imagined he spent his time in and around his croft, for even in the moonlight I could discern no other tracks incising the soft shape of the hill.

We reached his dwelling and he opened the

581

wooden door, allowing me to enter first. Then, seating me in front of the fire, he poured me a generous whisky before sitting down himself. I listened to the wind, locked outside the timber and turf croft, and waited for him to speak.

He said, "John, is't it? They told me on the radio."

"Yes—and you're Samual."

"Sam. You must call me Sam."

I told him I would and there was a period of silence while we regarded each other. Peat is not a consistent fuel, and tends to spurt and spit colorful plumes of flame as the gases escape, having been held prisoner from the seasons for God knows how long. Nevertheless, I was able to study my host in the brief periods of illumination that the fire afforded. He could have been any age, but I knew he was my senior by a great many years. The same thoughts must have been passing through his own head, for he remarked, "John, how old are you? I would guess at twenty."

"Nearer thirty, Sam. I was twenty-six last birthday." He nodded, saying that those who live a solitary life, away from others, have great difficulty in assessing the ages of people they do meet. Recent events slipped from his memory quite quickly, while the past seemed so close.

He leaned forward, into the hissing fire, as if drawing a breath from the ancient atmospheres it released into the room. Behind him, the earthen walls of the croft, held together by rough timbers and unhewn stones, seemed to move closer to his shoulder, as if ready to support his words with confirmation. I sensed a story coming. I recognized the pose from being in the company of sailors on long voyages and hoped he would finish before I had to leave.

"You're a good-looking boy," he said. "So was I, once upon a time." He paused to stir the flames and a blue-green cough from the peat illuminated his face. The skin was taut over the high cheekbones and there was a wanness to it, no doubt brought about by the inclement weather of the isles—the lack of sunshine and the constant misty rain that comes in as white veils from the north.

Yes, he had been handsome—still was. I was surprised by his youthful features and suspected that he was not as old as he implied.

"A long time ago," he began, "when we had horse-drawn vehicles and things were different, in more ways than one . . ."

A sharp whistling note—the wind squeezing through two tightly packed logs in the croft—distracted me. Horse-drawn vehicles? What was this? A second-hand tale, surely? Yet he continued in the first person.

". . . gas lighting in the streets. A different set of values. A different set of beliefs. We were more pagan then. Still had our roots buried in dark thoughts. Machines have changed all that. Those sort of pagan, mystical ideas can't share a world with machines. Unnatural beings can only exist close to the natural world and nature's been displaced.

"Yes, a different world—different things to fear. I was afraid as a young man—the reasons may seem trivial to you, now, in your time. I was afraid of, well, getting into something I couldn't get out of. Woman trouble, for instance—especially one not of my class. You understand?

"I got involved once. Must have been about your age, or maybe a bit younger since I'd only just finished my apprenticeship and was a journeyman at the time. Silversmith. You knew that? No, of course you didn't. A silversmith, and a good one too. My master trusted me with one of his three shops, which puffed my pride a bit, I don't mind telling you. Anyway, it happened that I was working late one evening, when I heard the basement doorbell jangle.

"I had just finished lighting the gas lamps in the workshop at the back, so I hurried to the counter where a customer was waiting. She had left the door open and the sounds from the street were distracting, the basement of course being on a level with the cobbled road. Coaches were rumbling by and the noise of street urchins and flower sellers was fighting for attention with the foghorns from the river. As politely as I could, I went behind the customer and closed the door. Then I turned to her and said, 'Yes madam? Can I be of service?'

"She was wearing one of those large satin cloaks that only ladies of quality could afford and she threw back the hood to reveal one of the most beautiful faces I have ever seen in my life. There was a purity to her complexion that went deeper than her flawless skin, much deeper. And her eyes—how can I describe her eyes?—they were like black mirrors and you felt you could see the reflection of your own soul in them. Her hair was dark—coiled on her head—and it contrasted sharply with that complexion, pale as a winter moon, and soft, soft as the velvet I used for polishing the silver.

"'Yes,' she replied. 'You may be of service. You are the silversmith, are you not?'

"'The journeyman, madam. I'm in charge of this shop.'

"She seemed a little agitated, her fingers playing nervously with her reticule.

"'I . . .' she faltered, then continued. 'I have a rather unusual request. Are you able to keep a secret, silversmith?'

"'My work is confidential, if the customer wishes it so. Is it some special design you require? Something to surprise a loved one with? I have some very fine filigree work here.' I removed a tray from beneath the counter. 'There's something for both the lady and the gentleman. A cigar case, perhaps? This one has a crest wrought into the case in fine silver wire—an eagle, as you can see. It has been fashioned especially for a particular customer, but I can do something similar if you require . . .'

"I stopped talking because she was shaking her head and seemed to be getting impatient with me.

"'Nothing like that. Something very personal. I want you to make me a collar—a silver collar. Is that possible?'

"'All things are possible.' I smiled. 'Given the time of course. A tore of some kind?'

"'No, you misunderstand me.' A small frown marred the ivory forehead and she glanced anxiously towards the shop door. 'Perhaps I made a mistake . . . ?'

"Worried, in case I lost her custom, I assured her that whatever was her request I should do my utmost to fulfill it. At the same time I told her that I could be trusted to keep the nature of the work to myself.

"'No one shall know about this but the craftsman and the customer—you and I.'

"She smiled at me then: a bewitching, spellbinding smile, and my heart melted within me. I would have done anything for her at that moment—I would have robbed my master—and I think she knew it.

"'I'm sorry,' she said. 'I should have realized I could trust you. You have a kind face. A gentle face. One should learn to trust in faces.

"'I want you—I want you to make me a collar which will cover my whole neck, especially the throat. I have a picture here, of some savages in Africa. The women have metal bands around their necks which envelop them from shoulder to chin. I want you to encase me in a similar fashion, except with one single piece of silver, do you understand? And I want it to fit tightly, so that not even your . . .' She took my hand in her own small gloved fingers. 'So that not even your little finger will be able to find its way beneath.'

"I was, of course, extremely perturbed at such a request. I tried to explain to her that she would have to take the collar off quite frequently, or the skin beneath would become diseased. Her neck would certainly become very ugly.

"'In any case, it will chafe and become quite sore. There will be constant irritation . . .'

"She dropped my hand and said, no, I still misunderstood. The collar was to be worn permanently. She had no desire to remove it, once I had fashioned it around her neck. There was to be no locking device or anything of that sort. She wanted me to seal the metal.

"'But?' I began, but she interrupted me in a firm voice.

"'Silversmith, I have stated my request, my requirements. Will you carry out my wishes, or do I find another craftsman? I should be loath to do so, for I feel we have reached a level of understanding which might be difficult elsewhere. I'm going to be frank with you. This device, well—its purpose is protective. My husband-to-be is not—not like other men, but I love him just the same. I don't wish to embarrass you with talk that's not proper between strangers, and personal to my situation, but the collar is necessary to ensure my marriage is happy—a limited happiness. Limited to a lifetime. I'm sure you *must* understand now. If you want me to leave your shop, I shall do so, but I am appealing to you because you are young and must know the pain of love—unfulfilled love. You are a handsome man and I don't doubt you have a young lady whom you adore. If she were suffering under some terrible affliction, a disease which you might contract from her, I'm sure it would make no difference to your feelings. You would strive to find a way in which you could live together, yet remain uncontaminated yourself. Am I right?'

"I managed to breathe the word 'Yes,' but at the time I was filled with visions of horror. Visions of this beautiful young woman being wooed by some foul creature of the night—a supernatural beast that had no right to be treading on the same earth, let alone touching that sacred skin, kissing—my mind reeled—kissing those soft, moist lips with his monstrous mouth. How could she? Even the thought of it made me shudder in revulsion.

"'Ah,' she smiled, knowingly. 'You want to save me from him. You think he is ugly and that I've been hypnotized, somehow, into believing otherwise? You're quite wrong. He's handsome in a way that you'd surely understand—and sensitive, kind, gentle—those things a woman finds important. He's also very cultured. His blood . . .'

"I winced and took a step backward, but she was lost in some kind of reverie as she listed his attributes and I'm sure was unaware of my presence for some time.

"'. . . his blood is unimpeachable, reaching back through a royal lineage to the most notable of European families. I love him, yet I do not want to become one of his kind, for that would destroy my love . . .'

"'And—he loves you of course,' I said, daringly.

"For a moment those bright eyes clouded over, but she replied, 'In his way. It's not important that we both feel the same *kind* of love. We want to be together, to share our lives. I prefer him to any man I have ever met and I *will not* be deterred by an obstacle that's neither his fault, nor mine. A barrier that's been placed in our way by the injustice of nature. He can't help the way he is—and I want to go to him. That's all there is to it.'

"For a long time neither of us said anything. My throat felt too dry and constricted for words, and deep inside me I could feel something struggling, like a small creature fighting the folds of a net. The situation was beyond my comprehension: that is, I did not wish to allow it to enter my full understanding or I would have run screaming from the shop and made myself look foolish to my neighbors.

"'Will you do it, silversmith?'

"'But,' I said, 'a collar covers only the throat . . .' I left the rest unsaid, but I was concerned that she was not protecting herself fully: the other parts of her anatomy—the wrists, the thighs.

"She became very angry. 'He isn't an *animal*. He's a gentleman. I'm merely guarding against—against moments of high passion. It's not just a matter of survival with him. The act is sensual and spiritual, as well as—as well as—what you're suggesting,' there was a note of loathing in her tone, 'is tantamount to rape.'

"She was so incensed that I did not dare say that her lover must have satisfied his need *somewhere*, and therefore had compromised the manners and morals of a gentleman many times.

"'Will you help me?' The eyes were pleading now. I tried to look out of the small, half-moon window, at the yellow-lighted streets, at the feet moving by on the pavement above, in an attempt to distract myself, but they were magnetic, those eyes, and they drew me back in less than a moment. I felt helpless—a trapped bird—in its unremitting gaze of anguish, and of course, I submitted.

"I agreed. I just heard myself saying, 'Yes,' and led her into the back of the shop where I began the work. It was not a difficult task to actually fashion the collar, though the sealing of it was somewhat painful to her and had to be carried out in stages, which took us well into the night hours. I must have, subconsciously perhaps, continued to glance through the workshop door at the window, for she said once, very quietly, 'He will not come here.'

"Such a beautiful throat she had too. Very long, and elegant. It seemed a sacrilege to encase such beauty in metal, though I made the collar as attractive as I made any silver ornament which might adorn a pretty woman. On the outside of the metal I engraved centripetal designs and at her request, some representational forms: Christ on the cross, immediately over her jugular vein, but also Zeus and Europa, and Zeus and Leda, with the Greek god in his bestial forms of the bull and the swan. I think she had been seduced by the thought that she was marrying some kind of deity.

"When I had finished, she paid me and left. I watched her walk out, into the early morning mists, with a heavy guilt in my heart. What could I have done? I was just a common craftsman and had no right interfering in the lives of others. Perhaps I should have tried harder to dissuade her, but I doubt she would have listened to my impertinence for more than a few moments. Besides, I had, during those few short hours, fallen in love with her—utterly—and when she realized she had made a mistake, she would have to come back to me again, to have the collar removed.

"I wanted desperately to see her again, though I knew that any chance of romance was impossible, hopeless. She was not of my class—or rather, I was not of hers, and her beauty was more than I could ever aspire to, though I knew myself to be a good-looking young man. Some had called *me* beautiful—it was that kind of handsomeness that I had been blessed with, rather than the rugged sort.

"But despite my physical advantages, I had nothing which would attract a lady of quality from her own kind. The most I could ever hope for—the very most—was perhaps to serve her in some way."

Three weeks later she was back, looking somewhat distraught.

"'I want it to come off,' she said. 'It must be removed.'

"My fingers trembled as I worked at cutting her free—a much simpler task than the previous one.

"'You've left him,' I said. 'Won't he follow?'

"'No, you're quite wrong.' There was a haunted look to her eyes which chilled me to the bone. 'It's not that. I was too mistrustful. I love him too much to withhold from him the very thing he desires. I must give myself to him—wholly and completely. I need him, you see. And he needs me—yet like this I cannot give him the kind of love he has to have. I've been selfish. Very selfish. I must go to him . . .'

"'Are you mad?' I cried, forgetting my position. 'You'll become like him—you'll become—'

"'How *dare* you! How dare you preach to *me*? Just do your work, silversmith. Remove the collar!'

"I was weak of course, as most of us are when confronted by a superior being. I cut the collar loose and put it aside. She rubbed her neck and complained loudly that flakes of skin were coming away in her hands.

"'It's ugly,' she said. 'Scrawny. He'll never want me like this.'

"'No—thank God!' I cried, gathering my courage.

"At that moment she looked me full in the eyes and a strange expression came over her face.

"'You're in love with me, aren't you? That's why you're so concerned, silversmith. Oh dear, I am so dreadfully sorry. I thought you were just being meddlesome. It was genuine concern for my welfare and I didn't recognize it at first. Dear man,' she touched my cheek. 'Don't look so sad. It cannot be, you know. You should find some nice girl and try to forget, because you'll never see me again after tonight. And don't worry about me. I know what I'm doing.'

"With that, she gathered up her skirts and was gone again, down toward the river. The sun was just coming up, since she had arrived not long before the dawn, and I thought: At least she will have a few hours more of natural life.

"After that I tried to follow her advice and put her out of my mind. I did my work, something I had always enjoyed, and rarely left the shop. I felt that if I could get over a few months without a change in my normal pattern of existence, I should be safe. There were nightmares of course, to be gone through after sunsets, but those I was able to cope with. I have always managed to keep my dreams at a respectable distance and not let them interfere with my normal activities.

"Then, one day, as I was working on a pendant—a butterfly requested by a banker for his wife—a small boy brought me a message. Though it was unsigned, I knew it was from her and my hands trembled as I read the words.

"They simply said, 'Come. I need you.'

"Underneath this request was scrawled an address, which I knew to be located down by one of the wharves, south of the river.

"She *needed* me—and I knew exactly what for. I touched my throat. I wanted her too, but for different reasons. I did not have the courage that she had—the kind of sacrificial courage that's produced by an overwhelming love. But I was not without strength. If there was a chance, just a chance, that I could meet with her and come away unscathed, then I was prepared to accept the risk.

"But I didn't see how that was possible. Her kind, as she had become, possessed a physical strength which would make any escape fraught with difficulty.

"I had no illusions about her being in love with me—or even fond of me. She wanted to use me for her own purposes, which were as far away from love as earth is from the stars. I remembered seeing deep gouges in the silver collar, the time she

had come to have it removed. They were like the claw marks of some beast, incised into the trunk of a tree. No wonder she had asked to have it sealed. Whoever, *what*ever, had made those marks would have had the strength to tear away any hinges or lock. The frenzy to get at what lay beneath the silver must have been appalling to witness—*experience*—yet she had gone back to him, without out the collar's protection.

"I wanted her. I dreamed about having her, warm and close to me. That she had become something other than the beautiful woman who had entered my shop was no deterrent. I knew she would be just as lovely in her new form and I desired her above all things. For nights I lay awake, running different schemes over in my mind, trying to find a path which would allow us to make love together, just once, and yet let me walk away safely afterward. Even as I schemed, I saw her beauty laid before me, willingly, and my body and soul ached for her presence.

"One chance. I had this one chance of loving a woman a dozen places above my station: a woman whose refined ways and manner of speech had captivated me from the moment I met her. A woman whose dignity, elegance, and gracefulness were without parallel. Whose form surpassed that of the finest silverwork figurine I had ever known.

"I had to find a way.

"Finally, I came up with a plan which seemed to suit my purposes, and taking my courage in both hands I wrote her a note which said, 'I'm waiting for you. *You* must come to *me*.' I found an urchin to carry it for me and told him to put it through the letter box of the address she had given me.

"That afternoon I visited the church and a purveyor of medical instruments.

"That evening I spent wandering the streets, alternately praising myself for dreaming up such a clever plan and cursing myself for my foolhardiness in carrying it through. As I strolled through the backstreets, stepping around the gin-soaked drunks and tipping my hat to the factory girls as they hurried home from a sixteen-hour day in some garment manufacturer's sweatshop, or a hosiery, I realized that for once I had allowed my emotions to overrule my intellect. I'm not saying I was an intelligent young man—not above the average—but I was wise enough to know that there was great danger in what I proposed to do, yet the force of my feelings was more powerful than fear. I could not deny them their expression. The heart has no reason, but its drive is stronger than sense dictates.

"The barges on the river ploughed slowly against the current as I leaned on the wrought-iron balustrade overlooking the water. I could see the gas lamps reflected on the dark surface and thought about the shadow world that lived alongside our own, where nothing was rigid, set, but could be warped and twisted, like those lights in the water when the ripples from the barges passed through them. Would it take me and twist me into something, not ugly, but insubstantial? Into something that has the appearance of the real thing, but which is evanescent in the daylight and can only make its appearance at night, when vacuous shapes and phantasms take on a semblance of life and mock it with their unreal forms?

"When the smell of the mud below me began to waft upward, as the tide retreated and the river diminished, I made my way homeward. There was a sharpness to the air which cut into my confidence and I was glad to be leaving it behind for the warmth and security of my rooms. Security? I laughed at myself, having voluntarily exposed my vulnerability.

"She came.

"There was a scratching at the casement windowpane in the early hours of the morning and I opened it and let her in. She had not changed. If anything, she was more beautiful than ever, with a paler color to her cheeks and a fuller red to her lips.

"No words were exchanged between us. I lay on the bed naked and she joined me after removing her garments. She stroked my hair and the nape of my neck as I sank into her soft young body. I cannot describe the ecstasy. It was—*unearthly*. She allowed me—encouraged me—and the happiness of those moments was worth all the risks of entering Hell for a taste of Heaven.

"Of course, the moment came when she low-

ered her head to the base of my throat. I felt the black coils of her hair against my cheek: smelled their sweet fragrance. I could sense the pulse in my neck, throbbing with blood. Her body was warm against mine—deliciously warm. I wanted her to stay there forever. There was just a hint of pain in my throat—a needleprick, no more, and then a feeling of drifting, floating on warm water, as if I had suddenly been transported to tropic seas and lay in the shallows of some sunbleached island's beaches. I felt no fear—only, *bliss*.

"Then, suddenly, she snorted, springing to her feet like no athlete I have ever seen. Her eyes were blazing and she spat and hissed into my face.

" 'What have you done?' she shrieked.

"Then the fear came, rushing to my heart. I cowered at the bedhead, pulling my legs up to my chest in an effort to get as far away from her as possible.

"Again she cried, 'What have you done?'

" 'Holy water,' I said. 'I've injected holy water into my veins.'

"She let out another wail which made my ears sing. Her hands reached for me and I saw those long nails, like talons, ready to slash at an artery, but the fear was gone from me. I just wanted her back in bed with me. I no longer cared for the consequences.

" 'Please?' I said, reaching for her. 'Help me? I want you to help me.' She withdrew from me then and sprang to the window. It was getting close to dawn: The first rays of the sun were sliding over the horizon.

" 'You fool,' she said, and then she was gone, out into the murk. I jumped up and looked for her through the window, but all I could see was the mist on the river, curling its way around the rotten stumps of an old jetty.

"Once I had recovered my common sense and was out of her influence, I remember thinking to myself that I would have to make a collar—a silver collar . . ."

The fire spat in the grate and I jerked upright. I had no idea how long Sam had been talking but the peat was almost all ashes.

"The tide," I said, alarmed. "I must leave."

"I haven't finished," he complained, but I was already on my feet. I opened the door and began to walk quickly down the narrow path we had made through the heather, to where my boat lay, but even as I approached it, I could see that it was lying on its side in the slick, glinting mud.

Angry, I looked back at the croft on the hillside. He must have known. He must have known. I was about to march back and take Sam to task, when I suddenly saw the croft in a new perspective. It was like most dwellings of its kind—timber framed, with sods of earth filling the cracks, and stones holding down the turf on the roof. But it was a peculiar shape—more of a mound than the normal four walls and a roof—and was without windows.

My mind suddenly ran wild with frightening images of wood, earth, and rocks. The wooden coffin goes inside the earth and the headstone weights it down. A mound—a burial mound. *He hadn't been able to stay away from her. The same trap that had caught her . . .*

I turned back to the boat and tried dragging it across the moonlit mud, toward the distant water, but it was too heavy. I could only inch it along, and rapidly became tired. The muscles in my arms and legs screamed at me. All the time I labored, one side of my mind kept telling me not to be so foolish, while the other was equally insistent regarding the need to get away. I could hear myself repeating the words. *"He couldn't stay away from her. He couldn't stay away."*

I had covered about six yards when I heard a voice at my shoulder—a soft, dry voice, full of concern.

"Here, John, let me help you . . ."

*Sam did help me that day, more than I wished him to. I don't hate him for that, especially now that so many years have passed. Since then I have obtained this job, of night ferryman on the loch, helping young ladies like the one I have in the skiff with me now—a runaway, off to join her lover.*

*"Don't worry," I try to reassure her, after telling her my story, "we sailors are fond of our tales. Come and join me by the tiller. I'll show you how to manage the boat. Do I frighten you? I don't mean to. I only want to help you . . ."*

## THE OLD MAN'S STORY

# Walter Starkie

Walter Fitzwilliam Starkie (1894–1976) was born in Ballybrack, Dublin, Ireland, and spent much of his life with gypsies. A scholar and academic, he spent his holidays among them, playing his fiddle and studying their language and folklore, leading *Time* magazine to profile him as a modern-day gypsy. He wrote about his own travels and transcribed gypsy tales in *Raggle-Taggle: Adventures with a Fiddle in Hungary and Roumania* (1933) and *Spanish Raggle-Taggle: Adventures with a Fiddle in North Spain* (1934). While the stories are allegedly true and autobiographical, there is more than a small possibility that there was embellishment. He wrote a more cohesive self-portrait in 1963, *Scholars and Gypsies: An Autobiography*.

Starkie was the first professor of Spanish at Trinity College, Dublin, beginning in 1926, and had a distinguished career as a translator of Spanish literature, notably a critically acclaimed unabridged edition of Miguel Cervantes's *Don Quixote*, published in 1957, which has remained in print for a half century.

Although not as famous as others who held the same position, such as Lady Augusta Gregory and William Butler Yeats, Starkie was the director of the renowned Abbey Theatre in Dublin, a position he held for seventeen years.

"The Old Man's Story" was first published in *Raggle-Taggle: Adventures with a Fiddle in Hungary and Roumania* (London: John Murray, 1933).

# The Old Man's Story

## WALTER STARKIE

It was now dark, and I determined to spend the night in the open, for the air was balmy and the moon made the country look like fairyland. In the daytime the meadows looked parched, the roads were dusty, and the heat was exhausting, but at night on the Hungarian plain there was a delightful, cool breeze and everything in nature seemed to awaken to life. The moonlight shining through the trees carved everything into queer, fantastic shapes. In some places the white light made the foliage look like silver filigree work; in other places the branches became shadowy, ghostly forms. It is difficult to explain in definite words the sensation of mystery and romance that the wayside traveller finds in Hungary. The scenery seen by the light of day is uninteresting, for the whole country is just a huge plain. But at night in the moonlight the fields of corn, the clumps of trees, the little knolls here and there become meeting-places of fairies. It is the mixture of races that has given to this countryside its poetical charm. To the Magyar mind all that country is inhabited by invisible beings that spring to life when the sun goes down, and I have met peasants who were afraid to wander in the light of the moon for, as they said, the fevers descend on the earth when the moon rides in the sky. The primitive Magyar is pantheistic in his attitude towards nature and translates this sentiment into the little folk-poems he improvises to the sound of his rustic flute or the gipsy's fiddle. The Hungarian projects his personality on to his external surroundings. The forest is in mourning because his love lies on her deathbed; Sari has sowed violets and awaits their growing because they symbolize the homecoming of her lover; the shepherd tending his flocks by the Tiza river looks up at the starry sky and thinks of his mother far away in Transylvania or his sister sweeping her room with rosemary boughs. In the northern countries of Europe the scenery is more majestic than the Hungarian plain, but the peasants do not look on their country through the veil of their own folk-lore or folk-music, nor do they associate each legend and melody with definite events in their country's history to the same extent as the Magyar does. Every step that the lonely traveller makes through the plain is accompanied by songs, dirges and dances until his mind echoes and re-echoes to a mighty symphony composed of countless fragmentary tunes.

I halted for the night at the foot of a knoll where there was a small rustic graveyard nestling peacefully in the moonlight. At the back of a big sheltering tombstone I made a fire of twigs and prepared to bivouac in Gipsy style in this desolate spot, feeling sure that no one would come to disturb me in a cemetery. I had some cheese and bread in my rucksack and my wine-skin was full. As the night continued and the fire burnt low I began to feel acute melancholy and loneliness. I was sorry that I had chosen a graveyard for a bivouacking ground, for graveyards brought thoughts of vampires and werewolves to the mind. I tried to dispel this attack of the shivers by music, but my violin sounded harsh and discordant like a *danse macabre*. I nearly dropped the bow in terror, for all of a sudden there was a soft whirr of wings and something brushed past my face: it was a bat. Round and round the bat circled like a spirit of evil omen and I thought of "Dracula" and shuddered.

When I settled down I found that sleeping out of doors, even on the torrid plain of Hungary, is not an unmixed enjoyment for the traveller whose skin is not as weather-beaten as that of a gipsy. The night became for me a series of hopeless struggles with mosquitoes and every other species of stinging insect. As long as the fire was burning merrily the insects gave me a wide berth, but later on in the shadows of the night I heard the ominous high note like the tuning of countless violins by a phantom orchestra and the hordes began their descent upon my unarmed flesh. Soon I felt my face swell under their attacks and sleep became an impossibility. At night, too, in Hungary, in contrast to the day, there were spells of cold and the sleeper in the open would feel his limbs stiffen. When I lie awake in the country all my senses become extraordinarily keen and sensitive to sounds. On that night I understood how the Hungarian peasants people their country graveyards with vampires: I heard the crackling of twigs and I imagined I saw two fiery eyes gleaming at me from behind some bushes. Then something dark darted beside my leg and I fancied it was a rat. Even in normal life at home the proximity of a rat would fill me with a sickening anguish, but here I felt inclined to shriek my helplessness. Another distressing feature of outdoor sleeping was the prevalence

of such crawling beasts as earwigs and woodlice, not to mention the sprightly flea. When I started to doze in a short period of respite from the mosquito orchestra, I felt an ominous tickling sensation on my neck. I found that a legion of ants was advancing in extended order over my body.

After a dreamless sleep I woke suddenly at the sound of a dog yelping near by. When I looked up above my tombstone I saw at the other side of the cemetery a light burning over one of the graves. For a moment I thought that I was still wandering through the halls of sleep, but then the horrible thought struck me that I might have been unlucky enough to enter a vampire-haunted graveyard. The yelping of dogs and the flickering lights over graves were sure signs of the dreaded vampire. My first thought was to take to my heels, but the whole scene seemed so eerie and unreal that my feelings of curiosity overmastered my fear and I stood my ground. The flickering light came nearer and nearer: I then saw that it was a small lantern carried by an old man who was hobbling on a stick and tugging after him at the end of a rope the dog I had heard yelping. He was a strange little old man like one of the goblins in Grimm's fairy stories. He walked with bent shoulders and his long white beard nearly touched the ground. His clothes were ragged and grimy, but here and there they were patched up with pieces of gaudy colours. So loosely did this ragged raiment hang on his cadaverous form that he seemed to be clothed in a garment of reeds mixed with the plumage of birds. So emaciated was his face that he looked like the figure of death in the mediaeval masquerade. He hobbled over to me and rasped out some unintelligible words in Magyar. I then answered in German and he continued in the latter language. "What are you doing in this graveyard?" said he. "Don't you know that the tomb you are resting on is haunted by a nachtoeher? When I saw you in the distance I took you for one of them and I made the sign of the Cross to drive you away. Look here, *mein Herr*, look on that tombstone and you will see two holes: that is the sign that the tomb is inhabited by a vampire: at any moment before dawn it might fly forth and attack you. Have you no garlic upon you to stop up those holes and prevent the foul demon from coming out?" The little old man's voice rose to a shriek as he spoke and his eyes were those of a madman. "I tell you no one can escape those vampires once they begin to go after you: I have striven for years to escape their visitation, but they have taken everything I have in the world and they would take me were it not for my prayers." So saying he pulled out of his coat a crucifix of black wood and blessed himself, muttering prayers in a low voice all the while. As he prayed, the dog kept up an accompaniment of snarling and growling, as though it was terrified of something. The old man then called out to the dog trying to soothe it, but the beast slunk behind him and began to tremble violently. "Look at my dog," said the old man; "he knows the werewolves are about and he won't approach that grave."

For a long time we stood motionless by the tomb, while the old man continued to ramble on in his rasping voice and told me his story. From time to time I had to interrupt him to say that the fire had burnt low and that it was necessary to add sticks. I was terrified to stay listening to stories of vampires without the protection of a fire, for the old man's superstitious nature had already infected me and I felt that all this experience had something supernatural about it. We sat by the fire and the old man's voice gradually droned me into a state of drowsiness and my eyes would close involuntarily. Then he would whine out in a shriller tone and I would awake with a start.

You wonder why I talk about vampires. My story will show you that I have good cause to fear their terrible vengeance.

"I was born in a village near Budapest, of peasant stock. As a young man I left my homestead and wandered afar, taking the rough with the smooth. I fought in the Turkish War of 1878, and as a legacy was left a wound which crippled my left leg, as you see. The soldier's life in those far-off days was a cruel one, and more than once I thought my greatcoat was to be my shroud. From being a soldier I became a commercial traveller and wandered from village to village in Turkey and Bulgaria. It was at the town of Rustchuk that I met a very beautiful Bulgarian farmer's daughter and paid court to her. I married her and we came to settle down in Hungary in the town of Szeged. Three children we had, a boy and two girls. The boy, who was called Sándor, grew into as fine and strapping a youth as you would see any day: why, he was as reckless and dare-devil as a young colt on the Hortobágy. Aye, it was horses ruined him, for he would wander off with dealers and the copers and there was no holding him at all. I was glad the day came when he put on the grey uniform and I thought army discipline would tame his spirit. After his service he returned home, bringing with him a stranger whom he introduced to the family as his benefactor. He confided to me that the stranger had helped him on more occasions than one when he was in difficulties through gaming debts and had lavished money on him. Naturally we all welcomed the stranger as the friend of Sándor, and he soon looked upon our house as a home. At first I was astonished at Sándor's infatuation for the stranger, seeing that he was at least twenty years older, but then I saw that it was the older man who pursued the younger. He monopolized my son's attention: not a thought would come into the latter's head which was not inspired by the stranger, and from being a wild, irresponsible youth he turned into a silent and thoughtful man, always day-dreaming. The stranger had something Mephistophelian about his appearance; he was tall and thin, with acquiline features and a small pointed beard. His eyes were strained and had a wild look in them like those of a cigány: his mouth coarse and brutal, with very red lips, and when he spoke he would frequently lick them and show his teeth, which were brilliantly white and sharply pointed like those of a dog or wolf.

"He was the life and soul of our family, for he had a soft, caressing manner, in spite of his sudden fits of passion when his eyes would blaze and he would show his canine teeth. He would come and visit us in the afternoon and delight us by his many accomplishments. He was the man of the world and we were the humble village folk whom he was pleased to honour. There was something fantastic about the stranger who had travelled all over the world enduring exciting adventures, and Julcsa, my eldest daughter, would call him the fairy prince, and she said that he was sent to our house by the Délibáb or Fata Morgana. We never knew when he would come, for he gave us no warning of his arrival in the town. He seemed to glide in unperceived, and after some days of consecutive visits he would suddenly depart on the pretext of urgent business. I could never find out what his business was, for he contented himself with telling me that he had to travel far and wide. As time went on Julcsa became more and more attracted towards him. She would sit for hours listening to his stories of travels and he seemed to hypnotize her by his cold, piercing grey eyes. Everything about the mysterious stranger thrilled her: his brown, close-fitting squire's costume, his polished top-boots, his purple necktie, which gave him the air of an Oriental prince, his long white fingers like those of a woman, with sharp nails cut to a point. Poor Julcsa, she was distracted with love for her cavalier, and she would confess to me with tears in her eyes that she loved him madly, but she was always terrified lest he might one day vanish away into the distance like Lohengrin on his fairy swan.

"My wife had always looked with misgivings on the stranger in spite of all his charm. 'He is an adventurer,' she cried, 'and he will seduce our Julcsa and then depart in the night like a thief.' In my mind I agreed with her, but I sympathized with Julcsa. When we tried to reason with Julcsa there were tears and lamentations. I could see she was hopelessly infatuated and I was afraid she might do something desperate. The best course seemed to me to say farewell to the stranger and forbid him to visit our house any more. Our leave-taking was stormy, and I saw a look of demoniacal hate in his grey eyes and his mouth was twisted into a grimace of sardonic triumph. In order to distract Julcsa's thoughts from her sufferings we closed our house and went to live for a while in the country near Temesvár.

"One night when all the household had retired to rest and all was as still as the grave, I heard the sound of horses' hoofs clattering on the road. The night was dark and misty, but when I looked out of the window I saw dimly in the distance a carriage drawn by four black horses galloping away in a cloud of dust. I was naturally superstitious and the sight of those four black horses paralysed me with horror, for I knew they were of evil omen. My first impulse was to rush into Julcsa's room. She was not there. The bed was tossed and one of the sheets twisted into a rope hung from the window. On the table I found a note saying: 'Dearest Father and Mother. Forgive me for what I am doing and pray for my soul. Julcsa."

"I cannot describe for you the grief of all of us. We searched high and low, we informed the police, we searched the country for miles round, but no definite news did we get of Julcsa. As so often happens in such cases of disappearance, many came forward to say that they had seen her here or there, accompanied by an elderly man, but the clues led to nothing. As for my wife, she was convinced that Julcsa had been carried away by a vampire and what agonized her more than the loss of her eldest daughter was the terrifying thought that Julcsa if she once came into the power of a vampire would turn into one herself. 'The stranger was a vampire,' she cried. 'Did you notice his pointed teeth, his red lips? The four black horses were his and he now possesses her body and soul. When he has sucked her blood she will become as he is and haunt us to our ruin." She spent her whole day in prayer. Each moment she thought she heard poor Julcsa crying out and she fancied that Julcsa would appear in the night in the form of a bat to haunt her remaining daughter Sari or else Sándor. She hung crucifixes in every room and at night she would insist on hanging garlic leaves over Sari's and Sándor's bed to protect them. Her mind gave way and she would wander aimlessly round the house with a vacant stare on her face calling out Julcsa's name and blessing herself as though to exorcise her. Some months after that I followed her hearse to the cemetery.

"As for Sándor, he left home after his mother's death and I was left alone with Sari in our house of mourning. From time to time Sándor wrote to me telling me of his life. He had obtained employment as a clerk in an office in Budapest and from his letters I inferred that he was satisfied with his humdrum life. Then for a long time I had no news of him until one day a letter came telling me to go at once to him as he was seriously ill. When I arrived at Budapest I went straight to his lodgings and I found him lying in a filthy room looking as if he would die any minute. He was as white as a sheet and he could just open his eyes and give me a sad, weary smile. The doctor, who was standing by his bedside, told me that Sándor had not many days to live for he was in the last stages of galloping consumption. All the life seemed to be ebbing fast from my son. At times he would cry out faintly for Julcsa and he told me of a strange dream he had had. He dreamt he met her outside the arched gate of a city and she stood within the arch and beckoned to enter. She was dressed in dazzling white and looked radiantly beautiful and happy, but her face was as white as her dress and her lips were like a scarlet wound. She beckoned again and again to him, but though he strove hard he was unable to cross the threshold of the gate. Then he awoke in a state of terrible anguish, and he felt so weak that he thought he was going to die. He could not understand the reason why he felt so sad, for the dream had been a happy one and Julcsa had seemed so radiant. Night after night the dream repeated itself and on each awakening he would feel the sense of overwhelming weakness. Then one night in the dream she had drawn him through the arch and he had followed her through the town and along a road until they came to a clump of trees where he saw tombstones dotted about. Sándor used to rave for hours incoherently, trying to recall the place where he had seen the tombstones. 'If I could only remember the name I should know where to find Julcsa,' he cried. Each day he became weaker in spite of the doctor's treatment and the drugs that he consumed. But I knew that all the medicine in the world would be of no avail, for it was Julcsa's spirit which was consuming him. Just as my dear wife had done, I placed garlic plants about his bed and a crucifix over his head. At night

I never left him alone and I would watch him tossing about in the bed trying in vain to find peace. There was a look of wild yearning in his face and he would mutter the name of Julcsa again and again. I knew that he was hypnotized by her spirit as a humming-bird is by the snake's eye. Every prayer that came into my mind I said over him and every incantation I had learnt from old gipsy women, but it was in vain. At a certain moment of the night I would feel drowsy, and a mist would gather before my eyes. After dozing off momentarily I would awake. Sándor would be sleeping peacefully, but his face would look still more deathly than before and from the corners of his mouth I saw a thin stream of blood trickle down his white neck. Each hour I watched by his deathbed became more terrifying than the last, for I watched him gradually change from my poor, dying son into the deathless vampire, ready to work evil on others. Then one night in the midst of a troubled sleep he suddenly shrieked out: 'The tombstones, the tombstones: I know where they are: I can see the trees and the low wall. The name of the town is Lepsény. Go through the town and then along the long road mile after mile until you come to the graveyard.' When he awoke he was so exhausted that he would not speak and he did not remember his dream. But my mind was made up. I determined to seek out the graveyard and discover Julcsa's tomb and rid the world of the terrible vampire. After handing over the care of Sándor to a trusted relative I set out from Budapest accompanied by an old gipsy woman I had known for many years. She was to be my confederate in the grim task which lay before me. She was one of the *cohalyi*, as the gipsies call the witches in Hungary, and as we tramped along the road she muttered incantations in the intervals of giving me advice how to rid myself of the vampire pest. When we reached Lepsény we turned back along the road and after a weary search we came to this cemetery where you and I are seated now, and I discovered that it tallied with the description my son had given in his dream. Tomb after tomb we examined and after a long search we came to one in a corner on whose stone the name

Julcsa was engraved in big letters. She had died the year before. How had she died? Who had closed her eyes? Did she die in poverty and if so who had raised the tombstone over her grave? Who knows?

"The night after I had discovered the grave I returned with the old woman to carry out my grim task of liberation. It was a stormy night, the wind was whistling through the trees, and rain and sleet lashed our faces. No moon was shining and I thanked God for that. A moon would have exposed our sinister work and perhaps drawn the suspicious peasantry after us. At midnight I started to dig down into the grave while the old woman stood by and muttered incantations. After digging for some time I knocked with my spade against the coffin. The sound of the spade striking the coffin filled me with such horror that I nearly fainted, but the old woman called sternly to me to break open the lid with the spade. With difficulty I did as she commanded, and when I had wrenched open the lid I gazed on all that remained of my poor Julcsa. For a moment I thought I was the victim of an hallucination, for Julcsa looked as if she were sleeping peacefully. Over her eyes there was spread a filmy substance and her lips were bright red as though she had recently fed on a loathsome repast in the land of the living. Again I hesitated, for my eyes were riveted on the corpse in the coffin. Again the old woman's sharp voice broke in upon my meditation: 'Make haste and use this knife. You must cut her head off and bury it in another part of the cemetery. If you do that her spirit will trouble you and your family no more.' The old hag with these words handed me a sharp knife she had brought with her and straitaway began to gather twigs to make a fire near by. Hardening my heart I tried to do her bidding, but my strength failed me. The witch then seized the knife from my hands and with one slash severed the head from the trunk. I shut my eyes, but it seemed to me as if the corpse moaned and the blood spurted over me. After fastening down the coffin lid and piling the earth over it we buried the head in the opposite side of the cemetery, and we departed on our way towards Budapest. Before she took leave of me the old woman said: 'Be sure to go back to that cemetery and pour wine on the grave of your daughter, for there is nothing like wine for laying the ghost to rest.' When I reached my son's bedside I found him at death's door, but he had no longer the wild look in his eye, only a serene peace, and he was just able to beg my prayers before he died. I buried him in the same cemetery as his sister, and once every month I come to the two graves. Tonight when I came in here I was frightened when I saw the fire, and I was afraid someone might have discovered my secret."

The old man, after finishing his story, led me over to the opposite side of the graveyard, where he pointed to a recently erected tombstone, and on it I read the name Sándor.

Dawn was now breaking and the air was grey and misty. The old man, pulling his dog after him, and I made our way out of the cemetery. At the top of the hill I saw a woman coming towards us. The old man said to me when he saw her: "There is my daughter Sari: she always comes to fetch me after my long night's vigil." The woman when she came near us ran up to the old man and kissed him. I then saw them depart on their way towards Lepsény.

## WILL

# Vincent O'Sullivan

Vincent O'Sullivan (1868–1940) was born to a wealthy family in New York City and attended Columbia Grammar School, then moved to England and studied at Oxford.

In 1894 he began to contribute stories and poems to *The Senate* magazine, resulting in a collection of poems; in 1896 *A Book of Bargains,* one of the most important early collections of supernatural fiction, was published by his friend Leonard Smithers, a key figure in *The Yellow Book* decade of the 1890s. O'Sullivan was the only American of significance in the aesthetic movement, which was led by Aubrey Beardsley, Oscar Wilde, and Ernest Dowson. Like that of so many of his circle, O'Sullivan's work was filled with morbidity and decadence.

O'Sullivan used his wealth to help friends, notably Wilde after his release from prison, and it was eventually dissipated. Of his friend O'Sullivan, Wilde once wrote that he is "really very pleasant, for one who treats life from the standpoint of the tomb." The strong negative reaction to his support of the despised Wilde resulted in a largely closed market for O'Sullivan's work. He was reduced to dire poverty late in life and died in a pauper's ward in Paris shortly after the German occupation.

"Will" was first published in book form in *The Green Window* (London: Leonard Smithers, 1899).

# Will

## VINCENT O'SULLIVAN

### I

Have the dead still power after they are laid in the earth? Do they rule us, by the power of the dead, from their awful thrones? Do their closed eyes become menacing beacons, and their paralyzed hands reach out to scourge our feet into the paths which they have marked out? Ah, surely when the dead are given to the dust, their power crumbles into the dust!

Often during the long summer afternoons, as they sat together in a deep window looking out at the Park of the Sombre Fountains, he thought of these things. For it was at the hour of sundown, when the gloomy house was splashed with crimson, that he most hated his wife. They had been together for some months now; and their days were always spent in the same manner—seated in the window of a great room with dark oak furniture, heavy tapestry, and rich purple hangings, in which a curious decaying scent of lavender ever lingered. For an hour at a time he would stare at her intensely as she sat before him—tall, and pale, and fragile, with her raven hair sweeping about her neck, and her languid hands turning over the leaves of an illuminated missal—and then he would look once more at the Park of the Sombre Fountains, where the river lay, like a silver dream, at the end. At sunset the river became for him turbulent and boding—a pool of blood; and the trees, clad in scarlet, brandished flaming swords. For long days they sat in that room, always silent, watching the shadows turn from steel to crimson, from crimson to grey, from grey to black. If by rare chance they wandered abroad, and moved beyond the gates of the Park of the Sombre Fountains, he might hear one passenger say to another, "How beautiful she is!" And then his hatred of his wife increased a hundred-fold.

So he was poisoning her surely and lingeringly—with a poison more wily and subtle than that of Cæsar Borgia's ring—with a poison distilled in his eyes. He was drawing out her life as he gazed at her; draining her veins, grudging the beats of her heart. He felt no need of the slow poisons which wither the flesh, of the dread poisons which set fire to the brain; for his hate was a poison which he poured over her white body, till it would no longer have the strength to hold back the escaping soul. With exultation he watched her growing weaker and weaker as the summer glided by: not a day, not an hour passed that she did not pay toll to his eyes: and when in the autumn there

597

came upon her two long faints which resembled catalepsy, he fortified his will to hate, for he felt that the end was at hand.

At length one evening, when the sky was grey in a winter sunset, she lay on a couch in the dark room, and he knew she was dying. The doctors had gone away with death on their lips, and they were left, for the moment, alone. Then she called him to her side from the deep window where he was seated looking out over the Park of the Sombre Fountains.

"You have your will," she said. "I am dying."

"My will?" he murmured, waving his hands.

"Hush!" she moaned. "Do you think I do not know? For days and months I have felt you drawing the life of my body into your life, that you might spill my soul on the ground. For days and months as I have sat with you, as I have walked by your side, you have seen me imploring pity. But you relented not, and you have your will; for I am going down to death. You have your will, and my body is dead; but my soul cannot die. No!" she cried, raising herself a little on the pillows. "My soul shall not die, but live, and sway an all-touching sceptre lighted at the stars."

"My wife!"

"You have thought to live without me, but you will never be without me. Through long nights when the moon is hid, through dreary days when the sun is dulled, I shall be at your side. In the deepest chaos illumined by lightning, on the loftiest mountain-top, do not seek to escape me. You are my bond-man: for this is the compact I have made with the Cardinals of Death."

At the noon of night she died; and two days later they carried her to a burying-place set about a ruined abbey, and there they laid her in the grave. When he had seen her buried, he left the Park of the Sombre Fountains and travelled to distant lands. He penetrated the most unknown and difficult countries; he lived for months amid Arctic seas; he took part in tragic and barbarous scenes. He used himself to sights of cruelty and terror: to the anguish of women and children, to the agony and fear of men. And when he returned after years of adventure, he went to live in a house the win-

dows of which overlooked the ruined abbey and the grave of his wife, even as the window where they had erewhile sat together overlooked the Park of the Sombre Fountains.

And here he spent dreaming days and sleepless nights—nights painted with monstrous and tumultuous pictures, and moved by waking dreams. Phantoms haggard and ghastly swept before him; ruined cities covered with a cold light edified themselves in his room; while in his ears resounded the trample of retreating and advancing armies, the clangour of squadrons, and noise of breaking war. He was haunted by women who prayed him to have mercy, stretching out beseeching hands—always women—and sometimes they were dead. And when the day came at last, and his tired eyes reverted to the lonely grave, he would soothe himself with some eastern drug, and let the hours slumber by as he fell into long reveries, murmuring at times to himself the rich, sonorous, lulling cadences of the poems in prose of Baudelaire, or dim meditative phrases, laden with the mysteries of the inner rooms of life and death, from the pages of Sir Thomas Browne.

On a night, which was the last of the moon, he heard a singular scraping noise at his window, and upon throwing open the casement he smelt the heavy odour which clings to vaults and catacombs where the dead are entombed. Then he saw that a beetle—a beetle, enormous and unreal—had crept up the wall of his house from the graveyard, and was now crawling across the floor of his room. With marvellous swiftness it climbed on a table placed near a couch on which he was used to lie, and as he approached, shuddering with loathing and disgust, he perceived to his horror that it had two red eyes like spots of blood. Sick with hatred of the thing as he was, those eyes fascinated him—held him like teeth. That night his other visions left him, but the beetle never let him go—nay! compelled him, as he sat weeping and helpless, to study its hideous conformation, to dwell upon its fangs, to ponder on its food. All through the night that was like a century—all through the pulsing hours—did he sit oppressed with horror gazing at that unutterable, slimy vermin. At the first streak of dawn it glided away, leaving in its trail the same smell of the charnel-house; but to him the day brought no rest, for his dreams were haunted by the abominable thing. All day in his ears a music sounded—a music thronged with passion and wailing of defeat, funereal and full of great alarums; all day he felt that he was engaged in a conflict with one in armour, while he himself was unharnessed and defenceless—all day, till the dark night came, when he observed the abhorred monster crawling slowly from the ruined abbey, and the calm, neglected Golgotha which lay there in his sight. Calm outwardly; but beneath perhaps—how disturbed, how swept by tempest! With trepidation, with a feeling of inexpiable guilt, he awaited the worm—the messenger of the dead. And this night and day were the type of nights and days to come. From the night of the new moon, indeed, till the night when it began to wane, the beetle remained in the grave; but so awful was the relief of those hours, the transition so poignant, that he could do nothing but shudder in a depression as of madness. And his circumstances were not merely those of physical horror and disgust: clouds of spiritual fear enveloped him: he felt that this abortion, this unspeakable visitor, was really an agent that claimed his life, and the flesh fell from his bones. So did he pass each day looking forward with anguish to the night; and then, at length, came the distorted night full of overwhelming anxiety and pain.

## II

At dawn, when the dew was still heavy on the grass, he would go forth into the graveyard and stand before the iron gates of the vault in which his wife was laid. And as he stood there, repeating wild litanies of supplication, he would cast into the vault things of priceless value: skins of man-eating tigers and of leopards; skins of beasts that drank from the Ganges, and of beasts that wallowed in the mud of the Nile; gems that were the ornament of the Pharaohs; tusks of elephants, and corals that men had given their lives to obtain. Then holding up his arms, in a voice that raged against heaven he would cry: "Take these, O avenging soul, and leave me in quiet! Are not these enough?"

And after some weeks he came to the vault again bringing with him a consecrated chalice studded with jewels which had been used by a priest at Mass, and a ciborium of the purest gold. These he filled with the rare wine of a lost vintage, and placing them within the vault he called in a voice of storm: "Take these, O implacable soul, and spare thy bondman! Are not these enough?"

And last he brought with him the bracelets of the woman he loved, whose heart he had broken by parting with her to propitiate the dead. He brought a long strand of her hair, and a handkerchief damp with her tears. And the vault was filled with the misery of his heart-quaking whisper: "O my wife, are not *these* enough?"

But it became plain to those who were about him that he had come to the end of his life. His hatred of death, his fear of its unyielding caress, gave him strength; and he seemed to be resisting with his thin hands some palpable assailant. Plainer and more deeply coloured than the visions of delirium, he saw the company which advanced to combat him: in the strongest light he contemplated the scenery which surrounds the portals of dissolution. And at the supreme moment, it was with a struggle far greater than that of the miser who is forcibly parted from his gold, with an anguish far more intense than that of the lover who is torn from his mistress, that he gave up his soul.

On a shrewd, grey evening in the autumn they carried him down to bury him in the vault by the side of his wife. This he had desired; for he thought that in no other vault however dark, would the darkness be quite still; in no other resting-place would he be allowed to repose. As they carried him they intoned a majestic threnody—a chaunt which had the deep tramp and surge of a triumphant march, which rode on the winds, and sobbed through the boughs of ancient trees. And having come to the vault they gave him to the grave, and knelt on the ground to pray for the ease of his spirit. *Requiem æternam dona ei, Domine!*

But as they prepared to leave the precincts of

the ruined abbey, a dialogue began within the vault—a dialogue so wonderful, so terrible, in its nature, its cause, that as they hearkened they gazed at one another in the twilight with wry and pallid faces.

And first a woman's voice.

"You are come."

"Yes, I am come," said the voice of a man. "I yield myself to you—the conqueror."

"Long have I awaited you," said the woman's voice. "For years I have lain here while the rain soaked through the stones, and snow was heavy on my breast. For years while the sun danced over the earth, and the moon smiled her mellow smile upon gardens and pleasant things. I have lain here in the company of the worm, and I have leagued with the worm. You did nothing but what I willed;

you were the toy of my dead hands. Ah, you stole my body from me, but I have stolen your soul from you!"

"And is there peace for me—now—at the last?"

The woman's voice became louder, and rang through the vault like a proclaiming trumpet. "Peace is not mine! You and I are at last together in the city of one who queens it over a mighty empire. Now shall we tremble before the queen of Death."

The watchers flung aside the gates of the vault and struck open two coffins. In a mouldy coffin they found the body of a woman having the countenance and warmth of one who has just died. But the body of the man was corrupt and most horrid, like a corpse that has lain for years in a place of graves.

## BLOOD-LUST

# Dion Fortune

Violet Mary Firth (1890–1946) took the pseudonym Dion Fortune from the family motto, *Deo, non Fortuna* (God, not Fate). Born in Llandudno, North Wales, Firth was the daughter of parents active in the Christian Science and Garden City movements. She became a member of the Hermetic Order of the Golden Dawn but left to found another society, the Fraternity of the Inner Light. Her interest in spiritualism and the occult was largely the result of encountering Dr. Theodore Moriarty, who became the inspiration for a series of stories about Dr. Taverner, a psychic detective much in the manner of Sherlock Holmes, whose adventures are narrated by his Watson-like assistant, Dr. Rhodes.

*The Secrets of Dr. Taverner* was her first work of fiction, though she had written and continued to write articles, books, and pamphlets on such subjects as spiritualism, vegetarianism, and contraception. Each Taverner story explores occult, magical, and psychological subjects, depicting a mystical path of life that passes through both good and evil veils of existence. Her fiction dealt with the lost city of Atlantis, the great god Pan, astral bodies, and reincarnation. When she died, her last novel, *Moon Magic,* was incomplete, but the final two chapters were reportedly dictated from beyond to one of the Inner Light mediums.

"Blood-Lust" was first published in *The Secrets of Dr. Taverner* (London: Douglas, 1926).

# Blood-Lust

## DION FORTUNE

### I

I have never been able to make up my mind whether Dr. Taverner should be the hero or the villain of these histories. That he was a man of the most selfless ideals could not be questioned, but in his methods of putting these ideals into practice he was absolutely unscrupulous. He did not evade the law, he merely ignored it, and though the exquisite tenderness with which he handled his cases was an education in itself, he would use that wonderful psychological method of his to break a soul to pieces, going to work as quietly and methodically and benevolently as if bent upon the cure of his patient.

The manner of my meeting with this strange man was quite simple. After being gazetted out of the R.A.M.C. I went to a medical agency and inquired what posts were available.

I said: "I have come out of the Army with my nerves shattered. I want some quiet place till I can pull myself together."

"So does everybody else," said the clerk.

He looked at me thoughtfully. "I wonder whether you would care to try a place we have had on our books for some time. We have sent several men down to it but none of them would stop."

He sent me round to one of the tributaries of Harley Street, and there I made the acquaintance of the man who, whether he was good or bad, I have always regarded as the greatest mind I ever met.

Tall and thin, with a parchment-like countenance, he might have been any age from thirty-five to sixty-five. I have seen him look both ages within the hour. He lost no time in coming to the point.

"I want a medical superintendent for my nursing home," he told me. "I understand that you have specialized, as far as the Army permitted you to, in mental cases. I am afraid you will find my methods very different from the orthodox ones. However, as I sometimes succeed where others fail, I consider I am justified in continuing to experiment, which I think, Dr. Rhodes, is all any of my colleagues can claim to do."

The man's cynical manner annoyed me, though I could not deny that mental treatment is not an exact science at the present moment. As if in answer to my thought he continued:

"My chief interest lies in those regions of psychology which orthodox science has not as yet ventured to explore. If you work with me you will see some queer things, but all I ask of you is, that you should keep an open mind and a shut mouth."

This I undertook to do, for, although I shrank instinctively from the man, yet there was about him such a curious attraction, such a sense of power and adventurous research, that I determined at least to give him the benefit of the doubt and see what it might lead to. His extraordinarily stimulating personality, which seemed to key my brain to concert pitch, made me feel that he might be a good tonic for a man who had lost his grip on life for the time being.

"Unless you have elaborate packing to do," he said, "I can motor you down to my place. If you will walk over with me to the garage I will drive you round to your lodgings, pick up your things, and we shall get in before dark."

We drove at a pretty high speed down the Portsmouth road till we came to Thursley, and, then, to my surprise, my companion turned off to the right and took the big car by a cart track over the heather.

"This is Thor's Ley, or field," he said, as the blighted country unrolled before us. "The old worship is still kept up about here."

"The Catholic faith?" I inquired.

"The Catholic faith, my dear sir, is an innovation. I was referring to the pagan worship. The peasants about here still retain bits of the old ritual; they think that it brings them luck, or some such superstition. They have no knowledge of its inner meaning." He paused a moment, and then turned to me and said with extraordinary emphasis: "Have you ever thought what it would mean if a man who had the Knowledge could piece that ritual together?"

I admitted I had not. I was frankly out of my depth, but he had certainly brought me to the most unchristian spot I had ever been in in my life.

His nursing home, however, was in delightful contrast to the wild and barren country that surrounded it. The garden was a mass of colour, and the house, old and rambling and covered with creepers, as charming within as without; it reminded me of the East, it reminded me of the Renaissance, and yet it had no style save that of warm rich colouring and comfort.

I soon settled down to my job, which I found exceedingly interesting. As I have already said, Taverner's work began where ordinary medicine ended, and I had under my care cases such as the ordinary doctor would have referred to the safe keeping of an asylum, as being nothing else but mad. Yet Taverner, by his peculiar methods of work, laid bare causes operating both within the soul and in the shadowy realm where the soul has its dwelling, that threw an entirely new light upon the problem, and often enabled him to rescue a man from the dark influences that were closing in upon him. The affair of the sheep-killing was an interesting example of his methods.

## II

One showery afternoon at the nursing home we had a call from a neighbour—not a very common occurrence, for Taverner and his ways were regarded somewhat askance. Our visitor shed her dripping mackintosh, but declined to loosen the scarf which, warm as the day was, she had twisted tightly round her neck.

"I believe you specialize in mental cases," she said to my colleague. "I should very much like to talk over with you a matter that is troubling me."

Taverner nodded, his keen eyes watching her for symptoms.

"It concerns a friend of mine—in fact, I think I may call him my *fiancé*, for, although he has asked me to release him from his engagement, I have refused to do so; not because I should wish to hold a man who no longer loved me, but because I am convinced that he still cares for me, and there is something which has come between us that he will not tell me of.

"I have begged him to be frank with me and let us share the trouble together, for the thing that seems an insuperable obstacle to him may not appear in that light to me; but you know what men are when they consider their honour is in question." She looked from one to the other of us smiling. No woman ever believes that her men folk are grown up; perhaps she is right. Then she leant forward and and clasped her hands eagerly. "I believe I have found the key to the mystery. I want you to tell me whether it is possible or not."

"Will you give me particulars?" said Taverner.

Clearly and concisely she gave us what was required.

"We got engaged while Donald was stationed here for his training (that would be nearly five years ago now), and there was always the most perfect harmony between us until he came out of the Army, when we all began to notice a change in him. He came to the house as often as ever, but he always seemed to want to avoid being alone with me. We used to take long walks over the moors together, but he has absolutely refused to do this recently. Then, without any warning, he wrote and told me he could not marry me and did not wish to see me again, and he put a curious thing in his letter. He said: 'Even if I should come to you and ask you to see me, I beg you not to do it.'

"My people thought he had got entangled with some other girl, and were furious with him for jilting me, but I believe there is something more in it than that. I wrote to him, but could get no answer, and I had come to the conclusion that I must try and put the whole thing out of my life, when he suddenly turned up again. Now, this is where the queer part comes in.

"We heard the fowls shrieking one night, and thought a fox was after them. My brothers turned out armed with golf clubs, and I went too. When we got to the hen-house we found several fowls with their throats torn as if a rat had been at them; but the boys discovered that the hen-house door had been forced open, a thing no rat could do. They said a gipsy must have been trying to steal the birds, and told me to go back to the house. I was returning by way of the shrubberies when someone suddenly stepped out in front of me. It was quite light, for the moon was nearly full, and I recognized Donald. He held out his arms and I

went to him, but, instead of kissing me, he suddenly bent his head and—look!"

She drew her scarf from her neck and showed us a semicircle of little blue marks on the skin just under the ear, the unmistakable print of human teeth.

"He was after the jugular," said Taverner. "Lucky for you he did not break the skin."

"I said to him: 'Donald, what are you doing?' My voice seemed to bring him to himself, for he let me go and tore off through the bushes. The boys chased him but did not catch him, and we have never seen him since."

"You have informed the police, I suppose?" said Tavener.

"Father told them someone had tried to rob the hen-roost, but they do not know who it was. You see, I did not tell them I had seen Donald."

"And you walk about the moors by yourself, knowing that he may be lurking in the neighbourhood?"

She nodded.

"I should advise you not to, Miss Wynter; the man is probably exceedingly dangerous, especially to you. We will send you back in the car."

"You think he has gone mad? That is exactly what I think. I believe he knew he was going mad, and that was why he broke off our engagement. Dr. Taverner, is there nothing that can be done for him? It seems to me that Donald is not mad in the ordinary way. We had a house-maid once who went off her head, and the whole of her seemed to be insane, if you can understand; but with Donald it seems as if only a little bit of him were crazy, as if his insanity were outside himself. Can you grasp what I mean?"

"It seems to me you have given a very clear description of a case of psychic interference—what was known in scriptural days as 'being possessed by a devil,'" said Taverner.

"Can you do anything for him?" the girl inquired eagerly.

"I may be able to do a good deal if you can get him to come to me."

On our next day at the Harley Street consulting-room we found that the butler had booked an appointment for a Captain Donald Craigie. We discovered him to be a personality of singular charm—one of those highly-strung, imaginative men who have the makings of an artist in them. In his normal state he must have been a delightful companion, but as he faced us across the consulting-room desk he was a man under a cloud.

"I may as well make a clean breast of this matter," he said. "I suppose Beryl told you about their chickens?"

"She told us that you tried to bite her."

"Did she tell you I bit the chickens?"

"No."

"Well, I did."

Silence fell for a moment. Then Taverner broke it.

"When did this trouble first start?"

"After I got shell shock. I was blown right out of a trench, and it shook me up pretty badly. I thought I had got off lightly, for I was only in hospital about ten days, but I suppose this is the aftermath."

"Are you one of those people who have a horror of blood?"

"Not especially so. I didn't like it, but I could put up with it. We had to get used to it in the trenches; someone was always getting wounded, even in the quietest times."

"And killed," put in Taverner.

"Yes, and killed," said our patient.

"So you developed a blood hunger?"

"That's about it."

"Underdone meat and all the rest of it, I suppose?"

"No, that is no use to me. It seems a horrible thing to say, but it is fresh blood that attracts me, blood as it comes from the veins of my victim."

"Ah!" said Taverner. "That puts a different complexion on the case."

"I shouldn't have thought it could have been much blacker."

"On the contrary, what you have just told me renders the outlook much more hopeful. You have not so much a blood lust, which might well be an effect of the subconscious mind, as a vitality hunger which is quite a different matter."

Craigie looked up quickly. "That's exactly it. I have never been able to put it into words before, but you have hit the nail on the head."

I saw that my colleague's perspicuity had given him great confidence.

"I should like you to come down to my nursing home for a time and be under my personal observation," said Taverner.

"I should like to very much, but I think there is something further you ought to know before I do so. This thing has begun to affect my character. At first it seemed something outside myself, but now I am responding to it, almost helping, and trying to find out ways of gratifying it without getting myself into trouble. That is why I went for the hens when I came down to the Wynters' house. I was afraid I should lose my self-control and go for Beryl. I did in the end, as it happened, so it was not much use. In fact I think it did more harm than good, for I seemed to get into much closer touch with 'It' after I had yielded to the impulse. I know that the best thing I could do would be to do away with myself, but I daren't. I feel that after I am dead I should have to meet—whatever it is—face to face."

"You need not be afraid to come down to the nursing home," said Taverner. "We will look after you."

After he had gone Taverner said to me: "Have you ever heard of vampires, Rhodes?"

"Yes, rather," I said. "I used to read myself to sleep with *Dracula* once when I had a spell of insomnia."

"That," nodding his head in the direction of the departing man, 'is a singularly good specimen."

"Do you mean to say you are going to take a revolting case like that down to Hindhead?"

"Not revolting, Rhodes, a soul in a dungeon. The soul may not be very savoury, but it is a fellow creature. Let it out and it will soon clean itself."

I often used to marvel at the wonderful tolerance and compassion Taverner had for erring humanity.

"The more you see of human nature," he said

to me once, "the less you feel inclined to condemn it, for you realize how hard it has struggled. No one does wrong because he likes it, but because it is the lesser of the two evils."

# III

A couple of days later I was called out of the nursing home office to receive a new patient. It was Craigie. He had got as far as the door-mat, and there he had stuck. He seemed so thoroughly ashamed of himself that I had not the heart to administer the judicious bullying which is usual under such circumstances.

"I feel as if I were driving a baulking horse," he said. "I want to come in, but I can't."

I called Taverner and the sight of him seemed to relieve our patient.

"Ah," he said, "you give me confidence. I feel that I can defy 'It,'" and he squared his shoulders and crossed the threshold. Once inside, a weight seemed lifted from his mind, and he settled down quite happily to the routine of the place. Beryl Wynter used to walk over almost every afternoon, unknown to her family, and cheer him up; in fact he seemed on the high road to recovery.

One morning I was strolling round the grounds with the head gardener, planning certain small improvements, when he made a remark to me which I had reason to remember later.

"You would think all the German prisoners should have been returned by now, wouldn't you, sir? But they haven't. I passed one the other night in the lane outside the back door. I never thought that I should see their filthy field-grey again."

I sympathized with his antipathy; he had been a prisoner in their hands, and the memory was not one to fade.

I thought no more of his remark, but a few days later I was reminded of it when one of our patients came to me and said:

"Dr. Rhodes, I think you are exceedingly unpatriotic to employ German prisoners in the garden when so many discharged soldiers cannot get work."

I assured her that we did not do so, no German being likely to survive a day's work under the superintendence of our ex-prisoner head gardener.

"But I distinctly saw the man going round the greenhouses at shutting-up time last night," she declared. "I recognized him by his flat cap and grey uniform."

I mentioned this to Taverner.

"Tell Craigie he is on no account to go out after sundown," he said, "and tell Miss Wynter she had better keep away for the present."

A night or two later, as I was strolling round the grounds smoking an after-dinner cigarette, I met Craigie hurrying through the shrubbery.

"You will have Dr. Taverner on your trail," I called after him.

"I missed the post-bag," he replied, "and I am going down to the pillar-box."

Next evening I again found Craigie in the grounds after dark. I bore down on him.

"Look here, Craigie," I said, "if you come to this place you must keep the rules, and Dr. Taverner wants you to indoors after sundown."

Craigie bared his teeth and snarled at me like a dog. I took him by the arm and marched him into the house, and reported the incident to Taverner.

"The creature has re-established its influence over him," he said. "We cannot evidently starve it out of existence by keeping it away from him; we shall have to use other methods. Where is Craigie at the present moment?"

"Playing the piano in the drawing-room," I replied.

"Then we will go up to his room and unseal it."

As I followed Taverner upstairs he said to me: "Did it ever occur to you to wonder why Craigie jibbed on the doorstep?"

"I paid no attention," I said. "Such a thing is common enough with mental cases."

"There is a sphere of influence, a kind of psychic bell-jar, over this house to keep out evil entities, what might in popular language be called a 'spell.' Craigie's familiar could not come inside, and did not like being left behind. I thought we might be able to tire it out by keeping Craigie away from its influences, but it has got too strong a hold over him, and he deliberately co-operates with it. Evil communications corrupt good manners, and you can't keep company with a thing like that and not be tainted, especially if you are a sensitive Celt like Craigie."

When we reached the room Taverner went over to the window and passed his hand across the sill, as if sweeping something aside.

"There," he said. "It can come in now and fetch him out, and we will see what it does."

At the doorway he paused again and made a sign on the lintel.

"I don't think it will pass that," he said.

When I returned to the office I found the village policeman waiting to see me.

"I should be glad if you would keep an eye on your dog, sir," he said. "We have been having complaints of sheep-killing lately, and whatever animal is doing it is working in a three-mile radius with this as the centre."

"Our dog is an Airedale," I said. "I should not think he is likely to be guilty. It is usually collies that take to sheep-killing."

At eleven o'clock we turned out the lights and herded our patients off to bed. At Taverner's request I changed into an old suit and rubber-soled tennis shoes and joined him in the smoking-room, which was under Craigie's bedroom. We sat in the darkness awaiting events.

"I don't want you to do anything," said Taverner, "but just to follow and see what happens."

We had not long to wait. In about a quarter-of-an-hour we heard a rustling in the creepers, and down came Craigie hand over fist, swinging himself along by the great ropes of wistaria that clothed the wall. As he disappeared into the shrubbery I slipped after him, keeping in the shadow of the house.

He moved at a stealthy dog-trot over the heather paths towards Frensham.

At first I ran and ducked, taking advantage of every patch of shadow, but presently I saw that this caution was unnecessary. Craigie was absorbed in his own affairs, and thereupon I drew up closer to him, following at a distance of some sixty yards.

He moved at a swinging pace, a kind of loping trot that put me in mind of a blood-hound. The wide, empty levels of that forsaken country stretched out on either side of us, belts of mist filled the hollows, and the heights of Hindhead stood out against the stars. I felt no nervousness; man for man, I reckoned I was a match for Craigie, and, in addition, I was armed with what is technically known as a "soother"—two feet of lead gas-piping inserted in a length of rubber hose-pipe. It is not included in the official equipment of the best asylums, but can frequently be found in a keeper's trouser-leg.

If I had known what I had to deal with I should not have put so much reliance on my "soother." Ignorance is sometimes an excellent substitute for courage.

Suddenly out of the heather ahead of us a sheep got up, then the chase began. Away went Craigie in pursuit, and away went the terrified wether. A sheep can move remarkably fast for a short distance, but the poor wool-encumbered beast could not keep the pace, and Craigie ran it down, working in gradually lessening circles. It stumbled, went to its knees, and he was on it. He pulled its head back, and whether he used a knife or not I could not see, a cloud passed over the moon, but dimly luminous in the shadow, I saw something that was semi-transparent pass between me and the dark, struggling mass among the heather. As the moon cleared the clouds I made out the flat-topped cap and field-grey uniform of the German Army.

I cannot possibly convey the sickening horror of that sight—the creature that was not a man assisting the man who, for the moment, was not human.

Gradually the sheep's struggles weakened and ceased. Craigie straightened his back and stood up; then he set off at his steady lope towards the east, his grey familiar at his heels.

How I made the homeward journey I do not know. I dared not look behind lest I should find a Presence at my elbow; every breath of wind that blew across the heather seemed to be cold fingers on my throat; fir trees reached out long arms to clutch me as I passed under them, and heather bushes rose up and assumed human shapes. I moved like a runner in a nightmare, making prodigious efforts after a receding goal.

At last I tore across the moonlit lawns of the house, regardless who might be looking from the windows, burst into the smoking-room and flung myself face downwards on the sofa.

# IV

"Tut, tut!" said Taverner. "Has it been as bad as all that?"

I could not tell him what I had seen, but he seemed to know.

"Which way did Craigie go after he left you?" he asked.

"Towards the moonrise," I told him.

"And you were on the way to Frensham? He is heading for the Wynters' house. This is very serious, Rhodes. We must go after him; it may be too late as it is. Do you feel equal to coming with me?"

He gave me a stiff glass of brandy, and we went to get the car out of the garage. In Taverner's company I felt secure. I could understand the confidence he inspired in his patients. Whatever that grey shadow might be, I felt he could deal with it and that I should be safe in his hands.

We were not long in approaching our destination.

"I think we will leave the car here," said Taverner, turning into a grass-grown lane. "We do not want to rouse them if we can help it."

We moved cautiously over the dew-soaked grass into the paddock that bounded one side of the Wynters' garden. It was separated from the lawn by a sunk fence, and we could command the whole front of the house and easily gain the terrace if we so desired. In the shadow of a rose pergola we paused. The great trusses of bloom, colourless in the moonlight, seemed a ghastly mockery of our business.

For some time we waited, and then a movement caught my eye.

Out in the meadow behind us something was moving at a slow lope; it followed a wide arc, of which the house formed the focus, and disappeared into a little coppice on the left. It might have been imagination, but I thought I saw a wisp of mist at its heels.

We remained where we were, and presently he came round once more, this time moving in a smaller circle—evidently closing in upon the house. The third time he reappeared more quickly, and this time he was between us and the terrace.

"Quick! Head him off," whispered Taverner. "He will be up the creepers next round."

We scrambled up the sunk fence and dashed across the lawn. As we did so a girl's figure appeared at one of the windows; it was Beryl Wynter. Taverner, plainly visible in the moonlight, laid his finger on his lips and beckoned her to come down.

"I am going to do a very risky thing," he whispered, "but she is a girl of courage, and if her nerve does not fail we shall be able to pull it off."

In a few seconds she slipped out of a side door and joined us, a cloak over her nightdress.

"Are you prepared to undertake an exceedingly unpleasant task?" Taverner asked her. "I can guarantee you will be perfectly safe so long as you keep your head, but if you lose your nerve you will be in grave danger."

"Is it to do with Donald?" she inquired.

"It is," said Taverner. "I hope to be able to rid him of the thing that is overshadowing him and trying to obsess him."

"I have seen it," she said. "It is like a wisp of grey vapour that floats just behind him. It has the most awful face you ever saw. It came up to the window last night, just the face only, while Donald was going round and round the house."

"What did you do?" asked Taverner.

"I didn't do anything. I was afraid that if someone found him he might be put in an asylum, and then we should have no chance of getting him well."

Taverner nodded.

"'Perfect love casteth out fear,'" he said. "You can do the thing that is required of you."

He placed Miss Wynter on the terrace in full moonlight.

"As soon as Craigie sees you," he said, "retreat round the corner of the house into the yard. Rhodes and I will wait for you there."

A narrow doorway led from the terrace to the back premises, and just inside its arch Taverner bade me take my stand.

"Pinion him as he comes past you and hang on for your life," he said. "Only mind he doesn't get his teeth into you; these things are infectious."

We had hardly taken up our positions when we heard the loping trot come round once more, this time on the terrace itself. Evidently he caught sight of Miss Wynter, for the stealthy padding changed to a wild scurry over the gravel, and the girl slipped quickly through the archway and sought refuge behind Taverner. Right on her heels came Craigie. Another yard and he would have had her, but I caught him by the elbows and pinioned him securely. For a moment we swayed and struggled across the dew-drenched flagstones, but I locked him in an old wrestling grip and held him.

"Now," said Taverner, "if you will keep hold of Craigie I will deal with the other. But first of all we must get it away from him, otherwise it will retreat on to him, and he may die of shock. Now, Miss Wynter, are you prepared to play your part?"

"I am prepared to do whatever is necessary," she replied. Taverner took a scalpel out of a pocket case and made a small incision in the skin of her neck, just under the ear. A drop of blood slowly gathered, showing black in the moonlight.

"That is the bait," he said. "Now go close up to Craigie and entice the creature away; get it to follow you and draw it out into the open."

As she approached us Craigie plunged and struggled in my arms like a wild beast, and then something grey and shadowy drew out of the gloom of the wall and hovered for a moment at my elbow. Miss Wynter came nearer, walking almost into it.

"Don't go too close," cried Taverner, and she paused.

Then the grey shape seemed to make up its mind; it drew clear of Craigie and advanced towards her. She retreated towards Taverner, and the Thing came out into the moonlight. We could see it quite clearly from its flat-topped cap to its knee-boots; its high cheek-bones and slit eyes pointed its origin to that south-eastern corner of Europe where strange tribes still defy civilization and keep up their still stranger beliefs.

The shadowy form drifted onwards, following the girl across the yard, and when it was some twenty feet from Craigie, Taverner stepped out quickly behind it, cutting off its retreat. Round it came in a moment, instantly conscious of his presence, and then began a game of "puss-in-the-corner." Taverner was trying to drive it into a kind of psychic killing-pen he had made for its reception. Invisible to me, the lines of psychic force which bounded it were evidently plainly perceptible to the creature we were hunting. This way and that way it slid in its efforts to escape, but Taverner all the time herded it towards the apex of the invisible triangle, where he could give it its *coup de grâce*.

Then the end came. Taverner leapt forward. There was a Sign then a Sound. The grey form commenced to spin like a top. Faster and faster it went, its outlines merging into a whirling spiral of mist; then it broke. Out into space went the particles that had composed its form, and with the almost soundless shriek of supreme speed the soul went to its appointed place.

Then something seemed to lift. From a cold hell of limitless horror the flagged space became a normal back yard, the trees ceased to be tentacled menaces, the gloom of the wall was no longer an ambuscade, and I knew that never again would a grey shadow drift out of the darkness upon its horrible hunting.

I released Craigie, who collapsed in a heap at my feet. Miss Wynter went to rouse her father, while Taverner and I got the insensible man into the house.

**W**hat masterly lies Taverner told to the family I have never known, but a couple of months later we received, instead of the conventional fragment of wedding cake, a really substantial chunk, with a note from the bride to say it was to go in the office cupboard, where she knew we kept provisions for those nocturnal meals that Taverner's peculiar habits imposed upon us.

It was during one of these midnight repasts that I questioned Taverner about the strange matter of Craigie and his familiar. For a long time I had not been able to refer to it; the memory of that horrible sheep-killing was a thing that would not bear recalling.

"You have heard of vampires," said Taverner. "That was a typical case. For close on a hundred years they have been practically unknown in Europe—Western Europe that is—but the War has caused a renewed outbreak, and quite a number of cases have been reported.

"When they were first observed—that is to say, when some wretched lad was caught attacking the wounded, they took him behind the lines and shot him, which is not a satisfactory way of dealing with a vampire, unless you also go to the trouble of burning his body, according to the good old-fashioned way of dealing with practitioners of black magic. Then our enlightened generation came to the conclusion that they were not dealing with a crime, but with a disease, and put the unfortunate individual afflicted with this horrible obsession into an asylum, where he did not usually live very long, the supply of his peculiar nourishment being cut off. But it never struck anybody that they might be dealing with more than one factor—that what they were really contending with was a gruesome partnership between the dead and the living."

"What in the world do you mean?" I asked.

"We have two physical bodies, you know," said Taverner, "the dense material one, with which we are all familiar, and the subtle etheric one, which inhabits it, and acts as the medium of the life forces, whose functioning would explain a very great deal if science would only condescend to investigate it. When a man dies, the etheric body, with his soul in it, draws out of the physical form and drifts about in its neighbourhood for about three days, or until decomposition sets in, and then the soul

draws out of the etheric body also, which in turn dies, and the man enters upon the first phase of his post mortem existence, the purgatorial one.

"Now, it is possible to keep the etheric body together almost indefinitely if a supply of vitality is available, but, having no stomach which can digest food and turn it into energy, the thing has to batten on someone who has, and develops into a spirit parasite which we call a vampire.

"There is a pretty good working knowledge of black magic in Eastern Europe. Now, supposing some man who has this knowledge gets shot, he knows that in three days time, at the death of the etheric body, he will have to face his reckoning, and with his record he naturally does not want to do it, so he establishes a connection with the subconscious mind of some other soul that still has a body, provided he can find one suitable for his purposes. A very positive type of character is useless; he has to find one of a negative type, such as the lower class of medium affords. Hence one of the many dangers of mediumship to the untrained. Such a negative condition may be temporarily induced by, say, shell-shock, and it is possible then for such a soul as we are considering to obtain an influence over a being of much higher type— Craigie, for instance—and use him as a means of obtaining its gratification."

"But why did not the creature confine its attentions to Craigie, instead of causing him to attack others?"

"Because Craigie would have been dead in a week if it had done so, and then it would have found itself minus its human feeding bottle. Instead of that it worked *through* Craigie, getting him to draw extra vitality from others and pass it on to itself; hence it was that Craigie had a vitality hunger rather than a blood hunger, though the fresh blood of a victim was the means of absorbing the vitality."

"Then that German we all saw—?"

"Was merely a corpse who was insufficiently dead."

# THE CANAL

# Everil Worrell

Mrs. Everil Worrell Murphy (1893–1969) graduated from George Washington University in Washington, D.C., in 1915.

Unlike most of her contemporary pulp writers, she was not at all prolific, though she did have nearly twenty stories published in the pulps between 1926 and 1954, mostly in *Weird Tales*. Among her most anthologized supernatural stories from *Weird Tales* are "From Beyond" (April 1928), "The Elemental Law" (July 1928), "Call Not Their Names" (March 1954), and the novelette "Once There Was a Little Girl" (January 1953). She also wrote a novelette for *Weird Tales* titled "Norn" (February 1936) using the pseudonym Lireve Monet. Her first published work appeared in the February 1916 issue of *Overland Monthly*.

Worrell's most famous story, the much-anthologized "The Canal," served as the basis for an episode of Rod Serling's television series *Night Gallery*, for which it was retitled "Death on a Barge," airing on NBC on March 4, 1973. The episode was directed by Leonard Nimoy and starred Lesley Ann Warren as the mysterious Hyacinth and Lou Antonio as the hopelessly smitten Jake.

"The Canal" was originally published in the December 1927 issue of *Weird Tales*.

# The Canal

## EVERIL WORRELL

Past the sleeping city the river sweeps; along its left bank the old canal creeps. I did not intend that to be poetry, although the scene is poetic—sombrely, gruesomely poetic, like the poems of Poe. I know it too well—I have walked too often over the grass-grown path beside the reflections of black trees and tumbledown shacks and distant factory chimneys in the sluggish waters that moved so slowly, and ceased to move at all.

I have always had a taste for nocturnal prowling. As a race we have grown too intelligent to take seriously any of the old, instinctive fears that preserved us through preceding generations. Our sole remaining salvation, then, has come to be our tendency to travel in herds. We wander at night—but our objective is somewhere on the brightly lighted streets, or still somewhere where men do not go alone. When we travel far afield, it is in company. Few of my acquaintances, few in the whole city here, would care to ramble at midnight over the grass-grown path I have spoken of—not because they would fear to do so, but because such things are not being done.

Well, it is dangerous to differ individually from one's fellows. It is dangerous to wander from the beaten road. And the fears that guarded the race in the dawn of time and through the centuries were founded on reality.

A month ago, I was a stranger here. I had just taken my first position—I was graduated from college only three months before, in the spring. I was lonely, and likely to remain so for some time, for I have always been of a solitary nature, making friends slowly.

I had received one invitation out, to visit the camp of a fellow employee in the firm for which I worked, a camp which was located on the farther side of the wide river, the side across from the city and the canal, where the bank was high and steep and heavily wooded, and little tents blossomed all along the water's edge. At night these camps were a string of sparkling lights and tiny, leaping camp fires, and the tinkle of music carried faintly across the calmly flowing water. That far bank of the river was no place for an eccentric, solitary man to love. But the near bank, which would have been an eyesore to the campers had not the river been so wide—the near bank attracted me from my first glimpse of it.

We embarked in a motor-boat at some distance

downstream, and swept up along the near bank, and then out and across the current. I turned my eyes backward. The murk of stagnant water that was the canal, the jumble of low buildings beyond it, the lonely, low-lying waste of the narrow strip of land between canal and river, the dark, scattered trees growing there—I intended to see more of these things.

That weekend bored me, but I repaid myself no later than Monday evening, the first evening when I was back in the city, alone and free. I ate a solitary dinner immediately after leaving the office. I went to my room and slept from seven until nearly midnight. I wakened naturally, then, for my whole heart was set on exploring the alluring solitude I had discovered. I dressed, slipped out of the house and into the street, started the motor in my roadster, and drove through the lighted streets.

When I parked my car on a rough, cobbled street that ran directly down into the inky waters of the canal, and crossed a narrow bridge, I was repaid. In a few minutes I set my feet on the old towpath where mules had drawn river-boats up and down only a year or so ago. As I walked upstream at a swinging pace, the miserable shacks where miserable people lived across the canal seemed to march with me, and then fell behind.

The bridge I had crossed was near the end of the city going north, as the canal marked its western extremity. Ten minutes of walking, and the dismal shacks were quite a distance behind, the river was farther away and the strip of waste land much wider and more wooded, and tall trees across the canal marched with me as the evil-looking houses had done before. Far and faint, the sound of a bell in the city reached my ears. It was midnight.

I stopped, enjoying the desolation around me. It had the savour I had expected and hoped for. I stood for some time looking up at the sky, watching the low drift of heavy clouds, which were visible in the dull reflected glow from distant lights in the heart of the city, so that they appeared to have a lurid phosphorescence of their own. The ground under my feet, on the contrary, was utterly devoid of light. I had felt my way carefully, knowing the edge of the canal partly by instinct, partly by the even more perfect blackness of the water in it, and even holding fairly well to the path, because it was perceptibly sunken below the ground beside it.

Now as I stood motionless in this spot, my eyes upcast, my mind adrift with strange fancies, suddenly my feelings of satisfaction and well-being gave way to something different. Fear was an emotion unknown to me—for I had always been drawn to those things which make men fear. But now along all the length of my spine I was conscious of a prickling, tingling sensation—such as my forefathers may have felt in the jungle when the hair on their backs stood up. I knew that there were eyes upon me, and that that was why I was afraid to move. I stood perfectly still, my face uptilted towards the sky. But with effort, mastered myself.

Slowly, slowly, with an attempt to propitiate the owner of the unseen eyes by my casual manner, I lowered my own. I looked straight ahead— at the softly swaying silhouette of the tree-tops across the canal as they moved gently in the cool night wind, at the mass of blackness that was those trees, and the opposite shore, at the shiny blackness that was the canal, where the reflections of the clouds glinted vaguely and disappeared. As I grew accustomed to the greater blackness and my pupils expanded, I dimly discerned the contours of an old boat or barge, half sunken in the water. An old, abandoned canal-boat. But was I dreaming or was there a white-clad figure seated on the roof of the low cabin aft, a pale, heart-shaped face gleaming strangely at me from the darkness, the glow of two eyes seeming to light up the face, and to detach it from the darkness?

Surely, there could be no doubt as to the eyes. They shone as the eyes of animals shine in the dark, with a phosphorescent gleam, and a glimmer of red! Well, I had heard that some human eyes have that quality at night.

But what a place for a human being to be—a girl, too, I was sure. That daintily heart-shaped face was the face of a girl, surely; I was seeing it clearer and clearer, either because my eyes were growing more accustomed to peering into the deeper shadows, or because of that phosphorescence in the eyes that stared back at me.

I raised my voice softly, not to break too much of the stillness of night.

"Hello! Who's there? Are you lost, or marooned, and can I help?"

There was a little pause. I was conscious of a soft lapping at my feet. A stronger night wind had sprung up, was ruffling the dark water. I had been overwarm, and where it struck me the perspiration turned cold on my body, so that I shivered uncontrollably.

"You can stay and talk awhile, if you will. I am lonely, but not lost. I—live here."

The voice was little more than a whisper, but it had carried clearly—a girl's voice. And she lived *there,* in an old, abandoned canal-boat, half submerged in the stagnant water.

"You are not *alone* there?"

"No, not alone. My father lives here with me, but he is deaf, and sleeps soundly."

Did the night wind blow still colder, as though it came to us from some unseen, frozen sea—or was there something in her tone that chilled me, even as a strange attraction drew me towards her? I wanted to draw near to her, to see closely the pale, heart-shaped face, to lose myself in the bright eyes that I had seen shining in the darkness. I wanted—I wanted to hold her in my arms, to find her mouth with mine, to kiss it . . .

I took a reckless step nearer the edge of the bank.

"Could I come over to you?" I asked. "It's warm and I don't mind a wetting. It's late, I know, but I'd like to sit and talk, if only for a few minutes before I go back to town. It's a lonely place here for a girl like you to live."

Was it the unconventionality of my request that made her next words sound like a long-drawn shudder of protest? There was a strangeness in the tones of her voice that held me wondering, every time she spoke.

"No, no. Oh, no! You must not come across."

"Then could I come tomorrow, or some day soon, in the daytime; and would you let me come on board then—or would you come on shore and talk to me, perhaps?"

"Not in the daytime—*never* in the daytime!"

Again the intensity of her low-toned negation held me spell-bound.

It was not her sense of the impropriety of the hour, then, that had dictated her manner. For surely, any girl with the slightest sense of the fitness of things would rather have a tryst by daytime than after midnight—yet there was an inference in her last words that if I came again it should be at night.

Still feeling the spell that had enthralled me, as one does not forget the presence of a drug in the air that is stealing one's senses, even when those senses begin to wander and to busy themselves with other things, I yet spoke shortly.

"Why do you say, 'Never in the daytime'? Do you mean that I may come more than this once at night, though now you won't let me cross the canal to you at the expense of my own clothes, and you won't put down your plank or drawbridge or whatever you come on shore with, and talk to me here for only a moment? I'll come again, if you'll let me talk to you instead of calling across the water. If I came in the daytime and met your father, wouldn't that be the best thing to do? Then we could be really acquainted; we could be friends."

"In the night-time, my father sleeps. In the daytime, I sleep. How could I talk to you, or introduce you to my father then? If you came on board this boat in the daytime, you would find my father—and you would be sorry. As for me, I would be sleeping. I could never introduce you to my father, do you see?"

"You sleep soundly, and your father." Again there was pique in my voice.

"Yes, we sleep soundly."

"And always at different times?"

"Always at different times. We are on guard— one of us is always on guard. We have been hardly used, down there in your city. And we have taken refuge here. And we are always—always—on guard."

My resentment vanished, and I felt my heart go out to her anew. She was so pale, so pitiful in the night. My eyes were learning better and better how to pierce the darkness; they were giving me a more definite picture of my companion—if I could think of her as a companion, between myself and whom stretched the black waters.

The sadness of the lonely scene, the perfection of the solitude itself, these things contributed to her pitifulness. Then there was that strangeness of atmosphere of which, even yet, I had only partly taken note. There was the strange, shivering chill, which yet did not seem like the healthful chill of a cool evening. In fact, it did not prevent me from feeling the oppression of the night, which was unusually sultry. It was like a little breath of deadly cold that came and went, and yet did not alter the temperature of the air itself, as the small ripples on the surface of the water do not concern the water even a foot down.

And even that was not all. There was an unwholesome smell about the night—a dank, mouldy smell that might have been the very breath of death and decay. Even I, a connoisseur in all things dismal and unwholesome, tried to keep my mind from dwelling overmuch upon that smell. What it must be to live breathing it constantly, I could not think. But no doubt the girl and her father were used to it; and no doubt it came from the stagnant water of the canal and from the rotting wood of the old, half-sunken boat that was their refuge.

My clearer vision of the girl showed me that she was pitifully thin, even though possessed of a strangely attractive face that drew me to her. Her clothes hung around her like old rags, but hers was no scarecrow aspect. I was sure the little, pale, heart-shaped face would be more beautiful still, if I could only see it closely. I must see it closely—I must establish some claim to consideration as a friend of the strange, lonely crew of the half-sunken wreck.

"This is a poor place to call a refuge," I said finally. "One might have very little money, and yet do somewhat better. Perhaps I might help you; I am sure I could. If your ill-treatment in the city was because of poverty—I am not rich, but I could

help that. I could help you a little with money, if you would let me; or, in any case, I could find a position for you. I'm sure I could do that."

The eyes that shone fitfully toward me like two small pools of water intermittently lit by a cloud-swept sky seemed to glow more brightly. She had been half crouching, half sitting on top of the cabin; now she leaped to her feet with one quick, sinuous, abrupt motion, and took a few rapid, restless steps to and fro before she answered.

"Do you think you would be helping me, to tie me to a desk, to shut me behind doors, away from freedom, away from the delight of doing my own will, of seeking my own way? Rather this old boat, rather a deserted grave under the stars for my home!"

A positive feeling of kinship with this strange being, whose face I had hardly seen, possessed me. So I myself might have spoken, so I had often felt, though I had never dreamed of putting my thoughts so forcibly. My regularized daytime life was a thing I thought little of; I really lived only in my nocturnal prowlings. This girl was right! All life should be free.

"I understand much better than you think," I answered. "I want to see you again, to come to know you. Surely, there must be some way in which I can be of use to you. All you have to do from tonight on for ever, is to command me, I swear it!"

"You swear *that*—do you swear it?"

"I swear it. From this night on, for ever—I swear it."

"Then listen. Tonight you may not come to me, or I to you. I do not want you to board this boat—not tonight, not any night. And most of all, not any day. But do not look so sad. I will come to you. No, not tonight, perhaps not for many nights, yet before very long. I will come to you there, on the bank of the canal, when the water in the canal ceases to flow."

I must have made a gesture of impatience, or of despair. It sounded like a way of saying "never"—for why should the water in the canal cease to flow? She read my thoughts in some way, for she answered them.

"You do not understand. I am speaking seriously; I am promising to meet you there on the bank, soon. The water is moving always slower. Higher up, the canal has been drained. Between these lower locks, the water still seeps in and drops slowly downstream. But there will come a night when it will be stagnant—and on that night I will come to you. And when I come, I will ask of you a favour."

It was all the assurance I could get that night. She had come back to the side of the cabin where she had sat crouched before, and she resumed again that posture and sat still and silent, watching me. Sometimes I could see her eyes upon me, and sometimes not. But I felt that their gaze was unwavering. The little cold breeze, which I had finally forgotten while I was talking with her, was blowing again, and the unwholesome smell of decay grew heavier before the dawn.

I went away, and in the first faint light of dawn I slipped up the stairs of my rooming-house, and into my room.

I was deadly tired at the office next day. And day after day slipped away and I grew more and more weary, for a man cannot wake day and night without suffering. I haunted the old towpath and waited, night after night, on the bank opposite the sunken boat. Sometimes I saw my lady of the darkness, and sometimes not. When I saw her, she spoke little; but sometimes she sat there on the top of the cabin and let me watch her till the dawn, or until the strange uneasiness that was like fright drove me from her and back to my room, where I tossed restlessly in the heat and dreamed strange dreams, half waking, till the sun shone in on my forehead and I tumbled into my clothes and down to the office again.

Once I asked her why she made the fanciful condition that she would not come ashore to meet me until the waters of the canal had ceased to run. (How eagerly I studied those waters! How I stole away at noontime more than once, not to approach the old boat, but to watch the almost imperceptible downdrift of bubbles, bits of straw, twigs, rubbish!) But my questioning displeased her, and I asked her that no more. It was enough that she chose to be whimsical. My part was to wait.

It was more than a week later that I questioned her again, this time on a different subject. And after that, I curbed my curiosity relentlessly.

"Never speak to me of things you do not understand about me, or you will not see me again."

I had asked her what form of persecution she and her father had suffered in the city, that had driven them out to this lonely place, and where in the city they had lived.

Frightened lest I lose the ground I was sure I had gained with her, I was about to speak of something else. But before I could find the words, her low voice came to me again.

"It was horrible, horrible! Those little houses below the bridge, those houses along the canal— tell me, are not they worse than my boat? Life there was shut in and furtive. I wasn't free as I am now, and the freedom I will soon have will make me forget the things I have not yet forgotten. The screaming, the reviling and cursing! Think how you would like to be shut up in one of those houses, and in fear of your life!"

I dared not answer her. I was surprised that she had vouchsafed me so much. But surely her words meant that before she had come to live on the decaying, water-rotted old boat, she had lived in one of those horrible houses I passed by on my way to her. Those houses, each of which looked like the predestined scene of dark crime!

As I left her that night, I felt that I was very daring.

And yet, the next day, for the first time my thoughts were definitely troubled. I had been living in a dream—I began to speculate concerning the end of the path on which my feet were set. I had conceived, from the first, such a horror of those old houses by the canal! Much as I loved all that was weird and eerie about the girl I was wooing so strangely, it was a little too much for my fancy that she had come from them.

By this time, I had become decidedly unpopular in my place of business. Not that I had made enemies, but my peculiar ways had caused too much adverse comment. It would have taken very little, I think, to have made the entire office force decide that I was mad. However, they were punctiliously polite to me, and merely let me alone as much as possible—which suited me perfectly. I dragged wearily through day after day, exhausted from lack of sleep, conscious of their speculative glances, living only for the night to come.

One day, I approached the man who had invited me to the camp across the river. "Have you ever noticed the row of tumbledown houses along the canal on the city side?" I asked.

He gave me an odd look. I suppose he sensed the significance of my breaking silence after so long to speak of them.

"You have odd tastes, Morton," he said after a moment. "I suppose you wander into strange places sometimes. But my advice to you is to keep away from those houses. They're unsavoury, and their reputation is pretty bad. You might very well be in danger of your life, if you go poking around there. They have been the scene of several murders, and a dope den or two has been cleaned out of them. Why in the world you should want to investigate them—"

"I don't expect to investigate them," I said. "I was merely interested in them—from the outside. To tell you the truth, I'd heard a story, a rumour—never mind where. But you say there have been murders there—I suppose this rumour I heard may have had to do with an attempted one. There was a girl who lived there with her father once, and they were set upon there, or something of the sort, and had to run away. Did you ever hear *that* story?"

Barrett gave me an odd look such as one gives in speaking of a past horror so dreadful that the mere speaking of it makes it live terribly again.

"What you say reminds me of something that was said to have happened down there once," he answered. "It was in all the papers. A little child disappeared in one of those houses, and a girl and her father were accused of having made away with it. They were accused of—oh, well, I don't like to talk about such things. It was pretty disagreeable.

The child's body was found—or, rather, *part* of it was found. It was mutilated, and the people seemed to believe it had been mutilated in order to conceal the manner of its death; there was an ugly wound in the throat, it finally came out, and it seemed as if this child might have been bled to death. It was found in the girl's room, hidden away. The old man and his daughter escaped before the police were called. The countryside was scoured, but they were never found. Why, you must have read it in the papers several years ago."

I *had* read it in the papers, I remembered now. And again, a terrible doubt came over me. Who was this girl, *what* was this girl, who seemed to have my heart in her keeping?

Befogged with exhaustion, bemused in a dire enchantment, my mind was incapable of thought. And yet, some soul-process akin to that which saves the sleepwalker poised at perilous heights sounded its warning now.

My mind was filled with doleful images. There were women, I had heard and read, who slew to satisfy a blood-lust. There were ghosts, spectres—call them what you will; their names have been legion in the dark pages of that lore which dates back to the infancy of the races of the earth—who retained even in death this blood-lust. Vampires—they had been called that. Corpses by day, spirits of evil by night, roaming abroad in their own forms or in the forms of bats or unclean beasts, killing body and soul of their victims—for whoever dies of the repeated "kiss" of the vampire, which leaves its mark on the throat and draws blood from the body, becomes a vampire also—of such beings I had read.

And, in that last day at the office, I remembered reading of those undead, that in their nocturnal flights they had one limitation—*they could not cross running water.*

That night I went my usual way, recognizing fully the misery of being the victim of an enchantment stronger than my feeble will. I approached the neighbourhood of the canal boat as the distant city clock chimed the first stroke of twelve. It was the dark of the moon and the sky was overcast.

Heat-lightning flickered low in the sky, seeming to come from every point of the compass and circumscribe the horizon, as if unseen fires burned behind the rim of the world. By its fitful glimmer, I saw a new thing: between the old boat and the canal bank stretched a long, slim, solid-looking shadow—a plank had been let down! In that moment, I realized that I had been playing with powers of evil which had no intention now to let me go, which were indeed about to lay hold upon me with an inexorable grasp. Why had I come tonight? Why, but that the spell of the enchantment laid upon me was a thing more potent and far more unbreakable, than any wholesome spell of love?

Behind me in the darkness there was a crackle of a twig, and something brushed against my arm.

This, then, was my fulfilment of my dream. I knew, without turning my head, that the pale, dainty face with its glowing eyes was near my own—that I had only to stretch out my arm to touch the slender grace of the girl I had so longed to draw near. I knew, and should have felt the rapture I had anticipated. Instead, the miasmic odours of the night, heavy and oppressive with heat and unrelieved by a breath of air, all but overcame me. The little waves of coldness I had felt often in this spot were possessing all my body, yet they were not from any breeze; the leaves on the trees hung down motionless, as though they were actually wilting on their branches.

With an effort, I turned my head.

Two hands caught me at my neck. The pale face was so near that I felt the warm breath from its nostrils fanning my cheek.

And, suddenly, all that was wholesome in my perverted nature rose uppermost. I longed for the touch of the red mouth, like a dark flower opening before me in the night, I longed for it—and yet more I dreaded it. I shrank back, catching in a powerful grip the fragile wrists of the hands that strove to hold me.

I was facing down the path towards the city. A low rumble of thunder broke the torrid hush of the summer night. A glare of lightning seemed to tear the night asunder, to light up the universe. Overhead, the clouds were careering madly in fan-tastic shapes, driven by a wind that swept the upper heavens without causing even a trembling in the air lower down. And far down the canal, that baleful glare seemed to play around and hover over the little row of shanties—murder-cursed and haunted by the ghost of a dead child.

My gaze was fixed on them, while I held away from me the pallid face and fought off the embrace that sought to overcome my resisting will. And so a long moment passed. The glare faded out of the sky, and a greater darkness took the world. But there was a near, more menacing light fastened upon my face—the light of two eyes that watched mine, that had watched me as I, unthinking, stared down at the dark houses.

This girl—this woman who had come to me at my own importunate requests, did not love me, since I had shrunk from her. She did not love me—but it was not only that. She had watched me as I gazed down at the houses that held her dark past, and I was sure that she divined my thoughts. She knew my horror of those houses—she knew my new-born horror of *her*. And she hated me for it, hated me more malignantly than I had believed a human being could hate.

Could a *human* being cherish such hatred as I read, trembling more and more, in those glowing fires lit with what seemed to me more like the fires of hell than any light that ought to shine in a woman's eyes?

At this point in the happenings of that night, my calmness deserted me; at this point I felt that I had been drawn into the midst of a horrible nightmare from which there was no escape, no waking! As I write, this feeling again overwhelms me, until I can hardly write at all—until, were it not for the thing which I must do, I would rush out into the street and run, screaming, until I was caught and dragged away, to be put behind strong bars. Perhaps I would feel safe there—perhaps!

I know that, terrified at the hate I saw confronting me in those red gleaming eyes, I would have slunk away. But the two thin hands that caught my arm again were strong enough to prevent that. I had been spared her kiss, but I was not to escape from the oath I had taken to serve her.

"You promised, you swore," she whispered at my ear. "And tonight you are to keep your oath."

My oath—yes, I had an oath to keep. I had lifted my hand towards the dark heavens and sworn to serve her in any way she chose. Freely, and of my own volition, I had sworn.

I sought to evade her.

"Let me help you back to your boat," I begged. "You have no kindly feeling for me, and—you have seen it—I love you no longer. I will go back to the city—you can go back to your father, and forget that I broke your peace."

The laughter that greeted my speech I shall never forget.

"So you do not love me, and I hate you! Have I waited these weary months for the water to stop, only to go back now? When the water was turned into the canal while I slept, so that I could never escape until its flow should cease, *because of the thing that I am*—when the imprisonment we shared ceased to matter to my father—come on board the deserted boat tomorrow, and see why, if you dare!—I dreamed of tonight! I have been lonely, desolate, starving—now the whole world shall be mine! And by *your* help!"

I asked her what she wanted of me. I knew that there was that on the opposite shore of the great river where the summer camps were, that she wanted to find. In the madness of my terror, she made me understand and obey her. I must carry her in my arms across the long bridge over the river, deserted in the small hours of the night.

The way back to the city was long tonight— long. She walked behind me, and I turned my eyes neither to right nor left. Only as I passed the tumbledown houses, I saw their reflection in the canal and trembled at the thought of the little child this woman had been accused of slaying there, and at the certainty I felt that she was reading my thoughts.

I know that we set our feet on the long, wide bridge that spanned the river. I know the storm broke there, so that I battled for my footing, almost for my life, it seemed, against the pelting deluge. And the horror I had invoked was in my arms, clinging to me, burying its head upon my shoulder. So increasingly dreadful had my pale-faced

companion become to me, that I hardly thought of her now as a woman at all.

The tempest raged still when she leaped down out of my arms on the other side. And again I walked with her against my will, while the trees lashed their branches around me, showing the pale undersides of their leaves in the vivid frequent flashes that rent the heavens.

On and on we went, branches flying through the air and missing us by a miracle of ill fortune. Such as she and I are not slain by falling branches. The river was a welter of whitecaps, flattened down into strange shapes by the pounding rain. The clouds as we glimpsed them were like devils flying through the sky.

Past dark tent after dark tent we stole, and past a few where lights burned dimly behind their canvas walls.

Outside a lighted tent she stopped, motioning me back. I saw her dark form silhouetted against the tent; saw it move stealthily toward the door-flap—saw it stand once more against the canvas wall and then grow in size and blur in outline as she moved away inside the tent. I heard her voice speak in those low, thrilling tones that had enchanted my soul at our first meeting.

"I'm so sorry. I lost my way in the storm. Please let me stay awhile; I'm so very tired, and cold."

I knew the nature of the woman I had carried across the river in my arms. I knew what was to follow. She would kiss him and then—

She had spared *me* the vampire kiss. She was so eager to use me as a tool, to get her away into the world of living men and women. And so now I might go free. Within this tent, tonight, she would satisfy the long-denied blood-lust. There had been that urgent hunger in her voice which told me so.

The two voices in the tent fell so low I lost their words; yet those low tones spoke for themselves. And there was nothing in the world that I could do in the way of giving an alarm. You can't bolt into a man's tent and warn him against a beautiful woman to whom he is about to make love, because she is a vampire. Having myself locked up in an asylum would save no one from the evil I had unwittingly loosed.

Head bent under the rain that fell more quietly now, I climbed down to the water's edge. The wind had fallen. Reeds sighed along the river bank. The crash of waves subsided to a sombre lapping against the rocks. The clouds parted and drifted away horizonward as I stood long in thought, and the gibbous moon shone far and dim behind a mist-veil.

And I knew what I must do. I know, as I write these last words, that it is what I *want* to do. If love and hate are akin, so, too, are enchantment and horror. When my terrible love crept into the tent of that other man, I knew that, abhor her as I might, I could not live without her.

She has spared me the vampire kiss. But I will have that from her, even as I save others from her curse. I have earned it with my soul. I will know that dark ecstasy, and I will insure that no other knows it after me.

It is strange how life leads one through the happy paths of childhood and of youth to an ordained destiny. I had a young uncle who loved tales of old knighthood, as I have loved the macabre.

He made me a sword out of oak, on a happy day in my boyhood. And when he went to volunteer in a war of one of the "little peoples," he tipped the sword with a point. He fell in his first action, far on foreign soil. The sword hangs on my wall. I have never taken it down since he went away.

The dawn broke at last, sick and storm-washed. I did not see them go; but I know that her victim lover will have carried her back across the bridge over the rushing water. For since she is what she is, she *must* go back to the old canal-boat. There she must sleep until tonight.

And there I will come to her then. I will take the tipped sword, and I will hold it behind me in the shadows.

"I have come back to be with you forever," I will say. "There can be no other woman's face before my eyes; only yours, heart-shaped and pale and beautiful. I would leave Heaven and go to Hell for your kiss, and be glad. Kiss me now—"

And then I will take the wooden sword, for wood is fatal to all vampires of whatever age, I will take the wooden sword and I will . . .

## *WHEN GRETCHEN WAS HUMAN*

# Mary A. Turzillo

Dr. Mary A. Turzillo was a professor of English at Kent State University, where she wrote critical articles and scholarly works, mainly on science-fiction subjects and themes. Under the pseudonym Mary T. Brizzi, she wrote *Starmont Reader's Guide to Philip Jose Farmer* (1980) and *Starmont Reader's Guide to Anne McCaffery* (1985). She has also written under the bylines Mary Turzillo and M. A. Turzillo.

An award-winning poet, she has been published in numerous journals nationally and has produced two collections of verse, *Your Cat and Other Space Aliens* (2007) and *Dragon Soup* (2008), a collaboration with artist and poet Marge Simon.

A longtime member of the Science Fiction and Fantasy Writers of America, she was given the Nebula Award by that organization for Best Novelette for *Mars Is No Place for Children*, originally published in *Science Fiction Age* (2000); her story "Pride" was nominated for a Nebula for Best Short Story of 2007; it was first published in *Fast Forward 1*. Her only novel to date, *An Old-Fashioned Martian Girl*, was serialized in *Analog* magazine (July–November 2004).

Turzillo is married to the science-fiction writer Geoffrey A. Landis; they live in Ohio.

"When Gretchen Was Human" was originally published in *The Mammoth Book of Vampire Stories by Women*, edited by Stephen Jones (London: Robinson, 2001).

# When Gretchen Was Human

## MARY A. TURZILLO

You're only human," said Nick Scuroforno, fanning the pages of a tattered first edition of *Image of the Beast*. The conversation had degenerated from half-hearted sales pitch, Gretchen trying to sell Nick Scuroforno an early Pang-born imprint. Now they sat cross-legged on the scarred wooden floor of Miss Trilby's Tomes, watching dust motes dance in August four o'clock sun. Gretchen was wallowing in self-disclosure and voluptuous self-pity.

"Sometimes I don't even feel human." Gretchen settled her back against the soft, dusty-smelling spines of a leather-bound 1910 imprint *Book of Knowledge*.

"I can identify."

"And given the choice, who'd really want to be?" asked Gretchen, tracing the grain of the wooden floor with chapped fingers.

"You have a choice?" asked Scuroforno.

"See, after Ashley was diagnosed, my ex got custody of her. Just as well." She rummaged her smock for a tissue. "I didn't have hospitalization after we split. And his would cover her, but only if she goes to a hospital way off in Seattle." Unbidden, a memory rose: Ashley's warm little body, wriggly as a puppy's, settling in her lap, opening *Where the Wild Things Are*, striking the page with her tiny pink index finger. *Mommy, read!*

Scuroforno nodded. "But can't they cure leukaemia now?"

"Sometimes. She's in remission at the moment. But how long will that last?" Gretchen kept sneaking looks at Scuroforno. Amazingly, she found him attractive. She thought depression had killed the sexual impulse in her. He was a big man, chunky but not actually fat, with evasive amber eyes and shaggy hair. Not bad looking, but not handsome either, in grey sweat pants, a brown T-shirt and beach sandals. He had a habit of twisting the band of his watch, revealing a strip of pale skin from which the fine hairs of his wrist had been worn.

"And yet cancer itself is immortal," he mused. "Why can't it make its host immortal too?"

"Cancer is immortal?" But of course cancer would be immortal. It was the ultimate predator. Why shouldn't it hold all the high cards?

"The cells are. There's some pancreatic cancer cells that have been growing in a lab fifty years since the man with the cancer died. And yet, cancer cells are not even as intelligent as a virus. A virus knows not to kill its host."

"But viruses do kill!"

He smiled. "That's true, lots do kill. Bacteria, too. But there are bacteria that millennia ago decided to infect every cell in our bodies. Turned into—let me think of the word. Organelles? Like the mitochondrion."

"What's a mitochondrion?"

He shrugged, slyly basking in his superior knowledge. "It's an energy-converting organ in animal cells. Different DNA from the host. You'd think you could design a mitochondrion that would make the host live for ever."

She stared at him. "No. I certainly wouldn't think that."

"Why not?"

"It would be horrible. A zombie. A vampire."

He was silent, a smile playing around his eyes.

She shuddered. "You get these ideas from Miss Trilby's Tomes?"

"The wisdom of the ages." He gestured at the high shelves, then stood. "And of course the world wide web. Here comes Madame Trilby herself. Does she like you lounging on the floor with customers?"

Gretchen flushed. "Oh, she never minds anything. My grandpa was friends with her father, and I've worked here off and on since I was little." She took Scuroforno's proffered hand and pulled herself to her feet.

Miss Trilby, frail and spry, wafting a fragrance of face powder and mouldy paper, lugged in a milk crate of pamphlets. She frowned at Gretchen. Strange, thought Gretchen. Yesterday she said I should find a new man, but now she's glaring at me. For sitting on the floor? I sit on the floor to do paperwork all the time. There's no room for chairs. It has to be for schmoozing with a male customer.

Miss Trilby dumped the mail on the counter and swept into the back room.

"Cheerful today, hmm?" said Scuroforno.

"Really, she's so good to me. She lends me money to go to Seattle and see my daughter. She's just nervous today."

"Ah. By the way, before I leave, do you have a cold, or were you crying?"

Gretchen reddened. "I have a chronic sinus infection." She suddenly saw herself objectively: stringy hair, bad posture, skinny. How could she be flirting with this man?

He touched her wrist. "Take care." And strode through the door into the street.

"Him you don't need," said Miss Trilby, bustling back in and firing up the shop's ancient Kaypro computer.

"Did I say I did?"

"Your face says you think you do. Did he buy anything?"

"I'm sorry. I can never predict what he'll be interested in."

"I'll die in the poorhouse. Sell him antique medical texts. Or detective novels. He stands reading historical novels right off the shelf and laughs. Pretends to be an expert, finds all the mistakes."

"What have you got against him, besides reading and not buying?"

"Oh, he buys. But Gretchen, lambkin, a man like that you don't need. Loner. Crazy."

"But he listens. He's so understanding."

"Like the butcher with the calf. What's this immortal cancer stuff he's feeding you?"

"Nothing. We were talking about Ashley."

"Sorry, lambkin. Life hasn't been kind to you. But be a little wise. This man has delusions he's a vampire."

Gretchen smoothed the dust jacket of *Euryanthe and Oberon at Covent Garden.* "Maybe he is."

Miss Trilby rounded her lips in mock horror. "Perhaps! Doesn't look much like Frank Langella, though, does he?"

No, he didn't, thought Gretchen, as she sorted orders for reprints of Kadensho's *Book of the Flowery Tradition* and de Honnecourt's *Fervor of Buenos Aires.*

But there was something appealing about Nick Scuroforno, something besides his empathy for a homely divorcee with a terminally ill child. His spare, dark humour, maybe that was it. Miss Trilby did not understand everything.

Why not make a play for him?

Even to herself, her efforts seemed pathetic. She got Keesha, the single mother across the hall in her apartment, to help her frost her hair. She bought a cheap cardigan trimmed with angora and dug out an old padded bra.

"Lambkin," said Miss Trilby dryly one afternoon when Gretchen came in dolled up in her desperate finery, "the man is not exactly a fashion plate himself."

But Scuroforno seemed flattered, if not impressed, by Gretchen's efforts, and took her out for coffee, then a late dinner. Mostly, however, he came into the bookstore an hour before closing and let her pretend to sell him some white elephant like the Reverend Wood's *Trespassers: How Inhabitants of Earth, Air, and Water Are Enabled to Trespass on Domains Not Their Own.* She would fiddle with the silver chain on her neck, and they would slide to the floor where she would pour out her troubles to him. Other customers seldom came in so late.

"You trust him with private details of your life," said Miss Trilby, "but what do you know of his?"

He did talk. He did. Philosophy, history, details of Gretchen's daughter's illness. One day, she asked, "What do you do?"

"I steal souls. Photographer."

Oh.

"Can't make much money on that artsy stuff," Miss Trilby commented when she heard this. "Rumour says he's got a private source of income."

"Illegal, you mean?"

"What a romantic you are, Gretchen. Ask him."

Gambling luck and investments, he told her.

One day, leaving for the shop, Gretchen opened her mail and found a letter—not even a phone call—that Ashley's remission was over. Her little girl was in the hospital again.

The grief was surreal, physical. She was afraid to go back into her apartment. She had bought a copy of Jan Pienkowski's *Haunted House,* full of diabolically funny pop-ups, for Ashley's birthday.

She couldn't bear to look at it now, waiting like a poisoned bait on the counter.

She went straight to the shop, began alphabetizing the new stock. Nothing made sense, she couldn't remember if O came after N. Miss Trilby had to drag her away, make her stop.

"What's wrong? Is it Ashley?"

Gretchen handed her the letter.

Miss Trilby read it through her thick lorgnette. Then, "Look at yourself. Your cheeks are flushed. Eyes bright. Disaster becomes you. Or is it the nearness of death bids us breed, like romance in a concentration camp?"

Gretchen shuddered. "Maybe my body is tricking me into reproducing again."

"To replace Ashley. Not funny, lambkin. But possibly true. I ask again, why this man? Doesn't madness frighten you?"

Next day, Gretchen followed him to his car. It seemed natural to get in, uninvited, ride home with him, follow him up two flights of stairs covered with cracked treads.

He let her perch on a stool in his kitchen darkroom while he printed peculiar old architectural photographs. The room smelled of chemicals, vinegary. An old Commodore 64 propped the pantry door open. She had seen a new computer in his living-room, running a screen saver of Giger babies holding grenades, and wraiths dancing an agony dance.

"I never eat here," he said. "As a kitchen, it's useless."

He emptied trays, washed solutions down the drain, rinsed. Her heart beat hard under the sleazy angora. His body, sleek as a lion's, gave off a male scent, faintly predatory.

While his back was turned, she undid her cardigan. The buttons too easily slipped out of the cheap fuzzy fabric, conspiring with lust.

She slipped it off as he turned around. And felt the draught of the cold kitchen and the surprise of his gaze on her inadequate chest.

He turned away, dried his hands on the kitchen towel. "Don't fall in love with me."

"Not at all arrogant, are you?" She wouldn't, wouldn't fall in love. No. That wasn't quite it.

"Not arrogance. A warning. I'm territorial; predators have to be. For a while, yes, I'd keep you around. But sooner or later, you'd interfere with my hunting. I'd kill you or drive you away to prevent myself from killing you."

"I won't fall in love with you." Level. Convincing.

"All right." He threw the towel into the sink, came to her. Covered her mouth with his.

She responded clumsily, overreacting after the long dry spell, clawing his back.

The kiss ended. He stroked her hair. "Don't worry. I won't draw blood. I can control the impulse."

She half pretended to play along with him. Half of her did believe. "It doesn't matter. I want to be like you." A joke?

He sat on the kitchen chair, pulled her to him and put his cheek against her breasts. "It doesn't work that way. You have to have the right genes to be susceptible."

"It really is an infection?" Still half pretending to believe, still almost joking.

"A virus that gives you cancer. All I know is that of all the thousands I've preyed upon, only a few have got the fever and lived to become—like me."

"Vampire?"

"As good a word as any. One who I infected and who lived on was my son. He got the fever and turned. That's why I think it's genetic." He pulled her nearer, as if for warmth.

"What happens if the prey doesn't have the genes?"

"Nothing. Nothing happens. I never take enough to kill. I haven't killed a human in over a hundred years. You're safe."

She slid to her knees, wrapping her arms around his waist. He held her head to him, stroking her bare arms and shoulders. "Silk," he said finally, pulling her up, touching her breast. She had nursed Ashley, but it hadn't stopped her from getting leukemia. Fire and ice sizzled across her breasts, as if her milk were letting down.

"Are you lonely?"

"God, yes. That's the only reason I was even tempted to let you do this. You know, I have the instincts of a predator, it does that. But I was born human."

"How did you infect your son?"

"Accident. I was infected soon after I was married. Pietra, my wife, is long dead."

"Pietra. Strange name."

"Not so strange in thirteenth-century Florence. I turned shortly after I was married. I was very ill. I knew I needed blood, but no knowledge of why or how to control my thirst. I took blood from a priest who came to give me last rites. My thirst was so voracious, I killed him. Not murder, Gretchen. I was no more guilty than a baby suckling at breast. The first thirst is overpowering. I took too much, and when I saw that he was dead, I put on my clothes and ran away."

"Leaving your wife."

"Never saw her again. But years later I encountered this young man at a gambling table. Pretended to befriend him. Overpowered him in a narrow dark street. Drank to slake my thirst. Later I encountered him, changed. As a rival for the blood of the neighbourhood. I had infected him, he had got the fever, developed into—what I am. Later I put the pieces together; I had left Pietra pregnant, this was our son, you see. He had the right genes. If he hadn't, he would have never even noticed that modest blood loss." His hand stroked her naked shoulder.

"Where is he now?"

"I often wonder. I drove him off soon after he finished the change. Vampires can't stand one another. They interfere with each other's hunting."

"Why have you chosen to tell me this?" She tried to control her voice, but heard it thicken.

"I tell people all the time what I am. Nobody ever believes it." He stood, pulling her to her feet, kissed her again, pressing his hips to her body. She ran her hands over his shoulders and loosened his shirt. "You don't believe me, either."

And then she smiled. "I want to believe you. I told you once, I don't want to be human."

He raised his eyebrows and smiled down at her.

"I doubt you have the right genes to be anything else."

His bedroom was neat, sparsely furnished. She recognized books from Miss Trilby's Tomes, *Red Dragon, Confessions of an English Opium Eater* on a low shelf near the bed. Unexpectedly, he lifted her off her feet and laid her on the quilt. They kissed again, a long, complicated kiss. He took her slowly. He didn't close the door, and from the bed she could see his computer screen in the living-room. The Giger wraiths in his screen saver danced slowly to their passion. And then she closed her eyes, and the wraiths danced behind her lids.

When they were finished, she knew that she had lied; if she did not feel love, then it was something as strong and as dangerous.

She traced a vein on the back of his hand. "You were born in Italy?"

He kissed the hand with which she had been tracing his veins. "Hundreds of years ago, yes. Before my flesh became numb."

"Then why don't you speak with an accent?"

He rolled on to his back, hands behind his head, and grinned. "I've been an American longer than you have. I made it a point to get rid of my accent. Aren't you going to ask me about the sun and garlic and silver bullets?"

"All just superstition?"

"It would seem." He smiled wryly. "But there is the gradual loss of feeling."

"You say you can't love."

He groped in the bedside table for a pen. He drove the tip into his arm. "You see?" Blood welled up slowly.

"Stop! My god, must you hurt yourself?"

"Just demonstrating. The flesh has been consumed by the—by the cancer, if that's what it is. It starts in the coldest parts of the body. No nerves. I don't *feel*. It has nothing to do with emotion."

"And because you are territorial—"

"Yes. But the emotions don't die, exactly. There's this horrible conflict. And physically, the metastasis continues, very slowly. I heard of a very old vampire whose brain had turned. He was worse than a shark, a feeding machine."

She pulled the sheets around her. The room seemed cold now that they were no longer entwined. "You seemed human enough, when you—"

"You didn't feel it when I kissed you?"

"Feel . . ."

He guided her index finger into his mouth, under the tongue. A bony little organ there, tiny spikes, retracted under the root of the tongue.

She jerked her hand away, suddenly afraid. He caught it and kissed it again, almost mockingly.

She shuddered, tenderness confounded with terror, and buried her face in the pillow. But wasn't this what she had secretly imagined, hoped for?

"Next time," she said, turning her face up to him, like a daisy to the sun, "draw blood, do."

The wraiths in his screen saver danced.

The idea of a bus trip to Seattle filled her with dread, and she put it off, as if somehow by staying in Warren she could stop the progress of reality. But a second letter, this from her ex-sister-in-law Miriam, forced her to face facts. The chemotherapy, Miriam wrote, was not working this time. Ashley was "fading."

"Fading!"

The same mail brought a postcard from Scuroforno. *Out of town on business, seeing to investments. Be well, human,* he wrote.

She told Miss Trilby she needed time off to see Ashley.

"Lambkin, you look awful. Don't go on the bus. I'll lend you the money for the plane, and you can pay me back when you marry some rich lawyer."

"No, Miss Trilby. I have a cold, that's all." Her skin itched, her throat and mouth were sore, her head throbbed.

They dusted books that afternoon. When Gretchen came down from the stepladder, she was so exhausted she curled up on the settee in the back room with a copy of *As You Desire*. The words swam before her eyes, but they might stop her from thinking, thinking about Ashley, about cancer, immortal cells killing their mortal host. Thinking, *immortal*. It might have worked. A different cancer. And then she stopped thinking.

And awoke in All Soul's Hospital, in pain and confusion.

"Drink. You're dehydrated," the nurse said. The room smelled of bleach and dead flowers.

Who had brought her in?

"I don't know. Your employer? An elderly woman. Doctor will be in to talk to you. Try to drink at least a glass every hour."

In lucid moments, Gretchen rejoiced. It was the change, surely it was the change. If she lived, she would be released from all the degrading baggage that being human hung upon her.

The tests showed nothing. Of course, the virus would not culture in agar, Gretchen thought. If it was a virus.

She awoke nights thinking of human blood. She whimpered when they took away her room-mate, an anorexic widow, nearly dry, but an alluring source of a few delicious drops, if only she could get to her while the nurses were away.

Miss Trilby visited, and only by iron will did Gretchen avoid leaping upon her. Gretchen screamed, "Get away from me! I'll kill you!" The doctors, unable to identify her illness, must have worried about her outburst; she didn't get another room-mate. And they didn't release her, though she had no insurance.

Miss Trilby did not come back.

They never thought of cancer. Cancer does not bring a fever and thirst, and bright, bright eyes, and a numbness in the fingers.

Finally, she realized she had waited too long. The few moments of each day that delirium left her, she was too weak to overpower anybody.

Scuroforno came in when she was almost gone. She was awake, floating, relishing death's sweet breath, the smell of disinfectants.

"I'm under quarantine," she whispered. This was not true, but nobody had come to see her since she had turned on Miss Trilby.

He waved that aside and unwrapped a large syringe. "What you need is blood. They wouldn't think of that, though."

"Where did you get that?" Blood was so beautiful. She wanted to press Scuroforno's wrists

against the delicate itching structure under her tongue, to faint in the heat from his veins.

"You're too weak to drink. Ideally, you should have several quarts of human blood. But mine will do."

She watched, sick with hunger, as he tourniqueted his arm, slipped the needle into the vein inside his elbow and drew blood.

She reached for the syringe. He held it away from her. She lunged with death-strength. He put the syringe on the table behind him, caught her wrists, held them together.

"You're stronger than I expected." He squeezed until the distant pain quelled her. She pretended to relax, still fixated on the sip of blood, so near. She darted at his throat, but he held her easily.

"Stop it! There isn't enough blood in the syringe to help you if you drink it! If I inject it, you'll get some relief. But my blood is forbidden."

Yes, she would have killed him, anybody, for blood. She sank back, shaking with desire. The needle entered her vein and she never felt the prick. She shuddered with pleasure as the blood trickled in. She could taste it. Old blood, sour with a hunger of its own, but the echo of satiety radiated from her arm.

"Here are some clothes. You should be just strong enough to walk to the car. I'll carry you from there."

She fumbled for his wrists. "No. Any more vampire blood would kill you. Or"—he laughed grimly—"you might be strong enough to kill me. On your feet." He lifted her like a child.

In his apartment, he carried her to the bedroom and laid her on the bed. She smelled blood. Next to her was an unconscious girl, perhaps twenty, very blonde, dressed in white suede jeans, boots, a black lace bra.

Ineptly, she went for the girl's jugular. The girl was wearing strong jasmine perfume, a cheap knock-off scent insistent and sexy.

"Wait. Don't slash her and waste it all. Be neat." He leaned over, pressed his mouth to the girl's neck.

Gretchen lunged.

She thrilled to sink her new blood-sucking

organ into the girl's neck, but discovered it was at the wrong place. Hissing with anger, she broke away and tried a third time. Salty, thick comfort seeped into her body like hot whisky.

In an instant, Gretchen felt Scuroforno slip his finger into her mouth, breaking the suction. She came away giddy with frustration. Scuroforno held her arms, hurting her. The pain was in another universe. She tried to twist away.

"You're going to kill her," he warned.

"Who is she?" She shook herself into self-control, gazed longingly at the girl, who seemed comatose.

"Nobody. A girl. I take her out now and then. I never take enough blood to harm her. I don't actually enjoy hurting people."

"She's drugged?"

"No, no. I—we have immunity to bacteria and so on, but drugs are bad. I hypnotized her."

"You hypnotized—she sleeps through all this?"

"She thinks she's dead drunk. Here, help me get her sweater back on."

"She thinks you made love to her?"

Scuroforno smiled.

"You did make love to her?"

He busied himself with adjusting the girl's clothes.

Gretchen lay back against the headboard. "I need more, God, I need more."

"I know. But you'll have to find your own from now on."

"How do I get them to submit?"

Scuroforno yawned. "That's your problem. Rescuing you was hard work. Now you'll have to find your own way. You're cleverer and stronger than humans now. Did you notice your sinus infection is gone?"

"Nick, help."

He did not look at her. "It would be better if you left town now."

"But you saved me."

"You're my competitor now. Leave before the rage for blood takes you, before we go after the same prey."

She held the hunger down inside her, remembering human emotions. "It makes no dif-ference that I love you?" And suddenly, she did love him.

"Tomorrow you'll know what hate is, too."

On the way out, she noticed he had a new screen saver: red blood cells floating on black, swelling, bursting apart.

On the bus to Seattle, she wept. Yes, she had loved him, and she had learned what hate was, too. She played with a sewing needle, stabbed her fingers. Numb. But her feelings were not numb, not yet. Would that happen? Was Nick emotionally dead?

Would the physical numbness spread? If her body was immortal, why would she need nerves, pain, to warn of danger?

Maybe she would regret the bargain she had made.

The numbness did spread. Her fingers and hands were immune to pain. But she still felt thirst. The cancer metastasized into her tongue and nerves, wanted to be fed.

Her seat-mate was a Mormon missionary, separated from his partner because the bus was crowded. In Chicago, he asked her to change seats, so he could sit with his partner. But she refused. It didn't fit her plan.

She stroked his cheek, held the back of his neck in a vice grip, all the while smiling, cat-like. Scarcely feeling her own skin, but vividly feeling the nourishment under his. He tried to repel her, laughing uneasily, taking it for an erotic game. A forward, sluttish gentile woman. Then he was fighting, uselessly. He twisted her thumb back, childish self-defence. She felt no pain. Then he was weeping, softening, falling into a trance. She kissed his throat with her open mouth. Drank from him. Drank again and again. Had he fought, she could have broken his neck. She was completely changed.

In Seattle, the floor nurse in Pediatrics challenged her. Sniffing phenol and the sweet, sick urine that could never quite be cleaned up, Gretchen glanced at her reflection in a dead computer screen behind the nurse. She did look predatory now. Like a wax manikin, but also like a cougar. Powerful. Not like anybody's mother. Two other nurses drifted up, as if sensing trouble.

She showed the nurse her driver's licence. They almost believed her, then. Let her go down the hall, to room 409. But still the nurses' eyes followed her. She had changed.

She opened the door. The floor nurse drifted in behind her. This balding, emaciated tyke, tangled in tubing, could not be her Ashley.

Ashley had changed, too. From a less benign cancer.

The nurse sniffed. "I'm sorry. She's gone downhill a lot in the last few weeks." The nurse clearly did not approve of noncustodial mothers. Maybe still did not believe this quiet, strong woman *was* the mother.

When Gretchen had been human, she would have been humiliated, would have tried to explain that Ashley had been taken from her by legal tricks. Now, she considered the nurse simply as a convenient beverage container from which, under suitable conditions, she might sip. She smiled, a cat smile, and the nurse could not hold her gaze.

"Ashley," said Gretchen, when they were alone. She had brought the Jan Pienkowski book, wrapped in red velvet paper with black cats on it. Ashley liked cats. She would love the scary haunted house pop-ups. They would read them together. Gretchen put the gift on the chair, because first she must tend to more important things. "Ashley, it's Mommy. Wake up, darling."

But the little girl only opened her eyes, huge and bruised in the pinched face, and sobbed feebly.

Gretchen lowered the rail on the bed and slid her arm under Ashley. The child was frighteningly light.

Gretchen felt the warmth of her feverish child, smelled the antiseptic of the room, the sweet girl-smell of her daughter's skin. But those were all at a distance. Gretchen was being subsumed by something immortal.

*We are very territorial.* Isn't that what Nick had said? *It's not an emotional numbness; it's physical.* And the memory of him jabbing the pen into his arm, the needle into his vein, her own numb fingers, how everything, even her daughter's warmth and the smell of the child and the room were all receding, distant. Immortal. Numb. Strong beyond human strength. Alone.

She touched her new, predatory mouth to her child's throat. Would Ashley thank her for this?

Now she must decide.

## THE STORY OF CHŪGORŌ

# Lafcadio Hearn

Patricio Lafcadio Tessima Carlos Hearn (1850–1904) was born on the Ionian island of Levkás, the son of a surgeon-major in the British army and his Greek wife,
Rosa. He moved to Dublin at six, then studied in England and Paris before moving to America, where he worked in a print shop and as a journalist.

He began to write grotesque tales, many with supernatural overtones, but earned
a living by writing newspaper columns and features. When he became involved
with a black woman, he lost his job and moved to New Orleans, where he wrote
stories of Creole life and tried to learn gombo French (a Louisiana Negro dialect).

His earliest books were a translation of works by Gautier (1882), *Leaves from
Strange Literature* (1884), and collections of Creole proverbs and Creole cuisine.
In 1890 he journeyed to Japan, where he married a twenty-two-year-old woman
of high samurai rank and spent the rest of his life. Although multinational, Hearn
is generally regarded as an American writer, though the bulk of his best work is
in the form of transcriptions and retellings of Japanese and Chinese folktales, frequently of a ghostly or macabre nature. His spare, terse prose antedates that of
Hemingway, though the similarities are not immediately apparent because of the
large differences in tone.

"The Story of Chūgorō" was first published in *Kotto: Japanese Curios with
Sundry Cobwebs* (New York: Macmillan, 1902).

# The Story of Chūgorō

## LAFCADIO HEARN

A long time ago there lived, in the Koishikawa quarter of Yedo, a *batamoto* named Suzuki, whose yashiki was situated on the bank of the Yedogawa, not far from the bridge called Naka-no-hashi. And among the retainers of this Suzuki there was an *ashigaru* named Chūgorō. Chūgorō was a handsome lad, very amiable and clever, and much liked by his comrades.

For several years Chūgorō remained in the service of Suzuki, conducting himself so well that no fault was found with him. But at last the other *ashigaru* discovered that Chūgorō was in the habit of leaving the yashiki every night, by way of the garden, and staying out until a little before dawn. At first they said nothing to him about this strange behavior; for his absences did not interfere with any regular duty, and were supposed to be caused by some love-affair. But after a time he began to look pale and weak; and his comrades, suspecting some serious folly, decided to interfere. Therefore, one evening, just as he was about to steal away from the house, an elderly retainer called him aside, and said:

"Chūgorō, my lad, we know that you go out every night and stay away until early morning, and we have observed that you are looking unwell. We fear that you are keeping bad company and injuring your health. And unless you can give a good reason for your conduct, we shall think that it is our duty to report this matter to the Chief Officer. In any case, since we are your comrades and friends, it is but right that we should know why you go out at night, contrary to the custom of this house."

Chūgorō appeared to be very much embarrassed and alarmed by these words. But after a short silence he passed into the garden, followed by his comrade. When the two found themselves well out of hearing of the rest, Chūgorō stopped, and said:

"I will now tell you everything; but I must entreat you to keep my secret. If you repeat what I tell you, some great misfortune may befall me.

"It was in the early part of last spring—about five months ago—that I first began to go out at night, on account of a love-affair. One evening, when I was returning to the yashiki after a visit to my parents, I saw a woman standing by the riverside, not far from the main gateway. She was dressed like a person of high rank; and I thought it strange that a woman so finely dressed should be standing there alone at such an hour. But I did not think that I had any right to question her; and I was about to pass her by, without speaking, when she stepped forward and pulled me by the sleeve. Then I saw that she was very young and handsome. 'Will you

631

not walk with me as far as the bridge?' she said. 'I have something to tell you.' Her voice was very soft and pleasant; and she smiled as she spoke; and her smile was hard to resist. So I walked with her toward the bridge; and on the way she told me that she had often seen me going in and out of the yash-hiki, and had taken a fancy to me. 'I wish to have you for my husband,' she said. 'If you can like me, we shall be able to make each other very happy.' I did not know how to answer her; but I thought her very charming. As we neared the bridge, she pulled my sleeve again, and led me down the bank to the very edge of the river. 'Come in with me,' she whispered, and pulled me toward the water. It is deep there, as you know; and I became all at once afraid of her, and tried to turn back. She smiled, and caught me by the wrist, and said, 'Oh, you must never be afraid with me!' And, somehow, at the touch of her hand, I became more helpless than a child. I felt like a person in a dream who tries to run, and cannot move hand or foot. Into the deep water she stepped, and drew me with her; and I nei-ther saw nor heard nor felt anything more until I found myself walking beside her through what seemed to be a great palace, full of light. I was nei-ther wet nor cold: everything around me was dry and warm and beautiful. I could not understand where I was, nor how I had come there. The woman led me by the hand: we passed through room after room—through ever so many rooms, all empty, but very fine—until we entered into a guest-room of a thousand mats. Before a great alcove, at the farther end, lights were burning, and cushions laid as for a feast; but I saw no guests. She led me to the place of honor, by the alcove, and seated herself in front of me, and said; 'This is my home: do you think that you could be happy with me here?' As she asked the question she smiled; and I thought that her smile was more beautiful than anything else in the world; and out of my heart I answered, 'Yes. . . .' In the same moment I remembered the story of Urashima; and I imagined that she might be the daughter of a god; but I feared to ask her any questions. . . . Presently maid-servants came in, bearing rice-wine and many dishes, which they set before us. Then she who sat before me said: 'To-night shall be our

bridal night, because you like me; and this is our wedding-feast.' We pledged ourselves to each other for the time of seven existences; and after the ban-quet we were conducted to a bridal chamber, which had been prepared for us.

"It was yet early in the morning when she awoke me, and said: 'My dear one, you are now indeed my husband. But for reasons which I cannot tell you, and which you must not ask, it is necessary that our marriage remain secret. To keep you here until daybreak would cost both of us our lives. Therefore do not, I beg of you, feel displeased be-cause I must now send you back to the house of your lord. You can come to me tonight again, and every night hereafter, at the same hour that we first met. Wait always for me by the bridge; and you will not have to wait long. But remember, above all things, that our marriage must be a se-cret, and that, if you talk about it, we shall prob-ably be separated forever.'

"I promised to obey her in all things—remem-bering the fate of Urashima—and she conducted me through many rooms, all empty and beautiful, to the entrance. There she again took me by the wrist, and everything suddenly became dark, and I knew nothing more until I found myself stand-ing alone on the river bank close to the Naka-no-hashi. When I got back to the yashiki, the temple bells had not yet begun to ring.

"In the evening I went again to the bridge at the hour she had named, and I found her waiting for me. She took me with her, as before into the deep water, and into the wonderful place where we had passed our bridal night. And every night, since then, I have met and parted from her in the same way. To-night she will certainly be waiting for me, and I would rather die than disappoint her: therefore I must go. . . . But let me again entreat you, my friend, never to speak to any one about what I have told you."

The elder *ashigaru* was surprised and alarmed by this story. He felt that Chūgorō had told him the truth; and the truth suggested un-pleasant possibilities. Probably the whole experience was an illusion, and an illusion produced by some evil power for a malevolent end. Nevertheless, if really bewitched, the lad was rather to be pitied than blamed; and any forcible interference would be likely to result in mischief. So the *ashigaru* answered kindly:

"I shall never speak of what you have told me— never, at least, while you remain alive and well. Go and meet the woman; but—beware of her! I fear that you are being deceived by some wicked spirit."

Chūgorō only smiled at the old man's warning, and hastened away. Several hours later he reentered the yashiki, with a strangely dejected look. "Did you meet her?" whispered his comrade. "No," replied Chūgorō, "she was not there. For the first time, she was not there. I think that she will never meet me again. I did wrong to tell you— I was very foolish to break my promise. . . ." The other vainly tried to console him. Chūgorō lay down, and spoke no word more. He was trembling from head to foot, as if he had caught a chill.

When the temple bells announced the hour of dawn, Chūgorō tried to get up, and fell back senseless. He was evidently sick—deathly sick. A Chinese physician was summoned.

"Why, the man has no blood!" exclaimed the doctor, after a careful examination. "There is nothing but water in his veins! It will be very difficult to save him. . . . What maleficence is this?"

Everything was done that could be done to save Chūgorō's life—but in vain. He died as the sun went down. Then his comrade related the whole story.

"Ah! I might have suspected as much!" exclaimed the doctor. . . . "No power could have saved him. He was not the first whom she destroyed."

."Who is she—or what is she?" the *ashigaru* asked. "A Fox-Woman?"

"No; she had been haunting this river from ancient time. She loves the blood of the young. . . ."

"A Serpent-Woman? A Dragon-Woman?"

"No, no! If you were to see her under that bridge by daylight, she would appear to you a very loathsome creature."

"But what kind of a creature?"

"Simply a Frog—a great and ugly Frog!"

## THE MEN & WOMEN OF RIVENDALE

# Steve Rasnic Tem

Steve Rasnic Tem (1950– ) was born in Jonesville, Virginia, in the middle of Appalachia. He went to college at Virginia Polytechnic Institute, Virginia State University, and Virginia Commonwealth University, receiving a B.A. in English education. He later earned a master's in creative writing from Colorado State University. He lives in Denver with his wife; they have four children and three grandchildren.

Tem's first work was poetry, followed by short fiction. Since 1980 he has produced more than two hundred mystery, science-fiction, dark fantasy, and horror short stories, many of which are difficult to categorize; they have been published in *The Saint*, *Rod Serling's Twilight Zone Magazine*, *Isaac Asimov, Science Fiction and Fantasy*, *Crimewave*, and other magazines. His stories have been nominated for a World Fantasy Award ("Firestorm" in 1983) and three Bram Stoker Awards ("Bodies and Heads," 1990, "Black Windows," 1991, and "Halloween Street," 2000). He also had Bram Stoker nominations for Best Novelette (*The Man on the Ceiling*, 2001) and Best Collection (*City Fishing*, 2001). He has written four novels: *Excavation* (1987), which was nominated for the Bram Stoker Best First Novel Award; *Daughters*, with Melanie Tem (2001); *The Book of Days* (2002), nominated for the International Horror Guild Award; and *Man on the Ceiling* (2008).

"The Men & Women of Rivendale" was first published in *Night Visions 1*, edited by Alan Ryan (Niles, IL: Dark Harvest, 1984).

# The Men & Women of Rivendale

## STEVE RASNIC TEM

The thing he would remember most about his days, his weeks at the Rivendale resort—had it really been weeks?—was not the enormous lobby and dining room, nor the elaborately carved mahogany woodwork framing the library, nor even the men and women of Rivendale themselves, with their bright eyes and pale, almost hairless, heads and hands. The thing he would remember most was the room he and Cathy stayed in, the way she looked when she curled up in bed, her bald head rising weakly over her shoulders, the way the dark brocade curtains hung so heavily, trapping dust and light in their intricate folds.

Frank thought he had spent days staring into those folds. He had only two places to look in that room: at the cancer-ridden sack his wife had become, her giant eyes, her grotesque, baby-like face, so stripped of age since she had begun her decline. Or at the curtains, adrift constantly with shadows. They were of a dark, burgundy-colored material, and he never knew if they had darkened with dust and age or if they were meant to be just that shade. If he examined the curtains at close range he could make out the tiny leaf and shell patterns embroidered over the entire surface. From a distance,

when he sat in the chair or lay on the bed, they looked like hundreds of tiny, hungry mouths.

Cathy had told him little about the place before they came—that it was a resort in Pennsylvania, in the countryside south of Erie, and that it used to have a hot springs. He hadn't asked, but he wondered what happened to the spring water when it left such a place. As if somebody somewhere had turned a tap. It didn't make any sense to him; natural things shouldn't work that way.

Her ancestors, the family Rivendale, had run the place when it was still a resort. Now many, perhaps all of her relatives lived in the Rivendale Resort Hotel, or in cottages spotted around the sprawling grounds. Probably several dozen cottages in all. It had been quite a jolt when Frank walked into the place, stumbling over the entrance rug with their luggage wedged under his arms, and saw all these Rivendales sitting around the fireplace in the lobby. It wasn't as if they were clones, or anything like that. But there was this uneasy sort of family resemblance. Something about the fleshtones, the shape of the hands, the perpetually arched eyebrows, the sharp angle at which they held their heads, the irregular pink splotches on their cheeks. It gave him a little chill.

After a few days at Rivendale he recognized part of the reason for that chill: the cancer had molded Cathy into a fuzzy copy of a Rivendale.

Frank remembered her as another woman entirely: her hair had been long and honey-brown, and there had been real color in her cheeks. She had been lively, her movements strong and fluid, an incredibly sleek, beautiful woman who could have been a model, though such a public display would have appalled her and, he knew without asking, would have disgraced the Rivendale name.

Cathy had told him that filling up with cancer was like roasting under a hot sun sometimes. The dusty rooms and dark chambers of Rivendale cooled her. They would stay at Rivendale as long as possible, she had said. She could hide from nurses and doctors there.

She wouldn't have surgery. She was a Rivendale; it didn't fit. She washed herself in radiation and, after Frank met these other Rivendales with their scrubbed and antiseptic flesh, the thought came to him: she'd over-bathed.

She never looked or smelled bad, as he'd expected. The distortions the growing cancer made within the skin that covered it were more subtle than that. Sometimes she complained of her legs suddenly weakening. Sometimes she would scream in the middle of the night. He'd look at her pale form and try to see through her translucent flesh, find the cancer feeding and thriving there.

One result of her treatments was that Cathy's belly blew up. She looked at least six months pregnant, maybe more. It had never occurred to either of them to have children. They'd always had too much to do; a child didn't have a place in the schedule. Sometimes now Frank dreamed he was wheeling her into the delivery room, running, trying to get her to the doctors before her terrible labor ceased. A tall doctor in a brilliant white mask always met him at the wide, swinging doors. The doctor took Cathy away from him but blocked Frank from seeing what kind of child they delivered from her heaving, discolored belly.

Nine months after the cancer was diagnosed, the invitation from the Rivendales was delivered.

Cathy, who'd barely mentioned her family in all the years they'd been married, welcomed it with a grim excitement he'd never seen in her before. Frank discovered the invitation in the trash later that afternoon. "Come to Rivendale" was all it said.

One of the uncles greeted her at the desk, although "greeted" was probably the wrong word. He checked her in, as if this were still a resort. Even gave her a room key with the resort tag still attached, although now the leather was cracked and the silver letting hard to read. Only a few of the relatives had bothered to look up from their reading, their mouths twitching as if they were attempting speech after years of muteness. But no one spoke; no one welcomed them. As far as Frank could tell, no one in the crowded, quiet lobby was speaking to anyone else.

They'd gone up to their room immediately; the trip had exhausted Cathy. Then Frank spent his first of many evenings sitting up in the old chair, staring at Cathy curled up on the bed, and staring at the curtains breathing the breeze from the window, the indecipherable embroidered patterns shifting restlessly.

The next morning they were awakened by a bell ringing downstairs. The sound was so soft Frank at first thought it was a dream, wind-chimes tinkling outside. But Cathy was up immediately, and dressing. Frank did the same, suddenly not wanting to initiate any action by himself. When another bell rang Cathy opened the door and started downstairs, and Frank followed her.

Two places were set for them at one of the long, linen-draped tables. "Cathy" and "Frank," the place cards read. He wondered briefly if there might be someone else staying here by those names, so surprised he was to see his name written on the card in floral script. But Cathy took her chair immediately, and he sat down beside her.

There was a silent toast. When the uncle who had met them at the desk tapped his glass of apple wine lightly with a fork the rest raised their glasses silently to the air, then a beat later tipped them back to drink. Cathy drank in time with the others, and that simple bit of coordination and exaggerated manners made Frank uneasy. He remained one step behind all the others, watching them over the lip of his glass. They didn't seem aware of each other, but they were almost, though not quite, synchronized.

He glanced at Cathy; her cheek had grown pale and taut as she drank. She wasn't eating real food anymore, only a special formula she took like medicine to sustain her. Although her skin was almost baby-smooth now, the lack of fat had left wrinkles that deepened as she moved. Death lines.

After breakfast they lingered by the enormous dining room window. Cathy watched as the Rivendales drifted across the front lawn in twos and threes. Their movements were slow and languid like ancient fish in shallow, sun-drenched waters.

"Shouldn't we introduce ourselves around?" Frank said softly. "I mean, we were invited by someone. How do these people even know who we are?"

"Oh, they know, Frank. Hush now; the Rivendales have always had their own way of doing things. Someone will come to us in time. Meanwhile, we enjoy ourselves."

"Sure."

They took a long walk around the grounds. The pool was closed and covered with canvas. The shuffleboard courts were cracked, the cracks pulled further apart by grass and tree roots. And the tennis courts . . . the tennis courts were his first inkling that perhaps he should be trying to convince her of the need to return home.

The tennis courts at Rivendale were built atop a slight, tree-shaded rise behind the main building. He heard the yowling and screeching as they climbed the rise, so loud that he couldn't make out any individual voices. It frightened him so that he grabbed Cathy by the arm and started back down. But she seemed unperturbed by the noise and shrugged away from him, continuing to walk toward the trees, her pace unchanging.

"Cathy . . . I don't think . . ." But she was oblivious to him.

So Frank followed her, reluctantly. As they neared the fenced enclosure the howling increased, and Frank knew that it wasn't people in there making all the noise, but animals, though he had never heard animal sounds quite like those.

As they passed the last tree Frank stopped, unable to proceed; Cathy walked right up to the fence. She pressed close to the wire, but not so close the outstretched paws could touch her.

The tennis courts had become a gigantic cage holding hundreds of cats. An old man stood on a ladder above the wire fence, dumping buckets of feed onto the snarling mass inside. Mesh with glass insulators attached—*electrified,* Frank thought—stretched across the top of the fence.

The old man turned to Frank and stared. He had the arched eyebrows, the pale skin and blotched cheeks. He smiled at Frank, and the shape of the lips seemed to match the shape of the eyebrows. A smile shaped like moth wings, or a bite-pattern in pale cheese, the teeth gleaming snow-white inside.

Cathy spent most of each day in the expansive Rivendale library, checking titles most of the time, but occasionally sitting down to read from a rare and privately-bound old volume. Every few hours one of the uncles, or cousins, would come in and speak to her in a low voice, nod, and leave. The longer he was here the more difficult it became to tell the Rivendales apart, other than male from female. The younger ones mirrored the older ones, and they were all very close in height, weight, and build.

When Cathy wasn't in the library she sat quietly in the parlor or dining room, or up in their own room catnapping or staring up at the ornate ceiling. She would say every day, almost ritualistically, that he was more than welcome to be with her, but he could see nothing here that he might participate in. Sitting in the parlor or dining room was made almost unbearable by the presence of the family, arranged mummy-like around the rooms. Sometimes he would pick up a volume in the library, but invariably discovered it was some sort of laborious tome on trellis and ornate gardening, French architecture, museum catalogs. Or sometimes an old leather-bound novel that read no better. It was impossible to peruse the books without thinking that whatever Cathy was studying must be far more interesting, but on the days he went he never could find the books she had been looking at, as if they had been kept somewhere special, out of his reach. And for some reason he hesitated to ask after them, or to look over his wife's shoulder as she read. As if he was afraid to.

This growing climate of awkwardness and fear angered Frank so that his neck muscles were always stiff, his head always aching. It was worse because it wasn't entirely unexpected. His relationship with Cathy had been going in this direction for some time. Until he'd met Cathy, he'd almost always been bored. As a child, always needing to be entertained. As an adult, constantly changing lovers and houses and jobs. Now it was happening again, and it frightened him.

The increasing boredom that was beginning to permeate his stay at Rivendale, in fact, had begun to impress on him how completely, utterly bored he had been in his married life. He'd almost forgotten, so preoccupied he'd become with her disease. When Cathy's cancer had first begun, and started to spread, that boredom had dissipated. Perversely, the cancer had brought something new and near-dramatic into their life together. He'd felt bad at first: Cathy, in her baldness, in her body that seemed, impossibly, both emaciated and swollen, had suddenly become sensuous to him again. He wanted to make love to her almost all the time. After the first few times, he had stopped the attempts, afraid to ask her. But as she approached death, his desire increased.

Sometimes Frank sat out on the broad resort lawn, his lounge chair positioned under a low-hanging tree only twenty or so feet away from the library window. He'd watch her as she sat at one of the enormous oak tables, poring over the books,

consulting with various elderly Rivendales who drifted in and out of that room in a seemingly endless stream. He'd heard one phrase outside the library, when the Rivendales didn't know he was near, or perhaps he had dreamed his eavesdropping while lying abed late one morning, or falling asleep midafternoon in his hiding place under the tree. "Family histories."

The pale face with the near-hairless pate that floated as if suspended in that library window bore no resemblance to the Cathy he had known, with her dark eyes and nervous gestures and narrow mouth quick to twist ugly and vituperative. They'd discovered it was so much easier to become excited by anger, rage, and all the small cruelties possible in married life, then by love. They'd had a bad fight on their very first date. He found himself asking her out again in the very heat of the argument. She'd stared at him wide-eyed and breathless for some time, then grudgingly accepted.

Throughout the following weeks their fights grew worse. Once he'd slapped her, something he would never have imagined himself doing, and she'd fallen sobbing into his arms. They made love for hours. It became a delirious pattern. The screams, the cries, the ineffectual hitting, then the sweet tickle and swallow of a lust that dragged them red-eyed through the night.

Marriage was a great institution. It gave you the opportunity to experience both sadism and masochism within the privacy and safety of your own home.

"What do you want from me, you bastard!" Cathy's teeth flashed, pinkly . . . her lipstick was running, he thought. Frank held her head down against the mattress, watching her tongue flicking back and forth over her teeth. He was trapped.

Her leg came up and knocked him off the bed. He tried to roll away but before he could move she had straddled him, pinning him to the floor. "Off! Get off!" He couldn't catch his breath. He suddenly realized her forearm was wedged between his neck and the floor, cutting off the air. His vision blurred quickly and the pressure began to build in his face.

"Frank . . ."

He could barely hear her. He thought he might actually die this time. It was another bad joke; he almost laughed. She was the one who was always talking about dying; she could be damned melodramatic about it. She was the one with the death wish.

He opened his eyes and stared up at her. She was fumbling with his shirt, pulling it loose, ripping the buttons off. Maybe she was trying to save him.

Then he got a better look at her: the feverish eyes, the slackening jawline, tongue flicking, eyes glazed. Now she was tugging frantically at his belt. It all seemed very familiar and ritualized. He searched her eyes and did not think she even saw him.

*"Frank . . ."*

He woke with a start and stared across the lawn at the library window. Cathy's pale face stared back at him, surrounded by her even paler brethren, their mouths moving soundlessly, fish-like. He thought he could hear the soft clinking of breaking glass, or hundreds of tiny mouths trying their teeth.

The thing he would remember most was this room, and the Rivendales watching. They had a peculiar way of watching; they were very polite about it, for if nothing else they were gentlemen and ladies, these Rivendales. Theirs was an ancient etiquette, developed through practice and interaction with human beings of all eras and climes. Long before he met Cathy they had known him, followed him, for they had intimate knowledge of his type. Or so he imagined it.

Each afternoon there was one who especially drew Frank's attention: an old one, his eyebrows fraying away with the heat like tattered moth wings. He walked the same path each day, wearing it down into a seamless pavement, and only by a slight pause at a particular point on the path did Frank know the old man Rivendale was watching him. Listening to him. And that old one's habitual, everyday patterns were what made Frank wonder if the world might be full of Rivendales, assigned to watch, and recruit.

He was beginning—with excitement—to recognize them, to guess at what they were. They would always feed, and feed viciously, but their hunger was so great they would never be filled, no matter how many lives they emptied, no matter how many dying relationships they so intimately observed. Like an internal cancer, their bland surfaces concealed an inner, parasitic excitement. They could not generate their own. They couldn't even generate their own kind; they had to infect others in order to multiply.

Frank had always imagined their type to be feral, with impossibly long teeth, and foul, blood-tainted breath. But they had manners, promising a better life, and a cold excitement one need not work for.

He was, after all, one of them. A Rivendale by habit, if not by blood. The thought terrified.

The thing he would remember most was the room, and the way she looked curled up in bed, her bald head rising weakly over her shoulders.

"I have to leave, Cathy. This is crazy."

He'd been packing for fifteen minutes, hoping she'd say something. But the only sounds in the room were those of the shirts and pants being pulled out from drawers and collapsed haphazardly into his suitcase. And the sound the breeze from the window made pushing out the heavy brocade curtains, making the tiny leaf and shell pattern breathe, sigh, the tiny mouths chatter.

And the sound of her last gasp, her last breath trying to escape the confines of the room, escape the family home before their mouths caught her and fed.

"Cathy . . ." Shadows moved behind the bed. It bothered him he couldn't see her eyes. "There was no love anyway . . . you understand what I'm saying?" Tiny red eyes flickered in the darkness. Dozens of pairs. "The fighting is the only thing that kept us together; it kept the boredom away. And I haven't felt like fighting you for some time." The quiet plucked at his nerves. "Cathy?"

He stopped putting his things into the suitcase. He let several pairs of socks fall to the floor. There were tiny red eyes fading into the shadows. And mouths. There was no other excitement out there for him; he couldn't do it on his own. No other defense against the awesome, all-encompassing boredom. The Rivendales had judged him well.

Cathy shifted in the bed. He could see the shadow of her terrible swollen belly as it pushed against the dusty sheets and raised the heavy covers. He could see the paleness of her skin. He could see her teeth. But he could not hear her breathe. He lifted his knee and began the long climb across the bedspread, his hands shaking, yet anxious to give themselves up for her.

He would remember the bite marks in the cool night air, the mouths in the dark brocade. He would remember his last moment of panic just before he gave himself up to this new excitement. The thing he would remember most was the room.

## WINTER FLOWERS

# Tanith Lee

For the past forty years, Tanith Lee has been a prodigiously productive author of fantasy, horror, gothic romance, historical fiction, and science fiction, both for children and adults, with more than fifty novels and nearly two hundred short stories to her credit.

It is not quantity, however, that has elevated her to the top of the writing world, but quality, as attested to by her numerous awards, including the following:

Nebula Award: *The Birthgrave*, nominated for Best Novel (1975); "Red as Blood," nominated for Best Short Story (1980). World Fantasy Award: *Night's Master*, nominated for Best Novel (1979); "The Gorgon," winner for Best Short Story (1983); "Elle Est Trois (La Mort)," winner for Best Short Story (1984); "Nunc Dimitis," nominated for Best Novella (1984); *Red as Blood, or, Tales from the Sisters Grimmer*, nominated for Best Anthology/Collection (1984); *Night Visions 1*, nominated for Best Anthology/Collection (1985); *Dreams of Dark and Light*, nominated for Best Anthology/Collection (1987); *Night's Sorceries*, nominated for Best Anthology/Collection (1988); *Scarlet and Gold*, nominated for Best Novella (1999); *Uous*, nominated for Best Novella (2006). British Fantasy Award: Five nominations, including *Death's Master*, which won for Best Novel (1980).

"Winter Flowers" was originally published in the June 1993 issue of *Asimov's Science Fiction* magazine.

# Winter Flowers

## TANITH LEE

**P**ierre was burned at Bethelmai; I helped them light the fire.

Parts of the town were already burning, and under cover of that, and the general sack, we had gone about our own business. There had been no real pay for months and Bethelmai was full of trinkets, particularly in the houses around the church, and there were the cellars of wine and the kitchens that still had chickens and loaves despite five weeks of siege. And there were the plump, cream-fed women. Duke Walf's boys were well occupied. There should have been room enough for anything.

I had found an old narrow house in a by-way that the onslaught had either missed or else run over and left behind. Probably not the latter, for though there were signs of upset, broken pots, a few coins scattered from a chest, the hurried household may have made a mess in getting out. Upstairs someone was moving, or maybe only breathing. I climbed the stair and pushed open the door. Into the gloom of the chamber from a slit of window a light ray fell from the smoking town, and lit a pair of brown-amber eyes wide with fright.

"Don't rape me," she said, and then a fragment of bad Latin, the kind you hear all over a camp before the assault, prayer in pieces. She was obviously a servant, abandoned, only about fourteen years old.

"No. I won't do that."

I went right over and sat beside her on the wooden bed of her deserting master and mistress. I took her hand. Of course I reeked of the fight, metal and blood and smoke, but not of lust. I was only thirsty.

There was a tiny silver ring on her wrist.

"Don't take it," she said. "It's all I've got."

"No, I won't take it."

I raised her hand to my mouth, and moved the ring up a little, away from the vein. I put my mouth there, and sucked at the flesh, letting my saliva numb her, the way it does. And I crooned in my throat. She became still and soft, and when I bit into the vein she never flinched, only sighed once.

It was some while since I had had blood. That is the way of it. The campaigns are often long and it will be difficult to get anything. The battles make up for this, affording as they usually do so many opportunities.

The nourishment went into me and I could feel it doing me good, better than wine and meat. But I did not take too much, and when I finished I tore her sleeve and bound up the wound. They rarely remember.

She was drowsy, and I kissed her forehead and put some of the coins from the chest downstairs into her hand.

"Stay up here till nightfall. Then go carefully, and you might sneak away." There was nowhere much for her to fly to, in fact, for the country side had been shaved bald by Walf's hungry vicious troops. Still, she must take her chance. It is all any of us can do.

Downstairs I worked a touch more damage on the hall, and gathered up the last coins from the chest, the lock of which I smashed with my dagger-hilt for good measure. It now looked for sure as though the soldiers had already been through and there could be nothing remaining to filch.

Outside I went looking for a drink of wine. I felt strong, alert, and clean now, the way we do after living blood. With bright clear eyes I viewed the smoldering roofs, and on the ground the occasional corpse, and many looted objects cast aside. Walf's happy men were throwing down treasures from upper windows and over walls. The mailed soldiers swaggered, drunk, round the streets, toasting the Duke, and now and then some of the captains rode by on their steaming horses, trailing Walf's colors proudly, as if something wonderful had been done. Dim intermittent thuds and crashes, shouts, and the continual high cries of women, thickened and smirched the air.

Bethelmai was hot from the fires, although outside winter had set in on the plains and hills. Bollo had said it would be snow before the week was out and he was seldom wrong. God help them then, all the towns and villages Duke Walf had cracked. Where next? There had been talk of Pax Pontis to the north. That was greater than Bethelmai and might require some months of siege. From somewhere Walf would have to get more cash and further provisions, or his toasting proud army would desert him. So I was thinking, idling along with a wine-skin I had pulled off an addled soldier, not realizing that none of this would presently concern me.

It was when I came out into the square before the church that I beheld a secondary commotion was going on, and Pierre was in the midst of it. Walf's men had him by both arms, and all across the distance I could see the scarlet marker, like the kiss of a rose, on his mouth.

Up on the church steps, before the broken gaping door, some of Walf's officers were standing, looking on. But all around the pillaging soldiers scurried, not noticing what happened with Pierre, supposing it possibly some breach of petty discipline peculiarly upheld, as often happens, in the middle of a riot.

Then big-bellied Captain Rotlam came at me, pushing his beaked, scarred, and scowling face forward like an angry, oddly-neckless goose.

"You, Maurs. That's your man there. You see, the one my fellows have got."

"I see, Captain. Yes, he's one of mine."

"Stinking mercenaries," said Rotlam. He spat at my boot. No matter. It had had worse on it today, and several times. "You God-cursed filthy thieves," he enlarged. "Taking the Duke's pay." I wondered what pay he meant, "skulking—have you even killed anything this morning, aside from your own fleas? Any enemy?"

I said, "Shall I bring you their severed hands?"

"Eh? Shut your mouth. That bastard there. Your scum. Do you know what we caught him at?"

I knew. Already and quite well I knew, and my heart, which had been high, was growing cold. It had happened before, and when it did, there was not much that could be done. We all understood that. Even Arpad the hothead, and Yens the gambler, and melancholy, colicky Festus. You must take your chance. All luck runs dry at last, like every river, now or tomorrow or at World's End.

But I said, scowling back, "What's Pierre done?"

"Pierre is it? Don't you know he's a stinking blasphemous witch?"

I crossed myself. I make my mistakes but am not a fool.

"Yes, God guard us—" Rotlam gestured at his men to bring my one forward, and they dragged Pierre, pulling him off his feet, so by the time they reached us he was kneeling.

His dark eyes moved up to mine above the red mouth. Poor lost Pierre. Dead brother to be. But I had my other brothers to consider, and my own damnable skin.

"Well," I said roughly, "What's this? What have you been doing in God's name?"

"Nothing, Maurs," said Pierre. He added expertly, and hopelessly, "There was this boy, he had a gold chain hidden, and when I tried to get it off him, he went for me like a mad dog. I fought him off but I couldn't get my knife—so I bit him. In the neck. It stopped him. Then the Captain's soldiers found us, and for some reason—"

"He was drinking the boy's blood," broke in the man who had Pierre by the left arm. He shook the arm as if to get it free of the socket and Pierre yelped. "Accursed demon shit!" the soldier shouted. He was terrified, all the drink gone to venom.

"He wanted to kill this bastard on the spot," said the other man, "but I said, bring him to the Captain."

"Oh, by God," I said, sounding amused, amazed, my heart like the snow Bollo had told me was coming. "By God, can't my fellow defend himself without—"

"He drank the boy's blood," said the calm soldier stolidly, staring at me. "If you'd seen, you'd believe. Or have you seen, sometime, and not minded?"

At that Rotlam punched me in the chest.

"Eh? Answer that, Maurs, you bit of muck."

I straightened up and shrugged. "These two are drunk out of their wits. What do they know?"

There was some shouting then, and the calmer of the soldiers drew his sword on me and I knocked him flat. Then Rotlam hit me and I had to take it, since he was one of the marvelous Duke's astounding captains. Pierre by this time had lowered his head. When the noise lessened, I heard him murmur, "Let me go, Maurs. My fault. Who cares. I've had enough."

"What's the devil say?" roared goose-face Rotlam, hissing and bubbling.

"God hears, not I," I said. "I don't know this man well. You'd better get a priest. See what he says."

So, like Peter before Cockcrow, I gave my friend over to oblivion. And like Peter I sweated chill and was full of darkness.

They made quite a show of it, calling all the troops they could prize from the sack, setting up a sort of court. Examining Pierre. There were three greasy priests, rats who had been busy enough themselves on Bethelmai's carcass until called off. The Duke's bastard looked in upon the "trial," but did not bother to stay. Bollo and I were asked questions, and Johan, who had been Pierre's companion on various forays, and Festus and Lutgeri, who had been with Pierre getting in over the fallen gates of the town. We all said we did not know Pierre that well, for he had not been with us very long. He had come out of the night to our fire that summer, just before we offered our swords to the Duke. And as we said this rubbish, I watched Pierre slightly nodding to himself. Once, long, long ago, at a similar scene, I had wept, and nearly implicated myself. But the tears dry like the luck and the fucking rivers.

In the end, Pierre was pronounced demon-possessed, a witch. He admitted it, because otherwise they would have broken his fingers, lashed him, done other choice things. They made up a makeshift but efficient pyre, with a pole in the center that had been a cross-beam of some house. They pushed Pierre up and bound him. He looked at me, and his eyes said *Curse me now.* So we cursed him, and asked the priests for help and penances, and what prayers to say, since we had been all summer and fall in Pierre's deadly company. The priests were sweet. They took our spoils of gold from Bethelmai and instructed us to abstain from wine and women, and meat. To beg from God morning and evening. And such clever methods.

When they set fire to the wood, I ran and flung a torch into the sticks, howling. My men cheered and spat upon Pierre. He looked down at us from beyond the smoke. He was a beautiful boy, seeming not more than twenty, with a face to charm the girls, and, come to that, the Dukes of this earth.

He knew every foul name we called him was a prayer, and every gob of spit a cry for his forgiveness.

In the end he screamed in agony, and forgot us all.

They say the fire is cold. I heard it once—*So cold! So cold!*

It would be easy to abstain from meat after all.

When he was gone and the flames sank and gave way, and they had raked about and made sure that nothing had lived in them, they sprinkled the place with holy water.

Soon after, Rotlam the goose told us to get going. We were to have no pay—what pay?—and to take nothing from the town—the priests had had most of it. I argued, since not to do so would seem strange and perhaps suspicious. "We fought hard and well for Duke Walf." But Rotlam laughed, and that in a ring of swords.

From the hills above the plain we glanced back, but Bethelmai was still burning, although Pierre had finished.

"May they eat their own flesh and vomit their own guts," said Arpad.

"They will," said Lutgeri. "They all do in the end."

I thought of the girl with a fawn's amber eyes, and if she would escape the town. To think of Pierre was a more terrible thing I must come to softly. For he was all the others who had died, and he was also all of us. No one spoke to me as we tramped across the hills, with the smut of Bethelmai upon our hides and the blood of Bethelmai in our bellies, and Pierre's death our banner.

**B**ollo had been right about the snow. It came like a great grey bird from the heart of the sky. The whiteness fell like petals. So cold. So cold.

"There'll be wolves," said Gilles.

"So, wolves are nothing," said Johan stoically.

There are always two schools of thought with wolves. One says they are fiends who will tear you up as you sleep and chew your genitals till you wake shrieking. The other school, which from ex-perience is mine, will tell that wolves seldom attack a moving man, or a sleeping man for that matter. Once Johan was relieving himself in a winter field and a wolf appeared and stared at him. The eyes of wolves are human, and Johan was costive for three days. But when he shouted at the wolf it fled.

In any case, we did not hear their song, up on the lean white hills. We heard nothing. The world had died. Good riddance.

Once, from a height, we saw a town far off, walls and towers, and when the dark began, that buzz of half-seen light, all the candles, torches, hearths, all the dreams and desires of the hive. Yens said that he thought the town was Musen, but we did not know, and hated it only dimly, like the distance.

After about two days, we began to talk of Pierre. We recalled things he had said and done, how he had been a friend, how he had enraged us. Those of us who recollected the first meeting between us spoke of that. It was true he had come to the campfire in the night, but that was a century ago. He found us by stealth and the magic of our kind. Our brotherhood of blood is old and uncanny, but we are like the wolves. Timid, lonely. Our pack cleaves to itself. We prey only where we can. And we too have human eyes.

In the dark white of the snow, Johan said to me, "You talked about bringing Rotlam the severed hands of those you killed. Was that unwise? Does it give away something? The Egyptians by the Nilus did that. Suppose you chatter to a scholar."

"Then I'm done for, Johan. One day."

Yes, no fool, but I make mistakes, and who does not?

Pierre. . . .

It was not that he had been my lover, or like some son I had never seen. He was myself. And to each of us, he was that.

Lutgeri may be the oldest of us. Sometimes he dreams of painted icons in a hut of logs, and smoke, and a hymn that brought the light.

As we age, we lose the nearer past a little, as any old man does.

For the rest, it is lies. The sun does not smite

us, nor the moon by night. Garlic is a fine flavor. Thorns rip but that is all. Iron and silver—we have had both, and lost both. And for the cross of the Christ? Well, He was one of us, or so Pierre once said. Did they not drink blood?

But kill us, we die. Burn us, we are ashes.

Ah, Pierre. . . .

And so, through the death of Pierre, we wandered, a band of mercenaries without a lord, scavengers on the winter land, wolves, crows. And so, we saw the castle.

Maybe we would have turned to it our shoulders, but the hour was sunset, and in the sunset we saw this place, on a sky as red as blood and threaded with gold like the robe of a priest.

The castle looked black. Not a light, not a glim to be glimpsed.

"Perhaps there is some count or duke there," said Arpad, "who wants men to serve him. Wants to take some city in the spring. The rotten old bastard. He'll feed us."

"And women," said Festus.

"Gorgeous women, white as the snow, with sweets for tits and cores of roses." This, Gilles.

We scanned the landscape for a village or town, some settlement to support the castle, and there was none. Under the snow, and the blood of crimson dying sun, nothing moved.

"A ruin," said Yens. "Taken, despoiled. Empty."

"We'll go and see." Arpad.

"Winter in a ruin. Not for the first." Johan.

But we sat on the hill, slept by the fire. In the dawn we looked down again, and now the castle was not black but warm, the sun's rays on it over the cloth of the snow.

If we had had his body, we would have buried him here, at this castle, our brother Pierre. But we did not have a mote of black dust.

Lutgeri said, "Pierre would have liked that place. He'd have waxed lyrical. Remember how well he sang. A troubadour."

We thought of Pierre under the long thin windows of the castle, singing to some princess of story.

As we descended we found the snow was deep. We were pulled in and hacked our way out. It was another battle. Under the snow, Hades, a Hell of ice.

When we began to get level with the castle, we looked it over again. It was not so large. Some big towers with crenellations, and an inner block, high-roofed and capped by snow, with one slender squinnying tower all its own. Up there, a stab of light went through a window, rose-red, deathly green as a dying thorn.

"By the Christ," said Johan.

We stopped.

"What's that, by the Mass?"

"Flowers," said Gilles.

"No."

There could be no flower in the snowlands.

"Remember—" said Arpad, "remember what Pierre called it—the battlefield—"

Memory again. We had once come to a place, the plain of a war, in the snow, years back. And on the plain, left to God and the carrion birds, were the dying men, and the blood leaking from their bodies, red on the white. A feast. A horrible and cursed feast we were then too desperate to ignore.

And Pierre had named the sight.

"The blood in the sunlight on the snow," he said. "Red roses. Winter flowers."

"Flowers in winter," said Arpad now, so low only we could have heard him, and we did.

There was something blooming along the walls of the castle, and it looked like flowers. Winter flowers. Roses.

"There's nothing like that," said Johan. "We—*we* are the legend."

We laughed.

We forced our way on towards the castle.

There is a tradition of Maryam, the Virgin Mother of the Christ: That she had a garden enclosed by high walls. And in the garden it is always summer and the flowers grow.

Had we come to the Garden of Maryam?

As the castle's barriers loomed up over us, we

searched walks and towers with our gaze. But there was no sentry. No one called a challenge. We came up to the doors—and they stood ajar. This was curious and foreboding in itself, but we had seen such things; the bizarre is not always dangerous, just as sometimes, the ordinary is.

They were huge heavy doors too, with valves of iron like black stone. We went in, and there was the castle yard, save it was not. It was this garden.

The snow was on the ground, and on the steps that went to the towers, and to the central place with its tall snowy roof. But out of the snow of the yard, the flowers climbed on their briars up the high walls, up to the very tops, a curtain of dark green and lavish reds, of smoky pinks and peaches too, of murrey and magenta and ivory. Here and there the snow had even touched the faces of these flowers, but it had not burnt them. It was only like a dusting of white spice. And they had scent. In the cold static air it was rich and heady.

Gilles said, "Oh God, it's beautiful. Will it poison us?"

"Yes," said Festus. He wrenched out his knife and made a move toward the rose-vines. Johan caught his arm. Lutgeri said softly, "Better not. You might anger . . . someone."

"Who?" snapped Festus.

"God, perhaps," said Lutgeri. "If He's gone to so much trouble."

In the middle of the yard was a stone well, or-namented with upright stone birds. I crossed to the well, Johan and Arpad coming with me. Deep down the water was shining green as a pope's jasper ring, though along the coping speared icicles.

Up on the battlements nothing stirred but a trace of wind, blowing off a spray of snow, and perfume.

"Is it magic?" said Gilles.

"Yes," said Bollo. "Like the virgin sleeping in her garden, and only the kiss of God can wake her."

"I don't like it," said Yens, "my guts are changing into snakes."

"That door is open too," said Arpad, pointing up at the central building just over from the well.

He strode off towards it. "A nice virgin in a bower. That's no threat to me."

Festus, knife still drawn, went after him.

Johan said, "What do you want to do, Maurs?"

"Look and see. Perhaps the inside is good, too."

Arpad and Festus had gone through the door. Then Arpad gave a shout, and we ran, all of us, getting the blades free as we did so.

As we burst through the door, it became a silly clowns' performance, for bringing up short Johan, Gilles, Lutgeri and I were collided with by Yens and Bollo.

Arpad and Festus were in the midst of the cas-tle hall, just standing there and gazing about. There was something to look at.

I have seen the house-halls of wealthy dukes and counts and other princes of the world, here and otherwise. But none better, and few so fine. And probably not one like that one.

There were carpets on the walls from the East, wonderful scarlets and saffrons, and high up the walls were carved, and the ceiling, with beasts and birds. And there were very strange, mythical, women things with the tails of fish and serpents, winged horses, lions with three heads, horned bears, birds with the faces of ancient bearded men. Out of the ceiling dropped brazen lamps on long chains, and they were alight, giving to the wide chamber a deep burnished glow broken only by the flutter of a large and burning hearth. The fire-place was fronted with rosy marble that ran off into a floor formed of squares of this rose marble and another that was of russet. A stair ascended between two statues. The figures were taller than a man, one of a woman holding up a gilded shield or mirror before her countenance, and one of King Death, a robed creature with the head of a skull crowned by gold. The windows that ran above the hall had glass in them, and in each pane was a sin-gle ruby jewel. The sun had got now behind three of these, and the bloody drops fell down to the room, directly on Death's diadem and robe. We took this sour omen in like vinegar.

Near the hearth, however, was a table set with chairs. The table was also laid with flagons and jars and jugs, with plates and knives, and the light danced on the gold-work. There were roasts on that table, pork and hare, a wide side of beef. And on the plates piled up the plaited pies and loaves, the sweetmeats you see and never taste, the mounded summer fruits like balls of enamel and gold. The fruit was fresh and ripe, the bread and meat were hot, you could smell them.

"What is it?" said Gilles.

"It's the Devil," said Yens.

Arpad had wandered to the table and stretched out his hands.

"No, fool," I shouted. *"No."*

Arpad put his hands down by his sides. He blushed.

Bollo said, "It's so miraculous it might be sound. It might be a gift from on high."

"But is it?" I said.

Bollo shrugged.

Festus said, "Well, what do we do?"

"We'll search this hold," I said, "and then we'll see if it's fit to banquet in."

And so we searched the building, the hub of the little castle on the plain of snow, the castle of summer and lit lamps and bright fire and new-cooked food.

It was uniformly splendid. It was beautiful. Everywhere the carvings, that had to do it seemed with every myth and fantasy of the earth. Wherever there was a window, it was glass, and in many of them was a gem of colored vitreous, or the delicate pattern of grisaille. Tapestries and carpets on the walls, gleaming with luster and tints as if sloughed from the loom only yesterday. Above the hall was a library with old, old books and scrolls in Latin and in Greek, and some even in the picture writing of earlier lands. An armory there was, its door open like all the rest. The weapons were antique and modern, well-cared for, the leather and lacquer oiled and rubbed, the iron shined. Bows of horn, bronze maces, lances notched like the swords from use. . . .

There were side chambers with sumptuous beds, and carved chests that, when they were easily undone, revealed the clothes of lords folded among herbs, and belts inlaid with gold. In caskets were found the jewelries of queens and kings, corals and pearls, amethysts like pigeons' blood, brooding garnets, crosses of silver pierced by green beryl, and from the East again armlets of heavy gold, headdresses of golden beads and discs, things the Herods might have looked on, worn.

"Take none of this."

"No, Maurs," they said.

Johan said, "I think it is a spell after all."

"Yes, a stink of a spell, to entrap us."

We said we would be better going at once, hunting the lean hills for mice, sleeping in the snow about a pale fire. Yet we were in love with the castle, as if with a beautiful woman. She may mean you no good and yet you hang about her. Perhaps you can charm the bitch, perhaps her heart is fair like her face, and needs only to be persuaded.

From the upper chambers we glared out beyond the castle walls and the snow was teeming once again. The day was dark now as evening, and how thoughtful the sorcery of the castle was, lighting all its lamps for us, in every room, and on the stairs the torches in their ornamented brackets.

At last we were weary of it, sick of it. Too many sweets and none to be eaten.

Then, we reached a door that did not give.

"What's *this*?"

"It could lead into that tower we spied," said Johan, "so I'd guess. With the pretty window."

Glancing up, I saw, carved in the stone above the door, the words: *Virgo pulchra, claustra recludens.*

"Lovely maiden, undo the bolt," translated Bollo.

"Does it only mean a girl?" said Yens. "Isn't it invoking the Mother of God?"

"It's all we need," said Gilles, "lovely maidens."

"No, one other thing," said Lutgeri.

"Blood," I said.

There was a silence, under the locked door.

"Perhaps this place will give us that, too," said Johan. "Since it offers everything else."

We examined each other.

Arpad's eyes glittered, and the eyes of Gilles were heavy. Yens frowned and gnawed his lip, Festus had turned away, and Bollo was blank as a worn page in one of the ancient books. Lutgeri and Johan seemed to be thinking, gazing down some tunnel of memory or the mind. And I? I recollected Pierre. And after him, the girl in the house at Bethelmai, who had wanted the impossible— to be spared rape, to keep her bracelet.

"We'll go down," I said.

"The food—" said Arpad, and Yens added, "I'm hungry enough I'd risk hemlock."

When we regained the hall, the fire was still as bright, its logs and sticks had not burnt up, and the lamps were glowing. But on the table, quite naturally, the feast had turned a little cold and greasy. We cut off chunks of meat and sliced the fruits and broke off the caps of the crystalline castle. There was no smell or appearance of anything bad, no taste, no evidence. We drew lots, and Arpad and Yens gladly tried the dishes, a mouthful of this and that. We would be likely to save them, if they had not had much. But then they did not sicken, and by the time the occluded sun had passed over to the other windows, we sat square at the table and gorged ourselves like the poor slaves of life we were.

I woke afraid. But that is not so unusual. There are dreams, unrecalled. There are noises heard in sleep, quite innocent, that remind the floating brain of other times when they were not—

I pushed myself up and my head rang slightly from the draughts of precious wine. Then it cleared and I remembered where I had lain down, and why, and that to fear might be quite wise.

Yes, the very image before me was one of alteration and so perhaps of warning.

The lamps had all gone out, and the changeless fire was sunken low, livid hovering lizard tongues on the remnants of the wood like blackened bones. Outside, beyond the enchanted castle, the weather seemed purified. The snow had been vomited out, and the sky was a sheer thin blackish-blue, threadbare with stars. This, through the high up windows of the hall, gave the light the lamps now withheld. The moon must be up.

I scrutinized the vast chamber and saw it all congealed in slabs of lunar ice. The great table ruined by our orgy of hunger. The carvings and the carved cupboards, the carpets hung on the walls with here and there some sequin of pallor, a hand, a unicorn, a skull.

No one in the room but I, yet someone had been there. Who? Most of my brotherhood had gone up to slumber in the haughty, luxurious beds of the castle. I had put Johan to watch at the stairhead, and Lutgeri and Festus to stroll the passages in a pair. The hall door we had bolted. And I had rolled myself to sleep before the fire in my cloak, with one of the fancy cushions under my head.

If something had happened, I would have heard a commotion.

But, by the Christ, something had happened. My heart and my soul knew it, if my stupid mind did not.

I got on my feet all the way, and went to the table. The wine had been unvenomous, and I took a drink of it, to steady me.

What had been in the hall with me was a whisper, a gliding sigh. Probably not that which had woken me at all, this cobweb of nothingness, this ghost. No, some deep instinct, clamoring, had reached me finally after a long while. It was as if a bell had been clanging in my blood and I had only just heard it—then, it stopped.

I did not call for the sentries, Lutgeri, Festus, Johan. Surely they should have woken me by now, and Yens and Bollo, to take our turn.

How silent the castle, and the land beyond. Rarely is anything so dumb. The wind calls, and the beasts that roam the night. And in the dwellings of men the rats and vermin move about, the timbers stir, the furniture creaks. Here—not a note. Only I had made a sound, and that not much.

I drew my sword, and my knife for the left hand. Then I climbed the stair, between Death and his Lady, noiseless, seeing.

Johan was not above. That was not like him. If he had gone from his post it was because something had summoned him. And then, certainly, he would have alerted me.

"Johan," I said, quietly. And he would have heard. But there was no answer, and beyond the windows there, the dark was full.

I went into it, that dark. One learns to use one's eyes, and so sight grudgingly came. I beheld the twisting passageway, and there a door. And there, something lay on the threshold.

For more than three hundred years, I knew him. He did not sleep unless he might. And now, he did not sleep. Across the door of the room Arpad had chosen, Johan lay dead.

This was not new to me. Yet never does it grow stale. To find your friend and brother is a corpse.

I bent over him, one ear, one eye upon the dark, and tried him.

Oh Christ—Oh, he was not a human thing anymore. No, no. He was a sack of emptiness. A rattling sack filled by loose bones. Like the picture of Death, whose cart is stacked by the skeletons of the dead that have a tiny, immodest fragment of skin on them. Like that. Johan. So.

I let go of him, and held down my screaming. I am practiced. And since that night, better.

There were no muscles left in his body, no *flesh*. I had no true light, and yet I *knew*. No *blood*.

In the dark, some demon had come, and sucked him dry. Oh, not as we do. Not like that. You give us sustenance like a maiden at a well, raising the bucket brimmed with water. Like the lord at the dinner, offering us wine. A drink. The drink of life. And with the woman or boy who sucks the smooth sword of our cock, tender and cunning, careful and fierce and honey in the dark, and with the girl who takes in our seed at her other mouth, and grows in the closed garden of her womb a rose: So it goes back to you. *But not like this.*

He had been drained. As the fire does it. Like Pierre. Save that burnt inward, and this, *out*.

No longer Johan.

I turned and opened Arpad's selected door, and stepped into the chamber.

Moonlight streamed here on the floor and over the bed, in a white mirror from the window, and in its heart a black cicatrix lay from the decaying window jewel the moon could not rouse.

Arpad sprawled half from the majestic bed he had chosen. His head drooped to the floor, and one arm, and when I tried him, Arpad, who had been sparks and pepper, hot iron and strong drink, Arpad was another flaccid sack on the cart of Death.

Then a fear came over me I had never felt. Not once, in all my long life. I have been pent and pinned, they have promised me all sorts of torture, and Hell after, and never once, no never had I felt this fear. It was born in me that night. Shall I ever be free of it?

I left Arpad, and Johan, and walked out along the passage.

In their brackets the kind torches had guttered out. Only the moon slid through the narrow slits, each with that mole of dark on it from its jewel, or else weird shapes from the painting on the flags. And then the corridor turned any way, and the moon had gone behind a wall. White Face they called her, long ago. She is fickle, and not your helpmeet. A betrayer, Dame Moon.

I came on Festus not long after. And then Lutgeri. Festus too was in the bone cart of Death. And I gave Lutgeri a shake, like a rat, but I hated him because he was dead. And then I heard him breathing, rasping and interrupted, like a rusty machine, some windmill, or thing of the old sieges they cannot make any more.

"Lutgeri—Lutgeri—"

"Hush," he said, "calmly, my boy."

I held him in my arms.

"If you die, you shit-rat, I'll kill you."

"I know you will, Maurs. I'll try not to."

I wept on his shoulder which had the feel of life and humanity. One whole second. Then I was myself again.

"What did this?"

"How many?" he gasped.

"Arpad, Festus—Johan—"

"Ah," he said, "Johan."

Then he lost consciousness and I squeezed on his neck, against the vein, to haul him back.

"Tell me, Lutgeri."

"I can't. I don't—something came from the shadow. It was like—no, it was like nothing at all. It didn't croon. And it hurt me. Christ's soul. Its teeth went into my breast—and the blood was ripped from me, Maurs, like my living organs, before I could struggle. And no voice in my throat."

"How do you survive?" I said. I was numb.

"God knows. Perhaps my old ichor wasn't to its taste, or a little did for more."

"The others," I said.

Lutgeri whispered, "Arpad? Festus—yes. Yens and Gilles—they must be gone if it came to them. Bollo, perhaps—old alligator. He might—"

His head fell back. He had fainted again, but still lived. I crushed my wrist between his teeth. "Drink it, you swine, you shit-heart. *Drink it.*"

In his stupor, he took a morsel from me.

Then, in my arms, he drew his sword.

"Leave me here, Maurs. I'm ready for it now. If it returns. But you must—"

"Yes." I got up. I raised him and slung him over my shoulder and took him into the library. Its lamp was out. I fetched down a book and pressed it on his hand. "When the weight changes, if it grows—"

"I know, Maurs. Then I'm lighter. I have the sword. Go find them. *Go.*"

Bollo had gone to sleep in the armory. That was, he had told me he would be there, to examine the weapons alone. He had not meant to sleep, and took with him a jar of the wine from the table. He could go days and nights, up to ten, without sleeping. I had seen it. But then, why battle the god of slumber here? I ran, up the stairs, up into the height of the place, to reach Bollo.

When I was near the door, something laid hold of me, and made me pause. I went slowly after that, the drawn sword and knife before me. I crept to the door of the armory, and it was partly open, as all the doors of the castle seemed to wish to be, but one, the virgin door to the tower.

I eased the armory door inward. So I saw.

Lovers making love cannot always stop.

There was a window, and the moon was in it, it was an arch of light, with only the dark Mark of Cain upon its forehead from the intercepting jewel. More than enough light to see.

Bollo sat at the table, one of the old books open in front of him from below, and a mace, and a candle that had been burning and which had gone out. Moonlight described the weapon, and the book, a great capital of gilding and indigo, and on it a gem of blackness that, in daylight, would have been red.

The eyes of Bollo were wide, and stiffly, like the cogs of a machine, they crawled in their sockets, till he could look at me. He knew me, he was coherent, but paralyzed.

While it bent over him, obscuring him as a cloud will the moon. It was so filmy, so wraith-like, yet so real.

What did I regard? The sight is printed on my mind. I can never forget, yet how to relate?

It was old, ancient as nothing in the castle was, not even the scrolls penned before the Flood. It was like something made of rags and bones, filaments and tendrils, pasted together, strung, like a harp of the air. Moonlight passed through its wrapping, but not through itself, though dimly in it, stones in a frozen river, you saw the elements of its skeleton like the teeth of a comb. It was, or had been, of human shape. But of what gender, God knew. It held Bollo, beneath the arms, and its head, from which a hank of gauzy hair spun out, was bowed upon his chest.

This looked like a deed of repentance. As if it had gone to him and sobbed in his breast. But I knew, for Lutgeri had told me, what it did.

I rammed my sword into its back, up into the spot where the heart is come on.

And it was like thrusting into snow.

But at the blow it left him, it straightened up, and turning like a snake it gazed on me.

Oh it had eyes. The eyes of wolves, our own, are human. But these were not. Like round black beads they shone, harder and more true than all the rest of it. Bits of night, but not this night. No night we will ever see.

And then it gaped its mouth, and its sharp yellow teeth were there, and the swarthy tongue, pointed and too long. It hissed at me, and I fell back.

My sword had come from it as if out of sticky vapor.

I hung before it, not knowing what I must do. And then it seemed to me I should strike that weaving insubstantial head from its shoulders. But as I drew my arm for the stroke, it smeared away. It slid, *rolled* at the wall, moving as the snake does. And the wall parted, to let it by.

Yes, like soft butter the stone gave way, and it slipped through. And then Bollo cried to me, as if he choked, "Maurs—there—there—"

And in his eyes I saw the deaths of Yens and Gilles. I saw King Death himself, on his fish-white charger, pacing slowly. Then I turned and flung myself through the wall before it closed. After the vampire.

I have done things in battle, many have, crazy things called after "brave." But they are the madness of war. And this, this was not like them, for I was afraid going in through that wall, and yet could not keep back.

It had come to me, this thing, or others of its kind. That had been the sigh, the whisper, in the dark. But I had woken, before its fangs could fasten into me. And why was that? But then, why ask? Each of us knows he alone is immortal, cannot die. And that whoever falls, he will survive it. Death may touch, but then he is gone.

The corridor inside the wall was black as pitch, and yet I could just see, for as I said I have learned to use my eyes, and besides, what went before me, invisible now in itself, gave off a faint luminescence, like the crests of waves, like fungus, such things.

It progressed quickly, but not as if it went on legs or feet. And the elf-light flowed behind it, and

now and then I was close enough a long trailing wisp of its garment, or perhaps *itself* billowed around a turn of the passage, and I might have plucked at it, but I did not.

How to kill it when I caught it. Would beheading do? We were vulnerable, but I had stabbed it through and it lived. Why then follow? I must. Or Bollo had put it on me that I must.

It went somewhere, evidently. To some lair.

Then the corridor began to branch. Constricted twisting routes led off this way and that, and it chose without hesitation, but now I was lost. We were inside the walls of the castle, in the very veins and arteries of it.

The passage ended at the foot of a sort of chimney. I dropped back, and beheld the aura of the being oozing up a flight of straight and narrow steps, directly up, and its glow abated as it vanished from sight.

The fear I felt was now so awful I could not for a moment or two more move or go after. And yet it was the fear itself, it seemed, that pushed me on.

Presently I eased out, and looking up into the shaft where the stairway went, saw the thing had completed its climb and gone in at a slender archway above. There was a hint of light inside the arch, but not like the other, the phosphorus of the vampire. This was warm.

I ran up the stair without a sound, and sprang into the arch. Within the vault of it, to the left, was another half-open door, and out of this stole the myrrh-soft shine. It was a gentle light, and by that I began to realize what might be there. Even so, when I had slunk to the doorway's edge, I peered around the door, and found I had not been prepared.

I grasped at once what chamber it was. None other than that upper room in the tower to which the lower outer door had refused us admittance. *Lovely girl, undo the bolt.* Up here, no doubt, she had done so, to let her creature in.

But the room was beautiful, like a painting, so neat and pleasant, every little accessory in its place. The slim white maiden's bed with its canopy of ashy rose, the tapestry of rainbow threads on its frame, the tiring table inlaid with different woods, the unguents and wooden combs, the trickle of a precious necklace from a carven box. There were little footstools with embroidered hounds and rabbits and birds, and on one of these, before her, the vampire I had pursued kneeled now, holding up its mealy hands. I learned here there had been others, three of them, who had taken the lives from my men. These vampires were like the first one, flimsy dolls of silver wire and thinnest samite, and crinkled now, folded over in strange shapes, like things that had no bones at all, like stiff clothing discarded.

She had had their messages and their gift already, she had emptied them in turn. And now she received the last of our ichor from the final creature, the one kneeling in front of her, lifting its hands so she might bow her head and bite the powdery wrists and drink, from that transferring vessel, *our blood*.

I moved into the doorway, and so into the room, and stood there, and looked on as she drained the wine-sack dry.

The ceiling was painted violet, with little golden stars. Under the stained glass window, which was black and moonless, only the brazen lamps to give their dulcet light, a rose bush grew in a pot. The great red blooms were open wide and I could smell their scent, and over that the perfume of the girl.

She had a skin like the snow, and hair like ebony, which fell all round her, with raven glints in it. Her gown was a pale sweet pink, the shade of fresh blood mixed into ice. There were rings on her fingers, gold emeralds, and as she lifted her head and let her servant go—it folded, discarded, lifeless, like the others—I saw that around her white forehead passed a golden chain fashioned into tiny flowers.

She had a lovely face. All of her was lovely. Not a flaw. There was not even any trace of blood on the petals of her lips, and her eyes were clear and innocent, the color of dark amber.

"At last you have come to me," she said. "I've waited so long."

"Have you, Lady?"

"Many, many years."

I believed that. I understood it all and did not need a lesson. Nor did I get one. The castle was her web. Probably it was a ruin, and every tasteful glamorous thing inside mildew and muck. God knew what we had eaten off that banquet table. For the rest, when we were lulled, her emissaries came. They filled themselves from us like jars, then glided back to her and gave up every drop to make her strong and fair. What had she been before? A desiccated insect lying, wheezing and murmuring on her charming bed, which maybe was a stinking gaping grave.

And one she wanted as her lover. Perhaps to continue her race through him, if she was the last of that particular kind. Or maybe only to ease her loneliness. Or to champion her, to take her out into the world beyond the web, where she could become a mighty sorceress, out in the thousand lands where blood runs in rivers.

Yet she looked at me and I loved her. Such adoration. She was the Virgin Queen and the fount of all delicious sin. She was my mother and my child, my sister, my soul.

Her magic was strong enough, and she had fed.

She held out her perfect hand to me, and I went forward.

And the lamplight shone through her amber eyes, and I remembered the girl in the upper room, her little ring of silver on her roughened hand. "Don't rape me. Don't take my bracelet." And it came to me as if I heard the words, that the soldiers had found her, or she had stumbled amongst them. They had raped her, they had stolen her solitary treasure, they had thrown her down in the mud among the reeking corpses. So then I saw the corpse of Pierre, his black dust raked over in the dying pyre. I saw the battlefield in the snow, where we had sucked out the life of dying, crying men, the crimson winter roses, since we must. And into us had passed with their life the despair of their death, so the tears froze on our faces with the blood cold against our lips. All that I saw, there in the eyes of the lovely maiden in the tower, and so I saw my brothers she had fed on. Arpad and Yens, Festus and Gilles. Johan. And Lutgeri with the sword, and the book on his hand to remind him to live, and Bollo staring. And I saw myself before her, tall and somber as a shadow, with the blade in my hand.

God knows, He had ordained it, we prey upon each other. As the lion on the deer, the cat upon the mouse. There is no penance we may do to right this wrong. There is no excuse for that we live by killing, save only that we must. To survive is all. And she, the maiden, like us was vulnerable, for unlike the automata of her slaves, she was a thing of flesh and blood. My sister, as Pierre had been my brother and myself. And, so beautiful—

The dawn was coming up, sluggish, like heavy iron. No color on the earth. The roses would be burnt papers and the books grey flour, like all the stuff in the upper chamber.

Lutgeri was sharpening his knife, slow. He did not speak to me of the cold grim rooms, the fallen areas and the rotted carpets. But Bollo, who had gone out and broken the thick corded ice of the well, informed me it stank, not fit to drink.

I told them of the girl in the tower. They listened. Before we went to bury our dead in the hard soil beyond the castle, they asked what I had done.

"I loved her, of course," I said. "I never loved any woman like that one. It was her spell."

"So you went to her," said Bollo, but Lutgeri held up his hand, mildly, as if to caution him.

"I went to her," I said.

"And then," Lutgeri said. "And then."

"With my sword I struck the head from her body."

# THE MAN WHO LOVED THE VAMPIRE LADY

# Brian Stableford

Brian Michael Stableford (1948– ) was born in Shipley, Yorkshire, and earned a B.A. in biology in 1969 and a Ph.D. in sociology ten years later, both from the University of York. He began writing short stories and teaching sociology at the University of Reading while also teaching courses in science fiction and fantasy literature. His first two novels were action-adventure science-fiction stories, *Cradle of the Sun* (1969) and *The Blind Worm* (1970). He then wrote a trilogy with the overall title *Dies Irae*, followed by a six-novel series with a misanthropic hero, Grainger, with the overall title *Hooded Swan*. These and subsequent novel cycles were structured as classic "space operas." Later works became more complex and incorporated elements of fantasy and horror.

Early (as well as a few later) works were published as Brian M. Stableford, and he also wrote as Brian Craig, employing his first name and that of his friend Craig A. Mackintosh, with whom he had collaborated on some early stories. In all, he has written more than fifty novels, as well as several scholarly works about the genre, including *The Mysteries of Science Fiction* (1977), *The Scientific Romance in Britain, 1890–1950* (1985), and *Opening Minds: Essays on Fantastic Literature* (1995). He has also translated numerous vampire and other dark fantasy fiction from the French.

"The Man Who Loved the Vampire Lady" was originally published in the August 1988 issue of *The Magazine of Fantasy & Science Fiction*.

# The Man Who Loved the Vampire Lady

## BRIAN STABLEFORD

*A man who loves a vampire lady may not die young, but cannot live forever.*
— WALACHIAN PROVERB

It was the thirteenth of June in the Year of Our Lord 1623. Grand Normandy was in the grip of an early spell of warm weather, and the streets of London bathed in sunlight. There were crowds everywhere, and the port was busy with ships, three having docked that very day. One of the ships, the *Freemartin*, was from the Moorish enclave and had produce from the heart of Africa, including ivory and the skins of exotic animals. There were rumors, too, of secret and more precious goods: jewels and magical charms; but such rumors always attended the docking of any vessel from remote parts of the world. Beggars and street urchins had flocked to the dockland, responsive as ever to such whisperings, and were plaguing every sailor in the streets, as anxious for gossip as for copper coins. It seemed that the only faces not animated by excitement were those worn by the severed heads that dressed the spikes atop the Southwark Gate. The Tower of London, though, stood quite aloof from the hubbub, its tall and forbidding turrets so remote from the streets that they belonged to a different world.

Edmund Cordery, mechanician to the court of the Archduke Girard, tilted the small concave mirror on the brass device that rested on his workbench, catching the rays of the afternoon sun and deflecting the light through the system of lenses.

He turned away and directed his son, Noell, to take his place. "Tell me if all is well," he said tiredly. "I can hardly focus my eyes, let alone the instrument."

Noell closed his left eye and put his other to the microscope. He turned the wheel that adjusted the height of the stage. "It's perfect," he said. "What is it?"

"The wing of a moth." Edmund scanned the polished tabletop, checking that the other slides were in readiness for the demonstration. The prospect of Lady Carmilla's visit filled him with a complex anxiety that he resented in himself. Even in the old days, she had not come to his laboratory often, but to see her here—on his own territory, as it were—would be bound to awaken memories that were untouched by the glimpses that he caught of her in the public parts of the Tower and on ceremonial occasions.

"The water slide isn't ready," Noell pointed out.

Edmund shook his head. "I'll make a fresh one when the time comes," he said. "Living things are fragile, and the world that is in a water drop is all too easily destroyed."

He looked farther along the bench-top, and moved a crucible, placing it out of sight behind a row of jars. It was impossible—and unnecessary—to make the place tidy, but he felt it important to conserve some sense of order and control. To discourage himself from fidgeting, he went to the window and looked out at the sparkling Thames and the strange gray sheen on the slate roofs of the houses beyond. From this high vantage point, the people were tiny; he was higher even than the cross on the steeple of the church beside the Leather-market. Edmund was not a devout man, but such was the agitation within him, yearning for expression in action, that the sight of the cross on the church made him cross himself, murmuring the ritual devotion. As soon as he had done it, he cursed himself for childishness.

*I am forty-four years old,* he thought, *and a mechanician. I am no longer the boy who was favored with the love of the lady, and there is no need for this stupid trepidation.*

He was being deliberately unfair to himself in this private scolding. It was not simply the fact that he had once been Carmilla's lover that made him anxious. There was the microscope, and the ship from the Moorish country. He hoped that he would be able to judge by the lady's reaction how much cause there really was for fear.

The door opened then, and the lady entered. She half turned to indicate by a flutter of her hand that her attendant need not come in with her, and he withdrew, closing the door behind him. She was alone, with no friend or favorite in tow. She came across the room carefully, lifting the hem of her skirt a little, though the floor was not dusty. Her gaze flicked from side to side, to take note of the shelves, the beakers, the furnace, and the numerous tools of the mechanician's craft. To a commoner, it would have seemed a threatening environment, redolent with unholiness, but her attitude was cool and controlled. She arrived to stand before the brass instrument that Edmund had recently completed, but did not look long at it before raising her eyes to look fully into Edmund's face.

"You look well, Master Cordery," she said calmly. "But you are pale. You should not shut yourself in your rooms now that summer is come to Normandy."

Edmund bowed slightly, but met her gaze. She had not changed in the slightest degree, of course, since the days when he had been intimate with her. She was six hundred years old—hardly younger than the archduke—and the years were impotent as far as her appearance was concerned. Her complexion was much darker than his, her eyes a deep liquid brown, and her hair jet black. He had not stood so close to her for several years, and he could not help the tide of memories rising in his mind. For her, it would be different: his hair was gray now, his skin creased; he must seem an altogether different person. As he met her gaze, though, it seemed to him that she, too, was remembering, and not without fondness.

"My lady," he said, his voice quite steady, "may I present my son and apprentice, Noell."

Noell bowed more deeply than his father, blushing with embarrassment.

The Lady Carmilla favored the youth with a smile. "He has the look of you, Master Cordery," she said—a casual compliment. She returned her attention then to the instrument.

"The designer was correct?" she asked.

"Yes, indeed," he replied. "The device is most ingenious. I would dearly like to meet the man who thought of it. A fine discovery—though it taxed the talents of my lens grinder severely. I think we might make a better one, with much care and skill; this is but a poor example, as one must expect from a first attempt."

The Lady Carmilla seated herself at the bench, and Edmund showed her how to apply her eye to the instrument, and how to adjust the focusing wheel and the mirror. She expressed surprise at the appearance of the magnified moth's wing, and Edmund took her through the series of prepared slides, which included other parts of insects' bodies, and sections through the stems and seeds of plants.

"I need a sharper knife and a steadier hand, my lady," he told her. "The device exposes the clumsiness of my cutting."

"Oh no, Master Cordery," she assured him politely. "These are quite pretty enough. But we were told that more interesting things might be seen. Living things too small for ordinary sight."

Edmund bowed in apology and explained about the preparation of water slides. He made a new one, using a pipette to take a drop from a jar full of dirty river water. Patiently, he helped the lady search the slide for the tiny creatures that human eyes were not equipped to perceive. He showed her one that flowed as if it were semiliquid itself, and tinier ones that moved by means of cilia. She was quite captivated, and watched for some time, moving the slide very gently with her painted fingernails.

Eventually she asked: "Have you looked at other fluids?"

"What kind of fluids?" he asked, though the question was quite clear to him and disturbed him.

She was not prepared to mince words with him. "Blood, Master Cordery," she said very softly. Her past acquaintance with him had taught her respect for his intelligence, and he half regretted it.

"Blood clots very quickly," he told her. "I could not produce a satisfactory slide. It would take unusual skill."

"I'm sure that it would," she replied.

"Noell has made drawings of many of the things we *have* looked at," said Edmund. "Would you like to see them?"

She accepted the change of subject, and indicated that she would. She moved to Noell's station and began sorting through the drawings, occasionally looking up at the boy to compliment him on his work. Edmund stood by, remembering how sensitive he once had been to her moods and desires, trying hard to work out now exactly what she was thinking. Something in one of her contemplative glances at Noell sent an icy pang of dread into Edmund's gut, and he found his more

important fears momentarily displaced by what might have been anxiety for his son, or simply jealousy. He cursed himself again for his weakness.

"May I take these to show the archduke?" asked the Lady Carmilla, addressing the question to Noell rather than to his father. The boy nodded, still too embarrassed to construct a proper reply. She took a selection of the drawings and rolled them into a scroll. She stood and faced Edmund again.

"We are most interested in this apparatus," she informed him. "We must consider carefully whether to provide you with new assistants, to encourage development of the appropriate skills. In the meantime, you may return to your ordinary work. I will send someone for the instrument, so that the archduke can inspect it at his leisure. Your son draws very well, and must be encouraged. You and he may visit me in my chambers on Monday next; we will dine at seven o'clock, and you may tell me about all your recent work."

Edmund bowed to signal his acquiescence—it was, of course, a command rather than an invitation. He moved before her to the door in order to hold it open for her. The two exchanged another brief glance as she went past him.

When she had gone, it was as though something taut unwound inside him, leaving him relaxed and emptied. He felt strangely cool and distant as he considered the possibility—stronger now—that his life was in peril.

When the twilight had faded, Edmund lit a single candle on the bench and sat staring into the flame while he drank dark wine from a flask. He did not look up when Noell came into the room, but when the boy brought another stool close to his and sat down upon it, he offered the flask. Noell took it, but sipped rather gingerly.

"I'm old enough to drink now?" he commented dryly.

"You're old enough," Edmund assured him. "But beware of excess, and never drink alone. Conventional fatherly advice, I believe."

Noell reached across the bench so that he could stroke the barrel of the microscope with slender fingers.

"What are you afraid of?" he asked.

Edmund sighed. "You're old enough for that, too, I suppose?"

"I think you ought to tell me."

Edmund looked at the brass instrument and said, "It were better to keep things like this dark secret. Some human mechanician, I daresay, eager to please the vampire lords and ladies, showed off his cleverness as proud as a peacock. Thoughtless. Inevitable, though, now that all this play with lenses has become fashionable."

"You'll be glad of eyeglasses when your sight begins to fail," Noell told him. "In any case, I can't see the danger in this new toy."

Edmund smiled. "New toys," he mused. "Clocks to tell the time, mills to grind the corn, lenses to aid human sight. Produced by human craftsmen for the delight of their masters. I think we've finally succeeded in proving to the vampires just how very clever we are—and how much more there is to know than we know already."

"You think the vampires are beginning to fear us?"

Edmund gulped wine from the flask and passed it again to his son. "Their rule is founded in fear and superstition," he said quietly. "They're long-lived, suffer only mild attacks of diseases that are fatal to us, and have marvelous powers of regeneration. But they're not immortal, and they're vastly outnumbered by humans. Terror keeps them safe, but terror is based in ignorance, and behind their haughtiness and arrogance, there's a gnawing fear of what might happen if humans ever lost their supernatural reverence for vampirekind. It's very difficult for them to die, but they don't fear death any the less for that."

"There've been rebellions against vampire rule. They've always failed."

Edmund nodded to concede the point. "There are three million people in Grand Normandy," he said, "and less than five thousand vampires. There are only forty thousand vampires in the entire imperium of Gaul, and about the same number in the imperium of Byzantium—no telling how many there may be in the khanate of Walachia and Cathay, but not so very many more. In Africa the vampires must be outnumbered three or four thousand to one. If people no longer saw them as demons and demi-gods, as unconquerable forces of evil, their empire would be fragile. The centuries through which they live give them wisdom, but longevity seems to be inimical to creative thought—they learn, but they don't *invent*. Humans remain the true masters of art and science, which are forces of change. They've tried to control that—to turn it to their advantage—but it remains a thorn in their side."

"But they do have power," insisted Noell. "They *are* vampires."

Edmund shrugged. "Their longevity is real— their powers of regeneration, too. But is it really their magic that makes them so? I don't know for sure what merit there is in their incantations and rituals, and I don't think even *they* know—they cling to their rites because they dare not abandon them, but where the power that makes humans into vampires really comes from, no one knows. From the devil? I think not. I don't believe in the devil—I think it's something in the blood. I think vampirism may be a kind of disease—but a disease that makes men stronger instead of weaker, insulates them against death instead of killing them. If that is the case—do you see now why the Lady Carmilla asked whether I had looked at blood beneath the microscope?"

Noell stared at the instrument for twenty seconds or so, mulling over the idea. Then he laughed.

"If we could *all* become vampires," he said lightly, "we'd have to suck one another's blood."

Edmund couldn't bring himself to look for such ironies. For him, the possibilities inherent in discovering the secrets of vampire nature were much more immediate, and utterly bleak.

"It's not true that they *need* to suck the blood of humans," he told the boy. "It's not nourishment. It gives them . . . a kind of pleasure that we can't understand. And it's part of the mystique that makes them so terrible . . . and hence so powerful." He stopped, feeling embarrassed. He did not know how much Noell knew about his sources of information. He and his wife never talked about the days of his affair with the Lady Carmilla, but there was no way to keep gossip and rumor from reaching the boy's ears.

Noell took the flask again, and this time took a deeper draft from it. "I've heard," he said distantly, "that humans find pleasure, too . . . in their blood being drunk."

"No," replied Edmund calmly. "That's untrue. Unless one counts the small pleasure of sacrifice. The pleasure that a human man takes from a vampire lady is the same pleasure that he takes from a human lover. It might be different for the girls who entertain vampire men, but I suspect it's just the excitement of hoping that they may become vampires themselves."

Noell hesitated, and would probably have dropped the subject, but Edmund realized suddenly that he did not want the subject dropped. The boy had a right to know, and perhaps might one day *need* to know.

"That's not entirely true," Edmund corrected himself. "When the Lady Carmilla used to taste my blood, it did give me pleasure, in a way. It pleased me because it pleased *her*. There *is* an excitement in loving a vampire lady, which makes it different from loving an ordinary woman . . . even though the chance that a vampire lady's lover may himself become a vampire is so remote as to be inconsiderable."

Noell blushed, not knowing how to react to this acceptance into his father's confidence. Finally he decided that it was best to pretend a purely academic interest.

"Why are there so many more vampire women than men?" he asked.

"No one knows for sure," Edmund said. "No humans, at any rate. I can tell you what I believe, from hearsay and from reasoning, but you must understand that it is a dangerous thing to think about, let alone to speak about."

Noell nodded.

"The vampires keep their history secret," said Edmund, "and they try to control the writing of human history, but the following facts are prob-

ably true. Vampirism came to western Europe in the fifth century, with the vampire-led horde of Attila. Attila must have known well enough how to make more vampires—he converted both Aëtius, who became ruler of the imperium of Gaul, and Theodosius II, the emperor of the east who was later murdered. Of all the vampires that now exist, the vast majority must be converts. I have heard reports of vampire children born to vampire ladies, but it must be an extremely rare occurrence. Vampire men seem to be much less virile than human men—it is said that they couple very rarely. Nevertheless, they frequently take human consorts, and these consorts often become vampires. Vampires usually claim that this is a gift, bestowed deliberately by magic, but I am not so sure they can control the process. I think the semen of vampire men carries some kind of seed that communicates vampirism much as the semen of humans makes women pregnant—and just as haphazardly. That's why the male lovers of vampire ladies don't become vampires."

Noell considered this, and then asked: "Then where do vampire lords come from?"

"They're converted by other male vampires," Edmund said. "Just as Attila converted Aëtius and Theodosius." He did not elaborate, but waited to see whether Noell understood the implication. An expression of disgust crossed the boy's face and Edmund did not know whether to be glad or sorry that his son could follow the argument through.

"Because it doesn't always happen," Edmund went on, "it's easy for the vampires to pretend that they have some special magic. But some women never become pregnant, though they lie with their husbands for years. It is said, though, that a human may also become a vampire by drinking vampire's blood—if he knows the appropriate magic spell. That's a rumor the vampires don't like, and they exact terrible penalties if anyone is caught trying the experiment. The ladies of our own court, of course, are for the most part onetime lovers of the archduke or his cousins. It would be indelicate to speculate about the conversion of the archduke, though he is certainly acquainted with Aëtius."

Noell reached out a hand, palm downward, and

made a few passes above the candle flame, making it flicker from side to side. He stared at the microscope.

"*Have* you looked at blood?" he asked.

"I have," replied Edmund. "And semen. Human blood, of course—and human semen."

"And?"

Edmund shook his head. "They're certainly not homogeneous fluids," he said, "but the instrument isn't good enough for really detailed inspection. There are small corpuscles—the ones in semen have long, writhing tails—but there's more . . . much more . . . to be seen, if I had the chance. By tomorrow this instrument will be gone—I don't think I'll be given the chance to build another."

"You're surely not in danger! You're an important man—and your loyalty has never been in question. People think of you as being almost a vampire yourself. A black magician. The kitchen girls are afraid of me because I'm your son—they cross themselves when they see me."

Edmund laughed, a little bitterly. "I've no doubt they suspect me of intercourse with demons, and avoid my gaze for fear of the spell of the evil eye. But none of that matters to the vampires. To them, I'm only a human, and for all that they value my skills, they'd kill me without a thought if they suspected that I might have dangerous knowledge."

Noell was clearly alarmed by this. "Wouldn't . . ." He stopped, but saw Edmund waiting for him to ask, and carried on after only a brief pause. "The Lady Carmilla . . . wouldn't she . . . ?"

"Protect me?" Edmund shook his head. "Not even if I were her favorite still. Vampire loyalty is to vampires."

"She was human once."

"It counts for nothing. She's been a vampire for nearly six hundred years, but it wouldn't be any different if she were no older than I."

"But . . . she did love you?"

"In her way," said Edmund sadly. "In her way." He stood up then, no longer feeling the urgent desire to help his son to understand. There were things the boy could find out only for himself and

might never have to. He took up the candle tray and shielded the flame with his hand as he walked to the door. Noel followed him, leaving the empty flask behind.

Edmund left the citadel by the so-called Traitor's Gate, and crossed the Thames by the Tower Bridge. The houses on the bridge were in darkness now, but there was still a trickle of traffic; even at two in the morning, the business of the great city did not come to a standstill. The night had clouded over, and a light drizzle had begun to fall. Some of the oil lamps that were supposed to keep the thoroughfare lit at all times had gone out, and there was not a lamplight in sight. Edmund did not mind the shadows, though.

He was aware before he reached the south bank that two men were dogging his footsteps, and he dawdled in order to give them the impression that he would be easy to track. Once he entered the network of streets surrounding the Leathermarket, though, he gave them the slip. He knew the maze of filthy streets well enough—he had lived here as a child. It was while he was apprenticed to a local clockmaker that he had learned the cleverness with tools that had eventually brought him to the notice of his predecessor, and had sent him on the road to fortune and celebrity. He had a brother and a sister still living and working in the district, though he saw them very rarely. Neither one of them was proud to have a reputed magician for a brother, and they had not forgiven him his association with the Lady Carmilla.

He picked his way carefully through the garbage in the dark alleys, unperturbed by the sound of scavenging rats. He kept his hands on the pommel of the dagger that was clasped to his belt, but he had no need to draw it. Because the stars were hidden, the night was pitch-dark, and few of the windows were lit from within by candlelight, but he was able to keep track of his progress by reaching out to touch familiar walls every now and again.

He came eventually to a tiny door set three steps down from a side street, and rapped upon it quickly, three times and then twice. There was a long pause before he felt the door yield beneath his fingers, and he stepped inside hurriedly. Until he relaxed when the door clicked shut again, he did not realize how tense he had been.

He waited for a candle to be lit.

The light, when it came, illuminated a thin face, crabbed and wrinkled, the eyes very pale and the wispy white hair gathered imperfectly behind a linen bonnet.

"The lord be with you," he whispered.

"And with you, Edmund Cordery," she croaked.

He frowned at the use of his name—it was a deliberate breach of etiquette, a feeble and meaningless gesture of independence. She did not like him, though he had never been less than kind to her. She did not fear him as so many others did, but she considered him tainted.

They had been bound together in the business of the Fraternity for nearly twenty years, but she would never completely trust him.

She led him into an inner room, and left him there to take care of his business.

A stranger stepped from the shadows. He was short, stout, and bald, perhaps sixty years old. He made the special sign of the cross, and Edmund responded.

"I'm Cordery," he said.

"Were you followed?" The older man's tone was deferential and fearful.

"Not here. They followed me from the Tower, but it was easy to shake them loose."

"That's bad."

"Perhaps—but it has to do with another matter, not with our business. There's no danger to you. Do you have what I asked for?"

The stout man nodded uncertainly. "My masters are unhappy," he said. "I have been asked to tell you that they do not want you to take risks. You are too valuable to place yourself in peril."

"I am in peril already. Events are overtaking us. In any case, it is neither your concern nor that of your . . . masters. It is for me to decide."

The stout man shook his head, but it was a gesture of resignation rather than a denial. He pulled something from beneath the chair where he had waited in the shadows. It was a large box, clad in leather. A row of small holes was set in the longer side, and there was a sound of scratching from within that testified to the presence of living creatures.

"You did exactly as I instructed?" asked Edmund.

The small man nodded, then put his hand on the mechanician's arm, fearfully. "Don't open it, sir, I beg you. Not here."

"There's nothing to fear," Edmund assured him.

"You haven't been in Africa, sir, as I have. Believe me, *everyone* is afraid—and not merely humans. They say that vampires are dying, too."

"Yes, I know," said Edmund distractedly. He shook off the older man's restraining hand and undid the straps that sealed the box. He lifted the lid, but not far—just enough to let the light in, and to let him see what was inside.

The box contained two big gray rats. They cowered from the light.

Edmund shut the lid again and fastened the straps.

"It's not my place, sir," said the little man hesitantly, "but I'm not sure that you really understand what you have there. I've seen the cities of West Africa—I've been in Corunna, too, and Marseilles. They remember other plagues in those cities, and all the horror stories are emerging again to haunt them. Sir, if any such thing ever came to London . . ."

Edmund tested the weight of the box to see whether he could carry it comfortably. "It's not your concern," he said. "Forget everything that has happened. I will communicate with your masters. It is in my hands now."

"Forgive me," said the other, "but I must say this: there is naught to be gained from destroying vampires, if we destroy ourselves, too. It would be a pity to wipe out half of Europe in the cause of attacking our oppressors."

Edmund stared at the stout man coldly. "You talk too much," he said. "Indeed, you talk a *deal* too much."

"I beg your pardon, sire."

Edmund hesitated for a moment, wondering

whether to reassure the messenger that his anxiety was understandable, but he had learned long ago that where the business of the Fraternity was concerned, it was best to say as little as possible. There was no way of knowing when this man would speak again of this affair, or to whom, or with what consequence.

The mechanician took up the box, making sure that he could carry it comfortably. The rats stirred inside, scrabbling with their small clawed feet. With his free hand, Edmund made the sign of the cross again.

"God go with you," said the messenger, with urgent sincerity.

"And with thy spirit," replied Edmund colorlessly.

Then he left, without pausing to exchange a ritual farewell with the crone. He had no difficulty in smuggling his burden back into the Tower, by means of a gate where the guard was long practiced in the art of turning a blind eye.

When Monday came, Edmund and Noell made their way to the Lady Carmilla's chambers. Noell had never been in such an apartment before, and it was a source of wonder to him. Edmund watched the boy's reactions to the carpets, the wall hangings, the mirrors and ornaments, and could not help but recall the first time *he* had entered these chambers. Nothing had changed here, and the rooms were full of provocations to stir and sharpen his faded memories.

Younger vampires tended to change their surroundings often, addicted to novelty, as if they feared the prospect of being changeless themselves. The Lady Carmilla had long since passed beyond this phase of her career. She had grown used to changelessness, had transcended the kind of attitude to the world that permitted boredom and ennui. She had adapted herself to a new aesthetic of existence, whereby her personal space became an extension of her own eternal sameness, and innovation was confined to tightly controlled areas of her life—including the irregular shifting of her erotic affections from one lover to another.

The sumptuousness of the lady's table was a further source of astonishment to Noell. Silver plates and forks he had imagined, and crystal goblets, and carved decanters of wine. But the lavishness of provision for just three diners—the casual waste—was something that obviously set him aback. He had always known that he was himself a member of a privileged elite, and that by the standards of the greater world, Master Cordery and his family ate well; the revelation that there was a further order of magnitude to distinguish the private world of the real aristocracy clearly made its impact upon him.

Edmund had been very careful in preparing his dress, fetching from his closet finery that he had not put on for many years. On official occasions he was always concerned to play the part of mechanician, and dressed in order to sustain that appearance. He never appeared as a courtier, always as a functionary. Now, though, he was reverting to a kind of performance that Noell had never seen him play, and though the boy had no idea of the subtleties of his father's performance, he clearly understood something of what was going on; he had complained acidly about the dull and plain way in which his father had made *him* dress.

Edmund ate and drank sparingly, and was pleased to note that Noell did likewise, obeying his father's instructions despite the obvious temptations of the lavish provision. For a while the lady was content to exchange routine courtesies, but she came quickly enough—by her standards—to the real business of the evening.

"My cousin Girard," she told Edmund, "Is quite enraptured by your clever device. He finds it most interesting."

"Then I am pleased to make him a gift of it," Edmund replied. "And I would be pleased to make another, as a gift for Your Ladyship."

"That is not our desire," she said coolly. "In fact, we have other matters in mind. The archduke and his seneschal have discussed certain tasks that you might profitably carry out. Instructions will be communicated to you in due time, I have no doubt."

"Thank you, my lady," said Edmund.

"The ladies of the court were pleased with the drawings that I showed to them," said the Lady Carmilla, turning to look at Noel. "They marveled at the thought that a cupful of Thames water might contain thousands of tiny living creatures. Do you think that our bodies, too, might be the habitation of countless invisible insects?"

Noell opened his mouth to reply, because the question was addressed to him, but Edmund interrupted smoothly.

"There are creatures that may live upon our bodies," he said, "and worms that may live within. We are told that the macrocosm reproduces in essence the microcosm of human beings; perhaps there is a small microcosm within us, where our natures are reproduced again, incalculably small. I have read . . ."

"I have read, Master Cordery," she cut in, "that the illnesses that afflict humankind might be carried from person to person by means of these tiny creatures."

"The idea that diseases were communicated from one person to another by tiny seeds was produced in antiquity," Edmund replied, "but I do not know how such seeds might be recognized, and I think it very unlikely that the creatures we have seen in river water could possibly be of that character."

"It is a disquieting thought," she insisted, "that our bodies might be inhabited by creatures of which we can know nothing, and that every breath we take might be carrying into us seeds of all kinds of change, too small to be seen or tasted. It makes me feel uneasy."

"But there is no need," Edmund protested. "Seeds of corruptibility take root in human flesh, but yours is inviolate."

"You know that is not so, Master Cordery," she said levelly. "You have seen me ill yourself."

"That was a pox that killed many humans, my lady—yet it gave to you no more than a mild fever."

"We have reports from the imperium of Byzantium, and from the Moorish enclave, too, that there is plague in Africa, and that it has now reached the southern regions of the imperium of Gaul. It is said that this plague makes little distinction between human and vampire."

"Rumors, my lady," said Edmund soothingly. "You know how news becomes blacker as it travels."

The Lady Carmilla turned again to Noell, and this time addressed him by name so that there could be no opportunity for Edmund to usurp the privilege of answering her. "Are you afraid of me, Noell?" she asked.

The boy was startled, and stumbled slightly over his reply, which was in the negative.

"You must not lie to me," she told him. "You *are* afraid of me, because I am a vampire. Master Cordery is a skeptic, and must have told you that vampires have less magic than is commonly credited to us, but he must also have told you that I can do you harm if I will. Would you like to be a vampire yourself, Noell?"

Noell was still confused by the correction, and hesitated over his reply, but he eventually said: "Yes, I would."

"Of course you would," she purred. "All humans would be vampires if they could, no matter how they might pretend when they bend the knee in church. And men *can* become vampires; immortality is within our gift. Because of this, we have always enjoyed the loyalty and devotion of the greater number of our human subjects. We have always rewarded that devotion in some measure. Few have joined our ranks, but the many have enjoyed centuries of order and stability. The vampires rescued Europe from a Dark Age, and as long as vampires rule, barbarism will always be held in check. Our rule has not always been kind, because we cannot tolerate defiance, but the alternative would have been far worse. Even so, there are men who would destroy us—did you know that?"

Noell did not know how to reply to this, so he simply stared, waiting for her to continue. She seemed a little impatient with his gracelessness, and Edmund deliberately let the awkward pause go on. He saw a certain advantage in allowing Noell to make a poor impression.

"There is an organization of rebels," the Lady

Carmilla went on. "A secret society, ambitious to discover the secret way by which vampires are made. They put about the idea that they would make all men immortal, but this is a lie, and foolish. The members of this brotherhood seek power for themselves."

The vampire lady paused to direct the clearing of one set of dishes and the bringing of another. She asked for a new wine, too. Her gaze wandered back and forth between the gauche youth and his self-assured father.

"The loyalty of your family is, of course, beyond question," she eventually continued. "No one understands the workings of society like a mechanician, who knows well enough how forces must be balanced and how the different parts of a machine must interlock and support one another. Master Cordery knows well how the cleverness of rulers resembles the cleverness of clockmakers, do you not?"

"Indeed, I do, my lady," replied Edmund.

"There might be a way," she said, in a strangely distant tone, "that a good mechanician might earn a conversion to vampirism."

Edmund was wise enough not to interpret this as an offer or a promise. He accepted a measure of the new wine and said: "My lady, there are matters that it would be as well for us to discuss in private. May I send my son to his room?"

The Lady Carmilla's eyes narrowed just a little, but there was hardly any expression in her finely etched features. Edmund held his breath, knowing that he had forced a decision upon her that she had not intended to make so soon.

"The poor boy has not quite finished his meal," she said.

"I think he has had enough, my lady," Edmund countered. Noell did not disagree, and, after a brief hesitation, the lady bowed to signal her permission. Edmund asked Noell to leave, and when he was gone, the Lady Carmilla rose from her seat and went from the dining room into an inner chamber. Edmund followed her.

"You were presumptuous, Master Cordery," she told him.

"I was carried away, my lady. There are too many memories here."

"The boy is mine," she said, "if I so choose. You do know that, do you not?"

Edmund bowed.

"I did not ask you here tonight to make you witness the seduction of your son. Nor do you think that I did. This matter that you would discuss with me—does it concern science or treason?"

"Science, my lady. As you have said yourself, my loyalty is not in question."

Carmilla laid herself upon a sofa and indicated that Edmund should take a chair nearby. This was the antechamber to her bedroom, and the air was sweet with the odor of cosmetics.

"Speak," she bade him.

"I believe that the archduke is afraid of what my little device might reveal," he said. "He fears that it will expose to the eye such seeds as carry vampirism from one person to another, just as it might expose the seeds that carry disease. I think that the man who devised the instrument may have been put to death already, but I think you know well enough that a discovery once made is likely to be made again and again. You are uncertain as to what course of action would best serve your ends, because you cannot tell whence the greater threat to your rule might come. There is the Fraternity, which is dedicated to your destruction; there is plague in Africa, from which even vampires may die; and there is the new sight, which renders visible what previously lurked unseen. Do you want my advice, Lady Carmilla?"

"Do you *have* any advice, Edmund?"

"Yes. Do not try to control by terror and persecution the things that are happening. Let your rule be unkind *now*, as it has been before, and it will open the way to destruction. Should you concede power gently, you might live for centuries yet, but if you strike out . . . your enemies will strike back."

The vampire lady leaned back her head, looking at the ceiling. She contrived a small laugh.

"I cannot take advice such as that to the archduke," she told him flatly.

"I thought not, my lady," Edmund replied very calmly.

"You humans have your own immortality," she complained. "Your faith promises it, and you all affirm it. Your faith tells you that you must not covet the immortality that is ours, and we do no more than agree with you when we guard it so jealously. You should look to your Christ for fortune, not to us. I think you know well enough that we could not convert the world if we wanted to. Our magic is such that it can be used only sparingly. Are you distressed because it has never been offered to you? Are you bitter? Are you becoming our enemy because you cannot become our kin?"

"You have nothing to fear from me, my lady," he lied. Then he added, not quite sure whether it was a lie or not: "I loved you faithfully. I still do."

She sat up straight then, and reached out a hand as though to stroke his cheek, though he was too far away for her to reach.

"That is what I told the archduke," she said, "when he suggested to me that you might be a traitor. I promised him that I could test your loyalty more keenly in my chambers than his officers in theirs. I do not think you could delude me, Edmund. Do you?"

"No, my lady," he replied.

"By morning," she told him gently, "I will know whether or not you are a traitor."

"That you will," he assured her. "That you will, my lady."

He woke before her, his mouth dry and his forehead burning. He was not sweating—indeed, he was possessed by a feeling of desiccation, as though the moisture were being squeezed out of his organs. His head was aching, and the light of the morning sun that streamed through the unshuttered window hurt his eyes.

He pulled himself up to a half-sitting position, pushing the coverlet back from his bare chest.

*So soon!* he thought. He had not expected to be consumed so quickly, but he was surprised to find that his reaction was one of relief rather than fear or regret. He had difficulty collecting his thoughts, and was perversely glad to accept that he did not need to.

He looked down at the cuts that she had made on his breast with her little silver knife; they were raw and red, and made a strange contrast with the faded scars whose crisscross pattern still engraved the story of unforgotten passions. He touched the new wounds gently with his fingers, and winced at the fiery pain.

She woke up then, and saw him inspecting the marks.

"Have you missed the knife?" she asked sleepily. "Were you hungry for its touch?"

There was no need to lie now, and there was a delicious sense of freedom in that knowledge. There was a joy in being able to face her, at last, quite naked in his thoughts as well as his flesh.

"Yes, my lady," he said with a slight croak in his voice. "I had missed the knife. Its touch . . . rekindled flames in my soul."

She had closed her eyes again, to allow herself to wake slowly. She laughed. "It is pleasant, sometimes, to return to forsaken pastures. You can have no notion how a particular *taste* may stir memories. I am glad to have seen you again, in this way. I had grown quite used to you as the gray mechanician. But now . . ."

He laughed, as lightly as she, but the laugh turned to a cough, and something in the sound alerted her to the fact that all was not as it should be. She opened her eyes and raised her head, turning toward him.

"Why, Edmund," she said, "you're as pale as death!"

She reached out to touch his cheek, and snatched her hand away again as she found it unexpectedly hot and dry. A blush of confusion spread across her own features. He took her hand and held it, looking steadily into her eyes.

"Edmund," she said softly. "What have you done?"

"I can't be sure," he said, "and I will not live to find out, but I have tried to kill you, my lady."

He was pleased by the way her mouth gaped

in astonishment. He watched disbelief and anxiety mingle in her expression, as though fighting for control. She did not call out for help.

"This is nonsense," she whispered.

"Perhaps," he admitted. "Perhaps it was also nonsense that we talked last evening. Nonsense about treason. Why did you ask me to make the microscope, my lady, when you knew that making me a party to such a secret was as good as signing my death warrant?"

"Oh Edmund," she said with a sigh. "You could not think that it was my own idea? I tried to protect you, Edmund, from Girard's fears and suspicions. It was because I was your protector that I was made to bear the message. What have you done, Edmund?"

He began to reply, but the words turned into a fit of coughing.

She sat upright, wrenching her hand away from his enfeebled grip, and looked down at him as he sank back upon the pillow.

"For the love of God!" she exclaimed, as fearfully as any true believer. "It is the plague—the plague out of Africa!"

He tried to confirm her suspicion, but could do so only with a nod of his head as he fought for breath.

"But they held the *Freemartin* by the Essex coast for a full fortnight's quarantine," she protested. "There was no trace of plague aboard."

"The disease kills men," said Edmund in a shallow whisper. "But animals can carry it, in their blood, without dying."

"You cannot know this!"

Edmund managed a small laugh. "My lady," he said, "I am a member of that Fraternity that interests itself in everything that might kill a vampire. The information came to me in good time for me to arrange delivery of the rats—though when I asked for them, I had not in mind the means of using them that I eventually employed. More recent events . . ." Again he was forced to stop, unable to draw sufficient breath even to sustain the thin whisper.

The Lady Camilla put her hand to her throat, swallowing as if she expected to feel evidence already of her infection.

"You would destroy me, Edmund?" she asked, as though she genuinely found it difficult to believe.

"I would destroy you all," he told her. "I would bring disaster, turn the world upside down, to end your rule. . . . We cannot allow you to stamp out learning itself to preserve your empire forever. Order must be fought with chaos, and chaos is come, my lady."

When she tried to rise from the bed, he reached out to restrain her, and though there was no power left in him, she allowed herself to be checked. The coverlet fell away from her, to expose her breasts as she sat upright.

"The boy will die for this, Master Cordery," she said. "His mother, too."

"They're gone," he told her. "Noell went from your table to the custody of the society that I serve. By now they're beyond your reach. The archduke will never catch them."

She stared at him, and now he could see the beginnings of hate and fear in her stare.

"You came here last night to bring me poisoned blood," she said. "In the hope that this new disease might kill even me, you condemned yourself to death. What did you do, Edmund?"

He reached out again to touch her arm, and was pleased to see her flinch and draw away: that he had become dreadful.

"Only vampires live forever," he told her hoarsely. "But anyone may drink blood, if they have the stomach for it. I took full measure from my two sick rats . . . and I pray to God that the seed of this fever is raging in my blood . . . and in my semen, too. You, too, have received full measure, my lady . . . and you are in God's hands now like any common mortal. I cannot know for sure whether you will catch the plague, or whether it will kill you, but I—an unbeliever—am not ashamed to pray. Perhaps you could pray, too, my lady, so that we may know how the Lord favors one unbeliever over another."

She looked down at him, her face gradually losing the expressions that had tugged at her features, becoming masklike in its steadiness.

"You could have taken our side, Edmund. I

trusted you, and I could have made the archduke trust you, too. You could have become a vampire. We could have shared the centuries, you and I."

This was dissimulation, and they both knew it. He had been her lover, and had ceased to be, and had grown older for so many years that now she remembered him as much in his son as in himself. The promises were all too obviously hollow now, and she realized that she could not even taunt him with them.

From beside the bed she took up the small silver knife that she had used to let his blood. She held it now as if it were a dagger, not a delicate instrument to be used with care and love.

"I thought you still loved me," she told him. "I really did."

That, at least, he thought, might be true.

He actually put his head farther back, to expose his throat to the expected thrust. He wanted her to strike him—angrily, brutally, passionately. He had nothing more to say, and would not confirm or deny that he did still love her.

He admitted to himself now that his motives had been mixed, and that he really did not know whether it was loyalty to the Fraternity that had made him submit to this extraordinary experiment. It did not matter.

She cut his throat, and he watched her, for a few long seconds while she stared at the blood gouting from the wound. When he saw her put stained fingers to her lips, knowing what she knew, he realized that after her own fashion, she still loved him.

# MIDNIGHT MASS

# F. Paul Wilson

Francis Paul Wilson (1946– ) was born in Jersey City, New Jersey, and received a medical degree, then worked as a part-time family physician. He sold his first short story to *Analog* magazine in 1970, and he continued to write science fiction; his first novel was *Healer* (1976). Of his more than thirty novels, six are in the science-fiction genre. His greatest success has come in the horror field, notably with the best-selling *The Keep* (1981), which was filmed by Paramount in 1983 with a screenplay by Michael Mann, who also directed, and *The Tomb* (1984), which introduced his antihero, the urban mercenary Repairman Jack, who subsequently appeared in several short stories and such novels as *Legacies* (1998) and *Conspiracies* (2000), with annual adventures ever since. In addition to other nonseries horror novels, he has written young-adult books, contemporary thrillers, the New Age thriller *The Fifth Harmonic* (2003), and novels that defy categorization. All his work reflects a libertarian political philosophy, most conspicuously in *An Enemy of the State* (1980) and the Repairman Jack series.

"Midnight Mass" was first published as a separate book by Axolotl Press/ Pulphouse in an edition of fewer than nine hundred copies in 1990. It was filmed in 2003, with a screenplay by F. Paul Wilson and Tony Mandile, who also directed. Both authors had small parts in the production, which is generally regarded as dreadful. A much-expanded novelization of the screenplay was written by Wilson and published in 2004 by Tor.

# Midnight Mass

## F. PAUL WILSON

### I

It had been almost a full minute since he'd slammed the brass knocker against the heavy oak door. That should have been proof enough. After all, wasn't the knocker in the shape of a cross? But no, they had to squint through their peephole and peer through the sidelights that framed the door.

Rabbi Zev Wolpin sighed and resigned himself to the scrutiny. He couldn't blame people for being cautious, but this seemed a bit overly so. The sun was in the west and shining full on his back; he was all but silhouetted in it. What more did they want?

*I should maybe take off my clothes and dance naked?*

He gave a mental shrug and savored the damp sea air. At least it was cool here. He'd bicycled from Lakewood, which was only ten miles inland from this same ocean but at least twenty degrees warmer. The bulk of the huge Tudor retreat house stood between him and the Atlantic, but the ocean's briny scent and rhythmic rumble were everywhere.

Spring Lake. An Irish Catholic seaside resort since before the turn of the century. He looked around at its carefully restored Victorian houses, the huge mansions arrayed here along the beach

front, the smaller homes set in neat rows running straight back from the ocean. Many of them were still occupied. Not like Lakewood. Lakewood was an empty shell.

Not such a bad place for a retreat, he thought. He wondered how many houses like this the Catholic Church owned.

A series of clicks and clacks drew his attention back to the door as numerous bolts were pulled in rapid succession. The door swung inward revealing a nervous-looking young man in a long black cassock. As he looked at Zev his mouth twisted and he rubbed the back of his wrist across it to hide a smile.

"And what should be so funny?" Zev asked.

"I'm sorry. It's just—"

"I know," Zev said, waving off any explanation as he glanced down at the wooden cross slung on a cord around his neck. "I know."

A bearded Jew in a baggy black serge suit wearing a yarmulke and a cross. Hilarious, no?

So, *nu?* This was what the times demanded, this was what it had come to if he wanted to survive. And Zev did want to survive. Someone had to live to carry on the traditions of the Talmud and the Torah, even if there were hardly any Jews left alive in the world.

Zev stood on the sunny porch, waiting. The priest watched him in silence.

Finally Zev said, "Well, may a wandering Jew come in?"

"I won't stop you," the priest said, "but surely you don't expect me to invite you."

Ah, yes. Another precaution. The vampire couldn't cross the threshold of a home unless he was invited in, so don't invite. A good habit to cultivate, he supposed.

He stepped inside and the priest immediately closed the door behind him, relatching all the locks one by one. When he turned around Zev held out his hand.

"Rabbi Zev Wolpin, Father. I thank you for allowing me in."

"Brother Christopher, sir," he said, smiling and shaking Zev's hand. His suspicions seemed to have been completely allayed. "I'm not a priest yet. We can't offer you much here, but—"

"Oh, I won't be staying long. I just came to talk to Father Joseph Cahill."

Brother Christopher frowned. "Father Cahill isn't here at the moment."

"When will he be back?"

"I—I'm not sure. You see—"

"Father Cahill is on another bender," said a stentorian voice behind Zev.

He turned to see an elderly priest facing him from the far end of the foyer. White-haired, heavy set, wearing a black cassock. "I'm Rabbi Wolpin."

"Father Adams," the priest said, stepping forward and extending his hand.

As they shook Zev said, "Did you say he was on 'another' bender? I never knew Father Cahill to be much of a drinker."

"Apparently there was a lot we never knew about Father Cahill," the priest said stiffly.

"If you're referring to that nastiness last year," Zev said, feeling the old anger rise in him, "I for one never believed it for a minute. I'm surprised anyone gave it the slightest credence."

"The veracity of the accusation was irrelevant in the final analysis. The damage to Father Cahill's reputation was a *fait accompli*. Father Palmeri was forced to request his removal for the good of St. Anthony's parish."

Zev was sure that sort of attitude had something to do with Father Joe being on "another bender."

"Where can I find Father Cahill?"

"He's in town somewhere, I suppose, making a spectacle of himself. If there's any way you can talk some sense into him, please do. Not only is he killing himself with drink but he's become quite an embarrassment to the priesthood and to the Church."

*Which bothers you more?* Zev wanted to ask but held his tongue. "I'll try."

He waited for Brother Christopher to undo all the locks, then stepped toward the sunlight.

"Try Morton's down on Seventy-one," the younger man whispered as Zev passed.

Zev rode his bicycle south on 71. It was almost strange to see people on the streets. Not many, but more than he'd ever see in Lakewood again. Yet he knew that as the vampires consolidated their grip on the world and infiltrated the Catholic communities, there'd be fewer and fewer day people here as well.

He thought he remembered passing a place named Morton's on his way to Spring Lake. And then up ahead he saw it, by the railroad track crossing, a white stucco one-story box of a building with "Morton's Liquors" painted in big black letters along the side.

Father Adams' words echoed back to him: . . . *on another bender* . . .

Zev pushed his bicycle to the front door and tried the knob. Locked up tight. A look inside showed a litter of trash and empty shelves. The windows were barred; the back door was steel and locked as securely as the front. So where was Father Joe?

Then he spotted the basement window at ground level by the overflowing trash dumpster. It wasn't latched. Zev went down on his knees and pushed it open.

Cool, damp, musty air wafted against his face

as he peered into the Stygian blackness. It occurred to him that he might be asking for trouble by sticking his head inside, but he had to give it a try. If Father Cahill wasn't here, Zev would begin the return trek to Lakewood and write this whole trip off as wasted effort.

"Father Joe?" he called. "Father Cahill?"

"That you again, Chris?" said a slightly slurred voice. "Go home, will you? I'll be all right. I'll be back later."

"It's me, Joe. Zev. From Lakewood."

He heard shoes scraping on the floor and then a familiar face appeared in the shaft of light from the window.

"Well I'll be damned. It *is* you! Thought you were Brother Chris come to drag me back to the retreat house. Gets scared I'm gonna get stuck out after dark. So how ya doin', Reb? Glad to see you're still alive. Come on in!"

Zev saw that Father Cahill's eyes were glassy and he swayed ever so slightly, like a skyscraper in the wind. He wore faded jeans and a black Bruce Springsteen *Tunnel of Love* Tour sweatshirt.

Zev's heart twisted at the sight of his friend in such condition. Such a mensch like Father Joe shouldn't be acting like a *shikker*. Maybe it was a mistake coming here. Zev didn't like seeing him like this.

"I don't have that much time, Joe. I came to tell you—"

"Get your bearded ass down here and have a drink or I'll come up and drag you down."

"All right," Zev said. "I'll come in but I won't have a drink."

He hid his bike behind the dumpster, then squeezed through the window. Father Joe helped him to the floor. They embraced, slapping each other on the back. Father Joe was a taller man, a giant from Zev's perspective. At six-four he was ten inches taller; at thirty-five he was a quarter-century younger; he had a muscular frame, thick brown hair, and—on better days—clear blue eyes.

"You're grayer, Zev, and you've lost weight."

"Kosher food is not so easily come by these days."

"All kinds of food is getting scarce." He touched the cross slung from Zev's neck and smiled. "Nice touch. Goes well with your zizith."

Zev fingered the fringe protruding from under his shirt. Old habits didn't die easily.

"Actually, I've grown rather fond of it."

"So what can I pour you?" the priest said, waving an arm at the crates of liquor stacked around him. "My own private reserve. Name your poison."

"I don't want a drink."

"Come on, Reb. I've got some nice hundred-proof Stoly here. You've got to have at least *one* drink—"

"Why? Because you think maybe you shouldn't drink alone?"

Father Joe smiled. "Touché."

"All right," Zev said. *"Bissel.* I'll have *one* drink on the condition that you *don't* have one. Because I wish to talk to you."

The priest considered that a moment, then reached for the vodka bottle.

"Deal."

He poured a generous amount into a paper cup and handed it over. Zev took a sip. He was not a drinker and when he did imbibe he preferred his vodka ice cold from a freezer. But this was tasty. Father Cahill sat back on a crate of Jack Daniel's and folded his arms.

*"Nu?"* the priest said with a Jackie Mason shrug.

Zev had to laugh. "Joe, I still say that somewhere in your family tree is Jewish blood."

For a moment he felt light, almost happy. When was the last time he had laughed? Probably more than a year now, probably at their table near the back of Horovitz's deli, shortly before the St. Anthony's nastiness began, well before the vampires came.

Zev thought of the day they'd met. He'd been standing at the counter at Horovitz's waiting for Yussel to wrap up the stuffed derma he had ordered when this young giant walked in. He towered over the other rabbis in the place, looked as Irish as Paddy's pig, and wore a Roman collar. He said he'd heard this was the only place on the whole Jersey Shore where you could get a decent corned beef sandwich. He ordered one and cheerfully warned that it better be good. Yussel asked him what could he know about good corned beef and the priest replied that he grew up in Bensonhurst. Well, about the half the people in Horovitz's on that day—and on any other day for that matter—grew up in Bensonhurst and before you knew it they were all asking him if he knew such-and-such a store and so-and-so's deli.

Zev then informed the priest—with all due respect to Yussel Horovitz behind the counter—that the best corned beef sandwich in the world was to be had at Shmuel Rosenberg's Jerusalem Deli in Bensonhurst. Father Cahill said he'd been there and agreed one hundred per cent.

Yussel served him his sandwich then. As he took a huge bite out of the corned beef on rye, the normal *tummel* of a deli at lunchtime died away until Horovitz's was as quiet as a *shoul* on Sunday morning. Everyone watched him chew, watched him swallow. Then they waited. Suddenly his face broke into this big Irish grin.

"I'm afraid I'm going to have to change my vote," he said. "Horovitz's of Lakewood makes the best corned beef sandwich in the world."

Amid cheers and warm laughter, Zev led Father Cahill to the rear table that would become theirs and sat with this canny and charming gentile who had so easily won over a roomful of strangers and provided such a *mechaieh* for Yussel. He learned that the young priest was the new assistant to Father Palmeri, the pastor at St. Anthony's Catholic church at the northern end of Lakewood. Father Palmeri had been there for years but Zev had never so much as seen his face. He asked Father Cahill—who wanted to be called Joe—about life in Brooklyn these days and they talked for an hour.

During the following months they would run into each other so often at Horovitz's that they decided to meet regularly for lunch, on Mondays and Thursdays. They did so for years, discussing religion—Oy, the religious discussions!—politics, economics, philosophy, life in general. During those lunchtimes they solved most of the world's problems. Zev was sure they'd have solved them all if the scandal at St. Anthony's hadn't resulted in Father Joe's removal from the parish.

But that was in another time, another world. The world before the vampires took over.

Zev shook his head as he considered the current state of Father Joe in the dusty basement of Morton's Liquors.

"It's about the vampires, Joe," he said, taking another sip of the Stoly. "They've taken over St. Anthony's."

Father Joe snorted and shrugged.

"They're in the majority now, Zev, remember? They've taken over everything. Why should St. Anthony's be different from any other parish in the world?"

"I didn't mean the parish. I meant the church."

The priest's eyes widened slightly. "The church? They've taken over the building itself?"

"Every night," Zev said. "Every night they are there."

"That's a holy place. How do they manage that?"

"They've desecrated the altar, destroyed all the crosses. St. Anthony's is no longer a holy place."

"Too bad," Father Joe said, looking down and shaking his head sadly. "It was a fine old church." He looked up again, at Zev. "How do you know about what's going on at St. Anthony's? It's not exactly in your neighborhood."

"A neighborhood I don't exactly have any more."

Father Joe reached over and gripped his shoulder with a huge hand.

"I'm sorry, Zev. I heard how your people got hit pretty hard over there. Sitting ducks, huh? I'm really sorry."

Sitting ducks. An appropriate description. Oh, they'd been smart, those bloodsuckers. They knew their easiest targets. Whenever they swooped into an area they singled out Jews as their first victims, and among Jews they picked the Orthodox first of the first. Smart. Where else would they be less likely to run up against a cross? It worked for them in Brooklyn, and so when they came south into New Jersey, spreading like a plague, they headed straight for the town with one of the largest collections of yeshivas in North America.

But after the Bensonhurst holocaust the people in the Lakewood communities did not take quite so long to figure out what was happening. The Reformed and Conservative synagogues started handing out crosses at Shabbes—too late for many but it saved a few. Did the Orthodox congregations follow suit? No. They hid in their homes and shules and yeshivas and read and prayed.

And were liquidated.

A cross, a crucifix—they held power over the vampires, drove them away. His fellow rabbis did not want to accept that simple fact because they could not face its devastating ramifications. To hold up a cross was to negate two thousand years of Jewish history, it was to say that the Messiah had come and they had missed him.

Did it say that? Zev didn't know. Argue about it later. Right now, people were dying. But the rabbis had to argue it now. And as they argued, their people were slaughtered like cattle.

How Zev railed at them, how he pleaded with them! Blind, stubborn fools! If a fire was consuming your house, would you refuse to throw water on it just because you'd always been taught not to believe in water? Zev had arrived at the rabbinical council wearing a cross and had been thrown out—literally sent hurtling through the front door. But at least he had managed to save a few of his own people. Too few.

He remembered his fellow Orthodox rabbis, though. All the ones who had refused to face the reality of the vampires' fear of crosses, who had forbidden their students and their congregations to wear crosses, who had watched those same students and congregations die en masse only to rise again and come for them. And soon those very same rabbis were roaming their own community, hunting the survivors, preying on other yeshivas, other congregations, until the entire community was liquidated and incorporated into the brotherhood of the vampire. The great fear had come to pass: they'd been assimilated.

The rabbis could have saved themselves, could have saved their people, but they would not bend to the reality of what was happening around them. Which, when Zev thought about it, was not at all out of character. Hadn't they spent generations learning to turn away from the rest of the world?

Those early days of anarchic slaughter were over. Now that the vampires held the ruling hand, the blood-letting had become more organized. But the damage to Zev's people had been done—and it was irreparable. Hitler would have been proud. His Nazi "final solution" was an afternoon picnic compared to the work of the vampires. They did in months what Hitler's Reich could not do in all the years of the Second World War.

*There's only a few of us now.* So few and so scattered. A final Diaspora.

For a moment Zev was almost overwhelmed by grief, but he pushed it down, locked it back into that place where he kept his sorrows, and thought of how fortunate it was for his wife Chana that she died of natural causes before the horror began. Her soul had been too gentle to weather what had happened to their community.

"Not as sorry as I, Joe," Zev said, dragging himself back to the present. "But since my neighbourhood is gone, and since I have hardly any friends left, I use the daylight hours to wander. So call me the Wandering Jew. And in my wanderings I meet some of your old parishioners."

The priest's face hardened. His voice became acid.

"Do you, now? And how fares the remnant of my devoted flock?"

"They've lost all hope, Joe. They wish you were back."

He laughed. "Sure they do! Just like they rallied behind me when my name and honor were being dragged through the muck last year. Yeah, they want me back. I'll bet!"

"Such anger, Joe. It doesn't become you."

"Bullshit. That was the old Joe Cahill, the naive turkey who believed all his faithful parishioners would back him up. But now Palmeri tells the bishop the heat is getting too much for him, the bishop removes me, and the people I dedicated my life to all stand by in silence as I'm railroaded out of my parish."

"It's hard for the commonfolk to buck a bishop."

"Maybe. But I can't forget how they stood quietly by while I was stripped of my position, my dignity, my integrity, of everything I wanted to be . . ."

Zev thought Joe's voice was going to break. He was about to reach out to him when the priest coughed and squared his shoulders. "Meanwhile, I'm a pariah over here in the retreat house. A goddam leper. Some of them actually believe—" He broke off in a growl. "Ah, what's the use? It's over and done. Most of the parish is dead anyway, I suppose. And if I'd stayed there I'd probably be dead too. So maybe it worked out for the best. And who gives a shit anyway."

He reached for the bottle of Glenlivet next to him.

"No-no!" Zev said. "You promised!"

Father Joe drew his hand back and crossed his arms across his chest.

"Talk on, oh, bearded one. I'm listening."

Father Joe had certainly changed for the worse. Morose, bitter, apathetic, self-pitying. Zev was beginning to wonder how he could have called this man a friend.

"They've taken over your church, desecrated it. Each night they further defile it with butchery and blasphemy. Doesn't that mean anything to you?"

"It's Palmeri's parish. I've been benched. Let him take care of it."

"Father Palmeri is their leader."

"He should be. He's their pastor."

"No. He leads the vampires in the obscenities they perform in the church."

Father Joe stiffened and the glassiness cleared from his eyes.

"Palmeri? He's one of them?"

Zev nodded. "More than that. He's the local leader. He orchestrates their rituals."

Zev saw rage flare in the priest's eyes, saw his hands ball into fists, and for a moment he thought the old Father Joe was going to burst through.

*Come on, Joe. Show me that old fire.*

But then he slumped back onto the crate.

"Is that all you came to tell me?"

Zev hid his disappointment and nodded. "Yes."

"Good." He grabbed the scotch bottle. "Because I need a drink."

Zev wanted to leave, yet he had to stay, had to probe a little bit deeper and see how much of his old friend was left, and how much had been replaced by this new, bitter, alien Joe Cahill. Maybe there was still hope. So they talked on.

Suddenly he noticed it was dark.

"Gevalt!" Zev said. "I didn't notice the time!"

Father Joe seemed surprised too. He ran to the window and peered out.

"Damn! Sun's gone down!" He turned to Zev. "Lakewood's out of the question for you, Reb. Even the retreat house is too far to risk now. Looks like we're stuck here for the night."

"We'll be safe?"

He shrugged. "Why not? As far as I can tell I'm the only one who's been in here for months, and only in the daytime. Be pretty odd if one of those human leeches should decide to wander in here tonight."

"I hope so."

"Don't worry. We're okay if we don't attract attention. I've got a flashlight if we need it, but we're better off sitting here in the dark and shooting the breeze till sunrise." Father Joe smiled and picked up a huge silver cross, at least a foot in length, from atop one of the crates. "Besides, we're armed. And frankly, I can think of worse places to spend the night."

He stepped over to the case of Glenlivet and opened a fresh bottle. His capacity for alcohol was enormous.

Zev could think of worse places too. In fact he had spent a number of nights in much worse places since the holocaust. He decided to put the time to good use.

"So, Joe. Maybe I should tell you some more about what's happening in Lakewood."

After a few hours their talk died of fatigue. Father Joe gave Zev the flashlight to hold and stretched out across a couple of crates to sleep. Zev tried to get comfortable enough to doze but found sleep impossible. So he listened to his friend snore in the darkness of the cellar.

Poor Joe. Such anger in the man. But more

than that—hurt. He felt betrayed, wronged. And with good reason. But with everything falling apart as it was, the wrong done to him would never be righted. He should forget about it already and go on with his life, but apparently he couldn't. Such a shame. He needed something to pull him out of his funk. Zev had thought news of what had happened to his old parish might rouse him, but it seemed only to make him want to drink more. Father Joe Cahill, he feared, was a hopeless case.

Zev closed his eyes and tried to rest. It was hard to get comfortable with the cross dangling in front of him so he took it off but laid it within easy reach. He was drifting toward a doze when he heard a noise outside. By the dumpster. Metal on metal.

*My bicycle!*

He slipped to the floor and tiptoed over to where Father Joe slept. He shook his shoulder and whispered.

"Someone's found my bicycle!"

The priest snorted but remained sleeping. A louder clatter outside made Zev turn, and as he moved his elbow struck a bottle. He grabbed for it in the darkness but missed. The sound of smashing glass echoed through the basement like a cannon shot. As the odor of scotch whiskey replaced the musty ambiance, Zev listened for further sounds from outside. None came.

Maybe it had been an animal. He remembered how raccoons used to raid his garbage at home . . . when he'd had a home . . . when he'd had garbage . . .

Zev stepped to the window and looked out. Probably an animal. He pulled the window open a few inches and felt cool night air wash across his face. He pulled the flashlight from his coat pocket and aimed it through the opening.

Zev almost dropped the light as the beam illuminated a pale, snarling demonic face, baring its fangs and hissing. He fell back as the thing's head and shoulders lunged through the window, its back curved fingers clawing at him, missing. Then it launched itself the rest of the way through, hurtling toward Zev.

He tried to dodge but he was too slow. The impact knocked the flashlight from his grasp and it

went rolling across the floor. Zev cried out as he went down under the snarling thing. Its ferocity was overpowering, irresistible. It straddled him and lashed at him, batting his fending arms aside, its clawed fingers tearing at his collar to free his throat, stretching his neck to expose the vulnerable flesh, its foul breath gagging him as it bent its fangs toward him. Zev screamed out his helplessness.

## II

Father Joe awoke to the cries of a terrified voice.

He shook his head to clear it and instantly regretted the move. His head weighed at least two hundred pounds, and his mouth was stuffed with foul-tasting cotton. Why did he keep doing this to himself? Not only did it leave him feeling lousy, it gave him bad dreams. Like now.

Another terrified shout, only a few feet away.

He looked toward the sound. In the faint light from the flashlight rolling across the floor he saw Zev on his back, fighting for his life against—

Damn! This was no dream! One of those bloodsuckers had got in here!

He leaped over to where the creature was lowering its fangs toward Zev's throat. He grabbed it by the back of the neck and lifted it clear of the floor. It was surprisingly heavy but that didn't slow him. Joe could feel the anger rising in him, surging into his muscles.

"Rotten piece of filth!"

He swung the vampire by its neck and let it fly against the cinderblock wall. It impacted with what should have been bone-crushing force, but it bounced off, rolled on the floor, and regained its feet in one motion, ready to attack again. Strong as he was, Joe knew he was no match for a vampire's power. He turned, grabbed his big silver crucifix, and charged the creature.

"Hungry? Eat this!"

As the creature bared its fangs and hissed at him, Joe shoved the long lower end of the cross into its open mouth. Blue-white light flickered along the silver length of the crucifix, reflecting in the creature's startled, agonized eyes as its flesh sizzled and crackled. The vampire let out a strangled cry and tried to turn away but Joe wasn't through with it yet. He was literally seeing red as rage poured out of a hidden well and swirled through him. He rammed the cross deeper down the thing's gullet. Light flashed deep in its throat, illuminating the pale tissues from within. It tried to grab the cross and pull it out but the flesh of its fingers burned and smoked wherever they came in contact with the cross.

Finally Joe stepped back and let the thing squirm and scrabble up the wall and out the window into the night. Then he turned to Zev. If anything had happened—

"Hey, Reb!" he said, kneeling beside the older man. "You all right?"

"Yes," Zev said, struggling to his feet. "Thanks to you."

Joe slumped onto a crate, momentarily weak as his rage dissipated. *This is not what I'm about,* he thought. But it had felt so damn good to let it loose on that vampire. Too good. And that worried him.

*I'm falling apart . . . like everything else in the world.*

"That was too close," he said to Zev, giving the older man's shoulder a fond squeeze.

"Too close for that vampire for sure," Zev said, replacing his yarmulke. "And would you please remind me, Father Joe, that in the future if ever I should maybe get my blood sucked and become a vampire that I should stay far away from you."

Joe laughed for the first time in too long. It felt good.

They climbed out at first light. Joe stretched his cramped muscles in the fresh air while Zev checked on his hidden bicycle.

"Oy," Zev said as he pulled it from behind the dumpster. The front wheel had been bent so far out of shape that half the spokes were broken. "Look what he did. Looks like I'll be walking back to Lakewood."

But Joe was less interested in the bike than in the whereabouts of their visitor from last night. He knew it couldn't have got far. And it hadn't. They found the vampire—or rather what was left of it—on the far side of the dumpster: a rotting, twisted corpse, blackened to a crisp and steaming in the morning sunlight. The silver crucifix still protruded from between its teeth.

Joe approached and gingerly yanked his cross free of the foul remains.

"Looks like you've sucked your last pint of blood," he said and immediately felt foolish.

Who was he putting on the macho act for? Zev certainly wasn't going to buy it. Too out of character. But then, what *was* his character these days? He used to be a parish priest. Now he was a nothing. A less than nothing.

He straightened up and turned to Zev.

"Come on back to the retreat house, Reb. I'll buy you breakfast."

But as Joe turned and began walking away, Zev stayed and stared down at the corpse.

"They say they don't wander far from where they spent their lives," Zev said. "Which means it's unlikely this fellow was Jewish if he lived around here. Probably Catholic. Irish Catholic, I'd imagine."

Joe stopped and turned. He stared at his long shadow. The hazy rising sun at his back cast a huge hulking shape before him, with a dark cross in one shadow hand and a smudge of amber light where it poured through the unopened bottle of Scotch in the other.

"What are you getting at?" he said.

"The Kaddish would probably not be so appropriate so I'm just wondering if maybe someone should give him the last rites or whatever it is you people do when one of you dies."

"He wasn't one of us," Joe said, feeling the bitterness rise in him. "He wasn't even human."

"Ah, but he used to be before he was killed and became one of them. So maybe now he could use a little help."

Joe didn't like the way this was going. He sensed he was being maneuvered.

"He doesn't deserve it," he said and knew in that instant he'd been trapped.

"I thought even the worst sinner deserved it," Zev said.

Joe knew when he was beaten. Zev was right. He shoved the cross and bottle into Zev's hands— a bit roughly, perhaps—then went and knelt by the twisted cadaver. He administered a form of the final sacrament. When he was through he returned to Zev and snatched back his belongings.

"You're a better man than I am, Gunga Din," he said as he passed.

"You act as if they're responsible for what they do after they become vampires," Zev said as he hurried along beside him, panting as he matched Joe's pace.

"Aren't they?"

"No."

"You're sure of that?"

"Well, not exactly. But they certainly aren't human anymore, so maybe we shouldn't hold them accountable on human terms."

Zev's reasoning tone flashed Joe back to the conversations they used to have in Horovitz's deli.

"But Zev, we know there's some of the old personality left. I mean, they stay in their home towns, usually in the basements of their old houses. They go after people they knew when they were alive. They're not just dumb predators, Zev. They've got the old consciousness they had when they were alive. Why can't they rise above it? Why can't they . . . resist?"

"I don't know. To tell the truth, the question has never occurred to me. A fascinating concept: an undead refusing to feed. Leave it to Father Joe to come up with something like that. We should discuss this on the trip back to Lakewood."

Joe had to smile. So *that* was what this was all about.

"I'm not going back to Lakewood."

"Fine. Then we'll discuss it now. Maybe the urge to feed is too strong to overcome."

"Maybe. And maybe they just don't try hard enough."

"This is a hard line you're taking, my friend."

"I'm a hard-line kind of guy."

"Well, you've become one."

Joe gave him a sharp look. "You don't know what I've become."

Zev shrugged. "Maybe true, maybe not. But do you truly think you'd be able to resist?"

"Damn straight."

Joe didn't know whether he was serious or not. Maybe he was just mentally preparing himself for the day when he might actually find himself in that situation.

"Interesting," Zev said as they climbed the front steps of the retreat house. "Well, I'd better be going. I've a long walk ahead of me. A long, *lonely* walk all the way back to Lakewood. A long, lonely, possibly *dangerous* walk back for a poor old man who—"

"All right, Zev! All *right*!" Joe said, biting back a laugh. "I get the point. You want me to go back to Lakewood. Why?"

"I just want the company," Zev said with pure innocence.

"No, really. What's going on in that Talmudic mind of yours? What are you cooking?"

"Nothing, Father Joe. Nothing at all."

Joe stared at him. Damn it all if his interest wasn't piqued. What was Zev up to? And what the hell? Why not go? He had nothing better to do.

"All right, Zev. You win. I'll come back to Lakewood with you. But just for today. Just to keep you company. And I'm not going anywhere near St. Anthony's, okay? Understood?"

"Understood, Joe. Perfectly understood."

"Good. Now wipe that smile off your face and we'll get something to eat."

# III

Under the climbing sun they walked south along the deserted beach, barefooting through the wet sand at the edge of the surf. Zev had never done this. He liked the feel of the sand between his toes, the coolness of the water as it sloshed over his ankles.

"Know what day it is?" Father Joe said. He had his sneakers slung over his shoulder. "Believe it or not, it's the Fourth of July."

"Oh, yes. Your Independence Day. We never made much of secular holidays. Too many religious ones to observe. Why should I not believe it's this date?"

Father Joe shook his head in dismay. "This is Manasquan Beach. You know what this place used to look like on the Fourth before the vampires took over? Wall-to-wall bodies."

"Really? I guess maybe sun-bathing is not the fad it used to be."

"Ah, Zev! Still the master of the understatement. I'll say one thing, though: the beach is cleaner than I've ever seen it. No beer cans or hypodermics." He pointed ahead. "But what's that up there?"

As they approached the spot, Zev saw a pair of naked bodies stretched out on the sand, one male, one female, both young and short-haired. Their skin was bronzed and glistened in the sun. The man lifted his head and stared at them. A blue crucifix was tattooed in the center of his forehead. He reached into the knapsack beside him and withdrew a huge, gleaming, nickel-plated revolver.

"Just keep walking," he said.

"Will do," Father Joe said. "Just passing through."

As they passed the couple, Zev noticed a similar tattoo on the girl's forehead. He noticed the rest of her too. He felt an almost-forgotten stirring deep inside him.

"A very popular tattoo," he said.

"Clever idea. That's one cross you can't drop or lose. Probably won't help you in the dark, but if there's a light on it might give you an edge."

They turned west and made their way inland, finding Route 70 and following it into Ocean County via the Brielle Bridge.

"I remember nightmare traffic jams right here every summer," Father Joe said as they trod the bridge's empty span. "Never thought I'd miss traffic jams."

They cut over to Route 88 and followed it all the way into Lakewood. Along the way they found a few people out and about in Bricktown and picking berries in Ocean County Park, but in the heart of Lakewood . . .

"A real ghost town," the priest said as they walked Forest Avenue's deserted length.

"Ghosts," Zev said, nodding sadly. It had been a long walk and he was tired. "Yes. Full of ghosts."

In his mind's eye he saw the shades of his fallen brother rabbis and all the yeshiva students, beards, black suits, black hats, crisscrossing back and forth at a determined pace on weekdays, strolling with their wives on Shabbes, their children trailing behind like ducklings.

Gone. All gone. Victims of the vampires. Vampires themselves now, most of them. It made him sick at heart to think of those good, gentle men, women, and children curled up in their basements now to avoid the light of day, venturing out in the dark to feed on others, spreading the disease . . .

He fingered the cross slung from his neck. *If only they had listened!*

"I know a place near St. Anthony's where we can hide," he told the priest.

"You've traveled enough today, Reb. And I told you, I don't care about St. Anthony's."

"Stay the night, Joe," Zev said, gripping the young priest's arm. He'd coaxed him this far; he couldn't let him get away now. "See what Father Palmeri's done."

"If he's one of them he's not a priest anymore. Don't call him Father."

"*They* still call him Father."

"Who?"

"The vampires."

Zev watched Father Joe's jaw muscles bunch.

Joe said, "Maybe I'll just take a quick trip over to St. Anthony's myself—"

"No. It's different here. The area is thick with them—maybe twenty times as many as in Spring Lake. They'll get you if your timing isn't just right. I'll take you."

"You need rest, pal."

Father Joe's expression showed genuine concern. Zev was detecting increasingly softer emotions in the man since their reunion last night. A good sign perhaps?

"And rest I'll get when we get to where I'm taking you."

# IV

Father Joe Cahill watched the moon rise over his old church and wondered at the wisdom of coming back. The casual decision made this morning in the full light of day seemed reckless and foolhardy now at the approach of midnight.

But there was no turning back. He'd followed Zev to the second floor of this two-story office building across the street from St. Anthony's, and here they'd waited for dark. Must have been a law office once. The place had been vandalized, the windows broken, the furniture trashed, but there was an old Temple University Law School degree on the wall, and the couch was still in one piece. So while Zev caught some Z's, Joe sat and sipped a little of his scotch and did some heavy thinking.

Mostly he thought about his drinking. He'd done too much of that lately, he knew; so much so that he was afraid to stop cold. So he was taking just a touch now, barely enough to take the edge off. He'd finish the rest later, after he came back from that church over there.

He'd stared at St. Anthony's since they'd arrived. It too had been extensively vandalized. Once it had been a beautiful little stone church, a miniature cathedral, really; very Gothic with all its pointed arches, steep roofs, crocketed spires, and multifoil stained glass windows. Now the windows were smashed, the crosses which had topped the steeple and each gable were gone, and anything resembling a cross in its granite exterior had been defaced beyond recognition.

As he'd known it would, the sight of St. Anthony's brought back memories of Gloria Sullivan, the young, pretty church volunteer whose husband worked for United Chemical International in New York, commuting in every day and trekking off overseas a little too often. Joe and Gloria had seen a lot of each other around the church offices and had become good friends. But Gloria had somehow got the idea that what they had went beyond friendship, so she showed up at the rectory one night when Joe was there alone. He tried to explain that as attractive as she was, she was not for him. He had taken certain vows and meant to stick by them. He did his best to let her down easy but she'd been hurt. And angry.

That might have been that, but then her six-year-old son Kevin had come home from altar boy practice with a story about a priest making him pull down his pants and touching him. Kevin was never clear on who the priest had been, but Gloria Sullivan was. Obviously it had been Father Cahill—any man who could turn down the heartfelt offer of her love and her body had to be either a queer or worse. And a child molester was worse.

She took it to the police and to the papers.

Joe groaned softly at the memory of how swiftly his life had become hell. But he had been determined to weather the storm, sure that the real culprit eventually would be revealed. He had no proof—still didn't—but if one of the priests at St. Anthony's was a pederast, he knew it wasn't him. That left Father Alberto Palmeri, St. Anthony's fifty-five-year-old pastor. Before Joe could get to the truth, however, Father Palmeri requested that Father Cahill be removed from the parish, and the bishop complied. Joe had left under a cloud that had followed him to the retreat house in the next county and hovered over him till this day. The only place he'd found even brief respite from the impotent anger and bitterness that roiled under his skin and soured his gut every minute of every day was in the bottle—and that was sure as hell a dead end.

So why had he agreed to come back here? To torture himself? Or to get a look at Palmeri and see how low he had sunk?

Maybe that was it. Maybe seeing Palmeri wallowing in his true element would give him the impetus to put the whole St. Anthony's incident behind him and rejoin what was left of the human race—which needed him now more than ever.

And maybe it wouldn't.

Getting back on track was a nice thought, but over the past few months Joe had found it increasingly difficult to give much of a damn about anyone or anything.

Except maybe Zev. He'd stuck by Joe through the worst of it, defending him to anyone who would listen. But an endorsement from an Orthodox rabbi had meant diddly in St Anthony's. And yesterday Zev had biked all the way to Spring Lake to see him. Old Zev was all right.

And he'd been right about the number of vampires here too. Lakewood was *crawling* with the things. Fascinated and repelled, Joe had watched the streets fill with them shortly after sundown.

But what had disturbed him more were the creatures who'd come out *before* sundown.

The humans. Live ones.

The collaborators.

If there was anything lower, anything that deserved true death more than the vampires themselves, it was the still-living humans who worked for them.

Someone touched his shoulder and he jumped. It was Zev. He was holding something out to him. Joe took it and held it up in the moonlight: a tiny crescent moon dangling from a chain on a ring.

"What's this?"

"An earring. The local Vichy wear them."

"Vichy? Like the Vichy French?"

"Yes. Very good. I'm glad to see that you're not as culturally illiterate as the rest of your generation. Vichy humans—that's what I call the collaborators. These earrings identify them to the local nest of vampires. They are spared."

"Where'd you get them?"

Zev's face was hidden in the shadows. "Their previous owners . . . lost them. Put it on."

"My ear's not pierced."

A gnarled hand moved into the moonlight. Joe saw a tong needle clasped between the thumb and index finger.

"That I can fix," Zev said.

**m**aybe you shouldn't see this," Zev whispered as they crouched in the deep shadows on St. Anthony's western flank. Joe squinted at him in the darkness, puzzled.

"You lay a guilt trip on me to get me here, now you're having second thoughts?"

"It is horrible like I can't tell you."

Joe thought about that. There was enough horror in the world outside St. Anthony's. What purpose did it serve to see what was going on inside?

*Because it used to be my church.*

Even though he'd only been an associate pastor, never fully in charge, and even though he'd been unceremoniously yanked from the post, St. Anthony's had been his first parish. He was here. He might as well know what they were doing inside.

"Show me."

Zev led him to a pile of rubble under a smashed stained glass window. He pointed up to where faint light flickered from inside.

"Look in there."

"You're not coming?"

"Once was enough, thank you."

Joe climbed as carefully, as quietly as he could, all the while becoming increasingly aware of a growing stench like putrid, rotting meat. It was coming from inside, wafting through the broken window. Steeling himself, he straightened up and peered over the sill.

For a moment he was disoriented, like someone peering out the window of a city apartment and seeing the rolling hills of a Kansas farm. This could not be the interior of St. Anthony's.

In the flickering light of hundreds of sacramental candles he saw that the walls were bare, stripped of all their ornaments, of the plaques for the stations of the cross; the dark wood along the wall was scarred and gouged wherever there had been anything remotely resembling a cross. The floor too was mostly bare, the pews ripped from their neat rows and hacked to pieces, their splintered remains piled high at the rear under the choir balcony.

And the giant crucifix that had dominated the space behind the altar—only a portion of it remained. The cross-pieces on each side had been sawed off and so now an armless, life-size Christ hung upside down against the rear wall of the sanctuary.

Joe took in all that in a flash, then his attention was drawn to the unholy congregation that peo-

pled St. Anthony's this night. The collaborators—
the Vichy humans, as Zev called them—made up
the periphery of the group. They looked like normal, everyday people but each was wearing a crescent moon earring.

But the others, the group gathered in the
sanctuary—Joe felt his hackles rise at the sight of
them. They surrounded the altar in a tight knot.
Their pale, bestial faces, bereft of the slightest
trace of human warmth, compassion, or decency,
were turned upward. His gorge rose when he saw
the object of their rapt attention.

A naked teenage boy—his hands tied behind
his back, was suspended over the altar by his ankles. He was sobbing and choking, his eyes wide
and vacant with shock, his mind all but gone. The
skin had been flayed from his forehead—apparently the Vichy had found an expedient solution
to the cross tattoo—and blood ran in a slow stream
down his abdomen and chest from his freshly trun-
cated genitals. And beside him, standing atop the
altar, a bloody-mouthed creature dressed in a long
cassock. Joe recognized the thin shoulders, the
graying hair trailing from the balding crown, but
was shocked at the crimson vulpine grin he flashed
to the things clustered below him.

"Now," said the creature in a lightly accented
voice Joe had heard hundreds of times from St.
Anthony's pulpit.

Father Alberto Palmeri.

And from the group a hand reached up with a
straight razor and drew it across the boy's throat.
As the blood flowed down over his face, those
below squeezed and struggled forward like hatch-
ling vultures to catch the falling drops and scarlet trickles in their open mouths.

Joe fell away from the window and vomited.
He felt Zev grab his arm and lead him away. He
was vaguely aware of crossing the street and heading toward the ruined legal office.

## V

"Why in God's name did you want me to see that?"

Zev looked across the office toward the source
of the words. He could see a vague outline where
Father Joe sat on the floor, his back against the
wall, the open bottle of scotch in his hand. The
priest had taken one drink since their return, no
more.

"I thought you should know what they were
doing to your church."

"So you've said. But what's the reason behind
that one?"

Zev shrugged in the darkness. "I'd heard you
weren't doing well, that even before everything
else began falling apart, you had already fallen
apart. So when I felt it safe to get away, I came to
see you. Just as I expected, I found a man who was
angry at everything and letting it eat up his *gud-
erim.* I thought maybe it would be good to give
that man something very specific to be angry at."

"You bastard!" Father Joe whispered. "Who
gave you the right?"

"Friendship gave me the right, Joe. I should
hear that you are rotting away and do nothing? I
have no congregation of my own anymore so I
turned my attention on you. Always I was a somewhat meddlesome rabbi."

"Still are. Out to save my soul, ay?"

"We rabbis don't save souls. Guide them maybe,
hopefully give them direction. But only you can
save your soul, Joe."

Silence hung in the air for awhile. Suddenly
the crescent-moon earring Zev had given Father
Joe landed in the puddle of moonlight on the floor
between them.

"Why do they do it?" the priest said. "The
Vichy—why do they collaborate?"

"The first were quite unwilling, believe me.
They cooperated because their wives and children
were held hostage by the vampires. But before too
long the dregs of humanity began to slither out
from under their rocks and offer their services in
exchange for the immortality of vampirism."

"Why bother working for them? Why not just
bare your throat to the nearest bloodsucker?"

"That's what I thought at first," Zev said. "But
as I witnessed the Lakewood holocaust I detected
the vampires' pattern. They can choose who joins
their ranks, so after they've fully infiltrated a pop-

ulation, they change their tactics. You see, they don't want too many of their kind concentrated in one area. It's like too many carnivores in one forest—when the herds of prey are wiped out, the predators starve. So they start to employ a different style of killing. For only when the vampire draws the life's blood from the throat with its fangs does the victim become one of them. Anyone drained as in the manner of that boy in the church tonight dies a true death. He's as dead now as someone run over by a truck. He will not rise tomorrow night."

"I get it," Father Joe said. "The Vichy trade their daylight services and dirty work to the vampires now for immortality later on."

"Correct."

There was no humor in the soft laugh that echoed across the room from Father Joe.

"Swell. I never cease to be amazed at our fellow human beings. Their capacity for good is exceeded only by their ability to debase themselves."

"Hopelessness does strange things, Joe. The vampires know that. So they rob us of hope. That's how they beat us. They transform our friends and neighbors and leaders into their own, leaving us feeling alone, completely cut off. Some of us can't take the despair and kill ourselves."

"Hopelessness," Joe said. "A potent weapon."

After a long silence, Zev said, "So what are you going to do now, Father Joe?"

Another bitter laugh from across the room.

"I suppose this is the place where I declare that I've found new purpose in life and will now go forth into the world as a fearless vampire killer."

"Such a thing would be nice."

"Well screw that. I'm only going as far as across the street."

"To St. Anthony's?"

Zev saw Father Joe take a swig from the Scotch bottle and then screw the cap on tight.

"Yeah. To see if there's anything I can do over there."

"Father Palmeri and his nest might not like that."

"I told you, don't call him Father. And screw him. Nobody can do what he's done and get away with it. I'm taking my church back."

In the dark, behind his beard, Zev smiled.

# VI

Joe stayed up the rest of the night and let Zev sleep. The old guy needed his rest. Sleep would have been impossible for Joe anyway. He was too wired. He sat up and watched St. Anthony's.

They left before first light, dark shapes drifting out the front doors and down the stone steps like parishioners leaving a predawn service. Joe felt his back teeth grind as he scanned the group for Palmeri, but he couldn't make him out in the dimness. By the time the sun began to peek over the rooftops and through the trees to the east, the street outside was deserted.

He woke Zev and together they approached the church. The heavy oak and iron front doors, each forming half of a pointed arch, were closed. He pulled them open and fastened the hooks to keep them open. Then he walked through the vestibule and into the nave.

Even though he was ready for it, the stench backed him up a few steps. When his stomach settled, he forced himself ahead, treading a path between the two piles of shattered and splintered pews. Zev walked beside him, a handkerchief pressed over his mouth.

Last night he had thought the place a shambles. He saw now that it was worse. The light of day poked into all the corners, revealing everything that had been hidden by the warm glow of the candles. Half a dozen rotting corpses hung from the ceiling—he hadn't noticed them last night—and others were sprawled on the floor against the walls. Some of the bodies were in pieces. Behind the chancel rail a headless female torso was draped over the front of the pulpit. To the left stood the statue of Mary. Someone had fitted her with foam rubber breasts and a huge dildo. And at the rear of the sanctuary was the armless Christ hanging head down on the upright of his cross.

"My church," he whispered as he moved along the path that had once been the center aisle, the aisle brides used to walk down with their fathers. "Look what they've done to my church!"

Joe approached the huge block of the altar. Once it had been backed against the far wall of the sanctuary, but he'd had it moved to the front so that he could celebrate Mass facing his parishioners. Solid Carrara marble, but you'd never know it now. So caked with dried blood, semen, and feces it could have been made of styrofoam.

His revulsion was fading, melting away in the growing heat of his rage, drawing the nausea with it. He had intended to clean up the place but there was so much to be done, too much for two men. It was hopeless.

"Fadda Joe?"

He spun at the sound of the strange voice. A thin figure stood uncertainly in the open doorway. A man of about fifty edged forward timidly.

"Fadda Joe, izat you?"

Joe recognized him now. Carl Edwards. A twitchy little man who used to help pass the collection basket at 10:30 Mass on Sundays. A transplantee from Jersey City—hardly anyone around here was originally from around here. His face was sunken, his eyes feverish as he stared at Joe.

"Yes, Carl. It's me."

"Oh, tank God!" He ran forward and dropped to his knees before Joe. He began to sob. "You come back! Tank God, you come back!"

Joe pulled him to his feet.

"Come on now, Carl. Get a grip."

"You come back ta save us, ain'tcha? God sent ya here to punish him, din't He?"

"Punish whom?"

"Fadda Palmeri! He's one a dem! He's da woist a alla dem! He—"

"I know," Joe said. "I know."

"Oh, it's so good to have ya back, Fadda Joe! We ain't knowed what to do since da suckers took ova. We been prayin fa someone like youse an now ya here. It's a freakin' miracle!"

Joe wanted to ask Carl where he and all these people who seemed to think they needed him now had been when he was being railroaded out of the parish. But that was ancient history.

"Not a miracle, Carl," Joe said, glancing at Zev. "Rabbi Wolpin brought me back." As Carl and Zev shook hands, Joe said, "And I'm just passing through."

"Passing t'rough? No. Dat can't be! Ya gotta stay!"

Joe saw the light of hope fading in the little man's eyes. Something twisted within him, tugging him.

"What can I do here, Carl? I'm just one man."

"I'll help! I'll do whatever ya want! Jes tell me!"

"Will you help me clean up?"

Carl looked around and seemed to see the cadavers for the first time. He cringed and turned a few shades paler.

"Yeah . . . sure. Anyting."

Joe looked at Zev. "Well? What do you think?"

Zev shrugged. "I should tell you what to do? My parish it's not."

"Not mine either."

Zev jutted his beard at Carl. "I think maybe he'd tell you differently."

Joe did a slow turn. The vaulted nave was utterly silent except for the buzzing of the flies around the cadavers.

A massive clean-up job. But if they worked all day they could make a decent dent in it. And then—

And then what?

Joe didn't know. He was playing this by ear. He'd wait and see what the night brought.

"Can you get us some food, Carl? I'd sell my soul for a cup of coffee."

Carl gave him a strange look.

"Just a figure of speech, Carl. We'll need some food if we're going to keep working."

The man's eyes lit again.

"Dat means ya staying?"

"For a while."

"I'll getcha some food," he said excitedly as he ran for the door. "An' coffee. I know someone who's still got coffee. She'll part wit' some of it for Fadda Joe." He stopped at the door and turned.

"Ay, an' Fadda, I neva believed any a dem tings dat was said aboutcha. Neva."

Joe tried but he couldn't hold it back.

"It would have meant a lot to have heard that from you last year, Carl."

The man lowered his eyes. "Yeah. I guess it woulda. But I'll make it up to ya, Fadda, I will. You can take dat to da bank."

Then he was out the door and gone. Joe turned to Zev and saw the old man rolling up his sleeves.

*"Nu?"* Zev said. "The bodies. Before we do anything else, I think maybe we should move the bodies."

# VII

By early afternoon, Zev was exhausted. The heat and the heavy work had taken their toll. He had to stop and rest. He sat on the chancel rail and looked around. Nearly eight hours' work and they'd barely scratched the surface. But the place did look and smell better.

Removing the flyblown corpses and scattered body parts had been the worst of it. A foul, gut-roiling task that had taken most of the morning. They'd carried the corpses out to the small grave-yard behind the church and left them there. Those people deserved a decent burial but there was no time for it today.

Once the corpses were gone, Father Joe had torn the defilements from the statue of Mary and then they'd turned their attention to the huge crucifix. It took a while but they finally found Christ's plaster arms in the pile of ruined pews. They were still nailed to the sawn-off cross-piece of the crucifix. While Zev and Father Joe worked at jury-rigging a series of braces to reattach the arms, Carl found a mop and bucket and began the long, slow process of washing the fouled floor of the nave.

Now the crucifix was intact again—the life-size plaster Jesus had his arms reattached and was once again nailed to his refurbished cross. Father Joe and Carl had restored him to his former position of dominance. The poor man was upright

again, hanging over the center of the sanctuary in all his tortured splendor.

A grisly sight. Zev could never understand the Catholic attachment to these gruesome statues. But if the vampires loathed them, then Zev was for them all the way.

His stomach rumbled with hunger. At least they'd had a good breakfast. Carl had returned from his food run this morning with bread, cheese, and two thermoses of hot coffee. He wished now they'd saved some. Maybe there was a crust of bread left in the sack. He headed back to the vestibule to check and found an aluminium pot and a paper bag sitting by the door. The pot was full of beef stew and the sack contained three cans of Pepsi.

He poked his head out the doors but no one was in sight on the street outside. It had been that way all day—he'd spy a figure or two peeking in the front doors; they'd hover there for a moment as if to confirm that what they had heard was true, then they'd scurry away. He looked at the meal that had been left. A group of the locals must have donated from their hoard of canned stew and precious soft drinks to fix this. Zev was touched.

He called Father Joe and Carl.

"Tastes like Dinty Moore," Father Joe said around a mouthful of the stew.

"It is," Carl said. "I recognize da little potatoes. Da ladies of the parish must really be excited about youse comin' back to break inta deir canned goods like dis."

They were feasting in the sacristy, the small room off the sanctuary where the priests had kept their vestments—a clerical Green Room, so to speak. Zev found the stew palatable but much too salty. He wasn't about to complain, though.

"I don't believe I've ever had anything like this before."

"I'd be real surprised if you had," said Father Joe. "I doubt very much that something that calls itself Dinty Moore is kosher."

Zev smiled but inside he was suddenly filled with a great sadness. Kosher . . . how meaningless now seemed all the observances which he had allowed to rule and circumscribe his life. Such a fierce proponent of strict dietary laws he'd been in the days before the Lakewood holocaust. But those days were gone, just as the Lakewood community was gone. And Zev was a changed man. If he hadn't changed, if he were still observing, he couldn't sit here and sup with these two men. He'd have to be elsewhere, eating special classes of specially prepared foods off separate sets of dishes. But really, wasn't division what holding to the dietary laws in modern times was all about? They served a purpose beyond mere observance of tradition. They placed another wall between observant Jews and outsiders, keeping them separate even from other Jews who didn't observe.

Zev forced himself to take a big bite of the stew. Time to break down all the walls between people . . . while there was still enough time and people left alive to make it matter.

"You okay, Zev?" Father Joe asked.

Zev nodded silently, afraid to speak for fear of sobbing. Despite all its anachronisms, he missed his life in the good old days of last year. Gone. It was all gone. The rich traditions, the culture, the friends, the prayers. He felt adrift—in time and in space. Nowhere was home.

"You sure?" The young priest seemed genuinely concerned.

"Yes, I'm okay. As okay as you could expect me to feel after spending the better part of the day repairing a crucifix and eating non-kosher food. And let me tell you, that's not so okay."

He put his bowl aside and straightened from his chair.

"Come on, already. Let's get back to work. There's much yet to do."

# VIII

"Sun's almost down," Carl said.

Joe straightened from scrubbing the altar and stared west through one of the smashed windows. The sun was out of sight behind the houses there.

"You can go now, Carl," he said to the little man. "Thanks for your help."

"Where youse gonna go, Fadda?"

"I'll be staying right here."

Carl's prominent Adam's apple bobbed convulsively as he swallowed.

"Yeah? Well den, I'm staying too. I tol' ya I'd make it up to ya, din't I? An besides, I don't tink the suckas'll like da new, improved St. Ant'ny's too much when dey come back tonight, d'you? I don't even tink dey'll get t'rough da doors."

Joe smiled at the man and looked around. Luckily it was July when the days were long. They'd had time to make a difference here. The floors were clean, the crucifix was restored and back in its proper position, as were most of the Stations of the Cross plaques. Zev had found them under the pews and had taken the ones not shattered beyond recognition and rehung them on the walls. Lots of new crosses littered those walls. Carl had found a hammer and nails and had made dozens of them from the remains of the pews.

"No, I don't think they'll like the new decor one bit. But there's something you can get us if you can, Carl. Guns. Pistols, rifles, shotguns, anything that shoots."

Carl nodded slowly. "I know a few guys who can help in dat department."

"And some wine. A little red wine if anybody's saved some."

"You got it."

He hurried off.

"You're planning Custer's last stand, maybe?" Zev said from where he was tacking the last of Carl's crude crosses to the east wall.

"More like the Alamo."

"Same result," Zev said with one of his shrugs.

Joe turned back to scrubbing the altar. He'd been at it for over an hour now. He was drenched with sweat and knew he smelled like a bear, but he couldn't stop until it was clean.

An hour later he was forced to give up. No use. It wouldn't come clean. The vampires must have done something to the blood and foulness to make the mixture seep into the surface of the marble like it had.

He sat on the floor with his back against the altar and rested. He didn't like resting because it gave him time to think. And when he started to think he realized that the odds were pretty high against his seeing tomorrow morning.

At least he'd die well fed. Their secret supplier had left them a dinner of fresh fried chicken by the front doors. Even the memory of it made his mouth water. Apparently someone was *really* glad he was back.

To tell the truth, though, as miserable as he'd been, he wasn't ready to die. Not tonight, not any night. He wasn't looking for an Alamo or a Little Big Horn. All he wanted to do was hold off the vampires till dawn. Keep them out of St. Anthony's for one night. That was all. That would be a statement—*his* statement. If he found an opportunity to ram a stake through Palmeri's rotten heart, so much the better, but he wasn't counting on that. One night. Just to let them know they couldn't have their way everywhere with everybody whenever they felt like it. He had surprise on his side tonight, so maybe it would work. One night. Then he'd be on his way.

"What the fuck have you *done?*"

Joe looked up at the shout. A burly, long-haired man in jeans and a flannel shirt stood in the vestibule staring at the partially restored nave. As he approached, Joe noticed his crescent moon earring.

A Vichy.

Joe balled his fists but didn't move.

"Hey, I'm talking to you, mister. Are you responsible for this?"

When all he got from Joe was a cold stare, he turned to Zev.

"Hey, you! Jew! What the hell do you think *you're* doing?" He started toward Zev. "You get those fucking crosses off—"

"Touch him and I'll break you in half," Joe said in a low voice.

The Vichy skidded to a halt and stared at him.

"Hey, asshole! Are you crazy? Do you know what Father Palmeri will do to you when he arrives?"

"*Father* Palmeri? Why do you still call him that?"

"It's what he wants to be called. And he's going to call you *dog meat* when he gets here!"

Joe pulled himself to his feet and looked down at the Vichy. The man took two steps back. Suddenly he didn't seem so sure of himself.

"Tell him I'll be waiting. Tell him Father Cahill is back."

"You're a priest? You don't look like one."

"Shut up and listen. Tell him Father Joe Cahill is back—and he's pissed. Tell him that. Now get out of here while you still can."

The man turned and hurried out into the growing darkness. Joe turned to Zev and found him grinning through his beard. "'Father Joe Cahill is back—and he's pissed.' I like that."

"We'll make it into a bumper sticker. Meanwhile let's close those doors. The criminal element is starting to wander in. I'll see if we can find some more candles. It's getting dark in here."

# IX

He wore the night like a tuxedo.

Dressed in a fresh cassock, Father Alberto Palmeri turned off County Line Road and strolled toward St. Anthony's. The night was lovely, especially when you owned it. And he owned the night in this area of Lakewood now. He loved the night. He felt at one with it, attuned to its harmonies and its discords. The darkness made him feel so alive. Strange to have to lose your life before you could really feel alive. But this was it. He'd found his niche, his métier.

Such a shame it had taken him so long. All those years trying to deny his appetites, trying to be a member of the other side, cursing himself when he allowed his appetites to win, as he had with increasing frequency toward the end of his mortal life. He should have given in to them completely long ago.

It had taken undeath to free him.

And to think he had been afraid of undeath, had cowered in fear each night in the cellar of the church, surrounded by crosses. Fortunately he had not been as safe as he'd thought and one of the beings he now called brother was able to slip in on him in the dark while he dozed. He saw now that he had lost nothing but his blood by that encounter.

And in trade he'd gained a world.

For now it was his world, at least this little corner of it, one in which he was completely free to indulge himself in any way he wished. Except for the blood. He had no choice about the blood. That was a new appetite, stronger than all the rest, one that would not be denied. But he did not mind the new appetite in the least. He'd found interesting ways to sate it.

Up ahead he spotted dear, defiled St. Anthony's. He wondered what his servants had prepared for him tonight. They were quite imaginative. They'd yet to bore him.

But as he drew nearer the church, Palmeri slowed. His skin prickled. The building had changed. Something was very wrong there, wrong inside. Something amiss with the light that beamed from the windows. This wasn't the old familiar candlelight, this was something else, something more. Something that made his insides tremble.

Figures raced up the street toward him. Live 'ones. His night vision picked out the earrings and familiar faces of some of his servants. As they neared he sensed the warmth of the blood coursing just beneath their skins. The hunger rose in him and he fought the urge to rip into one of their throats. He couldn't allow himself that pleasure. He had to keep the servants dangling, keep them working for him and the nest. They needed the services of the indentured living to remove whatever obstacles the cattle might put in their way.

"Father! Father!" they cried.

He loved it when they called him Father, loved being one of the undead and dressing like one of the enemy.

"Yes, my children. What sort of victim do you have for us tonight?"

"No victim, father—trouble!"

The edges of Palmeri's vision darkened with rage as he heard of the young priest and the Jew who had dared to try to turn St. Anthony's into a holy place again. When he heard the name of the priest, he nearly exploded.

"Cahill? Joseph Cahill is back in my church?"

"He was cleaning the altar!" one of the servants said.

Palmeri strode toward the church with the servants trailing behind. He knew that neither Cahill nor the Pope himself could clean that altar. Palmeri had desecrated it himself; he had learned how to do that when he became nest leader. But what else had the young pup dared to do?

Whatever it was, it would be undone. *Now!*

Palmeri strode up the steps and pulled the right door open—and screamed in agony.

The light! The *light*! The LIGHT! White agony lanced through Palmeri's eyes and seared his brain like two hot pokers. He retched and threw his arms across his face as he staggered back into the cool, comforting darkness.

It took a few minutes for the pain to drain off, for the nausea to pass, for vision to return.

He'd never understand it. He'd spent his entire life in the presence of crosses and crucifixes, surrounded by them. And yet as soon as he'd become undead, he was unable to bear the sight of one. As a matter of fact, since he'd become undead, he'd never even *seen* one. A cross was no longer an object. It was a light, a light so excruciatingly bright, so blazingly white that it was sheer agony to look at it. As a child in Naples he'd been told by his mother not to look at the sun, but when there'd been talk of an eclipse, he'd stared directly into its eye. The pain of looking at a cross was a hundred, no, a thousand times worse than that. And the bigger the cross or crucifix, the worse the pain.

He'd experienced monumental pain upon looking into St. Anthony's tonight. That could only mean that Joseph, that young bastard, had refurbished the giant crucifix. It was the only possible explanation.

He swung on his servants.

"Get in there! Get that crucifix down!"

"They've got guns!"

"Then get help. But get it *down*!"

"We'll get guns too! We can—"

"*No!* I want him! I want that priest alive! I want him for myself! Anyone who kills him will suffer a very painful, very long and lingering true death! Is that clear?"

It was clear. They scurried away without answering.

Palmeri went to gather the other members of the nest.

# X

Dressed in a cassock and a surplice, Joe came out of the sacristy and approached the altar. He noticed Zev keeping watch at one of the windows. He didn't tell him how ridiculous he looked carrying the shotgun Carl had brought back. He held it so gingerly, like it was full of nitroglycerine and would explode if he jiggled it.

Zev turned, and smiled when he saw him.

"*Now* you look like the old Father Joe we all used to know."

Joe gave him a little bow and proceeded toward the altar.

All right: He had everything he needed. He had the Missal they'd found in among the pew debris earlier today. He had the wine; Carl had brought back about four ounces of sour red babarone. He'd found a smudged surplice and a dusty cassock on the floor of one of the closets in the sacristy, and he wore them now. No hosts, though. A crust of bread left over from breakfast would have to do. No chalice, either. If he'd known he was going to be saying Mass he'd have come prepared. As a last resort he'd used the can opener in the rectory to remove the top from one of the Pepsi cans from lunch. Quite a stretch from the gold chalice he'd used since his ordination, but probably more in line with what Jesus had used at that first Mass—the Last Supper.

He was uncomfortable with the idea of weapons in St. Anthony's but he saw no alternative. He and Zev knew nothing about guns, and Carl knew little more; they'd probably do more damage to themselves than to the Vichy if they tried to use them. But maybe the sight of them would make the Vichy hesitate, slow them down. All he needed was a little time here, enough to get to the consecration.

*This is going to be the most unusual Mass in history,* he thought.

But he was going to get through it if it killed him. And that was a real possibility. This might well be his last Mass. But he wasn't afraid. He was too excited to be afraid. He'd had a slug of the Scotch—just enough to ward off the DTs—but it had done nothing to quell the buzz of the adrenalin humming along every nerve in his body.

He spread everything out on the white tablecloth he'd taken from the rectory and used to cover the filthy altar. He looked at Carl.

"Ready?"

Carl nodded and stuck the .38 caliber pistol he'd been examining in his belt.

"Been a while, Fadda. We did it in Latin when I was a kid but I tink I can swing it."

"Just do your best and don't worry about any mistakes."

*Some Mass.* A defiled altar, a crust for a host, a Pepsi can for a chalice, a fifty-year-old, pistol-packing altar boy, and a congregation consisting of a lone, shotgun-carrying Orthodox Jew.

Joe looked heavenward. *You do understand, don't you, Lord, that this was arranged on short notice?*

Time to begin.

He read the Gospel but dispensed with the homily. He tried to remember the Mass as it used to be said, to fit in better with Carl's outdated responses. As he was starting the Offertory the front doors flew open and a group of men entered—ten of them, all with crescent moons dangling from their ears. Out of the corner of his eye he saw Zev move away from the window toward the altar, pointing his shotgun at them.

As soon as they entered the nave and got past the broken pews, the Vichy fanned out toward the sides. They began pulling down the Stations of the Cross, ripping Carl's makeshift crosses from the walls and tearing them apart. Carl looked up at Joe from where he knelt, his eyes questioning, his hand reaching for the pistol in his belt.

Joe shook his head and kept up with the Offertory.

When all the little crosses were down, the Vichy swarmed behind the altar. Joe chanced a quick glance over his shoulder and saw them begin their attack on the newly repaired crucifix.

"Zev!" Carl said in a low voice, cocking his head toward the Vichy. "Stop 'em!"

Zev worked the pump on the shotgun. The sound echoed through the church. Joe heard the activity behind him come to a sudden halt. He braced himself for the shot . . .

But it never came.

He looked at Zev. The old man met his gaze and sadly shook his head. He couldn't do it. To the accompaniment of the sound of renewed activity and derisive laughter behind him, Joe gave Zev a tiny nod of reassurance and understanding, then hurried the Mass toward the Consecration.

As he held the crust of bread aloft, he started at the sound of the life-sized crucifix crashing to the floor, cringed as he heard the freshly buttressed arms and crosspiece being torn away again.

As he held the wine aloft in the Pepsi can, the swaggering, grinning Vichy surrounded the altar and brazenly tore the cross from around his neck. Zev and Carl put up a struggle to keep theirs but were overpowered.

And then Joe's skin began to crawl as a new group entered the nave. There had to be at least forty of them, all of them vampires.

And Palmeri was leading them.

# XI

Palmeri hid his hesitancy as he approached the altar. The crucifix and its intolerable whiteness were gone, yet something was not right. Something repellent here, something that urged him to flee. What?

Perhaps it was just the residual effect of the crucifix and all the crosses they had used to line the walls. That had to be it. The unsettling aftertaste would fade as the night wore on. Oh, yes. His night-brothers and sisters from the nest would see to that.

He focused his attention on the man behind the altar and laughed when he realized what he held in his hands.

"Pepsi, Joseph? You're trying to consecrate Pepsi?" He turned to his nest siblings. "Do you see this, my brothers and sisters? Is this the man

we are to fear? And look who he has with him! An old Jew and a parish hanger-on!"

He heard their hissing laughter as they fanned out around him, sweeping toward the altar in a wide phalanx. The Jew and Carl—he recognized Carl and wondered how he'd avoided capture for so long—retreated to the other side of the altar where they flanked Joseph. And Joseph . . . Joseph's handsome Irish face so pale and drawn, his mouth drawn into such a tight, grim line. He looked scared to death. And well he should be.

Palmeri put down his rage at Joseph's audacity. He was glad he had returned. He'd always hated the young priest for his easy manner with people, for the way the parishioners had flocked to him with their problems despite the fact that he had nowhere near the experience of their older and wiser pastor. But that was over now. That world was gone, replaced by a nightworld—Palmeri's world. And no one would be flocking to Father Joe for anything when Palmeri was through with him. "Father Joe"—how he'd hated it when the parishioners had started calling him that. Well, their Father Joe would provide superior entertainment tonight. This was going to be *fun*.

"Joseph, Joseph, Joseph," he said as he stopped and smiled at the young priest across the altar. "This futile gesture is so typical of your arrogance."

But Joseph only stared back at him, his expression a mixture of defiance and repugnance. And that only fueled Palmeri's rage.

"Do I repel you, Joseph? Does my new form offend your precious shanty-Irish sensibilities? Does my undeath disgust you?"

"You managed to do all that while you were still alive, Alberto."

Palmeri allowed himself to smile. Joseph probably thought he was putting on a brave front, but the tremor in his voice betrayed his fear.

"Always good with the quick retort, weren't you, Joseph. Always thinking you were better than me, always putting yourself above me."

"Not much of a climb where a child molester is concerned."

Palmeri's anger mounted.

"So superior. So self-righteous. What about

your appetites, Joseph? The secret ones? What are they? Do you always hold them in check? Are you so far above the rest of us that you never give in to an improper impulse? I'll bet you think that even if we made you one of us you could resist the blood hunger."

He saw by the startled look in Joseph's face that he had struck a nerve. He stepped closer, almost touching the altar.

"You do, don't you? You really think you could resist it! Well, we shall see about that, Joseph. By dawn you'll be drained—we'll each take a turn at you—and when the sun rises you'll have to hide from its light. When the night comes you'll be one of us. And then all the rules will be off. The night will be yours. You'll be able to do anything and everything you've ever wanted. But the blood hunger will be on you too. You won't be sipping your god's blood, as you've done so often, but *human* blood. You'll thirst for hot, human blood, Joseph. And you'll have to sate that thirst. There'll be no choice. And I want to be there when you do, Joseph. I want to be there to laugh in your face as you suck up the crimson nectar, and keep on laughing every night as the red hunger lures you into infinity."

And it *would* happen. Palmeri knew it as sure as he felt his own thirst. He hungered for the moment when he could rub dear Joseph's face in the muck of his own despair.

"I was about to finish saying Mass," Joseph said coolly. "Do you mind if I finish?"

Palmeri couldn't help laughing this time.

"Did you really think this charade would work? Did you really think you could celebrate Mass on *this*?"

He reached out and snatched the tablecloth from the altar, sending the Missal and the piece of bread to the floor and exposing the fouled surface of the marble.

"Did you really think you could effect the Transubstantiation here? Do you really believe any of that garbage? That the bread and wine actually take on the substance of "—he tried to say the name but it wouldn't form—"the Son's body and blood?"

One of the nest brothers, Frederick, stepped forward and leaned over the altar, smiling.

"Transubstantiation?" he said in his most unctuous voice, pulling the Pepsi can from Joseph's hands. "Does that mean that this is the blood of the Son?"

A whisper of warning slithered through Palmeri's mind. Something about the can, something about the way he found it difficult to bring its outline into focus . . .

"Brother Frederick, maybe you should—"

Frederick's grin broadened. "I've always wanted to sup on the blood of a deity."

The nest members hissed their laughter as Frederick raised the can and drank.

Palmeri was jolted by the explosion of intolerable brightness that burst from Frederick's mouth. The inside of his skull glowed beneath his scalp and shafts of pure white light shot from his ears, nose, eyes—every orifice in his head. The glow spread as it flowed down through his throat and chest and into his abdominal cavity, silhouetting his ribs before melting through his skin. Frederick was liquefying where he stood, his flesh steaming, softening, running like glowing molten lava.

No! This couldn't be happening! Not now when he had Joseph in his grasp!

Then the can fell from Frederick's dissolving fingers and landed on the altar top. Its contents splashed across the fouled surface, releasing another detonation of brilliance, this one more devastating than the first. The glare spread rapidly, extending over the upper surface and running down the sides, moving like a living thing, engulfing the entire altar, making it glow like a corpuscle of fire torn from the heart of the sun itself.

And with the light came blast-furnace heat that drove Palmeri back, back, back until he had to turn and follow the rest of his nest in a mad, headlong rush from St. Anthony's into the cool, welcoming safety of the outer darkness.

# XII

As the vampires fled into the night, their Vichy toadies behind them, Zev stared in horrid fascination at the puddle of putrescence that was all that remained of the vampire Palmeri had called Frederick. He glanced at Carl and caught the look of dazed wonderment on his face. Zev touched the top of the altar—clean, shiny, every whorl of the marble surface clearly visible.

There was fearsome power here. Incalculable power. But instead of elating him, the realization only depressed him. How long had this been going on? Did it happen at every Mass? Why had he spent his entire life ignorant of this?

He turned to Father Joe.

"What happened?"

"I—I don't know."

"A miracle!" Carl said, running his palm over the altar top.

"A miracle and a meltdown," Father Joe said. He picked up the empty Pepsi can and looked into it. "You know, you go through the seminary, through your ordination, through countless Masses *believing* in the Transubtantiation. But after all these years . . . to actually *know* . . ."

Zev saw him rub his finger along the inside of the can and taste it. He grimaced.

"What's wrong?" Zev asked.

"Still tastes like sour barbarone . . . with a hint of Pepsi."

"Doesn't matter what it tastes like. As far as Palmeri and his friends are concerned, it's the real thing."

"No," said the priest with a small smile. "That's Coke."

And then they started laughing. It wasn't that funny, but Zev found himself roaring along with other two. It was more a release of tension than anything else. His sides hurt. He had to lean against the altar to support himself.

It took the return of the Vichy to cure the laughter. They charged in carrying a heavy fire blanket. This time Father Joe did not stand by passively as they invaded his church. He stepped around the altar and met them head on.

He was great and terrible as he confronted them. His giant stature and raised fists cowed them for a few heartbeats. But then they must have remembered that they outnumbered him twelve to one and charged him. He swung a massive fist and caught the lead Vichy square on the jaw. The blow lifted him off his feet and he landed against another. Both went down.

Zev dropped to one knee and reached for the shotgun. He would use it this time, he would shoot these vermin, he swore it!

But then someone landed on his back and drove him to the floor. As he tried to get up he saw Father Joe, surrounded, swinging his fists, laying the Vichy out every time he connected. But there were too many. As the priest went down under the press of them, a heavy boot thudded against the side of Zev's head. He sank into darkness.

## XIII

. . . a throbbing in his head, stinging pain in his cheek, and a voice, sibilant yet harsh . . .

". . . now, Joseph. Come on. Wake up. I don't want you to miss this!"

Palmeri's sallow features swam into view, hovering over him, grinning like a skull. Joe tried to move but found his wrists and arms tied. His right hand throbbed, felt twice its normal size; he must have broken it on a Vichy jaw. He lifted his head and saw that he was tied spread-eagle on the altar, and that the altar had been covered with the fire blanket.

"Melodramatic, I admit," Palmeri said, "but fitting, don't you think? I mean, you and I used to sacrifice our god symbolically here every weekday and multiple times on Sundays, so why shouldn't this serve as *your* sacrificial altar?"

Joe shut his eyes against a wave of nausea. This couldn't be happening.

"Thought you'd won, didn't you?" When Joe wouldn't answer him, Palmeri went on. "And even if you'd chased me out of here for good, what would you have accomplished? The world is ours now, Joseph. Feeders and cattle—that is the hierarchy. We are the feeders. And tonight you'll join us. But *he* won't. *Voila!*"

He stepped aside and made a flourish toward the balcony. Joe searched the dim, candlelit space of the nave, not sure what he was supposed to see.

Then he picked out Zev's form and he groaned. The old man's feet were lashed to the balcony rail; he hung upside down, his reddened face and frightened eyes turned his way. Joe fell back and strained at the ropes but they wouldn't budge.

"Let him go!"

"What? And let all that good rich Jewish blood go to waste? Why, these people are the Chosen of God! They're a delicacy!"

"Bastard!"

If he could just get his hands on Palmeri, just for a minute.

"Tut-tut, Joseph. Not in the house of the Lord. The Jew should have been smart and run away like Carl."

Carl got away? Good. The poor guy would probably hate himself, call himself a coward the rest of his life, but he'd done what he could. Better to live on than get strung up like Zev.

*We're even, Carl.*

"But don't worry about your rabbi. None of us will lay a fang on him. He hasn't earned the right to join us. We'll use the razor to bleed him. And when he's dead, he'll be dead for keeps. But not you, Joseph. Oh no, not you." His smile broadened. "You're mine."

Joe wanted to spit in Palmeri's face—not so much as an act of defiance as to hide the waves of terror surging through him—but there was no saliva to be had in his parched mouth. The thought of being undead made him weak. To spend eternity like . . . he looked at the rapt faces of Palmeri's fellow vampires as they clustered under Zev's suspended form . . . like *them*?

He *wouldn't* be like them! He wouldn't allow it!

But what if there was no choice? What if becoming undead toppled a lifetime's worth of moral constraints, cut all the tethers on his human hungers, negated all his mortal concepts of how a life should be lived? Honor, justice, integrity, truth, decency, fairness, love—what if they became meaningless words instead of the footings for his life?

A thought struck him.

"A deal, Alberto," he said.

"You're hardly in a bargaining position, Joseph."

"I'm not? Answer me this: Do the undead ever kill each other? I mean, has one of them ever driven a stake through another's heart?"

"No. Of course not."

"Are you sure? You'd better be sure before you go through with your plans tonight. Because if I'm forced to become one of you, I'll be crossing over with just one thought in mind: to find you. And when I do I won't stake your heart, I'll stake your arms and legs to the pilings of the Point Pleasant boardwalk where you can watch the sun rise and feel it slowly crisp your skin to charcoal."

Palmeri's smile wavered. "Impossible. You'll be different. You'll want to thank me. You'll wonder why you ever resisted."

"You'd better be sure of that, Alberto . . . for your sake. Because I'll have all eternity to track you down. And I'll find you, Alberto. I swear it on my own grave. Think on that."

"Do you think an empty threat is going to cow me?"

"We'll find out how empty it is, won't we? But here's the deal: Let Zev go and I'll let you be."

"You care that much for an old Jew?"

"He's something you never knew in life, and never will know: He's a friend." *And he gave me back my soul.*

Palmeri leaned closer. His foul, nauseous breath wafted against Joe's face.

"A friend? How can you be friends with a dead man?" With that he straightened and turned toward the balcony. "Do him! *Now!*"

As Joe shouted out frantic pleas and protests, one of the vampires climbed up the rubble toward Zev. Zev did not struggle. Joe saw him close his eyes, waiting. As the vampire reached out with the straight razor, Joe bit back a sob of grief and rage and helplessness. He was about to squeeze his own eyes shut when he saw a flame arc through the air from one of the windows. It struck the floor with a crash of glass and a *woomp!* of exploding flame.

Joe had only heard of such things, but he immediately realized that he had just seen his first Molotov cocktail in action. The splattering gasoline caught the clothes of a nearby vampire who began running in circles, screaming as it beat at its flaming clothes. But its cries were drowned by the roar of other voices, a hundred or more. Joe looked around and saw people—men, women, teenagers—climbing in the windows, charging through the front doors. The women held crosses on high while the men wielded long wooden pikes—broom, rake, and shovel handles whittled to sharp points. Joe recognized most of the faces from the Sunday Masses he had held here for years.

St. Anthony's parishioners were back to reclaim their church.

"Yes!" he shouted, not sure of whether to laugh or cry. But when he saw the rage in Palmeri's face, he laughed. "Too bad, Alberto!"

Palmeri made a lunge at his throat but cringed away as a woman with an upheld crucifix and a man with a pike charged the altar—Carl and a woman Joe recognized as Mary O'Hare.

"Told ya I wun't letcha down, din't I, Fadda?" Carl said, grinning and pulling out a red Swiss Army knife. He began sawing at the rope around Joe's right wrist. "Din't I?"

"That you did, Carl. I don't think I've ever been so glad to see anyone in my entire life. But how—?"

"I told 'em. I run t'rough da parish, goin' house ta house. I told 'em dat Fadda Joe was in trouble an' dat we let him down before but we shoun't let him down again. He come back fa us, now we gotta go back fa him. Simple as dat. And den *dey* started runnin' house ta house, an afore ya knowed it, we had ourselfs a little army. We come ta kick ass, Fadda, if you'll excuse da expression."

"Kick all the ass you can, Carl."

Joe glanced at Mary O'Hare's terror-glazed eyes as she swiveled around, looking this way and that; he saw how the crucifix trembled in her hand. She wasn't going to kick too much ass in her state, but she was *here,* dear God, she was here for him and for St. Anthony's despite the terror that so obviously filled her. His heart swelled with love for these people and pride in their courage.

As soon as his arms were free, Joe sat up and took the knife from Carl. As he sawed at his leg ropes, he looked around the church.

The oldest and youngest members of the parish-

ioner army were stationed at the windows and doors where they held crosses aloft, cutting off the vampires' escape, while all across the nave—chaos. Screams, cries, and an occasional shot echoed through St. Anthony's. The vampires were outnumbered three to one and seemed blinded and confused by all the crosses around them. Despite their superhuman strength, it appeared that some were indeed getting their asses kicked. A number were already writhing on the floor, impaled on pikes. As Joe watched, he saw a pair of the women, crucifixes held before them, backing a vampire into a corner. As it cowered there with its arms across its face, one of the men charged in with a sharpened rake handle held like a lance and ran it through.

But a number of parishioners lay in inert, bloody heaps on the floor, proof that the vampires and the Vichy were claiming their share of victims too.

Joe freed his feet and hopped off the altar. He looked around for Palmeri—he *wanted* Palmeri—but the vampire priest had lost himself in the melée. Joe glanced up at the balcony and saw that Zev was still hanging there, struggling to free himself. He started across the nave to help him.

## XIV

Zev hated that he should be hung up here like a salami in a deli window. He tried again to pull his upper body up far enough to reach his leg ropes but he couldn't get close. He had never been one for exercise; doing a sit-up flat on the floor would have been difficult, so what made him think he could do the equivalent maneuver hanging upside down by his feet? He dropped back, exhausted, and felt the blood rush to his head again. His vision swam, his ears pounded, he felt like the skin of his face was going to burst open. Much more of this and he'd have a stroke or worse maybe.

He watched the upside-down battle below and was glad to see the vampires getting the worst of it. These people—seeing Carl among them, Zev assumed they were part of St. Anthony's parish—were ferocious, almost savage in their attacks on the vampires. Months' worth of pent-up rage and fear was being released upon their tormentors in a single burst. It was almost frightening.

Suddenly he felt a hand on his foot. Someone was untying his knots. Thank you, Lord. Soon he would be on his feet again. As the cords came loose he decided he should at least attempt to participate in his own rescue.

*Once more,* Zev thought. *Once more I'll try.*

With a grunt he levered himself up, straining, stretching to grasp something, anything. A hand came out of the darkness and he reached for it. But Zev's relief turned to horror when he felt the cold clamminess of the thing that clutched him, that pulled him up and over the balcony rail with inhuman strength. His bowels threatened to evacuate when Palmeri's grinning face loomed not six inches from his own.

"It's not over yet, Jew," he said softly, his foul breath clogging Zev's nose and throat. "Not by a long shot!"

He felt Palmeri's free hand ram into his belly and grip his belt at the buckle, then the other hand grab a handful of his shirt at the neck. Before he could struggle or cry out, he was lifted free of the floor and hoisted over the balcony rail.

And the demon's voice was in his ear.

"Joseph called you a friend, Jew. Let's see if he really meant it."

## XV

Joe was halfway across the floor of the nave when he heard Palmeri's voice echo above the madness.

"Stop them, Joseph! Stop them now or I drop your friend!"

Joe looked up and froze. Palmeri stood at the balcony rail, leaning over it, his eyes averted from the nave and all its newly arrived crosses. At the end of his outstretched arms was Zev, suspended in mid-air over the splintered remains of the pews, over a particularly large and ragged spire of wood that pointed directly at the middle of Zev's back. Zev's frightened eyes were flashing between Joe and the giant spike below.

Around him Joe heard the sounds of the melee

drop a notch, then drop another as all eyes were drawn to the tableau on the balcony.

"A human can die impaled on a wooden stake just as well as a vampire!" Palmeri cried. "And just as quickly if it goes through his heart. But it can take hours of agony if it rips through his gut."

St. Anthony's grew silent as the fighting stopped and each faction backed away to a different side of the church, leaving Joe alone in the middle.

"What do you want, Alberto?"

"First I want all those crosses put away so that I can see!"

Joe looked to his right where his parishioners stood.

"Put them away," he told them. When a murmur of dissent arose, he added, "Don't put them down, just out of sight. Please."

Slowly, one by one at first, then in groups, the crosses and crucifixes were placed behind backs or tucked out of sight within coats.

To his left, the vampires hissed their relief and the Vichy cheered. The sound was like hot needles being forced under Joe's fingernails. Above, Palmeri turned his face to Joe and smiled.

"That's better."

"What do you want?" Joe asked, knowing with a sick crawling in his gut exactly what the answer would be.

"A trade," Palmeri said.

"Me for him, I suppose?" Joe said.

Palmeri's smile broadened. "Of course."

"No, Joe!" Zev cried.

Palmeri shook the old man roughly. Joe heard him say, "Quiet, Jew, or I'll snap your spine!" Then he looked down at Joe again. "The other thing is to tell your rabble to let my people go." He laughed and shook Zev again. "Hear that, Jew? A Biblical reference—Old Testament, no less!"

"All right," Joe said without hesitation.

The parishioners on his right gasped as one and cries of "No!" and "You can't!" filled St. Anthony's. A particularly loud voice nearby shouted, "He's only a lousy kike!"

Joe wheeled on the man and recognized Gene Harrington, a carpenter. He jerked a thumb back over his shoulder at the vampires and their servants.

"You sound like you'd be more at home with them, Gene."

Harrington backed up a step and looked at his feet.

"Sorry, Father," he said in a voice that hovered on the verge of a sob. "But we just got you back!"

"I'll be all right," Joe said softly.

And he meant it. Deep inside he had a feeling that he would come through this, that if he could trade himself for Zev and face Palmeri one-on-one, he could come out the victor, or at least battle him to a draw. Now that he was no longer tied up like some sacrificial lamb, now that he was free, with full use of his arms and legs again, he could not imagine dying at the hands of the likes of Palmeri.

Besides, one of the parishioners had given him a tiny crucifix. He had it closed in the palm of his hand.

But he had to get Zev out of danger first. That above all else. He looked up at Palmeri.

"All right, Alberto. I'm on my way up."

"Wait!" Palmeri said. "Someone search him."

Joe gritted his teeth as one of the Vichy, a blubbery, unwashed slob, came forward and searched his pockets. Joe thought he might get away with the crucifix but at the last moment he was made to open his hands. The Vichy grinned in Joe's face as he snatched the tiny cross from his palm and shoved it into his pocket.

"He's clean now!" the slob said and gave Joe a shove toward the vestibule.

Joe hesitated. He was walking into the snake pit unarmed now. A glance at his parishioners told him he couldn't very well turn back now.

He continued on his way, clenching and unclenching his tense, sweaty fists as he walked. He still had a chance of coming out of this alive. He was too angry to die. He prayed that when he got within reach of the ex-priest the smoldering rage at how he had framed him when he'd been pastor, at what he'd done to St. Anthony's since then would explode and give him the strength to tear Palmeri to pieces.

"No!" Zev shouted from above. "Forget about me! You've started something here and you've got to see it through!"

Joe ignored his friend.

"Coming, Alberto."

*Father Joe's coming, Alberto. And he's pissed. Royally* pissed.

# XVI

Zev craned his neck around, watching Father Joe disappear beneath the balcony.

"Joe! Come back!"

Palmeri shook him again.

"Give it up, old Jew. Joseph never listened to anyone and he's not listening to you. He still believes in faith and virtue and honesty, in the power of goodness and truth over what he perceives as evil. He'll come up here ready to sacrifice himself for you, yet sure in his heart that he's going to win in the end. But he's wrong."

"No!" Zev said.

But in his heart he knew that Palmeri was right. How could Joe stand up against a creature with Palmeri's strength, who could hold Zev in the air like this for so long? Didn't his arms ever tire?

"Yes!" Palmeri hissed. "He's going to lose and we're going to win. We'll win for the same reason we'll always win. We don't let anything as silly and transient as sentiment stand in our way. If we'd been winning below and situations were reversed—if Joseph were holding one of my nest brothers over that wooden spike below—do you think I'd pause for a moment? For a second? Never! That's why this whole exercise by Joseph and these people is futile."

*Futile* . . . Zev thought. Like much of his life, it seemed. Like all of his future. Joe would die tonight and Zev would live on, a cross-wearing Jew, with the traditions of his past sacked and in flames, and nothing in his future but a vast, empty, limitless plain to wander alone.

There was a sound on the balcony stairs and Palmeri turned his head.

"Ah, Joseph," he said.

Zev couldn't see the priest but he shouted anyway.

"Go back Joe! Don't let him trick you!"

"Speaking of tricks," Palmeri said, leaning further over the balcony rail as an extra warning to Joe, "I hope you're not going to try anything foolish."

"No," said Joe's tired voice from somewhere behind Palmeri. "No tricks. Pull him in and let him go."

Zev could not let this happen. And suddenly he knew what he had to do. He twisted his body and grabbed the front of Palmeri's cassock while bringing his legs up and bracing his feet against one of the uprights of the brass balcony rail. As Palmeri turned his startled face toward him, Zev put all his strength into his legs for one convulsive backward push against the railing, pulling Palmeri with him. The vampire priest was overbalanced. Even his enormous strength could not help him once his feet came free of the floor. Zev saw his undead eyes widen with terror as his lower body slipped over the railing. As they fell free, Zev wrapped his arms around Palmeri and clutched his cold and surprisingly thin body tight against him.

"What goes through this old Jew goes through you!" he shouted into the vampire's ear.

For an instant he saw Joe's horrified face appear over the balcony's receding edge, heard Joe's faraway shout of *"No!"* mingle with Palmeri's nearer scream of the same word, then there was a spine-cracking jar and a tearing, wrenching pain beyond all comprehension in his chest. In an eyeblink he felt the sharp spire of wood rip through him and into Palmeri.

And then he felt no more.

As roaring blackness closed in he wondered if he'd done it, if this last desperate, foolish act had succeeded. He didn't want to die without finding out. He wanted to know—

But then he knew no more.

# XVII

Joe shouted incoherently as he hung over the rail and watched Zev's fall, gagged as he saw the bloody point of the pew remnant burst through the back of Palmeri's cassock directly below him. He saw Palmeri squirm and flop around like a speared fish, then go limp atop Zev's already inert form.

As cheers mixed with cries of horror and the sounds of renewed battle rose from the nave, Joe turned away from the balcony rail and dropped to his knees.

"Zev!" he cried aloud! "Good God, Zev!"

Forcing himself to his feet, he stumbled down the back stairs, through the vestibule, and into the nave. The vampires and the Vichy were on the run, as cowed and demoralized by their leader's death as the parishioners were buoyed by it. Slowly, steadily, they were falling before the relentless onslaught. But Joe paid them scant attention. He fought his way to where Zev lay impaled beneath Palmeri's already rotting corpse. He looked for a sign of life in his old friend's glazing eyes, a hint of a pulse in his throat under his beard, but there was nothing.

"Oh, Zev, you shouldn't have. You shouldn't have."

Suddenly he was surrounded by a cheering throng of St. Anthony's parishioners.

"We did it, Fadda Joe!" Carl cried, his face and hands splattered with blood. "We killed 'em all! We got our church back!"

"Thanks to this man here," Joe said, pointing to Zev.

"No!" someone shouted. "Thanks to *you!*"

Amid the cheers, Joe shook his head and said nothing. Let them celebrate. They deserved it. They'd reclaimed a small piece of the planet as their own, a toe-hold and nothing more. A small victory of minimal significance in the war, but a victory nonetheless. They had their church back, at least for tonight. And they intended to keep it.

Good. But there would be one change. If they wanted their Father Joe to stick around they were going to have to agree to rename the church.

St. Zev's.

Joe liked the sound of that.

# THE ADVENTURE OF THE SUSSEX VAMPIRE

# Arthur Conan Doyle

Doyle believed that his most important works of fiction were such historical novels and short-story collections as *Micah Clarke* (1889), *The White Company* (1892), *The Exploits of Brigadier Gerard* (1896), and *Sir Nigel* (1906). He believed his most significant nonfiction work was in the spiritualism field, to which he devoted the last twenty years of his life, a considerable portion of his fortune, and prodigious energy, producing many major and not-so-major works on the subject.

He was deluded, of course, as Sherlock Holmes was his supreme achievement, arguably the most famous fictional character ever created. His first appearance was in the novel *A Study in Scarlet* (1887), followed by *The Sign of Four* (1890), neither of which changed the course of the detective story. This occurred when the first short story, "A Scandal in Bohemia," was published in *The Strand Magazine* (July 1891), bringing the world's first private detective to a huge readership. Monthly publication of new Holmes stories became so widely anticipated that eager readers queued up at newsstands awaiting each new issue.

One of the most famous Holmes axioms was that when the impossible was eliminated, whatever remained must be the truth. This theory is in great evidence in the present story.

"The Adventure of the Sussex Vampire" was first published in the January 1924 issue of *The Strand Magazine*; it was first collected in book form in *The Case-Book of Sherlock Holmes* (London: John Murray, 1927).

# The Adventure of the Sussex Vampire

## ARTHUR CONAN DOYLE

Holmes had read carefully a note which the last post had brought him. Then, with the dry chuckle which was his nearest approach to a laugh, he tossed it over to me.

"For a mixture of the modern and the mediæval, of the practical and of the wildly fanciful, I think this is surely the limit," said he. "What do you make of it, Watson?"

I read as follows:

*46, Old Jewry*
*Nov. 19th*
*Re Vampires*
*Sir:*

*Our client, Mr. Robert Ferguson, of Ferguson and Murihead, tea brokers, of Mincing Lane, has made some inquiry from us in a communication of even date concerning vampires. As our firm specializes entirely upon the assessment of machinery the matter hardly comes within our purview, and we have therefore recommended Mr. Ferguson to call upon you and lay the matter before you. We have not forgotten your successful action in the case of Matilda Briggs.*

*We are, sir,*

FAITHFULLY YOURS,
MORRISON, MORRISON, AND
DODD
PER E. J. C.

"Matilda Briggs was not the name of a young woman, Watson," said Holmes in a reminiscent voice. "It was a ship which is associated with the giant rat of Sumatra, a story for which the world is not yet prepared. But what do we know about vampires? Does it come within our purview either? Anything is better than stagnation, but really we seem to have been switched on to a Grimms' fairy tale. Make a long arm, Watson, and see what V has to say."

I leaned back and took down the great index volume to which he referred. Holmes balanced it on his knee, and his eyes moved slowly and lovingly over the record of old cases, mixed with the accumulated information of a lifetime.

"Voyage of the *Gloria Scott*," he read. "That was a bad business. I have some recollection that you made a record of it, Watson, though I was unable to congratulate you upon the result. Victor Lynch, the forger. Venomous lizard or gila. Remarkable case, that! Vittoria, the circus belle. Vanderbilt and the Yeggman. Vipers. Vigor, the Hammersmith wonder. Hullo! Hullo! Good old index. You can't beat it. Listen to this, Watson. Vampirism in Hungary. And again, Vampires in Transylvania." He turned over the pages with eagerness, but after a short intent perusal he threw down the great book with a snarl of disappointment.

"Rubbish, Watson, rubbish! What have we to do with walking corpses who can only be held in their grave by stakes driven through their hearts? It's pure lunacy."

"But surely," said I, "the vampire was not necessarily a dead man? A living person might have the habit. I have read, for example, of the old sucking the blood of the young in order to retain their youth."

"You are right, Watson. It mentions the legend in one of these references. But are we to give serious attention to such things? This Agency stands flat-footed upon the ground, and there it must remain. The world is big enough for us. No ghosts need apply. I fear that we cannot take Mr. Robert Ferguson very seriously. Possibly this note may be from him, and may throw some light upon what is worrying him."

He took up a second letter which had lain unnoticed upon the table while he had been absorbed with the first. This he began to read with a smile of amusement upon his face which gradually faded away into an expression of intense interest and concentration. When he had finished, he sat for some little time lost in thought, with the letter dangling from his fingers. Finally, with a start, he aroused himself from his reverie.

"Cheeseman's, Lamberley. Where is Lamberley, Watson?"

"It is in Sussex, south of Horsham."

"Not very far, eh? And Cheeseman's?"

"I know that country, Holmes. It is full of old houses which are named after the men who built them centuries ago. You get Odley's and Harvey's and Carriton's—the folk are forgotten but their names live in their houses."

"Precisely," said Holmes coldly. It was one of the peculiarities of his proud, self-contained nature that though he docketed any fresh information very quietly and accurately in his brain, he seldom made any acknowledgment to the giver. "I rather fancy we shall know a good deal more about Cheeseman's, Lamberley, before we are through. The letter is, as I had hoped, from Robert Ferguson. By the way, he claims acquaintance with you."

"With me!"

"You had better read it."

He handed the letter across. It was headed with the address quoted.

*Dear Mr. Holmes* [it said]:

*I have been recommended to you by my lawyers, but indeed the matter is so extraordinarily delicate that it is most difficult to discuss. It concerns a friend for whom I am acting. This gentleman married some five years ago a Peruvian lady, the daughter of a Peruvian merchant, whom he had met in connection with the importation of nitrates. The lady was very beautiful, but the fact of her foreign birth and of her alien religion always caused a separation of interests and of feelings between husband and wife, so that after a time his love may have cooled towards her and he may have come to regard their union as a mistake. He felt there were sides of her character which he could never explore or understand. This was the more painful as she was as loving a wife as a man could have—to all appearance absolutely devoted.*

*Now for the point which I will make more plain when we meet. Indeed, this note is merely to give you a general idea of the situation and to ascertain whether you would care to interest yourself in the matter. The lady began to show some curious traits quite alien to her ordinarily sweet and gentle disposition. The gentleman had been married twice and he had one son by the first wife. This boy was now fifteen, a very charming and affectionate youth, though unhappily injured through an accident in child-*

hood. *Twice the wife was caught in the act of assaulting this poor lad in the most unprovoked way. Once she struck him with a stick and left a great weal on his arm.*

*This was a small matter, however, compared with her conduct to her own child, a dear boy just under one year of age. On one occasion about a month ago this child had been left by its nurse for a few minutes. A loud cry from the baby, as of pain, called the nurse back. As she ran into the room she saw her employer, the lady, leaning over the baby and apparently biting his neck. There was a small wound in the neck from which a stream of blood had escaped. The nurse was so horrified that she wished to call the husband, but the lady implored her not to do so and actually gave her five pounds as a price for her silence. No explanation was ever given, and for the moment the matter was passed over.*

*It left, however, a terrible impression upon the nurse's mind, and from that time she began to watch her mistress closely and to keep a closer guard upon the baby, whom she tenderly loved. It seemed to her that even as she watched the mother, so the mother watched her, and that every time she was compelled to leave the baby alone the mother was waiting to get at it. Day and night the nurse covered the child, and day and night the silent, watchful mother seemed to be lying in wait as a wolf waits for a lamb. It must read most incredible to you, and yet I beg you to take it seriously, for a child's life and a man's sanity may depend upon it.*

*At last there came one dreadful day when the facts could no longer be concealed from the husband. The nurse's nerve had given way; she could stand the strain no longer, and she made a clean breast of it all to the man. To him it seemed as wild a tale as it may now seem to you. He knew his wife to be a loving wife, and, save for the assaults upon her stepson, a loving mother. Why, then, should she wound her own dear little baby? He told the nurse that she was dreaming, that her suspicions were those of a lunatic, and that such libels upon her mistress*

*were not to be tolerated. While they were talking a sudden cry of pain was heard. Nurse and master rushed together to the nursery. Imagine his feelings, Mr. Holmes, as he saw his wife rise from a kneeling position beside the cot and saw blood upon the child's exposed neck and upon the sheet. With a cry of horror, he turned his wife's face to the light and saw blood all round her lips. It was she—she beyond all question—who had drunk the poor baby's blood.*

*So the matter stands. She is now confined to her room. There has been no explanation. The husband is half demented. He knows, and I know, little of vampirism beyond the name. We had thought it was some wild tale of foreign parts. And yet here in the very heart of the English Sussex—well, all this can be discussed with you in the morning. Will you see me? Will you use your great powers in aiding a distracted man? If so, kindly wire to Ferguson, Cheeseman's, Lamberley, and I will be at your rooms by ten o'clock.*

Yours faithfully,
Robert Ferguson

*P. S. I believe your friend Watson played Rugby for Blackheath when I was three-quarter for Richmond. It is the only personal introduction which I can give.*

"Of course I remembered him," said I as I laid down the letter. "Big Bob Ferguson, the finest three-quarter Richmond ever had. He was always a good-natured chap. It's like him to be so concerned over a friend's case."

Holmes looked at me thoughtfully and shook his head.

"I never get your limits, Watson," said he. "There are unexplored possibilities about you. Take a wire down, like a good fellow. 'Will examine your case with pleasure.'"

"*Your* case!"

"We must not let him think that this Agency is weak-minded. Of course it is his case. Send him that wire and let the matter rest till morning."

Promptly at ten o'clock next morning Ferguson strode into our room. I had remembered him as a long, slab-sided man with loose limbs and a fine turn of speed which had carried him round many an opposing back. There is surely nothing in life more painful than to meet the wreck of a fine athlete whom one has known in his prime. His great frame had fallen in, his flaxen hair was scanty, and his shoulders were bowed. I fear that I roused corresponding emotions in him.

"Hullo, Watson," said he, and his voice was still deep and hearty. "You don't look quite the man you did when I threw you over the ropes into the crowd at the Old Deer Park. I expect I have changed a bit also. But it's this last day or two that has aged me. I see by your telegram, Mr. Holmes, that it is no use my pretending to be anyone's deputy."

"It is simpler to deal direct," said Holmes.

"Of course it is. But you can imagine how difficult it is when you are speaking of the one woman whom you are bound to protect and help. What can I do? How am I to go to the police with such a story? And yet the kiddies have got to be protected. Is it madness, Mr. Holmes? Is it something in the blood? Have you any similar case in your experience? For God's sake, give me some advice, for I am at my wit's end."

"Very naturally, Mr. Ferguson. Now sit here and pull yourself together and give me a few clear answers. I can assure you that I am very far from being at my wit's end, and that I am confident we shall find some solution. First of all, tell me what steps you have taken. Is your wife still near the children?"

"We had a dreadful scene. She is a most loving woman, Mr. Holmes. If ever a woman loved a man with all her heart and soul, she loves me. She was cut to the heart that I should have discovered this horrible, this incredible, secret. She would not even speak. She gave no answer to my reproaches, save to gaze at me with a sort of wild, despairing look in her eyes. Then she rushed to her room and locked herself in. Since then she has refused to see me. She has a maid who was with her before her marriage, Dolores by name—a friend rather than a servant. She takes her food to her."

"Then the child is in no immediate danger?"

"Mrs. Mason, the nurse, has sworn that she will not leave it night or day. I can absolutely trust her. I am more uneasy about poor little Jack, for, as I told you in my note, he has twice been assaulted by her."

"But never wounded?"

"No, she struck him savagely. It is the more terrible as he is a poor little inoffensive cripple." Ferguson's gaunt features softened as he spoke of his boy. "You would think that the dear lad's condition would soften anyone's heart. A fall in childhood and a twisted spine, Mr. Holmes. But the dearest, most loving heart within."

Holmes had picked up the letter of yesterday and was reading it over. "What other inmates are there in your house, Mr. Ferguson?"

"Two servants who have not been long with us. One stable-hand, Michael, who sleeps in the house. My wife, myself, my boy Jack, baby, Dolores, and Mrs. Mason. That is all."

"I gather that you did not know your wife well at the time of your marriage?"

"I had only known her a few weeks."

"How long had this maid Dolores been with her?"

"Some years."

"Then your wife's character would really be better known by Dolores than by you?"

"Yes, you may say so."

Holmes made a note.

"I fancy," said he, "that I may be of more use at Lamberley than here. It is eminently a case for personal investigation. If the lady remains in her room, our presence could not annoy or inconvenience her. Of course, we would stay at the inn."

Ferguson gave a gesture of relief.

"It is what I hoped, Mr. Holmes. There is an excellent train at two from Victoria if you could come."

"Of course we could come. There is a lull at present. I can give you my undivided energies. Watson, of course, comes with us. But there are one or two points upon which I wish to be very sure before I start. This unhappy lady, as I understand it, has appeared to assault both the children, her own baby and your little son?"

"That is so."

"But the assaults take different forms, do they not? She has beaten your son."

"Once with a stick and once very savagely with her hands."

"Did she give no explanation why she struck him?"

"None save that she hated him. Again and again she said so."

"Well, that is not unknown among stepmothers. A posthumous jealousy, we will say. Is the lady jealous by nature?"

"Yes, she is very jealous—jealous with all the strength of her fiery tropical love."

"But the boy—he is fifteen, I understand, and probably very developed in mind, since his body has been circumscribed in action. Did he give you no explanation of these assaults?"

"No, he declared there was no reason."

"Were they good friends at other times?"

"No, there was never any love between them."

"Yet you say he is affectionate?"

"Never in the world could there be so devoted a son. My life is his life. He is absorbed in what I say or do."

Once again Holmes made a note. For some time he sat lost in thought.

"No doubt you and the boy were great comrades before this second marriage. You were thrown very close together, were you not?"

"Very much so."

"And the boy, having so affectionate a nature, was devoted, no doubt, to the memory of his mother?"

"Most devoted."

"He would certainly seem to be a most interesting lad. There is one other point about these assaults. Were the strange attacks upon the baby and the assaults upon your son at the same period?"

"In the first case it was so. It was as if some frenzy had seized her, and she had vented her rage upon both. In the second case it was only Jack who

suffered. Mrs. Mason had no complaint to make about the baby."

"That certainly complicates matters."

"I don't quite follow you, Mr. Holmes."

"Possibly not. One forms provisional theories and waits for time or fuller knowledge to explode them. A bad habit, Mr. Ferguson, but human nature is weak. I fear that your old friend here has given an exaggerated view of my scientific methods. However, I will only say at the present stage that your problem does not appear to me to be insoluble, and that you may expect to find us at Victoria at two o'clock."

It was evening of a dull, foggy November day when, having left our bags at the Chequers, Lamberley, we drove through the Sussex clay of a long winding lane and finally reached the isolated and ancient farmhouse in which Ferguson dwelt. It was a large, straggling building, very old in the centre, very new at the wings with towering Tudor chimneys and a lichen-spotted, high-pitched roof of Horsham slabs. The doorsteps were worn into curves, and the ancient tiles which lined the porch were marked with the rebus of a cheese and a man after the original builder. Within, the ceilings were corrugated with heavy oaken beams, and the uneven floors sagged into sharp curves. An odour of age and decay pervaded the whole crumbling building.

There was one very large central room into which Ferguson led us. Here, in a huge old-fashioned fireplace with an iron screen behind it dated 1670, there blazed and spluttered a splendid log fire.

The room, as I gazed round, was a most singular mixture of dates and of places. The half-panelled walls may well have belonged to the original yeoman farmer of the seventeenth century. They were ornamented, however, on the lower part by a line of well-chosen modern watercolours; while above, where yellow plaster took the place of oak, there was hung a fine collection of South American utensils and weapons, which had been brought, no doubt, by the Peruvian lady upstairs. Holmes rose, with that quick curiosity which sprang from his eager mind, and examined them with some care. He returned with his eyes full of thought.

"Hullo!" he cried. "Hullo!"

A spaniel had lain in a basket in the corner. It came slowly forward towards its master, walking with difficulty. Its hind legs moved irregularly and its tail was on the ground. It licked Ferguson's hand.

"What is it, Mr. Holmes?"

"The dog. What's the matter with it?"

"That's what puzzled the vet. A sort of paralysis. Spinal meningitis, he thought. But it is passing. He'll be all right soon—won't you, Carlo?"

A shiver of assent passed through the drooping tail. The dog's mournful eyes passed from one of us to the other. He knew that we were discussing his case.

"Did it come on suddenly?"

"In a single night."

"How long ago?"

"It may have been four months ago."

"Very remarkable. Very suggestive."

"What do you see in it, Mr. Holmes?"

"A confirmation of what I had already thought."

"For God's sake, what *do* you think, Mr. Holmes? It may be a mere intellectual puzzle to you, but it is life and death to me! My wife a would-be murderer—my child in constant danger! Don't play with me, Mr. Holmes. It is too terribly serious."

The big Rugby three-quarter was trembling all over. Holmes put his hand soothingly upon his arm.

"I fear that there is pain for you, Mr. Ferguson, whatever the solution may be," said he. "I would spare you all I can. I cannot say more for the instant, but before I leave this house I hope I may have something definite."

"Please God you may! If you will excuse me, gentlemen, I will go up to my wife's room and see if there has been any change."

He was away some minutes, during which Holmes resumed his examination of the curiosities upon the wall. When our host returned it was clear from his downcast face that he had made no progress. He brought with him a tall, slim, brown-faced girl.

"The tea is ready, Dolores," said Ferguson. "See that your mistress has everything she can wish."

"She verra ill," cried the girl, looking with indignant eyes at her master. "She no ask for food. She verra ill. She need doctor. I frightened stay alone with her without doctor."

Ferguson looked at me with a question in his eyes.

"I should be so glad if I could be of use."

"Would your mistress see Dr. Watson?"

"I take him. I no ask leave. She needs doctor."

"Then I'll come with you at once."

I followed the girl, who was quivering with strong emotion, up the staircase and down an ancient corridor. At the end was an iron-clamped and massive door. It struck me as I looked at it that if Ferguson tried to force his way to his wife he would find it no easy matter. The girl drew a key from her pocket, and the heavy oaken planks creaked upon their old hinges. I passed in and she swiftly followed, fastening the door behind her.

On the bed a woman was lying who was clearly in a high fever. She was only half conscious, but as I entered she raised a pair of frightened but beautiful eyes and glared at me in apprehension. Seeing a stranger, she appeared to be relieved and sank back with a sigh upon the pillow. I stepped up to her with a few reassuring words, and she lay still while I took her pulse and temperature. Both were high, and yet my impression was that the condition was rather that of mental and nervous excitement than of any actual seizure.

"She lie like that one day, two day. I 'fraid she die," said the girl.

The woman turned her flushed and handsome face towards me.

"Where is my husband?"

"He is below and would wish to see you."

"I will not see him. I will not see him." Then she seemed to wander off into delirium. "A fiend! A fiend! Oh, what shall I do with this devil?"

"Can I help you in any way?"

"No. No one can help. It is finished. All is destroyed. Do what I will, all is destroyed."

The woman must have some strange delusion. I could not see honest Bob Ferguson in the character of fiend or devil.

"Madame," I said, "your husband loves you dearly. He is deeply grieved at this happening."

Again she turned on me those glorious eyes.

"He loves me. Yes. But do I not love him? Do I not love him even to sacrifice myself rather than break his dear heart? That is how I love him. And yet he could think of me—he could speak to me so."

"He is full of grief, but he cannot understand."

"No, he cannot understand. But he should trust."

"Will you not see him?" I suggested.

"No, no, I cannot forget those terrible words nor the look upon his face. I will not see him. Go now. You can do nothing for me. Tell him only one thing. I want my child. I have a right to my child. That is the only message I can send him." She turned her face to the wall and would say no more.

I returned to the room downstairs, where Ferguson and Holmes still sat by the fire. Ferguson listened moodily to my account of the interview.

"How can I send her the child?" he said. "How do I know what strange impulse might come upon her? How can I ever forget how she rose from beside it with its blood upon her lips?" He shuddered at the recollection. "The child is safe with Mrs. Mason, and there he must remain."

A smart maid, the only modern thing which we had seen in the house, had brought in some tea. As she was serving it the door opened and a youth entered the room. He was a remarkable lad, pale-faced and fair-haired, with excitable light blue eyes which blazed into a sudden flame of emotion and joy as they rested upon his father. He rushed forward and threw his arms round his neck with the abandon of a loving girl.

"Oh, daddy," he cried, "I did not know that you were due yet. I should have been here to meet you. Oh, I am so glad to see you!"

Ferguson gently disengaged himself from the embrace with some little show of embarrassment.

"Dear old chap," said he, patting the flaxen head with a very tender hand. "I came early because my friends, Mr. Holmes and Dr. Watson, have been persuaded to come down and spend an evening with us."

"Is that Mr. Holmes, the detective?"

"Yes."

The youth looked at us with a very penetrating and, as it seemed to me, unfriendly gaze.

"What about your other child, Mr. Ferguson?" asked Holmes. "Might we make the acquaintance of the baby?"

"Ask Mrs. Mason to bring baby down," said Ferguson. The boy went off with a curious, shambling gait which told my surgical eyes that he was suffering from a weak spine. Presently he returned, and behind him came a tall, gaunt woman bearing in her arms a very beautiful child, dark-eyed, golden-haired, a wonderful mixture of the Saxon and the Latin. Ferguson was evidently devoted to it, for he took it into his arms and fondled it most tenderly.

"Fancy anyone having the heart to hurt him," he muttered as he glanced down at the small, angry red pucker upon the cherub throat.

It was at this moment that I chanced to glance at Holmes and saw a most singular intentness in his expression. His face was as set as if it had been carved out of old ivory, and his eyes, which had glanced for a moment at father and child, were now fixed with eager curiosity upon something at the other side of the room. Following his gaze I could only guess that he was looking out through the window at the melancholy, dripping garden. It is true that a shutter had half closed outside and obstructed the view, but none the less it was certainly at the window that Holmes was fixing his concentrated attention. Then he smiled, and his eyes came back to the baby. On its chubby neck there was this small puckered mark. Without speaking, Holmes examined it with care. Finally he shook one of the dimpled fists which waved in front of him.

"Good-bye, little man. You have made a strange

start in life. Nurse, I should wish to have a word with you in private."

He took her aside and spoke earnestly for a few minutes. I only heard the last words, which were: "Your anxiety will soon, I hope, be set at rest." The woman, who seemed to be a sour, silent kind of creature, withdrew with the child.

"What is Mrs. Mason like?" asked Holmes.

"Not very prepossessing externally, as you can see, but a heart of gold, and devoted to the child."

"Do you like her, Jack?" Holmes turned suddenly upon the boy. His expressive mobile face shadowed over, and he shook his head.

"Jacky has very strong likes and dislikes," said Ferguson, putting his arm round the boy. "Luckily I am one of his likes."

The boy cooed and nestled his head upon his father's breast. Ferguson gently disengaged him.

"Run away, little Jacky," said he, and he watched his son with loving eyes until he disappeared. "Now, Mr. Holmes," he continued when the boy was gone, "I really feel that I have brought you on a fool's errand, for what can you possibly do save give me your sympathy? It must be an exceedingly delicate and complex affair from your point of view."

"It is certainly delicate," said my friend with an amused smile, "but I have not been struck up to now with its complexity. It has been a case for intellectual deduction, but when this original intellectual deduction is confirmed point by point by quite a number of independent incidents, then the subjective becomes objective and we can say confidently that we have reached our goal. I had, in fact, reached it before we left Baker Street, and the rest has merely been observation and confirmation."

Ferguson put his big hand to his furrowed forehead.

"For heaven's sake, Holmes," he said hoarsely, "if you can see the truth in this matter, do not keep me in suspense. How do I stand? What shall I do? I care nothing as to how you have found your facts so long as you have really got them."

"Certainly I owe you an explanation, and you shall have it. But you will permit me to handle the matter in my own way? Is the lady capable of seeing us, Watson?"

"She is ill, but she is quite rational."

"Very good. It is only in her presence that we can clear the matter up. Let us go up to her."

"She will not see me," cried Ferguson.

"Oh, yes, she will," said Holmes. He scribbled a few lines upon a sheet of paper. "You at least have the entrée, Watson. Will you have the goodness to give the lady this note?"

I ascended again and handed the note to Dolores, who cautiously opened the door. A minute later I heard a cry from within, a cry in which joy and surprise seemed to be blended. Dolores looked out.

"She will see them. She will leesten," said she.

At my summons, Ferguson and Holmes came up. As we entered the room Ferguson took a step or two towards his wife, who had raised herself in the bed, but she held out her hand to repulse him. He sank into an armchair, while Holmes seated himself beside him, after bowing to the lady, who looked at him with wide-eyed amazement.

"I think we can dispense with Dolores," said Holmes. "Oh, very well, madame, if you would rather she stayed I can see no objection. Now, Mr. Ferguson, I am a busy man with many calls, and my methods have to be short and direct. The swiftest surgery is the least painful. Let me first say what will ease your mind. Your wife is a very good, a very loving, and a very ill-used woman."

Ferguson sat up with a cry of joy.

"Prove that, Mr. Holmes, and I am your debtor forever."

"I will do so, but in doing so I must wound you deeply in another direction."

"I care nothing so long as you clear my wife. Everything on earth is insignificant compared to that."

"Let me tell you, then, the train of reasoning which passed through my mind in Baker Street. The idea of a vampire was to me absurd. Such things do not happen in criminal practice in England. And yet your observation was precise. You had seen the lady rise from beside the child's cot with the blood upon her lips."

"I did."

"Did it not occur to you that a bleeding wound may be sucked for some other purpose than to draw the blood from it? Was there not a queen in English history who sucked such a wound to draw poison from it?"

"Poison!"

"A South American household. My instinct felt the presence of those weapons upon the wall before my eyes ever saw them. It might have been other poison, but that was what occurred to me. When I saw that little empty quiver beside the small bird-bow, it was just what I expected to see. If the child were pricked with one of those arrows dipped in curare or some other devilish drug, it would mean death if the venom were not sucked out.

"And the dog! If one were to use such a poison, would one not try it first in order to see that it had not lost its power? I did not foresee the dog, but at least I understand him and he fitted into my reconstruction.

"Now do you understand? Your wife feared such an attack. She saw it made and saved the child's life, and yet she shrank from telling you all the truth, for she knew how you loved the boy and feared lest it break your heart."

"Jacky!"

"I watched him as you fondled the child just now. His face was clearly reflected in the glass of the window where the shutter formed a background. I saw such jealousy, such cruel hatred, as I have seldom seen in a human face."

"My Jacky!"

"You have to face it, Mr. Ferguson. It is the more painful because it is a distorted love, a maniacal exaggerated love for you, and possibly for his dead mother, which has prompted his action. His very soul is consumed with hatred for this splendid child, whose health and beauty are a contrast to his own weakness."

"Good God! It is incredible!"

"Have I spoken the truth, madame?"

The lady was sobbing, with her face buried in the pillows. Now she turned to her husband.

"How could I tell you, Bob? I felt the blow it would be to you. It was better that I should wait and that it should come from some other lips than mine. When this gentleman, who seems to have powers of magic, wrote that he knew all, I was glad."

"I think a year at sea would be my prescription for Master Jacky," said Holmes, rising from his chair. "Only one thing is still clouded, madame. We can quite understand your attacks upon Master Jacky. There is a limit to a mother's patience. But how did you dare to leave the child these last two days?"

"I had told Mrs. Mason. She knew."

"Exactly. So I imagined."

Ferguson was standing by the bed, choking, his hands outstretched and quivering.

"This, I fancy, is the time for our exit, Watson," said Holmes in a whisper. "If you will take one elbow of the too faithful Dolores, I will take the other. There, now," he added as he closed the door behind him, "I think we may leave them to settle the rest among themselves."

I have only one further note of this case. It is the letter which Holmes wrote in final answer to that with which the narrative begins. It ran thus:

*Baker Street*
*Nov. 21st*
*Re Vampires*
*Sir:*

   *Referring to your letter of the 19th, I beg to state that I have looked into the inquiry of your client, Mr. Robert Ferguson, of Ferguson and Muirhead, tea brokers, of Mincing Lane, and that the matter has been brought to a satisfactory conclusion. With thanks for your recommendation, I am, sir,*

FAITHFULLY YOURS,
SHERLOCK HOLMES

## A DEAD FINGER

# Sabine Baring-Gould

Sabine Baring-Gould (1834–1924) was the son of a squire and the grandson of an admiral in North Devon, inheriting an estate of three thousand acres. After graduating with a B.A. and an M.A. from Clarke College, Cambridge University, he became curate in his mill town and fell in love with a beautiful sixteen-year-old mill hand. He paid for her education and married her in 1868; they had fifteen children. This transformation of the uneducated young girl served as the inspiration for George Bernard Shaw's play *Pygmalion* and the subsequent musical based on it, *My Fair Lady*.

While his somewhat stodgy and pious novels are no longer read today, his reputation could comfortably stand the test of time because of his contribution to collecting and preserving English folksongs and as the writer of such hymns as the justly famous "Onward, Christian Soldiers" and "Now the Day Is Done."

Perhaps strangely for a man of the cloth and author of religious works, he also produced scholarly works about fantastical medieval myths and lore, such as *The Book of Were-Wolves* and *Curious Myths of the Middle Ages*, leading to the authoring of several enduring works of horror and supernatural fiction.

"A Dead Finger" was first published in book form in *A Book of Ghosts* (London: Methuen, 1904).

# A Dead Finger

## SABINE BARING-GOULD

### I

Why the National Gallery should not attract so many visitors as, say, the British Museum, I cannot explain. The latter does not contain much that, one would suppose, appeals to the interest of the ordinary sightseer. What knows such of prehistoric flints and scratched bones? Of Assyrian sculpture? Of Egyptian hieroglyphics? The Greek and Roman statuary is cold and dead. The paintings in the National Gallery glow with colour, and are instinct with life. Yet, somehow, a few listless wanderers saunter yawning through the National Gallery, whereas swarms pour through the halls of the British Museum, and talk and pass remarks about the objects there exposed, of the date and meaning of which they have not the faintest conception.

I was thinking of this problem, and endeavouring to unravel it, one morning whilst sitting in the room for English masters at the great collection in Trafalgar Square. At the same time another thought forced itself upon me. I had been through the rooms devoted to foreign schools, and had then come into that given over to Reynolds, Morland, Gainsborough, Constable, and Hogarth. The morning had been for a while propitious, but towards noon a dense umber-tinted fog had come on, making it all but impossible to see the pictures, and quite impossible to do them justice. I was tired, and so seated myself on one of the chairs, and fell into the consideration first of all of—why the National Gallery is not as popular as it should be; and secondly, how it was that the British School had no beginnings, like those of Italy and the Netherlands. We can see the art of the painter from its first initiation in the Italian peninsula, and among the Flemings. It starts on its progress like a child, and we can trace every stage of its growth. Not so with English art. It springs to life in full and splendid maturity. Who were there before Reynolds and Gainsborough and Hogarth? The great names of those portrait and subject painters who have left their canvases upon the walls of our country houses were those of foreigners—Holbein, Kneller, Van Dyck, and Lely for portraits, and Monnoyer for flower and fruit pieces. Landscapes, figure subjects were all importations, none home-grown. How came that about? Was there no limner that was native? Was it that fashion trampled on home-grown pictorial beginnings as it flouted and spurned native music?

714

Here was food for contemplation. Dreaming in the brown fog, looking through it without seeing its beauties, at Hogarth's painting of Lavinia Fenton as Polly Peachum, without wondering how so indifferent a beauty could have captivated the Duke of Bolton and held him for thirty years, I was recalled to myself and my surroundings by the strange conduct of a lady who had seated herself on a chair near me, also discouraged by the fog, and awaiting its dispersion.

I had not noticed her particularly. At the present moment I do not remember particularly what she was like. So far as I can recollect she was middle-aged, and was quietly yet well dressed. It was not her face nor her dress that attracted my attention and disturbed the current of my thoughts; the effect I speak of was produced by her strange movements and behaviour.

She had been sitting listless, probably thinking of nothing at all, or nothing in particular, when, in turning her eyes round, and finding that she could see nothing of the paintings, she began to study me. This did concern me greatly. A cat may look at the king; but to be contemplated by a lady is a compliment sufficient to please any gentleman. It was not gratified vanity that troubled my thoughts, but the consciousness that my appearance produced—first of all a startled surprise, then undisguised alarm, and, finally, indescribable horror.

Now a man can sit quietly leaning on the head of his umbrella, and glow internally, warmed and illumined by the consciousness that he is being surveyed with admiration by a lovely woman, even when he is middle-aged and not fashionably dressed; but no man can maintain his composure when he discovers himself to be an object of aversion and terror.

What was it? I passed my hand over my chin and upper lip, thinking it not impossible that I might have forgotten to shave that morning, and in my confusion not considering that the fog would prevent the lady from discovering neglect in this particular, had it occurred, which it had not. I am a little careless, perhaps, about shaving when in the country; but when in town, never.

The next idea that occurred to me was—a smut. Had a London black, curdled in that dense pea-soup atmosphere, descended on my nose and blackened it? I hastily drew my silk handkerchief from my pocket, moistened it, and passed to my nose, and then each cheek. I then turned my eyes into the corners and looked at the lady, to see whether by this means I had got rid of what was objectionable in my personal appearance.

Then I saw that her eyes, dilated with horror, were riveted, not on my face, but on my leg.

My leg! What on earth could that harmless member have in it so terrifying? The morning had been dull; there had been rain in the night, and I admit that on leaving my hotel I had turned up the bottoms of my trousers. That is a proceeding not so uncommon, not so outrageous as to account for the stony stare of this woman's eyes.

If that were all I would turn my trousers down.

Then I saw her shrink from the chair on which she sat to one further removed from me, but still with her eyes fixed on my leg—about the level of my knee. She had let fall her umbrella, and was grasping the seat of her chair with both hands, as she backed from me.

I need hardly say that I was greatly disturbed in mind and feelings, and forgot all about the origin of the English schools of painters, and the question why the British Museum is more popular than the National Gallery.

Thinking that I might have been spattered by a hansom whilst crossing Oxford Street, I passed my hand down my side hastily, with a sense of annoyance, and all at once touched something, cold, clammy, that sent a thrill to my heart, and made me start and take a step forward. At the same moment, the lady, with a cry of horror, sprang to her feet, and with raised hands fled from the room, leaving her umbrella where it had fallen.

There were other visitors to the Picture Gallery besides ourselves, who had been passing through the saloon, and they turned at her cry, and looked in surprise after her.

The policeman stationed in the room came to me and asked what had happened. I was in such agitation that I hardly knew what to answer. I told him that I could explain what had occurred little better than himself. I had noticed that the lady had worn an odd expression, and had behaved in most extraordinary fashion, and that he had best take charge of her umbrella, and wait for her return to claim it.

This questioning by the official was vexing, as it prevented me from at once and on the spot investigating the cause of her alarm and mine—hers at something she must have seen on my leg, and mine at something I had distinctly felt creeping up my leg.

The numbing and sickening effect on me of the touch of the object I had not seen was not to be shaken off at once. Indeed, I felt as though my hand were contaminated, and that I could have no rest till I had thoroughly washed the hand, and, if possible, washed away the feeling that had been produced.

I looked on the floor, I examined my leg, but saw nothing. As I wore my overcoat, it was probable that in rising from my seat the skirt had fallen over my trousers and hidden the thing, whatever it was. I therefore hastily removed my overcoat and shook it, then I looked at my trousers. There was nothing whatever on my leg, and nothing fell from my overcoat when shaken.

Accordingly I reinvested myself, and hastily left the Gallery; then took my way as speedily as I could, without actually running, to Charing Cross Station and down the narrow way leading to the Metropolitan, where I went into Faulkner's bath and hairdressing establishment, and asked for hot water to thoroughly wash my hand and well soap it. I bathed my hand in water as hot as I could endure it, employed carbolic soap, and then, after having a good brush down, especially on my left side where my hand had encountered the object that had so affected me, I left. I had entertained the intention of going to the Princess's Theatre that evening, and of securing a ticket in the morning; but all thought of theatre-going was gone from me. I could not free my heart from the sense of nausea and cold that had been produced by the touch. I went into Gatti's to have lunch, and ordered something, I forget what, but, when served,

I found that my appetite was gone. I could eat nothing; the food inspired me with disgust. I thrust it from me untasted, and, after drinking a couple of glasses of claret, left the restaurant, and returned to my hotel.

Feeling sick and faint, I threw my overcoat over the sofa-back, and cast myself on my bed.

I do not know that there was any particular reason for my doing so, but as I lay my eyes were on my great-coat.

The density of the fog had passed away, and there was light again, not of first quality, but sufficient for a Londoner to swear by, so that I could see everything in my room, though through a veil, darkly.

I do not think my mind was occupied in any way. About the only occasions on which, to my knowledge, my mind is actually passive or inert is when crossing the Channel in *The Foam* from Dover to Calais, when I am always, in every weather, abjectly seasick—and thoughtless. But as I now lay on my bed, uncomfortable, squeamish, without knowing why—I was in the same inactive mental condition. But not for long.

I saw something that startled me.

First, it appeared to me as if the lappet of my overcoat pocket were in movement, being raised. I did not pay much attention to this, as I supposed that the garment was sliding down on to the seat of the sofa, from the back, and that this displacement of gravity caused the movement I observed. But this I soon saw was not the case. That which moved the lappet was something in the pocket that was struggling to get out. I could see now that it was working its way up the inside, and that when it reached the opening it lost balance and fell down again. I could make this out by the projections and indentations in the cloth; these moved as the creature, or whatever it was, worked its way up the lining.

"A mouse," I said, and forgot my seediness; I was interested. "The little rascal! However did he contrive to seat himself in my pocket? And I have worn that overcoat all the morning!" But no—it was not a mouse. I saw something white poke its way out from under the lappet; and in another moment an object was revealed that, though revealed, I could not understand, nor could I distinguish what it was.

Now roused by curiosity, I raised myself on my elbow. In doing this I made some noise, the bed creaked. Instantly the something dropped on the floor, lay outstretched for a moment, to recover itself, and then began, with the motions of a maggot, to run along the floor.

There is a caterpillar called "The Measurer," because, when it advances, it draws its tail up to where its head is and then throws forward its full length, and again draws up its extremity, forming at each time a loop, and with each step measuring its total length. The object I now saw on the floor was advancing precisely like the measuring caterpillar. It had the colour of a cheese-maggot, and in length was about three and a half inches. It was not, however, like a caterpillar, which is flexible throughout its entire length, but this was, as it seemed to me, jointed in two places, one joint being more conspicuous than the other. For some moments I was so completely paralysed by astonishment that I remained motionless, looking at the thing as it crawled along the carpet—a dull green carpet with darker green, almost black, flowers in it.

It had, as it seemed to me, a glossy head, distinctly marked; but, as the light was not brilliant, I could not make out very clearly, and, moreover, the rapid movements prevented close scrutiny.

Presently, with a shock still more startling than that produced by its apparition at the opening of the pocket of my great-coat, I became convinced that what I saw was a finger, a human forefinger, and that the glossy head was no other than the nail.

The finger did not seem to have been amputated. There was no sign of blood or laceration where the knuckle should be, but the extremity of the finger, or root rather, faded away to indistinctness, and I was unable to make out the root of the finger.

I could see no hand, no body behind this finger, nothing whatever except a finger that had little token of warm life in it, no coloration as though blood circulated in it; and this finger was in active

motion creeping along the carpet towards a wardrobe that stood against the wall by the fireplace.

I sprang off the bed and pursued it.

Evidently the finger was alarmed, for it redoubled its pace, reached the wardrobe, and went under it. By the time I had arrived at the article of furniture it had disappeared. I lit a vesta match and held it beneath the wardrobe, that was raised above the carpet by about two inches, on turned feet, but I could see nothing more of the finger.

I got my umbrella and thrust it beneath, and raked forwards and backwards, right and left, and raked out flue, and nothing more solid.

## II

I packed my portmanteau next day and returned to my home in the country. All desire for amusement in town was gone, and the faculty to transact business had departed as well.

A languor and qualms had come over me, and my head was in a maze. I was unable to fix my thoughts on anything. At times I was disposed to believe that my wits were deserting me, at others that I was on the verge of a severe illness. Anyhow, whether likely to go off my head or not, or take to my bed, home was the only place for me, and homeward I sped, accordingly. On reaching my country habitation, my servant, as usual, took my portmanteau to my bedroom, unstrapped it, but did not unpack it. I object to his throwing out the contents of my Gladstone bag; not that there is anything in it he may not see, but that he puts my things where I cannot find them again. My clothes—he is welcome to place them where he likes and where they belong, and this latter he knows better than I do; but, then, I carry about with me other things than a dress suit, and changes of linen and flannel. There are letters, papers, books—and the proper destinations of these are known only to myself. A servant has a singular and evil knack of putting away literary matter and odd volumes in such places that it takes the owner half a day to find them again. Although I was uncomfortable, and my head in a whirl, I opened and unpacked my own portmanteau. As I was thus engaged I saw something curled up in my collar-box, the lid of which had got broken in by a boot-heel impinging on it. I had pulled off the damaged cover to see if my collars had been spoiled, when something curled up inside suddenly rose on end and leapt, just like a cheese-jumper, out of the box, over the edge of the Gladstone bag, and scurried away across the floor in a manner already familiar to me.

I could not doubt for a moment what it was—here was the finger again. It had come with me from London to the country.

Whither it went in its run over the floor I do not know, I was too bewildered to observe.

Somewhat later, towards evening, I seated myself in my easy-chair, took up a book, and tried to read. I was tired with the journey, with the knocking about in town, and the discomfort and alarm produced by the apparition of the finger. I felt worn out. I was unable to give my attention to what I read, and before I was aware was asleep. Roused for an instant by the fall of the book from my hands, I speedily relapsed into unconsciousness. I am not sure that a doze in an armchair ever does good. It usually leaves me in a semi-stupid condition and with a headache. Five minutes in a horizontal position on my bed is worth thirty in a chair. That is my experience. In sleeping in a sedentary position the head is a difficulty; it drops forward or lolls on one side or the other, and has to be brought back into a position in which the line to the centre of gravity runs through the trunk, otherwise the head carries the body over in a sort of general capsize out of the chair on to the floor.

I slept, on the occasion of which I am speaking, pretty healthily, because deadly weary; but I was brought to waking, not by my head falling over the arm of the chair, and my trunk tumbling after it, but by a feeling of cold extending from my throat to my heart. When I awoke I was in a diagonal position, with my right ear resting on my right shoulder, and exposing the left side of my throat, and it was here—where the jugular vein throbs—that I felt the greatest intensity of cold. At once I shrugged my left shoulder, rubbing my neck with

the collar of my coat in so doing. Immediately something fell off, upon the floor, and I again saw the finger.

My disgust—horror, were intensified when I perceived that it was dragging something after it, which might have been an old stocking, and which I took at first glance for something of the sort.

The evening sun shone in through my window, in a brilliant golden ray that lighted the object as it scrambled along. With this illumination I was able to distinguish what the object was. It is not easy to describe it, but I will make the attempt.

The finger I saw was solid and material; what it drew after it was neither, or was in a nebulous, protoplasmic condition. The finger was attached to a hand that was curdling into matter and in process of acquiring solidity; attached to the hand was an arm in a very filmy condition, and this arm belonged to a human body in a still more vaporous, immaterial condition. This was being dragged along the floor by the finger, just as a silkworm might pull after it the tangle of its web. I could see legs and arms, and head, and coat-tail tumbling about and interlacing and disentangling again in a promiscuous manner. There were no bone, no muscle, no substance in the figure; the members were attached to the trunk, which was spineless, but they had evidently no functions, and were wholly dependent on the finger which pulled them along in a jumble of parts as it advanced.

In such confusion did the whole vaporous matter seem, that I think—I cannot say for certain it was so, but the impression left on my mind was—that one of the eyeballs was looking out at a nostril, and the tongue lolling out of one of the ears.

It was, however, only for a moment that I saw this germ-body; I cannot call by another name that which had not more substance than smoke. I saw it only so long as it was being dragged athwart the ray of sunlight. The moment it was pulled jerkily out of the beam into the shadow beyond, I could see nothing of it, only the crawling finger.

I had not sufficient moral energy or physical force in me to rise, pursue, and stamp on the finger, and grind it with my heel into the floor. Both seemed drained out of me. What became of the finger, whither it went, how it managed to secrete itself, I do not know. I had lost the power to inquire. I sat in my chair, chilled, staring before me into space.

"Please, sir," a voice said, "there's Mr. Square below, electrical engineer."

"Eh?" I looked dreamily round.

My valet was at the door.

"Please, sir, the gentleman would be glad to be allowed to go over the house and see that all the electrical apparatus is in order."

"Oh, indeed! Yes—show him up."

## III

I had recently placed the lighting of my house in the hands of an electrical engineer, a very intelligent man, Mr. Square, for whom I had contracted a sincere friendship.

He had built a shed with a dynamo out of sight, and had entrusted the laying of the wires to subordinates, as he had been busy with other orders and could not personally watch every detail. But he was not the man to let anything pass unobserved, and he knew that electricity was not a force to be played with. Bad or careless workmen will often insufficiently protect the wires, or neglect the insertion of the lead which serves as a safety-valve in the event of the current being too strong. Houses may be set on fire, human beings fatally shocked, by the neglect of a bad or slovenly workman.

The apparatus for my mansion was but just completed, and Mr. Square had come to inspect it and make sure that all was right.

He was an enthusiast in the matter of electricity, and saw for it a vast perspective, the limits of which could not be predicted.

"All forces," said he, "are correlated. When you have force in one form, you may just turn it into this or that, as you like. In one form it is motive power, in another it is light, in another heat. Now we have electricity for illumination. We employ it, but not as freely as in the States, for propelling vehicles. Why should we have horses drawing our buses? We should use only electric trams. Why do we burn coal to warm our shins? There is electricity, which throws out no filthy smoke as does coal. Why should we let the tides waste their energies in the Thames? In other estuaries? There we have Nature supplying us— free, gratis, and for nothing—with all the force we want for propelling, for heating, for lighting. I will tell you something more, my dear sir," said Mr. Square. "I have mentioned but three modes of force, and have instanced but a limited number of uses to which electricity may be turned. How is it with photography? Is not electric light becoming an artistic agent? I bet you," said he, "before long it will become a therapeutic agent as well."

"Oh, yes; I have heard of certain impostors with their life-belts."

Mr. Square did not relish this little dig I gave him. He winced, but returned to the charge. "We don't know how to direct it aright, that is all," said he. "I haven't taken the matter up, but others will, I bet; and we shall have electricity used as freely as now we use powders and pills. I don't believe in doctors' stuffs myself. I hold that disease lays hold of a man because he lacks physical force to resist it. Now, is it not obvious that you are beginning at the wrong end when you attack the disease? What you want is to supply force, make up for the lack of physical power, and force is force wherever you find it—here motive, there illuminating, and so on. I don't see why a physician should not utilize the tide rushing out under London Bridge for restoring the feeble vigour of all who are languid and a prey to disorder in the Metropolis. It will come to that, I bet, and that is not all. Force is force, everywhere. Political, moral force, physical force, dynamic force, heat, light, tidal waves, and so on—all are one, all is one. In time we shall know how to galvanize into aptitude and moral energy all the limp and crooked consciences and wills that need taking in hand, and such there always will be in modern civilisation. I don't know how to do it. I don't know how it will be done, but in the future the priest as well as the doctor will turn electricity on as his principal, nay, his only agent. And he can get his force anywhere, out of the running stream, out of the wind, out of the tidal wave.

"I'll give you an instance," continued Mr. Square, chuckling and rubbing his hands, "to show you the great possibilities in electricity, used in a crude fashion. In a certain great city away far west in the States, a go-ahead place, too, more so than New York, they had electric trams all up and down and along the roads to everywhere. The union men working for the company demanded that the non-unionists should be turned off. But the company didn't see it. Instead, it turned off the union men. It had up its sleeve a sufficiency of the others, and filled all places at once. Union men didn't like it, and passed word that at a given hour on a certain day every wire was to be cut. The company knew this by means of its spies, and turned on, ready for them, three times the power into all the wires. At the fixed moment, up the poles went the strikers to cut the cables, and down they came a dozen times quicker than they went up, I bet. Then there came wires to the hospitals from all quarters for stretchers to carry off the disabled men, some with broken legs, arms, ribs; two or three had their necks broken. I reckon the company was wonderfully merciful—it didn't put on sufficient force to make cinders of them then and there; possibly opinion might not have liked it. Stopped the strike, did that. Great moral effect—all done by electricity."

In this manner Mr. Square was wont to rattle on. He interested me, and I came to think that there might be something in what he said—that his suggestions were not mere nonsense. I was glad to see Mr. Square enter my room, shown in by my man. I did not rise from my chair to shake his hand, for I had not sufficient energy to do so. In a languid tone I welcomed him and signed to him to take a seat. Mr. Square looked at me with some surprise.

"Why, what's the matter?" he said. "You seem unwell. Not got the 'flu, have you?"

"I beg your pardon?"

"The influenza. Every third person is crying out that he has it, and the sale of eucalyptus is enor-mous, not that eucalyptus is any good. Influenza microbes indeed! What care they for eucalyptus? You've gone down some steps of the ladder of life since I saw you last, squire. How do you account for that?"

I hesitated about mentioning the extraordinary circumstances that had occurred; but Square was a man who would not allow any beating about the bush. He was downright and straight, and in ten minutes had got the entire story out of me.

"Rather boisterous for your nerves that—a crawling finger," said he. "It's a queer story taken on end."

Then he was silent, considering.

After a few minutes he rose, and said: "I'll go and look at the fittings, and then I'll turn this little matter of yours over again, and see if I can't knock the bottom out of it, I'm kinder fond of these sort of things."

Mr. Square was not a Yankee, but he had lived for some time in America, and affected to speak like an American. He used expressions, terms of speech common in the States, but had none of the Transatlantic twang. He was a man absolutely without affectation in every other particular; this was his sole weakness, and it was harmless.

The man was so thorough in all he did that I did not expect his return immediately. He was certain to examine every portion of the dynamo engine, and all the connections and burners. This would necessarily engage him for some hours. As the day was nearly done, I knew he could not accomplish what he wanted that evening, and accordingly gave orders that a room should be prepared for him. Then, as my head was full of pain, and my skin was burning, I told my servant to apologize for my absence from dinner, and tell Mr. Square that I was really forced to return to my bed by sickness, and that I believed I was about to be prostrated by an attack of influenza.

The valet—a worthy fellow, who has been with me for six years—was concerned at my appearance, and urged me to allow him to send for a doctor. I had no confidence in the local practitioner, and if I sent for another from the nearest town I should offend him, and a row would perhaps ensue, so I declined. If I were really in for an influenza attack, I knew about as much as any doctor how to deal with it. Quinine, quinine—that was all. I bade my man light a small lamp, lower it, so as to give sufficient illumination to enable me to find some lime-juice at my bed head, and my pocket-handkerchief, and to be able to read my watch. When he had done this, I bade him leave me.

I lay in bed, burning, racked with pain in my head, and with my eyeballs on fire.

Whether I fell asleep or went off my head for a while I cannot tell. I may have fainted. I have no recollection of anything after having gone to bed and taken a sip of lime-juice that tasted to me like soap—till I was roused by a sense of pain in my ribs—a slow, gnawing, torturing pain, waxing momentarily more intense. In half-consciousness I was partly dreaming and partly aware of actual suffering. The pain was real; but in my fancy I thought that a great maggot was working its way into my side between my ribs. I seemed to see it. It twisted itself half round, then reverted to its former position, and again twisted itself, moving like a bradawl, not like a gimlet, which latter forms a complete revolution.

This, obviously, must have been a dream, hallucination only, as I was lying on my back and my eyes were directed towards the bottom of the bed, and the coverlet and blankets and sheet intervened between my eyes and my side. But in fever one sees without eyes, and in every direction, and through all obstructions.

Roused thoroughly by an excruciating twinge, I tried to cry out, and succeeded in throwing myself over on my right side, that which was in pain. At once I felt the thing withdrawn that was awling—if I may use the word—in between my ribs.

And now I saw, standing beside the bed, a figure that had its arm under the bedclothes, and was slowly removing it. The hand was leisurely drawn from under the coverings and rested on the eiderdown coverlet, with the forefinger extended.

The figure was that of a man, in shabby clothes, with a sallow, mean face, a retreating forehead, with hair cut after the French fashion, and a moustache, dark. The jaws and chin were covered with a bristly growth, as if shaving had been neglected for a fortnight. The figure did not appear to be thoroughly solid, but to be of the consistency of curd, and the face was of the complexion of curd. As I looked at this object it withdrew, sliding backward in an odd sort of manner, and as though overweighted by the hand, which was the most substantial, indeed the only substantial portion of it. Though the figure retreated stooping, yet it was no longer huddled along by the finger, as if it had no material existence. If the same, it had acquired a consistency and a solidity which it did not possess before.

How it vanished I do not know, nor whither it went. The door opened, and Square came in.

"What!" he exclaimed with cheery voice. "Influenza is it?"

"I don't know—I think it's that finger again."

## IV

"Now, look here," said Square, "I'm not going to have that cuss at its pranks anymore. Tell me all about it."

I was now so exhausted, so feeble, that I was not able to give a connected account of what had taken place, but Square put to me just a few pointed questions and elicited the main facts. He pieced them together in his own orderly mind, so as to form a connected whole. "There is a feature in the case," said he, "that strikes me as remarkable and important. At first—a finger only, then a hand, then a nebulous figure attached to the hand, without backbone, without consistency. Lastly, a complete form, with consistency and with backbone, but the latter in a gelatinous condition, and the entire figure overweighted by the hand, just as hand and figure were previously overweighted by the finger. Simultaneously with this compacting and consolidating of the figure, came your degeneration and loss of vital force and, in a word, of health. What you lose, that object acquires, and what it acquires, it gains by contact with you. That's clear enough, is it not?"

"I dare say. I don't know. I can't think."

"I suppose not; the faculty of thought is drained out of you. Very well, I must think for you, and I will. Force is force, and see if I can't deal with your visitant in such a way as will prove just as truly a moral dissuasive as that employed on the union men on strike in—never mind where it was. That's not to the point."

"Will you kindly give me some lime-juice?" I entreated.

I sipped the acid draught, but without relief. I listened to Square, but without hope. I wanted to be left alone. I was weary of my pain, weary of everything, even of life. It was a matter of indifference to me whether I recovered or slipped out of existence.

"It will be here again shortly," said the engineer. "As the French say, *l'appetit vient en mangeant*. It has been at you thrice; it won't be content without another peck. And if it does get another, I guess it will pretty well about finish you."

Mr. Square rubbed his chin, and then put his hands into his trouser pockets. That also was a trick acquired in the States, an inelegant one. His hands, when not actively occupied, went into his pockets, inevitably they gravitated thither. Ladies did not like Square; they said he was not a gentleman. But it was not that he said or did anything "off colour," only he spoke to them, looked at them, walked with them, always with his hands in his pockets. I have seen a lady turn her back on him deliberately because of this trick.

Standing now with his hands in his pockets, he studied my bed, and said contemptuously: "Old-fashioned and bad, fourposter. Oughtn't to be allowed, I guess; unwholesome all the way round."

I was not in a condition to dispute this. I like a fourposter with curtains at head and feet; not that I ever draw them, but it gives a sense of privacy that is wanting in one of your half-tester beds.

If there is a window at one's feet, one can lie in bed without the glare in one's eyes, and yet without darkening the room by drawing the blinds. There is much to be said for a fourposter, but this is not the place in which to say it.

Mr. Square pulled his hands out of his pockets and began fiddling with the electric point near the head of my bed, attached a wire, swept it in a semicircle along the floor, and then thrust the knob at the end into my hand in the bed.

"Keep your eye open," said he, "and your hand shut and covered. If that finger comes again tickling your ribs, try it with the point. I'll manage the switch, from behind the curtain."

Then he disappeared.

I was too indifferent in my misery to turn my head and observe where he was. I remained inert, with the knob in my hand, and my eyes closed, suffering and thinking of nothing but the shooting pains through my head and the aches in my loins and back and legs.

Some time probably elapsed before I felt the finger again at work at my ribs; it groped, but no longer bored. I now felt the entire hand, not a single finger, and the hand was substantial, cold, and clammy. I was aware, how, I know not, that if the finger-point reached the region of my heart, on the left side, the hand would, so to speak, sit down on it, with the cold palm over it, and that then immediately my heart would cease to beat, and it would be, as Square might express it, "gone coon" with me.

In self-preservation I brought up the knob of the electric wire against the hand—against one of the fingers, I think—and at once was aware of a rapping, squealing noise. I turned my head languidly, and saw the form, now more substantial than before, capering in an ecstasy of pain, endeavouring fruitlessly to withdraw its arm from under the bedclothes, and the hand from the electric point.

At the same moment Square stepped from behind the curtain, with a dry laugh, and said: "I thought we should fix him. He has the coil about him, and can't escape. Now let us drop to particulars. But I shan't let you off till I know all about you."

The last sentence was addressed, not to me, but to the apparition.

Thereupon he bade me take the point away from the hand of the figure—being—whatever it was, but to be ready with it at a moment's notice. He then proceeded to catechize my visitor, who moved restlessly within the circle of wire, but could not escape from it. It replied in a thin, squealing voice that sounded as if it came from a distance, and had a querulous tone in it. I do not pretend to give all that was said. I cannot recollect everything that passed. My memory was affected by my illness, as well as my body. Yet I prefer giving the scraps that I recollect to what Square told me he had heard.

"Yes—I was unsuccessful, always was. Nothing answered with me. The world was against me. Society was. I hate Society. I don't like work neither, never did. But I like agitating against what is established. I hate the Royal Family, the landed interest, the parsons, everything that is, except the people—that is, the unemployed. I always did. I couldn't get work as suited me. When I died they buried me in a cheap coffin, dirt cheap, and gave me a nasty grave, cheap, and a service rattled away cheap, and no monument. Didn't want none. Oh! There are lots of us. All discontented. Discontent! That's a passion, it is—it gets into the veins, it fills the brain, it occupies the heart; it's a sort of divine cancer that takes possession of the entire man, and makes him dissatisfied with everything, and hate everybody. But we must have our share of happiness at some time. We all crave for it in one way or other. Some think there's a future state of blessedness and so have hope, and look to attain to it, for hope is a cable and anchor that attaches to what is real. But when you have no hope of that sort, don't believe in any future state, you must look for happiness in life here. We didn't get it when we were alive, so we seek to procure it after we are dead. We can do it, if we can get out of our cheap and nasty coffins. But not till the greater part of us is mouldered away. If a finger or two remains, that can work its way up to the surface, those cheap deal coffins go to pieces quick enough. Then the only solid part of us left can pull the rest of us that has gone to nothing after it. Then we grope about after the living. The well-to-do if we can get at them—the honest working poor if we can't—we hate them too, because they are content and happy. If we reach any of these, and can touch them, then

we can draw their vital force out of them into ourselves, and recuperate at their expense. That was about what I was going to do with you. Getting on famous. Nearly solidified into a new man; and given another chance in life. But I've missed it this time. Just like my luck. Miss everything. Always have, except misery and disappointment. Get plenty of that."

"What are you all?" asked Square. "Anarchists out of employ?"

"Some of us go by that name, some by other designations, but we are all one, and own allegiance to but one monarch—Sovereign discontent. We are bred to have a distaste for manual work; and we grow up loafers, grumbling at everything and quarrelling with Society that is around us and the Providence that is above us."

"And what do you call yourselves now?"

"Call ourselves? Nothing; we are the same, in another condition, that is all. Folk once called us Anarchists, Nihilists, Socialists, Levellers, now they call us the Influenza. The learned talk of microbes, and bacilli, and bacteria. Microbes, bacilli, and bacteria be blowed! We are the Influenza; we the social failures, the generally discontented, coming up out of our cheap and nasty graves in the form of physical disease. We are the Influenza."

"There you are, I guess!" exclaimed Square triumphantly. "Did I not say that all forces were correlated? If so, then all negations, deficiences of force are one in their several manifestations. Talk of Divine discontent as a force impelling to progress! Rubbish, it is a paralysis of energy. It turns all it absorbs to acid, to envy, spite, gall. It inspires nothing, but rots the whole moral system. Here you have it—moral, social, political discontent in another form, nay aspect—that is all. What Anarchism is in the body Politic, that Influenza is in the body Physical. Do you see that?"

"Ye-e-e-e-s," I believe I answered, and dropped away into the land of dreams.

I recovered. What Square did with the Thing I know not, but believe that he reduced it again to its former negative and self-decomposing condition.

## WAILING WELL

# M. R. James

Arguably the greatest writer of supernatural stories who ever lived, M. R. James had very specific notions of how a story should be constructed, what should be eschewed, and upon what it should focus.

The central character should be a quiet, naive, reclusive, scholarly gentleman (much as James himself was).

No sex. "Sex is tiresome enough in the novels," he wrote. "In a ghost story, or as the backbone of a ghost story, I have no patience with it." James's biographers and contemporaries have commented on the fact that the author's stories may be psychological manifestations of his repressed feelings for some of his students.

Stories should be set in an old, isolated building in a small, ancient town or at the seaside.

A rare book or other ancient artifact, meant to remain undisturbed, will open the door to a supernatural evil, usually manifested from beyond the grave.

The ghost must be malevolent, not amiable or possessed of humor.

Reticence and subtlety are vital, whereas blatancy ruins the horrific effect.

"Wailing Well" was first published in a limited edition of 157 copies under the Mill House Press imprint (Stanford Dingley, 1928), then in *The Collected Ghost Stories of M. R. James* (London: Arnold, 1932).

# Wailing Well

## M. R. JAMES

In the year 19— there were two members of the Troop of Scouts attached to a famous school, named respectively Arthur Wilcox and Stanley Judkins. They were the same age, boarded in the same house, were in the same division, and naturally were members of the same patrol. They were so much alike in appearance as to cause anxiety and trouble, and even irritation, to the masters who came in contact with them. But oh how different were they in their inward man, or boy!

It was to Arthur Wilcox that the Head Master said, looking up with a smile as the boy entered chambers, "Why, Wilcox, there will be a deficit in the prize fund if you stay here much longer! Here, take this handsomely bound copy of the *Life and Works of Bishop Ken*, and with it my hearty congratulations to yourself and your excellent parents." It was Wilcox again, whom the Provost noticed as he passed through the playing fields, and, pausing for a moment, observed to the Vice-Provost, "That lad has a remarkable brow!" "Indeed, yes," said the Vice-Provost. "It denotes either genius or water on the brain."

As a Scout, Wilcox secured every badge and distinction for which he competed. The Cookery Badge, the Map-making Badge, the Life-saving Badge, the Badge for picking up bits of newspaper, the Badge for not slamming the door when leaving the pupil-room, and many others. Of the Life-saving Badge I may have a word to say when we come to treat of Stanley Judkins.

You cannot be surprised to hear that Mr. Hope Jones added a special verse to each of his songs, in commendation of Arthur Wilcox, or that the Lower Master burst into tears when handing him the Good Conduct Medal in its handsome claret-coloured case: the medal which had been unanimously voted to him by the whole of Third Form. Unanimously, did I say? I am wrong. There was one dissentient, Judkins *mi.*, who said that he had excellent reasons for acting as he did. He shared, it seems, a room with his major. You cannot, again, wonder that in after years Arthur Wilcox was the first, and so far the only boy, to become Captain of both the School and of the Oppidans, or that the strain of carrying out the duties of both positions, coupled with the ordinary work of the school, was so severe that a complete rest for six months, followed by a voyage round the world, was pronounced an absolute necessity by the family doctor.

It would be a pleasant task to trace the steps by which he attained the giddy eminence he now occupies; but for the moment enough of Arthur Wilcox. Time presses, and we must turn to a very different matter; the career of Stanley Judkins— Judkins *ma*.

Stanley Judkins, like Arthur Wilcox, attracted the attention of the authorities; but in quite another fashion. It was to him that the Lower Master said, with no cheerful smile, "What, again, Judkins? A very little persistence in this course of conduct, my boy, and you will have cause to regret that you ever entered this academy. There, take that. and that, and think yourself very lucky you don't get that and that!" It was Judkins, again, whom the Provost had cause to notice as he passed through the playing fields, when a cricket ball struck him with considerable force on the ankle, and a voice from a short way off cried, "Thank you, cut-over!" "I think," said the Provost, pausing for a moment to rub his ankle, "that that boy had better fetch his cricket ball for himself!" "Indeed, yes," said the Vice-Provost, "and if he comes within reach, I will do my best to fetch him something else."

As a Scout, Stanley Judkins secured no badge save those which he was able to abstract from members of other patrols. In the cookery competition he was detected trying to introduce squibs into the Dutch oven of the next-door competitors. In the tailoring competition he succeeded in sewing two boys together very firmly, with disastrous effect when they tried to get up. For the Tidiness Badge he was disqualified, because, in the Midsummer schooltime, which chanced to be hot, he could not be dissuaded from sitting with his fingers in the ink: as he said, for coolness' sake. For one piece of paper which he picked up, he must have dropped at least six banana skins or orange peels. Aged women seeing him approaching would beg him with tears in their eyes not to carry their pails of water across the road. They knew too well what the result would inevitably be. But it was in the life-saving competition that Stanley Judkins's conduct was most blameable and had the most farreaching effects. The practice, as you know, was to throw a selected lower boy, of suitable dimen-

sions, fully dressed, with his hands and feet tied together, into the deepest part of Cuckoo Weir, and to time the Scout whose turn it was to rescue him. On every occasion when he was entered for this competition Stanley Judkins was seized, at the critical moment, with a severe fit of cramp, which caused him to roll on the ground and utter alarming cries. This naturally distracted the attention of those present from the boy in the water, and had it not been for the presence of Arthur Wilcox the death-roll would have been a heavy one. As it was, the Lower Master found it necessary to take a firm line and say that the competition must be discontinued. It was in vain that Mr. Beasley Robinson represented to him that in five competitions only four lower boys had actually succumbed. The Lower Master said that he would be the last to interfere in any way with the work of the Scouts; but that three of these boys had been valued members of his choir, and both he and Dr. Ley felt that the inconvenience caused by the losses outweighed the advantages of the competitions. Besides, the correspondence with the parents of these boys had become annoying, and even distressing: they were no longer satisfied with the printed form which he was in the habit of sending out, and more than one of them had actually visited Eton and taken up much of his valuable time with complaints. So the life-saving competition is now a thing of the past.

In short, Stanley Judkins was no credit to the Scouts, and there was talk on more than one occasion of informing him that his services were no longer required. This course was strongly advocated by Mr. Lambart: but in the end milder counsels prevailed, and it was decided to give him another chance.

So it is that we find him at the beginning of the Midsummer Holidays of 19— at the Scouts' camp in the beautiful district of W (or X) in the country of D (or Y).

It was a lovely morning, and Stanley Judkins and one or two of his friends—for he still had friends—lay basking on the top of the down. Stanley was lying on his stomach with his chin propped on his hands, staring into the distance.

"I wonder what that place is," he said.

"Which place?" said one of the others.

"That sort of clump in the middle of the field down there."

"Oh, ah! How should I know what it is?"

"What do you want to know for?" said another.

"I don't know: I like the look of it. What's it called? Nobody got a map?" said Stanley. "Call yourselves Scouts!"

"Here's a map all right," said Wilfred Pipsqueak, ever resourceful, "and there's the place marked on it. But it's inside the red ring. We can't go there."

"Who cares about a red ring?" said Stanley. "But it's got no name on your silly map."

"Well, you can ask this old chap what it's called if you're so keen to find out." "This old chap" was an old shepherd who had come up and was standing behind them.

"Good morning, young gents," he said, "you've got a fine day for your doin's, ain't you?"

"Yes, thank you," said Algernon de Montmorency, with native politeness. "Can you tell us what that clump over there's called? And what's that thing inside it?"

"Course I can tell you," said the shepherd. "That's Wailin' Well, that is. But you ain't got no call to worry about that."

"Is it a well in there?" said Algernon. "Who uses it?"

The shepherd laughed. "Bless you," he said, "there ain't from a man to a sheep in these parts uses Wailin' Well, nor haven't done all the years I've lived here."

"Well, there'll be a record broken today, then," said Stanley Judkins, "because I shall go and get some water out of it for tea!"

"Sakes alive, young gentleman!" said the shepherd in a startled voice. "Don't you get to talkin' that way! Why, ain't your masters give you notice not to go by there? They'd ought to have done."

"Yes, they have," said Wilfred Pipsqueak.

"Shut up, you ass!" said Stanley Judkins. "What's the matter with it? Isn't the water good? Anyhow, if it was boiled, it would be all right."

"I don't know as there's anything much wrong with the water," said the shepherd. "All I know is, my old dog wouldn't go through that field, let alone me or anyone else that's got a morsel of brains in their heads."

"More fool them," said Stanley Judkins, at once rudely and ungrammatically. "Who ever took any harm going there?" he added.

"Three women and a man," said the shepherd gravely. "Now just you listen to me. I know these 'ere parts and you don't, and I can tell you this much: for these ten years last past there ain't been a sheep fed in that field, nor a crop raised off of it—and it's good land, too. You can pretty well see from here what a state it's got into with brambles and suckers and trash of all kinds. *You've* got a glass, young gentleman," he said to Wilfred Pipsqueak, "you can tell with that anyway."

"Yes," said Wilfred, "but I see there's tracks in it. Someone must go through it sometimes."

"Tracks!" said the shepherd. "I believe you! Four tracks: three women and a man."

"What d'you mean, three women and a man?" said Stanley, turning over for the first time and looking at the shepherd (he had been talking with his back to him till this moment: he was an ill-mannered boy).

"Mean? Why, what I says: three women and a man."

"Who are they?" asked Algernon. "Why do they go there?"

"There's some p'r'aps could tell you who they *was*," said the shepherd, "but it was afore my time they come by their end. And why they goes there still is more than the children of men can tell: except I've heard they was all bad 'uns when they was alive."

"By George, what a rum thing!" Algernon and Wilfred muttered: but Stanley was scornful and bitter.

"Why, you don't mean they're deaders? What

rot! You must be a lot of fools to believe that. Who's ever seen them, I'd like to know?"

"*I've* seen 'em, young gentleman!" said the shepherd, "seen 'em from nearby on that bit of down: and my old dog, if he could speak, he'd tell you he've seen 'em, same time. About four o'clock of the day it was, much such a day as this. I see 'em, each one of 'em, come peerin' out of the bushes and stand up, and work their way slow by them tracks towards the trees in the middle where the well is."

"And what were they like? Do tell us!" said Algernon and Wilfred eagerly.

"Rags and bones, young gentlemen: all four of 'em: flutterin' rags and whitey bones. It seemed to me as if I could hear 'em clackin' as they got along. Very slow they went, and lookin' from side to side."

"What were their faces like? Could you see?"

"They hadn't much to call faces," said the shepherd, "but I could seem to see as they had teeth."

"Lor'!" said Wilfred. "And what did they do when they got to the trees?"

"I can't tell you that, sir," said the shepherd. "I wasn't for stayin' in that place, and if I had been, I was bound to look to my old dog: he'd gone! Such a thing he never done before as leave me; but gone he had, and when I came up with him in the end, he was in that state he didn't know me, and was fit to fly at my throat. But I kep' talkin' to him, and after a bit he remembered my voice and came creepin' up like a child askin' pardon. I never want to see him like that again, nor yet no other dog."

The dog, who had come up and was making friends all round, looked up at his master, and expressed agreement with what he was saying very fully.

The boys pondered for some moments on what they had heard: after which Wilfred said: "And why's it called Wailing Well?"

"If you was round here at dusk of a winter's evening, you wouldn't want to ask why," was all the shepherd said.

"Well, I don't believe a word of it," said Stanley Judkins, "and I'll go there next chance I get: blowed if I don't!"

"Then you won't be ruled by me?" said the shepherd. "Nor yet by your masters as warned you off? Come now, young gentleman, you don't want for sense, I should say. What should I want tellin' you a pack of lies? It ain't sixpence to me anyone goin' in that field: but I wouldn't like to see a young chap snuffed out like in his prime."

"I expect it's a lot more than sixpence to you," said Stanley. "I expect you've got a whisky still or something in there, and want to keep other people away. Rot I call it. Come on back, you boys."

So they turned away. The two others said, "Good evening" and "Thank you" to the shepherd, but Stanley said nothing. The shepherd shrugged his shoulders and stood where he was, looking after them rather sadly.

On the way back to the camp there was great argument about it all, and Stanley was told as plainly as he could be told all the sorts of fools he would be if he went to the Wailing Well.

That evening, among other notices, Mr. Beasley Robinson asked if all maps had got the red ring marked on them. "Be particular," he said, "not to trespass inside it."

Several voices—among them the sulky one of Stanley Judkins—said, "Why not, sir?"

"Because not," said Mr. Beasley Robinson, "and if that isn't enough for you, I can't help it." He turned and spoke to Mr. Lambart in a low voice, and then said, "I'll tell you this much: we've been asked to warn Scouts off that field. It's very good of the people to let us camp here at all, and the least we can do is to oblige them—I'm sure you'll agree to that."

Everybody said, "Yes, sir!" except Stanley Judkins, who was heard to mutter, "Oblige them be blowed!"

Early in the afternoon of the next day, the following dialogue was heard. "Wilcox, is all your tent there?"

"No, sir, Judkins isn't!"

"That boy is *the* most infernal nuisance ever invented! Where do you suppose he is?"

"I haven't an idea, sir."

"Does anybody else know?"

"Sir, I shouldn't wonder if he'd gone to the Wailing Well."

"Who's that? Pipsqueak? What's the Wailing Well?"

"Sir, it's that place in the field by—well, sir, it's in a clump of trees in a rough field."

"D'you mean inside the red ring? Good heavens! What makes you think he's gone there?"

"Why, he was terribly keen to know about it yesterday, and we were talking to a shepherd man, and he told us a lot about it and advised us not to go there: but Judkins didn't believe him, and said he meant to go."

"Young ass!" said Mr. Hope Jones. "Did he take anything with him?"

"Yes, I think he took some rope and a can. We did tell him he'd be a fool to go."

"Little brute! What the deuce does he mean by pinching stores like that! Well, come along, you three, we must see after him. Why can't people keep the simplest orders? What was it the man told you? No, don't wait, let's have it as we go along."

And off they started—Algernon and Wilfred talking rapidly and the other two listening with growing concern. At last they reached that spur of down overlooking the field of which the shepherd had spoken the day before. It commanded the place completely; the well inside the clump of bent and gnarled Scotch firs was plainly visible, and so were the four tracks winding about among the thorns and rough growth.

It was a wonderful day of shimmering heat. The sea looked like a floor of metal. There was no breath of wind. They were all exhausted when they got to the top, and flung themselves down on the hot grass.

"Nothing to be seen of him yet," said Mr. Hope Jones, "but we must stop here a bit. You're done up—not to speak of me. Keep a sharp look-out," he went on after a moment, "I thought I saw the bushes stir."

"Yes," said Wilcox, "so did I. Look . . . no, that can't be him. It's somebody though, putting their head up, isn't it?"

"I thought it was, but I'm not sure."

Silence for a moment. Then:

"That's him, sure enough," said Wilcox, "getting over the hedge on the far side. Don't you see? With a shiny thing. That's the can you said he had."

"Yes, it's him, and he's making straight for the trees," said Wilfred.

At this moment Algernon, who had been staring with all his might, broke into a scream.

"What's that on the track? On all fours—O, it's the woman. O, don't let me look at her! Don't let it happen!" And he rolled over, clutching at the grass and trying to bury his head in it.

"Stop that!" said Mr. Hope Jones loudly—but it was no use. "Look here," he said, "I must go down there. You stop here, Wilfred, and look after that boy. Wilcox, you run as hard as you can to the camp and get some help."

They ran off, both of them. Wilfred was left alone with Algernon, and did his best to calm him, but indeed he was not much happier himself. From time to time he glanced down the hill and into the field. He saw Mr. Hope Jones drawing nearer at a swift pace, and then, to his great surprise, he saw him stop, look up and round about him, and turn quickly off at an angle! What could be the reason? He looked at the field, and there he saw a terrible figure—something in ragged black—with whitish patches breaking out of it: the head, perched on a long thin neck, half hidden by a shapeless sort of blackened sun-bonnet. The creature was waving thin arms in the direction of the rescuer who was approaching, as if to ward him off: and between the two figures the air seemed to shake and shimmer as he had never seen it: and as he looked, he began himself to feel something of a waviness and confusion in his brain, which made him guess what might be the effect on someone within closer range of the influence. He looked away hastily, to see Stanley Judkins making his way pretty quickly towards the clump, and in proper Scout fashion;

evidently picking his steps with care to avoid treading on snapping sticks or being caught by arms of brambles. Evidently, though he saw nothing, he suspected some sort of ambush, and was trying to go noiselessly. Wilfred saw all that, and he saw more, too. With a sudden and dreadful sinking at the heart, he caught sight of someone among the trees, waiting: and again of someone—another of the hideous black figures—working slowly along the track from another side of the field, looking from side to side, as the shepherd had described it. Worst of all, he saw a fourth—unmistakably a man this time—rising out of the bushes a few yards behind the wretched Stanley, and painfully, as it seemed, crawling into the track. On all sides the miserable victim was cut off.

Wilfred was at his wits' end. He rushed at Algernon and shook him. "Get up," he said. "Yell! Yell as loud as you can. Oh, if we'd got a whistle!"

Algernon pulled himself together. "There's one," he said, "Wilcox's: he must have dropped it."

So one whistled, the other screamed. In the still air the sound carried. Stanley heard: he stopped: he turned round: and then indeed a cry was heard more piercing and dreadful than any that the boys on the hill could raise. It was too late. The crouched figure behind Stanley sprang at him and caught him about the waist. The dreadful one that was standing waving her arms waved them again but in exultation. The one that was lurking among the trees shuffled forward, and she too stretched out her arms as if to clutch at something coming her way; and the other, farthest off, quickened her pace and came on, nodding gleefully. The boys took it all in in an instant of terrible silence, and hardly could they breathe as they watched the horrid struggle between the man and his victim. Stanley struck with his can, the only weapon he had. The rim of a broken black hat fell off the creature's head and showed a white skull with stains that might be wisps of hair. By this time one of the women had reached the pair, and was pulling at the rope that was coiled about Stanley's neck. Between them they overpowered him in a

moment: the awful screaming ceased, and then the three passed within the circle of the clump of firs.

Yet for a moment it seemed as if rescue might come. Mr. Hope Jones, striding quickly along, suddenly stopped, turned, seemed to rub his eyes, and then started running *towards* the field. More: the boys glanced behind them, and saw not only a troop of figures from the camp coming over the top of the next down, but the shepherd running up the slope of their own hill. They beckoned, they shouted, they ran a few yards towards him and then back again. He mended his pace.

Once more the boys looked towards the field. There was nothing. Or, was there something among the trees? Why was there a mist about the trees? Mr. Hope Jones had scrambled over the hedge, and was plunging through the bushes.

The shepherd stood beside them, panting. They ran to him and clung to his arms. "They've got him! In the trees!" was as much as they could say, over and over again.

"What? Do you tell me he've gone in there after all I said to him yesterday? Poor young thing! Poor young thing!" He would have said more, but other voices broke in. The rescuers from the camp had arrived. A few hasty words, and all were dashing down the hill.

They had just entered the field when they met Mr. Hope Jones. Over his shoulder hung the corpse of Stanley Judkins. He had cut it from the branch to which he found it hanging, waving to and fro. There was not a drop of blood in the body.

On the following day Mr. Hope Jones sallied forth with an axe and with the expressed intention of cutting down every tree in the clump, and of burning every bush in the field. He returned with a nasty cut in his leg and a broken axe-helve. Not a spark of fire could he light, and on no single tree could he make the least impression.

I have heard that the present population of the Wailing Well field consists of three women, a man, and a boy.

The shock experienced by Algernon de Montmorency and Wilfred Pipsqueak was severe. Both of them left the camp at once; and the occurrence undoubtedly cast a gloom—if but a passing one—on those who remained. One of the first to recover his spirits was Judkins *mi.*

Such, gentlemen, is the story of the career of Stanley Judkins, and of a portion of the career of Arthur Wilcox. It has, I believe, never been told before. If it has a moral, that moral is, I trust, obvious: if it has none, I do not well know how to help it.

# HUMAN REMAINS

# Clive Barker

Clive Barker (1952– ) was born in Liverpool and studied English and philosophy at the University of Liverpool, achieving success as a short-story writer with the publication of his six-volume *Books of Blood* (1984–85) and as a screenwriter. His first screenplay, *Salome* (1973), was written when he was eighteen years old. He also wrote *The Forbidden* (1978), *Underworld* (1985, released in the United States as *Transmutations*), and the cult horror classic *Hellraiser* (1987, based on his 1986 novel *The Hellbound Heart*), the success of which inspired him to write the story for a sequel, *Hellbound: Hellraiser II* (1988). He then directed and wrote the screenplay for *Nightbreed* (1990, based on his best-selling 1988 novel, *Cabal*), receiving a Best Director nomination from the Academy of Science Fiction, Fantasy & Horror Films.

After writing exclusively in the horror genre early in his career, he moved into fantasy (although with horror overtones) with *Weaveworld* (1987), *The Great and Secret Show* (1989), *Imajica* (1991), and *Sacrament* (1996). Still later, he became a prolific comic book writer and created several computer games.

Barker received the 2004 Davidson/Valentini Award from GLAAD, presented to an openly lesbian, gay, bisexual, or transgender individual who has made a significant difference in promoting equal rights for any of those communities.

"Human Remains" was first published in *Books of Blood: Volume III* (London: Sphere, 1984).

# Human Remains

## CLIVE BARKER

Some trades are best practised by daylight, some by night. Gavin was a professional in the latter category. In midwinter, in midsummer, leaning against a wall, or poised in a doorway, a fire-fly cigarette hovering at his lips, he sold what sweated in his jeans to all comers.

Sometimes to visiting widows with more money than love, who'd hire him for a weekend of illicit meetings, sour, insistent kisses, and perhaps, if they could forget their dead partners, a dry hump on a lavender-scented bed. Sometimes to lost husbands, hungry for their own sex and desperate for an hour of coupling with a boy who wouldn't ask their name.

Gavin didn't much care which it was. Indifference was a trademark of his, even a part of his attraction. And it made leaving him, when the deed was done and the money exchanged, so much simpler. To say, "Ciao," or "Be seeing you," or nothing at all to a face that scarcely cared if you lived or died: that was an easy thing.

And for Gavin, the profession was not unpalatable, as professions went. One night out of four it even offered him a grain of physical pleasure. At worst it was a sexual abattoir, all steaming skins and lifeless eyes. But he'd got used to that over the years.

It was all profit. It kept him in good shoes.

By day he slept mostly, hollowing out a warm furrow in the bed, and mummifying himself in his sheets, head wrapped up in a tangle of arms to keep out the light. About three or so, he'd get up, shave, and shower, then spend half an hour in front of the mirror, inspecting himself. He was meticulously self-critical, never allowing his weight to fluctuate more than a pound or two to either side of his self-elected ideal, careful to feed his skin if it was dry, or swab it if it was oily, hunting for any pimple that might flaw his cheek. Strict watch was kept for the smallest sign of venereal disease—the only type of lovesickness he ever suffered. The occasional dose of crabs was easily dispatched, but gonorrhoea, which he'd caught twice, would keep him out of service for three weeks, and that was bad for business; so he policed his body obsessively, hurrying to the clinic at the merest sign of a rash.

It seldom happened. Uninvited crabs aside there was little to do in that half-hour of self-appraisal but admire the collision of genes that had made him. He was wonderful. People told him that all the time. Wonderful. The face, oh the face, they would say, holding him tight as if they could steal a piece of his glamour.

Of course there were other beauties available, through the agencies, even on the streets if you knew where to search. But most of the hustlers Gavin knew had faces that seemed, beside his, unmade. Faces that looked like the first workings of a sculptor rather than the finished article: unrefined, experimental. Whereas he was made, entire. All that could be done had been; it was just a question of preserving the perfection.

Inspection over, Gavin would dress, maybe regard himself for another five minutes, then take the packaged wares out to sell.

He worked the street less and less these days. It was chancey; there was always the law to avoid, and the occasional psycho with an urge to clean up Sodom. If he was feeling really lazy he could pick up a client through the Escort Agency, but they always creamed off a fat portion of the fee.

He had regulars of course, clients who booked his favours month after month. A widow from Fort Lauderdale always hired him for a few days on her annual trip to Europe; another woman whose face he'd seen once in a glossy magazine called him now and then, wanting only to dine with him and confide her marital problems. There was a man Gavin called Rover, after his car, who would buy him once every few weeks for a night of kisses and confessions.

But on nights without a booked client he was out on his own finding a spec and hustling. It was a craft he had pulled off perfectly. Nobody else working the street had caught the vocabulary of invitation better; the subtle blend of encouragement and detachment, of putto and wanton. The particular shift of weight from left foot to right that presented the groin at the best angle: so. Never too blatant: never whorish. Just casually promising.

He prided himself that there was seldom more than a few minutes between tricks, and never as much as an hour. If he made his play with his usual accuracy, eyeing the right disgruntled wife, the right regretful husband, he'd have them feed him (clothe him sometimes), bed him, and bid him a satisfied goodnight all before the last tube had run on the Metropolitan Line to Hammersmith. The years of half-hour assignations, three blow-jobs and a fuck in one evening, were over. For one thing he simply didn't have the hunger for it any longer, for another he was preparing for his career to change course in the coming years: from street hustler to gigolo, from gigolo to kept boy, from kept boy to husband. One of these days, he knew it, he'd marry one of the widows; maybe the matron from Florida. She'd told him how she could picture him spread out beside her pool in Fort Lauderdale, and it was a fantasy he kept warm for her. Perhaps he hadn't got there yet, but he'd turn the trick of it sooner or later. The problem was that these rich blooms needed a lot of tending, and the pity of it was that so many of them perished before they came to fruit.

Still, this year. Oh yes, this year for certain, it had to be this year. Something good was coming with the autumn, he knew it for sure.

Meanwhile he watched the lines deepen around his wonderful mouth (it was, without doubt, wonderful) and calculated the odds against him in the race between time and opportunity.

It was nine-fifteen at night. September 29th, and it was chilly, even in the foyer of the Imperial Hotel. No Indian summer to bless the streets this year: autumn had London in its jaws and was shaking the city bare.

The chill had got to his tooth, his wretched, crumbling tooth. If he'd gone to the dentist's, instead of turning over in his bed and sleeping another hour, he wouldn't be feeling this discomfort. Well, too late now, he'd go tomorrow. Plenty of time tomorrow. No need for an appointment. He'd just smile at the receptionist, she'd melt and tell him she could find a slot for him somewhere, he'd smile again, she'd blush, and he'd see the dentist then and there instead of waiting two weeks like the poor nerds who didn't have wonderful faces.

For tonight he'd just have to put up with it. All he needed was one lousy punter—a husband who'd pay through the nose for taking it in the mouth— then he could retire to an all-night club in Soho and content himself with reflections. As long as he didn't find himself with a confession-freak on his hands, he could spit his stuff and be done by half ten.

But tonight wasn't his night. There was a new face on the reception desk of the Imperial, a thin, shot-at face with a mismatched rug perched (glued) on his pate, and he'd been squinting at Gavin for almost half an hour.

The usual receptionist, Madox, was a closet-case Gavin had seen prowling the bars once or twice, an easy touch if you could handle that kind. Madox was putty in Gavin's hand; he'd even bought his company for an hour a couple of months back. He'd got a cheap rate too—that was good politics. But this new man was straight, and vicious, and he was on to Gavin's game.

Idly, Gavin sauntered across to the cigarette machine, his walk catching the beat of the muzack as he trod the maroon carpet. Lousy fucking night.

The receptionist was waiting for him as he turned from the machine, packet of Winston in hand.

"Excuse me . . . Sir." It was a practised pronounciation that was clearly not natural. Gavin looked sweetly back at him.

"Yes?"

"Are you actually a resident at this hotel . . . Sir?"

"Actually—"

"If not, the management would be obliged if you'd vacate the premises immediately."

"I'm waiting for somebody."

"Oh?"

The receptionist didn't believe a word of it.

"Well just give me the name—"

"No need."

"Give me the name," the man insisted, "and I'll gladly check to see if your . . . contact . . . is in the hotel."

The bastard was going to try and push it, which narrowed the options. Either Gavin could choose to play it cool, and leave the foyer, or play the outraged customer and stare the other man down. He chose, more to be bloodyminded than because it was good tactics, to do the latter.

"You don't have any right—" he began to bluster, but the receptionist wasn't moved.

"Look, sonny," he said, "I know what you're up to, so don't try and get snotty with me or I'll fetch the police." He'd lost control of his elocution: it was getting further south of the river with every syllable. "We've got a nice clientele here, and they don't want no truck with the likes of you, see?"

"Fucker," said Gavin very quietly.

"Well that's one up from a cocksucker, isn't it?"

Touché.

"Now, sonny—you want to mince out of here under your own steam or be carried out in cuffs by the boys in blue?"

Gavin played his last card.

"Where's Mr. Madox? I want to see Mr. Madox: he knows me."

"I'm sure he does," the receptionist snorted, "I'm bloody sure he does. He was dismissed for improper conduct—" the artificial accent was re-establishing itself "—so I wouldn't try dropping his name here if I were you. OK? On your way."

Upper hand well and truly secured, the receptionist stood back like a matador and gestured for the bull to go by.

"The management thanks you for your patronage. Please don't call again."

Game, set, and match to the man with the rug. What the hell; there were other hotels, other foyers, other receptionists. He didn't have to take all this shit.

As Gavin pushed the door open he threw a smiling "Be seeing you" over his shoulder. Perhaps that would make the tick sweat a little one of these nights when he was walking home and he heard a young man's step on the street behind him. It was a petty satisfaction, but it was something.

The door swung closed, sealing the warmth in and Gavin out. It was colder, substantially colder, than it had been when he'd stepped into the foyer. A thin drizzle had begun, which threatened to worsen as he hurried down Park Lane towards South Kensington. There were a couple of hotels on the High Street he could hole up in for a while; if nothing came of that he'd admit defeat.

The traffic surged around Hyde Park Corner,

speeding to Knightsbridge or Victoria, purposeful, shining. He pictured himself standing on the concrete island between the two contrary streams of cars, his fingertips thrust into his jeans (they were too tight for him to get more than the first joint into the pockets), solitary, forlorn.

A wave of unhappiness came up from some buried place in him. He was twenty-four and five months. He had hustled, on and off and on again, since he was seventeen, promising himself that he'd find a marriageable widow (the gigolo's pension) or a legitimate occupation before he was twenty-five.

But time passed and nothing came of his ambitions. He just lost momentum and gained another line beneath the eye.

And the traffic still came in shining streams, lights signalling this imperative or that, cars full of people with ladders to climb and snakes to wrestle, their passage isolating him from the bank, from safety, with its hunger for destination.

He was not what he'd dreamed he'd be, or promised his secret self.

And youth was yesterday.

Where was he to go now? The flat would feel like a prison tonight, even if he smoked a little dope to take the edge off the room. He wanted, no, he *needed* to be with somebody tonight. Just to see his beauty through somebody else's eyes. Be told how perfect his proportions were, be wined and dined and flattered stupid, even if it was by Quasimodo's richer, uglier brother. Tonight he needed a fix of affection.

The pick-up was so damned easy it almost made him forget the episode in the foyer of the Imperial. A guy of fifty-five or so, well-heeled: Gucci shoes, a very classy overcoat. In a word: quality.

Gavin was standing in the doorway of a tiny art-house cinema, looking over the times of the Truffaut movie they were showing, when he became aware of the punter staring at him. He glanced at the guy to be certain there was a pick-up in the offing. The direct look seemed to unnerve the punter; he moved on; then he seemed to change his mind, muttered something to himself, and retraced his steps, showing patently false interest in the movie schedule. Obviously not too familiar with this game, Gavin thought; a novice.

Casually Gavin took out a Winston and lit it, the flare of the match in his cupped hands glossing his cheekbones golden. He'd done it a thousand times, as often as not in the mirror for his own pleasure. He had the glance up from the tiny fire off pat: it always did the trick. This time when he met the nervous eyes of the punter, the other didn't back away.

He drew on the cigarette, flicking out the match and letting it drop. He hadn't made a pick-up like this in several months, but he was well satisfied that he still had the knack. The faultless recognition of a potential client, the implicit offer in eyes and lips, that could be construed as innocent friendliness if he'd made an error.

This was no error, however, this was the genuine article. The man's eyes were glued to Gavin, so enamoured of him he seemed to be hurting with it. His mouth was open, as though the words of introduction had failed him. Not much of a face, but far from ugly. Tanned too often, and too quickly: maybe he'd lived abroad. He was assuming the man was English: his prevarication suggested it.

Against habit, Gavin made the opening move. "You like French movies?"

The punter seemed to deflate with relief that the silence between them had been broken.

"Yes," he said.

"You going in?"

The man pulled a face.

"I . . . I . . . don't think I will."

"Bit cold . . ."

"Yes. It is."

"Bit cold for standing around, I mean."

"Oh—yes."

The punter took the bait.

"Maybe. . . you'd like a drink?"

Gavin smiled.

"Sure, why not?"

"My flat's not far."

"Sure."

"I was getting a bit cheesed off, you know, at home."

"I know the feeling."

Now the other man smiled. "You are . . . ?"

"Gavin."

The man offered his leather-gloved hand. Very formal, businesslike. The grip as they shook was strong, no trace of his earlier hesitation remaining.

"I'm Kenneth," he said, "Ken Reynolds."

"Ken."

"Shall we get out of the cold?"

"Suits me."

"I'm only a short walk from here."

A wave of musty, centrally-heated air hit them as Reynolds opened the door of his apartment. Climbing the three flights of stairs had snatched Gavin's breath, but Reynolds wasn't slowed at all. Health freak maybe. Occupation? Something in the city. The handshake, the leather gloves. Maybe Civil Service.

"Come in, come in."

There was money here. Underfoot the pile of the carpet was lush, hushing their steps as they entered. The hallway was almost bare: a calendar hung on the wall, a small table with telephone, a heap of directories, a coat-stand.

"It's warmer in here."

Reynolds was shrugging off his coat and hanging it up. His gloves remained on as he led Gavin a few yards down the hallway and into a large room.

"Let's have your jacket," he said.

"Oh . . . sure."

Gavin took off his jacket, and Reynolds slipped out into the hall with it. When he came in again he was working off his gloves; a slick of sweat made it a difficult job. The guy was still nervous: even on his home ground. Usually they started to calm down once they were safe behind locked doors. Not this one: he was a catalogue of fidgets.

"Can I get you a drink?"

"Yeah; that would be good."

"What's your poison?"

"Vodka."

"Surely. Anything with it?"

"Just a drop of water."

"Purist, eh?"

Gavin didn't quite understand the remark.

"Yeah," he said.

"Man after my own heart. Will you give me a moment—I'll just fetch some ice."

"No problem."

Reynolds dropped the gloves on a chair by the door, and left Gavin to the room. It, like the hallway, was almost stiflingly warm, but there was nothing homely or welcoming about it. Whatever his profession, Reynolds was a collector. The room was dominated by displays of antiquities, mounted on the walls, and lined up on shelves. There was very little furniture, and what there was seemed odd: battered tubular frame chairs had no place in an apartment this expensive. Maybe the man was a university don, or a museum governor, something academic. This was no stockbroker's living room.

Gavin knew nothing about art, and even less about history, so the displays meant very little to him, but he went to have a closer look, just to show he was willing. The guy was bound to ask him what he thought of the stuff. The shelves were deadly dull. Bits and pieces of pottery and sculpture: nothing in its entirety, just fragments. On some of the shards there remained a glimpse of design, though age had almost washed the colours out. Some of the sculpture was recognisably human: part of a torso, or foot (all five toes in place), a face that was all but eaten away, no longer male or female. Gavin stifled a yawn. The heat, the exhibits, and the thought of sex made him lethargic.

He turned his dulled attention to the wall-hung pieces. They were more impressive than the stuff on the shelves but they were still far from complete. He couldn't see why anyone would want to look at such broken things; what was the fascination? The stone reliefs mounted on the wall were pitted and eroded, so that the skins of the figures looked leprous, and the Latin inscriptions were almost wiped out. There was nothing beautiful about them: too spoiled for beauty. They made him feel dirty somehow, as though their condition was contagious.

Only one of the exhibits struck him as interesting: a tombstone, or what looked to him to be a tombstone, which was larger than the other reliefs and in slightly better condition. A man on a horse, carrying a sword, loomed over his headless enemy. Under the picture, a few words in Latin. The front legs of the horse had been broken off, and the pillars that bounded the design were badly defaced by age, otherwise the image made sense. There was even a trace of personality in the crudely made face: a long nose, a wide mouth; an individual.

Gavin reached to touch the inscription, but withdrew his fingers as he heard Reynolds enter.

"No, please touch it," said his host. "It's there to take pleasure in. Touch away."

Now that he'd been invited to touch the thing, the desire had melted away. He felt embarrassed; caught in the act.

"Go on," Reynolds insisted.

Gavin touched the carving. Cold stone, gritty under his fingertips.

"It's Roman," said Reynolds.

"Tombstone?"

"Yes. Found near Newcastle."

"Who was he?"

"His name was Flavinus. He was a regimental standard-bearer."

What Gavin had assumed to be a sword was, on closer inspection, a standard. It ended in an almost erased motif: maybe a bee, a flower, a wheel.

"You an archaeologist, then?"

"That's part of my business. I research sites, occasionally oversee digs; but most of the time I restore artifacts."

"Like these?"

"Roman Britain's my personal obsession."

He put down the glasses he was carrying and crossed to the pottery-laden shelves.

"This is stuff I've collected over the years. I've never quite got over the thrill of handling objects that haven't seen the light of day for centuries. It's like plugging into history. You know what I mean?"

"Yeah."

Reynolds picked a fragment of pottery off the shelf.

"Of course all the best finds are claimed by the major collections. But if one's canny, one manages to keep a few pieces back. They were an incredible influence, the Romans. Civil engineers, road-layers, bridge builders."

Reynolds gave a sudden laugh at his burst of enthusiasm.

"Oh hell," he said, "Reynolds is lecturing again. Sorry. I get carried away."

Replacing the pottery-shard in its niche on the shelf, he returned to the glasses, and started pouring drinks. With his back to Gavin, he managed to say: "Are you expensive?"

Gavin hesitated. The man's nervousness was catching and the sudden tilt of the conversation from the Romans to the price of a blow-job took some adjustment.

"It depends," he flannelled.

"Ah . . ." said the other, still busying himself with the glasses, "you mean what is the precise nature of my—er—requirement?"

"Yeah."

"Of course."

He turned and handed Gavin a healthy-sized glass of vodka. No ice.

"I won't be demanding of you," he said.

"I don't come cheap."

"I'm sure you don't," Reynolds tried a smile, but it wouldn't stick to his face, "and I'm prepared to pay you well. Will you be able to stay the night?"

"Do you want me to?"

Reynolds frowned into his glass.

"I suppose I do."

"Then yes."

The host's mood seemed to change, suddenly: indecision was replaced by a spurt of conviction.

"Cheers," he said, clinking his whisky-filled glass against Gavin's. "To love and life and anything else that's worth paying for."

The double-edged remark didn't escape Gavin: the guy was obviously tied up in knots about what he was doing.

"I'll drink to that," said Gavin and took a gulp of the vodka.

The drinks came fast after that, and just about his third vodka Gavin began to feel mellower than he'd felt in a hell of a long time, content to listen to Reynolds' talk of excavations and the glories of Rome with only one ear. His mind was drifting, an easy feeling. Obviously he was going to be here for the night, or at least until the early hours of the morning, so why not drink the punter's vodka and enjoy the experience for what it offered? Later, probably much later to judge by the way the guy was rambling, there'd be some drink-slurred sex in a darkened room, and that would be that. He'd had customers like this before. They were lonely, perhaps between lovers, and usually simple to please. It wasn't sex this guy was buying, it was company, another body to share his space awhile; easy money.

And then, the noise.

At first Gavin thought the beating sound was in his head, until Reynolds stood up, a twitch at his mouth. The air of well-being had disappeared.

"What's that?" asked Gavin, also getting up, dizzy with drink.

"It's all right—" Reynolds, palms were pressing him down into his chair. "Stay here—"

The sound intensified. A drummer in an oven, beating as he burned.

"Please, please stay here a moment. It's just somebody upstairs."

Reynolds was lying, the racket wasn't coming from upstairs. It was from somewhere else in the flat, a rhythmical thumping, that speeded up and slowed and speeded again.

"Help yourself to a drink," said Reynolds at the door, face flushed. "Damn neighbours . . ."

The summons, for that was surely what it was, was already subsiding.

"A moment only," Reynolds promised, and closed the door behind him.

Gavin had experienced bad scenes before: tricks whose lovers appeared at inappropriate moments; guys who wanted to beat him up for a price—one who got bitten by guilt in a hotel room and smashed the place to smithereens. These things happened. But Reynolds was different: nothing about him said weird. At the back of his mind, at the very back, Gavin was quietly reminding himself that the other guys hadn't seemed bad at the begin-

ning. Ah hell; he put the doubts away. If he started to get the jitters every time he went with a new face he'd soon stop working altogether. Somewhere along the line he had to trust to luck and his instinct, and his instinct told him that this punter was not given to throwing fits.

Taking a quick swipe from his glass, he refilled it, and waited.

The noise had stopped altogether, and it became increasingly easier to rearrange the facts: maybe it had been an upstairs neighbour after all. Certainly there was no sound of Reynolds moving around in the flat.

His attention wandered around the room looking for something to occupy it awhile, and came back to the tombstone on the wall.

Flavinus the Standard-Bearer.

There was something satisfying about the idea of having your likeness, however crude, carved in stone and put up on the spot where your bones lay, even if some historian was going to separate bones and stone in the fullness of time. Gavin's father had insisted on burial rather than cremation: How else, he'd always said, was he going to be remembered? Who'd ever go to an urn, in a wall, and cry? The irony was that nobody ever went to his grave either: Gavin had been perhaps twice in the years since his father's death. A plain stone bearing a name, a date, and a platitude. He couldn't even remember the year his father died.

People remembered Flavinus though; people who'd never known him, or a life like his, knew him now. Gavin stood up and touched the standard-bearer's name, the crudely chased "FLAV-INVS" that was the second word of the inscription.

Suddenly, the noise again, more frenzied than ever. Gavin turned away from the tombstone and looked at the door, half-expecting Reynolds to be standing there with a word of explanation. Nobody appeared.

"Damn it."

The noise continued, a tattoo. Somebody, somewhere, was very angry. And this time there could be no self-deception: the drummer was here, on this floor, a few yards away. Curiosity nibbled Gavin, a coaxing lover. He drained his glass and went out into the hall. The noise stopped as he closed the door behind him.

"Ken?" he ventured. The word seemed to die at his lips.

The hallway was in darkness, except for a wash of light from the far end. Perhaps an open door. Gavin found a switch to his right, but it didn't work.

"Ken?" he said again.

This time the enquiry met with a response. A moan, and the sound of a body rolling, or being rolled, over. Had Reynolds had an accident? Jesus, he could be lying incapacitated within spitting distance from where Gavin stood: he must help. Why were his feet so reluctant to move? He had the tingling in his balls that always came with nervous anticipation; it reminded him of childhood hide-and-seek: the thrill of the chase. It was almost pleasurable.

And pleasure apart, could he really leave now, without knowing what had become of the punter? He had to go down the corridor.

The first door was ajar; he pushed it open and the room beyond was a book-lined bedroom/study. Street lights through the curtainless window fell on a jumbled desk. No Reynolds, no thrasher. More confident now he'd made the first move Gavin explored further down the hallway. The next door—the kitchen—was also open. There was no light from inside. Gavin's hands had begun to sweat: he thought of Reynolds trying to pull his gloves off, though they stuck to his palm. What had he been afraid of? It was more than the pick-up: there was somebody else in the apartment: somebody with a violent temper.

Gavin's stomach turned as his eyes found the smeared hand-print on the door; it was blood.

He pushed the door, but it wouldn't open any further. There was something behind it. He slid through the available space, and into the kitchen. An unemptied waste bin, or a neglected vegetable rack, fouled the air. Gavin smoothed the wall with his palm to find the light switch, and the fluorescent tube spasmed into life.

Reynolds' Gucci shoes poked out from behind the door. Gavin pushed it to, and Reynolds rolled out of his hiding place. He'd obviously crawled behind the door to take refuge; there was something of the beaten animal in his tucked up body. When Gavin touched him he shuddered.

"It's all right . . . it's me." Gavin prised a bloody hand from Reynolds' face. There was a deep gouge running from his temple to his chin, and another, parallel with it but not as deep, across the middle of his forehead and his nose, as though he'd been raked by a two-pronged fork.

Reynolds opened his eyes. It took him a second only to focus on Gavin, before he said:

"Go away."

"You're hurt."

"Jesus' sake, go away. Quickly. I've changed my mind . . . You understand?"

"I'll fetch the police."

The man practically spat: "Get the fucking hell out of here, will you? Fucking bum-boy!"

Gavin stood up, trying to make sense out of all this. The guy was in pain, it made him aggressive. Ignore the insults and fetch something to cover the wound. That was it. Cover the wound, and then leave him to his own devices. If he didn't want the police that was his business. Probably he didn't want to explain the presence of a pretty-boy in his hot-house.

"Just let me get you a bandage—"

Gavin went back into the hallway.

Behind the kitchen door Reynolds said: "Don't," but the bum-boy didn't hear him. It wouldn't have made much difference if he had. Gavin liked disobedience. Don't was an invitation.

Reynolds put his back to the kitchen door, and tried to edge his way upright, using the door-handle as purchase. But his head was spinning: a carousel of horrors, round and round, each horse uglier than the last. His legs doubled up under him, and he fell down like the senile fool he was. Damn. Damn. Damn.

Gavin heard Reynolds fall, but he was too busy arming himself to hurry back into the kitchen. If the intruder who'd attacked Reynolds was still in the flat, he wanted to be ready to defend himself. He rummaged through the reports on the desk in the study and alighted on a paper knife which was lying beside a pile of unopened correspondence. Thanking God for it, he snatched it up. It was light, and the blade was thin and brittle, but properly placed it could surely kill.

Happier now, he went back into the hall and took a moment to work out his tactics. The first thing was to locate the bathroom, hopefully there he'd find a bandage for Reynolds. Even a clean towel would help. Maybe then he could get some sense out of the guy, even coax him into an explanation.

Beyond the kitchen the hallway made a sharp left. Gavin turned the corner, and dead ahead the door was ajar. A light burned inside: water shone on tiles. The bathroom.

Clamping his left hand over the right hand that held the knife, Gavin approached the door. The muscles of his arms had become rigid with fear: would that improve his strike if it was required? he wondered. He felt inept, graceless, slightly stupid.

There was blood on the door-jamb, a palm-print that was clearly Reynolds'. This was where it had happened—Reynolds had thrown out a hand to support himself as he reeled back from his assailant. If the attacker was still in the flat, he must be here. There was nowhere else for him to hide.

Later, if there was a later, he'd probably analyse this situation and call himself a fool for kicking the door open, for encouraging this confrontation. But even as he contemplated the idiocy of the action he was performing it, and the door was swinging open across tiles strewn with water-blood puddles, and any moment there'd be a figure there, hook-handed, screaming defiance.

No. Not at all. The assailant wasn't here; and if he wasn't here, he wasn't in the flat.

Galvin exhaled, long and slow. The knife sagged in his hand, denied its pricking. Now, despite the sweat, the terror, he was disappointed. Life had let him down, again—snuck his destiny out of the back door and left him with a mop in his hand not a medal. All he could do was play nurse to the old man and go on his way.

The bathroom was decorated in shades of lime; the blood and tiles clashed. The translucent shower curtain, sporting stylised fish and seaweed, was partially drawn. It looked like the scene of a movie murder: not quite real. Blood too bright: light too flat.

Gavin dropped the knife in the sink, and opened the mirrored cabinet. It was well-stocked with mouth-washes, vitamin supplements, and abandoned toothpaste tubes, but the only medication was a tin of Elastoplast. As he closed the cabinet door he met his own features in the mirror, a drained face. He turned on the cold tap full, and lowered his head to the sink; a splash of water would clear away the vodka and put some colour in his cheeks.

As he cupped the water to his face, something made a noise behind him. He stood up, his heart knocking against his ribs, and turned off the tap. Water dripped off his chin and his eyelashes, and gurgled down the waste pipe.

The knife was still in the sink, a hand's-length away. The sound was coming from the bath, from *in* the bath, the inoffensive slosh of water.

Alarm had triggered flows of adrenalin, and his senses distilled the air with new precision. The sharp scent of lemon soap, the brilliance of the turquoise angel-fish flitting through lavender kelp on the shower curtain, the cold droplets on his face, the warmth behind his eyes: all sudden experiences, details his mind had passed over 'til now, too lazy to see and smell and feel to the limits of its reach.

You're living in the real world, his head said (it was a revelation), and if you're not very careful you're going to die there.

Why hadn't he looked in the bath? Asshole. Why not the bath?

"Who's there?" he asked, hoping against hope that Reynolds had an otter that was taking a quiet swim. Ridiculous hope. There was blood here, for Christ's sake.

He turned from the mirror as the lapping subsided—do it! do it!—and slid back the shower curtain on its plastic hooks. In his haste to unveil the mystery he'd left the knife in the sink. Too late now: the turquoise angels concertinaed, and he was looking down into the water.

It was deep, coming up to within an inch or

two of the top of the bath, and murky. A brown scum spiralled on the surface, and the smell off it was faintly animal, like the wet fur of a dog. Nothing broke the surface of the water.

Gavin peered in, trying to work out the form at the bottom, his reflection floating amid the scum. He bent closer, unable to puzzle out the relation of shapes in the silt, until he recognised the crudely-formed fingers of a hand and he realised he was looking at a human form curled up into itself like a foetus, lying absolutely still in the filthy water.

He passed his hand over the surface to clear away the muck, his reflection shattered, and the occupant of the bath came clear. It was a statue, carved in the shape of a sleeping figure, only its head, instead of being tucked up tight, was cranked round to stare up out of the blur of sediment towards the surface. Its eyes were painted open, two crude blobs on a roughly carved face; its mouth was a slash, its ears ridiculous handles on its bald head. It was naked: its anatomy no better realised than its features: the work of an apprentice sculptor. In places the paint had been corrupted, perhaps by the soaking, and was lifting off the torso in grey, globular strands. Underneath, a core of dark wood was uncovered.

There was nothing to be frightened of here. An *objet d'art* in a bath, immersed in water to remove a crass paint-job. The lapping he'd heard behind him had been some bubbles rising from the thing, caused by a chemical reaction. There: the fright was explained. Nothing to panic over. Keep beating my heart, as the barman at the Ambassador used to say when a new beauty appeared on the scene.

Gavin smiled at the irony; this was no Adonis.

"Forget you ever saw it."

Reynolds was at the door. The bleeding had stopped, staunched by an unsavoury rag of a handkerchief pressed to the side of his face. The light of the tiles made his skin bilious: his pallor would have shamed a corpse.

"Are you all right? You don't look it."

"I'll be fine . . . just go, please."

"What happened?"

"I slipped. Water on the floor. I slipped, that's all."

"But the noise . . ."

Gavin was looking back into the bath. Something about the statue fascinated him. Maybe its nakedness, and that second strip it was slowly performing underwater: the ultimate strip: off with the skin.

"Neighbours, that's all."

"What is this?" Gavin asked, still looking at the unfetching doll-face in the water.

"It's nothing to do with you."

"Why's it all curled up like that? Is he dying?"

Gavin looked back to Reynolds to see the response to that question, the sourest of smiles, fading.

"You'll want money."

"No."

"Damn you! You're in business aren't you? There's notes beside the bed; take whatever you feel you deserve for your wasted time"—he was appraising Gavin—"and your silence."

Again the statue: Gavin couldn't keep his eyes off it, in all its crudity. His own face, puzzled, floated on the skin of the water, shaming the hand of the artist with its proportions.

"Don't wonder," said Reynolds.

"Can't help it."

"This is nothing to do with you."

"You stole it . . . is that right? This is worth a mint and you stole it."

Reynolds pondered the question and seemed, at last, too tired to start lying.

"Yes. I stole it."

"And tonight somebody came back for it—"

Reynolds shrugged.

"Is that it? Somebody came back for it?"

"That's right. I stole it . . ." Reynolds was saying the lines by rote, ". . . and somebody came back for it."

"That's all I wanted to know."

"Don't come back here, Gavin whoever-you-are. And don't try anything clever, because I won't be here."

"You mean extortion?" said Gavin, "I'm no thief."

Reynolds' look of appraisal rotted into contempt.

"Thief or not, be thankful. If it's in you." Reynolds stepped away from the door to let Gavin pass. Gavin didn't move.

"Thankful for what?" he demanded. There was an itch of anger in him; he felt, absurdly, rejected, as though he was being foisted off with a half-truth because he wasn't worthy enough to share this secret.

Reynolds had no more strength left for explanation. He was slumped against the door-frame, exhausted.

"Go," he said.

Gavin nodded and left the guy at the door. As he passed from bathroom into hallway a glob of paint must have been loosened from the statue. He heard it break surface, heard the lapping at the edge of the bath, could see, in his head, the way the ripples made the body shimmer.

"Goodnight," said Reynolds, calling after him.

Gavin didn't reply, nor did he pick up any money on his way out. Let him have his tombstones and his secrets.

On his way to the front door he stepped into the main room to pick up his jacket. The face of Flavinus the Standard-Bearer looked down at him from the wall. The man must have been a hero, Gavin thought. Only a hero would have been commemorated in such a fashion. He'd get no remembrance like that; no stone face to mark his passage.

He closed the front door behind him, aware once more that his tooth was aching, and as he did so the noise began again, the beating of a fist against a wall.

Or worse, the sudden fury of a woken heart.

The toothache was really biting the following day, and he went to the dentist midmorning, expecting to coax the girl on the desk into giving him an instant appointment. But his charm was at a low ebb, his eyes weren't sparkling quite as luxuriantly as usual. She told him he'd have to wait until the following Friday, unless it was an emergency. He told her it was: she told him it wasn't. It was going to be a bad day: an aching tooth, a lesbian dentist receptionist, ice on the puddles, nattering women on every street corner, ugly children, ugly sky.

That was the day the pursuit began.

Gavin had been chased by admirers before, but never quite like this. Never so subtle, so surreptitious. He'd had people follow him round for days, from bar to bar, from street to street, so dog-like it almost drove him mad. Seeing the same longing face night after night, screwing up the courage to buy him a drink, perhaps offering him a watch, cocaine, a week in Tunisia, whatever. He'd rapidly come to loathe that sticky adoration that went bad as quickly as milk, and stank to high Heaven once it had. One of his most ardent admirers, a knighted actor he'd been told, never actually came near him, just followed him around, looking and looking. At first the attention had been flattering, but the pleasure soon became irritation, and eventually he'd cornered the guy in a bar and threatened him with a broken head. He'd been so wound up that night, so sick of being devoured by looks, he'd have done some serious harm if the pitiful bastard hadn't taken the hint. He never saw the guy again; half thought he'd probably gone home and hanged himself.

But this pursuit was nowhere near as obvious, it was scarcely more than a feeling. There was no hard evidence that he had somebody on his tail. Just a prickly sense, every time he glanced round, that someone was slotting themselves into the shadows, or that on a night street a walker was keeping pace with him, matching every click of his heel, every hesitation in his step. It was like paranoia, except that he wasn't paranoid. If he was paranoid, he reasoned, somebody would tell him.

Besides, there were incidents. One morning the cat woman who lived on the landing below him idly enquired who his visitor was: the funny one who came in late at night and waited on the stairs hour after hour, watching his room. He'd had no such visitor: and knew no-one who fitted the description.

Another day, on a busy street, he'd ducked out of the throng into the doorway of an empty shop and was in the act of lighting a cigarette when somebody's reflection, distorted through the grime on the window, caught his eye. The match burned his finger, he looked down as he dropped it, and when he looked up again the crowd had closed round the watcher like an eager sea.

It was a bad, bad feeling: and there was more where that came from.

Gavin had never spoken with Preetorius, though they'd exchanged an occasional nod on the street, and each asked after the other in the company of mutual acquaintances as though they were dear friends. Preetorius was a black, somewhere between forty-five and assassination, a glorified pimp who claimed to be descended from Napoleon. He'd been running a circle of women, and three or four boys, for the best part of a decade, and doing well from the business. When he first began work, Gavin had been strongly advised to ask for Preetorius' patronage, but he'd always been too much of a maverick to want that kind of help. As a result he'd never been looked upon kindly by Preetorius or his clan. Nevertheless, once he became a fixture on the scene, no-one challenged his right to be his own man. The word was that Preetorius even admitted a grudging admiration for Gavin's greed.

Admiration or no, it was a chilly day in Hell when Preetorius actually broke the silence and spoke to him.

"White boy."

It was towards eleven, and Gavin was on his way from a bar off St. Martin's Lane to a club in Covent Garden. The street still buzzed: there were potential punters amongst the theatre and movie-goers, but he hadn't got the appetite for it tonight. He had a hundred in his pocket, which he'd made the day before and hadn't bothered to bank. Plenty to keep him going.

His first thought when he saw Preetorius and his pie-bald goons blocking his path was: they want my money.

"White boy."

Then he recognised the flat, shining face. Preetorius was no street thief; never had been, never would be.

"White boy, I'd like a word with you."

Preetorius took a nut from his pocket, shelled it in his palm, and popped the kernel into his ample mouth.

"You don't mind do you?"

"What do you want?"

"Like I said, just a word. Not too much to ask, is it?"

"OK. What?"

"Not here."

Gavin looked at Preetorius' cohorts. They weren't gorillas, that wasn't the black's style at all, but nor were they ninety-eight pound weaklings. This scene didn't look, on the whole, too healthy.

"Thanks, but no thanks." Gavin said, and began to walk, with as even a pace as he could muster, away from the trio. They followed. He prayed they wouldn't, but they followed. Preetorius talked at his back.

"Listen. I hear bad things about you," he said.

"Oh yes?"

"I'm afraid so. I'm told you attacked one of my boys."

Gavin took six paces before he answered. "Not me. You've got the wrong man."

"He recognised you, trash. You did him some serious mischief."

"I told you: not me."

"You're a lunatic, you know that? You should be put behind fucking bars."

Preetorius was raising his voice. People were crossing the street to avoid the escalating argument.

Without thinking, Gavin turned off St. Martin's Lane into Long Acre, and rapidly realised he'd made a tactical error. The crowds thinned substantially here, and it was a long trek through the streets of Covent Garden before he reached another centre of activity. He should have turned right instead of left, and he'd have stepped onto Charing Cross Road. There would have been some safety there. Damn it, he couldn't turn round, not and walk straight into them. All he could do was walk (not run; never run with a mad dog on your heels) and hope he could keep the conversation on an even keel.

Preetorius: "You've cost me a lot of money."

"I don't see—"

"You put some of my prime boy-meat out of commission. It's going to be a long time 'til I get that kid back on the market. He's shit scared, see?"

"Look . . . I didn't do anything to anybody."

"Why do you fucking lie to me, trash? What have I ever done to you, you treat me like this?"

Preetorius picked up his pace a little and came up level with Gavin, leaving his associates a few steps behind.

"Look . . ." he whispered to Gavin, "kids like that can be tempting, right? That's cool. I can get into that. You put a little boy-pussy on my plate I'm not going to turn my nose up at it. But you hurt him: and when you hurt one of my kids, I bleed too."

"If I'd done this like you say, you think I'd be walking the street?"

"Maybe you're not a well man, you know? We're not talking about a couple of bruises here, man. I'm talking about you taking a shower in a kid's blood, that's what I'm saying. Hanging him up and cutting him everywhere, then leaving him on my fuckin' stairs wearing a pair of fuckin' socks. You getting my message now, white boy? You read my message?"

Genuine rage had flared as Preetorius described the alleged crimes, and Gavin wasn't sure how to handle it. He kept his silence, and walked on.

"That kid idolised you, you know? Thought you were essential reading for an aspirant bumboy. How'd you like that?"

"Not much."

"You should be fuckin' flattered, man, 'cause that's about as much as you'll ever amount to."

"Thanks."

"You've had a good career. Pity it's over."

Gavin felt iced lead in his belly: he'd hoped Preetorius was going to be content with a warning. Apparently not. They were here to damage him: Jesus, they were going to hurt him, and for something he hadn't done, didn't even know anything about.

"We're going to take you off the street, white boy. Permanently."

"I did nothing."

"The kid knew you, even with a stocking over your head he knew you. The voice was the same, the clothes were the same. Face it, you were recognised. Now take the consequences."

"Fuck you."

Gavin broke into a run. As an eighteen-year-old he'd sprinted for his county: he needed that speed again now. Behind him Preetorius laughed (such sport!) and two sets of feet pounded the pavement in pursuit. They were close, closer—and Gavin was badly out of condition. His thighs were aching after a few dozen yards, and his jeans were too tight to run in easily. The chase was lost before it began.

"The man didn't tell you to leave," the white goon scolded, his bitten fingers digging into Gavin's biceps.

"Nice try." Preetorius smiled, sauntering towards the dogs and the panting hare. He nodded, almost imperceptibly, to the other goon.

"Christian?" he asked.

At the invitation Christian delivered a fist to Gavin's kidneys. The blow doubled him up, spitting curses.

Christian said: "Over there." Preetorius said: "Make it snappy," and suddenly they were dragging him out of the light into an alley. His shirt and his jacket tore, his expensive shoes were dragged through dirt, before he was pulled upright, groaning. The alley was dark and Preetorius' eyes hung in the air in front of him, dislocated.

"Here we are again," he said. "Happy as can be."

"I . . . didn't touch him," Gavin gasped.

The unnamed cohort, Not-Christian, put a ham hand in the middle of Gavin's chest, and pushed him back against the end wall of the alley. His heel slid in muck, and though he tried to stay upright his legs had turned to water. His ego too: this was no time to be courageous. He'd beg, he'd fall down on his knees and lick their soles if need be, anything to stop them doing a job on him. Anything to stop them spoiling his face.

That was Preetorius' favourite pastime, or so the street talk went: the spoiling of beauty. He had a rare way with him, could maim beyond hope of redemption in three strokes of his razor, and have the victim pocket his lips as a keepsake.

Gavin stumbled forward, palms slapping the wet ground. Something rotten-soft slid out of its skin beneath his hand.

Not-Christian exchanged a grin with Preetorius.

"Doesn't he look delightful?" he said.

Preetorius was crunching a nut. "Seems to me," he said, "the man's finally found his place in life."

"I didn't touch him," Gavin begged. There was nothing to do but deny and deny: and even then it was a lost cause.

"You're guilty as hell," said Not-Christian.

*"Please."*

"I'd really like to get this over with as soon as possible," said Preetorius, glancing at his watch. "I've got appointments to keep, people to pleasure."

Gavin looked up at his tormentors. The sodium-lit street was a twenty-five-yard dash away, if he could break through the cordon of their bodies.

"Allow me to rearrange your face for you. A little crime of fashion."

Preetorius had a knife in his hand. Not-Christian had taken a rope from his pocket, with a ball on it. The ball goes in the mouth, the rope goes round the head—you couldn't scream if your life depended on it. This was it.

Go!

Gavin broke from his grovelling position like a sprinter from his block, but the slops greased his heels, and threw him off balance. Instead of making a clean dash for safety he stumbled sideways and fell against Christian, who in turn fell back.

There was a breathless scrambling before Preetorius stepped in, dirtying his hands on the white trash, and hauling him to his feet.

"No way out, fucker," he said, pressing the point of the blade against Gavin's chin. The jut of the bone was clearest there, and he began the cut without further debate—tracing the jawline, too hot for the act to care if the trash was gagged or not. Gavin howled as blood washed down his neck, but his cries were cut short as somebody's fat fingers grappled with his tongue, and held it fast.

His pulse began to thud in his temples, and windows, one behind the other, opened and opened in front of him, and he was falling through them into unconsciousness.

Better to die. Better to die. They'd destroy his face: better to die.

Then he was screaming again, except that he wasn't aware of making the sound in his throat. Through the slush in his ears he tried to focus on the voice, and realised it was Preetorius' scream he was hearing, not his own.

His tongue was released; and he was spontaneously sick. He staggered back, puking, from a mess of struggling figures in front of him. A person, or persons, unknown had stepped in, and prevented the completion of his spoiling. There was a body sprawled on the floor, face up. Not-Christian, eyes open, life shut. God: someone had killed for him. *For him.*

Gingerly, he put his hand up to his face to feel the damage. The flesh was deeply lacerated along his jawbone, from the middle of his chin to within an inch of his ear. It was bad, but Preetorius, ever organised, had left the best delights to the last, and had been interrupted before he'd slit Gavin's nostrils or taken off his lips. A scar along his jawbone wouldn't be pretty, but it wasn't disastrous.

Somebody was staggering out of the mêlée towards him—Preetorius, tears on his face, eyes like golf-balls.

Beyond him Christian, his arms useless, was staggering towards the street.

Preetorius wasn't following: why?

His mouth opened; an elastic filament of saliva, strung with pearls, depended from his lower lip.

"Help me," he appealed, as though his life was in Gavin's power. One large hand was raised to squeeze a drop of mercy out of the air, but instead came the swoop of another arm, reaching over his shoulder and thrusting a weapon, a crude blade, into the black's mouth. He gargled it a moment, his throat trying to accommodate its edge, its width, before his attacker dragged the blade up and back, holding Preetorius' neck to steady him against the force of the stroke. The startled face divided, and heat bloomed from Preetorius' interior, warming Gavin in a cloud.

The weapon hit the alley floor, a dull clank. Gavin glanced at it. A short, wide-bladed sword. He looked back at the dead man.

Preetorius stood upright in front of him, supported now only by his executioner's arm. His gushing head fell forward, and the executioner took the bow as a sign, neatly dropping Preetorius' body at Gavin's feet. No longer eclipsed by the corpse, Gavin met his saviour face to face.

It took him only a moment to place those crude features: the startled, lifeless eyes, the gash of a mouth, the jug-handle ears. It was Reynolds' statue. It grinned, its teeth too small for its head. Milk-teeth, still to be shed before the adult form. There was, however, some improvement in its appearance, he could see that even in the gloom. The brow seemed to have swelled; the face was altogether better proportioned. It remained a painted doll, but it was a doll with aspirations.

The statue gave a stiff bow, its joints unmistakably creaking, and the absurdity, the sheer absurdity of this situation welled up in Gavin. It bowed, damn it, it smiled, it murdered: and yet it couldn't possibly be alive, could it? Later, he would disbelieve, he promised himself. Later he'd find a thousand reasons not to accept the reality in front of him: blame his blood-starved brain, his confusion, his panic. One way or another he'd argue himself out of this fantastic vision, and it would be as though it had never happened.

If he could just live with it a few minutes longer.

The vision reached across and touched Gavin's jaw, lightly, running its crudely carved fingers along the lips of the wound Preetorius had made. A ring on its smallest finger caught the light: a ring identical to his own.

"We're going to have a scar," it said.

Gavin knew its voice.

"Dear me: pity," it said. It was speaking with *his* voice. "Still, it could be worse."

*His voice.* God, his, his, his.

Gavin shook his head.

"Yes," it said, understanding that he'd understood.

"Not me."

"Yes."

"Why?"

It transferred its touch from Gavin's jawbone to its own, marking out the place where the wound should be, and even as it made the gesture its surface opened, and it grew a scar on the spot. No blood welled up: it had no blood.

Yet wasn't that his own, even brow it was emulating, and the piercing eyes, weren't they becoming his, and the wonderful mouth?

"The boy?" said Gavin, fitting the pieces together.

"Oh the boy . . ." It threw its unfinished glance to Heaven. "What a treasure he was. And how he snarled."

"You washed in his blood?"

"I need it." It knelt to the body of Preetorius and put its fingers in the split head. "This blood's old, but it'll do. The boy was better."

It daubed Preetorius' blood on its cheek, like war-paint. Gavin couldn't hide his disgust.

"Is he such a loss?" the effigy demanded.

The answer was no, of course. It was no loss at all that Preetorius was dead, no loss that some drugged, cocksucking kid had given up some blood and sleep because this painted miracle needed to feed its growth. There were worse things than this every day, somewhere; huge horrors. And yet—

"You can't condone me," it prompted, "it's not in your nature is it? Soon it won't be in mine either. I'll reject my life as a tormentor of children, because I'll see through *your* eyes, share *your* humanity. . ."

It stood up, its movements still lacking flexibility.

"Meanwhile, I must behave as I think fit."

On its cheek, where Preetorius' blood had been smeared, the skin was already waxier, less like painted wood.

"I am a thing without a proper name," it pronounced. "I am a wound in the flank of the world. But I am also that perfect stranger you always prayed for as a child, to come and take you, call you beauty, lift you naked out of the street and through Heaven's window. Aren't I? Aren't I?"

How did it know the dreams of his childhood? How could it have guessed that particular emblem, of being hoisted out of a street full of plague into a house that was Heaven?

"Because I am yourself," it said, in reply to the unspoken question, "made perfectable."

Gavin gestured towards the corpses.

"You can't be me. I'd never have done this."

It seemed ungracious to condemn it for its intervention, but the point stood.

"Wouldn't you?" said the other. "I think you would."

Gavin heard Preetorius' voice in his ear. "A crime of fashion." Felt again the knife at his chin, the nausea, the helplessness. Of course he'd have done it, a dozen times over he'd have done it, and called it justice.

It didn't need to hear his accession, it was plain.

"I'll come and see you again," said the painted face. "Meanwhile—if I were you"—it laughed— "I'd be going."

Gavin locked eyes with it a beat, probing it for doubt, then started towards the road.

"Not that way. This!"

It was pointing towards a door in the wall, almost hidden behind festering bags of refuse. That was how it had come so quickly, so quietly.

"Avoid the main streets, and keep yourself out of sight. I'll find you again, when I'm ready."

Gavin needed no further encouragement to leave. Whatever the explanations of the night's events, the deeds were done. Now wasn't the time for questions.

He slipped through the doorway without looking behind him: but he could hear enough to turn his stomach. The thud of fluid on the ground, the pleasurable moan of the miscreant: the sounds were enough for him to be able to picture its toilet.

**N**othing of the night before made any more sense the morning after. There was no sudden insight into the nature of the waking dream he'd dreamt. There was just a series of stark facts.

In the mirror, the fact of the cut on his jaw, gummed up and aching more badly than his rotted tooth.

In the newspapers, the reports of two bodies found in the Covent Garden area, known criminals viciously murdered in what the police described as a "gangland slaughter."

In his head, the inescapable knowledge that he would be found out sooner or later. Somebody would surely have seen him with Preetorius, and spill the beans to the police. Maybe even Christian, if he was so inclined, and they'd be there, on his step, with cuffs and warrants. Then what could he tell them, in reply to their accusations? That the man who did it was not a man at all, but an effigy of some kind, that was by degrees becoming a replica of himself? The question was not whether he'd be incarcerated, but which hole they'd lock him in, prison or asylum?

Juggling despair with disbelief, he went to the casualty department to have his face seen to, where he waited patiently for three and a half hours with dozens of similar walking wounded.

The doctor was unsympathetic. There was no use in stitches now, he said, the damage was done: the wound could and would be cleaned and covered, but a bad scar was now unavoidable. Why didn't you come last night, when it happened? the nurse asked. He shrugged: what the hell did they care? Artificial compassion didn't help him an iota.

As he turned the corner with his street, he saw the cars outside the house, the blue light, the cluster of neighbours grinning their gossip. Too late to claim anything of his previous life. By now they had possession of his clothes, his combs, his perfumes, his letters—and they'd be searching through them like apes after lice. He'd seen how thoroughgoing these bastards could be when it suited them, how completely they could seize and parcel up a man's identity. Eat it up, suck it up: they could erase you as surely as a shot, but leave you a living blank.

There was nothing to be done. His life was theirs now to sneer at and salivate over: even have a nervous moment, one or two of them, when they saw his photographs and wondered if perhaps they'd paid for this boy themselves, some horny night.

Let them have it all. They were welcome. From now on he would be lawless, because laws protect possessions and he had none. They'd wiped him clean, or as good as: he had no place to live, nor anything to call his own. He didn't even have fear: that was the strangest thing.

He turned his back on the street and the house he'd lived in for four years, and he felt something akin to relief, happy that his life had been stolen from him in its squalid entirety. He was the lighter for it.

Two hours later, and miles away, he took time to check his pockets. He was carrying a banker's card, almost a hundred pounds in cash, a small collection of photographs, some of his parents and sister, mostly of himself; a watch, a ring, and a gold chain round his neck. Using the card might be dangerous—they'd surely have warned his bank by now. The best thing might be to pawn the ring and the chain, then hitch North. He had friends in Aberdeen who'd hide him awhile.

But first—Reynolds.

I t took Gavin an hour to find the house where Ken Reynolds lived. It was the best part of twenty-four hours since he'd eaten and his belly complained as he stood outside Livingstone Mansions. He told it to keep its peace, and slipped into the building. The interior looked less impressive by daylight. The tread of the stair carpet was worn, and the paint on the balustrade filthied with use.

Taking his time he climbed the three flights to Reynolds' apartment, and knocked.

Nobody answered, nor was there any sound of movement from inside. Reynolds had told him of course: don't come back—I won't be here. Had he somehow guessed the consequences of sicking that thing into the world?

Gavin rapped on the door again, and this time he was certain he heard somebody breathing on the other side of the door.

"Reynolds . . ." he said, pressing to the door, "I can hear you."

Nobody replied, but there was somebody in

there, he was sure of it. Gavin slapped his palm on the door.

"Come on, open up. Open up, you bastard."

A short silence, then a muffled voice. "Go away."

"I want to speak to you."

"Go away, I told you, go away. I've nothing to say to you."

"You owe me an explanation, for God's sake. If you don't open this fucking door I'll fetch someone who will."

An empty threat, but Reynolds responded: "No! Wait. Wait."

There was the sound of a key in the lock, and the door was opened a few paltry inches. The flat was in darkness beyond the scabby face that peered out at Gavin. It was Reynolds sure enough, but unshaven and wretched. He smelt unwashed, even through the crack in the door, and he was wearing only a stained shirt and a pair of pants, hitched up with a knotted belt.

"I can't help you. Go away."

"If you'll let me explain—" Gavin pressed the door, and Reynolds was either too weak or too befuddled to stop him opening it. He stumbled back into the darkened hallway.

"What the fuck's going on in here?"

The place stank of rotten food. The air was evil with it. Reynolds let Gavin slam the door behind him before producing a knife from the pocket of his stained trousers.

"You don't fool me," Reynolds gleamed, "I know what you've done. Very fine. Very clever."

"You mean the murders? It wasn't me."

Reynolds poked the knife towards Gavin.

"How many blood-baths did it take?" he asked, tears in his eyes. "Six? Ten?"

"I didn't kill anybody."

". . . monster."

The knife in Reynolds' hand was the paper knife Gavin himself had wielded. He approached Gavin with it. There was no doubt: he had every intention of using it. Gavin flinched, and Reynolds seemed to take hope from his fear.

"Had you forgotten what it was like, being flesh and blood?"

The man had lost his marbles.

"Look . . . I just came here to talk."

"You came here to kill me. I could reveal you . . . so you came to kill me."

"Do you know who I am?" Gavin said.

Reynolds sneered: "You're not the queer boy. You look like him, but you're not."

"For pity's sake . . . I'm Gavin . . . Gavin—"

The words to explain, to prevent the knife pressing any closer, wouldn't come.

"Gavin, you remember?" was all he could say.

Reynolds faltered a moment, staring at Gavin's face.

"You're sweating," he said. The dangerous stare fading in his eyes.

Gavin's mouth had gone so dry he could only nod.

"I can see," said Reynolds, "you're sweating."

He dropped the point of the knife.

"It could never sweat," he said. "Never had, never would have, the knack of it. You're the boy . . . not it. The boy."

His face slackened, its flesh a sack which was almost emptied.

"I need help," said Gavin, his voice hoarse. "You've got to tell me what's going on."

"You want an explanation?" Reynolds replied. "You can have whatever you can find."

He led the way into the main room. The curtains were drawn, but even in the gloom Gavin could see that every antiquity it had contained had been smashed beyond repair. The pottery shards had been reduced to smaller shards, and those shards to dust. The stone reliefs were destroyed, the tombstone of Flavinus the Standard-Bearer was rubble.

"Who did this?"

"I did," said Reynolds.

"Why?"

Reynolds sluggishly picked his way through the destruction to the window, and peered through a slit in the velvet curtains.

"It'll come back, you see," he said, ignoring the question.

Gavin insisted: "Why destroy it all?"

"It's a sickness," Reynolds replied. "Needing to live in the past."

He turned from the window.

"I stole most of these pieces," he said, "over a period of many years. I was put in a position of trust, and I misused it."

He kicked over a sizeable chunk of rubble: dust rose.

"Flavinus lived and died. That's all there is to tell. Knowing his name means nothing, or next to nothing. It doesn't make Flavinus real again: he's dead and happy."

"The statue in the bath?"

Reynolds stopped breathing for a moment, his inner eye meeting the painted face.

"You thought I was it, didn't you? When I came to the door."

"Yes. I thought it had finished its business."

"It imitates."

Reynolds nodded. "As far as I understand its nature," he said, "yes, it imitates."

"Where did you find it?"

"Near Carlisle. I was in charge of the excavation there. We found it lying in the bathhouse, a statue curled up into a ball beside the remains of an adult male. It was a riddle. A dead man and a statue, lying together in a bathhouse. Don't ask me what drew me to the thing, I don't know. Perhaps it works its will through the mind as well as the physique. I stole it, brought it back here."

"And you fed it?"

Reynolds stiffened.

"Don't ask."

"I am asking. You fed it?"

"Yes."

"You intended to bleed me, didn't you? That's why you brought me here: to kill me, and let it wash itself—"

Gavin remembered the noise of the creature's fists on the sides of the bath, that angry demand for food, like a child beating on its cot. He'd been so close to being taken by it, lamb-like.

"Why didn't it attack me the way it did you? Why didn't it just jump out of the bath and feed on me?"

Reynolds wiped his mouth with the palm of his hand.

"It saw your face, of course."

Of course: it saw my face, and wanted it for itself, and it couldn't steal the face of a dead man, so it let me be. The rationale for its behaviour was fascinating, now it was revealed: Gavin felt a taste of Reynolds' passion, unveiling mysteries.

"The man in the bathhouse. The one you uncovered—"

"Yes . . . ?"

"He stopped it doing the same thing to him, is that right?"

"That's probably why his body was never moved, just sealed up. No-one understood that he'd died fighting a creature that was stealing his life."

The picture was near as damn it complete; just anger remaining to be answered.

This man had come close to murdering him to feed the effigy. Gavin's fury broke surface. He took hold of Reynolds by shirt and skin, and shook him. Was it his bones or teeth that rattled?

"It's almost got my face." He stared into Reynolds' bloodshot eyes. "What happens when it finally has the trick off pat?"

"I don't know."

"You tell me the worst—tell me!"

"It's all guesswork," Reynolds replied.

"Guess then!"

"When it's perfected its physical imitation, I think it'll steal the one thing it can't imitate: your soul."

Reynolds was past fearing Gavin. His voice had sweetened, as though he was talking to a condemned man. He even smiled.

"Fucker!"

Gavin hauled Reynolds' face yet closer to his. White spittle dotted the old man's cheek.

"You don't care! You don't give a shit, do you?"

He hit Reynolds across the face, once, twice, then again and again, until he was breathless.

The old man took the beating in absolute silence, turning his face up from one blow to receive another, brushing the blood out of his swelling eyes only to have them fill again.

Finally, the punches faltered.

Reynolds, on his knees, picked pieces of tooth off his tongue.

"I deserved that," he murmured.

"How do I stop it?" said Gavin.

Reynolds shook his head.

"Impossible," he whispered, plucking at Gavin's hand. "Please," he said, and taking the fist, opened it and kissed the lines.

Gavin left Reynolds in the ruins of Rome, and went into the street. The interview with Reynolds had told him little he hadn't guessed. The only thing he could do now was find this beast that had his beauty, and best it. If he failed, he failed attempting to secure his only certain attribute: a face that was wonderful. Talk of souls and humanity was for him so much wasted air. He wanted his face.

There was rare purpose in his step as he crossed Kensington. After years of being the victim of circumstance he saw circumstance embodied at last. He would shake sense from it, or die trying.

In his flat Reynolds drew aside the curtain to watch a picture of evening fall on a picture of a city.

No night he would live through, no city he'd walk in again. Out of sighs, he let the curtain drop, and picked up the short stabbing sword. The point he put to his chest.

"Come on," he told himself and the sword, and pressed the hilt. But the pain as the blade entered his body a mere half inch was enough to make his head reel: he knew he'd faint before the job was half-done. So he crossed to the wall, steadied the hilt against it, and let his own body-weight impale him. That did the trick. He wasn't sure if the sword had skewered him through entirely, but by the amount of blood he'd surely killed himself. Though he tried to arrange to turn, and so drive the blade all the way home as he fell on it, he fluffed the gesture, and instead fell on his side. The impact made him aware of the sword in his body, a stiff, uncharitable presence transfixing him utterly.

It took him well over ten minutes to die, but in that time, pain apart, he was content. Whatever the flaws of his fifty-seven years, and they were many, he felt he was perishing in a way his beloved Flavinus would not have been ashamed of.

Towards the end it began to rain, and the noise on the roof made him believe God was burying the house, sealing him up forever. And as the moment came, so did a splendid delusion: a hand, carrying a light, and escorted by voices, seemed to break through the wall, ghosts of the future come to excavate his history. He smiled to greet them, and was about to ask what year this was when he realised he was dead.

The creature was far better at avoiding Gavin than he'd been at avoiding it. Three days passed without its pursuer snatching sight of hide or hair of it.

But the fact of its presence, close, but never too close, was indisputable. In a bar someone would say: "Saw you last night on the Edgware Road" when he'd not been near the place, or "How'd you make out with that Arab then?" or "Don't you speak to your friends any longer?"

And God, he soon got to like the feeling. The distress gave way to a pleasure he'd not known since the age of two: ease.

So what if someone else was working his patch, dodging the law and the street-wise alike; so what if his friends (what friends? Leeches) were being cut by this supercilious copy; so what if his life had been taken from him and was being worn to its length and its breadth in lieu of him? He could sleep, and know that he, or something so like him it made no difference, was awake in the night and being adored. He began to see the creature not as a monster terrorising him, but as his tool, his public persona almost. It was substance: he shadow.

He woke, dreaming.

It was four-fifteen in the afternoon, and the whine of traffic was loud from the street below. A twilight room; the air breathed and rebreathed and breathed again so it smelt of his lungs. It was over a week since he'd left Reynolds to the ruins, and in that time he'd only ventured out from his new digs (one tiny bedroom, kitchen, bathroom) three times. Sleep was more important now than food or exercise. He had enough dope to keep him happy when sleep wouldn't come, which was seldom, and he'd grown to like the staleness of the air, the flux of light through the curtainless window, the sense of a world elsewhere which he had no part of or place in.

Today he'd told himself he ought to go out and get some fresh air, but he hadn't been able to raise the enthusiasm. Maybe later, much later, when the bars were emptying and he wouldn't be noticed, then he'd slip out of his cocoon and see what could be seen. For now, there were dreams—

Water.

He'd dreamt water; sitting beside a pool in Fort Lauderdale, a pool full of fish. And the splash of their leaps and dives was continuing, an overflow from sleep. Or was it the other way round? Yes; he had been hearing running water in his sleep and his dreaming mind had made an illustration to accompany the sound. Now awake, the sound continued.

It was coming from the adjacent bathroom, no longer running, but lapping. Somebody had obviously broken in while he was asleep, and was now taking a bath. He ran down the short list of possible intruders: the few who knew he was here. There was Paul: a nascent hustler who'd bedded down on the floor two nights before; there was Chink, the dope dealer; and a girl from downstairs he thought was called Michelle. Who was he kidding? None of these people would have broken the lock on the door to get in. He knew very well who it must be. He was just playing a game with himself, enjoying the process of elimination, before he narrowed the options to one.

Keen for reunion, he slid out from his skin of sheet and duvet. His body turned to a column of gooseflesh as the cold air encased him, his sleep-erection hid its head. As he crossed the room to where his dressing gown hung on the back of the door he caught sight of himself in the mirror, a freeze frame from an atrocity film, a wisp of a man, shrunk by cold, and lit by a rainwater light. His reflection almost flickered, he was so insubstantial.

Wrapping the dressing gown, his only freshly purchased garment, around him, he went to the bathroom door. There was no noise of water now. He pushed the door open.

The warped linoleum was icy beneath his feet; and all he wanted to do was to see his friend, then crawl back into bed. But he owed the tatters of his curiosity more than that: he had questions.

The light through the frosted glass had deteriorated rapidly in the three minutes since he'd woken: the onset of night and a rain-storm congealing the gloom. In front of him the bath was almost filled to overflowing, the water was oil-slick calm, and dark. As before, nothing broke surface. It was lying deep, hidden.

How long was it since he'd approached a lime-green bath in a lime-green bathroom, and peered into the water? It could have been yesterday: his life between then and now had become one long night. He looked down. It was there, tucked up, as before, and asleep, still wearing all its clothes as though it had had no time to undress before it hid itself. Where it had been bald it now sprouted a luxuriant head of hair, and its features were quite complete. No trace of a painted face remained: it had a plastic beauty that was his own absolutely, down to the last mole. Its perfectly finished hands were crossed on its chest.

The night deepened. There was nothing to do but watch it sleep, and he became bored with that. It had traced him here, it wasn't likely to run away again, he could go back to bed. Outside the rain had slowed the commuters' homeward journey to a crawl, there were accidents, some fatal; engines overheated, hearts too. He listened to the chase; sleep came and went. It was the middle of the evening when thirst woke him again: he was dreaming water, and there was the sound as it had been before. The creature was hauling itself out of the bath, was putting its hand to the door, opening it.

There it stood. The only light in the bedroom was coming from the street below; it barely began to illuminate the visitor.

"Gavin? Are you awake?"

"Yes," he said.

"Will you help me?" it asked. There was no trace of threat in its voice, it asked as a man might ask his brother, for kinship's sake.

"What do you want?"

"Time to heal."

"Heal?"

"Put on the light?"

Gavin switched on the lamp beside the bed and looked at the figure at the door. It no longer had its arms crossed on its chest, and Gavin saw that the position had been covering an appalling shot-gun wound. The flesh of its chest had been blown open, exposing its colourless innards. There was, of course, no blood: that it would never have. Nor, from this distance, could Gavin see anything in its interior that faintly resembled human anatomy.

"God Almighty," he said.

"Preetorius had friends," said the other, and its fingers touched the edge of the wound. The gesture recalled a picture on the wall of his mother's house. Christ in Glory—the Sacred Heart floating inside the Saviour—while his fingers, pointing to the agony he'd suffered, said: "This was for you."

"Why aren't you dead?"

"Because I'm not yet alive," it said.

Not yet: remember that, Gavin thought. It has intimations of mortality.

"Are you in pain?"

"No," it said sadly, as though it craved the experience, "I feel nothing. All the signs of life are cosmetic. But I'm learning." It smiled. "I've got the knack of the yawn, and the fart." The idea was both absurd and touching; that it would aspire to farting, that a farcical failure in the digestive system was for it a precious sign of humanity.

"And the wound?"

"—is healing. Will heal completely in time."

Gavin said nothing.

"Do I disgust you?" it asked, without inflection.

"No."

It was staring at Gavin with perfect eyes, his perfect eyes.

"What did Reynolds tell you?" it asked.

Gavin shrugged.

"Very little."

"That I'm a monster? That I suck out the human spirit?"

"Not exactly."

"More or less."

"More or less," Gavin conceded.

It nodded. "He's right," it said. "In his way, he's right. I need blood: that makes me monstrous. In my youth, a month ago, I bathed in it. Its touch gave wood the appearance of flesh. But I don't need it now: the process is almost finished. All I need now—"

It faltered; not, Gavin thought, because it intended to lie, but because the words to describe its condition wouldn't come.

"What do you need?" Gavin pressed it.

It shook its head, looking down at the carpet. "I've lived several times, you know. Sometimes I've stolen lives and got away with it. Lived a natural span, then shrugged off that face and found another. Sometimes, like the last time, I've been challenged, and lost—"

"Are you some kind of machine?"

"No."

"What then?"

"I am what I am. I know of no others like me; though why should I be the only one? Perhaps there *are* others, many others: I simply don't know of them yet. So I live and die and live again, and learn nothing"—the word was bitterly pronounced—"of myself. Understand? You know what you are because you see others like you. If you were alone on earth, what would you know? What the mirror told you, that's all. The rest would be myth and conjecture."

The summary was made without sentiment.

"May I lie down?" it asked.

It began to walk towards him, and Gavin could see more clearly the fluttering in its chest-cavity, the restless, incoherent forms that were mushrooming there in place of the heart. Sighing, it sank face-down on the bed, its clothes sodden, and closed its eyes.

"We'll heal," it said. "Just give us time."

Gavin went to the door of the flat and bolted it. Then he dragged a table over and wedged it under the handle. Nobody could get in and attack it in sleep: they would stay here together in safety, he and it, he and himself. The fortress secured, he brewed some coffee and sat in the chair across the room from the bed and watched the creature sleep.

The rain rushed against the window heavily one hour, lightly the next. Wind threw sodden leaves against the glass and they clung there like inquisitive moths; he watched them sometimes, when he tired of watching himself, but before long he'd want to look again, and he'd be back staring at the casual beauty of his outstretched arm, the light flicking the wrist-bone, the lashes. He fell asleep in the chair about midnight, with an ambulance complaining in the street outside, and the rain coming again.

It wasn't comfortable in the chair, and he'd surface from sleep every few minutes, his eyes opening a fraction. The creature was up: it was standing by the window, now in front of the mirror, now in the kitchen. Water ran: he dreamt water. The creature undressed: he dreamt sex. It stood over him, its chest whole, and he was reassured by its presence: he dreamt, it was for a moment only, himself lifted out of a street through a window into Heaven. It dressed in his clothes: he murmured his assent to the theft in his sleep. It was whistling: and there was a threat of day through the window, but he was too dozy to stir just yet, and quite content to have the whistling young man in his clothes live for him.

At last it leaned over the chair and kissed him on the lips, a brother's kiss, and left. He heard the door close behind it.

After that there were days, he wasn't sure how many, when he stayed in the room, and did nothing but drink water. This thirst had become unquenchable. Drinking and sleeping, drinking and sleeping, twin moons.

The bed he slept on was damp at the beginning from where the creature had laid, and he had no wish to change the sheets. On the contrary he enjoyed the wet linen, which his body dried out too soon. When it did he took a bath himself in the water the thing had lain in and returned to the bed dripping wet, his skin crawling with cold, and the scent of mildew all around. Later, too indifferent to move, he allowed his bladder free rein while he lay on the bed, and that water in time became cold, until he dried it with his dwindling body-heat.

But for some reason, despite the icy room, his nakedness, his hunger, he couldn't die.

He got up in the middle of the night of the sixth or seventh day, and sat on the edge of the bed to find the flaw in his resolve. When the solution didn't come he began to shamble around the room much as the creature had a week earlier, standing in front of the mirror to survey his pitifully changed body, watching the snow shimmer down and melt on the sill.

Eventually, by chance, he found a picture of his parents he remembered the creature staring at. Or had he dreamt that? He thought not: he had a distinct idea that it had picked up this picture and looked at it.

That was, of course, the bar to his suicide: that picture. There were respects to be paid. Until then how could he hope to die?

He walked to the Cemetery through the slush wearing only a pair of slacks and a tee-shirt. The remarks of middle-aged women and school-children went unheard. Whose business but his own was it if going barefoot was the death of him? The rain came and went, sometimes thickening towards snow, but never quite achieving its ambition.

There was a service going on at the church itself, a line of brittle coloured cars parked at the front. He slipped down the side into the churchyard. It boasted a good view, much spoiled today by the smoky veil of sleet, but he could see the trains and the high-rise flats; the endless rows of roofs. He ambled amongst the headstones, by no means certain of where to find his father's grave. It had been sixteen years: and the day hadn't been that memorable. Nobody had said anything illuminating about death in general, or his father's death specifically, there wasn't even a social gaff or two to mark the day: no aunt broke wind at the buffet table, no cousin took him aside to expose herself.

He wondered if the rest of the family ever came here: whether indeed they were still in the country. His sister had always threatened to move out: go to New Zealand, begin again. His mother was probably getting through her fourth husband by now, poor sod, though perhaps she was the pitiable one, with her endless chatter barely concealing the panic.

Here was the stone. And yes, there were fresh flowers in the marble urn that rested amongst the green marble chips. The old bugger had not lain here enjoying the view unnoticed. Obviously somebody, he guessed his sister, had come here seeking a little comfort from Father. Gavin ran his fingers over the name, the date, the platitude. Nothing exceptional, which was only right and proper, because there'd been nothing exceptional about him.

Staring at the stone, words came spilling out, as though Father was sitting on the edge of the grave, dangling his feet, raking his hair across his gleaming scalp, pretending, as he always pretended, to care.

"What do you think, eh?"

Father wasn't impressed.

"Not much, am I?" Gavin confessed.

You said it, son.

"Well I was always careful, like you told me. There aren't any bastards out there, going to come looking for me."

Damn pleased.

"I wouldn't be much to find, would I?"

Father blew his nose, wiped it three times. Once from left to right, again left to right, finishing right to left. Never failed. Then he slipped away.

"Old shithouse."

A toy train let out a long blast on its horn as it passed and Gavin looked up. There he was—himself—standing absolutely still a few yards away. He was wearing the same clothes he'd put on a week ago when he'd left the flat. They looked creased and shabby from constant wear. But the flesh! Oh, the flesh was more radiant than his own had ever been. It almost shone in the drizzling light; and the tears on the doppelganger's cheeks only made the features more exquisite.

"What's wrong?" said Gavin.

"It always makes me cry, coming here." It stepped over the graves towards him, its feet crunching on gravel, soft on grass. So real.

"You've been here before?"

"Oh yes. Many times, over the years—"

Over the years? What did it mean, over the years? Had it mourned here for people it had killed?

As if in answer:

"—I come to visit Father. Twice, maybe three times a year."

"This isn't your father," said Gavin, almost amused by the delusion. "It's mine."

"I don't see any tears on your face," said the other.

"I feel . . ."

"Nothing," his face told him. "You feel nothing at all, if you're honest."

That was the truth.

"Whereas I . . ." The tears began to flow again, its nose ran. "I will miss him until I die."

It was surely playacting, but if so why was there such grief in its eyes: and why were its features crumpled into ugliness as it wept. Gavin had seldom given in to tears: they'd always made him feel weak and ridiculous. But this thing was proud of tears, it gloried in them. They were its triumph.

And even then, knowing it had overtaken him, Gavin could find nothing in him that approximated grief.

"Have it," he said. "Have the snots. You're welcome."

The creature was hardly listening.

"Why is it all so painful?" it asked, after a pause. "Why is it loss that makes me human?"

Gavin shrugged. What did he know or care about the fine art of being human? The creature wiped its nose with its sleeve, sniffed, and tried to smile through its unhappiness.

"I'm sorry," it said, "I'm making a damn fool of myself. Please forgive me."

It inhaled deeply, trying to compose itself.

"That's all right," said Gavin. The display embarrassed him, and he was glad to be leaving.

"Your flowers?" he asked as he turned from the grave.

It nodded.

"He hated flowers."

The thing flinched.

"Ah."

"Still, what does he know?"

He didn't even look at the effigy again; just turned and started up the path that ran beside the church. A few yards on, the thing called after him:

"Can you recommend a dentist?"

Gavin grinned, and kept walking.

It was almost the commuter hour. The arterial road that ran by the church was already thick with speeding traffic: perhaps it was Friday, early escapees hurrying home. Lights blazed brilliantly, horns blared.

Gavin stepped into the middle of the flow without looking to right or left, ignoring the squeals of brakes, and the curses, and began to walk amongst the traffic as if he were idling in an open field.

The wing of a speeding car grazed his leg as it passed, another almost collided with him. Their eagerness to get somewhere, to arrive at a place they would presently be itching to depart from again, was comical. Let them rage at him, loathe him, let them glimpse his featureless face and go home haunted. If the circumstances were right, maybe one of them would panic, swerve, and run him down. Whatever. From now on he belonged to chance, whose Standard-Bearer he would surely be.

# THE VAMPIRE

# Sydney Horler

Sydney Henry Horler (1888–1954) was born in Leytonstone, London, and educated at the Redcliff School and Colston School in Bristol. He became a journalist for the Western Daily Press and Allied Newspapers in Bristol in 1905, leaving
to become a special features writer on the staff of Edward Hulton & Co. in Manchester in 1911. He moved to London to work on the *Daily Mail* and *Daily Citizen,* then joined the air force when World War I erupted, first as a clerk, then
writing propaganda for the Air Intelligence Agency; because of poor eyesight, he
never saw combat. After the war, he married and became the subeditor of *John
O'London's Weekly.* He had begun to write his own books and, when he was fired
in 1919, turned to a full-time career as a freelance writer of sports stories and books,
short stories and novels.

After his first mystery novel, *The Mystery of No. 1* (1925), was published, he
became one of the most prolific, popular, and successful thriller writers in the
United Kingdom over the next three decades. He went on to write 157 books,
mostly crime novels and some supernatural fiction as well. It became common for
his publisher to put the exclamatory "Horler for Excitement!" on his dust jackets. His most famous series character is the Honorable Timothy Overbury "Tiger"
Standish, a two-fisted adventurer in the mode of Bulldog Drummond.

"The Vampire" was first published in book form in *The Screaming Skull and
Other Stories* (London: Hodder & Stoughton, 1930).

# The Vampire

## SYDNEY HORLER

# TEN MINUTES OF HORROR

Until his death, quite recently, I used to visit at least once a week a Roman Catholic priest. The fact that I am a Protestant did nothing to shake our friendship. Father R—— was one of the finest characters I have ever known; he was capable of the broadest sympathies, and was, in the best sense of that frequently-abused term, "a man of the world." He was good enough to take considerable interest in my work as a novelist, and I often discussed plots and situations with him.

The story I am about to relate occurred about eighteen months ago—ten months before his illness. I was then writing my novel "The Curse of Doone." In this story I made the villain take advantage of a ghastly legend attached to an old manor-house in Devonshire and use it for his own ends.

Father R—— listened while I outlined the plot I had in mind, and then said, to my great surprise: "Certain people may scoff because they will not allow themselves to believe that there is any credence in the vampire tradition."

"Yes, that is so," I parried, "but, all the same, Bram Stoker stirred the public imagination with his 'Dracula'—one of the most horrible and yet fascinating books ever written—and I am hoping that my public will extend to me the customary 'author's licence.'"

My friend nodded.

"Quite," he replied. "As a matter of fact," he went on to say, "I believe in vampires myself."

"You do?" I felt the hair on the back of my neck commence to irritate. It is one thing to write about a horror, but quite another to begin to see it assume definite shape.

"Yes," said Father R——. "I am forced to believe in vampires for the very good but terrible reason that I have met one!"

I half-rose in my chair. There could be no questioning R——'s word, and yet—

"That, no doubt, my dear fellow," he continued, "may appear a very extraordinary statement to have made, and yet I assure you it is the truth. It happened many years ago and in another part of the country—exactly where I do not think I had better tell you."

"But this is amazing—you say you actually met a vampire face to face?"

"And talked to him. Until now I have never mentioned the matter to a living soul apart from a brother priest."

It was clearly an invitation to listen; I crammed tobacco into my pipe and leaned back in the chair on the opposite side of the crackling fire. I had heard that Truth was said to be stranger than fiction—but here I was about to have, it seemed, the strange experience of listening to my own most sensational imagining being hopelessly out-done by FACT!

The name of the small town does not matter (Father R—— started); let it suffice it was in the West of England and was inhabited by a good many people of superior means. There was a large city seventy-five miles away and business men, when they retired, often came to —— to wind up their lives. I was young and very happy there in my work until——. But I am a little previous.

I was on very friendly terms with a local doctor; he often used to come in and have a chat when he could spare the time. We used to try to thresh out many problems which later experience has convinced me are insoluble—in this world, at least.

One night, he looked at me rather curiously I thought.

"What do you think of that man, Farington?" he asked.

Now, it was a curious fact that he should have made that inquiry at that exact moment, for by some subconscious means I happened to be thinking of this very person myself.

The man who called himself "Joseph Faring-ton" was a stranger who had recently come to settle in ——. That circumstance alone would have caused comment, but when I say that he had bought the largest house on the hill overlooking the town on the south side (representing the best residential quarter) and had had it furnished apparently regardless of cost by one of the famous London houses, that he sought to entertain a great deal but that no one seemed anxious to go twice to "The Gables." Well, there was "something funny" about Farington, it was whispered.

I knew this, of course—the smallest fragment of gossip comes to a priest's ears—and so I hesitated before replying to the doctor's direct question.

"Confess now, Father," said my companion, "you are like all the rest of us—you don't like the man! He has made me his medical attendant, but I wish to goodness he had chosen someone else. There's 'something funny' about him."

"Something funny"—there it was again. As the doctor's words sounded in my ears I remembered Farington as I had last seen him walking up the main street with every other eye half-turned in his direction. He was a big-framed man, the essence of masculinity. He looked so robust that the thought came instinctively: This man will never die. He had a florid complexion; he walked with the elasticity of youth and his hair was jet-black. Yet from remarks he had made the impression in —— was that Farington must be at least sixty years of age.

"Well, there's one thing, Sanders," I replied. "If appearances are anything to go by, Farington will not be giving you much trouble. The fellow looks as strong as an ox."

"You haven't answered my question," persisted the doctor. "Forget your cloth, Father, and tell me exactly what you think of Joseph Farington. Don't you agree that he is a man to give you the shudders?"

"You—a doctor—talking about getting the shudders!" I gently scoffed because I did not want to give my real opinion of Joseph Farington.

"I can't help it—I have an instinctive horror of the fellow. This afternoon I was called up to 'The Gables.' Farington, like ever so many of his ox-like kind, is really a bit of a hypochondriac. He thought there was something wrong with his heart, he said."

"And was there?"

"The man ought to live to a hundred! But, I tell you, Father, I hated having to be near the fellow, there's something uncanny about him. I felt frightened—yes, frightened—all the time I was in the house. I had to talk to someone about it and as you are the safest person in —— I dropped in. . . . You haven't said anything yourself, I notice."

"I prefer to wait," I replied. It seemed the safest answer.

Two months after that conversation with Sanders, not only —— but the whole of the country was startled and horrified by a terrible crime. A girl of eighteen, the belle of the district, was found dead in a field. Her face, in life so beautiful, was revolting in death because of the expression of dreadful horror it held.

The poor girl had been murdered—but in a manner which sent shudders of fear racing up and down people's spines. . . . There was a great hole in the throat, as though a beast of the jungle had attacked. . . .

It is not difficult to say how suspicion for this fiendish crime first started to fasten itself on Joseph Farington, preposterous as the statement may seem. Although he had gone out of his way to become sociable, the man had made no real friends. Sanders, although a clever doctor, was not the most tactful of men and there is no doubt that his refusal to visit Farington professionally—he had hinted as much on the night of his visit to me, you will remember—got noised about. In any case, public opinion was strongly roused; without a shred of direct evidence to go upon, people began to talk of Farington as being the actual murderer. There was some talk among the wild young spirits of setting fire to "The Gables" one night, and burning Farington in his bed.

It was whilst this feeling was at its height that, very unwillingly, as you may imagine, I was brought into the affair. I received a note from Farington asking me to dine with him one night.

*I have something on my mind which I wish to talk over with you; so please do not fail me.*

These were the concluding words of the letter.

Such an appeal could not be ignored by a man of religion and so I replied accepting.

Farington was a good host; the food was excellent; on the surface there was nothing wrong. But—and here is the curious part—from the moment I faced the man I knew there *was* something wrong. I had the same uneasiness as Sanders, the doctor: *I felt afraid.* The man had an aura of evil; he was possessed of some devilish force or quality which chilled me to the marrow.

I did my best to hide my discomfiture, but when, after dinner, Farington began to speak about the murder of that poor, innocent girl, this feeling increased. And at once the terrible truth leaped into my mind: I knew it was Farington who had done this crime: the man was a monster!

Calling upon all my strength, I challenged him.

"You wished to see me to-night for the purpose of easing your soul of a terrible burden," I said. "You cannot deny that it was you who killed that unfortunate girl."

"Yes," he replied slowly, "that is the truth. I killed the girl. The demon which possesses me forced me to do it. But you, as a priest, must hold this confession sacred—you must preserve it as a secret. Give me a few more hours; then I will decide myself what to do."

I left shortly afterwards. The man would not say anything more.

"Give me a few hours," he repeated.

That night I had a horrible dream. I felt I was suffocating. Scarcely able to breathe, I rushed to the window, pulled it open—and then fell senseless to the floor. The next thing I remember was Dr. Sanders—who had been summoned by my faithful housekeeper—bending over me.

"What happened?" he asked. "You had a look on your face as though you had been staring into hell."

"So I had," I replied.

"Had it anything to do with Farington?" he asked bluntly.

"Sanders," and I clutched him by the arm in the intensity of my feeling, "does such a monstrosity as a vampire exist nowadays? Tell me, I implore you!"

The good fellow forced me to take another nip of brandy before he would reply.

Then he put a question himself.

"Why do you ask that?" he said.

"It sounds incredible—and I hope I really dreamed it—but I fainted to-night because I saw—or imagined I saw—the man Farington flying past the window that I had just opened."

"I am not surprised," he nodded. "Ever since I examined the mutilated body of that poor girl I came to the conclusion that she had come to her death through some terrible abnormality.

"Although we hear practically nothing about vampirism nowadays," he continued, "that is not to say that ghoulish spirits do not still take up their abode in a living man or woman, thus conferring upon them supernatural powers. What form was the shape you thought you saw?"

"It was like a huge bat," I replied, shuddering.

"To-morrow," said Sanders determinedly, "I'm going to London to see Scotland Yard. They may laugh at me at first, but—"

Scotland Yard did not laugh. But criminals with supernatural powers were rather out of their line, and, besides, as they told Sanders, they had to have *proof* before they could convict Farington. Even my testimony—had I dared to break my priestly pledge, which, of course, I couldn't in any circumstances do—would not have been sufficient.

Farington solved the terrible problem by committing suicide. He was found in bed with a bullet wound in his head.

But, according to Sanders, only the body is dead—the vile spirit is roaming free, looking for another human habitation.

God help its luckless victim.

## STRAGELLA

# Hugh B. Cave

Hugh Barnett Cave (1910–2004) was born in Chester, England, but his family moved to Boston when World War I broke out. He attended Boston University for a short time, taking a job at a vanity publishing house before becoming a full-time writer at the age of twenty. At nineteen he had sold his first short stories, "Island Ordeal" and "The Pool of Death," and went on to produce more than a thousand stories, mostly for the pulps but also with more than three hundred sales to national "slick" magazines such as *Collier's, Redbook, Good Housekeeping,* and *The Saturday Evening Post.* Although he wrote in virtually every genre, he is remembered most for his horror, supernatural, and science-fiction works. In addition to the numerous stories, he wrote forty novels, juveniles, and several volumes of nonfiction, including an authoritative study of voodoo. His best-selling novel, *Long Were the Nights* (1943), drew on his extensive reportage of World War II in the Pacific and featured the adventures of PT boats and those who captained them at Guadalcanal. He also wrote several nonfiction books chronicling World War II in the Pacific theater.

Cave was the recipient of numerous awards, including the Living Legend Award from the International Horror Guild, the Bram Stoker Lifetime Achievement Award from the Horror Writers Association, and the World Fantasy Life Achievement Award.

"Stragella" was first published in the June 1932 issue of *Strange Tales of Mystery and Terror.*

# Stragella

## HUGH B. CAVE

ight, black as pitch and filled with the wailing of a dead wind, sank like a shapeless specter into the oily waters of the Indian Ocean, leaving a great gray expanse of sullen sea, empty except for a solitary speck that rose and dropped in the long swell.

The forlorn thing was a ship's boat. For seven days and seven nights it had drifted through the waste, bearing its ghastly burden. Now, groping to his knees, one of the two survivors peered away into the East, where the first glare of a red sun filtered over the rim of the world.

Within arm's reach, in the bottom of the boat, lay a second figure, face down. All night long he had lain there. Even the torrential shower, descending in the dark hours and flooding the dory with life-giving water, had failed to move him.

The first man crawled forward. Scooping water out of the tarpaulin with a battered tin cup, he turned his companion over and forced the stuff through receded lips.

"Miggs!" The voice was a cracked whisper. "Miggs! Good God, you ain't dead, Miggs? I ain't left all alone out here—"

John Miggs opened his eyes feebly.

"What—what's wrong?" he muttered.

"We got water, Miggs! Water!"

"You're dreamin' again, Yancy. It—it ain't water. It's nothin' but sea—"

"It rained!" Yancy screeched. "Last night it rained. I stretched the tarpaulin. All night long I been lyin' face up, lettin' it rain in my mouth!"

Miggs touched the tin cup to his tongue and lapped its contents suspiciously. With a mumbled cry he gulped the water down. Then, gibbering like a monkey, he was crawling toward the tarpaulin.

Yancy flung him back, snarling.

"No you won't!" Yancy rasped. "We got to save it, see? We got to get out of here."

Miggs glowered at him from the opposite end of the dory. Yancy sprawled down beside the tarpaulin and stared once again over the abandoned sea, struggling to reason things out.

They were somewhere in the Bay of Bengal. A week ago they had been on board the *Cardigan*, a tiny tramp freighter carrying its handful of passengers from Maulmain to Georgetown. The *Cardigan* had foundered in the typhoon off the Mergui Archipelago. For twelve hours she had heaved and groaned through an inferno of swirling seas. Then she had gone under.

Yancy's memory of the succeeding events was

763

a twisted, unreal parade of horrors. At first there had been five men in the little boat. Four days of terrific heat, no water, no food, had driven the little Persian priest mad; and he had jumped overboard. The other two had drunk salt water and died in agony. Now he and Miggs were alone.

The sun was incandescent in a white hot sky. The sea was calm, greasy, unbroken except for the slow, patient black fins that had been following the boat for days. But something else, during the night, had joined the sharks in their hellish pursuit. Sea snakes, hydrophiinae, wriggling out of nowhere, had come to haunt the dory, gliding in circles round and round, venomous, vivid, vindictive. And overhead were gulls wheeling, swooping in erratic arcs, cackling fiendishly and watching the two men with relentless eyes.

Yancy glanced up at them. Gulls and snakes could mean only one thing—land! He supposed they had come from the Andamans, the prison isles of India. It didn't much matter. They were here. Hideous, menacing harbingers of hope!

His shirt, filthy and ragged, hung open to the belt, revealing a lean chest tattooed with grotesque figures. A long time ago—too long to remember— he had gone on a drunken binge in Goa. Jap rum had done it. In company with two others of the *Cardigan*'s crew he had shambled into a tattooing establishment and ordered the Jap, in a bloated voice, to "paint anything you damned well like, professor. Anything at all!" And the Jap, being of a religious mind and sentimental, had decorated Yancy's chest with a most beautiful Crucifix, large, ornate, and colorful.

It brought a grim smile to Yancy's lips as he peered down at it. But presently his attention was centered on something else—something unnatural, bewildering, on the horizon. The thing was a narrow bank of fog lying low on the water, as if a distorted cloud had sunk out of the sky and was floating heavily, half submerged in the sea. And the small boat was drifting toward it.

In a little while the fog bank hung dense on all sides. Yancy groped to his feet, gazing about him. John Miggs muttered something beneath his breath and crossed himself.

The thing was shapeless, grayish-white, clammy. It reeked—not with the dank smell of sea fog, but with the sickly, pungent stench of a buried jungle or a subterranean mushroom cellar. The sun seemed unable to penetrate it. Yancy could see the red ball above him, a feeble, smothered eye of crimson fire, blotted by swirling vapor.

"The gulls," mumbled Miggs. "They're gone."

"I know it. The sharks, too—and the snakes. We're all alone, Miggs."

An eternity passed, while the dory drifted deeper and deeper into the cone. And then there was something else—something that came like a moaning voice out of the fog. The muted, irregular, singsong clangor of a ship's bell!

"Listen!" Miggs cackled. "You hear—"

But Yancy's trembling arm had come up abruptly, pointing ahead.

"By God, Miggs! Look!"

Miggs scrambled up, rocking the boat beneath him. His bony fingers gripped Yancy's arm. They stood there, the two of them, staring at the massive black shape that loomed up, like an ethereal phantom of another world, a hundred feet before them.

"We're saved," Miggs said incoherently. "Thank God, Nels—"

Yancy called out shrilly. His voice rang through the fog with a hoarse jangle, like the scream of a caged tiger. It choked into silence. And there was no answer, no responsive outcry—nothing so much as a whisper.

The dory drifted closer. No sound came from the lips of the two men as they drew alongside. There was nothing—nothing but the intermittent tolling of that mysterious, muted bell.

Then they realized the truth—a truth that brought a moan from Miggs' lips. The thing was a derelict, frowning out of the water, inanimate, sullen, buried in its winding-sheet of unearthly fog. Its stern was high, exposing a propeller red with rust and matted with clinging weeds. Across the bow, nearly obliterated by age, appeared the words: *Golconda—Cardiff*.

"Yancy, it ain't no real ship! It ain't of this world—"

Yancy stooped with a snarl, and picked up the oar in the bottom of the dory. A rope dangled within reach, hanging like a black serpent over the scarred hull. With clumsy strokes he drove the small boat beneath it; then, reaching up, he seized the line and made the boat fast.

"You're—goin' aboard?" Miggs said fearfully.

Yancy hesitated, staring up with bleary eyes. He was afraid, without knowing why. The *Golconda* frightened him. The mist clung to her tenaciously. She rolled heavily, ponderously in the long swell; and the bell was still tolling softly somewhere within the lost vessel.

"Well, why not?" Yancy growled. "There may be food aboard. What's there to be afraid of?"

Miggs was silent. Grasping the ropes, Yancy clambered up them. His body swung like a gibbet-corpse against the side. Clutching the rail, he heaved himself over; then stood there, peering into the layers of thick fog, as Miggs climbed up and dropped down beside him.

"I—don't like it," Miggs whispered. "It ain't—"

Yancy groped forward. The deck planks creaked dismally under him. With Miggs clinging close, he led the way into the waist, then into the bow. The cold fog seemed to have accumulated here in a sluggish mass, as if some magnetic force had drawn it. Through it, with arms outheld in front of him, Yancy moved with shuffling steps, a blind man in a strange world.

Suddenly he stopped—stopped so abruptly that Miggs lurched headlong into him. Yancy's body stiffened. His eyes were wide, glaring at the deck before him. A hollow, unintelligible sound parted his lips.

Miggs cringed back with a livid screech, clawing at his shoulder.

"What—what is it?" he said thickly.

At their feet were bones. Skeletons—lying there in the swirl of vapor. Yancy shuddered as he examined them. Dead things they were, dead and harmless, yet they were given new life by the motion of the mist. They seemed to crawl, to wriggle, to slither toward him and away from him.

He recognized some of them as portions of human frames. Others were weird, unshapely things. A tiger skull grinned up at him with jaws that seemed to widen hungrily. The vertebrae of a huge python lay in disjointed coils on the planks, twisted as if in agony. He discerned the skeletonic remains of tigers, tapirs, and jungle beasts of unknown identity. And human heads, many of them, scattered about like an assembly of mocking, dead-alive faces, leering at him, watching him with hellish anticipation. The place was a morgue—a charnel house!

Yancy fell back, stumbling. His terror had returned with triple intensity. He felt cold perspiration forming on his forehead, on his chest, trickling down the tattooed Crucifix.

Frantically he swung about in his tracks and made for the welcome solitude of the stern deck, only to have Miggs clutch feverishly at his arm.

"I'm goin' to get out of here, Nels! That damned bell—these here things—"

Yancy flung the groping hands away. He tried to control his terror. This ship—this *Golconda*—was nothing but a tramp trader. She'd been carrying a cargo of jungle animals for some expedition. The beasts had got loose, gone amuck, in a storm. There was nothing fantastic about it!

In answer, came the intermittent clang of the hidden bell below decks and the soft lapping sound of the water swishing through the thick weeds which clung to the ship's bottom.

"Come on," Yancy said grimly. "I'm goin' to have a look around. We need food."

He strode back through the waist of the ship, with Miggs shuffling behind. Feeling his way to the towering stern, he found the fog thinner, less pungent.

The hatch leading down into the stern hold was open. It hung before his face like an uplifted hand, scarred, bloated, as if in mute warning. And out of the aperture at its base straggled a spidery thing that was strangely out of place here on this abandoned derelict—a curious, menacing, crawling vine with mottled triangular leaves and immense orange-hued blossoms. Like a living snake, intertwined about itself, it coiled out of the hold and wormed over the deck.

Yancy stepped closer, hestitantly. Bending down, he reached to grasp one of the blooms, only to turn his face away and fall back with an involuntary mutter. The flowers were sickly sweet, nauseating. They repelled him with their savage odor.

"Somethin'—" Miggs whispered sibilantly, "is watchin' us, Nels! I can feel it."

Yancy peered all about him. He, too, felt a third presence close at hand. Something malignant, evil, unearthly. He could not name it.

"It's your imagination," he snapped. "Shut up, will you?"

"We ain't alone, Nels. This ain't no ship at all!"

"Shut *up*!"

"But the flowers there—they ain't right. Flowers don't grow aboard a Christian ship, Nels!"

"This hulk's been here long enough for trees to grow on it," Yancy said curtly. "The seeds probably took root in the filth below."

"Well, I don't like it."

"Go forward and see what you can find. I'm goin' below to look around."

Miggs shrugged helplessly and moved away. Alone, Yancy descended to the lower levels. It was dark down here, full of shadows and huge gaunt forms that lost their substance in the coils of thick, sinuous fog. He felt his way along the passage, pawing the wall with both hands. Deeper and deeper into the labyrinth he went, until he found the galley.

The galley was a dungeon, reeking of dead, decayed food, as if the stench had hung there for an eternity without being molested; as if the entire ship lay in an atmosphere of its own—an atmosphere of the grave—through which the clean outer air never broke.

But there was food here; canned food that stared down at him from the rotted shelves. The labels were blurred, illegible. Some of the cans crumbled in Yancy's fingers as he seized them—disintegrated into brown, dry dust and trickled to the floor. Others were in fair condition, air-tight. He stuffed four of them into his pockets and turned away.

Eagerly now, he stumbled back along the passage. The prospects of food took some of those other thoughts out of his mind, and he was in better humor when he finally found the captain's cabin.

Here, too, the evident age of the place gripped him. The walls were gray with mold, falling into a broken, warped floor. A single table stood on the far side near the bunk, a blackened, grimy table bearing an upright oil lamp and a single black book.

He picked the lamp up timidly and shook it. The circular base was yet half full of oil, and he set it down carefully. It would come in handy later. Frowning, he peered at the book beside it.

It was a seaman's Bible, a small one, lying there, coated with cracked dust, dismal with age. Around it, as if some crawling slug had examined it on all sides, leaving a trail of excretion, lay a peculiar line of black pitch, irregular but unbroken.

Yancy picked the book up and flipped it open. The pages slid under his fingers, allowing a scrap of loose paper to flutter to the floor. He stooped to retrieve it; then, seeing that it bore a line of penciled script, he peered closely at it.

The writing was an apparently irrelevant scrawl—a meaningless memorandum which said crudely:

*It's the bats and the crates. I know it now, but it is too late. God help me!*

With a shrug, he replaced it and thrust the Bible into his belt, where it pressed comfortingly against his body. Then he continued his exploration.

In the wall cupboard he found two full bottles of liquor, which proved to be brandy. Leaving them there, he groped out of the cabin and returned to the upper deck in search of Miggs.

Miggs was leaning on the rail, watching something below. Yancy trudged toward him, calling out shrilly:

"Say, I got food, Miggs! Food and brand—"

He did not finish. Mechanically his eyes followed the direction of Miggs' stare, and he recoiled involuntarily as his words clipped into stifled silence. On the surface of the oily water below, huge sea snakes paddled against the ship's side—enormous slithering shapes, banded with streaks of black and red and yellow, vicious and repulsive.

"They're back," Miggs said quickly. "They know this ain't no proper ship. They come here out of their hell-hole, to wait for us."

Yancy glanced at him curiously. The inflection of Miggs' voice was peculiar—not at all the phlegmatic, guttural tone that usually grumbled through the little man's lips. It was almost eager!

"What did you find?" Yancy faltered.

"Nothin'. All the ship's boats are hangin' in their davits. Never been touched."

"I found food," Yancy said abruptly, gripping his arm. "We'll eat; then we'll feel better. What the hell are we, anyhow—a couple of fools? Soon as we eat, we'll stock the dory and get off this blasted death ship and clear out of this stinkin' fog. We got water in the tarpaulin."

"We'll clear out? Will we, Nels?"

"Yah. Let's eat."

Once again, Yancy led the way below decks to the galley. There, after a twenty-minute effort in building a fire in the rusty stove, he and Miggs prepared a meal, carrying the food into the captain's cabin, where Yancy lighted the lamp.

They ate slowly, sucking the taste hungrily out of every mouthful, reluctant to finish. The lamplight, flickering in their faces, made gaunt masks of features that were already haggard and full of anticipation.

The brandy, which Yancy fetched out of the cupboard, brought back strength and reason—and confidence. It brought back, too, that unnatural sheen to Miggs' twitching eyes.

"We'd be damned fools to clear out of here right off," Miggs said suddenly. "The fog's got to lift sooner or later. I ain't trustin' myself to no small boat again, Nels—not when we don't know where we're at."

Yancy looked at him sharply. The little man turned away with a guilty shrug. Then hesitantly:

"I—I kinda like it here, Nels."

Yancy caught the odd gleam in those small eyes. He bent forward quickly.

"Where'd you go when I left you alone?" he demanded.

"Me? I didn't go nowhere. I—I just looked around a bit, and I picked a couple of them flowers. See."

Miggs groped in his shirt pocket and held up one of the livid, orange-colored blooms. His face took on an unholy brilliance as he held the thing close to his lips and inhaled its deadly aroma. His eyes, glittering across the table, were on fire with sudden fanatic lust.

For an instant Yancy did not move. Then, with a savage oath, he lurched up and snatched the flower out of Miggs' fingers. Whirling, he flung it to the floor and ground it under his boot.

"You damned thick-headed fool!" he screeched. "You—God help you!"

Then he went limp, muttering incoherently. With faltering steps he stumbled out of the cabin and along the black passageway, and up on the abandoned deck. He staggered to the rail and stood there, holding himself erect with nerveless hands.

"God!" he whispered hoarsely. "God—what did I do that for? Am I goin' crazy?"

No answer came out of the silence. But he knew the answer. The thing he had done down there in the skipper's cabin—those mad words that had spewed from his mouth—had been involuntary. Something inside him, some sense of danger that was all about him, had hurled the words out of his mouth before he could control them. And his nerves were on edge, too; they felt as though they were ready to crack.

But he knew instinctively that Miggs had made a terrible mistake. There was something unearthly and wicked about those sickly sweet flowers. Flowers didn't grow aboard ships. Not real flowers. Real flowers had to take root somewhere, and, besides, they didn't have that drunken, etherish odour. Miggs should have left the vine alone. Clinging at the rail there, Yancy *knew* it, without knowing why.

He stayed there for a long time, trying to think and get his nerves back again. In a little while he began to feel frightened, being alone, and he returned below decks to the cabin.

He stopped in the doorway, and stared.

Miggs was still there, slumped grotesquely over

the table. The bottle was empty. Miggs was drunk, unconscious, mercifully oblivious of his surroundings.

For a moment Yancy glared at him morosely. For a moment, too, a new fear tugged at Yancy's heart—fear of being left alone through the coming night. He yanked Miggs' arm and shook him savagely; but there was no response. It would be hours, long, dreary, sinister hours, before Miggs regained his senses.

Bitterly Yancy took the lamp and set about exploring the rest of the ship. If he could find the ship's papers, he considered, they might dispel his terror. He might learn the truth.

With this in mind, he sought the mate's quarters. The papers had not been in the captain's cabin where they belonged; therefore they might be here.

But they were not. There was nothing—nothing but a chronometer, sextant, and other nautical instruments lying in curious positions on the mate's table, rusted beyond repair. And there were flags, signal flags, thrown down as if they had been used at the last moment. And, lying in a distorted heap on the floor, was a human skeleton.

Avoiding this last horror, Yancy searched the room thoroughly. Evidently, he reasoned, the captain had died early in the *Golconda*'s unknown plague. The mate had brought these instruments, these flags, to his own cabin, only to succumb before he could use them.

Only one thing Yancy took with him when he went out: a lantern, rusty and brittle, but still serviceable. It was empty, but he poured oil into it from the lamp. Then, returning the lamp to the captain's quarters where Miggs lay unconscious, he went on deck.

He climbed the bridge and set the lantern beside him. Night was coming. Already the fog was lifting, allowing darkness to creep in beneath it. And so Yancy stood there, alone and helpless, while blackness settled with uncanny quickness over the entire ship.

He was being watched. He felt it. Invisible eyes, hungry and menacing, were keeping check on his movements. On the deck beneath him were those inexplicable flowers, trailing out of the unexplored

hold, glowing like phosphorescent faces in the gloom.

"By God," Yancy mumbled, "I'm goin' to get out of here!"

His own voice startled him and caused him to stiffen and peer about him, as if someone else had uttered the words. And then, very suddenly, his eyes became fixed on the far horizon to starboard. His lips twitched open, spitting out a shrill cry.

"Miggs! Miggs! A light! Look, Miggs—"

Frantically he stumbled down from the bridge and clawed his way below decks to the mate's cabin. Feverishly he seized the signal flags. Then, clutching them in his hand, he moaned helplessly and let them fall. He realized that they were no good, no good in the dark. Gibbering to himself, he searched for rockets. There were none.

Suddenly he remembered the lantern. Back again he raced through the passage, on deck, up on the bridge. In another moment, with the lantern dangling from his arm, he was clambering higher and higher into the black spars of the mainmast. Again and again he slipped and caught himself with outflung hands. And at length he stood high above the deck, feet braced, swinging the lantern back and forth. . . .

Below him, the deck was no longer silent, no longer abandoned. From bow to stern it was trembling, creaking, whispering up at him. He peered down fearfully. Blurred shadows seemed to be prowling through the darkness, coming out of nowhere, pacing dolefully back and forth through the gloom. They were watching him with a furtive interest.

He called out feebly. The muted echo of his own voice came back up to him. He was aware that the bell was tolling again, and the swish of the sea was louder, more persistent.

With an effort he caught a grip on himself.

"Damned fool," he rasped. "Drivin' yourself crazy—"

The moon was rising. It blurred the blinking light on the horizon and penetrated the darkness like a livid yellow finger. Yancy lowered the lantern with a sob. It was no good now. In the glare of the moonlight, this puny flame would be invisible to the men aboard that other ship. Slowly, cautiously, he climbed down to the deck.

He tried to think of something to do, to take his mind off the fear. Striding to the rail, he hauled up the water butts from the dory. Then he stretched the tarpaulin to catch the precipitation of the night dew. No telling how long he and Miggs would be forced to remain aboard the hulk.

He turned, then, to explore the forecastle. On his way across the deck, he stopped and held the light over the creeping vine. The curious flowers had become fragrant, heady, with the fumes of an intoxicating drug. He followed the coils to where they vanished into the hold, and he looked down. He saw only a tumbled pile of boxes and crates. Barred boxes which must have been cages at one time.

Again he turned away. The ship was trying to tell him something. He felt it—felt the movements of the deck planks beneath his feet. The moonlight, too, had made hideous white things of the scattered bones in the bow. Yancy stared at them with a shiver. He stared again, and grotesque thoughts obtruded into his consciousness. The bones were moving. Slithering, sliding over the deck, assembling themselves, gathering into definite shapes. He could have sworn it!

Cursing, he wrenched his eyes away. Damned fool, thinking such thoughts! With clenched fists he advanced to the forecastle; but before he reached it, he stopped again.

It was the sound of flapping wings that brought him about. Turning quickly, with a jerk, he was aware that the sound emanated from the open hold. Hesitantly he stepped forward—and stood rigid with an involuntary scream.

Out of the aperture came two horrible shapes—two inhuman things with immense, clapping wings and glittering eyes. Hideous; enormous. *Bats!*

Instinctively he flung his arm up to protect himself. But the creatures did not attack. They hung for an instant, poised over the hatch, eyeing him with something that was fiendishly like intelligence. Then they flapped over the deck, over the rail, and away into the night. As they sped away towards the west, where he had seen the light of that other ship twinkling, they clung together like witches hell-bent on some evil mission. And below them, in the bloated sea, huge snakes weaved smoky, golden patterns—waiting! . . .

He stood fast, squinting after the bats. Like two hellish black eyes they grew smaller and smaller, became pinpoints in the moon-glow, and finally vanished. Still he did not stir. His lips were dry, his body stiff and unnatural. He licked his mouth. Then he was conscious of something more. From somewhere behind him came a thin, throbbing thread of harmony—a lovely, utterly sweet musical note that fascinated him.

He turned slowly. His heart was hammering, surging. His eyes went suddenly wide.

There, not five feet from him, stood a human form. Not his imagination. Real!

But he had never seen a girl like her before. She was too beautiful. She was wild, almost savage, with her great dark eyes boring into him. Her skin was white, smooth as alabaster. Her hair was jet black; and a waving coil of it, like a broken cobweb of pitch strings, framed her face. Grotesque hoops of gold dangled from her ears. In her hair, above them, gleamed two of those sinister flowers from the straggling vine.

He did not speak; he simply gaped. The girl was bare-footed, bare-legged. A short, dark skirt covered her slender thighs. A ragged white waist, open at the throat, revealed the full curve of her breast. In one hand she held a long wooden reed, a flute-like instrument fashioned out of crude wood. And about her middle, dangling almost to the deck, twined a scarlet, silken sash, brilliant as the sun, but not so scarlet as her lips, which were parted in a faint, suggestive smile, showing teeth of marble whiteness!

"Who—who are you?" Yancy mumbled.

She shook her head. Yet she smiled with her eyes, and he felt, somehow, that she understood him. He tried again, in such tongues as he knew. Still she shook her head, and still he felt that she was mocking him. Not until he chanced upon a scattered, faltering greeting in Serbian, did she nod her head.

"Dobra!" she replied, in a husky rich voice which sounded, somehow, as if it were rarely used.

He stepped closer then. She was a gipsy evidently. A Tzany of the Serbian hills. She moved very close to him with a floating, almost ethereal movement of her slender body. Peering into his face, flashing her haunting smile at him, she lifted the flute-like instrument and, as if it were nothing at all unnatural or out of place, began to play again the song which had first attracted his attention.

He listened in silence until she had finished. Then, with a cunning smile, she touched her fingers to her lips and whispered softly:

"You—mine. Yes?"

He did not understand. She clutched his arm and glanced fearfully toward the west, out over the sea.

"You—mine!" she said again, fiercely. "Papa Bocito—Seraphino—they no have you. You—not go—to them!"

He thought he understood then. She turned away from him and went silently across the deck. He watched her disappear into the forecastle, and would have followed her, but once again the ship—the whole ship—seemed to be struggling to whisper a warning.

Presently she returned, holding in her white hand a battered silver goblet, very old and very tarnished, brimming with scarlet fluid. He took it silently. It was impossible to refuse her. Her eyes had grown into lakes of night, lit by the burning moon. Her lips were soft, searching, undeniable.

"Who are you?" he whispered.

"Stragella," she smiled.

"Stragella . . . Stragella . . ."

The name itself was compelling. He drank the liquid slowly, without taking his eyes from her lovely face. The stuff had the taste of wine—strong, sweet wine. It was intoxicating, with the same weird effect that was contained in the orange blooms which she wore in her hair and which groveled over the deck behind her.

Yancy's hands groped up weakly. He rubbed his eyes, feeling suddenly weak, powerless, as if the very blood had been drained from his veins.

Struggling futilely, he staggered back, moaning half inaudibly.

Stragella's arms went about him, caressing him with sensuous touch. He felt them, and they were powerful, irresistible. The girl's smile maddened him. Her crimson lips hung before his face, drawing nearer, mocking him. Then, all at once, she was seeking his throat. Those warm, passionate, deliriously pleasant lips were searching to touch him.

He sensed his danger. Frantically he strove to lift his arms and push her away. Deep in his mind some struggling intuition, some half-alive idea, warned him that he was in terrible peril. This girl, Stragella, was not of his kind; she was a creature of the darkness, a denizen of a different, frightful world of her own! Those lips, wanting his flesh, were inhuman, too fervid—

Suddenly she shrank away from him, releasing him with a jerk. A snarling animal-like sound surged through her flaming mouth. Her hand lashed out, rigid, pointing to the thing that hung in his belt. Talonic fingers pointed to the Bible that defied her!

But the scarlet fluid had taken its full effect. Yancy slumped down, unable to cry out. In a heap he lay there, paralyzed, powerless to stir.

He knew that she was commanding him to rise. Her lips, moving in pantomime, formed soundless words. Her glittering eyes were fixed upon him, hypnotic. The Bible—she wanted him to cast it over the rail! She wanted him to stand up and go into her arms. Then her lips would find a hold. . . .

But he could not obey. He could not raise his arms to support himself. She, in turn, stood at bay and refused to advance. Then, whirling about, her lips drawn into a diabolical curve, beautiful but bestial, she retreated. He saw her dart back, saw her tapering body whip about, with the crimson sash outflung behind her as she raced across the deck.

Yancy closed his eyes to blot out the sight. When he opened them again, they opened to a new, more intense horror. On the *Golconda*'s deck, Stragella was darting erratically among those piles of gleaming bones. But they were bones no longer. They had gathered into shapes, taken on flesh, blood. Before his very eyes they assumed substance, men and beasts alike. And then began an orgy such as Nels Yancy had never before looked upon—an orgy of the undead.

Monkeys, giant apes, lunged about the deck. A huge python reared its sinuous head to glare. On the hatch cover a snow-leopard, snarling furiously, crouched to spring. Tigers, tapirs, crocodiles—fought together in the bow. A great brown bear, of the type found in the lofty plateaus of the Pamirs, clawed at the rail.

And the men! Most of them were dark-skinned— dark enough to have come from the same region, from Madras. With them crouched Chinamen, and some Anglo-Saxons. Starved, all of them. Lean, gaunt, mad!

Pandemonium raged then. Animals and men alike were insane with hunger. In a little struggling knot, the men were gathered about the number-two hatch, defending themselves. They were wielding firearms—firing pointblank with desperation into the writhing mass that confronted them. And always, between them and around them and among, darted the girl who called herself Stragella.

They cast no shadows, those ghost shapes. Not even the girl, whose arms he had felt about him only a moment ago. There was nothing real in the scene, nothing human. Even the sounds of the shots and the screams of the cornered men, even the roaring growls of the big cats, were smothered as if they came to him through heavy glass windows, from a sealed chamber.

He was powerless to move. He lay in a cataleptic condition, conscious of the entire pantomime, yet unable to flee from it. And his senses were horribly acute—so acute that he turned his eyes upward with an abrupt twitch, instinctively; and then shrank into himself with a new fear as he discerned the two huge bats which had winged their way across the sea. . . .

They were returning now. Circling above him, they flapped down one after the other and settled with heavy, sullen thuds upon the hatch, close to that weird vine of flowers. They seemed to have lost their shape, these nocturnal monstrosities, to have become fantastic blurs, enveloped in an unearthly bluish radiance. Even as he stared at them, they vanished altogether for a moment; and then the strange vapor cleared to reveal the two creatures who stood there!

Not bats! Humans! Inhumans! They were gipsies, attired in moldy, decayed garments which stamped them as Balkans. Man and woman. Lean, emaciated, ancient man with fierce white mustache; plump old woman with black, rat-like eyes that seemed unused to the light of day. And they spoke to Stragella—spoke to her eagerly. She, in turn, swung about with enraged face and pointed to the Bible in Yancy's belt.

But the pantomime was not finished. On the deck the men and animals lay moaning, sobbing. Stragella turned noiselessly, calling the old man and woman after her. Calling them by name.

"Come—Papa Bocito, Seraphino!"

The tragedy of the ghost-ship was being reenacted. Yancy knew it, and shuddered at the thought. Starvation, cholera had driven the *Golconda*'s crew mad. The jungle beasts, unfed, hideously savage, had escaped out of their confinement. And now— now that the final conflict was over—Stragella and Papa Bocito and Seraphino were proceeding about their ghastly work.

Stragella was leading them. Her charm, her beauty, gave her a hold on the men. They were in love with her. She had *made* them love her, madly and without reason. Now she was moving from one to another, loving them and holding them close to her. And as she stepped away from each man, he went limp, faint, while she laughed terribly and passed on to the next. Her lips were parted. She licked them hungrily—licked the blood from them with a sharp, crimson tongue.

How long it lasted, Yancy did not know. Hours, hours on end. He was aware, suddenly, that a high wind was screeching and wailing in the upper reaches of the ship; and, peering up, he saw that the spars were no longer bare and rotten with age. Great gray sails stood out against the black sky— fantastic things without any definite form or outline. And the moon above them had vanished utterly. The howling wind was bringing a storm with it, filling the sails to bulging proportions. Beneath the decks the ship was groaning like a creature in agony. The seas were lashing her, slashing her, carrying her forward with amazing speed.

Of a sudden came a mighty grinding sound. The *Golconda* hurtled back, as if a huge, jagged reef of submerged rock had bored into her bottom. She listed. Her stern rose high in the air. And Stragella with her two fellow fiends, was standing in the bow, screaming in mad laughter in the teeth of the wind. The other two laughed with her.

Yancy saw them turn toward him, but they did not stop. Somehow, he did not expect them to stop. This scene, this mad pantomime, was not the present; it was the past. He was not here at all. All this had happened years ago! Forgotten, buried in the past!

But he heard them talking, in a mongrel dialect full of Serbian words.

"It is done. Papa Bocito! We shall stay here forever now. There is land within an hour's flight, where fresh blood abounds and will always abound. And here, on this wretched hulk, they will never find our graves to destroy us!"

The horrible trio passed close. Stragella turned, to stare out across the water, and raised her hand in silent warning. Yancy, turning wearily to stare in the same direction, saw that the first streaks of daylight were beginning to filter over the sea.

With a curious floating, drifting movement the three undead creatures moved toward the open hatch. They descended out of sight. Yancy, jerking himself erect and surprised to find that the effects of the drug had worn off with the coming of dawn, crept to the hatch and peered down—in time to see those fiendish forms enter their coffins. He knew then what the crates were. In the dim light, now that he was staring directly into the aperture, he saw what he had not noticed before. Three of those oblong boxes were filled with dank grave-earth!

He knew then the secret of the unnatural flowers. They *had* roots! They were rooted in the soil which harbored those undead bodies!

Then, like a groping finger, the dawn came out of the sea. Yancy walked to the rail, dazed. It was over now—all over. They orgy was ended. The *Golconda* was once more an abandoned, rotted hulk.

For an hour he stood at the rail, sucking in the warmth and glory of the sunlight. Once again that wall of unsightly mist was rising out of the water on all sides. Presently it would bury the ship, and Yancy shuddered.

He thought of Miggs. With quick steps he paced to the companionway and descended to the lower passage. Hesitantly he prowled through the thickening layers of dank fog. A queer sense of foreboding crept over him.

He called out even before he reached the door. There was no answer. Thrusting the barrier open, he stepped across the sill—and then he stood still while a sudden harsh cry broke from his lips.

Miggs was lying there, half across the table, his arms flung out, his head turned grotesquely on its side, staring up at the ceiling.

"Miggs! Miggs!" The sound came choking through Yancy's lips. "Oh, God, Miggs—what's happened?"

He reeled forward. Miggs was cold and stiff, and quite dead. All the blood was gone out of his face and arms. His eyes were glassy, wide open. He was as white as marble, shrunken horribly. In his throat were two parallel marks, as if a sharp-pointed staple had been hammered into the flesh and then withdrawn. The marks of the vampire.

For a long time Yancy did not retreat. The room swayed and lurched before him. He was alone. Alone! The whole ghastly thing was too sudden, too unexpected.

Then he stumbled forward and went down on his knees, clawing at Miggs' dangling arm.

"Oh God, Miggs," he mumbled incoherently. "You got to help me. I can't stand it!"

He clung there, white-faced, staring, sobbing thickly—and presently slumped in a pitiful heap, dragging Miggs over on top of him.

It was later afternoon when he regained consciousness. He stood up, fighting away the fear that overwhelmed him. He had to get away, get away! The thought hammered into his head with monotonous force. Get away!

He found his way to the upper deck. There was nothing he could do for Miggs. He would have to leave him here. Stumbling, he moved along the rail and reached down to draw the small boat closer, where he could provision it and make it ready for his departure.

His fingers clutched emptiness. The ropes were gone. The dory was gone. He hung limp, staring down at a flat expanse of oily sea.

For an hour he did not move. He fought to throw off his fear long enough to think of a way out. Then he stiffened with a sudden jerk and pushed himself away from the rail.

The ship's boats offered the only chance. He groped to the nearest one and labored feverishly over it.

But the task was hopeless. The life boats were of metal, rusted through and through, wedged in their davits. The wire cables were knotted and immovable. He tore his hands on them, wringing blood from his scarred fingers. Even while he worked, he knew that the boats would not float. They were rotten, through and through.

He had to stop, at last, from exhaustion.

After that, knowing that there was no escape, he had to do something, anything, to keep sane. First he would clear those horrible bones from the deck, then explore the rest of the ship. . . .

It was a repulsive task, but he drove himself to it. If he could get rid of the bones, perhaps Stragella and the other two creatures would not return. He did not know. It was merely a faint hope, something to cling to.

With grim, tight-pressed lips he dragged the bleached skeletons over the deck and kicked them over the side, and stood watching them as they sank from sight. Then he went to the hold, smothering his terror, and descended into the gloomy belly of the vessel. He avoided the crates with a shudder of revulsion. Ripping up that evil vine-thing by the roots, he carried it to the rail and flung it away, with the mold of grave-earth still clinging to it.

After that he went over the entire ship, end to end, but found nothing.

He slipped the anchor chains then, in the hopes that the ship would drift away from that vindictive bank of fog. Then he paced back and forth, muttering to himself and trying to force courage for the most hideous task of all.

The sea was growing dark, and with dusk came increasing terror. He knew the *Golconda* was drifting. Knew, too, that the undead inhabitants of the vessel were furious with him for allowing the boat to drift away from their source of food. Or they *would* be furious when they came alive again after their interim of forced sleep.

And there was only one method of defeating them. It was a horrible method, and he was already frightened. Nevertheless he searched the deck for a marlin spike and found one; and, turning sluggishly, he went back to the hold.

A stake, driven through the heart of each of the horrible trio . . .

The rickety stairs were deep in shadow. Already the dying sun, buried behind its wreath of evil fog, was a ring of bloody mist. He glanced at it and realized that he must hurry. He cursed himself for having waited so long.

It was hard, lowering himself into the pitch-black hold when he could only feel his footing and trust to fate. His boots scraped ominously on the steps. He held his hands above him, gripping the deck timbers.

And suddenly he slipped.

His foot caught on the edge of a lower step, twisted abruptly, and pitched him forward. He cried out. The marlin spike dropped from his hands and clattered on one of the crates below. He tumbled in a heap, clawing for support. The impact knocked something out of his belt. And he realized, even as his head came in sharp contact with the foremost oblong box, that the Bible, which had heretofore protected him, was no longer a part of him.

He did not lose complete control of his senses. Frantically he sought to regain his knees and grope for the black book in the gloom of the hold. A sobbing, choking sound came pitifully from his lips.

A soft, triumphant laugh came out of the darkness close to him. He swung about heavily—so heavily that the movement sent him sprawling again in an inert heap.

He was too late. She was already there on her knees, glaring at him hungrily. A peculiar bluish glow welled about her face. She was ghastly beautiful as she reached behind her into the oblong crate and began to trace a circle about the Bible with a chunk of soft, tarry, pitch-like substance clutched in her white fingers.

Yancy stumbled toward her, finding strength in desperation. She straightened to meet him. Her lips, curled back, exposed white teeth. Her arms coiled out, enveloping him, stifling his struggles. God, they were strong. He could not resist them. The same languid, resigned feeling came over him. He would have fallen, but she held him erect.

She did not touch him with her lips. Behind her he saw two other shapes take form in the darkness. The savage features of Papa Bocito glowered at him; and Seraphino's ratty, smoldering eyes, full of hunger, bored into him. Stragella was obviously afraid of them.

Yancy was lifted from his feet. He was carried out on deck and borne swiftly, easily, down the companionway, along the lower passage, through a swirling blanket of hellish fog and darkness, to the cabin where Miggs lay dead. And he lost consciousness while they carried him.

He could not tell, when he opened his eyes, how long he had been asleep. It seemed a long, long interlude. Stragella was sitting beside him. He lay on the bunk in the cabin, and the lamp was burning on the table, revealing Miggs' limp body in full detail.

Yancy reached up fearfully to touch his throat. There were no marks there; not yet.

He was aware of voices, then. Papa Bocito and the ferret-faced woman were arguing with the girl beside him. The savage old man in particular was being angered by her cool, possessive smile.

"We are drifting away from the prison isles," Papa Bocito snarled, glancing at Yancy with unmasked hate. "It is his work, lifting the anchor. Unless you share him with us until we drift ashore, we shall perish!"

"He is mine," Stragella shrugged, modulating her voice to a persuasive whisper. "You had the other. This one is mine. I shall have him!"

"He belongs to us all!"

"Why?" Stragella smiled. "Because he has looked upon the resurrection night? Ah, he is the first to learn our secret."

Seraphino's eyes narrowed at that, almost to pinpoints. She jerked forward, clutching the girl's shoulder.

"We have quarreled enough," she hissed. "Soon it will be daylight. He belongs to us all because he has taken us away from the isles and learned our secrets."

The words drilled their way into Yancy's brain. "The resurrection night!" There was an ominous significance in it, and he thought he knew its meaning. His eyes, or his face, must have revealed his thoughts, for Papa Bocito drew near to him and pointed into his face with a long, bony forefinger, muttering triumphantly.

"You have seen what no other eyes have seen," the ancient man growled bitterly. "Now, for that, you shall become one of us. Stragella wants you. She shall have you for eternity—for a life without death. Do you know what that means?"

Yancy shook his head dumbly, fearfully.

"We are the undead," Bocito leered. "Our victims become creatures of the blood, like us. At night we are free. During the day we must return to our graves. That is why"—he cast his arm toward the upper deck in a hideous gesture—"those other victims of ours have not yet become like us. They were never buried; they have no graves to return to. Each night we give them life for our own amusement, but they are not of the brotherhood—yet."

Yancy licked his lips and said nothing. He understood then. Every night it happened. A nightly pantomime, when the dead become alive again, reenacting the events of the night when the *Golconda* had become a ship of hell.

"We are gipsies," the old man gloated. "Once we were human, living in our pleasant little camp in the shadow of the Pobyezdin Potok's crusty peaks, in the Morava Valley of Serbia. That was in the time of Milutin, six hundreds of years ago. Then the vampires of the hills came for us and took us to them. We lived the undead life, until there was no more blood in the valley. So we went to the coast, we three, transporting our grave-earth with us. And we lived there, alive by night and dead by day, in the coastal villages of the Black Sea, until the time came when we wished to go to the far places."

Seraphino's guttural voice interrupted him, saying harshly:

"Hurry. It is nearly dawn!"

"And we obtained passage on this *Golconda*, arranging to have our crates of grave-earth carried secretly to the hold. And the ship fell into cholera and starvation and storm. She went aground. And—here we are. Ah, but there is blood upon the islands, my pretty one, and so we anchored the *Golconda* on the reef, where life was close at hand!"

Yancy closed his eyes with a shudder. He did not understand all of the words; they were in a jargon of gipsy tongue. But he knew enough to horrify him.

Then the old man ceased gloating. He fell back, glowering at Stragella. And the girl laughed, a mad, cackling, triumphant laugh of possession. She leaned forward, and the movement brought her out of the line of the lamplight, so that the feeble glow fell full over Yancy's prostrate body.

At that, with an angry snarl, she recoiled. Her eyes went wide with abhorrence. Upon his chest gleamed the Crucifix—the tattooed Cross and Savior which had been indelibly printed there. Stragella held her face away, shielding her eyes. She cursed him horribly. Backing away, she seized the arms of her companions and pointed with trembling finger to the thing which had repulsed her.

The fog seemed to seep deeper and deeper into the cabin during the ensuing silence. Yancy struggled to a sitting posture and cringed back against the wall, waiting for them to attack him. It would be finished in a moment, he knew. Then he would join Miggs, with those awful marks on his throat and Stragella's lips crimson with his sucked blood.

But they held their distance. The fog enveloped them, made them almost indistinct. He could see only three pairs of glaring, staring, phosphorescent eyes that grew larger and wider and more intensely terrible.

He buried his face in his hands, waiting. They did not come. He heard them mumbling, whispering. Vaguely he was conscious of another sound, far off and barely audible. The howl of wolves.

Beneath him the bunk was swaying from side to side with the movement of the ship. The *Golconda* was drifting swiftly. A storm had risen out of nowhere, and the wind was singing its dead dirge in the rotten spars high above decks. He could hear it moaning, wheezing, like a human being in torment.

Then the three pairs of glittering orbs moved nearer. The whispered voices ceased, and a cunning smile passed over Stragella's features. Yancy screamed, and flattened against the wall. He watched her in fascination as she crept upon him. One arm was flung across her eyes to protect them from the sight of the Crucifix. In the other hand, outstretched, groping ever nearer, she clutched that hellish chunk of pitch-like substance with which she had encircled the Bible!

He knew what she would do. The thought struck him like an icy blast, full of fear and madness. She would slink closer, closer, until her hand touched his flesh. Then she would place the black substance around the tattooed cross and kill its powers. His defense would be gone. Then—those cruel lips on his throat . . .

There was no avenue of escape. Papa Bocito and the plump old woman, grinning malignantly, had slid to one side, between him and the doorway. And Stragella writhed forward with one alabaster arm feeling . . . feeling. . . .

He was conscious of the roar of surf, very close, very loud, outside the walls of the fog-filled enclosure. The ship was lurching, reeling heavily, pitching in the swell. Hours must have passed. Hours and hours of darkness and horror.

Then she touched him. The sticky stuff was hot on his chest, moving in a slow circle. He hurled himself back, stumbled, went down, and she fell upon him.

Under his tormented body the floor of the cabin split asunder. The ship buckled from top to bottom with a grinding, roaring impact. A terrific shock burst through the ancient hulk, shattering its rotted timbers.

The lamp caromed off the table, plunging the cabin in semidarkness. Through the port-holes filtered a gray glare. Stragella's face, thrust into Yancy's, became a mask of beautiful fury. She whirled back. She stood rigid, screaming lividly to Papa Bocito and the old hag.

"Go back! Go back!" she railed. "We have waited too long! It is dawn!"

She ran across the floor, grappling with them. Her lips were distorted. Her body trembled. She hurled her companions to the door. Then, as she followed them into the gloom of the passage, she turned upon Yancy with a last unholy snarl of defeated rage. And she was gone.

**Y**ancy lay limp. When he struggled to his feet at last and went on deck, the sun was high in the sky, bloated and crimson, struggling to penetrate the cone of fog which swirled about the ship.

The ship lay far over, careened on her side. A hundred yards distant over the port rail lay the heaven-sent sight of land—a bleak, vacant expanse of jungle-rimmed shore line.

He went deliberately to work—a task that had to be finished quickly, lest he be discovered by the inhabitants of the shore and be considered stark mad. Returning to the cabin, he took the oil lamp and carried it to the open hold. There, sprinkling the liquid over the ancient wood, he set fire to it.

Turning, he stepped to the rail. A scream of agony, unearthly and prolonged, rose up behind him. Then he was over the rail, battling in the surf.

When he staggered up on the beach, twenty minutes later, the *Golconda* was a roaring furnace. On all sides of her the flames snarled skyward, spewing through that hellish cone of vapor. Grimly Yancy turned away and trudged along the beach.

He looked back after an hour of steady plodding. The lagoon was empty. The fog had vanished. The sun gleamed down with warm brilliance on a broad, empty expanse of sea.

Hours later he reached a settlement. Men came and talked to him, and asked curious questions. They pointed to his hair which was stark white. They told him he had reached Port Blair, on the southern island of the Andamans. After that, noticing the peculiar gleam of his blood-shot eyes, they took him to the home of the governor.

There he told his story—told hesitantly, because he expected to be disbelieved, mocked.

The governor looked at him cryptically.

"You don't expect me to understand?" the governor said. "I am not so sure, sir. This is a penal colony, a prison isle. During the past few years, more than two hundred of our convicts have died in the most curious way. Two tiny punctures in the throat. Loss of blood."

"You—you must destroy the graves," Yancy muttered.

The governor nodded silently, significantly.

After that, Yancy returned to the world, alone. Always alone. Men peered into his face and shrank away from the haunted stare of his eyes. They saw the Crucifix upon his chest and wondered why, day and night, he wore his shirt flapping open, so that the brilliant design glared forth.

But their curiosity was never appeased. Only Yancy knew; and Yancy was silent.

## MARSYAS IN FLANDERS

# Vernon Lee

Vernon Lee is the pseudonym of Violet Paget (1856–1935), a British writer who was born in Boulogne, France. She was the half sister of Eugene Lee-Hamilton, from whose surname she took her nom de plume. She lived for a time in London but moved to a hillside outside Florence in 1889 and lived there until her death.

She wrote prodigiously on eighteenth-century Italian art, music, and architecture, and became a member of the Aesthetic movement, meeting both the movement's effective leader, Walter Pater, and its most renowned member, Oscar Wilde; she contributed poems to its most famous publication, *The Yellow Book*. She is, however, mainly remembered today for her supernatural fiction. The most important scholar of gothic and supernatural fiction Montague Summers wrote that she should be ranked ahead of M. R. James as the greatest modern exponent of the supernatural in fiction. Her reputation would undoubtedly have been enhanced had she written more stories, of which there are fewer than twenty. Perhaps her most famous is the novella *A Phantom Lover,* often reprinted as *Oke of Okehurst*. Her most important short-story collection is *Hauntings* (1890).

"Marsyas in Flanders" was first published in a magazine in 1900, then was collected in *For Maurice: Five Unlikely Tales* (London: John Lane, The Bodley Head, 1927).

# Marsyas in Flanders

## VERNON LEE

### I

**Y**ou are right. This is not the original crucifix at all. Another one has been put instead. *Il y a eu substitution*," and the little old Antiquary of Dunes nodded mysteriously, fixing his ghost-seer's eyes upon mine.

He said it in a scarce audible whisper. For it happened to be the vigil of the Feast of the Crucifix, and the once famous church was full of semi-clerical persons decorating it for the morrow, and of old ladies in strange caps, clattering about with pails and brooms. The Antiquary had brought me there the very moment of my arrival, lest the crowd of faithful should prevent his showing me everything next morning.

The famous crucifix was exhibited behind rows and rows of unlit candles, and surrounded by strings of paper flowers and coloured muslin, and garlands of sweet resinous maritime pine; and two lighted chandeliers illumined it.

"There has been an exchange," he repeated, looking round that no one might hear him. *"Il y a eu substitution."*

For I had remarked, as anyone would have done, at the first glance, that the crucifix had every appearance of French work of the thirteenth century, boldly realistic, whereas the crucifix of the legend, which was a work of St. Luke, which had hung for centuries in the Holy Sepulchre at Jerusalem and been miraculously cast ashore at Dunes in 1195, would surely have been a more or less Byzantine image, like its miraculous companion of Lucca.

"But why should there have been a substitution?" I inquired innocently.

"Hush, hush," answered the Antiquary, frowning, "not here—later, later—"

He took me all over the church, once so famous for pilgrimages; but from which, even like the sea which has left it in a salt marsh beneath the cliffs, the tide of devotion has receded for centuries. It is a very dignified little church, of charmingly restrained and shapely Gothic, built of a delicate pale stone, which the sea damp has picked out, in bases and capitals and carved foliation, with stains of a lovely bright green. The Antiquary showed me where the transept and belfry had been left unfinished when the miracles had diminished in the fourteenth century. And he took me up to the curious warder's chamber, a large room up some steps in the triforium; with a fireplace and stone seats for the men who guarded the precious crucifix day and night. There had even been beehives in the window, he told me, and he remembered seeing them still as a child.

"Was it usual, here in Flanders, to have a guard-room in churches containing important relics?" I asked, for I could not remember having seen anything similar before.

"By no means," he answered, looking round to make sure we were alone, "but it was necessary here. You have never heard in what the chief miracles of this church consisted?"

"No," I whispered back, gradually infected by his mysteriousness, "unless you allude to the legend that the figure of the Saviour broke all the crosses until the right one was cast up by the sea?"

He shook his head but did not answer, and descended the steep stairs into the nave, while I lingered a moment looking down into it from the warder's chamber. I have never had so curious an impression of a church. The chandeliers on either side of the crucifix swirled slowly round, making great pools of light which were broken by the shadows of the clustered columns, and among the pews of the nave moved the flicker of the sacristan's lamp. The place was full of the scent of resinous pine branches, evoking dunes and mountainsides; and from the busy groups below rose a subdued chatter of women's voices, and a splash of water and clatter of pattens. It vaguely suggested preparations for a witches' sabbath.

"What sort of miracles did they have in this church?" I asked, when we had passed into the dusky square, "and what did you mean about their having exchanged the crucifix—about a *substitution*?"

It seemed quite dark outside. The church rose black, a vague lopsided mass of buttresses and high-pitched roofs, against the watery, moonlit sky; the big trees of the churchyard behind wavering about in the seawind; and the windows shone yellow, like flaming portals, in the darkness.

"Please remark the bold effect of the gargoyles," said the Antiquary pointing upwards.

They jutted out, vague wild beasts, from the roof-line; and, what was positively frightening, you saw the moonlight, yellow and blue through the open jaws of some of them. A gust swept through the trees, making the weathercock clatter and groan.

"Why, those gargoyle wolves seem positively to howl," I exclaimed.

The old Antiquary chuckled. "Aha," he answered, "did I not tell you that this church has witnessed things like no other church in Christendom? And it still remembers them! There— have you ever known such a wild, savage church before?"

And as he spoke there suddenly mingled with the sough of the wind and the groans of the weather-vane, a shrill quavering sound as of pipers inside.

"The organist trying his vox humana for tomorrow," remarked the Antiquary.

## II

Next day I bought one of the printed histories of the miraculous crucifix which they were hawking all round the church; and next day also, my friend the Antiquary was good enough to tell me all that he knew of the matter. Between my two informants, the following may be said to be the true story.

In the autumn of 1195, after a night of frightful storm, a boat was found cast upon the shore of Dunes, which was at that time a fishing village at the mouth of the Nys, and exactly opposite a terrible sunken reef.

The boat was broken and upset; and close to it, on the sand and bent grass, lay a stone figure of the crucified Saviour, without its cross and, as seems probable, also without its arms, which had been made of separate blocks. A variety of persons immediately came forward to claim it; the little church of Dunes, on whose glebe it was found; the Barons of Cröy, who had the right of jetsam on that coast, and also the great Abbey of St. Loup of Arras, as possessing the spiritual overlordship of the place. But a holy man, who lived close by in the cliffs, had a vision which settled the dispute. St. Luke in person appeared and told him that he was the original maker of the figure; that it had been one of three which had hung round the Holy

Sepulchre of Jerusalem; that three knights, a Norman, a Tuscan, and a man of Arras, had with the permission of Heaven stolen them from the Infidels and placed them on unmanned boats; that one of the images had been cast upon the Norman coast near Salenelles; that the second had run aground not far from the city of Lucca, in Italy, and that this third was the one which had been embarked by the knight from Artois. As regarded its final resting place, the hermit, on the authority of St. Luke, recommended that the statue should be left to decide the matter itself. Accordingly, the crucified figure was solemly cast back into the sea. The very next day it was found once more in the same spot, among the sand and bent grass at the mouth of the Nys. It was therefore deposited in the little church of Dunes; and very soon indeed the flocks of pious persons who brought it offerings from all parts made it necessary and possible to rebuild the church thus sanctified by its presence.

The Holy Effigy of Dunes—*Sacra Dunarum Effigies* as it was called—did not work the ordinary sort of miracles. But its fame spread far and wide by the unexampled wonders which became the constant accompaniment of its existence. The Effigy, as above mentioned, had been discovered without the cross to which it had evidently been fastened, nor had any researches or any subsequent storms brought the missing blocks to light, despite the many prayers which were offered for the purpose. After some time therefore, and a deal of discussion, it was decided that a new cross should be provided for the effigy to hang upon. And certain skilful stonemasons of Arras were called to Dunes for this purpose. But behold! The very day after the cross had been solemnly erected in the church, an unheard of and terrifying fact was discovered. The Effigy, which had been hanging perfectly straight the previous evening, had shifted its position, and was bent violently to the right, as if in an effort to break loose.

This was attested not merely by hundreds of laymen, but by the priests of the place, who notified the fact in a document, existing in the episcopal archives of Arras until 1790, to the Abbot of St. Loup their spiritual overlord.

This was the beginning of a series of mysterious occurrences which spread the fame of the marvellous crucifix all over Christendom. The Effigy did not remain in the position into which it had miraculously worked itself: it was found, at intervals of time, shifted in some other manner upon its cross, and always as if it had gone through violent contortions. And one day, about ten years after it had been cast up by the sea, the priests of the church and the burghers of Dunes discovered the Effigy hanging in its original outstretched, symmetrical attitude, but O wonder! with the cross, broken in three pieces, lying on the steps of its chapel.

Certain persons, who lived in the end of the town nearest the church, reported to have been roused in the middle of the night by what they had taken for a violent clap of thunder, but which was doubtless the crash of the cross falling down; or perhaps, who knows? the noise with which the terrible Effigy had broken loose and spurned the alien cross from it. For that was the secret: the Effigy, made by a saint and come to Dunes by miracle, had evidently found some trace of unholiness in the stone to which it had been fastened. Such was the ready explanation afforded by the Prior of the church, in answer to an angry summons of the Abbot of St. Loup, who expressed his disapproval of such unusual miracles. Indeed, it was discovered that the piece of marble had not been cleaned from sinful human touch with the necessary rites before the figure was fastened on; a most grave, though excusable oversight. So a new cross was ordered, although it was noticed that much time was lost about it; and the consecration took place only some years later.

Meanwhile the Prior had built the warder's chamber, with the fireplace and recess, and obtained permission from the Pope himself that a clerk in orders should watch day and night, on the score that so wonderful a relic might be stolen. For the relic had by this time entirely cut out all similar crucifixes, and the village of Dunes, through the concourse of pilgrims, had rapidly grown into a town, the property of the now fabulously wealthy Priory of the Holy Cross.

The Abbots of St. Loup, however, looked upon the matter with an unfavourable eye. Although nominally remaining their vassals, the Priors of Dunes had contrived to obtain gradually from the Pope privileges which rendered them virtually independent, and in particular, immunities which sent to the treasury of St. Loup only a small proportion of the tribute money brought by the pilgrims. Abbot Walterius in particular, showed himself actively hostile. He accused the Prior of Dunes of having employed his warders to trump up stories of strange movements and sounds on the part of the still crossless Effigy, and of suggesting, to the ignorant, changes in its attitude which were more credulously believed in now that there was no longer the straight line of the cross by which to verify. So finally the new cross was made, and consecrated, and on Holy Cross Day of the year, the Effigy was fastened to it in the presence of an immense concourse of clergy and laity. The Effigy, it was now supposed, would be satisfied, and no unusual occurrences would increase or perhaps fatally compromise its reputation for sanctity.

These expectations were violently dispelled. In November, 1293, after a year of strange rumours concerning the Effigy, the figure was again discovered to have moved, and continued moving, or rather (judging from the position on the cross) writhing; and on Christmas Eve of the same year, the cross was a second time thrown down and dashed in pieces. The priest on duty was, at the same time, found, it was thought, dead, in his warder's chamber. Another cross was made and this time privately consecrated and put in place, and a hole in the roof made a pretext to close the church for a while, and to perform the rites of purification necessary after its pollution by workmen. Indeed, it was remarked that on this occasion the Prior of Dunes took as much trouble to diminish and if possible to hide away the miracles, as his predecessor had done his best to blazon the preceding ones abroad. The priest who had been on duty on the eventful Christmas Eve disappeared mysteriously, and it was thought by many persons that he had gone mad and was confined in the Prior's prison, for fear of the revelations he might make. For by this time, and not without some encouragement from the Abbots at Arras, extraordinary stories had begun to circulate about the goings-on in the church of Dunes. This church, be it remembered, stood a little above the town, isolated and surrounded by big trees. It was surrounded by the precincts of the Priory and, save on the water side, by high walls. Nevertheless, persons there were who affirmed that, the wind having been in that direction, they had heard strange noises come from the church of nights. During storms, particularly, sounds had been heard which were variously described as howls, groans, and the music of rustic dancing. A master mariner affirmed that one Halloween, as his boat approached the mouth of the Nys, he had seen the church of Dunes brilliantly lit up, its immense windows flaming. But he was suspected of being drunk and of having exaggerated the effect of the small light shining from the warder's chamber. The interest of the townsfolk of Dunes coincided with that of the Priory, since they prospered greatly by the pilgrimages, so these tales were promptly hushed up. Yet they undoubtedly reached the ear of the Abbot of St. Loup. And at last there came an event which brought them all back to the surface.

For, on the Vigil of All Saints, 1299, the church was struck by lightning. The new warder was found dead in the middle of the nave, the cross broken in two; and oh, horror! the Effigy was missing. The indescribable fear which overcame everyone was merely increased by the discovery of the Effigy lying behind the high altar, in an attitude of frightful convulsion, and, it was whispered, blackened by lightning.

This was the end of the strange doings at Dunes.

An ecclesiastical council was held at Arras, and the church shut once more for nearly a year. It was opened this time and re-consecrated by the Abbot of St. Loup, whom the Prior of Holy Cross served humbly at mass. A new chapel had been built, and in it the miraculous crucifix was displayed, dressed in more splendid brocade and gems than usual, and its head nearly hidden by one of the most gorgeous crowns ever seen before; a gift, it was said, of the Duke of Burgundy.

All this new splendour, and the presence of the great Abbot himself, was presently explained to the faithful, when the Prior came forward to announce that a last and greatest miracle had now taken place. The original cross, on which the figure had hung in the Church of the Holy Sepulchre, and for which the Effigy had spurned all others made by less holy hands, had been cast on the shore of Dunes, on the very spot where, a hundred years before, the figure of the Saviour had been discovered in the sands. "This," said the Prior, "was the explanation of the terrible occurrences which had filled all hearts with anguish. The Holy Effigy was now satisfied, it would rest in peace and its miraculous powers would be engaged only in granting the prayers of the faithful."

One half of the forecast came true: from that day forward the Effigy never shifted its position; but from that day forward also, no considerable miracle was ever registered; the devotion of Dunes diminished, other relics threw the Sacred Effigy into the shade; and the pilgrimages dwindling to mere local gatherings, the church was never brought to completion.

What had happened? No one ever knew, guessed, or perhaps even asked. But, when in 1790 the Archiepiscopal palace of Arras was sacked, a certain notary of the neighbourhood bought a large portion of the archives at the price of waste paper, either from historical curiosity, or expecting to obtain thereby facts which might gratify his aversion to the clergy. These documents lay unexamined for many years, till my friend the Antiquary bought them. Among them taken helter skelter from the Archbishop's palace, were sundry papers referring to the suppressed Abbey of St. Loup

of Arras, and among these latter, a series of notes concerning the affairs of the church of Dunes; they were, so far as their fragmentary nature explained, the minutes of an inquest made in 1309, and contained the deposition of sundry witnesses. To understand their meaning it is necessary to remember that this was the time when witch trials had begun, and when the proceedings against the Templars had set the fashion of inquests which could help the finances of the country while furthering the interests of religion.

What appears to have happened is that after the catastrophe of the Vigil of All Saints, October, 1299, the Prior, Urbain de Luc, found himself suddenly threatened with a charge of sacrilege and witchcraft, of obtaining miracles of the Effigy by devilish means, and of converting his church into a chapel of the Evil One.

Instead of appealing to high ecclesiastical tribunals, as the privileges obtained from the Holy See would have warranted, Prior Urbain guessed that this charge came originally from the wrathful Abbot of St. Loup, and, dropping all his pretensions in order to save himself, he threw himself upon the mercy of the Abbot whom he had hitherto flouted. The Abbot appears to have been satisfied by his submission, and the matter to have dropped after a few legal preliminaries, of which the notes found among the Archiepiscopal archives of Arras represented a portion. Some of these notes my friend the Antiquary kindly allowed me to translate from the Latin, and I give them here, leaving the reader to make what he can of them.

I tem. The Abbot expresses himself satisfied that His Reverence the Prior has had no personal knowledge of or dealings with the Evil One (Diabolus). Nevertheless, the gravity of the charge requires . . ."—here the page is torn.

"Hugues Jacquot, Simon le Couvreur, Pierre Denis, burghers of Dunes, being interrogated, witness.

"That the noises from the Church of the Holy

Cross always happened on nights of bad storms, and foreboded shipwrecks on the coast; and were very various, such as terrible rattling, groans, howls as of wolves, and occasional flute playing. A certain Jehan, who has twice been branded and flogged for lighting fires on the coast and otherwise causing ships to wreck at the mouth of the Nys, being promised immunity, after two or three slight pulls on the rack, witnesses as follows: That the band of wreckers to which he belongs always knew when a dangerous storm was brewing, on account of the noises which issued from the church of Dunes. Witness has often climbed the walls and prowled round in the churchyard, waiting to hear such noises. He was not unfamiliar with the howlings and roarings mentioned by the previous witnesses. He has heard tell by a countryman who passed in the night that the howling was such that the countryman thought himself pursued by a pack of wolves, although it is well known that no wolf has been seen in these parts for thirty years. But the witness himself is of the opinion that the most singular of all the noises, and the one which always accompanied or foretold the worst storms, was a noise of flutes and pipes *(quod vulgo dicuntur flustes et musettes)* so sweet that the King of France could not have sweeter at his Court. Being interrogated whether he had ever seen anything? the witness answers: 'That he has seen the church brightly lit up from the sands; but on approaching found all dark, save the light from the warder's chamber. That once, by moonlight, the piping and fluting and howling being uncommonly loud, he thought he had seen wolves, and a human figure on the roof, but that he ran away from fear, and cannot be sure.'

"Item. His Lordship the Abbot desires the Right Reverend Prior to answer truly, placing his hand on the Gospels, whether or not he had himself heard such noises.

"The Right Reverend Prior denies ever having heard anything similar. But, being threatened with further proceedings (the rack?) acknowledges that he had frequently been told of these noises by the Warder on duty.

"*Query:* Whether the Right Reverend Prior was ever told anything else by the Warder?

"*Answer:* Yes; but under the seal of confession. The last Warder, moreover, the one killed by lightning, had been a reprobate priest, having committed the greatest crimes and obliged to take asylum, whom the Prior had kept there on account of the difficulty of finding a man sufficiently courageous for the office.

"*Query:* Whether the Prior has ever questioned previous Warders?

"*Answer:* That the Warders were bound to reveal only in confession whatever they had heard; that the Prior's predecessors had kept the seal of confession inviolate, and that though unworthy, the Prior himself desired to do alike.

"*Query:* What had become of the Warder who had been found in a swoon after the occurrences of Halloween?

"*Answer:* That the Prior does not know. The Warder was crazy. The Prior believes he was secluded for that reason."

A disagreeable surprise had been, apparently, arranged for Prior Urban de Luc. For the next entry states that:

"Item. By order of His Magnificence the Lord Abbot, certain servants of the Lord Abbot aforesaid introduce Robert Baudouin, priest, once Warder in the Church of the Holy Cross, who has been kept ten years in prison by His Reverence the Prior, as being of unsound mind. Witness manifests great terror on finding himself in the presence of their Lordships, and particularly of His Reverence the Prior. And refuses to speak, hiding his face in his hands and uttering shrieks. Being comforted with kind words by those present, nay even most graciously by My Lord the Abbot himself, *etiam* threatened with the rack if he continue obdurate, this witness deposes as follows, not without much lamentation, shrieking, and senseless jabber after the manner of mad men.

"*Query:* Can he remember what happened on the Vigil of All Saints, in the church of Dunes, before he swooned on the floor of the church?

"*Answer:* He cannot. It would be sin to speak

of such things before great spiritual Lords. More-over he is but an ignorant man, and also mad. Moreover his hunger is great.

"Being given white bread from the Lord Abbot's own table, witness is again cross-questioned.

"*Query:* What can he remember of the events of the Vigil of All Saints?

"*Answer:* Thinks he was not always mad. Thinks he has not always been in prison. Thinks he once went in a boat on sea, etc.

"*Query:* Does witness think he has ever been in the church of Dunes?

"*Answer:* Cannot remember. But is sure that he was not always in prison.

"*Query:* Has witness ever heard anything like that? (My Lord the Abbot having secretly ordered that a certain fool in his service, an excellent mu-sician, should suddenly play the pipes behind the Arras.)

"At which sound witness began to tremble and sob and fall on his knees, and catch hold of the robe even of My Lord the Abbot, hiding his head therein.

"*Query:* Wherefore does he feel such terror, being in the fatherly presence of so clement a prince as the Lord Abbot?

"*Answer:* That witness cannot stand that pip-ing any longer. That it freezes his blood. That he has told the Prior many times that he will not re-main any longer in the warder's chamber. That he is afraid for his life. That he dare not make the sign of the Cross nor say his prayers for fear of the Great Wild Man. That the Great Wild Man took the Cross and broke it in two and played at quoits with it in the nave. That all the wolves trooped down from the roof howling, and danced on their hind legs while the Great Wild Man played the pipes on the high altar. That witness had sur-rounded himself with a hedge of little crosses, made of broken rye straw, to keep off the Great Wild Man from the warder's chamber. Ah—ah—ah! He is piping again! The wolves are howling! He is raising the tempest.

"*Item:* That no further information can be ex-tracted from witness, who falls on the floor like one possessed and has to be removed from the presence of His Lordship the Abbot and His Rev-erence the Prior."

# III

Here the minutes of the inquest break off. Did those great spiritual dignitaries ever get to learn more about the terrible doings in the church of Dunes? Did they ever guess at their cause?

"For there was a cause," said the Antiquary, folding his spectacles after reading me these notes, "or more strictly the cause still exists. And you will understand, though those learned priests of six centuries ago could not."

And rising, he fetched a key from a shelf and preceded me into the yard of his house, situated on the Nys, a mile below Dunes.

Between the low steadings one saw the salt marsh, lilac with sea lavender, the Island of Birds, a great sandbank at the mouth of the Nys, where every kind of sea fowl gathers; and beyond, the angry white-crested sea under an angry orange af-terglow. On the other side, inland, and appearing above the farm roofs, stood the church of Dunes, its pointed belfry and jagged outlines of gables and buttresses and gargoyles and wind-warped pines black against the easterly sky of ominous livid red.

"I told you," said the Antiquary, stopping with the key in the lock of a big outhouse, "that there had been a *substitution*; that the crucifix at present at Dunes is not the one miraculously cast up by the storm of 1195. I believe the present one may be identified as a life-size statue, for which a re-ceipt exists in the archives of Arras, furnished to the Abbot of St. Loup by Estienne Le Mas and Guillaume Pernel, stonemasons, in the year 1299, that is to say the year of the inquest and of the ces-sation of all supernatural occurrences at Dunes. As to the original effigy, you shall see it and un-derstand everything."

The Antiquary opened the door of a sloping, vaulted passage, lit a lantern, and led the way. It was evidently the cellar of some mediæval build-ing; and a scent of wine, of damp wood, and of fir branches from innumerable stacked up faggots, filled the darkness among thickset columns.

"Here," said the Antiquary, raising his lantern, "he was buried beneath this vault and they had run an iron stake through his middle, like a vampire, to prevent his rising."

The Effigy was erect against the dark wall, surrounded by brushwood. It was more than life-size, nude, the arms broken off at the shoulders, the head, with stubbly beard and clotted hair, drawn up with an effort, the face contracted with agony; the muscles dragged as of one hanging crucified, the feet bound together with a rope. The figure was familiar to me in various galleries. I came forward to examine the ear: it was leaf-shaped.

"Ah, you have understood the whole mystery," said the Antiquary.

"I have understood," I answered, not knowing how far his thought really went, "that this supposed statue of Christ is an antique satyr, a Marsyas awaiting his punishment."

The Antiquary nodded. "Exactly," he said drily, "that is the whole explanation. Only I think the Abbot and the Prior were not so wrong to drive the iron stake through him when they removed him from the church."

## *THE HORLA*

# Guy de Maupassant

Guy de Maupassant (1850–93) was born in Normandy, France, to an old and distinguished family. His parents divorced when he was eleven, and his mother was befriended by Gustave Flaubert, who took an interest in her elder son, becoming his literary mentor. Immediately after graduating high school, Maupassant served with distinction in the Franco-Prussian War, then took a job as a civil servant for nearly ten years. He was beginning to write, first poetry, which was undistinguished, then short stories, most of which Flaubert forced him to discard as unworthy. When his first story was published in a collection with the work of such literary lions of the day as Émile Zola, it outshone them all and his future was secured. Over the next decade, he wrote more than three hundred short stories, six novels, three travel books, poetry, several plays, and more than three hundred magazine articles.

His naturalistic style was a powerful influence on other great short-story writers, including O. Henry and W. Somerset Maugham. Unfortunately, Maupassant died before his forty-third birthday. As an ardent womanizer, he contracted syphilis when he was quite young and suffered from other ailments as well. His brother died in an insane asylum, and when Maupassant felt he was losing his mind, he twice attempted suicide; he died a lunatic.

"Le Horla" was first published in *Gil Blas*, October 26, 1886; its first publication in book form was in 1887 (Paris: Paul Ollendorff).

# The Horla

## GUY DE MAUPASSANT

*ay 8.* What a lovely day. I have spent all the morning lying in the grass in front of my house, under the enormous plane tree that shades the whole of it. I like this part of the country and I like to live here because I am attached to it by old associations, by those deep and delicate roots which attach man to the soil on which his ancestors were born and died, which attach him to the ideas and usages of the place as well as to the food, to local expressions, to the peculiar twang of the peasants, to the smell of the soil, of the villages, and of the atmosphere itself.

I love my house in which I grew up. From my windows I can see the Seine which flows alongside my garden, on the other side of the high road, almost through my grounds, the great and wide Seine, which goes to Rouen and Havre, and is covered with boats passing to and fro.

On the left, down yonder, lies Rouen, that large town, with its blue roofs, under its pointed Gothic towers. These are innumerable, slender or broad, dominated by the spire of the cathedral, and full of bells which sound through the blue air on fine mornings, sending their sweet and distant iron clang even as far as my home; that song of the metal, which the breeze wafts in my direction, now stronger and now weaker, according as the wind is stronger or lighter.

What a delicious morning it was!

About eleven o'clock, a long line of boats drawn by a steam tug as big as a fly, and which scarcely puffed while emitting its thick smoke, passed my gate.

After two English schooners, whose red flag fluttered in space, there came a magnificent Brazilian three-master; it was perfectly white, and wonderfully clean and shining. I saluted it, I hardly knew why, except that the sight of the vessel gave me great pleasure.

*May 12.* I have had a slight feverish attack for the last few days, and I feel ill, or rather I feel low-spirited.

Whence come those mysterious influences which change our happiness into discouragement, and our self-confidence into diffidence? One might almost say that the air, the invisible air, is full of unknowable Powers whose mysterious presence we have to endure. I wake up in the best spirits, with an inclination to sing. Why? I go down to the edge of the water, and suddenly, after walking a short distance, I return home wretched, as if some misfortune were awaiting me there. Why? Is it a

787

cold shiver which, passing over my skin, has upset my nerves and given me low spirits? Is it the form of the clouds, the color of the sky, or the color of the surrounding objects which is so changeable, that has troubled my thoughts as they passed before my eyes? Who can tell? Everything that we touch, without knowing it, everything that we handle, without feeling it, all that we meet, without clearly distinguishing it, has a rapid, surprising, and inexplicable effect upon us and upon our senses, and, through them, on our ideas and on our heart itself.

How profound that mystery of the Invisible is! We cannot fathom it with our miserable senses, with our eyes which are unable to perceive what is either too small or too great, too near to us, or too far from us—neither the inhabitants of a star nor of a drop of water; nor with our ears that deceive us, for they transmit to us the vibrations of the air in sonorous notes. They are fairies who work the miracle of changing these vibrations into sounds, and by that metamorphosis give birth to music, which makes the silent motion of nature musical . . . with our sense of smell which is less keen than that of a dog, . . . with our sense of taste which can scarcely distinguish the age of wine!

Oh! If we only had other organs which would work other miracles in our favor, what a number of fresh things we might discover around us!

*May 16.* I am ill, decidedly! I was so well last month! I am feverish, horribly feverish, or rather I am in a state of feverish enervation, which makes my mind suffer as much as my body. I have, continually, that horrible sensation of some impending danger, that apprehension of some coming misfortune, or of approaching death; that presentiment which is, no doubt, an attack of some illness which is still unknown, which germinates in the flesh and in the blood.

*May 17.* I have just come from consulting my physician, for I could no longer get any sleep. He said my pulse was rapid, my eyes dilated, my nerves highly strung, but there were no alarming symptoms. I must take a course of shower baths and of bromide of potassium.

*May 25.* No change! My condition is really very

peculiar. As the evening comes on, an incomprehensible feeling of disquietude seizes me, just as if night concealed some threatening disaster. I dine hurriedly, and then try to read, but I do not understand the words, and can scarcely distinguish the letters. Then I walk up and down my drawing-room, oppressed by a feeling of confused and irresistible fear, the fear of sleep and fear of my bed.

About ten o'clock I go up to my room. As soon as I enter it I double-lock and bolt the door; I am afraid . . . of what? Up to the present time I have been afraid of nothing . . . I open my cupboards, and look under my bed; I listen . . . to what? How strange it is that a simple feeling of discomfort, impeded or heightened circulation, perhaps the irritation of a nerve filament, a slight congestion, a small disturbance in the imperfect delicate functioning of our living machinery, may turn the most light-hearted of men into a melancholy one, and make a coward of the bravest? Then, I go to bed, and wait for sleep as a man might wait for the executioner. I wait for its coming with dread, and my heart beats and my legs tremble, while my whole body shivers beneath the warmth of the bed-clothes, until all at once I fall asleep, as though one should plunge into a pool of stagnant water in order to drown. I do not feel it coming on as I did formerly, this perfidious sleep which is close to me and watching me, which is going to seize me by the head, to close my eyes and annihilate me.

I sleep—a long time—two or three hours perhaps—then a dream—no—a nightmare lays hold on me. I feel that I am in bed and asleep . . . I feel it and I know it . . . and I feel also that somebody is coming close to me, is looking at me, touching me, is getting on to my bed, is kneeling on my chest, is taking my neck between his hands and squeezing it . . . squeezing it with all his might in order to strangle me.

I struggle, bound by that terrible sense of powerlessness which paralyzes us in our dreams; I try to cry out—but I cannot; I want to move—I cannot do so; I try, with the most violent efforts and breathing hard, to turn over and throw off this being who is crushing and suffocating me—I cannot!

And then, suddenly, I wake up, trembling and bathed in perspiration. I light a candle and find that I am alone, and after that crisis, which occurs every night, I at length fall asleep and slumber tranquilly till morning.

*June 2.* My condition has grown worse. What is the matter with me? The bromide does me no good, and the shower baths have no effect. Sometimes, in order to tire myself thoroughly, though I am fatigued enough already, I go for a walk in the forest of Roumare. I used to think first that the fresh light and soft air, impregnated with the odor of herbs and leaves, would instill new blood into my veins and impart fresh energy to my heart. I turned into a broad hunting road, and then turned toward La Bouille, through a narrow path, between two rows of exceedingly tall trees, which placed a thick green, almost black, roof between the sky and me.

A sudden shiver ran through me, not a cold shiver, but a strange shiver of agony, and I hastened my steps, uneasy at being alone in the forest, afraid, stupidly and without reason, of the profound solitude. Suddenly it seemed to me as if I were being followed, that somebody was walking at my heels, close, quite close to me, near enough to touch me.

I turned round suddenly, but I was alone. I saw nothing behind me except the straight, broad path, empty and bordered by high trees, horribly empty; before me it also extended until it was lost in the distance, and looked just the same, terrible.

I closed my eyes. Why? And then I began to turn round on one heel very quickly, just like a top. I nearly fell down, and opened my eyes; the trees were dancing round me and the earth heaved; I was obliged to sit down. Then ah! I no longer remembered how I had come! What a strange idea! What a strange, strange idea! I did not in the least know. I started off to the right, and got back into the avenue which had led me into the middle of the forest.

*June 3.* I have had a terrible night. I shall go away for a few weeks, for no doubt a journey will set me up again.

*July 2.* I have come back, quite cured, and have had a most delightful trip into the bargain. I have been to Mont Saint-Michel, which I had not seen before.

What a sight, when one arrives, as I did, at Avranches, toward the end of the day! The town stands on a hill, and I was taken into the public garden at the extremity of the town. I uttered a cry of astonishment. An extraordinarily large bay lay extended before me, as far as my eyes could reach, between two hills which were lost to sight in the mist; and in the middle of this immense yellow bay, under a clear, golden sky, a peculiar hill rose up, sombre and pointed in the midst of the sand. The sun had just disappeared, and under the still flaming sky appeared the outline of that fantastic rock which bears on its summit a fantastic monument.

At daybreak I went out to it. The tide was low, as it had been the night before, and I saw that wonderful abbey rise up before me as I approached it. After several hours' walking, I reached the enormous mass of rocks which supports the little town, dominated by the great church. Having climbed the steep and narrow street, I entered the most wonderful Gothic building that has ever been built to God on earth, as large as a town, full of low rooms which seem buried beneath vaulted roofs, and lofty galleries supported by delicate columns.

I entered this gigantic granite gem, which is as light as a bit of lace, covered with towers, with slender belfries with spiral staircases, which raise their strange heads that bristle with chimeras, with devils, with fantastic animals, with monstrous flowers, to the blue sky by day, and to the black sky by night, and are connected by finely carved arches.

When I had reached the summit I said to the monk who accompanied me: "Father, how happy you must be here!" And he replied: "It is very windy here, monsieur"; and so we began to talk while watching the rising tide, which ran over the sand and covered it as with a steel cuirass.

And then the monk told me stories, all the old stories belonging to the place, legends, nothing but legends.

One of them struck me forcibly. The country

people, those belonging to the Mount, declare that at night one can hear voices talking on the sands, and then that one hears two goats bleating, one with a strong, the other with a weak voice. Incredulous people declare that it is nothing but the cry of the sea birds, which occasionally resembles bleatings, and occasionally, human lamentations; but belated fishermen swear that they have met an old shepherd wandering between tides on the sands around the little town. His head is completely concealed by his cloak and he is followed by a billy goat with a man's face, and a nanny goat with a woman's face, both having long, white hair and talking incessantly and quarreling in an unknown tongue. Then suddenly they cease and begin to bleat with all their might.

"Do you believe it?" I asked the monk. "I scarcely know," he replied, and I continued: "If there are other beings beside ourselves on this earth, how comes it that we have not known it long since, or why have *you* not seen them? How is that *I* have not seen them?" He replied: "Do we see the hundred-thousandth part of what exists? Look here; there is the wind, which is the strongest force in nature, which knocks down men, and blows down buildings, destroys cliffs and casts great ships on the rocks; the wind which kills, which whistles, which sighs, which roars—have you ever seen it, and can you see it? It exists for all that, however."

I was silent before this simple reasoning. That man was a philosopher, or perhaps a fool; I could not say which exactly, so I held my tongue. What he had said had often been in my own thoughts.

*July 3.* I have slept badly; certainly there is some feverish influence here, for my coachman is suffering in the same way as I am. When I went back home yesterday, I noticed his singular paleness, and I asked him: "What is the matter with you, Jean?" "The matter is that I never get any rest, and my nights devour my days. Since your departure, monsieur, there has been a spell over me."

However, the other servants are all well, but I am very much afraid of having another attack myself.

*July 4.* I am decidedly ill again; for my old nightmares have returned. Last night I felt somebody leaning on me and sucking my life from between my lips. Yes, he was sucking it out of my throat, like a leech. Then he got up, satiated, and I woke up, so exhausted, crushed, and weak that I could not move. If this continues for a few days, I shall certainly go away again.

*July 5.* Have I lost my reason? What happened last night is so strange that my head wanders when I think of it!

I had locked my door, as I do now every evening, and then, being thirsty, I drank half a glass of water, and accidentally noticed that the water bottle was full up to the cut-glass stopper.

Then I went to bed and fell into one of my terrible sleeps, from which I was aroused in about two hours by a still more frightful shock.

Picture to yourself a sleeping man who is being murdered and who wakes up with a knife in his lung, and whose breath rattles, who is covered with blood, and who can no longer breathe and is about to die, and does not understand—there you have it.

Having recovered my senses, I was thirsty again, so I lit a candle and went to the table on which stood my water bottle. I lifted it up and tilted it over my glass, but nothing came out. It was empty! It was completely empty! At first I could not understand it at all, and then suddenly I was seized by such a terrible feeling that I had to sit down, or rather I fell into a chair! Then I sprang up suddenly to look about me; then I sat down again, overcome by astonishment and fear, in front of the transparent glass bottle! I looked at it with fixed eyes, trying to conjecture, and my hands trembled! Somebody had drunk the water, but who? I? I without any doubt. It could surely only be I. In that case I was a somnambulist; I lived, without knowing it, that mysterious double life which makes us doubt whether there are not two beings in us, or whether a strange, unknowable, and invisible being does not at such moments, when our soul is in a state of torpor, animate our captive body, which obeys this other being, as it obeys us, and more than it obeys ourselves.

Oh! Who will understand my horrible agony?

Who will understand the emotion of a man who is sound in mind, wide awake, full of common sense, who looks in horror through the glass of a water bottle for a little water that disappeared while he was asleep? I remained thus until it was daylight, without venturing to go to bed again.

*July 6.* I am going mad. Again all the contents of my water bottle have been drunk during the night—or rather, I have drunk it!

But is it I? Is it I? Who could it be? Who? Oh! God! Am I going mad? Who will save me?

*July 10.* I have just been through some surprising ordeals. Decidedly I am mad! And yet! . . .

On July 6, before going to bed, I put some wine, milk, water, bread, and strawberries on my table. Somebody drank—I drank—all the water and a little of the milk, but neither the wine, bread, nor the strawberries were touched.

On the seventh of July I renewed the same experiment, with the same results, and on July 8, I left out the water and the milk, and nothing was touched.

Lastly, on July 9, I put only water and milk on my table, taking care to wrap up the bottles in white muslin and to tie down the stoppers. Then I rubbed my lips, my beard and my hands with pencil lead, and went to bed.

Irresistible sleep seized me, which was soon followed by a terrible awakening. I had not moved, and there was no mark of lead on the sheets. I rushed to the table. The muslin round the bottles remained intact; I undid the string, trembling with fear. All the water had been drunk, and so had the milk! Ah! Great God! . . .

I must start for Paris immediately.

*July 12.* Paris. I must have lost my head during the last few days! I must be the plaything of my enervated imagination, unless I am really a somnambulist, or that I have been under the power of one of those hitherto unexplained influences which are called suggestions. In any case, my mental state bordered on madness, and twenty-four hours of Paris sufficed to restore my equilibrium.

Yesterday, after doing some business and paying some visits which instilled fresh and invigorating air into my soul, I wound up the evening at the *Théâtre-Français.* A play by Alexandre Dumas the younger was being acted, and his active and powerful imagination completed my cure. Certainly solitude is dangerous for active minds. We require around us men who can think and talk. When we are alone for a long time, we people space with phantoms.

I returned along the boulevards to my hotel in excellent spirits. Amid the jostling of the crowd I thought, not without irony, of my terrors and surmises of the previous week, because I had believed—yes, I had believed—that an invisible being lived beneath my roof. How weak our brains are, and how quickly they are terrified and led into error by a small incomprehensible fact.

Instead of saying simply: "I do not understand because I do not know the cause," we immediately imagine terrible mysteries and supernatural powers.

*July 14.* Fête of the Republic. I walked through the streets, amused as a child at the firecrackers and flags. Still it is very foolish to be merry on a fixed date, by Government decree. The populace is an imbecile flock of sheep, now stupidly patient, and now in ferocious revolt. Say to it: "Amuse yourself," and it amuses itself. Say to it: "Vote for the Emperor," and it votes for the Emperor, and then say to it: "Vote for the Republic," and it votes for the Republic.

Those who direct it are also stupid; only, instead of obeying men, they obey principles which can only be stupid, sterile, and false, for the very reason that they are principles, that is to say, ideas which are considered as certain and unchangeable, in this world where one is certain of nothing, since light is an illusion and noise is an illusion.

*July 16.* I saw some things yesterday that troubled me very much.

I was dining at the house of my cousin, Madame Sable, whose husband is colonel of the 76th Chasseurs at Limoges. There were two young women there, one of whom had married a medical man, Dr. Parent, who devotes much attention to nervous diseases and to the remarkable manifestations taking place at this moment under the influence of hypnotism and suggestion.

He related to us at some length the wonderful results obtained by English scientists and by the doctors of the Nancy school; and the facts which he adduced appeared to me so strange that I declared that I was altogether incredulous.

"We are," he declared, "on the point of discovering one of the most important secrets of nature; I mean to say, one of its most important secrets on this earth, for there are certainly others of a different kind of importance up in the stars, yonder. Ever since man has thought, ever since he has been able to express and write down his thoughts, he has felt himself close to a mystery which is impenetrable to his gross and imperfect senses, and he endeavors to supplement through his intellect the inefficiency of his senses. As long as that intellect remained in its elementary stage, these apparitions of invisible spirits assumed forms that were commonplace, though terrifying. Thence sprang the popular belief in the supernatural, the legends of wandering spirits, of fairies, of gnomes, ghosts, I might even say the legend of God; for our conceptions of the workman-creator, from whatever religion they may have come down to us, are certainly the most mediocre, the most stupid, and the most incredible inventions that ever sprang from the terrified brain of any human beings. Nothing is truer than what Voltaire says: 'God made man in His own image, but man has certainly paid Him back in his own coin.'

"However, for rather more than a century men seem to have had a presentiment of something new. Mesmer and some others have put us on an unexpected track, and, especially within the last two or three years, we have arrived at really surprising results."

My cousin, who is also very incredulous, smiled, and Dr. Parent said to her: "Would you like me to try and send you to sleep, madame?" "Yes, certainly."

She sat down in an easy chair, and he began to look at her fixedly, so as to fascinate her. I suddenly felt myself growing uncomfortable, my heart beating rapidly and a choking sensation in my throat. I saw Madame Sable's eyes becoming heavy, her mouth twitching and her bosom heaving, and at the end of ten minutes she was asleep.

"Go behind her," the doctor said to me, and I took a seat behind her. He put a visiting card into her hands, and said to her: "This is a looking-glass; what do you see in it?" And she replied: "I see my cousin." "What is he doing?" "He is twisting his mustache." "And now?" "He is taking a photograph out of his pocket." "Whose photograph is it?" "His own."

That was true, and the photograph had been given me that same evening at the hotel.

"What is his attitude in this portrait?" "He is standing up with his hat in his hand."

She saw, therefore, on that card, on that piece of white pasteboard, as if she had seen it in a mirror.

The young women were frightened, and exclaimed: "That is enough! Quite, quite enough!"

But the doctor said to Madame Sable authoritatively: "You will rise at eight o'clock tomorrow morning; then you will go and call on your cousin at his hotel and ask him to lend you five thousand francs which your husband demands of you, and which he will ask for when he sets out on his coming journey."

Then he woke her up.

On returning to my hotel, I thought over this curious séance, and I was assailed by doubts, not as to my cousin's absolute and undoubted good faith, for I had known her as well as if she were my own sister ever since she was a child, but as to a possible trick on the doctor's part. Had he not, perhaps, kept a glass hidden in his hand, which he showed to the young woman in her sleep, at the same time as he did the card? Professional conjurors do things that are just as singular.

So I went home and to bed, and this morning, at about half-past eight, I was awakened by my valet, who said to me: "Madame Sable has asked to see you immediately, monsieur." I dressed hastily and went to her.

She sat down in some agitation, with her eyes on the floor, and without raising her veil she said to me: "My dear cousin, I am going to ask a great favor of you." "What is it, cousin?" "I do not like to tell you, and yet I must. I am in absolute need of five thousand francs." "What, you?" "Yes, I, or rather my husband, who has asked me to procure them for him."

I was so thunderstruck that I stammered out my answers. I asked myself whether she had not really been making fun of me with Dr. Parent, if it was not merely a very well-acted farce which had been rehearsed beforehand. On looking at her attentively, however, all my doubts disappeared. She was trembling with grief, so painful was this step to her, and I was convinced that her throat was full of sobs.

I knew that she was very rich and I continued: "What! Has not your husband five thousand francs at his disposal? Come, think. Are you sure that he commissioned you to ask me for them?"

She hesitated for a few seconds, as if she were making a great effort to search her memory, and then she replied: "Yes . . . yes, I am quite sure of it." "He has written to you?"

She hesitated again and reflected, and I guessed the torture of her thoughts. She did not know. She only knew that she was to borrow five thousand francs of me for her husband. So she told a lie. "Yes, he had written to me." "When, pray? You did not mention it to me yesterday." "I received his letter this morning." "Can you show it me?" "No; no . . . no . . . it contained private matters . . . things too personal to ourselves . . . I burned it." "So your husband runs into debt?"

She hesitated again, and then murmured: "I do not know." Thereupon I said bluntly: "I have not five thousand francs at my disposal at this moment, my dear cousin."

She uttered a kind of cry as if she were in pain and said: "Oh! Oh! I beseech you, I beseech you to get them for me. . . ."

She got excited and clasped her hands as if she were praying to me! I heard her voice change its tone; she wept and stammered, harassed and dominated by the irresistible order that she had received.

"Oh! Oh! I beg you to . . . if you knew what I am suffering . . . I want them today."

I had pity on her: "You shall have them by and by, I swear to you." "Oh! Thank you! Thank you! How kind you are."

I continued: "Do you remember what took place at your house last night?" "Yes." "Do you remember that Dr. Parent sent you to sleep?" "Yes." "Oh! Very well, then; he ordered you to come to me this morning to borrow five thousand francs, and at this moment you are obeying that suggestion."

She considered for a few moments, and then replied: "But as it is my husband who wants them—"

For a whole hour I tried to convince her, but could not succeed, and when she had gone I went to the doctor. He was just going out, and he listened to me with a smile, and said: "Do you believe now?" "Yes, I cannot help it." "Let us go to your cousin's."

She was already half asleep on a reclining chair, overcome with fatigue. The doctor felt her pulse, looked at her for some time with one hand raised toward her eyes, which she closed by degrees under the irresistible power of this magnetic influence, and when she was asleep, he said:

"Your husband does not require the five thousand francs any longer! You must, therefore, forget that you asked your cousin to lend them to you, and, if he speaks to you about it, you will not understand him."

Then he woke her up, and I took out a pocket book and said: "Here is what you asked me for this morning, my dear cousin." But she was so surprised that I did not venture to persist; nevertheless, I tried to recall the circumstance to her, but she denied it vigorously, thought I was making fun of her, and, in the end, very nearly lost her temper.

There! I have just come back, and I have not been able to eat any lunch, for this experiment has altogether upset me.

*July 19.* Many people to whom I told the adventure laughed at me. I no longer know what to think. The wise man says: "It may be!"

*July 21.* I dined at Bougival, and then I spent the evening at a boatmen's ball. Decidedly everything depends on place and surroundings. It would be the height of folly to believe in the supernatural on the Ile de la Grenouillière . . . but on top of Mont Saint-Michel? . . . And in India? We are terribly influenced by our surroundings. I shall return home next week.

*July 30.* I came back to my own house yesterday. Everything is going on well.

*August 2.* Nothing new; it is splendid weather, and I spend my days in watching the Seine flowing past.

*August 4.* Quarrels among my servants. They declare that the glasses are broken in the cupboards at night. The footman accuses the cook, who accuses the seamstress, who accuses the other two. Who is the culprit? It is a clever person who can tell.

*August 6.* This time I am not mad. I have seen . . . I have seen . . . I have seen! . . . I can doubt no longer . . . I have seen it! . . .

I was walking at two o'clock among my rose trees, in the full sunlight . . . in the walk bordered by autumn roses which are beginning to fall. As I stopped to look at a Géant de Bataille, which had three splendid blossoms, I distinctly saw the stalk of one of the roses near me bend, as if an invisible hand had bent it, and then break, as if that hand had picked it! Then the flower raised itself, following the curve which a hand would have described in carrying it toward a mouth, and it remained suspended in the transparent air, all alone and motionless, a terrible red spot, three yards from my eyes. In desperation I rushed at it to take it! I found nothing; it had disappeared. Then I was seized with furious rage against myself, for a reasonable and serious man should not have such hallucinations.

But was it an hallucination? I turned round to look for the stalk, and I found it at once, on the bush, freshly broken, between two other roses which remained on the branch. I returned home then, my mind greatly disturbed; for I am certain now, as certain as I am of the alternation of day and night, that there exists close to me an invisible being that lives on milk and water, that can touch objects, take them and change their places; that is, consequently, endowed with a material na-

ture, although it is imperceptible to our senses, and that lives as I do, under my roof—

*August 7.* I slept tranquilly. He drank the water out of my decanter, but did not disturb my sleep.

I wonder if I am mad. As I was walking just now in the sun by the river side, doubts as to my sanity arose in me; not vague doubts such as I have had hitherto, but definite, absolute doubts. I have seen mad people, and I have known some who have been quite intelligent, lucid, even clear-sighted in every concern of life, except on one point. They spoke readily, clearly, profoundly on everything, when suddenly their mind struck upon the shoals of their madness and broke to pieces there, and scattered and floundered in that furious and terrible sea, full of rolling waves, fogs, and squalls, which is called *madness.*

I certainly should think that I was mad, absolutely mad, if I were not conscious, did not perfectly know my condition, did not fathom it by analyzing it with the most complete lucidity. I should, in fact, be only a rational man who was laboring under an hallucination. Some unknown disturbance must have arisen in my brain, one of those disturbances which physiologists of the present day try to note and to verify; and that disturbance must have caused a deep gap in my mind and in the sequence and logic of my ideas. Similar phenomena occur in dreams which lead us among the most unlikely phantasmagoria, without causing us any surprise, because our verifying apparatus and our organ of control are asleep, while our imaginative faculty is awake and active. Is it not possible that one of the imperceptible notes of the cerebral keyboard had been paralyzed in me? Some men lose the recollection of proper names, of verbs, or of numbers, or merely of dates, in consequence of an accident. The localization of all the variations of thought has been established nowadays; why, then, should it be surprising if my faculty of controlling the unreality of certain hallucinations were dormant in me for the time being?

I thought of all this as I walked by the side of the water. The sun shone brightly on the river and made earth delightful, while it filled me with a love for life, for the swallows, whose agility always delights my eye, for the plants by the river side, the rustle of whose leaves is a pleasure to my ears.

By degrees, however, an inexplicable feeling of discomfort seized me. It seemed as if some unknown force were numbing and stopping me, were preventing me from going further, and were calling me back. I felt that painful wish to return which oppresses you when you have left a beloved invalid at home, and when you are seized with a presentiment that he is worse.

I, therefore, returned in spite of myself, feeling certain that I should find some bad news awaiting me, a letter or a telegram. There was nothing, however, and I was more surprised and uneasy than if I had had another fantastic vision.

*August 8.* I spent a terrible evening yesterday. He does not show himself any more, but I feel that he is near me, watching me, looking at me, penetrating me, dominating me, and more redoubtable when he hides himself thus than if he were to manifest his constant and invisible presence by supernatural phenomena. However, I slept.

*August 9.* Nothing, but I am afraid.

*August 10.* Nothing; what will happen tomorrow?

*August 11.* Still nothing; I cannot stop at home with this fear hanging over me and these thoughts in my mind; I shall go away.

*August 12.* Ten o'clock at night. All day long I have been trying to get away, and have not been able. I wish to accomplish this simple and easy act of freedom—to go out—to get into my carriage in order to go to Rouen—and I have not been able to do it. What is the reason?

*August 13.* When one is attacked by certain maladies, all the springs of our physical being appear to be broken, all our energies destroyed, all our muscles relaxed; our bones, too, have become as soft as flesh, and our blood as liquid as water. I am experiencing these sensations in my moral being in a strange and distressing manner. I have no longer any strength, any courage, any self-control, not even any power to set my own will in motion. I have no power left to will anything; but someone does it for me and I obey.

*August 14.* I am lost. Somebody possesses my soul and dominates it. Someday orders all my acts, all my movements, all my thoughts. I am no longer anything in myself, nothing except an enslaved and terrified spectator of all the things I do. I wish to go out; I cannot. He does not wish to, and so I remain, trembling and distracted, in the armchair in which he keeps me sitting. I merely wish to get up and to rouse myself; I cannot! I am riveted to my chair, and my chair adheres to the ground in such a manner that no power could move us.

Then, suddenly, I must, I must go to the bottom of my garden to pick some strawberries and eat them, and I go there. I pick the strawberries and eat them! Oh, my God! My God! Is there a God? If there be one, deliver me! Save me! Succor me! Pardon! Pity! Mercy! Save me! Oh, what sufferings! What torture! What horror!

*August 15.* This is certainly the way in which my poor cousin was possessed and controlled when she came to borrow five thousand francs of me. She was under the power of a strange will which had entered into her, like another soul, like another parasitic and dominating soul. Is the world coming to an end?

But who is he, this invisible being that rules me? This unknowable being, this rover of a supernatural race?

Invisible beings exist, then! How is it, then, that since the beginning of the world they have never manifested themselves precisely as they do to me? I have never read of anything that resembles what goes on in my house. Oh, if I could only leave it, if I could only go away, escape, and never return! I should be saved, but I cannot.

*August 16.* I managed to escape today for two hours, like a prisoner who finds the door of his dungeon accidentally open. I suddenly felt that I was free and that he was far away, and so I gave orders to harness the horses as quickly as possible, and I drove to Rouen. Oh, how delightful to be able to say to a man who obeys you: "Go to Rouen!"

I made him pull up before the library, and I begged them to lend me Dr. Herrmann Herestauss' treatise on the unknown inhabitants of the ancient and modern world.

Then, as I was getting into my carriage, I intended to say: "To the railway station!" but instead of this I shouted—I did not say, I shouted—in such a loud voice that all the passersby turned round: "Home!" and I fell back on the cushion of my carriage, overcome by mental agony. He had found me again and regained possession of me.

*August 17.* Oh, what a night! What a night! And yet it seems to me that I ought to rejoice. I read until one o'clock in the morning! Herestauss, doctor of philosophy and theogony, wrote the history of the manifestation of all those invisible beings which hover round man, or of whom he dreams. He describes their origin, their domain, their power; but none of them resembles the one which haunts me. One might say that man, ever since he began to think, has had a foreboding fear of a new being, stronger than himself, his successor in this new world, and that, feeling his presence, and not being able to foresee the nature of that master, he has, in his terror, created the whole race of occult beings, of vague phantoms born of fear.

Having, therefore, read until one o'clock in the morning, I went and sat down at the open window, in order to cool my forehead and my thoughts, in the calm night air. It was very pleasant and warm! How I should have enjoyed such a night formerly!

There was no moon, but the stars darted out their rays in the dark heavens. Who inhabits those worlds? What forms, what living beings, what animals are there yonder? What can they do more than we can? What do they see which we do not know? Will not one of them, some day or other, traversing space, appear on our earth to conquer it, just as the Norsemen formerly crossed the sea in order to subjugate nations more feeble than themselves?

We are so weak, so defenseless, so ignorant, so small, we who live on this particle of mud which revolves in a drop of water.

I fell asleep, dreaming thus in the cool night air, and when I had slept for about three-quarters of an hour, I opened my eyes without moving, awakened by I know not what confused and strange sensation. At first I saw nothing, and then suddenly it appeared to me as if a page of a book which had remained open on my table turned over of its own accord. Not a breath of air had come in at my window, and I was surprised, and waited. In about four minutes, I saw, I saw, yes, I saw with my own eyes, another page lift itself up and fall down on the others, as if a finger had turned it over. My armchair was empty, appeared empty, but I knew that he was there, he, and sitting in my place, and that he was reading. With a furious bound, the bound of an enraged wild beast that springs at its tamer, I crossed my room to seize him, to strangle him, to kill him! But before I could reach it, the chair fell over as if somebody had run away from me—my table rocked, my lamp fell and went out, and my window closed as if some thief had been surprised and had fled out into the night, shutting it behind him.

So he had run away; he had been afraid; he, afraid of me!

But—but—tomorrow—or later—some day or other—I should be able to hold him in my clutches and crush him against the ground! Do not dogs occasionally bite and strangle their masters?

*August 18.* I have been thinking the whole day long. Oh, yes, I will obey him, follow his impulses, fulfill all his wishes, show myself humble, submissive, a coward. He is the stronger; but the hour will come—

*August 19.* I know—I know—I know all! I have just read the following in the *Revue du Monde Scientifique:* "A curious piece of news comes to us from Rio de Janeiro. Madness, an epidemic of madness, which may be compared to that contagious madness which attacked the people of Europe in the Middle Ages, is at this moment raging in the Province of San-Paolo. The terrified inhabitants are leaving their houses, saying that they are pursued, possessed, dominated like human cattle by invisible, though tangible beings, a species of vampire, which feed on their life while they are asleep, and who, besides, drink water and milk without appearing to touch any other nourishment.

"Professor Don Pedro Henriquez, accompanied by several medical savants, has gone to the Province of San-Paolo, in order to study the origin and the manifestations of this surprising madness on the spot, and to propose such measures to the Emperor as may appear to him to be most fitted to restore the mad population to reason."

Ah! Ah! I remember now that fine Brazilian three-master which passed in front of my windows as it was going up the Seine, on the 8th day of last May! I thought it looked so pretty, so white and bright! That Being was on board of her, coming from there, where its race originated. And it saw me! It saw my house which was also white, and it sprang from the ship onto the land. Oh, merciful heaven!

Now I know, I can divine. The reign of man is over, and he has come. He who was feared by primitive man; whom disquieted priests exorcised; whom sorcerers evoked on dark nights, without having seen him appear, to whom the imagination of the transient masters of the world lent all the monstrous or graceful forms of gnomes, spirits, genii, fairies, and familiar spirits. After the coarse conceptions of primitive fear, more clear-sighted men foresaw it more clearly. Mesmer divined it, and ten years ago physicians accurately discovered the nature of his power, even before he exercised it himself. They played with this new weapon of the Lord, the sway of a mysterious will over the human soul, which had become a slave. They called it magnetism, hypnotism, suggestion—what do I know? I have seen them amusing themselves like rash children with this horrible power! Woe to us! Woe to man! He has come, the—the—what does he call himself—the—I fancy that he is shouting out his name to me and I do not hear him—the—yes—he is shouting it out—I am listening—I cannot—he repeats it—the—Horla—I hear—the Horla—it is he—the Horla—he has come!

Ah! The vulture has eaten the pigeon; the wolf has eaten the lamb; the lion has devoured the sharp-horned buffalo; man has killed the lion with an arrow, with sword, with gunpowder; but the Horla will make of man what we have made of the horse and of the ox; his chattel, his slave, and his food, by the mere power of his will. Woe to us!

But, nevertheless, the animal sometimes revolts and kills the man who has subjugated it. I should also like—I shall be able to—but I must know him, touch him, see him! Scientists say that animals' eyes, being different from ours, do not distinguish objects as ours do. And my eye cannot distinguish this newcomer who is oppressing me.

Why? Oh, now I remember the words of the monk at Mont Saint-Michel: "Can we see the hundred-thousandth part of what exists? See here; there is the wind, which is the strongest force in nature, which knocks men, and bowls down buildings, uproots trees, raises the sea into mountains of water, destroys cliffs and casts great ships on the breakers; the wind which kills, which whistles, which sighs, which roars—have you ever seen it, and can you see it? It exists for all that, however!"

And I went on thinking; my eyes are so weak, so imperfect, that they do not even distinguish hard bodies, if they are as transparent as glass! If a glass without tinfoil behind it were to bar my way, I should run into it, just as a bird which has flown into a room breaks its head against the window-panes. A thousand things, moreover, deceive man and lead astray. Why should it then be surprising that he cannot perceive an unknown body through which the light passes?

A new being! Why not? It was assuredly bound to come! Why should we be the last? We do not distinguish it any more than all the others created before us! The reason is, that its nature is more perfect, its body finer and more finished than ours, that ours is so weak, so awkwardly constructed, encumbered with organs that are always tired, always on the strain like machinery that is too complicated, which lives like a plant and like a beast, nourishing itself on air, herbs, and flesh, an animal machine which is a prey to maladies, to malformations, to decay; broken-winded, badly regulated, simple and eccentric, ingeniously badly made, at once a coarse and a delicate piece of workmanship, the rough sketch of a being that might become intelligent and grand.

We are only a few, so few in this world, from the oyster up to man. Why should there not be one more, once that period is passed which separates the successive apparitions from all the different species?

Why not one more? Why not, also, other trees with immense, splendid flowers, perfuming whole regions? Why not other elements besides fire, air, earth, and water? There are four, only four, those nursing fathers of various beings! What a pity! Why are there not forty, four hundred, four thousand? How poor everything is, how mean and wretched! Grudgingly produced, roughly constructed, clumsily made! Ah, the elephant and the hippopotamus, what grace! And the camel, what elegance!

But the butterfly, you will say, a flying flower? I dream of one that should be as large as a hundred worlds, with wings whose shape, beauty, colors and motion I cannot even express. But I see it—it flutters from star to star, refreshing them and perfuming them with the light and harmonious breath of its flight! And the people up there look at it as it passes in an ecstasy of delight!

What is the matter with me? It is he, the Horla, who haunts me, and who makes me think of these foolish things! He is within me, he is becoming my soul; I shall kill him!

*August 19.* I shall kill him. I have seen him! Yesterday I sat down at my table and pretended to write very assiduously. I knew quite well that he would come prowling round me, quite close to me, so close that I might perhaps be able to touch him, to seize him. And then—then I should have the strength of desperation; I should have my hands, my knees, my chest, my forehead, my teeth to strangle him, to crush him, to bite him, to tear him to pieces. And I watched for him with all my over-excited senses.

I had lighted my two lamps and the eight wax candles on my mantelpiece, as if with this light I could discover him.

My bedstead, my old oak post bedstead, stood opposite to me; on my right was the fireplace; on my left, the door which was carefully closed, after I had left it open for some time in order to attract him; behind me was a very high wardrobe with a looking-glass in it, before which I stood to shave and dress every day, and in which I was in the habit of glancing at myself from head to foot every time I passed it.

I pretended to be writing in order to deceive him, for he also was watching me, and suddenly I felt—I was certain that he was reading over my shoulder, that he was there, touching my ear.

I got up, my hands extended, and turned round so quickly that I almost fell. Eh! Well? It was as bright as at midday, but I did not see my reflection in the mirror! It was empty, clear, profound, full of light! But my figure was not reflected in it—and I, I was opposite to it! I saw the large, clear glass from top to bottom, and I looked at it with unsteady eyes; and I did not dare to advance; I did not venture to make a movement, feeling that he was there, but that he would escape me again, he whose imperceptible body had absorbed my reflection.

How frightened I was! And then, suddenly, I began to see myself in a mist in the depths of the looking-glass, in a mist as it were a sheet of water; and it seemed to me as if this water were flowing clearer every moment. It was like the end of an eclipse. Whatever it was that hid me did not appear to possess any clearly defined outlines, but a sort of opaque transparency which gradually grew clearer.

At last I was able to distinguish myself completely, as I do every day when I look at myself.

I had seen it! And the horror of it remained with me, and makes me shudder even now.

*August 20.* How could I kill it, as I could not get hold of it? Poison? But it would see me mix it with the water; and then, would our poisons have any effect on its impalpable body? No—no—no doubt about the matter—Then—then?—

*August 21.* I sent for a blacksmith from Rouen, and ordered iron shutters for my room, such as some private hotels in Paris have on the ground floor, for fear of burglars, and he is going to make me an iron door as well. I have made myself out a coward, but I do not care about that!

*September 10*. Rouen, Hôtel Continental. It is done—it is done—but is he dead? My mind is thoroughly upset by what I have seen.

Well then, yesterday, the locksmith having put on the iron shutters and door, I left everything until midnight, although it was getting cold.

Suddenly I felt that he was there, and joy, mad joy, took possession of me. I got up softly, and walked up and down for some time, so that he might not suspect anything; then I took off my boots and put on my slippers carelessly; then I fastened the iron shutters, and, going back to the door, quickly double-locked it with a padlock, putting the key into my pocket.

Suddenly I noticed that he was moving restlessly round me, that in his turn he was frightened and was ordering me to let him out. I nearly yielded; I did not, however, but putting my back to the door, I half opened it, just enough to allow me to go out backward, and as I am very tall my head touched the casing. I was sure that he had not been able to escape, and I shut him up alone, quite alone. What happiness! I had him fast. Then I ran downstairs; in the drawing-room, which was under my bedroom, I took the two lamps and I poured all the oil on the carpet, the furniture, everywhere; then I set fire to it and made my escape, after having carefully double-locked the door.

I went and hid myself at the bottom of the garden, in a clump of laurel bushes. How long it seemed! How long it seemed! Everything was dark, silent, motionless, not a breath of air and not a star, but heavy banks of clouds which one could not see, but which weighed, oh, so heavily on my soul.

I looked at my house and waited. How long it was! I already began to think that the fire had gone out of its own accord, or that he had extinguished it, when one of the lower windows gave way under the violence of the flames, and a long, soft, caressing sheet of red flame mounted up the white wall, and enveloped it as far as the roof. The light fell on the trees, the branches, and the leaves, and a shiver of fear pervaded them also! The birds awoke, a dog began to howl, and it seemed to me as if the day were breaking! Almost immediately two other windows flew into fragments, and I saw that the whole of the lower part of my house was nothing but a terrible furnace. But a cry, a horrible, shrill, heartrending cry, a woman's cry, sounded through the night, and two garret windows were opened! I had forgotten the servants! I saw their terror-stricken faces, and their arms waving frantically.

Then overwhelmed with horror, I set off to run to the village, shouting: "Help! Help! Fire! Fire!" I met some people who were already coming to the scene, and I returned with them.

By this time the house was nothing but a horrible and magnificent funeral pile, a monstrous funeral pile which lit up the whole country, a funeral pile where men were burning, and where he was burning also, He, He, my prisoner, that new Being, the new master, the Horla!

Suddenly the whole roof fell in between the walls, and a volcano of flames darted up to the sky. Through all the windows which opened on that furnace, I saw the flames darting, and I thought that he was there, in that kiln, dead.

Dead? Perhaps?—His body? Was not his body, which was transparent, indestructible by such means as would kill ours?

If he were not dead?—Perhaps time alone has power over that Invisible and Redoubtable Being. Why this transparent, unrecognizable body, this body belonging to a spirit, if it also has to fear ills, infirmities, and premature destruction?

Premature destruction? All human terror springs from that! After man, the Horla. After him who can die every day, at any hour, at any moment, by any accident, came the one who would die only at his own proper hour, day, and minute, because he had touched the limits of his existence!

No—no—without any doubt—he is not dead— Then—then—I suppose I must kill myself! . . .

# THE GIRL WITH THE HUNGRY EYES

# Fritz Leiber

Fritz Reuter Leiber (1910–92) was born in Chicago, the son of two famous Shakespearean actors, Fritz Sr. and Virginia (nee Bronson). He graduated from the University of Chicago with a degree in biology and briefly followed in his parents' footsteps as a thespian, appearing in several films, including the 1937 classic *Camille*, with Greta Garbo and Robert Taylor, and *The Hunchback of Notre Dame* (1939), in which his father also appeared. Leiber also studied at the General Theological Seminary in New York City. After World War II, he became an associate editor at *Science Digest* magazine, which inspired him to write science fiction and fantasy.

His prolific career included the sword-and-sorcery (a term he created) series about Fafhrd (a hero based on himself) and the Gray Mouser (based on his friend Harry Otto Fischer), which spanned fifty years. Among his works to have been made into feature films, perhaps the best known is *Conjure Wife* (1943), filmed three times, most famously as *Burn, Witch, Burn* (1962), with a screenplay by George Baxt, Charles Beaumont, and Richard Matheson. It was also filmed as *Weird Woman* (1944) and *Witches' Brew* (1980).

Leiber won eight Hugo Awards and two Nebulas.

"The Girl with the Hungry Eyes" was originally published in *The Girl with the Hungry Eyes and Other Stories*, edited by Donald Wollheim (New York: Avon, 1949). It was filmed in 1995; Jon Jacobs directed.

# The Girl with the Hungry Eyes

## FRITZ LEIBER

All right, I'll tell you why the Girl gives me the creeps. Why I can't stand to go downtown and see the mob slavering up at her on the tower, with that pop bottle or pack of cigarettes or whatever it is beside her. Why I hate to look at magazines any more because I know she'll turn up somewhere in a brassiere or a bubble bath. Why I don't like to think of millions of Americans drinking in that poisonous half-smile. It's quite a story—more story than you're expecting.

No, I haven't suddenly developed any long-haired indignation at the evils of advertising and the national glamour-girl complex. That'd be a laugh for a man in my racket, wouldn't it? Though I think you'll agree there's something a little perverted about trying to capitalize on sex that way. But it's okay with me. And I know we've had the Face and the Body and the Look and what not else, so why shouldn't someone come along who sums it all up so completely, that we have to call her the Girl and blazon her on all the billboards from Times Square to Telegraph Hill?

But the Girl isn't like any of the others. She's unnatural. She's morbid. She's unholy.

Oh it's 1948, is it, and the sort of thing I'm hint-ing at went out with witchcraft? But you see I'm not altogether sure myself what I'm hinting at, beyond a certain point. There are vampires and vampires, and not all of them suck blood.

And there were the murders, if they were murders.

Besides, let me ask you this. Why, when America is obsessed with the Girl, don't we find out more about her? Why doesn't she rate a *Time* cover with a droll biography inside? Why hasn't there been a feature in *Life* or the *Post*? A profile in *The New Yorker*? Why hasn't *Charm* or *Mademoiselle* done her career saga? Not ready for it? Nuts!

Why haven't the movies snapped her up? Why hasn't she been on *Information, Please*? Why don't we see her kissing candidates at political rallies? Why isn't she chosen queen of some sort of junk or other at a convention?

Why don't we read about her tastes and hobbies, her views of the Russian situation? Why haven't the columnists interviewed her in a kimono on the top floor of the tallest hotel in Manhattan, and told us who her boyfriends are?

Finally—and this is the real killer—why hasn't she ever been drawn or painted?

Oh, no she hasn't. If you knew anything about commercial art you'd know that. Every blessed one of those pictures was worked up from a photograph. Expertly? Of course. They've got the top artists on it. But that's how it's done.

And now I'll tell you the *why* of all that. It's because from the top to the bottom of the whole world of advertising, news, and business, there isn't a solitary soul who knows where the Girl came from, where she lives, what she does, who she is, even what her name is.

You heard me. What's more, not a single solitary soul ever *sees* her—except one poor damned photographer, who's making more money off her than he ever hoped to in his life and who's scared and miserable as hell every minute of the day.

No, I haven't the faintest idea who he is or where he has his studio. But I know there has to be such a man and I'm morally certain he feels just like I *said*.

Yes, I might be able to find her, if I tried. I'm not sure though—by now she probably has other safeguards. Besides, I don't want to.

Oh, I'm off my rocker, am I? That sort of thing can't happen in this Year of our Atom 1948? People can't keep out of sight that way, not even Garbo?

Well I happen to know they can, because last year I was that poor damned photographer I was telling you about. Yes, last year, in 1947, when the Girl made her first poisonous splash right here in this big little city of ours.

Yes, I knew you weren't here last year and you don't know about it. Even the Girl had to start small. But if you hunted through the files of the local newspapers, you'd find some ads, and I might be able to locate you some of the old displays—I think Lovelybelt is still using one of them. I used to have a mountain of photos myself, until I burned them.

Yes, I made my cut off her. Nothing like what that other photographer must be making, but enough so it still bought this whiskey. She was funny about money. I'll tell you about that.

But first picture me in 1947. I had a fourth-floor studio in that rathole the Hauser Building, catty-corner from Ardleigh Park.

I'd been working at the Marsh-Mason studios until I'd got my bellyful of it and decided to start in for myself. The Hauser Building was crummy—I'll never forget how the stairs creaked—but it was cheap and there was a skylight.

Business was lousy. I kept making the rounds of all the advertisers and agencies, and some of them didn't object to me too much personally, but my stuff never clicked. I was pretty near broke. I was behind on my rent. Hell, I didn't even have enough money to have a girl.

It was one of those dark gray afternoons. The building was awfully quiet—even with the storage they can't half rent the Hauser. I'd just finished developing some pix I was doing on speculation for Lovelybelt Girdles and Buford's Pool and Playground—the last a faked-up beach scene. My model had left. A Miss Leon. She was a civics teacher at one of the high schools and modeled for me on the side, just lately on speculation too. After one look at the prints, I decided that Miss Leon probably wasn't just what Lovelybelt was looking for—or my photography either. I was about to call it a day.

And then the street door slammed four storeys down and there were steps on the stairs and she came in.

She was wearing a cheap, shiny black dress. Black pumps. No stockings. And except that she had a gray cloth coat over one of them, those skinny arms of hers were bare. Her arms are pretty skinny, you know, or can you see things like that any more?

And then the thin neck, the slightly gaunt, almost prim face, the tumbling mass of dark hair, and looking out from under it the hungriest eyes in the world.

That's the real reason she's plastered all over the country today, you know—those eyes. Nothing vulgar, but just the same they're looking at you with a hunger that's all sex and something more than sex. That's what everybody's been looking for since the Year One—something a little more than sex.

Well, boys, there I was, along with the Girl, in an office that was getting shadowy, in a nearly empty building. A situation that a million male

Americans have undoubtedly pictured to themselves with various lush details. How was I feeling? Scared.

I know sex can be frightening. That cold, heart-thumping when you're alone with a girl and feel you're going to touch her. But if it was sex this time, it was overlaid with something else.

At least I wasn't thinking about sex.

I remember that I took a backward step and that my hand jerked so that the photos I was looking at sailed to the floor.

There was the faintest dizzy feeling like something was being drawn out of me. Just a little bit.

That was all. Then she opened her mouth and everything was back to normal for a while.

"I see you're a photographer, mister," she said. "Could you use a model?"

Her voice wasn't very cultivated.

"I doubt it," I told her, picking up the pix. You see, I wasn't impressed. The commercial possibilities of her eyes hadn't registered on me yet, by a long shot. "What have you done?"

Well, she gave me a vague sort of story and I began to check her knowledge of model agencies and studios and rates and what not and pretty soon I said to her, "Look here, you never modeled for a photographer in your life. You just walked in here cold."

Well, she admitted that was more or less so.

All along through our talk I got the idea she was feeling her way, like someone in a strange place. Not that she was uncertain of herself, or of me, but just of the general situation.

"And you think anyone can model?" I asked her pityingly.

"Sure," she said.

"Look," I said, "a photographer can waste a dozen negatives trying to get one halfway human photo of an average woman. How many do you think he'd have to waste before he got a real catchy, glamorous pix of her?"

"I think I could do it," she said.

Well, I should have kicked her out right then. Maybe I admired the cool way she stuck to her dumb little guns. Maybe I was touched by her un-derfed look. More likely I was feeling mean on account of the way my pix had been snubbed by everybody and I wanted to take it out on her by showing her up.

"Okay, I'm going to put you on the spot," I told her. "I'm going to try a couple of shots of you. Understand, it's strictly on spec. If somebody should ever want to use a photo of you, which is about one chance in two million, I'll pay you regular rates for your time. Not otherwise."

She gave me a smile. The first. "That's swell by me," she said.

Well, I took three or four shots, close-ups of her face since I didn't fancy her cheap dress, and at least she stood up to my sarcasm. Then I remembered I still had the Lovelybelt stuff and I guess the meanness was still working in me because I handed her a girdle and told her to go behind the screen and get into it and she did, without getting flustered as I'd expected, and since we'd gone that far I figured we might as well shoot the beach scene to round it out, and that was that.

All this time I wasn't feeling anything particular in one way or the other except every once in a while I'd get one of those faint dizzy flashes and wonder if there was something wrong with my stomach or if I could have been a bit careless with my chemicals.

Still, you know, I think the uneasiness was in me all the while.

I tossed her a card and pencil. "Write your name and address and phone," I told her and made for the darkroom.

A little later she walked out. I didn't call any good-byes. I was irked because she hadn't fussed around or seemed anxious about her poses, or even thanked me, except for that one smile.

I finished developing the negatives, made some prints, glanced at them, decided they weren't a great deal worse than Miss Leon. On an impulse I slipped them in with the pix I was going to take on the rounds next morning.

By now I'd worked long enough so I was a bit fagged and nervous, but I didn't dare waste enough money on liquor to help that. I wasn't very hungry. I think I went to a cheap movie.

I didn't think of the Girl at all, except maybe to wonder faintly why in my present womanless state I hadn't made a pass at her. She had seemed to belong to a, well, distinctly more approachable social stratum than Miss Leon. But then of course there were all sorts of arguable reasons for my not doing that.

Next morning I made the rounds. My first step was Munsch's Brewery. They were looking for a "Munsch Girl." Papa Munsch had a sort of affection for me, though he razzed my photography. He had a good natural judgment about that, too. Fifty years ago he might have been one of the shoestring boys who made Hollywood.

Right now he was out in the plant pursuing his favorite occupation. He put down the beaded can, smacked his lips, gabbled something technical to someone about hops, wiped his fat hands on the big apron he was wearing, and grabbed my thin stack of pix.

He was about halfway through, making noises with his tongue and teeth, when he came to her. I kicked myself for even having stuck her in.

"That's her," he said. "The photography's not so hot, but that's the girl."

It was all decided. I wondered now why Papa Munsch sensed what the girl had right away, while I didn't. I think it was because I saw her first in the flesh, if that's the right word.

At the time I just felt faint.

"Who is she?" he asked.

"One of my new models." I tried to make it casual.

"Bring her out tomorrow morning," he told me. "And your stuff. We'll photograph her here. I want to show you.

"Here, don't look so sick," he added. "Have some beer."

Well, I went away telling myself it was just a fluke, so that she'd probably blow it tomorrow with her inexperience, and so on.

Just the same, when I reverently laid my next stack of pix on Mr. Fitch, of Lovelybelt's rose-colored blotter, I had hers on top.

Mr. Fitch went through the motions of being an art critic. He leaned over backward, squinted his eyes, waved his long fingers, and said, "Hmmm. What do you think, Miss Willow? Here, in this light. Of course the photograph doesn't show the bias cut. And perhaps we should use the Lovelybelt Imp instead of the Angel. Still, the girl . . . Come over here, Binns." More finger-waving. "I want a married man's reaction."

He couldn't hide the fact that he was hooked.

Exactly the same thing happened at Buford's Pool and Playground, except that Da Costa didn't need a married man's say-so.

"Hot stuff," he said, sucking his lips. "Oh, boy, you photographers!"

I hot-footed it back to the office and grabbed up the card I'd given to her to put down her name and address.

It was blank.

I don't mind telling you that the next five minutes were about the worst I ever went through, in an ordinary way. When next morning rolled around and I still hadn't got hold of her, I had to start stalling.

"She's sick," I told Papa Munsch over the phone.

"She's at a hospital?" he asked me.

"Nothing that serious," I told him.

"Get her out here then. What's a little headache?"

"Sorry, I can't."

Papa Munsch got suspicious. "You really got this girl?"

"Of course I have."

"Well, I don't know. I'd think it was some New York model, except I recognized your lousy photography."

I laughed.

"Well, look, you get her here tomorrow morning, you hear?"

"I'll try."

"Try nothing. You get her out here."

He didn't know half of what I tried. I went around to all the model and employment agencies. I did some slick detective work at the photographic and art studios. I used up some of my last dimes putting advertisements in all three papers. I looked at high school yearbooks and at employee photos in local house organs. I went to restaurants and drugstores, looking for waitresses, and to dime stores and department stores, looking at clerks. I watched the crowds coming out of movie theaters. I roamed the streets.

Evenings I spent quite a bit of time along Pick-up Row. Somehow that seemed the right place.

The fifth afternoon I knew I was licked. Papa Munsch's deadline—he'd given me several, but this was it—was due to run out at six o'clock. Mr. Fitch had already canceled.

I was at the studio window, looking out at Ardleigh Park.

She walked in.

I'd gone over this moment so often in my mind that I had no trouble putting on my act. Even the faint dizzy feeling didn't throw me off.

"Hello," I said, hardly looking at her.

"Hello," she said.

"Not discouraged yet?"

"No." It didn't sound uneasy or defiant. It was just a statement.

I snapped a look at my watch, and got up and said curtly, "Look here, I'm going to give you a chance. There's a client of mine looking for a girl your general type. If you do a real good job you may break into the modeling business.

"We can see him this afternoon if we hurry," I said. I picked up my stuff. "Come on. And next time, if you expect favors, don't forget to leave your phone number."

"Uh, uh," she said, not moving.

"What do you mean?" I said.

"I'm not going to see any client of yours."

"The hell you aren't," I said. "You little nut, I'm giving you a break."

She shook her head slowly. "You're not fooling me, baby, you're not fooling me at all. They *want* me." And she gave me the second smile.

At the time I thought she must have seen my newspaper ad. Now I'm not so sure.

"And now I'll tell you how we're going to work," she went on. "You aren't going to have my name or address or phone number. Nobody is. And we're

going to do all the pictures right here. Just you and me."

You can imagine the roar I raised at that. I was everything—angry, sarcastic, patiently explanatory, off my nut, threatening, pleading.

I would have slapped her face off, except it was photographic capital.

In the end all I could do was phone Papa Munsch and tell him her conditions. I knew I didn't have a chance, but I had to take it.

He gave me a really angry bawling out, said "no" several times, and hung up.

It didn't faze her. "We'll start shooting at ten o'clock tomorrow," she said.

It was just like her, using that corny line from the movie magazines.

About midnight Papa Munsch called me up.

"I don't know what insane asylum you're renting this girl from," he said, "but I'll take her. Come around tomorrow morning and I'll try to get it through your head just how I want the pictures. And I'm glad I got you out of bed!"

After that it was a breeze. Even Mr. Fitch reconsidered and after taking two days to tell me it was quite impossible, he accepted the conditions too.

Of course you're all under the spell of the Girl, so you can't understand how much self-sacrifice it represented on Mr. Fitch's part when he agreed to forgo supervising the photography of my model in the Lovelybelt Imp or Vixen or whatever it was we finally used.

Next morning she turned up on time according to her schedule, and we went to work. I'll say one thing for her, she never got tired and she never kicked at the way I fussed over shots. I got along okay except I still had the feeling of something being shoved away gently. Maybe you've felt it just a little, looking at her picture.

When we finished I found out there were still more rules. It was about the middle of the afternoon. I started down with her to get a sandwich and coffee.

"Uh uh," she said, "I'm going down alone. And look, baby, if you ever try to follow me, if you ever so much as stick your head out that window when I go, you can hire yourself another model."

You can imagine how all this crazy stuff strained my temper—and my imagination. I remember opening the window after she was gone—I waited a few minutes first—and standing there getting some fresh air and trying to figure out what could be back of it, whether she was hiding from the police, or was somebody's ruined daughter, or maybe had got the idea it was smart to be temperamental, or more likely Papa Munsch was right and she was partly nuts.

But I had my pix to finish up.

Looking back it's amazing to think how fast her magic began to take hold of the city after that. Remembering what came after I'm frightened of what's happening to the whole country—and maybe the world. Yesterday I read something in *Time* about the Girl's picture turning up on billboards in Egypt.

The rest of my story will help show you why I'm frightened in that big general way. But I have a theory, too, that helps explain, though it's one of those things that's beyond that "certain point." It's about the Girl. I'll give it to you in a few words.

You know how modern advertising gets everybody's mind set in the same direction, wanting the same things, imagining the same things. And you know the psychologists aren't so skeptical of telepathy as they used to be.

Add up the two ideas. Suppose the identical desires of millions of people focused on one telepathic person. Say a girl. Shaped her in their image.

Imagine her knowing the hiddenmost hungers of millions of men. Imagine her seeing deeper into those hungers than the people that had them, seeing the hatred and the wish for death behind the lust. Imagine her shaping herself in that complete image, keeping herself as aloof as marble. Yet imagine the hunger she might feel in answer to their hunger.

But that's getting a long way from the facts of my story. And some of those facts are darn solid. Like money. We made money.

That was the funny thing I was going to tell you. I was afraid the Girl was going to hold me up. She really had me over a barrel, you know.

But she didn't ask for anything but the regular rates. Later on I insisted on pushing more money at her, a whole lot. But she always took it with that same contemptuous look, as if she were going to toss it down the first drain when she got outside.

Maybe she did.

At any rate, I had money. For the first time in months I had money enough to get drunk, buy new clothes, take taxicabs. I could make a play for any girl I wanted to. I only had to pick.

And so of course I had to go and pick—

But first let me tell you about Papa Munsch.

Papa Munsch wasn't the first of the boys to try to meet my model but I think he was the first to really go soft on her. I could watch the change in his eyes as he looked at her pictures. They began to get sentimental, reverent. Mama Munsch had been dead for two years.

He was smart about the way he planned it. He got me to drop some information which told him when she came to work, and then one morning he came pounding up the stairs a few minutes before.

"I've got to see her, Dave," he told me.

I argued with him, I kidded him. I explained he didn't know just how serious she was about her crazy ideas. I pointed out he was cutting both our throats. I even amazed myself by bawling him out.

He didn't take any of it in his usual way. He just kept repeating, "But, Dave, I've got to see her."

The street door slammed.

"That's her," I said, lowering my voice. "You've got to get out."

He wouldn't, so I shoved him in the darkroom. "And keep quiet," I whispered. "I'll tell her I can't work today."

I knew he'd try to look at her and probably come busting in, but there wasn't anything else I could do.

The footsteps came to the fourth floor. But she never showed at the door. I got uneasy.

"Get that bum out of there!" she yelled suddenly from beyond the door. Not very loud, but in her commonest voice.

"I'm going up to the next landing," she said, "and if that fat-bellied bum doesn't march straight down to the street, he'll never get another pix of me except spitting in his lousy beer."

Papa Munsch came out of the darkroom. He was white. He didn't look at me as he went out. He never looked at her pictures in front of me again.

That was Papa Munsch. Now it's me I'm telling about. I talked about the subject with her, I hinted, eventually I made my pass.

She lifted my hand off her as if it were a damp rag.

"Nix, baby," she said. "This is working time."

"But afterward . . ." I pressed.

"The rules still hold." And I got what I think was the fifth smile.

It's hard to believe, but she never budged an inch from that crazy line. I mustn't make a pass at her in the office, because our work was very important and she loved it and there mustn't be any distractions. And I couldn't see her anywhere else, because if I tried to, I'd never snap another picture of her—and all this with more money coming in all the time and me never so stupid as to think my photography had anything to do with it.

Of course I wouldn't have been human if I hadn't made more passes. But they always got the wet-rag treatment and there weren't any more smiles.

I changed. I went sort of crazy and light-headed—only sometimes I felt my head was going to burst. And I started to talk to her all the time. About myself.

It was like being in a constant delirium that never interfered with business. I didn't pay attention to the dizzy feeling. It seemed natural.

I'd walk around and for a moment the reflector would look like a sheet of white-hot steel, or the shadows would seem like armies of moths, or the camera would be a big black coal car. But the next instant they'd come all right again.

I think sometimes I was scared to death of her. She'd seem the strangest, horriblest person in the world. But other times . . .

And I talked. It didn't matter what I was doing—lighting her, posing her, fussing with props, snapping my pix—or where she was—on the platform, behind the screen, relaxing with a magazine—I kept up a steady gab.

I told her everything I knew about myself. I told her about my first girl. I told her about my brother Bob's bicycle. I told her about running away on a freight and the licking Pa gave me when I came home. I told her about shipping to South America and the blue sky at night. I told her about Betty. I told her about my mother dying of cancer. I told her about being beaten up in a fight in an alley behind a bar. I told her about Mildred. I told her about the first picture I ever sold. I told her how Chicago looked from a sailboat. I told her about the longest drunk I was ever on. I told her about Marsh-Mason. I told her about Gwen. I told her about how I met Papa Munsch. I told her about hunting her. I told her about how I felt now.

She never paid the slightest attention to what I said. I couldn't even tell if she heard me.

It was when we were getting our first nibble from national advertisers that I decided to follow her when she went home.

Wait, I can place it better than that. Something you'll remember from the out-of-town papers—those maybe-murders I mentioned. I think there were six.

I say "maybe" because the police could never be sure they weren't heart attacks. But there's bound to be suspicion when heart attacks happen to people whose hearts have been okay, and always at night when they're alone and away from home and there's a question of what they were doing.

The six deaths created one of those "mystery poisoner" scares. And afterward there was a feeling that they hadn't really stopped, but were being continued in a less suspicious way.

That's one of the things that scares me now.

But at that time my only feeling was relief that I'd decided to follow her.

I made her work until dark one afternoon. I didn't need any excuses, we were snowed under with orders. I waited until the street door slammed, then I ran down. I was wearing rubber-soled shoes. I'd slipped on a dark coat she'd never seen me in, and a dark hat.

I stood in the doorway until I spotted her. She was walking by Ardleigh Park toward the heart of town. It was one of those warm fall nights. I followed her on the other side of the street. My idea for tonight was just to find out where she lived. That would give me a hold on her.

She stopped in front of a display window of Everly's department store, standing back from the glow. She stood there looking in.

I remembered we'd done a big photograph of her for Everly's, to make a flat model for a lingerie display. That was what she was looking at.

At that time it seemed all right to me that she should adore herself, if that was what she was doing.

When people passed she'd turn away a little or drift back farther into the shadows.

Then a man came by alone. I couldn't see his face very well, but he looked middle-aged. He stopped and stood looking in the window.

She came out of the shadows and stepped up beside him.

How would you boys feel if you were looking at a poster of the Girl and suddenly she was there beside you, her arm linked with yours?

This fellow's reaction showed plain as day. A crazy dream had come to life for him.

They talked for a moment. Then he waved a taxi to the curb. They got in and drove off.

I got drunk that night. It was almost as if she'd known I was following her and had picked that way to hurt me. Maybe she had. Maybe this was the finish.

But the next morning she turned up at the usual time and I was back in the delirium, only now with some new angles added.

That night when I followed her she picked a spot under a street lamp, opposite one of the Munsch Girl billboards.

Now it frightens me to think of her lurking that way.

After about twenty minutes a convertible slowed down going past her, backed up, swung in to the curb.

I was closer this time. I got a good look at the fellow's face. He was a little younger, about my age.

Next morning the same face looked up at me from the front page of the paper. The convertible had been found parked on a side street. He had been in it. As in the other maybe-murders, the cause of death was uncertain.

All kinds of thoughts were spinning in my head that day, but there were only two things I knew for sure. That I'd got the first real offer from a national advertiser, and that I was going to take the Girl's arm and walk down the stairs with her when we quit work.

She didn't seem surprised. "You know what you're doing?" she said.

"I know."

She smiled. "I was wondering when you'd get around to it."

I began to feel good. I was kissing everything good-bye, but I had my arm around hers.

It was another of those warm fall evenings. We cut across into Ardleigh Park. It was dark there, but all around the sky was a sallow pink from the advertising signs.

We walked for a long time in the park. She didn't say anything and she didn't look at me, but I could see her lips twitching and after a while her hand tightened on my arm.

We stopped. We'd been walking across the grass. She dropped down and pulled me after her. She put her hands on my shoulders. I was looking down at her face. It was the faintest sallow pink from the glow in the sky. The hungry eyes were dark smudges.

I was fumbling with her blouse. She took my hand away, not like she had in the studio. "I don't want that," she said.

First I'll tell you what I did afterward. Then I'll tell you why I did it. Then I'll tell you what she said.

What I did was run away. I don't remember all of that because I was dizzy, and the pink sky was swinging against the dark trees. But after a while I staggered into the lights of the street. The next day I closed up the studio. The telephone was ringing when I locked the door and there were unopened letters on the floor. I never saw the Girl again in the flesh, if that's the right word.

I did it because I didn't want to die. I didn't want the life drawn out of me. There are vampires and vampires, and the ones that suck blood aren't the worst. If it hadn't been for the warning of those dizzy flashes, and Papa Munsch and the face in the morning paper, I'd have gone the way the others did. But I realized what I was up against while there was still time to tear myself away. I realized that wherever she came from, whatever shaped her, she's the quintessence of the horror behind the bright billboard. She's the smile that tricks you into throwing away your money and your life. She's the eyes that lead you on and on, and then show you death. She's the creature you give everything for and never really get. She's the being that takes everything you've got and gives nothing in return. When you yearn toward her face on the billboards, remember that. She's the lure. She's the bait. She's the Girl.

And this is what she said, "I want you. I want your high spots. I want everything that's made you happy and everything that's hurt you bad. I want your first girl. I want that shiny bicycle. I want that licking. I want that pinhole camera. I want Betty's legs. I want the blue sky filled with stars. I want your mother's death. I want your blood on the cobblestones. I want Mildred's mouth. I want the first picture you sold. I want the lights of Chicago. I want the gin. I want Gwen's hands. I want your wanting me. I want your life. Feed me, baby, feed me."

## THE LIVING DEAD

# Robert Bloch

Robert Albert Bloch (1917–94) was born in Chicago and began a successful and prolific writing career at an early age. An avid reader of the most successful pulp magazine in the science-fiction and horror genres, *Weird Tales,* he especially liked the work of H. P. Lovecraft and began a correspondence with him. Lovecraft encouraged Bloch's writing ambitions, resulting in two stories being sold to *Weird Tales* at the age of seventeen.

Bloch went on to write hundreds of short stories and twenty novels, the most famous being *Psycho* (1959), which was memorably filmed by Alfred Hitchcock. While his early work was virtually a pastiche of Lovecraft, he went on to develop his own style. Much of his work was exceptionally dark, gory, and violent for its time, but a plethora of his short fiction has elements of humor—often relying on a pun or wordplay in the last line. A famously warm, friendly, and humorous man in real life, he defended himself against charges of being a macabre writer by saying that he wasn't that way at all. "Why, I have the heart of a small boy," he said. "It's in a jar, on my desk." He commonly created a short story by inventing a good pun for the last line, then writing a story to accompany it.

"The Living Dead" was first published in the April 1967 issue of *Ellery Queen's Mystery Magazine*; it was first published in book form in *The King of Terrors* (New York: Mysterious Press, 1977).

# The Living Dead

## ROBERT BLOCH

All day long he rested, while the guns thundered in the village below. Then, in the slanting shadows of the late afternoon, the rumbling echoes faded into the distance and he knew it was over. The American advance had crossed the river. They were gone at last, and it was safe once more.

Above the village, in the crumbling ruins of the great château atop the wooded hillside, Count Barsac emerged from the crypt.

The Count was tall and thin—cadaverously thin, in a manner most hideously appropriate. His face and hands had a waxen pallor; his hair was dark, but not as dark as his eyes and the hollows beneath them. His cloak was black, and the sole touch of color about his person was the vivid redness of his lips when they curled in a smile.

He was smiling now, in the twilight, for it was time to play the game.

The name of the game was Death, and the Count had played it many times.

He had played it in Paris on the stage of the Grand Guignol; his name had been plain Eric Karon then, but still he'd won a certain renown for his interpretation of bizarre roles. Then the war had come and, with it, his opportunity.

Long before the Germans took Paris, he'd joined their Underground, working long and well. As an actor he'd been invaluable.

And this, of course, was his ultimate reward—to play the supreme role, not on the stage, but in real life. To play without the artifice of spotlights, in true darkness; this was the actor's dream come true. He had even helped to fashion the plot.

"Simplicity itself," he told his German superiors. "Château Barsac has been deserted since the Revolution. None of the peasants from the village dare to venture near it, even in daylight, because of the legend. It is said, you see, that the last Count Barsac was a vampire."

And so it was arranged. The shortwave transmitter had been set up the large crypt beneath the château, with three skilled operators in attendance, working in shifts. And he, "Count Barsac," in charge of the entire operation, as guardian angel. Rather, as guardian demon.

"There is a graveyard on the hillside below," he informed them. "A humble resting place for poor and ignorant people. It contains a single imposing crypt—the ancestral tomb of the Barsacs. We shall open that crypt, remove the remains of the last Count, and allow the villagers to discover that the coffin is empty. They will never dare come near the spot or the château again, because this will prove that the legend is true—Count Barsac is a vampire, and walks once more."

The question came then. "What if there are sceptics? What if someone does not believe?"

And he had his answer ready. "They will believe. For at night I shall walk—I, Count Barsac."

After they saw him in the makeup, wearing the black cloak, there were no more questions. The role was his.

The role was his, and he'd played it well. The Count nodded to himself as he climbed the stairs and entered the roofless foyer of the château, where only a configuration of cobwebs veiled the radiance of the rising moon.

Now, of course, the curtain must come down. If the American advance had swept past the village below, it was time to make one's bow and exit. And that too had been well arranged.

During the German withdrawal another advantageous use had been made of the tomb in the graveyard. A cache of Air Marshal Goering's art treasures now rested safely and undisturbed within the crypt. A truck had been placed in the château. Even now the three wireless operators would be playing new parts—driving the truck down the hillside to the tomb, placing the *objets d'art* in it.

By the time the Count arrived there, everything would be packed. They would then don the stolen American Army uniforms, carry the forged identifications and permits, drive through the lines across the river, and rejoin the German forces at a predesignated spot. Nothing had been left to chance. Someday, when he wrote his memoirs . . .

But there was not time to consider that now. The Count glanced up through the gaping aperture in the ruined roof. The moon was high. It was time to leave.

In a way he hated to go. Where others saw only dust and cobwebs he saw a stage—the setting of his finest performance. Playing a vampire's role had not addicted him to the taste of blood—but as an actor he enjoyed the taste of triumph. And he had triumphed here.

"Parting is such sweet sorrow." Shakespeare's line. Shakespeare, who had written of ghosts and witches, of bloody apparitions. Because Shakespeare knew that his audiences, the stupid masses, believed in such things—just as they still believed today. A great actor could always make them believe.

The Count moved into the shadowy darkness outside the entrance of the château. He started down the pathway toward the beckoning trees.

It was here, amid the trees, that he had come upon Raymond, one evening weeks ago. Raymond had been his most appreciative audience—a stern, dignified, white-haired elderly man, mayor of the village of Barsac. But there had been nothing dignified about the old fool when he'd caught sight of the Count looming up before him out of the night. He'd screamed like a woman and run.

Probably Raymond had been prowling around, intent on poaching, but all that had been forgotten after his encounter in the woods. The mayor was the one to thank for spreading the rumors that the Count was again abroad. He and Clodez, the oafish miller, had then led an armed band to the graveyard and entered the Barsac tomb. What a fright they got when they discovered the Count's coffin open and empty!

The coffin had contained only dust that had been scattered to the winds, but they could not know that. Nor could they know about what had happened to Suzanne.

The Count was passing the banks of a small stream now. Here, on another evening, he'd found the girl—Raymond's daughter, as luck would have it—in an embrace with young Antoine LeFevre, her lover. Antoine's shattered leg had invalided him out of the army, but he ran like a deer when he glimpsed the cloaked and grinning Count. Suzanne had been left behind and that was unfortunate, because it was necessary to dispose of her. Her body had been buried in the woods, beneath great stones, and there was no question of discovery; still, it was a regrettable incident.

In the end, however, everything was for the best. Now silly superstitious Raymond was doubly convinced that the vampire walked. He had seen the creature himself, had seen the empty tomb and the open coffin; his own daughter had disappeared. At his command none dared venture near the graveyard, the woods, or the château beyond.

Poor Raymond! He was not even a mayor any more—his village had been destroyed in the bombardment. Just an ignorant, broken old man, mumbling his idiotic nonsense about the "living dead."

The Count smiled and walked on, his cloak fluttering in the breeze, casting a batlike shadow on the pathway before him. He could see the graveyard now, the tilted tombstones rising from the earth like leprous fingers rotting in the moonlight. His smile faded; he did not like such thoughts. Perhaps the greatest tribute to his talent as an actor lay in his actual aversion to death, to darkness and what lurked in the night. He hated the sight of blood, had developed within himself an almost claustrophobic dread of the confinement of the crypt.

Yes, it had been a great role, but he was thankful it was ending. It would be good to play the man once more, and cast off the creature he had created.

As he approached the crypt he saw the truck waiting in the shadows. The entrance to the tomb was open, but no sounds issued from it. That meant his colleagues had completed their task of loading and were ready to go. All that remained now was to change his clothing, remove the makeup, and depart.

The Count moved to the darkened truck. And then . . .

Then they were upon him, and he felt the tines of the pitchfork bite into his back, and as the flash of lanterns dazzled his eyes he heard the stern command. "Don't move!"

He didn't move. He could only stare as they surrounded him—Antoine, Clodez, Raymond, and the others, a dozen peasants from the village. A dozen armed peasants, glaring at him in mingled rage and fear, holding him at bay.

But how could they dare?

The American corporal stepped forward. That was the answer, of course—the American corporal and another man in uniform, armed with a sniper's rifle. They were responsible. He didn't

even have to see the riddled corpses of the three shortwave operators piled in the back of the truck to understand what had happened. They'd stumbled on his men while they worked, shot them down, then summoned the villagers.

Now they were jabbering questions at him, in English, of course. He understood English, but he knew better than to reply. "Who are you? Were these men working under your orders? Where were you going with this truck?"

The Count smiled and shook his head. After a while they stopped, as he knew they would.

The corporal turned to his companion. "Okay," he said. "Let's go." The other man nodded and climbed into the cab of the truck as the motor coughed into life. The corporal moved to join him, then turned to Raymond.

"We're taking this across the river," he said. "Hang on to our friend here—they'll be sending a guard detail for him within an hour."

Raymond nodded.

The truck drove off into the darkness.

And as it was dark now—the moon had vanished behind a cloud. The Count's smile vanished, too, as he glanced around at his captors. A rabble of stupid clods, surly and ignorant. But armed. No chance of escaping. And they kept staring at him, and mumbling.

"Take him into the tomb."

It was Raymond who spoke, and they obeyed, prodding their captive forward with pitchforks. That was when the Count recognized the first faint ray of hope. For they prodded him most gingerly, no man coming close, and when he glared at them their eyes dropped.

They were putting him in the crypt because they were afraid of him. Now the Americans were gone, they feared him once more—feared his presence and his power. After all, in their eyes he was a vampire—he might turn into a bat and vanish entirely. So they wanted him in the tomb for safekeeping.

The Count shrugged, smiled his most sinister smile, and bared his teeth. They shrank back as he entered the doorway. He turned and, on impulse, furled his cape. It was an instinctive final gesture, in keeping with his role—and it provoked the appropriate response. They moaned and old Raymond crossed himself. It was better, in a way, than any applause.

In the darkness of the crypt the Count permitted himself to relax a trifle. He was offstage now. A pity he'd not been able to make his exit the way he'd planned, but such were the fortunes of war. Soon he'd be taken to the American headquarters and interrogated. Undoubtedly there would be some unpleasant moments, but the worst that could befall him was a few months in a prison camp. And even the Americans must bow to him in appreciation when they heard the story of his masterful deception.

It was dark in the crypt, and musty. The Count moved about restlessly. His knee grazed the edge of the empty coffin set on a trestle in the tomb. He shuddered involuntarily, loosening his cape at the throat. It would be good to remove it, good to be out of here, good to shed the role of vampire forever. He'd played it well, but now he was anxious to be gone.

There was a mumbling audible from outside, mingled with another and less identifiable noise—a scraping sound. The Count moved to the closed door of the crypt and listened intently; but now there was only silence.

What were the fools doing out there? He wished the Americans would hurry back. It was too hot in here. And why the sudden silence?

Perhaps they'd gone.

Yes. That was it. The Americans had told them to wait and guard him, but they were afraid. They really believed he was a vampire—old Raymond had convinced them of that. So they'd run off. They'd run off, and he was free, he could escape now . . .

So the Count opened the door.

And he saw them then, saw them standing and waiting, old Raymond staring sternly for a moment before he moved forward. He was holding something in his hand, and the Count recognized it, remembering the scraping sound that he'd heard.

It was a long wooden stake with a sharp point.

Then he opened his mouth to scream, telling them it was only a trick, he was no vampire, they were a pack of superstitious fools . . .

But all the while they bore him back into the crypt, lifting him up and thrusting him into the open coffin, holding him there as the grim-faced Raymond raised the pointed stake above his heart.

It was only when the stake came down that he realized there's such a thing as playing a role too well.

# DOWN AMONG THE DEAD MEN

# Gardner Dozois and Jack Dann

Gardner Dozois (1947– ) grew up in Salem, Massachusetts, and, following service in the army, became active in the science-fiction and fantasy community. He was the editor of *Isaac Asimov's Science Fiction Magazine* from 1984 to 2004, winning an astonishing fifteen Hugo Awards as Best Professional Editor. He has also edited *The Year's Best Science Fiction* annually since 1984. With Jack Dann, he has edited many single-subject anthologies with such themes as unicorns, mermaids, dinosaurs, angels, and cats. Dozois also writes novels, including *Strangers* (1978) and *Nightmare Blue* (1977), in collaboration with George Alec Effinger; two of his many short stories have won Nebula Awards.

Jack Dann (1945– ), an American author living in Australia, has written or edited more than seventy books in various genres that have been translated into thirteen languages, and has been compared with Jorge Luis Borges, Roald Dahl, Lewis Carroll, and Mark Twain while winning numerous awards, including a Nebula, the Australian Aurealis (twice), and World Fantasy. He has written a historical novel about Leonardo da Vinci, *The Memory Cathedral* (1995); a Civil War novel, *The Silent* (1998); a road novel, *Bad Medicine* (2001), described as the best since Jack Kerouac's *On the Road*; *The Rebel: An Imagined Life of James Dean* (2004); and a sequel, *Promised Land* (2007).

"Down Among the Dead Men" was first published in *Oui* magazine in July 1982.

# Down Among the Dead Men

## GARDNER DOZOIS AND JACK DANN

Bruckman first discovered that Wernecke was a vampire when they went to the quarry that morning.

He was bending down to pick up a large rock when he thought he heard something in the gully nearby. He looked around and saw Wernecke huddled over a *Musselmänn*, one of the walking dead, a new man who had not been able to wake up to the terrible reality of the camp.

"Do you need any help?" Bruckman asked Wernecke in a low voice.

Wernecke looked up, startled, and covered his mouth with his hand, as if he were signing to Bruckman to be quiet.

But Bruckman was certain that he had glimpsed blood smeared on Wernecke's mouth. "The Musselmänn, is he alive?" Wernecke had often risked his own life to save one or another of the men in his barracks. But to risk one's life for a Musselmänn? "What's wrong?"

"Get away."

All right, Bruckman thought. Best to leave him alone. He looked pale, perhaps it was typhus. The guards were working him hard enough, and Wernecke was older than the rest of the men in the work gang. Let him sit for a moment and rest. But what about that blood? . . .

"Hey, you, what are you doing?" one of the young SS guards shouted to Bruckman.

Bruckman picked up the rock and, as if he had not heard the guard, began to walk away from the gully, toward the rusty brown cart on the tracks that led back to the barbed-wire fence of the camp. He would try to draw the guard's attention away from Wernecke.

But the guard shouted at him to halt. "Were you taking a little rest, is that it?" he asked, and Bruckman tensed, ready for a beating. This guard was new, neatly and cleanly dressed—and an unknown quantity. He walked over to the gully and, seeing Wernecke and the Musselmänn, said, "Aha, so your friend is taking care of the sick." He motioned Bruckman to follow him into the gully.

Bruckman had done the unpardonable—he had brought it on Wernecke. He swore at himself. He had been in this camp long enough to know to keep his mouth shut.

The guard kicked Wernecke sharply in the ribs. "I want you to put the Musselmänn in the cart. Now!" He kicked Wernecke again, as if as an afterthought. Wernecke groaned, but got to his feet.

"Help him put the Musselmänn in the cart," the guard said to Bruckman; then he smiled and drew a circle in the air—the sign of smoke, the smoke which rose from the tall gray chimneys behind them. This Musselmänn would be in the oven within an hour, his ashes soon to be floating in the hot, stale air, as if they were the very particles of his soul.

Wernecke kicked the Musselmänn, and the guard chuckled, waved to another guard who had been watching, and stepped back a few feet. He stood with his hands on his hips. "Come on, dead man, get up or you're going to die in the oven," Wernecke whispered as he tried to pull the man to his feet. Bruckman supported the unsteady Musselmänn, who began to wail softly. Wernecke slapped him hard. "Do you want to live, Musselmänn? Do you want to see your family again, feel the touch of a woman, smell grass after it's been mowed? Then *move*." The Musselmänn shambled forward between Wernecke and Bruckman. "You're dead, aren't you Musselmänn," goaded Wernecke. "As dead as your father and mother, as dead as your sweet wife, if you ever had one, aren't you? Dead!"

The Musselmänn groaned, shook his head, and whispered, "Not dead, my wife . . ."

"Ah, it talks," Wernecke said, loud enough so the guard walking a step behind them could hear. "Do you have a name, corpse?"

"Josef, and I'm not a Musselmänn."

"The corpse says he's alive," Wernecke said, again loud enough for the SS guard to hear. Then in a whisper, he said, "Josef, if you're not a Musselmänn, then you must work now, do you understand?" Josef tripped, and Bruckman caught him. "Let him be," said Wernecke. "Let him walk to the cart himself."

"Not the cart," Josef mumbled. "Not to die, not—"

"Then get down and pick up stones, show the fart-eating guard you can work."

"Can't. I'm sick, I'm . . ."

"Musselmänn!"

Josef bent down, fell to his knees, but took hold of a stone and stood up.

"You see," Wernecke said to the guard, "it's not dead yet. It can still work."

"I told you to carry him to the cart, didn't I," the guard said petulantly.

"Show him you can work," Wernecke said to Josef, "or you'll surely be smoke."

And Josef stumbled away from Wernecke and Bruckman, leaning forward, as if following the rock he was carrying.

"Bring him *back*!" shouted the guard, but his attention was distracted from Josef by some other prisoners, who, sensing the trouble, began to mill about. One of the other guards began to shout and kick at the men on the periphery, and the new guard joined him. For the moment, he had forgotten about Josef.

"Let's get to work, lest they notice us again," Wernecke said.

"I'm sorry that I—"

Wernecke laughed and made a fluttering gesture with his hand—smoke rising. "It's all hazard, my friend. All luck." Again the laugh. "It was a venial sin," and his face seemed to darken. "Never do it again, though, lest I think of you as bad luck."

"Carl, are you all right?" Bruckman asked. "I noticed some blood when—"

"Do the sores on your feet bleed in the morning?" Wernecke countered angrily. Bruckman nodded, feeling foolish and embarrassed. "And so it is with my gums. Now go away, unlucky one, and let me live."

At dusk, the guards broke the hypnosis of lifting and grunting and sweating and formed the prisoners into ranks. They marched back to the camp through the fields, beside the railroad tracks, the electrified wire, conical towers, and into the main gate of the camp.

Josef walked beside them, but he kept stumbling, as he was once again slipping back into death, becoming a Musselmänn. Wernecke helped him walk, pushed him along. "We should let this man become dead," Wernecke said to Bruckman.

Bruckman only nodded, but he felt a chill sweep

over his sweating back. He was seeing Wernecke's face again as it was for that instant in the morning. Smeared with blood.

Yes, Bruckman thought, we should let the Musselmänn become dead. We should all be dead. . . .

**W**ernecke served up the lukewarm water with bits of spoiled turnip floating on the top, what passed as soup for the prisoners. Everyone sat or kneeled on the rough-planked floor, as there were no chairs.

Bruckman ate his portion, counting the sips and bites, forcing himself to take his time. Later, he would take a very small bite of the bread he had in his pocket. He always saved a small morsel of food for later—in the endless world of the camp, he had learned to give himself things to look forward to. Better to dream of bread than to get lost in the present. That was the fate of the Musselmänner.

But he always dreamed of food. Hunger was with him every moment of the day and night. Those times when he actually ate were in a way the most difficult, for there was never enough to satisfy him. There was the taste of softness in his mouth, and then in an instant it was gone. The emptiness took the form of pain—it *hurt* to eat. For bread, he thought, he would have killed his father, or his wife. God forgive me, and he watched Wernecke—Wernecke, who had shared his bread with him, who had died a little so he could live. He's a better man than I, Bruckman thought.

It was dim inside the barracks. A bare light bulb hung from the ceiling and cast sharp shadows across the cavernous room. Two tiers of five-foot-deep shelves ran around the room on three sides, bare wooden shelves where the men slept without blankets or mattresses. Set high in the northern wall was a slatted window, which let in the stark white light of the kliegs. Outside, the lights turned the grounds into a deathly imitation of day; only inside the barracks was it night.

"Do you know what tonight is, my friends?"

Wernecke asked. He sat in the far corner of the room with Josef, who, hour by hour, was reverting back into a Musselmänn. Wernecke's face looked hollow and drawn in the light from the window and the light bulb; his eyes were deep-set and his face was long with deep creases running from his nose to the corners of his thin mouth. His hair was black, and even since Bruckman had known him, quite a bit of it had fallen out. He was a very tall man, almost six feet four, and that made him stand out in a crowd, which was dangerous in a death camp. But Wernecke had his own secret ways of blending with the crowd, of making himself invisible.

"No, tell us what tonight is," crazy old Bohme said. That men such as Bohme could survive was a miracle—or, as Bruckman thought—a testament to men such as Wernecke who somehow found the strength to help the others live.

"It's Passover," Wernecke said.

"How does he know that?" someone mumbled, but it didn't matter how Wernecke knew because he *knew*—even if it really wasn't Passover by the calendar. In this dimly lit barrack, it *was* Passover, the feast of freedom, the time of thanksgiving.

"But how can we have Passover without a *seder*?" asked Bohme. "We don't even have any *matzoh*," he whined.

"Nor do we have candles, or a silver cup for Elijah, or the shankbone, or *haroset*—nor would I make a *seder* over the *traif* the Nazis are so generous in giving us," replied Wernecke with a smile. "But we can pray, can't we? And when we all get out of here, when we're in our own homes in the coming year with God's help, then we'll have twice as much food—two *afikomens*, a bottle of wine for Elijah, and the *haggadahs* that out fathers and our fathers' fathers used."

It *was* Passover.

"Isadore, do you remember the four questions?" Wernecke asked Bruckman.

And Bruckman heard himself speaking. He was twelve years old again at the long table beside his father, who sat in the seat of honor. To sit next to him was itself an honor, "How does this night differ from all other nights? On all other nights we eat bread and *matzoh*; why on this night do we eat only *matzoh*?

"*M'a nisht' ana halylah hazeah. . . .*"

Sleep would not come to Bruckman that night, although he was so tired that he felt as if the marrow of his bones had been sucked away and replaced with lead.

He lay there in the semidarkness, feeling his muscles ache, feeling the acid biting of his hunger. Usually he was numb enough with exhaustion that he could empty his mind, close himself down, and fall rapidly into oblivion, but not tonight. Tonight he was noticing things again, his surroundings were getting through to him again, in a way that they had not since he had been new in camp. It was smotheringly hot, and the air was filled with the stinks of death and sweat and fever, of stale urine and drying blood. The sleepers thrashed and turned, as though they fought with sleep, and as they slept, many of them talked or muttered or screamed aloud; they lived other lives in their dreams, intensely compressed lives dreamed quickly, for soon it would be dawn, and once more they would be thrust into hell. Cramped in the midst of them, sleepers squeezed in all around him, it suddenly seemed to Bruckman that these pallid white bodies were already dead, that he was sleeping in a graveyard. Suddenly it was the boxcar again. And his wife Miriam was dead again, dead and rotting unburied. . . .

Resolutely, Bruckman emptied his mind. He felt feverish and shaky, and wondered if the typhus were coming back, but he couldn't afford to worry about it. Those who couldn't sleep couldn't survive. Regulate your breathing, force your muscles to relax, don't think. Don't think.

For some reason, after he had managed to banish even the memory of his dead wife, he couldn't shake the image of the blood on Wernecke's mouth.

There were other images mixed in with it: Wernecke's uplifted arms and upturned face as he led them in prayer; the pale strained face of the stumbling Musselmänn; Wernecke looking up, startled, as he crouched over Josef . . . but it was the

blood to which Bruckman's feverish thoughts returned, and he pictured it again and again as he lay in the rustling, fart-smelling darkness, the watery sheen of blood over Wernecke's lips, the tarry trickle of blood in the corner of his mouth, like a tiny scarlet worm. . . .

Just then a shadow crossed in front of the window, silhouetted blackly for an instant against the harsh white glare, and Bruckman knew from the shadow's height and its curious forward stoop that it was Wernecke.

Where could he be going? Sometimes a prisoner would be unable to wait until morning, when the Germans would let them out to visit the slit-trench latrine again, and would slink shamefacedly into a far corner to piss against a wall, but surely Wernecke was too much of an old hand for that. . . . Most of the prisoners slept on the sleeping platforms, especially during the cold nights when they would huddle together for warmth, but sometimes during the hot weather, people would drift away and sleep on the floor instead; Bruckman had been thinking of doing that, as the jostling bodies of the sleepers around him helped to keep him from sleep. Perhaps Wernecke, who always had trouble fitting into the cramped sleeping niches, was merely looking for a place where he could lie down and stretch his legs. . . .

Then Bruckman remembered that Josef had fallen asleep in the corner of the room where Wernecke had sat and prayed, and that they had left him there alone.

Without knowing why, Bruckman found himself on his feet. As silently as the ghost he sometimes felt he was becoming, he walked across the room in the direction Wernecke had gone, not understanding what he was doing nor why he was doing it. The face of the Musselmänn, Josef, seemed to float behind his eyes. Bruckman's feet hurt, and he knew, without looking, that they were bleeding, leaving faint tracks behind him. It was dimmer here in the far corner, away from the window, but Bruckman knew that he must be near the wall by now, and he stopped to let his eyes readjust.

When his eyes had adapted to the dimmer light,

he saw Josef sitting on the floor, propped up against the wall. Wernecke was hunched over the Musselmänn. Kissing him. One of Josef's hands was tangled in Wernecke's thinning hair.

Before Bruckman could react—such things had been known to happen once or twice before, although it shocked him deeply that *Wernecke* would be involved in such filth—Josef released his grip on Wernecke's hair. Josef's upraised arm fell limply to the side, his hand hitting the floor with a muffled but solid impact that should have been painful—but Josef made no sound.

Wernecke straightened up and turned around. Stronger light from the high window caught him as he straightened to his full height, momentarily illuminating his face.

Wernecke's mouth was smeared with blood.

"My God," Bruckman cried.

Startled, Wernecke flinched, then took two quick steps forward and seized Bruckman by the arm. "Quiet!" Wernecke hissed. His fingers were cold and hard.

At that moment, as though Wernecke's sudden movement were a cue, Josef began to slip down sideways along the wall. As Wernecke and Bruckman watched, both momentarily riveted by the sight, Josef toppled over to the floor, his head striking against the floorboards with a sound such as a dropped melon might make. He had made no attempt to break his fall or cushion his head, and lay now unmoving.

"My *God*," Bruckman said again.

"Quiet, I'll explain," Wernecke said, his lips still glazed with the Musselmänn blood. "Do you want to ruin us all? For the love of God, be *quiet*."

But Bruckman had shaken free of Wernecke's grip and crossed to kneel by Josef, leaning over him as Wernecke had done, placing a hand flat on Josef's chest for a moment, then touching the side of Josef's neck. Bruckman looked slowly up at Wernecke. "He's dead," Bruckman said, more quietly.

Wernecke squatted on the other side of Josef's body, and the rest of their conversation was carried out in whispers over Josef's chest, like friends conversing at the sickbed of another friend who has finally fallen into a fitful doze.

"Yes, he's dead," Wernecke said. "He was dead yesterday, wasn't he? Today he had just stopped walking." His eyes were hidden here, in the deeper shadow nearer to the floor, but there was still enough light for Bruckman to see that Wernecke had wiped his lips clean. Or licked them clean, Bruckman thought, and felt a spasm of nausea go through him.

"But *you*," Bruckman said, haltingly. "You were . . ."

"Drinking his blood?" Wernecke said. "Yes, I was drinking his blood."

Bruckman's mind was numb. He couldn't deal with this, he couldn't understand it at all. "But *why*, Eduard? Why?"

"To live, of course. Why do any of us do anything here? If I am to live, I must have blood. Without it, I'd face a death even more certain than that doled out by the Nazis."

Bruckman opened and closed his mouth, but no sound came out, as if the words he wished to speak were too jagged to fit through his throat. At last he managed to croak, "A vampire? You're a vampire? Like in the old stories?"

Wernecke said calmly, "Men would call me that." He paused, then nodded. "Yes, that's what men would call me. . . . As though they can understand something simply by giving it a name."

"But Eduard," Bruckman said weakly, almost petulantly. "The Musselmänn . . ."

"Remember that he *was* a Musselmänn," Wernecke said, leaning forward and speaking more fiercely. "His strength was going, he was sinking. He would have been dead by morning anyway. I took from him something that he no longer needed, but that I needed in order to live. Does it matter? Starving men in lifeboats have eaten the bodies of their dead companions in order to live. Is what I've done any worse than that?"

"But he didn't just die. You *killed* him. . . ."

Wernecke was silent for a moment, and then said, quietly, "What better thing could I have done for him? I won't apologize for what I do, Isadore; I do what I have to do to live. Usually I take only a little blood from a number of men, just enough to survive. And that's fair, isn't it? Haven't I given food to others, to help them survive? To you, Isadore? Only very rarely do I take more than a minimum from any one man, although I'm weak and hungry all the time, believe me. And never have I drained the life from someone who wished to live. Instead I've helped them fight for survival in every way I can, you know that."

He reached out as though to touch Bruckman, then thought better of it and put his hand back on his own knee. He shook his head. "But these Musselmänner, the ones who have given up on life, the walking dead—it is a favor to them to take them, to give them the solace of death. Can you honestly say it is not, *here*? That it is better for them to walk around while they are dead, being beaten and abused by the Nazis until their bodies cannot go on, and then to be thrown into the ovens and burned like trash? Can you say that? Would *they* say that, if they knew what was going on? Or would they thank me?"

Wernecke suddenly stood up, and Bruckman stood up with him. As Wernecke's face came again into the stronger light, Bruckman could see that his eyes had filled with tears. "You have lived under the Nazis," Wernecke said. "Can you really call me a monster? Aren't I still a Jew, whatever else I might be? Aren't I *here*, in a death camp? Aren't I being persecuted, too, as much as any other? Aren't I in as much danger as anyone else? If I'm not a Jew, then tell the Nazis—they seem to think so." He paused for a moment, and then smiled wryly. "And forget your superstitious boogey tales. I'm no night spirit. If I could turn myself into a bat and fly away from here, I would have done it long before now, believe me."

Bruckman smiled reflectively, then grimaced. The two men avoided each other's eyes, Bruckman looking at the floor, and there was an uneasy silence, punctured only by the sighing and moaning of the sleepers on the other side of the cabin. Then, without looking up, in tacit surrender, Bruckman said, "What about *him*? The Nazis will find the body and cause trouble. . . ."

"Don't worry," Wernecke said. "There are no obvious marks. And nobody performs autopsies

in a death camp. To the Nazis, he'll be just another Jew who had died of the heat, or from starvation or sickness, or from a broken heart."

Bruckman raised his head then and they stared eye to eye for a moment. Even knowing what he knew, Bruckman found it hard to see Wernecke as anything other than what he appeared to be: an aging, balding Jew, stooping and thin, with sad eyes and a tired, compassionate face.

"Well, then, Isadore," Wernecke said at last, matter-of-factly. "My life is in your hands. I will not be indelicate enough to remind you of how many times your life has been in mine."

Then he was gone, walking back toward the sleeping platforms, a shadow soon lost among other shadows.

Bruckman stood by himself in the gloom for a long time, and then followed him. It took all of his will not to look back over his shoulder at the corner where Josef lay, and even so Bruckman imagined that he could feel Josef's dead eyes watching him, watching reproachfully as he walked away abandoning Josef to the cold and isolated company of the dead.

Bruckman got no more sleep that night, and in the morning, when the Nazis shattered the gray predawn stillness by bursting into the shack with shouts and shrill whistles and barking police dogs, he felt as if he were a thousand years old.

They were formed into two lines, shivering in the raw morning air, and marched off to the quarry. The clammy dawn mist had yet to burn off, and marching through it, through a white shadowless void, with only the back of the man in front of him dimly visible, Bruckman felt more than ever like a ghost, suspended bodiless in some limbo between Heaven and Earth. Only the bite of pebbles and cinders into his raw, bleeding feet kept him anchored to the world, and he clung to the pain as a lifeline, fighting to shake off a feeling of numbness and unreality. However strange, however outré, the events of the previous night had *happened*. To doubt it, to wonder now if it had all been a feverish dream brought on by starvation and exhaustion, was to take the first step on the road to becoming a Musselmänn.

Wernecke is a vampire, he told himself. That was the harsh, unyielding reality that, like the reality of the camp itself, must be faced. Was it any more surreal, any more impossible than the nightmare around them? He must forget the tales that his grandmother had told him as a boy, "boogey tales" as Wernecke himself had called them, half-remembered tales that turned his knees to water whenever he thought of the blood smeared on Wernecke's mouth, whenever he thought of Wernecke's eyes watching him in the dark. . . .

"Wake up, Jew!" the guard alongside him snarled, whacking him lightly on the arm with his rifle butt. Bruckman stumbled, managed to stay upright and keep going. Yes, he thought, wake up. Wake up to the reality of this, just as you once had to wake up to the reality of the camp. It was just one more unpleasant fact he would have to adapt to, learn to deal with. . . .

Deal with how? he thought, and shivered.

By the time they reached the quarry, the mist had burned off, swirling past them in rags and tatters, and it was already beginning to get hot. There was Wernecke, his balding head gleaming dully in the harsh morning light. He didn't dissolve in the sunlight—there was one boogey tale disproved. . . .

They set to work, like golems, like ragtag clockwork automatons.

Lack of sleep had drained what small reserves of strength Bruckman had, and the work was very hard for him that day. He had learned long ago all the tricks of timing and misdirection, the safe way to snatch short moments of rest, the ways to do a minimum of work with the maximum display of effort, the ways to keep the guards from noticing you, to fade into the faceless crowd of prisoners and not be singled out, but today his head was muzzy and slow, and none of the tricks seemed to work.

His body felt like a sheet of glass, fragile, ready to shatter into dust, and the painful, arthritic slowness of his movements got him first shouted at, and then knocked down. The guard kicked him twice for good measure before he could get up. When Bruckman had climbed back to his feet again, he saw that Wernecke was watching him, face blank, eyes expressionless, a look that could have meant anything at all.

Bruckman felt the blood trickling from the corner of his mouth and thought, *the blood . . . he's watching the blood . . .* and once again he shivered.

Somehow, Bruckman forced himself to work faster, and although his muscles blazed with pain, he wasn't hit again, and the day passed.

When they formed up to go back to camp, Bruckman, almost unconsciously, made sure that he was in a different line than Wernecke.

That night in the cabin, Bruckman watched as Wernecke talked with the other men, here trying to help a new man named Melnick—no more than a boy—adjust to the dreadful reality of the camp, there exhorting someone who was slipping into despair to live and spite his tormentors, joking with old hands in the flat, black, bitter way that passed for humor among them, eliciting a wan smile or occasionally even a laugh from them, finally leading them all in prayer again, his strong, calm voice raised in the ancient words, giving meaning to those words again. . . .

He keeps us together, Bruckman thought, he keeps us going. Without him, we wouldn't last a week. Surely that's worth a little blood, a bit from each man, not even enough to hurt. . . . Surely they wouldn't even begrudge him it, if they knew and really understood. . . . No, he is a good man, better than the rest of us, in spite of his terrible affliction.

Bruckman had been avoiding Wernecke's eyes, hadn't spoken to him at all that day, and suddenly felt a wave of shame go through him at the thought of how shabbily he had been treating his friend. Yes, his friend, regardless, the man who had saved his life. . . . Deliberately, he caught Wernecke's eyes, and nodded, and then somewhat sheepishly, smiled. After a moment, Wernecke smiled back, and Bruckman felt a spreading warmth and relief uncoil his guts. Everything was going to be all right, as all right as it could be, here. . . .

Nevertheless, as soon as the inside lights clicked off that night, and Bruckman found himself lying alone in the darkness, his flesh began to crawl.

He had been unable to keep his eyes open a moment before, but now, in the sudden darkness, he found himself tensely and tickingly awake. Where was Wernecke? What was he doing, whom was he visiting tonight? Was he out there in the darkness even now, creeping closer, creeping nearer? . . . Stop it, Bruckman told himself uneasily, forget the boogey tales. This is your friend, a good man, not a monster. . . . But he couldn't control the fear that made the small hairs on his arms stand bristlingly erect, couldn't stop the grisly images from coming. . . .

Wernecke's eyes, gleaming in the darkness . . . was the blood already glistening on Wernecke's lips, as he drank? . . . The thought of the blood staining Wernecke's yellowing teeth made Bruckman cold and nauseous, but the image that he couldn't get out of his mind tonight was an image of Josef toppling over in that sinister boneless way, striking his head against the floor. . . . Bruckman had seen people die in many more gruesome ways during this time at the camp, seen people shot, beaten to death, seen them die in convulsions from high fevers or cough their lungs up in bloody tatters from pneumonia, seen them hanging like charred-black scarecrows from the electrified fences, seen them torn apart by dogs . . . but somehow it was Josef's soft, passive, almost restful slumping into death that bothered him. That, and the obscene limpness of Josef's limbs as he sprawled there like a discarded rag doll, his pale and haggard face gleaming reproachfully in the dark. . . .

When Bruckman could stand it no longer, he got shakily to his feet and moved off through the shadows, once again not knowing where he was going or what he was going to do, but drawn forward by some obscure instinct he himself did not understand. This time he went cautiously, feeling his way and trying to be silent, expecting every second to see Wernecke's coal-black shadow rise up before him.

He paused, a faint noise scratching at his ears, then went on again, even more cautiously, crouching low, almost crawling across the grimy floor.

Whatever instinct had guided him—sounds heard and interpreted subliminally, perhaps?—it had timed his arrival well. Wernecke had someone down on the floor there, perhaps someone he seized and dragged away from the huddled mass of sleepers on one of the sleeping platforms, someone from the outer edge of bodies whose presence would not be missed, or perhaps someone who had gone to sleep on the floor, seeking solitude or greater comfort.

Whoever he was, he struggled in Wernecke's grip, but Wernecke handled him easily, almost negligently, in a manner that spoke of great physical power. Bruckman could hear the man trying to scream, but Wernecke had one hand on his throat, half-throttling him, and all that would come out was a sort of whistling gasp. The man thrashed in Wernecke's hands like a kite in a child's hands flapping in the wind, and, moving deliberately, Wernecke smoothed him out like a kite, pressing him slowly flat on the floor.

Then Wernecke bent over him, and lowered his mouth to his throat.

Bruckman watched in horror, knowing that he should shout, scream, try to rouse the other prisoners, but somehow unable to move, unable to make his mouth open, his lungs pump. He was paralyzed by fear, like a rabbit in the presence of a predator, a terror sharper and more intense than any he'd ever known.

The man's struggles were growing weaker, and Wernecke must have eased up some on the throttling pressure of his hand, because the man moaned "Don't . . . please don't . . ." in a weaker, slurred voice. The man had been drumming his fists against Wernecke's back and sides, but now the tempo of the drumming slowed, slowed, and then stopped, the man's arms falling laxly to the floor. "Don't . . ." the man whispered; he groaned and muttered incomprehensively for a moment or two longer, then became silent. The silence stretched out for a minute, two, three, and Wernecke still crouched over his victim, who was now not moving at all. . . .

Wernecke stirred, a kind of shudder going through him, like a cat stretching. He stood up. His face became visible as he straightened up into the full light from the window, and there was blood on it, glistening black under the harsh glare of the kliegs. As Bruckman watched, Wernecke began to lick his lips clean, his tongue, also black in this light, sliding like some sort of sinuous ebony snake around the rim of his mouth, darting and probing for the last lingering drops. . . .

How smug he looks, Bruckman thought, like a cat who has found the cream, and the anger that flashed through him at the thought enabled him to move and speak again. "Wernecke," he said harshly.

Wernecke glanced casually in his direction. "You again, Isadore?" Wernecke said. "Don't you ever sleep?" Wernecke spoke lazily, quizzically, without surprise, and Bruckman wondered if Wernecke had known all along that he was there. "Or do you just enjoy watching me?"

"Lies," Bruckman said. "You told me nothing but lies. Why did you bother?"

"You were excited," Wernecke said. "You had surprised me. It seemed best to tell you what you wanted to hear. If it satisfied you, then that was an easy solution to the problem."

"Never have I drained the life from someone who wanted to live," Bruckman said bitterly, mimicking Wernecke. "Only a little from each man! My God—and I believed you! I even felt sorry for you!"

Wernecke shrugged. "Most of it was true. Usually I only take a little from each man, softly and carefully, so that they never know, so that in the morning they are only a little weaker than they would have been anyway. . . ."

"Like Josef?" Bruckman said angrily. "Like the poor devil you killed tonight?"

Wernecke shrugged again. "I have been careless the last few nights, I admit. But I need to build up my strength again." His eyes gleamed in the darkness. "Events are coming to a head here. Can't you feel it, Isadore, can't you sense it? Soon the war will be over, everyone knows that. Before then, this camp will be shut down, and the Nazis will move us back into the interior—either that, or kill us. I have grown weak here, and I will soon need all my strength to survive, to take whatever op-

portunity presents itself to escape. I *must* be ready. And so I have let myself drink deeply again, drink my fill for the first time in months. . . ." Wernecke licked his lips again, perhaps unconsciously, then smiled bleakly at Bruckman. "You don't appreciate my restraint, Isadore. You don't understand how hard it has been for me to hold back, to take only a little each night. You don't understand how much that restraint has cost me. . . ."

"You are gracious," Bruckman sneered.

Wernecke laughed. "No, but I am a rational man; I pride myself on that. You other prisoners were my only source of food, and I have had to be very careful to make sure that you would last. I have no access to the Nazis, after all. I am trapped here, a prisoner just like you, whatever else you may believe—and I have not only had to find ways to survive here in the camp, I have had to procure my own food as well! No shepherd has ever watched over his flock more tenderly than I."

"Is that all we are to you—sheep? Animals to be slaughtered?"

Wernecke smiled. "Precisely."

When he could control his voice enough to speak, Bruckman said, "You're worse than the Nazis."

"I hardly think so," Wernecke said quietly, and for a moment he looked tired, as though something unimaginably old and unutterably weary had looked out through his eyes. "This camp was built by the Nazis—it wasn't my doing. The Nazis sent you here—not I. The Nazis have tried to kill you every day since, in one way or another—and I have tried to keep you alive, even at some risk to myself. No one has more of a vested interest in the survival of his livestock than the farmer, after all, even if he does occasionally slaughter an inferior animal. I have given you food—"

"Food you had no use for yourself! You sacrificed nothing!"

"That's true, of course. But *you* needed it, remember that. Whatever my motives, I have helped you to survive here—you and many others. By doing so I also acted in my own self-interest, of course, but can you have experienced this camp and still believe in things like altruism? What difference does it make what my reason for helping was—I still helped you, didn't I?"

"Sophistries!" Bruckman said. "Rationalizations! You twist words to justify yourself, but you can't disguise what you really are—a monster!"

Wernecke smiled gently, as though Bruckman's words amused him, and made as if to pass by, but Bruckman raised an arm to bar his way. They did not touch each other, but Wernecke stopped short, and a new quivering kind of tension sprung into existence in the air between them.

"I'll stop you," Bruckman said. "Somehow I'll stop you, I'll keep you from doing this terrible thing—"

"You'll do nothing," Wernecke said. His voice was hard and cold and flat, like a rock speaking. "What can you do? Tell the other prisoners? Who would believe you? They'd think you'd gone insane. Tell the *Nazis,* then?" Wernecke laughed harshly. "They'd think you'd gone crazy, too, and they'd take you to the hospital—and I don't have to tell you what your chances of getting out of there alive are, do I? No, you'll do *nothing.*"

Wernecke took a step forward; his eyes were shiny and black and hard, like ice, like the pitiless eyes of a predatory bird, and Bruckman felt a sick rush of fear cut through his anger. Bruckman gave way, stepping backward involuntarily, and Wernecke pushed past him, seeming to brush him aside without touching him.

Once past, Wernecke turned to stare at Bruckman, and Bruckman had to summon up all the defiance that remained in him not to look uneasily away from Wernecke's agate-hard eyes. "You are the strongest and cleverest of all the other animals, Isadore," Wernecke said in a calm, conversational voice. "You have been useful to me. Every shepherd needs a good sheepdog. I still need you, to help me manage the others, and to help me keep them going long enough to serve my needs. This is the reason why I have taken so much time with you, instead of just killing you outright." He shrugged. "So let us both be rational about this—you leave me alone, Isadore, and I will leave you

alone also. We will stay away from each other and look after our own affairs. Yes?"

"The others . . ." Bruckman said weakly.

"They must look after themselves," Wernecke said. He smiled, a thin and almost invisible motion of his lips. "What did I teach you, Isadore? Here everyone must look after themselves. What difference does it make what happens to the others? In a few weeks almost all of them will be dead anyway."

"You *are* a monster," Bruckman said.

"I'm not much different from you, Isadore. The strong survive, whatever the cost."

"I am *nothing* like you," Bruckman said, with loathing.

"No?" Wernecke asked, ironically, and moved away; within a few paces he was hobbling and stooping, vanishing into the shadows, once more the harmless old Jew.

Bruckman stood motionless for a moment, and then, moving slowly and reluctantly, he stepped across to where Wernecke's victim lay.

It was one of the new men Wernecke had been talking to earlier in the evening, and, of course, he was quite dead.

Shame and guilt took Bruckman then, emotions he thought he had forgotten—black and strong and bitter, they shook him by the throat the way Wernecke had shaken the new man.

Bruckman couldn't remember returning across the room to his sleeping platform, but suddenly he was there, lying on his back and staring into the stifling darkness, surrounded by the moaning, thrashing, stinking mass of sleepers. His hands were clasped protectively over his throat, although he couldn't remember putting them there, and he was shivering convulsively. How many mornings had he awoken with a dull ache in his neck, thinking it was no more than the habitual bodyaches and strained muscles they had all learned to take for granted? How many nights had Wernecke fed on *him?*

Every time Bruckman closed his eyes he would see Wernecke's face floating there in the luminous darkness behind his eyelids . . . Wernecke with his eyes half-closed, his face vulpine and cruel and satiated . . . Wernecke's face moving closer and closer to him, his eyes opening like black pits, his lips smiling back from his teeth . . . Wernecke's lips, sticky and red with blood . . . and then Bruckman would seem to feel the wet touch of Wernecke's lips on *his* throat, feel Wernecke's teeth biting into *his* flesh, and Bruckman's eyes would fly open again. Staring into the darkness. Nothing there. Nothing there *yet* . . .

Dawn was a dirty gray imminence against the cabin window before Bruckman could force himself to lower his shielding arms from his throat, and once again he had not slept at all.

That day's work was a nightmare of pain and exhaustion for Bruckman, harder than anything he had known since his first few days at the camp. Somehow he forced himself to get up, somehow he stumbled outside and up the path to the quarry, seeming to float along high off the ground, his head a bloated balloon, his feet a thousand miles away at the end of boneless beanstalk legs he could barely control at all. Twice he fell, and was kicked several times before he could drag himself back to his feet and lurch forward again. The sun was coming up in front of them, a hard red disk in a sickly yellow sky, and to Bruckman it seemed to be a glazed and lidless eye staring dispassionately into the world to watch them flail and struggle and die, like the eye of a scientist peering into a laboratory maze.

He watched the disk of the sun as he stumbled towards it; it seemed to bob and shimmer with every painful step, expanding, swelling, and bloating until it swallowed the sky. . . .

Then he was picking up a rock, moaning with the effort, feeling the rough stone tear his hands. . . .

Reality began to slide away from Bruckman. There were long periods when the world was blank, and he would come slowly back to himself as if from a great distance, and hear his own voice speaking words that he could not understand, or keen-

ing mindlessly, or grunting in a hoarse, animalistic way, and he would find that his body was working mechanically, stooping and lifting and carrying, all without volition. . . .

A Musselmänn, Bruckman thought, I'm becoming a Musselmänn . . . and felt a chill of fear sweep through him. He fought to hold onto the world, afraid that the next time he slipped away from himself he would not come back, deliberately banging his hands into the rocks, cutting himself, clearing his head with pain.

The world steadied around him. A guard shouted a hoarse admonishment at him and slapped his rifle butt, and Bruckman forced himself to work faster, although he could not keep himself from weeping silently with the pain his movements cost him.

He discovered that Wernecke was watching him, and stared back defiantly, the bitter tears still runneling his dirty cheeks, thinking, *I won't become a Musselmänn for you, I won't make it easy for you, I won't provide another helpless victim for you.* . . . Wernecke met Bruckman's gaze for a moment, and then shrugged and turned away.

Bruckman bent for another stone, feeling the muscles in his back crack and the pain drive in like knives. What had Wernecke been thinking behind the blankness of his expressionless face? Had Wernecke, sensing weakness, marked Bruckman for his next victim? Had Wernecke been disappointed or dismayed by the strength of Bruckman's will to survive? Would Wernecke now settle upon someone else?

The morning passed, and Bruckman grew feverish again. He could feel the fever in his face, making his eyes feel sandy and hot, pulling the skin taut over his cheekbones, and he wondered how long he could manage to stay on his feet. To falter, to grow weak and insensible, was certain death; if the Nazis didn't kill him, Wernecke would. . . . Wernecke was out of sight now, on the other side of the quarry, but it seemed to Bruckman that Wernecke's hard and flinty eyes were everywhere, floating in the air around him, looking out momentarily from the back of a Nazi soldier's head, watching him from the dulled iron side of a quarry cart, peering at him from a dozen different angles. He bent ponderously for another rock, and when he had pried it up from the earth he found Wernecke's eyes beneath it, staring unblinkingly up at him from the damp and pallid soil. . . .

That afternoon there were great flashes of light on the eastern horizon, out across the endless flat expanse of the steppe, flares in rapid sequence that lit up the sullen gray sky, all without sound. The Nazi guards had gathered in a group, looking to the east and talking in subdued voices, ignoring the prisoners for the moment. For the first time Bruckman noticed how disheveled and unshaven the guards had become in the last few days, as though they had given up, as though they no longer cared. Their faces were strained and tight, and more than one of them seemed to be fascinated by the leaping fires on the distant edge of the world.

Melnick said that it was only a thunderstorm, but old Bohme said that it was an artillery battle being fought, and that that meant that the Russians were coming, that soon they would all be liberated.

Bohme grew so excited at the thought that he began shouting, "The Russians! It's the Russians! The Russians are coming to free us!" Dichstein, another one of the new prisoners, and Melnick tried to hush him, but Bohme continued to caper and shout—doing a grotesque kind of jig while he yelled and flapped his arms—until he had attracted the attention of the guards. Infuriated, two of the guards fell upon Bohme and beat him severely, striking him with their rifle butts with more than usual force, knocking him to the ground, continuing to flail at him and kick him while he was down, Bohme writhing like an injured worm under their stamping boots. They probably would have beaten Bohme to death on the spot, but Wernecke organized a distraction among some of the other prisoners, and when the guards moved away to deal with it, Wernecke helped Bohme to stand up and hobble away to the other side of the quarry, where the rest of the prisoners shielded him from sight with their bodies as best they could for the rest of the afternoon.

Something about the way Wernecke urged Bohme to his feet and helped him to limp and lurch away, something about the protective, possessive curve of Wernecke's arm around Bohme's shoulders, told Bruckman that Wernecke had selected his next victim.

That night Bruckman vomited up the meager and rancid meal that they were allowed, his stomach convulsing uncontrollably after the first few bites. Trembling with hunger and exhaustion and fever, he leaned against the wall and watched as Wernecke fussed over Bohme, nursing him as a man might nurse a sick child, talking gently to him, wiping away some of the blood that still oozed from the corner of Bohme's mouth, coaxing Bohme to drink a few sips of soup, finally arranging that Bohme should stretch out on the floor away from the sleeping platforms, where he would not be jostled by the others. . . .

As soon as the interior lights went out that night, Bruckman got up, crossed the floor quickly and unhesitantly, and lay down in the shadows near the spot where Bohme muttered and twitched and groaned.

Shivering, Bruckman lay in the darkness, the strong smell of the earth in his nostrils, waiting for Wernecke to come. . . .

In Bruckman's hand, held close to his chest, was a spoon that had been sharpened to a jagged needle point, a spoon he had stolen and begun to sharpen while he was still in a civilian prison in Cologne, so long ago that he almost couldn't remember, scraping it back and forth against the stone wall of his cell every night for hours, managing to keep it hidden on his person during the nightmarish ride in the sweltering boxcar, the first few terrible days at the camp, telling no one about it, not even Wernecke during the months when he'd thought of Wernecke as a kind of saint, keeping it hidden long after the possibility of escape had become too remote even to fantasize about, retaining it then more as a tangible link with the daydream country of his past than as a tool he ever actually hoped to employ, cherishing it almost as a holy relic, as a remnant of a vanished world that he otherwise might almost believe had never existed at all. . . .

And now that it was time to use it at last, he was almost reluctant to do so, to soil it with another man's blood. . . .

He fingered the spoon compulsively, turning it over and over; it was hard and smooth and cold, and he clenched it as tightly as he could, trying to ignore the fine tremoring of his hands.

He had to kill Wernecke. . . .

Nausea and an odd feeling of panic flashed through Bruckman at the thought, but there was no other choice, there was no other way. . . . He couldn't go on like this, his strength was failing; Wernecke was killing him, as surely as he had killed the others, just by keeping him from sleeping. . . . And as long as Wernecke lived, he would never be safe: always there would be the chance that Wernecke would come for him, that Wernecke would strike as soon as his guard was down. . . . Would Wernecke scruple for a second to kill *him*, after all, if he thought that he could do it safely? . . . No, of course not. . . . Given the chance, Wernecke would kill him without a moment's further thought. . . . No, he must strike *first*. . . .

Bruckman licked his lips uneasily. Tonight. He had to kill Wernecke *tonight*. . . .

There was a stirring, a rustling: Someone was getting up, working his way free from the mass of sleepers on one of the platforms. A shadowy figure crossed the room toward Bruckman, and Bruckman tensed, reflexively running his thumb along the jagged end of the spoon, readying himself to rise, to strike—but at the last second, the figure veered aside and stumbled toward another corner. There was a sound like rain drumming on cloth; the man swayed there for a moment, mumbling, and then slowly returned to his pallet, dragging his feet, as if he had pissed his very life away against the wall. It was not Wernecke.

Bruckman eased himself back down to the floor, his heart seeming to shake his wasted body back and forth with the force of its beating. His hand was damp with sweat. He wiped it against his tattered pants, and then clutched the spoon again. . . .

Time seemed to stop. Bruckman waited, stretched out along the hard floorboards, the raw wood rasp-ing his skin, dust clogging his mouth and nose, feeling as though he were already dead, a corpse laid out in the rough pine coffin, feeling eternity pile up on his chest like heavy clots of wet black earth. . . . Outside the hut, the kliegs blazed, banishing night, abolishing it, but here inside the hut it was night, here night survived, perhaps the only pocket of night remaining on a klieg-lit planet, the shafts of light that came in through the slatted windows only serving to accentuate the surrounding darkness, to make it greater and more puissant by comparison. . . . Here in the darkness, nothing ever changed . . . there was only the smothering heat, and the weight of eternal darkness, and the changeless moments that could not pass because there was nothing to differentiate them one from the other. . . .

Many times as he waited Bruckman's eyes would grow heavy and slowly close, but each time his eyes would spring open again at once, and he would find himself staring into the shadows for Wernecke. Sleep would no longer have him, it was a kingdom closed to him now; it spat him out each time he tried to enter it, just as his stomach now spat out the food he placed in it. . . .

The thought of food brought Bruckman to a sharper awareness, and there in the darkness he huddled around his hunger, momentarily forgetting everything else. Never had he been so hungry. . . . He thought of the food he had wasted earlier in the evening, and only the last few shreds of his self-control kept him from moaning aloud.

Bohme did moan aloud then, as though unease were contagious. As Bruckman glanced at him, Bohme said, "Anya," in a clear calm voice; he mumbled a little, and then, a bit more loudly, said, "Tseitel, have you set the table yet?" and Bruckman realized that Bohme was no longer in the camp, that Bohme was back in Dusseldorf in the tiny apartment with his fat wife and his four healthy children, and Bruckman felt a pang of envy go through him, for Bohme, who had escaped.

It was at that moment that Bruckman realized that Wernecke was standing there, just beyond Bohme.

There had been no movement that Bruckman

had seen. Wernecke had seemed to slowly materialize from the darkness, atom by atom, bit by incremental bit, until at some point he had been solid enough for his presence to register on Bruckman's consciousness, so that what had been only a shadow a moment before was now unmistakably Wernecke as well, however much a shadow it remained.

Bruckman's mouth went dry with terror, and it almost seemed that he could hear the voice of his dead grandmother whispering in his ears. Boogey tales . . . Wernecke had said *I'm no night spirit*. Remember that he had said that. . . .

Wernecke was almost close enough to touch. He was staring down at Bohme; his face, lit by a dusty shaft of light from the window, was cold and remote, only the total lack of expression hinting at the passion that strained and quivered behind the mask. Slowly, lingeringly, Wernecke stooped over Bohme. "Anya," Bohme said again, caressingly, and then Wernecke's mouth was on his throat.

Let him feed, said a cold remorseless voice in Bruckman's mind. It will be easier to take him when he's nearly sated, when he's fully preoccupied and growing lethargic and logy . . . growing *full*. . . .

Slowly, with infinite caution, Bruckman gathered himself to spring, watching in horror and fascination as Wernecke fed. He could hear Wernecke sucking the juice out of Bohme, as if there were not enough blood in the foolish old man to satiate him, as if there were not enough blood in the whole camp . . . or perhaps, the whole world. . . . And now Bohme was ceasing his feeble struggling, was becoming still. . . .

Bruckman flung himself upon Wernecke, stabbing him twice in the back before his weight bowled them both over. There was a moment of confusion as they rolled and struggled together, all without sound, and then Bruckman found himself sitting atop Wernecke, Wernecke's white face turned up to him. Bruckman drove his weapon into Wernecke again, the shock of the blow jarring Bruckman's arm to the shoulder. Wernecke made no outcry; his eyes were already glazing, but they looked at Bruckman with recognition, with

cold anger, with bitter irony and, oddly, with what might have been resignation or relief, with what might almost have been pity. . . .

Bruckman stabbed again and again, driving the blows home with hysterical strength, panting, rocking atop his victim, feeling Wernecke's blood spatter against his face, wrapped in the heat and steam that rose from Wernecke's torn-open body like a smothering black cloud, coughing and choking on it for a moment, feeling the steam seep in through his pores and sink deep into the marrow of his bones, feeling the world seem to pulse and shimmer and change around him, as though he were suddenly seeing through new eyes, as though something had been born anew inside him, and then abruptly he was *smelling* Wernecke's blood, the hot organic reek of it, leaning closer to drink in that sudden overpowering smell, better than the smell of freshly baked bread, better than anything he could remember, rich and heady and strong beyond imagining.

There was a moment of revulsion and horror, and he tried to wonder how long the ancient contamination had been passing from man to man to man, how far into the past the chain of lives stretched, how Wernecke himself had been trapped, and then his parched lips touched wetness, and he was drinking, drinking deeply and greedily, and his mouth was filled with the strong clean taste of copper.

T he following night, after Bruckman led the memorial prayers for Wernecke and Bohme, Melnick came to him. Melnick's eyes were bright with tears. "How can we go on without Eduard? He was everything to us. What will we do now? . . ."

"It will be all right, Moishe," Bruckman said. "I promise you, everything will be all right." He put his arm around Melnick for a moment to comfort him, and at the touch sensed the hot blood that pumped through the intricate network of the boy's veins, just under the skin, rich and warm and nourishing, waiting there inviolate for him to set it free.

## NECROS

# Brian Lumley

Brian Lumley was born in County Durham in the northeast part of England, nine months after the death of his greatest early literary influence, H. P. Lovecraft. He joined the Corps of Royal Military Police and served for twenty-two years, retiring in 1980 as a warrant officer.

He wrote stories while serving in the army, mainly in the style of Lovecraft, often expanding on the Cthulhu mythos, though he noted a difference between his Cthulhu and that of Lovecraft: "My guys fight back," he wrote, "also, they like to have a laugh now and then." After he left the RMP, Lumley devoted his full time to writing. Encouraged by August Derleth, he had already produced several Lovecraftian short stories, which were published by Arkham House, then the first of his six Titus Crow novels, *The Burrowers Beneath* (1974), and the stand-alone novel *Khai of Ancient Khem* (1981), followed by a series of four books about Lovecraft's *Dreamlands* milieu, then the Psychomech trilogy (1981–84). In 1984 he wrote his breakout book, *Necroscope,* which featured Harry Keogh, the man who could talk to dead people, beginning a best-selling series that has sold more than a million copies. As the guest of honor at the World Horror Convention in 1998, he was given the Grand Master Award for lifetime achievement.

"Necros" (not part of the Necroscope series) was first published in *The Second Book of After Midnight Stories,* edited by Amy Myers (London: William Kimber, 1986). The story was adapted for Ridley Scott's Showtime television series, *The Hunger.*

# Necros

## BRIAN LUMLEY

### I

An old woman in a faded blue frock and black head-square paused in the shade of Mario's awning and nodded good-day. She smiled a gap-toothed smile. A bulky, slouch-shouldered youth in jeans and a stained yellow T-shirt—a slope-headed idiot, probably her grandson—held her hand, drooling vacantly and fidgeting beside her.

Mario nodded good-naturedly, smiled, wrapped a piece of stale *fucaccia* in greaseproof paper and came from behind the bar to give it to her. She clasped his hand, thanked him, turned to go.

Her attention was suddenly arrested by something she saw across the road. She started, cursed vividly, harshly, and despite my meager knowledge of Italian I picked up something of the hatred in her tone. "Devil's spawn!" She said it again. "Dog! Swine!" She pointed a shaking hand and finger, said yet again: "Devil's spawn!" before making the two-fingered, double-handed stabbing sign with which the Italians ward off evil. To do this it was first necessary that she drop her salted bread, which the idiot youth at once snatched up.

Then, still mouthing low, guttural imprecations, dragging the shuffling, *fucaccia*-munching cretin behind her, she hurried off along the street and disappeared into an alley. One word that she had repeated over and over again stayed in my mind: *"Necros! Necros!"* Though the word was new to me, I took it for a curse-word. The accent she put on it had been poisonous.

I sipped at my Negroni, remained seated at the small circular table beneath Mario's awning and stared at the object of the crone's distaste. It was a motorcar, a white convertible Rover and this year's model, inching slowly forward in a stream of holiday traffic. And it was worth looking at it only for the girl behind the wheel. The little man in the floppy white hat beside her—well, he was something else, too. But *she* was—just something else.

I caught just a glimpse, sufficient to feel stunned. That was good. I had thought it was something I could never know again: that feeling a man gets looking at a beautiful girl. Not after Linda. And yet—

She was young, say twenty-four or -five, some three or four years my junior. She sat tall at the wheel, slim, raven-haired under a white, wide-

836

brimmed summer hat which just missed matching that of her companion, with a complexion cool and creamy enough to pour over peaches. I stood up—yes, to get a better look—and right then the traffic came to a momentary standstill. At that moment, too, she turned her head and looked at me. And if the profile had stunned me . . . well, the full frontal knocked me dead. The girl was simply, classically, beautiful.

Her eyes were of a dark green but very bright, slightly tilted and perfectly oval under straight, thin brows. Her cheeks were high, her lips a red Cupid's bow, her neck long and white against the glowing yellow of her blouse. And her smile—

—Oh, yes, she smiled.

Her glance, at first cool, became curious in a moment, then a little angry, until finally, seeing my confusion—that smile. And as she turned her attention back to the road and followed the stream of traffic out of sight, I saw a blush of color spreading on the creamy surface of her cheek. Then she was gone.

Then, too, I remembered the little man who sat beside her. Actually, I hadn't seen a great deal of him, but what I had seen had given me the creeps. He too had turned his head to stare at me, leaving in my mind's eye an impression of beady bird eyes, sharp and intelligent in the shade of his hat. He had stared at me for only a moment, and then his head had slowly turned away; but even when he no longer looked at me, when he stared straight ahead, it seemed to me I could feel those raven's eyes upon me, and that a query had been written in them.

I believed I could understand it, that look. He must have seen a good many young men staring at him like that—or rather, at the girl. His look had been a threat in answer to my threat—and because he was practiced in it I had certainly felt the more threatened!

I turned to Mario, whose English was excellent. "She has something against expensive cars and rich people?"

"Who?" he busied himself behind his bar.

"The old lady, the woman with the idiot boy."

"Ah!" he nodded. "Mainly against the little man, I suspect."

"Oh?"

"You want another Negroni?"

"OK—and one for yourself—but tell me about this other thing, won't you?"

"If you like—but you're only interested in the girl, yes?" He grinned.

I shrugged. "She's a good-looker . . ."

"Yes, I saw her." Now he shrugged. "That other thing—just old myths and legends, that's all. Like your English Dracula, eh?"

"Transylvanian Dracula," I corrected him.

"Whatever you like. And Necros: that's the name of the spook, see?"

"Necros is the name of a vampire?"

"A spook, yes."

"And this is a real legend? I mean, historical?"

He made a fifty-fifty face, his hands palms-up. "Local, I guess. Ligurian. I remember it from when I was a kid. If I was bad, old Necros sure to come and get me. Today," again the shrug, "it's forgotten."

"Like the bogeyman," I nodded.

"Eh?"

"Nothing. But why did the old girl go on like that?"

Again he shrugged. "Maybe she think that old man Necros, eh? She crazy, you know? Very backward. The whole family."

I was still interested. "How does the legend go?"

"The spook takes the life out of you. You grow old, spook grows young. It's a bargain you make: he gives you something you want, gets what he wants. What he wants is your youth. Except he uses it up quick and needs more. All the time, more youth."

"What kind of bargain is that?" I asked. "What does the victim get out of it?"

"Gets what he wants," said Mario, his brown face cracking into another grin. "In your case the girl, eh? If the little man was Necros . . ."

He got on with his work and I sat there sipping my Negroni. End of conversation. I thought no more about it—until later.

## II

Of course, I should have been in Italy with Linda, but . . . I had kept her "Dear John" for a fortnight before shredding it, getting mindlessly drunk and starting in on the process of forgetting. That had been a month ago. The holiday had already been booked and I wasn't about to miss out on my trip to the sun. And so I had come out on my own. It was hot, the swimming was good, life was easy and the food superb. With just two days left to enjoy it, I told myself it hadn't been bad. But it would have been better with Linda.

Linda . . . She was still on my mind—at the back of it, anyway—later that night as I sat in the bar of my hotel beside an open bougainvillaea-decked balcony that looked down on the bay and the seafront lights of the town. And maybe she wasn't all that far back in my mind—maybe she was right there in front—or else I was just plain daydreaming. Whichever, I missed the entry of the lovely lady and her shriveled companion, failing to spot and recognize them until they were taking their seats at a little table just the other side of the balcony's sweep.

This was the closest I'd been to her, and—

Well, first impressions hadn't lied. This girl *was* beautiful. She didn't look quite as young as she'd first seemed—my own age, maybe—but beautiful she certainly was. And the old boy? He must be, could only be, her father. Maybe it sounds like I was a little naive, but with her looks this lady really didn't need an old man. And if she did need one it didn't have to be *this* one.

By now she'd seen me and my fascination with her must have been obvious. Seeing it she smiled and blushed at one and the same time, and for a moment turned her eyes away—but only for a moment. Fortunately her companion had his back to me or he must have known my feelings at once; for as she looked at me again—fully upon me this time—I could have sworn I read an invitation in her eyes, and in that same moment any bitter vows I may have made melted away completely and were forgotten. God, *please* let him be her father!

For an hour I sat there, drinking a few too many cocktails, eating olives and potato crisps from little bowls on the bar, keeping my eyes off the girl as best I could, if only for common decency's sake. But . . . all the time I worried frantically at the problem of how to introduce myself, and as the minutes ticked by it seemed to me that the most obvious way must also be the best.

But how obvious would it be to the old boy?

And the damnable thing was that the girl hadn't given me another glance since her original—invitation? Had I mistaken that look of hers?—or was she simply waiting for me to make the first move? *God, let him be her father!*

She was sipping Martinis, slowly; he drank a rich red wine, in some quantity. I asked a waiter to replenish their glasses and charge it to me. I had already spoken to the bar steward, a swarthy, friendly little chap from the South called Francesco, but he hadn't been able to enlighten me. The pair were not resident, he assured me; but being resident myself I was already pretty sure of that.

Anyway, my drinks were delivered to their table; they looked surprised; the girl put on a perfectly innocent expression, questioned the waiter, nodded in my direction and gave me a cautious smile, and the old boy turned his head to stare at me. I found myself smiling in return but avoiding his eyes, which were like coals now, sunken deep in his brown-wrinkled face. Time seemed suspended—if only for a second—then the girl spoke again to the waiter and he came across to me.

"Mr. Collins, sir, the gentleman and the young lady thank you and request that you join them." Which was everything I had dared hope for—for the moment.

Standing up I suddenly realized how much I'd had to drink. I willed sobriety on myself and walked across to their table. They didn't stand up but the little chap said, "Please sit." His voice was a rustle of dried grass. The waiter was behind me with a chair. I sat.

"Peter Collins," I said. "How do you do, Mr.—er?—"

"Karpethes," he answered. "Nichos Karpethes. And this is my wife, Adrienne." Neither one of them had made the effort to extend their hands, but that didn't dismay me. Only the fact that they were married dismayed me. He must be very, very rich, this Nichos Karpethes.

"I'm delighted you invited me over," I said, forcing a smile, "but I see that I was mistaken. You see, I thought I heard you speaking English, and I—"

"Thought we were English?" she finished it for me. "A natural error. Originally I am Armenian, Nichos is Greek, of course. We do not speak each other's tongue, but we do both speak English. Are you staying here, Mr. Collins?"

"Er, yes—for one more day and night. Then"—I shrugged and put on a sad look—"back to England, I'm afraid."

"Afraid?" the old boy whispered. "There is something to fear in a return to your homeland?"

"Just an expression," I answered. "I meant I'm afraid that my holiday is coming to an end."

He smiled. It was a strange, wistful sort of smile, wrinkling his face up like a little walnut. "But your friends will be glad to see you again. Your loved ones—?"

I shook my head. "Only a handful of friends—none of them really close—and no loved ones. I'm a loner, Mr. Karpethes."

"A loner?" His eyes glowed deep in their sockets and his hands began to tremble where they gripped the table's rim. "Mr. Collins, you don't—"

"We understand," she cut him off. "For although we are together, we too, in our way, are loners. Money has made Nichos lonely, you see? Also, he is not a well man and time is short. He will not waste what time he has on frivolous friendships. As for myself—people do not understand our being together, Nichos and I. They pry, and I withdraw. And so I too am a loner."

There was no accusation in her voice, but still I felt obliged to say: "I certainly didn't intend to pry, Mrs.—"

"Adrienne," she smiled. "Please. No, of course you didn't. I would not want you to think we thought that of you. Anyway I will *tell* you why we are together, and then it will be put aside."

Her husband coughed, seemed to choke, struggled to his feet. I stood up and took his arm. He at once shook me off—with some distaste, I thought—but Adrienne had already signaled to a waiter. "Assist Mr. Karpethes to the gentleman's room," she quickly instructed in very good Italian. "And please help him back to the table when he has recovered."

As he went Karpethes gesticulated, probably tried to say something to me by way of an apology, choked again, and reeled as he allowed the waiter to help him from the room.

"I'm . . . sorry," I said, not knowing what else to say.

"He has attacks." She was cool. "Do not concern yourself. I am used to it."

We sat in silence for a moment. Finally I began. "You were going to tell me—"

"Ah, yes! I had forgotten. It is a symbiosis."

"Oh?"

"Yes. I need the good life he can give me, and he needs . . . my youth? We supply each other's needs." And so, in a way, the old woman with the idiot boy hadn't been wrong after all. A sort of bargain had indeed been struck. Between Karpethes and his wife. As that thought crossed my mind I felt the short hairs at the back of my neck stiffen for a moment. Gooseflesh crawled on my arms. After all, "Nichos" was pretty close to "Necros," and now this youth thing again. Coincidence, of course. And after all, aren't all relationships bargains of sorts? Bargains struck for better or for worse.

"But for how long?" I asked. "I mean, how long will it work for you?"

She shrugged. "I have been provided for. And he will have me all the days of his life."

I coughed, cleared my throat, gave a strained, self-conscious laugh. "And here's me, the non-pryer!"

"No, not at all, I wanted you to know."

"Well," I shrugged, "—but it's been a pretty deep first conversation."

"First? Did you believe that buying me a drink would entitle you to more than one conversation?"

I almost winced. "Actually, I—"

But then she smiled and my world lit up. "You did not need to buy the drinks," she said. "There would have been some other way."

I looked at her inquiringly. "Some other way to—?"

"To find out if we were English or not."

"Oh!"

"Here comes Nichos now," she smiled across the room. "And we must be leaving. He's not well. Tell me, will you be on the beach tomorrow?"

"Oh—yes!" I answered after a moment's hesitation. "I like to swim."

"So do I. Perhaps we can swim out to the raft . . . ?"

"I'd like that very much."

Her husband arrived back at the table under his own steam. He looked a little stronger now, not quite so shriveled somehow. He did not sit but gripped the back of his chair with parchment fingers, knuckles white where the skin stretched over old bones. "Mr. Collins," he rustled, "—Adrienne, I'm sorry. . . ."

"There's really no need," I said, rising.

"We really must be going." She also stood. "No, you stay here, er, Peter? It's kind of you, but we can manage. Perhaps we'll see you on the beach." And she helped him to the door of the bar and through it without once looking back.

## III

They weren't staying at my hotel, had simply dropped in for a drink. That was understandable (though I would have preferred to think that she had been looking for me) for *my* hotel was middling tourist-class while theirs was something else. They were up on the hill, high on the crest of a Ligurian spur where a smaller, much more exclusive place nested in Mediterranean pines. A place whose lights spelled money when they shone up there at night, whose music came floating down from a tiny open-air disco like the laughter of high-living elementals of the air. If I was poetic it was because of her. I mean, that beautiful girl and that

weary, wrinkled dried up walnut of an old man. If anything I was sorry for him. And yet in another way I wasn't.

And let's make no pretense about it—if I haven't said it already, let me say it right now—I wanted her. Moreover, there had been that about our conversation, her beach invitation, which told me that she was available.

The thought of it kept me awake half the night. . . .

I was on the beach at 9:00 a.m.—they didn't show until 11:00. When they did, and when she came out of her tiny changing cubicle—

There wasn't a male head on the beach that didn't turn at least twice. Who could blame them? That girl, in *that* costume, would have turned the head of a sphynx. But—there was something, some little nagging thing different about her. A maturity beyond her years? She held herself like a model, a princess. But who was it for? Karpethes or me?

As for the old man: he was in a crumpled lightweight summer suit and sunshade hat as usual, but he seemed a bit more perky this morning. Unlike myself he'd doubtless had a good night's sleep. While his wife had been changing he had made his way unsteadily across the pebbly beach to my table and sun umbrella, taking the seat directly opposite me; and before his wife could appear he had opened with:

"Good morning, Mr. Collins."

"Good morning," I answered. "Please call me Peter."

"Peter, then," he nodded. He seemed out of breath, either from his stumbling walk over the beach or a certain urgency which I could detect in his movements, his hurried, almost rude "let's get down to it" manner.

"Peter, you said you would be here for one more day?"

"That's right," I answered, for the first time studying him closely where he sat like some strange garden gnome half in the shade of the beach umbrella. "This is my last day."

He was a bundle of dry wood, a pallid prune, a small, umber scarecrow. And his voice, too, was of straw, or autumn leaves blown across a shady path. Only his eyes were alive. "And you said you have no family, few friends, no one to miss you back in England?"

Warning bells rang in my head. Maybe it wasn't so much urgency in him—which usually implies a goal or ambition still to be realized—but eagerness in that the goal was in sight. "That's correct. I am, was, a student doctor. When I get home I shall seek a position. Other than that there's nothing, no one, no ties."

He leaned forward, bird eyes very bright, claw hand reaching across the table, trembling, and—

Her shadow suddenly fell across us as she stood there in that costume. Karpethes jerked back in his chair. His face was working, strange emotions twisting the folds and wrinkles of his flesh into stranger contours. I could feel my heart thumping against my ribs . . . why I couldn't say. I calmed myself, looked up at her, and smiled.

She stood with her back to the sun, which made a dark silhouette of her head and face. But in that blot of darkness her oval eyes were green jewels. "Shall we swim, Peter?"

She turned and ran down the beach, and of course I ran after her. She had a head start and beat me to the water, beat me to the raft, too. It wasn't until I hauled myself up beside her that I thought of Karpethes: how I hadn't even excused myself before plunging after her. But at least the water had cleared my head, bringing me completely awake and aware.

Aware of her incredible body where it stretched almost touching mine, on the fiber deck of the gently bobbing raft.

I mentioned her husband's line of inquiry, gasping a little for breath as I recovered from the frantic exercise of our race. She, on the other hand, already seemed completely recovered. She carefully arranged her hair about her shoulders like a fan, to dry in the sunlight, before answering.

"Nichos is not really my husband," she finally said, not looking at me. "I am his companion, that's all. I could have told you last night, but . . . there was the chance that you really were curious only about our nationality. As for any veiled threats he might have issued: that is not unusual. He might not have the vitality of younger men, but jealousy is ageless."

"No," I answered, "he didn't threaten—not that I noticed. But jealousy? Knowing I have only one more day to spend here, what has he to fear from me?"

Her shoulders twitched a little, a shrug. She turned her face to me, her lips inches away. Her eyelashes were like silken shutters over green pools, hiding whatever swam in the deeps. "I am young, Peter, and so are you. And you are very attractive, very . . . eager? Holiday romances are not uncommon."

My blood was on fire. "I have very little money," I said. "We are staying at different hotels. He already suspects me. It is impossible."

"What is?" she innocently asked, leaving me at a complete loss.

But then she laughed, tossed back her hair, already dry, dangled her hands and arms in the water. "Where there's a will . . . " she said.

"You know that I want you—" The words spilled out before I could control or change them.

"Oh, yes. And I want you." She said it so simply, and yet suddenly I felt seared. A moth brushing the magnet candle's flame.

I lifted my head, looked toward the beach. Across seventy-five yards of sparkling water the beach umbrellas looked very large and close. Karpethes sat in the shade just as I had last seen him, his face hidden in shadow. But I knew that he watched.

"You can do nothing here," she said, her voice languid—but I noticed now that she, too, seemed short of breath.

"This," I told her with a groan, "is going to kill me!"

She laughed, laughter that sparkled more than the sun on the sea. "I'm sorry," she sobered. "It's unfair of me to laugh. But—your case is not hopeless."

"Oh?"

"Tomorrow morning, early, Nichos has an appointment with a specialist in Genova. I am to drive him into the city tonight. We'll stay at a hotel overnight."

I groaned my misery. "Then my case *is* quite hopeless. I fly tomorrow."

"But if I sprained my wrist," she said, "and so could not drive . . . and if he went into Genova by taxi while I stayed behind with a headache—because of the pain from my wrist—" Like a flash she was on her feet, the raft tilting, her body diving, striking the water into a spray of diamonds.

Seconds for it all to sink in—and then I was following her, laboring through the water in her churning wake. And as she splashed from the sea, seeing her stumble, go to her hands and knees in Ligurian shingle—and the pained look on her face, the way she held her wrist as she came to her feet. As easy as that!

Karpethes, struggling to rise from his seat, stared at her with his mouth agape. Her face screwed up now as I followed her up the beach. And Adrienne holding her "sprained" wrist and shaking it, her mouth forming an elongated "O." The sinuous motion of her body and limbs, mobile marble with dew of ocean clinging saltily. . . .

If the tiny man had said to me: "I am Necros. I want ten years of your life for one night with her," at that moment I might have sealed the bargain. Gladly. But legends are legends and he wasn't Necros, and he didn't, and I didn't. After all, there was no need. . . .

# IV

I suppose my greatest fear was that she might be "having me on," amusing herself at my expense. She was, of course, "safe" with me—insofar as I would be gone tomorrow and the "romance" forgotten, for her, anyway—and I could also see how she was starved for young companionship, a fact she had brought right out in the open from the word go.

But why me? Why should I be so lucky?

Attractive? Was I? I had never thought so. Perhaps it was because I *was* so safe: here today and gone tomorrow, with little or no chance of complications. Yes, that must be it. *If* she wasn't simply making a fool of me. She might be just a tease—

—But she wasn't.

At 8:30 that evening I was in the bar of my hotel—had been there for an hour, careful not to drink too much, unable to eat—when the waiter came to me and said there was a call for me on the reception telephone. I hurried out to reception where the clerk discreetly excused himself and left me alone.

"Peter?" Her voice was a deep well of promise. "He's gone. I've booked us a table, to dine at 9:00. Is that all right for you?"

"A table? Where?" my own voice breathless.

"Why, up here, of course! Oh, don't worry, it's perfectly safe. And anyway, Nichos knows."

"Knows?" I was taken aback, a little panicked. "What does he know?"

"That we're dining together. In fact he suggested it. He didn't want me to eat alone—and since this is your last night . . ."

"I'll get a taxi right away," I told her.

"Good. I look forward to . . . seeing you. I shall be in the bar."

I replaced the telephone in its cradle, wondering if she always took an *apéritif* before the main course. . . .

I had smartened myself up. That is to say, I was immaculate. Black bow tie, white evening jacket (courtesy of C & A), black trousers, and a lightly-frilled white shirt, the only one I had ever owned. But I might have known that my appearance would never match up to hers. It seemed that everything she did was just perfectly right. I could only hope that that meant literally everything.

But in her black lace evening gown with its plunging neckline, short wide sleeves, and delicate silver embroidery, she was stunning. Sitting with her in the bar, sipping our drinks—for me a large whiskey and for her a tall Cinzano—I couldn't take my eyes off her. Twice I reached out for her hand and twice she drew back from me.

"Discreet they may well be," she said, letting her oval green eyes flicker toward the bar, where guests stood and chatted, and back to me, "but there's really no need to give them occasion to gossip."

"I'm sorry, Adrienne," I told her, my voice husky and close to trembling, "but—"

"How is it," she demurely cut me off, "that a good-looking man like you is—how do you say it?—going short?"

I sat back, chuckled. "That's a rather unladylike expression," I told her.

"Oh? And what I've planned for tonight is ladylike?"

My voice went huskier still. "Just what is your plan?"

"While we eat," she answered, her voice low, "I shall tell you." At which point a waiter loomed, towel over his arm, inviting us to accompany him to the dining room.

A drienne's portions were tiny, mine huge. She sipped a slender, light white wine, I gulped blocky rich red from a glass the waiter couldn't seem to leave alone. Mercifully I was hungry—I hadn't eaten all day—else that meal must surely have bloated me out. And all of it ordered in advance, the very best in quality cuisine.

"This," she eventually said, handling me her key, "fits the door of our suite." We were sitting back, enjoying liqueurs and cigarettes. "The rooms are on the ground floor. Tonight you enter through the door, tomorrow morning you leave via the window. A slow walk down to the seafront will refresh you. How is that for a plan?"

"Unbelievable!"

"You don't believe it?"

"Not my good fortune, no."

"Shall we say that we both have our needs?"

"I think," I said, "that I may be falling in love

with you. What if I don't wish to leave in the morning?"

She shrugged, smiled, said: "Who knows what tomorrow may bring?"

h ow could I ever have thought of her simply as another girl? Or even an ordinary young woman? Girl she certainly was, woman, too, but so . . . *knowing*! Beautiful as a princess and knowing as a whore.

If Mario's old myths and legends were reality, and if Nichos Karpethes were really Necros, then he'd surely picked the right companion. No man born could ever have resisted Adrienne, of that I was quite certain. These thoughts were in my mind—but dimly, at the back of my mind—as I left her smoking in the dining room and followed her directions to the suite of rooms at the rear of the hotel. In the front of my mind were other thoughts, much more vivid and completely erotic.

I found the suite, entered, left the door slightly ajar behind me.

The thing about an Italian room is its size. An entire suite of rooms is vast. As it happened I was only interested in one room, and Adrienne had obligingly left the door to that one open.

I was sweating. And yet . . . I shivered.

Adrienne had said fifteen minutes, time enough for her to smoke another cigarette and finish her drink. Then she would come to me. By now the entire staff of the hotel probably knew I was in here, but this was Italy.

## V

I shivered again. Excitement? Probably.

I threw off my clothes, found my way to the bathroom, took the quickest shower of my life. Drying myself off, I padded back to the bedroom.

Between the main bedroom and the bathroom a smaller door stood ajar. I froze as I reached it, my senses suddenly alert, my ears seeming to stretch themselves into vast receivers to pick up any slightest sound. For there had been a sound, I was sure of it, from that room. . . .

A scratching? A rustle? A whisper? I couldn't say. But a sound, anyway.

Adrienne would be coming soon. Standing outside that door I slowly recommenced toweling myself dry. My naked feet were still firmly rooted, but my hands automatically worked with the towel. It was nerves, only nerves. There had been no sound, or at worst only the night breeze off the sea, whispering in through an open window.

I stopped toweling, took another step toward the main bedroom, heard the sound again. A small, choking rasp. A tiny gasping for air.

Karpethes? What the hell was going on?

I shivered violently, my suddenly chill flesh shuddering in an uncontrollable spasm. But . . . I forced myself to action, returned to the main bedroom, quickly dressed (with the exceptions of my tie and jacket), and crept back to the small room.

Adrienne must be on her way to me even now. She mustn't find me poking my nose into things, like a suspicious kid. I must kill off this silly feeling that had my skin crawling. Not that an attack of nerves was unnatural in the circumstances, on the contrary, but I wasn't about to let it spoil the night. I pushed open the door of the room, entered into darkness, found the lightswitch. Then—

—I held my breath, flipped the switch.

The room was only half as big as the others. It contained a small single bed, a bedside table, a wardrobe. Nothing more, or at least nothing immediately apparent to my wildly darting eyes. My heart, which was racing, slowed and began to settle toward a steadier beat. The window was open, external shutters closed—but small night sounds were finding their way in through the louvers. The distant sounds of traffic, the toot of horns—holiday sounds from below.

I breathed deeply and gratefully, and saw something projecting from beneath the pillow on the bed. A corner of card or of dark leather, like a wallet or—

—Or a passport!

A Greek passport, Karpethes', when I opened it. But how could it be? The man in the photograph was young, no older than me. His birthdate proved it. And there was his name: Nichos Karpethes. Printed in Greek, of course, but still plain enough. His son?

Puzzling over the passport had served to distract me. My nerves had steadied up. I tossed the passport down, frowned at it where it lay upon the bed, breathed deeply once more . . . and froze solid!

A scratching, a hissing, a dry grunting—from the wardrobe.

Mice? Or did I in fact smell a rat?

Even as the short hairs bristled on the back of my neck I knew anger. There were too many unexplained things here. Too much I didn't understand. And what was it I feared? Old Mario's myths and legends? No, for in my experience the Italians are notorious for getting things wrong. Oh, yes, notorious . . .

I reached out, turned the wardrobe's doorknob, yanked the doors open.

At first I saw nothing of any importance or significance. My eyes didn't know what they sought. Shoes, patent leather, two pairs, stood side by side below. Tiny suits, no bigger than boys' sizes, hung above on steel hangers. And—my God, my God— a waistcoat!

I backed out of that little room on rubber legs, with the silence of the suite shrieking all about me, my eyes bugging, my jaw hanging slack—

"Peter?"

She came in through the suite's main door, came floating toward me, eager, smiling, her green eyes blazing. Then blazing their suspicion, their anger as they saw my condition. "Peter!"

I lurched away as her hands reached for me, those hands I had never yet touched, which had never touched me. Then I was into the main bedroom, snatching my tie and jacket from the bed, (don't ask me why!) and out of the window, yelling some inarticulate, choking thing at her and lashing out frenziedly with my foot as she reached after me. Her eyes were bubbling green hells. *Peter!*

Her fingers closed on my forearm, bands of steel containing a fierce, hungry heat. And strong as two men she began to lift me back into her lair!

I put my feet against the wall, kicked, came

free, and crashed backward into shrubbery. Then up on my feet, gasping for air, running, tumbling, crashing into the night, down madly tilting slopes, through black chasms of mountain pine with the Mediterranean stars winking overhead, and the beckoning, friendly lights of the village seen occasionally below . . .

In the morning, looking up at the way I had descended and remembering the nightmare of my panic-flight, I counted myself lucky to have survived it. The place was precipitous. In the end I *had* fallen, but only for a short distance. All in utter darkness, and my head striking something hard. But . . .

I did survive. Survived both Adrienne and my flight from her.

And waking with the dawn, and gently fingering my bruises and the massive bump on my forehead, I made my staggering way back to my still slumbering hotel, let myself in, and *locked* myself in my room—then sat there trembling and moaning until it was time for the coach.

Weak? Maybe I was, maybe I am.

But on my way into Genova, with people round me and the sun hot through the coach's windows, I could think again. I could roll up my sleeve and examine that claw mark of four slim fingers and a thumb, branded white into my suntanned flesh, where hair would never more grow on skin sere and wrinkled.

And seeing those marks I could also remember the wardrobe and the waistcoat—and what the waistcoat contained.

That tiny puppet of a man, alive still but barely, his stick-arms dangling through the waistcoat's armholes, his baby's head projecting, its chin supported by the tightly buttoned waistcoat's breast. And the large bull-dog clip over the hanger's bar, its teeth fastened in the loose, wrinkled skin of his walnut head, holding it up. And his skinny little legs dangling, twig-things twitching there; and his pleading, pleading eyes!

But eyes are something I mustn't dwell upon. And green is a color I can no longer bear. . . .

# THE MAN UPSTAIRS

# Ray Bradbury

Ray Douglas Bradbury (1920– ) was born in Waukegan, Illinois, and moved to California as a young boy, graduating from Los Angeles High School and, eschewing college, got his first job as a newsboy. He sold his first short story to a pulp magazine, *Super Science Stories*, in 1941 and became a full-time writer the following year. His first book was a collection, *Dark Carnival* (1947). He has since produced more than six hundred stories and sixty books, including such modern classics as *The Martian Chronicles* (1950), *The Illustrated Man* (1951), *Fahrenheit 451* (1953), *The October Country* (1955), *Dandelion Wine* (1957), and *I Sing the Body Electric* (1969).

Many of his works have been filmed for television, most notably the sixty-five stories that he adapted for *The Ray Bradbury Theater* and the three-part miniseries, *The Martian Chronicles*, which starred Rock Hudson in 1980. Films based on his novels include *It Came from Outer Space* (1953), *The Beast from 20,000 Fathoms* (1953), *The Illustrated Man* (1969), and the excellent *Fahrenheit 451* (1966), which starred Oskar Werner and Julie Christie. He has won too many awards to count, including a special Pulitzer citation, a star on Hollywood Boulevard's Hollywood Walk of Fame, the Bram Stoker Award, the World Fantasy and SFWA lifetime achievement awards, and the National Book Foundation Medal for Distinguished Contribution to American Letters.

"The Man Upstairs" was originally published in the March 1947 issue of *Harper's Magazine*.

# The Man Upstairs

## RAY BRADBURY

he remembered how carefully and expertly Grandmother would fondle the cold cut guts of the chicken and withdraw the marvels therein; the wet shining loops of meat-smelling intestine, the muscled lump of heart, the gizzard with the collection of seeds in it. How neatly and nicely Grandma would slit the chicken and push her fat little hand in to deprive it of its medals. These would be segregated, some in pans of water, others in paper to be thrown to the dog later, perhaps. And then the ritual of taxidermy, stuffing the bird with watered, seasoned bread, and performing surgery with a swift, bright needle, stitch after pulled-tight stitch.

This was one of the prime thrills of Douglas's eleven-year-old life span.

Altogether, he counted twenty knives in the various squeaking drawers of the magic kitchen table from which Grandma, a kindly, gentle-faced, white-haired old witch, drew paraphernalia for her miracles.

Douglas was to be quiet. He could stand across the table from Grandma, his freckled nose tucked over the edge, watching, but any loose boy-talk might interfere with the spell. It was a wonder when Grandma brandished silver shakers over the bird, supposedly sprinkling showers of mummy-dust and pulverized Indian bones, muttering mystical verses under her toothless breath.

"Grammy," said Douglas at last, breaking the silence. "Am I like that inside?" He pointed at the chicken.

"Yes," said Grandma. "A little more orderly and presentable, but just about the same. . . ."

"And more *of* it!" added Douglas, proud of his guts.

"Yes," said Grandma. "More of it."

"Grandpa has lots more'n me. His sticks out in front so he can rest his elbows on it."

Grandma laughed and shook her head.

Douglas said, "And Lucie Williams, down the street, she . . ."

"Hush, child!" cried Grandma.

"But she's got . . ."

"Never you mind what she's got! That's different."

"But why is *she* different?"

"A darning-needle dragon-fly is coming by some day and sew up your mouth," said Grandma firmly.

Douglas waited, then asked, "How do you know I've got insides like that, Grandma?"

"Oh, go 'way, now!"

The front doorbell rang.

Through the front-door glass as he ran down the hall, Douglas saw a straw hat. The bell jangled again and again. Douglas opened the door.

"Good morning, child, is the landlady at home?"

Cold gray eyes in a long, smooth, walnut-colored face gazed upon Douglas. The man was tall, thin, and carried a suitcase, a briefcase, an umbrella under one bent arm, gloves rich and thick and gray on his thin fingers, and wore a horribly new straw hat.

Douglas backed up. "She's busy."

"I wish to rent her upstairs room, as advertised."

"We've got ten boarders, and it's already rented; go away!"

"Douglas!" Grandma was behind him suddenly. "How do you do?" she said to the stranger. "Never mind this child."

Unsmiling, the man stepped stiffly in. Douglas watched them ascend out of sight up the stairs, heard Grandma detailing the conveniences of the upstairs room. Soon she hurried down to pile linens from the linen closet on Douglas and send him scooting up with them.

Douglas paused at the room's threshold. The room was changed oddly, simply because the stranger had been in it a moment. The straw hat lay brittle and terrible upon the bed, the umbrella leaned stiff against one wall like a dead bat with dark wings folded.

Douglas blinked at the umbrella.

The stranger stood in the center of the changed room, tall, tall.

"Here!" Douglas littered the bed with supplies. "We eat at noon sharp, and if you're late coming down the soup'll get cold. Grandma fixes it so it will, every time!"

The tall strange man counted out ten new copper pennies and tinkled them in Douglas's blouse pocket. "We shall be friends," he said, grimly.

It was funny, the man having nothing but pennies. Lots of them. No silver at all, no dimes, no quarters. Just new copper pennies.

Douglas thanked him glumly. "I'll drop these in my dime bank when I get them changed into a dime. I got six dollars and fifty cents in dimes all ready for my camp trip in August."

"I must wash now," said the tall strange man.

Once, at midnight, Douglas had wakened to hear a storm rumbling outside—the cold hard wind shaking the house, the rain driving against the window. And then a lightning bolt had landed outside the window with a silent, terrific concussion. He remembered that fear of looking about at his room, seeing it strange and awful in the instantaneous light.

So it was, now, in this room. He stood looking up at the stranger. This room was no longer the same, but changed indefinably because this man, quick as a lightning bolt, had shed his light about it. Douglas backed up slowly as the stranger advanced.

The door closed in his face.

T he wooden fork went up with mashed potatoes, came down empty. Mr. Koberman, for that was his name, had brought the wooden fork and wooden knife and spoon with him when Grandma called lunch.

"Mrs. Spaulding," he said, quietly, "my own cutlery; please use it. I will have lunch today, but from tomorrow on, only breakfast and supper."

Grandma bustled in and out, bearing steaming tureens of soup and beans and mashed potatoes to impress her new boarder, while Douglas sat rattling his silverware on his plate, because he had discovered it irritated Mr. Koberman.

"I know a trick," said Douglas. "Watch." He picked a fork-tine with his fingernail. He pointed at various sectors of the table, like a magician. Wherever he pointed, the sound of the vibrating fork-tine emerged, like a metal elfin voice. Simply done, of course. He pressed the fork handle on the table-top, secretly. The vibration came from the wood like a sounding board. It looked quite magical. "There, there, and *there*!" exclaimed Douglas, happily plucking the fork again. He pointed at Mr. Koberman's soup and the noise came from it.

Mr. Koberman's walnut-colored face became

hard and firm and awful. He pushed the soup bowl away violently, his lips twisting. He fell back in his chair.

Grandma appeared. "Why, what's wrong, Mr. Koberman?"

"I cannot eat this soup."

"Why?"

"Because I am full and can eat no more. Thank you."

Mr. Koberman left the room, glaring.

"What did you do, just then?" asked Grandma at Douglas, sharply.

"Nothing. Grandma, why does he eat with *wooden* spoons?"

"Yours not to question! When do you go back to school, anyway?"

"Seven weeks."

"Oh, my lord!" said Grandma.

M r. Koberman worked nights. Each morning at eight he arrived mysteriously home, devoured a very small breakfast, and then slept soundlessly in his room all through the dreaming hot daytime, until the huge supper with all the other boarders at night.

Mr. Koberman's sleeping habits made it necessary for Douglas to be quiet. This was unbearable. So, whenever Grandma visited down the street, Douglas stomped up and down stairs beating a drum, bouncing golf balls, or just screaming for three minutes outside Mr. Koberman's door, or flushing the toilet seven times in succession.

Mr. Koberman never moved. His room was silent, dark. He did not complain. There was no sound. He slept on and on. It was very strange.

Douglas felt a pure white flame of hatred burn inside himself with a steady, unflickering beauty. Now that room was Koberman Land. Once it had been flowery bright when Miss Sadlowe lived there. Now it was stark, bare, cold, clean, everything in its place, alien and brittle.

Douglas climbed upstairs on the fourth morning.

Halfway to the second floor was a large sun-filled window, framed by six-inch panes of orange, purple, blue, red, and burgundy glass. In the enchanted early mornings when the sun fell through to strike the landing and slide down the stair banister, Douglas stood entranced at this window peering at the world through the multi-colored panes.

Now a blue world, a blue sky, blue people, blue streetcars, and blue trotting dogs.

He shifted panes. Now—an amber world! Two lemonish women glided by, resembling the daughters of Fu Manchu! Douglas giggled. This pane made even the sunlight more purely golden.

It was eight a.m. Mr. Koberman strolled by below, on the sidewalk, returning from his night's work, his umbrella looped over his elbow, straw hat glued to his head with patent oil.

Douglas shifted panes again. Mr. Koberman was a red man walking through a red world with red trees and red flowers and—something else.

Something about—Mr. Koberman.

Douglas squinted.

The red glass *did* things to Mr. Koberman. His face, his suit, his hands. The clothes seemed to melt away. Douglas almost believed, for one terrible instant, that he could see *inside* Mr. Koberman. And what he saw made him lean wildly against the small red pane, blinking.

Mr. Koberman glanced up just then, saw Douglas, and raised his umbrella angrily, as if to strike. He ran swiftly across the red lawn to the front door.

"Young man!" he cried, running up the stairs. "What were you doing?"

"Just looking," said Douglas, numbly.

"That's all, is it?" cried Mr. Koberman.

"Yes, sir. I look through all the glasses. All kinds of worlds. Blue ones, red ones, yellow ones. All different."

"All kinds of worlds, is it!" Mr. Koberman glanced at the little panes of glass, his face pale. He got hold of himself. He wiped his face with a handkerchief and pretended to laugh. "Yes. All kinds of worlds. All different." He walked to the door of his room. "Go right ahead; play," he said.

The door closed. The hall was empty. Mr. Koberman had gone in.

Douglas shrugged and found a new pane. "Oh, everything's violet!"

half an hour later, while playing in his sandbox behind the house, Douglas heard the crash and the shattering tinkle. He leaped up.

A moment later, Grandma appeared on the back porch, the old razor strop trembling in her hand.

"Douglas! I told you time and again never fling your basketball against the house! Oh, I could just cry!"

"I been sitting right here," he protested.

"Come see what you've done, you nasty boy!"

The great colored window panes lay shattered in a rainbow chaos on the upstairs landing. His basketball lay in the ruins.

Before he could even begin telling his innocence, Douglas was struck a dozen stinging blows upon his rump. Wherever he landed, screaming, the razor strop struck again.

Later, hiding his mind in the sandpile like an ostrich, Douglas nursed his dreadful pains. He knew who'd thrown that basketball. A man with a straw hat and a stiff umbrella and a cold, gray room. Yeah, yeah, yeah. He dribbled tears. Just wait. Just *wait*.

He heard Grandma sweeping up the broken glass. She brought it out and threw it in the trash bin. Blue, pink, yellow meteors of glass dropped brightly down.

When she was gone, Douglas dragged himself, whimpering, over to save out three pieces of the incredible glass. Mr. Koberman disliked the colored windows. These—he clinked them in his fingers—would be worth saving.

grandfather arrived from his newspaper office each night, shortly ahead of the other boarders, at five o'clock. When a slow, heavy tread filled the hall, and a thick, mahogany cane thumped in the cane-rack, Douglas ran to embrace the large stomach and sit on Grandpa's knee while he read the evening paper.

"Hi, Grampa!"

"Hello, down there!"

"Grandma cut chickens again today. It's fun watching," said Douglas.

Grandpa kept reading. "That's twice this week, chickens. She's the chickenist woman. You like to watch her cut 'em, eh? Cold-blooded little pepper! Ha!"

"I'm just curious."

"You are," rumbled Grandpa, scowling. "Remember that day when that young lady was killed at the rail station? You just walked over and looked at her, blood and all." He laughed. "Queer duck. Stay that way. Fear nothing, ever in your life. I guess you get it from your father, him being a military man and all, and you so close to him before you came here to live last year." Grandpa returned to his paper.

A long pause. "Gramps?"

"Yes?"

"What if a man didn't have a heart or lungs or stomach but still walked around, alive?"

"That," rumbled Gramps, "would be a miracle."

"I don't mean a—a miracle. I mean, what if he was all *different* inside? Not like me."

"Well, he wouldn't be quite human then, would he, boy?"

"Guess not, Gramps. Gramps, you got a heart and lungs?"

Gramps chuckled. "Well, tell the truth, I don't *know*. Never seen them. Never had an X-ray, never been to a doctor. Might as well be potato-solid for all I know."

"Have *I* got a stomach?"

"You certainly have!" cried Grandma from the parlor entry. "'Cause I feed it! And you've lungs, you scream loud enough to wake the crumblees. And you've dirty hands, go wash them! Dinner's ready. Grandpa, come on. Douglas, git!"

In the rush of boarders streaming downstairs, Grandpa, if he intended questioning Douglas further about the weird conversation, lost his opportunity. If dinner delayed an instant more, Grandma and the potatoes would develop simultaneous lumps.

The boarders, laughing and talking at the table—Mr. Koberman silent and sullen among them—were silenced when Grandfather cleared his throat. He talked politics a few minutes and then shifted over into the intriguing topic of the recent peculiar deaths in the town.

"It's enough to make an old newspaper editor prick up his ears," he said, eying them all. "That young Miss Larson, lived across the ravine, now. Found her dead three days ago for no reason, just funny kinds of tattoos all over her, and a facial expression that would make Dante cringe. And that other young lady, what was her name? Whitely? She disappeared and *never did* come back."

"Them things happen alla time," said Mr. Britz, the garage mechanic, chewing. "Ever peek inna Missing Peoples Bureau file? It's *that* long." He illustrated. "Can't tell *what* happens to most of 'em."

"Anyone want more dressing?" Grandma ladled liberal portions from the chicken's interior. Douglas watched, thinking about how that chicken had had two kinds of guts—God-made and Man-made.

Well, how about *three* kinds of guts?

Eh?

Why not?

Conversation continued about the mysterious death of so-and-so, and, oh, yes, remember a week ago, Marion Barsumian died of heart failure, but maybe that didn't connect up? or did it? you're crazy! forget it, why talk about it at the dinner table? So.

"Never can tell," said Mr. Britz. "Maybe we got a vampire in town."

Mr. Koberman stopped eating.

"In the year 1927?" said Grandma. "A vampire? Oh go on, now."

"Sure," said Mr. Britz. "Kill 'em with silver bullets. Anything silver for that matter. Vampires

*hate* silver. I read it in a book somewhere, once. Sure, I did."

Douglas looked at Mr. Koberman who ate with wooden knives and forks and carried only new copper pennies in his pocket.

"It's poor judgment," said Grandpa, "to call anything by a name. We don't know what a hobgoblin or a vampire or a troll is. Could be lots of things. You can't heave them into categories with labels and say they'll act one way or another. That'd be silly. They're people. People who do things. Yes, that's the way to put it: people who *do* things."

"Excuse me," said Mr. Koberman, who got up and went out for his evening walk to work.

The stars, the moon, the wind, the clock ticking, and the chiming of the hours into dawn, the sun rising, and here it was another morning, another day, and Mr. Koberman coming along the sidewalk from his night's work. Douglas stood off like a small mechanism whirring and watching with carefully microscopic eyes.

At noon, Grandma went to the store to buy groceries.

As was his custom every day when Grandma was gone, Douglas yelled outside Mr. Koberman's door for a full three minutes. As usual, there was no response. The silence was horrible.

He ran downstairs, got the pass-key, a silver fork, and the three pieces of colored glass he had saved from the shattered window. He fitted the key to the lock and swung the door slowly open.

The room was in half light, the shades drawn. Mr. Koberman lay atop his bedcovers, in slumber clothes, breathing gently, up and down. He didn't move. His face was motionless.

"Hello, Mr. Koberman!"

The colorless walls echoed the man's regular breathing.

"Mr. Koberman, hello!"

Bouncing a golf ball, Douglas advanced. He yelled. Still no answer. "Mr. Koberman!"

Bending over Mr. Koberman, Douglas picked

the tines of the silver fork in the sleeping man's face.

Mr. Koberman winced. He twisted. He groaned bitterly.

Response. Good. Swell.

Douglas drew a piece of blue glass from his pocket. Looking through the blue glass fragment he found himself in a blue room, in a blue world different from the world he knew. As different as was the red world. Blue furniture, blue bed, blue ceiling and walls, blue wooden eating utensils atop the blue bureau, and the sullen dark blue of Mr. Koberman's face and arms and his blue chest rising, falling. Also . . .

Mr. Koberman's eyes were wide, staring at him with a hungry darkness.

Douglas fell back, pulled the blue glass from his eyes.

Mr. Koberman's eyes were shut.

Blue glass again—open. Blue glass away—shut. Blue glass again—open. Away—shut. Funny. Douglas experimented, trembling. Through the glass the eyes seemed to peer hungrily, avidly, through Mr. Koberman's closed lids. Without the blue glass they seemed tightly shut.

But it was the rest of Mr. Koberman's body . . .

Mr. Koberman's bedclothes dissolved off him. The blue glass had something to do with it. Or perhaps it was the clothes themselves, just being *on* Mr. Koberman. Douglas cried out.

He was looking through the wall of Mr. Koberman's stomach, right *inside* him!

Mr. Koberman was solid.

Or, nearly so, anyway.

There were strange shapes and sizes within him.

Douglas must have stood amazed for five minutes, thinking about the blue worlds, the red worlds, the yellow worlds side by side, living together like glass panes around the big white stair window. Side by side, the colored panes, the different worlds; Mr. Koberman had said so himself.

So this was why the colored window had been broken.

"Mr. Koberman, wake up!"

No answer.

"Mr. Koberman, where do you work at night? Mr. Koberman, where do you work?"

A little breeze stirred the blue window shade.

"In a red world or a green world or a yellow one, Mr. Koberman?"

Over everything was a blue glass silence.

"Wait there," said Douglas.

He walked down to the kitchen, pulled open the great squeaking drawer and picked out the sharpest, biggest knife.

Very calmly he walked into the hall, climbed back up the stairs again, opened the door to Mr. Koberman's room, went in, and closed it, holding the sharp knife in one hand.

**G**randma was busy fingering a piecrust into a pan when Douglas entered the kitchen to place something on the table.

"Grandma, what's this?"

She glanced up briefly, over her glasses. "I don't know."

It was square, like a box, and elastic. It was bright orange in color. It had four square tubes, colored blue, attached to it. It smelled funny.

"Ever see anything like it, Grandma?"

"No."

"That's what *I* thought."

Douglas left it there, went from the kitchen. Five minutes later he returned with something else. "How about *this*?"

He laid down a bright pink linked chain with a purple triangle at one end.

"Don't bother me," said Grandma. "It's only a chain."

Next time he returned with two hands full. A ring, a square, a triangle, a pyramid, a rectangle, and—other shapes. All of them were pliable, resilient, and looked as if they were made of gelatin. "This isn't all," said Douglas, putting them down. "There's more where this came from."

Grandma said, "Yes, yes," in a far-off tone, very busy.

"You were wrong, Grandma."

"About what?"

"About all people being the same inside."

"Stop talking nonsense."

"Where's my piggy-bank?"

"On the mantel, where you left it."

"Thanks."

He tromped into the parlor, reached up for his piggy-bank.

Grandpa came home from the office at five.

"Grandpa, come upstairs."

"Sure, son. Why?"

"Something to show you. It's not nice; but it's interesting."

Grandpa chuckled, following his grandson's feet up to Mr. Koberman's room.

"Grandma mustn't know about this; she wouldn't like it," said Douglas. He pushed the door wide open. "There."

Grandfather gasped.

D ouglas remembered the next few hours all the rest of his life. Standing over Mr. Koberman's naked body, the coroner and his assistants. Grandma, downstairs, asking somebody, "What's going on up there?" and Grandpa saying, shakily, "I'll take Douglas away on a long vacation so he can forget this whole ghastly affair. Ghastly, ghastly affair!"

Douglas said, "Why should it be bad? I don't see anything bad. I don't feel bad."

The coroner shivered and said, "Koberman's dead, all right."

His assistant sweated. "Did you see those *things* in the pans of water and in the wrapping paper?"

"Oh, my God, my God, yes, I saw them."

"Christ."

The coroner bent over Mr. Koberman's body again. "This better be kept secret, boys. It wasn't murder. It was a mercy the boy acted. God knows what might have happened if he hadn't."

"What was Koberman? A vampire? A monster?"

"Maybe. I don't know. Something—not human." The coroner moved his hands deftly over the suture.

Douglas was proud of his work. He'd gone to much trouble. He had watched Grandmother carefully and remembered. Needle and thread and all. All in all, Mr. Koberman was as neat a job as any chicken ever popped into hell by Grandma.

"I heard the boy say that Koberman lived even after all those *things* were taken out of him." The coroner looked at the triangles and chains and pyramids floating in the pans of water. "Kept on *living*. God."

"Did the boy say that?"

"He did."

"Then, what *did* kill Koberman?"

The coroner drew a few strands of sewing thread from their bedding.

"This. . . ." he said.

Sunlight blinked coldly off a half-revealed treasure trove; six dollars and sixty cents' worth of silver dimes inside Mr. Koberman's chest.

"I think Douglas made a wise investment," said the coroner, sewing the flesh back up over the "dressing" quickly.

# CHASTEL

# Manly Wade Wellman

Manly Wade Wellman (1903–86) was born in Kamundongo, Portuguese West Africa (now Angola), the son of a physician at a British medical outpost. He moved to Washington, D.C., as a child, eventually graduating with a B.A. in English from what is now Wichita State University, then receiving an LL.B. from Columbia Law School. He worked as a reporter for two Wichita newspapers, the *Beacon* and the *Eagle,* then moved to New York in 1939 to become the assistant director of the WPA's Folklore Project.

He began writing, mainly in the horror field, in the 1920s and by the 1930s was selling stories to the leading pulps in the genre: *Weird Tales, Wonder Stories,* and *Astounding Stories.* He had three series running simultaneously in *Weird Tales,* featuring the characters Silver John, also know as John the Balladeer, the backwoods minstrel with a silver-stringed guitar; John Thunstone, the New York playboy and adventurer who was also a psychic detective; and Judge Keith Hilary Persuivant, an elderly occult detective, which he wrote under the pseudonym Gans T. Fields.

Wellman also wrote for the comic books, producing the first Captain Marvel issue for Fawcett Publications. When DC Comics sued Fawcett for plagiarizing their Superman character, Wellman testified against Fawcett, and DC won the case after three years of litigation.

"Chastel" was originally published in *The Year's Best Horror Stories VII,* edited by Gerald W. Page (New York: DAW, 1979).

# Chastel

## MANLY WADE WELLMAN

**T**hen you won't let Count Dracula rest in his tomb?" inquired Lee Cobbett, his square face creasing with a grin.

Five of them sat in the parlor of Judge Keith Hilary Pursuivant's hotel suite on Central Park West. The Judge lounged in an armchair, a wineglass in his big old hand. On this, his eighty-seventh birthday, his blue eyes were clear, penetrating. His once tawny hair and mustache had gone blizzard-white, but both grew thick, and his square face showed rosy. In his tailored blue leisure suit, he still looked powerfully deep-chested and broad-shouldered.

Blocky Lee Cobbett wore jacket and slacks almost as brown as his face. Next to him sat Laurel Parcher, small and young and cinnamon-haired. The others were natty Phil Drumm the summer theater producer, and Isobel Arrington from a wire press service. She was blond, expensively dressed, she smoked a dark cigarette with a white tip. Her pen scribbled swiftly.

"Dracula's as much alive as Sherlock Holmes," argued Drumm. "All the revivals of the play, all the films—"

"Your musical should wake the dead, anyway," said Cobbett, drinking. "What's your main number, Phil? 'Garlic Time?' 'Gory, Gory Hallelujah'?"

"Let's have Christian charity here, Lee," Pursuivant came to Drumm's rescue. "Anyway, Miss Arrington came to interview me. Pour her some wine and let me try to answer her questions."

"I'm interested in Mr. Cobbett's remarks," said Isobel Arrington, her voice deliberately throaty. "He's an authority on the supernatural."

"Well, perhaps," admitted Cobbett, "and Miss Parcher has had some experiences. But Judge Pursuivant is the true authority, the author of *Vampiricon*."

"I've read it, in paperback," said Isobel Arrington. "Phil, it mentions a vampire belief up in Connecticut, where you're having your show. What's that town again?"

"Deslow," he told her. "We're making a wonderful old stone barn into a theater. I've invited Lee and Miss Parcher to visit."

She looked at Drumm. "Is Deslow a resort town?"

"Not yet, but maybe the show will bring tourists. In Deslow, up to now, peace and quiet is the chief business. If you drop your shoe, everybody in town will think somebody's blowing the safe."

855

"Deslow's not far from Jewett City," observed Pursuivant. "There were vampires there about a century and a quarter ago. A family named Ray was afflicted. And to the east, in Rhode Island, there was a lively vampire folklore in recent years."

"Let's leave Rhode Island to H. P. Lovecraft's imitators," suggested Cobbett. "What do you call your show, Phil?"

"*The Land Beyond the Forest,*" said Drumm. "We're casting it now. Using locals in bit parts. But we have Gonda Chastel to play Dracula's countess."

"I never knew that Dracula had a countess," said Laurel Parcher.

"There was a stage star named Chastel, long ago when I was young," said Pursuivant. "Just the one name—Chastel."

"Gonda's her daughter, and a year or so ago Gonda came to live in Deslow," Drumm told them. "Her mother's buried there. Gonda has invested in our production."

"Is that why she has a part in it?" asked Isobel Arrington.

"She has a part in it because she's beautiful and gifted," replied Drumm, rather stuffily. "Old people say she's the very picture of her mother. Speaking of pictures, here are some to prove it."

He offered two glossy prints to Isobel Arrington, who murmured "Very sweet," and passed them to Laurel Parcher. Cobbett leaned to see.

One picture seemed copied from an older one. It showed a woman who stood with unconscious stateliness, in a gracefully draped robe with a tiara binding her rich flow of dark hair. The other picture was of a woman in fashionable evening dress, her hair ordered in modern fashion, with a face strikingly like that of the woman in the other photograph.

"Oh, she's lovely," said Laurel. "Isn't she, Lee?"

"Isn't she?" echoed Drumm.

"Magnificent," said Cobbett, handing the pictures to Pursuivant, who studied them gravely.

"Chastel was in Richmond, just after the First World War," he said slowly. "A dazzling Lady Macbeth. I was in love with her. Everyone was."

"Did you tell her you loved her?" asked Laurel.

"Yes. We had supper together, twice. Then she went ahead with her tour, and I sailed to England and studied at Oxford. I never saw her again, but she's more or less why I never married."

Silence a moment. Then: "*The Land Beyond the Forest,*" Laurel repeated. "Isn't there a book called that?"

"There is indeed, my child," said the Judge. "By Emily de Laszowska Gerard. About Transylvania, where Dracula came from."

"That's why we use the title, that's what Transylvania means," put in Drumm. "It's all right, the book's out of copyright. But I'm surprised to find someone who's heard of it."

"I'll protect your guilty secret, Phil," promised Isobel Arrington. "What's over there in your window, Judge?"

Pursuivant turned to look. "Whatever it is," he said, "it's not Peter Pan."

Cobbett sprang up and ran toward the half-draped window. A silhouette with head and shoulders hung in the June night. He had a glimpse of a face, rich-mouthed, with bright eyes. Then it was gone. Laurel had hurried up behind him. He hoisted the window sash and leaned out.

Nothing. The street was fourteen stories down. The lights of moving cars crawled distantly. The wall below was course after course of dull brick, with recesses of other windows to right and left, below, above. Cobbett studied the wall, his hands braced on the sill.

"Be careful, Lee," Laurel's voice besought him.

He came back to face the others. "Nobody out there," he said evenly. "Nobody could have been. It's just a wall—nothing to hang to. Even that sill would be tricky to stand on."

"But I saw something, and so did Judge Pursuivant," said Isobel Arrington, the cigarette trembling in her fingers.

"So did I," said Cobbett. "Didn't you, Laurel?"

"Only a face."

Isobel Arrington was calm again. "If it's a trick, Phil, you played a good one. But don't expect me to put it in my story."

Drumm shook his head nervously. "I didn't play any trick, I swear."

"Don't try this on old friends," she jabbed at him. "First those pictures, then whatever was up against the glass. I'll use the pictures, but I won't write that a weird vision presided over this birthday party."

"How about a drink all around?" suggested Pursuivant.

He poured for them. Isobel Arrington wrote down answers to more questions, then said she must go. Drumm rose to escort her. "You'll be at Deslow tomorrow, Lee?" he asked.

"And Laurel, too. You said we could find quarters there."

"The Mapletree's a good auto court," said Drumm. "I've already reserved cabins for the two of you."

"On the spur of the moment," said Pursuivant suddenly, "I think I'll come along, if there's space for me."

"I'll check it out for you, Judge," said Drumm.

He departed with Isobel Arrington. Cobbett spoke to Pursuivant. "Isn't that rather offhand?" he asked. "Deciding to come with us?"

"I was thinking about Chastel." Pursuivant smiled gently. "About making a pilgrimage to her grave."

"We'll drive up about nine tomorrow morning."

"I'll be ready, Lee."

Cobbett and Laurel, too, went out. They walked down a flight of stairs to the floor below, where both their rooms were located. "Do you think Phil Drumm rigged up that illusion for us?" asked Cobbett.

"If he did, he used the face of that actress, Chastel."

He glanced keenly at her. "You saw that."

"I thought I did, and so did you."

They kissed good night at the door to her room.

Pursuivant was ready next morning when Cobbett knocked. He had only one suitcase and a thick, brown-blotched malacca cane, banded with silver below its curved handle.

"I'm taking only a few necessaries, I'll buy socks and such things in Deslow if we stay more than a couple of days," he said. "No, don't carry it for me, I'm quite capable."

When they reached the hotel garage, Laurel was putting her luggage in the trunk of Cobbett's black sedan. Judge Pursuivant declined the front seat beside Cobbett, held the door for Laurel to get in, and sat in the rear. They rolled out into bright June sunlight.

Cobbett drove them east on Interstate 95, mile after mile along the Connecticut shore, past service stations, markets, sandwich shops. Now and then they glimpsed Long Island Sound to the right. At toll gates, Cobbett threw quarters into hoppers and drove on.

"New Rochelle to Port Chester," Laurel half chanted, "Norwalk, Bridgeport, Stratford—"

"Where, in 1851, devils plagued a minister's home," put in Pursuivant.

"The names make a poem," said Laurel.

"You can get that effect by reading any timetable," said Cobbett. "We miss a couple of good names—Mystic and Giants Neck, though they aren't far off from our route. And Griswold—that means Gray Woods—where the Judge's book says Horace Ray was born."

"There's no Griswold on the Connecticut map anymore," said the Judge.

"Vanished?" said Laurel. "Maybe it appears at just a certain time of the day, along about sundown."

She laughed, but the Judge was grave.

"Here we'll pass by New Haven," he said. "I was at Yale here, seventy years ago."

They rolled across the Connecticut River between Old Saybrook and Old Lyme. Outside New London, Cobbett turned them north on State Highway 82 and, near Jewett City, took a two-lane road that brought them into Deslow, not long after noon.

There were pleasant clapboard cottages among elm trees and flower beds. Main Street had bright shops with, farther along, the belfry of a sturdy old church. Cobbett drove them to a sign saying MAPLETREE COURT. A row of cabins faced along a cement-floored colonnade, their fronts painted white with blue doors and window frames. In the office, Phil Drumm stood at the desk, talking to the plump proprietress.

"Welcome home," he greeted them. "Judge, I was asking Mrs. Simpson here to reserve you a cabin."

"At the far end of the row, sir," the lady said. "I'd have put you next to your two friends, but so many theater folks have already moved in."

"Long ago I learned to be happy with any shelter," the Judge assured her.

They saw Laurel to her cabin and put her suitcases inside, then walked to the farthest cabin where Pursuivant would stay. Finally Drumm followed Cobbett to the space next to Laurel's. Inside, Cobbett produced a fifth of bourbon from his briefcase. Drumm trotted away to fetch ice. Pursuivant came to join them.

"It's good of you to look after us," Cobbett said to Drumm above his glass.

"Oh, I'll get my own back," Drumm assured him. "The Judge and you, distinguished folklore experts—I'll have you in all the papers."

"Whatever you like," said Cobbett. "Let's have lunch, as soon as Laurel is freshened up."

The four ate crab cakes and flounder at a little restaurant while Drumm talked about *The Land Beyond the Forest*. He had signed the minor film star Caspar Merrick to play Dracula. "He has a fine baritone singing voice," said Drumm. "He'll be at afternoon rehearsal."

"And Gonda Chastel?" inquired Pursuivant, buttering a roll.

"She'll be there tonight." Drumm sounded happy about that. "This afternoon's mostly for bits and chorus numbers. I'm directing as well as producing." They finished their lunch, and Drumm rose. "If you're not tired, come see our theater."

It was only a short walk through town to the converted barn. Cobbett judged it had been built in Colonial times, with a recent roof of composition tile, but with walls of stubborn, brown-gray New England stone. Across a narrow side street stood the old white church, with a hedge-bordered cemetery.

"Quaint, that old burying ground," commented Drumm. "Nobody's spaded under there now, there's a modern cemetery on the far side, but Chastel's tomb is there. Quite a picturesque one."

"I'd like to see it," said Pursuivant, leaning on his silver-banded cane.

The barn's interior was set with rows of folding chairs, enough for several hundred spectators. On a stage at the far end, workmen moved here and there under lights. Drumm led his guests up steps at the side.

High in the loft, catwalks zigzagged and a dark curtain hung like a broad guillotine blade. Drumm pointed out canvas flats, painted to resemble grim castle walls. Pursuivant nodded and questioned.

"I'm no authority on what you might find in Transylvania," he said, "but this looks convincing."

A man walked from the wings toward them. "Hello, Caspar," Drumm greeted him. "I want you to meet Judge Pursuivant and Lee Cobbett. And Miss Laurel Parcher, of course." He gestured the introductions. "This is Mr. Caspar Merrick, our Count Dracula."

Merrick was elegantly tall, handsome, with carefully groomed black hair. Sweepingly he bowed above Laurel's hand and smiled at them all. "Judge Pursuivant's writings I know, of course," he said richly. "I read what I can about vampires, inasmuch as I'm to be one."

"Places for the Delusion number!" called a stage manager.

Cobbett, Pursuivant, and Laurel went down the steps and sat on chairs. Eight men and eight girls hurried into view, dressed in knockabout summer clothes. Someone struck chords on a piano, Drumm gestured importantly, and the chorus sang. Merritt, coming downstage, took solo on a verse. All joined in the refrain. Then Drumm made them sing it over again.

After that, two comedians made much of confusing the words vampire and empire. Cobbett found it tedious. He excused himself to his companions and strolled out and across to the old, tree-crowded churchyard.

The gravestones bore interesting epitaphs: not only the familiar PAUSE O STRANGER PASSING BY/AS YOU ARE NOW SO ONCE WAS I, and A BUD ON EARTH TO BLOOM IN HEAVEN, but several of more originality. One bewailed a man who, since he had been lost at sea, could hardly have been there at all. Another bore, beneath a bat-winged face, the declaration DEATH PAYS ALL DEBTS and the date 1907, which Cobbett associated with a financial panic.

Toward the center of the graveyard, under a drooping willow, stood a shedlike structure of heavy granite blocks. Cobbett picked his way to the door of heavy grillwork, which was fastened with a rusty padlock the size of a sardine can. On the lintel were strongly carved letters: CHASTEL.

Here, then, was the tomb of the stage beauty Pursuivant remembered so romantically. Cobbett peered through the bars.

It was murkily dusty in there. The floor was coarsely flagged, and among sooty shadows at the rear stood a sort of stone chest that must contain the body. Cobbett turned and went back to the theater. Inside, piano music rang wildly and the people of the chorus desperately rehearsed what must be meant for a folk dance.

"Oh, it's exciting," said Laurel as Cobbett sat down beside her. "Where have you been?"

"Visiting the tomb of Chastel."

"Chastel?" echoed Pursuivant. "I must see that tomb."

Songs and dance ensembles went on. In the midst of them, a brisk reporter from Hartford appeared, to interview Pursuivant and Cobbett. At last Drumm resoundingly dismissed the players on stage and joined his guests.

"Principals rehearse at eight o'clock," he announced. "Gonda Chastel will be here, she'll want to meet you. Could I count on you then?"

"Count on me, at least," said Pursuivant. "Just now, I feel like resting before dinner, and so, I think, does Laurel here."

"Yes, I'd like to lie down for a little," said Laurel.

"Why don't we all meet for dinner at the place where we had lunch?" said Cobbett. "You come too, Phil."

"Thanks, I have a date with some backers from New London."

It was half-past five when they went out.

Cobbett went to his quarters, stretched out on the bed, and gave himself to thought.

He hadn't come to Deslow because of this musical interpretation of the Dracula legend. Laurel had come because he was coming, and Pursuivant on a sudden impulse that might have been more than a wish to visit the grave of Chastel. But Cobbett was here because this, he knew, had been vampire country, maybe still was vampire country.

He remembered the story in Pursuivant's book about vampires at Jewett City, as reported in the Norwich *Courier* for 1854. Horace Ray, from the now vanished town of Griswold, had died of a "wasting disease." Thereafter his oldest son, then his second son had also gone to their graves. When a third son sickened, friends and relatives dug up Horace Ray and the two dead brothers and burned the bodies in a roaring fire. The surviving son got well. And something like that had happened in Exeter, near Providence in Rhode Island. Very well, why organize and present the Dracula musical here in Deslow, so near those places?

Cobbett had met Phil Drumm in the South the year before, knew him for a brilliant if erratic producer, who relished tales of devils and the dead who walk by night. Drumm might have known enough stage magic to have rigged that seeming appearance at Pursuivant's window in New York. That is, if indeed it was only a seeming appearance, not a real face. Might it have been real, a manifestation of the unreal? Cobbett had seen enough of what people dismissed as unreal, impossible, to wonder.

A soft knock came at the door. It was Laurel. She wore green slacks, a green jacket, and she smiled, as always, at sight of Cobbett's face. They sought Pursuivant's cabin. A note on the door said: MEET ME AT THE CAFÉ.

When they entered there, Pursuivant hailed them from the kitchen door. "Dinner's ready," he hailed them. "I've been supervising in person, and I paid well for the privilege."

A waiter brought a laden tray. He arranged platters of red-drenched spaghetti and bowls of salad on a table. Pursuivant himself sprinkled Parmesan cheese. "No salt or pepper," he warned. "I seasoned it myself, and you can take my word it's exactly right."

Cobbett poured red wine into glasses. Laurel took a forkful of spaghetti. "Delicious," she cried. "What's in it, Judge?"

"Not only ground beef and tomatoes and onions and garlic," replied Pursuivant. "I added marjoram and green pepper and chile and thyme and bay leaf and oregano and parsley and a couple of other important ingredients. And I also minced in some Italian sausage."

Cobbett, too, ate with enthusiastic appetite. "I won't order any dessert," he declared. "I want to keep the taste of this in my mouth."

"There's more in the kitchen for dessert if you want it," the Judge assured him. "But here, I have a couple of keepsakes for you."

He handed each of them a small, silvery object. Cobbett examined his. It was smoothly wrapped in foil. He wondered if it was a nutmeat.

"You have pockets, I perceive," the Judge said. "Put those into them. And don't open them, or my wish for you won't come true."

When they had finished eating, a full moon had begun to rise in the darkening sky. They headed for the theater.

A number of visitors sat in the chairs and the stage lights looked bright. Drumm stood beside the piano, talking to two plump men in summer business suits. As Pursuivant and the others came down the aisle, Drumm eagerly beckoned them and introduced them to his companions, the financial backers with whom he had taken dinner.

"We're very much interested," said one. "This vampire legend intrigues anyone, if you forget that a vampire's motivation is simply nourishment."

"No, something more than that," offered Pursuivant. "A social motivation."

"Social motivation," repeated the other backer.

"A vampire wants company of its own kind. A victim infected becomes a vampire, too, and an associate. Otherwise the original vampire would be a disconsolate loner."

"There's a lot in what you say," said Drumm, impressed.

After that there was financial talk, something in which Cobbett could not intelligently join. Then someone else approached, and both the backers stared.

It was a tall, supremely graceful woman with red-lighted black hair in a bun at her nape, a woman of impressive figure and assurance. She wore a sweeping blue dress, fitted to her slim waist, with a frill-edged neckline. Her arms were bare and white and sweetly turned, with jeweled bracelets on them. Drumm almost ran to bring her close to the group.

"Gonda Chastel," he said, half-prayerfully. "Gonda, you'll want to meet these people."

The two backers stuttered admiringly at her. Pursuivant bowed and Laurel smiled. Gonda Chastel gave Cobbett her slim, cool hand. "You know so much about this thing we're trying to do here," she said, in a voice like cream.

Drumm watched them. His face looked plaintive.

"Judge Pursuivant has taught me a lot, Miss Chastel," said Cobbett. "He'll tell you that once he knew your mother."

"I remember her, not very clearly," said Gonda Chastel. "She died when I was just a little thing, thirty years ago. And I followed her here, now I make my home here."

"You look very like her," said Pursuivant.

"I'm proud to be like my mother in any way," she smiled at them. She could be overwhelming, Cobbett told himself.

"And Miss Parcher," went on Gonda Chastel, turning toward Laurel. "What a little presence she is. She should be in our show—I don't know what part, but she should." She smiled dazzlingly. "Now then, Phil wants me on stage."

"Knock-at-the-door number, Gonda," said Drumm.

Gracefully she mounted the steps. The piano sounded, and she sang. It was the best song, felt Cobbett, that he had heard so far in the rehearsals. "Are they seeking for a shelter from the night?" Gonda Chastel sang richly. Caspar Merritt entered, to join in a recitative. Then the chorus streamed on, singing somewhat shrilly.

Pursuivant and Laurel had sat down. Cobbett strode back up the aisle and out under a moon that rained silver-blue light.

He found his way to the churchyard. The trees that had offered pleasant afternoon shade now made a dubious darkness. He walked underneath branches that seemed to lower like hovering wings as he approached the tomb structure at the center.

The barred door that had been massively locked now stood open. He peered into the gloom within. After a moment he stepped across the threshold upon the flagged floor.

He had to grope, with one hand upon the rough wall. At last he almost stumbled upon the great stone chest at the rear.

It, too, was flung open, its lid heaved back against the wall.

There was, of course, complete darkness within it. He flicked on his cigar lighter. The flame showed him the inside of the stone coffer, solidly made and about ten feet long. Its sides of gray marble were snugly fitted. Inside lay a coffin of rich dark wood with silver fittings and here, yet again, was an open lid.

Bending close to the smudged silk lining, Cobbett seemed to catch an odor of stuffy sharpness, like dried herbs. He snapped off his light and frowned in the dark. Then he groped back to the door, emerged into the open, and headed for the theater again.

"Mr. Cobbett," said the beautiful voice of Gonda Chastel.

She stood at the graveyard's edge, beside a sagging willow. She was almost as tall as he. Her eyes glowed in the moonlight.

"You came to find the truth about my mother," she half-accused.

"I was bound to try," he replied. "Ever since I saw a certain face at a certain window of a certain New York hotel."

She stepped back from him. "You know that she's a—"

"A vampire," Cobbett finished for her. "Yes."

"I beg you to be helpful—merciful." But there was no supplication in her voice. "I already realized, long ago. That's why I live in little Deslow. I want to find a way to give her rest. Night after night, I wonder how."

"I understand that," said Cobbett.

Gonda Chastel breathed deeply. "You know all about these things. I think there's something about you that could daunt a vampire."

"If so, I don't know what it is," said Cobbett truthfully.

"Make me a solemn promise. That you won't return to her tomb, that you won't tell others what you and I know about her. I—I want to think how we two together can do something for her."

"If you wish, I'll say nothing," he promised.

Her hand clutched his.

"The cast took a five-minute break, it must be time to go to work again," she said, suddenly bright. "Let's go back and help the thing along."

They went.

Inside, the performers were gathering on stage. Drumm stared unhappily as Gonda Chastel and Cobbett came down the aisle. Cobbett sat with Laurel and Pursuivant and listened to the rehearsal.

Adaptation from Bram Stoker's novel was free, to say the least. Dracula's eerie plottings were much hampered by his having a countess, a walking dead beauty who strove to become a spirit of good. There were some songs, in interesting minor keys. There was a dance, in which men and women leaped like kangaroos. Finally Drumm called a halt, and the performers trooped wearily to the wings.

Gonda Chastel lingered, talking to Laurel. "I wonder, my dear, if you haven't had acting experience," she said.

"Only in school entertainments down South, when I was little."

"Phil," said Gonda Chastel, "Miss Parcher is

a good type, has good presence. There ought to be something for her in the show."

"You're very kind, but I'm afraid that's impossible," said Laurel, smiling.

"You may change your mind, Miss Parcher. Will you and your friends come to my house for a nightcap?"

"Thank you," said Pursuivant. "We have some notes to make, and we must make them together."

"Until tomorrow evening, then Mr. Cobbett, we'll remember our agreement."

She went away toward the back of the stage. Pursuivant and Laurel walked out. Drumm hurried up the aisle and caught Cobbett's elbow.

"I saw you," he said harshly. "Saw you both as you came in."

"And we saw you, Phil. What's this about?"

"She likes you." It was half an accusation. "Fawns on you, almost."

Cobbett grinned and twitched his arm free. "What's the matter, Phil, are you in love with her?"

"Yes, God damn it, I am. I'm in love with her. She knows it but she won't let me come to her house. And you—the first time she meets you, she invites you."

"Easy does it, Phil," said Cobbett. "If it'll do you any good, I'm in love with someone else, and that takes just about all my spare time."

He hurried out to overtake his companions.

Pursuivant swung his cane almost jauntily as they returned through the moonlight to the auto court.

"What notes are you talking about, Judge?" asked Cobbett.

"I'll tell you at my quarters. What do you think of the show?"

"Perhaps I'll like it better after they've rehearsed more," said Laurel. "I don't follow it at present."

"Here and there, it strikes me as limp," added Cobbett.

They sat down in the Judge's cabin. He poured them drinks. "Now," he said, "there are certain things to recognize here. Things I more or less expected to find."

"A mystery, Judge?" asked Laurel.

"Not so much that, if I expected to find them. How far are we from Jewett City?"

"Twelve or fifteen miles as the crow flies," estimated Cobbett. "And Jewett City is where that vampire family, the Rays, lived and died."

"Died twice, you might say," nodded Pursuivant, stroking his white mustache. "Back about a century and a quarter ago. And here's what might be a matter of Ray family history. I've been thinking about Chastel, whom once I greatly admired. About her full name."

"But she had only one name, didn't she?" asked Laurel.

"On the stage she used one name, yes. So did Bernhardt, so did Duse, so later did Garbo. But all of them had full names. Now, before we went to dinner, I made two telephone calls to theatrical historians I know. To learn Chastel's full name."

"And she had a full name," prompted Cobbett.

"Indeed she did. Her full name was Chastel Ray."

Cobbett and Laurel looked at him in deep silence.

"Not apt to be just coincidence," elaborated Pursuivant. "Now then, I gave you some keepsakes today."

"Here's mine," said Cobbett, pulling the foil-wrapped bit from his shirt pocket.

"And I have mine here," said Laurel, her hand at her throat. "In a little locket I have on this chain."

"Keep it there," Pursuivant urged her. "Wear it around your neck at all times. Lee, have yours always on your person. Those are garlic cloves, and you know what they're good for. You can also guess why I cut up a lot of garlic in our spaghetti for dinner."

"You think there's a vampire here," offered Laurel.

"A specific vampire." The Judge took a deep breath into his broad chest. "Chastel. Chastel Ray."

"I believe it, too," declared Cobbett tonelessly, and Laurel nodded. Cobbett looked at the watch on his wrist.

"It's past one in the morning," he said. "Perhaps we'd all be better off if we had some sleep."

They said their good nights and Laurel and Cobbett walked to where their two doors stood side by side. Laurel put her key into the lock, but did not turn it at once. She peered across the moonlit street.

"Who's that over there?" she whispered. "Maybe I ought to say, what's that?"

Cobbett looked. "Nothing, you're just nervous. Good night, dear."

She went in and shut the door. Cobbett quickly crossed the street.

"Mr. Cobbett," said the voice of Gonda Chastel.

"I wondered what you wanted, so late at night," he said, walking close to her.

She had undone her dark hair and let it flow to her shoulders. She was, Cobbett thought, as beautiful a woman as he had ever seen.

"I wanted to be sure about you," she said. "That you'd respect your promise to me, not to go into the churchyard."

"I keep my promises, Miss Chastel."

He felt a deep, hushed silence all around them. Not even the leaves rustled in the trees.

"I had hoped you wouldn't venture even this far," she went on. "You and your friends are new in town, you might tempt her specially." Her eyes burned at him. "You know I don't mean that as a compliment."

She turned to walk away. He fell into step beside her. "But you're not afraid of her," he said.

"Of my own mother?"

"She was a Ray," said Cobbett. "Each Ray sapped the blood of his kinsmen. Judge Pursuivant told me all about it."

Again the gaze of her dark, brilliant eyes. "Nothing like that has ever happened between my mother and me." She stopped, and so did he. Her slim, strong hand took him by the wrist.

"You're wise and brave," she said. "I think you may have come here for a good purpose, not just about the show."

"I try to have good purposes."

The light of the moon soaked through the overhead branches as they walked on. "Will you come to my house?" she invited.

"I'll walk to the churchyard," replied Cobbett. "I said I wouldn't go into it, but I can stand at the edge."

"Don't go in."

"I've promised that I wouldn't, Miss Chastel."

She walked back the way they had come. He followed the street under silent elms until he reached the border of the churchyard. Moonlight flecked and spattered the tombstones. Deep shadows lay like pools. He had a sense of being watched from within.

As he gazed, he saw movement among the graves. He could not define it, but it was there. He glimpsed, or fancied he glimpsed, a head, indistinct in outline as though swathed in dark fabric. Then another. Another. They huddled in a group, as though to gaze at him.

"I wish you'd go back to your quarters," said Gonda Chastel beside him. She had drifted after him, silent as a shadow herself.

"Miss Chastel," he said, "tell me something if you can. Whatever happened to the town or village of Griswold?"

"Griswold?" she echoed. "What's Griswold? That means gray woods."

"Your ancestor, or your relative, Horace Ray, came from Griswold to die in Jewett City. And I've told you that I knew your mother was born a Ray."

Her shining eyes seemed to flood upon him. "I didn't know that," she said.

He gazed into the churchyard, at those hints of furtive movement.

"The hands of the dead reach out for the living," murmured Gonda Chastel.

"Reach out for me?" he asked.

"Perhaps for both of us. Just now, we may be the only living souls awake in Deslow." She gazed at him again. "But you're able to defend yourself, somehow."

"What makes you think that?" he inquired, aware of the clove of garlic in his shirt pocket.

"Because they—in the churchyard there—they

watch, but they hold away from you. You don't invite them."

"Nor do you, apparently," said Cobbett.

"I hope you're not trying to make fun of me," she said, her voice barely audible.

"On my soul, I'm not."

"On your soul," she repeated. "Good night, Mr. Cobbett."

Again she moved away, tall and proud and graceful. He watched her out of sight. Then he headed back toward the motor court.

Nothing moved in the empty street. Only one or two lights shone here and there in closed shops. He thought he heard a soft rustle behind him, but did not look back.

As he reached his own door, he heard Laurel scream behind hers.

Judge Pursuivant sat in his cubicle, his jacket off, studying a worn little brown book. Skinner, said letters on the spine, and *Myths and Legends of Our Own Land*. He had read the passage so often that he could almost repeat it from memory:

"To lay this monster he must be taken up and burned; at least his heart must be; and he must be disinterred in the daytime when he is asleep and unaware."

There were other ways, reflected Pursuivant.

It must be very late by now, rather it must be early. But he had no intention of going to sleep. Not when stirs of motion sounded outside, along the concrete walkway in front of his cabin. Did motion stand still, just beyond the door there? Pursuivant's great, veined hand touched the front of his shirt, beneath which a bag of garlic hung like an amulet. Garlic—was that enough? He himself was fond of garlic, judiciously employed in sauces and salads. But then, he could see himself in the mirror of the bureau yonder, could see his broad old face with its white sweep of mustache like a wreath of snow on a sill. It was a clear image of a face, not a calm face just then, but a determined one. Pursuivant smiled at

it, with a glimpse of even teeth that were still his own.

He flicked up his shirt cuff and looked at his watch. Half past one, about. In June, even with daylight savings time, dawn would come early. Dawn sent vampires back to the tombs that were their melancholy refuges, "asleep and unaware," as Skinner had specified.

Putting the book aside, he poured himself a small drink of bourbon, dropped in cubes of ice and a trickle of water, and sipped. He had drunk several times during that day, when on most days he partook of only a single highball, by advice of his doctor; but just now he was grateful for the pungent, walnutty taste of the liquor. It was one of earth's natural things, a good companion when not abused. From the table he took a folder of scribbled notes. He looked at jottings from the works of Montague Summers.

These offered the proposition that a plague of vampires usually stemmed from a single source of infection, a king or queen vampire whose feasts of blood drove victims to their graves, to rise in their turn. If the original vampires were found and destroyed, the others relaxed to rest as normally dead bodies. Bram Stoker had followed the same gospel when he wrote *Dracula*, and doubtless Bram Stoker had known. Pursuivant looked at another page, this time a poem copied from James Grant's curious *Mysteries of All Nations*. It was a ballad in archaic language, that dealt with baleful happenings in "The Towne of Peste"—Budapest?

*It was the Corpses that our Churchyardes*
  *filled*
*That did at midnight lumberr up our Stayres;*
*They suck'd our Bloud, the gorie Banquet*
  *swilled,*
*And harried everie Soule with hydeous*
  *Feares . . .*

Several verses down:

*They barr'd with Boltes of Iron the*
  *Churchyard-pale*

*To keep them out; but all this wold not doe;*
*For when a Dead-Man has learn'd to draw*
*  a naile,*
*He can also burst an iron Bolte in two.*

Many times Pursuivant had tried to trace the author of that verse. He wondered if it was not something quaintly confected not long before 1880, when Grant published his work. At any rate, the Judge felt that he knew what it meant, the experience that it remembered.

He put aside the notes, too, and picked up his spotted walking stick. Clamping the balance of it firmly in his left hand, he twisted the handle with his right and pulled. Out of the hollow shank slid a pale, bright blade, keen and lean and edged on both front and back.

Pursuivant permitted himself a smile above it. This was one of his most cherished possessions, this silver weapon said to have been forged a thousand years ago by St. Dunstan. Bending, he spelled out the runic writing upon it: *Sic pereant omnes inimici tui, Domine.*

That was the end of the fiercely triumphant song of Deborah in the Book of Judges: So perish all thine enemies, O Lord. Whether the work of St. Dunstan or not, the metal was silver, the writing was a warrior's prayer. Silver and writing had proved their strength against evil in the past.

Then, outside, a loud, tremulous cry of mortal terror.

Pursuivant sprang out of his chair on the instant. Blade in hand, he fairly ripped his door open and ran out. He saw Cobbett in front of Laurel's door, wrenching at the knob, and hurried there like a man half his age.

"Open up, Laurel," he heard Cobbett call. "It's Lee out here!"

The door gave inward as Pursuivant reached it, and he and Cobbett pressed into the lighted room.

Laurel half-crouched in the middle of the floor. Her trembling hand pointed to a rear window. "She tried to come in," Laurel stammered.

"There's nothing at that window," said Cobbett, but even as he spoke, there was. A face, pale as tallow, crowded against the glass. They saw wide, staring eyes, a mouth that opened and squirmed. Teeth twinkled sharply.

Cobbett started forward, but Pursuivant caught him by the shoulder. "Let me," he said, advancing toward the window, the point of his blade lifted.

The face at the window writhed convulsively as the silver weapon came against the pane with a clink. The mouth opened as though to shout, but no sound came. The face fell back and vanished from their sight.

"I've seen that face before," said Cobbett hoarsely.

"Yes," said Pursuivant. "At my hotel window. And since."

He dropped the point of the blade to the floor. Outside came a whirring rush of sound, like feet, many of them.

"We ought to wake up the people at the office," said Cobbett.

"I doubt if anyone in this little town could be wakened," Pursuivant told him evenly. "I have it in mind that every living soul, except the three of us, is sound asleep. Entranced."

"But out there—"Laurel gestured at the door, where something seemed to be pressing.

"I said, every living soul," Pursuivant looked from her to Cobbett. "Living," he repeated.

He paced across the floor, and with his point scratched a perpendicular line upon it. Across this he carefully drove a horizontal line, making a cross. The pushing abruptly ceased.

"There it is, at the window again," breathed Laurel.

Pursuivant took long steps back to where the face hovered, with black hair streaming about it. He scraped the glass with his silver blade, up and down, then across, making lines upon it. The face drew away. He moved to mark similar crosses on the other windows.

"You see," he said, quietly triumphant, "the force of old, old charms."

He sat down in a chair, heavily. His face was weary, but he looked at Laurel and smiled.

"It might help if we managed to pity those poor things out there," he said.

"Pity?" she almost cried out.

"Yes," he said, and quoted:

*. . . Think how sad it must be*
*To thirst always for a scorned elixir,*
*The salt of quotidian blood.*

"I know that," volunteered Cobbett. "It's from a poem by Richard Wilbur, a damned unhappy poet."

"Quotidian," repeated Laurel to herself.

"That means something that keeps coming back, that returns daily," Cobbett said.

"It's a term used to refer to a recurrent fever," added Pursuivant.

Laurel and Cobbett sat down together on the bed.

"I would say that for the time being we're safe here," declared Pursuivant. "Not at ease, but at least safe. At dawn, danger will go to sleep and we can open the door."

"But why are we safe, and nobody else?" Laurel cried out. "Why are we awake, with everyone else in this town asleep and helpless?"

"Apparently because we all of us wear garlic," replied Pursuivant patiently, "and because we ate garlic, plenty of it, at dinnertime. And because there are crosses—crude, but unmistakable—wherever something might try to come in. I won't ask you to be calm, but I'll ask you to be resolute."

"I'm resolute," said Cobbett between clenched teeth. "I'm ready to go out there and face them."

"If you did that, even with the garlic," said Pursuivant, "you'd last about as long as a pint of whiskey in a five-handed poker game. No, Lee, relax as much as you can, and let's talk."

They talked, while outside strange presences could be felt rather than heard. Their talk was of anything and everything but where they were and why. Cobbett remembered strange things he had encountered, in towns, among mountains, along desolate roads, and what he had been able to do about them. Pursuivant told of a vampire he had known and defeated in upstate New York, of a werewolf in his own Southern countryside. Laurel, at Cobbett's urging, sang songs, old songs,

from her own rustic home place. Her voice was sweet. When she sang "Round Is the Ring," faces came and hung like smudges outside the cross-scored windows. She saw, and sang again, an old Appalachian carol called "Mary She Heared a Knock in the Night." The faces drifted away again. And the hours, too, drifted away, one by one.

"There's a horde of vampires on the night street here, then." Cobbett at last brought up the subject of their problem.

"And they lull the people of Deslow to sleep, to be helpless victims," agreed Pursuivant. "About this show, *The Land Beyond the Forest,* mightn't it be welcomed as a chance to spread the infection? Even a townful of sleepers couldn't feed a growing community of blood drinkers."

"If we could deal with the source, the original infection—" began Cobbett.

"The mistress of them, the queen," said Pursuivant. "Yes. The one whose walking by night rouses them all. If she could be destroyed, they'd all die properly."

He glanced at the front window. The moonlight had a touch of slaty gray.

"Almost morning," he pronounced. "Time for a visit to her tomb."

"I gave my promise I wouldn't go there," said Cobbett.

"But I didn't promise," said Pursuivant, rising. "You stay here with Laurel."

His silver blade in hand, he stepped out into darkness from which the moon had all but dropped away. Overhead, stars were fading out. Dawn was at hand.

He sensed a flutter of movement on the far side of the street, an almost inaudible gibbering of sound. Steadily he walked across. He saw nothing along the sidewalk there, heard nothing. Resolutely he tramped to the churchyard, his weapon poised. More grayness had come to dilute the dark.

He pushed his way through the hedge of shrubs, stepped in upon the grass, and paused at the side of a grave. Above it hung an eddy of soft mist, no larger than the swirl of water draining from a sink. As Pursuivant watched, it seemed to soak into the earth and disappear. That, he said to himself, is what a soul looks like when it seeks to regain its coffin.

On he walked, step by weary, purposeful step, toward the central crypt. A ray of the early sun, stealing between heavily leafed boughs, made his way more visible. In this dawn, he would find what he would find. He knew that.

The crypt's door of open bars was held shut by its heavy padlock. He examined that lock closely. After a moment, he slid the point of his blade into the rusted keyhole and judiciously pressed this way, then that, and back again the first way. The spring creakily relaxed and he dragged the door open. Holding his breath, he entered.

The lid of the great stone vault was closed down. He took hold of the edge and heaved. The lid was heavy, but rose with a complaining grate of the hinges. Inside he saw a dark, closed coffin. He lifted the lid of that, too.

She lay there, calm-faced, the eyes half shut as though dozing.

"Chastel," said Pursuivant to her. "Not Gonda. Chastel."

The eyelids fluttered. That was all, but he knew that she heard what he said.

"Now you can rest," he said. "Rest in peace, really in peace."

He set the point of his silver blade at the swell of her left breast. Leaning both his broad hands upon the curved handle, he drove downward with all his strength.

She made a faint squeak of sound.

Blood sprang up as he cleared his weapon. More light shone in. He could see a dark moisture fading from the blade, like evaporating dew.

In the coffin, Chastel's proud shape shrivelled, darkened. Quickly he slammed the coffin shut, then lowered the lid of the vault into place and went quickly out. He pushed the door shut again and fastened the stubborn old lock. As he walked back through the churchyard among the graves, a bird twittered over his head. More distantly, he heard the hum of a car's motor. The town was waking up.

In the growing radiance, he walked back across the street. By now, his steps were the steps of an old man, old and very tired.

Inside Laurel's cabin, Laurel and Cobbett were stirring instant coffee into hot water in plastic cups. They questioned the Judge with their tired eyes.

"She's finished," he said shortly.

"What will you tell Gonda?" asked Cobbett.

"Chastel was Gonda."

"But—"

"She was Gonda," said Pursuivant again, sitting down. "Chastel died. The infection wakened her out of her tomb, and she told people she was Gonda, and naturally they believed her." He sagged wearily. "Now that she's finished and at rest, those others—the ones she had bled, who also rose at night—will rest, too."

Laurel took a sip of coffee. Above the cup, her face was pale.

"Why do you say Chastel was Gonda?" she asked the Judge. "How can you know that?"

"I wondered from the very beginning. I was utterly sure just now."

"Sure?" said Laurel. "How can you be sure?"

Pursuivant smiled at her, the very faintest of smiles.

"My dear, don't you think a man always recognizes a woman he has loved?"

He seemed to recover his characteristic defiant vigor. He rose and went to the door and put his hand on the knob. "Now, if you'll just excuse me for a while."

"Don't you think we'd better hurry and leave?" Cobbett asked him. "Before people miss her and ask questions?"

"Not at all," said Pursuivant, his voice strong again. "If we're gone, they'll ask questions about us, too, possibly embarrassing questions. No, we'll stay. We'll eat a good breakfast, or at least pretend to eat it. And we'll be as surprised as the rest of them about the disappearance of their leading lady."

"I'll do my best," vowed Laurel.

"I know you will, my child," said Pursuivant, and went out the door.

# Peter Tremayne

Peter Berresford Ellis (1943– ) was born in Coventry, Warwickshire, England, the son of a Cork-born journalist whose family can be traced back in the area to 1288. Ellis, most of whose fiction has been published under the Peter Tremayne pseudonym, earned his B.A. and master's degrees in Celtic studies, then followed in his father's footsteps to become a journalist. His first book, published in 1968, was a history of the Welsh struggle for independence, followed by popular titles in Celtic studies. He has served as international chairman of the Celtic League (1988–90) and is the honorary life president of The 1820 Society and an honorary life member of the Irish Literary Society.

He has produced eighty-eight full-length books, a similar number of short stories, and numerous scholarly pamphlets. As Tremayne he has written eighteen worldwide best-selling novels about the seventh-century Irish nun detective, Sister Fidelma, with more than three million copies in print. As Peter MacAlan he produced eight thrillers (1983–93). In the horror field he has written more than two dozen novels, mostly inspired by Celtic myths and legends, including *Dracula Unborn* (1977), *The Revenge of Dracula* (1978), and *Dracula, My Love* (1980).

"Dracula's Chair" was planned as an epilogue to his novel *The Revenge of Dracula*, but the author decided it was overkill. It was first published in *The Count Dracula Fan Club Book of Vampires* (1980).

# Dracula's Chair

## PETER TREMAYNE

aybe this is an hallucination. Perhaps I am mad. How else can this be explained?

I sit here alone and helpless! So utterly alone! Alone in an age which is not mine, in a body which is not mine. Oh God! I am slowly being killed—or worse! Yet what is worse than death? That terrifying limbo that is the borderland of Hell, that state that is neither the restful sleep of death nor the perplexities of life but is the nightmare of undeath.

He is draining me of life and yet, *yet is it me who is the victim*? How can I tell him that the person he thinks I am, the person whose body my mind inhabits, is no longer in that body? How can I tell him that *I* am in the body of his victim? *I* . . . a person from another time, another age, another place!

God help me! He is draining me of life and I cannot prevent him!

When did this nightmare begin? An age away. I suppose it began when my wife and I saw the chair.

We were driving back to London one hot July Sunday afternoon, having been picnicking in Essex. We were returning about mid-afternoon down the A11, through the village of Newport, when my wife suddenly called upon me to pull over and stop.

"I've just seen the most exquisite chair in the window of an antique shop."

I was somewhat annoyed because I wanted to get home early that evening to see a vintage Humphrey Bogart film on the television, one I'd never seen before even though I have been a Bogart fan for years.

"What's the point?" I muttered grumpily, getting out of the car and trailing after her. "The shop's shut anyway."

But the shop wasn't shut. Passing trade on a Sunday from Londoners was apparently very lucrative and most antique shops in the area opened during the afternoons.

The chair stood like a lone sentinel in the window. It was square in shape, a wooden straight-backed chair with sturdy arms. It was of a plain and simple design, dark oak wood yet with none of the ornate woodwork that is commonly associated with such items. The seat was upholstered in a faded tapestry work which was obviously the original. It was a very unattractive upholstery for it was in a faded black with a number of once white exotic dragon's heads. The same upholstery was reflected in a piece which provided a narrow back rest—a strip a foot deep thrust across the middle of the frame. My impression of the chair was hardly "exquisite"—it was a squat, ugly, and aggressive piece. Certainly it did not seem worth the £100 price ticket which was attached by string to one arm.

My wife had contrary ideas. It was, she felt, exactly the right piece to fill a corner in my study and provide a spare chair for extra guests. It could, she assured me, easily be re-upholstered to fit in with our general colour scheme of greens and golds. What was wanted, she said, was a functional chair and this was it. She was adamant and so I resigned myself to a minimum of grumbling, one eye on my watch to ensure I would not miss the Bogart film. The transaction was concluded fairly quickly by comparison with my wife's usual standard of detailed questioning and examination. Perhaps the vendor was rather more loquacious than the average antique dealer.

"It's a very nice chair," said the dealer with summoned enthusiasm. "It's a Victorian piece of eastern European origin. Look, on the back you can actually see a date of manufacture and the place of origin." He pointed to the back of the chair where, carved into the wood with small letters was the word "Bistritz" and the date "1887." The dealer smiled in the surety of knowledge. "That makes it Romanian in origin. Actually, I purchased the piece from the old Purfleet Art Gallery."

"The Purfleet Art Gallery?" said I, thinking it time to make some contribution to the conversation. "Isn't that the old gallery and museum over which there were some protests a few months ago?"

"Yes, do you know the place? Purfleet in Essex? The gallery was housed in an ancient building, a manor house called Carfax, which was said to date back to medieval times. The old gallery had been there since the late Victorian period but had to close through lack of government subsidies, and the building is being carved up into apartments."

I nodded, feeling I had, perhaps, made too much of a contribution.

The antique dealer went on obliviously.

"When the gallery closed, a lot of its *objets d'art* were auctioned and I bought this chair. Accord-ing to the auctioneer's catalogue it had been in the old house when the gallery first opened and had belonged to the previous owner. He was said to have been a foreign nobleman . . . probably a Romanian by the workmanship of the chair."

Finally, having had her fears assuaged over matters of woodworm, methods of upholstery, and the like, the purchase was concluded by my wife. The chair was strapped to the roofrack of my car and we headed homewards.

The next day was Monday. My wife, who is in research, had gone to her office while I spent the morning in my study doodling on pieces of paper and vainly waiting for a new plot to mature for the television soap-opera that I was scripting at the time. At mid-day my wife telephoned to remind me to check around for some price quotations for re-upholstering our purchase. I had forgotten all about the chair, still strapped to the roofrack of my car. Feeling a little guilty, I went down to the garage and untied it, carrying it up to my study and placing it in the alloted corner with a critical eye. I confess, I did not like the thing; it was so square and seemed to somehow challenge me. It is hard to define what I mean but you have, I suppose, seen certain types of people with thrust out jaws, square and aggressive? Well, the chair gave the same impression.

After a while, perhaps in response to its challenge, I decided to sit down in the chair, and as I sat, a sudden coldness spread up my spine and a weird feeling of unease came over me. So strong was it that I immediately jumped up. I stood there looking down at the chair and feeling a trifle self-conscious. I laughed nervously. Ridiculous! What would my friend Philip, who was a psychiatrist, say to such behaviour? I did not like the chair but there was no need to create physical illusions around my distaste.

I sat down again and, as expected, the cold feelings of unease were gone—a mere shadow in my mind. In fact, I was surprised at the comfort of the chair. I sat well back, arms and hands resting on the wooden arm rests, head leaning against the back, legs spread out. It was extremely comfortable.

So comfortable was it that a feeling of deep relaxation came over me, and with the relaxation came the desire to have a cat-nap. I must confess, I tend to enjoy a ten minute nap just after lunch. It relaxes me and stimulates the mind. I sat back, closed my drooping eyelids, and gently let myself drift, drift . . .

It was dark when I awoke.

For an instant I struggled with the remnants of my dreams. Then my mind cleared and I looked about me. My first thought was the question—how long had I slept? I could see the dark hue of early evening through the tall windows. Then I started *for there were no tall windows in my study nor anywhere in our house*!

Blinking my eyes rapidly to focus them in the darkened room, I abruptly perceived that I was not in my study, nor was I in any room that I had ever seen before. I tried to rise in my surprise and found that I could not move—some sluggish feeling in my body prevented me from coordinating my limbs. My mind had clarity and will but below my neck my whole body seemed numb. And so I just sat there, staring wildly at the unfamiliar room in a cold sweat of fear and panic. I tried to blink away the nightmare, tried to rationalize.

I could move my head around and doing so I found that I was sitting in the same chair—that accursed chair! Yet it seemed strangely newer than I remembered it. I thought, perhaps it was a trick of the light. But I discovered that around my legs was tucked a woolen blanket while the top half of me was clad in a pajama jacket over which was a velvet smoking jacket, a garment that I knew I had never owned. My eyes wandered around the room from object to unfamiliar object, each unfamiliar item causing the terror to mount in my veins, now surging with adrenalin. I was in a lounge filled with some fine pieces of Victoriana. The chair in which I sat now stood before an open hearth in which a few coals faintly glimmered. In one corner stood a lean, tall grandfather clock, whose steady tick-tock added to the oppressiveness of the scene. There was, so far as I could see, nothing modern in the room at all.

But for me the greatest horror was the strange paralysis which kept me anchored in that chair. I tried to move until the sweat poured from my face with the effort. I even tried to shout, opening my mouth wide to emit strange choking-like noises. What in God's name had happened to me?

Suddenly a door opened. Into the room came a young girl of about seventeen holding aloft one of those old brass oil lamps, the sort you see converted into electric lamps these days by "trendy" people. Yet this was no converted lamp but a lamp from which a flame spluttered and emitted the odour of burning paraffin. And the girl! She wore a long black dress with a high button collar, with a white linen apron over it. Her fair hair was tucked inside a small white cap set at a jaunty angle on her head. In fact, she looked like a serving maid straight out of those Victorian drama serials we get so often on the television these days. She came forward and placed the lamp on a table near me, and then started, seeing my eyes wide open and upon her. I tried to speak to her, to demand, to exhort some explanation, to ask what the meaning of this trickery was, but only a strangled gasp came from my throat.

The girl was clearly frightened and bobbed what was supposed to be a curtsy in my direction before turning to the door.

"Ma'am! Ma'am!" Her strong Cockney accent made the word sound like "Mum!" "Master's awake, ma'am. What'll I do?"

Another figure moved into the room, tall, graceful, wearing an elegant Victorian dress hung low at the shoulders, and leaving very little of her bust to the imagination. A black ribbon with a cameo was fastened to her pale throat. Her raven black hair was done up in a bun at the back of her head. Her face was small, heart-shaped, and pretty. The lips were naturally red though a trifle sullen for her features. The eyes were deep green and seemed a little sad. She came towards me, bent over me, and gave a wan smile. There was a strange, almost unnatural pallor to her complexion.

"That's all, Fanny," she said. "I'll see to him now."

"Yes, ma'am." The girl bobbed another curtsy and was gone through the door.

"Poor Upton," whispered the woman before me. "Poor Upton. I wish I knew whether you hurt at all? No one seems to know from what strange malady you suffer."

She stood back and sighed sorrowfully and deeply.

"It's time for your medication."

She picked up a bottle and a spoon, pouring a bitter smelling amber liquid which she forced down my throat. I felt a numbing bitterness searing down my gullet.

"Poor Upton," she sighed again. "It's bitter I know but the doctor says it will take away any pain."

I tried to speak; tried to tell her that I was not Upton, that I did not want her medicine, that I wanted this play-acting to cease. I succeeded only in gnashing my teeth and making inarticulate cries like some wild beast at bay. The woman took a step backwards, her eyes widening in fright. Then she seemed to regain her composure.

"Come, Upton," she chided. "This won't do at all. Try to relax."

The girl, Fanny, reappeared.

"Doctor Seward is here, ma'am."

A stocky man in a brown tweed suit, looking like some character out of a Dickens novel, stepped into the room and bowed over the woman's proffered hand.

"John," smiled the woman. "I'm so glad you've come."

"How are you, Clara," smiled the man. "You look a trifle weary, a little pale."

"I'm alright, John. But I worry about Upton."

The man turned to me.

"Yes, how is the patient? I swear he looks a little more alert today."

The woman, Clara, spread her hands and shrugged.

"To me he seems little better, John. Even when he seems more alert physically he can only growl like a beast. I try my best but I fear . . . I fear that . . ."

The man called John patted her hand and gestured her to silence. Then he came and bent over me with a friendly smile.

"Strange," he murmured. "Indeed, a strange affliction. And yet . . . yet I do detect a more intelligent gleam in the eyes today. Hello, old friend, do you know me. It's John . . . John Seward? Do you recognise me?"

He leaned close to my face, so close I could smell the scent of oranges on his breath.

I struggled to break the paralysis which gripped me and only succeeded in issuing a number of snarls and grunts. The man drew back.

"Upon my word, Clara, has he been violent at all?"

"Not really, John. He does excite himself so with visitors. But perhaps it is his way of trying to communicate with us."

The man grunted and nodded.

"Well, the only remedy for pain is to keep dosing him with the laudanum as I prescribed it. I think he is a little better. However, I shall call again tomorrow to see if there is a significant improvement. If not, I will ask your permission to consult a specialist, perhaps a doctor from Harley Street. There are a number of factors that still puzzle me—the anaemia, the apparent lack of red blood corpuscles or hemoglobin. His paleness and languor. And these strange wounds on his neck do not seem to be healing at all."

The woman bit her lip and lowered her voice.

"You may be frank with me, John. You have known Upton and me for some years now. I am resigned to the fact that there can only be a worsening of his condition. I do fear for his life."

The man glanced at me nervously.

"Should you talk like this in front of him?"

The woman sighed. "He cannot understand, of that I am sure. Poor Upton. Just to think that a few short days ago he was so full of life, so active, and now this strange disease has cut him down . . ."

The man nodded.

"You have been a veritable goddess, Clara, charity herself, nursing him constantly day and night. I shall look in again tomorrow, but if there is no improvement I shall seek permission to call in a specialist."

Clara lowered her head as if in resignation.

The man turned to me and forced a smile.

"So long, old fellow . . ."

I tried to call, desperately tried to plead for help. Then he was gone.

The minutes dragged into hours as the woman, Clara, who was supposed to be my wife, sat gazing into the fire, while I sat pinioned in my accursed chair opposite to her. How long we sat thus I do not truly know. From time to time I felt her gaze, sad and thoughtful, upon me. Then I became aware, somewhere in the house, of a clock commencing to strike. A few seconds later it was followed by the resonant and hollow sounds of the grandfather clock. Without raising my head I counted slowly to twelve. Midnight.

The woman Clara abruptly sprung from her chair and stood upright before the fire.

As I looked up she seemed to change slightly—it is hard to explain. Her face seemed to grow coarser, more bloated. Her tongue, a red glistening object, darted nervously over her lips making them moist and of a deeper red than before, contrasting starkly to the sharp whiteness of her teeth. A strange lustre began to sparkle in her eyes. She raised a languid hand and began to massage her neck slowly, sensually.

Then, abruptly, she laughed—a low voluptuous chuckle that made the hairs on my neck bristle.

She gazed down at me with a wanton expression, a lascivious smile.

"Poor Upton." Her tone was a gloating caress. "He'll be coming soon. You'll like that won't you? Yet why he takes you first, I cannot understand. Why *you*? Am I not full of the warmth of life—does not warm, rich young blood flow in my veins? Why *you*?"

She made an obscene, seductive gesture with her body.

The way she crooned, the saliva trickling from a corner of those red—oh, so red—lips, made my heart beat faster yet at the same time, the blood seemed to deny its very warmth and pump like some ice-cold liquid in my veins.

What new nightmare was this?

How *he* appeared I do not know.

One minute there was just the woman and myself in the room. Then he was standing there.

A tall man, apparently elderly although his pale face held no aging of the skin, only the long white moustache which drooped over his otherwise clean-shaven face gave the impression of age. His face was strong—extremely strong, aquiline with a high-bridged nose and peculiarly arched nostrils. His forehead was loftily domed and hair grew scantily round the temples but profusely elsewhere. The eyebrows were massive and nearly met across the bridge of the nose.

It was his mouth which captured my attention—a mouth set in the long pale face, fixed and cruel looking, with teeth that protruded over the remarkably ruddy lips whose redness had the effect of highlighting his white skin and giving the impression of an extraordinary pallor. And where the teeth protruded over the lips, they were white and sharp.

His eyes seemed a ghastly red in the glow of the flickering fire.

The woman, Clara, took a step toward him, hands out as if imploring, a glad cry on her red wanton lips, her breasts heaving as if with some wild ecstasy.

"My Lord," she cried, "you have come!"

The tall man ignored her. His red eyes were upon mine, seeming to devour me.

The woman raised a hand to massage her throat.

"Lord, take me first! Take me now!"

The tall man took a stride towards me, drawing back an arm and pushing her roughly aside.

"It is he that I shall take first," he said sibilantly, with a strange accent to his English. "You shall wait your turn which shall be in a little while."

The woman made to protest but he stopped her with an upraised hand.

"Dare you question me?" he said mildly. "Have no fear. You shall be my bountiful wine press in a while. But first I shall slake my thirst with him."

He towered over me as I remained helpless in that chair, that accursed chair. A smile edged his face.

"Is it not just?" whispered the tall man. "Is it not just that having thwarted me, you Upton Welsford, now become everything that you abhorred and feared?"

And while part of my mind was witnessing this obscene hallucination, another part of it began to experience a strange excitement—almost a sexual excitement as the man lowered his face to mine . . . closer came those awful red eyes to gaze deep into my soul. His mouth was open slightly, I could smell a vile reek of corruption. There was a deliberate voluptuousness about his movements that was both thrilling and appalling—he licked his lips like some animal, the scarlet tongue flickering over the white sharp teeth.

Lower came his head, lower, until it passed from my sight and I could hear the churning sound of his tongue against his teeth and could feel his hot breath on my neck. The skin of my throat began to tingle. Then I felt the soft shivering touch of his cold lips on my throat, the hard indent of two sharp white teeth!

For a while, how long I could not measure, I seemed to fall into a languorous ecstasy.

Then he was standing above me, smiling down sardonically, a trickle of blood on his chin. My blood!

"There is one more night to feast with him," he said softly. "One night more and then, Upton Welsford, you shall be my brother."

The woman exclaimed in anger.

"But you promised! You promised! When am I to be called?"

The tall man turned and laughed.

"Aye, I promised, my slender vine. You already bear my mark. You belong to me. You shall be one with me, never fear. Immortality will soon be yours and we shall share in the drinking. You will provide me with the wine of life. Have patience, for the greatest wines are long in the savouring. I shall return."

Then to my horror the man was gone. Simply gone, as if he had dissolved into elemental dust.

For some time I sat in horror staring at the woman who seemed to have retreated into a strange trance. Then the grandfather clock began to chime and the woman started, as if waking from a deep sleep. She stared in amazement at the clock and then towards the window where the faint light of early dawn was beginning to show.

"Good Lord, Upton," she exclaimed, "we seemed to have been up all night. I must have fallen asleep, I'm sorry."

She shook herself.

"I've had a strange dream. Ah well, no matter. I'd better get you up to bed. I'll go and wake poor Fanny to help me."

She smiled softly at me as she left the room; there was no trace of the wanton seductress left on her delicate features.

She left me sitting alone, alone in my prison of a chair.

I sit here alone and helpless. So utterly alone! Alone in an age which is not mine, in a body which is not mine. Oh God! I am slowly being killed—or worse! Yet what is worse than death? That terrifying limbo that is the borderland of Hell, that state that is neither the restful sleep of death nor the perplexities of life but is the nightmare of undeath.

And where is this person . . . the Upton Welsford whose body I now inhabit? Where is he? Has he, by some great effort of will, exchanged his body with mine? Is he even now awakening from that cat-nap sometime in the future? Awakening in my body, in my study, to resume my life? Is he doing even as I have done? What does it all mean?

Maybe this is an hallucination. Perhaps I am mad. How else can all this be explained?

# SPECIAL

# Richard Laymon

Richard Carl Laymon (1947–2001) was born in Chicago, moving to California as a child. He received a B.A. in English literature from Willamette University in Oregon and an M.A. in English literature from Marymount Loyola University in Los Angeles. He worked as a schoolteacher, a librarian, and a report writer for a law firm before becoming a full-time novelist and short-story writer. While mainly known as a horror writer, he also wrote other fiction, notably mysteries, having stories published in *Ellery Queen's Mystery Magazine*, *Alfred Hitchcock's Mystery Magazine*, *The Second Black Lizard Anthology of Crime Fiction*, and elsewhere.

In his primary writing genre, horror, he produced about sixty short stories and thirty novels, achieving far greater success in England and Europe than in his own country. His work has received numerous awards, including four nominations for Bram Stoker Awards from the Horror Writers Association: for *Flesh*, nominated for Best Novel in 1988; *Funland*, nominated for Best Novel in 1990; *Bad News*, nominated for Best Anthology in 2000; and *The Traveling Vampire Show*, which won as Best Novel in 2000. In addition, *Flesh* was named the Best Horror Novel of the Year by *Science Fiction Chronicle*. He also wrote several novels under the names Richard Kelly and Carl Laymon.

"Special" was originally published in *Under the Fang*, edited by Robert R. Mc-Cammon (New York: Pocket Books, 1991).

# Special

## RICHARD LAYMON

The outlaw women, wailing and shrieking, fled from the encampment. All but one, who stayed to fight.

She stood by the campfire, a sleek arm reaching up to pull an arrow from the quiver on her back. She stood alone as the men began to fall beneath the quick fangs of the dozen raiding vampires.

"She's mine!" Jim shouted.

None of his fellow Guardians gave him argument. Maybe they wanted no part of her. They raced into the darkness of the woods to chase down the others.

Jim rushed the woman.

*You get her and you get her.*

She looked innocent, fierce, glorious. Calmly nocking the arrow. Her thick hair was golden in the firelight. Her legs gleamed beneath the short leather skirt that hung low on her hips. Her vest spread open as she drew back her bowstring, sliding away from the tawny mound of her right breast.

Jim had never seen such a woman.

*Get her!*

She glanced at him. Without an instant of hesitation, she pivoted away and loosed her arrow.

Jim snapped his head sideways. The shaft flew at Strang's back. Hit him with a thunk. The vampire hurled the flapping body of an outlaw from his arms and whirled around, his black eyes fixing on the woman, blood spewing from his wide mouth as he bellowed, "Mine!"

Jim lurched to a halt.

Eyes narrowed, lips a tight line, the woman reached up for another arrow as Strang staggered toward her. Jim was near enough to hear breath hissing through her nostrils. He gazed at her, fascinated, as she fit the arrow onto the bowstring. Her eyes were on Strang. She pulled the string back to her jaw. Her naked breast rose and fell as she panted for air.

She didn't let the arrow fly.

Strang took one more stumbling stride, foamy blood gushing from his mouth, arms outstretched as if to reach beyond the campfire and grab her head. Then he pitched forward. His face crushed the flaming heap of wood, sending up a flurry of sparks. His hair began to blaze.

The woman met Jim's eyes.

*Get her and you get her.*

He'd never wanted any woman so much.

"Run!" he whispered. "Save yourself."

"Eat shit and die," she muttered, and released her arrow. It whizzed past his arm.

Going for her, Jim couldn't believe that she

876

had missed. But he heard the arrow punch into someone, heard the roar of a wounded vampire, and knew that she'd found her target. For the second time, she had chosen to take down a vampire rather than protect herself from him. And she hadn't run when he'd given her the chance. What kind of woman *is* this?

With his left hand, he knocked the bow aside. With his right, he swung at her face. His fist clubbed her cheek. Her head snapped sideways, mouth dropping open, spit spraying out. The punch spun her. The bow flew from her hand. Her legs tangled and she went down. She pushed at the ground, got to her hands and knees, and scurried away from Jim.

Let her go?

He hurried after her, staring at her legs. Shadows and firelight fluttered on them. Sweat glistened. The skirt was so short it barely covered her rump and groin.

*You get her and you get her.*

She thrust herself up.

I'm gonna let her go, Jim thought. They'll kill me, and they'll probably get her anyway, but . . .

Instead of making a break for the woods, she whirled around, jerked a knife from the sheath at her hip, and threw herself at Jim. The blade ripped the front of his shirt. Before she could bring it back across, he caught her wrist. He yanked her arm up high and drove a fist into her belly. Her breath exploded out. The blow picked her up. The power of it would've hurled her backward and slammed her to the ground, but Jim kept his grip on her wrist. She dangled in front of him, writhing and wheezing. Her sweaty face was twisted with agony.

One side of her vest hung open.

*She might've had a chance.*

*I got her, I get her.*

Jim cupped her warm, moist breast, felt its nipple pushing against his palm.

Her fist crashed into his nose. He saw it coming, but had no time to block it. Pain exploded behind his eyes. But he kept his grip, stretched her high by the trapped arm, and punched her belly until he could no longer hold her up.

Blinking tears from his eyes, sniffing up blood,

he let her go. She dropped to her knees in front of him and slumped forward, her face hitting the ground between his feet. Crouching, he pulled a pair of handcuffs from his belt. Blood splashed the back of her vest as he picked up her limp arms, pulled them behind her, and snapped the cuffs around her wrists.

"That one put up a hell of a scrap," Roger said.

Jim, sitting on the ground beside the crumpled body of the woman, looked up at the grinning vampire. "She was pretty tough," he said. He sniffed and swallowed some more blood. "Sorry I couldn't stop her quicker."

Roger patted him on the head. "Think nothing of it. Strang was always a pain in the ass, anyway, and Winthrop was such an atrocious brown-noser. I'm better off without them. I'd say, taken all 'round, that we've had a banner night."

Roger crouched in front of the woman, clutched the hair on top of her head, and lifted her to her knees. Her eyes were shut. By the limp way she hung there, Jim guessed she must still be unconscious.

"A looker," Roger said. "Well worth a broken nose, if you ask me." He chuckled. "Of course, it's not *my* nose. But if I were you, I'd be a pretty damn happy fellow about now." He eased her down gently and walked off to join the other vampires.

While they waited for all the Guardians to return with the female prisoners, they searched the bodies of the outlaws, took whatever possessions they found interesting, and stripped the corpses. They tossed the clothing into the campfire, not one of them bothering to remove Strang from the flames.

Joking and laughing quite a bit, they hacked the bodies to pieces. The banter died away as they began to suck the remaining blood from severed heads, stumps of necks and arms and legs, from various limbs and organs. Jim turned his eyes away. He looked at the woman. She was lucky to be out cold. She couldn't see the horrible carnage. She couldn't hear the grunts and sighs of pleasure, the sloppy wet sounds, the occasional belch from the vampires relishing their feast. Nor could she hear the women who'd been captured and brought in by the other Guardians. They were weeping, pleading, screaming, vomiting.

When he finally looked away from her, he saw that all the Guardians had returned. Each had a prisoner. Bart and Harry both had two. Most of the women looked as if they'd been beaten. Most had been stripped of their clothes.

They looked to Jim like a sorry bunch.

Not one stood proud and defiant.

I got the best of the lot, he thought.

Roger rose to his feet, tossed a head into the fire, and rubbed the back of his hand across his mouth. "Well, folks," he said, "how's about heading on back to the old homestead?"

Jim picked up the woman. Carrying her on his shoulder, he joined the procession through the woods. Other Guardians complimented him on his catch. Some made lewd suggestions about her. A few peeked under her skirt. Several offered to trade, and grumbled when Jim refused.

At last, they found their way to the road. They hiked up its moonlit center until they came to the bus. Biff and Steve, Guardians who'd stayed behind to protect it from outlaws and vampire gangs, waved greetings from its roof.

On the side of the black bus, in huge gold letters that glimmered with moonlight, was painted: ROGER'S ROWDY RAIDERS.

The vampires, Guardians, and prisoners climbed aboard.

Roger drove.

An hour later, they passed through the gates of his fortified estate.

The next day, Jim slept late. When he woke up, he lay in bed for a long time, thinking about the woman. Remembering her courage and beauty, the way her breast had felt in his hand, her weight and warmth and smoothness while she hung over his shoulder on the way to the bus.

He hoped she was all right. She'd seemed to be unconscious during the entire trip. Of course, she might've been pretending. Jim, sitting beside her, had savored the way she looked in the darkness and felt quick rushes of excitement each time a break in the trees permitted moonlight to wash across her.

The other Guardians were all busy ravishing their prisoners during the bus ride. Some had poked fun of him, asked if he'd gone queer like Biff and Steve, offered to pay him for a chance to screw Sleeping Beauty.

He wasn't sure why he had left her alone during the trip. In the past, he'd never hesitated to enjoy his prisoners.

But this woman was different. Special. Proud and strong. She deserved better than to be molested while out cold and in the presence of others.

Jim would have her soon. In privacy. She would be alert, brave, and fierce.

Soon.

But not today.

For today, the new arrivals would be in the care of Doc and his crew. They would be deloused and showered, then examined. Those judged incapable of bearing children would go to the Doner Ward. Each Doner had a two-fold job: to give a pint of blood daily for the estate's stockroom, and to provide sexual services not only for the Guardian who captured her but also for any others, so inclined, once he'd finished.

The other prisoners would find themselves in the Specialty Suite.

It wasn't a suite, just a barracklike room similar to the Doner Ward. But those assigned to it did receive special treatment. They weren't milked for blood. They were fed well.

And each Special could only be used by the Guardian who had captured her.

Mine will be a Special, Jim thought. She's gotta be. She *will* be. She's young and strong.

She'll be mine. All mine.

At least till Delivery Day.

He felt a cold, spreading heaviness.

That's a long time from now, he told himself. Don't think about it.

Moaning, he climbed out of bed.

h e was standing guard in the north tower at ten the next morning when the two-way radio squawked and Doc's voice came through the speaker. "Harmon, you're up. Specialty Suite, Honors Room Three. Bennington's on his way to relieve you."

Jim thumbed the speak button on his mike. "Roger," he said.

Heart pounding, he waited for Bennington. He'd found out last night that his prisoner, named Diane, had been designated a Special. He'd hoped this would be the day, but he hadn't counted on it; Doc only gave the okay if the timing was right. In Doc's opinion, it was only right during about two weeks of each woman's monthly cycle.

Jim couldn't believe his luck.

Finally, Bennington arrived. Jim climbed down from the tower and made his way across the courtyard toward the Specialty Suite. He had a hard time breathing. His legs felt weak and shaky.

He'd been in Honor Rooms before. With many different outlaw women. But he'd never felt like this: excited, horribly excited, but also nervous. Petrified.

h onors Room Three had a single large bed with red satin sheets. The plush carpet was red. So were the curtains that draped the barred windows, and the shades of the twin lamps on either side of the bed.

Jim sat down on a soft, upholstered armchair. And waited. Trembling.

Calm down, he told himself. This is crazy. She's just a woman.

Yeah, sure.

Hearing footfalls from the corridor, he leapt to his feet. He turned to the door. Watched it open.

Diane stumbled in, shoved from behind by Morgan and Donner, Doc's burly assistants. She glared at Jim.

"Key," Jim said.

Morgan shook his head. "I wouldn't, if were you."

"I brought her in, didn't I?"

"She'll bust more than your nose, you give her half a chance."

Jim held out his hand. Morgan, shrugging, tossed him the key to the shackles. Then the two men left the room. The door bumped shut, locking automatically.

And he was alone with Diane.

From the looks of her, she'd struggled on the way to the Honors Room. Her thick hair was mussed, golden wisps hanging down her face. Her blue satin robe had fallen off one shoulder. Its cloth belt was loose, allowing a narrow gap from her waist to the hem at her knees. She was naked beneath the robe.

Jim slipped a finger under the belt. He pulled until its half-knot came apart. Then he spread the robe and slipped it down her arms until it was stopped by the wrist shackles.

Guilt subdued his excitement when he saw the livid smudges on her belly. "I'm sorry about that," he murmured.

"Do what you're going to do," she said. Though she was trying to sound tough, he heard a slight tremor in her voice.

"I'll take these shackles off," he said. "But if you fight me, I'll be forced to hurt you again. I don't want to do that."

"Then don't take them off."

"It'll be easier on you without them."

"Easier *for* you."

"Do you know why you're here?"

"It seems pretty obvious."

"It's not that obvious," Jim said, warning himself to speak with care. The room was bugged. A Guardian in the Security Center would be eavesdropping, and Roger himself was fond of listening to the Honors Room tapes. "This isn't . . . just so I can have fun and games with you. The thing is . . . I've got to make you pregnant."

Her eyes narrowed. She caught her lower lip between her teeth. She said nothing.

"What that means," Jim went on, "is that we'll be seeing each other every day. At least during your fertile times. Every day until you conceive. Do you understand?"

"Why do they want me pregnant?" she asked.

"They need more humans. For guards and staff and things. As it is, there aren't enough of us."

She gazed into his eyes. He couldn't tell whether or not she believed the lie.

"If you don't become pregnant, they'll put you in with the Doners. It's much better for you here. The Doners . . . all the Guardians can have them whenever they want."

"So, it's either you or the whole gang, huh?"

"That's right."

"Okay."

"Okay?"

She nodded.

Jim began taking off his clothes, excited but uncomfortably aware of the scorn in her eyes.

"You must be a terrible coward," she said.

He felt heat spread over his skin.

"You don't seem evil. So you must be a coward. To serve such beasts."

"Roger treats us very well," he said.

"If you were a man, you'd kill him and all his kind. Or die trying."

"I have a good life here."

"The life of a dog."

Naked, he crouched in front of Diane. His face was inches from her tuft of golden down. Aching with a hot confusion of lust and shame, he lowered his eyes to the short length of chain stretched taut between her feet. "I'm no coward," he said, and removed the steel cuffs.

As the shackles fell to the carpet, she pumped a knee into his forehead. Not a powerful blow, but enough to knock him off balance. His rump hit the floor. He caught himself with both hands while Diane dropped backward, curling, jamming her thighs tight against her chest. Before he could get up, she somehow slipped the hand shackles and trapped robe under her but-

tocks and up the backs of her legs. They cleared her feet. Her hands were suddenly in front of her, cuffs and chain hidden under the draping robe.

As her heels thudded the floor, Jim rushed her. She spread her legs wide, raised her knees, and stretched her arms out straight overhead. The robe was a glossy curtain molded to her face and breasts.

Jim dove, slamming down on her. She grunted. Clamped her legs around him. He reached for her arms. They were too quick for him. The covered chain swept past his eyes. Went tight around his throat. Squeezed.

Choking, he found her wrists. They were crossed behind his head. He tugged at them. Parted them. Felt the chain loosen. Forced them down until the chain pressed into Diane's throat.

Her face had come uncovered. Her eyes bulged. Her lips peeled back. She twisted and bucked and squirmed.

When he entered her, tears shimmered in her eyes.

The next day, Jim let Morgan and Donner chain her to the bed frame before leaving. She didn't say a word. She didn't struggle. She lay motionless and glared at Jim as he took her.

When he was done but still buried in her tight heat, he whispered, "I'm sorry." He hoped the microphone didn't pick it up.

For an instant, the look of hatred in her eyes changed to something else. Curiosity? Hope?

What are you sorry about, Jim?"

"Sorry?"

"You apologized. What did you apologize for?"

"To who?"

"You've gone soft on her," Roger said. "Can't say I blame you. She's quite a looker. Feisty too. But she's obviously messing you up. I'm afraid someone else'll have to take over. We'll work a trade with Phil. You can do his gal, and he'll do yours. It'll be better for everyone."

"Yes, sir."

**P**hil's gal was named Betsy. She was a brunette. She was pretty. She was stacked. She was not just compliant, but enthusiastic. She said that she'd hated being an outlaw, living in the wilds, often hungry and always afraid. This, she said, was like paradise.

Jim had her once a day.

Each time, he closed his eyes and made believe she was Diane.

**H**e longed for her. He dreamed about her. But she was confined to the Specialty Suite, available only to Phil, so he would probably never have a chance to see her again. It ate at him. He began to hope she would fail to conceive. In that case, she would eventually be sent to the Doner Ward.

A terrible fate for someone with her spirit. But at least Jim would be able to see her, go to her, touch her, have her. And she would be spared the final horror which awaited the Specials. Doc had judged her to be fertile, however, so Jim knew there was little chance of ever seeing her again.

Jim was in the Mess Hall a week after being reassigned to Betsy, trying to eat lunch though he had no appetite, when the alarm suddenly blared. The PA boomed, "Guardian down, Honor Room One! Make it snappy, men!"

Jim and six others ran from the Mess Hall. Sprinting across the courtyard, he took over the lead. He found Donner waiting in the corridor. The man, gray and shaky, pointed at the closed door of Honor Room One.

Jim threw the door open.

Instead of a bed, this room was equipped with a network of steel bars from which the Special could be suspended, stretched, and spread in a variety of positions.

Diane hung by her wrists from a high bar. There were no restraints on her feet. She was swinging and twisting at the ends of her chains as she kicked at Morgan. Her face wore a fierce grimace. Her hair clung to her face. Her skin, apparently oiled by Phil, gleamed and poured sweat. The shackles had cut into her wrists, and blood streamed down her arms and sides.

Phil lay motionless on the floor beneath her wild, kicking body. His head was turned. Too much.

*She'd broken his neck?*

How could she?

Even as Jim wondered, he saw Morgan lurch forward and grab one of her darting ankles. Diane shot her other leg high. With a cry of pain, she twisted her body and hooked her foot behind Morgan's head. The big man stumbled toward her, gasping with alarm. He lost his hold on her ankle. That leg flew up. In an instant, he was on his knees, his head trapped between her thighs.

Morgan's dilemma seemed to snap the audience of Guardians out of their stunned fascination.

Jim joined the others in their rush to the rescue.

He grabbed one leg. Bart grabbed the other. They forced her thighs apart, freeing Morgan. The man slumped on top of Phil's body, made a quick little whimpery sound, and scurried backward.

"Take Phil out of here," said Rooney, the head Guardian.

The body was dragged from under Diane and taken from the room.

"What'll we do with her?" Jim asked.

"Let her hang," Rooney said. "We'll wait for tonight and let Roger take care of her."

They released her legs and backed up quickly.

She dangled, swaying back and forth, her eyes fixed on Jim.

He paused in the doorway. He knew he would never see her again.

**H**e was wrong.

He saw her a month later when he relieved Biff and began his new duty of monitoring video screens in the Security Center. Diane was on one of the dozen small screens. Alone. In the Punishment Room.

Jim couldn't believe his eyes. He'd been certain that Roger had killed her—probably torturing her, allowing the other vampires small samples of her blood before draining her himself. Jim had seen that done, once, to a Doner who tried to escape. Diane's crime had been much worse. She'd murdered a Guardian.

Instead of taking her life, however, Roger had merely sent her to the Punishment Room. Which amounted to little more than solitary confinement.

Incredible. Wonderful.

Night after night, alone in the Security Center, Jim watched her.

He watched her sleep on the concrete floor, a sheet wrapped around her naked body. He watched her sit motionless, crosslegged, gazing at the walls. He watched her squat on a metal bucket to relieve herself. Sometimes, she gave herself sponge baths.

Frequently, she exercised. For hours at a time, she would stretch, run in place, kick and leap, do sit-ups and push-ups and handstands. Jim loved to watch her quick, graceful motions, the flow of her sleek muscles, the way her hair danced and how her breasts jiggled and swayed. He loved the sheen of sweat that made her body glisten.

He could never see enough of her.

Every day, he waited eagerly for the hour when he could relieve Biff and be alone with Diane.

When he had to go on night raids, he was miserable. But he did his duty. He rounded up outlaw women. Some became Specials, and he visited them in Honor Rooms, but when he was with them he always tried to pretend they were Diane.

Then one night, watching her exercise, he noticed that her belly didn't look quite flat.

"No," he murmured.

Throughout the winter, he watched her grow. Every night, she seemed larger. Her breasts swelled and her belly became a bulging mound.

He often wondered whose child she was bearing. It might be his. It might be Phil's.

He worried, always, about Delivery Day.

During his free time, he began making solitary treks into the woods surrounding the estate.

He took his submachine gun and machete.

He often came back with game, which he delivered afterward to Jones in the kitchen. The grinning chef was always delighted to receive the fresh meat. He was glad to have Jim's company while he prepared it for the Guardians' evening meal.

Spring came. One morning at six, just as Bart entered the Security Center to relieve Jim of his watch, Diane flinched awake grimacing. She drew her knees up. She clutched her huge belly through the sheet.

"What gives?" Bart asked.

Jim shook his bead.

Bart studied the monitor. "She's starting contractions. I'd better ring up Doc."

Bart made the call. Then he took over Jim's seat in front of the video screens.

"I think I'll stick around," Jim said.

Bart chuckled. "Help yourself."

He stayed. He watched the monitor. Soon, Doc and Morgan and Donner entered the cell. They flung the sheet aside. Morgan and Donner forced Diane's legs apart. Doc inspected her. Then they lifted her onto a gurney and strapped her down. They rolled the gurney out of the cell.

"I'll pick 'em up in the Prep Room," Bart muttered. "That's what you want to see, right?" He leered over his shoulder.

Jim forced a smile. "You got it."

Bart fingered some buttons. The deserted Punishment Room vanished from the screen, and the Prep Room appeared.

Doc and his assistants rolled the gurney in.

He soaked a pad with chloroform and pressed it against Diane's nose and mouth until she passed out. Then the straps were unfastened.

After being sprayed with water, she was rubbed with white foam. All three men went at her with razors.

"Wouldn't mind that job," Bart said.

Jim watched the razors sweep paths through the foam, cutting away not only Diane's thick golden hair, but also the fine down. The passage of the blades left her skin shiny and pink. After a while, she was turned over so the rest of her body could be lathered and shaved.

Then the men rinsed her and dried her with towels.

They carried her from the gurney to the wheeled, oak serving table. The table, a rectangle large enough to seat only six, was bordered by brass gutters for catching the runoff. At the corners of one end—Roger's end—were brass stirrups.

Feeling sick, Jim watched the men lift Diane's limp body onto the table. They bent her legs. They strapped her feet into the stirrups. They slid her forward to put her within easy reach of Roger. Then they cinched a belt across her chest, just beneath her breasts. They stretched her arms overhead and strapped her wrists to the table.

"That's about it for now," Bart said. "If you drop by around seven tonight, that's about when they'll be basting her. She'll be awake then too. That's about the time the panic really hits them. It's usually quite a sight to behold."

"I've seen," Jim muttered, and left the room.

he returned to the barracks and tried to sleep. It was no use. Finally, he got up and armed himself. Steve let him out the front gate. He wandered the woods for hours. With his submachine gun, he bagged three squirrels.

In the late afternoon, he ducked into the hiding place he'd found in a clump of bushes. He lashed together the twenty wooden spears which he'd fashioned during the past weeks. He pocketed the small pouch containing the nightcap mushrooms which he had gathered and ground to fine powder.

He carried the spears to the edge of the forest. Leaving them propped against a tree, he stepped into the open. He smiled and waved his squirrels at the north tower. The gate opened, and he entered the estate.

He took the squirrels to Jones in the kitchen. And helped the cheerful chef prepare stew for the Guardians' supper.

Just after sunset, Jim went to the Security Center and knocked.

"Yo." Biff's voice.

"It's Jim. I want to see the basting."

"You're a little early," Biff said. Moments later, he opened the door. He exhaled sharply and folded over as Jim rammed a knife into his stomach.

Diane was awake, sweaty and grunting, struggling against the restraints, gritting her teeth and flinching rigid each time a contraction hit her.

Jim stared at the screen. Without hair and eyebrows, she looked so *odd*. Freakish. Even her figure, misshapen by the distended belly and swollen breasts, seemed alien. But her eyes were pure Diane. In spite of her pain and terror, they were proud, unyielding.

Doc entered the Prep Room, examined her for a few moments, then went away.

Jim checked the other screens.

In the Doner Ward, the women had been locked down for the Guardians' evening mealtime. Some slept. Others chatted with friends in neighboring beds. Jim made a quick count.

In the Specialty Suite, Morgan and Donner were just returning a woman from an Honors Room. They led her to one of the ten empty beds, shoved her down on it, and shackled her feet to the metal frame. Jim counted heads.

Thirty-two Doners. Only sixteen Specials. Generally, however, the Doners were older women who'd been weakened by the daily loss of blood and by regular mistreatment at the hands of the Guardians. The Specials were fewer in number, but younger and stronger. Though some appeared to be in the late stages of their pregnancies, most were not very far along, and many of the newer ones had probably not even conceived yet.

It'll be the Specials, Jim decided.

He watched Morgan and Donner leave the suite.

In the mess hall, Guardians began to eat their stew.

In the floodlit courtyard, Steven and Bennington climbed stairs to the north and west towers, carrying pots of dinner to the men on watch duty. When they finished there, they should be heading for the other two towers.

Morgan and Donner entered the mess hall. They sat down, and Jones brought them pots of stew.

Doc entered the Prep Room. He sat a bowl of shimmering red fluid onto the table beside Diane's hip. He dipped in a brush. He began to paint her body. The blood coated her like paint.

In the mess hall, Baxter groaned and staggered away from the table, clutching his belly.

In the Banquet Room, there was no camera. But Jim knew that Roger and his pals would be there, waiting and eager. The absence of the usual table would've already tipped them off that tonight would be special. Even now, Roger was probably picking five to sit with him at the serving table. The unfortunate four would only get to watch and dine on their usual fare of Doner blood.

In the mess hall, Guardians were stumbling about, falling down, rolling on the floor.

In the Prep Room, Doc set aside the brush and bowl. He rolled the serving table toward the door. Diane shook her crimson, hairless head from side to side and writhed against the restraints.

Jim rushed out of the Security Center.

**A**ll hell's broken loose!" he shouted as he raced up the stairs to the north tower. "Don't touch your food! Jones poisoned it!"

"Oh shit!" Harris blurted, and spat out a mouthful.

"Did you swallow any?" Jim asked, rushing toward him.

"Not much, but . . ."

Jim jerked the knife from the back of his belt and slashed Harris's throat. He punched a button on the control panel.

By the time he reached the front gate, it was open. He ran out, dashed across the clear area beyond the wall, and grabbed the bundle of spears.

The gate remained open for him. Apparently, the poison had taken care of the Guardian on the west tower.

Rushing across the courtyard, he saw two Guardians squirming on the ground.

At the outer door of the Specialty Suite, Jim snatched the master key off its nail. He threw the door open and rushed in.

"All right, ladies! Listen up! We're gonna kill some vampires!"

**B**lasts pounding his ears, Jim blew apart the lock. He threw his gun aside, kicked the door, and charged into the Banquet Room.

Followed by sixteen naked Specials yelling and brandishing spears.

For just an instant, the vampires around the serving table continued to go about their business—greedily lapping the brown, dry blood from Diane's face and breasts and legs as Roger groped between her thighs. The four who watched, goblets in hand, were the first to respond.

Then, roaring, they all abandoned the table and attacked.

All except Roger.

Roger stood where he was. He met Jim's eyes. *"You dumb fuck!"* he shouted. "Take care of him, guys!"

The vampires tried. They all rushed Jim.

But were met, first, by Specials. Some went down with spears in their chests while others tossed the women away or slammed them to the floor or snapped their spines or ripped out their throats.

Jim rushed through the melee. He halted at the near end of the table as Roger cried out, "Is *this* why you're here?" His hands delved. Came up a moment later with a tiny, gleaming infant. "Not enough to share, I'm afraid." Grinning, he raised the child to his mouth. With a quick nip, he severed its umbilical cord.

One hand clutching the baby's feet, he raised it high and tilted back his head. His mouth opened wide. His other hand grasped the top of its head.

Ready to twist it off. Ready to enjoy his special, rare treat.

"No!" Diane shrieked.

Jim hurled his spear. Roger's hand darted down. He caught the shaft, stopping its flight even as the wooden point touched his chest. "Dickhead," he said. "You didn't really think . . ."

Jim launched himself at Diane. He flew over her body, smashed down on her, slid through the wide V of her spread legs and reached high and grabbed the spear and rammed it deep into Roger's chest.

The vampire bellowed. He staggered backward. Coughed. Blood exploded from his mouth, spraying Jim's face and arms. He dropped to his knees and looked up at the infant that he still held high. He lowered its head toward his wide, gushing mouth.

Jim flung himself off the end of the table and landed on the spear. As its shaft snapped under his weight, bloody vomit cascaded over his head. Pushing himself up, he saw the baby dangling over Roger's mouth. The vampire snapped futilely at its head. Jim scurried forward and grabbed the child as Roger let go and slumped against the floor.

Afterward, the Doners were released. They helped with the burials.

Eleven dead Specials were buried in the courtyard, their graves marked by crosses fashioned of spears.

Morgan, Donner, and the Guardians, who'd all succumbed to the poison, were buried beyond the south wall of the estate.

The corpses of Roger and his fellow vampires were taken into the woods to a clearing where two trails crossed. The heads were severed. The torsos were buried with the spears still in place. The heads were carried a mile away to another crossing in the trail. There, they were burned. The charred skulls were crushed, then buried.

After a vote by the women, Doc and three Guardians who'd missed the poisoned squirrels were put to death. Jones had also missed the meal. But the women seemed to like him. He was appointed chef. Jim was appointed leader.

He chose Diane to be his assistant.

The child was a girl. They named her Glory. She had Diane's eyes, and ears that stuck out in very much the same way as Jim's.

The small army lived in Roger's estate, and seemed happy.

Frequently, when the weather was good, a squad of well-armed volunteers would board the bus. Jim driving, they would follow roads deep into the woods. They would park the bus and wander about, searching. Sometimes they found vampires and took them down with a shower of arrows. Sometimes they found bands of outlaws and welcomed these strangers into their ranks.

One morning, when a commotion in the courtyard drew Jim's attention, he looked down from the north tower and saw Diane gathered around the bus with half a dozen other women. Instead of their usual leather skirts and vests, they were dressed in rags.

Diane saw him watching, and waved. Her hair had grown, but it was still quite short. It shone like gold in the sunlight.

She looked innocent, glorious.

She and her friends were painting the bus pink.

## CARRION COMFORT

# Dan Simmons

Dan Simmons (1948– ) was born in Peoria, Illinois, then lived in various cities and small towns in the Midwest. He received his B.A. in English from Wabash College in 1970 and his master's in education from Washington University in St. Louis a year later, working in elementary education for eighteen years. His first published short story, "The River Styx Runs Upstream," written with the assistance of Harlan Ellison, won first prize in a *Rod Serling's Twilight Zone Magazine* competition in 1982; it was published on the same day that his daughter was born.

Most of Simmons's early work was in the horror genre, beginning with his first novel, *Song of Kali* (1985), which won the World Fantasy Award. After *Summer of Night* (1991), he began to focus on science fiction, though *Children of the Night* (1992) won the Locus Award (one of his three) in the Best Horror category. His novel *Hyperion* (1989) won both the Hugo and Locus awards. The basic structure of this, one of his most successful novels, is taken from Geoffrey Chaucer's *Canterbury Tales,* with a group of individuals on a pilgrimage to the planet Hyperion to seek the demon-god called the Shrike, each explaining his reason for the journey.

"Carrion Comfort" was originally published in the September/October 1983 issue of *Omni* magazine. It derives its title from a Gerard Manley Hopkins poem. Simmons later expanded the short story into a novel of the same title, winning the Bram Stoker Award from the Horror Writers of America in 1989.

# Carrion Comfort

## DAN SIMMONS

ina was going to take credit for the death of the Beatle, John. I thought that was in very bad taste. She had her scrapbook laid out on my mahogany coffee table, newspaper clippings neatly arranged in chronological order, the bald statements of death recording all of her Feedings. Nina Drayton's smile was radiant, but her pale-blue eyes showed no hint of warmth.

"We should wait for Willi," I said.

"Of course, Melanie. You're right, as always. How silly of me. I know the rules." Nina stood and began walking around the room, idly touching the furnishings or exclaiming softly over a ceramic statuette or piece of needlepoint. This part of the house had once been the conservatory, but now I used it as my sewing room. Green plants still caught the morning light. The light made it a warm, cozy place in the daytime, but now that winter had come the room was too chilly to use at night. Nor did I like the sense of darkness closing in against all those panes of glass.

"I love this house," said Nina.

She turned and smiled at me. "I can't tell you how much I look forward to coming back to Charleston. We should hold all of our reunions here."

I knew how much Nina loathed this city and this house.

"Willi would be hurt," I said. "You know how he likes to show off his place in Beverly Hills—and his new girlfriends."

"And boyfriends," Nina said, laughing. Of all the changes and darkenings in Nina, her laugh has been least affected. It was still the husky but childish laugh that I had first heard so long ago. It had drawn me to her then—one lonely, adolescent girl responding to the warmth of another as a moth to a flame. Now it served only to chill me and put me even more on guard. Enough moths had been drawn to Nina's flame over the many decades.

"I'll send for tea," I said.

Mr. Thorne brought the tea in my best Wedgwood china. Nina and I sat in the slowly moving squares of sunlight and spoke softly of nothing important: mutually ignorant comments on the economy, references to books that the other had not gotten around to reading, and sympathetic murmurs about the low class of persons one meets while flying these days. Someone peering in from the garden might have thought he was seeing an aging but attractive niece visiting her favorite aunt. (I drew the line at suggesting that anyone would mistake us for mother and daughter.) People usually consider me a well-dressed if not stylish person. Heaven knows I have paid enough to have the wool skirts and silk blouses mailed from Scotland and France. But next to Nina I've always felt dowdy.

This day she wore an elegant, light-blue dress that must have cost several thousand dollars. The color made her complexion seem even more perfect than usual and brought out the blue of her eyes. Her hair had gone as gray as mine, but somehow she managed to get away with wearing it long and tied back with a single barrette. It looked youthful and chic on Nina and made me feel that my short artificial curls were glowing with a blue rinse.

Few would suspect that I was four years younger than Nina. Time had been kind to her. And she had Fed more often.

She set down her cup and saucer and moved aimlessly around the room again. It was not like Nina to show such signs of nervousness. She stopped in front of the glass display case. Her gaze passed over the Hummels and the pewter pieces and then stopped in surprise.

"Good heavens, Melanie. A pistol! What an odd place to put an old pistol."

"It's an heirloom," I said. "A Colt Peacemaker from right after the War Between the States. Quite expensive. And you're right, it *is* a silly place to keep it. But it's the only case I have in the house with a lock on it and Mrs. Hodges often brings her grandchildren when she visits—"

"You mean it's *loaded*?"

"No, of course not," I lied. "But children should not play with such things . . ." I trailed off lamely. Nina nodded but did not bother to conceal the condescension in her smile. She went to look out the south window into the garden.

*Damn her.* It said volumes about Nina that she did not recognize that pistol.

On the day he was killed, Charles Edgar Larchmont had been my beau for precisely five months and two days. There had been no formal announcement, but we were to be married. Those five months had been a microcosm of the

era itself—naive, flirtatious, formal to the point of preciosity, and romantic. Most of all, romantic. Romantic in the worst sense of the word: dedicated to saccharine or insipid ideals that only an adolescent—or an adolescent society—would strive to maintain. We were children playing with loaded weapons.

Nina, she was Nina Hawkins then, had her own beau—a tall, awkward, but well-meaning Englishman named Roger Harrison. Mr. Harrison had met Nina in London a year earlier, during the first stages of the Hawkinses' Grand Tour. Declaring himself smitten—another absurdity of those times—the tall Englishman had followed her from one European capital to another until, after being firmly reprimanded by Nina's father (an unimaginative little milliner who was constantly on the defensive about his doubtful social status), Harrison returned to London to "settle his affairs." Some months later he showed up in New York just as Nina was being packed off to her aunt's home in Charleston in order to terminate yet another flirtation. Still undaunted, the clumsy Englishman followed her south, ever mindful of the protocols and restrictions of the day.

We were a gay group. The day after I met Nina at Cousin Celia's June ball, the four of us were taking a hired boat up the Cooper River for a picnic on Daniel Island. Roger Harrison, serious and solemn on every topic, was a perfect foil for Charles's irreverent sense of humor. Nor did Roger seem to mind the good-natured jesting, since he was soon joining in the laughter with his peculiar *haw-haw-haw*.

Nina loved it all. Both gentlemen showered attention on her, and although Charles never failed to show the primacy of his affection for me, it was understood by all that Nina Hawkins was one of those young women who invariably becomes the center of male gallantry and attention in any gathering. Nor were the social strata of Charleston blind to the combined charm of our foursome. For two months of that now-distant summer, no party was complete, no excursion adequately planned, and no occasion considered a success unless we four were invited and had chosen to attend. Our

happy dominance of the youthful social scene was so pronounced that Cousins Celia and Loraine wheedled their parents into leaving two weeks early for their annual August sojourn in Maine.

I am not sure when Nina and I came up with the idea of the duel. Perhaps it was during one of the long, hot nights when the other "slept over"—creeping into the other's bed, whispering and giggling, stifling our laughter when the rustling of starched uniforms betrayed the presence of our colored maids moving through the darkened halls. In any case, the idea was the natural outgrowth of the romantic pretensions of the time. The picture of Charles and Roger actually dueling over some abstract point of honor relating to *us* thrilled both of us in a physical way that I recognize now as a simple form of sexual titillation.

It would have been harmless except for the Ability. We had been so successful in our manipulation of male behavior—a manipulation that was both expected and encouraged in those days—that neither of us had yet suspected that there was anything beyond the ordinary in the way we could translate our whims into other people's actions. The field of parapsychology did not exist then; or rather, it existed only in the rappings and knockings of parlor-game séances. At any rate, we amused ourselves for several weeks with whispered fantasies, and then one of us—or perhaps both of us—used the Ability to translate the fantasy into reality.

In a sense, it was our first Feeding.

I do not remember the purported cause of the quarrel, perhaps some deliberate misinterpretation of one of Charles's jokes. I cannot recall who Charles and Roger arranged to have serve as seconds on that illegal outing. I do remember the hurt and confused expression on Roger Harrison's face during those few days. It was a caricature of ponderous dullness, the confusion of a man who finds himself in a situation not of his making and from which he cannot escape. I remember Charles and his mercurial swings of mood—the bouts of humor, periods of black anger, and the tears and kisses the night before the duel.

I remember with great clarity the beauty of that morning. Mists were floating up from the river and diffusing the rays of the rising sun as we rode out to the dueling field. I remember Nina reaching over and squeezing my hand with an impetuous excitement that was communicated through my body like an electric shock.

Much of the rest of that morning is missing. Perhaps in the intensity of that first, subconscious Feeding, I literally lost consciousness as I was engulfed in the waves of fear, excitement, pride—of *maleness*—emanating from our two beaus as they faced death on that lovely morning. I remember experiencing the shock of realizing, *this is really happening,* as I shared the tread of high boots through the grass. Someone was calling off the paces. I dimly recall the weight of the pistol in my hand—Charles's hand, I think; I will never know for sure—and a second of cold clarity before an explosion broke the connection, and the acrid smell of gunpowder brought me back to myself.

It was Charles who died. I have never been able to forget the incredible quantities of blood that poured from the small, round hole in his breast. His white shirt was crimson by the time I reached him. There had been no blood in our fantasies. Nor had there been the sight of Charles with his head lolling, mouth dribbling saliva onto his bloodied chest while his eyes rolled back to show the whites like two eggs embedded in his skull.

Roger Harrison was sobbing as Charles breathed his final, shuddering gasps on that field of innocence.

I remember nothing at all about the confused hours that followed. The next morning I opened my cloth bag to find Charles's pistol lying with my things. Why would I have kept that revolver? If I had wished to take something from my fallen lover as a sign of remembrance, why that alien piece of metal? Why pry from his dead fingers the symbol of our thoughtless sin?

It said volumes about Nina that she did not recognize that pistol.

"Willi's here," announced Nina's amanuensis, the loathsome Miss Barrett Kramer. Kramer's appearance was as unisex as her name: short-cropped, black hair, powerful shoulders, and a blank, aggressive gaze that I associated with lesbians and criminals. She looked to be in her mid-thirties.

"Thank you, Barrett dear," said Nina.

Both of us went out to greet Willi, but Mr. Thorne had already let him in, and we met in the hallway.

"Melanie! You look marvelous! You grow younger each time I see you. Nina!" The change in Willi's voice was evident. Men continued to be overpowered by their first sight of Nina after an absence. There were hugs and kisses. Willi himself looked more dissolute than ever. His alpaca sport coat was exquisitely tailored, his turtleneck sweater successfully concealed the eroded lines of his wattled neck, but when he swept off his jaunty sports-car cap the long strands of white hair he had brushed forward to hide his encroaching baldness were knocked into disarray. Willi's face was flushed with excitement, but there was also the telltale capillary redness about the nose and cheeks that spoke of too much liquor, too many drugs.

"Ladies, I think you've met my associates, Tom Luhar and Jenson Reynolds?" The two men added to the crowd in my narrow hall. Mr. Luhar was thin and blond, smiling with perfectly capped teeth. Mr. Reynolds was a gigantic Negro, hulking forward with a sullen, bruised look on his coarse face. I was sure that neither Nina nor I had encountered these specific cat's-paws of Willi's before. It did not matter.

"Why don't we go into the parlor?" I suggested. It was an awkward procession ending with the three of us seated on the heavily upholstered chairs surrounding the Georgian tea table that had been my grandmother's. "More tea, please, Mr. Thorne." Miss Kramer took that as her cue to leave, but Willi's two pawns stood uncertainly by the door, shifting from foot to foot and glancing at the crystal on display as if their mere proximity could break something. I would not have been surprised if that had proved to be the case.

"Jense!" Willi snapped his fingers. The Negro hesitated and then brought forward an expensive leather attaché case. Willi set it on the tea table

and clicked the catches open with his short, broad fingers. "Why don't you two see Mrs. Fuller's man about getting something to drink?"

When they were gone Willi shook his head and smiled apologetically at Nina. "Sorry about that, Love."

Nina put her hand on Willi's sleeve. She leaned forward with an air of expectancy. "Melanie wouldn't let me begin the Game without you. Wasn't that *awful* of me to want to start without you, Willi dear?"

Willi frowned. After fifty years he still bridled at being called Willi. In Los Angeles he was Big Bill Borden. When he returned to his native Germany—which was not often because of the dangers involved—he was once again Wilhelm von Borchert, lord of dark manor, forest, and hunt. But Nina had called him Willi when they had first met in 1931 in Vienna, and Willi he had remained.

"You begin, Willi dear," said Nina. "You go first."

I could remember the time when we would have spent the first few days of our reunion in conversation and catching up with one another's lives. Now there was not even time for small talk.

Willi showed his teeth and removed news clippings, notebooks, and a stack of cassettes from his briefcase. No sooner had he covered the small table with his material than Mr. Thorne arrived with the tea and Nina's scrapbook from the sewing room. Willi brusquely cleared a small space.

At first glance one might see certain similarities between Willi Borchert and Mr. Thorne. One would be mistaken. Both men tended to the florid, but Willi's complexion was the result of excess and emotion; Mr. Thorne had known neither of these for many years. Willi's balding was a patchy, self-consciously concealed thing—a weasel with mange; Mr. Thorne's bare head was smooth and unwrinkled. One could not imagine Mr. Thorne ever having *had* hair. Both men had gray eyes—what a novelist would call cold, gray eyes—but Mr. Thorne's eyes were cold with indifference, cold with a clarity coming from an absolute absence of troublesome emotion or thought. Willi's eyes were the cold of a blustery North Sea winter and were often clouded with shifting curtains of the emotions that controlled him—pride, hatred, love of pain, the pleasures of destruction.

Willi never referred to his use of the Ability as *Feedings*—I was evidently the only one who thought in those terms—but Willi sometimes talked of The Hunt. Perhaps it was the dark forests of his homeland that he thought of as he stalked his human quarry through the sterile streets of Los Angeles. Did Willi dream of the forest, I wondered. Did he look back to green wool hunting jackets, the applause of retainers, the gouts of blood from the dying boar? Or did Willi remember the slam of jack-boots on cobblestones and the pounding of his lieutenants' fists on doors? Perhaps Willi still associated his Hunt with the dark European night of the ovens that he had helped to oversee.

I called it Feeding. Willi called it The Hunt. I had never heard Nina call it anything.

"Where is your VCR?" Willi asked. "I have put them all on tape."

"Oh, Willi," said Nina in an exasperated tone. "You know Melanie. She's *so* old-fashioned. You know she wouldn't have a video player."

"I don't even have a television," I said. Nina laughed.

"Goddamn it," muttered Willi. "It doesn't matter. I have other records here." He snapped rubber bands from around the small, black notebooks. "It just would have been better on tape. The Los Angeles stations gave much coverage to the Hollywood Strangler, and I edited in the . . . Ach! Never mind."

He tossed the videocassettes into his briefcase and slammed the lid shut.

"Twenty-three," he said. "Twenty-three since we met twelve months ago. It doesn't seem that long, does it?"

"Show us," said Nina. She was leaning forward, and her blue eyes seemed very bright. "I've been wondering since I saw the Strangler interviewed on *Sixty Minutes*. He *was* yours, Willi? He seemed so—"

"*Ja, ja,* he was mine. A nobody. A timid little man. He was the gardener of a neighbor of mine. I left him alive so that the police could question

him, erase any doubts. He will hang himself in his cell next month after the press loses interest. But this is more interesting. Look at this." Willi slid across several glossy black-and-white photographs. The NBC executive had murdered the five members of his family and drowned a visiting soap-opera actress in his pool. He had then stabbed himself repeatedly and written 50 SHARE in blood on the wall of the bathhouse.

"Reliving old glories, Willi?" asked Nina. "DEATH TO THE PIGS and all that?"

"No, goddamn it. I think it should receive points for irony. The girl had been scheduled to drown on the program. It was already in the script outline."

"Was he hard to Use?" It was my question. I was curious despite myself.

Willi lifted one eyebrow. "Not really. He was an alcoholic and heavily into cocaine. There was not much left. And he hated his family. Most people do."

"Most people in California, perhaps," said Nina primly. It was an odd comment from Nina. Years ago her father had committed suicide by throwing himself in front of a trolley car.

"Where did you make contact?" I asked.

"A party. The usual place. He bought the coke from a director who had ruined one of my—"

"Did you have to repeat the contact?"

Willi frowned at me. He kept his anger under control, but his face grew redder. "*Ja, ja.* I saw him twice more. Once I just watched from my car as he played tennis."

"Points for irony," said Nina. "But you lose points for repeated contact. If he were as empty as you say, you should have been able to Use him after only one touch. What else do you have?"

He had his usual assortment. Pathetic skid-row murders. Two domestic slayings. A highway collision that turned into a fatal shooting. "I was in the crowd," said Willi. "I made contact. He had a gun in the glove compartment."

"Two points," said Nina.

Willi had saved a good one for last. A once-famous child star had suffered a bizarre accident. He had left his Bel Air apartment while it filled with gas and then returned to light a match. Two others had died in the ensuing fire.

"You get credit only for him," said Nina.

"*Ja, ja.*"

"Are you absolutely sure about this one? It *could* have been an accident."

"Don't be ridiculous," snapped Willi. He turned toward me. "*This* one was very hard to Use. Very strong. I blocked his memory of turning on the gas. Had to hold it away for two hours. Then forced him into the room. He struggled not to strike the match."

"You should have had him use his lighter," said Nina.

"He didn't smoke," growled Willi. "He gave it up last year."

"Yes," smiled Nina. "I seem to remember him saying that to Johnny Carson." I could not tell whether Nina was jesting.

The three of us went through the ritual of assigning points. Nina did most of the talking. Willi went from being sullen to expansive to sullen again. At one point he reached over and patted my knee as he laughingly asked for my support. I said nothing. Finally he gave up, crossed the parlor to the liquor cabinet, and poured himself a tall glass of bourbon from father's decanter. The evening light was sending its final, horizontal rays through the stained-glass panels of the bay windows, and it cast a red hue on Willi as he stood next to the oak cupboard. His eyes were small, red embers in a bloody mask.

"Forty-one," said Nina at last.

She looked up brightly and showed the calculator as if it verified some objective fact. "I count forty-one points. What do you have, Melanie?"

"*Ja,*" interrupted Willi. "That is fine. Now let us see your claims, Nina." His voice was flat and empty. Even Willi had lost some interest in the Game.

Before Nina could begin, Mr. Thorne entered and motioned that dinner was served. We adjourned to the dining room—Willi pouring himself another glass of bourbon and Nina fluttering her hands in mock frustration at the interruption of the Game. Once seated at the long, mahogany table, I worked at being a hostess. From decades of tradition, talk of the Game was banned from the dinner table. Over soup we discussed Willi's new movie and the purchase of another store for Nina's line of boutiques. It seemed that Nina's monthly column in *Vogue* was to be discontinued but that a newspaper syndicate was interested in picking it up.

Both of my guests exclaimed over the perfection of the baked ham, but I thought that Mr. Thorne had made the gravy a trifle too sweet. Darkness had filled the windows before we finished our chocolate mousse. The refracted light from the chandelier made Nina's hair dance with highlights while I feared that mine glowed more bluely than ever.

Suddenly there was a sound from the kitchen. The huge Negro's face appeared at the swinging door. His shoulder was hunched against white hands and his expression was that of a querulous child.

". . . the hell you think we are sittin' here like goddamned—" The white hands pulled him out of sight.

"Excuse me, ladies." Willi dabbed linen at his lips and stood up. He still moved gracefully for all of his years.

Nina poked at her chocolate. There was one sharp, barked command from the kitchen and the sound of a slap. It was the slap of a man's hand—hard and flat as a small-caliber-rifle shot. I looked up and Mr. Thorne was at my elbow, clearing away the dessert dishes.

"Coffee, please, Mr. Thorne. For all of us." He nodded and his smile was gentle.

Franz Anton Mesmer had known of it even if he had not understood it. I suspect that Mesmer must have had some small touch of the Ability. Modern pseudosciences have studied it and renamed it, removed most of its power, confused its uses and origins, but it remains the shadow of what Mesmer discovered. They have no idea of what it is like to Feed.

I despair at the rise of modern violence. I truly

give in to despair at times, that deep, futureless pit of despair that poet Gerard Manley Hopkins called carrion comfort. I watch the American slaughterhouse, the casual attacks on popes, presidents, and uncounted others, and I wonder whether there are many more out there with the Ability or whether butchery has simply become the modern way of life.

All humans feed on violence, on the small exercises of power over another. Bur few have tasted—as we have—the ultimate power. And without the Ability, few know the unequaled pleasure of taking a human life. Without the Ability, even those who do feed on life cannot savor the flow of emotions in stalker and victim, the total exhilaration of the attacker who has moved beyond all rules and punishments, the strange, almost sexual submission of the victim in that final second of truth when all options are canceled, all futures denied, all possibilities erased in an exercise of absolute power over another.

I despair at modern violence. I despair at the impersonal nature of it and the casual quality that has made it accessible to so many. I had a television set until I sold it at the height of the Vietnam War. Those sanitized snippets of death—made distant by the camera's lens—meant nothing to me. But I believe it meant something to these cattle that surround me. When the war and the nightly televised body counts ended, they demanded more, *more,* and the movie screens and streets of this sweet and dying nation have provided it in mediocre, mob abundance. It is an addiction I know well.

They miss the point. Merely observed, violent death is a sad and sullied tapestry of confusion. But to those of us who have Fed, death can be a *sacrament.*

"M y turn! My turn!" Nina's voice still resembled that of the visiting belle who had just filled her dance card at Cousin Celia's June ball.

We had returned to the parlor. Willi had finished his coffee and requested a brandy from Mr. Thorne. I was embarrassed for Willi. To have

one's closest associates show any hint of unplanned behavior was certainly a sign of weakening Ability. Nina did not appear to have noticed.

"I have them all in order," said Nina. She opened the scrapbook on the now-empty tea table. Willi went through them carefully, sometimes asking a question, more often grunting assent. I murmured occasional agreement although I had heard of none of them. Except for the Beatle, of course. Nina saved that for near the end.

"Good God, Nina, that was you?" Willi seemed near anger. Nina's Feedings had always run to Park Avenue suicides and matrimonial disagreements ending in shots fired from expensive, small-caliber ladies' guns. This type of thing was more in Willi's crude style. Perhaps he felt that his territory was being invaded. "I mean . . . you were risking a lot, weren't you? It's so . . . damn it . . . so *public.*"

Nina laughed and set down the calculator. "Willi *dear,* that's what the Game is *about,* is it not?"

Willi strode to the liquor cabinet and refilled his brandy snifter. The wind tossed bare branches against the leaded glass of the bay window. I do not like winter. Even in the South it takes its toll on the spirit.

"Didn't this guy . . . what's his name . . . buy the gun in Hawaii or someplace?" asked Willi from across the room. "That sounds like his initiative to me. I mean, if he was *already* stalking the fellow—"

"Willie dear." Nina's voice had gone as cold as the wind that raked the branches. "No one said he was *stable.* How many of yours are stable, Willi? But I made it *happen,* darling. I chose the place and the time. Don't you see the irony of the *place,* Willi? After that little prank on the director of that witchcraft movie a few years ago? It was straight from the script—"

"I don't know," said Willi. He sat heavily on the divan, spilling brandy on his expensive sport coat. He did not notice. The lamplight reflected from his balding skull. The mottles of age were more visible at night, and his neck, where it disappeared into his turtleneck, was all ropes and tendons. "I don't know." He looked up at me and smiled suddenly, as if we shared a conspiracy. "It could be like that writer fellow, eh, Melanie? It could be like that."

Nina looked down at the hands in her lap. They were clenched and the well-manicured fingers were white at the tips.

*The Mind Vampires.* That's what the writer was going to call his book.

I sometimes wonder if he really would have written anything. What was his name? Something Russian.

Willi and I received telegrams from Nina: COME QUICKLY YOU ARE NEEDED. That was enough. I was on the next morning's flight to New York. The plane was a noisy, propeller-driven Constellation, and I spent much of the flight assuring the overly solicitous stewardess that I needed nothing, that, indeed, I felt fine. She obviously had decided that I was someone's grandmother, who was flying for the first time.

Willi managed to arrive twenty minutes before me. Nina was distraught and as close to hysteria as I had ever seen her. She had been at a party in lower Manhattan two days before—she was not so distraught that she forgot to tell us what important names had been there—when she found herself sharing a corner, a fondue pot, and confidences with a young writer. Or rather, the writer was sharing confidences. Nina described him as a scruffy sort with a wispy little beard, thick glasses, a corduroy sport coat worn over an old plaid shirt—one of the type invariably sprinkled around successful parties of that era, according to Nina. She knew enough not to call him a beatnik, for that term had just become passé, but no one had yet heard the term *hippie,* and it wouldn't have applied to him anyway. He was a writer of the sort that barely ekes out a living, these days at least, by selling blood and doing novelizations of television series. Alexander something.

His idea for a book—he told Nina that he had been working on it for some time—was that many of the murders then being committed were actu-

ally the result of a small group of psychic killers, he called them *mind vampires,* who used others to carry out their grisly deeds.

He said that a paperback publisher had already shown interest in his outline and would offer him a contract tomorrow if he would change the title to *The Zombie Factor* and put in more sex.

"So what?" Willi had said to Nina in disgust. "You have me fly across the continent for this? I might buy the idea myself."

That turned out to be the excuse we used to interrogate this Alexander somebody during an impromptu party given by Nina the next evening. I did not attend. The party was not overly successful according to Nina but it gave Willi the chance to have a long chat with the young would-be novelist. In the writer's almost pitiable eagerness to do business with Bill Borden, producer of *Paris Memories, Three on a Swing,* and at least two other completely forgettable Technicolor features touring the drive-ins that summer, he revealed that the book consisted of a well-worn outline and a dozen pages of notes.

He was sure, however, that he could do a treatment for Mr. Borden in five weeks, perhaps even as fast as three weeks if he were flown out to Hollywood to get the proper creative stimulation.

Later that evening we discussed the possibility of Willi simply buying an option on the treatment, but Willi was short on cash at the time and Nina was insistent. In the end the young writer opened his femoral artery with a Gillette blade and ran screaming into a narrow Greenwich Village side street to die. I don't believe that anyone ever bothered to sort through the clutter and debris of his remaining notes.

It could be like that writer, *ja,* Melanie?" Willi patted my knee. I nodded. "He was mine," continued Willi, "and Nina tried to take credit. Remember?"

Again I nodded. Actually he had been neither Nina's nor Willi's. I had avoided the party so that I could make contact later without the young man noticing he was being followed. I did so easily. I remember sitting in an overheated little delicatessen across the street from the apartment building. It was over so quickly that there was almost no sense of Feeding. Then I was aware once again of the sputtering radiators and the smell of salami as people rushed to the door to see what the screaming was about. I remember finishing my tea slowly so that I did not have to leave before the ambulance was gone.

"Nonsense," said Nina. She busied herself with her little calculator. "How many points?" She looked at me. I looked at Willi.

"Six," he said with a shrug. Nina made a small show of totaling the numbers.

"Thirty-eight," she said and sighed theatrically. "You win again, Willi. Or rather, you beat *me* again. We must hear from Melanie. You've been so quiet, dear. You must have some surprise for us."

"Yes," said Willi, "it is your turn to win. It has been several years."

"None," I said. I had expected an explosion of questions, but the silence was broken only by the ticking of the clock on the mantelpiece. Nina was looking away from me, at something hidden by the shadows in the corner.

"None?" echoed Willi.

"There was . . . one," I said at last. "But it was by accident. I came across them robbing an old man behind . . . but it was completely by accident."

Willi was agitated. He stood up, walked to the window, turned an old straight-back chair around, and straddled it, arms folded. "What does this mean?"

"You're quitting the Game?" Nina asked as she turned to look at me. I let the question serve as the answer.

"Why?" snapped Willi. In his excitement it came out with a hard *v*.

If I had been raised in an era when young ladies were allowed to shrug, I would have done so. As it was, I contented myself with running my fingers along an imaginary seam on my skirt.

Willi had asked the question, but I stared straight into Nina's eyes when I finally answered, "I'm tired. It's been too long. I guess I'm getting old."

"You'll get a lot *older* if you do not Hunt," said Willi. His body, his voice, the red mask of his face, everything signaled great anger just kept in check. "My God, Melanie, you *already* look older! You look terrible. This is *why* we hunt, woman. Look at yourself in the mirror! Do you want to die an old woman just because you're tired of using *them*?" Willi stood and turned his back.

"Nonsense!" Nina's voice was strong, confident, in command once more. "Melanie's *tired,* Willi. Be nice. We all have times like that. I remember how *you* were after the war. Like a whipped puppy. You wouldn't even go outside your miserable little flat in Baden. Even after we helped you get to New Jersey you just sulked around feeling sorry for yourself. Melanie *made up* the Game to help you feel better. So quiet! *Never* tell a lady who feels tired and depressed that she looks terrible. Honestly, Willi, you're such a *Schwachsinniger* sometimes. And a crashing boor to boot."

I had anticipated many reactions to my announcement, but this was the one I feared most. It meant that Nina had also tired of the Game. It meant that she was ready to move to another level of play.

It had to mean that.

"Thank you, Nina darling," I said. "I knew you would understand."

She reached across and touched my knee reassuringly. Even through my wool skirt, I could feel the cold of her fingers.

My guests would not stay the night. I implored. I remonstrated. I pointed out that their rooms were ready, that Mr. Thorne had already turned down the quilts.

"Next time," said Willi. "Next time, Melanie, my little love. We'll make a weekend of it as we used to. A week!" Willi was in a much better mood since he had been paid his thousand-dollar prize by each of us. He had sulked, but I had insisted. It soothed his ego when Mr. Thorne brought in a check already made out to WILLIAM D. BORDEN.

Again I asked him to stay, but he protested that he had a midnight flight to Chicago. He had to see a prizewinning author about a screenplay. Then he was hugging me good-bye, his companions were in the hall behind me, and I had a brief moment of terror.

But they left. The blond young man showed his white smile, and the Negro bobbed his head in what I took as a farewell. Then we were alone.

Nina and I were alone.

Not quite alone. Miss Kramer was standing next to Nina at the end of the hall. Mr. Thorne was out of sight behind the swinging door to the kitchen. I left him there.

Miss Kramer took three steps forward. I felt my breath stop for an instant. Mr. Thorne put his hand on the swinging door. Then the husky little brunette opened the door to the hall closet, removed Nina's coat, and stepped back to help her into it.

"Are you sure you won't stay?"

"No, thank you, darling. I've promised Barrett that we would drive to Hilton Head tonight."

"But it's late—"

"We have reservations. Thank you anyway, Melanie. I *will* be in touch."

"Yes."

"I mean it, dear. We must talk. I understand *exactly* how you feel, but you have to remember that the Game is still important to Willi. We'll have to find a way to end it without hurting his feelings. Perhaps we could visit him next spring in Karinhall or whatever he calls that gloomy old Bavarian place of his. A trip to the Continent would do wonders for you, dear."

"Yes."

"I *will* be in touch. After this deal with the new store is settled. We need to spend some time together, Melanie . . . just the two of us . . . like old times." Her lips kissed the air next to my cheek. She held my forearms tightly. "Good-bye, darling."

"Good-bye, Nina."

I carried the brandy glass to the kitchen. Mr. Thorne took it in silence.

"Make sure the house is secure," I said. He nodded and went to check the locks and alarm system. It was only nine forty-five, but I was very tired. *Age,* I thought. I went up the wide staircase, perhaps the finest feature of the house, and dressed for bed. It had begun to storm, and the sound of the cold raindrops on the window carried a sad rhythm to it.

Mr. Thorne looked in as I was brushing my hair and wishing it were longer. I turned to him. He reached into the pocket of his dark vest. When his hand emerged a slim blade flicked out. I nodded. He palmed the blade shut and closed the door behind him. I listened to his footsteps recede down the stairs to the chair in the front hall, where he would spend the night.

I believe I dreamed of vampires that night. Or perhaps I was thinking about them just prior to falling asleep, and a fragment had stayed with me until morning. Of all mankind's self-inflicted terrors, of all its pathetic little monsters, only the myth of the vampire had any vestige of dignity. Like the humans it feeds on, the vampire must respond to its own dark compulsions. But unlike its petty human prey, the vampire carries out its sordid means to the only possible ends that could justify such actions—the goal of literal immortality. There is a nobility there. And a sadness.

Before sleeping I thought of that summer long ago in Vienna. I saw Willi young again—blond, flushed with youth, and filled with pride at escorting two such independent American ladies.

I remembered Willi's high, stiff collars and the short dresses that Nina helped to bring into style that summer. I remembered the friendly sounds of crowded *Biergartens* and the shadowy dance of leaves in front of gas lamps.

I remembered the footsteps on wet cobblestones, the shouts, the distant whistles, and the silences.

Willi was right; I had aged. The past year had taken a greater toll than the preceding decade. But I had not Fed. Despite the hunger, despite the aging reflection in the mirror, *I had not Fed.*

I fell asleep trying to think of that writer's last name. I fell asleep hungry.

**M**orning. Bright sunlight through bare branches. It was one of those crystalline, warming winter days that make living in the South so much less depressing than merely surviving a Yankee winter. I had Mr. Thorne open the window a crack when he brought in my breakfast tray. As I sipped my coffee I could hear children playing in the courtyard. Once Mr. Thorne would have brought the morning paper with the tray, but I had long since learned that to read about the follies and scandals of the world was to desecrate the morning. I was growing less and less interested in the affairs of men. I had done without a newspaper, telephone, or television for twelve years and had suffered no ill effects unless one were to count a growing self-contentment as an ill thing. I smiled as I remembered Willi's disappointment at not being able to play his video cassettes. He was such a child.

"It is Saturday, is it not, Mr. Thorne?" At his nod I gestured for the tray to be taken away. "We will go out today," I said. "A walk. Perhaps a trip to the fort. Then dinner at Henry's and home. I have arrangements to make."

Mr. Thorne hesitated and half-stumbled as he was leaving the room. I paused in the act of belting my robe. It was not like Mr. Thorne to commit an ungraceful movement. I realized that he too was getting old. He straightened the tray and dishes, nodded his head, and left for the kitchen.

I would not let thoughts of aging disturb me on such a beautiful morning. I felt charged with a new energy and resolve. The reunion the night before had not gone well but neither had it gone as badly as it might have. I had been honest with

Nina and Willi about my intention of quitting the Game. In the weeks and months to come, they—or at least Nina—would begin to brood over the ramifications of that, but by the time they chose to react, separately or together, I would be long gone. Already I had new (and old) identities waiting for me in Florida, Michigan, London, southern France, and even in New Delhi. Michigan was out for the time being. I had grown unused to the harsh climate. New Delhi was no longer the hospitable place for foreigners it had been when I resided there briefly before the war.

Nina had been right about one thing—a return to Europe would be good for me. Already I longed for the rich light and cordial *savoir vivre* of the villagers near my old summer house outside of Toulon.

The air outside was bracing. I wore a simple print dress and my spring coat. The trace of arthritis in my right leg had bothered me coming down the stairs, but I used my father's old walking stick as a cane. A young Negro servant had cut it for father the summer we moved from Greenville to Charleston. I smiled as we emerged into the warm air of the courtyard.

Mrs. Hodges came out of her doorway into the light. It was her grandchildren and their friends who were playing around the dry fountain. For two centuries the courtyard had been shared by the three brick buildings. Only my home had not been parceled into expensive town houses or fancy apartments.

"Good morning, Miz Fuller."

"Good morning, Mrs. Hodges. A beautiful day, isn't it?"

"It is that. Are you off shopping?"

"Just for a walk, Mrs. Hodges. I'm surprised that Mr. Hodges isn't out today. He always seems to be working in the yard on Saturdays."

Mrs. Hodges frowned as one of the little girls ran between us. Her friend came squealing after her, sweater flying. "Oh, George is at the marina already."

"In the daytime?" I had often been amused by Mr. Hodges's departure for work in the evening, his security-guard uniform neatly pressed, gray hair jutting out from under his cap, black lunch pail gripped firmly under his arm.

Mr. Hodges was as leathery and bowlegged as an aged cowboy. He was one of those men who were always on the verge of retiring but who probably realized that to be suddenly inactive would be a form of death sentence.

"Oh, yes. One of those colored men on the day shift down at the storage building quit, and they asked George to fill in. I told him that he was too old to work four nights a week and then go back on the weekend, but you know George. He'll never retire."

"Well, give him my best," I said.

The girls running around the fountain made me nervous.

Mrs. Hodges followed me to the wrought-iron gate. "Will you be going away for the holidays, Miz Fuller?"

"Probably, Mrs. Hodges. Most probably." Then Mr. Thorne and I were out on the sidewalk and strolling toward the Battery. A few cars drove slowly down the narrow streets, some tourists stared at the houses of our Old Section, but the day was serene and quiet.

I saw the masts of the yachts and sailboats before we came in sight of the water as we emerged onto Broad Street.

"Please acquire tickets for us, Mr. Thorne," I said. "I believe I would like to see the fort."

As is typical of most people who live in close proximity to a popular tourist attraction, I had not taken notice of it for many years. It was an act of sentimentality to visit the fort now. An act brought on by my increasing acceptance of the fact that I would have to leave these parts forever. It is one thing to plan a move; it is something altogether different to be faced with the imperative reality of it.

There were few tourists. The ferry moved away from the marina and into the placid waters of the harbor. The combination of warm sunlight and the steady throb of the diesel caused me to doze briefly. I awoke as we were putting in at the dark hulk of the island fort.

For a while I moved with the tour group, en-joying the catacomb silences of the lower levels and the mindless singsong of the young woman from the Park Service. But as we came back to the museum, with its dusty dioramas and tawdry little trays of slides, I climbed the stairs back to the outer walls. I motioned for Mr. Thorne to stay at the top of the stairs and moved out onto the ramparts.

Only one other couple—a young pair with a cheap camera and a baby in an uncomfortable-looking papoose carrier—were in sight along the wall.

It was a pleasant moment. A midday storm was approaching from the west and it set a dark backdrop to the still-sunlit church spires, brick towers, and bare branches of the city.

Even from two miles away I could see the movement of people strolling along the Battery walkway. The wind was blowing in ahead of the dark clouds and tossing whitecaps against the rocking ferry and wooden dock. The air smelled of river and winter and rain by nightfall.

It was not hard to imagine that day long ago. The shells had dropped onto the fort until the upper layers were little more than protective piles of rubble. People had cheered from the rooftops behind the Battery. The bright colors of dresses and silk parasols must have been maddening to the Yankee gunners. Finally one had fired a shot above the crowded rooftops. The ensuing confusion must have been amusing from this vantage point.

A movement down below caught my attention. Something dark was sliding through the gray water—something dark and shark silent. I was jolted out of thoughts of the past as I recognized it as a Polaris submarine, old but obviously still operational, slipping through the dark water without a sound. Waves curled and rippled over the porpoise-smooth hull, sliding to either side in a white wake. There were several men on the tower. They were muffled in heavy coats, their hats pulled low. An improbably large pair of binoculars hung from the neck of one man, whom I assumed to be the captain. He pointed at something beyond Sullivan's Island. I stared. The periphery of my vision began to fade as I made contact. Sounds and sensations came to me as from a distance.

*Tension. The pleasure of salt spray, breeze from the north, northwest. Anxiety of the sealed orders below. Awareness of the sandy shallows just coming into sight on the port side.*

I was startled as someone came up behind me. The dots flickering at the edge of my vision fled as I turned.

Mr. Thorne was there. At my elbow. Unbidden. I had opened my mouth to command him back to the top of the stairs when I saw the cause of his approach. The youth who had been taking pictures of his pale wife was now walking toward me. Mr. Thorne moved to intercept him.

"Hey, excuse me, ma'am. Would you or your husband mind taking our picture?"

I nodded and Mr. Thorne took the proffered camera. It looked minuscule in his long-fingered hands. Two snaps and the couple were satisfied that their presence there was documented for posterity. The young man grinned idiotically and bobbed his head. Their baby began to cry as the cold wind blew in.

I looked back to the submarine, but already it had passed on, its gray tower a thin stripe connecting the sea and sky.

We were almost back to town, the ferry was swinging in toward the ship, when a stranger told me of Willi's death.

"It's awful, isn't it?" The garrulous old woman had followed me out onto the exposed section of deck. Even though the wind had grown chilly and I had moved twice to escape her mindless chatter, the woman had obviously chosen me as her conversational target for the final stages of the tour. Neither my reticence nor Mr. Thorne's glowering presence had discouraged her. "It must have been terrible," she continued. "In the dark and all."

"What was that?" A dark premonition prompted my question.

"Why, the airplane crash. Haven't you heard about it? It must have been awful, falling into the swamp and all. I told my daugher this morning—"

"What airplane crash? When?" The old woman cringed a bit at the sharpness of my tone, but the vacuous smile stayed on her face.

"Why last night. This morning I told my daughter—"

"Where? What aircraft are you talking about?" Mr. Thorne came closer as he heard the tone of my voice.

"The one last night," she quavered. "The one from Charleston. The paper in the lounge told all about it. Isn't it terrible? Eighty-five people. I told my daughter—"

I left her standing there by the railing. There was a crumpled newspaper near the snack bar, and under the four-word headline were the sparse details of Willi's death. Flight 417, bound for Chicago, had left Charleston International Airport at twelve-eighteen a.m. Twenty minutes later the aircraft had exploded in midair not far from the city of Columbia. Fragments of fuselage and parts of bodies had fallen into Congaree Swamp, where fishermen had found them. There had been no survivors. The FAA and FBI were investigating.

There was a loud rushing in my ears, and I had to sit down or faint. My hands were clammy against the green-vinyl upholstery. People moved past me on their way to the exits.

Willi was dead. Murdered. Nina had killed him. For a few dizzy seconds I considered the possibility of a conspiracy—an elaborate ploy by Nina and Willi to confuse me into thinking that only one threat remained. But no. There would be no reason. If Nina had included Willi in her plans, there would be no need for such absurd machinations.

Willi was dead. His remains were spread over a smelly, obscure marshland. I could imagine his last moments. He would have been leaning back in first-class comfort, a drink in his hand, perhaps whispering to one of his loutish companions.

Then the explosion. Screams. Sudden darkness. A brutal tilting and the final fall to oblivion. I shuddered and gripped the metal arm of the chair.

How had Nina done it? Almost certainly not one of Willi's entourage. It was not beyond Nina's powers to Use Willi's own cat's-paws, especially in light of his failing Ability, but there would have been no reason to do so. She could have Used anyone on that flight. It *would* have been difficult. The elaborate step of preparing the bomb. The supreme effort of blocking all memory of it, and the almost unbelievable feat of Using someone even as we sat together drinking coffee and brandy.

But Nina could have done it. Yes, she *could* have. And the timing. The timing could mean only one thing.

The last of the tourists had filed out of the cabin. I felt the slight bump that meant we had tied up to the dock. Mr. Thorne stood by the door.

Nina's timing meant that she was attempting to deal with both of us at once. She obviously had planned it long before the reunion and my timorous announcement of withdrawal. How amused Nina must have been. No wonder she had reacted so generously! Yet, she had made one great mistake. By dealing with Willi first, Nina had banked everything on my not hearing the news before she could turn on me. She knew that I had no access to daily news and only rarely left the house anymore. Still, it was unlike Nina to leave anything to chance. Was it possible that she thought I had lost the Ability completely and that Willi was the greater threat?

I shook my head as we emerged from the cabin into the gray afternoon light. The wind sliced at me through my thin coat. The view of the gangplank was blurry, and I realized that tears had filled my eyes. For Willi? He had been a pompous, weak old fool. For Nina's betrayal? Perhaps it was only the cold wind.

The streets of the Old Section were almost empty of pedestrians. Bare branches clicked together in front of the windows of fine homes. Mr. Thorne stayed by my side. The cold air sent needles of arthritic pain up my right leg to my hip. I leaned more heavily upon father's walking stick.

What would her next move be? I stopped. A fragment of newspaper, caught by the wind, wrapped itself around my ankle and then blew on.

How would she come at me? Not from a distance. She was somewhere in town. I knew that.

While it is possible to Use someone from a great distance, it would involve great rapport, an almost intimate knowledge of that person. And if contact were lost, it would be difficult if not impossible to reestablish at a distance. None of us had known why this was so. It did not matter now. But the thought of Nina still here, nearby, made my heart begin to race.

Not from a distance. I would see my assailant. If I knew Nina at all, I knew that. Certainly Willi's death had been the least personal Feeding imaginable, but that had been a mere technical operation. Nina obviously had decided to settle old scores with *me*, and Willi had become an obstacle to her, a minor but measurable threat that had to be eliminated before she could proceed. I could easily imagine that in Nina's own mind her choice of death for Willi would be interpreted as an act of compassion, almost a sign of affection. Not so with me. I felt that Nina would want me to know, however briefly, that she was behind the attack. In a sense, her own vanity would be my warning. Or so I hoped.

I was tempted to leave immediately. I could have Mr. Thorne get the Audi out of storage, and we could be beyond Nina's influence in an hour—away to a new life within a few more hours. There were important items in the house, of course, but the funds that I had stored elsewhere would replace most of them. It would be almost welcome to leave everything behind with the discarded identity that had accumulated them.

No. I could not leave. Not yet.

From across the street the house looked dark and malevolent. Had *I* closed those blinds on the second floor? There was a shadowy movement in the courtyard, and I saw Mrs. Hodges's granddaughter and a friend scamper from one doorway to another. I stood irresolutely on the curb and tapped father's stick against the black-barked tree. It was foolish to dither so—I knew it was—but it had been a long time since I had been forced to make a decision under stress.

"Mr. Thorne, please check the house. Look in each room. Return quickly."

A cold wind came up as I watched Mr. Thorne's

black coat blend into the gloom of the courtyard. I felt terribly exposed standing there alone. I found myself glancing up and down the street, looking for Miss Kramer's dark hair, but the only sign of movement was a young woman pushing a perambulator far down the street.

The blinds on the second floor shot up, and Mr. Thorne's face stared out whitely for a minute. Then he turned away, and I remained staring at the dark rectangle of window. A shout from the courtyard startled me, but it was only the little girl—what was her name?—calling to her friend. Kathleen, that was it. The two sat on the edge of the fountain and opened a box of animal crackers. I stared intently at them and then relaxed. I even managed to smile a little at the extent of my paranoia. For a second I considered using Mr. Thorne directly, but the thought of being helpless on the street dissuaded me. When one is in complete contact, the senses still function but are a distant thing at best.

*Hurry*. The thought was sent almost without volition. Two bearded men were walking down the sidewalk on my side of the street. I crossed to stand in front of my own gate. The men were laughing and gesturing at each other. One looked over at me. *Hurry*.

Mr. Thorne came out of the house, locked the door behind him, and crossed the courtyard toward me. One of the girls said something to him and held out the box of crackers, but he ignored her. Across the street the two men continued walking. Mr. Thorne handed me the large front-door key. I dropped it in my coat pocket and looked sharply at him. He nodded. His placid smile unconsciously mocked my consternation.

"You're sure?" I asked. Again the nod. "You checked all of the rooms?" Nod. "The alarms?" Nod. "You looked in the basement?" Nod. "No sign of disturbance?" Mr. Thorne shook his head.

My hand went to the metal of the gate, but I hesitated. Anxiety filled my throat like bile. I was a silly old woman, tired and aching from the chill, but I could not bring myself to open that gate.

"Come." I crossed the street and walked briskly away from the house. "We will have dinner at Henry's and return later." Only I was not walking toward the old restaurant. I was heading away from the house in what I knew was a blind, directionless panic. It was not until we reached the waterfront and were walking along the Battery wall that I began to calm down.

No one else was in sight. A few cars moved along the street, but to approach us someone would have to cross a wide, empty space. The gray clouds were quite low and blended with the choppy, white-crested waves in the bay.

The open air and fading evening light served to revive me, and I began to think more clearly. Whatever Nina's plans had been, they certainly had been thrown into disarray by my day-long absence. I doubted that Nina would stay if there were the slightest risk to herself. No, she would be returning to New York by plane even as I stood shivering on the Battery walk. In the morning I would receive a telegram, I could see it. MELANIE ISN'T IT TERRIBLE ABOUT WILLI? TERRIBLY SAD. CAN YOU TRAVEL WITH ME TO THE FUNERAL? LOVE, NINA.

I began to realize that my reluctance to leave immediately had come from a desire to return to the warmth and comfort of my home. I simply had been afraid to shuck off this old cocoon. I could do so now. I would wait in a safe place while Mr. Thorne returned to the house to pick up the one thing I could not leave behind. Then he would get the car out of storage, and by the time Nina's telegram arrived I would be far away. It would be *Nina* who would be starting at shadows in the months and years to come. I smiled and began to frame the necessary commands.

"Melanie."

My head snapped around. Mr. Thorne had not spoken in twenty-eight years. He spoke now.

"Melanie." His face was distorted in a rictus that showed his back teeth. The knife was in his right hand. The blade flicked out as I stared. I looked into his empty, gray eyes, and I knew.

"Melanie."

The long blade came around in a powerful arc. I could do nothing to stop it. It cut through the fabric of my coat sleeve and continued into my side. But in the act of turning, my purse had swung with me. The knife tore through the leather, ripped through the jumbled contents, pierced my coat, and drew blood above my lowest left rib. The purse had saved my life.

I raised father's heavy walking stick and struck Mr. Thorne squarely in his left eye. He reeled but did not make a sound. Again he swept the air with the knife, but I had taken two steps back and his vision was clouded. I took a two-handed grip on the cane and swung sideways again, bringing the stick around in an awkward chop. Incredibly, it again found the eye socket. I took three more steps back.

Blood streamed down the left side of Mr. Thorne's face, and the damaged eye protruded onto his cheek. The rictal grin remained. His head came up, he raised his left hand slowly, plucked out the eye with a soft snapping of a gray cord, and thew it into the water of the bay. He came toward me. I turned and ran.

I *tried* to run. The ache in my right leg slowed me to a walk after twenty paces. Fifteen more hurried steps and my lungs were out of air, my heart threatening to burst. I could feel a wetness seeping down my left side and there was a tingling—like an ice cube held against the skin—where the knife blade had touched me. One glance back showed me that Mr. Thorne was striding toward me faster than I was moving. Normally he could have overtaken me in four strides. But it is hard to make someone run when you are Using him. Especially when that person's body is reacting to shock and trauma. I glanced back again, almost slipping on the slick pavement. Mr. Thorne was grinning widely. Blood poured from the empty socket and stained his teeth. No one else was in sight.

Down the stairs, clutching at the rail so as not to fall. Down the twisting walk and up the asphalt path to the street. Pole lamps flickered and went on as I passed. Behind me Mr. Thorne took the steps in two jumps. As I hurried up the path, I thanked God that I had worn low-heel shoes for the boat ride. What would an observer think seeing this bizarre, slow-motion chase between two old people? There were no observers.

I turned onto a side street. Closed shops, empty warehouses. Going left would take me to Broad Street, but to the right, half a block away, a lone figure had emerged from a dark storefront. I moved that way, no longer able to run, close to fainting. The arthritic cramps in my leg hurt more than I could ever have imagined and threatened to collapse me on the sidewalk. Mr. Thorne was twenty paces behind me and quickly closing the distance.

The man I was approaching was a tall, thin Negro wearing a brown nylon jacket. He was carrying a box of what looked like framed sepia photographs.

He glanced at me as I approached and then looked over my shoulder at the apparition ten steps behind.

"Hey!" The man had time to shout the single syllable and then I reached out with my mind and *shoved*. He twitched like a poorly handled marionette. His jaw dropped, and his eyes glazed over, and he lurched past me just as Mr. Thorne reached for the back of my coat.

The box flew into the air, and glass shattered on the brick sidewalk. Long, brown fingers reached for a white throat. Mr. Thorne backhanded him away, but the Negro clung tenaciously, and the two swung around like awkward dance partners. I reached the opening to an alley and leaned my face against the cold brick to revive myself. The effort of concentration while Using this stranger did not afford me the luxury of resting even for a second.

I watched the clumsy stumblings of the two tall men for a while and resisted an absurd impulse to laugh.

Mr. Thorne plunged the knife into the other's stomach, withdrew it, plunged it in again. The Negro's fingernails were clawing at Mr. Thorne's good eye now. Strong teeth were snapping in search of the blade for a third time, but the heart was still beating and he was still usable. The man jumped, scissoring his legs around Mr. Thorne's middle while his jaws closed on the muscular throat. Fingernails raked bloody streaks across white skin. The two went down in a tumble.

*Kill him.* Fingers groped for an eye, but Mr.

Thorne reached up with his left hand and snapped the thin wrist. Limp fingers continued to flail. With a tremendous exertion, Mr. Thorne lodged his forearm against the other's chest and lifted him bodily as a reclining father tosses a child above him. Teeth tore away a piece of flesh, but there was no vital damage. Mr. Thorne brought the knife between them, up, left, then right. He severed half the Negro's throat with the second swing, and blood fountained over both of them. The smaller man's legs spasmed twice, Mr. Thorne threw him to one side, and I turned and walked quickly down the alley.

Out into the light again, the fading evening light, and I realized that I had run myself into a dead end. Backs of warehouses and the window-less, metal side of the Battery Marina pushed right up against the waters of the bay. A street wound away to the left, but it was dark, deserted, and far too long to try.

I looked back in time to see the black silhou-ette enter the alley behind me.

I tried to make contact, but there was nothing there. Nothing. Mr. Thorne might as well have been a hole in the air. I would worry later how Nina had done this thing.

The side door to the marina was locked. The main door was almost a hundred yards away and would also be locked. Mr. Thorne emerged from the alley and swung his head left and right in search of me. In the dim light his heavily streaked face looked almost black. He began lurching toward me.

I raised father's walking stick, broke the lower pane of the window, and reached in through the jagged shards. If there was a bottom or top bolt I was dead. There was a simple doorknob lock and crossbolt. My fingers slipped on the cold metal, but the bolt slid back as Mr. Thorne stepped up on the walk behind me. Then I was inside and throwing the bolt.

It was very dark. Cold seeped up from the con-crete floor and there was a sound of many small boats rising and falling at their moorings. Fifty yards away light spilled out of the office windows. I had hoped there would be an alarm system, but the building was too old and the marina too cheap to have one. I walked toward the light as Mr. Thorne's forearm shattered the remaining glass in the door behind me. The arm withdrew. A great kick broke off the top hinge and splintered wood around the bolt. I glanced at the office, but only the sound of a radio talk show came out of the im-possibly distant door. Another kick.

I turned to my right and stepped to the bow of a bobbing inboard cruiser. Five steps and I was in the small, covered space that passed for a forward cabin. I closed the flimsy access panel behind me and peered out through the Plexiglas.

Mr. Thorne's third kick sent the door flying inward, dangling from long strips of splintered wood. His dark form filled the doorway. Light from a distant streetlight glinted off the blade in his right hand.

*Please. Please hear the noise.* But there was no movement from the office, only the metallic voices from the radio. Mr. Thorne took four paces, paused, and stepped down onto the first boat in line. It was an open outboard, and he was back up on the con-crete in six seconds. The second boat had a small cabin. There was a ripping sound as Mr. Thorne kicked open the tiny hatch door, and then he was back up on the walkway. My boat was the eighth in line. I wondered why he couldn't just hear the wild hammering of my heart.

I shifted position and looked through the star-board port. The murky Plexiglas threw the light into streaks and patterns. I caught a brief glimpse of white hair through the window, and the radio was switched to another station. Loud music echoed in the long room. I slid back to the other porthole. Mr. Thorne was stepping off the fourth boat.

I closed my eyes, forced my ragged breathing to slow, and tried to remember countless evenings watching a bowlegged old figure shuffle down the street. Mr. Thorne finished his inspection of the fifth boat, a longer cabin cruiser with several dark recesses, and pulled himself back onto the walk-way.

*Forget the coffee in the thermos. Forget the cross-word puzzle. Go look!*

The sixth boat was a small outboard. Mr. Thorne

glanced at it but did not step onto it. The seventh was a low sailboat, mast folded down, canvas stretched across the cockpit. Mr. Thorne's knife slashed through the thick material. Blood-streaked hands pulled back the canvas like a shroud being torn away. He jumped back to the walkway.

*Forget the coffee. Go look! Now!*

Mr. Thorne stepped onto the bow of my boat. I felt it rock to his weight. There was nowhere to hide, only a tiny storage locker under the seat, much too small to squeeze into. I untied the canvas strips that held the seat cushion to the bench. The sound of my ragged breathing seemed to echo in the little space. I curled into a fetal position behind the cushion as Mr. Thorne's leg moved past the starboard port. *Now.* Suddenly his face filled the Plexiglas strip not a foot from my head. His impossibly wide grimace grew even wider. *Now.* He stepped into the cockpit.

*Now. Now. Now.*

Mr. Thorne crouched at the cabin door. I tried to brace the tiny louvered door with my legs, but my right leg would not obey. Mr. Thorne's fist slammed through the thin wooden strips and grabbed my ankle.

"Hey there!"

It was Mr. Hodges's shaky voice. His flashlight bobbed in our direction.

Mr. Thorne shoved against the door. My left leg folded painfully. Mr. Thorne's left hand firmly held my ankle through the shattered slats while the hand with the knife blade came through the opening hatch.

"Hey—" My mind shoved. Very hard. The old man stopped. He dropped the flashlight and unstrapped the buckle over the grip of his revolver.

Mr. Thorne slashed the knife back and forth. The cushion was almost knocked out of my hands as shreds of foam filled the cabin. The blade caught the tip of my little finger as the knife swung back again.

*Do it. Now. Do it.* Mr. Hodges gripped the revolver in both hands and fired. The shot went wide in the dark as the sound echoed off concrete and water. *Closer, you fool. Move!* Mr. Thorne shoved again and his body squeezed into the open hatch.

He released my ankle to free his left arm, but almost instantly his hand was back in the cabin, grasping for me. I reached up and turned on the overhead light. Darkness stared at me from his empty eye socket. Light through the broken shutters spilled yellow strips across his ruined face. I slid to the left, but Mr. Thorne's hand, which had my coat, was pulling me off the bench. He was on his knees, freeing his right hand for the knife thrust.

*Now!* Mr. Hodges's second shot caught Mr. Thorne in the right hip. He grunted as the impact shoved him backward into a sitting position. My coat ripped, and buttons rattled on the deck.

The knife slashed the bulkhead near my ear before it pulled away.

Mr. Hodges stepped shakily onto the bow, almost fell, and inched his way around the starboard side. I pushed the hatch against Mr. Thorne's arm, but he continued to grip my coat and drag me toward him. I fell to my knees. The blade swung back, ripped through foam, and slashed at my coat. What was left of the cushion flew out of my hands. I had Mr. Hodges stop four feet away and brace the gun on the roof of the cabin.

Mr. Thorne pulled the blade back and poised it like a matador's sword. I could sense the silent scream of triumph that poured out over the stained teeth like a noxious vapor. The light of Nina's madness burned behind the single, staring eye.

Mr. Hodges fired. The bullet severed Mr. Thorne's spine and continued on into the port scupper. Mr. Thorne arched backward, splayed out his arms, and flopped onto the deck like a great fish that just been landed. The knife fell to the floor of the cabin, while stiff, white fingers continued to slap nervelessly against the deck. I had Mr. Hodges step forward, brace the muzzle against Mr. Thorne's temple just above the remaining eye, and fire again. The sound was muted and hollow.

There was a first-aid kit in the office bathroom. I had the old man stand by the door while I bandaged my little finger and took three aspirin.

My coat was ruined, and blood had stained my print dress. I had never cared very much for the dress—I thought it made me look dowdy—but the coat had been a favorite of mine. My hair was a mess. Small, moist bits of gray matter flecked it. I splashed water on my face and brushed my hair as best I could. Incredibly, my tattered purse had stayed with me although many of the contents had spilled out. I transferred keys, billfold, reading glasses, and Kleenex to my large coat pocket and dropped the purse behind the toilet. I no longer had father's walking stick, but I could not remember where I had dropped it.

Gingerly I removed the heavy revolver from Mr. Hodges's grip. The old man's arm remained extended, fingers curled around air. After fumbling for a few seconds I managed to click open the cylinder. Two cartridges remained unfired. The old fool had been walking around with all six chambers loaded! *Always leave an empty chamber under the hammer.* That is what Charles had taught me that gay and distant summer so long ago when such weapons were merely excuses for trips to the island for target practice punctuated by the shrill shrieks of our nervous laughter as Nina and I allowed ourselves to be held, arms supported, bodies shrinking back into the firm support of our so-serious tutors' arms. *One must always count the cartridges,* lectured Charles, as I half-swooned against him, smelling the sweet, masculine shaving soap and tobacco smell rising from him on that warm, bright day.

Mr. Hodges stirred slightly as my attention wandered. His mouth gaped, and his dentures hung loosely. I glanced at the worn leather belt, but there were no extra bullets there, and I had no idea where he kept any. I probed, but there was little left in the old man's jumble of thoughts except for a swirling tape-loop replay of the muzzle being laid against Mr. Thorne's temple, the explosion, the—

"Come," I said. I adjusted the glasses on Mr. Hodges's vacant face, returned the revolver to the holster, and let him lead me out of the building.

It was very dark out. We had gone six blocks before the old man's violent shivering reminded me that I had forgotten to have him put on his coat. I tightened my mental vise, and he stopped shaking.

The house looked just as it had . . . my God . . . only forty-five minutes earlier. There were no lights. I let us into the courtyard and searched my overstuffed coat pocket for the key. My coat hung loose and the cold night air nipped at me. From behind lighted windows across the courtyard came the laughter of little girls, and I hurried so that Kathleen would not see her grandfather entering my house.

Mr. Hodges went in first, with the revolver extended. I had him switch on the light before I entered.

The parlor was empty, undisturbed. The light from the chandelier in the dining room reflected off polished surfaces. I sat down for a minute on the Williamsburg reproduction chair in the hall to let my heart rate return to normal. I did not have Mr. Hodges lower the hammer on the still-raised pistol. His arm began to shake from the strain of holding it. Finally, I rose and we moved down the hall toward the conservatory.

Miss Kramer exploded out of the swinging door from the kitchen with the heavy iron poker already coming down in an arc. The gun fired harmlessly into the polished floor as the old man's arm snapped from the impact. The gun fell from limp fingers as Miss Kramer raised the poker for a second blow.

I turned and ran back down the hallway. Behind me I heard the crushed-melon sound of the poker contacting Mr. Hodges's skull. Rather than run into the courtyard I went up the stairway. A mistake. Miss Kramer bounded up the stairs and reached the bedroom door only a few seconds after me. I caught one glimpse of her widened, maddened eyes and of the upraised poker before I slammed and locked the heavy door. The latch clicked just as the brunette on the other side began to throw herself against the wood. The thick oak did not budge. Then I heard the concussion of metal against the door and frame. Again.

Cursing my stupidity, I turned to the familiar room, but there was nothing there to help me.

There was not as much as a closet to hide in, only the antique wardrobe. I moved quickly to the window and threw up the sash. My screams would attract attention but not before that monstrosity had gained access. She was prying at the edges of the door now. I looked out, saw the shadows in the window across the way, and did what I had to do.

Two minutes later I was barely conscious of the wood giving away around the latch. I heard the distant grating of the poker as it pried at the recalcitrant metal plate. The door swung inward.

Miss Kramer was covered with sweat. Her mouth hung slack, and drool slid from her chin. Her eyes were not human. Neither she nor I heard the soft tread of sneakers on the stairs behind her.

*Keep moving. Lift it. Pull it back—all the way back. Use both hands. Aim it.*

Something warned Miss Kramer. Warned Nina, I should say; there was no more Miss Kramer. The brunette turned to see little Kathleen standing on the top stair, her grandfather's heavy weapon aimed and cocked. The other girl was in the courtyard shouting for her friend.

This time Nina knew she had to deal with the threat. Miss Kramer hefted the poker and turned into the hall just as the pistol fired. The recoil tumbled Kathleen backward down the stairs as a red corsage blossomed above Miss Kramer's left breast. She spun but grasped the railing with her left hand and lurched down the stairs after the child. I released the ten-year-old just as the poker fell, rose, fell again. I moved to the head of the stairway. I had to see.

Miss Kramer looked up from her grim work. Only the whites of her eyes were visible in her spattered face. Her masculine shirt was soaked with her own blood, but still she moved, functioned. She picked up the gun in her left hand. Her mouth opened wider, and a sound emerged like steam leaking from an old radiator.

"Melanie . . ." I closed my eyes as the thing started up the stairs for me.

Kathleen's friend came in through the open door, her small legs pumping. She took the stairs in six jumps and wrapped her thin, white arms around Miss Kramer's neck in a tight embrace.

The two went over backward, across Kathleen, all the way down the wide stairs to the polished wood below.

The girl appeared to be little more than bruised. I went down and moved her to one side. A blue stain was spreading along one cheekbone, and there were cuts on her arms and forehead. Her blue eyes blinked uncomprehendingly.

Miss Kramer's neck was broken. I picked up the pistol on the way to her and kicked the poker to one side. Her head was at an impossible angle, but she was still alive. Her body was paralyzed, urine already stained the wood, but her eyes still blinked and her teeth clicked together obscenely. I had to hurry. There were adult voices calling from the Hodgeses' town house. The door to the courtyard was wide open. I turned to the girl. "Get up." She blinked once and rose painfully to her feet.

I shut the door and lifted a tan raincoat from the coatrack.

It took only a minute to transfer the contents of my pockets to the raincoat and to discard my ruined spring coat. Voices were calling in the courtyard now.

I kneeled down next to Miss Kramer and seized her face in my hands, exerting pressure to keep the jaws still. Her eyes had rolled upward again, but I shook her head until the irises were visible. I leaned forward until our cheeks were touching. My whisper was louder than a shout.

"I'm coming for you, Nina."

I dropped her head onto the wood and walked quickly to the conservatory, my sewing room. I did not have time to get the key from upstairs; so I raised a Windsor side chair and smashed the glass of the cabinet. My coat pocket was barely large enough.

The girl remained standing in the hall. I handed her Mr. Hodges's pistol. Her left arm hung at a strange angle and I wondered if she had broken something after all. There was a knock at the door, and someone tried the knob.

"This way," I whispered, and led the girl into the dining room.

We stepped across Miss Kramer on the way,

walked through the dark kitchen as the pounding grew louder, and then were out, into the alley, into the night.

There were three hotels in this part of the Old Section. One was a modern, expensive motor hotel some ten blocks away, comfortable but commercial. I rejected it immediately. The second was a small, homey lodging house only a block from my home. It was a pleasant but nonexclusive little place, exactly the type I would choose when visiting another town. I rejected it also. The third was two and a half blocks farther, an old Broad Street mansion done over into a small hotel, expensive antiques in every room, absurdly overpriced. I hurried there. The girl moved quickly at my side. The pistol was still in her hand, but I had her remove her sweater and carry it over the weapon. My leg ached, and I frequently leaned on the girl as we hurried down the street.

The manager of the Mansard House recognized me. His eyebrows went up a fraction of an inch as he noticed my disheveled appearance. The girl stood ten feet away in the foyer, half-hidden in the shadows.

"I'm looking for a friend of mine," I said brightly. "A Mrs. Drayton."

The manager started to speak, paused, frowned without being aware of it, and tried again. "I'm sorry. No one under that name is registered here."

"Perhaps she registered under her maiden name," I said. "Nina Hawkins. She's an older woman but very attractive. A few years younger than I. Long, gray hair. Her friend may have registered for her . . . an attractive, young, dark-haired lady named Barrett Kramer—"

"No, I'm sorry," said the manager in a strangely flat tone. "No one under that name has registered. Would you like to leave a message in case your party arrives later?"

"No," I said. "No message."

I brought the girl into the lobby, and we turned down a corridor leading to the restrooms and side stairs. "Excuse me, please," I said to a passing porter. "Perhaps you can help me."

"Yes, ma'am." He stopped, annoyed, and brushed back his long hair. It would be tricky. If I was not to lose the girl, I would have to act quickly.

"I'm looking for a friend," I said. "She's an older lady but quite attractive. Blue eyes. Long, gray hair. She travels with a young woman who has dark, curly hair."

"No, ma'am. No one like that is registered here."

I reached out and grabbed hold of his forearm tightly. I released the girl and focused on the boy. "Are you sure?"

"Mrs. Harrison," he said. His eyes looked past me. "Room 207. North front."

I smiled. *Mrs. Harrison.* Good God, what a fool Nina was. Suddenly the girl let out a small whimper and slumped against the wall. I made a quick decision. I like to think that it was compassion, but I sometimes remember that her left arm was useless.

"What's your name?" I asked the child, gently stroking her bangs. Her eyes moved left and right in confusion. "Your name!"

"Alicia." It was only a whisper.

"All right, Alicia. I want you to go home now. Hurry, but don't run."

"My *arm* hurts," she said. Her lips began to quiver. I touched her forehead again and *pushed.*

"You're going home," I said. "Your arm does not hurt. You won't remember anything. This is like a dream that you will forget. Go home. Hurry, but do not run." I took the pistol from her but left it wrapped in the sweater. "Bye-bye, Alicia."

She blinked and crossed the lobby to the doors. I handed the gun to the bellhop. "Put it under your vest," I said.

Who is it?" Nina's voice was light.
"Albert, ma'am. The porter. Your car's out front, and I'll take your bags down."

There was the sound of a lock clicking and the door opened the width of a still-secured chain. Albert blinked in the glare, smiled shyly, and brushed his hair back. I pressed against the wall.

"Very well." She undid the chain and moved back. She had already turned and was latching her suitcase when I stepped into the room.

"Hello, Nina," I said softly. Her back straightened, but even that move was graceful. I could see the imprint on the bedspread where she had been lying. She turned slowly. She was wearing a pink dress I had never seen before.

"Hello, Melanie." She smiled. Her eyes were the softest, purest blue I had ever seen. I had the porter take Mr. Hodges's gun out and aim it. His arm was steady. He pulled back the hammer and held it with his thumb. Nina folded her hands in front of her. Her eyes never left mine.

"Why?" I asked.

Nina shrugged ever so slightly. For a second I thought she was going to laugh. I could not have borne it if she had laughed—that husky, childlike laugh that had touched me so many times. Instead she closed her eyes. Her smile remained.

"Why Mrs. Harrison?" I asked.

"Why, darling, I felt I owed him *something*. I mean, poor Roger. Did I ever tell you how he died? No, of course I didn't. And you never asked." Her eyes opened. I glanced at the porter, but his aim was steady. It only remained for him to exert a little more pressure on the trigger.

"He *drowned*, darling," said Nina. "Poor Roger threw himself from that steamship—what was its name?—the one that was taking him back to England. So strange. And he had just written me a letter promising marriage. Isn't that a *terribly* sad story, Melanie? Why do you think he did a thing like that? I guess we'll never know, will we?"

"I guess we never will," I said. I silently ordered the porter to pull the trigger.

Nothing.

I looked quickly to my right. The young man's head was turning toward me. *I had not made him do that.* The stiffly extended arm began to swing in my direction. The pistol moved smoothly like the tip of a weather vane swinging in the wind.

*No!* I strained until the cords in my neck stood out. The turning slowed but did not stop until the muzzle was pointing at my face. Nina laughed now. The sound was very loud in the little room.

"Good-bye, Melanie *dear*," Nina said, and laughed again. She laughed and nodded at the porter. I stared into the black hole as the hammer fell. On an empty chamber. And another. And another.

"Good-bye, Nina," I said as I pulled Charles's long pistol from the raincoat pocket. The explosion jarred my wrist and filled the room with blue smoke. A small hole, smaller than a dime but as perfectly round, appeared in the precise center of Nina's forehead. For the briefest second she remained standing as if nothing had happened. Then she fell backward, recoiled from the high bed, and dropped face forward onto the floor.

I turned to the porter and replaced his useless weapon with the ancient but well-maintained revolver. For the first time I noticed that the boy was not much younger than Charles had been. His hair was almost exactly the same color. I leaned forward and kissed him lightly on the lips.

"Albert," I whispered, "there are four cartridges left. One must always count the cartridges, mustn't one? Go to the lobby. Kill the manager. Shoot one other person, the nearest. Put the barrel in your mouth and pull the trigger. If it misfires, pull it again. Keep the gun concealed until you are in the lobby."

We emerged into general confusion in the hallway.

"Call for an ambulance!" I cried. "There's been an accident. Someone call for an ambulance!" Several people rushed to comply. I swooned and leaned against a white-haired gentleman. People milled around, some peering into the room and exclaiming. Suddenly there was the sound of three gunshots from the lobby. In the renewed confusion I slipped down the back stairs, out the fire door, into the night.

Time has passed. I am very happy here. I live in southern France now, between Cannes and Toulon, but not, I am happy to say, too near St. Tropez.

I rarely go out. Henri and Claude do my shopping in the village. I never go to the beach. Occasionally I go to the townhouse in Paris or to my pensione in Italy, south of Pescara, on the Adriatic. But even those trips have become less and less frequent.

There is an abandoned abbey in the hills, and I often go there to sit and think among the stones and wild flowers. I think about isolation and abstinence and how each is so cruelly dependent upon the other.

I feel younger these days. I tell myself that this is because of the climate and my freedom and not as a result of that final Feeding. But sometimes I dream about the familiar streets of Charleston and the people there. They are dreams of hunger.

On some days I rise to the sound of singing as girls from the village cycle by our place on their way to the dairy. On those days the sun is marvelously warm as it shines on the small white flowers growing between the tumbled stones of the abbey, and I am content simply to be there and to share the sunlight and silence with them.

But on other days—cold, dark days when the clouds move in from the north—I remember the shark-silent shape of a submarine moving through the dark waters of the bay, and I wonder whether my self-imposed abstinence will be for nothing. I wonder whether those I dream of in my isolation will indulge in their own gigantic, final Feeding.

It is warm today. I am happy. But I am also alone. And I am very, very hungry.

# THE SEA WAS WET AS WET COULD BE

# Gahan Wilson

Gahan Wilson (1930– ) was born in Evanston, Illinois. A self-described loner and weird kid, he was a fan of science fiction and fantasy, but was especially taken with the horror stories in *Weird Tales*. Influenced by the fiction of H. P. Lovecraft and the cartoons of Charles Addams, his earliest bizarre cartoons sold to *Weird Tales*, then to the higher-paying *Collier's*, *Look*, and eventually *National Lampoon*, *The New Yorker*, and *Playboy*. The latter two still publish his original, hilarious cartoons of gigantic and grotesque monsters and other macabre visitations.

Wilson has also shown himself to be a gifted writer, producing such humorous novels as *Eddy Deco's Last Caper* (1987) and *Everybody's Favorite Duck* (1988); children's fantasy novels, including *Harry, the Fat Bear Spy* (1973), *Harry and the Sea Serpent* (1976), and *Harry and the Snow Melting Ray* (1978); more than fifteen collections of his cartoons; and highly popular stories for Harlan Ellison's famous anthology, *Again, Dangerous Visions* (1972), *Playboy*, *The Magazine of Fantasy & Science Fiction*, and others. He also created a computer game titled *Gahan Wilson's The Ultimate Haunted House*. He received the World Fantasy Convention Award in 1981 and the National Cartoonists Society's Milton Caniff Lifetime Achievement Award in 2005.

"The Sea Was Wet as Wet Could Be" was originally published in the May 1967 issue of *Playboy*.

# The Sea Was Wet as Wet Could Be

## GAHAN WILSON

I felt we made an embarrassing contrast to the open serenity of the scene around us. The pure blue of the sky was unmarked by a single cloud or bird, and nothing stirred on the vast stretch of beach except ourselves. The sea, sparkling under the freshness of the early morning sun, looked invitingly clean. I wanted to wade into it and wash myself, but I was afraid I would contaminate it.

We are a contamination here, I thought. We're like a group of sticky bugs crawling in an ugly little crowd over polished marble. If I were God and looked down and saw us, lugging our baskets and our silly, bright blankets, I would step on us and squash us with my foot.

We should have been lovers or monks in such a place, but we were only a crowd of bored and boring drunks. You were always drunk when you were with Carl. Good old, mean old Carl was the greatest little drink pourer in the world. He used drinks like other types of sadists used whips. He kept beating you with them until you dropped or sobbed or went mad, and he enjoyed every step of the process.

We'd been drinking all night, and when the morning came, somebody, I think it was Mandie, got the great idea that we should all go out on a picnic. Naturally, we thought it was an inspiration, we were nothing if not real sports, and so we'd packed some goodies, not forgetting the liquor, and we'd piled into the car, and there we were, weaving across the beach, looking for a place to spread our tacky banquet.

We located a broad, low rock, decided it would serve for our table, and loaded it with the latest in plastic chinaware, a haphazard collection of food, and a quantity of bottles.

Someone had packed a tin of Spam among the other offerings and, when I saw it, I was suddenly overwhelmed with an absurd feeling of nostalgia. It reminded me of the war and of myself soldier-boying up through Italy. It also reminded me of how long ago the whole thing had been and how little I'd done of what I'd dreamed I'd do back then.

I opened the Spam and sat down to be alone with it and my memories, but it wasn't to be for long. The kind of people who run with people like Carl don't like to be alone, ever, especially with their memories, and they can't imagine any-one else might, at least now and then, have a taste for it.

My rescuer was Irene. Irene was particularly sensitive about seeing people alone because being alone had several times nearly produced fatal results for her. Being alone and taking pills to end the being alone.

"What's wrong, Phil?" she asked.

"Nothing's wrong," I said, holding up a forkful of the pink Spam in the sunlight. "It tastes just like it always did. They haven't lost their touch."

She sat down on the sand beside me, very carefully, so as to avoid spilling the least drop of what must have been her millionth Scotch.

"Phil," she said, "I'm worried about Mandie. I really am. She looks so unhappy!"

I glanced over at Mandie. She had her head thrown back and she was laughing uproariously at some joke Carl had just made. Carl was smiling at her with his teeth glistening and his eyes deep down dead as ever.

"Why should Mandie be happy?" I asked. "What, in God's name, has she got to be happy about?"

"Oh, Phil," said Irene. "You pretend to be such an awful cynic. She's *alive*, isn't she?"

I looked at her and wondered what such a statement meant, coming from someone who'd tried to do herself in as earnestly and as frequently as Irene. I decided that I did not know and that I would probably never know. I also decided I didn't want anymore of the Spam. I turned to throw it away, doing my bit to litter up the beach, and then I saw them.

They were far away, barely bigger than two dots, but you could tell there was something odd about them even then.

"We've got company," I said.

Irene peered in the direction of my point.

"Look, everybody," she cried, "we've got company!"

Everybody looked, just as she had asked them to.

"What the hell is this?" asked Carl. "Don't they know this is my private property?" And then he laughed.

Carl had fantasies about owning things and having power. Now and then he got drunk enough to have little flashes of believing he was king of the world.

"You tell 'em, Carl!" said Horace.

Horace had sparkling quips like that for almost every occasion. He was tall and bald and he had a huge Adam's apple and, like myself, he worked for Carl. I would have felt sorrier for Horace than I did if I hadn't had a sneaky suspicion that he was really happier when groveling. He lifted one scrawny fist and shook it in the direction of the distant pair.

"You guys better beat it," he shouted. "This is private property!"

"Will you shut up and stop being such an ass?" Mandie asked him. "It's not polite to yell at strangers, dear, and this may damn well be *their* beach for all you know."

Mandie happens to be Horace's wife. Horace's children treat him about the same way. He busied himself with zipping up his windbreaker, because it was getting cold and because he had received an order to be quiet.

I watched the two approaching figures. The one was tall and bulky, and he moved with a peculiar, swaying gait. The other was short and hunched into himself, and he walked in a fretful, zigzag line beside his towering companion.

"They're heading straight for us," I said.

The combination of the cool wind that had come up and the approach of the two strangers had put a damper on our little group. We sat quietly and watched them coming closer. The nearer they got, the odder they looked.

"For heaven's sake!" said Irene. "The little one's wearing a square hat!"

"I think it's made of paper," said Mandie, squinting, "folded newspaper."

"Will you look at the mustache on the big bastard?" asked Carl. "I don't think I've ever seen a bigger bush in my life."

"They remind me of something," I said.

The others turned to look at me.

*The Walrus and the Carpenter . . .*

"They remind me of the Walrus and the Carpenter," I said.

"The who?" asked Mandie.

"Don't tell me you never heard of the Walrus and the Carpenter?" asked Carl.

"Never once," said Mandie.

"Disgusting," said Carl. "You're an uncultured bitch. The Walrus and the Carpenter are probably two of the most famous characters in literature. They're in a poem by Lewis Carroll in one of the *Alice* books."

"In *Through the Looking Glass*," I said, and then I recited their introduction:

*The Walrus and the Carpenter*
*Were walking close at hand*
*They wept like anything to see*
*Such quantities of sand . . .*

Mandie shrugged. "Well, you'll just have to excuse my ignorance and concentrate on my charm," she said.

"I don't know how to break this to you all," said Irene, "but the little one *does* have a handkerchief."

We stared at them. The little one did indeed have a handkerchief, a huge handkerchief, and he was using it to dab at his eyes.

"Is the little one supposed to be the Carpenter?" asked Mandie.

"Yes," I said.

"Then it's all right," she said, "because he's the one that's carrying the saw."

"He is, so help me, God," said Carl. "And, to make the whole thing perfect, he's even wearing an apron."

"So the Carpenter in the poem has to wear an apron, right?" asked Mandie.

"Carroll doesn't say whether he does or not," I said, "but the illustrations by Tenniel show him wearing one. They also show him with the same square jaw and the same big nose this guy's got."

"They're goddamn doubles," said Carl. "The only thing wrong is that the Walrus isn't a walrus, he just looks like one."

"You watch," said Mandie. "Any minute now he's going to sprout fur all over and grow long fangs."

Then, for the first time, the approaching pair noticed us. It seemed to give them quite a start. They stood and gaped at us and the little one furtively stuffed his handkerchief out of sight.

"We can't be as surprising as all that!" whispered Irene.

The big one began moving forward, then, in a hesitant, tentative kind of shuffle. The little one edged ahead, too, but he was careful to keep the bulk of his companion between himself and us.

"First contact with the aliens," said Mandie, and Irene and Horace giggled nervously. I didn't respond. I had come to the decision that I was going to quit working for Carl, that I didn't like any of these people about me, except, maybe, Irene, and that these two strangers gave me the honest creeps.

Then the big one smiled, and everything was changed.

I've worked in the entertainment field, in advertising, and in public relations. This means I have come in contact with some of the prime charm boys and girls in our proud land. I have become, therefore, not only a connoisseur of smiles, I am a being equipped with numerous automatic safeguards against them. When a talcumed smoothie comes at me with his brilliant ivories exposed, it only shows he's got something he can bite me with, that's all.

But the smile of the Walrus was something else.

The smile of the Walrus did what a smile hasn't done for me in years—it melted my heart. I use the corn-ball phrase very much on purpose. When I saw his smile, I knew I could trust him; I felt in my marrow that he was gentle and sweet and had nothing but the best intentions. His resemblance to the Walrus in the poem ceased being vaguely chilling and became warmly comical. I loved him as I had loved the teddy bear of my childhood.

"Oh, I *say*," he said, and his voice was an embarrassed boom, "I *do* hope we're not intruding!"

"I daresay we are," squeaked the Carpenter, peeping out from behind his companion.

"The, uhm, fact is," boomed the Walrus, "we didn't even notice you until just back then, you see."

"We were talking, is what," said the Carpenter.

*They wept like anything to see*
*Such quantities of sand . . .*

"About sand?" I asked.

The Walrus looked at me with a startled air.

"We *were*, actually, now you come to mention it."

He lifted one huge foot and shook it so that a little trickle of sand spilled out of his shoe.

"The stuff's impossible," he said. "Gets in your clothes, tracks up the carpet."

"Ought to be swept away, it ought," said the Carpenter.

*"If seven maids with seven mops*
*Swept it for half a year,*
*Do you suppose," the Walrus said,*
*"That they could get it clear?"*

"It's too much!" said Carl.

"Yes, indeed," said the Walrus, eying the sand around him with vague disapproval, "altogether too much."

Then he turned to us again and we all basked in that smile.

"Permit me to introduce my companion and myself," he said.

"You'll have to excuse George," said the Carpenter, "as he's a bit of a stuffed shirt, don't you know?"

"Be that as it may," said the Walrus, patting the Carpenter on the flat top of his paper hat, "this is Edward Farr, and I am George Tweedy, both at your service. We are, uhm, both a trifle drunk, I'm afraid."

"We are, indeed. We are that."

"As we have just come from a really delightful party, to which we shall soon return."

"Once we've found the fuel, that is," said Farr, waving his saw in the air. By now he had found the courage to come out and face us directly.

"Which brings me to the question," said Tweedy.

"Have you seen any *driftwood* lying about the premises? We've been looking high and low and we can't seem to find *any* of the blasted stuff."

"Thought there'd be piles of it," said Farr, "but all there is is sand, don't you see?"

"I would have sworn you were looking for oysters," said Carl.

Again, Tweedy appeared startled.

*"O Oysters, come and walk with us!"*
*The Walrus did beseech . . .*

"Oysters?" he asked. "Oh, no, we've *got* the oysters. All we lack is the means to cook 'em."

"'Course we could always use a few more," said Farr, looking at his companion.

"I suppose we *could*, at that," said Tweedy thoughtfully.

"I'm afraid we can't help you fellows with the driftwood problem," said Carl, "but you're more than welcome to a drink."

There was something unfamiliar about the tone of Carl's voice that made my ears perk up. I turned to look at him, and then had difficulty covering up my astonishment.

It was his eyes. For once, for the first time, they were really friendly.

I'm not saying Carl had fishy eyes, blank eyes—not at all. On the surface, that is. On the surface, with his eyes, with his face, with the handling of his entire body, Carl was a master of animation and expression. From sympathetic, heartfelt warmth, all the way to icy rage, and on every stop in-between, Carl was completely convincing.

But only on the surface. Once you got to know Carl, and it took a while, you realized that none of it was really happening. That was because Carl had died, or been killed, long ago. Possibly in childhood. Possibly he had been born dead. So, under the actor's warmth and rage, the eyes were always the eyes of a corpse.

But now it was different. The friendliness here was genuine, I was sure of it. The smile of Tweedy, of the Walrus, had performed a miracle. Carl had risen from his tomb. I was in honest awe.

*"Delighted,* old chap!" said Tweedy.

They accepted their drinks with obvious pleasure, and we completed the introductions as they sat down to join us. I detected a strong smell of fish when Tweedy sat down beside me but, oddly, I didn't find it offensive in the least. I was glad he'd chosen me to sit by. He turned and smiled at me, and my heart melted a little more.

It soon turned out that the drinking we'd done before had only scratched the surface. Tweedy and Farr were magnificent boozers, and their gusto encouraged us all to follow suit.

We drank absurd toasts and were delighted to discover that Tweedy was an incredible raconteur. His specialty was outrageous fantasy: wild tales involving incongruous objects, events, and characters. His invention was endless.

> *"The time has come," the Walrus said,*
> *"To talk of many things:*
> *Of shoes—and ships—and sealing-wax—*
> *Of cabbages—and kings—*
> *And why the sea is boiling hot—*
> *And whether pigs have wings."*

We laughed and drank, and drank and laughed, and I began to wonder why in hell I'd spent my life being such a gloomy, moody son of a bitch, been such a distrustful and suspicious bastard, when the whole secret of everything, the whole core secret, was simply to enjoy it, to take it as it came.

I looked around and grinned, and I didn't care if it was a foolish grin. Everybody looked all right, everybody looked swell, everybody looked better than I'd ever seen them look before.

Irene looked happy, honestly and truly happy. She, too, had found the secret. No more pills for Irene, I thought. Now that she knows the secret, now that she's met Tweedy who's given her the secret, she'll have no more need of those goddamn pills.

And I couldn't believe Horace and Mandie. They had their arms around each other, and their bodies were pressed close together, and they rocked as one being when they laughed at Tweedy's wonderful stories. No more nagging for Mandie, I thought, and no more cringing for Horace, now they've learned the secret.

And then I looked at Carl, laughing and relaxed and absolutely free of care, absolutely unchilled, finally, at last, after years of—

And then I looked at Carl again.

And then I looked down at my drink, and then I looked at my knees, and then I looked out at the sea, sparkling, clean, remote and impersonal.

And then I realized it had grown cold, quite cold, and that there wasn't a bird or a cloud in the sky.

> *The sea was wet as wet could be,*
> *The sands were dry as dry.*
> *You could not see a cloud, because*
> *No cloud was in the sky:*
> *No birds were flying overhead—*
> *There were no birds to fly.*

That part of the poem was, after all, a perfect description of a lifeless earth. It sounded beautiful at first, it sounded benign. But then you read it again and you realized that Carroll was describing barrenness and desolation.

Suddenly Carl's voice broke through and I heard him say:

"Hey, that's a hell of an idea, Tweedy! By God, we'd love to! Wouldn't we, gang?"

The others broke out in an affirmative chorus and they all started scrambling to their feet around me. I looked up at them, like someone who's been awakened from sleep in a strange place, and they grinned down at me like loons.

"Come on, Phil!" cried Irene.

Her eyes were bright and shining, but it wasn't with happiness. I could see that now.

> *"It seems a shame," the Walrus said,*
> *"To play them such a trick . . ."*

I blinked my eyes and stared at them, one after the other.

"Old Phil's had a little too much to drink!" cried Mandie, laughing. "Come on, old Phil! Come on and join the party!"

"What party?" I asked.

I couldn't seem to get located. Everything seemed disorientated and grotesque.

"For Christ's sake, Phil," said Carl, "Tweedy and Farr, here, have invited us to join their party. There's no more drinks left, and they've got plenty!"

I set my plastic cup down carefully on the sand. If they would just shut up for a moment, I thought, I might be able to get the fuzz out of my head.

"Come *along*, sir!" boomed Tweedy jovially. "It's only a pleasant walk!"

*"O oysters come and walk with us,"*
*The walrus did beseech.*
*"A pleasant walk, a pleasant talk,*
*Along the briny beach . . ."*

He was smiling at me, but the smile didn't work anymore.

"You cannot do with more than four," I told him.

"*Uhm?* What's that?"

*". . . we cannot do with more than four,*
*And give a hand to each."*

"I said, 'You cannot do with more than four.'"

"He's right, you know," said Farr, the Carpenter.

"Well, uhm, then," said the Walrus, "if you feel you really *can't* come, old chap . . ."

"What, in Christ's name, are you all talking about?" asked Mandie.

"He's hung up on that goddamn poem," said Carl. "Lewis Carroll's got the yellow bastard scared."

"Don't be such a party pooper, Phil!" said Mandie.

"To hell with him," said Carl. And he started off, and all the others followed him. Except Irene.

"Are you sure you really don't want to come, Phil?" she asked.

She looked frail and thin against the sunlight. I realized there really wasn't much of her, and that what there was had taken a terrible beating.

"No," I said. "I don't. Are you sure you want to go?"

"Of course I do, Phil."

I thought of the pills.

"I suppose you do," I said. "I suppose there's really no stopping you."

"No, Phil, there isn't."

And then she stooped and kissed me. Kissed me very gently, and I could feel the dry, chapped surface of her lips and the faint warmth of her breath.

I stood.

"I wish you'd stay," I said.

"I can't," she said.

And then she turned and ran after the others.

I watched them growing smaller and smaller on the beach, following the Walrus and the Carpenter. I watched them come to where the beach curved around the bluff, and watched them disappear behind the bluff.

I looked up at the sky. Pure blue. Impersonal.

"What do you think of this?" I asked it.

Nothing. It hadn't even noticed.

*"Now, if you're ready, oysters dear,*
*We can begin to feed."*
*"But not on us!" the oysters cried,*
*Turning a little blue,*
*"After such kindness, that would be*
*A dismal thing to do!"*

A dismal thing to do.

I began to run up the beach, toward the bluff. I stumbled now and then because I had had too much to drink. Far too much to drink. I heard small shells crack under my shoes, and the sand made whipping noises.

I fell, heavily, and lay there gasping on the beach. My heart pounded in my chest. I was too old for this sort of footwork. I hadn't had any real exercise in years. I smoked too much and I drank too much. I did all the wrong things. I didn't do any of the right things.

I pushed myself up a little and then I let myself down again. My heart was pounding hard enough to frighten me. I could feel it in my chest, frantically pumping, squeezing blood in and spurting blood out.

Like an oyster pulsing in the sea.

*"Shall we be trotting home again?"*

My heart was like an oyster.

I got up, fell up, and began to run again, weaving widely, my mouth open and the air burning my throat. I was coated with sweat, streaming with it, and it felt icy in the cold wind.

*"Shall we be trotting home again?"*

I rounded the bluff and then I stopped and stood swaying, and then I dropped to my knees.

The pure blue of the sky was unmarked by a single bird or cloud, and nothing stirred on the whole vast stretch of the beach.

*But answer came there none—*
*And this was scarcely odd, because . . .*

Nothing stirred, but they were there. Irene and Mandie and Carl and Horace were there, and four others, too. Just around the bluff.

*"We cannot do with more than four . . ."*

But the Walrus and the Carpenter had taken two trips.

I began to crawl toward them on my knees. My heart, my oyster heart, was pounding too hard to allow me to stand.

The other four had had a picnic, too, very like our own. They, too, had plastic cups and plates, and they, too, had brought bottles. They had sat and waited for the return of the Walrus and the Carpenter.

Irene was right in front of me. Her eyes were open and stared at, but did not see, the sky. The pure blue uncluttered sky. There were a few grains of sand in her left eye. Her face was almost clear of blood. There were only a few flecks of it on her lower chin. The spray from the huge wound in her chest seemed to have traveled mainly downward and to the right. I stretched out my arm and touched her hand.

"Irene," I said.

*But answer came there none—*
*And this was scarcely odd, because*
*They'd eaten every one.*

I looked up at the others. Like Irene, they were, all of them, dead. The Walrus and the Carpenter had eaten the oysters and left the shells.

The Carpenter never found any firewood, and so they'd eaten them raw. You can eat oysters raw if you want to.

I said her name once more, just for the record, and then I stood and turned from them and walked to the bluff. I rounded the bluff and the beach stretched before me, vast, smooth, empty, and remote.

Even as I ran upon it, away from them, it was remote.

# The Vampire

## A BIBLIOGRAPHY

### Compiled by
### *DANIEL SEITLER*

This is a comprehensive listing of vampire novels and short stories, including juvenile fiction, but not including comics, games, movies, plays, television, or radio programs. It provides first printing information (place, publisher, and date). In most cases, if no place is indicated, the story or novel was published electronically.

**Abbott, Tony.** *Trapped in Transylvania: Dracula: Cracked Classics #1.* New York: Hyperion, 2002 (juvenile).

**Acevedo, Mario.** *The Nymphos of Rocky Flats.* New York: Rayo, 2006 (erotica).

———. *X-Rated Bloodsuckers.* New York: Eos, 2007 (erotica).

———. *The Undead Kama Sutra.* New York: Eos, 2008 (erotica).

**Achilli, Justin.** *Vampire Masquerade: Kindred of the Ebony Kingdom.* Clarkston, GA: White Wolf, 1998.

**Ackerman, Forrest J.** "Countdown to Doom." *Famous Monsters,* 1966.

———. "The Man Who Was Thirsty." In *The Science Fiction Worlds of Forrest J. Ackerman and Friends.* Reseda, CA: Powell Publications, 1969.

**Acosta, Marta.** *Happy Hour at Casa Dracula.* New York: Pocket Books, 2006.

———. *Midnight Brunch.* New York: Pocket Books, 2007.

———. *The Bride of Casa Dracula.* New York: Pocket Books, 2008.

**Acres, Mark.** *Dark Divide (Runesworld, No. 5).* New York: Ace, 2001.

**Adair, Dominique.** "Last Kiss." In *Dark Dreams.* Akron, OH: Ellora's Cave, 2001 (erotica).

———. "Blood Law." In *Lady Jaided's Virile Vampires.* Akron, OH: Ellora's Cave, 2007 (erotica).

**Adams, Baylor.** "As Vampires Sleep." *Prisoners of the Night 2,* 1988.

———. "Whatever Happened to Candice?" *Prisoners of the Night 3,* 1989.

**Adams, C. T., and Cathy Clamp.** *Touch of Evil: Thrall Series #1.* New York: Tor, 2006.

———. *Touch of Madness: Thrall Series #2.* New York: Tor, 2007.

**Adams, Carmen.** *The Band.* New York: Avon Flare, 1994 (juvenile).

———. *Song of the Vampire.* New York: Avon Flare, 1996 (juvenile).

**Adams, Elisa.** *Midnight: Dark Promises #1.* Akron, OH: Ellora's Cave, 2003 (erotica).

————. *In Darkness.* Akron, OH: Ellora's Cave, 2004 (erotica).

————. *Demonic Obsession: Dark Promises #2.* Akron, OH: Ellora's Cave, 2005 (erotica).

————. *Shift of Fate: Dark Promises #3.* Akron, OH: Ellora's Cave, 2005 (erotica).

**Adams, Nicholas.** *Vampire's Kiss.* New York: HarperPaperbacks, 1994 (juvenile).

**Adams, Scott Charles.** . . . *Never Dream.* Charleston, SC: BookSurge, 1999.

**Addison, Linda.** "Whispers During Still Moments." In *Dark Thirst.* New York: Simon & Schuster, 2004.

**Addleman, David R.** "So Long to Love." *The Vampire's Crypt 6* (Fall 1992).

**Adrian, Lara.** *Kiss the Midnight: The Midnight Breed #1.* New York: Dell, 2007.

————. *Kiss the Crimson: The Midnight Breed #2.* New York: Dell, 2007.

————. *Midnight Awakening: The Midnight Breed #3.* New York: Dell, 2007.

————. *Midnight Rising: The Midnight Breed #4.* New York: Dell, 2008.

**Agnew, Denise A.** *Dark Fire: Deep Is the Night Book 1.* Akron, OH: Ellora's Cave, 2003 (erotica).

————. *Night Watch: Deep Is the Night Book 2.* Akron, OH: Ellora's Cave, 2004 (erotica).

————. *Haunted Souls: Deep Is the Night Book 3.* Akron, OH: Ellora's Cave, 2004 (erotica).

————. "Special Investigations Agency—Night Scream." In *Ellora's Cavemen: Tales from the Temple IV.* Akron, OH: Ellora's Cave, 2004 (erotica).

**Aickman, Robert.** "The Insufficient Answer." In *We Are for the Dark: Six Ghost Stories.* London: Jonathan Cape, 1951.

————. "Pages from a Young Girl's Journal." *The Magazine of Fantasy & Science Fiction,* February 1973.

**Airies, Rebecca.** "Devon's Vix." In *Season of Seduction #2.* Akron, OH: Ellora's Cave, 2007 (erotica).

**Aislinn, Erin.** *The Night of Maya.* Akron, OH: Ellora's Cave, 2005 (erotica).

————. *Earthly Possession.* Akron, OH: Ellora's Cave, 2007.

**Aldiss, Brian W.** "The Saliva Tree." *The Magazine of Fantasy & Science Fiction,* September 1965.

————. *Dracula Unbound.* New York: HarperCollins, 1991.

**Alecsandi, Vasile.** "The Vampire." *English Illustrated Magazine,* November 1886 (poem).

**Aletti, Steffen B.** "The Last Work of Pietro of Apono." *The Magazine of Horror,* May 1969.

————. "The Cellar Room." *Weird Terror Tales,* Fall 1970.

**Alexander, Jan.** *Blood Moon.* New York: Lancer, 1970.

————. *The Glass Painting.* New York: Popular Library, 1972.

**Alexander, Karl.** *The Curse of the Vampire.* New York: Pinnacle, 1982.

**Alexander, Leslie Jean.** "Christmas Eve." *Count Dracula Fan Club Newsletter,* Christmas 1982.

**Alexander, Stacey.** "Shades." *The Vampire Journal 1,* Summer 1985.

————. "Contract." *The Vampire Journal 2,* Fall 1985.

————. "Survivor." *The Vampire Journal 2,* Fall 1985.

**Allan, Luman.** *The Pharoah's Treasure.* Chicago, IL: Donahue & Henneberry, 1891.

**Allan, Peter.** "Domdaniel." In *The Vampire's Bedside Companion.* London: Leslie Frewin, 1975.

**Allen, Angela C.** "Vamp Noir." In *Dark Thirst.* New York: Simon & Schuster, 2004.

**Allen, Harper.** *Dressed to Slay: Darkheart and Crosse #1.* Toronto: Silhouette Bombshell, 2006.

———. *Vampaholic: Darkheart and Crosse #2.* Toronto: Silhouette Bombshell, 2006.

———. *Dead Is the New Black: Darkheart and Crosse #3.* Toronto: Silhouette Bombshell, 2007.

**Allen, Wilford.** "Night-Thing." *Weird Tales,* July 1929.

**Allen, Woody.** "Count Dracula." In *Getting Even.* New York: Random House, 1971.

**Altman, Steven-Elliot.** *Zen in the Art of Slaying Vampires.* New York: Hell's Kitchen Books, 1994.

**Ambrus, Victor G.** *Dracula's Bedtime Story Book.* London: Oxford University Press, 1983 (juvenile).

———. *Dracula's Late-Night TV Show.* London: Oxford University Press, 1990 (juvenile).

**Amis, Kingsley.** "To See the Sun." In *Collected Short Stories.* London: Hutchinson, 1980.

**Amsbary, Jonathan Howard.** *Cyberblood.* Philadelphia: Xlibris, 2000.

———. *Kit: The Cyberblood Chronicles.* Philadelphia: Xlibris, 2001.

**Anderson, Colleen.** "Lover's Triangle." *On Spec,* Summer 2001.

**Anderson, Evalyn.** *Vampires Don't Backpack.* Frederick, MD: PublishAmerica, 2004.

**Anderson, Evangeline.** *Secret Thirst.* Akron, OH: Ellora's Cave, 2005 (erotica).

**Anderson, Kevin J.** "Much at Stake." In *The Ultimate Dracula.* New York: Dell, 1991.

**Anderson, M. T.** *Thirsty.* Westminster, MD: Candlewick, 1997 (juvenile).

**Anderson, Mary.** *Leipzig Vampire: Mostly Ghosts #2.* New York: Yearling Books, 1987 (juvenile).

**Anderson, Paul Dale.** "The Best." In *Hotter Blood.* New York: Pocket Books, 1991.

**Andersson, C. Dean.** *Raw Pain Max.* New York: Popular Library, 1988.

———. *I Am Dracula.* New York: Zebra, 1993.

**Andrews, Christopher.** *Pandora's Game.* Philadelphia: Xlibris, 1999.

**Andrews, Ilona.** *Magic Bites: Kate Daniels #1.* New York: Ace, 2007.

**Andrews, Val.** *Sherlock Holmes and the Longacre Vampire.* Brighton, East Sussex, UK: Breese Books, 2000.

**Andreyev, Leonid.** "Lazarus." In *The Gentlemen from San Francisco.* Boston: Stratford, 1918.

**Angeleno.** *A Working Class Vampire Is Something to Be.* Seattle, WA: Ice Dragon, 1992.

**Anna, Vivi.** *Goddess of the Dead.* Garibaldi Highlands, BC, Canada: eXtasybooks.com, 2001.

———. *Blood Secrets.* Toronto: Silhouette Nocturne, 2007.

**Anonymous.** "The Mysterious Stranger." *Odds and Ends,* 1860.

———. "The Last Ride." *Ghostly Haunts,* October 1975.

———. "The Bridegroom." *The Many Ghosts of Dr. Graves,* December 1975.

———. "Death Flew into Darkness." *The Many Ghosts of Dr. Graves,* April 1976.

———. "Evil Encounter." *The Many Ghosts of Dr. Graves,* October 1976.

———. "The T-Shirt." *Count Dracula Fan Club Bi-Annual 2,* Spring/Summer 1979.

———. "The Fire Chief." *Count Dracula Fan Club Bi-Annual 3,* 1980.

———. "Future Shock." *Secret Order of the Undead Annual,* September/October 1991.

———. "You Wanted to Know How I Felt, Here It Is." *Secret Order of the Undead Annual,* September/October, 1991.

———. "Ancient Predator, Modern Times." *Secret Order of the Undead Annual,* Fall 1992.

————. "Foresight Future Shock, Ch. 4." *Secret Order of the Undead Annual,* Fall 1992.

Anscombe, Roderick. *The Secret Life of Laszlo: Count Dracula.* New York: Harper, 1995.

Anthony, Piers. *Pornucopia.* Houston, TX: Tafford Publishing, 1989.

Antieau, Kim. "Medusa's Child." In *Final Shadows.* New York: Doubleday, 1991.

Anwar, Celeste. *Carnal Thirst.* Lake Park, GA: New Concepts, 2004 (erotica).

Apps, Roy. *A Vampire in the Family.* London: Hodder Wayland, 1993 (juvenile).

————. *My Vampire Grandad (The Fang Gang).* London: Bloomsbury, 2006 (juvenile).

————. *The Vampire Slaying Competition (The Fang Gang).* London: Bloomsbury, 2007 (juvenile).

Armae, Angelique. *Come the Night.* Indian Hills, CA: Amber Quill, 2002.

————. *The Tangled Web.* Indian Hills, CA: Amber Quill, 2002.

————. *The Blood Ruby.* Indian Hills, CA: Amber Quill, 2003 (erotica).

————. *Night of the Shadows.* Indian Hills, CA: Amber Quill, 2003.

————. *The Protectorate: Dead Walkers #1.* Hickory Corners, MI: ImaJinn Books, 2005.

————. *Blood Sword: Dead Walkers #2.* Hickory Corners, MI: ImaJinn Books, 2006.

————. *Blood Line: Dead Walkers #3.* Hickory Corners, MI: ImaJinn Books, 2007.

Armintrout, Jennifer. *The Turning: Blood Ties #1.* Toronto: Mira, 2006.

————. *Possession: Blood Ties #2.* Toronto: Mira, 2007.

————. *Ashes to Ashes: Blood Ties #3.* Toronto: Mira, 2007.

Armstead, Joseph. *Nocturnes and Neon.* Lincoln, NE: Writer's Club, 2001.

————. *Darkness Fears.* Lincoln, NE: Writer's Club, 2002.

————. *Nightflesh: The Porphyrricon Vol. 1.* Lincoln, NE: iUniverse, 2006.

————. *Endless Nocturnes.* Lincoln, NE: iUniverse, 2007.

Armstrong, F. W. *Devouring.* New York: Tor, 1987.

Armstrong, Kelley. "Twilight." In *Many Bloody Returns.* New York: Ace, 2007.

Armstrong, Michelle. *Blood Kiss.* Scottsdale, AZ: Loose Id, 2005 (erotica).

————. *Blood Lines: Conduit.* Scottsdale, AZ: Loose Id, 2006 (erotica).

————. *Blood Lines: Crimson Rose.* Scottsdale, AZ: Loose Id, 2006 (erotica).

————. *Blood Lines: Currents.* Scottsdale, AZ: Loose Id, 2007 (erotica).

————. *Blood Lines: Night's Journey.* Scottsdale, AZ: Loose Id, 2007 (erotica).

Arnes, William. "Shrieking Victim of the Vampire's Curse." *Adventures in Horror,* October 1971.

Arneson, D. J. "Interrupted Voyage." *Dark Shadows Story Digest Magazine,* June 1970.

Arnzen, Michael A. "Baby Teeth." *Dead of Night 5,* April 1990.

Arsenault, Jeff. "Surrounded by Dark Shadows." *World of Dark Shadows,* June 1978.

Arsenault, Jeff, and Kathy Resch. "Blood in the Night." *World of Dark Shadows,* February 1981.

Arter, Janice. "The Innkeeper." In *Count Dracula and the Unicorn.* Chicago: Adams, 1978.

Arthur, Keri. *Hearts in Darkness.* Hickory Corners, MI: ImaJinn Books, 2001.

————. *Chasing the Shadows.* Hickory Corners, MI: ImaJinn Books, 2002.

————. *Circle of Death.* Hickory Corners, MI: ImaJinn Books, 2002.

————. *Dancing with the Devil.* Hickory Corners, MI: ImaJinn Books, 2002.

————. *Kiss the Night Goodbye.* Hickory Corners, MI: ImaJinn Books, 2004.

————. *Full Moon Rising: Riley Jenson Guardian #1.* New York: Bantam Dell, 2006.

————. *Kissing Sin: Riley Jenson Guardian #2.* New York: Dell, 2007.

———. *Tempting Evil: Riley Jenson Guardian #3*. New York: Dell, 2007.

———. *Dangerous Games: Riley Jenson Guardian #4*. New York: Dell, 2007.

———. *Embraced by Darkness: Riley Jenson Guardian #5*. New York: Dell, 2007.

———. *The Darkest Kiss: Riley Jenson Guardian #6*. New York: Dell, 2008.

**Ascher, Eugene.** *There Were No Asper Ladies*. London: Mitre, 1946.

**Ashley, Amanda.** *Embrace the Night*. New York: Love Spell, 1995.

———. *Deeper Than the Night*. New York: Love Spell, 1996.

———. *A Darker Dream*. New York: Love Spell, 1997.

———. *Sunlight Moonlight*. New York: Love Spell, 1997.

———. *Shades of Gray*. New York: Love Spell, 1998.

———. "Jessie's Girl." In *Paradise*. New York: Leisure Books, 1999.

———. "Masquerade." In *After Twilight*. New York: Love Spell, 2001.

———. *Midnight Embrace*. New York: Love Spell, 2002.

———. *After Sundown*. New York: Zebra, 2003.

———. *A Whisper of Eternity*. New York: Zebra, 2004.

———. *Night's Kiss*. New York: Zebra, 2005.

———. *Desire After Dark*. New York: Zebra, 2006.

———. *Dead Sexy*. New York: Zebra, 2007.

———. *Night's Touch*. New York: Zebra, 2007.

———. *Dead Perfect*. New York: Zebra, 2008.

———. *Night's Master*. New York: Zebra, 2008.

**Ashley, Jennifer.** "Viva Las Vampires." In *Just One Slip*. New York: Leisure Books, 2006.

**Ashmore, Annie.** *The Sweet Sisters of Inchvarra: or, The Vampire of Guillamores*. New York: Street and Smith, 1890.

**Asimov, Janet.** "The Contagion." In *The Ultimate Dracula*. New York: Dell, 1991.

**Askegren, Pierce.** "The House Where Death Stood Still." In *The Longest Night Vol. 1 (Angel)*. New York: Pocket Books, 2002.

———. *After Image (Buffy the Vampire Slayer)*. New York: Pocket Books, 2006.

**Askew, Alice, and Claude Askew.** "Aylmer Vance and the Vampire." *Weekly Tale-Teller*, 1914.

**Asprin, Robert.** *Myth-ing Persons*. Norfolk, VA: Donning, 1984.

**Asquith, Cynthia.** "God Grant That She Lye Stille." In *This Mortal Coil*. Sauk City, WI: Arkham House, 1947.

**Atherton, Nancy.** *Aunt Dimity: Vampire Hunter*. New York: Viking, 2008.

**Athkins, D. E.** "Blood Kiss." In *Thirteen*. New York: Scholastic, 1991 (juvenile).

**Atkins, Gerald.** "The Midnight Lover." In *Pan Book of Horror Stories No. 11*. London: Pan, 1970.

**Atkins, Peter.** *Morningstar*. New York: HarperPaperbacks, 1992.

**Atlas, Kelly Gunter.** "The Park." *Night Mountains 6*, Winter 1991.

———. "The Garden Wall." *Miss Lucy Westenra Society of the Undead 3*, Spring 1992.

**Atwater-Rhodes, Amelia.** *In the Forests of the Night*. New York: Delacorte, 1999 (juvenile).

———. *Demon in My View*. New York: Delacorte, 2000 (juvenile).

———. *Shattered Mirror*. New York: Delacorte, 2001 (juvenile).

———. *Midnight Predator*. New York: Delacorte, 2002 (juvenile).

**Atypus, P. L.** "Mother's Blood." *Dead of Night 3*, Fall 1989.

**Aubin, Etienne.** *Dracula and the Virgin of the Undead*. London: New English Library, 1974.

**Aubrey, Frank.** "A Queen of Atlantis." *Argosy*, February–August 1898.

**Auerback, Lloyd M.** "Vampire?" *Vampirella*, August 1972.

Augustyn, Michael. *Vlad Dracula: The Dragon Prince.* Lincoln, NE: iUniverse, 1995.

Aulden, W. L. "The Mystery of Elias G. Roebuck." London: A.D. Innes, 1896.

Ault, J. L. *A Thorned Rose.* Frederick, MD: PublishAmerica, 2004.

———. *Chosen of the Night.* Frederick, MD: PublishAmerica, 2005.

Autrey, Jimmy. *What Big Teeth You Have: A Vampire Tale.* Lincoln, NE: iUniverse, 2004.

Avallone, Michael. *One More Time.* New York: Popular Library, 1970.

Avison, A. D. "The Horror in the Pond." In *Tales of Fear: A Collection of Uneasy Tales.* London: Phillip Allen, 1935.

Aycliffe, Jonathan. *The Lost: A Novel of Dark Discoveries.* New York: HarperPrism, 1996.

Aylmer, Arthur Stafford. "The Thing in the Pit." In *Tales of Fear: A Collection of Uneasy Tales.* London: Phillip Allen, 1935.

Babson, Marian. *Shadows in Their Blood.* New York: St. Martin's, 1993.

Baglini, Lisa. "Equus Vampyre." *Nightmist 1,* Spring 1991, and *Nocturnal Extacy 1,* July 1991.

Bainbridge, Sharon. *Blood and Roses.* New York: Diamond Books, 1993.

Baird, Meredith Suzanne. "They Have No Faces." In *Night Bites: Vampire Stories by Women.* Seattle, WA: Seal, 1996.

Baker, Mike. "Love Me Forever." In *Love in Vein.* New York: HarperCollins, 1994 (erotica).

Baker, Nancy. *The Night Inside.* New York: Fawcett, 1993.

———. *Blood and Chrysanthemums.* Canada: Penguin, 1995.

———. *Terrible Beauty.* Canada: Penguin, 1996.

Baker, Nicki. "Backlash." In *Night Bites: Vampire Stories by Women.* Seattle, WA: Seal, 1996.

Baker, Scott. *Nightchild.* New York: Berkley, 1979.

———. *Dhampire.* New York: Pocket Books, 1982.

———. "Varicose Worms." In *Blood Is Not Enough.* New York: William Morrow, 1989.

———. *Ancestral Hungers.* New York: Tor, 1995.

Baker, Trisha. *Crimson Kiss.* New York: Pinnacle, 2001.

———. *Crimson Night.* New York: Pinnacle, 2002.

———. *Crimson Shadows.* New York: Pinnacle, 2003.

Baldwin, Dick. "Money Talks." In *Ghosts.* New York: Doubleday, 1981.

Baldwin, E. E. *The Strange Story of Dr. Senex.* London: Minerva, 1891.

Baldwin, Robert. "Swampire." *Dead of Night 6,* July 1990.

———. "Refuge." *Bloodreams 3,* January 1992.

Ball, Brian. *The Venomous Serpent.* New York: Baen, 1991.

Ballard, J. G. *The Day of Forever.* London: Panther, 1967.

Ballou, Mardi. *Young Vampires in Love.* Akron, OH: Ellora's Cave, 2004 (erotica).

———. "Fangs N' Foxes." In *Nibbles N' Bits.* Akron, OH: Ellora's Cave, 2005 (erotica).

———. *Heliotropic I: From the Light.* Martinsburg, WV: Changeling, 2006.

———. *Young Vampires in France.* Akron, OH: Ellora's Cave, 2006 (erotica).

———. *Reunions Dangereuses,* Akron, OH: Ellora's Cave, 2007 (erotica).

Balzen, Jerrod. *The Oak Clan.* Bloomington, IN: AuthorHouse, 2004.

Bangs, Nina. *Master of Ecstasy.* New York: Love Spell, 2004.

———. *Night Bites.* New York: Love Spell, 2005.

———. *Wicked Bites.* New York: Berkley, 2005.

———. *A Taste of Darkness.* New York: Leisure Books, 2006.

————. *Wicked Fantasy.* New York: Berkley, 2007.

————. *One Bite Stand.* New York: Leisure Books, 2008.

**Banks, L. A.** *Minion: Vampire Huntress Legends #1.* New York: St. Martin's, 2003.

————. *The Awakening: Vampire Huntress Legends #2.* New York: St. Martin's Griffin, 2004.

————. *The Hunted: Vampire Huntress Legends #3.* New York: St. Martin's Griffin, 2004.

————. *The Bitten: Vampire Huntress Legends #4.* New York: St. Martin's Griffin, 2005.

————. *The Forbidden: Vampire Huntress Legends #5.* New York: St. Martin's Griffin, 2005.

————. *The Damned: Vampire Huntress Legends #6.* New York: St. Martin's Griffin, 2006.

————. *The Forsaken: Vampire Huntress Legends #7.* New York: St. Martin's Griffin, 2006.

————. *The Wicked: Vampire Huntress Legends #8.* New York: St. Martin's Griffin, 2007.

————. *The Cursed: Vampire Huntress Legends #9.* New York: St. Martin's Griffin, 2007.

————. *The Darkness: Vampire Huntress Legends #10.* New York: St. Martin's Griffin, 2008.

**Barbanica, Sherry.** *Kindred Spirits-Tortured Souls.* Philadelphia: Xlibris, 2001.

**Bardsley, Michele.** *I'm the Vampire That's Why.* New York: Signet, 2006.

————. *Don't Talk Back to Your Vampire.* New York: Signet, 2007.

————. *Because Your Vampire Said So.* New York: Signet, 2008.

**Baring-Gould, Sabine.** "Glamr." In *Iceland: Its Scenes and Sagas.* London: Smith, Elder, 1863.

————. "A Dead Finger." In *A Book of Ghosts.* London: Methuen, 1904.

————. "A Professional Secret." In *A Book of Ghosts.* London: Methuen, 1904.

**Barker, Clive.** "Sex, Death, and Starshine." In *Clive Barker's Books of Blood, Volume 1.* London: Sphere, 1984.

————. "Human Remains." In *Clive Barker's Books of Blood, Volume 3.* London: Sphere, 1984.

————. "Son of Celluloid." In *Clive Barker's Books of Blood, Volume 3.* London: Sphere, 1984.

————. "Cabal." In *Cabal,* New York: Poseidon, 1988.

**Barker, Lawrence.** "Not Damned." In *Dark Tyrants.* Clarkston, GA: White Wolf, 1997.

————. *Renfield.* Marietta Publishing, 2005.

**Barker, Sonny.** *Vampire's Kiss.* Phoenix: A Pleasure Reader, 1970.

**Barlow, Linda.** *Midnight Rambler.* Toronto: Silhouette Desire, 1987.

**Barnes, Linda.** *Blood Will Have Blood.* New York: Avon, 1982.

**Barnhill, Sheila.** "It was raining for the second week . . ." (untitled story). *Society of the Undead Annual Issue 2,* Fall 1992.

**Baron, Nick.** *Castle of the Undead (Endless Quest Ravenloft).* Lake Geneva, WI: TSR, 1994 (juvenile).

**Barone, Jessica.** *Eternal Night.* Frederick, MD: PublishAmerica, 2001.

————. *The Requiem.* Frederick, MD: PublishAmerica, 2002.

————. *The Legendary.* Frederick, MD: PublishAmerica, 2004.

**Barrie, James Matthew.** *Farewell Miss Julie Logan: A Wintry Tale.* London: Hodder & Stoughton, 1932.

Barron, William P. "Jungle Beasts." *Weird Tales,* May 1923.

Bartlett, Gerry. *Real Vampires Have Curves: Glory St. Clair #1.* New York: Berkley, 2007.

———. *Real Vampires Live Large: Glory St. Clair #2.* New York: Berkley, 2007.

———. *Real Vampires Get Lucky: Glory St. Clair #3.* New York: Berkley, 2008.

Barton, Lee. *The Unseen.* London: Badger Books, 1963.

Bassingthwaite, Don. *Pomegranates Full and Fine.* Clarkston, GA: White Wolf, 1995.

———. "Three Days or Six." In *Dark Tyrants.* Clarkston, GA: White Wolf, 1997.

Bassingthwaite, Don, and Nancy Kilpatrick. *As One Dead (Vampire-The Masquerade).* Clarkston, GA: White Wolf, 1996.

Basso, Adrienne. "His Eternal Bride." In *Highland Vampire.* New York: Brava, 2005.

Bast, Anya. *Blood of the Rose: The Embraced #1.* Akron, OH: Ellora's Cave, 2004 (erotica).

———. *Blood of the Raven: The Embraced #2.* Akron, OH: Ellora's Cave, 2004 (erotica).

———. *Blood of the Angel: The Embraced #3.* Akron, OH: Ellora's Cave, 2005 (erotica).

———. "Scarlet Sweet." In *Ellora's Cavemen #3.* Akron, OH: Ellora's Cave, 2005 (erotica).

Bates, Andrew. *Dark Ages Cappadocian.* Clarkston, GA: White Wolf, 2002.

Baugh, Bruce. *Sacrifices.* Clarkston, GA: White Wolf, 2002.

———. *Vampire: Shadows.* Clarkston, GA: White Wolf, 2002.

Baumbach, Laura. "Sin and Salvation." In *The Bite Before Christmas.* Scottsdale, AZ: Loose Id, 2007.

Beath, Warren Newton. *Bloodletter.* New York: Tor, 1994.

Beaty, Tanya. "Slave to the Sword." In *Sword and Sorceress IX.* New York: DAW, 1992.

Beaufort, Roxanne. *Stranger in Venice.* Waterlooville, Hampshire, UK: Chimera, 1998 (erotica).

———. *Forever Chained.* Waterlooville, Hampshire, UK: Chimera, 2001 (erotica).

Beaumont, Charles. "Place of Meeting." *Orbit Science Fiction,* February 1953.

———. "Perchance to Dream." *Playboy,* October 1958.

———. "Blood Brother." *Playboy,* April 1961.

Beaver, Lorrie. "Wysteria: The Vampire Chronicles." *Bloodreams 3–4,* January, April 1992.

Bedwell-Grime, Stephanie. *The Bleeding Sun.* Lake Park, GA: New Concepts, 2002 (erotica).

Behm, Mark. *The Ice Maiden.* London: Zomba Books, 1982.

Bell, Earl Leaston. "The Land of Lur." *Weird Tales,* May 1930.

Bellamy, Dodie. *Real: The Letters of Mina Harker and Sam D'Allesandro.* Kingston, RI: Talisman House, 1994.

Bellero, Antonia T. "The Hunt." In *Legends in Blood.* West Hollywood, CA: Fantaseas, 1991.

———. "Taproot." In *Legends in Blood.* West Hollywood, CA: Fantaseas, 1991.

Benda, Richard, and Henry Hamarck. "Transylvania, Here We Come." *Famous Monsters,* January 1964.

Bennett, Janice. "The Full of the Moon." In *Lords of the Night.* New York: Zebra, 1997.

Bennett, Nigel, and P. N. Elrod. *Keeper of the King.* New York: Baen, 1997.

———. *His Father's Son.* New York: Baen, 2002.

————. *Siege Perilous.* New York: Baen, 2004.

**Benson, Edward Frederic.** "The Room in the Tower." In *The Room in the Tower and Other Stories.* London: Mills and Boon, 1912.

————. "The Thing in the Hall." In *The Room in the Tower and Other Stories.* London: Mills and Boon, 1912.

————. "Mrs. Amworth." In *Visible and Invisible.* London: Hutchinson, 1923.

————. "Negotium Perambulans." In *Visible and Invisible.* London: Hutchinson, 1923.

————. "And No Bird Sings." In *Spook Stories.* London: Hutchinson, 1928.

————. "The Face." In *Spook Stories.* London: Hutchinson, 1928.

**Berberick, Nancy Varian.** "Ransom Cowl Walks the Road." In *Women of Darkness.* New York: Tor, 1988.

**Beret, Renee.** "Coffee Vampire." *Children of the Night Coven Journal 4,* 1990.

**Bergstrom, Elaine.** "Ebb Tide." *The Vampire's Crypt 1,* 1989.

————. *Shattered Glass.* New York: Jove, 1989.

————. *Blood Alone.* New York: Jove, 1990.

————. *Blood Rites.* New York: Jove, 1991.

————. *Daughter of the Night.* New York: Jove, 1992.

————. *Tapestry of Dark Souls (Ravenloft).* Lake Geneva, WI: TSR, 1993.

————. *Mina: A Survivor's Tale.* New York: Berkley, 1994.

————. *Baroness of Blood (Ravenloft).* Lake Geneva, WI: TSR, 1995.

————. *Blood to Blood: The Dracula Story Continues.* New York: Ace, 2000.

————. "The Three Boxes." In *Dracula in London.* New York: Ace, 2001.

————. *Nocturne.* New York: Jove, 2003.

**Berliner, Janet.** "Aftermath." In *Jerusalem by Night.* Clarkston, GA: White Wolf, 1999.

**Bernal, A. W.** "Vampires of the Moon." *Weird Tales,* May 1934.

**Bernard, David.** "Jekal's Lesson." *Weird Tales,* October 1938.

**Berry, Amanda.** *Vampire's Revenge.* Bloomington, IN: 1st Books Library, 2004.

**Berry, T.** "A Unique Vintage." *Inside the Old House 9/10,* February/May 1980.

**Bertin, Eddie C.** "The Whispering Horror." In *Pan Book of Horror Stories No. 9.* London: Pan, 1968.

————. "A House with a Garden." *Weirdbook 5,* 1972.

————. "The Price to Pay." *Fantasy Tales,* Summer 1977.

————. "Something Small, Something Hungry." *Weirdbook,* May 1978.

**Betencourt, John Gregory.** "In the Cusp of the Hour." In *The Ultimate Dracula.* New York: Dell, 1991.

————. "By Moonlight." In *I, Vampire.* Stamford, CT: Longmeadow, 1995.

**Bethke, Bruce.** "The Final Death of the Comeback King." *Weird Tales,* Summer 1991.

**Bethlen, Julianna.** *Dracula Junior and the Fake Fangs: A 3-D Picture Book.* London: Tango Books, 1996 (juvenile).

**Bianchi, John.** *A Vampire's Halloween.* New York: Grosset & Dunlap, 2002 (juvenile).

**Bierce, Ambrose.** "The Death of Halpin Fraser." In *Can Such Things Be?* New York: Cassell, 1893.

**Bigley, Leo.** "Blessed Are the Dead." *Prisoners of the Night 2,* 1988.

**Billson, Anne.** *Suckers.* New York: Macmillan, 1993.

**Binder, E., and O. Binder.** "In a Graveyard." *Weird Tales,* October 1935.

**Bischoff, David.** *Nightworld.* New York: Ballantine, 1979.

————. *Vampires of Nightworld.* New York: Ballantine, 1981.

**Bischoff, David, and C. Lampton.** "Feeding Time." In *The Fifty-Meter Monsters and Other Horrors.* New York: Pocket, 1976.

**Bishop, David.** *Fiends of the Eastern Front 1: Operation Vampyr.* Nottingham, UK: Games Workshop, 2005.

———. *Fiends of the Eastern Front 2: Blood Red Army.* Nottingham, UK: Games Workshop, 2006.

———. *Fiends of the Eastern Front 3: Twilight of the Dead.* Nottingham, UK: Games Workshop, 2006.

———. *Fiends of the Rising Sun.* Nottingham, UK: Black Flame, 2007.

**Bishop, Rosemarie E.** *A Matter of Conscience.* Philadelphia: Xlibris, 1999.

———. *Search for a Soul.* Philadelphia: Xlibris, 1999.

———. *Spiritual Vengeance.* Philadelphia: Xlibris, 2001.

**Bishop, Zealia B.** "Medusa's Coil." *Weird Tales,* January 1939.

**Bixby, Jerome, and Joe E. Dean.** "Share Alike." *Beyond,* July 1953.

**Black, Campbell.** *The Wanting.* New York: McGraw-Hill, 1986.

**Black, J. R.** *The Undead Express.* New York: Random House, 1994 (juvenile).

**Black, Jaid.** *The Hunger.* Akron, OH: Ellora's Cave, 2006.

**Black, Jenna.** *Watchers in the Night: Guardians of the Night #1.* New York: Tor, 2006.

———. *Secrets in the Shadows: Guardians of the Night #2.* New York: Tor, 2007.

———. *Shadows of the Soul: Guardians of the Night #3.* New York: Tor, 2007.

**Blackburn, John.** *Children of the Night.* London: Jonathan Cape, 1966.

———. *Our Lady of Pain.* London: Jonathan Cape, 1974.

**Blackburn, Thomas.** *The Feast of the Wolf.* London: MacGibbon & Kee, 1971.

**Blacker, Terence.** *Ms. Wiz Loves Dracula.* London: Picadilly, 1993.

**Blackwood, Algernon.** "With Intent to Steal." In *The Empty House.* London: Eveleigh Nash, 1906.

———. "The Terror of the Twins." *The Westminster Gazette,* 1910.

———. "The Singular Death of Morton." *The Tramp,* December 1910.

———. "The Transfer." In *Pan's Garden.* London: Macmillan, 1912.

**Blackwood, Tyler.** *Prophesy of the Seventh Dragon.* Garibaldi Highlands, BC, Canada: eXtasy Books, 2003.

**Blacque, Dovya.** "Orinoco Flow." In *Dyad: The Vampire Stories.* Poway, CA: Mkashef Enterprises, 1991.

———. *South of Heaven.* Poway, CA: Mkashef Enterprises, 1997.

**Blake, Kathryn R.** *Mortal Illusions.* Lake Park, GA: New Concepts, 2003.

**Blake, Rebecca.** "Sleepless Shelter." In *Dead of Night 2,* July 1989.

**Blassingame, Wyatt.** "Goddess of Crawling Horrors." *Horror Stories,* February–March 1937.

**Blau, Gala.** "Outfangthief." In *The Mammoth Book of Vampire Stories by Women.* New York: Carroll & Graf, 2001.

**Blayne, Sara.** "Dark Shadows." In *Lords of the Night.* New York: Zebra, 1997.

———. "Stranger in the Night." In *His Immortal Embrace.* New York: Kensington, 2003.

**Blayre, Christopher (aka E. Heron-Allen).** "Zum Wildbad." In *Some Women at the University.* London: R. Stockwell, 1934.

**Blazer, Melani.** "Haunted Redemption." In *Things That Go Bump in the Night V.* Akron, OH: Ellora's Cave, 2006.

**Blessing, Caroline.** "Anna's Last Day." *Screem 2–3,* September/October 1991.

**Blish, James.** "The Unreal McCoy." In *Star Trek 1.* New York: Bantam, 1967.

**Blish, James, and Judith Ann Lawrence.** "Getting Along." In *Again, Dangerous Visions.* Garden City, NY: Doubleday, 1972.

**Bloch, Robert.** "The Feast in the Abbey." *Weird Tales*, 1934.

———. "The Shambler from the Stars." *Weird Tales*, September 1935.

———. "The Opener of the Way." *Weird Tales*, October 1936.

———. "The Cloak." *Unknown Worlds*, May 1939.

———. "Nursemaid to Nightmares." *Weird Tales*, November 1942.

———. "Fear Planet." *Super Science Stories*, February 1943.

———. "Yours Truly, Jack the Ripper." *Weird Tales*, July 1943.

———. "Black Barter." *Weird Tales*, September 1943.

———. "Death Is a Vampire." *Thrilling Mystery*, September 1944.

———. "The Bat Is My Brother." *Weird Tales*, November 1944.

———. "The Skull of the Marquis de Sade." *Weird Tales*, September 1945.

———. "The Bogeyman Will Get You." *Weird Tales*, March 1946.

———. "Tooth or Consequences." *Amazing Stories*, May 1950.

———. "The Hungry House." *Imagination 2*, April 1951.

———. "The Man Who Collected Poe." *Famous Fantastic Mysteries*, October 1951.

———. "I Kiss Your Shadow." *The Magazine of Fantasy & Science Fiction*, April 1956.

———. "Dig That Crazy Grave." *Ellery Queen Mystery Magazine*, June 1957.

———. "The Sleeping Redheads." *Swank*, March 1958.

———. "Hungarian Rhapsody." *Fantastic*, June 1958.

———. "The Living Dead." *Ellery Queen Mystery Magazine*, April 1967.

———. "A Case of the Stubborns." *The Magazine of Fantasy & Science Fiction*, October 1976.

———. "The Undead." *The Book Sail 16th Anniversary Catalog*, 1984.

———. "The Yugoslaves." *Night Cry*, Spring 1986.

———. "The Bedposts of Life." *Weird Tales*, Summer 1991.

**Bloch, Robert, and Edgar Allan Poe.** "The Light-House." *Fantastic*, January/February 1953.

**Block, Lawrence.** "I'll Love You to Death." *Monster Parade*, September 1958.

**Bloom, Hanya.** *School Ghoul: Vic the Vampire #1*. New York: HarperCollins, 1990 (juvenile).

**Blosser, John.** *Mariah (Vampire: The Redemption Book 1)*. Frederick, MD: PublishAmerica, 2006.

**Blue, Lucy.** *My Demon's Kiss: Bound in Darkness #1*. New York: Pocket, 2005.

———. *The Devil's Knight: Bound in Darkness #2*. New York: Pocket, 2006.

———. *Dark Angel: Bound in Darkness #3*. New York: Pocket, 2006.

**Blysse, Annalee.** "Never a Sunset." In *Immortal Lover*. Lake Park, GA: New Concepts, 2006.

**Bodner, Hal.** *Bite Club: A West Hollywood Vampire Novel*. Los Angeles: Alyson, 2005.

**Bone, Patrick.** *The Aliens of Transylvania County*. Johnson City, TN: Overmountain, 2002.

**Bonnefoux, Melanie.** *Blood and Mind*. Frederick, MD: PublishAmerica, 2003.

———. *Tainted Blood*. Frederick, MD: PublishAmerica, 2004.

**Booth, Bob.** "Still Life." In *After Midnight*. New York: Tor, 1986.

**Borland, Carroll.** *Countess Dracula*. Absecon MagicImage, 1994.

**Borton, Douglas.** "Voivode." In *Dracula: Prince of Darkness*. New York: DAW, 1992.

**Boucher, Anthony.** "They Bite." *Unknown Worlds*, June 1942.

———. "Summer's Cloud." *The Acolyte*, Summer 1944.

———. "The Ambassadors." *Startling Stories*, April 1952.

**Boucher, Brad J.** "Nocturne." *Night Mountains 6*, Winter 1991.

**Boucher, Page.** "Light Harvest." *The Vampire Journal 5,* 1989.

**Boulle, Phillipe.** *A Morbid Initiation.* Clarkston, GA: White Wolf, 2002.

———. *Vampire: Madness of Priests.* Clarkston, GA: White Wolf, 2003.

———. *Vampire: The Wounded King.* Clarkston, GA: White Wolf, 2003.

**Bounds, Sydney J.** "Young Blood." In *The Fourth Fontana Book of Great Horror Stories.* London: Fontana, 1969.

———. "The Circus." In *The Thirteenth Fontana Book of Great Horror Stories.* London: Fontana, 1980.

**Bousfield, H. T. W.** "Death and the Duchess." In *Vinegar and Cream.* London: John Murray, 1941.

**Bowen, Gary.** *Diary of a Vampire.* New York: Masquerade Books, 1996 (erotica).

**Boyett, Steven R.** "Like Pavlov's Dogs." In *Book of the Dead.* New York: Bantam, 1989.

**Boyett-Compo, Charlotte.** *Bloodwind.* Redwood City, CA: Romance Foretold, 1999.

**Brackett, Leigh.** "The Veil of Astellar." *Thrilling Wonder Stories,* Spring 1944.

**Bradbury, Ray.** "The Crowd." *Weird Tales,* May 1943.

———. "The Dead Man." *Weird Tales,* July 1945.

———. "Skeleton." *Weird Tales,* September 1945.

———. "The Traveller." *Weird Tales,* March 1946.

———. "Homecoming." *Mademoiselle,* October 1946.

———. "Uncle Einer." In *Dark Carnival.* Sauk City, WI: Arkham House, 1947.

———. "The Man Upstairs." *Harper's,* March 1947.

———. "Interim." *Weird Tales,* July 1947.

———. "Pillar of Fire." *Planet Stories,* Summer 1948.

———. "The Exiles." In *The Illustrated Man.* New York: Doubleday, 1951.

———. "A Medicine for Melancholy." In *A Medicine for Melancholy.* New York: Doubleday, 1959.

———. "West of October." In *The Toynbee Convector.* New York: Alfred A. Knopf, 1988.

———. *From the Dust Returned.* New York: William Morrow, 2001.

**Braddon, Mary Elizabeth.** *Lady Audley's Secret.* London: Tinsley Bros., 1862.

———. "Good Lady Ducayne." *The Strand,* February 1896.

**Bradley, Marion Zimmer.** "Treason of the Blood." *Web of Horror 1,* 1962.

———. *Falcons of Narabedia.* New York: Ace Books, 1964.

———. "The Waterfall." In *The Planet Savers/The Sword of Aldones.* New York: Ace, 1976.

**Brand, Chris.** *Trail of the Vampire.* London: Grayling Publishing Company, n.d.

**Brand, Rebecca: See Charnas, Suzy McKee.**

**Brandewyne, Rebecca.** "Devil's Keep." In *Bewitching Love Stories.* New York: Avon, 1992.

**Brandon, Marion.** "The Dark Castle." *Strange Tales of Mystery and Terror,* September 1931.

**Braunbeck, Gary A.** "Curtain Call." In *Dracula in London.* New York: Ace, 2001.

**Brennan, Joseph Payne.** "The Hunt." In *Nine Horrors and a Dream.* Sauk City, WI: Arkham House, 1958.

———. "On the Elevator." In *Nine Horrors and a Dream.* Sauk City, WI: Arkham House, 1958.

———. "The Corpse of Charlie Rull." In *The Dark Returners.* New Haven, CT: Macabre House, 1959.

———. "The Horror at Chilton Castle." In *Scream at Midnight.* New Haven, CT: Macabre House, 1963.

————. "The Vampire Bat." In *Scream at Midnight*. New Haven, CT: Macabre House, 1963.

————. "Vampires from the Void." In *The Borders Just Beyond*. West Kingston, RI: Donald M. Grant, 1986.

Brennert, Alan. "Cradle." In *The Mammoth Book of Best New Horror Vol. 7*. New York: Carroll & Graf, 1996.

Bretnor, Reginald. "How Sweet, How Silently She Sleeps." *Weird Tales*, Spring–Fall 1989.

Brett, Leo. "The Lamia." *Supernatural Stories*, January 1959.

Brett, Stephen. *The Vampire Chase*. New York: Manor Books, 1979.

Brewer, Heather. *The Chronicles of Vladimir Tod: Eighth Grade Bites*. New York: Dutton Juvenile, 2007 (juvenile).

Bridger, Denyse M. *A World of Darkness*. Indian Hills, CA: Amber Quill, 2006.

————. *A Whisper of Humanity*. East Prairie, MO: Forbidden Publications, 2007 (erotica).

Briery, Traci. *The Vampire Journals*. New York: Zebra, 1996.

Briery, Traci, and Mara McCuniff. *The Vampire Memoirs*. New York: Zebra, 1991.

Briggs, Greta. "The Undead." *Phantom 2*, May 1957.

Briggs, Patricia. *Moon Called*. New York: Ace, 2006.

Bright, Crystal B. *Revamped*. Lake Park, GA: New Concepts, 2007.

Brinson-Untiet, J. C. *Blood Red: A Vampire's Love Story*. Frederick, MD: PublishAmerica, 2004.

Briscoe, Pat. *The Other People*. Reseda, CA: Powell Publications, 1970.

Brite, Poppy Z. "A Taste of Blood and Altars." *The Horror Show*, Summer 1988.

————. *Lost Souls*. New York: Delacorte, 1992.

————. *Drawing Blood*. New York: Delacorte, 1993.

————. *The Seed of Lost Souls*. Burton, MI: Subterranean, 1999 (chapbook).

————. "Homewrecker." In *The Mammoth Book of Vampire Stories by Women*. New York: Carroll & Graf, 2001.

Brizzolara, John, and Diane Brizzolara. "The Opposite House." In *Weird Tales Number 3*. New York: Kensington, 1981.

Brockenbrough, Kevin S. "The Family Business." In *Dark Thirst*. New York: Simon & Schuster, 2006.

Brondos, Sharon. "Fragrant Suicide." *Dead of Night 4*, January 1990.

————. *Kiss of Shadows*. Toronto: Silhouette Shadows, 1994.

Brook, Meljean. *Demon Moon*. New York: Berkley Sensation, 2007.

Brooker, Alan. *The Battle for Barnstable*. Philadelphia: Xlibris, 1998.

Brookes, Alyssa. "Sexual Feeding." In *Vamprotica 2005*. Chippewa, 2005 (erotica).

Brooks, Clifford V. "There Are No Nightclubs in East Palo Alto." In *Under the Fang*. New York: Pocket Books, 1991.

Brown, Carter. *So What Killed the Vampire?* New York: Signet, 1966.

Brown, Fredric. "Blood." *The Magazine of Fantasy & Science Fiction*, February 1954.

Brown, Molly. "Agents of Darkness." *Interzone*, October 1992.

Brown, Sherrie. "Diet of Death." *Children of the Night Coven Journal 4*, 1990.

————. "Reading Is Believing." *Children of the Night Coven Journal 4*, 1990.

————. "Ladies' Night." *Night Mountains 6*, Winter 1991.

Brown, Toni. "Immunity." In *Night Bites: Vampire Stories by Women*. Seattle, WA: Seal, 1996.

Brownworth, Victoria. "Twelfth Night." In *Night Bites: Vampire Stories by Women*. Seattle, WA: Seal, 1996.

Bruecker, Liz. "Just a Dream." *Loyalists of the Vampire Realm Newsletter*, Summer 1991.

Brunner, John. "Such Stuff." *The Magazine of Fantasy & Science Fiction*, June 1962.

———. "The Dead Man." *The Magazine of Fantasy & Science Fiction*, October/November 1992.

Brust, Steven. *Agyar*. New York: Tor, 1993.

Bruton, Heather. "The Shinji." *Book of Shadows 1*, 1990.

———. "Step Softly in the Fog." *Book of Shadows 4*, 1992.

Bryant, Edward. "Good Kids." In *Blood is Not Enough*. New York: William Morrow, 1989.

———. "A Sad Last Love at the Diner of the Damned." In *Book of the Dead*. New York: Bantam, 1989.

———. "Country Mouse." *The Magazine of Fantasy & Science Fiction*, March 1992.

Bryant, Taerie. "Vampire's Consort." *Prisoners of the Night 3*, 1988.

———. "The Demon." *Prisoners of the Night 4*, 1990.

———. "In the Dark." *Prisoners of the Night 4*, 1990.

———. "The Visitor." *Prisoners of the Night 4*, 1990.

———. "The Vampire Child." *Prisoners of the Night 5*, 1991.

———. "The Sybarite." *Prisoners of the Night 6*, 1992.

Buchanan, Kelly. *Rasputin's Vintage*. Santa Barbara, CA: Xaxi, 1987.

Buckner, Marie. "The Vakulia Promise." *The Vampire's Crypt 4*, Fall 1991.

———. "Transmutation." *Night Mountains 6*, Winter 1991.

Bumberger, Otto. "Toby and the Vampire." *The Vampire Journal 4*, 1988.

———. "Getting Even." *The Vampire Journal 5*, 1989.

Bunch, Chris. *The Vampires of Malibu High*. Wilder Publications, 2007.

Buonocore, Julia. "Homesick." *The Vampire Journal 4*, 1988.

———. "Like a Virgin." *The Vampire Journal 4*, 1988.

Burbank, L. G. *The Soulless: Lords of Darkness #1*. Palm Beach, FL: Medallion, 2004.

———. *The Ruthless: Lords of Darkness #2*. Palm Beach, FL: Medallion, 2005.

———. *The Heartless: Lords of Darkness #3*. Palm Beach, FL: Medallion, 2006.

Burchett, Jan. *Little Terrors 5: Vampire for Hire*. New York: Macmillan Children's Books, 1999 (juvenile).

Burchett, M. H. "Partners." In *Shadows 6*. New York: Doubleday, 1983.

Burden, Elisabeth Erica. "Dreams." In *Shadows 6*. New York: Doubleday, 1983.

Burgess, Mason. *Blood Moon*. New York: Leisure Books, 1986.

Burke, Stephanie. *Lucavarious*. Akron, OH: Ellora's Cave, 2002, (erotica).

———. *The Slayer*. Akron, OH: Ellora's Cave, 2002 (erotica).

Burks, Arthur J. "Murder Brides." *Horror Stories*, 1935.

———. "The Room of Shadows." *Weird Tales*, May 1936.

Burnell, Mark. *Glittering Savages*. London: Hodder & Stoughton, 1995.

Burns, Laura J., and Melinda Metz. *Apocalypse Memories (Buffy the Vampire Slayer)*. New York: Simon Pulse, 2004.

Burstein, Michael. "Hunger." *Fictionwise*, November 2000.

Burton, Jaci. *Bite Me*. Akron, OH: Ellora's Cave, 2004 (erotica).

———. *Out of the Darkness*. Akron, OH: Ellora's Cave 2006 (erotica).

Burton, Sir Richard F. *Vikram and the Vampire: Tales of Hindu Devilry*. London: Longman, Green, 1870.

Busch, Charles. *Vampire Lesbians of Sodom and Sleeping Beauty or Coma*. New York: Samuel French, 1986 (play).

**Busiek, Kurt.** "Confession." In *Hotter Blood*. New York: Pocket Books, 1991.

**Butcher, Jim.** *Storm Front*. New York: Roc, 2000.

———. *Full Moon*. New York: Roc, 2001.

———. *Grave Peril*. New York: Roc, 2001.

———. *Death Masks*. New York: Roc, 2003.

———. *Blood Rites*. New York: Roc, 2004.

———. *Dead Beat*. New York: Roc, 2005.

———. *Proven Guilty*. New York: Roc, 2006.

———. "It's My Birthday Too." In *Many Bloody Returns*. New York: Ace, 2007.

———. *White Night*. New York: Roc, 2007.

———. *Small Favor*. New York: Roc, 2008.

**Butler, Octavia.** "Bloodchild." *Isaac Asimov's Science Fiction Magazine*, June 1984.

———. *Fledgling*. New York: Seven Stories, 2005.

**Byers, Richard Lee.** *The Vampire Apprentice*. New York: Zebra, 1992.

———. *Netherworld*. New York: HarperCollins, 1995.

———. *On the Darkling Plain*. Clarkston, GA: White Wolf, 1995.

———. "The Winged Child." In *Dark Tyrants*. Clarkston, GA: White Wolf, 1997.

———. *Dark Kingdoms*. Clarkston, GA: White Wolf, 1998.

———. *X-Men: Soul Killer*. New York: Berkley, 1999.

**Byrne, John L.** "Hide in Plain Sight." In *Shock Rock*. New York: Pocket Books, 1991.

**Byrne, Lora.** "One Curse, with Love." *The Tomb of Dracula*, February 1980.

**Byron, Lord.** "The Giaour." London: John Murray, 1813 (poem).

**Cable, Dorian.** "The Devil's Own Undead." *Screem 3*, October 1991.

**Cabos, Llewellyn M.** "The Wreck of the Alatair." *Space and Time*, September 1973.

**Cabot, Meg.** "The Exterminator's Daughter." In *Prom Dates from Hell*. New York: Harper Teen, 2007 (juvenile).

**Cacek, P. D.** *Night Prayers*. Darien, IL: Design Image Group, 1998.

———. *Night Players*. Darien, IL: Design Image Group, 2001.

**Cadigan, Pat.** "My Brother's Keeper." *Isaac Asimov's Science Fiction Magazine*, January 1988.

———. "Dirty Work." In *Blood is Not Enough*. New York: William Morrow, 1989.

———. "The Power and His Passion." In *Patterns*. Kansas City, MO: Ursus Imprints, 1989.

———. "Home by Sea." In *A Whisper of Blood*. New York: William Morrow, 1991.

**Cadnum, Michael.** *The Judas Glass*. New York: Carroll & Graf, 1996.

**Caillou, Alan.** "Odile." *Coven 13*, September 1969.

**Caine, Geoffrey.** *Curse of the Vampire*. New York: Diamond Books, 1991.

**Caine, Rachel.** *Glass Houses: The Morganville Vampires #1*. New York: Signet, 2006 (juvenile).

———. *Dead Girl's Dance: The Morganville Vampires #2*. New York: Signet, 2007 (juvenile).

———. "The First Day of the Rest of Your Life." In *Many Bloody Returns*. New York: Ace, 2007.

———. *Midnight Alley: The Morganville Vampires #3*. New York: Signet, 2007 (juvenile).

———. *Feast of Fools: The Morganville Vampires #4*. New York: Signet, 2008 (juvenile).

**Calchman, J. B.** *Kiss of the Vampire: Dark Enchantments #1*. New York: Puffin Books, 1996 (juvenile).

———. *Dance with the Vampire: Dark Enchantments #2*. New York: Puffin Books, 1996 (juvenile).

———. *Vampire Heart*. London: Penguin, 1999 (juvenile).

**Caldecott, Andrew.** "Authorship Disputed." In *Fires Burn Blue*. London: Longmans, 1948.

**Calder, A. W.** "Song of Death." *Weird Tales,* June 1938.

**Calder, Dave.** *A Garden for Dracula*. London: Headland Publications, 1988 (juvenile).

**Caldwell, Christopher.** *Vampire Annihilation Methods Project*. Roseland, NJ: DynaTainment, 2002.

**Califia, Patrick.** *Mortal Companion*. San Francisco, CA: Suspect Thoughts, 2004 (erotica).

**Calloway, Paula.** *Dark Hope*. Garibaldi Highlands, BC, Canada: eXtasy Books, 2005.

**Calvani, Mayra.** *Dark Hunger*. Indian Hills, CA: Amber Quill, 2003.

**Calvino, Italo.** "The Tale of the Vampires' Kingdom." In *The Castle of Crossed Destinies*. New York: Harcourt, 1977.

**Camden, Dani A.** *Vampire Slayer: One Foot in Darkness*. Frederick, MD: PublishAmerica, 2006.

**Campbell, Brian.** *Transylvania Saga 1*. Clarkston, GA: White Wolf, 2001.

**Campbell, Ramsey.** "The Insects from Shaggai." In *The Inhabitant of the Lake and Less Welcome Tenants*. Sauk City, WI: Arkham House, 1964.

———. "Conversion." In *The Rivals of Dracula*. London: Corgi, 1977.

———. "The Pit of Wings." In *Swords against Darkness 3*. New York: Zebra, 1978.

———. "To Wake the Dead." *Dark Horizons*, 1979.

———. "The Brood." *Dark Forces*, 1980.

———. "Again." *Rod Serling's Twilight Zone Magazine*, 1981.

———. "The Sunshine Club." In *The Dodd Mead Gallery of Horror*. New York: Dodd, Mead, 1983.

———. "Jack in the Box." *Dark Horizons*, 1986.

**Cantrell, Lisa W.** "Cruising." In *Hotter Blood*. New York: Pocket Books, 1991.

———. "Juice." In *Under the Fang*. New York: Pocket Books, 1991.

**Capes, Bernard.** "The Mask." In *The Fabulists*. London: Mills and Boon, 1915.

**Capuano, Luigi.** "A Vampire." Rome: Enrico Voghere, 1907.

**Cara, Dyanna.** "This Old Castle." *Marion Zimmer Bradley's Fantasy Magazine*, Summer 1990.

**Caraker, Mary.** "The Vampires Who Loved Beowulf." *Analog*, 1982.

**Cardiff, Larry G.** "Beware the Hills of Vjeszczi." *Dead of Night 5*, April 1990.

**Carew, Henry.** *The Vampire of the Andes*. London: Jarrold, 1925.

**Carey, Peter.** "He Found Her in Late Summer." In *Winter's Tales 25*. New York: St. Martin's, 1980.

**Carleton, Gordon.** "Trekula." *Warped Space 39*, 1978.

**Carleton, Patrick.** "Doctor Horder's Room." In *Thrills*. London: Philip Allan, 1935.

**Carlisle, Jo.** *Raina's Fantasy*. Akron, OH: Ellora's Cave, 2007.

**Carlson, Dale, and Danny Carlson.** *The Shining Pool*. New York: Athenaeum, 1979 (juvenile).

**Carmen, Edward.** "The Burden." In *Dark Tyrants*. Clarkston, GA: White Wolf, 1997.

**Carr, A. A.** *Eye Killers*. Norman, OK: University of Oklahoma Press, 1996.

**Carr, Carol.** "Tooth Fairy." *Omni*, September 1984.

**Carr, Jan.** "Apologia." In *Night Bites: Vampire Stories by Women*. Seattle, WA: Seal, 1996.

**Carr, John Dickson.** *The Three Coffins*. New York: Harper and Brothers, 1935.

———. *He Who Whispers*. New York: Harper and Row, 1946.

Carr, Terry. "Sleeping Beauty." *The Magazine of Fantasy & Science Fiction*, May 1967.

Carrington, Leonora. "The Sisters." In *A Night with Jupiter and Other Fantastic Stories*. New York: View Editions, 1945.

Carrington, Rachel. *Sin's Touch*. Akron, OH: Ellora's Cave, 2005 (erotica).

Carroll, Jonathan. "The Moose Church." In *A Whisper of Blood*. New York: William Morrow, 1991.

Carter, Angela. "The Lady of the House of Love." *Iowa Review*, Summer/Fall 1975.

Carter, Caryn. *The Vampire Julian: The Whitcombe Legacy #1*. Hickory Corners, MI: ImaJinn Books, 2007.

Carter, Margaret L. "A Call in the Blood." In *Voices from the Vaults*. Toronto: Key Porter, 1987.

———. "Matter of Semantics." *Promises/Pro- Mss 2*, 1987.

———. "Demon on the Hill." *The Vampire Journal 4*, 1988.

———. "The Devourer from Within." In *Four Moons of Darkover*. New York: DAW, 1988.

———. "Sorcerer's Pet." In *Sword and Sorceress V*. New York: DAW, 1988.

———. "Caged." *The Vampire's Crypt 1*, 1989.

———. "Rites of Passage." *The Vampire Journal 5*, 1989.

———. "Brother's Keeper." *Newsletter of the Miss Lucy Westenra Society of the Undead 2*, December 1989.

———. "Snow Waif." *Children of the Night Coven Journal 1*, 1990.

———. "Tame Demon." *Book of Shadows 1*, 1990.

———. "Incunabula." *Good Guys Wear Fangs 1*, May 1992.

———. "Cold Magic." *After Hours 15*, Summer 1992.

———. "Debtor's Payment." *The Vampire's Crypt 6*, Fall 1992.

———. *Dark Changeling*. Amherst Junction, WI: Hardshell Word Factory, 1999.

———. *Sealed in Blood*. Tempe, AZ: RFI West, 2001.

———. *Night Flight*. Akron, OH: Ellora's Cave, 2002 (erotica).

———. "Tall, Dark and Deadly." In *Things That Go Bump in the Night 2*. Akron, OH: Ellora's Cave, 2002 (erotica).

———. *Child of Twilight*. Amherst Junction, WI: Hardshell Word Factory, 2003.

———. *Crimson Dreams*. Indian Hills, CA: Amber Quill, 2003.

———. "Night Flight." In *Dark Dreams*. Akron OH: Ellora's Cave, 2004 (erotica).

———. *Embracing Darkness*. Toronto: Silhouette, 2005.

———. *Virgin Blood*. Akron, OH: Ellora's Cave, 2005 (erotica).

Carter, Margaret L., and Sandra Robinson. "Midnight Visitor." *The Vampire's Crypt 2*, 1990.

Carter, Natalie, and Teresia Craig. *Nathaniel Leary: A Vampire's Odyssey*. Bloomington, IN: AuthorHouse, 2002.

Cartier, Annee. *Redemption*. New York: Zebra, 1997.

Cartier, Crystal. *Immortal Obsession Book One: The Prophecy*. Love Story, 2004.

Carver, Jeffrey A. "Love Rogo." In *Futurelove*. New York: Bobbs-Merrill, 1977.

Cary, Kate. *Bloodline*. New York: Razorbill, 2005 (juvenile).

———. *Reckoning: Bloodline #2*. New York: Razorbill, 2007 (juvenile).

Cascio, Mary Lee. "To Die, to Sleep." In *Dracula*. East Lansing, MI: T'Kuhtian, 1980.

Casper, Susan. "Under Her Skin." *Amazing*, March 1987.

———. "A Child of Darkness." In *Blood Is Not Enough*. New York: William Morrow, 1989.

Cassada, Jackie. "Toujours." In *Dark Tyrants*. Clarkston, GA: White Wolf, 1997.

**Cassidy, Colin.** "Revenge of the Jukebox Vampire." *Monster Parade*, September 1958.

**Cassidy, Dakota.** *It's a Vampire Thing*. Indianapolis, IN: Liquid Silver Books, 2003 (erotica).

————. *Blood Lite*. Akron, OH: Ellora's Cave, 2004 (erotica).

**Cast, P. C., and Kristin Cast.** *Marked: A House of Night #1*. New York: St. Martin's Griffin, 2007 (juvenile).

————. *Betrayed: A House of Night #2*. New York: St. Martin's Griffin, 2007 (juvenile).

————. *Chosen: A House of Night #3*. New York: St. Martin's Griffin, 2008 (juvenile).

————. *Untamed: A House of Night #4*. New York: St. Martin's Griffin, 2008 (juvenile).

**Catling, Patrick Skere.** *John Midas and the Vampires*. London: Methuen, 1994 (juvenile).

**Cave, Hugh B.** "The Brotherhood of Blood." *Weird Tales*, May 1932.

————. "Stragella." *Strange Tales of Mystery and Terror*, June 1932.

————. "Murgunstrumm." *Strange Tales of Mystery and Terror*, January 1933.

————. "Prey of the Nightborn." *Spicy Mystery Stories*, 1942.

————. *Disciples of Dread*. New York: Tor, 1989.

————. "The Second Time Around." In *The Mammoth Book of Dracula*. London: Robinson, 1997.

**Caveney, Philip.** *Love Bites*. Philadelphia: Xlibris, 2000.

**Cecilione, Michael.** *Domination*. New York: Zebra, 1993.

————. *Thirst*. New York: Zebra, 1995.

**Chakoian, Linda S.** *So You Want to Be a Vampire*. Philadelphia: Xlibris, 2003.

**Chalker, Jack L.** *And the Devil Will Drag You Under*. New York: Del Rey, 1979.

**Chambers, Patricia A.** "Changeover." *Bloodreams 1*, July 1991.

————. "The Draining." *Bloodreams 2*, October 1991.

**Chance, Karen.** *Touch the Dark: Cassandra Palmer #1*. New York: Roc, 2006.

————. *Claimed by Shadow: Cassandra Palmer #2*. New York: Roc, 2007.

————. *Embrace the Truth: Cassandra Palmer #3*. New York: Roc, 2008.

**Chappell, Fred.** "The Adder." *Deathrealm 9*, 1989.

————. "The Flame." In *100 Vicious Little Vampire Stories*. New York: Barnes and Noble, 1995.

**Chappelle-Marriott, Glenn.** *Nentres Drystan: Journal of a Vampir*. Morrisville, NC: Lulu.com, 2005.

**Charles, Robert.** *Flowers of Evil*. London: Futura Publications, 1981.

**Charlton, Reno.** *The Secret Portal II: The Vampire Returns*. Bewrite Books, 2002 (juvenile).

**Charnas, Suzy McKee.** "The Ancient Mind at Work." *Omni*, February 1979.

————. "Unicorn Tapestry." In *New Dimensions 11*. New York: Pocket Books, 1980.

————. *The Vampire Tapestry*. New York: Simon & Schuster, 1980.

————. "Now I Lay Me Down to Sleep." In *A Whisper of Blood*. New York: William Morrow, 1991.

————. (as Rebecca Brand). *The Ruby Tear*. New York: Forge, 1997.

**Charnas, Suzy McKee, and Chelsea Quinn Yarbro.** "Advocates." In *Under the Fang*. New York: Pocket Books, 1991.

**Chatillon, Celine.** *Help! I'm Falling for the Vampire Next Door*. Indianapolis, IN: Atlantic Bridge, 2007.

**Cheever, John.** "Torch Song." In *The Stories of John Cheever*. New York: Alfred A. Knopf, 1947.

**Cherry, James.** "A Very Important Date." *Dead of Night 3,* Fall 1989.

**Chetwynd-Hayes, R.** "Looking for Something to Suck." In *The Fourth Fontana Book of Great Horror Stories.* London: Fontana, 1969.

———. "A Family Welcome." In *The Unbidden.* London: Tandem, 1971.

———. "Great Grandad Walks Again." In *Cold Terror.* London: Tandem, 1973.

———. "Neighbors." In *Cold Terror.* London: Tandem, 1973.

———. "Birth." In *The Elemental.* London: Fontana, 1974.

———. "The Jumpity-Jim." In *The Elemental.* London: Fontana, 1974.

———. "The Labyrinth." In *The Elemental.* London: Fontana, 1974.

———. "The Sad Vampire." In *The First Armada Monster Book.* London: Armada, 1975.

———. "Keep the Gaslight Burning." In *Gaslight Tales of Terror.* London: Fontana, 1976.

———. "The Werewolf and the Vampire." In *The Monster Club.* London: New English Library, 1976.

———. "My Mother Married a Vampire." In *The Cradle Demon and Other Stories.* London: William Kimber, 1978.

———. "Amelia." In *The Fantastic World of Kamteller.* London: William Kimber, 1980.

———. *The Partaker.* London: William Kimber, 1980 (juvenile).

———. "Acquiring a Family." In *Tales from the Shadows.* London: William Kimber, 1986.

———. "Benjamin." In *Dracula's Children.* London: William Kimber, 1987 (juvenile).

———. "Caroline." In *The House of Dracula.* London: William Kimber, 1987.

———. "Cuthbert." In *Dracula's Children.* London: William Kimber, 1987 (juvenile).

———. *Dracula's Children.* London: William Kimber, 1987 (juvenile).

———. "Gilbert." In *The House of Dracula.* London: William Kimber, 1987.

———. "Irma." In *Dracula's Children.* London: William Kimber, 1987 (juvenile).

———. "Karl." In *The House of Dracula.* London: William Kimber, 1987.

———. "Louis." In *The House of Dracula.* London: William Kimber, 1987.

———. "Marcus." In *Dracula's Children.* London: William Kimber, 1987 (juvenile).

———. "Marikova" In *The House of Dracula.* London: William Kimber, 1987.

———. "Rudolph." In *Dracula's Children.* London: William Kimber, 1987 (juvenile).

———. "Zena." In *Dracula's Children.* London: William Kimber, 1987 (juvenile).

———. "The Fundamental Elemental." In *The Vampire Stories of R. Chetwynd-Hayes.* Fedogen & Bremer, 1997.

**Child, Maureen.** "Christmas Cravings." In *Holiday with a Vampire.* Toronto: Silhouette Nocturne, 2007.

**Childe of the Night, A.** *Existence as a Vampire.* Morrisville, NC: Lulu.com, 2006.

**Chilton, Athan Yugao.** "Catching Cat." *Good Guys Wear Fangs 1,* May 1992.

**Chinn, Mike.** "Blood of Eden." In *The Mammoth Book of Dracula.* London: Robinson, 1997.

**Chizmar, Richard T.** "Uncle Manny." *Dead of Night 5,* April 1990.

**Cholmondeley, Mary.** "Let Loose." *Temple Bar: A London Magazine for Town and Country Readers,* April 1890.

**Christian, M.** *The Very Bloody Marys.* Binghamton, NY: Harrington Park, 2007.

**Christie, Agatha.** "The Last Seance." In *Double Sin and Other Stories.* New York: Dodd, Mead, 1926.

**Ciencin, Scott.** *Parliament of Blood.* New York: Zebra, 1992.

————. *The Vampire Odyssey*. New York: Zebra, 1992

————. *The Wildings*. New York: Zebra, 1992.

————. *Sweet Sixteen (Buffy the Vampire Slayer)*. New York: Pocket Books, 2002.

**Ciencin, Scott, and Dan Jolley.** *Vengeance (Angel 14)*. New York: Pocket Books, 2002 (juvenile).

**Ciencin, Scott, and Denise Ciencin.** "It Can Happen to You." In *The Longest Night Vol. 1 (Angel)*. New York: Pocket Books, 2002.

————. *Mortal Fear (Buffy the Vampire Slayer)*. New York: Pocket Books, 2003.

————. *Nemesis (Angel)*. New York: Simon Spotlight, 2004.

**Cilescu, Valentina.** *Kiss of Death*. London: Headline Book, 1992.

————. *Empire of Lust*. London: Headline Book, 1993.

————. *The Phallus Osiris*. London: Headline Book, 1993.

————. *Masque of Death*. London: Headline Book, 1995.

————. *Vixens of Night*. London: Headline Book, 1997.

**Citro, Joseph.** "Them Balde-Headed Snays." In *Masques 3*. New York: St. Martin's, 1989.

————. *The Unseen*. New York: Warner, 1990.

————. *Dark Twilight*. New York: Warner, 1991.

**Claire, Suzon.** *From Darkness Forth*. Charleston, SC: BookSurge, 2001.

**Claremont, Chris.** "Who Is Bram Stoker and Why Is He Saying Those Terrible Things about Me?" *Dracula Lives*, August 1973.

————. "I Was Once a Gentle Man." *Dracula Lives*, October 1973.

————. "Child of the Sun." *Dracula Lives*, September 1974.

**Clark, Dale.** "Peace Denied." In *Decades*. Santa Clara, CA: Pentagram, 1977.

————. "Altered Destiny." *Inside the Old House*, February/May 1980.

————. *Resolutions in Time*. North Riverside, IL: Pandora Publications, 1980.

————. *Payer of Tribute*. Matairie, LA: Baker Street Publications, 1989.

**Clark, Simon.** *Vampyrrhic*. London: Hodder & Stoughton, 1998.

————. *London after Midnight*. Sutton, Surrey: Severn House, 2007.

**Clay, Michelle.** *Blood Donor*. Frederick, MD: PublishAmerica, 2004.

**Clayton, Ash.** "The Gradual Seduction of the Night." *Prisoners of the Night 5*, 1991.

————. "Stand Not Alone Against Eternity." *Prisoners of the Night 6*, 1992.

**Clegg, Douglas.** "White Chapel." In *Love in Vein*. New York: HarperCollins, 1994 (erotica).

————. *The Priest of Blood (Vampyricon)*. New York: Shocklines, 2003.

————. *Lady of Serpents*. New York: Penguin, 2006.

————. *The Queen of the Witches*. New York: Ace, 2007.

**Clement, Hal.** "Assumption Unjustified." *Astounding Science Fiction*, October 1946.

————. "A Question of Guilt." In *The Year's Best Horror Stories Series IV*. New York: DAW, 1976.

**Clewitt, George Charles.** *Blood Dynasty*. London: New English Library, 1973.

**Cochran, Connor Freff: see Freff.**

**Codrescu, Andrei.** *The Blood Countess*. New York: Simon & Schuster, 1995.

**Cody, Morrill.** *Passing Stranger*. New York: Macauly, 1933.

**Coffin, M. T.** *My Dentist Is a Vampire: Spinetingler #29*. New York: Harper, 1998.

**Coffman, Virginia.** *The Vampyre of Moura*. New York: Ace, 1970.

————. *The Devil's Mistress*. New York: Pinnacle, 1987.

**Cogswell, Theodore R.** "The Masters." *Thrilling Wonder Stories*, Summer 1944.

**Cohen, Daniel.** *Real Vampires*. New York: Apple, 1995 (juvenile).

**Cole, Adrian.** "All Things Dark and Evil." *Weirdbook*, 1978.

Cole, Jennifer. "The Hunter and the Hunted." In *Legends in Blood*. West Hollywood, CA: Fantaseas, 1991.

Cole, Kresley. *A Hunger Like No Other: Immortals After Dark #1*. New York: Pocket Star, 2006.

———. *No Rest for the Wicked: Immortals After Dark #2*. New York: Pocket Star, 2006.

———. "The Warlord Wants Forever." In *Playing Easy to Get*. New York: Pocket Books, 2006.

Colgan, Jennifer. "Bonfire of the Vampires." In *Hunters*. Lake Park, GA: New Concepts, 2005.

———. "Fresh Blood." In *Immortal Lovers*. Lake Park, GA: New Concepts, 2006.

Collins, Charles, editor. *A Feast of Blood*. New York: Avon, 1967.

Collins, Clint. "Stoker's Mistress." In *Under the Fang*. New York: Pocket Books, 1991.

Collins, Nancy A. *Sunglasses after Dark*. New York: Onyx, 1989.

———. *Tempter*. New York: Onyx, 1990.

———. "Dancing Nitley." In *Under the Fang*. New York: Pocket Books, 1991.

———. *In the Blood*. New York: Roc, 1992.

———. *Paint It Black*. Clarkston, GA: White Wolf, 1995.

———. *A Dozen Black Roses*. Clarkston, GA: White Wolf, 1996.

———. "Vampire King of the Goth Chicks." *Cemetary Dance*, Fall 1998.

———. "Some Velvet Morning." In *The Vampire Sextette*. Garden City, NY: Guild-America Books, 2000.

———. *The Darkest Heart*. Clarkston, GA: White Wolf, 2002.

———. *Dead Roses for a Blue Lady*. Clarkston, GA: White Wolf, 2003.

Collins, Toni. *Something Old*. Toronto: Silhouette Romance, 1993.

Combs, David. *The Intrusion*. New York: Avon, 1981.

Conde, Philip. *Skyway Vampire*. London: Wright & Brown, 1938.

Condenzio, John. *The Shadow of the Succubus*. Bloomington, IN: 1st Books Library, 2001.

———. *The Eternal Thirst*. Bloomington, IN: 1st Books Library, 2004.

Conner, Michael. *Arkangel*. New York: Tor, 1996.

Connolly, Lynne. *The Hunting: The Curse of the Midnight Star #3*. Surprise, AZ: Triskelion, 2005.

———. *Rubies of Fire: Department 57 #3*. Surprise, AZ: Triskelion, 2007.

Connors, Cheryl L. "Dry Ice." *Sherwood Tunnels 7*, 1992.

———. "Running." *Good Guys Wear Fangs 1*, May 1992.

Connors, R. J. "The Reluctant Vampire." *Yankee*, October 1981.

Conrad, Cheryl. "Dark Thoughts." In *Legends in Blood*. West Hollywood, CA: Fantaseas, 1991.

Conrad, Liza. *High School Bites: The Lucy Chronicles*. New York: Penguin, 2006 (juvenile).

Constantine, Storm. *Burying the Shadow*. London: Headline Book Publications, 1992.

———. *Stalking Tender Prey: The Gregori Trilogy #1*. Decatur, GA: Meisha Merlin, 1998.

———. *Scenting Hallowed Blood: The Gregori Trilogy #2*. Decatur, GA: Meisha Merlin, 1999.

———. "Just His Type." In *The Mammoth Book of Vampire Stories by Women*. New York: Carroll & Graf, 2001.

Conway, Gerry. "Demons in Darkness." *Dracula Lives*, March 1974.

Cook, Glen. *Sweet Silver Blues*. New York: Signet, 1987.

Cook, Robert E. "Some Enchanted Evening." *Dead of Night 4*, January 1990.

**Cooke, Catherine.** "The Bat-Winged Knight." *The Magazine of Fantasy & Science Fiction*, March 1990.

**Cooke, Cynthia.** *Rising Darkness: Dark Enchantments #2*. Toronto: Silhouette Nocturne, 2007.

**Cooke, Dorothy Norman.** "The Parasitic." *Startling Mystery Stories*, Winter 1969.

**Cooke, John Peyton.** *Out for Blood*. New York: Avon, 1991.

**Coolidge-Rask, Marie.** *London after Midnight*. New York: Grosset and Dunlap, 1928.

**Cooney, Caroline B.** *The Return of the Vampire (Point Horror)*. London: Hippo Books, 1992 (juvenile).

———. *The Vampire's Promise*. London: Hippo Books, 1993 (juvenile).

———. *Deadly Fear: The Vampire's Promise #1*. New York: Scholastic, 2003 (juvenile).

———. *Evil Returns: The Vampire's Promise #2*. New York: Scholastic, 2003 (juvenile).

———. *Fatal Bargain: The Vampire's Promise #3*. New York: Scholastic, 2003 (juvenile).

**Cooper, Astrid.** "Night's Kiss." In *Sugar and Spice*. London: Virgin Books, 1998.

———. *Shadow's Embrace*. Marleston, SA, Australia: JB Books, 1998.

**Cooper, Louise.** *Blood Summer*. London: New English Library, 1976.

———. *In Memory of Sarah Bailey*. London: New English Library, 1977.

———. "Services Rendered." In *The Mammoth Book of Vampire Stories by Women*. New York: Carroll & Graf, 2001.

**Copper, Basil.** "Dr. Porthos." In *The Midnight People*. London: Leslie Frewin, 1968.

———. "The Grey House." In *From Evil's Pillow*. Sauk City, WI: Arkham House, 1973.

———. "When Greek Meets Greek." In *The Mammoth Book of Dracula*. London: Robinson, 1997.

**Corby, Michael, and Michael Geare.** *Dracula's Diary*. New York: Beaufort Books, 1982.

**Cortázar, Julio.** *62: A Model Kit*. New York: Bard Books, 1973.

**Cory, Ann.** *Private Dancer*. Casper, WY: Whiskey Creek, 2006 (erotica).

**Costello, Matthew J.** "Deep Sleep." In *Dracula: Prince of Darkness*. New York: DAW, 1992.

**Coultes, Sybille.** "Expedition." *Newsletter of the Lucy Westenra Society of the Undead 3*, Summer 1990.

**Counsil, Wendy.** "How to Tame a Vampire." *The Magazine of Fantasy & Science Fiction*, February 1992.

**Countess, The.** *Here I Shall Stay: Memoirs of a Vampire*. Frederick, MD: PublishAmerica, 2006 (poetry).

**Courtney, Vincent.** *Vampire Beat*. New York: Pinnacle, 1991.

———. *Harvest of Blood*. New York: Pinnacle, 1992.

**Cover, Arthur Byron.** *Night of the Living Rerun (Buffy the Vampire Slayer)*. New York: Pocket Books, 1998.

**Cowan, Steven R.** *Gothica: Romance of the Immortals*. Hampton, GA: Southern Charm, 2001.

**Cowen, Geoffrey.** *Jinny Jampire*. Hauppauge, NY: Barrons Educational Series Inc., 1996 (juvenile).

**Cowles, Frederick.** "The Horror of Abbot's Grange." In *The Horror of Abbot's Grange and Other Stories*. London: Frederick Muller, 1937.

————. "The Vampire of Kaldenstein." In *The Nightwind Howls*. London: Frederick Muller, 1938.

————. "Princess of Darkness." In *Dracula's Brood*. Wellingborough, Northamptonshire: Aquarian, 1987.

Cox, Deidra. "Yesterday's Prayer." *Bloodreams 1*, July 1991.

————. "Bread and Circuses." *Bloodreams 2*, October 1991.

Cox, Greg. "Credibility Problem." *Fantasy Book*, March 1985.

————. "Fortress Memory." *Argos*, Summer 1988.

————. *Underworld: Book 1*. New York: Pocket Star, 2003 (movie tie-in).

————. *Blood Enemy: Underworld Book 2*. New York: Pocket Star, 2004 (movie tie-in).

Cox, Michael. *Invasion of the Sausage Snatchers: Vampire Vigilantes #1*. London: Hodder & Stoughton, 2003 (juvenile).

————. *Nightmare on Eck Street: Vampire Vigilantes #2*. London: Hodder & Stoughton, 2003 (juvenile).

————. *The Fall of the House of Bloodvat: Vampire Vigilantes #3*. London: Hodder & Stoughton, 2003 (juvenile).

Coyne, John. *Hunting Season*. New York: Warner, 1988.

Craig, Jamie. *Master of Obsidian*. Indian Hills, CA: Amber Quill, 2007 (erotica).

Crase, Chris. *Never Fall in Love with a Vampire: It Is a Pain in the Neck*. Bloomington, IN: AuthorHouse, 2002.

Crawford, Anne. "Mystery of the Campagna." *Unwin's Annual*, 1887.

Crawford, F. Marion. "For the Blood Is the Life." *Collier's*, Dec. 16, 1905.

————. "The Screaming Skull." *Collier's*, July 11 and July 18, 1908.

Cresswell, Jasmine. *Prince of the Night*. New York: Topaz, 1995.

Crews, Heather. *Prince of Misery*. Frederick, MD: PublishAmerica, 2006.

Crider, Bill. "I Was a Teenage Vampire." In *Many Bloody Returns*, New York: Ace, 2007.

Crispin, A. C. "Bloodspell." In *Tales of the Witch World 1*. New York: Tor, 1987.

Crombie, Elaine Cole. "Annie's Stranger." *Prisoners of the Night 4*, 1990.

Crook, William F. "Night Class." *Prisoner of the Night 2*, 1988.

Cross, Michael. *After Human*. New York: Pinnacle, 2004.

Crow, Florence. "The Nightmare Road." *Weird Tales*, March 1934.

Crowther, Peter. "The Last Vampire." In *The Mammoth Book of Dracula*. London: Robinson, 1997.

Crozier, Ouida. *Shadows after Dark*. Tucson, AZ: Rising Tide, 1993.

Cruceanu, Irina. *In the Shadow of the Vampire*. Frederick, MD: PublishAmerica, 2005.

Csernica, Lillian. "Fallen Idol." *After Hours 13*, Winter 1992.

Culotta, Paul. *Children of the Night: Vampires*. Lake Geneva, WI: TSR, 1996.

Cummings, J. A. *Nightchild: A Clan's Novel*. Dublin, OH: Kresnak, 1999.

Curley, Jason. *The Vampire's Rose: An Unseen Society*. Bloomington, IN: AuthorHouse, 2005.

Curtin, Joseph. *Daughters of the Moon*. New York: Pinnacle, 2002.

Cusick, Richie Tankersley. *Buffy the Vampire Slayer*. New York: Simon Spotlight Entertainment, 1992.

————. *The Harvest (Buffy the Vampire Slayer)*. New York: Pocket Books, 1997.

Custer, Barbara. *Twilight Healer*. Bloomington, IN: 1st Books Library, 2003.

D'Arc, Bianca. *One & Only*. Chippewa, 2006 (erotica).

da Costa, Lima. "Sun of Dracula." *Famous Monsters*, June 1961.

Da Foe, Sierra. "Make Me." In *Tricks & Treats Quickies*. Akron, OH: Ellora's Cave, 2007 (erotica).

**Dadey, Debbie.** *Dracula Doesn't Drink Lemonade*. New York: Little Apple, 1995 (juvenile).

————. *Vampires Don't Wear Polka Dots*. New York: Little Apple, 1997 (juvenile).

————. *Vampire Trouble (Bailey City Monsters #3)*. New York: Little Apple, 1998 (juvenile).

————. *Vampire Baby (Bailey City Monsters #7)*. New York: Little Apple, 1999 (juvenile).

————. *Dracula Doesn't Rock and Roll (Bailey Kids #39)*. New York: Little Apple, 2000 (juvenile).

————. *Mrs. Jeepers on Vampire Island (Adv. Bailey Kids Super #6)*. New York: Scholastic, 2002 (juvenile).

**Dahme, Jeanne.** "The Vampire's Baby." In *Night Bites: Vampire Stories by Women*. Seattle, WA: Seal, 1996.

**Dalman, Max.** *Vampire Abroad*. London: Ward, Lock, 1938.

**Dalton, Trevor.** *The Possession Legacy*. Spain: Libros International, 2007.

**Daly, Carroll Jones.** *The Legion of the Living Dead*. New York: Popular Library, 1947.

**Damien, Anisa.** *Scarlet Ties: Tempted*. Martinsburg, WV: Changeling, 2007.

**Damon, Ron.** "This Night." *Count Ken Fan Club Newsletter 92*, March 1992.

————. "The Alcoholic Bite." *Count Ken Fan Club Newsletter 94*, June 1992.

**Dancey, Sandra P.** *Concerto in Crimson*. Canada: Self-published, 1996.

**Dane, Adrianna.** *Vampyre Falls: Morganna's Sacrifice*. Indian Hills, CA: Amber Quill, 2008 (erotica).

**Dane, Deveraux.** "Corruption." In *Dryad: The Vampire Stories*. Poway, CA: Mkashef Enterprises, 1991.

**Dane, Raven.** *Blood Tears: Legacy of the Dark Kind #1*. Charlston, SC: BookSurge, 2007.

————. *Blood Laments: Legacy of the Dark Kind #2*, Charleston, SC: BookSurge, 2007.

**Daniels, Cora Linn.** *Sardia: A Story of Love*. Boston: Lee and Shepard, 1881.

**Daniels, Les.** *The Black Castle*. New York: Charles Scribner's Sons, 1978.

————. *The Silver Skull*. New York: Charles Scribner's Sons, 1979.

————. *Citizen Vampire*. New York: Charles Scribner's Sons, 1981.

————. *Yellow Fog*. West Kingston, RI: Donald M. Grant, 1986.

————. "The Good Parts." In *Book of the Dead*. New York: Bantam, 1989.

————. "They're Coming for You." In *Cutting Edge*. New York: Bantam, 1989.

————. *No Blood Spilled*. New York: Tor, 1991.

**Daniels, Philip.** *The Dracula Murders*. New York: Critic's Choice Paperbacks, 1983.

**Dann, Jack, and Gardner Dozois.** "Down among the Dead Men." *Oui*, July 1982.

**Dansky, Richard E.** "Bearer of Ill News." In *Dark Tyrants*. Clarkston, GA: White Wolf, 1997.

**Danu, Sophia.** *Kentucky Hunger*. Garibaldi Highlands, BC, Canada: eXtasy Books, 2007.

**Dare, M. P.** "The Demoniac Goat." In *Unholy Relics*. London: Edward Arnold, 1947.

**Darke, David.** *Blind Hunger*. New York: Pinnacle, 1993.

————. *Shade*. New York: Zebra, 1994.

————. *Last Rites*. New York: Zebra, 1996.

**Darling, T. L.** *Autobiography of an Online Vampire: Tealie's Story*. Frederick, MD: PublishAmerica, 2006.

**Dartt, Jewel.** *Enemy Mine*. Dark Star Publications, 2000.

**Daubeny, Ulric.** "The Sumach." In *The Elemental: Tales of the Supernormal and the Inexplicable*. London: G. Routledge, 1919.

**David, Michael.** *Nighthag.* Huntington, WV: University Editions, 1992.

**David, Peter.** *Howling Mad.* New York: Ace, 1989.

**Davidson, Hugh.** "Vampire Village." *Weird Tales,* November 1932.

———. "The Vampire Master." *Weird Tales,* October 1933.

**Davidson, MaryJanice.** "Monster Love." In *Things That Go Bump in the Night.* Akron, OH: Ellora's Cave, 2002 (erotica).

———. "Biting in Plain Sight." In *Bite.* New York: Jove, 2004.

———. "Dead Girls Don't Dance." In *Cravings.* New York: Jove, 2004.

———. *Undead and Unwed: Queen Betsy #1.* New York: Berkley, 2004.

———. *Undead and Unemployed: Queen Betsy #2.* New York: Berkley, 2004.

———. "The Incredible Misadventures of Boo and the Boy Blunder." In *Kick Ass.* New York: Berkley, 2005.

———. *Undead and Unappreciated: Queen Betsy #3.* New York: Berkley, 2005.

———. *Undead and Unreturnable: Queen Betsy #4.* New York: Berkley, 2005.

———. *Undead and Unpopular: Queen Betsy #5.* New York: Berkley, 2006.

———. "Driftwood." In *Over the Moon.* New York: Berkley, 2007.

———. *Undead and Uneasy: Queen Betsy #6.* New York: Berkley, 2007.

———. *Undead and Unworthy: Queen Betsy #7.* New York: Berkley, 2008.

**Davis, F. D.** *In the Beginning.* Mira Loma, CA: Parker, 2007.

**Davis, Grania.** "Tree of Life, Book of Death." *The Magazine of Fantasy & Science Fiction,* March 1992.

**Davis, Jay, and Don Davis.** *Bring on the Night.* New York: Tor, 1993.

**Davis, Laura.** *Lifeshades.* Victoria, BC, Canada: Treeside, 2006.

**Davy, S. (Pseud. Sean Ryan).** *Gay Vampire.* New York: 101 Enterprises, 1969.

**Day, J. L.** "In the Shadows." In *Vamprotica 2005.* Chippewa, 2005 (erotica).

**Day, L. A.** *Double Penetration.* Akron, OH: Ellora's Cave, 2007 (erotica).

**Day, Sylvia.** *Dangerous: Kiss of the Night.* Akron, OH: Ellora's Cave, 2005 (erotica).

———. *Dangerous: Misled.* Akron, OH: Ellora's Cave, 2005 (erotica).

———. *Declassified: Dark Kisses.* Akron, OH: Ellora's Cave, 2006 (erotica).

**De Bate, Betty.** "Mirror Image." *The Vampire's Crypt 4,* Fall 1991.

**de Camp, L. Sprague.** "Castle of Terror." In *Conan of Cimmeria.* New York: Lancer, 1969.

**de Camp, L. Sprague, and Lin Carter.** "Black Tears." In *Conan the Wanderer.* New York: Lancer, 1968.

**de la Cruz, Melissa.** *Blue Bloods.* New York: Hyperion, 2006 (juvenile).

———. *Masquerade: Blue Bloods #2.* New York: Hyperion, 2007 (juvenile).

**de la Mare, Walter.** "Seaton's Aunt." In *The Riddle and Other Stories.* London: Selwyn and Blount, 1923.

**de la Peña, Terri.** "Refugio." In *Night Bites: Vampire Stories by Women.* Seattle, WA: Seal, 1996.

**de Lint, Charles.** "The Sacred Fire." In *Stalkers.* New York: New American Library, 1990.

———. "There's No Such Thing." In *Vampires: A Collection of Original Stories.* New York: HarperCollins, 1991.

———. "We Are Dead Together." In *Under the Fang.* New York: Pocket Books, 1991.

———. "The Graceless Child." *The Magazine of Fantasy & Science Fiction,* February 1992.

———. "In the Soul of a Woman." In *Love in Vein.* New York: HarperCollins, 1994 (erotica).

de Lioncourt, Gabrielle. "Wednesday Night, August 26th." *Vamps 1 and 2*, 1990 and 1991.

de Maupassant, Guy. "The Horla." *Gil Blas*, October 26, 1886.

De Sade, Madame Elisandrya. *Memoires of a Mad Vampire*. Bloomington, IN: AuthorHouse, 2005.

de Winter, Morganna. *Red as Blood*. Lake Park, GA: New Concepts, 2004 (erotica).

Dean, Cameron. *Passionate Thirst: A Candace Steele Vampire Killer Novel #1*. New York: Ballantine, 2006.

———. *Luscious Craving: A Candance Steele Vampire Killer Novel #2*. New York: Ballantine, 2006.

———. *Eternal Hunger: A Candace Steele Vampire Killer Novel #3*. New York: Ballantine, 2006.

Deane, Hamilton, and John L. Balderston. *Dracula: A Play in Three Acts*. New York: Samuel French, 1933.

Dear, Ian. *Village of Blood*. London: New English Library, 1975.

Deason, Lisa. "Freeing Souls." In *Swords and Sorceress IX*. New York: DAW, 1992.

Deaubl, C. J. "Wanted." *Prisoners of the Night 2*, 1988.

DeBill, Walter C. "Where Yidhra Walks." In *The Disciples of Cthulhu*. New York: DAW, 1976.

DeBrandt, Don. *Shakedown (Angel)*. New York: Pocket Books, 2000.

DeCandido, Keith R. A. *The Xander Years, Vol. 1 (Buffy the Vampire Slayer)*. New York: Pocket Books, 1999.

———. *Blackout (Buffy the Vampire Slayer)*. New York: Simon Spotlight Entertainment, 2006.

———. *The Deathless (Buffy the Vampire Slayer)*. New York: Simon Spotlight Entertainment, 2007.

Dedman, Stephen. *Shadows Bite*. New York: Tor, 2001.

———. "Waste Land." In *Never Seen by Waking Eyes*. Akron, OH: Infrapress, 2005.

Dedopulos, Tim. *The Overseer*. Clarkston, GA: White Wolf, 2003.

———. *The Puppet-Masters*. Clarkston, GA: White Wolf, 2003.

———. *Vampire: Slave Ring*. Clarkston, GA: White Wolf, 2003.

Dee, Ron. *Blood Lust*. New York: Dell, 1990.

———. *Dusk*. New York: Dell Abyss, 1991.

———. "A Matter of Style." In *The Ultimate Dracula*. New York: Dell, 1991.

———. *Blood*. New York: Pocket Books, 1993.

———. *Sex and Blood*. Leesburg, VA: TAL Chapbook, 1994.

Dekelb-Rittenhouse, Diane. "To Die For." In *Night Bites: Vampire Stories by Women*. Seattle, WA: Seal, 1996.

Del Rey, Lester. "Cross of Fire." *Weird Tales*, May 1939.

Delany, Joseph. "An Ill Wind." *Analog*, December 1986.

Delany, Samuel R., and James Sallis. "They Fly at Ciron." *The Magazine of Fantasy & Science Fiction*, June 1971.

Dennis, K. C. *Blood Red!* New York: Vantage, 1983.

Dent, Sue. *Never Ceese*. Fairfield, OH: Journey Stone Creations, 2006 (juvenile).

Derby, Crispin. "To Claim His Own." In *The Vampire's Bedside Companion*. London: Frewin, 1975.

Derby, Kathleen. *Tale of the Nightly Neighbors (Are You Afraid of the Dark? #4)*. New York: Minstrel Books, 1995 (juvenile).

Derleth, August. "Bat's Belfry." *Weird Tales*, May 1926.

———. "Those Who Seek." *Weird Tales*, January 1932.

———. "In the Left Wing." *Weird Tales*, June 1932.

———. "Red Hands." *Weird Tales*, October 1932.

———. "Nellie Foster." *Weird Tales*, June 1933.

———. "The Metronome." *Weird Tales*, 1935.

———. "The Satin Mask." *Weird Tales*, January 1936.

———. "The Drifting Snow." *Weird Tales*, February 1939.

———. "Mrs. Lannisfree." *Weird Tales*, November 1945.

———. "Revenants." In *The Shuttered Room and Other Pieces*. Sauk City, WI: Arkham House, 1949.

———. "Keeper of the Key." *Weird Tales*, May 1951.

———. "Who Shall I Say is Calling." *Magazine of Fantasy & Science Fiction*, August 1952.

**Derleth, August, and Mark Schorer.** "The Occupant of the Crypt." In *Colonel Markeson and Less Pleasant People*. Sauk City, WI: Arkham House, 1966.

**Derwydd, Kay.** "Novel Visions." In *Vamprotica 2005*. Chippewa, 2005 (erotica).

**Desjardin, Teresa.** "Untitled." In *Bewitched by Love*. New York: Zebra, 1996.

**Dessing, Jim.** *Vampires*. New York: HarperCollins, 1993 (juvenile).

**Devereaux, Robert.** "A Slow Red Whisper of Sand." In *Love in Vein*. New York: HarperCollins, 1994.

**Devine, Thea.** *Sinful Secrets*. New York: Zebra, 1996.

———. *The Forever Kiss*. New York: Kensington, 2003.

**Devlin, Delilah.** *My Immortal Knight 1: All Hallow's Heartbreaker*. Akron, OH: Ellora's Cave, 2003 (erotica).

———. *My Immortal Knight 2: Love Bites*. Akron, OH: Ellora's Cave, 2004 (erotica).

———. *My Immortal Knight 3: All Knight Long*. Akron, OH: Ellora's Cave, 2004 (erotica).

———. *My Immortal Knight 4: Relentless*. Akron, OH: Ellora's Cave, 2004 (erotica).

———. *My Immortal Knight 5: Uncovering Navarro*. Akron, OH: Ellora's Cave, 2005 (erotica).

———. "Darkest Knight." In *Vamprotica 2005*. Chippewa, 2005 (erotica).

———. "Frannie N' the Private Dick." In *Nibbles N' Bits*. Akron, OH: Ellora's Cave, 2005 (erotica).

———. *My Immortal Knight 6: Silver Bullet*. Akron, OH: Ellora's Cave, 2005 (erotica).

———. *Into the Darkness: The Otherkin #1*. New York: Avon Red, 2007.

———. *Seduced by Darkness: The Otherkin #2*. New York: Avon Red, 2008.

**DeWeese, Gene.** "An Essay on Containment." In *Dracula in London*. New York: Ace, 2001.

**Diamante, Saundra.** *Dracula's Vampires*. Bloomington, IN: AuthorHouse, 2001.

**Dick, Philip K.** "The Cookie Lady." In *Fantasy Fiction*, June 1953.

**Dicks, Terrance.** *Doctor Who and the State of Decay*. London: Target, 1981.

**Dietz, Ulysses.** *Desmond: A Novel of Love and the Modern Vampire*. Los Angeles: Alyson Publications, 1998.

**Dillard, J. M.** *Star Trek #37: Bloodthirst*. New York: Pocket Books, 1987.

**Dimitra, Ria.** *Fiend Angelical*. New Market, AL: Ragnell, 2005.

**Disch, Thomas M.** "The Vamp." *Fantastic Stories of the Imagination*, February 1965.

**Dixon, Franklin W.** *Danger on Vampire Trail (Hardy Boys #50)*. East Rutherford, NJ: Price Stern Sloan, 1971 (juvenile).

**Dobie, Charles Caldwell.** "The Elder Brother." *Harper's Magazine*, February 1925.

**Doherty, Robert.** *Area 51: Nosferatu*. New York: Dell, 2003.

**Dokey, Cameron.** *Here Be Monsters (Buffy the Vampire Slayer)*. New York: Simon Spotlight Entertainment, 2000.

————. "Looks Can Kill." In *How I Survived My Summer Vacation (Buffy the Vampire Slayer)*. New York: Pocket Books, 2000.

————. "No Place Like..." In *How I Survived My Summer Vacation (Buffy the Vampire Slayer)*. New York: Pocket Books, 2000.

————. *The Summoned (Angel)*. New York: Pocket Books, 2001.

**Dole, D. M.** *The Vampire's Daughter*. Frederick, MD: PublishAmerica, 2004.

**Dominie, Fay.** "One Night Stand." *The Vampire's Crypt 2*, 1990.

————. "Twenty-fifth Reunion." *The Vampire's Crypt 4*, Fall 1991.

**Donald, Elizabeth.** *Nocturnal Urges*. Akron, OH: Ellora's Cave, 2004 (erotica).

**Donovan, Dick.** "The Woman with the Oily Eyes." In *Tales of Terror*. London: Chattoo & Windus, 1899.

**Dorr, James S.** "The Hawk and the Slipper." In *Dark Tyrants*. Clarkston, GA: White Wolf, 1997.

**Dougan, Nolene-Patricia.** *Vrolock*. Bloomington, IN: AuthorHouse, 2005.

**Douglas, Carol Nelson.** *Dracula on the Rocks*. New York: DAW, 1995.

**Douglas, Jack.** "The Traitor." *Amazing Stories*, July 1959.

**Douglas, John Scott.** "The Spider's Web." *Weird Tales*, June 1935.

**Douglas, Theo.** *Nemo*. London: Smith, Elder, 1900.

**Dow, Packard.** "The Winged Menace." *Wonder Stories Quarterly*, Spring 1931.

**Doyle, Arthur Conan.** "John Barrington Cowles." *Cassell's Saturday Journal*, April 1884.

————. *The Parasite, Constable's Acme Library Volume 1*. London: Constable, 1894.

————. "The Adventure of the Sussex Vampire." *The Strand*, January 1924.

**Dozois, Gardner, and Jack Dann.** "Down among the Dead Men." *Oui*, July 1982.

**Drake, Asa.** *Crimson Kisses*. New York: Avon, 1981.

**Drake, David.** "The Shortest Way." *Whispers*, 1974.

————. "Something Had to be Done." *The Magazine of Fantasy & Science Fiction*, February 1975.

**Drake, Douglas.** *Creature*. New York: Leisure Books, 1985.

**Drake, Shannon.** "Vanquish the Night." In *Bewitching Love Stories*. New York: Avon, 1992.

————. *Beneath a Blood Red Moon*. New York: Zebra, 1999.

————. *When Darkness Falls*. New York: Zebra, 2000.

————. *Deep Midnight*. New York: Zebra, 2001.

————. *Realm of Shadows*. New York: Zebra, 2002.

————. *Dead by Dusk*. New York: Zebra, 2005.

**Draven, Alan.** *Bitternest*. Lincoln, NE: iUniverse, 2007.

**Drax, Michael.** "Electric Night." *Prisoners of the Night 2*, 1988.

**Dreadstone, Carl.** *Dracula's Daughter*. New York: Berkley Medallion, 1977.

**Drippe, Colleen.** "The Women of Rattlesnake Hill." *Alpha Adventures*, January 1986.

**DuBarry, M. A.** *The Blood Ruby*. Indian Hills, CA: Amber Quill, 2003.

————. *In the Shadow of the Selkie*. Macon, GA: Samhain, 2008.

**Due, Tananarive.** *My Soul to Keep*. London: Piatkus Books, 1995.

————. *The Living Blood*. New York: Atria, 2001.

**Duigon, Lee.** *Lifeblood*. New York: Pinnacle, 1988.

**Duncan, Ronald.** "Consanguinity." In *The Fourth Ghost Book*. London: Barrie and Rockliff, 1965.

**Dundas, Susan K.** "Night Sun." In *Dryad: The Vampire Stories*. Poway, CA: Mkashef Enterprises, 1991.

**Dunn, Gertrude.** *The Mark of the Bat: A Tale of Vampires Living and Dead*. London: T. Butterworth, 1928.

Dunn, Helen M. "Vampyre." *Haunts 19,* Summer 1990.

Dunne, Jennifer. *Dark Salvation.* Amherst Junction, WI: Hard Shell Word Factory, 2001.

Duprae, Livant. *The Vampires: Sodom.* Bloomington, IN: 1st Books Library, 2004.

Durgin, Doranna. "Bummed Out." In *The Longest Night, Vol. 1 (Angel).* New York: Pocket Books, 2002.

———. "Yoke of the Soul." In *The Longest Night, Vol. 1 (Angel).* New York: Pocket Books, 2002.

———. *Fearless (Angel).* New York: Pocket Books, 2003.

———. *Impressions (Angel).* New York: Pocket Books, 2003.

Duval, Alex. *Bloodlust: Vampire Beach #1.* New York: Simon & Schuster, 2006 (juvenile).

———. *Initiation: Vampire Beach #2.* New York: Simon & Schuster, 2006 (juvenile).

———. *Ritual: Vampire Beach #3.* New York: Simon & Schuster, 2007 (juvenile).

———. *Legacy: Vampire Beach #4.* New York: Simon & Schuster, 2007 (juvenile).

Duval, Cheryl W. "Serenata Notturna." *Heart's Blood 1,* May 1992.

Dvorkin, David. *Insatiable.* New York: Pinnacle, 1993.

———. "Reign of Blood." In *Love Bites.* New York: Masquerade Books, 1995.

———. *Unquenchable.* New York: Zebra, 1995.

Dyan, Sheila. *Love Bites.* London: Hodder & Stoughton, 1993.

Eadie, Arlton. "The White Vampire." *Weird Tales,* September 1928.

———. *The Veiled Vampire,* London: Fiction House, 1930.

———. "The Vampire Airplane." *Weird Tales,* 1933.

Easton, Kathy. "The Only Way to Fly." *Vampire Junction 5,* 1992.

Eccarius, J. G. *The Last Days of Christ the Vampire.* Gualala, CA: III, 1988.

Ecker, Don. *Past Sins.* Dark Realm Press, 2004.

Eddy, C. M. "The Loved Dead." *Weird Tales,* May/June/July 1924.

———. "Miscreant from Muriana." In *Exit into Eternity.* Providence, RI: Oxford, 1973.

Eden, Cynthia. *The Vampire's Kiss.* Hickory Corners, MI: ImaJinn Books, 2005.

Edwards, G. John. "Rip Van Dracula." *Famous Monsters,* December 1965.

Edwards, Jan. "A Taste of Culture." In *The Mammoth Book of Dracula.* London: Robinson, 1997.

Elflandsson, Galad. "An Overruling Passion." In *Greystone Bay.* New York: Tor, 1985.

———. "The Last Time I Saw Harris." In *Shadows 9.* New York: Doubleday, 1986.

Elg, Stefan. *Beyond Belief.* New York: Tower Books, 1970.

Eliade, Mircea. "Miss Christina." In *Mystic Stories.* New York: Columbia University Press, 1993.

Elias, Amelia. *Hunter: Guardian's League #1.* Macon, GA: Samhain, 2006.

———. *Outcast: Guardian's League #2.* Macon, GA: Samhain, 2006.

Eliot, Marc. *How Dear the Dawn.* New York: Ballantine, 1987.

Elliott, Jacqueline. *Full Moon Inheritance.* Treble Heart Books, 2003.

Ellis, Carol. *Overnight Bite.* New York: Random House, 1996 (juvenile).

Ellis, Jack. *Nightlife.* New York: Kensington, 1996.

Ellis, Monique. "The DeVille Inheritance." In *Lords in the Night.* New York: Zebra, 1997.

Ellis, Tangi. *Bite: A Modern Gothic Vampire Tale.* Augusta, GA: Harbor House, 2001.

Ellison, Harlan. "The Hungry One." *The Gent Magazine,* May 1957.

———. "Try a Dull Knife." *The Magazine of Fantasy & Science Fiction,* October 1968.

————. "V Is for the Vordalake." *The Magazine of Fantasy & Science Fiction,* 1975.

————. "Lonely Women Are the Vessels of Time." *MidAmeriCon Program Book,* 1976.

————. "Footsteps." *Gallery,* December 1980.

Ellwood, Leigh. *The Healing.* Hillsborough, NC: Venus, 2006 (erotica).

Elrod, P. N. *Vampire Files: Bloodcircle.* New York: Ace, 1990.

————. *Vampire Files: Bloodlist.* New York: Ace, 1990.

————. *Vampire Files: Lifeblood.* New York: Ace, 1990.

————. *Vampire Files: Art in the Blood.* New York: Ace, 1991.

————. *Vampire Files: Fire in the Blood.* New York: Ace, 1991.

————. "Partners in Time." *Good Guys Wear Fangs 1,* May 1992.

————. *Vampire Files: Blood on the Water.* New York: Ace, 1992.

————. "The Wind Breathes Cold." In *Dracula: Prince of Darkness.* New York: DAW, 1992.

————. *I, Strahd: The Memoirs of a Vampire.* Lake Geneva, WI: TSR, 1993.

————. *Red Death.* New York: Ace, 1993.

————. "Caretaker." In *Tales of the Ravenloft.* Lake Geneva, WI: TSR, 1994.

————. *Death and the Maiden.* New York: Ace, 1994.

————. *Death Masque.* New York: Ace, 1995.

————. "Fugitives." In *Women at War.* New York: Tor, 1995.

————. "A Night at the (Horse) Opera." In *Celebrity Vampires.* New York: DAW, 1995.

————. "You'll Catch Your Death." In *Vampire Detectives.* New York: DAW, 1995.

————. *Dance of Death.* New York: Ace, 1996.

————. "The Witches' Mark." In *Time of the Vampires.* New York: DAW, 1996.

————. *I, Strahd: The War Against Azalin.* Lake Geneva, WI: TSR, 1998.

————. "The Quick Way Down." In *Mob Magic.* New York: DAW, 1998.

————. *Vampire Files: Chill in the Blood.* New York: Ace, 1998.

————. *Vampire Files: Dark Sleep.* New York: Ace, 2000.

————. *Quincey Morris, Vampire.* New York: Baen, 2001.

————. *Vampire Files: Lady Crymsyn.* New York: Ace, 2001.

————. "Slaughter." In *The Repentant.* New York: DAW, 2003.

————. *Vampire Files: Cold Streets.* New York: Ace, 2003.

————. *Vampire Files: Song in the Dark.* New York: Ace, 2005.

————. "Grave-Robbed." In *Many Bloody Returns.* New York: Ace, 2007.

Elrod, P. N., and Nigel Bennett. *Keeper of the King.* New York: Baen Books, 1996.

————. *His Father's Son.* New York: Baen Books, 2001.

————. *Siege Perilous.* New York: Baen Books, 2004.

Elsen, Rudolf. "Thing of Abomination." *Dead of Night 5,* April 1990.

————. "Changes." *Dead of Night 6,* July 1990.

Elwood, Roger. "Future Love." Indianapolis, IN: Bobbs-Merrill, 1977.

Emerson, Kevin. *Oliver Nocturne: The Vampire's Photograph.* New York: Scholastic, 2008.

Emerson, Shirley. "Initiation Night." In *Dracula.* East Lansing, MI: T'Kuhtian, 1980.

Enfield, Hugh. *Kronos.* London: Fontana, 1972.

England, C. J. *Don't Spank the Vamp.* Mardi Gras, 2006 (erotica).

Engstrom, Elizabeth. *Black Ambrosia.* New York: Tor, 1988.

————. "Elixer." In *Love in Vein.* New York: HarperCollins, 1994 (erotica).

Erickson, John R. *The Case of the Vampire Cat: Hank the Cowdog #21.* New York: Puffin, 1993 (juvenile).

———. *The Case of the Vampire Vacuum Sweeper: Hank the Cowdog #29*. New York: Puffin, 1997 (juvenile).

Erickson, Lynne. *Out of the Darkness*. Toronto: Harlequin Super-Romance, 1994.

Erotique, Desiree. *The Bindmaster's Collar*. Garibaldi Highlands, BC, Canada: eXtasy Books, 2003 (erotica).

———. *Diabolique*. Scottsdale, AZ: Loose Id, (erotica).

Erwin, Alan. *Skeleton Dancer*. New York: Dell, 1989.

Eshbach, Lloyd Arthur. "Isle of the Undead." *Weird Tales*, October 1936.

Essence. *Tempting Reynaldo*. Scottsdale, AZ: Loose Id, 2007.

Estleman, Loren D. *Sherlock Holmes vs. Dracula: The Adventure of the Sanguinary Count*. New York: Doubleday, 1978.

Estes, James. *The Inquisition*. Clarkston, GA: White Wolf, 1995.

———. *No Vein Glory: Redemption of a Young Vampire*. Philadelphia: Xlibris, 2003.

Etchison, Dennis. "It Only Comes at Night." In *Frights*. New York: St. Martin's, 1976.

Eulo, Ken. *The House of Caine*. New York: Tor, 1988.

Evans, Angelina. *Night Stalker*. Martinsburg, WV: Changeling, 2004 (erotica).

Evans, Anna. "Fang Dysfunction." In *Vamprotica 2005*. Chippewa, 2005 (erotica).

Evans, E. Everett. "The Undead Die." *Weird Tales*, July 1948.

———. "Food for Demons." In *Food for Demons*. San Diego: Shroud, 1971.

———. "The Martian and the Vampire." In *Food for Demons*. San Diego: Shroud, 1971.

———. "Operation Almost." In *Food for Demons*. San Diego: Shroud, 1971.

———. "The Sun Shines Bright." In *Food for Demons*. San Diego: Shroud, 1971.

———. "The Undead Die." In *Food for Demons*. San Diego: Shroud, 1971.

———. "The Unusual Model." In *Food for Demons*. San Diego: Shroud, 1971.

Evans, Gloria. *Meh'yam: The Vampire*. Gainesville, FL: Tibo, 2000.

Evans, Tim. *Vampire of the Sierra*. London: Reynolds, 1979.

Ewers, Hanns Heinz. "The Spider," 1921.

———. *Vampire*. New York: John Day, 1934.

Fahy, Christopher. *The Lyssa Syndrome*. New York: Zebra, 1990.

Fairfield, Henry W. A. "Only by Mortal Hands." *Ghost Stories*, October 1927.

Falk, Lee. *The Phantom #12: The Vampires and the Witch*. New York: Avon Books and King Features, 1974.

Fallon, Martin. "Mass Production." *The Vampire's Crypt 5*, Spring 1992.

Farber, Erica. *My Teacher Is a Vampire*. Racine, WI: Golden Book, 1994 (juvenile).

———. *Kiss of the Vampire*. Racine, WI: Golden Book, 1996 (juvenile).

———. *Vampire Brides*. New York: Random House, 1996 (juvenile).

———. *The Vampire Barbecue*. New York: Random House, 1997 (juvenile).

Farber, Sharon. "Born Again." *Isaac Asimov's Science Fiction Magazine*, 1978.

———. "A Surfeit of Melancholic Humours." *Issac Asimov's Science Fiction Magazine*, March 1984.

———. "Return of the Dust Vampires." In *Whispers V*. New York: Doubleday, 1985.

———. "Ice Dreams." *Isaac Asimov's Science Fiction Magazine*, March 1987.

Farley, Ralphe Milne. "Another Dracula?" *Weird Tales*, September/October 1930.

Farmer, Philip Jose. *Image of the Beast*. North Hollywood, CA: Essex House, 1968.

———. *Blown*. North Hollywood, CA: Essex House, 1969.

———. "Nobody's Perfect." In *The Ultimate Dracula*. New York: Dell, 1991.

Farrar, Stewart. *The Dance of Blood*. London: Arrow Books, 1977.

Farren, Mick. *The Time of Feasting*. New York: Tor, 1996.

———. *Darklost*. New York: Tor, 2000.

————. *More Than Mortal*. New York: Forge, 2001.

————. *Underland*. New York: Tor, 2002.

Farrington, Geoffrey. *The Revenants*. UK: Dedalus, 1983.

Farris, John. *All Heads Turn When the Hunt Goes By*. New York: Playboy, 1977.

————. *The Catacombs*. New York: Delacorte, 1981.

————. *Nightfall*. New York: Tor, 1987.

Farshtey, Greg. *Hell's Feast*. Honesdale, PA: West End Games, 1994.

Faulkner, Colleen. "Highland Blood." In *After Midnight*. New York: Zebra, 1998.

Faust, Christa. "Cherry." In *Love in Vein*. New York: HarperCollins, 1994 (erotica).

————. "Bootleg." In *The Mammoth Book of Vampire Fiction by Women*. New York: Carroll & Graf, 2001.

Fearn, John Russell. *No Grave Need I*. Philip Harbottle, 1984.

Feehan, Christine. *Dark Prince: The Carpathians #1*. New York: Love Spell, 1999.

————. *Dark Desire: The Carpathians #2*. New York: Love Spell, 1999.

————. *Dark Gold: The Carpathians #3*. New York: Love Spell, 2000.

————. *Dark Magic: The Carpathians #4*. New York: Love Spell, 2000.

————. *Dark Challenge: The Carpathians #5*. New York: Love Spell, 2000.

————. "Dark Dream." In *After Twilight*. New York: Love Spell, 2001.

————. *Dark Fire: The Carpathians #6*. New York: Love Spell, 2001.

————. *Dark Legend: The Carpathians #7*. New York: Love Spell, 2002.

————. *Dark Guardian: The Carpathians #8*. New York: Love Spell, 2002.

————. "Dark Descent." In *The Only One*. New York: Leisure Books, 2003.

————. *Dark Symphony: The Carpathians #9*. New York: Jove, 2003.

————. *Dark Melody: The Carpathians #10*. New York: Leisure Books, 2003.

————. *Dark Destiny: The Carpathians #11*. New York: Leisure Books, 2004.

————. "Dark Hunger." In *Hot Blooded*. New York: Jove, 2004.

————. *Dark Secret: The Carpathians #12*. New York: Jove, 2005.

————. *Dark Demon: The Carpathians #13*. New York: Jove, 2006.

————. *Dark Celebration: A Carpathian Reunion: The Carpathians #14*. New York: Berkley, 2006.

————. *Dark Possession: The Carpathians #15*. New York: Berkley, 2007.

Feinleib, Yvonne. "Hunting." *The Vampire's Crypt 6*, Fall 1992.

Fenn, Lionel. *The Mark of the Moderately Vicious Vampire*. New York: Ace, 1992.

Fenyvesi, Angela S. *Pilare the Vampire: The Untold Existance*. Frederick, MD: PublishAmerica, 2002.

Feval, Paul. *Knightshade*. Encino, CA: Black Coat, 2003.

————. *Vampire City*. Encino, CA: Black Coat, 2003.

————. *The Vampire Countess*. Encino, CA: Black Coat, 2003.

Fiddler, Angela. *Lineage*. Scottsdale, AZ: Loose Id, 2007 (erotica).

Files, Gemma. "Year Zero." In *The Mammoth Book of Vampire Stories by Women*. New York: Carroll & Graf, 2001.

Finch, Carol. "Red Moon Rising." In *After Midnight*. New York: Zebra, 1998.

Firth, Wesley. *Spawn of the Vampire*. London: Bear 1945.

Fish, B. N. "Choices." *Good Guys Wear Fangs 1*, May 1992.

————. "Instinct." *Good Guys Wear Fangs 1*, May 1992.

————. "The LaCroix Chronicles." *Just My Type*, 1992.

Fitch, Ed. *Castle of Deception*. St. Paul, MN: Llewellyn, 1983.

Fite, Jason P. *The Vampire of Suburbia*. Lincoln, NE: Writers Club, 2001.

Flagg, Francis. "The Smell." *Strange Tales*, January 1932.

Flanders, Eric. *To Love a Vampire*. Toronto: World-Wide Publications, 1980.

————. *Night Blood*. New York: Zebra, 1993.

Flanders, John. "The Graveyard Duchess." In *Weird Tales*, December 1934.

Fleming, Gherbod. *The Devil's Advocate*. Clarkston, GA: White Wolf, 1997.

————. *The Winnowing*. Clarkston, GA: White Wolf, 1998.

————. *Gangrel*. Clarkston, GA: White Wolf, 1999.

————. *Venture*. Clarkston, GA: White Wolf, 1999.

————. *Assamite*. Clarkston, GA: White Wolf, 2000.

————. *Brujah*. Clarkston, GA: White Wolf, 2000.

————. *Nosferatu*. Clarkston, GA: White Wolf, 2000.

————. *Dark Ages: Nosferatu*. Clarkston, GA: White Wolf, 2002.

————. *Dark Ages: Lasombra*. Clarkston, GA: White Wolf, 2003.

Fleming, Nigel. *To Love a Vampire*. Encino, CA: World-Wide, 1980 (erotica).

Fletcher, Jo. "Lord of the Undead." In *The Mammoth Book of Dracula*. London: Robinson, 1997.

Florian, Z. P. "Vampirritation." *Heart's Blood 1*, May 1992.

Floyd, Mike. "The Meadow and Beyond." *Dead of Night 2*, July 1989.

Floyd, Trevor. "Defender." *Dead of Night 5*, April 1990.

Flynn, Michael F. "Dragons." *Weird Tales*, Spring–Fall 1989.

Foley, Louise Munro. *Vampire Cat: My Substitute Teacher's Gone Batty (Vampire Cat #1)*. New York: Tor Kids, 1996 (juvenile).

————. *Vampire Cat: Bird Brained Fiasco (Vampire Cat #2)*. New York: Tor Kids, 1996 (juvenile).

————. *Vampire Cat: Phoney-Baloney Professor (Vampire Cat #3)*. New York: Tor Kids, 1996 (juvenile).

————. *Vampire Cat: The Catnip Cat-Astrophe (Vampire Cat #4)*. New York: Tor Kids, 1999 (juvenile).

Ford, Arthur. "The Mark on the Seaman's Throat." *Ghost Stories*, March 1992.

Ford, John M. *The Dragon Waiting*. New York: Simon & Schuster, 1983.

Ford, Michael Thomas. "Sting." In *Masters of Midnight: Erotic Tales of the Vampire*. New York: Kensington, 2003.

Forest, Salambo. *Witch Power*. New York: Olympia Press, 1971.

Forrest, Katherine V. "O Captain, My Captain." In *Dreams and Swords*. Tallahassee, FL: Naiad, 1987.

Forrest, V. K. *Eternal*. New York: Kensington, 2007.

Fortune, Dion. "Blood-Lust." In *The Secrets of Dr. Taverner*. London: Noel Douglas, 1926.

————. *The Demon Lover*. London: Noel Douglas, 1927.

Foster, Prudence. *Blood Legacy*. New York: Pocket Books, 1971.

Fowler, Christopher. "Dracula's Library." In *The Mammoth Book of Dracula*. London: Robinson, 1997.

Fox, Andrew. *Fat White Vampire Blues*. New York: Ballantine, 2003.

————. *Bride of the Fat White Vampire*. New York: Ballantine, 2004.

Fox, Janet. "Creeper." *Moonbroth 7*, 1972.

————. "Eyes of the Laemi." In *Sword and Sorceress V*. New York: DAW, 1988.

Fox, Leslie H. "The Vampire." In *The Vampire and Sixteen Other Stories*. London: Alliance, 1945.

Fox, Marion. *Ape's Face*. New York: John Lane Company, 1914.

Foxxe, Chaste. *Bite Me If You Can*. Lake Park, GA: New Concepts, 2003 (erotica).

Frances, A. D. *Scent of a Vampire*. Richardson, TX: Lyric Studios, 2001.

Francis, Gregory. "High Moon." *Weirdbook*, January 1971.

Francis, JennaKay. *From the Heart*. Indian Hills, CA: Amber Quill, 2002.

————. *A Gift of Blood*. Indian Hills, CA: Amber Quill, 2002.

Francis, Lee. "The Chemical Vampire." *Amazing Stories,* March 1949.

Frank, Jacquelyn. *Jacob: The Nightwalkers #1*. New York: Kensington, 2006.

————. *Gideon: The Nightwalkers #2*. New York: Kensington, 2007.

Frank, Janrae. "Visiting the Neighbors." In *I, Vampire*. Stamford, CT: Longmeadow, 1995.

Frasier, Anne. *Pale Immortal*. New York: Onyx, 2006.

————. *Garden of Darkness*. New York: Onyx, 2007.

Frederick, Otto. *Count Dracula's Canadian Affair*. New York: Pageant, 1960.

Freed, L. A. *Blood Thirst*. New York: Pinnacle, 1989.

Freff (Connor Freff Cochran). "A Night on the Docks." *Whispers,* August 1982.

Fremont, Eleanor. "Bats in the Belfry." In *Tales from the Crypt Vol. 1*. New York: Random House, 1990.

————. "By the Dawn's Early Light." In *Tales from the Crypt Vol. 2*. New York: Random House, 1991.

————. "Fare Tonight, Followed by Increasing Clottiness." In *Tales from the Crypt Vol. 2*. New York: Random House, 1991.

Friedman, C. S. *The Madness Season*. New York: DAW, 1990.

————. *Black Sun Rising*. New York: DAW, 1991.

————. *When True Night Falls*. New York: DAW, 1993.

————. *Crown of Shadows*. New York: DAW, 1995.

Friesner, Esther M. "The Vampire of Gretna Green." *Fantasy Book,* December 1985.

————. "The Blood-Ghoul of Scarsdale." In *Vampires: A Collection of Original Stories*. New York: HarperCollins, 1991.

————. "Claim-Jumpin' Woman You Got a Stake in My Heart." *The Magazine of Fantasy & Science Fiction,* July 1991.

————. "Puss." In *Snow White, Blood Red*. New York: Morrow, 1993.

————. "Werotica." In *Single White Vampire Seeks Same*. New York: DAW, 2001.

Friswell, James Hain. "The Dead Man's Story." In *Ghost Stories and Phantom Fancies*. London: 1858.

Fritch, Charles E. "Much Ado about Plenty." *Fantasy Magazine,* August 1953.

Frost, Gregory. "Some Things Are Better Left." *Isaac Asimov's Science Fiction Magazine,* February 1993.

Frost, Jeaniene. *Halfway to the Grave: A Night Huntress Novel #1*. New York: Avon, 2007.

————. *One Foot in the Grave: A Night Huntress Novel #2*. New York: Avon, 2008.

Fulilove, J. B. S. "Ghouls of the Sea." *Weird Tales,* March 1934.

Gallagher, Diana G. "Tipping Is Not a Name of a City in China." In *I, Vampire*. Stamford, CT: Longmeadow, 1995.

————. *Obsidian Fate (Buffy the Vampire Slayer)*. Riverside, NJ: Simon Spotlight Entertainment, 1999.

————. *Doomsday Deck (Buffy the Vampire Slayer)*. Riverside, NJ: Simon Spotlight Entertainment, 2000.

————. *Prime Evil (Buffy the Vampire Slayer)*. Riverside, NJ: Simon Spotlight Entertainment, 2000.

————. *Spark and Burn (Buffy the Vampire Slayer)*. Riverside, NJ: Simon Spotlight Entertainment, 2005.

Gallagher, Stephen. "River of Darkness, Over Me." *The Magazine of Fantasy & Science Fiction,* August 1989.

Galvin, George W. *A Thousand Faces*. Boston: Four Seas, 1920.

**Gannett, Lewis.** *The Living One.* New York: Random House, 1993.

**Garden, Nancy.** *Prisoner of Vampires.* New York: Dell, 1984 (juvenile).

———. *My Sister the Vampire.* New York: Alfred A. Knopf, 1992 (juvenile).

**Gardiner, Lina.** *Grave Illusions: The Jess Vandemire Vampire Hunter Series.* Hickory Corners, MI: ImaJinn, 2007.

**Gardner, Craig Shaw.** "Aim for the Heart." In *The Dodd, Mead Gallery of Horror.* New York: Dodd, Mead, 1983.

———. "Three Faces of the Night." In *Halloween Horrors.* New York: Doubleday, 1986.

———. *The Lost Boys.* New York: Berkley, 1987 (movie novelization).

———. *Return to Chaos (Buffy the Vampire Slayer).* London: Pocket Books, 1998.

———. *Dark Mirror (Angel).* New York: Simon Spotlight, 2004.

**Garfield, Frances.** "The House at Evening." *Whispers,* March 1982.

**Garnett, David S.** "Together." In *Final Shadows.* New York: Doubleday, 1991.

**Garrett, Michael.** "Reunion." *Chic Magazine,* 1987.

**Garrett, Randall.** "League of the Living Dead." *Mystic Magazine,* November 1953.

**Garrison, Joan.** "The Yearning." *Undinal Songs 5,* October 1982.

**Garton, Ray.** *Live Girls.* London: MacDonald, 1987.

———. *Lot Lizards.* Mark V. Ziesing, 1991.

———. *Resurrecting Ravana (Buffy the Vampire Slayer).* New York: Simon Spotlight Entertainment, 2000.

———. *Night Life.* Burton, MI: Subterranean, 2005.

**Gaskell, Jane.** *The Shiny Narrow Grin.* London: Hodder & Stoughton, 1964.

**Gauthier, Theophile.** *The Beautiful Vampire.* London: A. M. Philpot, 1926.

**Gelb, Jeff.** "Suzie Sucks." *Hustler Letters Magazine,* 1987 (erotica).

**Gelfland, Alayne.** "The Night Keeper." *Prisoners of the Night 1,* 1987.

———. "Dancing with the Dead." *Prisoners of the Night 2,* 1988.

———. "A Terrible Fruit." *Prisoners of the Night 3,* 1989.

———. "To Sacrifice the Sun." *Prisoners of the Night 4,* 1990.

**Geller, Ruth.** "Dreckula." In *Pictures from the Past and Other Stories.* Buffalo, NY: Imp, 1980.

**Gelotte, Mark.** "A Bride of Darkness." *Space and Time,* February 1972.

**Gelsey, James.** *Scooby-Doo and the Vampire's Revenge (Scooby-Doo Mysteries #6).* New York: Scholastic, 1999 (juvenile).

**Gembeck, Frank, Jr.** "Forever Young." *Book of Shadows 1,* 1990.

**Gengler, Cindy.** *Fallen Angels: Rafe's Heart.* Round Lake Park, IL: Gardenia, 2002.

**Gerwolds, Richard David.** *Neverafter: A Vampire Tragedy.* Frederick, MD: PublishAmerica, 2003.

**Ghoul, Jule.** "Vampire's Life." *Bloodreams 3–4,* January and April 1992.

**Gibbons, Cromwell.** *The Bat Woman.* Cleveland: World, 1938.

**Gideon, John.** *Greeley's Cove.* New York: Jove, 1991.

———. *Golden Eyes.* New York: Berkley, 1994.

———. *Kindred.* New York: Jove, 1996.

**Gideon, Nancy.** *Midnight Kiss.* New York: Pinnacle, 1994.

———. *Midnight Temptation.* Hickory Corners, MI: ImaJinn Books, 1994.

———. *Midnight Surrender.* Hickory Corners, MI: ImaJinn Books, 1995.

———. *Midnight Enchantment.* Hickory Corners, MI: ImaJinn Books, 1999.

———. *Midnight Gamble.* Hickory Corners, MI: ImaJinn Books, 2000.

———. *Midnight Redeemer.* Hickory Corners, MI: ImaJinn Books, 2000.

———. *Midnight Shadows.* Hickory Corners, MI: ImaJinn Books, 2001.

———. *Midnight Masquerade.* Hickory Corners, MI: ImaJinn Books, 2001.

————. *Midnight Crusader*. Hickory Corners, MI: ImaJinn Books, 2002.

Gilbert, J. *Blood Hunt: The Legend*. Surprise, AZ: Triskelion, 2006.

Gilbert, William. "The Last Lords of Gardonal." *Argosy*, July–September 1867.

Gilbreath, Allan. *Galen*. Memphis, TN: Ronin Enterprises, 1997.

Gilchrist, R. Murray. "The Crimson Weaver." *The Yellow Book 6*, July 1985.

Gilden, Mel. *M Is for Monster*. New York: Avon, 1987 (juvenile).

————. *Born to Howl*. New York: Avon, 1987 (juvenile).

————. *There's a Batwing in My Lunchbox*. New York: Avon, 1988 (juvenile).

————. *The Pet of Frankenstein*. New York: Avon, 1988 (juvenile).

————. *Z Is for Zombie*. New York: Avon, 1988 (juvenile).

Giles, Raymond. *Night of the Vampire*. New York: Avon, 1969.

Gillman, Laura Anne. "Exposure." In *Blood Muse*. New York: Donald I. Fine, 1995.

Gillman, Laura Anne, and Joseph Sherman. *Visitors (Buffy the Vampire Slayer)*. New York: Pocket Books, 1999.

————. *Deep Water (Buffy the Vampire Slayer)*. New York: Pocket Books, 2000.

Gilmore, Sheri. *Maslow's Needs*. Scottsdale, AZ: Loose Id, 2005.

Gissendaner, Christy. *The Vampire Scrolls: Damien and Charisse*. Surprise, AZ: Triskelion, 2005.

Gittens, Allen J. "Killer Instinct." *Nightmist 1*, Spring 1991.

Glad, Victoria. "Each Man Kills." *Weird Tales*, March 1951.

Glass, Lorena. *Fiery Roses*. Frederick, MD: PublishAmerica, 2002.

Gleason, Colleen. *The Rest Falls Away: The Gordella Vampire Chronicles*. New York: Signet, 2007.

————. *Rises the Night: The Gordella Vampire Chronicles #2*. New York: Signet, 2007.

————. *The Bleeding Dusk: The Gordella Vampire Chronicles #3*. New York: Signet, 2008.

————. *When Twilight Burns: The Gordella Vampire Chronicles #4*. New York: Signet, 2008.

Gloag, J. "Lady without Appetite." *Magpie*, March 1952.

Glut, Donald F. "Dr. Karnstein's Creation." *The New Adventures of Frankenstein*, May 2004.

Goddin, Jeffrey. *The Living Dead*. New York: Leisure Books, 1987.

———— "A Scent of Roses." *Dark Infinity*, Spring 1991.

Godwin, John B. L. "The Cocoon." *Story Magazine*, October 1946.

Goethe, Johann Wolfgang Von. "The Bride of Corinth." *Haven* by Friedrich Schiller, 1797 (poem).

Gogol, Nikolai. "Viy." 1835.

Gold, E. J. "Rock and Roll Will Never Die." In *I, Vampire*. Stamford, CT: Longmeadow, 1995.

Golden, Christie. *Vampire of the Mists*. Lake Geneva, WI: TSR Hobbies, 1991.

————. *Dance of the Dead*. Lake Geneva, WI: TSR Hobbies, 1992.

————. *The Enemy Within*. Lake Geneva, WI: TSR Hobbies, 1994.

————. "The Sun Child." In *The Longest Night Vol. 1 (Angel)*. New York: Pocket Books, 2002.

Golden, Christopher. *Of Saints and Sinners (The Shadow Saga Book 1)*. New York: Jove, 1994.

————. *Angel Souls and Devil Hearts (The Shadow Saga Book 2)*. New York: Berkley, 1995.

————. *Of Masques and Martyrs (The Shadow Saga Book 3)*. New York: Ace, 1998.

————. *Sins of the Father (Buffy the Vampire Slayer)*. New York: Pocket Books, 1999.

———. *Spike & Dru: Pretty Maids All in a Row (Buffy the Vampire Slayer)*. New York: Pocket Books, 2000.

———. *Prophecies: The Lost Slayer Book 1 (Buffy the Vampire Slayer)*. New York: Pocket Books, 2001.

———. *Dark Times: The Lost Slayer Book 2 (Buffy the Vampire Slayer)*. New York: Pocket Books, 2001.

———. *King of the Dead: The Lost Slayer Book 3 (Buffy the Vampire Slayer)*. New York: Pocket Books, 2001.

———. *Original Sins: The Lost Slayer Book 4 (Buffy the Vampire Slayer)*. New York: Pocket Books, 2001.

———. "I Still Believe." In *The Longest Night Vol. 1 (Angel)*. New York: Pocket Books, 2002.

———. *Oz: Into the Wild (Buffy the Vampire Slayer)*. New York: Pocket Books, 2002.

———. *The Wisdom of War (Buffy the Vampire Slayer)*. New York: Pocket Books, 2002.

———. *The Gathering Dark (The Shadow Saga Book 4)*. New York: Ace, 2003.

———. *Dark Congress (Buffy the Vampire Slayer)*. Riverside, NJ: Simon Spotlight Entertainment, 2007.

———. "The Mournful Cry of Owls." In *Many Bloody Returns*. New York: Ace, 2007.

**Golden, Christopher, and James A. Moore.** *Bloodstained Oz*. Northborough, MA: Earthling Publications, 2006.

**Golden, Christopher, and Nancy Holder.** *Halloween Rain (Buffy the Vampire Slayer)*. New York: Pocket Books, 1997.

———. *Blooded (Buffy the Vampire Slayer)*. New York: Pocket Books, 1998.

———. *Child of the Hunt (Buffy the Vampire Slayer)*. Riverside, NJ: Simon Spotlight Entertainment, 1998.

———. *Ghost Roads (Buffy the Vampire Slayer)*. New York: Pocket Books, 1999.

———. *The Gatekeeper Trilogy 1: Out of the Madhouse (Buffy the Vampire Slayer)*. Riverside, NJ: Simon Spotlight Entertainment, 1999.

———. *The Gatekeeper Trilogy 2: Ghost Roads (Buffy the Vampire Slayer)*. Riverside, NJ: Simon Spotlight Entertainment, 1999.

———. *The Gatekeeper Trilogy 3: Sons of Entropy (Buffy the Vampire Slayer)*. Riverside, NJ: Simon Spotlight Entertainment, 1999.

———. *Immortal (Buffy the Vampire Slayer)*. Riverside, NJ: Simon Spotlight Entertainment, 1999.

———. *The Xander Years Vol.1 (Buffy the Vampire Slayer)*. London: Pocket Books, 1999.

**Golden, Christopher, and Tom Sniegoski.** *Force Majeure*. New York: Pocket Books, 2002.

———. *Monster Island (Buffy the Vampire Slayer/Angel)*. New York: Simon Pulse, 2003.

**Gomez, Jewelle.** "No Day Too Long." In *Lesbian Fiction*. Watertown, MA: Persephone, 1981.

———. *The Gilda Stories: A Novel*. Ithaca, NY: Firebrand Books, 1991.

———. "Joe Louis Was a Heck of a Fighter." In *Embracing the Dark*. Los Angeles: Alyson Publications, 1991.

**Gordon, Charles J., Jr.** "Mr. Lucky." *The Vampire's Crypt 4*, Fall 1991.

———. "What Are Friends For?" *Bloodreams 4*, April 1992.

**Gordon, John.** "Black Beads." In *The Mammoth Book of Dracula*. London: Robinson, 1997.

Gordon, Julien. "Vampires." In *Lippincott's Monthly Magazine*. Philadelphia: J. B. Lippincott, May 1891.

Gorman, Ed. "Duty." In *Under the Fang*. New York: Pocket Books, 1991.

———. "Selection Process." In *The Ultimate Dracula*. New York: Dell, 1991.

Gosse, Douglas. *The Celtic Cross: The Vampire's Journal*. St. John's, NF, Canada: Jesperson, 1995.

Gottlieb, Sherry. *Love Bite*. White Rock: Transylvania Press, 1994.

———. *Worse Than Death*. New York: Tor, 2000.

Goulart, Ron. *The Avengers #33: The Blood Countess* (as Kenneth Robeson). New York: Warner Books, 1975.

———. *Vampirella #1: Bloodstalk*. New York: Warner Books, 1975.

———. *Vampirella #2: On Alien Wings*. New York: Warner Books, 1975.

———. *Vampirella #3: Deadwalk*. New York: Warner Books, 1976.

———. *Vampirella #4, Blood Wedding*. New York: Warner Books, 1976.

———. *Vampirella #5: Deathgame*. New York: Warner Books, 1976.

———. *Vampirella #6: Snakegod*. New York: Warner Books, 1976.

———. *The Prisoner of Blackwood Castle*. New York: Avon, 1984.

———. "Glory." *The Magazine of Fantasy & Science Fiction*, December 1986.

———. *The Curse of the Obelisk*. New York: Avon, 1987.

Gouveia, Keith. *The Eternal Battle*. Bloomington, IN: 1st Books Library, 2002.

Grabowski, Geoffrey, and Jason Langlors. *Wolves of the Sea*. Clarkston, GA: White Wolf, 1999.

Graham, Heather. "The Vampire in His Closet." In *The Ultimate Dracula*. New York: Dell, 1991.

———. *Kiss of Darkness*. Toronto: Mira, 2006.

———. *Blood Red*. Toronto: Mira, 2007.

Graham, Jean. *Dark Angel*. Pentagram Publications, 1977.

———. *Dark Lord*. New York: Peacock, 1980.

Gralley, Jean. *Hogula: Dread Pig of the Night*. New York: Henry Holt, 1999 (juvenile).

Gramlich, Charles A. "Clowns in the Dark." *Prisoners of the Night 4*, 1990.

———. "Messiah." *Dead of Night 5*, April 1990.

———. "In Memory of the Sun." *The Vampire's Crypt 4*, Fall 1991.

———. "The Lady Wore Black." *Prisoners of the Night 6*, 1992.

Grant, Charles L. "The House of Evil." *The Magazine of Fantasy & Science Fiction*, December 1968.

———. *The Hour of the Oxrun Dead*. New York: Popular Library, 1977.

———. "Love Starved." *The Mystery of Fantasy & Science Fiction*, August 1979.

———. *The Nestling*. New York: Pocket Books, 1982.

———. *The Soft Whisper of the Dead*. West Kingston: Donald M. Grant Publisher, 1982.

———. "The Generation Waltz." *Fantasy Tales*, Winter 1984.

———. "Crystal." *The Magazine of Fantasy & Science Fiction*, December 1986.

———. *Doom City*. New York: Tor, 1988.

Grant, Chris Marie. *Night Rising: Vampire Babylon #1*. New York: Ace, 2007.

———. *Midnight Reign: Vampire Babylon #2*. New York: Ace, 2008.

———. *Break of Dawn: Vampire Babylon #3*. New York: Ace, 2008.

Grant, Cynthia. *Uncle Vampire*. New York: Atheneum Books, 1993 (juvenile).

Grant, Kenneth. *Gamaliel: The Diary of the Vampire and Dance, Doll, Dance*. London: Starfire, 2003.

Graverson, Pat. *Sweet Blood*. New York: Zebra, 1992.

————. *Precious Blood*. New York: Zebra, 1993.

**Graves, Warren.** *Mors Draculae*. Toronto: Playwright's Canada, 1979 (play).

**Gray, Claudia.** *Evernight*. New York: HarperTeen, 2008 (juvenile).

**Gray, Dulcie.** "The Fur Brooch." In *Pan Book of Horror Stories No. 7*. London: Pan, 1966.

**Gray, Nathalie.** *DamNATION*. Akron, OH: Ellora's Cave, 2007 (erotica).

**Green, Crystal.** *The Huntress*. Toronto: Silhouette Bombshell, 2005.

————. *The Ultimate Bite*, Toronto: Harlequin Blaze, 2007.

**Greenburg, Dan.** *Don't Count on Dracula (Zack Files #21)*. New York: Grosset & Dunlap, 2000 (juvenile).

————. *Secrets of Dripping Fang: The Vampire's Curse #3*. New York: Harcourt Children's Books, 2006 (juvenile).

**Greene, Vincent.** "One Man's Meat." In *1955 Anthology of Best Original Short-Shorts*. Ocean City, NJ: Oberfirst Publications, 1955.

**Greer, Morag.** "Under the Flagstone." In *Pan Book of Horror Stories No. 15*. London: Pan, 1974.

**Greifendorff, J. L.** *A Working Class Vampire Is Something to Be #1: Coming into Blood*. Booklocker.com, 2001.

**Gresham, Stephen.** *Bloodwings*. New York: Zebra, 1990.

————. *In the Blood*. New York: Pinnacle, 2001.

————. *The Fraternity*. New York: Pinnacle, 2004.

**Grey, John.** "Mix-Up." *Dead of Night 2*, July 1989.

————. "Three on Montague." *Prisoners of the Night 3*, 1989.

————. "From a Need to Linger." *Prisoners of the Night 4*, 1990.

————. "Another Small Town Night." *The Vampire's Crypt 3*, Spring 1991.

————. "Bat." *Book of Shadows 4*, 1992.

**Grey, Robert.** "Sing I Die." *Prisoners of the Night 5*, 1991.

**Griffin, Adele.** *Vampire Island*. New York: Putnam, 2007 (juvenile).

————. *The Knaveheart's Curse: Vampire Island #2*. New York: Putnam, 2008 (juvenile).

**Griffin, Lawrence R.** "The Girl in 218." *Macabre*, 1970.

**Griffith, Kathryn Meyer.** *Vampire Blood*. New York: Zebra, 1991.

————. *The Last Vampire*. New York: Zebra, 1992.

**Grimly, Gris, and Carolyn Crimi.** *Boris and Bella*. New York: Harcourt Children's Books, 2004 (juvenile).

**Grimson, Todd.** *Stainless*. New York: Harper Prism, 1996.

**Gruesome, Gertrude.** *Drak's Slumber Party: Monster Kids #1*. New York: Harper-Collins, 1995 (juvenile).

**Guest, Elizabeth.** *Night Life: Pharoahs Rising #1*. New York: Berkley Sensation, 2007.

————. *Night Hunger: Pharoahs Rising #2*. New York: Berkley Sensation, 2008.

**Guffey, Vincent.** "A Letter." *Miss Lucy Westenra Society of the Undead*, Spring 1992.

**Guillone, Sedonia.** *Darelle's Trinity*. Akron, OH: Ellora's Cave, 2007 (erotica).

————. "A Vampire for Christmas." In *The Bite Before Christmas*. Scottsdale, AZ: Loose Id, 2007.

**Gunn, Derek.** *Vampire Apocalypse: A World Torn Asunder*. Effort, PA: KHP Publisher, 2006.

**Gurnett, Dee L.** "The Unending Night." *World of Dark Shadows*, June 1977.

**Haddock, Nancy.** *La Vida Vampire: Oldest City Vampire*. New York: Berkley, 2008.

**Hadley, Patrick.** "Eating Medusa." In *Dark Tyrants*. Clarkston, GA: White Wolf, 1997.

# BIBLIOGRAPHY

Haeuser, Mark. *Hunters of the Shadows*. Crystal Dreams, 2002.

Hahn, Mary Downing. *Look for Me by Moonlight*. New York: HarperTeen, 1997 (juvenile).

Haines, Carolyn. "The Wish." In *Many Bloody Returns*. New York: Ace, 2007.

Haining, Peter. "The Beefstaking Room." In *The Vampire Hunter's Casebook*. New York: Barnes & Noble, 1996.

Haldeman, Joe. "Time Lapse." In *Blood Is Not Enough*. New York: William Morrow, 1989.

———. "Graves." *The Magazine of Fantasy & Science Fiction,* October/November 1992.

Haley, Wendy. *This Dark Paradise*. New York: Diamond Books, 1994.

———. *These Fallen Angels*. New York: Diamond Books, 1995.

Halidom, M. Y. *The Woman in Black*. London: Greening, 1906.

Hall, Angus. *Scars of Dracula*. New York: Beacon Books, 1971 (movie novelization).

Hall, Diane. "The Contributor." *Dead of Night 1,* Spring 1989.

Hall, Dorothy Dian. *Into the Light*. Bloomigton, IN: 1st Books Library, 2000.

Hall, Melissa Mia. "Rapture." In *Shadows 7*. New York: Doubleday, 1984.

Hallaway, Tate. *Tall, Dark and Dead: Garnet Legacy #1*. New York: Berkley, 2006.

———. *Dead Sexy: Garnet Legacy #2*. New York: Berkley, 2007.

———. "Fire and Ice and Linguini for Two." In *Many Bloody Returns*. New York: Ace, 2007.

———. *Romancing the Dead: Garnet Legacy #3*. New York: Berkley, 2008.

Hallowell, Madelyne. *Ancestral Blood*. Bloomington, IN: 1st Blood Library, 1999.

Hambly, Barbara. *Those Who Hunt by Night*. New York: Del Rey, 1988.

———. *Traveling with the Dead*. New York: Del Rey, 1995.

Hamilton, Edmond. "The Earth-Owners." *Weird Tales,* August 1931.

Hamilton, Laurell K. "Stealing Souls." In *Spells of Wonder*. New York: DAW, 1989.

———. *Pleasures: Anita Blake: Vampire Hunter #1*. New York: Ace, 1993.

———. *The Laughing Corpse: Anita Blake: Vampire Hunter #2*. New York: Ace, 1994.

———. *Circus of the Damned: Anita Blake: Vampire Hunter #3*. New York: Ace, 1995.

———. *The Lunatic Cafe: Anita Blake: Vampire Hunter #4*. New York: Ace, 1996.

———. *Bloody Bones: Anita Blake: Vampire Hunter #5*. New York: Ace, 1996.

———. *The Killing Dance: Anita Blake: Vampire Hunter #6*. New York: Ace, 1997.

———. *Burnt Offerings: Anita Blake: Vampire Hunter #7*. New York: Ace, 1998.

———. *Blue Moon: Anita Blake: Vampire Hunter #8*. New York: Ace, 1998.

———. *Obsidian Butterfly: Anita Blake: Vampire Hunter #9*. New York: Ace, 2000.

———. *Narcissus in Chains: Anita Blake: Vampire Hunter #10*. New York: Berkley, 2001.

———. *Cerulean Sins: Anita Blake: Vampire Hunter #11*. New York: Berkley, 2003.

———. "Blood Upon My Lips." In *Cravings*. New York: Jove, 2004.

———. "The Girl Who Was Infatuated with Death." In *Bite*. New York: Jove, 2004.

———. *Incubus Dreams: Anita Blake: Vampire Hunter #12*. New York: Berkley, 2004.

———. *Micah: Anita Blake: Vampire Hunter #13*. New York: Jove, 2006.

———. *Danse Macabre: Anita Blake: Vampire Hunter #14*. New York: Berkley, 2006.

———. *The Harlequin: Anita Blake: Vampire Hunter #15*. New York: Berkley, 2007.

———. *Blood Noir*. New York: Berkley, 2008.

Hammer, Charles D. "The Man Believed in Vampires." *Monster Parade,* 1958.

Hampton, A. J. *Bending to Break*. Cacoethes Publishing House, 2007 (erotica).

Hampton, L. F. *Winged Victory*. Hickory Corners, MI: ImaJinn Books, 2004.

Hand, Elizabeth. "Prince of Flowers." *Rod Serling's Twilight Zone Magazine,* February 1988.

**Harbaugh, Karen.** *The Vampire Viscount.* New York: Signet, 1995.

————. *Dark Enchantment.* New York: Dell, 2003.

————. *Night Fires.* New York: Bantam, 2003.

————. *The Vampire Viscount / The Devil's Bargain.* New York: Signet, 2004.

**Hare, Augustus.** "The Vampire of Croglin Grange." In *The Midnight People.* London: Leslie Frewin, 1968.

**Harper, Elaina.** *No Release: A Vampire's Tale.* Haverford, PA: Infinity, 2001.

**Harrell, Janice.** *Blood Lines: Vampire Twins #1.* New York: Harper, 1994 (juvenile).

————. *Blood Lust: Vampire Twins #2.* New York: Harper, 1994 (juvenile).

————. *Blood Choice: Vampire Twins #3.* New York: Harper, 1994 (juvenile).

————. *Blood Curse: Vampire's Love #1.* New York: Scholastic, 1995 (juvenile).

————. *Blood Reunion: Vampire Twins #4.* New York: Harper, 1995 (juvenile).

————. *Blood Spell: Vampire's Love #2.* New York: Scholastic, 1995 (juvenile).

**Harris, Charlaine.** *Dead until Dark.* New York: Ace, 2001.

————. *Living Dead in Dallas.* New York: Ace, 2002.

————. *Club Dead.* New York: Ace, 2003.

————. "Dancers in the Dark." In *Night's Edge.* Toronto: Harlequin, 2004.

————. *Dead to the World.* New York: Ace, 2004.

————. "Fairy Dust." In *Powers of Detection.* New York: Ace, 2004.

————. *Dead as a Doornail.* New York: Ace, 2005.

————. "One Word Answer." In *Bite.* New York: Jove, 2005.

————. *Definitely Dead.* New York: Ace, 2006.

————. "Tacky." In *My Big, Fat Supernatural Wedding.* New York: St. Martin's, 2006.

————. *All Together Dead.* New York: Ace, 2007.

————. "Dracula Night." In *Many Bloody Returns.* New York: Ace, 2007.

————. *From Dead to Worse.* New York: Ace, 2008.

**Harris, Jesse.** *The Power: The Vampire's Kiss.* New York: Borzoi Sprinters, 1993.

**Harris, Larry M.** "Mex." *Fantastic Universe,* January 1957.

**Harrison, Jane.** *Dark Dreams.* New York: Zebra, 1996.

**Harrison, Kim.** *Dead Witch Walking.* New York: HarperTorch, 2004.

————. *Every Which Way but Dead.* New York: HarperTorch, 2005.

————. *The Good, The Bad and the Undead.* New York: HarperTorch, 2005.

————. *A Fistfull of Charms.* New York: HarperTorch, 2006.

————. "Undead in the Garden of Good and Evil." In *Dates from Hell.* New York: Avon Books, 2006.

————. *For a Few Demons More.* New York: HarperCollins, 2007.

————. "Two Ghosts for Sister Rachel." In *Holidays Are Hell.* New York: Harper-Collins, 2007.

————. *The Outlaw Demon Wails.* New York: HarperCollins, 2008.

**Harrison, Michael.** "At the Heart of It." *The Magazine of Fantasy & Science Fiction,* June 1968.

**Hart, Crymsyn R.** *Immortal Desires.* Stardust, 2007.

**Hart, James S.** "The Traitor." *The Magazine of Fantasy & Science Fiction,* Fall 1950.

**Hart, Raven.** *Masquerade.* Awe-Struck Books, 2006.

————. *The Vampire's Seduction.* New York: Ballantine, 2006.

————. *The Vampire's Secret.* New York: Ballantine, 2007.

————. *The Vampire's Betrayal.* New York: Ballantine, 2008.

————. *The Vampire's Kiss.* New York: Ballantine, 2008.

**Hartman, Franz.** "An Authenticated Vampire Story." *The Occult Review,* September 1909.

Hartt, David. "Supression." *Night Mountains 6,* Winter 1991.

Hartwick, Sue-Anne. "No Choice at All." *Prisoners of the Night 1,* 1987.

———. "Curtain Call." *Prisoner of the Night 2,* 1988.

———. "Long in the Tooth." In *Dryad: The Vampire Stories.* Poway, CA: Mkashef Enterprises, 1991.

Harvey, Jayne. *Great Uncle Dracula.* New York: Random House, 1992 (juvenile).

———. *Great Uncle Dracula and the Dirty Rat.* New York: Random House, 1993 (juvenile).

Haskell, Owen. *If Books Could Kill.* Cranston, RI: Lazarus Press, 1995.

Hatchigan, Jessica. *Count Dracula, Me and Norma D.* New York: Avon Books, 1987 (juvenile).

Hauf, Michele. *Dark Rapture.* New York: Zebra, 1997.

———. *From the Dark: Bewitch the Dark #1.* Toronto: Silhouette Nocturne, 2006.

———. *Kiss Me Deadly: Bewitch the Dark #2.* Toronto: Silhouette Nocturne, 2007.

———. *Wicked Angels.* Surprise, AZ: Triskelion, 2007.

———. *His Forgotten Forever: Bewitch the Dark #3.* Toronto: Silhouette Nocturne, 2008.

———. *The Devil to Pay: Bewitch the Dark #4.* Toronto: Silhouette Nocturne, 2009.

Hautala, Rick. "The Source of the Nile." In *Masques IV.* Baltimore: Maclay and Associates, 1991.

Hautman, Pete. *Sweetblood.* New York: Simon & Schuster, 2003 (juvenile).

Haviland, Naima. *Bloodroom.* Catalyst Books, 2002.

Hawes, Neal. "The Staple." *Desert Sun,* Spring 1989.

———. ". . . And Now the News. . . ." *Encounters Magazine,* Winter 1990.

Hawke, Morgan. *House of Shadows Book 1: Enchantment in Crimson.* Garibaldi Highlands, BC, Canada: eXtasy Books, 2004 (erotica).

———. *Passion's Vintage—Tarot: The Star.* Garibaldi Highlands, BC, Canada: eXtasy Books, 2004 (erotica).

———. *Kiss of the Wolf.* New York: Aphrodisia, 2007 (erotica).

Hawke, Simon. *The Dracula Caper: Time Wars #8.* New York: Berkley Ace, 1988 (juvenile).

Hawkins, Kerri. *Blood Legacy: The Story of Ryan.* Image Comics/Top Cow, 2002.

———. *Blood Legacy: The House of Alexander.* Red Raptor Productions, 2005.

Hawthorn, Libby. *The Linski Kids and Dracula.* New York: Puffin, 1992 (juvenile).

Hawthorne, Julian. "Ken's Mystery." *Harper's New Monthly,* November 1883.

Hawthorne, Nathaniel. "Rappacini's Daughter." *United States Magazine and Democratic Review,* December 1844.

Hayden, Chris. *A Vampyre's Blues: The Passion of Varnado.* Hemet Mountain, CA: Door of Kush, 2004.

Hays, Clark. *Cowboy and the Vampire: A Very Unusual Romance.* St. Paul, MN: Llewellyn Publications, 1999.

Hazleton, Philip. "After Sunset." *Strange Tales,* November 1931.

Heald, Hazel (with H. P. Lovecraft). "The Horror in the Museum." *Weird Tales,* July 1933.

Hearn, Lafcadio. "The Story of Ming-Y." In *Some Chinese Ghosts.* Boston: Robert Brothers, 1887.

———. "The Story of Chūgorō." In *Kotto: Being Japanese Curios with Sundry Cobwebs.* New York: Macmillan, 1902.

Hecht, Jeff. "Aunt Horrible's Last Visit." In *Vampires: A Collection of Original Stories.* New York: HarperCollins, 1991.

Hecker, Howard. *Vampire Wasps.* Cheshire Press, 2000.

Heisey, Johann Wolfe. *Tepes*. Frederick, MD: PublishAmerica, 2006.

Helou, Brenda. "The Car." *Count Dracula Fan Club Newsletter*, 1979.

Hemp, Ray. "Voyage of Dracula." *Monster Sex Tales 1*, August/September 1972 (erotica).

Hendee, Barb. "Night and Day." *After Hours 5*, 1990.

———. *Blood Memories*. Flushing, NY: Vision Novels, 1999.

Hendee, Barb, and J. C. Hendee. *Dhampir*. New York: Roc, 2003.

———. *Thief of Lives*. New York: Roc, 2004.

———. *Sister of the Dead*. New York: Roc, 2005.

———. *Traitor to the Blood*. New York: Roc, 2006.

———. *Rebel Frey*. New York: Roc, 2007.

———. *Child of a Dead God*. New York: Roc, 2008.

Henderson, Alice. *Night Terrors (Buffy the Vampire Slayer)*. New York: Pocket Books, 2005.

Henderson, Christian L. "That Part Which Governs." *Vampire Junction 4*, 1992.

Henderson, Patty G. *Blood Scent*. Spanaway, WA: Justice House Publishing, 2001.

———. *So Dead My Love*. Lincoln, NE: iUniverse, 2001.

Henrick, Richard. *St. John the Pursuer, Book 1: Vampire in Moscow*. Lake Geneva, WI: TSR, 1988.

Henry, Philip. *Vampire Dawn*. Effort, PA: KHP Publisher, 2004.

Hensley, Joe L. "And Not Quite Human." *Beyond*, September 1951.

———. "Argent Blood." *The Magazine of Fantasy & Science Fiction*, August 1967.

Henson, Debra. *The Lives of the Vampires*. Frederick, MD: PublishAmerica, 2004.

Heron, E. and H. (Hesketh and Kate Prichard). "The Story of the Moor Road." *Pearson's Magazine*, March 1898.

———. "The Story of Baelbrow." *Pearson's Magazine*, April 1898.

———. "The Story of the Gray House." *Pearson's Magazine*, May 1898.

———. "The Story of the Yand Manor House." *Pearson's Magazine*, June 1898.

Heron-Allen, Edward. *The Princess Daphne*. London: H. J. Drane, 1888.

———. "Another Squaw?" In *Some Women at the University*. London: R. Stockwell, 1934.

———. "Zum Wildbad." In *Some Women at the University*. London: R. Stockwell, 1934.

Herter, Lori. *Obsession*. New York: Berkley, 1991.

———. *Confession*. New York: Berkley, 1992.

———. *Possession*. New York: Berkley, 1992.

———. *Eternity*. New York: Berkley, 1993.

Hetherington, Grant. *Evolution of the Vampire*. Philadelphia: Xlibris, 1998.

Hewitt, Douglas. "Niagra." *The Vampire's Crypt 4*, Fall 1991.

Heyse, Paul. *The Fair Abigail*. New York: Dodd, Mead, 1894.

Hichens, Robert. "How Love Came to Professor Guildea." In *Tongues of Conscience*. London: Methuen, 1900.

Higney, Gene Michael. "All the Hungry Guardians." *Dead of Night 6*, July 1990.

Hilburn, Lynda. *Diary of a Narcissistic Bloodsucker*. Wild Rose, 2006.

———. *The Vampire Shrink*. New York: Medallion, 2007.

Hiles, William J. "The Hangman's Beautiful Daughter." *Dead of Night 5*, April 1990.

———. "Crows in a Field of Dawn." *Dead of Night 6*, July 1990.

Hill, Donna. "The Touch." In *Dark Thirst*. New York: Simon & Schuster, 2006.

Hill, Joey W. *The Mark of the Vampire Queen*. New York: Berkley, 2008.

Hill, Kate. *Moonlust Privateer*. Akron, OH: Ellora's Cave, 2002 (erotica).

———. *Vampire Master: Blood and Soul #1*. Martinsburg, WV: Changeling, 2004 (erotica).

———. *Ancient Blood—Infernal*. Akron, OH: Ellora's Cave, 2005 (erotica).

———. *Unquenchable: Ancient Blood*. Akron OH: Ellora's Cave, 2007 (erotica).

Hill, Kate, and Claudia Rose. *Vampires at Heart*. Akron, OH: Ellora's Cave, 2003 (erotica).

Hill, Kate, and Sherri L. King. *Midnight Desires*. Akron, OH: Ellora's Cave, 2002 (erotica).

Hill, William. *Dawn of the Vampire*. New York: Pinnacle, 1991.

———. *Vampire's Kiss*. New York: Pinnacle, 1994.

———. *The Vampire Hunters*. Doctor's Inlet, FL: Otter Creek, 1998 (juvenile).

———. *The Stalked: The Vampire Hunters #2*. Doctor's Inlet, FL: Otter Creek, 2006 (juvenile).

Hillyer, James R. "Sleep Well, Teresa." *Weirdbook 5*, 1972.

Hinton, S. E. *Hawke's Harbor*. New York: Tor, 2004.

Hirsch, Janet. "The Seeking Thing." *Magazine of Horror*, February 1964.

H.M.P. *A Vampire of Souls*. Alexander Grant, 1904.

Hoch, Edward D. "Dracula 1944." In *The Ultimate Dracula*. New York: Dell, 1991.

Hochstein, Dale. "Metamorphosis." *The Vampire's Crypt 3*, Spring 1991.

———. "Don't Double Cross a Vampire." *Bloodreams 4*, April 1992.

Hocker, Karla. "A Lady of the Night." In *His Eternal Kiss*. New York: Kensington, 2002.

Hodge, Brian. "Dead Giveaway." In *Book of the Dead*. New York: Bantam, 1989.

———. "Midnight Sun." In *Under the Fang*. New York: Pocket Books, 1991.

———. "Like a Pilgrim to the Shrine." In *Dracula: Prince of Darkness*. New York: DAW, 1992.

———. "The Alchemy of the Throat." In *Love in Vein*. New York: HarperCollins, 1994 (erotica).

———. *Shrines and Desecrations*. Leesburg, VA: TAL Chapbook, 1994.

———. "The Last Testament." In *The Mammoth Book of Dracula*. London: Robinson, 1997.

Hodgman, Ann. *My Babysitter Is a Vampire*. New York: Aladdin, 1991 (juvenile).

———. *My Babysitter Has Fangs*. New York: Aladdin, 1992 (juvenile).

———. *My Babysitter Bites Again*. New York: Aladdin, 1993 (juvenile).

———. *My Babysitter Flies by Night*. New York: Aladdin, 1994 (juvenile).

———. *My Babysitter Goes Bats*. New York: Aladdin, 1994 (juvenile).

———. *My Babysitter Is a Movie Monster*. New York: Aladdin, 1995 (juvenile).

Hoffman, E. T. A. "Aurelia." *The Serapion Brethren*, 1820.

Hoffman, Karla. *Wicked Ways*. Toronto: Harlequin Temptation, 1996.

Hoffman, Mallory. *Touched by a Vampire*. Frederick, MD: PublishAmerica, 2005 (juvenile).

Hoffman, Mary. *Yelban: Dracula's Daughter*. Egmont Children's Books, 2002 (juvenile).

Hoffman, Nina Kiriki. "Waiting for the Hunger." In *Greystone Bay*. New York: Tor, 1985.

———. "Zombies for Jesus." In *Strained Relations*. Eugene: Hypatia, 1989.

Hoffman, Valerie. *The Rebellion: Vampire Royalty #1*. American Legacy Books, 2006.

———. *Resurrection: Vampire Royalty #2*. Lincoln, NE: iUniverse, 2007.

Hoffman, Wynette A. *Blood Is Thicker Than Water: The Reilly Vampire Chronicles*. Aurora, CO: Alien Perspectives, 2002.

**Hoh, Diana.** *The Vampire's Kiss (Nightmare Hall No. 22).* New York: Scholastic, 1995 (juvenile).

**Holder, Nancy.** "Blood Gothic." In *Shadows 8.* New York: Doubleday, 1985.

———. "Cafe Endless: Spring Rain." In *Love in Vein.* New York: HarperCollins, 1994 (erotica).

———. "Blood Freak." In *The Mammoth Book of Dracula.* London: Robinson, 1997.

———. *The Angel Chronicles: A Novelization (Angel).* Riverside, NJ: Simon Spotlight Entertainment, 1998.

———. *The Angel Chronicles Vol. 2 (Angel).* Riverside, NJ: Simon Spotlight Entertainment, 1999.

———. *The Angel Chronicles Vol. 3 (Angel).* Riverside, NJ: Simon Spotlight Entertainment, 1999.

———. "Absalom Rising." In *How I Survived My Summer Vacation (Buffy the Vampire Slayer).* New York: Pocket Books, 2000.

———. *The Evil That Men Do (Buffy the Vampire Slayer).* New York: Pocket Books, 2000.

———. *Not Forgotten (Angel).* New York: Pocket Books, 2000.

———. *The Book of Fours (Buffy the Vampire Slayer).* New York: Pocket Star, 2001.

———. "The Anchoress." In *The Longest Night Vol. 1 (Angel).* New York: Pocket Books, 2002.

———. "Have Gunn, Will Travel." In *The Longest Night Vol. 1 (Angel).* New York: Pocket Books, 2002.

———. *Blood and Fog (Buffy the Vampire Slayer).* New York: Simon Pulse, 2003.

———. *Heat (Buffy the Vampire Slayer/Angel).* Riverside, NJ: Simon Spotlight Entertainment, 2004.

———. *Daughter of the Flames.* Toronto: Silhouette Bombshell, 2005.

———. *Keep Me in Mind (Buffy the Vampire Slayer).* Riverside, NJ: Simon Spotlight Entertainment, 2005.

———. *Queen of the Slayers (Buffy the Vampire Slayer).* Riverside, NJ: Simon Spotlight Entertainment, 2005.

———. *Carnival of Souls (Buffy the Vampire Slayer).* Riverside, NJ: Simon Spotlight Entertainment, 2006.

———. *Daughter of the Blood.* Toronto: Silhouette Bombshell, 2006.

**Holder, Nancy, and Jeff Mariotte.** *Unseen Book 1, The Burning (Buffy the Vampire Slayer/Angel).* Riverside NJ: Simon Spotlight 2001.

———. *Unseen Book 2, Door to Alternity (Buffy the Vampire Slayer/Angel).* New York: Pocket Books, 2001.

———. *Unseen Book 3, Long Way Home (Buffy the Vampire Slayer/Angel).* New York: Pocket Books, 2001.

———. *Endangered Species (Angel).* New York: Pocket Star, 2003.

**Holdstock, Robert, and Garry Kilworth.** "The Ragthorn." In *A Whisper of Blood.* New York: William Morrow, 1991.

**Holland, Clive.** *An Egyptian Coquette.* C. Arthur Pearson, 1898.

**Holland, Tom.** *Lord of the Dead.* New York: Pocket Books, 1996.

———. *Deliver Us From Evil.* London: Little, Brown, 1997.

———. *Slave of My Thirst.* New York: Pocket Books, 1997.

**Holleyman, Sonia, and Hiawyn Oram.** *Mona the Vampire.* London: Orchard Books, 1991 (juvenile).

———. *Little Vampire's Diary.* London: Orchard Books, 1995 (juvenile).

———. *Mona the Vampire and the Hairy Hands.* London: Orchard Books, 1996 (juvenile).

————. *Mona the Vampire and the School Fete Skulduggery*. London: Orchard Books, 1996 (juvenile).

————. *Mona the Vampire and the Big Brown Bap Monster*. London: Orchard Books, 2001 (juvenile).

————. *Mona the Vampire and the Book of Slimy*. London: Orchard Books, 2001 (juvenile).

————. *Mona the Vampire and the Jackpot Disaster*. London: Orchard Books, 2001 (juvenile).

————. *Mona the Vampire and the Jurassic Parking Lot*. London: Orchard Books, 2001 (juvenile).

————. *Mona the Vampire and the Men in Dark Suits*. London: Orchard Books, 2001 (juvenile).

————. *Mona the Vampire and Miss Gotto's Haunted House*. London: Orchard Books, 2001 (juvenile).

————. *Mona the Vampire and the Tinned Poltergeist*. London: Orchard Books, 2001 (juvenile).

————. *Mona the Vampire and the Vampire Hunter*. London: Orchard Books, 2001 (juvenile).

————. *Mona the Vampire's Diary*. London: Orchard Books, 2001 (juvenile).

Holly, Emma. "Luisa's Desire." In *Fantasy*. New York: Jove, 2002.

————. *Catching Midnight*. New York: Jove, 2003.

————. *Hunting Midnight*. New York: Berkley, 2003.

————. "The Night Owl." In *Hot Blooded*. New York: Jove, 2004.

————. *Courting Midnight*. New York: Berkley, 2005.

Hood, Robin. "Shadows in October." *Prisoners of the Night 1*, 1987.

————. "Bloodfire." *Prisoners of the Night 2*, 1988.

Hooks, Wayne. "Servitude." *Space and Time*, January 1976.

Hopkins, Brian. *The Licking Valley Coon Hunters Club*. Alma, AR: Yard Dog, 2000.

Hopkins, Howard. *The Dark Riders*. Golden Perils, 2007.

Hopkins, Robert Thurston. "The Vampire of Woolpit Grange." In *The Girl with the Velvet Eyes*. Angold, 1924.

Hopkinson, Nalo. *Brown Girl in the Ring*. London: Get a Grip, 1998.

Horler, Sydney. "The Vampire." In *The Screaming Skull and Other Stories*. London: Hodder and Stoughton, 1930.

————. "The Believer: Ten Minutes of Horror." In *The Vampire*. London: Hutchinson, 1935.

————. "The Bloodsucker of Portland Place." In *The Vampire*. London: Hutchinson, 1935.

Howard, Richard. "Dies Irae." In *The Vampire's Bedside Companion*. London: Leslie Frewin, 1975.

Howard, Robert E. "The Moon of Skulls." *Weird Tales*, June/July 1930.

————. "The Hills of the Dead." *Weird Tales*, August 1930.

————. "The Horror from the Mound." *Weird Tales*, May 1932.

————. "Wings in the Night." *Weird Tales*, July 1932.

————. "The Garden of Fear." *Marvel Tales*, July/August 1934.

————. "Red Nails." *Weird Tales*, July–October 1936.

Howard, Robert E., and Lin Carter. "The Hand of Nergel." In *Conan*. New York: Ace, 1967.

Howard, Robert E., and L. Sprague De Camp. "The Road of the Eagles." In *Conan the Freebooter*. New York: Lancer, 1968.

**Howe, James.** *Bunnicula: A Rabbit-Tale of Mystery.* New York: Atheneum, 1979 (juvenile).

————. *Howliday Inn.* New York: Atheneum, 1982 (juvenile).

————. *The Celery Stalks at Midnight.* New York: Atheneum, 1983 (juvenile).

————. *Nighty-Nightmare.* New York: Atheneum, 1987 (juvenile).

————. *The Fright Before Christmas.* New York: William Morrow, 1988 (juvenile).

————. *Scared Silly.* New York: William Morrow, 1989 (juvenile).

————. *Hot Fudge.* New York: William Morrow, 1990 (juvenile).

————. *Creepy-Crawly Birthday.* New York: William Morrow, 1991 (juvenile).

————. *Return to Howliday Inn.* New York: Atheneum, 1992 (juvenile).

————. *Bunnicula Escapes.* Fairfield, NJ: Tupelo Books, 1994 (juvenile, pop-up book).

————. *Bunnicula Strikes Again!* New York: Atheneum, 1999 (juvenile).

————. *Bud Barkin, Private Eye: Tales from the House of Bunnicula.* New York: Atheneum, 2003 (juvenile).

————. *Howie Monroe and the Doghouse of Doom: Tales from the House of Bunnicula.* New York: Atheneum, 2003 (juvenile).

————. *Invasion of the Mind Swappers from Asteroid 6!: Tales from the House of Bunnicula.* New York: Atheneum, 2003 (juvenile).

————. *It Came from Beneath the Bed!: Tales from the House of Bunnicula.* New York: Atheneum, 2003 (juvenile).

————. *Screaming Mummies of the Pharoah's Tomb: Tales from the House of Bunnicula.* New York: Atheneum, 2003 (juvenile).

————. *Odorous Adventures of Stinky Dog: Tales from the House of Bunnicula.* New York: Atheneum, 2004 (juvenile).

————. *Bunnicula Meets Edgar Allan Crow.* New York: Atheneum, 2006 (juvenile).

**Howell, Hannah.** "The Yearning." In *His Immortal Embrace.* New York: Kensington, 2003.

————. "Kiss of the Vampire." In *Highland Vampire.* New York: Brava, 2005.

**Howell, Hannah, and Lynsay Sands.** *Highland Thirst.* New York: Kensington, 2007.

**Hubbard, Susan.** *The Society of "S."* New York: Simon & Schuster, 2007.

————. *The Year of Disappearances.* New York: Simon & Schuster, 2008.

**Huff, Tanya.** *Blood Price.* New York: DAW, 1991.

————. *Blood Trail.* New York: DAW, 1992.

————. *Blood Lines.* New York: DAW, 1993.

————. *Blood Pact.* New York: DAW, 1993.

————. "This Town Ain't Big Enough." In *Vampire Detectives.* New York: DAW, 1995.

————. *Blood Debt.* New York: DAW, 1997.

————. "Someone to Share the Night." In *Single White Vampire Seeks Same.* New York: DAW, 2001.

————. "To Each His Own Kind." In *Dracula in London.* New York: Ace, 2001.

————. "The Vengeful Spirit of Lake Nepeakea." In *The Mammoth Book of Vampire Stories by Women.* New York: Carroll and Graf, 2001.

————. *Smoke and Shadows.* New York: DAW, 2004.

————. *Smoke and Mirrors.* New York: DAW, 2005.

————. *Blood Bank.* New York: DAW, 2006.

————. *Smoke and Ashes.* New York: DAW, 2006.

————. "Blood Wrapped." In *Many Bloody Returns.* New York: Ace, 2007.

**Huffman, Marlys.** "All in Evil Time." *Night Mountains 6,* Winter 1991.

————. "A Change of Diet." *The Vampire's Crypt 5,* Spring 1992.

Hughes, A. L. "Of a Time." *Prisoners of the Night 1*, 1987.

Hughes, Charlotte. "Too Many Husbands." In *Moonlight, Madness and Magic*. Fanfare, 1993.

Hughes, Naomi, and Sonia Hughes. "The Language of the Hot Plates." *Prisoners of the Night 3*, 1989.

———. "Life Support." *Prisoners of the Night 4*, 1990.

———. "Wooden Eyes." *Prisoners of the Night 4*, 1990.

Hughes, Ted. *Ffangs the Vampire Bat and the Kiss of Truth*. London: Faber & Faber, 1986 (juvenile).

Hughes, William. *Lust for a Vampire*. London: Sphere, 1971.

Hull, Helen R. "Clay-Shuttered Doors: A Story." *Harper's Monthly Magazine*, May 1926.

Hume, Fergus. *A Creature of the Night*. R. E. King, 1891.

Humphries, Dwight E. "A Letter to Renee." *Prisoners of the Night 2*, 1988.

Hunt, Lee. *The Vampire of New York*. New York: Signet, 2008.

Hunt, Violet. "The Story of a Ghost." *Chapman's Magazine*, December 1895.

Hunter, C. L. *Internal Anomaly*. Morrisville, NC: Lulu.com, 2007.

Huntington, Kate. "The Awakening." In *His Immortal Embrace*. New York: Kensington, 2003.

Hurley, Mike. "Vameleon." *SPWAO Showcase 6*, 1987.

Hurn, Mlyn. *Blood Dreams*. Akron, OH: Ellora's Cave, 2004 (erotica).

———. *Hunter's Legacy: Blood Dreams 2*. Akron, OH: Ellora's Cave, 2004 (erotica).

———. *Endless Night: Blood Dreams 3*. Akron, OH: Ellora's Cave, 2005 (erotica).

Hurwood, Bernhardt J. *By Blood Alone*. New York: Charter Books, 1979.

Hussey, Leigh Ann. "Blood Libel." In *Vampires: A Collection of Original Stories*. New York: HarperCollins, 1991.

Huston, Charlie. *Already Dead*. New York: Del Rey, 2005.

———. *No Dominion*. New York: Del Rey, 2006.

———. *Half the Blood of Brooklyn*. New York: Del Rey, 2007.

Hutson, Shaun. *Erebus*. UK: Star, 1984.

———. *Renegades*. London: Macdonald, 1990.

Hyder, Alan. *Vampires Overhead*. London: Philip Allan, 1935.

Hyttinen, Roger. *A Clash of Fangs*. Lincoln, NE: Writer's Club Press, 2001.

Ideus, Roberta. *Unholy Penance*. Frederick, MD: PublishAmerica, 2007.

Ingraham, Prentiss. *The Ocean Vampire or The Heiress of Castle Curse*. New York: Beadle and Adams, 1882.

Inman, Arthur Crew. *Of Castle Terror*. Boston: B. J. Brimmer, 1923 (play).

Ireland, Kenneth. "The Empty Tomb." In *The Werewolf Mask*. London: Hodder and Stoughton, 1983.

Ironside, Virginia. *Vampire Master at Burlap Hall*. London: Walker Books, 1997 (juvenile).

Irving, Washington. "The Adventure of the German Student." In *Tales of a Traveller*. Philadelphia: H. C. Carey and I. Lea, 1824.

Irwin, Sarita. *To Love a Vampire*. London: Carousel, 1982.

Isilwath, T. *Blood Origins*. Lincoln, NE: Writer's Showcase Press, 2000.

Ivanhoe, Mark. *Virgintooth*. San Francisco, CA: III, 1991.

Ivy, Alexandra. *When Darkness Comes: Guardians of Eternity*. New York: Zebra, 2007.

Jablonski, Carla. *Van Helsing: The Junior Novel*. New York: Harper Festival, 2004 (juvenile).

———. *Thicker Than Water*. New York: Penguin, 2007 (juvenile).

Jac, Cherlyn. *Night's Immortal Kiss.* New York: Zebra, 1994.
———. *Night's Immortal Touch.* New York: Zebra, 1995.
Jackson, Lynn. *Logan: The Birth of a Vampire.* Lincoln, NE: iUniverse, 2006.
Jackson, Melanie. *Divine Madness.* New York: Love Spell, 2006.
Jackson, Monica. "The Ultimate Diet." In *Dark Thirst.* New York: Simon & Schuster, 2006.
———. "Vamped." In *Creepin'.* Kimani, 2007.
Jackson, Myla. "Out of the Shadows." In *Alluring Tales: Awaken the Fantasy.* New York: Avon Red, 2007 (erotica).
Jacob, Charlee. "The Ophelias." *Prisoners of the Night 6,* 1992.
———. *The Indigo People: A Vampire Collection.* Wilder Publications, 2007.
Jacob, Laine. *Irma: Memoirs of a Vampire Gone Dry.* Stillwater: River's Bend, 2004.
Jacobi, Carl. "Revelations in Black." *Weird Tales,* April 1933.
Jacobs, David. *The Devil's Night: The New Adventures of Dracula, Frankenstein & The Universal Monsters.* New York: Berkley Boulevard Books, 2001.
Jacobs, Harvey. "L'Chaim!." In *Blood Is Not Enough.* New York: William Morrow, 1989.
James, Dean. *Posted to Death: Simon Kirby-Jones #1.* New York: Kensington, 2002.
———. *Faked to Death: Simon Kirby-Jones #2.* New York: Kensington, 2003.
———. *Decorated to Death: Simon Kirby-Jones #3.* New York: Kensington, 2004.
———. *Baked to Death: Simon Kirby-Jones #4.* New York: Kensington, 2005.
James, Henry. "De Grey: A Romance." *Atlantic Monthly,* 1868.
———. "Longstaff's Marriage." *Scribner's Monthly,* August 1878.
———. "Maud-Evelyn." *Atlantic Monthly,* April 1890.
James, J. W. *Sorrow: A Vampire's Tale.* Morrisville, NC: Lulu.com, 2005.
James, M. R. "Count Magnus." In *Ghost Stories of an Antiquary.* London: Edward Arnold, 1904.
———. "An Episode of Cathedral History." *Cambridge Review,* June 10, 1914.
———. "Wailing Wall." *Stanford Dingley: The Mill House,* 1928.
James, Patrick. *Vampire Stripper.* Bangor, ME: Booklocker.com, 2002.
James, Philip. "Carillon of Skulls." *Unknown,* February 1941.
James, Robert. *Blood Mist.* New York: Leisure Books, 1987.
Jarrell, Patty. "Toshu." *Loyalists of the Vampire Realm Newsletter,* Summer 1991.
Jasper, Liz. *Underdead.* Akron, OH: Cerridwen, 2007.
Jean, Lorraine A. "Nightlover's Tour of London." *Prisoners of the Night 6,* 1992.
Jefferson, Jemiah. *Voice of the Blood.* New York: Leisure Books, 2001.
———. *Wounds.* New York: Dorchester, 2002.
———. *Fiend.* New York: Dorchester, 2005.
———. *A Drop of Scarlet.* New York: Dorchester, 2007.
Jeffries, J. M. *Blood Lust.* Genesis Books, 2005.
———. *Blood Seduction.* Genesis Books, 2007.
———. *Vegas Strikes Back.* Genesis Books, 2007.
Jennings, Gary. "Let Us Prey." *The Magazine of Fantasy & Science Fiction,* June 1978.
Jennings, Jan. *Vampyr.* New York: Pinnacle, 1981.
Jensen, Ruby Jean. *Vampire Child.* New York: Zebra, 1990.
Jenson, Jeya. *Flesh and the Devil.* Garibaldi Highlands, BC, Canada: eXtasy Books, 2003 (erotica).
———. *Before the Night Falls.* Garibaldi Highlands, BC, Canada: eXtasy Books, 2003 (erotica).

Jeter, K. W. "The First Time." In *Alien Sex*. New York: Dutton, 1990 (erotica).

———. "True Love." In *A Whisper of Blood*. New York: William Morrow, 1991.

Jewel, Carolyn. *A Darker Crimson*. New York: Love Spell, 2005.

Jewell, Elizabeth. *Dark Callings: Bloodlines*. Martinsburg, WV: Changeling, 2004.

Jimerson, Royal W. "Medusa." *Weird Tales*, April 1928.

John, Anthony. *The Predator*. New York: Ballantine, 1983.

John, Laurie. *Kiss of the Vampire: Sweet Valley University Thriller #3*. New York: Bantam, 1996 (juvenile).

Johnson, Bill. "Business as Usual." *The Magazine of Fantasy & Science Fiction*, September 1986.

———. "Vote Early, Vote Often." *The Magazine of Fantasy & Science Fiction*, September 1990.

Johnson, Caroline. "Vampires and Lovers." In *Legends in Blood*. West Hollywood, CA: Fantaseas, 1991.

Johnson, Ken. *Hounds of Dracula*. New York: Signet, 1977.

Johnson, Kij. "Ferata." In *Embracing the Dark*. Boston: Alyson, 1991.

Johnson, Robert Barbour. "The Silver Coffin." *Weird Tales*, January 1939.

Johnson, V. M. *Dhampir: Child of Blood*. Mystic Rose Books, 1996.

Johnston, David A. "Mr. Alucard." In *Over the Edge*. Sauk City, WI: Arkham House, 1964.

Johnstone, William W. *The Devil's Kiss*. New York: Zebra, 1980.

———. *Wolfsbane*. New York: Zebra, 1982.

———. *The Devil's Heart*. New York: Zebra, 1983.

———. *The Nursery*. New York: Zebra, 1983.

———. *The Devil's Touch*. New York: Zebra, 1984.

———. *The Devil's Cat*. New York: Zebra, 1987.

———. *Bats*. New York: Zebra, 1993.

Jolly, Stratford D. *The Soul of the Moor*. London: William Rider & Son, 1911.

Jones, A. Leigh. *Forever Crossed*. Hickory Corners, MI: ImaJinn Books, 2004.

Jones, E. Carter. *Absence of Faith: A Vampire's Lesson in Betrayal*. Lincoln, NE: iUniverse, 2000.

Jones, Gwyneth. "A North Light." In *The Mammoth Book of Vampire Stories by Women*. New York: Carroll & Graf, 2001.

Jones, Matt R. *Hollywood Vampires: Unholy War*. Bloomington, IN: AuthorHouse, 2001.

———. *Hollywood Vampires: Sex, Blood & Rock 'n Roll*. Bloomington, IN: AuthorHouse, 2004.

Jones, Neil R. "Vampire of the Void." *Planet Stories*, Fall 1942.

Jones, Prof. P. *The Pobratim: A Slav Novel*. London: H. S. Nicols, 1895.

Jorgensen, H. F. *The Hall of the Vampires*. Lincoln, NE: Writer's Club, 2002 (juvenile).

Judd, A. M. *The White Vampire*. London: John Long, 1914.

Juers, Stephen L. *Eternally Yours*. Bloomington, IN: AuthorHouse, 2005.

Jungman, Ann. *Vlad the Drac*. London: Grenada, 1982 (juvenile).

———. *Vlad the Drac Returns*. London: Dragon, 1984 (juvenile).

———. *Vlad the Drac: Superstar*. London: Dragon, 1986 (juvenile).

———. *Vlad the Drac Vampire*. London: Young Lions, 1988 (juvenile).

———. *Count Dracula and the Ghost*. London: Collins Educational, 1989 (juvenile).

———. *Count Dracula and the Monster*. London: Collins Educational, 1989 (juvenile).

———. *Count Dracula and the Victim*. London: Collins Educational, 1989 (juvenile).

————. *Count Dracula Meets His Match*. London: Collins Educational, 1989 (juvenile).

————. *Dracula Play*. London: Collins Educational, 1989 (juvenile).

————. *Vlad the Drac Down Under*. London: Young Lions, 1989 (juvenile).

————. *Count Dracula and the Vampire*. London: Collins Educational, 1995 (juvenile).

————. *Count Dracula and the Wedding*. London: Collins Educational, 1995 (juvenile).

————. *Count Dracula and the Witch*. London: Collins Educational, 1995 (juvenile).

————. *Count Dracula Gets a Shock*. London: Collins Educational, 1995 (juvenile).

————. *Vlad the Drac Goes Traveling*. London: Collins Educational, 1996 (juvenile).

————. *Dracula Is Backula*. London: Anderson, 1999 (juvenile).

Kadushin, Rachel. "Moonshine." *Good Guys Wear Fangs 1*, May 1992.

Kagan, Susan R. "Once Upon a Time. . . ." *Children of the Night Coven Journal 4*, 1990.

Kahn, James. *World Enough and Time*. New York: Del Rey, 1980.

————. *Time's Dark Laughter*. New York: Del Rey, 1982.

————. *Timefall*. New York: St. Martin's, 1987.

Kaip, Jason. "The Day After." *Loyalists of the Vampire Realm Newsletter*, Summer 1991.

Kalis, Myranda. *Dark Ages: Brujah*. Clarkston, GA: White Wolf, 2003.

Kalogridis, Jeanne. *Covenant with the Vampire: The Diaries of the Family Dracul #1*. New York: Delacorte, 1994.

————. *Children of the Vampire: The Diaries of the Family Dracul #2*. New York: Delacorte, 1995.

————. *Lord of the Vampires: The Diaries of the Family Dracul #3*. New York: Delacorte, 1996.

Kaminsky, Stuart M. *Never Cross a Vampire*. New York: St. Martin's, 1980.

Kanemann, Sol. "I'll Conserve You." *Moonbroth 8*, 1973.

Kaplan, S. *Vampires Are*. Palm Springs, CA: ETC Productions, 1984.

Kapralov, Yuri. *Castle Dubrava*. New York: E. P. Dutton, 1982.

Karpova, Daria. *Loose Diamonds*. Scottsdale, AZ: Loose Id, 2004.

Karr, Phyllis Ann. "A Cold Stake." In *Vampires: A Collection of Original Stories*. New York: HarperCollins, 1991.

Kast, P. *The Vampires of Alfama*. London: W. H. Allen, 1976.

Katt, Katharina. *A Female Vampire*. Markham, ON, Canada: Double Dragon, 2002.

Katz, Judith. "Anita, Polish Vampire, Holds Forth at the Jewish Cafe of the Dead." In *Night Bites: Vampire Stories by Women*. Seattle, WA: Seal, 1996.

Kaye, Erika. "Love Sucks." In *Vamprotica 2005*. Chippewa, 2005 (erotica).

Kaye, Marvin. *The Incredible Umbrella*. New York: Doubleday, 1979.

Kearney, Maxwell. *Dracula Sucks*. New York: Zebra, 1981.

Keats, John. "La Belle Dame sans Merci." *The Indicator*, May 1820 (poem).

Keeper, Laurie. "Black Dawn." *Good Guys Wear Fangs 1*, May 1992.

Kei, Atira. "Bloodbond." In *Dyad: The Vampire Stories*. Poway, CA: Mkashef Enterprises, 1991.

Keller, David H. "The Damsel and Her Cat." *Weird Tales*, April 1929.

————. "The Ivy War." *Amazing Science Fiction Stories*, May 1930.

————. "The Moon Artist." *Stirring Science Fiction Stories*, June 1941.

————. "Heredity." In *Life Everlasting and Other Tales of Science, Fantasy and Horror*. Newark, NJ: Avalon, 1947.

Kelley, Thomas P. "A Million Years in the Future." *Weird Tales*, January-July 1940.

Kells, Sabine. *A Deeper Hunger*. New York: Leisure Books, 1994.

Kelly, Ronald. "The Cistern." *Cemetery Dance 2*, 1990.

———. "Blood Suede Shoes." In *Shock Rock*. New York: Pocket Books, 1992.

———. *Blood Kin*. New York: Zebra, 1996.

Kelly, Sahara. "Beating Level Nine." In *Lasy Jaided's Virile Vampires*. Akron, OH: Ellora's Cave, 2004 (erotica).

———. *Sucks to Be You*. Martinsburg, WV: Changeling, 2004 (erotica).

Kelly, Tim. *The Dracula Kidds: The House on Blood Pudding Lane*. Schulenburg, TX: I. E. Clark, 1986.

Kelner, Toni L. P. "How Stella Got Her Grave Back." In *Many Bloody Returns*. New York: Ace, 2007.

Kemp, Obadiah. "Fangs of the Fiend for the Girl Who Died Twice." *Adventures in Horror*, August 1971.

Kemp-Jones, Diana. "Eyes Like Limpid Pools." *Dead of Night 6*, July 1990.

Kemske, Floyd. *Human Resources*. North Haven, CT: Catbird Press, 1995.

Kenner, Julie. *Good Ghouls Do*. New York: Berkley, 2007 (juvenile).

Kenson, Steve. *Thousand Whispers*. Clarkston, GA: White Wolf, 2001.

Kenyon, Sherrilyn. "Dragonswan." In *Tapestry*. New York: Jove, 2002.

———. *Fantasy Lover: Dark Hunter #1*. New York: St. Martin's, 2002.

———. *Night Pleasures: Dark Hunter #2*. New York: St. Martin's, 2002.

———. *Night Embrace: Dark Hunter #3*. New York: St. Martin's, 2003.

———. *Dance with the Devil: Dark Hunter #4*. New York: St. Martin's, 2003.

———. "A Dark-Hunter Christmas." In *Dance with the Devil*. New York: St. Martin's, 2003.

———. "Phantom Lover." In *Midnight Pleasures*. New York: St. Martin's, 2003.

———. *Kiss of the Night: Dark Hunter #5*. New York: St. Martin's, 2004.

———. *Night Play: Dark Hunter #6*. New York: St. Martin's, 2004.

———. "Winter Born." In *Stroke of Midnight*. New York: St. Martin's, 2004.

———. "The Beginning." In *Sins of the Night*. New York: St. Martin's, 2005.

———. "Second Chances." An Exclusive Dark-Hunter Collectible Booklet. New York: St. Martin's, 2005 (free giveaway).

———. *Seize the Night: Dark Hunter #7*. New York: St. Martin's, 2005.

———. *Sins of the Night: Dark Hunter #8*. New York: St. Martin's, 2005.

———. *Unleash the Night: Dark Hunter #9*. New York: St. Martin's, 2005.

———. *Dark Side of the Moon: Dark Hunter #10*. New York: St. Martin's, 2006.

———. "A Hard Day's Night-Searcher." In *My Big Fat Supernatural Wedding*. New York: St. Martin's Griffin, 2006.

———. "Until Death We Do Part." In *Love at First Bite*. New York: St. Martin's, 2006.

———. *Devil May Cry: Dark Hunter #11*. New York: St. Martin's, 2007.

———. *The Dream-Hunter*. New York: St. Martin's, 2007.

———. *Upon the Midnight Clear*. New York: St. Martin's, 2007.

———. *Acheron: Dark Hunter #12*. New York: St. Martin's, 2008.

———. *Dream Chaser*. New York: St. Martin's, 2008.

Kersten, Shayla. *The Cost of Eternity*. Akron, OH: Ellora's Cave, 2008 (erotica).

Kerwath, Pauline. "Hard Drive." *Dead of Night 5*, April 1990.

———. "Preservation of a Species." *Prisoners of the Night 5*, 1991.

Ketchum, Jack. *She Wakes*. New York: Berkley, 1989.

Kewitz, Mary Deball. *Little Vampire and the Midnight Bear*. New York: Dial Books, 1995 (juvenile).

Key, Samuel M. *Angels of Darkness*. New York: Jove, 1990.

Key, Uel. "The Broken Fang." In *The Broken Fang and Other Experiences of a Specialist in Spooks*. London: Hodder and Stoughton, 1920.

Kidd, A. F. "The Bellfounder's Wife." In *In and Out of the Belfry*. Self-published, 1987.

Kiernan, Caitlan R. "So Runs the World Away." In *The Mammoth Book of Vampire Stories by Women*. New York: Carroll & Graf, 2001.

———. *The Five of Cups*. Burton, MI: Subterranean, 2003.

Kikuchi, Hideyuki. *Raiser of Gales D*. Milwaukie, OR: DH, 2005.

———. *Vampire Hunter D*. Milwaukie, OR: DH, 2005.

———. *D- Demon Deathchase*. Milwaukie, OR: DH, 2006.

———. *D- Pilgrimage of the Sacred and the Profane*. Milwaukie, OR: DH, 2006.

———. *D- Tale of the Dead Town*. Milwaukie, OR: DH, 2006.

———. *The Stuff of Dreams D*. Milwaukie, OR: DH, 2006.

———. *Mysterious Journey to the North Sea Part One*. Milwaukie, OR: DH, 2007.

———. *Mysterious Journey to the North Sea Part Two*. Milwaukie, OR: DH, 2007.

———. *Rose Princess*. Milwaukie, OR: DH, 2007.

———. *Dark Nocturne*. Milwaukie, OR: DH, 2008.

Killough, Lee. *Blood Hunt*. New York: Tor, 1987.

———. *Bloodlinks*. New York: Tor, 1988.

———. *BloodWalk*. Decatur, GA: Meisha Merlin, 1997.

———. *Blood Games*. Decatur, GA: Meisha Merlin, 2001.

Kilpatrick, Nancy. "Dark Seduction." *Prisoners of the Night 2*, 1988.

———. "Root Cellar." *The Vampire's Crypt 4*, Fall 1991.

———. "Farm Wife." *The Vampire's Crypt 5*, Spring 1992.

———. "Vampire Lovers." *The Vampire's Crypt 6*, Fall 1992.

———. *Near Death*. New York: Pocket Books, 1994.

———. *Sex and the Single Vampire*. Leesburg, VA: TAL Chapbook, 1994.

———. *As One Dead: Vampire: The Masquerade*. Clarkston, GA: White Wolf, 1995.

———. *Child of the Night*. London: Raven, 1996.

———. *Endorphins*. Norfolk, VA: Macabre, 1997.

———. "Teaserama." In *The Mammoth Book of Dracula*. London: Robinson, 1997.

———. *Dracul: An Eternal Love Story*. San Diego, CA: Lucard, 1998.

———. *Reborn*. Nottingham, UK: Pumpkin Books, 1998.

———. "Berserker." In *Dracula in London*. New York: Ace, 2001.

———. *Blood Lover: The Power of the Blood*. Baskerville, 2001.

———. "La Diente." In *The Mammoth Book of Vampire Stories by Women*. New York: Carroll & Graf, 2001.

Kilpatrick, Nancy, as Amarantha Knight. *The Darker Passions: Dracula*. New York: Masquerade, 1993.

———. *The Darker Passions: Carmilla*. New York: Masquerade, 1998.

Kilworth, Garry. "Dogfaerie." In *Hidden Turnings*. Modern Children's Books, 1989.

———. "The Silver Collar." In *Blood Is Not Enough*. New York: William Morrow, 1989.

Kimberly, Gail. *Dracula Began*. New York: Pyramid Books, 1976.

Kimbriel, Katharine Eliska. "Triad." *The Magazine of Fantasy & Science Fiction*, August 1991.

King, Kenneth. "The Marndyke Evil." *The Vampire Journal 4*, 1988.

———. "They Must Feed." *The Velvet Vampyre (Journal of the Campire Society, Surrey, England) 8*, Winter 1989.

King, Samara. *Flirting with Danger*. Scottsdale, AZ: Loose Id, 2007.

King, Sherri L. "Icarus." In *Fever: Hot Dreams*. Akron, OH: Ellora's Cave, 2007 (erotica).

King, Stephen. *Salem's Lot*. Garden City: Doubleday, 1975.

———. "One for the Road." *Maine Magazine*, March/April 1977.

———. "Jerusalem's Lot." In *Night Shift*. New York: Doubleday, 1978.

———. "The Oracle and the Mountains." *The Magazine of Fantasy & Science Fiction*, February 1981.

———. "Popsy." In *Masques II*. Baltimore: Maclay and Associates, 1987.

———. "The Night Flier." In *Prime Evil*. New American Library, 1988.

———. "The Library Policeman." In *Four Past Midnight*. New York: Viking, 1990.

———. "You Know They Got a Hell of a Band." In *Shock Rock*. New York: Pocket Books, 1992.

King, T. Stanleyan. *Vampire City*. London: Mellifont, 1935.

King, Valerie. "Vampire Rogue." In *Bewitched by Love*. New York: Zebra, 1996.

King, William. *Vampire Slayer*. New York: Pocket Books, 2001.

Kingston, W. H. "The Vampire; or, Pedro Pacheco and the Bruxa." In *Tales for All Ages*. London: Bickers & Bush, 1863.

Kinkopf, Vlad. "Nellie's Grave." In *Voices from the Vaults*. Toronto: Key Porter, 1987.

Kiraly, Marie. *Mina: The Dracula Story Continues*. New York: Berkley, 1994.

Kirk, Damion. *Reflections of a Vampire*. Superior, CO: RahuBooks, 2002.

Kisner, James Martin. "Migration." *Dead of Night 4*, January 1990.

———. "The God-Less Men." In *Vampire Detectives*. New York: DAW, 1995.

Klause, Annette Curtis. *The Silver Kiss*. New York: Delacorte, 1990 (juvenile).

———. "Summer of Love." In *The Color of Absense*. Pulse, 2003 (juvenile).

Klein, Rachel. *The Moth Diaries*. Washington, D.C.: Counterpoint, 2002.

Klein, Victor C. *Soul Shadows*. Metairie, LA: Lycanthrope, 1996.

Kline, Otis Adelbert, and Frank Belknap Long. "Lord of the Lamia." *Weird Tales*, March–May 1935.

———. "Return of the Undead." *Weird Tales*, July 1943.

Knight, Angela. "Blood & Kisses." In *Secrets Vol. 3*. Seminole, FL: Red Sage, 1997.

———. "A Candidate for a Kiss." In *Secrets Vol. 6*. Seminole, FL: Red Sage, 1999.

———. "Kissing the Hunter." In *Secrets Vol. 8*. Seminole, FL: Red Sage, 2002.

———. *The Forever Kiss*. Seminole, FL: Red Sage, 2004.

———. "Galahad." In *Bite*. New York: Jove, 2004.

———. *Master of the Night*. New York: Berkley, 2004.

———. "Seduction's Gift." In *Hot Blooded*. New York: Berkley, 2004.

———. *Master of the Moon*. New York: Berkley, 2005.

———. *Master of Swords*. New York: Berkley, 2006.

Knight, Damon. "Eripmav." *The Magazine of Fantasy & Science Fiction*, June 1958.

Knight, E. E. *Way of the Wolf*. New York: Roc, 2003.

———. *Choice of the Cat*. New York: Roc, 2004.

———. *Tale of the Thunderbolt*. New York: Roc, 2005.

———. *Valentine's Rising*. New York: Roc, 2005.

———. *Valentine's Exile*. New York: Roc, 2006.

———. *Valentine's Resolve*. New York: Roc, 2007.

———. *Fall with Honor*. New York: Roc, 2008.

Knight, Mallory T. *Dracutwig*. New York: Award Books, 1969.

Knight, Tracy A. "Blessed by His Dying Tongue." In *Celebrity Vampires*. New York: DAW, 1995.

Knights, Katriena. *Vampire Apocalypse Book 1: Revelations*. Hickory Corners, MI: ImaJinn Books, 2002.

———. *Vampire Apocalypse Book 2: Apotheosis*. Hickory Corners, MI: ImaJinn Books, 2003.

Knox, Elizabeth. *Daylight*. New York: Ballantine, 2003.

Knox, John H. "Men without Blood." *Horror Stories,* January 1935.

Knudsen, Michelle. *The Case of Vampire Vivian*. New York: Kane, 2003 (juvenile).

Koehler, Karen. "Immortal." In *Slayer: Black Miracles*. Effort, PA: KHP, 2002.

———. *Slayer: Stigmata*. Effort, PA: Black Death Books, 2002.

———. "The Sign of the Six." In *The Blackburn & Scarletti Mysteries, Vol. 1*. Effort, PA: KHP, 2006.

Kofmel, Kim. "Beast." *Book of Shadows 4,* 1992.

Koja, Kate, and Barry Malzberg. "In the Green House." In *Love in Vein*. New York: HarperCollins, 1994.

Koja, Kathe. "The Prince of Nox." In *Still Dead: Book of the Dead 2*. New York: Bantam, 1992.

Kolbe, John A. *Vampires of Vengeance*. London: Fiction House, 1935.

Kolometz, Dawn. "White Rose, Dark Knight." *The Vampire's Crypt 1,* 1989.

Kolometz, Dawn, and Toby Lancelotti. "In for the Kill." *The Vampire's Crypt 2,* 1990.

Koltz, Tony. *Vampire Express (Choose Your Own Adventure #31)*. New York: Bantam, 1984.

Komroff, Manuel. "A Red Coat for Night." *Argosy,* December 1944.

Koogler, Dori, and Ashley McConnell. *These Our Actors (Buffy the Vampire Slayer)*. New York: Pocket Books, 2002.

Kornbluth, C. M. "The Mindworm." *Worlds Beyond,* December 1950.

Kostova, Elizabeth. *The Historian: A Novel*. New York: Little, Brown, 2005.

Kraft, Jim. *The Vampire Hound*. Mahwah, NJ: Troll Communications, 2002 (juvenile).

Krinard, Susan. *Chasing Midnight*. Toronto: Harlequin, 2007.

———. *Dark of the Moon*. Toronto: Harlequin, 2008.

Kriske, Anne. "Widow." *Vampire Quarterly 8,* May 1987.

———. "Midnight Snack." *Dead of Night 3,* Fall 1989.

Krulik, Nancy, and Jim Jinkins. *Doug's Vampire Caper*. New York: Disney Press, 1997 (juvenile).

Kupfer, Allen C. *The Journal of Professor Abraham Van Helsing*. New York: Forge, 2004.

Kurtinski, Pyotyr. *Thirst*. New York: Leisure Books, 1995.

Kurtz, Katherine. *The Legacy of Lehr*. New York: Walker, 1986.

Kushner, Ellen. "Night Laughter." In *After Midnight*. New York: Tor, 1986.

Kuttner, Henry. "The Graveyard Rats." *Weird Tales,* March 1936.

———. "The Secret of Kralitz." *Weird Tales,* October 1936.

———. "I, the Vampire." *Weird Tales,* February 1937.

———. "Hydra." *Weird Tales,* April 1939.

———. "The Masquerade." *Weird Tales,* May 1942.

———. "The Dark World." *Startling Stories,* Summer 1946.

———. "Call Him Demon." *Thrilling Wonder Stories,* Fall 1946.

Kwiatkowski, Kat. *The Last Vampire Bringer*. Morrisville, NC: Lulu.com, 2006.

L.J.A. "Free Gifts." *Count Dracula Fan Club Bi-Annual 2,* Spring/Summer 1979.

L. X. (Julian Osgood Field). "A Kiss of Judas." *The Pall Mall Magazine,* July 1893.

La Spina, Greye. "Fettered." *Weird Tales,* July–October 1926.

———. "Vampire Bite." *Bulls-Eye Detective,* Spring 1930.

———. "The Antimacassar." *Weird Tales,* May 1949.

Labatt, Mary. *Spying on Dracula*. New York: Kids Can, 1999 (juvenile).

Lach, Jane. "The Stranger." *World of Dark Shadows,* February 1981.

**Lacher, Chris B.** "Kings." *The Vampire Journal 3*, 1986.

**Lackey, Mercedes.** "Nightside." *Marion Zimmer Bradley's Fantasy Magazine*, Autumn 1989.

———. *Children of the Night.* New York: Tor, 1990.

———. "Satanic, Versus. . . ." *Marion Zimmer Bradley's Fantasy Magazine*, Autumn 1990.

———. *Jinx High.* New York: Tor, 1991.

**Lackey, Mercedes, Eric Flint, and Dave Freer.** *This Rough Magic.* New York: Baen, 2005.

**LaCroix, Marianne.** *Descendants of Darkness.* Akron, OH: Ellora's Cave, 2005 (erotica).

———. "The Hunted." In *Vamprotica 2005.* Chippewa, 2005 (erotica).

———. *The Hunted: The Hunters #1.* Chippewa, 2005 (erotica).

———. *Eternal Embrace: Descendants of Darkness 2.* Akron, OH: Ellora's Cave, 2006 (erotica).

———. *Captive Embrace: Descendants of Darkness 3.* Akron, OH: Ellora's Cave, 2006 (erotica).

**Ladd, Ashley.** *Blessed Be.* Akron, OH: Ellora's Cave, 2005 (erotica).

**Laffer, Jax.** *The Blood Within.* Alma, AR: Yard Dog, 2002.

**Lafferty, R. A.** "This Grand Carcass." *Amazing Stories,* November 1968.

**Laico, Kim Elizabeth.** "Indian Lover." *Screem 2,* September 1991.

———. "Into the Night." *The Miss Lucy Westenra Society of the Undead 2,* 1991.

**Laidlaw, Marc.** *The 37th Mandala.* New York: St. Martin's, 1996.

**Laing, Charles Richard.** "Preypretty." *Dead of Night 4,* January 1990.

**Lake, Paul.** *Among the Immortals.* Ashland, OR: Story Line, 1994.

**Lalique, Josephine.** *Scarlet: The Secret Diaries.* Sanguine, 1998.

**Lamb, Charlotte.** *Vampire Lover.* London: Mills and Boon, 1994.

**Lamb, Marilyn.** *Blood Covenant.* Minneapolis: Free Spirit, 1999.

**Lamb, Nancy.** *The Vampire Went Thataway!* Mahwah, NJ: Troll Association, 1997 (juvenile).

**Lamsley, Terry.** "Volunteers." In *The Mammoth Book of Dracula.* London: Robinson, 1997.

**Lanai, Norma K.** "The Night Trilogy." *Children of the Night Coven Journal 4,* 1990.

**Landolfi, Thomas.** "The Kiss." In *Words in Commotion and Other Stories.* New York: Viking, 1986.

**Lane, Amy.** *Vulnerable.* Lincoln, NE: iUniverse, 2005.

**Lane, Joel.** "Your European Son." In *The Mammoth Book of Dracula.* London: Robinson, 1997.

**Lane, Jourdan.** *Soulmates: Bound by Blood.* Torquere, 2007 (erotica).

———. *Soulmates: Deceptions.* Torquere, 2007 (erotica).

**Lang, Andrew.** *The Disentanglers.* London: Longmans, Green, 1901.

**Langu, Radu.** *Dracula.* Parkstone, 2000.

**Lannes, Roberta.** "I Walk Alone." In *Still Dead: Book of the Dead 2.* New York: Bantam, 1992.

———. "Melancholia." In *The Mammoth Book of Dracula.* London: Robinson, 1997.

———. "Turkish Delight." In *The Mammoth Book of Vampire Stories by Women.* New York: Carroll & Graf, 2001.

**Lansdale, Joe R.** "Shadow Time." In *For a Few Stories More.* Burton, MI: Subterranean, 2001.

**Lansdowne, Judith.** "The Cossack." In *His Eternal Kiss.* East Rutherford, NJ: Kensington, 2002.

Larson, Kristine K. "Father Exhumed." *Night Mountains 6,* Winter 1991.

LaSalle, Robyn. "Keep Me in the Dark." In *Dyad: The Vampire Tales.* Poway, CA: Mkashef Enterprises, 1991.

Laurey, Rosemary. *Walk in Moonlight: Forever Vampire #1.* Brighton, MI: Avid, 2000.

————. *Rapture in Moonlight: Forever Vampire #2.* Brighton, MI: Avid, 2001.

————. *Mystery in Moonlight.* Brighton, MI: Avid, 2002.

————. "The Legacy." In *Conventional Vampires.* Dracula Society UK, 2003.

————. "Turkish Delight." In *Winter Warriors.* Akron, OH: Ellora's Cave, 2003 (erotica).

————. "Velvet Nights." In *Immortal Bad Boys.* East Rutherford, NJ: Brava, 2004.

————. *Be Mine Forever: Forever Vampire #3.* New York: Zebra, 2005.

————. *Keep Me Forever: Forever Vampire #4.* New York: Kensington, 2006.

————. *Midnight Lover: Forever Vampire #5.* New York: Zebra, 2007.

————. *Super Natural Acts.* New York: Kensington, 2007.

————. *Super Natural Spies.* New York: Zebra, 2008.

Lauria, Frank. *Raga Six.* New York: Bantam Books, 1972.

LaVoie, Philip M. *Legacy of the Vampire.* Lincoln, NE: iUniverse, 2005.

Lawes, Henry. "Feast of Blood in the House of the Vampire." *Adventures in Horror,* June 1971.

Lawrence, Brittany Anne. *Misty Nights.* Bloomington, IN: AuthorHouse, 2005.

Lawrence, D. H. "The Lovely Lady." In *The Black Cap: New Stories of Murder and Mystery.* London: Hutchinson, 1927.

Laws, Stephen. *Fear Me.* New York: Leisure Books, 2005.

Lawson, Brad. *Twilight Hour.* Frederick, MD: PublishAmerica, 2005.

Lawson, W. B. *Diamond Dick's Vampire Trail: Or, The Mad Horseman of Thunder Mountain.* New York: Street and Smith, 1906.

Laymon, Carl. *Nightmare Lake.* New York: Dell, 1983.

Laymon, Richard. *Lonely One.* London: Fearon/Janus/Quercus, 1985.

————. "Special." In *Under the Fang.* New York: Pocket Books, 1991.

————. *Blood Games.* London: Headline, 1992.

————. "Dracuson's Driver." In *Dracula: Prince of Darkness.* New York: DAW, 1992.

————. *The Stake.* New York: Zebra, 1995.

————. *Bite.* New York: Leisure Books, 1999.

————. *The Traveling Vampire Show.* New York: Leisure Books, 2001.

Le Blanc, Richard. *The Fangs of the Vampire.* New York: Vantage, 1979.

Le Fanu, Sheridan Joseph. "Carmilla." *The Dark Blue,* December 1871, January–March 1872.

Lecale, Errol. *Castle Doom.* London: New English Library, 1974.

————. *Blood of My Blood.* London: New English Library, 1975.

Leconte, Marianne. "Femme Fatale." In *New Terrors II.* London: Pan, 1980.

Lee, Diana. *A Taste for Blood.* Binghamton, NY: Haworth, 2003.

Lee, Earl. *Drakulya: The Lost Journal of Mircea Drakulya, Lord of the Undead.* Tuscon, AZ: Sharp, 1991.

Lee, Edward. "Almost Never." *Cemetary Dance,* Fall 1991.

Lee, Mara. *Turned Innocence.* Indianapolis, IN: Liquid Silver Books, 2003 (erotica).

Lee, Marilyn. "Bloodlust." In *Things That Go Bump in the Night.* Akron, OH: Ellora's Cave, 2001 (erotica).

————. *Bloodlust II: The Taming of Serge Dumont.* Akron, OH: Ellora's Cave, 2002 (erotica).

————. *Bloodlust III: Forbidden Desires.* Akron, OH: Ellora's Cave, 2002 (erotica).

——. *The Talisman*. Akron, OH: Ellora's Cave, 2002 (erotica).

——. *Bloodlust: All in the Family*. Akron, OH: Ellora's Cave, 2004 (erotica).

——. *Bloodlust: Conquering Mikhel Dumont*. Akron, OH: Ellora's Cave, 2004 (erotica).

——. *Daughters of Takira 1: One Night in Vegas*. Martinsburg, WV: Changeling, 2004 (erotica).

Lee, Michael. "Et Sans Reproche." In *Dark Tyrants*. Clarkston, GA: White Wolf, 1997.

Lee, Shizuko. *Raiders of Vampyra*. Lake Park, GA: New Concepts, 2005.

Lee, Tanith. "The Demoness." In *Year's Best Fantasy 2*. New York: DAW, 1976.

——. "Red as Blood." *The Magazine of Fantasy & Science Fiction*, July 1979.

——. "Cyrion in Bronze." *The Magazine of Fantasy & Science Fiction*, February 1980.

——. *Sabella or The Bloodstone*. New York: DAW, 1980.

——. "The Squire's Tale." *Sorcerer's Apprentice 7*, 1980.

——. "Sirriamnis." In *Unsilent Night*. Cambridge, MA: New England Science Fiction Association, 1981.

——. "A Lynx with Lions." In *Cyrion*. New York: DAW, 1982.

——. "Il Bacio (Il Chiave)." *Amazing*, 1983.

——. "Nunc Dimittis." In *The Dodd, Mead Gallery of Horror Stories*. New York: Dodd, Mead, 1983.

——. "Bite-Me-Not or, Fleur de Feu." *Isaac Asimov's Science Fiction Magazine*, October 1984.

——. "The Vampire Lover." *Night Visions I*. Arlington Heights, IL: Dark Harvest, 1984.

——. "Quatt-Sup." In *The Gorgon and Other Beastly Tales*. New York: DAW, 1985.

——. "The Janfia Tree." In *Blood is Not Enough*. New York: William Morrow, 1989.

——. "White as Sin, Now." In *The Forests of the Night*. London: Unwin-Hyman, 1989.

——. *Blood of Roses*. London: Legend, 1990.

——. "Venus Rising on Water." *Isaac Asimov's Science Fiction Magazine*, October 1991.

——. *Dark Dance: First in the Blood Opera Sequence*. New York: Dell, 1992.

——. "Winter Flowers." *Isaac Asimov's Science Fiction Magazine*, June 1993.

——. *Personal Darkness: Second in the Blood Opera Sequence*. New York: Dell, 1994.

——. *Darkness, I: Third in the Blood Opera Sequence*. New York: St. Martin's, 1996.

——. "The Isle Is Full of Noises." In *The Vampire Sextette*. Garden City, NY: GuildAmerica Books, 2000.

——. "Isabel." *Realms in Fantasy*, 2004.

Lee, Vernon. "Amour Dure." In *Hauntings: Fantastic Stories*. London: William Heineman, 1890.

——. "Marsyas in Flanders." In *For Maurice: Five Unlikely Stories*. London: John Lane, 1927.

Lee, Warner. "Cult." In *Dracula: Prince of Darkness*. New York: DAW, 1992.

Lee, Wendi, and Terry Beatty. "The Black Wolf." In *Dracula: Prince of Darkness*. New York: DAW, 1992.

Leeds, Arthur. "Return of the Undead." *Weird Tales*, November 1925.

Lehti, Steve. "With the Rising of the Morning Sun." *World of Dark Shadows*, December 1977.

Leiber, Fritz. "The Girl with the Hungry Eyes." In *The Girl with the Hungry Eyes and Other Stories*. New York: Avon, 1949.

———. "The Dead Man." *Weird Tales*, November 1950.

———. "Dr. Adams' Garden of Evil." *Strange Fantasy*, Spring 1969.

———. "Ship of Shadows." *The Magazine of Fantasy & Science Fiction*, July 1969.

Leigh, Lora. "Blood Ties—Knight Stalker." In *Manaconda*. Akron, OH: Ellora's Cave, 2004 (erotica).

Leigh, Shannon, and Ivona Knight. *Vampyress*. Chippewa, 2005.

Leinster, Murray. "The Man with the Iron Cap." *Startling Stories*, November 1947.

Leith, Kay. "The Sanguivites." In *The 9th Fontana Book of Great Horror Stories*. London: Fontana, 1975.

Leman, Bob. "The Pilgrimage of Clifford M." *The Magazine of Fantasy & Science Fiction*, May 1984.

Lemon, Don M. "The Scarlet Planet." *Wonder Stories Quarterly*, Winter 1931.

Leomax, Oxborne. *Vampires & Virgins*. San Francisco: Last Gasp, 2003 (erotica).

Leroux, Gaston. *The Kiss That Killed*. New York: Macaulay Co., 1934.

Levinson, Mark. "Kletch's Rib." *Space and Time*, November 1976.

Levy, Elizabeth. *Dracula Is a Pain in the Neck*. New York: Harper & Row, 1984 (juvenile).

Levy, Robert Joseph. *The Suicide King (Buffy the Vampire Slayer)*. New York: Simon Spotlight, 2005.

———. *Go Ask Malice: A Slayer's Diary (Buffy the Vampire Slayer)*. New York: Simon Spotlight, 2006.

Lewis, D. F. "Debutante." *The Vampire's Crypt 4*, Fall 1991.

———. "Like Eve's Apples." *The Vampire's Crypt 6*, Fall 1992.

Lewis, Geoffrey Wyndham. "The Silent Inn." In *Tales of Fear*. London: Philip Allan, 1935.

Lewis, Jack. *Blood Money*. London: Headline Book, 1960.

Lewis, Jeremy F. *Staked*. New York: Pocket Books, 2008.

Libby, Alisa M. *The Blood Confession*. New York: Dutton, 2006 (juvenile).

Liberty. *Turnbull Bay: A Traditional Vampire Story*. Philadelphia: Xlibris, 2001.

———. *Dark Revenge: A Vampire Story*. Lincoln, NE: Writer's Club, 2002.

Lichtenberg, Jacqueline. "Through the Moon Gate." In *Tales of the Witchcraft #2*. New York: Tor, 1988.

———. *Those of My Blood*. New York: St. Martin's, 1988.

———. *Dreamspy*. New York: St. Martin's, 1989.

———. "False Prophecy." In *Tarot Tales*. London: Century Hutchinson, 1989.

———. "Vampire's Friend." In *Heaven and Hell: An Anthology of Whimsical Stories*. Kingston, IL: Speculation, 2002.

Ligotti, Thomas. "The Lost Art of Twilight." *Dark Horizons*, Summer 1986.

———. "Mrs. Rinaldi's Angel." In *Whisper in Blood*. New York: William Morrow, 1991.

———. "The Unnatural Persecution by a Vampire of Mr. Jacob J." *The Agonizing Resurrection of Victor Frankenstein and Other Gothic Tales*. Eugene, OR: Silver Salamander, 1994.

———. "The Heart of Count Dracula, Descendant of Attila, Scourge of God." In *Songs of a Dead Dreamer*. Albuquerque, NM: Silver Scarab, 1995.

Linczy, Eva. *Vampire Desire*. London: New English Library, 1996.

Lindqvist, John Ajvade. *Let Me In*. New York: Thomas Dunne Books, 2007.

———. *Let the Right One In*. London: Quercus, 2007.

Linssen, John. *Tabitha fffoulkes*. New York: Arbor House, 1978.

**Linton, Eliza Lynn.** "The Fate of Madame Cabanel." In *Within a Silken Thread and Other Stories.* London: Chatto & Windus, 1880.

**Linzer, Gordon.** "You Only Die Twice." *Space and Time,* June 1971.

———. "Moonfever." *Space and Time,* September 1975.

———. "Thunderboomer." *Space and Time,* March 1977.

———. "Demons Are Forever." *Space and Time,* July 1978.

———. "The Man with the Silver Stake." *Space and Time,* January 1979.

———. "The Great Wet Hope." *Space and Time,* January 1980.

———. "The Spy Who Drank Blood." *Space and Time,* 1984.

———. "Children of Glory." *Space and Time,* Winter 1984–85.

———. "Night Stalkers." *Space and Time,* Summer 1986.

———. "Butterball." *Space and Time,* Fall 1987.

**Lisle, Holly.** *Fire in the Mist.* New York: Baen, 1992.

**Little, Bentley.** "Hard Times." In *Dracula: Prince of Darkness.* New York: DAW, 1992.

———. *The Summoning.* New York: Zebra, 1993.

**Little John, Dana.** *Mikhail's Hunt: The Dioni Chronicles #1.* Red Rose, 2007.

**Liu, Marjorie M.** *A Taste of Crimson: Crimson City #2.* New York: Love Spell, 2005.

**Livia, Anna.** *Minimax.* Portland, OR: Eighth Mountain, 1991.

**Lloyd, Charles.** "Special Diet." In *Pan Book of Horror Stories No. 3.* London: Pan, 1959.

**Lochte, Dick.** "Vampire Dreams." In *The Ultimate Dracula.* New York: Dell, 1991.

**Locke, Joseph.** *Vampire Heart: Blood and Lace #1.* New York: Starfire, 1994 (juvenile).

———. *Deadly Relations: Blood and Lace #2.* New York: Bantam, 1994 (juvenile).

**Lodi, Ed.** "Maude's Home Eatery." *Dead of Night 3,* Fall 1989.

**Logston, Anne.** "Twighlight (sic) Time." *Children of the Night Coven Journal 1,* 1990.

**Long, Amelia Reynolds.** "The Thought-Monster." *Weird Tales,* March 1930.

———. "The Undead." *Weird Tales,* August 1931.

———. "Flapping Wings of Death." *Weird Tales,* June 1935.

**Long, Frank Belknap.** "The Ocean Leech." *Weird Tales,* January 1925.

———. "The Sea Thing." *Weird Tales,* December 1925.

———. "The Brain Eaters." *Weird Tales,* June 1932.

———. "Second Night Out." *Weird Tales,* 1933.

———. "The Black, Dead Thing." *Weird Tales,* October 1933.

———. "Stellar Vampire." *Science Fiction Stories,* June 1943.

**Long, Frank Belknap, and Otis Adelbert Kline.** "Return of the Undead." *Weird Tales,* July 1943.

**Long, Richard.** *Unholy Thirst.* Frederick, MD: PublishAmerica, 2004.

**Longstreet, Roxanne.** *The Undead.* New York: Zebra, 1993.

———. *Cold Kiss.* New York: Zebra, 1994.

**LoProto, Frank.** "Night Battles." *The Vampire Journal 4,* 1988.

**Lord, David Thomas.** *Bound in Blood: The Erotic Journey of a Vampire.* New York: Kensington, 2001.

———. *Bound in Flesh.* New York: Kensington, 2006.

**Lord-Wolff, Peter.** *The Silence in Heaven.* New York: Tor, 2000.

**Loring, F. G.** "The Tomb of Sarah." *The Pall Mall Magazine,* December 1887.

**Lorrah, Jean.** "Paradox Lost." *World of Dark Shadows,* March 1979.

———. *Blood Will Tell.* Dallas, TX: BenBella Books, 2003.

**Lortz, Richard.** *Children of the Night.* New York: Dell, 1974.

**Lory, Ann.** *Eternal Embrace: Eternal #1.* Scottsdale, AZ: Loose Id, 2007.

**Lory, Robert.** *Dracula Returns (Dracula Horror Series #1).* New York: Pinnacle, 1973.

————. *The Hand of Dracula (Dracula Horror Series #2).* New York: Pinnacle, 1973.

————. *Dracula's Brother (Dracula Horror Series #3).* New York: Pinnacle, 1973.

————. *Dracula's Gold (Dracula Horror Series #4).* New York: Pinnacle, 1973.

————. *The Witching of Dracula (Dracula Horror Series #5).* New York: Pinnacle, 1974.

————. *The Drums of Dracula (Dracula Horror Series #6).* New York: Pinnacle, 1974.

————. *Dracula's Lost World (Dracula Horror Series #7).* New York: Pinnacle, 1974.

————. "The Beat of Leather Wings." In *Boris Karloff Presents More Tales of the Frightened.* New York: Pyramid, 1975.

————. *Dracula's Disciple (Dracula Horror Series #8).* New York: Pinnacle, 1975.

————. *Challenge to Dracula (Dracula Horror Series #9).* New York: Pinnacle, 1975.

————. "There's Something in the Soup." In *Boris Karloff Presents More Tales of the Frightened.* New York: Pyramid, 1975.

**Love, Kathy.** *Fangs for the Memories: The Young Brothers #1.* New York: Kensington, 2005.

————. *Fangs but No Fangs: The Young Brothers #2.* New York: Brava, 2006.

————. *I Only Have Fangs for You: The Young Brothers #3.* New York: Brava, 2006.

————. *Any Way You Want It.* New York: Kensington, 2008.

**Lovecraft, H. P.** "The Hound." *Weird Tales,* February 1924.

————. "The Tomb." *Weird Tales,* January 1926.

————. "The Thing on the Doorstep." *Weird Tales,* January 1937.

————. "The Shunned House." *Weird Tales,* October 1937.

**Lovell, Marc.** *Vampire in the Shadows.* London: Coronet, 1977.

**Lovko, Buzz.** "Lugosi Wannabe." *The Vampire's Crypt 5,* Spring 1992.

————. "Signed in Blood." *The Vampire's Crypt 6,* Fall 1992.

**Lowell, Marc.** *An Enquiry into the Existance of Vampires.* New York: Doubleday, 1974.

**Lowery, Fawn.** *Jaharis #2: The Witch and the Vampire.* Garibaldi Highlands, BC, Canada: eXtasy Books, 2008.

**Lubar, David.** *The Vanishing Vampire: The Accidental Monsters #1.* New York: Scholastic, 1997 (juvenile).

**Lucas, Tim.** *The Book of Renfield: A Gospel of Dracula.* New York: Touchstone, 2005.

**Ludwick, Kathleen.** "Dr. Immortelle." *Fantastic,* May 1968.

**Lukyanenko, Sergei.** *The Night Watch: The Others #1.* London: Heineman, 2006.

————. *Day Watch: The Others #2.* London: Heineman, 2007.

————. *Twilight Watch: The Others #3.* London: Heineman, 2007.

**Lumley, Brian.** "Cement Surroundings." In *Tales of Cthulu Mythos Vol. 2.* Sauk City, WI: Arkham House, 1969.

————. "Haggopian." *The Magazine of Fantasy & Science Fiction,* June 1973.

————. "Tharquest and the Lamia Orbiquita." *Fantastic,* November 1976.

————. "Zack Phalanx Is Vlad the Impaler." *Weirdbook 11,* 1977.

————. "The House of the Temple." *Weird Tales,* Fall 1981.

————. "Necros." In *The Second Book of After Midnight Stories.* London: William Kimber, 1986.

————. *Necroscope.* New York: Tor, 1986.

————. *Necroscope II: Wamphyri!* New York: Tor, 1988.

————. *Necroscope II: The Source.* New York: Tor, 1989.

————. *Necroscope IV: Deadspeak.* New York: Tor, 1990.

————. "The Thief Immortal." *Weirdbook 25,* Autumn 1990.

————. *Necroscope V: Deadspawn.* New York: Tor, 1991.

————. "The Picnickers." In *Final Shadows.* New York: Doubleday, 1991.

————. *Vampire World 1: Blood Brothers.* New York: Tor, 1992.

————. *Vampire World 2: The Last Aerie.* New York: Tor, 1993.

————. *Vampire World 3: Bloodwars.* New York: Tor, 1994.

————. *Necroscope: The Lost Years #1.* New York: Tor, 1995.

————. *Necroscope: Resurgence: The Lost Years #2.* New York: Tor, 1996.

————. *Invaders (E-Branch 1).* New York: Tor, 2000.

————. *Defilers (E-Branch 2).* New York: Tor, 2001.

————. *Avengers (E-Branch 3).* New York: Tor, 2001.

————. *Harry Keogh: Necroscope and Other Heroes.* New York: Tor, 2003.

————. *Necroscope: The Touch.* New York: Tor, 2006.

**Luna, Claire.** *Ebony Blood.* Northwest, 1993.

**Lundenmuth, K.** "In Control." *Nocturnal Extacy 2,* 1992 (erotica).

**Lupoff, Richard A.** "A Freeway for Draculas." In *The Berserkers.* New York: Simon & Schuster, 1973.

————. *Sandworld.* New York: Berkley Medalion, 1976.

**Lutz, John.** "Mr. Lucrada." In *The Ultimate Dracula.* New York: Dell, 1991.

————. "After the Ball." In *Dracula: Prince of Darkness.* New York: DAW, 1992.

**Lutzen, Hanna.** *Vlad the Undead.* Toronto: Groundwood Books, 1998 (juvenile).

**Lyman, Russ.** *Record of Nightly Occurences: Diary of a Vampire.* Russ Lyman, 1991.

**Lyons, Brenna.** *Remember Me.* Garibaldi Highlands, BC, Canada: eXtasy Books, 2003 (erotica).

————. *The Konig Cursebreakers—Night Warriors Book 2.* Garibaldi Highlands, BC, Canada: eXtasy Books, 2004 (erotica).

**Lyons, Rene.** *Midnight Sun: Templar Vampires #1.* Macon, GA: Samhain, 2006.

————. *The Daystar: Templar Vampires #2.* Macon, GA: Samhain, 2007.

**Lytle, C. Alan.** *American Vampire.* Lincoln, NE: iUniverse.com, 2000.

**Lytton, E. K.** *Dracula's Daughter,* 1977.

**Lytton, Edward Bulwer.** "A Strange Story." *All the Year Round,* 10 August 1891 and 8 March 1862.

**MacAlister, Katie.** *A Girl's Guide to Vampires.* New York: Love Spell, 2003.

————. *Sex and the Single Vampire.* New York: Love Spell, 2004.

————. *Sex, Lies and Vampires.* New York: Love Spell, 2005.

————. "Bring Out Your Dead." In *Just One Sip.* New York: Love Spell, 2006.

————. *Even Vampires Get the Blues.* New York: Signet Eclipse, 2006.

————. *Holy Smokes: Aisling Gray Guardian #5.* New York: Berkley, 2007.

————. *Last of the Red Hot Vampires.* New York: Signet, 2007.

**McAllister, Bruce.** "When the Fathers Go." In *Universe 12.* Garden City, NY: Doubleday, 1982.

**McAuley, Paul J.** "The Worst Place in the World." In *The Mammoth Book of Dracula.* London: Robinson, 1997.

**McCall, B. J.** "Embrace Forever." In *Things That Go Bump in the Night V.* Akron, OH: Ellora's Cave, 2006 (erotica).

**McCammon, Robert R.** *They Thirst: A Novel.* New York: Avon, 1981.

————. "Eat Me." In *Book of the Dead.* New York: Bantam, 1989.

————. "The Miracle Mile." In *Under the Fang.* New York: Pocket Books, 1991.

**McCann, Jesse Leon.** *Scooby-Doo and the Legend of the Vampire Rock.* New York: Scholastic, 2003 (juvenile).

McCarthy, Erin. *High Stakes: Vegas Vampires Book 1.* New York: Berkley Sensation, 2006.

———. *Bit the Jackpot: Vegas Vampires Book 2.* New York: Berkley Sensation, 2006.

———. *Bled Dry: Vegas Vampires Book 3.* New York: Berkley Sensation, 2007.

———. *Sucker Bet: Vegas Vampires Book 4.* New York: Berkley Sensation, 2008.

McCarthy, Justin Huntley. *Our Sensational Novel.* London: Chatto & Windus, 1886.

McCarty, Sarah. *Shadow Wranglers.* Toronto: Harlequin, 2008.

McClaine, Jenna. *The Wages of Sin.* Morrisville, NC: Lulu, 2006.

McClusky, Thorp. "Loot of the Vampire." *Weird Tales,* June–July 1936.

———. "The Crawling Horror." *Weird Tales,* November 1936.

———. "The Woman in Room 607." *Weird Tales,* January 1937.

———. "The Graveyard Horror." *Weird Tales,* March 1941.

———. "The Lamia in the Penthouse." *Weird Tales,* May 1952.

McConnell, Ashley. *Book of the Dead (Angel).* New York: Pocket Books, 2004.

McConnell, Ashley, and Dori Koogler. *These Our Actors (Buffy the Vampire Slayer).* New York: Pocket Books, 2002.

McCoy, Judi. *Making Over Mr. Right.* New York: Avon, 2008.

McCoy, Renee. "Circus of Vampires." *Loyalists of the Vampire Realm Newsletter,* October 1991.

McCray, Cheyenne, and Annie Windsor. *Vampire Dreams.* Akron, OH: Ellora's Cave, 2004 (erotica).

McCullough, Karen. "A Vampire's Christmas Carol." In *Beneath a Christmas Moon.* Akron, OH: Cerridwen, 2007.

McDaniel, David. *The Man From U.N.C.L.E. #6: The Vampire Affair.* New York: Ace, 1966.

McDaniels, Abigail. *The Uprising.* New York: Zebra, 1994.

Macdonald, James D., and Debra Doyle. "Nobody Has to Know." In *Vampires: A Collection of Original Stories.* New York: HarperCollins, 1991.

McDonley, Dudley. "Lust of the Vampire." *Monster Sex Tales 1,* August–September 1972.

MacDougall, Lyle. "Moondance." *Good Guys Wear Fangs 1,* May 1992.

McDowell, Ian. "Geraldine." In *Love in Vein.* New York: HarperCollins, 1994 (erotica).

McDowell, Michael. "Halley's Passing." *Twilight Zone,* June 1987.

MacEwen, P. H. "A Winter's Night." In *Writers of the Future Volume IV.* Los Angeles: Bridge, 1988.

McGonegal, Richard F. "When Darkness Comes." *Dead of Night 3,* Fall 1989.

———. "Double Cross." *Dead of Night 4,* January 1990.

McGowan, Michael. *Shadowlands.* Martinsburg, VA: Quiet Storm Publications, 2005.

McGrath, Patrick. "Blood Disease." In *Blood and Water and Other Tales.* New York: Poseidon, 1988.

———. "Cleave the Vampire, or, A Gothic Pastorale." In *I Shudder at Your Touch.* New York: Penguin, 1991.

McGrew, Leah. "Vengeance." *Vampire Quarterly 5,* August 1986.

McKade, Mackenzie. *Six Feet Under.* Macon, GA: Samhain, 2006 (erotica).

McKean, Thomas. *Vampire Vacation.* New York: Avon-Camelot, 1986.

MacKeever, Maggie. *Waltz with a Vampire.* New York: Zebra, 2005.

McKinley, Robin. *Sunshine.* New York: Berkley, 2003.

McKnight, Ava. *The Invitation.* Phaze.com, 2005 (erotica).

McKnight, Cari. *Akhkharu: House of the Vampire*. Lincoln, NE: iUniverse, 2003.

Maclaine, Jenna. *The Wages of Sin*. Morrisville, NC: Lulu.com, 2006.

McMahan, F. A. "Welcome to the Dream." *Prisoners of the Night 6*, 1992.

McMahan, Jeffrey. "Hell Is for Children." In *Somewhere in the Night*. Boston: Alyson, 1989.

———. "Somewhere in the Night." In *Somewhere in the Night*. Boston: Alyson, 1989.

———. "Blood Relations." In *Embracing the Dark*. Boston: Alyson, 1991.

McMillan, Scott, and Katherine Kurtz. *Knights of the Blood*. E. Rutherford, NJ: New American Library, 1993.

———. *At Sword's Point: Knights of the Blood #2*. E. Rutherford, NJ: New American Library, 1994.

McMullen, Sean. *Voyage of the Shadowmoon*. New York: Tor, 2002.

———. *Glass Dragons*. New York: Tor, 2004.

McNaughton, Colin. *Dracula's Tomb*. Westminster, MD: Candlewick, 1998 (juvenile).

McShane, M. *Vampire in the Shadows*. London: Robert Hale, 1977.

Machen, Arthur. "The Inmost Light." In *The Great God Pan and the Inmost Light*. London: J. Lane, 1894.

Mack, Barbara A. *Blood Worship*. Booklocker.com, 2003.

Maclay, John. "The Reason Why." *Dead of Night 2*, July 1989.

———. "A Case of Misjudgement." *Dead of Night 6*, July 1990.

———. "The Hand That Feeds." *Bloodreams 3*, July 1992.

Madigan, Dawn. "Ryality Bites." In *Lady Jaided's Virile Vampires*. Akron, OH: Ellora's Cave, 2007 (erotica).

Madison, David. "Tower of Darkness." *Space and Time 28*, January 1975.

Madison, J. J. *Oooooh, It Feels Like Dying*. Monument, CO: Peacock, 1971.

Mahn, Inga. "House of Pleasure." In *Vamprotica 2005*. Chippewa, 2005 (erotica).

Mahoney, Shawn P. *Slayer Team Alpha*. Frederick, MD: PublishAmerica, 2007.

Malgadi, Roberto. *The Eleventh Sephiroth: Saga of the Vampire*. Bloomington, IN: AuthorHouse, 2006.

Mallory, Lewis. *The Nursery*. London: Hamlyn, 1981.

Malzberg, Barry. "Trial of Blood." In *The Berserkers*. New York: Simon & Schuster, 1973.

———. "The Student." In *Vampires, Werewolves and Other Monsters*. New York: Curtis, 1974.

———. "Indigestion." *Fantastic*, September 1977.

Malzberg, Barry, and Bill Pronzini. "Opening a Vein." In *Shadows 3*. New York: Doubleday, 1980.

Manchester, Sean. *Carmel: A Vampire's Tale*. Gothic Press, 2000.

Mancusi, Mari. *Boys That Bite: Blood Coven #1*. New York: Penguin, 2006 (juvenile).

———. *Stake That!: Blood Coven #2*. New York: Berkley, 2006 (juvenile).

———. *Girls That Growl: Blood Coven #3*. New York: Berkley, 2007 (juvenile).

Maney, Mabel. "Almost the Color of Summer Sky." In *Night Bites: Vampire Stories by Women*. Seattle, WA: Seal, 1996.

Mann, Jeff. "Devoured." In *Masters of Midnight*. New York: Kensington, 2003 (erotica).

Mann, William J. "His Hunger." In *Masters of Midnight*. New York: Kensington, 2003 (erotica).

Mannheim, Karl. *Vampires of Venus*. Manchester, England: Five Star, 1973.

**Marffin, Kyle.** *Carmilla: The Return, Darien II.* Burr Ridge, IL: Design Image Group, 1998.

———. *Gothique.* Burr Ridge, IL: Design Image Group, 2000.

———. *Waiting for the 400.* Burr Ridge, IL: Design Image Group, 2002.

**Mariotte, Jeff.** *Close to the Ground (Angel).* New York: Pocket Books, 2000.

———. *Hollywood Noir (Angel).* New York: Pocket Books, 2001.

———. *Haunted (Angel).* New York: Pocket Books, 2002.

———. "A Joyful Noise." In *The Longest Night Vol. 1 (Angel).* New York: Pocket Books, 2002.

———. *Stranger to the Sun (Angel).* New York: Pocket Books, 2002.

———. *Sanctuary (Angel).* New York: Simon Pulse, 2003.

———. *Solitary Man (Angel).* New York: Simon Pulse, 2003.

———. *Love and Death (Angel).* New York: Simon Spotlight, 2004.

**Markham, Harold.** "The Second-Hand Limousine." *Weird Tales,* November 1931.

**Marks, John.** *Fangland.* New York: Penguin, 2007.

**Markusen, Bruce.** *Haunted House of the Vampire: Coopersville Creepers #1.* Indian Hills, CA: Amber Quill, 2004.

**Marjanovic, Barbara.** "One Night Stand." In *Tabloid Purposes IV.* Lake Fossil, 2007.

**Marley, Stephen.** *Spirit Mirror.* New York: HarperCollins, 1988.

———. *Mortal Mask.* New York: Random House, 1991.

———. *Shadow Sisters.* New York: Random House, 1993.

**Marmell, Ari.** *Gehenna: The Final Night.* Clarkston, GA: White Wolf, 2004.

**Marra, Sue.** "Hannah's Hitchhiker." *Beyond 7,* 1987.

**Marryat, Florence.** *The Blood of the Vampire.* London: Hutchinson, 1897.

**Marsh, Geoffrey.** *The Fangs of the Hooded Demon.* New York: Tor, 1988.

**Marsh, Richard.** "The Mask." In *Marvels and Mysteries.* London: Methuen, 1900.

**Martin, Ann M.** *Ma and Pa Dracula.* New York: Holiday House, 1989 (juvenile).

———. *Kristy and the Vampire.* New York: Scholastic, 1994 (juvenile).

**Martin, David.** *Tap Tap: A Novel.* New York: Random House, 1995.

**Martin, Eve.** "Dark Love." *Vampire Junction 3,* 1992.

**Martin, George R. R.** *Fevre Dream.* New York: Poseidon, 1982.

**Martin, Ian.** "Time and Again or, the Vampire Clock." In *Strange Tales from CBS Mystery Theater.* New York: Popular Library, 1976.

**Martin, Lisa M.** "Remembering Michael." *Dead of Night 5,* April 1990.

———. "Love Me Forever." *Newsletter of the Miss Lucy Westenra Society of the Undead 3,* Summer 1990.

**Martin, Mario, Jr.** "Precious Bodily Fluids." In *Monster Tales.* New York: Rand McNally, 1973.

**Martin, Michael.** *The Vampire King.* ION Systems, 2002.

**Martin, Shirley.** *One More Tomorrow.* Lake Park, GA: New Concepts, 2003.

**Martin-Barnes, Adrienne.** "The Wolf Creek Fragment." In *I, Vampire.* Stamford, CT: Longmeadow, 1995.

**Martindale, T. Chris.** *Nightblood.* New York: Warner, 1990.

**Martinez, A. Lee.** *Gil's All Fright Diner.* New York: Tor, 2005 (juvenile).

**Martinez-Byrne, Dawn.** "The Cage." In *I, Vampire.* Stamford, CT: Longmeadow, 1995.

**Martone, Eric.** *Alexandre Dumas' The Vampire.* Lincoln, NE: iUniverse, 2003.

**Masek, Carrie S.** *Twice Damned.* Cincinnati, OH: Mundania, 2005.

**Mashburn, Kirk.** "Placide's Wife." *Weird Tales,* November 1931.

———. "The Vengeance of Ixmal." *Weird Tales,* March 1932.

———. "The Last of Placide's Wife." *Weird Tales,* September 1932.

———. "De Brignac's Lady." *Weird Tales,* February 1933.

Mason, Catharine. "Red Waters." *Miss Lucy Westenra Society of the Undead 2,* December 1991.

Massey, Brandon. *Dark Corner.* New York: Kensington, 2004.

Massie, Elizabeth. *Power of Persuasion (Buffy the Vampire Slayer).* Riverside, NJ: Simon Spotlight Entertainment, 1999.

———. "Forever, Amen." In *The Mammoth Book of Vampire Stories by Women.* New York: Carroll & Graf, 2001.

Masterson, Graham. "Bridal Suite." In *New Terrors I.* London: Pan, 1980.

———. "Changeling." In *Scare Care.* New York: Tor, 1989.

———. "Grease Monkey." *Gauntlet 2,* 1991.

———. "Laird of Dunain." In *Book of Vampires.* New York: Barnes & Noble, 1992.

Masterson, John. *A Scarlet Peccadillo.* Morrisville, NC: Lulu, 2004.

Masterton, Graham. "Roadkill." In *The Mammoth Book of Dracula.* London: Robinson, 1997.

———. *Manitou Blood.* New York: Leisure Books, 2005.

———. *Descendant.* London: Severn House, 2007.

Matheson, Richard. "Drink My Red Blood." *Imagination,* April 1951.

———. "Dress of White Silk." *The Magazine of Fantasy & Science Fiction,* October 1951.

———. *I Am Legend.* New York: Fawcett, 1954.

———. "The Funeral." *The Magazine of Fantasy & Science Fiction,* April 1955.

———. "No Such Thing as a Vampire." *Playboy,* October 1959.

———. "First Anniversary." *Playboy,* July 1960.

Matheson, Richard Christian. "Vampire." In *Cutting Edge.* New York: Doubleday, 1986.

Mathews, Gene. "The Kiss." *Dead of Night 4,* January 1990.

Matthews, Richard. "Pen Pals." *Dead of Night 1,* Spring 1989.

Mauro, Sherry Hall. *The Darkest Hour.* Garibaldi Highlands, BC, Canada: eXtasy Books, 2004.

Maverick, Liz. *Crimson City.* New York: Love Spell, 2005.

Maxey, Sue. "Teeth." *The Vampire Journal 4,* 1988.

Maxwell, Katie. *Got Fangs?* New York: Leisure Smooch, 2005 (juvenile).

———. *Circus of the Darned.* New York: Leisure Smooch, 2006 (juvenile).

Mayer, Mercer. *My Teacher Is a Vampire.* Racine, WI: Western, 1994 (juvenile).

Mayor, Flora. "Fifteen Charlotte Street." In *The Room Opposite and Other Tales of Mystery and Imagination.* London: Longman, 1935.

Mayotte, Raymond. *Khufu: The Legendary Immortal.* Self-published, 2003.

Mays, Judy. "Rednecks N' Roses." In *Nibbles N' Bits.* Akron, OH: Ellora's Cave, 2005 (erotica).

Meachum, Valerie. "Little Girl Lost." *Heart's Blood 1,* May 1992.

Mead, Richelle. *Vampire Academy #1.* New York: Razorbill, 2007 (juvenile).

———. *Frostbite: Vampire Academy #2.* New York: Razorbill, 2008 (juvenile).

———. *Shadow. Kiss: Vampire Academy #3.* New York: Razorbill, 2008 (juvenile).

Medeiros, Teresa. *After Midnight.* New York: Avon, 2005.

———. *The Vampire Who Loved Me.* New York: Avon, 2006.

———. *Some Like it Wicked.* New York: Avon, 2008.

Meik, Vivian. "The Two Old Women." In *Monsters: A Collection of Uneasy Tales.* London: Philip Allan, 1934.

**Meikle, William.** *The Coming of the King: The Watchers Trilogy #1*. Effort, PA: Black Death Books, 2003.

———. *The Battle for the Throne: The Watchers Trilogy #2*. Effort, PA: KHP, 2004.

———. *Culloden!: The Watchers Trilogy #3*. Effort, PA: KHP, 2004.

———. *Eldren: The Book of the Dark*. Effort, PA: Black Death Books, 2007.

**Mercer, Sienna.** *Switched!: My Sister the Vampire #1*. New York: HarperCollins, 2007 (juvenile).

———. *Fangtastic!: My Sister the Vampire #2*. New York: HarperTrophy, 2007 (juvenile).

———. *Re-Vamped!: My Sister the Vampire #3*. New York: HarperTrophy, 2007 (juvenile).

———. *Vampalicious!; My Sister the Vampire #4*. New York: HarperTrophy, 2008 (juvenile).

**Merlyn.** "Night Hunter." In *Dyad: The Vampire Stories*. Poway, CA: Mkashef Enterprises, 1991.

———. "Rough Boys." In *Dyad: The Vampire Stories*. Poway, CA: Mkashef Enterprises, 1991.

**Merz, Jon F.** *The Fixer*. New York: Pinnacle, 2002.

———. *The Invoker*. New York: Pinnacle, 2002.

———. *The Destructor*. New York: Pinnacle, 2003.

———. *The Syndicate*. New York: Pinnacle, 2003.

**Metcalfe, John.** *Feasting Dead*. Sauk City, WI: Arkham House, 1954.

**Metz, Melinda, and Laura J. Burns.** *Colony (Buffy the Vampire Slayer)*. New York: Pocket Books, 2005.

**Meyer, Adam.** "The Boardwalk." *The Vampire's Crypt 4*, Fall 1991.

**Meyer, David N., III.** "A Bloodsucker." In *Under the Fang*. New York: Pocket Books, 1991.

**Meyer, Stephanie.** *Twilight*. New York: Little, Brown, 2005 (juvenile).

———. *New Moon*. New York: Little, Brown, 2006 (juvenile).

———. *Eclipse*. New York: Little, Brown, 2007 (juvenile).

———. *Breaking Dawn*. New York: Little, Brown, 2008 (juvenile).

**Michael, Sean.** *Need*. Round Rock, TX: Torquere, 2005 (erotica).

**Michaels, Lynn.** *Nightwing*. Toronto: Harlequin Temptation, 1995.

**Michaels, Monette.** *The Case of the Virtuous Vampire*. LTD Books, 2004.

**Michaels, T. J.** *Carinian's Seeker: Vampire Council of Ethics #1*. Macon, GA: Samhain, 2007.

———. *Serati's Flame: Vampire Council of Ethics #2*. Macon, GA: Samhain, 2007.

**Michelle, Patrice.** *A Taste of Passion: Kendrians #1*. Akron, OH: Ellora's Cave, 2003 (erotica).

———. *A Taste of Revenge: Kendrians #2*. Akron, OH: Ellora's Cave, 2003 (erotica).

———. *A Taste for Control: Kendrians #3*. Akron, OH: Ellora's Cave, 2005 (erotica).

———. *Resurrection: Scions #1*. Toronto: Silhouette Nocturne, 2008.

———. *Insurrection: Scions #2*. Toronto: Silhouette Nocturne, 2008.

**Michelman, Jeffrey L.** "Revenge." *Count Dracula Fan Club News Journal*, May 1987.

**Middleton, Haydn.** "Psychopomp." In *I Shudder at Your Touch*. New York: Penguin, 1991.

**Miller, Beverly.** *Blood Lust*. Reseda, CA: Academy, 1974.

**Miller, Brian.** "The Disinternment." *The Vampire Journal 5*, 1989.

**Miller, Janet.** *All Night Inn*. Akron, OH: Cerridwen, 2005.

———. *Tasting Nightwalker Wine*. Akron, OH: Cerridwen, 2006.

**Miller, Kenneth.** *To Be Damned.* Edmonton, AB, Canada: Commonwealth Publications, 1995.

**Miller, Linda Lael.** *Forever and the Night.* New York: Berkley, 1993.

———. *For All Eternity.* New York: Berkley, 1994.

———. *Time without End.* New York: Berkley, 1995.

———. *Tonight and Always.* New York: Berkley, 1996.

———. *Into the Night.* New York: Berkley, 2002.

———. *Out of the Shadows.* New York: Berkley, 2002.

**Miller, P. Schuyler.** "Spawn." *Weird Tales,* August 1939.

———. "Over the River." *Unknown Worlds,* April 1941.

———. "The Titan." *Fantastic,* August 1962.

**Miller, Rex.** "Interview with a CENSORED Vampire." *Gauntlet 2,* 1991.

———. "Blood Drive." In *Dracula: Prince of Darkness.* New York: DAW, 1992.

**Millitello, Deborah.** "The Reluctant Vampire." *Marion Zimmer Bradley's Fantasy Magazine,* Autumn 1990.

**Miner, Suzy.** *Blood Bond.* Frederick, MD: PublishAmerica, 2006.

**Minns, Karen.** *Virago.* Tallahassee, FL: Naiad Press, 1990.

———. *Bloodsong: A Novel.* Bluestocking Press, 1997.

**Mintz, Leon.** *Memoir of the Masses.* Erie Harbor Productions, 2006.

**Minyard, R. Edward.** *In the Misty Moonlight.* Philadelphia: Xlibris, 2001.

**Mitchell, Mary Ann.** "Blameless." *The Haunted Sun 1,* October 1990.

———. *Sips of Blood.* New York: Leisure Books, 1999.

———. *Quenched.* New York: Leisure Books, 2000.

———. *Cathedral of Vampires.* New York: Leisure Books, 2002.

———. *Tainted Blood.* New York: Dorchester, 2003.

———. *The Vampire de Sade.* New York: Leisure Books, 2004.

———. *In the Name of the Vampire.* New York: Leisure Books, 2005.

**M'Lady, K. A.** *To Tell of Darkness: Book 1.* Mojocastle, 2007 (erotica).

**Moesta, Rebecca.** *Little Things (Buffy the Vampire Slayer).* New York: Pocket Books, 2002.

**Monahan, Brent.** *Book of Common Dread.* New York: St. Martin's, 1993.

———. *Blood of the Covenant: A Novel of the Vampire.* New York: St. Martin's, 1995.

**Monday, Donna.** *The Best Black Vampire Story You've Ever Read.* Booklocker.com, 2006.

**Monette, Paul.** *Nosferatu, the Vampyre.* New York: Avon, 1979 (movie novelization).

**Moning, Karen Marie.** *Darkfever.* New York: Delacorte, 2006.

———. *Bloodfever.* New York: Delacorte, 2007.

**Monteleone, Thomas.** "Prodigal Sun." In *Under the Fang.* New York: Pocket Books, 1991.

———. "Triptych Di Amore." In *Love in Vein.* New York: HarperCollins, 1994 (erotica).

**Mooers, DeSacia.** *The Blonde Vampire.* New York: Moffat, Yard, 1920.

**Mooney, Brian.** "Endangered Species." In *The Mammoth Book of Dracula.* London: Robinson, 1997.

**Moore, C. L.** "Shambleau." *Weird Tales,* November 1933.

———. "Black Thirst." *Weird Tales,* April 1934.

———. "Scarlet Dream." *Weird Tales,* May 1934.

———. "Julhi." *Weird Tales,* March 1935.

———. "The Cold Gray God." *Weird Tales,* October 1935.

———. "Yvala." *Weird Tales,* February 1936.

———. "Lost Paradise." *Weird Tales,* July 1936.

———. "The Tree of Life." *Weird Tales,* October 1936.

———. "Hellsgarde." *Weird Tales,* April 1939.

Moore, Christopher. *Bloodsucking Fiends.* New York: Simon & Schuster, 1995.

———. *You Suck: A Love Story.* New York: William Morrow, 2007.

Moore, Elaine. *Madonna of the Dark.* Irving, TX: Authorlink, 1999.

———. *Retribution: Dark Madonna 2.* Irving, TX: Authorlink, 2002.

———. *Dark Desire: Dark Madonna 3.* New York: iBooks, 2004.

Moore, James A. *Blood Red.* Northborough, MA: Earthling, 2005.

Mooser, Stephen. *Hitchhiking Vampire.* New York: Dell, 1991 (juvenile).

Moran, Chris. "Two-Spirits." In *I, Vampire.* Stamford, CT: Longmeadow, 1995.

Morecambe, Eric. *The Reluctant Vampire.* London: Methuen's Children's Books, 1982 (juvenile).

———. *The Vampire's Revenge.* London: Methuen, 1983.

Morel, Melina. *Devour.* New York: Signet Eclipse, 2007.

Morgan, Bassett. "The Wolf Woman." *Weird Tales,* September 1927.

———. "The Devils of Po Sung." *Weird Tales,* December 1927.

Morgan, Chris. "Windows '99 of the Soul." In *The Mammoth Book of Dracula.* London: Robinson, 1997.

Morgan, Jill. *Blood Brothers.* New York: Harper Trophy, 1996 (juvenile).

Morgan, John Thomas. *The Night Usher: A Vampire's Tale.* Philadelphia: Xlibris, 2001.

Morgan, Robert. *Some Things Never Die.* New York: Diamond Books, 1993.

———. *Some Things Come Back.* New York: Berkley, 1995.

Moriarty, Timothy. *Vampire Nights.* New York: Pinnacle, 1988.

Morlan, A. R. "Of Vampires and Gentlemen." *Prisoners of the Night 1,* 1987.

———. ". . . And the Horses Hiss at Midnight." In *Love in Vein.* New York: HarperCollins, 1994 (erotica).

Morris, E. G. "Vampires Can't Die!" *Dime Mystery Stories,* February 1935.

Morris, Gwendolyn R. *Vampire: A Sensual Romance Novella.* Lincoln, NE: iUniverse, 2005.

Morris, Jeff. *The Vampire Janine.* Bandersnatch Press, 1991.

Morris, Joshua. *Vampires (Scary Pop-Up Books).* Santa Monica, CA: Reader's Digest, 1994 (juvenile).

Morrison, Kevin. *The Accursed Realm.* Frederick, MD: PublishAmerica, 2007.

Morrison, Michael Leo. *Undeadly Spring.* Morrisville, NC: Lulu.com, 2006.

Morrow, Christopher. "I Am." *Loyalists of the Vampire Realm Newsletter,* October 1991.

Morrow, Sonora. "Hard Times." *Ellery Queen Mystery Magazine,* December 1974.

Morse, Jody A. "The Coffin Caper." In *Legends in Blood.* West Hollywood, CA: Fantaseas, 1991.

———. "The Hungry Hour." In *Legends in Blood.* West Hollywood, CA: Fantaseas, 1991.

———. "The Stuff of Life." In *Legends in Blood.* West Hollywood, CA: Fantaseas, 1991.

Morton, Gary Lynn. "Ain't No Vampires Anymore." *Tekeli-Li! 4,* Winter/Spring 1992.

Morton, Lisa. "Children of the Long Night." In *The Mammoth Book of Dracula.* London: Robinson, 1997.

Mosiman, Billie Sue. *Red Moon Rising.* New York: DAW, 2001.

———. *Malachi's Moon.* New York: DAW, 2002.

———. *The Ancient Path.* New York: DAW, 2003.

———. *Craven Moon.* New York: DAW, 2003.

Mosley, Cathy S. "Afterwards." *Heart's Blood 1,* May 1992.

Mucia, Monique. *Prince Eternal: Sacred Soul.* Lincoln, NE: iUniverse, 2000.

Mudryk, Theresa. "Come Join Me in Death." *World of Dark Shadows,* July 1982.

Muir, Maxwell M. "The Invisible War." *Vampire Junction 2,* 1992.

Mulvany, Catherine. *Something Wicked.* New York: Pocket Star, 2007.

Munro, Alix. "Resurrection Man." *After Hours,* Winter 1992.

Munton, Gill. *Dear Vampire.* Oxford: Oxford University Press, 2006 (juvenile).

Murphy, Kevin Andrew. "The Croquet Mallet Murders." In *I, Vampire.* Stamford, CT: Longmeadow, 1995.

———. "The Red Elixir." In *Dark Tyrants.* Clarkston, GA: White Wolf, 1997.

Murphy, Shannon K. "Wedded to the Night." *Nocturnal Extacy 2,* 1992.

Murphy, Warren, and Richard Sapir. *Destroyer #29: The Final Death.* New York: Pinnacle, 1977.

———. *Destroyer #88, The Ultimate Death.* New York: Penguin, 1992.

Murray, Hannah. *Tooth and Nailed.* Akron, OH: Ellora's Cave, 2007 (erotica).

Muss-Barnes, Eric. *The Gothic Rainbow.* Brooklyn, OH: Dubh Sith Ink, 1997.

Myers, Bill, and David Wimbish. *Fangs for the Memories: Bloodhounds, Inc. #5.* Bloomington, MN: Bethany House, 1999 (juvenile).

Myers, James. "Warrior of the Night." In *Chosen Haunts.* North Riverside, IL: Pandora, 1981.

Myers, Robert J. *The Virgin and the Vampire.* New York: Pocket Books, 1977.

Myles, Douglas. *Prince Dracula: Son of the Devil.* New York: McGraw-Hill, 1988.

Namioka, Lensey. *Village of the Vampire Cat.* New York: Delacorte, 1981 (juvenile).

Nasaw, Jonathan. *The World on Blood.* New York: Dutton, 1996.

———. *Shadows.* New York: Signet, 1998.

Nastassia, Countess. "The Promise." *The Vampire Journal 3,* 1986.

Navarro, Yvonne. "Rosedust." *The Vampire's Crypt 3,* Spring 1991.

———. "Feeding the Masses." In *Eldritch Tales.* Yith, 1992.

———. *Afterimage.* New York: Bantam, 1993.

———. "The Best Years of My Life." In *100 Vicious Little Vampire Stories.* New York: Barnes & Noble, 1995.

———. "Folds of the Faithful." In *100 Vicious Little Vampire Stories.* New York: Barnes & Noble, 1995.

———. "One Among Millions." In *The Many Faces of Fantasy: The 22nd World Fantasy Convention Souvenir Book,* 1996.

———. *Paleo (Buffy the Vampire Slayer).* Riverside, NJ: Simon Spotlight Entertainment, 2000.

———. "Uncle Dead and the Fourth of July." In *How I Survived My Summer Vacation (Buffy the Vampire Slayer).* New York: Pocket Books, 2000.

———. "Generous Presence." In *The Longest Night Vol. 1 (Angel).* New York: Pocket Books, 2002.

———. "Icicle Memories." In *The Longest Night Vol. 1 (Angel).* New York: Pocket Books, 2002.

———. *Tempted Champions (Buffy the Vampire Slayer).* New York: Pocket Books, 2002.

———. *The Darkening: Wicked Willow Book 1 (Buffy the Vampire Slayer).* Riverside, NJ: Simon Spotlight Entertainment, 2004.

———. *Shattered Twilight: Wicked Willow Book 2 (Buffy the Vampire Slayer).* Riverside, NJ: Simon Spotlight Entertainment, 2004.

———. *Broken Sunrise: Wicked Willow Book 3 (Buffy the Vampire Slayer)*. Riverside, NJ: Simon Spotlight Entertainment, 2004.

Neeley, Rhiannon. *John the Deliverer*. Indianapolis, IN: Liquid Silver Books, 2003 (erotica).

———. *Dirk the Savior*. Indianapolis, IN: Liquid Silver Books, 2003 (erotica).

———. *Drake the Defender*. Indianapolis, IN: Liquid Silver Books, 2003 (erotica).

———. *Eric the Guardian*. Indianapolis, IN: Liquid Silver Books, 2004 (erotica).

Neiderman, Andrew. *Blood Child*. New York: Berkley, 1990.

———. *The Need*. New York: G. P. Putnam, 1992.

———. *The Immortals*. New York: Pocket Star, 1993.

Nelson, K. H. "Your Soul to Keep." *Space and Time*, Winter 1988.

Neruda, Jan. "The Vampire." In *Czechoslavak Stories*. New York: Duffield, 1920.

Nesbit, E. "The Haunted House." *The Strand Magazine*, December 1913.

———. "The Pavilion." In *To the Adventurous*. London: Hutchinson, 1923.

Newman, Kim. *Bad Dreams*. London: Simon & Schuster, 1990.

———. *Anno Dracula*. London: Simon & Schuster, 1992.

———. "Red Reign." In *The Mammoth Book of Vampires*. London: Robinson, 1992.

———. *The Bloody Red Baron*. New York: Carroll & Graf, 1995.

———. "Coppola's Dracula." In *The Mammoth Book of Dracula*. London: Robinson, 1997.

———. *Judgement of Tears: Anno Dracula 1959*. New York: Carroll & Graf, 1998.

———. *Andy Warhol's Dracula*. PS, 1999 (chapbook).

———. "Dead Travel Fast." In *Unforgivable Stories*. London: Pocket Books, 2000.

———. *Dracula Cha Cha Cha*. London: Simon & Schuster, 2000.

———. "The Other Side of Midnight." In *The Vampire Sextette*. Garden City, NY: GuildAmerica Books, 2000.

———. "Castle in the Desert: Anno Dracula 1977." In *Mammoth Book of Best New Horror, Vol 12*. London: Robinson, 2001.

———. "You Are the Wind Beneath My Wings." *Horror Garage 3*, 2001.

Niall, David. "A Candle in the Sun." *Starshore*, Winter 1990.

———. "Undying Love." *Dead of Night 4*, January 1990.

Nicholson, Scott. *They Hunger*. New York: Pinnacle, 2007.

Nicke, Adam. "The Lake." *Miss Lucy Westenra Society of the Undead*, Spring 1992.

Nickles, Jason. *Immortal*. New York: Zebra, 1996.

Nicolson, J. U. *Fingers of Fear*. New York: Covis-Friede, 1937.

Nile, Dorathea. *The Vampire Cameo*. New York: Lancer Books, 1968.

Nisbet, Hume. "The Old Portrait." In *Stories Weird and Wonderful*. London: F. V. White, 1900.

———. "The Vampire Maid." In *Stories Weird and Wonderful*. London: F. V. White, 1900.

Nolan, William. "Fair Trade." *Whispers*, 1982.

———. "The Ceremony." In *Midnight*. New York: Tor, 1985.

———. "Getting Dead." *Iniquities*, 1991.

———. "Vympyre." In *I, Vampire*. Stamford, CT: Longmeadow, 1995.

Nordin, Ruth Ann. *The Vampire's Kiss*. Lincoln, NE: iUniverse, 2004 (juvenile).

Norris, Frank. "Grettir at Thorhall-Stead." *Everybody's Magazine*, April 1903.

Norris, Gregory L. "If by Night." *Bloodreams 2*, October 1991.

———. "Those Magnificent Blackberries." *Bloodreams 3*, January 1992.

Norton, Andre. "Sword of Unbelief." In *Swords Against Darkness II*. New York: Zebra Books, 1977.

Nottestad, Roy M. "Vienna." *The Vampire Journal 4*, 1988.

**Nour, Myra.** *A Vampire's Kiss.* Lake Park, GA: New Concepts, 2003 (erotica).
**Nox, Abraham R.** *Bloodfellow 1: Separation.* Philadelphia: Xlibris, 2000.
————. *Bloodfellow 2: Transformation.* Philadelphia: Xlibris, 2000.
**Noyes, Deborah.** *It's Vladimir!* New York: Cavendish Children's Books, 2001 (juvenile).
**Nyarlathotep, Frater.** *Ardeth: The Made Vampire.* Morrisville, NC: Lulu.com, 2006.
**Nyman, Gregory.** "Confession." *Dead of Night 3,* Fall 1989.
————. "Respects." *The Vampire's Crypt 6,* Fall 1992.
**Oates, Joyce Carol.** *Bellefleur.* Franklin Center, PA: Franklin Library, 1980.
————. "The Vampire." *Murder and Obsession.* New York: Delacorte, 1999.
**O'Brien, Fitz-James.** "What Was It? A Mystery." *Harper's New Monthly Magazine,* March 1859.
**O'Connor, William.** *Three Pillars.* Clarkston, GA: White Wolf, 1997.
**Odom, Mel.** *Unnatural Selection (Buffy the Vampire Slayer).* Riverside, NJ: Simon Spotlight Entertainment, 1999.
————. *Redemption (Angel).* New York: Pocket Books, 2000.
————. *Bruja (Angel).* New York: Pocket Books, 2001.
————. *Revenant (Buffy the Vampire Slayer).* Riverside, NJ: Simon Spotlight Entertainment, 2001.
————. *Crossings (Buffy the Vampire Slayer).* Riverside, NJ: Simon Spotlight Entertainment, 2002.
————. *Image (Angel).* New York: Pocket Books, 2002.
————. *Cursed (Buffy the Vampire Slayer/Angel).* New York: Simon Pulse, 2003.
**Offen, Jody.** *Garden of Stones.* Frederick, MD: PublishAmerica, 2004.
————. *To Love a Vampire.* Frederick, MD: PublishAmerica, 2004.
————. *To Love a Vampire: Book 2.* Frederick, MD: PublishAmerica, 2005.
**O'Grady, Leslie.** *The Grateful Undead.* Pride's Crossing, MA: Larcom, 2002.
**O'Halloran, Shane.** *Green Trees.* Frederick, MD: PublishAmerica, 2003.
**O'Keefe, M. Timothy.** "Blood Money." *The London Mystery Selection.* London: Norman Kark.
**Oleck, Jack.** *The Vault of Horror.* New York: Bantam, 1973.
**Oliver, Martin.** *Attack of the Vampire.* London: Andre Deutsch Children's Books, 1993 (juvenile).
**Oliver, Sherry.** *Mandrake.* London: Jarrolds, 1929.
**Olson, Paul F.** *Night Prophets.* New York: Onyx, 1989.
**Oppel, Kenneth.** *Silverwing.* New York: Aladdin Paperbacks, 1999 (juvenile).
————. *Sunwing.* New York: Simon & Schuster, 2000 (juvenile).
————. *Firewing.* New York: Simon & Schuster, 2003 (juvenile).
**Orloff, Erica.** *Urban Legend.* Toronto: Silhouette Bombshell, 2004.
————. *Blood Son.* Toronto: Silhouette Nocturne, 2007.
**O'Rourke, Thompson.** "Blood Moon." *Dracula Lives,* May 1974.
**Orsini, Doreen.** *Hunting Diana.* Surprise, AZ: Triskelion, 2007.
**Osburn, Jesse.** "Peppermint Kisses." In *Shadows 6.* New York: Doubleday, 1983.
**O'Shea, Patti.** *Through a Crimson Veil.* New York: Love Spell, 2005.
**Oshii, Mamoru.** *Blood: The Last Vampire: Night of the Beasts.* Milwaukie, OR: DH, 2005.
**O'Sullivan, Vincent.** "Will." In *The Green Willow.* London: Leonard Smithers, 1899.
————. "Verschoyles House." In *Human Affairs.* London: David Nutt, 1907.
**Otfinoski, Steven.** *Village of the Vampires.* Chicago: Children's Press, 1979 (juvenile).
**Otter, Mark.** "Dance of Dawn." *Moonbroth 17,* 1974.

Ouglie, Archie E. *Bloody Kisses: The Trials and Tribulations of Anton the Vampire.* Philadelphia: Xlibris, 2001.

Overman, Ben, and Mary Overman. *Ungentled Darkness.* Booklocker.com, 2002.

Owen, Dean. *The Brides of Dracula.* Derby, CT: Monarch, 1960.

Owen, Frank. "The Tinkle of the Camel's Bell." *Weird Tales,* December 1928.

———. "Monk's Blood." In *The Porcelain Magician.* New York: Gnome, 1949.

Owens, Thomas. "Blood Moon." *Whispers,* October 1979.

Oz, Emily. "Model Behavior." In *The Longest Night Vol. 1 (Angel).* New York: Pocket Books, 2002.

Pacione, Nickolaus A. "Among Shadows." In *Collectives in a Forsaken Landscape.* Morrisville, NC: Lulu.com, 2004.

Pacione, Nickolaus A., and Barbara Marjanovic. *House of Spiders 3.* NSP Books, 2007.

Packard, Edward. *Vampire Invaders (Choose Your Own Adventure #118).* New York: Bantam, 1991 (juvenile).

———. *Biting for Blood (Choose Your Own Nightmare #7).* New York: Bantam, 1997 (juvenile).

Page, Gerald W. "The Tree." *Magazine of Horror,* August 1965.

———. "Thirst." *Witchcraft and Sorcery 7,* 1972.

Page, Norvell. "They Drink Blood." *Dime Mystery Stories,* August 1934.

Page, Sharon. "Midnight Man." In *Wild Nights.* New York: Aphrodisia, 2006.

———. *Blood Red.* New York: Aphrodisia, 2007.

Painter, Sally. *All I Need.* Akron, OH: Ellora's Cave, 2005 (erotica).

———. *Last Resort.* Akron, OH: Ellora's Cave, 2007 (erotica).

Painton, Fred C. "Vampire Meat." *Doctor Death,* April 1935.

Palmer, Andrew. "The Vampire's Fangs Were Red with My Woman's Blood." *Adventures in Horror,* February 1971.

Palwick, Susan. "Ever After." *Isaac Asimov's Science Fiction Magazine,* November 1987.

Pantaleo, Jack. *Mother Julian and the Gentle Vampire.* Roseville, CA: Dry Bone, 2000.

Panzer, Lance. *Vampire Seductress.* CrossroadsPub.com, 2001.

Papineau, Lucie. *Gulp!, Baby Vampire.* Quebec, Canada: Heritage Editions, 1999 (juvenile).

Paragon, John. *Elvira: Transylvania 90210.* New York: Boulevard Books, 1996.

———. *Elvira 2: Camp Vamp.* New York: Boulevard Books, 1997.

———. *Elvira 3: The Boy Who Cried Werewolf.* New York: Boulevard Books, 1998.

Parker, Barbara. "A Fan to the End." *Dead of Night 2,* July 1989.

———. "The Tribunal." *Dead of Night 3,* Fall 1989.

Parker, Lara. *Dark Shadows: Angelique's Descent.* New York: HarperEntertainment, 1998.

———. *Dark Shadows: The Salem Branch.* New York: Tor, 2006.

Parker, Percy Spurlark. "The Vampire Man." *Mike Shane Mystery Magazine,* November 1980.

Parks, Lydia. *All Night Long.* Garibaldi Highlands, BC, Canada: eXtasy Books, 2003 (erotica).

———. *Dark Desires.* Garibaldi Highlands, BC, Canada: eXtasy Books, 2003 (erotica).

———. *A New Year's Bite.* Garibaldi Highlands, BC, Canada: eXtasy Books, 2003 (erotica).

———. "Novella." In *Blood Bonds.* Garibaldi Highlands, BC, Canada: eXtasy Books, 2003 (erotica).

———. *The Truth about Vampires.* Garibaldi Highlands, BC, Canada: eXtasy Books, 2004 (erotica).

Parry, Dennis, and H. M. Chapman. *The Bishop's Move.* London: Robert Hale, 1938.

Parry, Michael. *Countess Dracula.* London: Sphere, 1971.

———. *The Rivals of Dracula.* London: Corgi, 1977.

Partridge, Norman. "Apotropaics." *Cemetary Dance,* Winter 1992.

———. "Do Not Hasten to Bid Me Adieu." In *Love in Vein.* New York: Harper-Collins, 1994 (erotica).

Pascal, Francine. *Dance of Death (Sweet Valley High #127).* New York: Bantam, 1996 (juvenile).

Passarella, John. *Ghoul Trouble (Buffy the Vampire Slayer).* New York: Pocket Books, 2000.

———. *Avatar (Angel).* New York: Pocket Books, 2001.

———. *Monolith (Buffy the Vampire Slayer).* New York: Simon Spotlight, 2004.

Patrick, David A. *Nero Demare and the Legend of the Vampire.* Lincoln, NE: iUniverse, 2007 (juvenile).

Patrick, James. "The Provender." *The Vampire Journal 4,* 1988.

Patrick, Susan M. "In the Sorcerer's Garden." *Witchcraft and Sorcery 7,* 1972.

Patterson, Kathleen J. "The Abbot." In *Ghosts and Scholars 12.* Chester, England: Haunted Library, 1990.

Patton, Linda. "Over and Done." *Screem 3,* October 1991.

Paul, F. W. *The Orgy at Madame Dracula's.* New York: Lancer Books, 1968.

Paulding, James Kirke. "The Vroucalacas: A Tale." *Graham's Magazine,* June 1846.

Pauley, Kimberly. *Sucks to Be Me: The All True Confessions of Mina Hamilton, Teen Vampire (Maybe).* Renton, WA: Mirrorstone, 2008 (juvenile).

Paulsen, Gary. *Amos and the Vampire (Culpepper Adventures #26).* New York: Yearling, 1996 (juvenile).

Peel, John. *The Last Drop.* New York: Pocket Books, 1995 (juvenile).

Pelcher, Anthony. "Vampires of Venus." *Astounding Stories of Super-Science,* April 1930.

Pendarves, G. G. "The Eight Green Man." *Weird Tales,* March 1928.

———. "The Withered Heart." *Weird Tales,* November 1939.

Pendelton, Casey. "High Heels and Bloodsuckers." In *Vamprotica 2005.* Chippewa, 2005 (erotica).

Penrose, Valentine. *The Bloody Countess.* London: Calder & Boyers, 1970.

Perez, Dan. "Behind Enemy Lines." In *Under the Fang.* New York: Pocket Books, 1991.

Perkins, Muriel. "Eucharist." *Children of the Night Coven Journal 4,* 1990.

Persons, Dan. "The Better Feast." *Prisoners of the Night 3,* 1989.

Perucho, Joan. *Natural History.* New York: Alfred A. Knopf, 1988.

Peters, Othello. "Experiment." *Moonbroth 5,* 1972.

Peters, Roman. *Vampire World.* Lincoln, NE: iUniverse, 2006.

Petersen, Gail. *The Making of a Monster.* New York: Dell Abyss, 1993.

Peterson, Margaret. *Moonflowers.* London: Hutchinson, 1926.

Petrey, Susan C. "Spareen Among the Tartars." *The Magazine of Fantasy & Science Fiction,* September 1979.

———. "Spareen Among the Cossacks." *The Magazine of Fantasy & Science Fiction,* May 1981.

———. "The Healer's Touch." *The Magazine of Fantasy & Science Fiction,* February 1982.

———. "Leechcraft." *The Magazine of Fantasy & Science Fiction*, May 1982.

———. "Small Changes." *The Magazine of Fantasy & Science Fiction*, February 1983.

———. "Spareen and Old Turk." *The Magazine of Fantasy & Science Fiction*, August 1983.

Phelan, Susan. *The Cure: The Blood Tapestry*. Akron, OH: Cerridwen, 2006.

Philbrick, W. R. "The Dark Rising." In *The Ultimate Dracula*. New York: Dell, 1991.

———. "The Cure." In *Dracula: Prince of Darkness*. New York: DAW, 1992.

Phillips, Mike. *Blood Rare*. London: Michael Joseph, 1963.

Phillips, Rog. "Vampire of the Deep." *Amazing Stories*, May 1951.

Phoenix, Adrian. "Sacrament." In *Embracing the Dark*. Boston: Alyson, 1991.

———. *A Rush of Wings*. New York: Pocket Books, 2008.

Piasecki, Jerry. *Teacher Vic Is a Vampire . . . Retired*. New York: Skylark, 1995 (juvenile).

Pickens, Michael. "The Adamson Family and Friends." *Space and Time*, 1989.

Pierce, Diana J. *An Uncommon Valentine*. Charleston, SC: BookSurge, 2006.

Pierce, Earl. "Doom of the House of Duryea." *Weird Tales*, October 1936.

Pierce, Meredith Ann. *The Dark Angel*. New York: Little, Brown, 1982 (juvenile).

———. *A Gathering of Gargoyles (The Darkangel Trilogy Book 2)*. Boston: Little, Brown, 1984 (juvenile).

Pierce, Racheal. *Kiss of the Sun*. Phaze Books, 2007 (erotica).

Pierson, Roxana. "The Price of the Gods." In *Sword and Sorceress IX*. New York: DAW, 1992.

Pike, Christopher. *The Season of Passage*. New York: Tor, 1992 (juvenile).

———. *The Last Vampire*. London: Hodder Children's Book, 1994 (juvenile).

———. *The Last Vampire 2: Black Blood*. London: Hodder Children's Book, 1994 (juvenile).

———. *The Last Vampire 3: Red Dice*. London: Hodder Children's Book, 1995 (juvenile).

———. *The Last Vampire 4: Phantom*. London: Hodder Children's Book, 1996 (juvenile).

———. *The Last Vampire 5: Evil Thirst*. London: Hodder Children's Book, 1997 (juvenile).

———. *The Last Vampire 6: Creatures of Forever*. London: Hodder Children's Books, 1997 (juvenile).

———. *Night of the Vampire: Spooksville #19*. New York: Aladdin, 1997 (juvenile).

Pillow, Michelle M. *The Jaded Hunter*. Lake Park, GA: New Concepts, 2004 (erotica).

———. *Redeemer of Shadows: The Tribes of the Vampires*. Lake Park, GA: New Concepts, 2004 (erotica).

Pine, T. H. *Dawn of the Blood Moon: A Vampire's Tale*. Creation Books, 1999.

Pineiro, Caridad. *Darkness Calls: The Calling #1*. Toronto: Silhouette, 2004.

———. *Danger Calls: The Calling #2*. Toronto: Silhouette, 2005.

———. *Temptation Calls: The Calling #3*. Toronto: Silhouette, 2005.

———. *Death Calls: The Calling #4*. Toronto: Silhouette, 2006.

———. *Devotion Calls: The Calling #5*. Toronto: Silhouette, 2007.

———. *Blood Calls: The Calling #6*. Toronto: Silhouette, 2007.

———. "Fate Calls." In *Holiday with a Vampire*. Toronto: Silhouette, 2007.

Pinkwater, Daniel Manus. *The Moosepire*. Boston: Little, Brown, 1986 (juvenile).

———. *Wempire*. New York: Macmillan, 1991 (juvenile).

Piper, Danielle. "The Brief Romance of Augustine." *Loyalists of the Vampire Realm Newsletter*, October 1991.

**Pitt, Ingrid.** "Hisako San." In *The Mammoth Book of Vampire Stories by Women*. New York: Carroll & Graf, 2001.

**Pizarnik, Alejandra.** "The Bloody Countess." In *Other Fires*. New York: Clarkson N. Potter, 1986.

**Platt, Kin.** *Dracula, Go Home*. Danbury, CT: Franklin Watts, 1979 (juvenile).

**Poe, Edgar Allan.** "Berenice." *Southern Literary Messenger*, March 1835.

———. "Morella." *Southern Literary Messenger*, April 1835.

———. "Ligea." *American Museum*, September 1838.

———. "The Fall of the House of Usher." *Burton's Gentleman's Magazine*, September 1839.

———. "Life in Death." *Graham's Magazine*, April 1842.

**Poff, Christy.** *Dante's Flame: Eyes of Darkness #1*. Swanbeauty Publications, 2004.

———. *Love Hurts: Eyes of Darkness #3*. Casper, WY: Whiskey Creek, 2005.

———. "Scarlet Love." In *War in Darkness*. Casper, WY: Whiskey Creek, 2006.

**Poli, Evelyn O.** "Blood Donor." *Count Dracula Fan Club Newsletter*.

**Polidori, John William.** "The Vampyre." *The New Monthly Magazine*, April 1819.

**Ponce, Sean.** "I Know Who You Are." *Bloodreams 3*, January 1992.

**Popescu, Petru.** *In Hot Blood*. New York: Fawcett, 1986.

**Poplaff, Michelle.** *Roses Are Dread, Violets Are Boo: A Vampire Valentine Story*. New York: Little Apple, 2002 (juvenile).

**Popp, Robin T.** *Out of the Night: Night Slayer #1*. New York: Warner, 2005.

———. *Seduced by the Night: Night Slayer #2*. New York: Warner, 2006.

———. *The Darkening: Immortals #1*. New York: Leisure Books, 2007.

———. *Lord of the Night*. New York: Grand Central, 2007.

———. *Tempted in the Night: Night Slayer #3*. New York: Warner, 2007.

**Porges, Arthur.** "Mop-Up." *The Magazine of Fantasy & Science Fiction*, July 1953.

———. The Arrogant Vampire." *Fantastic*, May 1961.

**Porter, Barry.** *Dark Souls*. New York: Zebra, 1989.

**Povhe, Tim.** "One Night at Rosie's Cantina." *Onyx 2*, November 1992.

**Powell, Denise.** "Night Flight." *Vampire Quarterly 8*, May 1987.

**Power, F. H.** "The Electric Vampire." *London Magazine*, October 1910.

**Powers, Mae.** "Vampyrus." In *Vamprotica 2005*. Chippewa, 2005 (erotica).

**Powers, Tim.** *Dinner at Deviant's Palace*. New York: Berkley, 1985.

———. *The Stress of Her Regard*. Lynbrook, NY: Charnel House, 1989.

**Powling, Chris.** *Dracula in Sunlight*. London: Blackie Children's Books, 1990 (juvenile).

**Poyer, D. C.** "The Report of the All-Union Committee on Recent Rumors Concerning the Moldavian SSR." *Analog*, December 1987.

**Pozzessere, Heather Graham.** *This Rough Magic*. Toronto: Silhouette Intimate Moments, 1988.

**Praed, Mrs. Campbell.** *The Soul of the Countess Adrian*. London: Trischler, 1891.

**Pratchett, Terry.** *Carpe Jugulum*. London: Doubleday, 1998.

**Prebler, Christine.** *Vampires at the Opera*. L & L Dreamspell, 2007.

**Preiss, Byron.** *The Vampire State Building*. New York: Skylark, 1992.

**Prest, Thomas Preskett.** "The Storm Visitor." In *The Midnight People*. London: Leslie Frewin Publishing, 1968.

**Prestin, Eliza.** "Ely." *Book of Shadows 1*, 1990.

**Preston, Arthur C. A.** *A Royal Revenge*. London: Hutchinson, 1899.

**Preston, Guy.** "The Inn." In *The "Not at Night" Omnibus*. London: Selwyn and Blount, 1925.

**Price, Daimon.** *Embrace of the Sun*. Palo Alto, CA: Fultus, 2004.

Price, E. Hoffman. "Spanish Vampire." *Weird Tales,* September 1939.

Pridgeon, William. *Night of the Dragon's Blood.* Palatka, FL: Hodge & Braddock, 1997.

Proctor, Judith. "Dear Mr. Bernard Shaw." In *Dracula in London.* New York: Ace, 2001.

Pronzini, Bill. "I, Vampire." *Coven 13,* March 1970.

———. "Thirst." *The Magazine of Fantasy & Science Fiction,* November 1973.

Pronzini, Bill, and Barry N. Malzberg. "Opening a Vein." In *Shadows 3.* New York: Doubleday, 1980.

Proulx, Lisa V. *Puncture.* Frederick, MD: PublishAmerica, 2004.

Prout, Mearle. "The House of the Worm." *Weird Tales,* October 1933.

Ptacek, Kathryn. *Shadow Eyes.* New York: Tor, 1984.

———. *Blood Autumn.* New York: Tor, 1985.

———. *In Silence Sealed.* New York: Tor, 1988.

Pugmire, W. H. "The Boy with the Bloodstained Mouth." In *Nocturne.* Secundus, 1989.

———. "The Isolated Dead." *Sozoryoku 2,* Summer 1991.

Pugmire, William. "Delicious Antique Whore." In *Love in Vein.* New York: Harper-Collins, 1994 (erotica).

Pullinger, Kate. *Where Does the Kissing End?* London: Serpent's Tail, 1995.

Pumilia, Joseph. "Forever Stand the Stones." In *Jack the Knife: Tales of Jack the Ripper.* St. Albans: Mayflower, 1975.

Punshon, E. R. "The Living Stone." *Cornhill Magazine,* September 1939.

Purtill, Richard R. "Something in the Blood." *The Magazine of Fantasy & Science Fiction,* August 1986.

Quednau, Walter. "The Gates." *Weird Tales,* April 1968.

Quijano, Mary L. *Bloodmaster.* New York: Windsor, 1989.

Quiller-Couch, A. T. "Old Aeson." *The Speaker,* February 1890.

———. "The Legend of Sir Dinar." In *Wandering Heath.* London: Cassell, 1895.

Quinn, December. *Blood Will Tell.* Akron, OH: Ellora's Cave, 2007 (erotica).

Quinn, Devyn. *Flesh and the Devil.* New York: Kensington Aphrodisia, 2007 (erotica).

———. *Sins of the Flesh.* New York: Kensington Aphrodisia, 2007 (erotica).

Quinn, Seabury. "The Blood-Flower." *Weird Tales,* March 1927.

———. "The Man Who Cast No Shadows." *Weird Tales,* March 1927.

———. "Restless Souls." *Weird Tales,* October 1928.

———. "The Silver Countess." *Weird Tales,* October 1929.

———. "Children of Ubasti." *Weird Tales,* December 1929.

———. "Daughter of the Moonlight." *Weird Tales,* August 1930.

———. "Malay Horror." *Weird Tales,* September 1933.

———. "The Black Orchid." *Weird Tales,* August 1935.

———. "A Rival from the Grave." *Weird Tales,* January 1936.

———. "Witch-House." *Weird Tales,* November 1936.

———. "Body and Soul." *Weird Tales,* January 1937.

———. "Children of the Bat." *Weird Tales,* January 1937.

———. "Pledged to the Dead." *Weird Tales,* October 1937.

———. "The Poltergeist of Swan Upping." *Weird Tales,* February 1939.

———. "Uncanonized." *Weird Tales,* November 1939.

———. "Mortman." *Weird Tales,* January 1940.

———. "Mrs. Pellington Assists." *Weird Tales,* September 1947.

———. "Vampire Kith & Kin." *Weird Tales,* May 1949.

———. "Dark O' the Moon." *Weird Tales,* July 1949.

Quiroga, Horacio. "The Feather Pillow." In *Tales of Love, Madness and Death,* 1907.

Ragan, Jacie. "Orientation." *Dead of Night 5,* April 1990.

Raget, Bill. "Renfield or Dining at the Bug House." In *Dracula in London.* New York: Ace, 2001.

Raisor, Gary. *Less Than Human.* Woodstock, GA: Overlook Connection, 1992.

Raleigh, Deborah. *My Lord Eternity.* New York: Zebra, 2003.

———. *My Lord Immortality.* New York: Zebra, 2003.

———. *My Lord Vampire.* New York: Zebra, 2003.

———. "To Tame the Beast." In *Highland Vampire.* New York: Brava, 2005.

Ramsland, Katherine. "Path of Least Resistance." *The Vampire Journal 4,* 1988.

———. "Reverse Chain." *Dead of Night 4,* January 1990.

———. *The Heat Seekers.* New York: Pinnacle, 2002.

———. *The Blood Hunters.* New York: Pinnacle, 2004.

Rand, William. *That Way Lies Madness.* Lincoln, NE: Writer's Club Press, 2000.

Randolphe, Arabella. *The Vampire Tapes.* New York: Berkley Medallion, 1977.

Ranney, Karen. "Dance in the Dark." In *After Midnight.* New York: Zebra, 1998.

Ransom, Daniel. "Night Cries." In *Dracula: Prince of Darkness.* New York: DAW, 1992.

———. "Valentine for a Vampire." In *14 Vicious Valentines.* New York: Avon, 1988.

Rardin, Jennifer. *Once Bitten, Twice Shy, Jaz Parks #1.* New York: Orbit, 2007.

———. *Another One Bites the Dust, Jaz Parks #2.* New York: Orbit, 2007.

———. *Biting the Bullet: Jaz Parks #3.* New York: Orbit, 2008.

———. *Bitten to Death: Jaz Parks #4.* New York: Orbit, 2008.

Rasey, Patricia A. *Deadly Obsession.* Dark Star Publications, 1999.

———. *The Hour Before Dawn.* Amherst Junction, WI: Hard Shell Word Factory, 2003.

Rath, Tina. "Miss Massingberd and the Vampire." *Women's Realm,* January 1986.

Rathbone, Wendy. "Vampire Weather." *Prisoners of the Night 1,* 1987.

———. "A Vampire's Madness." *Prisoners of the Night 2,* 1988.

———. "Waking the Vampire." *Prisoners of the Night 2,* 1988.

———. "Love and Forgiveness." *Prisoners of the Night 3,* 1989.

———. "Hello Lilianne." *Prisoners of the Night 4,* 1990.

———. "Nightcast." *Prisoners of the Night 4,* 1990.

———. "Obligation." *Prisoners of the Night 4,* 1990.

———. "The Host." *Prisoners of the Night 5,* 1991.

———. "Partner Immortalis." *Prisoners of the Night 6,* 1992.

Ratnett, Michael. *Dracula Steps Out.* London: Orchard Books, 1998 (juvenile).

Rattray, Joyce M. "Obligation." *Prisoners of the Night 4,* 1990.

Raven, Simon. *Doctors Wear Scarlet.* London: Anthony Blond, 1960.

Ray, Ron. *The Vampire's Vacation.* New York: Random House, 2004.

Raye, Kimberly. *Dead End Dating: A Novel of Vampire Love.* New York: Ivy Books, 2006.

———. *Dead and Dateless: Dead End Dating #2.* New York: Ballantine, 2007.

———. *Dead Sexy.* Toronto: Harlequin Blaze, 2007.

———. *Your Coffin or Mine? Dead End Dating #3.* New York: Ballantine, 2007.

———. *Just One Bite: Dead End Dating #4.* New York: Ballantine, 2008.

Reamy, Tom. "The Detweiler Boy." *The Magazine of Fantasy & Science Fiction,* April 1977.

Rebara, Altheda. "Life after Life-Force." *Vampire Quarterly 1,* August 1985.

Rechy, John. *The Vampires.* New York: Grove, 1973.

Reck, Katherine. "Black Rose, Black Violet." *After Hours,* Summer 1992.

Redd, David. "The Old Man of Munnington." *Isaac Asimov's Science Fiction Magazine,* 1993.

Redding, Judith M. "Unexpurgated Notes from a Homicide Case File." In *Night Bites: Vampire Stories by Women.* Seattle, WA: Seal, 1996.

Reed, Rick R. *In the Blood.* Quest, 2007.

Reed, Shelby. *Midnight Rose.* Akron, OH: Ellora's Cave, 2005 (erotica).

Reed, Vance. "Red Pencil." *Dead of Night 4,* January 1990.

Reedman, Janet P. "Exodus." *Good Guys Wear Fangs 1,* May 1992.

Rees, Douglas. *Vampire High.* New York: Delacorte, 2003 (juvenile).

Reeve, Arthur B. *The Exploits of Elaine.* New York: Hearst's, 1915.

Reeve-Stevens, Garfield. *Bloodshift.* Toronto: Virgo, 1981.

Reeve-Stevens, Garfield, and Judith Reeve-Stevens. *Nightfeeder.* New York: Roc, 1991.

Reeves, Peter. "Web." In *Chosen Haunts.* North Riverside, IL: Pandora, 1981.

Regan, Dian Curtis. *The Vampire Who Came for Christmas.* New York: Apple, 1994 (juvenile).

———. *Fangs-Giving.* New York: Apple, 1997 (juvenile).

Rehan, Sathanas, and Viktor Vesperto. "Dracula 2000." *Famous Monsters,* May 1969.

Reid, Moira. *Sunlight: The Vampire Oracle.* Cobblestone, 2008.

Reidy, Tom. "Weedkiller." *The Vampire's Crypt 3,* Spring 1991.

Reines, Kathryn. *The Kiss.* New York: Avon, 1996.

Reinke, Sara. *Dark Thirst.* New York: Zebra, 2007.

———. *Dark Hunger.* New York: Zebra, 2008.

Reiss, Eric. "The Dangers of a One Night Stand in the 90's." *Vampire Junction 1,* 1991.

Reitz, Bonnie. "Night Life." *Book of Shadows 4,* 1992.

Reliford, Ardella. *Lacroix.* Sea-J-Press, 2000.

Relling, William, Jr. "Blood." *Night Cry,* Spring 1987.

———. "Night Games." *Cemetary Dance 2,* June 1989.

———. "The Obsession." In *The Bradbury Chronicles.* New York: Penguin, 1991.

Resch, Katherine. "Kitt's Choice." *World of Dark Shadows,* November 1975 and January 1976.

———. "Edge." In *Decades.* Santa Clara, CA: Pentagram, 1977.

Resch, Kathleen. "The Dark." In *New Terrors 2.* London: Pan, 1980.

Resnick, Mike. "A Little Night Music." In *The Ultimate Dracula.* New York: Dell, 1991.

———. *Stalking the Vampire: A Fable of Twilight.* Pyr, 2008.

Reventlow, Ernst Zu. *The Vampire of the Continent.* Kessinger, 2005.

Reynolds, Kay. "Loose Change." *Prisoners of the Night 5,* 1991.

Reynolds, Mack. "Dead End." In *Microcosmic Tales.* New York: Taplinger, 1980.

Rhea, Tina. "Alteration." *Prisoners of the Night 1,* 1987.

———. "Darkness." *Prisoners of the Night 1,* 1987.

———. "The First Time Ever." *Prisoners of the Night 1,* 1987.

———. "Of Dark and Bright." *Prisoners of the Night 1,* 1987.

———. "The Adventure of the Gentleman in Black." *The Holmesian Federation 8,* 1991.

———. "Nothing Like the Sun." *Heart's Blood 1,* May 1992.

Rhodes, Daniel. *The Kiss of Death.* New York: Tor, 1990.

**Rhodes, Natasha.** *Blade: Trinity.* Nottingham, UK: Games Workshop, 2004 (movie tie-in).

———. *Dante's Girl.* Nottingham, UK: Solaris, 2007.

**Riccardo, Martin V.** "A Message to Mortals." *Children of the Night Coven Journal 4,* 1990.

**Rice, Anne.** *Interview with the Vampire.* New York: Alfred A. Knopf, 1976.

———. "The Master of Rampling Gate." *Redbook,* February 1984.

———. *The Vampire Lestat.* New York: Alfred A. Knopf, 1985.

———. *The Queen of the Damned.* New York: Alfred A. Knopf, 1988.

———. *The Tale of the Body Thief.* New York: Alfred A. Knopf, 1992.

———. *Memnoch the Devil.* New York: Alfred A. Knopf, 1995.

———. *Pandora.* New York: Alfred A. Knopf, 1998.

———. *The Vampire Armand.* New York: Alfred A. Knopf, 1998.

———. *Vittorio the Vampire.* New York: Alfred A. Knopf, 1999.

———. *Merrick.* New York: Alfred A. Knopf, 2000.

———. *Blood and Gold.* New York: Alfred A. Knopf, 2001.

———. *Blackwood Farm.* New York: Alfred A. Knopf, 2002.

———. *Blood Canticle.* New York: Alfred A. Knopf, 2003.

**Rice, Bebe Faas.** *The Vampire (Doomsday Mall #5).* New York: Skylark, 1996 (juvenile).

**Rice, Doug.** *Blood of Mugwump: A Tiresian Tale of Incest.* Black Ice Books, 1996.

**Rice, Jeff.** *The Night Stalker.* New York: Pocket Books, 1973.

**Richards, Kel.** *The Vampire Serpent (Sherlock Holmes Tales of Terror #3).* Australia: Beacon Communications, 1997.

**Richardson, A. L.** *Thirst for Love.* Lake Park, GA: New Concepts, 2003.

**Richardson, Frederick Louis.** *Black Rush.* Washington, D.C.: DreaMerchant, 2003.

**Richardson, Nikki Key.** *Vampires of Oz.* Philadelphia: Xlibris, 2000.

**Richerson, Carrie.** "A Dying Breed." *The Magazine of Fantasy & Science Fiction,* October–November 1992.

**Rickert, Ken.** "We've Been Expecting You." *Castle Rock,* December 1987/January 1988.

**Ringo, Renardo.** *Prodigy Vampire.* Lincoln, NE: iUniverse, 2007.

**Ritchie, Jack.** "Kid Cardula." *Alfred Hitchcock's Mystery Magazine,* June 1976.

———. "The Cardula Detective Agency." *Alfred Hitchcock's Mystery Magazine,* March 1977.

———. "Cardula to the Rescue." *Alfred Hitchcock's Mystery Magazine,* December 1977.

———. "Cardula and the Kleptomaniac." *Alfred Hitchcock's Mystery Magazine,* April 1978.

———. "Cardula's Revenge." *Alfred Hitchcock's Mystery Magazine,* November 1978.

———. "The Return of Cardula." *Alfred Hitchcock's Mystery Magazine,* February 3, 1982.

———. "Cardula and the Locked Rooms." *Alfred Hitchcock's Mystery Magazine,* March 3, 1982.

———. "Cardula and the Briefcase." *Mike Shayne Mystery Magazine,* June 1983.

**Rives, Amelie.** "The Ghost Garden." *Harper's Bazaar,* 1917.

**Roark, Sarah.** *Dark Ages: Ravnos.* Clarkston, GA: White Wolf, 2003.

**Roark, Sarah, and Dean Shomshak.** *Time of Thin Blood: Vampire the Masquerade.* Clarkston, GA: White Wolf, 1999.

**Robar, Serana.** *Braced 2 Bite.* New York: Penguin, 2006 (juvenile).

———. *Fangs 4 Freaks.* New York: Berkley, 2006 (juvenile).

**Robards, Karen.** "Sugar and Spice and. . . ." In *The Ultimate Dracula.* New York: Dell, 1991.

**Robbie.** "Time of Truth." In *Dyad: The Vampire Stories.* Poway, CA: Mkashef Enterprises, 1991.

**Robbing, David.** *Vampire Strike.* New York: Leisure Books, 1989.

**Robbins, Clement.** *Vampires of New York.* Self-published, 1831.

**Robers, Donald, Jr.** "Whispers Like the Falling Snow." *Night Mountains 6,* Winter 1991.

**Roberts, James P.** "The Moon Has Turned Red and I Cannot Sleep." *Elegia 2,* 1992.

**Roberts, Keith.** "The Scarlet Lady." *SF Impulse,* August 1966.

———. "Kaeti's Nights." *The Magazine of Fantasy & Science Fiction,* 1981.

**Roberts, Morley.** "The Blood Fetish." In *Midsummer Madness.* London: Eveleigh Nash, 1909.

**Roberts, Nora.** *Morrigan's Cross: The Circle Trilogy #1.* New York: Jove, 2006.

———. *Dance of the Gods: The Circle Trilogy #2.* New York: Jove, 2006.

———. *Valley of Silence: The Circle Trilogy #3.* New York: Jove, 2006.

**Roberts, P. J.** "The Dead of Night." *Nocturnal Extacy 2,* 1992.

**Robin, Marcy.** "Farewell Memories." In *Decades.* Santa Clara, CA: Pentagram, 1977.

———. "Premonition." In *Decades.* Santa Clara, CA: Pentagram, 1977.

———. "The Time for Grief." In *Decades.* Santa Clara, CA: Pentagram, 1977.

———. "Transition." In *Decades.* Santa Clara, CA: Pentagram, 1977.

———. "The Taste of Death." *World of Dark Shadows 9,* February 1977.

———. "In the Light of a Candle." *World of Dark Shadows,* October 1977.

———. "Purgatory." *World of Dark Shadows,* May 1978.

———. "Cursed." *World of Dark Shadows,* July 1978.

———. "Eternity Now." In *Dark Fires: Impressions from Dark Shadows.* Lawndale, CA: Phantom, 1980.

———. "The Final Truth." *World of Dark Shadows,* February 1980.

———. "Just Brushing Up, Ma'am." In *Die Laughing.* North Riverside, IL: Phoenix Publications, 1981.

———. "Shadowed Soul." In *Chosen Haunts.* North Riverside, IL: Pandora, 1981.

**Robins, Eden.** *Redemption (After Sundown).* Akron, OH: Cerridwen, 2006.

**Robinson, Philip.** "The Man-Eating Tree." In *Under the Punkah.* London: Sampson Low, 1881.

———. "The Last of the Vampires." *The Contemporary Review,* March 1893.

**Robinson, Sandra.** "Bathroom Guest." *The Vampire's Crypt 1,* 1989.

———. "Trick 'R Treat." *The Vampire's Crypt 4,* Fall 1991.

**Robinson, Spider.** "Pyotr's Story." *Analog,* October 12, 1981.

———. "The Immediate Family." *Analog,* January 1993.

**Robson, Ruthann.** "Women's Music." In *Night Bites: Vampire Stories by Women.* Seattle, WA: Seal, 1996.

**Rodman, Eric.** "The Insidious Invaders." *Super-Science Fiction,* October 1959.

**Rogers, Cameron.** *The Vampires: After Dark Series #21.* Melbourne, Australia: Lothian, 2000 (juvenile).

**Rogers, Wayne.** "Dracula's Brides." *Horror Stories,* February 1941.

**Rollin, Jean.** *Little Orphan Vampires.* London: Redemption Books, 1995.

**Rolls, B. A.** "Cholin of Camel." In *Sword and Sorceress V.* New York: DAW, 1988.

**Roman, Victor.** "Four Wooden Stakes." *Weird Tales,* February 1925.

Romeo, Melodie. *Vlad, a Novel*. Bloomington, IN: 1st Books Library, 2002.

Romero, George A., and Susanna Sparrow. *Martin*. New York: Stein & Day, 1977 (movie novelization).

Romkey, Michael. *I, Vampire*. New York: Fawcett, 1990.

———. *The Vampire Papers*. New York: Fawcett, 1994.

———. *The Vampire Princess*. New York: Fawcett, 1995.

———. *The Vampire Virus*. New York: Fawcett Gold Medal, 1997.

———. *Vampire Hunter*. New York: Fawcett Gold Medal, 1998.

———. *The London Vampire Panic*. New York: Ballantine, 2001.

———. *The Vampire's Violin*. New York: Del Rey, 2003.

———. *American Gothic*. New York: Random House, 2004.

Ronson, Mark. *Bloodthirst*. London: Century, 1979.

Rooke, Sebastian. *The Vampire Plagues I: London 1850*. New York: Scholastic, 2005 (juvenile).

———. *The Vampire Plagues II: Paris, 1850*. New York: Scholastic, 2005 (juvenile).

———. *The Vampire Plagues III: Mexico 1851*. New York: Scholastic, 2005 (juvenile).

Rooney, Anne. *Vampire Castle*. Saint Catharines, ON, Canada: Crabtree, 2008 (juvenile).

Roorie, Douglas Derek. "The Root." *Space and Time*, August 1972.

Rose, Jeanne. *Good Night, My Love*. Toronto: Silhouette Shadows, 1996.

Rosemoor, Patricia. *Hot Case*. Toronto: Silhouette Bombshell, 2004.

Rosemoor, Patricia, and Marc Paoletti. *The Last Vampire*. New York: Del Rey, 2008.

Rosen, Selina. "They Never Approve." *Marion Zimmer Bradley's Fantasy Magazine*, Spring 1991.

———. *The Host: The Host Series 1*. Alma, AR: Yard Dog Press, 1997.

———. *Fright-Eater: The Host Series 2*. Alma, AR: Yard Dog Press, 1998.

———. *Gang Approval: The Host Series 3*. Alma, AR: Yard Dog Press, 1999.

Rosenman, John B. "Future Shock." *The Vampire Journal 4*, 1988.

———. "A Sense of Vocation." *The Vampire Journal 4*, 1988.

Rosenquist, J. Wesley. "Return to Death." *Weird Tales*, January 1936.

———. "Horror in Space." *Super-Science Fiction*, February 1959.

———. "Creatures of Green Slime." *Super-Science Fiction*, June 1959.

Ross, Barbara. *The Mortal Indiscretion*. Frederick, MD: PublishAmerica, 2005.

Ross, Clarissa. *Secret of the Pale Lover*. New York: Lancer Books, 1969.

———. *The Corridors of Fear*. New York: Avon, 1971.

Ross, Laverne. *Night Travels of the Elvin Vampire*. Frederick, MD: PublishAmerica, 2003.

Ross, Marilyn. *Dark Shadows*. New York: Paperback Library, 1966.

———. *Victoria Winters (Dark Shadows 2)*. New York: Paperback Library, 1967.

———. *Strangers at Collins House (Dark Shadows 3)*. New York: Paperback Library, 1967.

———. *The Mystery of Collinwood (Dark Shadows 4)*. New York: Paperback Library, 1968.

———. *The Curse of Collinwood (Dark Shadows 5)*. New York: Paperback Library, 1968.

———. *Barnabas Collins (Dark Shadows 6)*. New York: Paperback Library, 1968.

———. *The Secret of Barnabas Collins (Dark Shadows 7)*. New York: Paperback Library, 1969.

———. *The Demon of Barnabas Collins (Dark Shadows 8)*. New York: Paperback Library, 1969.

————. *The Foe of Barnabas Collins (Dark Shadows 9)*. New York: Paperback Library, 1969.

————. *The Phantom and Barnabas Collins (Dark Shadows 10)*. New York: Paperback Library, 1969.

————. *Barnabas Collins vs. The Warlock (Dark Shadows 11)*. New York: Paperback Library, 1969.

————. *The Peril of Barnabas Collins (Dark Shadows 12)*. New York: Paperback Library, 1969.

————. *Barnabas Collins and the Mysterious Ghost (Dark Shadows 13)*. New York: Paperback Library, 1970.

————. *Barnabas Collins and Quentin's Demon (Dark Shadows 14)*. New York: Paperback Library, 1970.

————. *Barnabas Collins and the Gypsy Witch (Dark Shadows 15)*. New York: Paperback Library, 1970.

————. *Barnabas, Quentin and the Mummy's Curse (Dark Shadows 16)*. New York: Paperback Library, 1970.

————. *Barnabas, Quentin and the Avenging Ghost (Dark Shadows 17)*. New York: Paperback Library, 1970.

————. *Barnabas, Quentin and the Nightmare Assassin (Dark Shadows 18)*. New York: Paperback Library, 1970.

————. *Barnabas, Quentin and the Crystal Coffin (Dark Shadows 19)*. New York: Paperback Library, 1970.

————. *Barnabas, Quentin and the Witch's Curse (Dark Shadows 20)*. New York: Paperback Library, 1970.

————. *Barnabas, Quentin and the Haunted Cave (Dark Shadows 21)*. New York: Paperback Library, 1970.

————. *Barnabas, Quentin and the Frightened Bride (Dark Shadows 22)*. New York: Paperback Library, 1970.

————. *House of Dark Shadows*. New York: Paperback Library, 1970 (movie novelization).

————. *Barnabas, Quentin and the Scorpio Curse (Dark Shadows 23)*. New York: Paperback Library, 1970.

————. *Barnabas, Quentin and the Serpent (Dark Shadows 24)*. New York: Paperback Library, 1970.

————. *Barnabas, Quentin and the Magic Potion (Dark Shadows 25)*. New York: Paperback Library, 1971.

————. *Barnabas, Quentin and the Body Snatchers (Dark Shadows 26)*. New York: Paperback Library, 1971.

————. *Barnabas, Quentin and Dr. Jekyll's Son (Dark Shadows 27)*. New York: Paperback Library, 1971.

————. *Barnabas, Quentin and the Grave Robbers (Dark Shadows 28)*. New York: Paperback Library, 1971.

————. *Barnabas, Quentin and the Sea Ghost (Dark Shadows 29)*. New York: Paperback Library, 1971.

————. *Barnabas, Quentin and the Mad Magician (Dark Shadows 30)*. New York: Paperback Library, 1971.

————. *Barnabas, Quentin and the Hidden Tomb (Dark Shadows 31)*. New York: Paperback Library, 1971.

————. *Barnabas, Quentin and the Vampire Beauty (Dark Shadows 32)*. New York: Paperback Library, 1972.

———. *The Vampire Contessa: From the Journal of Jeremy Quentain*. New York: Pinnacle, 1974.

Ross, Rebecca. "Amid the Curse Goes On." *Moonbroth 7*, 1972.

Rossi, Mary Lynn. "Free Spirit." In *Die Laughing*. North Riverside, IL: Phoenix, 1981.

Roth, Mandy M. *Daughters of Darkness*. Lake Park, GA: New Concepts, 2004 (erotica).

———. *Valhalla: The Valkyrie's Beginnings*. Lake Park, GA: New Concepts, 2004 (erotica).

———. *Vampyre Productions: The Valkyrie #1*. Lake Park, GA: New Concepts, 2004 (erotica).

———. *The Enchantress*. Lake Park, GA: New Concepts, 2005 (erotica).

———. *Paranormal Payload: Project Exorcism #1*. Lake Park, GA: New Concepts, 2005.

———. *Force of Attraction: Project Exorcism #2*. Lake Park, GA: New Concepts, 2005.

———. *Wicked Lucidity*. Lake Park, GA: New Concepts, 2005.

Rothe, William B. "Ashes." In *Legends in Blood*. West Hollywood, CA: Fantaseas, 1991.

Rothman, Chuck. "Curse of the Undead." In *Vampires: A Collection of Original Stories*. New York: HarperCollins, 1991.

Rousseau, Victor. "A Cry from Beyond." *Strange Tales of Mystery and Terror*, September 1931.

Rowan, Victor. "Four Wooden Stakes." *Weird Tales*, February 1925.

Rowen, Michelle. *Bitten & Smitten: Immortality Bites #1*. New York: Warner Forever, 2006.

———. *Fanged and Fabulous: Immortality Bites #2*. New York: Warner Forever, 2007.

———. *Lady and the Vamp: Immortality Bites #3*. New York: Warner Forever, 2008.

Roy, Archie. *Devil in Darkness*. London: John Lang, 1978.

Roy, Ron. *The Vampire's Vacation (A to Z Mysteries)*. New York: Random House, 2004 (juvenile).

Roycraft, Jaye. *Double Image*. Hickory Corners, MI: ImaJinn Books, 2001.

———. *Afterimage*. Hickory Corners, MI: ImaJinn Books, 2002.

———. *Shadow Image*. Hickory Corners, MI: ImaJinn Books, 2002.

———. *Immortal Image*. Hickory Corners, MI: ImaJinn Books, 2003.

Royle, Nicholas. "Saxophone." In *Books of the Dead*. New York: Bantam, 1989.

———. "Mbo." In *The Mammoth Book of Dracula*. London: Robinson, 1997.

Rozanski, J. M. "The V-Plague." *Bloodreams 4*, April 1992.

Ruddy, John. *The Bargain*. New York: Knightsbridge, 1990.

Ruditis, Paul. "The Show Must Go On." In *How I Survived My Summer Vacation (Buffy the Vampire Slayer)*. New York: Pocket Books, 2000.

Rudorff, Raymond. *The Dracula Archives*. New York: Arbor House, 1971.

Ruggiero, Tony. *Team of Darkness*. Amherst Junction, WV: Hard Shell Word Factory, 2002.

Rusch, Kristine Kathryn. "Children of the Night." In *The Ultimate Dracula*. New York: Dell, 1991.

———. *Sins of the Blood*. New York: Dell Abyss, 1994.

Rushton, Jesse. *Love Letters from a Vampire*. Frederick, MD: PublishAmerica, 2004.

Russ, Joanna. "My Dear Emily." *The Magazine of Fantasy & Science Fiction*, July 1962.

———. "There Is Another Shore, You Know, Upon the Other Side." *The Magazine of Fantasy & Science Fiction*, September 1963.

———. "The New Men." *The Magazine of Fantasy & Science Fiction*, February 1966.

**Russe, Savannah.** *Beyond the Pale: The Darkwing Chronicles Book One*. New York: Signet, 2005.

———. *Past Redemption: The Darkwing Chronicles Book Two*. New York: Signet, 2006.

———. *Beneath the Skin: The Darkwing Chronicles Book Three*. New York: Signet, 2007.

———. *In the Blood: The Darkwing Chronicles Book Four*. New York: Signet, 2007.

———. *Under Darkness: The Darkwing Chronicles Book Five*. New York: Signet, 2008.

**Russell, Eric Frank.** "Sinister Barrier." *Unknown*, March 1939.

———. "Vampire from the Void." *Fantasy*, 1939.

**Russell, Ray.** "The Exploits of Argo." *Rogue*, April 1961.

———. "Sagitarius." *Playboy*, March 1962.

———. "Comet Wine." *Playboy*, March 1967.

———. "Sanguinarius." In *Unholy Trinity*. New York: Bantam, 1967.

———. "Reflections." In *Masques 3*. New York: St. Martin's, 1989.

**Russell, Robert Leonard.** "The Amulet of Hell." *Weird Tales*, October 1935.

**Russo, Arlene.** *Vampire Nation*. London: John Blake, 2005.

**Russo, John.** *The Awakening*. New York: Pocket Books, 1983.

**Russo, Patricia.** "Night Game." *Count Dracula Fan Club Newsletter*, Autumn 1984.

———. "The Bottler." *Haunts 1*, October 1984.

———. "To Be Worthy." *The Vampire Journal 1*, Summer 1985.

**Rutherford, Michael.** "Knights of Darkness, Knight of Light." *Weird Tales*, Spring 1990.

**Rutter, Owen.** "The Vampires of Tempassuk." In *Monsters, Monsters, Monsters*. New York: Franklin Watts, 1975.

**Ryan, Alan.** "Following the Way." In *Shadows 5*. New York: Doubleday, 1982.

———. "Onawa." In *Death*. Chicago: Playboy, 1982.

———. "Baby's Blood." In *Terrors*. New York: Berkley, 1984.

———. "I Shall Not Leave England Now." In *Shadows 7*. New York: Doubleday, 1984.

———. "Kiss the Vampire Goodbye." *Alfred Hitchcock's Mystery Magazine*, June 1985.

**Ryan, Franklin W.** "The Last Earl." *Amazing Stories*, January 1933.

**Ryan, Kathleen.** *Setite*. Clarkston, GA: White Wolf, 1999.

———. *Ravnos*. Clarkston, GA: White Wolf, 2000.

**Ryan, Kevin.** *Van Helsing*. New York: Pocket, 2004 (movie novelization).

**Ryan, Rachel.** *Echo of a Curse*. London: H. Jenkins, 1939.

**Ryan, Sean: See Davy, S.**

**Ryan, Shawn.** *Nocturnas*. New York: Pocket Books, 1995.

**Rylien, Katherine X.** "A Visit from Paulie." *The Vampire's Crypt 3*, Spring 1991.

———. "No Such Thing as a Free Lunch." *The Vampire's Crypt 4*, 1991.

———. "County Fair 2092." *The Vampire's Crypt 5*, Spring 1992.

———. "Chasing the Twilight." *The Vampire's Crypt 6*, Fall 1992.

———. "For Sale." *Book of Shadows 4*, 1992.

**Rymer, James Malcolm.** *Varney the Vampire or The Feast of Blood*. London: E. Lloyd, 1847.

**Saberhagen, Fred.** *The Dracula Tape*. New York: Warner, 1975.

———. *The Holmes/Dracula File*. New York: Ace, 1978.

———. *An Old Friend in the Family*. New York: Ace, 1979.

———. *Thorn*. New York: Ace, 1980.

———. *Dominion*. New York: Tor, 1982.

———. "From the Tree of Time." *The Sorcerer's Apprentice*, Spring 1982.

———. *A Matter of Taste*. New York: Tor, 1990.

———. *A Question of Time*. New York: Tor, 1992.

———. *Seance for a Vampire*. New York: Tor, 1994.

———. *A Sharpness on the Neck*. New York: Tor, 1996.

———. *The Vlad Tapes*. New York: Baen, 2000.

———. "Box Number Fifty." In *Dracula in London*. New York: Ace, 2001.

———. *A Coldness in the Blood*. New York: Forge, 2002.

**Saberhagen, Fred, and James V. Hart.** *Bram Stoker's Dracula: A Francis Ford Coppola Film*. New York: Signet, 1992 (movie novelization).

**Sacher-Masoch, Leopold von.** "Eternal Youth." 1874.

**Sackett, Jeffrey.** *Blood of the Impaler*. New York: Bantam, 1989.

**Sacksteder, Ruth M.** "The Matter of Dr. Moraven." *The Vampire's Crypt 2*, 1990.

———. "Solstice Vigil." *The Vampire's Crypt 3*, Spring 1991.

**Sadler, Thomas D.** "Himeros's Daughter." In *Lovers and Other Monsters*. New York: Doubleday, 1992.

**Sagara, Michelle.** *Children of the Blood*. New York: Del Rey, 1992.

**Sallee, Wayne Allen.** "The Vampire at the Galleria." *The Vampire Journal 3*, Fall/Winter 1986.

———. "Blood from a Turnip." In *Dracula: Prince of Darkness*. New York: DAW, 1992.

———. "From Hunger." In *Love in Vein*. New York: HarperCollins, 1994 (erotica).

**Salmon, Michael.** *Count Munch: The Vampire Who Loved Chocolate*. New York: Viking, 2004 (juvenile).

**Salmonson, Jessica Amanda.** "The Final Fete of Abba Adi." In *Love in Vein*. New York: HarperCollins, 1994.

**Salonia, John, and Traci Salonia.** "The Imp in the Bottle." *Space and Time*, Winter 1988.

**St. Clair, Margaret.** "The Family." *Weird Tales*, January 1950.

**St. George, Margaret.** *Love Bites*. New York: Harlequin, 1995.

**Samiels, Minda.** *Soul of the Vampire*. San Diego, CA: Clocktower Books, 2001.

**Sams, Candace.** *Watchkeepers*. Hickory Corners, MI: ImaJinn Books, 2004.

**Samuels, Victor.** *The Vampire Women*. New York: Popular Library, 1973.

**San Souci, Robert D.** *The Dreaming*. New York: Berkley, 1989.

**Sanchez, Gail, and Michael Williams.** *Vampires: Chill Mode*. Delavan, WI: Pacesetter, 1985.

**Sandison, Robert C.** "River of Lost Souls." *Weird Tales*, May 1930.

———. "The Vrykolakas." *Weird Tales*, April 1932.

**Sands, Lynsay.** "Bitten." In *His Immortal Embrace*. New York: Kensington, 2003.

———. *Single White Vampire: Argeneau #1*. New York: Love Spell, 2003.

———. *Love Bites: Argeneau #2*. New York: Love Spell, 2004.

———. *Tall, Dark & Hungry: Argeneau #3*. New York: Love Spells, 2004.

———. *A Quick Bite: Argeneau #4*. New York: Avon, 2005.

———. *A Bite to Remember: Argeneau #5*. New York: Avon, 2006.

———. *Bite Me if You Can: Argeneau #6*. New York: Avon, 2007.

———. "Capture." In *Highland Thirst*. New York: Kensington, 2007.

———. *The Accidental Vampire: Argeneau #7*. New York: Avon, 2008.

———. "Bitten." In *Eternal Lover*. New York: Kensington, 2008.

———. *Vampires Are Forever: Argeneau #8*. New York: Avon, 2008.

———. *Vampire, Interrupted: Argeneau #9*. New York: Avon, 2008.

**Sanford, William, and Karl Green.** *Dracula's Daughter.* Mankato, MN: Crestwood House, 1985 (juvenile).

**Santiago, Cinsearae R.** *Welcome to the Gratista Vampire Clan: Blood Touch #1.* Frederick, MD: PublishAmerica, 2004.

———. *Desires Unleashed: Blood Touch #2.* Frederick, MD: PublishAmerica, 2005.

**Sanulescu, Jacques, and Anne Gottlieb.** *Carpathian Caper.* New York: Putnam, 1975.

**Sanvoisin, Eric.** *The Ink Drinker.* New York: Delacorte Press, 1998 (juvenile).

———. *A Straw for Two: The Companion to the Ink Drinker.* New York: Delacorte, 1999 (juvenile).

———. *The City of Darkness.* New York: Delacorte, 2001 (juvenile).

———. *Little Red Ink Drinker.* New York: Delacorte, 2003 (juvenile).

**Saplak, Charles M.** "The Storyteller Syndrome." *Prisoners of the Night 5,* 1991.

———. "Why We Shun Reflection, Why We Fear the Light." *Prisoners of the Night 6,* 1992.

**Saralegui, Jorge.** *Last Rites.* New York: Charter, 1985.

**Sargent, Carl, and Marc Gascione.** *Shadowrun: Nosferatu.* New York: Roc, 1994.

**Sarrantonio, Al.** "Red Eve." In *Under the Fang.* New York: Pocket Books, 1991.

**Satterthwait, Walter.** "Territorial Imperative." *The Magazine of Fantasy & Science Fiction,* April 1983.

**Savage, Chad.** "Cowboy's Lament (or Pas de Dude)." *Children of the Night Coven Journal 4,* 1990.

———. "Takes One to Know One." *Children of the Night Coven Journal 4,* 1990.

**Savage, Lacey.** *Fighting Chance.* Akron, OH: Ellora's Cave, 2008.

**Savery, Jeanne.** "Dark Seduction." In *His Eternal Kiss.* New York: Zebra, 2002.

**Savignano, Lisa.** "In the Beginning." *Good Guys Wear Fangs 1,* May 1992.

**Saville, Susanne.** *Vampire Close.* Lake Park, GA: New Concepts Publishing, 2006.

**Saville, Susanne, and Teri Adkins.** *The Crimson Fold.* Lake Park, GA: New Concepts, 2006.

**Savory, Gerald.** *Count Dracula: A Gothic Romance.* London: Corgi, 1977.

**Sawbridge, M. C.** *The Vampire.* London: George Allen and Unwin, 1920.

**Saxby, Chester L.** "The Death Touch." *Weird Tales,* July 1929.

**Saxon, Peter.** *The Disoriented Man.* London: Mayflower, 1966.

———. *The Torturer.* London: Mayflower, 1966.

———. *Vampire's Moon.* New York: Belmont, 1970.

———. *The Vampires of Finistere: The Guardians #4.* London: Howard Baker, 1970.

**Scarborough, Elizabeth.** *The Goldcamp Vampire, or, The Sanguinary Sourdough.* New York: Bantam Spectra, 1987.

———. "An Invitation to the Great White North." *Argos,* Spring 1988.

**Schachner, Nat.** "Thirst of the Ancients." *Terror Tales,* February 1935.

**Schiefelbein, Michael.** *Vampire Vow.* Los Angeles: Alyson, 2001.

———. *Vampire Thrall.* Los Angeles: Alyson, 2003.

———. *Vampire Transgression.* New York: St. Martin's, 2005.

**Schimel, Lawrence.** "The Last Bite." *Dead of Night 6,* July 1990.

———. "Secret Societies." In *Blood Lines: Vampire Stories from New England.* Cumberland House, 1997.

**Schimel, Lawrence, and Billie Sue Mosiman.** "The Scent of Magnolias." In *Southern Blood: Vampire Stories from the American South.* Nashville, TN: Cumberland House, 1997.

**Schindler, William.** *Blood of the Goddess.* Philadelphia: Xlibris, 2001.

**Schliessmann, Larry.** *Templar's Fate.* Morrisville, NC: Lulu.com, 2006.

**Schmaaeka, Reid.** *Ill Omens.* Clarkston, GA: White Wolf, 1999.

**Schmitz, James H.** "The Vampirate." *Science Fiction Plus,* December 1953.

**Schoder, Judith.** *Blood Suckers.* Englewood Cliffs, NJ: Julian Messner, 1981 (juvenile).

**Schoun, Edward.** "Blood Relatives." *Onyx 2,* August 1992.

**Schow, David J.** "Red Light." *Twilight Zone,* December 1986.

———. "Night Bloomer." *Weird Tales,* Spring 1990.

———. "A Week in the Unlife." In *A Whisper of Blood.* New York: William Morrow, 1991.

———. Dusting the Flowers." In *Love in Vein II.* New York: Harper, 1997 (erotica).

**Schreiber, Ellen.** *Vampire Kisses.* New York: HarperCollins, 2003 (juvenile).

———. *Kissing Cousins: Vampire Kisses #2.* New York: KatherineTegan Books, 2005 (juvenile).

———. *Vampireville: Vampire Kisses #3.* New York: Katherine Tegan Books, 2006 (juvenile).

———. *Dance with a Vampire: Vampire Kisses #4.* New York: Harper Teen, 2007 (juvenile).

———. *The Coffin Club: Vampire Kisses #5.* New York: Harper Teen, 2008 (juvenile).

**Schultz, J. T.** *More Than Illusions.* New York: Wild Rose, 2008.

**Schwader, Ann K.** "Alternates." *Prisoners of the Night 4,* 1990.

———. "Angeleyes." *Book of Shadows 1,* 1990.

———. "Crossing Over." *The Vampire's Crypt 3,* 1991.

**Schwartz, Ellen.** *Starshine and the Fanged Vampire Spider.* Vancouver, BC, Canada: Polestar, 2000 (juvenile).

**Schwartz, Kim Mathias.** *Confessions of the Vampire.* Grand Prairie, TX: Apage2You Book Publishing, 2002.

**Schwartz, Susan.** "The Carpetbagger." In *South from Midnight.* New Orleans: Southern Fried Press, 1994.

**Schweitzer, Darrell.** "The Lady of the Fountain." *Void 5,* 1977.

———. "Runaway." In *I, Vampire.* Stamford, CT: Longmeadow, 1995.

**Schweitzer, Darrell, and Jason Van Hollander.** "Men without Maps." *Marion Zimmer Bradley's Fantasy Magazine,* Winter 1991.

**Schwob, Marcel.** "Septima." In *Imaginary Lives.* New York: Boni and Liveright, 1924.

**Scopilo, Ella.** "Of Elves and Vampires: The Beginning." In *Vamprotica 2005.* Chippewa, 2005 (erotica).

**Scott, Alan.** *Project Dracula.* London: Sphere, 1971.

**Scott, Jody.** *I, Vampire.* New York: Ace, 1984.

**Scott, Martha.** "Feast of Blood for the Girl Who Couldn't Die." *Adventures in Horror,* April 1971.

**Scott, R. C.** *Dark Forces #14: Blood Sport.* New York: Bantam, 1984.

**Scott-Moncrieff, D.** "Schloss Wappenburg." In *Not for the Squeamish.* London: Background, 1948.

**Scotten, H. F.** "The Thing in the House." *Weird Tales,* May 1929.

**Scovitch, Joseph.** *Jerusalem Vampire.* Palo Alto, CA: Fultus, 2006.

**Scram, Arthur N.** *Werewolf vs. the Vampire Woman.* Beverly Hills, CA: Guild Hartford Books, 1972 (movie novelization).

**Scroggs, Kirk.** *Wiley & Grampa's Creature Features: Dracula vs. Grampa at the Monster Truck Spectacular.* Boston: Little, Brown, 2006 (juvenile).

**Seabrooke, Brenda.** *The Vampire in My Bathtub.* New York: Holiday House, 1999 (juvenile).

**Searight, Richard F.** "The Sealed Casket." *Weird Tales,* March 1935.

**Sebastian, Uma.** *The Enticing Bite Chronicles: Vampire RX.* Bloomington, IN: AuthorHouse, 2006.

**Seibold, Vivian.** *Vunce Upon a Time.* San Francisco: Chronicle Books, 2008 (juvenile).

**Selby, Curt.** *Blood Country.* New York: Popular Library, 1976.

**Serling, Rod.** "The Riddle of the Crypt." In *The Twilight Zone.* New York: Grosset and Dunlap, 1963.

**Serra, Louis.** *The Reluctant Vampire.* Oklahoma City, OK: Capri, 2006 (juvenile).

**Seymour, Miranda.** *Count Manfred.* New York: Popular Library, 1976.

————. *Vampire of Verdonia.* Knight Books, 1987.

**Shafer, Sam, and Dennis Logan Miller.** *Vampire High Council.* Charleston, SC: BookSurge, 2001.

**Shan, Darren.** *Cirque Du Freak: The Saga of Darren Shan Book 1.* London: HarperCollins, 2000 (juvenile).

————. *The Vampire's Assistant: The Saga of Darren Shan Book 2.* London: HarperCollins, 2000 (juvenile).

————. *Tunnels of Blood: The Saga of Darren Shan Book 3.* London: HarperCollins, 2000 (juvenile).

————. *Vampire Mountain: The Saga of Darren Shan Book 4.* London: HarperCollins, 2001 (juvenile).

————. *Trials of Death: The Saga of Darren Shan Book 5.* London: HarperCollins, 2001 (juvenile).

————. *The Vampire Prince: The Saga of Darren Shan Book 6.* London: HarperCollins, 2002 (juvenile).

————. *Hunters of the Dusk: The Saga of Darren Shan Book 7.* London: HarperCollins, 2002 (juvenile).

————. *Allies of the Night: The Saga of Darren Shan Book 8.* London: HarperCollins, 2002 (juvenile).

————. *Killers of the Dawn: The Saga of Darren Shan Book 9.* London: HarperCollins 2003 (juvenile).

————. *The Lake of Souls: The Saga of Darren Shan Book 10.* London: HarperCollins, 2003 (juvenile).

————. *Lord of the Shadows: The Saga of Darren Shan Book 11.* London: HarperCollins, 2004 (juvenile).

————. *Sons of Destiny: The Saga of Darren Shan Book 12.* London: HarperCollins, 2004 (juvenile).

**Shannon, Colleen.** *The Trelayne Inheritance.* New York: Leisure Books, 2002.

**Sharp, Allen.** *Return of the Undead: Can You Destroy the Vampire of Valdah.* Cambridge: Cambridge University Press, 1984.

**Sharp, Steven.** "Jet Lag." *The Vampire's Crypt 5,* Spring 1992.

**Sharpless, Richard.** "Darkness, My Companion." *Elegia 2,* 1992.

————. "Local Legend." *The Vampire's Crypt 5,* Spring 1992.

**Shaurette, Dan.** *Lilith's Love.* Charleston, SC: BookSurge, 2002.

**Shaver, Edward F.** "The Third Effect." *The Magazine of Fantasy & Science Fiction,* September 1989.

**Shaw, Christopher.** *Vampire Apocolypse: The Chaotic Brood.* Bloomington, IN: AuthorHouse, 2002.

**Shayne, Maggie.** *Twilight Phantasies: The Twilight Series #1.* New York: Silhouette, 1993.

————. *Twilight Memories: The Twilight Series #2.* New York: Silhouette, 1994.

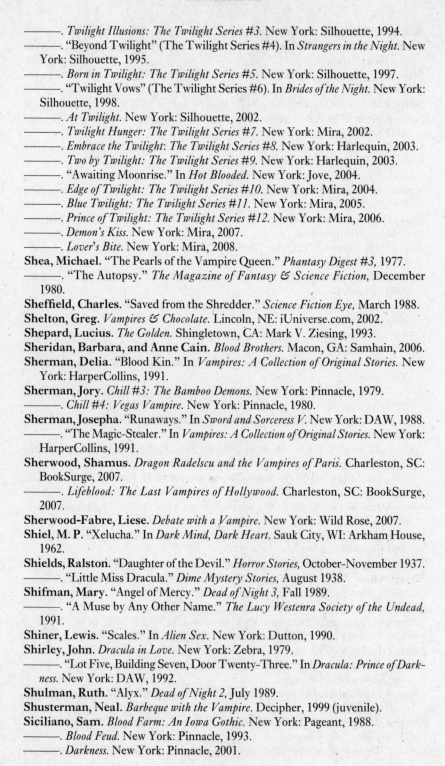
————. *Twilight Illusions: The Twilight Series #3*. New York: Silhouette, 1994.

————. "Beyond Twilight" (The Twilight Series #4). In *Strangers in the Night*. New York: Silhouette, 1995.

————. *Born in Twilight: The Twilight Series #5*. New York: Silhouette, 1997.

————. "Twilight Vows" (The Twilight Series #6). In *Brides of the Night*. New York: Silhouette, 1998.

————. *At Twilight*. New York: Silhouette, 2002.

————. *Twilight Hunger: The Twilight Series #7*. New York: Mira, 2002.

————. *Embrace the Twilight: The Twilight Series #8*. New York: Harlequin, 2003.

————. *Two by Twilight: The Twilight Series #9*. New York: Harlequin, 2003.

————. "Awaiting Moonrise." In *Hot Blooded*. New York: Jove, 2004.

————. *Edge of Twilight: The Twilight Series #10*. New York: Mira, 2004.

————. *Blue Twilight: The Twilight Series #11*. New York: Mira, 2005.

————. *Prince of Twilight: The Twilight Series #12*. New York: Mira, 2006.

————. *Demon's Kiss*. New York: Mira, 2007.

————. *Lover's Bite*. New York: Mira, 2008.

**Shea, Michael.** "The Pearls of the Vampire Queen." *Phantasy Digest #3*, 1977.

————. "The Autopsy." *The Magazine of Fantasy & Science Fiction*, December 1980.

**Sheffield, Charles.** "Saved from the Shredder." *Science Fiction Eye*, March 1988.

**Shelton, Greg.** *Vampires & Chocolate*. Lincoln, NE: iUniverse.com, 2002.

**Shepard, Lucius.** *The Golden*. Shingletown, CA: Mark V. Ziesing, 1993.

**Sheridan, Barbara, and Anne Cain.** *Blood Brothers*. Macon, GA: Samhain, 2006.

**Sherman, Delia.** "Blood Kin." In *Vampires: A Collection of Original Stories*. New York: HarperCollins, 1991.

**Sherman, Jory.** *Chill #3: The Bamboo Demons*. New York: Pinnacle, 1979.

————. *Chill #4: Vegas Vampire*. New York: Pinnacle, 1980.

**Sherman, Josepha.** "Runaways." In *Sword and Sorceress V*. New York: DAW, 1988.

————. "The Magic-Stealer." In *Vampires: A Collection of Original Stories*. New York: HarperCollins, 1991.

**Sherwood, Shamus.** *Dragon Radelscu and the Vampires of Paris*. Charleston, SC: BookSurge, 2007.

————. *Lifeblood: The Last Vampires of Hollywood*. Charleston, SC: BookSurge, 2007.

**Sherwood-Fabre, Liese.** *Debate with a Vampire*. New York: Wild Rose, 2007.

**Shiel, M. P.** "Xelucha." In *Dark Mind, Dark Heart*. Sauk City, WI: Arkham House, 1962.

**Shields, Ralston.** "Daughter of the Devil." *Horror Stories*, October–November 1937.

————. "Little Miss Dracula." *Dime Mystery Stories*, August 1938.

**Shifman, Mary.** "Angel of Mercy." *Dead of Night 3*, Fall 1989.

————. "A Muse by Any Other Name." *The Lucy Westenra Society of the Undead*, 1991.

**Shiner, Lewis.** "Scales." In *Alien Sex*. New York: Dutton, 1990.

**Shirley, John.** *Dracula in Love*. New York: Zebra, 1979.

————. "Lot Five, Building Seven, Door Twenty-Three." In *Dracula: Prince of Darkness*. New York: DAW, 1992.

**Shulman, Ruth.** "Alyx." *Dead of Night 2*, July 1989.

**Shusterman, Neal.** *Barbeque with the Vampire*. Decipher, 1999 (juvenile).

**Siciliano, Sam.** *Blood Farm: An Iowa Gothic*. New York: Pageant, 1988.

————. *Blood Feud*. New York: Pinnacle, 1993.

————. *Darkness*. New York: Pinnacle, 2001.

**Signorelli, Sam, and Sandra Signorelli.** "Dreamweb." In *Legends in Blood*. West Hollywood, CA: Fantaseas, 1991.

**Silva, David.** "Empty Vessels." In *Love in Vein*. New York: HarperCollins, 1994.

**Silver, Drew.** *The Beginning: The Vampire Within #1.* Charleston, SC: BookSurge, 2006.

———. *New Blood: The Vampire Within #2.* Charleston, SC: BookSurge, 2007.

**Silverberg, Robert.** "Warm Man." *The Magazine of Fantasy & Science Fiction*, May 1957.

———. "The Shadow of Wings." *Worlds of If*, July 1963.

———. "Born with the Dead." *The Magazine of Fantasy & Science Fiction*, April 1974.

———. "The Werewolf Gambit." In *The Ultimate Werewolf*. New York: Dell, 1991.

**Simmons, D. N.** *Desires Unleashed: Knights of the Darkness Chronicles #1.* Bloomington, IN: AuthorHouse, 2004.

———. *The Guilty Innocent: Knights of the Darkness Chronicles #2.* Bloomington, IN: AuthorHouse, 2005.

———. *The Royal Flush: Knights of the Darkness Chronicles #3.* Bloomington, IN: AuthorHouse, 2006.

**Simmons, Dan.** "The River Styx Runs Upstream." *Twilight Zone Magazine*, February 1982.

———. "Carrion Comfort." *Omni*, September–October 1983.

———. "Metastasis." In *Night Visions V*. Arlington Heights, IL: Dark Harvest, 1988.

———. *Carrion Comfort*. Arlington Heights, IL: Dark Harvest, 1989.

———. "Shave and a Haircut, Two Bites." In *Masques III*. New York: St. Martin's, 1989.

———. "All Dracula's Children." In *The Ultimate Dracula*, New York: Dell, 1991.

———. *Children of the Night*. New York: G. P. Putnam and Sons, 1992.

**Simmons, Suzanne.** *Night Life*. New York: Berkley, 2007.

**Simmons, Wm. Mark.** *One Foot in the Grave*. New York: Baen, 1996.

———. *Dead on My Feet*. New York: Baen, 2003.

———. *Habeas Corpses*. New York: Baen, 2005.

———. *Dead Easy*. New York: Baen, 2007.

**Sims, Kassandra.** *The Midnight Work*. New York: Tor, 2005.

**Sims, Shimon.** "There Once Lived a King Who Was a Hypocrite." *Pandora 1*, n.d.

**Sinclaire, T. L.** *Silver Dagger*. Hickory Corners, MI: ImaJinn Books, 2002.

**Siodmak, Curt.** "Experiment with Evil." In *Vampire*. London: Target, 1985.

**Sipos, Thomas M.** *Vampire Nation*. Philadelphia: Xlibris, 2000.

**Siral.** "The Vampire Was a Sucker." *Thriller*, February 1962.

**Sisk, Frank.** "The Leech." *The Magazine of Fantasy & Science Fiction*, June 1978.

**Sizemore, Susan.** *Forever Knight: A Stirring of Dust*. New York: Boulevard, 1997.

———. *The Hunt: Laws of the Blood #1.* New York: Ace, 1999.

———. *Partners: Laws of the Blood #2.* New York: Ace, 2000.

———. *Companions: Laws of the Blood #3.* New York: Ace, 2001.

———. *Deceptions: Laws of the Blood #4.* New York: Ace, 2002.

———. *Heroes: Laws of the Blood #5.* New York. Ace, 2003.

———. *I Burn for You: Primal Desires #1.* New York: Pocket Star, 2003.

———. *I Thirst for You: Primal Desires #2.* New York: Pocket Star, 2004.

———. *I Hunger for You: Primal Desires #3.* New York: Pocket Star, 2005.

———. *Master of Darkness: Primal Desires #4.* New York: Pocket Star, 2006.

———. *Primal Heat: Primal Desires #5.* New York: Pocket Star, 2006.

———. *Primal Desires: Primal Desires #6.* New York: Pocket Star, 2007.

———. "Tempting Fate." In *Moon Fever*. New York: Pocket Books, 2007.

———. *Primal Needs*. New York: Pocket Star, 2008.

**Skipp, John, and Craig Spector.** *Fright Night*. New York: Tor, 1985 (movie novelization).

———. *The Light at the End*. New York: Bantam, 1986.

**Slama, Caroledith.** "Anniversary." *Dead of Night 6*, July 1990.

**Slater, Mandy.** "Daddy's Little Girl." In *The Mammoth Book of Dracula*. London: Robinson, 1997.

**Smeds, Dave.** "The Flower That Does Not Wither." In *Sword and Sorceress IX*. New York: DAW, 1992.

**Smith, Ariel, Amanda Clay, and Melissa Bosco-Torchio.** "The Vampire Letters." *Children of the Night Coven Journal*, 1990.

**Smith, Basil A.** "The Scallion Stone." In *Whispers*. New York: Doubleday, 1977.

**Smith, Beecher.** *The Guardian*. Memphis, TN: Hot Bisquit, 1999.

**Smith, Clark Ashton.** "The End of the Story." *Weird Tales*, May 1930.

———. "Marooned on Andromeda." *Wonder Stories*, October 1930.

———. "A Rendezvous in Averoigne." *Weird Tales*, April/May 1931.

———. "The Vaults of Yoh-Vombis." *Weird Tales*, May 1932.

———. "The Invisible City." *Wonder Stories*, June 1932.

———. "The Hunters from Beyond." *Strange Tales*, October 1932.

———. "The Testament of Athammaus." *Weird Tales*, October 1932.

———. "Genius Loci." *Weird Tales*, June 1933.

———. "The Seed from the Sepulcher." *Weird Tales*, October 1933.

———. "The Demon of the Flower." *Astounding Stories*, December 1933.

———. "The Witchcraft of Ulua." *Weird Tales*, February 1934.

———. "The Epiphany of Death." *The Fantasy Fan*, July 1934.

———. "The Flower-Women." *Weird Tales*, May 1935.

———. "The Black Abbot of Puthuum." *Weird Tales*, March 1936.

———. "The Death of Ilalotha." *Weird Tales*, September 1937.

———. "The Enchantress of Sylaire." *Weird Tales*, May 1941.

———. "Morthylla." *Weird Tales*, May 1953.

**Smith, Clark Ashton, and Lin Carter.** "The Stairs in the Crypt." *Fantastic Stories*, August 1976.

**Smith, Cynthia Leitich.** *Tantalize*. Westminster, MD: Candlewick, 2007 (juvenile).

**Smith, Diana, and Pat Dunn.** "The Fellowship." *The Memory Flame 2*, 1990.

———. "The Strangers." *A Different Drum*, 1990.

———. "Queen of the Night." *Faded Roses 3*, 1991.

———. "The Adventure of the Abducted Wife." *Heart's Blood 1*, May 1992.

———. "The Intrepid Vampire Killer." *Good Guys Wear Fangs 1*, May 1992.

———. "Lucky Night." *Heart's Blood 1*, May 1992.

———. "Of Wooden Stakes and Silver Crosses." *Good Guys Wear Fangs 1*, May 1992.

———. "Secrets." *Heart's Blood 1*, May 1992.

———. "The Truth About Murdoc." *Good Guys Wear Fangs 1*, May 1992.

———. "On the Cold Hill's Side." *The Turn of the Wheel*, 1992.

———. "The Singing Señorita." *Zorro, Blade of Justice*, 1992.

———. "To Kill a Vampire." *Time Knight*, 1992.

**Smith, Diana, and Valerie Meachum.** "Angel of Darkness, Angel of Light." *Good Guys Wear Fangs 1*, May 1992.

**Smith, Dona.** *Shock Shots #4: Vampires*. New York: Scholastic, 1993 (juvenile).

**Smith, Eleanor.** "Satan Circus." *Weird Tales*, October 1931.

Smith, Evelyn E. "The Good Husband." *Fantastic Universe,* August 1955.

———. "Softly, While You're Sleeping." *The Magazine of Fantasy & Science Fiction,* April 1961.

Smith, George K. *Scourge of the Blood Cult.* Los Angeles: Epic, 1961.

Smith, Guy N. *Bats Out of Hell.* London: New English Library, 1978.

———. *Doom Fright.* London: Hamlyn, 1981.

———. *The Blood Merchants.* London: New English Library, 1982.

———. *The Undead.* London: New English Library, 1983.

———. *The Knighton Vampires.* London: Piatkus Books, 1993.

———. "Larry's Guest." In *The Mammoth Book of Dracula.* London: Robinson, 1997.

Smith, J. *An Odd Collection.* Philadelphia: Xlibris, 1997.

Smith, Kathryn. *Be Mine Tonight: Brotherhood of Blood #1.* New York: Avon, 2006.

———. *Night of the Huntress: Brotherhood of Blood #2.* New York: Avon, 2007.

———. *Taken by the Night: Brotherhood of Blood #3.* New York: Avon, 2007.

———. *Let the Night Begin: Brotherhood of Blood #4.* New York: Avon, 2008.

Smith, Lady Eleanor. "Satan's Circus." In *Satan's Circus and Other Stories.* London: Victor Gollancz, 1932.

Smith, L. J. *The Vampire Diaries #1: The Awakening.* New York: HarperPrism, 1991 (juvenile).

———. *The Vampire Diaries #2: The Struggle.* New York: HarperPrism, 1991 (juvenile).

———. *The Vampire Diaries #3: The Fury.* New York: HarperPrism, 1991 (juvenile).

———. *The Vampire Diaries #4: Dark Reunion.* New York: HarperPrism, 1991 (juvenile).

———. *Dark Vision Vol. 3: The Passion.* New York: Pocket Books, 1995 (juvenile).

———. *Secret Vampire: Night World #1.* New York: Pocket Books, 1996 (juvenile).

———. *Daughters of Darkness: Night World #2.* New York: Pocket Books, 1996 (juvenile).

———. *Spellbinder: Night World #3.* New York: Pocket Books, 1996 (juvenile).

———. *Dark Angel: Night World #4.* New York: Pocket Books, 1996 (juvenile).

———. *The Chosen: Night World #5.* New York: Pocket Books, 1997 (juvenile).

———. *Soul Mate: Night World #6.* New York: Pocket Books, 1997 (juvenile).

———. *Huntress: Night World #7.* New York: Pocket Books, 1997 (juvenile).

———. *Black Dawn: Night World #8.* New York: Pocket Books, 1998 (juvenile).

———. *Witchlight: Night World #9.* New York: Pocket Books, 1998 (juvenile).

Smith, Lisa Rene. *Chaos the Vampire Child.* Houston, TX: L & L Dreamspell, 2007.

Smith, Martin Cruz. *Nightwing.* Scranton: PA: W. W. Norton, 1977.

Smith, Michael Marshall. "Dear Alison." In *The Mammoth Book of Dracula.* London: Robinson, 1997.

Smith, Robert Arthur. *Vampire Notes.* New York: Fawcett, 1990.

Smith, Sandy. "Home to Collinwood." *World of Dark Shadows,* July 1978.

Smith, Shelli. *Vampire and His Ghoul.* Daytona Beach, FL: Denlinger's, 2005.

Smith, Susan. *Confessions of a Teenage Frog.* New York: Archway, 1987 (juvenile).

Smith, Will, and R. J. Robbins. "Swamp Horror." *Weird Tales,* March 1926.

Smith-Ready, Jeri. *Wicked Game.* New York: Pocket, 2008.

Smythe, Julie Anne. *The Burning Blood Chronicles: Vampires.* Frederick, MD: PublishAmerica, 2003.

Sneddon, Robert W. "The Vampire of Oakdale Ridge." *Ghost Stories,* December 1926.

Snell, D. L. *Roses of Blood on Barbwire Vines.* Mena, AR: Permuted, 2007.

**Sneyd, Steve.** "Milk of Kindness." *Space and Time,* Winter 1981–82.

**Sniegoski, Thomas E.** *Soul Trade (Angel).* New York: Pocket Books, 2001.

**Snodgrass, Melinda M.** "Requiem." In *A Very Large Array.* Albuquerque, NM: University of New Mexico Press, 1987.

**Snow, K. Z.** *Plagued.* Akron: OH: Ellora's Cave, 2007 (erotica).

**Sommer-Bodenburg, Angela.** *The Little Vampire Moves In.* London: Hippo Books, 1982 (juvenile).

————. *The Little Vampire Takes a Trip.* London: Hippo Books, 1984 (juvenile).

————. *The Little Vampire.* London: Hippo Books, 1986 (juvenile).

————. *The Little Vampire in Love.* London: Hippo Books, 1986 (juvenile).

————. *The Little Vampire on the Farm.* London: Hippo Books, 1986 (juvenile).

————. *The Little Vampire in the Vale of Doom.* London: Simon & Schuster, 1991 (juvenile).

————. *The Little Vampire and the Mystery Planet.* London: Simon & Schuster, 1992 (juvenile).

————. *The Little Vampire in Danger.* London: Simon & Schuster, 1992 (juvenile).

————. *The Little Vampire in Despair.* London: Simon & Schuster, 1992 (juvenile).

————. *The Little Vampire and the Wicked Plot.* London: Simon & Schuster, 1993 (juvenile).

————. *The Little Vampire Gets a Surprise.* London: Simon & Schuster, 1993 (juvenile).

————. *The Little Vampire in the Lion's Den.* London: Simon & Schuster, 1993 (juvenile).

————. *The Little Vampire Learns to Be Brave.* London: Simon & Schuster, 1993 (juvenile).

————. *The Little Vampire and the Christmas Surprise.* London: Hodder Wayland, 1994 (juvenile).

————. *The Little Vampire and the School Trip.* London: Simon & Schuster, 1994 (juvenile).

————. *The Little Vampire and the Summer Surprise.* London: Simon & Schuster, 1994 (juvenile).

————. *The Little Vampire Meets Count Dracula.* London: Hodder Wayland, 1995 (juvenile).

**Sommersby, Samantha.** *Forbidden: The Claim.* Linden Bay Romance, 2006.

————. *Forbidden: The Awakening.* Linden Bay Romance, 2007.

————. *Forbidden: The Revolution.* Linden Bay Romance, 2008.

**Somper, Justin.** *Demons of the Ocean: Vampirates 1.* London: Simon & Schuster, 2005 (juvenile).

————. *Tide of Terror: Vampirates 2.* London: Little, Brown Young Readers, 2006 (juvenile).

————. *Blood Captain: Vampirates 3.* London: Simon & Schuster, 2006 (juvenile).

————. *Dead Deep: Vampirates 4.* London: Simon & Schuster, 2007 (juvenile).

**Somtow, S. P.** "The Vampire of Mallworld." *Amazing,* May 1981.

————. *Vampire Junction.* Norfolk, VA: Starblaze/ Donning, 1984.

————. *Valentine.* New York: Tor, 1992.

————. "The Captive Angel." In *I, Vampire.* Longmeadow, 1995.

————. *Vanitas: Escape from Vampire Junction.* White Rock: Transylvania, 1995.

————. *The Riverrun Trilogy.* New York: Doubleday Books, 1996.

————. *The Vampire's Beautiful Daughter.* New York: Atheneum, 1997 (juvenile).

————. "Vanilla Blood." In *The Vampire Sextette.* Garden City, NY: GuildAmerica Books, 2000.

**Somtow, S. P., and Gary Lippincott.** *The Vampire's Beautiful Daughter.* New York: Atheneum Books, 1997 (juvenile).

**Sontheimer, Lee Ann.** "Flame." *The Vampire Journal 4,* 1988.

**Sosnowski, David.** *Vamped: A Novel.* New York: Simon & Schuster, 2004.

**Soule, John.** "Dream Journal." *Prisoners of the Night 2,* 1988.

**Spangler, Catherine.** "Street Corners and Halos." In *Demon's Delight.* New York: Berkley Sensation, 2007.

**Sparks, Kerrelyn.** *How to Marry a Vampire Millionaire: Love at Stake #1.* New York: Avon, 2005.

———. *Vamps and the City: Love at Stake #2.* New York: Avon, 2006.

———. "A Very Vampy Christmas." In *Sugarplums and Scandal.* New York: Avon, 2006.

———. *Be Still My Vampire Heart: Love at Stake #3.* New York: Avon, 2007.

———. *The Undead Next Door: Love at Stake #4.* New York: Avon, 2008.

———. *All I Want for Christmas Is a Vampire: Love at Stake #5.* New York: Avon, 2008.

**Spear, Terry.** *Killing the Bloodlust.* Surprise, AZ: Triskelion, 2005.

———. *Seducing the Huntress.* Surprise, AZ: Triskelion, 2005.

———. "Vampiric Calling." In *Vamprotica 2005.* Chippewa, 2005 (erotica).

**Specht, Robert.** "The Real Thing." *Alfred Hitchcock's Mystery Magazine,* April 1966.

**Spehner, Norbert.** *Dracula: Opus 300.* Ashem Fictions, 1996 (chapbook).

**Spence, J. Lewis Thomas Chalmers.** "The Red Flasket." In *The Archer in the Arras and Other Tales of Mystery.* Edinburgh: Grant and Murray, 1932.

**Spicer, Dorothy G.** "Vanna and the Vampire." In *Thirteen Ghosts.* New York: Coward, McCann, 1965.

**Spinrod, Norman.** *Vampire Junkies.* Brooklyn, NY: Gryphon Publications, 1994.

**Spoor, Ryk E.** *Digital Knight.* New York: Baen, 2003.

**Spriggs, Robin, and Brent L. Glenn.** *Dracula Poems: A Poetic Encounter with the Lord of Vampires.* Murrayville, GA: Circle Myth, 1992.

**Spruill, Steven.** *Rulers of Darkness.* New York: St. Martin's, 1995.

———. *Daughters of Darkness.* New York: Doubleday, 1997.

———. *Lords of Light.* London: Hodder & Stoughton, 1999.

**Squires, Susan.** *Sacrament.* New York: Love Spell, 2002.

———. "Sacrilege." In *The Only One.* New York: Dorchester, 2003.

———. *The Companion.* New York: St. Martin's, 2005.

———. *The Hunger: The Companion #2.* New York: St. Martin's, 2005.

———. *The Burning: The Companion #3.* New York: St. Martin's, 2006 (erotica).

———. "The Gift." In *Love at First Bite.* New York: St. Martin's, 2006.

———. *One with the Night: The Companion #4.* New York: St. Martin's, 2007.

———. *One with the Shadows: The Companion #5.* New York: St. Martin's, 2007.

———. *One with the Darkness: The Companion #6.* New York: St. Martin's, 2008.

**Staab, Thomas.** *Vampire's Waltz.* Seattle, WA: Crazy Wolf, 1999.

**Stableford, Brian.** *The Empire of Fear.* London: Simon & Schuster, 1988.

———. "The Man Who Loved the Vampire Lady." *The Magazine of Fantasy & Science Fiction,* August 1988.

———. *Young Blood.* London: Simon & Schuster, 1992.

———. *The Hunger and Ecstasy of Vampires.* Shingleton: Mark V. Ziesing, 1996.

———. "Quality Control." In *The Mammoth Book of Dracula.* London: Robinson, 1997.

———. "Sheena." In *The Vampire Sextette.* Garden City, NY: GuildAmerica Books, 2000.

———. "Hot Blood." In *Asimov's Science Fiction*, September 2002.

**Stadt, Jeffrey A.** "Windchill." *Bloodreams 3*, January 1992.

———. "The Dark Man's Children." *The Vampire's Crypt 6*, Fall 1992.

**Stamper, J. B.** "The Train through Transylvania." In *Tales of the Midnight Hour*. New York: Scholastic, 1977 (juvenile).

———. "Trick or Treat." In *More Tales for the Midnight Hour*. New York: Scholastic, 1987 (juvenile).

———. "The Masked Ball." In *Still More Tales of the Midnight Hour*. New York: Scholastic, 1989 (juvenile).

**Stanley, George Edward.** *The Vampire Kittens of Count Dracula (Scaredy Cats #8)*. New York: Aladdin Paperbacks, 1997 (juvenile).

**Stanton, Edward.** *Dreams of the Dead*. Boston: Lee and Shepard, 1892.

**Stanwyck, Michael.** *In the Drift*. New York: Berkley, 1985.

**Stark, Richard.** "Birth of a Monster." *Super-Science Fiction*, August 1959.

**Starkie, Walter.** "The Old Man's Story." In *Raggle Taggle*. London: John Murray, 1933.

**Starr, Crickett.** "Dark Pilot's Bride." In *Ellora's Cavemen: Legendary Tails 1*. Akron: OH: Ellora's Cave, 2005 (erotica).

———. *Fangs for the Memories*. Akron: OH: Ellora's Cave, 2005 (erotica).

**Starrett, Vincent.** "The Quick and the Dead." *Weird Tales*, December 1932.

**Steakley, John.** *Vampire$*. New York: Roc, 1990.

**Steele, Kate.** *By Blood's Decree*. Scottsdale: AZ: Loose Id, n.d.

**Steele, Kimberly.** *Forever Fifteen*. Morrisville, NC: Lulu.com, 2005 (juvenile).

**Steele, Wilbur Daniel.** "The Woman at Seven Brothers." *Golden Book Magazine*, July 1929.

**Steiger, Brad.** "Three Tales for the Horrid at Heart." *Fantastic*, January 1963.

**Stein, Jeanne C.** *The Becoming: The Anna Strong Chronicles #1*. Hickory Corners, MI: ImaJinn Books, 2004.

———. *Blood Drive: The Anna Strong Chronicles #2*. Hickory Corners, MI: ImaJinn Books, 2006.

———. "The Witch and the Wicked." In *Many Bloody Returns*. New York: Ace, 2007.

———. *The Watcher: The Anna Strong Chronicles #3*. New York: Ace, 2007.

**Steiner, Barbara.** *The Calling (Dark Chronicles #3)*. New York: Flare, 1995 (juvenile).

**Stenbock, Count Stanislau Eric.** "The Sad Story of a Vampire." In *Studies of Death: Romantic Tales*. London: Nutt, 1894.

**Stevens, Amanda.** *The Perfect Kiss*. Toronto: Silhouette Shadows, 1993.

———. *Dark Obsession*. Toronto: Silhouette Shadows, 1994.

**Stevenson, Florence.** *The Curse of the Concullens*. New York: Signet, 1970.

———. *Dark Encounter*. New York: New American Library, 1976.

———. *Moonlight Variations*. New York: Jove, 1981.

———. *Household*. New York: Leisure Books, 1989.

**Stevenson, Robert Louis.** "Thrawn Janet." *Cornhill Magazine*, October 1881.

———. "Olalla." *Court and Society Review*, December 1885.

**Steward, Lindsay.** "Jolly Uncle." In *Pan Book of Horror Stories No. 9*. London: Pan, 1968.

**Stewardson, Dawn.** *Hunter's Moon*. Toronto: Harlequin Intrigue, 1994.

**Stewart, Desmond.** *The Vampire of Mons*. New York: Harper & Row, 1976.

**Stine, R. L.** *The Goodnight Kiss (Fear Street Super Chillers)*. Simon Pulse, 1993 (juvenile).

———. *The Goodnight Kiss #2 (Fear Street Super Chillers)*. Simon Pulse, 1996 (juvenile).

———. *Vampire Breath (Goosebumps No. 49)*. New York: Scholastic, 1996 (juvenile).

———. *Please Don't Feed the Vampires (Give Yourself Goosebumps #15)*. Apple, 1997 (juvenile).

———. *Attack of the Vampire Worms (Ghosts of Fear Street No. 33)*. Westminster, MD: Goldenbooks, 1998 (juvenile).

———. *One Last Kiss (Fear Street Sagas No. 14)*. Westminster, MD: Goldenbooks, 1998 (juvenile).

———. *Dangerous Girls*. New York: HarperCollins, 2003 (juvenile).

———. *The Taste of Night*. New York: HarperCollins, 2004 (juvenile).

Stivers, Valerie. *Blood Is the New Black*. New York: Three Rivers, 2007.

Stockmyer, John. *The Gentleman Vampire*. Lincoln, NE: iUniverse, 2004.

Stoker, Bram. *Dracula*. Westminster: Archibald Constable & Co., 1897.

———. *The Lair of the White Worm*. London: William Rider & Son, 1907.

———. *The Lady of the Shroud*. London: William Rider & Son, 1909.

———. "Dracula's Guest." In *Dracula's Guest and Other Weird Stories*. London: George Routledge and Sons, 1914.

———. "The Fate of Fenella." *Cassell's Magazine*, 1892.

Stone, Leslie F. "When the Flame-Flowers Blossomed." *Weird Tales*, November 1935.

Stone, Tom B. *Camp Dracula (Graveyard School #6)*. New York: Skylark, 1995 (juvenile).

———. *Escape From Vampire Park (Graveyard School #25)*. New York: Skylark, 1998 (juvenile).

Stooker, Richard. "Bloodfire." *The Vampire's Crypt 5*, Spring 1992.

Storm, Derek. *Vampire Island (Shivers #1)*. New York: Family Vision, 1993 (juvenile).

Storme, Sarah. *Flight of the Raven*. Echelon, 2002.

Strasser, Todd. *Help! I'm Trapped in a Vampire's Body*. New York: Apple, 2000 (juvenile).

Strauch, Thomas J. "Angel." *Children of the Night Coven Journal 1*, 1990.

———. "Pas de Deux." *Children of the Night Coven Journal 3*, 1990.

Straum, Niel. "Vanishing Breed." In *The Curse of the Undead*. New York: Fawcett, 1970.

Streiber, Whitley. *The Hunger*. New York: William Morrow, 1981.

———. "Pain." In *Cutting Edge*. New York: Doubleday, 1986.

———. *The Last Vampire*. New York: Pocket Star, 2001.

———. *The Last Vampire 2*. New York: Pocket Books, 2002.

———. *Lilith's Dream: A Tale of the Vampire Life*. New York: Atria, 2002.

Strickland, Brad. "Her Wild Wild Eyes." *The Magazine of Fantasy & Science Fiction*, April 1991.

Strong, Jeremy. *Living the Vampires*. Edinburgh: Barrington Stoke, 2000 (juvenile).

Strong, Jory. *Skye's Trail: The Angelini Series #1*. Akron, OH: Ellora's Cave, 2005 (erotica).

———. *Syndelle's Possession: The Angelini Series #2*. Akron, OH: Ellora's Cave, 2005 (erotica).

Strong, Louise J. "An Unscientific Story." *Cosmopolitan*, February 1903.

Stuart, Kiel. "Juice." In *Hotter Blood*. New York: Pocket Books, 1991.

Sturgeon, Theodore. "The Professor's Teddy Bear." *Weird Tales*, March 1948.

———. "The Music." In *E. Pluribus Unicorn*. New York: Abelard, 1953.

———. "So Near the Darkness." *Fantastic Universe*, November 1955.

————. *Some of Your Blood.* New York: Ballantine, 1961.

Sturgis, Susanna J. "Sustenance." In *Night Bites: Vampire Stories by Women.* Seattle, WA: Seal, 1996.

Sturm, Robbie. "Inevah." *Vampire Quarterly 3,* February 1986.

Sucharitkul, Somtow. "The Vampire of Mallworld." *Amazing Science Fiction Stories,* May 1981.

Sullivan, Tim. "Los Niños de la Noche." In *The Ultimate Dracula.* New York: Dell, 1991.

Summers, David Lee. *Vampires of the Scarlet Order.* Kingston, NS, Canada: LBF Books, 2005.

Summers, Jack. "April's Dream." *Good Guys Wear Fangs 1,* May 1992.

————. "Caleb." *Miss Lucy Westenra Society of the Undead,* Spring 1992.

————. "The Resting Place." *Vlad the Impaler Volume 3,* July 1992.

Summers, Jordan. *Gothic Passions.* Akron, OH: Ellora's Cave, 2003 (erotica).

Summers, Sultry. *Gift of the Nightflyer.* Casper, WY: Whiskey Creek, 2008 (erotica).

Sumner, M. C. *The Coach.* New York: HarperCollins, 1994 (juvenile).

————. *The Principal.* New York: HarperCollins, 1994 (juvenile).

————. *The Substitute.* New York: HarperCollins, 1994 (juvenile).

Sumner, Mark. *News from the Edge: Vampires of Vermont.* New York: Ace, 1999.

Sutcliffe, Barbara. "Woodacres." *Children of the Night Coven Journal 4,* 1990.

Sutcliffe, Katherine. "Forever Yours." In *Haunting Love Stories.* New York: Avon, 1991.

Suzane, Linda. *Eyes of Truth.* Kingsport, TN: Twilight Times Books, 2004.

Swain, Robyn D. *Dhampir.* Lincoln, NE: iUniverse.com, 2001.

Swann, Cara. *Shadow Walking.* TrueFire.com, 2000.

Swiniarski, S. A. *Raven.* New York: DAW, 1996.

————. *The Flesh, the Blood and the Fire.* Bergenfield, NJ: DAW, 1998.

Sylvestre, George. *The House of the Vampires.* New York: Moffat, Yard, 1907.

Talbot, Michael. *The Delicate Dependency: A Novel of Vampire Life.* New York: Avon, 1982.

Tammerie. "Bat in the Belfry." *The Vampire's Crypt 2,* 1990.

Tanis, Jennifer. *Forgotten Vampire.* Frederick, MD: PublishAmerica, 2004.

Tankersley, Richie. *The Angel Chronicles, Vol. 2 (Buffy the Vampire Slayer).* New York: Simon Spotlight Entertainment, 1998.

Tarleton, J. P. "Love Is the Color of Blood." *Adventures in Horror,* October 1970.

Tate, Richard. *The Dead Travel Fast.* London: Constable, 1971.

Tatro, Edgar F. "Schlecht." *The Vampire Journal 4,* 1988.

————. "A Breath of Fresh Air." *Cemetary Dance 1,* December 1988.

Tattunigma. *In the Shadow of the Arch.* Shadowstone, 2001.

Tavano, Noel Lana. *Suicide Surprise: It Could Always Be Worse #1.* CreateSpace: 2008.

Taylor, Alvin, and Len J. Moffatt. "Father's Vampire." *Weird Tales,* May 1952.

Taylor, Drew Hayden. *The Night Wanderer.* Toronto: Annick, 2007 (juvenile).

Taylor, J. Lee. *Cinderella and the Vampire.* Amherst Junction, WI: Hard Shell Word Factory, 2006.

Taylor, Karen E. *Blood Secrets (The Vampire Legacy No. 1).* New York: Zebra, 1993.

————. *Bitter Blood (The Vampire Legacy No. 2).* New York: Zebra, 1994.

————. *Blood Ties (The Vampire Legacy No. 3).* New York: Zebra, 1995.

————. *Blood of My Blood (The Vampire Legacy No. 4).* New York: Pinnacle, 2000.

———. *The Vampire Vivienne (The Vampire Legacy No. 5)*. New York: Pinnacle, 2001.

———. *Resurrection (The Vampire Legacy No. 6)*. New York: Pinnacle, 2002.

———. *Fangs and Angel Wings*. Doylestown, PA: Betancourt, 2003.

———. *From the Ruins (The Vampire Legacy No. 7)*. New York: Pinnacle, 2004.

———. *Blood Red Dawn (The Vampire Legacy No. 8)*. New York: Pinnacle, 2004.

———. *Blood Red Dawn: The Vampire Legacy*. New York: Kensington, 2004.

**Taylor, Keith.** "The Haunting of Mara." *Weird Tales,* Fall 1988.

———. "Men from the Plain of Lir." *Weird Tales,* Fall 1988.

**Taylor, Lucy.** *Eternal Hearts*. Clarkston, GA: White Wolf, 1999.

**Taylor, Michael.** *Adam's Undead: Darke Lyfe Eternal: Tome 1*. Philadelphia: Xlibris, 2004.

———. *Absolute Evil: Darke Lyfe Eternal: Tome 2*. Philadelphia: Xlibris, 2004.

———. *Arcanum of Abbadon: Darke Lyfe Eternal: Tome 3*. Philadelphia: Xlibris, 2005.

**Taylor, Tawney.** *Burning Hunger*. Akron, OH: Ellora's Cave, 2007 (erotica).

**Taylor, Vickie.** "Blood Lust." In *Bite*. New York: Jove, 2004.

**Tedford, William.** *Liquid Diet*. New York: Diamond Books, 1992.

**Tegen, Katherine.** *Dracula and Frankenstein are Friends*. New York: HarperCollins, 2003 (juvenile).

**Teglia, Charlene.** "Night Music." In *Beginnings*. Macon, GA: Samhain, 2007.

**Tem, Melanie.** "The Better Half." *Isaac Asimov's Science Fiction Magazine,* December 1989.

———. "Lightning Rod." In *Skin of the Soul*. London: Women's Press, 1990.

———. *Desmodus*. New York: Dell, 1995.

———. "Lunch at Charon's." *The Mammoth Book of Vampire Stories by Women*. New York: Carroll & Graf, 2001.

**Tem, Steve Rasnic.** "The Men and Women of Rivendale." In *Night Visions I*. Arlington Heights, IL: Dark Harvest, 1984.

———. "Be Mine." In *14 Vicious Valentines*. New York: Avon, 1988.

———. "Carnal House." In *Hot Blood*. New York: Pocket Books, 1989.

———. "Nocturne." In *Blood is Not Enough*. New York: William Morrow, 1989.

———. "Vintage Domestic." In *The Mammoth Book of Vampires*. London: Robinson, 1992.

**Tem, Steve, and Melanie Tem.** "The Tenth Scholar." In *The Ultimate Dracula*. New York: Dell, 1991.

———. "The Marriage." In *Love in Vein*. New York: HarperCollins, 1994 (erotica).

**Templeton, Julia.** *Return to Me*. New York: Berkley, 2007.

**Ten-Eyck, Glen, and Connie Ten-Eyck.** "Stand By Me." *Marion Zimmer Bradley's Fantasy Magazine,* Fall 1991.

**Tenebrae, Catharina.** "Blood Sisters." *Children of the Night Coven Journal 4,* 1990.

———. "Mother Stands for Comfort." *Nightmist 1,* Spring 1991.

**Tenn, William.** "The Human Angle." *Famous Fantastic Mysteries,* October 1948.

———. "She Only Goes Out at Night." *Fantastic Universe,* October 1956.

**Tepper, Sheri S.** "The Gardener." In *Night Visions 6*. Arlington Heights, IL: Dark Harvest, 1988.

———. "The Gazebo." *The Magazine of Fantasy & Science Fiction,* October 1990.

**Tessier, Thomas.** "Infidel." In *A Whisper of Blood*. New York: William Morrow, 1991.

**Thiel, James II.** "The Enforcer." *Newsletter of the Miss Lucy Westenra Society of the Undead,* Summer 1990.

**Thomas, Jeffrey.** "The White Bat." *Dead of Night 4*, January 1990.

**Thomas, Roger M.** "The Bradley Vampire." *Weird Tales*, May 1951.

**Thomas-Sundstorm, Linda.** "Midnight Court." In *Immortal Bad Boys*. New York: Brava, 2001.

**Thompson, Claire.** *Sacred Circle*. Akron, OH: Ellora's Cave, 2005 (erotica).

**Thompson, David.** "Beauty in a Shadow's Desire." *Loyalists of the Vampire Realm Newsletter*, October 1991.

**Thompson, Dawn.** *Blood Moon*. New York: Love Spell, 2007.

———. *The Brotherhood: Blood Moon #2*. New York: Love Spell, 2007.

———. *The Ravening: Blood Moon #3*. New York: Love Spell, 2008.

**Thompson, James M.** *Night Blood*. New York: Pinnacle, 2001.

———. *Dark Blood*. New York: Pinnacle, 2002.

———. *Immortal Blood*. New York: Pinnacle, 2003.

———. *Tainted Blood*. New York: Pinnacle, 2004.

**Thompson, Kate.** *Midnight's Choice*. New York: Hyperion, 1999 (juvenile).

**Thompson, Ronda.** "Midnight Serenade." In *After Twilight*. New York: Love Spell, 2001.

**Thompson, Russell.** "Terror of the Undead Corpses." *Super-Science Fiction*, June 1959.

**Thorne, Tamara.** *Candle Bay*. New York: Pinnacle, 2001.

**Thurlo, David, and Aimee Thurlo.** *Second Sunrise: A Lee Nez Novel #1*. New York: Forge, 2002.

———. *Blood Retribution: A Lee Nez Novel #2*. New York: Forge, 2004.

———. *Pale Death: A Lee Nez Novel #3*. New York: Forge, 2005.

**Thurman, Rob.** *Nightlife*. New York: Roc, 2006.

———. *Moonshine*. New York: Roc, 2007.

**Tieck, John.** *Wake Not the Dead*, 1823.

**Tiedmann, Mark W.** "Drink." *Isaac Asimov's Science Fiction Magazine*, 1994.

**Tigges, John.** *Vessel*. New York: Leisure Books, 1988.

**Tignor, Beth.** *Tryst of Dark Shadows*. North Riverside, IL: Pandora Publications, 1981.

**Tilton, Lois.** "In the Service of Evil." In *Bringing Down the Moon*. New York: Space and Time, 1985.

———. *Vampire Winter*. New York: Pinnacle, 1990.

———. *Darkness on the Ice*. New York: Pinnacle, 1993.

———. *Darkspawn*. Tulsa, OK: Hawk Publishing Group, 2000.

**Tofte, Arthur.** "A Thirst for Blood." In *More Science Fiction Tales*. New York: Rand McNally, 1974.

**Tolson, Dana.** "Nice Old House." *Startling Mystery Stories*, Winter 1967–68.

**Tolstoy, Alexei.** "The Family of the Vourdalak" (originally "Sem'ya Vurdalaka," 1839), 1841.

———. "The Vampire" (originally "Upyr"), 1841.

**Tonkin, Peter.** *The Journal of Edwin Underhill*. London: Hodder & Stoughton, 1981.

**Tooker, Richard.** "Thorda, Queen of Vampires." *Unusual Stories*, March 1934.

**Topping, Keith.** *Hollywood Vampire (Buffy the Vampire Slayer)*. London: Virgin, 2004.

**Tozer, Basil John.** "The Vampire." In *Around the World with a Millionaire*. London: R. A. Everett, 1902.

**Tracy, Marilyn.** "Married by Dawn. In *Brides of the Night*. Toronto: Silhouette, 1998.

**Trautvetter, Janet.** *World of Darkness: Dark Ages*. Clarkston, GA: White Wolf, 2003.

**Treanor, Marie.** *Undead Men Wear Plaid.* Surprise, AZ: Triskelion, 2006 (erotica).

———. *Loving the Man.* Martinsburg, WV: Changeling, 2007 (erotica).

———. *Loving the Vampire.* Martinsburg, WV: Changeling, 2007 (erotica).

**Tredinnick, William.** "Legend of a Vampire." *Moonbroth 8,* 1973.

**Tremayne, Peter.** *Dracula Unborn.* Folkestone, Kent, UK: Bailey Brothers and Swinfen, 1977.

———. *The Revenge of Dracula.* Folkestone, Kent, UK: Bailey Brothers and Swinfen, 1978.

———. *Dracula, My Love.* Folkestone, Kent, UK: Bailey Brothers and Swinfen, 1980.

———. "Dracula's Chair." In *The Count Dracula Fan Club Book of Vampire Stories.* Chicago: Adams, 1980.

———. "The Hungry Grass." In *Freak Show Vampire and the Hungry Grass.* Chicago: Adams, 1981.

———. "The Samhain Feis." In *Halloween Horrors.* New York: Doubleday, 1986.

———. "My Name Upon the Wind." In *The Vampire Hunter's Casebook.* New York: Barnes & Noble, 1996.

**Trexler, Roger Dale.** "Looking for a Hot Meal." *The Vampire Journal 4,* 1988.

**Tubb, E. C.** "Fresh Guy." *Science Fantasy,* June 1958.

**Tunstall, Kit.** *Blood Challenge.* Akron, OH: Ellora's Cave, 2003 (erotica).

———. *Heart of Midnight.* Akron, OH: Ellora's Cave, 2003 (erotica).

———. *Beloved Forever.* Akron, OH: Ellora's Cave, 2004 (erotica).

———. "Heart of Midnight." In *Dark Dreams.* Akron, OH: Ellora's Cave, 2004 (erotica).

———. *Blood Oath: Bloodlines #1.* Akron, OH: Ellora's Cave, 2005 (erotica).

———. *Hunter's Prey.* Scottsdale, AZ: Loose Id, 2005 (erotica).

———. "The Master's Gift." In *The Bite before Christmas.* Scottsdale, AZ: Loose Id, 2007 (erotica).

**Turner, James.** "Mirror without Image." In *The Vampire's Bedside Companion.* London: Leslie Frewin, 1975.

**Turtledove, Harry.** "Thicker Than Water." *Fantasy Book,* March 1986.

———. "Gentlemen of the Shade." In *Ripper.* New York: Tor, 1988.

———. "Batboy." *Magazine of Fantasy & Science Fiction,* December 1988.

**Turzillo, Mary A.** "When Gretchen Was Human." In *The Mammoth Book of Vampire Stories by Women.* New York: Carroll & Graf, 2001.

**Tuttle, Lisa.** "Sangre." *Fantastic,* July 1977.

———. "Jamie's Grave." In *Shadows 10.* New York: Doubleday, 1987.

———. "Replacements." In *Memories of the Body: Tales of Desire and Transformation.* London: Grafton/Collins, 1992.

**Tweed, Jack Hamilton.** *The Blood of Dracula.* London: Mills and Boon, 1971.

**Tyler, Tim.** "Blood Brothers." *Blood Reign 1,* July 1991.

**Tyree, Omar.** "Human Heat: The Confessions of an Addicted Vampire." In *Dark Thirst.* New York: Simon & Schuster, 2004.

**Ulrichs, Karl Heinrich.** "Manor," 1884.

**Umansky, Kaye.** *The Night I Was Chased by a Vampire.* London: Dolphin Paperbacks, 1996 (juvenile).

**Underwood, Laura.** "Tangled Webs." In *Swords and Sorceress IX.* New York: DAW, 1992.

**Underwood, Peter.** "The Italian Count." In *Voices from the Vault.* Toronto: Key Porter, 1987.

**Utley, Steven.** "Night Life." In *The Rivals of Dracula.* London: Corgi, 1977.

**Vachss, Andrew.** *Strega.* New York: Alfred A. Knopf, 1995.

**Valdemi, Maria.** *The Demon Lover.* New York: Tor, 1981.

**Valentine, Blair.** "Surrender the Night." In *Lady Jaided's Virile Vampires.* Akron, OH: Ellora's Cave, 2007 (erotica).

**Vallejo, Doris.** "Seduction." In *Enchantment.* New York: Ballantine, 1984.

———. "Thirst" In *Enchantment.* New York: Ballantine, 1984.

**Van Belkom, Edo.** "Lip-O-Suction." *The Vampire's Crypt 4,* Fall 1991.

———. "Blood Bait." *The Vampire's Crypt 6,* Fall 1992.

**Van der Elst, Violet.** "The Immortal Soul." In *The Torture Chamber and Other Stories.* London: Doge, 1937.

**Van Hise, Della.** "More Rare Than Blood." *Prisoners of the Night 3,* 1989.

———. *Ragged Angels.* Yucca Valley, CA: Eye Scrye Publications, 1997.

**Van Hise, James.** "Dark Embrace." In *Midnight Graffiti.* New York: Warner, 1992.

**Van Horne, Hollie.** *Beneath the Wings of Isis.* Miami, FL: Time Travelers, 2004.

**Van Lustbader, Eric.** "In Darkness, Angels." In *The Dodd, Mead Gallery of Horror.* New York: Dodd, Mead, 1983.

**Van Over, Raymond.** *The Twelfth Child.* New York: Pinnacle, 1990.

**Van Vogt, A. E.** "Asylum." *Astounding,* May 1942.

———. "The Proxy Intelligence." *Worlds of If,* October 1968.

**Vance, Gerald.** "Reggie and the Vampire." *Fantastic Adventures,* September 1948.

**Vance, Jack.** "Rumfuddle." In *Three Trips in Time and Space.* New York: Hawthorn, 1973.

**Vandevelde, Vivian.** *Companions of the Night.* New York: Jane Yolen Books, 1995 (juvenile).

**Vanore, James.** *Beware the Leaven.* Lincoln, NE: Writers Club Press, 1999.

**Vaughn, Carrie.** *Kitty and the Midnight Hour.* New York: Warner Aspect, 2005 (juvenile).

———. *Kitty Goes to Washington.* New York: Warner Books, 2006 (juvenile).

———. *Kitty Takes a Holiday.* New York: Warner Books, 2007 (juvenile).

**Veinglory, Emily.** "Thanates." In *Vamprotica 2005.* Chippewa, 2005 (erotica).

**Veley, Charles.** *Night Whispers.* New York: Doubleday, 1980.

**Verner, G.** *The Vampire Men.* London: Wright & Brown, 1941.

**Verrill, A. Hyatt.** "The Plague of the Living Dead." *Amazing Stories,* April 1927.

———. "Vampires of the Desert." *Amazing Stories,* December 1929.

**Veselik, William A.** *Weep Not for the Vampire.* Mundania Press, 2006.

**Viehl, Lynn.** *If Angels Burn: Darkyn #1.* New York: Signet, 2005.

———. *Private Demon: Darkyn #2.* New York: Signet, 2005.

———. *Dark Need: Darkyn #3.* New York: Signet, 2006.

———. *Night Lost: Darkyn #4.* New York: Signet, 2007.

———. *Evermore: Darkyn #5.* New York: Signet, 2008.

———. *Twilight Fall: Darkyn #6.* New York: Signet, 2008.

**Viereck, George Sylvester.** *The House of the Vampire.* New York: Moffat, Yard, 1907.

**Viets, Elaine.** "Vampire Hours." In *Many Bloody Returns.* New York: Ace, 2007.

**Vitola, Denise.** *The Winter Man.* New York: Berkley, 1995.

**Vivian, Steve.** *A Self-Made Monster.* Raleigh, NC: Boson Books, 2000.

**Vivigatz, Melissa J.** *Hunting Shadows.* Middleton, CT: Dragon Vine, 2001.

**Voltz, Don.** "Filler." *Prisoners of the Night 2,* 1988.

**Von Cosel, Karl Tanzler.** "The Secret of Elena's Tomb." *Fantastic Adventures,* September 1947.

**Von Rabe, Baroness Anne Crawford.** "A Mystery of the Campagna." *Unwin's Annual,* 1887.

**Vornholt, John.** *Coyote Moon (Buffy the Vampire Slayer).* New York: Pocket Books, 1998.

———. *Seven Crows (Buffy the Vampire Slayer/Angel).* New York: Simon Pulse, 2003.

**Vremont, Ann.** *Harnessed Angels: The Quickening.* Yoni Books, 2003 (erotica).

**Waddell, Martin.** "Bloodthirsty." In *Pan Book of Horror Stories No. 9.* London: Pan, 1968.

———. *Little Dracula's Christmas.* London: Walker Books, 1986 (juvenile).

———. *Little Dracula's First Bite.* London: Walker Books, 1986 (juvenile).

———. *Little Dracula at the Seaside.* London: Walker Books, 1987 (juvenile).

———. *Little Dracula Goes to School.* London: Walker Books, 1987 (juvenile).

———. *Little Dracula's Fangtastic Fun Book.* London: Walker Books, 1992 (juvenile).

**Wade, Darryl.** *Boys of the Night: The Second Vampire/Wolf War.* Bloomington, IN: 1st Books Library, 2002.

**Wagar, A. Warren.** "A Woman's Life." In *Afterlives: An Anthology of Stories about Life after Death.* New York: Vintage, 1986.

**Waggoner, Jayne.** *Celic.* Frederick, MD: PublishAmerica, 2008.

**Waggoner, Tim.** "Seeker." In *Dark Tyrants.* Clarkston, GA: White Wolf, 1997.

———. *Necropolis.* Marlton, N.J.: Gale Group, 2004.

**Wagner, Bobby G.** "Sister." *Dead of Night 6,* July 1990.

**Wagner, Esther.** "Miss Weird-O." *Ellery Queen Mystery Magazine,* December 1960.

**Wagner, Joyce.** "Bad Company." In *Night Bites: Vampire Stories by Women.* Seattle, WA: Seal, 1996.

**Wagner, Karl Edward.** *Death's Angel's Shadow.* New York: Warner, 1973.

———. "Sticks." *Whispers,* March 1974.

———. "Beyond Any Measure." *Whispers,* March 1982.

———. "Neither Brute Nor Human." *World Fantasy Convention Program Book,* 1983.

———. "The Kind Men Like." In *Hotter Blood.* New York: Pocket Books, 1991.

———. "The Slug." In *A Whisper of Blood.* New York: William Morrow, 1991.

**Wahl, Jan.** *Dracula's Cat.* Englewood Cliffs, NJ: Prentice-Hall, 1978 (juvenile).

**Wakefield, H. Russell.** "And He Shall Sing. . . ." In *They Return at Evening.* New York: D. Appleton, 1928.

———. "The Seventeenth Hole at Duncaster." In *They Return at Evening.* New York: D. Appleton, 1928.

———. "Monstrous Regiment." In *Strayers from Sheol.* Sauk City, WI: Arkham House, 1961.

———. "The Sepulchre of Jasper Sarasen." In *Strayers from Sheol.* Sauk City, WI: Arkham House, 1961.

**Walder, Cassie.** *Dream Lover.* Akron, OH: Ellora's Cave, 2003 (erotica).

**Waldron, Virginia.** "Whence No Man Steers." *World of Dark Shadows,* July 1982.

———. "The Scars of Betrayal." *Karlenzine,* 1984.

**Waldrop, Howard.** "Der Untertag des Abendlandesmenshen." *Chacal 1,* Winter 1976.

**Walker, John Edward.** *The Origin of the Vampire: How It Started.* Pittsburgh, PA: Dorrance, 1999.

**Walker, Shiloh.** *The Beginning: The Hunters #1 and #2.* Akron, OH: Ellora's Cave, 2004 (erotica).

———. *Interlude: The Hunters #3 and #4.* Akron, OH: Ellora's Cave, 2005 (erotica).

———. *Ben and Shadoe: The Hunters #5.* Akron, OH: Ellora's Cave, 2005 (erotica).

————. *Rafe and Sheila: The Hunters #6*. Akron, OH: Ellora's Cave, 2005 (erotica).

————. *I'll Be Hunting You: The Hunters #7*. Akron, OH: Ellora's Cave, 2005 (erotica).

————. *Mythe-Vampire*. Akron, OH: Ellora's Cave, 2005 (erotica).

————. *Heart and Soul: The Hunters #8*. New York: Berkley, 2006.

————. *Hunting the Hunter: The Hunters #9*. New York: Berkley, 2006.

————. *Hunter's Salvation: The Hunters #10*. New York: Berkley, 2007.

Wallace, F. L. "Bolden's Pets." *Galaxy 11*, October 1955.

Wallace, Patricia. *Monday's Child*. New York: Zebra, 1989.

Walters, N. J. *Harker's Journey*. Akron, OH: Ellora's Cave, 2005 (erotica).

————. *Lucian's Delight*. Akron, OH: Ellora's Cave, 2006 (erotica).

Walters, R. R. *Ludlow's Mill*. New York: Pinnacle, 1981.

Walton, Evangeline. "At the End of the Corridor." *Weird Tales*, May 1950.

Waltz, Anne. *Swedish Lutheran Vampires of Brainerd*. St. Paul, MN: Sidecare Preservation Society, 2001.

Wandrei, Donald. "The Fire Vampires." *Weird Tales*, February 1933.

Wandrei, Howard. "Vine Terror." *Weird Tales*, September 1934.

Ward, Howard. "The House of the Living Dead." *Weird Tales*, March 1932.

————. "The Thing from the Grave." *Weird Tales*, July 1933.

————. "The Life-Eater." *Weird Tales*, June 1937.

Ward, J. R. *Dark Lover: The Black Dagger Brotherhood #1*. New York: Signet, 2005.

————. *Lover Eternal: The Black Dagger Brotherhood #2*. New York: Signet, 2006.

————. *Lover Awakened: The Black Dagger Brotherhood #3*. New York: Signet, 2006.

————. *Lover Revealed: The Black Dagger Brotherhood #4*. New York: Onyx, 2007.

————. *Lover Unbound: The Black Dagger Brotherhood #5*. New York: Signet, 2007.

————. *Lover Enshrined: The Black Dagger Brotherhood #6*. New York: Signet, 2008.

Wardlaw, James C. *Dracul: The Vampire Returns*. Frederick, MD: PublishAmerica, 2002.

Warner, Bobby G. "Deathwatch." *Dead of Night 3*, Fall 1989.

————. "Back Home Again." *The Vampire's Crypt 3*, Spring 1991.

Warner, Scarlet. "The Dark Side of the Sun." *Prisoners of the Night 1*, 1987.

————. "Against a Full Moon." *Prisoners of the Night 2*, 1988.

Warren, Bill. "Death Is a Lonely Place." *Worlds of Fantasy 1*, 1968.

Warren, Charles. "Coyote Women." *Ace Mystery*, July 1936.

Warren, Christine. *Fantasy Fix*. Akron, OH: Ellora's Cave, 2003 (erotica).

Warren, Lynn. *Eternal Flame*. Surprise, AZ: Triskelion, 2005 (erotica).

————. *Moonlight, Wine and Stakes*. Surprise, AZ: Triskelion, 2005 (erotica).

Warrington, Freda. "The Raven Bound." In *The Mammoth Book of Vampire Stories by Women*. New York: Carroll & Graf, 2001.

Warrington, Sheila. *A Taste of Blood Wine*. London: Pan Books, 1992.

————. *A Dance in Black Velvet*. London: Pan Books, 1994.

————. *The Dark Blood of Poppies*. London: Pan Books, 1995.

————. *Dracula the Undead*. London: Pan Books, 1997.

Wartell, Matthew L. *Blood of Our Children*. Westminster, CO: WEB, 1996.

Watkins, E. F. *Dance with the Dragon*. Indian Hills, CA: Amber Quill, 2003.

Watson, H. B. Mariott. *The Amber*. London: John Lane, 1899.

————. "The Stone Chamber." In *The Heart of Miranda and Other Stories*. London: John Lane, 1899.

Watson, Ian. "Cold Light." *The Magazine of Fantasy & Science Fiction*, April 1986.

————. "Aid from a Vampire." *Science Fiction Eye*, March 1988.

Watson, Richard F. "Vampires from Outer Space." *Super-Science Fiction,* April 1959.

Watt-Evans, Lawrence. "Richie." In *Vampires: A Collection of Original Stories.* New York: HarperCollins, 1991.

———. "The Name of Fear." In *The Ultimate Dracula.* New York: Dell, 1991.

Watts, Peter. *Blindsight.* New York: Tor, 2006.

Waugh, Michael. *Fangs of the Vampire.* Sydney, Australia: Cleveland, 1954.

———. *Back from the Dead.* Sydney, Australia: Cleveland, 1955.

———. *The Living Dead.* Sydney, Australia: Cleveland, 1955.

Wayne, Teresa. *Eternal Bonds: Blood Brothers.* Mardi Gras, 2007.

Weathersby, Lee. *Kiss of the Vampire.* New York: Zebra, 1992.

Weaver, Debra. "A Lower Deep." *Dead of Night 5,* April 1990.

Webb, W. T. "Grimjank." In *Vampires, Werewolves and Other Monsters.* New York: Curtis, 1974.

Webb, Wendy. "Sleeping Cities." In *The Mammoth Book of Vampire Stories by Women.* New York: Carroll & Graf, 2001.

Webber, Minda. *The Remarkable Miss Frankenstein.* New York: Leisure Books, 2005.

———. "Lucy and the Crypt Casanova." In *Just One Slip.* New York: Leisure Books, 2006.

———. *The Reluctant Miss Van Helsing.* New York: Leisure Books, 2006.

Weinberg, Robert. "They Drink Blood." *Space and Time,* September 1971.

———. *Bloodwar: Masquerade of Death.* Clarkston, GA: White Wolf, 1995.

———. *Unholy Allies.* Clarkston, GA: White Wolf, 1995.

———. *The Unbeholden.* Clarkston, GA: White Wolf, 1996.

Weinberg, Robert, and Rein-Hagen, Mark. *Vampire Diary: The Embrace.* Stone Mountain, GA: White Wolf, 1994.

Wellington, David. *13 Bullets.* New York: Three Rivers, 2007.

———. *99 Coffins: A Historical Vampire Tale.* New York: Three Rivers, 2007.

———. *Vampire Zero.* New York: Three Rivers, 2008.

Wellman, Mac. *The Land beyond the Forest: Dracula and Swoop.* Sun and Moon, 1995 (juvenile).

Wellman, Manly Wade. "The Horror Undying." *Weird Tales,* May 1936.

———. "School for the Unspeakable." *Weird Tales,* September 1937.

———. "The Black Drama." *Weird Tales,* June–August 1938.

———. "Fearful Rock." *Weird Tales,* February 1939.

———. "When it Was Midnight." *Unknown Worlds,* February 1940.

———. "Coven." *Weird Tales,* July 1942.

———. "The Vampire of Shiloh." *Weird Tales,* July 1942.

———. "The Devil Is Not Mocked." *Unknown Worlds,* June 1943.

———. "Come into My Parlor." In *The Girl with the Hungry Eyes.* New York: Avon, 1949.

———. "The Last Grave of Lil Warran." *Weird Tales,* May 1951.

———. "Hundred Years Gone." *The Magazine of Fantasy & Science Fiction,* March 1978.

———. "Chaste!" in *The Year's Best Horror Stories: Series VII.* New York: DAW, 1979.

———. "Where Did She Wander?" In *Whispers VI.* New York: Doubleday, 1987.

———. "The Cursed Damozel." In *Southern Blood: Vampire Stories from the American South.* Cumberland House, 1997.

Wells, H. G. "The Flowering of the Strange Orchid." *The Pall Mall Magazine,* August 1894.

Wells, J. A. "Like Cats." *Prisoners of the Night 6*, 1992.

Wells, Sharon. "A Curse in Time." *Good Guys Wear Fangs 1*, May 1992.

Wenk, Richard. "Midnight Mess." *Tales from the Crypt Volume 3*. New York: Random House, 1991.

West, Michelle Sagara. "Dust." In *How I Survived My Summer Vacation*. New York: Pocket Books, 2000.

West, Summer. *The Pirate's Secret*. Dover, NH: RuneStone, 2005.

West, Terry. *The Turning: Confessions of a Teen-age Vampire #1*. New York: Scholastic Paperbacks, 1997 (juvenile).

———. *Zombie Saturday Night: Confessions of a Teen-age Vampire #2*. New York: Scholastic Paperbacks, 1997 (juvenile).

Westerfield, Scott. *Peeps*. New York: Razorbill, 2005 (juvenile).

———. *The Last Days*. New York: Razorbill, 2006 (juvenile).

Westerly, Lark. *Dangerous Lovers (Roses and Thorns)*. Garibaldi Highlands, BC, Canada: eXtasy Books, 2004.

Westfield, Morven. *Darksome Thirst*. Southborough, MA: Harvest Shadows Publications, 2003.

———. *The Old Power Returns*. Southborough, MA: Harvest Shadows Publications, 2007.

Westlake, Donald, and Abby Westlake. *Transylvania Station*. Miami Beach, FL: Dennis McMillan, 1987.

Whalen, Patrick. *Monastery*. New York: Pocket Books, 1988.

———. *Night Thirst*. New York: Pocket Books, 1991.

Wharton, Edith. "Bewitched." In *Here and Beyond*. New York: D. Appleton, 1926.

———. "Miss Mary Pask." In *Here and Beyond*. New York: D. Appleton, 1926.

Wheeler, Deborah. "Under the Skin." *Marion Zimmer Bradley's Fantasy Magazine*, Spring 1989.

Wheeler, Wendy. "Desiree's Shadow." *Dead of Night 3*, Fall 1989.

Whetstone, Raymond. "The Thirsty Dead." *Terror Tales*, March 1935.

Whipple, Chandler W. "Brother Lucifer." *Weird Tales*, November 1936.

White, Fred M. "The Purple Terror." *The Strand Magazine*, September 1899.

Whiteside, Diane. *The Hunter's Prey*. Akron, OH: Ellora's Cave, 2002 (erotica).

———. *Bond of Blood: Texas Vampires #1*. New York: Berkley, 2006.

———. "Red Skies at Night." In *Unleashed*. New York: Berkley, 2006.

———. *Bond of Fire: Texas Vampires #2*. New York: Berkley, 2008.

———. *Bond of Darkness: Texas Vampires #3*. New York: Berkley, 2008.

Whitfield, Timothy. *Witchblood*. Effort, PA: KHP Industries, 2003.

Whitley, George. "And Not in Peace." *Famous Fantastic Mysteries*, December 1946.

Whitley, Strieber. *The Hunger*. New York: William Morrow, 1981.

———. *The Last Vampire*. New York: Atria Books, 2001.

———. *Lilith's Dream*. New York: Atria Books, 2002.

Whitten, Leslie H. *Progeny of the Adder*. New York: Doubleday, 1965.

———. *The Fangs of Morning*. New York: Leisure Books, 1994.

Whittington, Don. *Vampire Mom*. New York: Avon Camelot, 1995 (juvenile).

Whittington, Mary K. "Ahvel." In *Vampires: A Collection of Original Stories*. New York: HarperCollins, 1991.

Whyte-Mellville, George John. "The Vampire." In *Bones and I or The Skeleton at Home*. London: Chapman and Hall, 1868.

Wieck, Stewart. *Toreador (The Clan Novel Series, No. 1)*. Clarkston, GA: White Wolf, 1999.

———. *The Beast Within*. Clarkston, GA: White Wolf, 2001.

———. *The Eye of Gehanna (The Clan Novel Series, No. 2)*. Clarkston, GA: White Wolf, 2003.

———. *Bloody September (The Clan Novel Series, No. 3)*. Clarkston, GA: White Wolf, 2004.

Wiesner, Karen. *Sweet Dreams*. Brighton, MI: Avid, 2001.

Wightman, Wayne. "The Touch." In *Shadows 6*. New York: Doubleday, 1983.

Wilde, D. C. *Love Poems to a Vampire*. Vancouver, BC: Privately printed, 1996.

Wilde, Kelley. *Mastery*. New York: Dell, 1991.

Wilde, Terry. *Vampire of My Dreams*. Palm Beach, FL: Medallion, 2005.

———. *Vampire . . . in My Dreams*. Macon, GA: Samhain, 2007 (juvenile).

Wilder, Craig. "The Guest." *The Vampire Journal 1*, Summer 1985.

———. "Just Wait Until Dark." *The Vampire Journal 2*, Fall 1985.

———. "Free at Last." *The Vampire Journal 3*, 1986.

Wilder, J. C. *One with the Hunger: Shadow Dwellers Series #1*. Akron, OH: Ellora's Cave, 1998 (erotica).

———. "One Night Stand." In *Ellora's Caveman: Tales from the Temple II*. Akron, OH: Ellora's Cave, 2004 (erotica).

Wiley, Carol A. "Just a Few More Pounds." *The Vampire's Crypt 3*, Spring 1991.

Wilkens, Bob. *Lowell Lehrer: Vampire Killer*. San Mateo, CA: Publishers Circulation, 1997.

Wilkerson, Cherie. "Echos from a Darkened Shore." In *Shadows 4*. New York: Doubleday, 1981.

Wilkins-Freeman, Mary E. "Luella Miller." *Everybody's Magazine*, December 1902.

Willems, S. F. "Vampyr." *Miss Lucy Westenra Society of the Undead*, December 1991.

William, Kate. *Tall, Dark and Deadly (Sweet Valley University #126)*. New York: Bantam, 1996 (juvenile).

Williams, Conrad. "Bloodlines." In *The Mammoth Book of Dracula*. London: Robinson, 1997.

Williams, Harlan. "Trapped in the Vampire's Web of Icy Death." *Adventures of Horror*, December 1970.

Williams, Mark. "Native Soil." *Onyx 1*, 1991–92.

Williams, Sidney. *Night Brothers*. New York: Pinnacle, 1990.

———. "Sojourners: A Love Story." *House Carfax 6*, Fall 1990.

Williams, Sidney, and Robert Petit. "Does the Blood Line Run on Time?" In *Under the Fang*. New York: Pocket Books, 1991.

Williams, Tad. "Child in an Ancient City." *Weird Tales*, Fall 1988.

———. *Child of an Ancient City*. New York: St. Martin's, 1999 (juvenile).

Williams, Thadeus. *In Quest of Life*. New York: F. T. Neely, 1898.

Williams, Wayne Rile. "One More Customer." *Prisoner of the Night 1*, 1987.

Williamson, Chet. ". . . To Feel Another's Woe." In *Blood Is Not Enough*. New York: William Morrow, 1989.

———. "Calm Sea and Prosperous Voyage." In *Under the Fang*. New York: Pocket Books, 1991.

Williamson, Diane Lisa D. "Best of Friends." In *Night Bites: Vampire Stories by Women*. Berkeley, CA: Seal, 1995.

Williamson, J. N. *Death-Angel*. New York: Zebra, 1981.

———. *Death-Couch*. New York: Zebra, 1981.

———. *Death-Doctor*. New York: Zebra, 1982.

———. *Death-School*. New York: Zebra, 1982.

———. *Brotherkind*. New York: Leisure Books, 1987.

————. "Everyone Must Know." *Dead of Night 2*, July 1989.

————. "Vampire Nostalgia." *Dead of Night 2*, July 1989.

————. "Herrenrasse." In *Under the Fang*. New York: Pocket Books, 1991.

————. *Bloodlines*. New York: Leisure Books, 1998.

Williamson, Jack. "The Plutonian Terror." *Weird Tales*, October 1933.

————. "The Ruler of Fate." *Weird Tales*, April-June 1936.

————. "Darker Than You Think." *Unknown Worlds*, December 1940.

Williamson, Lisa D. "Best of Friends." In *Night Bites: Vampire Stories by Women*. Seattle, WA: Seal, 1996.

Willis, Connie. "Jack." *Isaac Asimov's Science Fiction Magazine*, October 1991.

Willis, Danielle. "The Gift of Neptune." In *Love in Vein*. New York: HarperCollins, 1994 (erotica).

Wilson, Ann. "The Chosen One." *Antithesis 9*, 1980.

————. "Touch of the Dragon." *Apex! 2*, August 1987.

Wilson, Ann, and Colleen Drippe. "Not Quite Human." *Book of Shadows 4*, 1992.

Wilson, Barbara. *Trouble in Transylvania: A Cassandra Reilly Mystery*. Berkeley, CA: Seal, 1993.

Wilson, Colin. "The Return of the Lloigar." In *Tales of the Cthulhu Mythos Volume 2*. Sauk City, WI: Arkham House, 1969.

————. *The Space Vampires*. New York: Random House, 1976.

Wilson, David Niall. *To Sift Through Bitter Ashes: The Grail Covenant 1*. Clarkston, GA: White Wolf, 1997.

————. *To Dream of Dreamers Lost: The Grail Covenant 2*. Clarkston, GA: White Wolf, 1998.

————. *To Speak in Lifeless Tongues: The Grail Covenant 3*. Clarkston, GA: White Wolf, 1998.

————. *This Is My Blood*. Black River, NY: Terminal Fright, 1999.

Wilson, David Niall, and Lisanne Lake. *This Is My Blood*. Black River, NY: Terminal Fright, 1999.

Wilson, Eric. *Vampires of Ottawa*. Victoria, BC, Canada: Orca Book, 2001 (juvenile).

Wilson, F. Paul. *The Keep*. New York: William Morrow, 1981.

————. "Tenants." In *Night Visions 6*. Arlington Heights, IL: Dark Harvest, 1988.

————. *Reborn*. New York: Dark Harvest, 1990.

————. *Midnight Mass*. Eugene, OR: Axoloti Press/Pulphouse, 1990.

————. *Reprisal*. New York: Dark Harvest, 1991.

————. *Nightworld*. New York: Dark Harvest, 1992.

————. "The Lord's Work." In *Dracula: Prince of Darkness*. New York: DAW, 1992.

Wilson, Gahan. "Phyllis." In "Horror Trio." *Playboy*, June 1962.

————. "The Sea Was Wet as Wet Could Be." *Playboy*, May 1967.

Wilson, Jacqueline. *Stevie Day—Vampire*. London: Lions/Armada, 1988.

Wilson, K. R. *Crimson Wings*. Garibaldi Highlands, BC, Canada: eXtasy Books, 2004.

————. *Of Blood and Orchids*. Garibaldi Highlands, BC, Canada: eXtasy Books, 2005.

Windsor, Annie. *Redevence 1: The Edge*. Akron, OH: Ellora's Cave, 2003 (erotica).

Winfield, Chester. "Castle of Dracula." *Monster Sex Tales 1*, August–September 1972 (erotica).

Winrow, Everett L. *Night of the Harvest Moon: Vampire: A Tale of the Living and the Undead*. Lincoln, NE: iUniverse, 2003.

Winston, Daoma. *The Vampire Curse*. New York: Paperback Library, 1971.

Winston, Samantha. *My Fair Pixie*. Akron, OH: Ellora's Cave, 2005 (erotica).

Wolfe, Gene. "Queen of the Night." In *Love in Vein*. New York: HarperCollins, 1994.

Wolfe, Sean. "Brandon's Bite." In *Masters of Midnight*. New York: Kensington, 2003.

Womack, Jack. "Lifeblood." In *A Whisper of Blood*. New York: William Morrow, 1991.

Wong, Victor James. *Matthew Piper and the Vampire Hunter*. Bloomington, IN: 1st Books Library, 2003.

———. *Vampire Hunter*. Bloomington, IN: 1st Books Library, 2003.

Woolrich, Cornell. "Vampire's Honeymoon." *Horror Stories*, August 1939.

———. "My Lips Destroy." In *Beyond the Night*. New York: Avon, 1959.

Workman, Grant, and Mary Grant. *The Guide*. Bloomington, IN: 1st Books Library, 1996.

Worrell, Everil. "The Canal." *Weird Tales*, December 1927.

———. "The Hollow Moon." *Weird Tales*, May 1939.

Wray, Roger. *The Dweller in the Half-Light*. London: Oldhams, 1920.

Wright, Linda K. "The Last Train." In *Night Bites: Vampire Stories by Women*. Seattle, WA: Seal, 1996.

Wright, Sean. *Jesse Jameson and the Vampire Vault*. King's Lynn, Norfolk, UK: Crowswing Books, 2004.

Wright, Sewell Peaslee. "Vampires of Space." *Astounding Stories*, March 1932.

———. "The Dead Walk Softly." *Strange Tales*, October 1932.

Wright, T. Lucien. *The Hunt*. New York: Pinnacle, 1991.

———. *Blood Brothers*. New York: Pinnacle, 1992.

———. *Thirst of the Vampire*. New York: Pinnacle, 1992.

Wright, T. M. *The Last Vampire*. London: Victor Gollancz, 1990.

Wyndham, John. "Close Behind Him." *Fantastic*, January/February 1953.

Wysocki, John. "Vourdalak." *Weirdbook*, 1983.

X.L. "The Kiss of Judas." *Pall Mall Magazine*, July 1893.

X, Madeline. *I Am a Vampire*. Privately printed, 1974.

Yarbro, Chelsea Quinn. "Disturb Not My Slumbering Fair." In *Cautionary Tales*. New York: Doubleday, 1978.

———. *Hotel Transylvania (Saint-Germain)*. New York: St. Martin's, 1978.

———. *The Palace (Saint-Germain)*. New York: St. Martin's, 1979.

———. "Seat Partner." In *Nightmares*. New York: Playboy, 1979.

———. *Blood Games (Saint-Germain)*. New York: St. Martin's, 1980.

———. "Cabin 33" (Saint Germain). In *Shadows 3*. New York: Doubleday, 1980.

———. *The Path of the Eclipse (Saint-Germain)*. New York: St. Martin's, 1981.

———. "The Spider Glass." In *Shadows 4*. New York: Doubleday, 1981.

———. "Renewal." In *Shadows 5*. New York: Doubleday, 1982.

———. *Tempting Fate (Saint-Germain)*. New York: St. Martin's, 1982.

———. *A Flame in Byzantium (Atta Olivia Clemens)*. New York: Tor, 1986.

———. *Crusader's Torch (Atta Olivia Clemens)*. New York: Tor, 1988.

———. *A Candle for D'Artagnan (Atta Olivia Clemens)*. New York: Tor, 1989.

———. *Out of the House of Life (Saint-Germain)*. New York: Tor, 1990.

———. "Salome." In *The Bradbury Chronicles*. New York: Penguin, 1991.

———. "Investigating Jericho." *The Magazine of Fantasy & Science Fiction*, April 1992.

———. *Better in the Dark (Saint-Germain)*. New York: Tor, 1993.

———. *Darker Jewels (Saint-Germain)*. New York: Tor, 1993.

———. "A Question of Patronage." In *The Vampire Stories of Chelsea Quinn Yarbro*. BC, Canada: Transylvania, 1994.

———. *Mansions in the Darkness (Saint-Germain)*. New York: Tor, 1996.

———. *Writ in Blood (Saint-Germain)*. New York: Tor, 1997.

———. *The Angry Angels (Sisters of the Night)*. New York: Avon, 1998.

————. *Blood Roses (Saint-Germain)*. New York: Tor, 1998.

————. *Communion Blood (Saint-Germain)*. New York: Tor, 1999.

————. *The Soul of an Angel (Sisters of the Night)*. New York: Avon, 1999.

————. *Come Twilight (Saint-Germain)*. New York: Tor, 2000.

————. "In the Face of Death." In *The Vampire Sextette*. Garden City, NY: Guild-America Books, 2000.

————. *A Feast in Exile (Saint Germain)*. New York: Tor, 2001.

————. *In the Face of Death (Saint-Germain)*. California: Hidden Knowledge Publications, 2001.

————. *Night Blooming (Saint-Germain)*. New York: Warner, 2002.

————. *Midnight Harvest*. New York: Warner, 2003.

————. *Dark of the Son*. New York: Tor, 2004.

————. *States of Grace (Saint-Germain)*. New York: Tor, 2005.

————. *Roman Dusk (Saint-Germain)*. New York: Tor, 2006.

————. *Borne in Blood (Saint-Germain)*. New York: Tor, 2007.

**Yarbro, Chelsea Quinn, and Suzy McKee Charnas.** "Advocates" (Saint-Germain). In *Under the Fang*. New York: Pocket Books, 1991.

**Yeovil, Jack.** *Drachenfels*. New York: Pocket Books, 2001.

————. *Genevieve Undead*. New York: Pocket Books, 2002.

————. *The Vampire Genevieve*. Glen Burnie, MD: Games Workshop, 2005.

**Yolen, Jane.** "Mama Gone." In *Vampires: A Collection of Original Stories*. New York: HarperCollins, 1991.

————. "Vampyr." In *The Mammoth Book of Vampire Stories by Women*. New York: Carroll & Graf, 2001.

**York, James E.** *Cross: Vampire Hunter*. Bloomington, IN: AuthorHouse, 2004.

**York, Rebecca.** "Night Ecstasy." In *Immortal Bad Boys*. New York: Brava, 2004.

**Youngson, Jeanne.** "Count Dracula and the Unicorn." In *Count Dracula and the Unicorn*. Chicago: Adams, 1978.

————. "The Lycanthrope." In *Count Dracula and the Unicorn*. Chicago: Adams, 1978.

————. "The S.O.B.: A Vampire Western." In *The Count Dracula Fan Club Book of Vampire Stories*. Chicago: Adams, 1980.

————. "Freak Show Vampire." In *Freak Show Vampire and the Hungry Glass*. Chicago: Adams, 1981.

————. "Another Good Story Spoiled by an Eye Witness." *Count Dracula Fan Club Letterzine*, Spring 1988.

————. "Beating the Odds." *Children of the Night Coven Journal 4*, 1990.

————. *Case Histories From the Private Files of a Vampirologist*. Chicago: Adams, 1997.

**Zagat, Arthur Leo.** "Thirst of the Living Dead." *Terror Tales*, November 1934.

**Zagoren, Kimberly.** *Mina's Journal (The Mina St. Claire Series)*. Lincoln, NE: Writer's Club, 2002.

————. *Thicker Than Water (The Mina St. Claire Series)*. Lincoln, NE: iUniverse, 2004.

**Zambreno, Mary Frances.** "Miss Emily's Roses." In *Vampires: A Collection of Original Vampire Stories*. New York: HarperCollins, 1991.

**Zapata, Luis.** *Adonis Garcia: A Picaresque Novel*. San Francisco: Gay Sunshine, 1981.

**Zeek, Anne Elizabeth.** "Life-Line." In *Dracula*. East Lansing, MI: T'Kuhtian, 1980.

————. "Blood Line." *Kessel Run 4*, 1984.

**Zelanko, Harry.** *Vampire Blood Bank*. ZAI Publications, 1999.

**Zelazny, Roger.** "On the Road to Splenoba." *Fantastic Stories of the Imagination,* January 1963.

————. The Stainless Steel Leech." *Fantastic,* April 1963.

————. "The Graveyard Heart." *Fantastic Stories of Imagination,* March 1964.

————. "Dayblood." *Rod Serling's Twilight Zone Magazine,* June 1985.

————. "Night Kings." *Worlds of If,* Fall 1986.

**Zeuli, Cynthia.** *Bound by Blood.* Las Vegas: ArcheBooks, 2003.

**Zimmer, Paul Edwin.** "A Swordsman from Carcosa." *Fantasy Book 5,* March, June 1986.

**Zinger, Steve.** *Ray McMickle and the Kentucky Vampire Clan.* Bloomington, IN: 1st Books Library, 2004.

————. *The Sab.* Bloomington, IN: 1st Books Library, 2004.

**Zoon, Susan.** *Vampire Lover: What Doesn't Kill Me, Makes Me Stronger.* Superior, WA: Port Town, 2004.

# Permissions Acknowledgments

Clive Barker: "Human Remains" by Clive Barker, copyright © 1984 by Clive Barker. Originally published in *Books of Blood, Vol. 3* (London: Sphere, 1984). Reprinted by permission of the author.

Charles Beaumont: "Place of Meeting" by Charles Beaumont, copyright © 1953 by Hanro Corporation, copyright renewed 1981 by Christopher Beaumont. Originally published in *Orbit Magazine*, published by Hanro Corporation, December 30, 1953. Reprinted by permission of Don Congdon Associates, Inc.

Robert Bloch: "The Living Dead" by Robert Bloch, copyright © 1967, copyright renewed 1995 by The Estate of Robert Bloch. Originally published in *Ellery Queen's Mystery Magazine*, April 1967. Reprinted by permission of the Estate of Robert Bloch and Ralph M. Vicanza, Inc.

Ray Bradbury: "The Man Upstairs" by Ray Bradbury, copyright © 1947 by *Harper's Magazine*, copyright renewed 1974 by Minneapolis Star and Tribune Co., Inc. Originally published in *Harper's Magazine*, March 1947. Reprinted by permission of Don Congdon Associates, Inc.

Joseph Payne Brennan: "The Horror of Chilton Castle" by Joseph Payne Brennan, copyright © 1963 by Cynthia P. Torello. Originally published in *Screams at Midnight* (New Haven: Macabre House, 1963). Reprinted by permission of Cynthia P. Torello.

Fredric Brown: "Blood" by Fredric Brown, copyright © 1954 by Fredric Brown. Originally published in *The Magazine of Fantasy & Science Fiction*, February 1954. Reprinted by permission of Barry Malzberg for the Estate of Fredric Brown.

Hugh B. Cave: "Stragella" by Hugh B. Cave, copyright © 1932 by *Strange Tales*. Originally published in *Strange Tales of Mystery and Terror*, June 1932. Reprinted by permission of the Estate of Hugh B. Cave.

R. Chetwynd-Hayes: "The Werewolf and the Vampire" by R. Chetwynd-Hayes, copyright © 1975 by R. Chetwynd-Hayes. Originally published in *The Monster Club* (New English Library, 1975). Reprinted by permission of the Dorian Literary Agency, acting on behalf of the author's estate, Linda Smith.

Frederick Cowles: "Princess of Darkness" by Frederick Cowles, copyright © 1993 by Michael W. Cowles. Originally published in *Fear Walks the Night* (London: Ghost Story Press, 1993). "The Vampire of Kaldenstein" by Frederick Cowles, copyright © 1999 by Michael W. Cowles. Originally published in *The Night Wind Howls* (London: Frederick Muller, 1999). Reprinted by permission of Michael W. Cowles.

August Derleth: "The Drifting Snow" by August Derleth, copyright © 1948 by August Derleth, copyright renewed 1976 by April R. Derleth and Walden W. Derleth. Originally published in *Weird Tales*, February 1939. Reprinted by permission of April R. Derleth for Arkham House Publishers Inc.

Gardner Dozois and Jack Dann: "Down Among the Dead Men" by Gardner Dozois with Jack Dann. Copyright © 1982 by Gardner Dozois and Jack Dann. Originally published in *Oui*, July 1982. Reprinted by permission of Gardner Dozois.

Harlan Ellison: "Lonely Women Are the Vessels of Time" by Harlan Ellison, copyright © 1976 by Harlan Ellison, copyright renewed 2004 by The Kilimanjaro Corporation. Originally published in *Strange Wine* (New York: Harper & Row, 1978). All rights reserved. Reprinted by arrangement with, and permission of, the author and the author's agent Richard Curtis Associates, Inc., New York. Harlan Ellison is a registered trademark of The Kilimanjaro Corporation.

Ed Gorman: "Duty" by Ed Gorman, copyright © 1991 by Ed Gorman. Originally published in *Under the Fang*, edited by Robert R. McCammon (New York: Pocket Books, 1991). Reprinted by permission of Ed Gorman.

Carl Jacobi: "Revelations in Black" by Carl Jacobi, copyright © 1947 by Carl Jacobi, copyright renewed 1975. Originally published in *Weird Tales*, April 1933. Reprinted by permission of Arkham House Publishers Inc.

Garry Kilworth: "The Silver Collar" by Garry Kilworth. Copyright © 1989 by Garry Kilworth. Originally published in *Blood Is Not Enough*, edited by Ellen Datlow (New York: Morrow, 1989). Reprinted by permission of Garry Kilworth.

Stephen King: "Popsy" by Stephen King, copyright © 1987 by Stephen King. Originally published in *Masques II : All-New Stories of Horror and the Supernatural*, edited by J. N. Williamson (Baltimore: Maclay, 1989). All rights reserved. Reprinted by permission of Stephen King.

Richard Laymon: "Special" by Richard Laymon, copyright © 1991 by Richard Laymon. Originally published in *Under the Fang*, edited by Robert R. McCammon (New York: Pocket Books, 1991). Reprinted by permission of Ann Laymon.

Tanith Lee: "Bite-Me-Not or, Fleur de Fur" by Tanith Lee, copyright © 1984 by Tanith Lee. Originally published in *Isaac Asimov's Science Fiction Magazine*, October 1984. "Winter Flowers" by Tanith Lee, copyright © 1993 by Tanith Lee. Originally published in *Isaac Asimov's Science Fiction Magazine*, June 1993. Reprinted by permission of Tanith Lee.

Fritz Leiber: "The Girl with the Hungry Eyes" by Fritz Leiber, copyright © 1949 by Fritz Leiber, copyright renewed. Originally published in The *Girl with the Hungry Eyes*, edited by Donald Wollheim (New York: Avon, 1949). Reprinted by permission of the Estate of Fritz Leiber.

Brian Lumley: "Necros" by Brian Lumley, copyright © 1998 by Brian Lumley. Originally published in *The Second Book of After Midnight Stories*, edited by Amy Myers (William Kimber, 1986). Reprinted by permission of Brian Lumley.

Richard Matheson: "Drink My Red Blood" by Richard Matheson, copyright © 1951, copyright renewed 1979 by Richard Matheson. Originally published in *Imagination*, April 1951. Reprinted by permission of Don Congdon Associates, Inc.

Anne Rice: "The Master of Rampling Gate" by Anne Rice, copyright © 1984 by Anne O'Brien Rice. Originally published in *Redbook*, February 1984. Reprinted by permission of Anne Rice.

David J. Schow: "A Week in the Unlife" by David J. Schow, copyright © 1991 by David J. Schow. Originally published in *A Whisper of Blood*, edited by Ellen Datlow (New York: William Morrow & Co., 1991). Reprinted by permission of David J. Schow.

Dan Simmons: "Carrion Comfort" by Dan Simmons, copyright © 1983 by Dan Simmons. Originally published in *Omni*, Sept./Oct. 1983. Reprinted by permission of Dan Simmons.

Clark Ashton Smith: "The Death of Ilalotha" by Clark Ashton Smith, copyright © 1937 by Clark Ashton Smith, copyright renewed 1965 by Caslana Literary Ent. Originally published in *Weird Tales*, Sept. 1937. "The End of the Story" by Clark Ashton Smith, copyright © 1930 by Clark Ashton Smith, copyright renewed 1958 by Caslana Literary Ent. Originally published in *Weird Tales*, May 1930. Reprinted by permission of Arkham House, Inc.

Brian Stableford: "The Man Who Loved the Vampire Lady" by Brian Stableford, copyright © 1988 by Brian Stableford. Originally published in *The Magazine of Fantasy & Science Fiction*, August 1988. Reprinted by permission of Brian Stableford.

Steve Rasnic Tem: "The Men & Women of Rivendale" by Steve Rasnic Tem, copyright © 1984 by Steve Rasnic Tem. Originally published in *Night Visions* (Dark Harvest, 1984). Reprinted by permission of Steve Rasnic Tem.

Peter Tremayne: "Dracula's Chair" by Peter Tremayne, copyright © 1980 by Peter Tremayne. Originally published in *The Count Dracula Fan Club Book of Vampires* (1981). Reprinted by permission of Brandt & Hochman Literary Agents, Inc.

Mary A. Turzillo: "When Gretchen Was Human" by Mary A. Turzillo, copyright © 2001 by Mary A. Turzillo. Originally published in *The Mammoth Book of Vampire Stories by Women* (Carroll & Graf, 2001). Reprinted by permission of Mary A. Turzillo.

Lisa Tuttle: "Replacements" by Lisa Tuttle, copyright © 1992 by Lisa Tuttle. Reprinted by permission of Lisa Tuttle.

Manly Wade Wellman: "Chastel" by Manly Wade Wellman, copyright © 1979 by Manly Wade Wellman. Originally published in *The Year's Best Horror Stories, Series VII* (DAW Books, 1979). "When It Was Moonlight" by Manly Wade Wellman, copyright © 1940 by Street & Smith, copyright renewed 1968 by Conde Nast. Originally published in *Unknown Worlds*, February 1940. Reprinted by permission of David Drake.

F. Paul Wilson: "Midnight Mass" by F. Paul Wilson, copyright © 1990 by F. Paul Wilson. Reprinted by permission of F. Paul Wilson.

Gahan Wilson: "When the Sea Was Wet as Wet Could Be" by Gahan Wilson, copyright © 1967 by Gahan Wilson. Originally published in *Playboy*, May 1967. Reprinted by permission of Gahan Wilson.

Roger Zelazny: "Dayblood" by Roger Zelazny, copyright © 1985 by Amber Ltd.. Originally published in *Twilight Zone*, May/June 1985. Reprinted by permission of The Pimlico Agency.

# ALSO EDITED BY OTTO PENZLER

THE BLACK LIZARD BIG BOOK OF PULPS
*The Best Crime Stories from the Pulps During Their
Golden Age—The '20s, '30s, & '40s*

Weighing in at over a thousand pages, containing more
than fifty stories and two novels, this book is big, baby,
bigger and more powerful than a freight train—a bullet
couldn't pass through it. Here are the best stories and every
major writer who ever appeared in celebrated pulps like
*Black Mask, Dime Detective, Detective Fiction Weekly,*
and more. These are the classic tales that created the genre
and gave birth to hard-hitting detectives who smoke criminals like cheap cigars; sultry dames whose looks are as
lethal as a dagger to the chest; and gin-soaked hideouts
where conversations are just preludes to murder. This is
crime fiction at its gritty best.

Crime Fiction/978-0-307-28048-0

VINTAGE CRIME/BLACK LIZARD
Available at your local bookstore, or visit
www.randomhouse.com